Of Time and the River

OF TIME AND THE RIVER

A LEGEND OF MAN'S HUNGER
IN HIS YOUTH

By

Thomas Wolfe

*"Who knoweth that spirit of man that goeth upward, and
the spirit of the beast that goeth downward to the earth?"*

THE SUN DIAL PRESS
GARDEN CITY, NEW YORK

1944
THE SUN DIAL PRESS

COPYRIGHT, 1935, BY
CHARLES SCRIBNER'S SONS

Printed in the United States of America

19051

To

MAXWELL EVARTS PERKINS

A GREAT EDITOR AND A BRAVE AND HONEST MAN, WHO STUCK TO
THE WRITER OF THIS BOOK THROUGH TIMES OF BITTER HOPELESS-
NESS AND DOUBT AND WOULD NOT LET HIM GIVE IN TO HIS OWN
DESPAIR, A WORK TO BE KNOWN AS "OF TIME AND THE RIVER" IS
DEDICATED WITH THE HOPE THAT ALL OF IT MAY BE IN SOME WAY
WORTHY OF THE LOYAL DEVOTION AND THE PATIENT CARE WHICH
A DAUNTLESS AND UNSHAKEN FRIEND HAS GIVEN TO EACH PART OF
IT, AND WITHOUT WHICH NONE OF IT COULD HAVE BEEN WRITTEN

"Crito, my dear friend Crito, that, be-
lieve me, that is what I seem to hear, as
the Corybants hear flutes in the air, and
the sound of those words rings and
echoes in my ears and I can listen to
nothing else."

Contents

BOOK ONE
PAGE

ORESTES: FLIGHT BEFORE FURY   1

BOOK TWO
YOUNG FAUSTUS   87

BOOK THREE
TELEMACHUS   325

BOOK FOUR
PROTEUS: THE CITY   405

BOOK FIVE
JASON'S VOYAGE   599

BOOK SIX
ANTÆUS: EARTH AGAIN   795

BOOK SEVEN
KRONOS AND RHEA: THE DREAM OF TIME   851

BOOK EIGHT
FAUST AND HELEN   901

Of Time and the River

"Kennst du das Land, wo die Zitronen blühn,
Im dunkeln Laub die Gold-Orangen glühn,
Ein sanfter Wind vom blauen Himmel weht,
Die Myrte still und hoch der Lorbeer steht,
Kennst du es wohl?
                    Dahin! Dahin
Möcht' ich mit dir, O mein Geliebter, ziehn!

Kennst du das Haus, auf Säulen ruht sein Dach,
Es glänzt der Saal, es schimmert das Gemach,
Und Marmorbilder stehn und sehn mich an:
Was hat man dir, du armes Kind, getan?
Kennst du es wohl?
                    Dahin! Dahin
Möcht' ich mit dir, O mein Beschützer, ziehn!

Kennst du den Berg und seinen Wolkensteg?
Das Maultier sucht im Nebel seinen Weg,
In Höhlen wohnt der Drachen alte Brut,
Es stürzt der Fels und über ihn die Flut:
Kennst du ihn wohl?
                    Dahin! Dahin
Geht unser Weg; *O Vater, lass uns ziehn!*"

BOOK 1

ORESTES: FLIGHT BEFORE FURY

. . . of wandering forever and the earth again . . . of seed-time, bloom, and the mellow-dropping harvest. And of the big flowers, the rich flowers, the strange unknown flowers.

Where shall the weary rest? When shall the lonely of heart come home? What doors are open for the wanderer? And which of us shall find his father, know his face, and in what place, and in what time, and in what land? Where? Where the weary of heart can abide forever, where the weary of wandering can find peace, where the tumult, the fever, and the fret shall be forever stilled.

Who owns the earth? Did we want the earth that we should wander on it? Did we need the earth that we were never still upon it? Whoever needs the earth shall have the earth: he shall be still upon it, he shall rest within a little place, he shall dwell in one small room forever.

Did he feel the need of a thousand tongues that he sought thus through the moil and horror of a thousand furious streets? He shall need a tongue no longer, he shall need no tongue for silence and the earth: he shall speak no word through the rooted lips, the snake's cold eye will peer for him through sockets of the brain, there will be no cry out of the heart where wells the vine.

The tarantula is crawling through the rotted oak, the adder lisps against the breast, cups fall: but the earth will endure forever. The flower of love is living in the wilderness, and the elmroot threads the bones of buried lovers.

The dead tongue withers and the dead heart rots, blind mouths crawl tunnels through the buried flesh, but the earth will endure forever; hair grows like April on the buried breast and from the sockets of the brain the death flowers grow and will not perish.

O flower of love whose strong lips drink us downward into death, in all things far and fleeting, enchantress of our twenty thousand days, the brain will madden and the heart be twisted, broken by her kiss, but glory, glory, glory, she remains: Immortal love, alone and aching in the wilderness, we cried to you: You were not absent from our loneliness.

I

ABOUT fifteen years ago, at the end of the second decade of this century, four people were standing together on the platform of the railway station of a town in the hills of western Catawba. This little station, really just a suburban adjunct of the larger town which, behind the concealing barrier of a rising ground, swept away a mile or two to the west and north, had become in recent years the popular point of arrival and departure for travellers to and from the cities of the east, and now, in fact, accommodated a much larger traffic than did the central station of the town, which was situated two miles westward around the powerful bend of the rails. For this reason a considerable number of people were now assembled here, and from their words and gestures, a quietly suppressed excitement that somehow seemed to infuse the drowsy mid-October afternoon with an electric vitality, it was possible to feel the thrill and menace of the coming train.

An observer would have felt in the complexion of this gathering a somewhat mixed quality—a quality that was at once strange and familiar, alien and native, cosmopolitan and provincial. It was not the single native quality of the usual crowd that one saw on the station platforms of the typical Catawba town as the trains passed through. This crowd was more mixed and varied, and it had a strong coloring of worldly smartness, the element of fashionable sophistication that one sometimes finds in a place where a native and alien population have come together. And such an inference was here warranted: the town of Altamont a mile or so away was a well-known resort and the mixed gathering on the station platform was fairly representative of its population. But all of these people, both strange and native, had been drawn here by a common experience, an event which has always been of first interest in the lives of all Americans. This event is the coming of the train.

It would have been evident to an observer that of the four people who were standing together at one end of the platform three—the two women and the boy—were connected by the relationship of blood. A stranger would have known instantly that the boy and the young woman were brother and sister and that the woman was their mother. The relation-

3

ship was somehow one of tone, texture, time, and energy, and of the grain and temper of the spirit. The mother was a woman of small but strong and solid figure. Although she was near her sixtieth year, her hair was jet black and her face, full of energy and power, was almost as smooth and unlined as the face of a girl. Her hair was brushed back from a forehead which was high, white, full, and naked-looking, and which, together with the expression of her eyes, which were brown, and rather worn and weak, but constantly thoughtful, constantly reflective, gave her face the expression of straight grave innocence that children have, and also of strong native intelligence and integrity. Her skin was milk white, soft of texture, completely colorless save for the nose, which was red, broad and fleshy at the base, and curiously masculine.

A stranger seeing her for the first time would have known somehow that the woman was a member of a numerous family, and that her face had the tribal look. He would somehow have felt certain that the woman had brothers and that if he could see them, they would look like her. Yet, this masculine quality was not a quality of sex, for the woman, save for the broad manlike nose, was as thoroughly female as a woman could be. It was rather a quality of tribe and character—a tribe and character that was decisively masculine.

The final impression of the woman might have been this:—that her life was somehow above and beyond a moral judgment, that no matter what the course or chronicle of her life may have been, no matter what crimes of error, avarice, ignorance, or thoughtlessness might be charged to her, no matter what suffering or evil consequences may have resulted to other people through any act of hers, her life was somehow beyond these accidents of time, training, and occasion, and the woman was as guiltless as a child, a river, an avalanche, or any force of nature whatsoever.

The younger of the two women was about thirty years old. She was a big woman, nearly six feet tall, large, and loose of bone and limb, almost gaunt. Both women were evidently creatures of tremendous energy, but where the mother suggested a constant, calm, and almost tireless force, the daughter was plainly one of those big, impulsive creatures of the earth who possess a terrific but undisciplined vitality, which they are ready to expend with a whole-souled and almost frenzied prodigality on any person, enterprise, or object which appeals to their grand affections.

This difference between the two women was also reflected in their faces. The face of the mother, for all its amazing flexibility, the startled animal-like intentness with which her glance darted from one object to another, and the mobility of her powerful and delicate mouth, which she pursed and convolved with astonishing flexibility in such a way as to show the constant reflective effort of her mind, was nevertheless the face of a woman whose spirit had an almost elemental quality of patience, fortitude and calm.

The face of the younger woman was large, high-boned, and generous and already marked by the frenzy and unrest of her own life. At moments it bore legibly and terribly the tortured stain of hysteria, of nerves stretched to the breaking point, of the furious impatience, unrest and dissonance of her own tormented spirit, and of impending exhaustion and collapse for her overwrought vitality. Yet, in an instant, this gaunt, strained, tortured, and almost hysterical face could be transformed by an expression of serenity, wisdom, and repose that would work unbelievably a miracle of calm and radiant beauty on the nervous, gaunt, and tortured features.

Now, each in her own way, the two women were surveying the other people on the platform and the new arrivals with a ravenous and absorptive interest, bestowing on each a wealth of information, comment, and speculation which suggested an encyclopædic knowledge of the history of every one in the community.

"—Why, yes, child," the mother was saying impatiently, as she turned her quick glance from a group of people who at the moment were the subject of discussion—"that's what I'm telling you!—Don't I know? . . . Didn't I grow up with all those people? . . . Wasn't Emma Smathers one of my girlhood friends? . . . That boy's not this woman's child at all. He's Emma Smathers' child by that first marriage."

"Well, that's news to me," the younger woman answered. "That's certainly news to me. I never knew Steve Randolph had been married more than once. I'd always thought that all that bunch were Mrs. Randolph's children."

"Why, of course not!" the mother cried impatiently. "She never had any of them except Lucille. All the rest of them were Emma's children. Steve Randolph was a man of forty-five when he married her. He'd been a widower for years—poor Emma died in childbirth when Bernice was born—nobody ever thought he'd marry again and nobody ever expected this woman to have any children of her own for she was almost as old as he was—why, yes!—hadn't she been married before, a widow, you know, when she met him, came here after her first husband's death from some place way out West—oh, Wyoming, or Nevada or Idaho, one of those States, you know—and had never had chick nor child, as the saying goes—till she married Steve. And that woman was every day of forty-four years old when Lucille was born."

"Uh-huh! . . . Ah-hah!" the younger woman muttered absently, in a tone of rapt and fascinated interest, as she looked distantly at the people in the other group, and reflectively stroked her large chin with a big, bony hand. "So Lucille, then, is really John's half-sister?"

"Why, of course!" the mother cried. "I thought every one knew that. Lucille's the only one that this woman can lay claim to. The rest of them were Emma's."

"—Well, that's certainly news to me," the younger woman said slowly as before. "It's the first *I* ever heard of it. . . . And you say she was forty-four when Lucille was born?"

"Now, she was all of *that*," the mother said. "I know. And she may have been even older."

"Well," the younger woman said, and now she turned to her silent husband, Barton, with a hoarse snigger, "it just goes to show that while there's life there's hope, doesn't it? So cheer up, honey," she said to him, "we may have a chance yet." But despite her air of rough banter her clear eyes for a moment had a look of deep pain and sadness in them.

"Chance!" the mother cried strongly, with a little scornful pucker of the lips—"why, of course there is! If I was your age again I'd have a dozen—and never think a thing of it." For a moment she was silent, pursing her reflective lips. Suddenly a faint sly smile began to flicker at the edges of her lips, and turning the boy, she addressed him with an air of sly and bantering mystery:

"Now, boy," she said—"there's lots of things that you don't know . . . you always thought you were the last—the youngest—didn't you?"

"Well, wasn't I?" he said.

"H'm!" she said with a little scornful smile and an air of great mystery — "There's lots that I could tell you——"

"Oh, my God!" he groaned, turning towards his sister with an imploring face. "More mysteries! . . . The next thing I'll find that there were five sets of triplets after I was born— Well, come on, Mama," he cried impatiently. "Don't hint around all day about it. . . . What's the secret now—how many were there?"

"H'm!" she said with a little bantering, scornful, and significant smile.

"O Lord!" he groaned again— "Did she ever tell you what it was?" Again he turned imploringly to his sister.

She snickered hoarsely, a strange high-husky and derisive falsetto laugh, at the same time prodding him stiffly in the ribs with her big fingers:

"Hi, hi, hi, hi, hi," she laughed. "More spooky business, hey? You don't know the half of it. She'll be telling you next you were only the fourteenth."

"H'm!" the older woman said, with a little scornful smile of her pursed lips. "Now I could tell him more than that! The fourteenth! Pshaw!" she said contemptuously—"I could tell him——"

"O God!" he groaned miserably. "I knew it! . . . I don't want to hear it."

"K, k, k, k, k," the younger woman snickered derisively, prodding him in the ribs again.

"No, sir," the older woman went on strongly—"and that's not all either!— Now, boy, I want to tell you something that you didn't know," and as she spoke she turned the strange and worn stare of her serious brown eyes on him, and levelled a half-clasped hand, fingers pointing, a gesture loose, casual, and instinctive and powerful as a man's.— "There's a lot I could tell you that you never heard. Long years after you were born, child—why, at the time I took you children to the Saint Louis Fair—" here her face grew stern and sad, she pursed her lips strongly and shook her head with a short convulsive movement—"oh, when I think of it—to think what I went through—oh, awful, awful, you know," she whispered ominously.

"Now, Mama, for God's sake, I don't want to hear it!" he fairly shouted, beside himself with exasperation and foreboding. "God-damn it, can we have no peace—even when I go away!" he cried bitterly and illogically. "Always these damned gloomy hints and revelations—this Pentland spooky stuff," he yelled—"this damned I-could-if-I-wanted-to-tell-you air of mystery, horror, and damnation!" he shouted incoherently. "Who cares? What does it matter?" he cried, adding desperately, "I don't want to hear about it— No one cares."

"Why, child, now, I was only saying—" she began hastily and diplomatically.

"All right, all right, all right," he muttered. "I don't care——"

"But, as I say, now," she resumed.

"I don't care!" he shouted. "Peace, peace. peace, peace, peace," he muttered in a crazy tone as he turned to his sister. "A moment's peace for all of us before we die. A moment of peace, peace, peace."

"Why, boy, I'll vow," the mother said in a vexed tone, fixing her reproving glance on him, "what on earth's come over you? You act like a regular crazy man. I'll vow you do."

"A moment's peace!" he muttered again, thrusting one hand wildly through his hair. "I beg and beseech you for a moment's peace before we perish!"

"K, k, k, k, k," the younger woman snickered derisively, as she poked him stiffly in the ribs— "There's no peace for the weary. It's like that river that goes on forever," she said with a faint loose curving of lewd humor around the edges of her generous big mouth— "Now you see, don't you?" she said, looking at him with this lewd and challenging look. "You see what it's like now, don't you? . . . You're the lucky one! You got away! You're smart enough to go way off somewhere to college—to Boston—Harvard—anywhere—but you're away from it. You get it for a short time when you come home. How do you think I stand it?" she said challengingly. "I have to hear it all the time. . . . Oh, all the time, and all the time, and all the time!" she said with a kind of weary desperation. "If they'd only leave me alone for five minutes some time I think I'd be able to pull myself together, but it's this way all the time and all the time and all the time. You see, don't you?"

But now, having finished, in a tone of hoarse and panting exasperation, her frenzied protest, she relapsed immediately into a state of marked, weary, and dejected resignation.

"Well, I know, I know," she said in a weary and indifferent voice. ". . . Forget about it. . . . Talking does no good. . . . Just try to make the best of it the little time you're here. . . . I used to think something could be done about it . . . but I know different now," she muttered, although she would have been unable to explain the logical meaning of these incoherent and disjointed phrases.

"Hah? . . . What say?" the mother now cried sharply, darting her glances from one to another with the quick, startled, curiously puzzled intentness of an animal or a bird. "What say?" she cried sharply again, as no one answered. "I thought——"

But fortunately, at this moment, this strange and disturbing flash in which had been revealed the blind and tangled purposes, the powerful and obscure impulses, the tormented nerves, the whole tragic perplexity of soul which was of the very fabric of their lives, was interrupted by a

commotion in one of the groups upon the platform, and by a great guffaw of laughter which instantly roused these three people from this
painful and perplexing scene, and directed their startled attention to the
place from which the laughter came.

And now again they heard the great guffaw—a solid "Haw! Haw!
Haw!" which was full of such an infectious exuberance of animal good-
nature that other people on the platform began to smile instinctively,
and to look affectionately towards the owner of the laugh.

Already, at the sound of the laugh, the young woman had forgotten
the weary and dejected resignation of the moment before, and with
an absent and yet eager look of curiosity in her eyes, she was staring
towards the group from which the laugh had come, and herself now
laughing absently, she was stroking her big chin in a gesture of meditative curiosity, saying:

"Hah! Hah! Hah! . . . That's George Pentland. . . . You can tell
him anywhere by his laugh."

"Why, yes," the mother was saying briskly, with satisfaction. "That's
George all right. I'd know him in the dark the minute that I heard that
laugh.— And say, what about it? He's always had it—why, ever since he
was a kid-boy—and was going around with Steve. . . . Oh, he'd come
right out with it anywhere, you know, in Sunday school, church, or
while the preacher was sayin' prayers before collection—that big, loud
laugh, you know, that you could hear, from here to yonder, as the sayin'
goes. . . . Now I don't know where it comes from—none of the others
ever had it in our family; now we all liked to laugh well enough, but I
never heard no such laugh as that from any of 'em—there's one thing
sure, Will Pentland never laughed like that in his life— Oh, Pett, you
know! Pett!"—a scornful and somewhat malicious look appeared on the
woman's face as she referred to her brother's wife in that whining and
affected tone with which women imitate the speech of other women
whom they do not like—"Pett got so mad at him one time when he
laughed right out in church that she was goin' to take the child right
home an' whip him.—Told me, says to me, you know—'Oh, I could
wring his neck! He'll disgrace us all,' she says, 'unless I cure him of it,'
says, 'He burst right out in that great roar of his while Doctor Baines
was sayin' his prayers this morning until you couldn't hear a word the
preacher said.' Said, 'I was so mortified to think he could do a thing like
that that I'd a-beat the blood right out of him if I'd had my buggy whip,'
says, 'I don't know where it comes from'—oh, sneerin'-like, you know,"

the woman said, imitating the other woman's voice with a sneering and viperous dislike—" 'I don't know where it comes from unless it's some of that common Pentland blood comin' out in him'—'Now you listen to me,' I says; oh, I looked her in the eye, you know"—here the woman looked at her daughter with the straight steady stare of her worn brown eyes, illustrating her speech with the loose and powerful gesture of the half-clasped finger-pointing hand—" 'you listen to me. I don't know where that child gets his laugh,' I says, 'but you can bet your bottom dollar that he never got it from his father—or any other Pentland that I ever heard of—for none of them ever laughed that way—Will, or Jim, or Sam, or George, or Ed, or Father, or even Uncle Bacchus,' I said—'no, nor old Bill Pentland either, who was that child's great-grandfather—for I've seen an' heard 'em all,' I says. 'And as for this common Pentland blood you speak of, Pett'—oh, I guess I talked to her pretty straight, you know," she said with a little bitter smile, and the short, powerful, and convulsive tremor of her strong pursed lips—" 'as for that common Pentland blood you speak of, Pett,' I says, 'I never heard of that either—for we stood high in the community' I says, 'and we all felt that Will was lowerin' himself when he married a Creasman!' "

"Oh, you didn't say that, Mama, surely not," the young woman said with a hoarse, protesting, and yet abstracted laugh, continuing to survey the people on the platform with a bemused and meditative curiosity, and stroking her big chin thoughtfully as she looked at them, pausing from time to time to grin in a comical and rather formal manner, bow graciously, and murmur:

"How-do-you-do? ah-hah? How-do-you-do, Mrs. Willis?"

"Haw! Haw! Haw!" Again the great laugh of empty animal good nature burst out across the station platform, and this time George Pentland turned from the group of which he was a member and looked vacantly around him, his teeth bared with savage joy, as, with two brown fingers of his strong left hand, he dug vigorously into the muscular surface of his hard thigh. It was an animal reflex, instinctive and unconscious, habitual to him in moments of strong mirth.

He was a powerful and handsome young man in his early thirties, with coal-black hair, a strong thick neck, powerful shoulders, and the bull vitality of the athlete. He had a red, sensual, curiously animal and passionate face, and when he laughed his great guffaw, his red lips were bared over two rows of teeth that were white and regular and solid as ivory.

—But now, the paroxysm of that savage and mindless laughter having left him, George Pentland had suddenly espied the mother and her children, waved to them in genial greeting, and excusing himself from his companions—a group of young men and women who wore the sporting look and costume of "the country club crowd"—he was walking towards his kinsmen at an indolent swinging stride, pausing to acknowledge heartily the greetings of people on every side, with whom he was obviously a great favorite.

As he approached, he bared his strong white teeth again in greeting, and in a drawling, rich-fibred voice, which had unmistakably the Pentland quality of sensual fulness, humor, and assurance, and a subtle but gloating note of pleased self-satisfaction, he said:

"Hello, Aunt Eliza, how are you? Hello, Helen—how are you, Hugh?" he said in his high, somewhat accusing, but very strong and masculine voice, putting his big hand in an easy affectionate way on Barton's arm. "Where the hell you been keepin' yourself anyway?" he said accusingly. "Why don't some of you folks come over to see us sometime? Ella was askin' about you all the other day—wanted to know why Helen didn't come around more often."

"Well, George, I tell you how it is," the young woman said with an air of great sincerity and earnestness. "Hugh and I have intended to come over a hundred times, but life has been just one damned thing after another all summer long. If I could only have a moment's peace—if I could only get away by myself for a moment—if *they* would only leave me *alone* for an hour at a time, I think I could get myself together again—do you know what I mean, George?" she said hoarsely and eagerly, trying to enlist him in her sympathetic confidence—"If they'd only do something for *themselves* once in a while—but they *all* come to me when anything goes wrong—they never let me have a moment's peace—until at times I think I'm going crazy—I get *queer*—funny, you know," she said vaguely and incoherently. "I don't know whether something happened Tuesday or last week or if I just imagined it." And for a moment her big gaunt face had the dull strained look of hysteria.

"The strain on her has been very great this summer," said Barton in a deep and grave tone. "It's—it's," he paused carefully, deeply, searching for a word, and looked down as he flicked an ash from his long cigar, "it's—been too much for her. Everything's on her shoulders," he concluded in his deep grave voice.

"My God, George, what is it?" she said quietly and simply, in the tone of one begging for enlightenment. "Is it going to be this way all our lives? Is there never going to be any peace or happiness for us? Does it always have to be this way? Now I want to ask you—is there nothing in the world but trouble?"

"Trouble!" he said derisively. "Why, I've had more trouble than any one of you ever heard of. . . . I've had enough to kill a dozen people . . . but when I saw it wasn't goin' to kill me, I quit worryin'. . . . So you do the same thing," he advised heartily. "Hell, don't *worry*, Helen! . . . It never got you anywhere. . . . You'll be all right," he said. "You got nothin' to worry over. You don't know what trouble is."

"Oh, I'd be all right, George—I think I could stand anything—all the rest of it—if it wasn't for Papa. . . . I'm almost crazy from worrying about him this summer. There were three times there when I knew he was gone. . . . And I honestly believe I pulled him back each time by main strength and determination—do you know what I mean?" she said hoarsely and eagerly—"I was just determined not to let him go. If his heart had stopped beating I believe I could have done something to make it start again—I'd have stood over him and blown my breath into him— got my blood into him—shook him," she said with a powerful, nervous movement of her big hands—"anything just to keep him alive."

"She's—she's—saved his life—time after time," said Barton slowly, flicking his cigar ash carefully away, and looking down deeply, searching for a word.

"He'd—he'd—have been a dead man long ago—if it hadn't been for her."

"Yeah—I know she has," George Pentland drawled agreeably. "I know you've sure stuck by Uncle Will—I guess he knows it, too."

"It's not that I mind it, George—you know what I mean?" she said eagerly. "Good heavens! I believe I could give away a dozen lives if I thought it was going to save his life! . . . But it's the *strain* of it. . . . Month after month . . . year after year . . . lying awake at night wondering if he's all right over there in that back room in Mama's house— wondering if he's keeping warm in that old cold house——"

"Why, no, child," the older woman said hastily. "I kept a good fire burnin' in that room all last winter—that was the warmest room in the whole place—there wasn't a warmer——"

But immediately she was engulfed, swept aside, obliterated in the flood-tide of the other's speech.

"—Wondering if he's sick or needs me—if he's begun to bleed again—

oh! George, it makes me sick to think about it—that poor old man left there all alone, rotting away with that awful cancer, with that horrible smell about him all the time—everything he wears gets simply *stiff* with that rotten corrupt matter— Do you know what it is to wait, wait, wait, year after year, and year after year, never knowing when he's going to die, to have him hang on by a thread until it seems you've lived forever—that there'll never be an end—that you'll never have a chance to live your own life—to have a moment's peace or rest or happiness yourself? My God, does it always have to be this way? . . . Can I never have a moment's happiness? . . . Must they *always* come to me? Does *everything* have to be put on my shoulders? . . . Will you tell me that?" Her voice had risen to a note of frenzied despair. She was glaring at her cousin with a look of desperate and frantic entreaty, her whole gaunt figure tense and strained with the stress of her hysteria.

"That's—that's the trouble now," said Barton, looking down and searching for the word. "She's . . . She's . . . made the goat for every one. . . . She . . . she has to do it all. . . . That's . . . that's the thing that's got her down."

"Not that I mind—if it will do any good. . . . Good heavens, Papa's life means more to me than anything on earth. . . . I'd keep him alive at any cost as long as there was a breath left in him. . . . But it's the strain of it, the *strain* of it—to wait, to wait year after year, to feel it hanging over you all the time, never to know when he will die—always the *strain,* the strain—do you see what I mean, George?" she said hoarsely, eagerly, and pleadingly. "You see, don't you?"

"I sure do, Helen," he said sympathetically, digging at his thigh, and with a swift, cat-like grimace of his features. "I know it's been mighty tough on you. . . . How is Uncle Will now?" he said. "Is he any better?"

"Why, yes," the mother was saying, "he seemed to improve—" but she was cut off immediately.

"Oh, yes," the daughter said in a tone of weary dejection. "He pulled out of this last spell and got well enough to make the trip to Baltimore— we sent him back a week ago to take another course of treatments. . . . But it does no real good, George. . . . They can't cure him. . . . We know that now. . . . They've told us that. . . . It only prolongs the agony. . . . They help him for a little while and then it all begins again. . . . Poor old man!" she said, and her eyes were wet. "I'd give everything I have—my own blood, my own life—if it would do him any good—but,

George, he's gone!" she said desperately. "Can't you understand that? . . . They can't save him! . . . Nothing can save him! . . . Papa's a dead man now!"

George looked gravely sympathetic for a moment, winced swiftly, dug hard fingers in his thigh, and then said:

"Who went to Baltimore with him?"

"Why, Luke's up there," the mother said. "We had a letter from him yesterday—said Mr. Gant looks much better already—eats well, you know, has a good appetite—and Luke says he's in good spirits. Now——"

"Oh, Mama, for heaven's sake!" the daughter cried. "What's the use of talking that way? . . . He's not getting any better. . . . Papa's a sick man—dying—good God! Can no one ever get that into their heads!" she burst out furiously. "Am I the only one that realizes how sick he is?"

"No, now I was only sayin'," the mother began hastily— "Well, as I say, then," she went on, "Luke's up there with him—and Gene's on his way there now—he's goin' to stop off there tomorrow on his way up north to school."

"Gene!" cried George Pentland in a high, hearty, bantering tone, turning to address the boy directly for the first time. "What's all this I hear about you, son?" He clasped his muscular hand around the boy's arm in a friendly but powerful grip. "Ain't one college enough for you, boy?" he drawled, becoming deliberately ungrammatical and speaking good-naturedly but with a trace of the mockery which the wastrel and ne'er-do-well sometimes feels towards people who have had the energy and application required for steady or concentrated effort. "Are you one of those fellers who needs two or three colleges to hold him down?"

The boy flushed, grinned uncertainly, and said nothing.

"Why, son," drawled George in his hearty, friendly and yet bantering tone, in which a note of malice was evident, "you'll be gettin' so educated an' high brow here before long that you won't be able to talk to the rest of us at all. . . . You'll be floatin' around there so far up in the clouds that you won't even see a roughneck like me, much less talk to him"—As he went on with this kind of sarcasm, his speech had become almost deliberately illiterate, as if trying to emphasize the superior virtue of the rough, hearty, home-grown fellow in comparison with the bookish scholar.

"—Where's he goin' to this time, Aunt Eliza?" he said, turning to her questioningly, but still holding the boy's arm in his strong grip. "Where's he headin' for now?"

"Why," she said, stroking her pursed serious mouth with a slightly puzzled movement, "he says he's goin' to Harvard. I reckon," she said, in the same puzzled tone, "it's all right—I guess he knows what he's about. Says he's made up his mind to go—I told him," she said, and shook her head again, "that I'd send him for a year if he wanted to try it—an' then he'll have to get out an' shift for himself. We'll see," she said. "I reckon it's all right."

"Harvard, eh?" said George Pentland. "Boy, you *are* flyin' high! . . . What you goin' to do up there?"

The boy, furiously red of face, squirmed, and finally stammered: "Why . . . I . . . guess . . . I guess I'll do some studying!"

"You *guess* you will!" roared George. "You'd damn well *better* do some studying—I bet your mother'll take it out of your hide if she finds you loafin' on her money."

"Why, yes," the mother said, nodding seriously, "I told him it was up to him to make the most of this——"

"Harvard, eh!" George Pentland said again, slowly looking his cousin over from head to foot. "Son, you're flyin' high, you are! . . . Now don't fly so high you never get back to earth again! . . . You know the rest of us who didn't go to Harvard still have to walk around upon the ground down here," he said. "So don't fly too high or we may not even be able to see you!"

"George! George!" said the young woman in a low tone, holding one hand to her mouth, and bending over to whisper loudly as she looked at her young brother. "Do you think any one could fly very high with a pair of feet like that?"

George Pentland looked at the boy's big feet for a moment, shaking his head slowly in much wonderment.

"Hell, no!" he said at length. "He'd never get off the ground! . . . But if you cut 'em off," he said, "he'd go right up like a balloon, wouldn't he? Haw! Haw! Haw! Haw!" The great guffaw burst from him, and grinning with his solid teeth, he dug blindly at his thigh.

"Hi, hi, hi, hi, hi," the sister jeered, seeing the boy's flushed and angry face and prodding him derisively in the ribs— "This is our Harvard boy! k, k, k, k!"

"Don't let 'em kid you, son," said George now in an amiable and friendly manner. "Good luck to you! Give 'em hell when you get up there! . . . You're the only one of us who ever had guts enough to go through college, and we're proud of you! . . . Tell Uncle Bascom and

Aunt Louise and all the rest of 'em hello for me when you get to Boston. . . . And remember me to your father and Luke when you get to Baltimore. . . . Good-bye, 'Gene—I've got to leave you now. Good luck, son," and with a friendly grip of his powerful hand he turned to go. "You folks come over sometime—all of you," he said in parting. "We'd like to see you." And he went away.

At this moment, all up and down the platform, people had turned to listen to the deep excited voice of a young man who was saying in a staccato tone of astounded discovery:

"You *don't* mean it! . . . You *swear* she did! . . . And *you* were there and saw it with your *own* eyes! . . . Well, if that don't beat all I ever heard of! . . . I'll be *damned!*" after which ejaculation, with an astounded falsetto laugh, he looked about him in an abstracted and unseeing manner, thrust one hand quickly and nervously into his trouser's pocket in such a way that his fine brown coat came back, and the large diamond-shaped pin of the Delta Kappa Epsilon fraternity was revealed, and at the same time passing one thin nervous hand repeatedly over the lank brown hair that covered his small and well-shaped head, and still muttering in tones of stupefied disbelief—"Lord! Lord! . . . What do you know about that?" suddenly espied the woman and her two children at the other end of the platform, and without a moment's pause, turned on his heel, and walked towards them, at the same time muttering to his astonished friends:

"Wait a minute! . . . Some one over here I've got to speak to! . . . Back in a minute!"

He approached the mother and her children rapidly, at his stiff, prim and somewhat lunging stride, his thin face fixed eagerly upon them, bearing towards them with a driving intensity of purpose as if the whole interest and energy of his life was focussed on them, as if some matter of the most vital consequence depended on his reaching them as soon as possible. Arrived, he immediately began to address the other youth without a word of greeting or explanation, bursting out with the sudden fragmentary explosiveness that was part of him:

"Are you taking this train, too? . . . Are you going today? . . . Well, what did you decide to do?" he demanded mysteriously in an accusing and challenging fashion. "Have you made up your mind yet? . . ."

"Pett Barnes says you've decided on Harvard. Is that it?"

"Yes, it is."

"Lord, Lord!" said the youth, laughing his falsetto laugh again. "I don't see how you can! . . . You'd better come on with me. . . . What ever got into your head to do a thing like that?" he said in a challenging tone. "Why do you want to go to a place like that?"

"Hah? What say?" The mother who had been looking from one to the other of the two boys with the quick and startled attentiveness of an animal, now broke in:

"You know each other. . . . Hah? . . . You're taking this train, too, you say?" she said sharply.

"Ah-hah-hah!" the young man laughed abruptly, nervously; grinned, made a quick stiff little bow, and said with nervous engaging respectfulness: "Yes, Ma'am! . . . Ah-hah-hah! . . . How d'ye do! . . . How d'ye do, Mrs. Gant?" He shook hands with her quickly, still laughing his broken and nervous "ah-hah-hah"—"How d'ye do," he said, grinning nervously at the younger woman and at Barton. "Ah-hah-hah! How d'ye do!"

The older woman still holding his hand in her rough worn clasp looked up at him a moment calmly, her lips puckered in tranquil meditation:

"Now," she said quietly, in the tone of a person who refuses to admit failure, "I know you. I know your face. Just give me a moment and I'll call you by your name."

The young man grinned quickly, nervously, and then said respectfully in his staccato speech:

"Yes, Ma'am. . . . Ah-hah-hah. . . . Robert Weaver."

"*Ah-h,* that's *so!*" she cried, and shook his hand with sudden warmth. "You're Robert Weaver's boy, of course."

"Ah-hah-hah!" said Robert, with his quick nervous laugh. "Yes, Ma'am. . . . That's right. . . . Ah-hah-hah. . . . Gene and I went to school together. We were in the same class at the University."

"Why, of course!" she cried in a tone of complete enlightenment, and then went on in a rather vexed manner, "I'll *vow!* I knew you all along! I knew that I'd seen you just as soon as I saw your face! Your name just slipped my mind a moment—and then, of course, it all flashed over me. . . . You're Robert Weaver's boy! . . . And you *are,*" she still held his hand in her strong, motherly and friendly clasp, and looking at him with a little sly smile hovering about the corners of her mouth, she was silent a moment, regarding him quizzically—"now, boy," she said quietly, "you may think I've got a pretty poor memory for names and faces—but I want to tell you something that may surprise you. . . . I

know more about you than you think I do. Now," she said, "I'm going
to tell you something and you can tell me if I'm right."

"Ah-hah-hah!" said Robert respectfully. "Yes, Ma'am."

"You were born," she went on slowly and deliberately, "on September 2nd, 1898, and you are just two years and one month and one day
older than this boy here—" she nodded to her own son. "Now you can
tell me if I'm right or wrong."

"Ah-hah-hah!" said Robert. "Yes, Ma'am. . . . That's right. . . .
You're absolutely right," he cried, and then in an astounded and admiring tone, he said: "Well, I'll declare. . . . If that don't beat all! . . .
How on earth did you ever remember it!" he cried in an astonished
tone that obviously was very gratifying to her vanity.

"Well, now, I'll tell you," she said with a little complacent smile—
"I'll tell you how I *know*. . . . I remember the day you were born, boy—
because it was on that very day that one of my own children—my son,
Luke—was allowed to get up out of bed after havin' typhoid fever. . . .
That very day, sir, when Mr. Gant came home to dinner, he said—'Well,
I was just talking to Robert Weaver on the street and everything's all
right. His wife gave birth to a baby boy this morning and he says she's
out of danger.' And I know I said to him, 'Well, then, it's been a lucky
day for both of us. McGuire was here this morning and he said Luke
is now well enough to be up and about. He's out of danger.'—And I
reckon," she went on quietly, "that's why the date made such an impression on me—of course, Luke had been awfully sick," she said
gravely, and shook her head, "we thought he was goin' to die more than
once—so when the doctor came and told me he was out of danger—
well, it was a day of rejoicin' for me, sure enough. But that's how I
know—September 2nd, 1898—that's when it was, all right, the very day
when you were born."

"Ah-hah-hah!" said Robert. "That is certainly right. . . . Well, if
that don't beat all!" he cried with his astounded and engaging air of surprise. "The most remarkable thing I ever heard of!" he said solemnly.

"So the next time you see your father," the woman said, with the
tranquil satisfaction of omniscience, "you tell him that you met Eliza
Pentland—he'll know who *I* am, boy—I can assure you—for we were
born and brought up within five miles from each other and you can
tell him that she knew you right away, and even told you to the hour
and minute the day when you were born! . . . You tell him that," she
said.

"Yes, Ma'am!" said Robert respectfully, "I certainly will! . . . I'll tell him! . . . That is certainly a remarkable thing. . . . Ah-hah-hah! . . . Beats all I ever heard of! . . . Ah-hah-hah," he kept bowing and smiling to the young woman and her husband, and muttering "ah-hah-hah! . . . Pleased to have met you. . . . Got to go now: some one over here I've got to see . . . but I'll certainly tell him . . . ah-hah-hah. . . . Gene, I'll see you on the train. . . . Good-bye. . . . Good-bye. . . . Glad to have met you all . . . Ah-hah-hah. . . . Certainly a remarkable thing. . . . Good-bye!" and turning abruptly, he left them, walking rapidly along at his stiff, prim, curiously lunging stride.

The younger woman looked after the boy's tall form as he departed, stroking her chin in a reflective and abstracted manner:

"So that's Judge Robert Weaver's son, is it? . . . Well," she went on, nodding her head vigorously in a movement of affirmation. "He's all right. . . . He's got good manners. . . . He looks and acts like a gentleman. . . . You can see he's had a good bringing up. . . . I like him!" she declared positively again.

"Why, yes," said the mother, who had been following the tall retreating form with a reflective look, her hands loose-folded at her waist—"Why, yes," she continued, nodding her head in a thoughtful and conceding manner that was a little comical in its implications—"He's a good-looking all-right sort of a boy. . . . And he certainly seems to be intelligent enough." She was silent for a moment, pursing her lips thoughtfully and then concluded with a little nod—"Well, now, the boy may be all right. . . . I'm not saying that he isn't. . . . He may turn out all right, after all."

"All right?" her daughter said, frowning a little and showing a little annoyance, but with a faint lewd grin around the corners of her mouth —"what do you mean by all right, Mama? Why, of course he's all right. . . . What makes you think he's not?"

The other woman was silent for another moment: when she spoke again, her manner was tinged with portent, and she turned and looked at her daughter a moment in a sudden, straight and deadly fashion before she spoke:

"Now, child," she said, "I'm going to tell you: perhaps everything will turn out all right for that boy—I hope it does—but——"

"Oh, my God!" the younger woman laughed hoarsely but with a shade of anger, and turning, prodded her brother stiffly in the ribs. "Now we'll get it!" she sniggered, prodding him, "k-k-k-k-k! What do you call it?" she said with a lewd frowning grin that was indescribably comic in its evocations of coarse humor—"the low down?—the dirt?— Did you ever know it to fail?—The moment that you meet any one, and up comes the family corpse."

"—Well, now, child, I'm not saying anything against the boy—perhaps it won't touch him—maybe he'll be the one to escape—to turn out all right—but——"

"Oh, my God!" the younger woman groaned, rolling her eyes around in a comical and imploring fashion. "Here it comes."

"You are too young to know about it yourself," the other went on gravely—"you belong to another generation—you don't know about it— but I *do*." She paused again, shook her pursed lips with a convulsive pucker of distaste, and then looking at her daughter again in her straight and deadly fashion, said slowly, with a powerful movement of the hand:

"There's been insanity in that boy's family for generations back!"

"Oh, my God! I knew it!" the other groaned.

"Yes, sir!" the mother said implacably—"and two of his aunts—Robert Weaver's own sisters died raving maniacs—and Robert Weaver's mother herself was insane for the last twenty years of her life up to the hour of her death—and I've heard tell that it went back——"

"Well, deliver me," the younger woman checked her, frowning, speaking almost sullenly. "I don't want to hear any more about it. . . . It's a mighty funny thing that they all seem to get along now—better than we do . . . so let's let bygones be bygones . . . don't dig up the past."

Turning to her brother with a little frowning smile, she said wearily: "Did you ever know it to fail? . . . They know it all, don't they?" she said mysteriously. "The minute you meet any one you like, they spill the dirt. . . . Well, I don't care," she muttered. "You stick to people like that. . . . He looks like a nice boy and—" with an impressed look over towards Robert's friends, she concluded, "he goes with a nice crowd. . . . You stick to that kind of people. I'm all for him."

Now the mother was talking again: the boy could see her powerful and delicate mouth convolving with astonishing rapidity in a series of pursed thoughtful lips, tremulous smiles, bantering and quizzical jocosities, old sorrow and memory, quiet gravity, the swift easy fluency of tears that the coming of a train always induced in her, thoughtful seriousness, and sudden hopeful speculation.

"Well, boy," she was now saying gravely, "you are going—as the sayin' goes—" here she shook her head slightly, strongly, rapidly with powerful puckered lips, and instantly her weak worn eyes of brown were wet with tears "—as the sayin' goes—to a strange land—a stranger among strange people.—It may be a long long time," she whispered in an old husky tone, her eyes tear-wet as she shook her head mysteriously with a brave pathetic smile that suddenly filled the boy with rending pity, anguish of the soul, and a choking sense of exasperation and of woman's unfairness "—I hope we are all here when you come back again. . . . I hope you find us all alive. . . ." She smiled bravely, mysteriously, tearfully. "You never know," she whispered, "you never know."

"Mama," he could hear his voice sound hoarsely and remotely in his throat, choked with anguish and exasperation at her easy fluency of sorrow, "—Mama—in Christ's name! Why do you have to act like this every time some one goes away! . . . I beg of you, for God's sake, not to do it!"

"Oh, stop it! Stop it!" his sister said in a rough, peremptory and yet kindly tone to the mother, her eyes grave and troubled, but with a faint rough smile about the edges of her generous mouth. "He's not going away forever! Why, good heavens, you act as if some one is dead! Boston's not so far away you'll never see him again! The trains are running every day, you know. . . . Besides," she said abruptly and with an assurance that infuriated the boy, "he's not going today, anyway. Why, you haven't any intention of going today, you know you haven't," she said to him. "He's been fooling you all along," she now said, turning to the mother with an air of maddening assurance. "He has no idea of taking that train. He's going to wait over until tomorrow. I've known it all along."

The boy went stamping away from them up the platform, and then came stamping back at them while the other people on the platform grinned and stared.

"Helen, in God's name!" he croaked frantically. "Why do you start that when I'm all packed up and waiting here at the God-damned station for the train! You *know* I'm going away today!" he yelled, with a sudden sick desperate terror in his heart as he thought that something might now come in the way of going. "You *know* I am! Why did we come here? What in Christ's name are we waiting for if you don't think I'm going?"

The young woman laughed her high, husky laugh which was almost deliberately irritating and derisive—"Hi! Hi! Hi! Hi! Hi!"—and prodded him in the ribs with her large stiff fingers. Then, almost wearily, she turned away, plucking at her large chin absently, and said: "Well, have it your own way! It's your own funeral! If you're determined to go today, no one can stop you. But I don't see why you can't just as well wait over till tomorrow."

"Why, yes!" the mother now said briskly and confidently. "That's exactly what I'd do if I were you! . . . Now, it's not going to do a bit of harm to any one if you're a day or so late in gettin' there. . . . Now I've never been there myself," she went on in her tone of tranquil sarcasm, "but I've always heard that Harvard University was a good big sort of place—and I'll bet you'll find," the mother now said gravely, with a strong slow nod of conviction—"I'll bet you'll find that it's right there where it always was when you get there. I'll bet you find they haven't moved a foot," she said, "and let me tell you something, boy," she now continued, looking at him almost sternly, but with the ghost of a smile about her powerful and delicate mouth "—now I haven't had your education and I reckon I don't know as much about universities as you do— but I've never heard of one yet that would run a feller away for bein' a day late as long as he's got money enough to pay his tuition. . . . Now you'll find 'em waitin' for you when you get there—and *you'll get in,*" she said slowly and powerfully. "You don't have to worry about that— they'll be glad to see you, and they'll take you in a hurry when they see you've got the price."

"Now, Mama," he said in a quiet frenzied tone, "I beg of you, for God's sake, please, not to——"

"All right, all right," the mother answered hastily in a placating tone, "I was only sayin'——"

"If you will kindly, please, for God's sake——"

"K-k-k-k-k!" his sister snickered, poking him in the ribs.

But now the train was coming. Down the powerful shining tracks a half mile away, the huge black snout of the locomotive swung slowly round the magnificent bend and flare of the rails that went into the railway yards of Altamont two miles away, and with short explosive thunders of its squat funnel came barging slowly forward. Across the golden pollenated haze of the warm autumnal afternoon they watched it with numb lips and an empty hollowness of fear, delight, and sorrow in their hearts.

And from the sensual terror, the ecstatic tension of that train's approach, all things before, around, about the boy came to instant life, to such sensuous and intolerable poignancy of life as a doomed man might feel who looks upon the world for the last time from the platform of the scaffold where he is to die. He could feel, taste, smell, and see everything with an instant still intensity, the animate fixation of a vision seen instantly, fixed forever in the mind of him who sees it, and sense the clumped dusty autumn masses of the trees that bordered the tracks upon the left, and smell the thick exciting hot tarred caulking of the tracks, the dry warmth and good worn wooden smell of the powerful railway ties, and see the dull rusty red, the gaping emptiness and joy of a freight car, its rough floor whitened with soft siltings of thick flour, drawn in upon a spur of rusty track behind a warehouse of raw concrete blocks, and see with sudden desolation, the warehouse flung down rawly, newly, there among the hot, humid, spermy, nameless, thick-leaved field-growth of the South.

Then the locomotive drew in upon them, loomed enormously above them, and slowly swept by them with a terrific drive of eight-locked pistoned wheels, all higher than their heads, a savage furnace-flare of heat, a hard hose-thick hiss of steam, a moment's vision of a lean old head, an old gloved hand of cunning on the throttle, a glint of demon hawk-eyes fixed forever on the rails, a huge tangle of gauges, levers, valves, and throttles, and the goggled blackened face of the fireman, lit by an intermittent hell of flame, as he bent and swayed with rhythmic swing of laden shovel at his furnace doors.

The locomotive passed above them, darkening the sunlight from their faces, engulfing them at once and filling them with terror, drawing the souls out through their mouths with the God-head of its instant absoluteness, and leaving them there, emptied, frightened, fixed forever, a cluster of huddled figures, a bough of small white staring faces, upturned, silent, and submissive, small, lonely, and afraid.

Then as the heavy rust-black coaches rumbled past, and the wheels ground slowly to a halt, the boy could see his mother's white stunned face beside him, the naked startled innocence of her eyes, and feel her rough worn clasp upon his arm, and hear her startled voice, full of apprehension, terror, and surprise, as she said sharply:

"Hah? What say? Is this his train? I thought——"

It was his train and it had come to take him to the strange and secret heart of the great North that he had never known, but whose austere and lonely image, whose frozen heat and glacial fire, and dark stern beauty had blazed in his vision since he was a child. For he had dreamed and hungered for the proud unknown North with that wild ecstasy, that intolerable and wordless joy of longing and desire, which only a Southerner can feel. With a heart of fire, a brain possessed, a spirit haunted by the strange, secret and unvisited magic of the proud North, he had always known that some day he should find it—his heart's hope and his father's country, the lost but unforgotten half of his own soul,—and take it for his own.

And now that day had come, and these two images—call them rather lights and weathers of man's soul—of the world-far, lost and lonely South, and the fierce, the splendid, strange and secret North were swarming like a madness through his blood. And just as he had seen a thousand images of the buried and silent South which he had known all his life, so now he had a vision of the proud fierce North with all its shining cities, and its tides of life. He saw the rocky sweetness of its soil and its green loveliness, and he knew its numb soft prescience, its entrail-stirring ecstasy of coming snow, its smell of harbors and its traffic of proud ships.

He could not utter what he wished to say and yet the wild and powerful music of those two images kept swelling in him and it seemed that the passion of their song must burst his heart, explode the tenement of bright blood and agony in which they surged, and tear the sinews of his life asunder unless he found some means to utter them.

But no words came. He only knew the image of man's loneliness, a feeling of sorrow, desolation, and wild mournful secret joy, longing and desire, as sultry, moveless and mysterious in its slow lust as the great rivers of the South themselves. And at the same moment that he fel this wild and mournful sorrow, the slow, hot, secret pulsings of desire, and breathed the heavy and mysterious fragrance of the lost South again, he felt suddenly and terribly, its wild strange pull, the fatal absoluteness of its world-lost resignation.

Then, with a sudden feeling of release, a realization of the incredible escape that now impended for him, he knew that he was waiting for the train, and that the great life of the North, the road to freedom, solitude and the enchanted promise of the golden cities was now before him. Like a dream made real, a magic come to life, he knew that in another hour he would be speeding world-ward, life-ward, North-ward out of the enchanted, time-far hills, out of the dark heart and mournful mystery of the South forever.

And as that overwhelming knowledge came to him, a song of triumph, joy, and victory so savage and unutterable, that he could no longer hold it in his heart was torn from his lips in a bestial cry of fury, pain, and ecstasy. He struck his arms out in the shining air for loss, for agony, for joy. The whole earth reeled about him in a kaleidoscopic blur of shining rail, massed heavy greens, and white empetalled faces of the staring people.

And suddenly he was standing there among his people on the platform of the little station. All things and shapes on earth swam back into their proper shape again, and he could hear his mother's voice, the broken clatter of the telegraph, and see, there on the tracks, the blunt black snout, the short hard blasts of steam from its squat funnel, the imminent presence, the enormous bigness of the train.

II

THE journey from the mountain town of Altamont to the tower-masted island of Manhattan is not, as journeys are conceived in America, a long one. The distance is somewhat more than 700 miles, the time required to make the journey a little more than twenty hours. But so relative are the qualities of space and time, and so complex and multiple their shifting images, that in the brief passage of this journey one may live a life, share instantly in 10,000,000 other ones, and see pass before his eyes the infinite panorama of shifting images that make a nation's history.

First of all, the physical changes and transitions of the journey are strange and wonderful enough. In the afternoon one gets on the train and with a sense of disbelief and wonder sees the familiar faces, shapes, and structures of his native town recede out of the last fierce clasp of life and vision. Then, all through the waning afternoon, the train is toiling down around the mountain curves and passes. The great shapes of the hills, embrowned and glowing with the molten hues of autumn, are all about him: the towering summits, wild and lonely, full of joy and strangeness and their haunting premonitions of oncoming winter soar above him, the gulches, gorges, gaps, and wild ravines, fall sheer and suddenly away with a dizzy terrifying steepness, and all the time the great train toils slowly down from the mountain summits with the sinu-ous turnings of an enormous snake. And from the very toiling slowness of the train, together with the terrific stillness and nearness of the mar-vellous hills, a relation is established, an emotion evoked, which it is impossible to define, but which, in all its strange and poignant mingling of wild sorrow and joy, grief for the world that one is losing, swelling triumph at the thought of the strange new world that one will find, is instantly familiar, and has been felt by every one.

The train toils slowly round the mountain grades, the short and powerful blasts of its squat funnel sound harsh and metallic against the sides of rocky cuts. One looks out the window and sees cut, bank, and gorge slide slowly past, the old rock wet and gleaming with the water of some buried mountain spring. The train goes slowly over the perilous and dizzy height of a wooden trestle; far below, the traveller can see and hear the clean foaming clamors of rock-bright mountain water; beside the track, before his little hut, a switchman stands looking at the train with the slow wondering gaze of the mountaineer. The little shack in which he lives is stuck to the very edge of the track above the steep and perilous ravine. His wife, a slattern with a hank of tight drawn hair, a snuff-stick in her mouth, and the same gaunt, slow wondering stare her husband has, stands in the doorway of the shack, holding a dirty little baby in her arms.

It is all so strange, so near, so far, so terrible, beautiful, and instantly familiar, that it seems to the traveller that he must have known these people forever, that he must now stretch forth his hand to them from the windows and the rich and sumptuous luxury of the pullman car, that he must speak to them. And it seems to him that all the strange and bitter miracle of life—how, why, or in what way, he does not know—is in that instant greeting and farewell; for once seen, and lost the moment that he sees it, it is his forever and he can never forget it. And then the slow toiling train has passed these lives and faces and is gone, and there is something in his heart he cannot say.

At length the train has breached the last great wall of the soaring ranges, has made its slow and sinuous descent around the powerful bends and cork-screws of the shining rails (which now he sees above him seven times) and towards dark, the lowland country has been reached. The sun goes down behind the train a tremendous globe of orange and pollen, the soaring ranges melt swiftly into shapes of smoky and enchanted purple, night comes—great-starred and velvet-breasted night—and now the train takes up its level pounding rhythm across the piedmont swell and convolution of the mighty State.

Towards nine o'clock at night there is a pause to switch cars and change engines at a junction town. The traveller, with the same feeling of wild unrest, wonder, nameless excitement and wordless expectancy, leaves the train, walks back and forth upon the platform, rushes into the little station lunch room or out into the streets to buy cigarettes, a sandwich—really just to feel this moment's contact with another town. He sees vast flares and steamings of gigantic locomotives on the rails, the seamed, blackened, lonely faces of the engineers in the cabs of their great engines, and a little later he is rushing again across the rude, mysterious visage of the powerful, dark, and lonely earth of old Catawba.

Toward midnight there is another pause at a larger town—the last stop in Catawba—again the feeling of wild unrest and nameless joy and sorrow. The traveller gets out, walks up and down the platform, sees the vast slow flare and steaming of the mighty engine, rushes into the station, and looks into the faces of all the people passing with the same sense of instant familiarity, greeting, and farewell,—that lonely, strange, and poignantly wordless feeling that Americans know so well. Then he is in the pullman again, the last outposts of the town have slipped away from him and the great train which all through the afternoon has travelled eastward from the mountains half across the mighty State, is now for the first time pointed northward, worldward, towards the secret borders of Virginia, towards the great world cities of his hope, the fable of his childhood legendry, and the wild and secret hunger of his heart, his spirit and his life.

Already the little town from which he came in the great hills, the faces of his kinsmen and his friends, their most familiar voices, the shapes of things he knew seem far and strange as dreams, lost at the bottom of the million-visaged sea-depth of dark time, the strange and bitter miracle of life. He cannot think that he has ever lived there in the far lost hills, or ever left them, and all his life seems stranger than the dream of time, and the great train moves on across the immense and lonely visage of America, making its great monotone that is the sound of silence and forever. And in the train, and in ten thousand little towns, the sleepers sleep upon the earth.

Then bitter sorrow, loneliness and joy come swelling to his throat—quenchless hunger rises from the adyts of his life and conquers him, and with wild wordless fury horsed upon his life, he comes at length, in dark mid-watches of the night, up to the borders of the old earth of Virginia.

Who has seen fury riding in the mountains? Who has known fury striding in the storm? Who has been mad with fury in his youth, given no rest or peace or certitude by fury, driven on across the earth by fury, until the great vine of the heart was broke, the sinews wrenched, the little tenement of bone, blood, marrow, brain, and feeling in which great fury raged, was twisted, wrung, depleted, worn out, and exhausted by the fury which it could not lose or put away? Who has known fury, how it came?

How have we breathed him, drunk him, eaten fury to the core, until we have him in us now and cannot lose him anywhere we go? It is a strange and subtle worm that will be forever feeding at our heart. It is a madness working in our brain, a hunger growing from the food it feeds upon, a devil moving in the conduits of our blood, it is a spirit wild and dark and uncontrollable forever swelling in our soul, and it is in the saddle now, horsed upon our lives, rowelling the spurs of its insatiate desire into our naked and defenseless sides, our owner, master, and the mad and cruel tyrant who goads us on forever down the blind and brutal tunnel of kaleidoscopic days at the end of which is nothing but the blind mouth of the pit and darkness and no more.

Then, then, will fury leave us, he will cease from those red channels of our life he has so often run, another sort of worm will work at that great vine, whereat he fed. Then, then, indeed, he must give over, fold his camp, retreat; there is no place for madness in a dead man's brain, no place for hunger in a dead man's flesh, and in a dead man's heart there is a place for no desire.

At what place of velvet-breasted night long long ago, and in what leafy darkened street of mountain summer, hearing the footsteps of approaching lovers in the night, the man's voice, low, hushed, casual, confiding, suddenly the low rich welling of a woman's laughter, tender and sensual in the dark, going, receding, fading, and then the million-noted silence of the night again? In what ancient light of fading day in a late summer; what wordless passion then of sorrow, joy, and ecstasy—was he betrayed to fury when it came?

Or in the black dark of some forgotten winter's morning, child of the storm and brother to the dark, alone and wild and secret in the night as he leaned down against the wind's strong wall towards Niggertown, blocking his folded papers as he went, and shooting them terrifically in the wind's wild blast against the shack-walls of the jungle-sleeping blacks, himself alone awake, wild, secret, free and stormy as the wild wind's blast, giving it howl for howl and yell for yell, with madness, and a demon's savage and exultant joy, up-welling in his throat! Oh, was he then, on such a night, betrayed to fury—was it then, on such a night, that fury came?

He never knew; it may have been a rock, a stone, a leaf, the moths of golden light as warm and moving in a place of magic green, it may have been the storm-wind howling in the barren trees, the ancient fading light of day in some forgotten summer, the huge unfolding mystery of undulant, on-coming night.

Oh, it might have been all this in the April and most lilac darkness of some forgotten morning as he saw the clean line of the East cleave into morning at the mountain's ridge. It may have been the first light, bird-song, an end to labor and the sweet ache and pure fatigue of the lightened shoulder as he came home at morning hearing the single lonely hoof, the jinking bottles, and the wheel upon the street again, and smelled the early morning breakfast smells, the smoking wheat-cakes, and the pungent sausages, the steaks, biscuits, grits, and fried green apples, and the brains and eggs. It may have been the coil of pungent smoke upcurling from his father's chimney, the clean sweet gardens and the peach-bloom, apples, crinkled lettuce wet with dew, bloom and cherry bloom down drifting in their magic snow within his father's orchard, and his father's giant figure awake now and astir, and moving in his house!

Oh, ever to wake at morning knowing he was there! To feel the fire-full chimney-throat roar up a-tremble with the blast of his terrific fires, to hear the first fire crackling in the kitchen range, to hear the sounds of morning in the house, the smells of breakfast and the feeling of security never to be changed! Oh, to hear him prowling like a wakened lion below, the stertorous hoarse frenzy of his furious breath; to hear the ominous muttering mounting to faint howls as with infuriated relish he prepared the roaring invective of the morning's tirade, to hear him muttering as the coal went rattling out upon the fire, to hear him growling as savagely the flame shot up the trembling chimney-throat, to hear him muttering back and forth now like a raging beast, finally to hear his giant stride racing through the house prepared now, storming to the charge, and the well-remembered howl of his awakened fury as springing to the door-way of the back-room stairs he flung it open, yelling at them to awake.

Was it in such a way, one time as he awoke, and heard below his father's lion-ramp of morning that fury came? He never knew, no more than one could weave the great web of his life back through the brutal chaos of ten thousand furious days, unwind the great vexed pattern of his life to silence, peace, and certitude in the magic land of new beginnings, no return.

He never knew if fury had lain dormant all those years, had worked secret, silent, like a madness in the blood. But later it would seem to him that fury had first filled his life, exploded, conquered, and possessed him, that he first felt it, saw it, knew the dark illimitable madness of its power, one night years later on a train across Virginia.

III

It was a little before midnight when the youth entered the smoking room of the pullman where, despite the lateness of the hour, several men still sat. At just this moment the train had entered the State of Virginia although, of course, none of the men who sat there talking knew this.

It is true that some of them might have known had their interest and attention been directed toward this geographic fact, had they been looking for it. Just at this moment, indeed, as the train, scarcely slackening its speed, was running through the last of the Catawba towns, one of the men glanced up suddenly from the conversation in which he and the others were earnestly engaged, which was exclusively concerned with the fascinating, ever mounting prices of their property and the tempting profits undoubtedly to be derived from real-estate speculation in their native town. He had looked up quickly, casually, and absently, with that staggering indifference of prosperous men who have been so far, so often, on such splendid trains, that a trip across the continent at night toward the terrific city is no longer a grand adventure of their lives, but just a thing of custom, need, and even weariness, and who, therefore, rarely look out windows any more:

"What is this?" he said quickly. "Oh, Maysville, probably. Yes, I guess this must be Maysville," and had then returned vigorously from his brief inspection of the continent of night, a few lights, and a little town, to the enticing topic which had for several hours absorbed the interests of the group.

Nor was there any good reason why this traveller who had glanced so swiftly and indifferently from the window of the train should feel any greater interest than he showed. Certainly the briefest and most casual

inspection would have convinced the observer that, in Baedeker's celebrated phrase, there was "little here that need detain the tourist."
What the man saw in the few seconds of his observation was the quiet,
dusty and sparsely lighted street of a little town in the upper South. The
street was shaded by large trees and there were some level lawns, more
trees, and some white frame houses with spacious porches, gables, occasionally the wooden magnificence of Georgian columns.

On everything—trees, houses, foliage, yards, and street there was a
curious loneliness of departure and October, an attentive almost mournful waiting. And yet this dark and dusty street of the tall trees left
a haunting, curiously pleasant feeling of strangeness and familiarity.
One viewed it with a queer sudden ache in the heart, a feeling of friendship and farewell, and this feeling was probably intensified by the swift
and powerful movement of the train which seemed to slide past the town
almost noiselessly, its wheels turning without friction, sound, or vibrance
on the pressed steel ribbons of the rails, giving to a traveller, and particularly to a youth who was going into the secret North for the first time, a
feeling of illimitable and exultant power, evoking for him the huge
mystery of the night and darkness, and the image of ten thousand lonely
little towns like this across the continent.

Then the train slides by the darkened vacant-looking little station and
for a moment one has a glimpse of the town's chief square and business
centre. And as he sees it he is filled again with the same feeling of loneliness, instant familiarity, and departure. The square is one of those
anomalous, shabby-ornate, inept, and pitifully pretentious places that
one finds in little towns like these. But once seen, if only for this fraction of a moment, from the windows of a train, the memory of it will
haunt one forever after.

And this haunting and lonely memory is due probably to the combination of two things: the ghastly imitation of swarming life and metropolitan gaiety in the scene, and the almost total absence of life itself. The
impression one gets, in fact, from that brief vision is one of frozen cataleptic silence in a world from which all life has recently been extinguished by some appalling catastrophe. The lights burn, the electric
signs wink and flash, the place is still horribly intact in all its bleak
prognathous newness, but all the people are dead, gone, vanished. The
place is a tomb of frozen silence, as terrifying in its empty bleakness as
those advertising backdrops one saw formerly in theatres, where the
splendid buildings, stores, and shops of a great street are painted in the

richest and most flattering colors, and where there is no sign of life whatever.

So was it here, save that here the illusion of the dead world gained a hideous physical reality by its stark, staring, nakedly concrete dimensions.

All this the boy had seen, or rather sensed, in the wink of an eye, a moment's vision of a dusty little street, a fleeting glimpse of a silent little square, a few hard lights, and then the darkness of the earth again —these half-splintered glimpses were all the boy could really see in the eye-wink that it took the train to pass the town. And yet, all these fragmentary things belonged so completely to all the life of little towns which he had known, that it was not as if he had seen only a few splintered images, but rather as if the whole nocturnal picture of the town was instantly whole and living in his mind.

Beyond the station, parked in a line against the curb is a row of empty motor cars, and he knows instantly that they have been left there by the patrons of the little moving-picture theatre which explodes out of the cataleptic silence of the left-hand side of the square into a blaze of hard white and flaming posters which seem to cover the entire façade. Even here, no movement of life is visible, but one who has lived and known towns like these feels for the first time an emotion of warmth and life as he looks at the gaudy, blazing bill-beplastered silence of that front.

For suddenly he seems to see the bluish blaze of carbon light that comes from the small slit-like vent-hole cut into the wall and can hear again—one of the loneliest and most haunting of all sounds—the rapid shuttering sound of the projection camera late at night, a sound lonely, hurried, unforgettable, coming out into those cataleptic squares of silence in the little towns—as if the operator is fairly racing through the last performance of the night like a weary and exhausted creature whose stale, over-driven life can find no joy in what is giving so much joy to others, and who is pressing desperately ahead toward the merciful rewards of food, sleep, and oblivion which are already almost in his grasp.

And as he remembers this, he also suddenly sees and knows the people in the theatre, and in that instant greets them, feels his lonely kinship with them, with the whole family of the earth, and says farewell. Small, dark, lonely, silent, thirsty, and insatiate, the people of the little town are gathered there in that one small cell of radiance, warmth, and joy. There for a little space they are united by the magic spell the theatre casts upon them. They are all dark and silent leaning forward like a single mind and congeries of life, and yet they are all separate too.

Yes, lonely, silent, for a moment beautiful, he knows the people of the town are there, lifting the small white petals of their faces, thirsty and insatiate, to that magic screen: now they laugh exultantly as their hero triumphs, weep quietly as the mother dies, the little boys cheer wildly as the rascal gets his due—they are all there in darkness, under immense immortal skies of time, small nameless creatures in a lost town on the mighty continent, and for an instant we have seen them, known them, said farewell.

Around the four sides of the square at even intervals, the new standards of the five-bulbed lamps cast down implacably upon those cataleptic pavements the cataleptic silence of their hard white light. And this, he knows, is called "the Great White Way," of which the town is proud. Somehow the ghastly, lifeless silence of that little square is imaged nowhere else so cruelly as in the harsh, white silence of these lights. For they evoke terribly, as nothing else can do, the ghastly vacancy of light without life. And poignantly, pitifully, and unutterably their harsh, white silence evokes the moth-like hunger of the American for hard, brilliant, blazing incandescence.

It is as if there may be in his soul the horror of the ancient darkness, the terror of the old immortal silences, which will not down and must be heard. It is as if he feels again the ancient fear of—what? Of the wilderness, the wet and lidless eye of shame and desolation feeding always on unhoused and naked sides. It is as if he fears the brutal revelation of his loss and loneliness, the furious, irremediable confusion of his huge unrest, his desperate and unceasing flight from the immense and timeless skies that bend above him, the huge, doorless and unmeasured vacancies of distance, on which he lives, on which, as helpless as a leaf upon a hurricane, he is driven on forever, and on which he cannot pause, which he cannot fence, wall, conquer, make his own.

Then the train, running always with its smooth, powerful, almost noiseless movement, has left the station and the square behind it. The last outposts of the town appear and vanish in patterns of small, lonely light, and there is nothing but huge and secret night before us, the lonely, everlasting earth, and presently Virginia.

And surely, now, there is little more to be seen. Surely, now, there is almost nothing that by day would be worthy of more than a glance from those great travellers who have ranged the earth, and known all its wild and stormy seas, and seen its rarest glories. And by night, now, there is nothing, nothing by night but darkness and a space we call Virginia through which the huge projectile of the train is hurtling onward in the dark.

Field and fold and gulch and hill and hollow, forest and stream and bridge and bank and cut, the huge earth, the rude earth, the wild, formless, infinitely various, most familiar, ever haunting earth, the grand and casual earth that is so brown, so harsh, so dusty, so familiar, the strange and homely earth wrought in our blood, our brain, our heart, the earth that can never be forgotten or described, is flowing by us, by us, by us in the night.

What is it that we know so well and cannot speak? What is it that we want to say and cannot tell? What is it that keeps swelling in our hearts its grand and solemn music, that is aching in our throats, that is pulsing like a strange wild grape through all the conduits of our blood, that maddens us with its exultant and intolerable joy and that leaves us tongueless, wordless, maddened by our fury to the end?

We do not know. All that we know is that we lack a tongue that could reveal, a language that could perfectly express the wild joy swelling to a music in our heart, the wild pain welling to a strong ache in our throat, the wild cry mounting to a madness in our brain, the thing, the word, the joy we know so well, and cannot speak! All that we know is that the little stations whip by in the night, the straggling little towns whip by with all that is casual, rude, familiar, ugly, and unutterable. All that we know is that the earth is flowing by us in the darkness, and that this is the way the world goes—with a field and a wood and a field! And of the huge and secret earth all we know is that we feel with all our life its texture with our foot upon it.

All that we know is that having everything we yet hold nothing, that feeling the wild song of this great earth upwelling in us we have no words to give it utterance. All that we know is that here the passionate enigma of our lives is so bitterly expressed, the furious hunger that so haunts and hurts Americans so desperately felt—that being rich, we all are yet so poor, that having an incalculable wealth we have no way of spending it, that feeling an illimitable power we yet have found no way of using it.

Therefore we hurtle onward in the dark across Virginia, we hurtle onward in the darkness down a million roads, we hurtle onward driven by our hunger down the blind and brutal tunnel of ten thousand furious and kaleidoscopic days, the victims of the cruel impulse of a million chance and fleeting moments, without a wall at which to thrust the shoulder of our strength, a roof to hide us in our nakedness, a place to build on, or a door.

IV

As the boy entered the smoking compartment, the men who were talking together paused, and looked up at him briefly with the intent, curious, momentary stare of men interrupted in a conversation. The boy, a leggy creature racing into unfledged lengths of shank and arm and shoulder, fumbled nervously in his coat pocket for a package of cigarettes and then sat down abruptly on the upholstered leather seat beside one of the men.

The boy's manner betrayed that mixture of defiance and diffidence which a young man going out into the world for the first time feels in the presence of older and more experienced men. And this was the way he felt. And for this reason in the sharp and casual stare which the men fixed briefly on him there may have been unconsciously something affectionate and tender as each one recalled a moment of his own lost youth.

The boy felt the powerful movement of the train beneath him and the lonely austerity and mystery of the dark earth outside that swept past forever with a fanlike stroke, an immortal and imperturbable stillness. It seemed to him that these two terrific negatives of speed and stillness, the hurtling and projectile movement of the train and the calm silence of the everlasting earth, were poles of a single unity—a unity coherent with his destiny, whose source was somehow in himself.

It seemed to him that this incredible and fortunate miracle of his own life and fate had ordered all these accidental facts into coherent and related meanings. He felt that everything—the powerful movement of the train, the infinite mystery and lonely wildness of the earth, the feeling of luxury, abundance, and unlimited wealth that was stimulated by the rich furnishings of the pullman, and the general air of affluence of these prosperous men—belonged to him, had come out of his own life, and were ready to serve him at his own behest and control.

It seemed to him that the glorious moment for which his whole life had been shaped, and toward which every energy and desire in his spirit had been turned, was now here.

As that incredible knowledge came to him, a fury, wild, savage, wordless, pulsed through his blood and filled him with such a swelling and exultant joy as he had never known before. He felt the savage tongueless cry of pain and joy swell up and thicken in his throat, he felt a rending and illimitable power in him as if he could twist steel between his fingers, and he felt an almost uncontrollable impulse to yell into the faces of the men with a demonic glee.

Instead he just sat down quickly with an abrupt, half-defiant movement, lit his cigarette, and spoke to one of the men quickly and diffidently, saying:

"Hello, Mr. Flood."

For a moment, the man thus addressed said nothing, but sat staring at the boy stupidly with an expression of heavy surprise. He was a well-dressed but bloated-looking man in his fifties whose gross figure even in repose betrayed a gouty tenderness. His face, which had the satiny rosy texture, veinous and tender, that alcoholism and a daily massage can give, was brutally coarse and sensual, but was given a disturbing and decisive character by his bulging yellow eyeballs and the gross lewd mouth which, because of several large buck teeth whose discolored surfaces protruded under the upper lip, seemed always to be half opened and half smiling. And it was not a pleasant smile. It was a smile, faint, unmistakably sensual, and rather sly. It seemed to come from some huge choking secret glee and there was in it a quality that was jubilantly obscene.

For a moment more Mr. Flood stared through his bulging eyes at the boy who had just spoken to him, with an air of comical and stupid surprise. Then amiably, but with a puzzled undertone, he said gruffly:

"Hello. Oh, hello, son! How are you?"

And after looking at the boy a moment longer, he turned his attention to the other men again.

It was at just that season of the year when two events which are dear to the speculations of the American had absorbed the public interest. These events were baseball and politics, and at that moment both were thrillingly imminent. The annual baseball contests for "the championship of the world" were to begin within another day or two, and the national campaign for the election of the American president, which would be held in another month, was moving daily to its furious apogee of speeches, accusations, dire predictions, and impassioned promises. Both events gave the average American a thrill of pleasurable anticipation: his approach to both was essentially the same. It was the desire of a man to see a good show, to "take sides" vigorously in an exciting con-test—to be amused, involved as an interested spectator is involved, but not to be too deeply troubled or concerned by the result.

It was just natural, therefore, that at the moment when the boy en-tered the smoking compartment of the train, the conversation of the men assembled there should be chiefly concerned with these twin sports. As he came in, there was a hum of voices, a sound of argument, and then he could see the hearty red-faced man—the politician—shaking his head dubiously and heard him say, with a protesting laugh:

"Ah-h, I don't know about that. From what I hear it's just the other way. I was talking to a man from Tennessee the other day, and from what he says, Cox is gaining everywhere. He said that a month ago he wouldn't have given two cents for his chances, but now he thinks he's going to carry the State."

"It's going to be close," another conceded. "He may win yet—but it looks to me as if he's got a hard uphill fight on his hands. Tennessee al-ways polls a big Republican vote—in some of those mountain districts they vote two to one Republican—and this year it looks as if they're all set for a change. . . . What do you think about it, Emmet?" he said, appealing to the small, swarthy and important-looking little man, who sat there, swinging his short little legs and chewing on a fat cigar with an air of wise reflection.

"Well," that person answered slowly after a thoughtful moment, tak-ing his cigar in his pudgy fingers and looking at it studiously—"it may be—it may be—that the country's ready for a change—now don't mis-understand me," he went on hastily, as if eager to set their perturbed minds at rest— "I'm not saying that I want to see Harding elected—that I'm going to cast my vote for him—as you know, I'm a party man and have voted the Democratic ticket ever since I came of age—but," again he paused, frowned importantly at his cigar, and spoke with careful deliberation—"it may just be that we are due for a change this year— that the country is ready for it—that we need it. . . . Now, I supported Wilson twice, in 1912, when he got elected to his first term of office, and again in 1916——"

"The time he kept us out of war," some one said ironically.

"And," the little man said deliberately—"if he was running again—if he was well enough to run—if he wanted a third term—(although I'm against the third term in principle)," he amended hastily again—"why, I believe I'd go ahead and vote for him. That's how much I think of

him. But," again he paused, and meditated his chewed cigar profoundly—"it may be we're due now for a change. Wilson was a great
president—in my opinion, the greatest man we've had since Lincoln—I
don't believe any other man could have done the job he did as well as
he—*but*," the word came out impressively, "the job is done! The war is
over——"

"Yes, thank God!" some one murmured softly but fervently.

"The people want to forget about the war—they want to forget all
their sacrifices and suffering—" said this little man who had sacrificed
and suffered nothing—"they are looking forward to better times. . . .
And in my opinion," he spoke again with his air of slow deliberation,
important carefulness—"in my opinion, better times are before us. I
think that after this election, we are going to witness one of the greatest
periods of national development and expansion that the world has ever
known. . . . Why, we haven't begun yet! We haven't even started!" he
cried suddenly, with a note of passionate conviction in his voice— "Do
you realize that this country is only a little more than a hundred years
old? Why, we haven't even begun to show what we can do yet! We've
spent all that time in getting started—in building cities—settling the
country—building railroads and factories—developing the means of
production—making the tools with which to work. . . . The resources
of this country are scarcely tapped as yet. And in my opinion we are on
the eve of the greatest period of prosperity and growth the world has
ever known. . . . Look at Altamont, for example," he went on cogently.
"Ten years ago, in 1910, the census gave us a population of 18,000. . . .
Now, we have thirty, according to government figures, and that doesn't
begin to take the whole thing in: it doesn't take in Biltburn, Lunn's
Cove, Beaver Hills, Sunset Parkway—a dozen other places I can mention, all really part of the town but not included in the census figures.
. . . If all the suburbs were included we'd have a population of at least
40,000 inhabitants——"

"I'd call it nearer fifty," said another patriot.

"And within another ten years we'll go to seventy-five, perhaps a
hundred. . . . Why, that town hasn't begun to grow yet!" he said, bending his short body forward in his enthusiasm and tapping his fat knee—
"It has been less than eight years since we established the Citizen's Bank
and Trust Company with a capital of $25,000 and capital stock at $100 a
share. . . . Now," he paused a moment, and looked around him, his
swarthy face packed with strong conviction—"*now,* we have a capital of

$2,000,000—deposits totalling more than $18,000,000—and as for the stock
—" for a moment the little man's swarthy face was touched with a faint
complacent smile, he said smugly, "I don't know exactly how much stock
you gentlemen may hold among you, but if any of you wants to sell what
he has, I will pay you $1000 a share—here and now," he slapped a fat
small hand down upon a fat small knee—"here and now! for every share
you own."

And he looked at them steadily for a moment with an air of challenge.

"Not for mine!" the florid heavy man cried heartily. "No sir! I've
only got ten shares, Emmet, but you can't buy it from me at any price! I
won't sell!"

And the swarthy little man, pleased by the answer, smiled complacently about him before he spoke again.

"Yes, sir!" he said. "That's the way it is. And the thing that's begun
to happen at home already is going to happen everywhere—all over the
country. From now on you're going to see a period of rising prices and
high wages—increased production, a boom in real estate, stocks, investments, business of all kinds—rising values everywhere such as you never
saw before and never hoped to see."

"And where is it going to stop?"

"Stop!" the swarthy little man spoke almost curtly, and then barked,
"It's not going to stop! Not during *our* lifetime, anyway! I tell you,
man, we're just beginning! How can there be any talk of stopping
when we haven't *started* yet! . . . There's been nothing like it before,"
he cried with passionate earnestness—"nothing to match it in the history
of the world. We've had wars, booms, good times, hard times, slumps,
periods of prosperity—but, I tell you, gentlemen!" and here he smote
himself sharply on the knee and his voice rose with the strength of an
unshakable conviction—"this thing is different! We have reached a
stage in our development that no other country in the world has ever
known—that was never dreamed of before—a stage that is beyond
booms, depressions, good times, hard times—anything——"

"You mean that after this we shall never be affected by those things?"

"Yes, sir!" he cried emphatically. "I mean just that! I mean that we
have learned the causes for each of those conditions. I mean that we
have learned how to check them, how to control them. I mean that so
far as we are concerned they don't *exist* any more!" His voice had become almost shrill with the force of his persuasive argument, and sud-

denly whipping a sheaf of envelopes, tied with a rubber band, out of his inner pocket, and gripping a stub of pencil in his stubby hand, he crossed his short fat legs with an energetic movement, bent forward poised above the envelopes, and said quietly but urgently:

"See here, now!— I'd like to show you a few figures! My business, as you know, is to look after other people's money—your money, the town's money, everybody's money—I've got to keep my fingers on the pulse of business at every moment of the day—my business is to *know* —to *know*—and let me tell you something," he said quietly, looking directly in their eyes, "I *do* know—so pay attention just a moment while I show these figures to you."

And for some moments he spoke quietly, persuasively, his dark features packed with an energy of powerful conviction, while he rapidly jotted figures down upon the backs of the soiled envelopes, and they bent around him—their medicine-man of magic numerals—in an attitude of awed and rapt attentiveness. And when he had finished, there was silence for a moment, save for the rhythmic clack of wheels, the rocketing sound of the great train. Then one of the men, stroking his chin thoughtfully, and with an impressed air, said:

"I see. . . . And you think, then, that in view of these conditions it would be better for the country if Harding is elected."

The little man's manner became instantly cautious, non-committal, "conservative":

"I don't say that," he said, shaking his head in a movement of denial— "I only say that whoever gets elected we're in for a period of unparalleled ' development. . . . Now both of them are good men—as I say, I shall probably vote for Cox—but you can rest assured," he spoke deliberately and looked around him in his compelling way—"you can rest assured that no matter which one gets elected the country will be in good hands. There's no question about that."

"Yes, sir," said the florid-faced politician in his amiable and hearty way. "I agree with you. . . . I'm a Democrat myself, both in practice and in principle. I'm going to vote for Cox, but if Harding gets elected I won't shed any tears over his election. We'll have to give the Republicans credit for a good deed this time—they couldn't have made a wiser or a better decision. He has a long and honorable career in the service of his country,"—as he spoke his voice unconsciously took on the sententious ring and lilt of the professional politician—"no breath of scandal has ever touched his name: in public and in private life he has remained as he began—a statesman loyal to the institutions of his country, a husband devoted to his family life, a plain American of simple tastes who loves his neighbors as himself, and prefers the quiet life of a little town, the democracy of the front porch, to the marble arches of the capitol—so, whatever the result may be," the orator concluded, "this nation need fear nothing: it has chosen well and wisely in both cases, its future is secure."

Mr. Flood, during the course of this impassioned flight, had remained ponderously unmoved. In the pause that followed, he sat impassively, his coarse jowled face and bulging yellowed eyes fixed on the orator in their customary expression of comic stupefaction. Now, breathing hoarsely and stertorously, he coughed chokingly and with an alarming rattling noise into his handkerchief, peered intently at his wadded handkerchief for a moment, and then said coarsely:

"Hell! What all of you are saying is that you are goin' to vote for Cox but that you hope that Harding wins."

"No, now, Jim—" the politician, Mr. Candler, said in a protesting tone— "I never said——"

"Yes, you did!" Mr. Flood wheezed bluntly. "You meant it, anyhow, every one of you is sayin' how he always was a Democrat and what a great man Wilson is, and how he's goin' to vote for Cox—and every God-damn one of you is praying that the other feller gets elected. . . . Why? I'll tell you why," he wheezed coarsely, "—it's because we're sick an' tired of Woodrow, all of us—we want to put the rollers under him an' see the last of him! Oh, yes, we are," he went on brutally as some one started to protest—"we're tired of Woodrow's flowery speeches, an' we're tired of hearin' about wars an' ideals an' democracy an' how fine an' noble we all are an' 'Mister won't you please subscribe.' We're tired of hearin' bunk that doesn't pay an' we want to hear some bunk that does—an' we're goin' to vote for the crook that gives it to us. . . . Do you know what we all want—what we're lookin' for?" he demanded, glowering brutally around at them. "We want a piece of the breast with lots of gravy—an' the boy that promises us the most is the one we're for! . . . Cox! Hell! All of you know Cox has no more chance of getting in than a snowball has in hell. When they get through with him he won't know whether he was run over by a five-ton truck or chewed up in a sausage mill. . . . Nothing has changed, the world's no different, we're just the same as we always were—and I've watched 'em come an' go for forty years—Blaine, Cleveland, Taft, McKinley, Roosevelt—the whole damned

lot of 'em—an' what we want from them is just the same: all we can get
for ourselves, a free grab with no holts barred, and to hell with the other
fellow."

"So who are you going to vote for, Jim?" said Mr. Candler smiling.

"Who? Me?" said Mr. Flood with a coarse grin. "Why, hell, you
ought to know that without asking. Me—I'm a Democrat, ain't I?—
don't I publish a Democratic newspaper? I'm going to vote for Cox, of
course."

And, in the burst of laughter that followed, some one could be heard,
saying jestingly:

"And who's going to win the Series, Jim? Some one told me you're
for Brooklyn!"

"Brooklyn!" Mr. Flood jeered wheezingly. "Brooklyn has just the
same kind of chance Cox has—the chance a snowball has in hell!
Brooklyn! They're in just the same fix the Democrats are in—they've
got nothing on the ball. When Speaker and that Cleveland gang get
through with them, Brooklyn is going to look just like Cox the day after
the election. Brooklyn," he concluded with brutal conviction, "hasn't
got a chance."

And again the debate between the men grew eager, animated and
vociferous: they shouted, laughed, denied, debated, jeered good-naturedly, and the great train hurtled onward in the darkness, and the
everlasting earth was still.

And other men, and other voices, words, and moments such as these
would come, would pass, would vanish and would be forgotten in the
huge record and abyss of time. And the great trains of America would
hurtle on through darkness over the lonely, everlasting earth—the earth
which only was eternal—and on which our fathers and our brothers had
wandered, their lives so brief, so lonely, and so strange—into whose
substance at length they all would be compacted. And the great trains
would hurtle on forever over the silent and eternal earth—fixed in that
design of everlasting stillness and unceasing change. The trains would
hurtle onward bearing other lives like these, all brought together for an
instant between two points of time—and then all lost, all vanished,
broken and forgotten. The trains would bear them onward to their million destinations—each to the fortune, fame, or happiness he wished,
whatever it was that he was looking for—but whether any to a sure
success, a certain purpose, or the thing he sought—what man could say?
All that he knew was that these men, these words, this moment would

vanish, be forgotten—and that great wheels would hurtle on forever. And the earth be still.

Mr. Flood shifted his gouty weight carefully with a movement of his fat arm, grunting painfully as he did so. This delicate operation completed, he stared sharply and intently at the boy again and at length said bluntly:

"You're one of those Gant boys, ain't you? Ain't you Ben's brother?"

"Yes, sir," the boy answered. "That's right."

"Which one are you?" Mr. Flood said with this same brutal directness. "You ain't the one that stutters, are you?"

"No," one of the other men interrupted with a laugh, but in a decided tone. "He's not the one. You're thinking of Luke."

"Oh," said Mr. Flood stupidly. "Is Luke the one that stutters?"

"Yes," the boy said, "that's Luke. I'm Eugene."

"Oh," Mr. Flood said heavily. "I reckon you're the youngest one."

"Yes, sir," the boy answered.

"Well," said Mr. Flood with an air of finality, "I didn't know which one you were but I knew you were one of them. I knew I'd seen you somewhere."

"Yes, sir," the boy answered. He was about to go on, hesitated for a moment, and suddenly blurted out: "I used to carry a route on *The Courier* when you owned it. I guess that's how you remembered me."

"Oh," said Mr. Flood stupidly, "you did? Yes, that's it, all right. I remember now." And he continued to look at the boy with his bulging stare of comic stupefaction and for a moment there was silence save for the pounding of the wheels upon the rail.

"How many of you boys are there?" The swarthy and important-looking man who had previously been addressed as Emmet now spoke curiously: "There must be five or six in all."

"No," the boy said, "there's only three now. There's Luke and Steve and me."

"Oh, Steve, Steve," the little man said with an air of crisp finality, as if this was the name that had been at the tip of his tongue all the time. "Steve was the oldest, wasn't he?"

"Yes, sir," said the boy.

"Whatever became of Steve, anyway?" the man said. "I don't believe I've seen him in ten or fifteen years. He doesn't live at home any more, does he?"

"No, sir," the boy said. "He lives in Indiana."

"Does he for a fact?" said the little man, as if this was a rare and curious bit of information. "What's Steve doing out there? Is he in business?"

For a moment the boy was going to say, "No, he runs a pool room and lives up over it with his wife and children," but feeling ashamed to say this, he said:

"I think he runs some kind of cigar store out there."

"Is that so?" the man answered with an air of great interest. "Well," he went on in a moment in a conciliatory tone, "Steve was always smart enough. He had brains enough to do almost anything if he tried."

Emmet Wade, the man who had asked the boy all these questions, was a quick, pompous little figure, corpulently built, but so short in stature as to be almost dwarfish-looking. His skin was curiously and unpleasantly swarthy, and save for a fringe of thin black hair at either side, his head was completely bald. In that squat figure, the suggestion of pompous authority and mountainous conceit was so pronounced that even in repose, as now, the whole man seemed to strut. He was, by virtue of that fortuitous chance and opportunity which has put so many small men in great positions, the president of the leading bank of the community. Even as he sat there in the smoking compartment, with his short fat legs crossed, the boy could see him sitting at his desk in the bank, swinging back and forth in his swivel chair thoughtfully, his pudgy hands folded behind his head as he dictated a letter to his obsequious secretary.

"Where's old Luke? What's he doing, anyway?" another of the men demanded suddenly, beginning to chuckle even as he spoke. The speaker was the florid-faced, somewhat countrified-looking man already noted, who wore the string neck-tie and spoke with the rhetorical severity of the small-town politician. He was one of the town commissioners and in his hearty voice and easy manner there was a more genial quality than any of the others had. "I haven't seen that boy in years," he continued. "Some one was asking me just the other day what had become of him."

"He's got a job selling farm machinery and lighting equipment," the boy answered.

"Is that so?" the man replied with this same air of friendly interest. "Where is he located? He doesn't get home very often, does he?"

"No, sir," the boy said, "not very often. He comes in every two or three weeks, but he doesn't stay home long at a time. His territory is down through South Carolina and Georgia—all through there."

"What did you say he was selling?" said Mr. Flood, who had been staring at the boy fixedly during all this conversation with his heavy expression of a slow, intent and brutal stupefaction.

"He sells lighting systems and pumps and farm equipment and machinery—for farms," the boy said awkwardly.

"That's Luke—who does that?" said Mr. Flood after a moment, when this information had had time to penetrate.

"Yes, sir. That's Luke."

"And he's the one that stutters?"

"Yes, sir."

"The one that used to have the agency for *The Saturday Evening Post* and did all that talking when he sold 'em to you?"

"Yes, sir. That's Luke."

"And what d'you say he's doing now?" said Mr. Flood heavily. "Selling farm machinery?"

"Yes, sir. That's what he's doing."

"Then, by God," said Mr. Flood, with a sudden and explosive emphasis which, after his former attitude of heavy, brutal stupefaction, was startling, "he'll do it!" The other men laughed and Mr. Flood shook his ponderous, crimson head slowly from side to side to emphasize his conviction in the matter.

"If any one can sell 'em, he'll do it," he said positively. "That boy could sell Palm Beach suits to the Esquimaux. They'd have to buy 'em just to keep him from talking them to death."

"I'll tell you what I saw him do one time," said the politician, shifting his weight a little in order to accommodate himself more comfortably to the motion of the train. "I was standing in front of the post office one day talking to Dave Redmond about some property he owned out on the Haw Creek Road—oh, it must have been almost fifteen years ago—when here he comes hustling along, you know, with a big bundle of his papers under his arm. Well, he sails right into us, talking about a mile a minute and going so fast neither of us had a chance to get a word in edgeways. 'Here you are, gentlemen,' he says, 'hot off the press, just the thing you've been waiting for, this week's edition of *The Saturday Evening Post,* five cents, only a nickel, the twentieth part of a dollar.' By that time," said Mr. Candler, "he had the thing all opened up and shoved up right under Dave Redmond's nose, and he was turning the pages and telling him all about the different pieces it had in it and who wrote them and what was in them, and what a bargain it was for five cents. 'W-w-w-why,' he says, 'if you b-b-b-bought it in a book, why it'd cost you á d-d-d-dollar and a half and then,' he says, 'it wouldn't be half as good.' Well, Dave was getting sort of red in the face by that time," Mr. Candler said, "and I could see he was sort of annoyed at being interrupted, but the boy kept right on with his spiel and wouldn't give up. 'I don't want it,' says Dave, 'I'm busy' and he tries to turn away from him, but Luke moves right around to the other side and goes after him about twice as hard as before. 'Go on, go on,' says Dave. 'We're busy! I don't want it! I can't read!' he says. 'All right,' says Luke, 'then you can look at the p-p-p-pictures. Why, the pictures alone,' he says, 'are w-w-w-worth a half a dollar. It's the b-b-b-bargain of a life time,' he says. Well, the boy was pressing him pretty hard and I guess Dave lost his temper. He sort of knocked the magazine away from him and shouted, 'Damn it, I told you that I didn't want it, and I mean it! Now go on! We're busy.' Well," said Mr. Candler, "Luke didn't say a word for a moment. He took his magazine and put it under his arm again, and he just stood there looking at Dave Redmond for a moment, and then he said, just as quiet as you please, 'All right, sir. You're the doctor. But I think you're going to regret it!' And then he turned and walked away from us. Well, sir," said Mr. Candler, laughing, "Dave Redmond's face was a study. You could see he felt pretty small to think he had shouted at the boy like that, and acted as he did. And Luke hadn't gone twenty feet before Dave Redmond called him back. 'Here, son,' he says, diving his hand down into his pocket, 'give me one of those things! I may never read it but it's worth a dollar just to hear you talk.' And he gave him a dollar, too, and made him take it," Mr. Candler said, "and from that day on Dave Redmond was one of the biggest boosters that Luke had. . . . 'I think you're going to regret it,'" said Mr. Candler again, laughing at the memory. "That's the thing that did it—that's what got him—the way the boy just looked at him and said, 'All right, sir, but I think you're going to regret it.' That did the trick, all right." And pleased with his story and the memory it evoked, Mr. Candler looked mildly out the window for a moment, smiling.

"That was Luke that done that?" Mr. Flood demanded hoarsely after a moment, with his air of brutal and rather stunned surprise. "The one that stutters?"

"Yes, that's the one all right," said Mr. Candler. "That's who it was."

Mr. Flood pondered this information for a moment with his bulging eyes still fastened on Mr. Candler in their look of stupefied curiosity. Then, as the full import of what he had heard at length soaked into his intelligence, he shook his great coarse head once, slowly, in a movement of ponderous but emphatic satisfaction, and said with hoarse conviction:

"Well, he's a good 'un! If any one can sell 'em, he's the one."

This judgment was followed by a brief but heavy pause, which was broken in a moment by the voice of the pompous, swarthy little man who, in a tone of detached curiosity, said:

"Whatever became of that other boy—the one who used to work there in *The Courier* office when you owned it? What was his name, anyway?"

"Ben," said Mr. Flood heavily, but without hesitation. "That was Ben." Here he coughed in an alarming, phlegmy sort of way, cleared his throat and spat chokingly into the spittoon at his feet, wiped his mouth with his wadded handkerchief and in a moment, panting for breath, wheezed:

"Ben was the one that worked for me."

"Oh, yes, yes, yes!" the swarthy little man said rapidly, as if now it all came back to him. "Ben! That was the one! What ever became of him? I haven't seen him recently."

"He's dead," said Mr. Flood, still wheezing rapidly for breath and gazing at the spittoon. "That's the reason you haven't seen him," he said seriously. And suddenly, as if the long-awaited moment had come, he bent over, torn by a fit of choking and phlegmy sounds of really astounding proportions. When it was over, he raised himself, settled back slowly and painfully in his seat, and for a moment with closed eyes, did nothing but wheeze rapidly. In a moment, still with closed eyes, he gasped almost inaudibly:

"Ben was the one that died."

"Oh, yes! I do remember now," the pompous little man declared, nodding his head sharply with an air of conviction. "That's been some time ago, hasn't it?" he said to the boy.

"He died two years ago," the boy replied, "during the war."

"Oh, that's so, he did! I remember now!" the man cried instantly, with an air of recollection that somehow said that he remembered nothing. "He was overseas at the time, wasn't he?" he asked smoothly.

"No, sir," the boy answered. "He was at home. He died of pneumonia —during that big epidemic."

"I know," the man said regretfully. "That got a lot of the boys. Ben was in service at the time, wasn't he?"

"No," the boy answered. "He never got in. Luke was the one who was in service. Ben tried to get in twice but he couldn't pass the examinations."

"Is that so?" the man said vaguely. "Well, I was mighty sorry to hear about his death. Old Ben was one fine boy!"

Nothing was said for a moment.

"I'll tell you how fine he was," Mr. Flood, who had been wheezing with closed eyes, now grunted suddenly, glaring solemnly about him with an air of brutal earnestness. "Now I think I knew that boy about as well as any man alive—he worked for me for almost fifteen years—started out when he was ten years old as a route-boy on *The Courier* and kept right on working for my paper until just a year or two before he died! And I'm here to tell you," he wheezed solemnly, "that they don't come any better than Ben!" Here he glowered around him pugnaciously as if the character of a dead saint had been called in question. "Now he wasn't one of your big talkers who'd promise everything and do nothing. Ben was a do-er, not a talker. You could depend on him," said Mr. Flood, hoarsely and impressively. "When he told you he'd do a thing, you'd know it was going to get done! As regular as a clock and as steady as the day is long! And as quiet a fellow as you ever saw," said Mr. Flood. "That was Ben for you! Am I right?" he demanded, suddenly turning to the boy. "Was that Ben?"

"Yes, sir," the boy answered. "That was Ben."

"And until you asked him something he'd go for days at a time without speaking to you, but I knew he didn't mean anything by it, it was just his way. He believed in tending to his own business and he expected every one else to do the same." And for a moment, exhausted by these eulogies, he wheezed rapidly.

"Well, the world would be a lot better off if there were more like him," the pompous, swarthy little man now said virtuously, as if this sentiment expressed his own pious belief and practice. "There are too many people sticking their noses in other people's business, as it is."

"Well, they didn't stick their noses in Ben's business," said Mr. Flood with grim emphasis, "not after the first time, anyway. But they didn't come any better than that boy. I couldn't have thought more of him if he'd been my own son," he concluded piously and then gasped stertorously, lifted his cigar slowly to his lips with the thick, gouty tenderness that characterized all his movements and for a moment puffed slowly, wheezing reflectively over it.

"Not that he was ever much like a boy," he grunted suddenly, with a surprising flash of insight. "He was always more like an old man— didn't ever seem to be a kid like the others. Why," suddenly he chuckled with a phlegmy hoarseness, "I remember when he first began to come down there in the morning as a carrier, the other kids all called him 'Pop.' That was Ben for you. Always had that scowl on his face, even when he was laughing—as serious and earnest as an old man. But he was one of the best—as good as they come." Again he coughed chokingly, bent over with a painful grunt, and cleared his throat phlegmily into the polished brass spittoon beside him. Then, wheezing a little, he drew the wadded silk handkerchief from a side-pocket, wiped his mouth with it, raised himself up in his seat a little, and settled back slowly, tenderly, wheezing, with a sigh! Then for a moment he labored painfully, eyes closed, with his rapid wheezing breath and finally, when it seemed he must be exhausted by his efforts and done with conversation for the evening, he wheezed faintly and unexpectedly:

"That was Ben."

"Oh, I remember that boy now," the swarthy pompous-looking man suddenly broke in with a flash of recollective inspiration—"Wasn't Ben the boy who used to stand in the windows of *The Courier* offices when the World Series was being played, and post the score up on the scoreboard as they phoned it in to him?"

"Yes," wheezed Mr. Flood, nodding heavily, "You got him now, all right. That was Ben."

"I remember now," the swarthy little man said thoughtfully, with a far-away look in his eye. "I was thinking about him the other day when I went by *The Courier* office. They were playing the Series then. They had another fellow in the window and I wondered what had become of him. So that was Ben?"

"Yes," Mr. Flood wheezed hoarsely again. "That was Ben."

For a moment as the gouty old rake had spoken of the boy's dead brother, the boy had felt within him a sense of warmth: a wakening of dead time, a stir of grateful affection for the gross old man as if there might have been in this bloated carcass some trace of understanding for the dead boy of whom he spoke—an understanding faint and groping as a dog who bays the moon might have of the sidereal universe, and yet genuine and recognizable.

And for a moment present time fades out and the boy sits there staring blindly out at the dark earth that strokes forever past the train, and now he has the watch out and feels it in his hands. . . . And suddenly Ben is standing there before his vision, smoking, and scowls down through the window of the office at the boy.

He jerks his head in a peremptory gesture: the boy, obedient to his brother's command, enters the office and stands there waiting at the counter. Ben steps down from the platform in the window, puts the earphones on a table and walks over to the place where the boy is standing. For a moment, scowling fiercely, he stands there looking at the boy across the counter. The scowl deepens, he makes a sudden threatening gesture of his hard white hand as if to strike the boy, but instead he reaches across the counter quickly, seizes the boy by the shoulders, pulls him closer, and with rough but skillful fingers tugs, pulls and jerks the frayed string of neck-tie which the boy is wearing into a more orderly and presentable shape.

The boy starts to go.

"Wait!" says Ben, quietly, in a deliberately off-hand kind of tone. He opens a drawer below the counter, takes out a small square package, and scowling irritably, and without looking at the boy, he thrusts it at him. "Here's something for you," he says, and walks away.

"What is it?" The boy takes the package and examines it with a queer numb sense of expectancy and growing joy.

"Why don't you open it and see?" Ben says, his back still turned, and scowling down into a paper on the desk.

"Open it?" the boy says, staring at him stupidly.

"Yes, open it, fool!" Ben snarls. "It's not going to bite you!"

While the boy fumbles with the cords that tie the package, Ben prowls over toward the counter with his curious, loping, pigeon-toed stride, leans on it with his elbows and, scowling, begins to look up and down the want-ad columns, while blue, pungent smoke coils slowly from his nostrils. By this time, the boy has taken off the outer wrapping of the package, and is holding a small case, beautifully heavy, of sumptuous blue velvet, in his hands.

"Well, did you look at it?" Ben says, still scowling up and down the want-ads of the paper, without looking at the boy.

The boy finds the spring and presses it, the top opens, inside upon its rich cushion of white satin is a gold watch, and a fine gold chain. It is a miracle of design, almost as thin and delicate as a wafer. The boy stares at it with bulging eyes and in a moment stammers:

"It's—it's a watch!"

"Does it look like an alarm clock?" Ben jeers quietly, as he turns a page and begins to scowl up and down the advertisements of another column.

"It's—for me?" the boy says thickly, slowly, as he stares at it.

"No," Ben says, "it's for Napoleon Bonaparte, of course! . . . You little idiot! Don't you know what day this is? Have I got to do all the thinking for you? Don't you ever use your head for anything except a hat-rack? . . . Well," he goes on quietly in a moment, still looking at his paper, "what do you think of it? . . . There's a spring in the back that opens up," he goes on casually. "Why don't you look at it?"

The boy turns the watch over, feels the smooth golden surface of that shining wafer, finds the spring, and opens it. The back of the watch springs out, upon the inner surface is engraved, in delicate small words, this inscription:

> "To Eugene Gant
> Presented To Him On His Twelfth Birthday
> By His Brother
> B. H. Gant
> October 3, 1912"

"Well," Ben says quietly in a moment. "Did you read what it says?"

"I'd just like to say—" the boy begins in a thick, strange voice, staring blindly down at the still open watch.

"Oh, for God's sake!" Ben says, lifting his scowling head in the direction of his unknown demon, and jerking his head derisively towards the boy. "Listen to this, won't you? . . . Now, for God's sake, try to take good care of it and don't abuse it!" he says quickly and irritably. "You've got to look after a watch the same as anything else. Old man Enderby" —this is the name of the jeweller from whom he has bought the watch—"told me that a watch like that was good for fifty years, if you take care of it. . . . You know," he goes on quietly, insultingly "you're not supposed to drive nails with it or use it for a hammer. You know that, don't you?" he says, and for the first time turns and looks quietly at the boy. "Do you know what a watch is for?"

"Yes."

"What is it for?"

"To keep time with," says the boy.

Ben says nothing for a moment, but looks at him.

"Yes," he says quietly at length, with all the bitter weariness of a fathomless resignation and despair, the infinite revulsion, scorn, disgust which life has caused in him. "That's it. That's what it's for. To keep time with." The weary irony in his voice has deepened to a note of passionate despair. "And I hope to God you keep it better than the rest of us! Better than Mama or the old man—better than me! God help you if you don't! . . . Now go on home," he says quietly in a moment, "before I kill you."

"To keep time with!"

What is this dream of time, this strange and bitter miracle of living? Is it the wind that drives the leaves down bare paths fleeing? Is it the storm-wild flight of furious days, the storm-swift passing of the million faces, all lost, forgotten, vanished as a dream? Is it the wind that howls above the earth, is it the wind that drives all things before its lash, is it the wind that drives all men like dead ghosts fleeing? Is it the one red leaf that strains there on the bough and that forever will be fleeing? All things are lost and broken in the wind: the dry leaves scamper down the path before us, in their swift-winged dance of death the dead souls flee along before us driven with rusty scuffle before the fury of the demented wind. And October has come again, has come again.

What is this strange and bitter miracle of life? Is it to feel, when furious day is done, the evening hush, the sorrow of lost, fading light, far sounds and broken cries, and footsteps, voices, music, and all lost—and something murmurous, immense and mighty in the air?

And we have walked the pavements of a little town and known the passages of barren night, and heard the wheel, the whistle and the tolling bell, and lain in the darkness waiting, giving to silence the huge prayer of our intolerable desire. And we have heard the sorrowful silence of the river in October—and what is there to say? October has come again, has come again, and this world, this life, this time are stranger than a dream.

May it not be that some day from this dream of time, this chronicle of smoke, this strange and bitter miracle of life in which we are the moving and phantasmal figures, we shall wake? Knowing our father's voice upon the porch again, the flowers, the grapevines, the low rich moons of waning August, and the tolling bell—and instantly to know we live, that we have dreamed and have awakened, and find then in our hands some object, like this real and palpable, some gift out of the lost land and the unknown world as token that it was no dream—that we have really been there? And there is no more to say.

For now October has come back again, the strange and lonely month comes back again, and you will not return.

Up on the mountain, down in the valley, deep, deep, in the hill, Ben— cold, cold, cold.

"To keep time with!"

And suddenly the scene, the shapes, the voices of the men about him swam back into their focus, and he could hear the rhythmed pounding of the wheels below him, and in his palm the frail-numbered visage of the watch stared blank and plain at him its legend. It was one minute after twelve o'clock, Sunday morning, October the third, 1920, and he was hurtling across Virginia, and this world. this life, this time were stranger than a dream.

The train had halted for a moment at one of the Virginia towns, and for a moment the people were conscious of the strange yet casual familiarity of all those sounds which suddenly will intercept the rhythmic spell of time and memory which a journey in a train can cast upon its passengers. Suddenly this spell was broken by the intrusion of peculiar things—of sounds and voices—the sense of instant recognition, union to a town, a life which they had never known, but with which they now felt immediately familiar. A trainman was coming swiftly down the station platform beneath the windows of the train, pausing from time to time to hammer on the car-wheels of each truck. A negro toiled past below them with a heavy rattling truck in tow, piled high with baggage.

And elsewhere there were the casual voices of the train men—conductors, porters, baggage masters, station men—greeting each other with friendly words, without surprise, speaking of weather, work, plans for the future, saying farewell in the same way. Then the bell tolled, the whistle blew, the slow panting of the engine came back to them, the train was again in motion; the station, and the station lights, a glimpse of streets, the thrilling, haunting, white-glazed incandescence of a cotton mill at night, the hard last lights of town, slid past the windows of the train. The train was in full speed now, and they were rushing on across the dark and lonely earth again.

Then one of the men in the compartment, the politician, who had been looking curiously out the window at this town and station scene, turned and spoke with a casual interest to the boy:

"Your father's in Baltimore now, isn't he, son?" he said.

"Yes, sir. He's at Hopkins. Luke's up there with him."

"Well, I thought I read something in the paper a week or two back about his being there," said the man with the florid face.

"What's wrong with him?" Mr. Flood demanded coarsely in a moment, after he had absorbed this information. "Ain't he feeling good?"

The boy shifted nervously in his seat before he answered. His father was dying of cancer, but for some reason it did not seem possible or proper for him to say this to these men. He said:

"He's got some kind of kidney trouble, I think. He goes up there for radium treatments."

"It's the same thing John Rankin had," the florid-faced man glibly interposed at this moment. "Some sort of prostate trouble, isn't it?" he said.

"Yes, sir, that's it," the boy said. For some reason he felt a sense of relief and gratefulness towards the man with the florid face. The easy, glib and false assurance that his father's "trouble" was "the same thing John Rankin had" seemed to give the disease a respectable standing and to divest the cancer of its fatal, shameful and putrescent horror.

"I know what it is," the florid-faced man was saying, nodding his head in a confident manner. "It's the same thing John Rankin had. A lot of men get it after they're fifty. John told me he went through agony with it for ten years. Said he used to be up with it a dozen times a night. It got so he couldn't sleep, he couldn't rest, he couldn't do anything but walk the floor with it. It got him down so that he was nothing but skin and bones, he was walking around like a dead man. Then he went up there and had that operation and he's been a new man ever since. He looks better than he's looked in twenty years. I was talking to him the other day and he told me he didn't have an ache or a pain in the world. He said he was going to live to be a hundred and he looked it—the picture of health.

"Well," he said in a friendly tone, now turning to the boy, "remember me to your father when you see him. Tell him Frank Candler asked to be remembered to him."

"Are you and him good friends?" Mr. Flood demanded heavily, after another staring pause, with the brutal, patient, and somehow formidable curiosity which belonged to him. "You know him well?"

"Who? Mr. Gant?" Mr. Candler cried with the hearty geniality of the politician, which seemed to suggest he knew the man so well that the very question was amusing to him. "Why, I've known him all my life— I've known him ever since he first came to Altamont—let's see, that's all of forty years ago when he first came there?" Mr. Candler went on reflectively, "or no, maybe a little less than that. Wait a minute." He considered seriously for a moment. "The first time I ever saw your father," said Mr. Candler very slowly and impressively, with a frown on his face and not looking at any one, but staring straight before him, "was in October, 1882—and I believe—I believe," he said strongly, "that was the very year he came to town—yes, sir! I'm positive of it!" he cried. "For Altamont was nothing but a cross-roads village in those days—I don't believe we had 2000 people there—why, that's all in the world it was." Mr. Candler now interrupted himself heartily. "The courthouse up there on the square and a few stores around it—when you got two blocks away you were right out in the country. Didn't Captain Bob Porter offer me three lots he owned down there on Pisgah Avenue, not a block from the square, for a thousand dollars, and didn't I laugh at him to think he was fool enough to ask such a price as that and expect to get it! Why!" Mr. Candler declared, with a full countrified laugh, "it was nothing but a mud-hole down in the holler. I've seen old Captain Porter's hawgs wallerin' around in it many's the time. 'And you,' I said to him, 'you—do you think I'd pay you a price like that for a mud-hole? Why, you must think I'm crazy, sure enough.' 'All right,' he says, 'have it your own way, but you'll live to see the day you'll regret not buying it. You'll live to see the day when you can't buy *one* of those lots for a thousand dollars!' *One* of them!" Mr. Candler now cried in hearty self-derision. "Why, if I owned one of those lots today, I'd be a rich man! I don't believe you could buy a foot of that land today for less than a thousand dollars, could you, Bruce?" he said, addressing himself to the swarthy, pompous-looking man who sat beside the boy.

"Five thousand a front foot would come closer to it, I should think," the pompous little man replied, with the crisp, brisk and almost strutting assurance that characterized all his words and gestures. He crossed and uncrossed his fat little legs briskly as he uttered these words and then sat there "all reared back" as the saying goes, unable even to reach the floor with his fat little legs, but smiling a complacent smile and simply exud-

ing conceit and strutting self-satisfaction from every pore. "Yes, sir!"
the swarthy little man continued, pompously, "I should doubt very
much if you could buy a foot of that property for less than $5000 today!"

"Well," said Mr. Candler with a satisfied air. "That's what I thought!
I knew it would be way up there somewheres. But I could have had the
whole thing once for a thousand dollars. I've kicked myself in the seat
of the pants a thousand times since to think what a fool I was for not
taking it when I had the chance! I'd be a rich man today if I had! It
just goes to show you, doesn't it?" he concluded indefinitely.

"Yes, sir," the pompous, swarthy little man replied, in his dry, briskly
assured tones, "it goes to show that our hindsight is usually a great deal
better than our foresight!" And he glanced about him complacently,
obviously pleased with his wit and convinced that he had said something
remarkably pungent and original.

"It was about that time when I first met your father," said Mr. Candler, turning to the boy again. "Along there in the fall of '82—that's
when it was all right—and I don't think he'd been in town then more
than a month, for in a town that size, I'd have known if he'd been there
longer. And, yes, of course!" he cried sharply, struck by sudden recollection, "that very first day I saw him he was standing there in front
of his shop with two nigger men, unloading some blocks of marble and
granite and tombstones, I reckon, and moving them back into his shop.
I guess he was just moving in at the time. He'd rented an old shack over
there at the northeast corner of the square where the Sluder building is
now. That's where it was, all right. I was working for old man Weaver at
the time—he had a grocery and general-goods store there opposite the
old courthouse about where the Blue Ridge Coal and Ice Company is
now. I was going back to work after dinner and had just turned the
corner at the Square there from Academy Street when I saw your father.
I remember stopping to watch him for a moment because there was
something about his appearance—I don't know what it was, but if you
saw him once you'd never forget him—there was something about the
way he looked and talked and worked that was different from any one
I'd ever seen. Of course, he was an awful tall, big-boned, powerful-looking sort of man—how tall is your father, son?"

"He was about six feet five," the boy answered, "but I guess he's not
that much now—he's stooped over some since he got old."

"Well, he didn't stoop in those days," said Mr. Candler. "He always
carried himself as straight as an arrow. I noticed that. He was an awful

big man—not that he had much weight on him—he was always lean and *skinny* like—but he *looked* big—he had big bones—his *frame* was big!" cried Mr. Candler. "You'll make a big man too when you fill out," he continued, giving the boy an appraising look. "Of course, you look like your mother's people, you're a Pentland and they're fleshy people, but you've got the old man's frame. You may make a bigger man than he is when you put on weight and widen out—but it wasn't that your father was so big—I think he looked bigger than he really was—it was something else about him—about the way he gave orders to the niggers and went about his work," said Mr. Candler, in a rather puzzled tone. "I don't know what it was, but I'd never seen any one like him before. For one thing he was dressed so good!" he said suddenly. "He always wore his good clothes when he worked—I'd never seen a man who did hard labor with his hands who dressed that way. Here he was, you know, sweating over those big blocks of stone with those two niggers and wearing better clothes than you and me would go to church in. Of course, he had his coat off, and his cuffs rolled back, and he was wearing one of those big striped aprons that go the whole way up across the shoulders—but you could see his clothes was *good*," said Mr. Candler. "Looked like black broadcloth that had been made by a tailor and wearing a *boiled* shirt, mind you, and one of those wing collars with a black silk neck-tie—and not afraid to work, either! Why, the first thing I saw him do," said Mr. Candler, laughing, "he let out a string of words at those niggers you could have heard from here to yonder because they were sweating and straining to get a big hunk of marble up on the rollers, that they hadn't been able to budge an inch. 'Merciful God,' he says, that's just the way he talked, you know—'Merciful God! Has it come to this that I must do everything for myself while you stand there gloating at my agony? I could as soon look for help from a couple of God-damned wooden Indians! In the name of God, stand back. I'll do it myself, sick and feeble as I am!' Well," said Mr. Candler, chuckling with the recollection, "with that he reaches down and gets a grip on that big hunk of stone and gives a heave and up she comes on to the rolling pins as nice and easy as anything you ever saw. Well, sir, you should have seen the look upon those niggers' faces—I thought their eyes were going to pop out of their heads. And that's the first time I ever spoke to him, you know. I can remember the very words I said. I said to him, 'Well, if you call that being sick and feeble, most of the folks up in this part of the country are already dead and in their graves.' "

The man's story had stirred in the boy's mind a thousand living memories of his father. For a moment it seems to him that the lost world which these words evoked has never died, lives yet in all the radiant and enchanted color of his childhood, in all its proud, dense, and single fabric of passion, fury, certitude and joy. Every memory that the story brought to life is part of him. There are a thousand buried, nameless and forgotten lives, ten thousand strange and secret tongues alive now, urgent, swarming in his blood, and thronging at the gateways of his memory. They are the lives of the lost wilderness, his mother's people; they are the tongues, the faces of the secret land, the dark half of his heart's desire, the fertile golden earth from which his father came.

He knows the farmer boy who stood beside the road and watched the dusty rebels marching past towards Gettysburg. He smells the sweet fragrance of that lavish countryside, he hears the oaths, the jests, the laughter of the marching soldiers, he hears the cricketing stitch of noon in drowsy fields, the myriad woodnotes, secret, green, and cool, the thrumming noises. He feels the brooding wait and murmur of hot afternoon, the trembling of the distant guns in the hot air, and the vast, oncoming hush and peace and silence of the dusk.

And then he is lying beside his father in the little gabled room upstairs. He is there beside his father and his father's brothers in the darkness—waiting, silent, waiting—with an unspoken single question in their hearts. They are thinking of an older brother who that night is lying twelve miles away, shot through the lungs. He sees his father's gaunt, long form in darkness, the big-boned hands, the gaunt, long face, the cold, green-gray, restless and weary eyes, so deep and untelling, so strangely lonely, and the slanting, almost reptilian large formation of the skull that has, somehow, its own strange dignity—as of some one lost. And the great stars of America blaze over them, the vast and lonely earth broods round them, then as now, with its secret and mysterious presences, and then as now the million-noted ululation of the night throngs up from silence the song of all its savage, dark and measureless fecundity. And he lies there in the darkness with his father and the brothers—silent, waiting—their cold, gray eyes turned upward to the loneliness of night, the blazing stars, having no words to say the thing they feel, the dream of time and the dark wonder of man's destiny which has drenched with blood the old earth, the familiar wheat, and fused that day the image of immortal history in a sleepy country town twelve miles away.

He sees the gaunt figure of the stonecutter coming across the square at his earth-devouring stride. He hears him muttering underneath his breath the mounting preludes of his huge invective. He sees him striding on forever, bent forward in his haste, wetting his thumb and clearing his throat with an infuriated and anticipatory relish as he comes. He sees him striding round the corner, racing up-hill towards the house, bearing huge packages of meat beneath his arm. He sees him take the high front steps four at a time, hasten like a hurricane into the house, lay down the meat upon the kitchen table, and then without a pause or introduction, comes the storm—fire, frenzy, curses, woes and lamentations, and then news out of the streets, the morning's joy, the smoking and abundant dinner.

A thousand memories of that life of constant and unresting fury brim in the boy's mind in an instant. At this moment, with telescopic force, all of these memories of his father's life become fused and blurred to one terrific image, in which it seems that the whole packed chronicle, from first to last, is perfectly comprised.

At the same moment the boy became conscious that the men were getting up around him, preparatory to departure, and that the florid-faced man, who had been speaking of his father, had laid his hand upon his shoulder in a friendly gesture, and was speaking to him.

"Good-night, son," the man was saying. "I'm getting off at Washington. If I don't see you again, good-luck to you. I suppose you'll be getting off at Baltimore to see your father before you go on, won't you?"

"Yes. Yes, sir," the boy stammered confusedly, getting to his feet.

"Remember me to him, won't you? Tell him you saw Frank Candler on the train and he sent his best regards."

"Yes, sir—thank you— I will," the boy said.

"All right. And good luck to you, boy," the politician said, giving him his broad, fleshy and rather tender hand. "Give 'em hell when you get up there," he said quietly, with a firm, friendly clasp and a good-natured wink.

"Yes—I certainly will—thank you—" the boy stammered, flaming in the face, with a feeling of proud hope, and with affection for the man who had spoken to him.

Then the man had gone, but his words had brought back to the boy suddenly the knowledge that in the morning he was to see his father. And that knowledge instantly destroyed all the exultancy of flight and darkness, the incredible realization of his escape, the image of new lands, the new life, and the shining city that had been swelling in his spirit all night long. It had interposed its leaden face between him and this image of wild joy towards which he was rushing onward in the darkness, and its gray oppressive cloud weighed down upon him suddenly a measureless weight of dull weariness, horror and disgust.

He knew that next day he must meet his brother and his father, he knew that the dreaded pause and interruption of his flight would last but two short days, and that in this brief time he might see and know for the last time all that was living of his father, and yet the knowledge of this hated meeting filled him with loathing, a terrible desire to get away from it as quickly as possible, to forget it, to escape from it forever.

He knew in his heart that for the wretched, feeble, whining old man whom he must meet next day, he felt no love whatever. He knew, indeed, that he felt instead a kind of hate—the wretched kind of hatred that comes from intolerable pity without love, from suffering and disgust, from the agony of heart and brain and nerves, the poisonous and morbid infection of our own lives, which a man dying of a loathsome disease awakes in us, and from the self-hate, the self-loathing that it makes us feel because of our terrible desire to escape him, to desert him, to blot out the horrible memory we have for him, utterly to forget him.

Now the three men remaining in the compartment were rising to depart. Old Flood got up with a painful grunt, carefully dropped the chewed butt of his cigar into the brass spittoon, and walked tenderly with a gouty and flat-footed shuffle across the little room to the mirrored door of the latrine. He opened it, entered, and closed it behind him. The pompous swarthy little man got up, stretched his short fat arms out stiffly, and said, "Well, I'll be turning in. I'll see you in the morning, won't I, Jim?"

The man with the thin, tight, palely freckled face, to whom these words had been addressed, looked up quickly from the magazine he was reading, and said sharply, in a rather cold, surprised and distant tone:

"What? . . . Oh! Yes. Good-night, Wade."

He got up then, carefully detached the horn-rimmed spectacles from his long, pointed nose, folded them carefully and put them in the breast pocket of his coat, and then took up the brief-case at his side. At this moment, a man, accompanied by Robert Weaver and by another youth who was about the same age as the boy, entered the smoking-room.

The man, who was in his middle thirties, was a tall lean Englishman, already bald, with bitten and incisive features, a cropped mustache, and the high hard flush of the steady drinker.

His name was John Hugh William Macpherson Marriott. He was the youngest son of an ancient family of the English nobility and just a year or two before he had married the great heiress, Virginia Willets. To the boy, and to all the other men in the train, except the man with the cold thin face and pointed nose, the Englishman was known only by sight and rumor, and his sudden entrance into the smoking-room had much the same effect as would the appearance of a figure from some legendary world of which they had often heard, but which they had never seen.

The reason for this feeling was that the Englishman and his wife lived on the great estate near town which her father had built and left to her. All the people in the town had seen this immense estate, had driven over some of its 90,000 acres, had seen its farms, its fields, its pastures, and its forests, its dairies, buildings, and its ranges of wild, smoke-blue mountains. And finally they had all seen from a distance its great mansion house, the gables, roof, and spires of a huge stone structure modelled on one of the great châteaux of France. But few of them had ever been inside the place or known the wonderful people who lived there.

All the lives of these fortunate people had become, therefore, as strange and wonderful to the people of the town as the lives of legendary heroes. And in a curious way that great estate had shaped the whole life of the town. To be a part of that life, to be admitted there, to know the people who belonged to it would have been the highest success, the greatest triumph that most of the people in the town could imagine. They could not admit it, but it was the truth. At the heart of the town's desire was the life of that great house.

The Englishman had entered the smoking compartment with the driving movement of a man who has been drinking hard, but is used to it. The moment that he entered, however, and saw the other people there he stopped short, with a kind of stunned abruptness. In a moment, after an astounded silence, he spoke to them, greeting them with the rough, brief, blurted-out friendliness of a shy and reticent man:

"Hello! . . . Oh, hello! . . . How do!" He grinned formally and suddenly began to stare with an astounded expression at the gouty figure of old Flood who at just this moment had opened the door of the latrine

and was shuffling painfully out into the compartment. Mr. Flood
stopped and returned his look in kind, with his bulging and bejowled
stare of comic stupefaction.

In a moment more the Englishman recovered himself, grimaced with
his shy, quick, toothy grin, and blurted out at Flood, as to the other men:
"Oh, hello! Hello! How d'ye do!"

"I'm pretty good, thank you!" old Flood said hoarsely and slowly,
after a heavy pause. "How are you?" and continued to stare heavily and
stupidly at him.

But already the Englishman had turned abruptly from him, his face
and lean neck reddening instantly and fiercely with the angry embarrassment of a shy man. And with the same air of astonished discovery
he now addressed himself to the man with the long thin nose and palely
freckled face, blurting his words out rapidly and by rushes as before,
but somehow conveying to the others the sense of his intimacy and
friendship with this man and of their own exclusion.

"Oh! . . . There you are, Jim!" he was saying in his astounded and
explosive fashion. "Where the devil have you been all night? . . . I
say!" he went on rapidly without waiting for an answer, "won't you
come in and have a spot with me before you turn in?"

Every suggestion of the disdain and cold aloofness which had characterized the other man's manner towards his fellow passengers, had now
vanished at the Englishman's words. Indeed, in the way he now came
forward, smiling, and put his hand in a friendly manner on the Englishman's arm, there was something almost scrambling in its effusive eagerness. "Why yes, Hugh," he said hastily. "I'd be delighted, of course!
. . . Just a minute," he said in an almost confused tone of voice, "till I
get my brief-case. . . . Where did I leave it? Oh, here it is!" he cried,
picking it up, and making for the door with his companion, "I'm all
ready now! Let's go!"

"Hugh! Hugh!" cried Robert who had accompanied the Englishman
when he entered the compartment, and whom the Englishman now
seemed to have forgotten entirely, "will I see you tomorrow before you
get off? The words were spoken in a deep, rapid, eager tone of voice,
and in the tone and manner of the youth who spoke them there was
the same suggestion of almost fawning eagerness that had characterized
the older man.

"Eh! What's that?" the Englishman cried in a startled tone, turning
abruptly and staring at the young man who had addressed him. "Oh!

Yes, Robert! I'm stopping at Washington! Look in for a moment, won't you, if you're up!"

Something in his tone and manner plainly and definitely said that the young man's company was no longer wanted for the evening, but the youth immediately nodded his head energetically and decisively, saying in a satisfied manner:

"Good! Good! I'll do that! I'll be in to say good-bye tomorrow morning."

"Right!" the Englishman said curtly. "Good-night! . . . Good-night! . . . Good-night!" he blurted out, turning around and addressing every one, yet seeing no one, in a series of toothy grimaces. "Oh—good-night!" he said suddenly, before going out, grinning and shaking hands briefly, in a gesture of permanent dismissal, with the other young man, who was a blond insignificant-looking youth, obviously a "hanger-on," with whom the Englishman evidently cared to have no further acquaintance. Then, pushing his companion before him through the green curtain, he went out suddenly with the same desperate shy abruptness, and in a moment the other men, saying good-night all around, had followed him, and the three young men were left alone in the compartment. It was now after one o'clock. Outside, the moon was up, flooding the dark earth of Virginia with a haunting light. That grand, moon-haunted earth stroked calmly past and, through the media of its changeless and unceasing change, the recession and recurrent movement of the enchanted scene, the train made on forever its tremendous monotone that was itself the rhythm of suspended time, the sound of silence and forever.

For a moment, after the men had gone, Robert stared down sternly and quizzically at the boy, with an expression of mock gravity, and then, in his rapid, eager, deep-toned and rather engaging voice, said:

"Well, Colonel? . . . What have you to say for yourself? . . . Was there grass on the back of her back, or was the foul deed perpetrated in your Hudson Super Six? . . . Come, sir! Explain yourself! Were you drunk or sober?" And suddenly lifting his thin, young, yet almost tortured-looking face and his restless eyes, which were inflamed with drink, and in whose haggard depths the incipient flashes of the madness which later would destroy him were already visible, he laughed suddenly, a strange, small, hoarsely falsetto kind of laugh, jerking his head towards the boy, and saying in an annoying and indefinite way:

"Crazy! Crazy! Crazy! . . . The craziest man I ever saw!" He stopped suddenly and, looking down at the boy for a moment with this same expression of haggard, over-driven restlessness, demanded impatiently:

"What have you been doing by yourself all night? Just sitting there all alone and doing nothing? . . . I'll swear, I don't see how you do it! . . . I'd go crazy sitting in one place like that without any one to talk to!" he said in an accusing and impatient tone of voice, as if the other youth had really done some extraordinary and unreasonable thing. He thrust one hand quickly and impatiently into the trousers' pocket of his well-cut clothes in such a way that his Delta Kappa Epsilon pin was for a moment visible. Then he stood there, jingling some coins about in his pocket and looking at the boy with his inflamed, restless, furiously desperate eyes. Turning away suddenly, with a movement of impatience, he shook his head in a gesture of astounded disbelief, laughed his little hoarse falsetto laugh again, and said:

"It beats me! . . . Don't see how he does it! . . . Damnedest man I ever saw! . . . It'd drive me crazy to be alone like that!"

He turned abruptly again, thrust both hands into his pockets, and for a moment stood looking at the boy with the old expression of mock gravity, and with a faintly malicious smile hovering about the edges of his thin, nervous, strongly modelled mouth.

"Do you know what they're saying about you at home? . . . Do you know what those people think of you? . . . Do you know what all those old women up there are doing now?" he said hoarsely and accusingly, in his deep, sonorous, and rapid tone.

"Now, Robert!" the boy suddenly shouted, in a choking and furious tone, getting to his feet. "Don't you start that stuff! I'm not going to listen to it! You can't fool me! They're not saying anything!"

Robert lifted his thin, finely drawn face and laughed again, his little annoying hoarse-falsetto laugh, in which a note of malice and triumph was audible.

"Why, they *are!*" he said solemnly. "It's the truth! . . . I think you ought to know about it! . . . I heard it everywhere, all over town!"

"Oh, Robert, you're a liar!" the boy cried furiously. *"What* did you hear all over town? You heard nothing!"

"Why, I *did!*" said Robert solemnly, as before. "I'll swear it to you. . . . Do you know what I heard the other day?" he went on in a blunt, accusing tone. "I heard that one of those women up there—some old sister in the Baptist Church—said she grew up with your mother and has known her all her life—well, she's praying for you!" said Robert solemnly. "I'll swear she is!"

"Praying for me!" the boy cried in an exasperated tone, but at the same time, feeling the numb white nauseous sickness of the heart which the intolerable thought that people are talking in a disparaging manner about him, his talents, or the success or failure of his life, can always bring to a young man. "Praying for me!" he fiercely shouted. "Why the hell should any one pray for me?"

"I know! I know!" said Robert, nodding his head vigorously, and speaking with grave agreement. "That's what I told them. That's just the way I felt about it! . . . But some of those people down there think you've gone to hell for good. . . . Do you know what I heard a woman say the other day? She said that Eugene Gant had gone straight to the devil since he went away to the State University——"

"Robert, I don't believe you!" the boy shouted. "You're making all this up!"

"Why, she did! So help me God, I heard her say it, as sure as I'm standing here," swore Robert solemnly. "She said you'd gone down there and taken Vergil Weldon's courses in philosophy and that you were ruined for life! She said you had turned into a regular infidel—didn't believe in God or anything any more. . . . Said she certainly did feel sorry for your mother," said Robert maliciously.

"Feel sorry for my mother!" the boy fairly howled, dancing around now like a maniac. "Why the hell should the old bitch feel sorry for my mother! My mother can take care of herself; she doesn't need any one to feel sorry for her! . . . All right, then!" he cried bitterly, with sudden acceptation of the other's story. "Let 'em pray! If that's the way they feel, let 'em pray till they wear corns on their God-damned knees! The dirty hypocrites!" he cried bitterly. "I'll show them! Sneaking around behind your back to tell their rotten lies about you—and their talk of praying for your soul! I'm glad I'm out of that damned town! The two-faced bastards! I wouldn't trust any of them as far as I could throw an elephant by his tail!"

"I know! I know!" said Robert, wagging his head in solemn agreement. "I agree with you absolutely. It's awful—that's what it is."

It was extraordinary that this absurd story, whether true or not, should have had such a violent effect on the emotions of the boy. Yet now that he had been told of some unknown woman's concern for the salvation of his soul, and that certain people of the praying sort already thought that he was "lost" the words were fastened in his flesh like rankling and envenomed barbs. And instantly, the moment that he heard this story and had cursed it, he thought that it was true. Now his mind could no longer remember the time just a moment before when Robert's words had seemed only an idle and malicious fabrication, probably designed to goad him, or, even if true, of no great importance.

But now, as if the idle gossip of the other youth had really pronounced some fatal and inexorable judgment against his whole life, the boy's spirit was set against "them" blindly, as against a nameless and hostile antagonist. Plunged suddenly into a dark weather of fatality and grim resolution, something in him was saying grimly and desperately:

"All right, then. If that's the way they feel about me, I'll show them." And seeing the lonely earth outside that went stroking past the windows of the train, he suddenly felt the dark and brooding joy of desperation and escape, and thought again: "Thank God, I've got away at last. Now there's a new land, a new life, new people like myself who will see and know me as I am and value me—and, by God, I'll show them! I'll show *them,* all right."

And at just this moment of his gloomy thoughts, he muttered sombrely, aloud, with sullen face:

"All right! To hell with them! I'll show them!"

—And was instantly aware that Robert was looking at him, laughing his little, malicious, hoarse, falsetto laugh, and that the other youth, who was a fair-haired, red-cheeked and pleasant-featured boy named Creasman, obviously somewhat inflamed by drink and by his social triumphs of the evening, was now, with an eager excessiveness of good-fellowship, slapping him on the back and saying boisterously:

"Don't let him kid you, Gene! To hell with them! What do you care what they say, anyway?"

With these words, he produced from his pocket a flask of the raw, colorless, savagely instant corn whiskey, of which both of them apparently had been partaking pretty freely, and tendering it to the boy, said:

"Here, take a drink!"

The boy took the flask, pulled out the cork, and putting the bottle to his lips, instantly gulped down two or three powerful swallows of the fiery stuff. For a moment, he stood there blind and choking, instantly robbed of breath, his throat muscles swelling, working, swallowing convulsively in an aching struggle to keep down the revolting and nauseous tasting stuff, and on no account to show the effort it was costing him.

"Is that the kick of the mule, or not?" said the Creasman boy, grinning and taking back his flask. "How is it?"

"Good!" the boy said hoarsely, gasping. "Fine! Best I ever tasted!" And he blinked his eyes rapidly to keep the tears from coming.

"Well, there's lots more where that came from, boy," said Creasman. "I've got two pint jars of it in my berth. Let me know when you want some more." And putting the bottle to his lips with a smile, he tilted his head, and drank in long easy swallows which showed he was no novice to the act.

"Damn!" cried Robert, staring at him, in his familiar tone of astounded disbelief. "Do you mean to tell me you can stand there drinking that stuff straight! Phew!" he said, shuddering, and making a face. "That old pukey stuff! Why, it'd rot the guts of a brass monkey! . . . I don't see how you people do it!" he cried protestingly, as he took the bottle. In three gulps he had drained it to the last drop, and even as he was looking around for a place to throw the empty flask, he shuddered convulsively again, made a contracted grimace of disgust, and said to the others accusingly, with his small falsetto laugh of astounded protest:

"Why, you'll kill yourself drinking that stuff raw! Don't you know that? You must be crazy! . . . Wait a minute," he muttered suddenly, comically, dropping the bottle deftly into his pocket, as the swarthy, pompous little man named Wade entered, attired in blue pajamas and a dressing gown, and holding a tooth-brush and a tube of tooth paste in his hand:

"Good-evening, sir! . . . Ah-hah! . . . How d'ye do!" said Robert, bowing slightly and stiffly, and speaking in his grave, staccato, curiously engaging tone.

"Still up, are you, boys?" the pompous little man remarked, with his usual telling aptness.

"Ah-hah-hah!" said Robert appreciatively. "Yes, sir! . . . Just fixin' to go! . . . Come on," he muttered to the others, jerking his head towards the little man warningly. "Not here! . . . Well, good-night, sir! . . . Goin' now."

"Good-night, boys," said the little man, who now had his back turned to them, and was standing at the silvery basin with his toothbrush held in readiness. "See you in the morning."

"Ah-hah-hah!" said Robert. "Yes, sir. That's right. Good-night."

And frowning in a meaningful way at his companions, he jerked his head toward the corridor, and, with an air of great severity, led them out.

"Didn't want him to see us with that bottle," he muttered when they were outside in the corridor. "Hell! He's got the biggest bank in town! Where'd you be if Emmet Wade ever got the idea you're a liquor-head! . . . Wait a minute!" he said, with the dissonant abruptness that characterized so much of his speech and action. "Come outside here—on the platform: nobody to see you there!"

"I'll meet you out there. I'll go and get another bottle," whispered Creasman, and disappeared along the darkened corridor in the direction of his berth. In a moment he returned, and the three of them went out upon the platform at the car-end, closed the door behind them and there, among the rocking and galloping noises of the pounding wheels, they took another long drink of the savage liquor. By this time the fiery stuff was leaping, pulsing, pounding the mounting and exuberant illusions of its power and strength through every tissue of their blood and life.

And outside, floating past their vision the huge pageant of its enchanted and immortal stillness, the old earth of Virginia now lay dreaming in the moon's white light.

So here they are now, three atoms on the huge breast of the indifferent earth, three youths out of a little town walled far away within the great rim of the silent mountains, already a distant, lonely dot upon the immense and sleeping visage of the continent. Here they are—three youths bound for the first time towards their image of the distant and enchanted city, sure that even though so many of their comrades had found there only dust and bitterness, the shining victory will be theirs. Here they are hurled onward in the great projectile of the train across the lonely visage of the everlasting earth. Here they are—three nameless grains of life among the manswarm ciphers of the earth, three faces of the million faces, three drops in the unceasing flood—and each of them a flame, a light, a glory, sure that his destiny is written in the blazing stars, his life shone over by the fortunate watches of the moon, his fame nourished and sustained by the huge earth, whose single darling charge he is, on whose immortal stillness he is flung onward in the night, his glorious fate set in the very brain and forehead of the fabulous, the unceasing city, of whose million-footed life he will tomorrow be a part.

Therefore they stand upon the rocking platform of the train, wild and dark and jubilant from the fierce liquor they have drunk, but more wild and dark and jubilant from the fury swelling in their hearts, the mad fury pounding in their veins, the savage, exultant and unutterable fury working like a madness in the adyts of their soul. And the great wheels smash and pound beneath their feet, the great wheels pound and smash and give a rhyme to madness, a tongue to hunger and desire, a certitude to all the savage, drunken, and exultant fury that keeps mounting, rising, swelling in them all the time!

Click, clack, clackety-clack; click, clack, clackety-clack; click, clack, clackety-clack; clackety-clackety-clack!

Hip, hop, hackety-hack; stip, step, rackety-rack; come and fetch it, come and fetch it, hickety hickety hack!

Rock, reel, smash, and swerve; hit it, hit it, on the curve; steady, steady, does the trick, keep her steady as a stick; eat the earth, eat the earth, slam and slug and beat the earth, and let her whir-r, and let her pur-r, at eighty per-r!

—Whew-w!

—Wow!

—God-dam!

—Put 'er there, boy!

—Put 'er there—whah!—*whah-h!* you ole long-legged frowsle-headed son-of-a-bitch!

—Whoop-ee! Whah—*whah-h!* Why, Go-d-d-dam!

—Whee! Vealer rog?

—Wadja say? Gant hearya!

—I say 'ja vealer rog? Wow! Pour it to her, son! Give 'er the gas! We're out to see the world! Run her off the god-damn track, boy! We don't need no rail, do we?

—Hell no! Which way does this damn train go, anyway, after it leaves Virginia?

—Maryland.

—Maryland my—! I don't want to go to Maryland! To hell with Mary's land! Also to hell with Mary's lamb and Mary's calf and Mary's blue silk underdrawers! Good old Lucy's the girl for me—the loosier the better! Give me Lucy any day! Good old Lucy Bowles, God bless her—she's the pick of the crowd, boys! Here's to Lucy!

Robert! Art there, boy?

—Aye, aye, sir! Present!

—Hast seen the damsel down in Lower Seven?

—I' sooth, sir, that I have! A comely wench, I trow!

—Peace, fool! Don't think, proud Princocke, thou canst snare this dove of innocence into the nets of infamous desire with stale reversions of thy wit! Out, out, vile lendings! An but thou carried'st at thy shrunken waist that monstrous tun of guts thou takest for a brain 'twould so beslubber this receiving earth with lard as was not seen twixt here and Nottingham since butter shrove! Out, out upon you, scrapings of the pot! A dove, a doe, it is a faultless swan, I say, a pretty thing!

Now Virginia lay dreaming in the moonlight. In Louisiana bayous the broken moonlight shivers the broken moonlight quivers the light of many rivers lay dreaming in the moonlight beaming in the moonlight dreaming in the moonlight moonlight moonlight seeming in the moonlight moonlight moonlight to be gleaming to be streaming in the moonlight moonlight moonlight moonlight moonlight moonlight moonlight moonlight

—Mo-hoo-oonlight-oonlight oonlight oonlight oonlight oonlight oonlight oonlight oonlight oonlight

—To be seeming to be dreaming in the moonlight!

WHAM!
SMASH!

—Now! God-dam, let her have it! Wow-w!

With slamming roar, hoarse waugh, and thunderbolted light, the southbound train is gone in one projectile smash of wind-like fury, and the open empty silence of its passing fills us, thrills us, stills us with the vision of Virginia in the moonlight, with the dream-still magic of Virginia in the moon.

And now, as if with recollected force, the train gains power from the train it passed, leaps, gathers, springs beneath them, smashes on with recollected demon's fury in the dark . . .

With slam-bang of devil's racket and God-dam of curse—give us the bottle, drink, boys, drink!—the power of Virginia lies compacted in the moon. To you, God-dam of devil's magic and slam-bang of drive, fire-flame of the terrific furnace, slam of rod, storm-stroke of pistoned wheel and thunderbolt of speed, great earth-devourer, city-bringer—hail!

To you, also, old glint of demon hawkeyes on the rail and the dark

gloved hand of cunning—you, there, old bristle-crops!—Tom Wilson,
H. F. Cline, or T. J. Johnson—whatever the hell your name is——
CASEY JONES! Open the throttle, boy, and let her rip! Boys, I'm a
belly-busting bastard from the State of old Catawba—a rootin' tootin'
shootin' son-of-a-bitch from Saw Tooth Gap in Buncombe—why, God
help this lovely bastard of a train—it is the best damned train that ever
turned a wheel since Casey Jones's father was a pup—why, you sweet
bastard, run! Eat up Virginia!—Give her the throttle, you old goggle-
eyed son-of-a-bitch up there!—Pour it to her! Let 'er have it, you nigger-
Baptist bastard of a shovelling fireman—let 'er rip!—Wow! By God,
we'll be in Washington for breakfast!

—Why, God bless this lovely bastard of a train! It is the best damned
train that ever pulled a car since Grant took Richmond!—Which way
does the damn thing go?—Pennsylvania?—Well, that's all right! Don't
you say a word against Pennsylvania! My father came from Pennsylvania, boys, he was the best damned man that ever lived—He was
a stonecutter and he's better than any son-of-a-bitch of a plumber you
ever saw—He's got a cancer and six doctors and they can't kill him!—
But to hell with going where we go!—We're out to see the world, boy!
—To hell with Baltimore, New York, Boston! Run her off the God-
damn rails! We're going West! Run her through the woods—cross
fields—rivers, through the hills! Hell's pecker! But I'll shove her up the
grade and through the gap, no double-header needed!—Let's see the
world now! Through Nebraska, boy! Let's shove her through, now,
you can do it!—Let's run her through Ohio, Kansas, and the unknown
plains! Come on, you hogger, let's see the great plains and the fields of
wheat—Stop off in Dakota, Minnesota, and the fertile places—Give us a
minute while you breathe to put our foot upon it, to feel it spring back
with the deep elastic feeling, 8000 miles below, unrolled and lavish,
depthless, different from the East.

Now Virginia lay dreaming in the moonlight! And on Florida's
bright waters the fair and lovely daughters of the Wilsons and the Potters; the Cabots and the Lowells; the Weisbergs and O'Hares; the Astors
and the Goulds; the Ransoms and the Rands; the Westalls and the Pat-
tons and the Webbs; the Reynolds and McRaes; the Spanglers and the
Beams; the Gudgers and the Blakes; the Pedersons and Craigs—all the
lovely daughters, the Robinsons and Waters, the millionaires' sweet
daughters, the Boston maids, the Beacon Slades, the Back Bay Wades,

all of the merchant, lawyer, railroad and well-monied grades of Hudson
River daughters in the moon's bright living waters—lay dreaming in the
moonlight, beaming in the moonlight, seeming in the moonlight, to be
dreaming to be gleaming in the moon.

—Give 'em hell, son!

—Here, give him another drink!—Attaboy! Drink her down!

—Drink her down—drink her down—drink her down—damn your
soul—drink her down!

—By God, I'll drink her down and flood the whole end of Virginia,
I'll drown out Maryland, make a flood in Pennsylvania—I tell you boys
I'll float 'em, I'll raise 'em up, I'll bring 'em down stream, now—I mean
the Potters and the Waters, the rich men's lovely daughters, the city's
tender daughters, the Hudson river daughters——

Lay dreaming in the moonlight, beaming in the moonlight, to be
seeming to be beaming in the moonlight moonlight moonlight oonlight
oonlight oonlight oonlight oonlight.

And Virginia lay dreaming in the moon.

Then the moon blazed down upon the vast desolation of the American coasts, and on all the glut and hiss of tides, on all the surge and
foaming slide of waters on lone beaches. The moon blazed down on
18,000 miles of coast, on the million sucks and scoops and hollows of the
shore, and on the great wink of the sea, that ate the earth minutely and
eternally. The moon blazed down upon the wilderness, it fell on sleeping woods, it dripped through moving leaves, it swarmed in weaving
patterns on the earth, and it filled the cat's still eye with blazing yellow.
The moon slept over mountains and lay like silence in the desert, and it
carved the shadows of great rocks like time. The moon was mixed with
flowing rivers, and it was buried in the heart of lakes, and it trembled on
the water like bright fish. The moon steeped all the earth in its living
and unearthly substance, it had a thousand visages, it painted continental
space with ghostly light; and its light was proper to the nature of all the
things it touched: it came in with the sea, it flowed with the rivers, and
it was still and living on clear spaces in the forest where no men watched.

And in woodland darkness great birds fluttered to their sleep—in
sleeping woodlands strange and secret birds, the teal, the nightjar, and
the flying rail went to their sleep with flutterings dark as hearts of sleeping men. In fronded beds and on the leaves of unfamiliar plants where
the tarantula, the adder, and the asp had fed themselves asleep on their

own poisons, and on lush jungle depths where green-golden, bitter red and glossy blue proud tufted birds cried out with brainless scream, the moonlight slept.

The moonlight slept above dark herds moving with slow grazings in the night, it covered lonely little villages; but most of all it fell upon the unbroken undulation of the wilderness, and it blazed on windows, and moved across the face of sleeping men.

Sleep lay upon the wilderness, it lay across the faces of the nations, it lay like silence on the hearts of sleeping men; and low upon lowlands, and high upon hills, flowed gently sleep, smooth-sliding sleep—sleep—sleep.

—Robert——

—Go on to bed, Gene, go to bed now, go to bed.

—There's shump'n I mush shay t'you——

—Damn fool! Go to bed!

—Go to bed, my balls! I'll go to bed when I'm God-damn good and ready! I'll not go to bed when there's shump'n I mush shay t'you——

—Go on to bed now, Gene. You've had enough.

—Creasman, you're a good fellow maybe but I don't know you. . . . You keep out of this. . . . Robert . . . I'm gonna tell y' shump'n. . . . You made a remark t'night I didn' like—Prayin' for me, are they, Robert?

—You damn fool!—You don't know what you're talkin' 'bout! Go on to bed!——

—I'll go to bed, you bastard—I got shump'n to shay t'you!—Prayin' for me, are yuh?—Pray for yourself, y' bloody little Deke!

—Damn fool's crazy! Go on to bed now——

—I'll bed yuh, you son-of-a-bitch! What was it that y' said that day?——

—What day? You damned fool, you don't know what you're saying!

—I'll tell yuh what day!—Coming along Chestnut Street that day after school with you and me and Sunny Jim Curtis and Ed Petrie and Bob Pegram and Carl Hartshorn and Monk Paul—and the rest of those boys——

—You damn fool! Chestnut Street! I don't know what you're talking about!

—Yes, you do!— You and me and Bob and Carl and Irwin and Jim Homes and some other boys— 'Member what y' said, yuh son-of-a-bitch?

Old man English was in his yard there burning up some leaves and it was October and we were comin' along there after school and you could smell the leaves and it was after school and you said, "Here's Mr. Gant the tomb-stone cutter's son."

—You damn fool! I don't know what you're talking about!——

—Yes, you do, you cheap Deke son-of-a-bitch— Too good to talk to us on the street when you were sucking around after Bruce Martin or Steve Patton or Jack Marriott—but a life-long brother—oh! couldn't see enough of us, could you, when you were alone?

—The damn fool's crazy!

—Crazy, am I?—Well, we never had any old gummy grannies tied down and hidden in the attic—which is more than some people that I know can say!—you son-of-a-bitch—who do you think you are with your big airs and big Deke pin!—My people were better people than your crowd ever hoped to be—we've been here longer and we're better people —and as for the tombstone cutter's son, my father was the best damned stonecutter that ever lived—he's dying of cancer and all the doctors in the world can't kill him—he's a better man than any little ex-police court magistrate who calls himself a judge will ever be—and that goes for you too—you——

Why, you crazy fool! I never said anything about your father——

To hell with you, you damn little bootlicking——

Come on Gene come on you've had enough you're drunk now come on.

Why God-damn you to hell, I hate your guts you——

All right, all right—He's drunk! He's crazy—Come on, Bill! Leave him alone!—He don't know what he's doing——.

All right. Good night, Gene. . . . Be careful now—See you in the morning, boy.

All right, Robert, I mean nothing against you—you——

All right!—All right!—Come on, Bill. Let him alone! Good night, Gene—Come on—let's go to bed!——

To bed to bed to bed to bed to bed! So, so, so, so, so! Make no noise, make no noise, draw the curtains; so, so, so. We'll go to supper i' the morning: so so, so.

And Ile goe to bedde at noone.

Alone, alone now, down the dark, the green, the jungle aisle between the dark drugged snorings of the sleepers. The pause, the stir, the sigh, the sudden shift, the train that now rumbles on through the dark forests of the dream-charged moon-enchanted mind its monotone of silence and forever: Out of these prison bands of clothes, now, rip, tear, toss, and haul while the green-curtained sleepers move from jungle depths and the even-pounding silence of eternity—into the stiff white sheets, the close, hot air, his long body crookedly athwart, lights out, to see it shining faintly in the coffined under-surface of the berth above—and sleepless, Virginia floating, dreamlike, in the still white haunting of the moon——

—At night, great trains will pass us in the timeless spell of an un-sleeping hypnosis, an endless, and unfathomable stupefaction. Then suddenly in the unwaking never sleeping century of the night, the sensual limbs of carnal whited nakedness that stir with drowsy silken warmth in the green secrecies of Lower Seven, the slow swelling and lonely and swarmhaunted land—and suddenly, suddenly, silence and thick hardening lust of dark exultant joy, the dreamlike passage of Virginia!—Then in the watches of the night a pause, the sudden silence of up-welling night, and unseen faces, voices, laughter, and farewells upon a lonely little night-time station—the lost and lonely voices of Americans:—"Good-bye! Good-bye, now! Write us when you get there, Helen! Tell Bob he's got to write!—Give my love to Emily!—Good-bye, good-bye now—write us, soon!"— And then the secret, silken and sub-dued rustling past the thick green curtains and the sleepers, the low respectful negroid tones of the black porter—and then the whistle cry, the tolling bell, the great train mounting to its classic monotone again, and presently the last lights of a little town, the floating void and lone-liness of moon-haunted earth—Virginia!

Also, in the dream—thickets of eternal night—there will be huge steamings on the rail, the sudden smash, the wall of light, the sudden flarings of wild, roaring light upon the moon-haunted and dream-tortured faces of the sleepers!

—And finally, in that dark jungle of the night, through all the visions, memories, and enchanted weavings of the timeless and eternal spell of time, the moment of forever—there are two horsemen, riding, riding, riding in the night.

Who are they? Oh, we know them with our life and they will ride across the land, the moon-haunted passage of our lives forever. Their names are Death and Pity, and we know their face: our brother and our father ride ever beside us in the dream-enchanted spell and vista of the night; the hooves keep level time beside the rhythms of the train.

Horsed on the black and moon-maned steeds of fury, cloaked in the dark of night, the spell of time, dream-pale, eternal, they are rushing on across the haunted land, the moon-enchanted wilderness, and their hooves make level thunder with the train.

Pale Pity and Lean Death their names are, and they will ride forever-more the moon-plantations of Virginia keeping time time time to the level thunder of the train pounding time time time as with four-hooved thunder of phantasmal hooves they pound forever level with the train across the moon-plantations of Virginia.

Quadrupedante putrem sonitu quatit ungula campum as with storm-phantasmal hooves Lean Death and Pale Pity with quadrupedante putrem sonitu quatit ungula campum . . . campum . . . quadrupe-dante . . . putrem . . . putrem . . . putrem putrem putrem as with sonitu quatit ungula campum quadrupedante putrem . . . putrem . . . putrem putrem putrem . . . putrem . . . putrem . . . putrem putrem putrem quadrupedante quadrupedante quadrupedante putrem putrem as with sonitu quatit ungula campum quadrupedante putrem . . . pu-trem . . . putrem putrem putrem . . . as with sonitu quatit ungula campum quadrupedante putrem . . . ungula campum . . . campum . . . ungula . ungula campum . . .

V

At day-break suddenly, he awoke. The first light of the day, faint, gray-white, shone through the windows of his berth. The faint gray light fell on the stiff white linen, feverishly scuffed and rumpled in the distressful visions of the night, on the hot pillows and on the long cramped figure of the boy, where dim reflection already could be seen on the polished surface of the berth above his head. Outside, that smoke-gray light had stolen almost imperceptibly through the darkness. The air now shone gray-blue and faintly luminous with day, and the old brown earth was just beginning to emerge in that faint light. Slowly, the old brown earth was coming from the darkness with that strange and awful stillness which the first light of the day has always brought.

The earth emerged with all its ancient and eternal quality: stately and solemn and lonely-looking in that first light, it filled men's hearts with all its ancient wonder. It seemed to have been there forever, and, though they had never seen it before, to be more familiar to them than their mother's face. And at the same time it seemed they had discovered it once more, and if they had been the first men who ever saw the earth, the solemn joy of this discovery could not have seemed more strange or more familiar. Seeing it, they felt nothing but silence and wonder in their hearts, and were naked and alone and stripped down to their bare selves, as near to truth as men can ever come. They knew that they would die and that the earth would last forever. And with that feeling of joy, wonder, and sorrow in their hearts, they knew that another day had gone, another day had come, and they knew how brief and lonely are man's days.

The old earth went floating past then in that first gaunt light of the morning, and it seemed to be the face of time itself, and the noise the train made was the noise of silence. They were fixed there in that classic design of time and silence. The engine smoke went striding out upon the air, the old earth—field and wood and hill and stream and wood and field and hill—went stroking, floating past with a kind of everlasting repetitiveness, and the train kept making on its steady noise that was like silence and forever—until it almost seemed that they were poised there in that image of eternity forever—in moveless movement, unsilent silence, spaceless flight.

All of the noises, rhythms, sounds and variations of the train seemed to belong to all the visions, images, wild cries and oaths and songs and haunting memories of the night before, and now the train itself seemed united to this infinite monotone of silence, and the boy felt that this land now possessed his life, that he had known it forever, and could now think only with a feeling of unbelief and wonder that yesterday—just yesterday—he had left his home in the far mountains and now was stroking eastward, northward towards the sea.

And against the borders of the East, pure, radiant, for the first time seen in the unbelievable wonder of its new discovery, bringing to all of us, as it had always done, the first life that was ever known on this earth, the golden banner of the day appeared.

VI

IN morning sunlight on a hospital porch, five flights above the ground, an old dying spectre of a man was sitting, looking mournfully out across the sun-hazed sweep of the city he had known in his youth. He sat there, a rusty, creaking hinge, an almost severed thread of life, a shockingly wasted integument of skin and bone, of which every fibre and sinew was almost utterly rotted out, consumed and honey-combed by the great plant of the cancer. which flowered from his entrails and had now spread its fibrous roots to every tissue of his life. Everything was gone: everything was wasted from him: the face was drawn tight and boney as a beak, the skin was clean, tinged with a fatal cancerous yellow, and almost delicately transparent. The great thin blade of nose cut down across the face with knife-like sharpness and in the bony, slant· ing, almost reptilian cage-formation of the skull, the smallish cold-gray-green eyes were set wearily, with a wretched and enfeebled dullness, out across the great space of the city which swept away and melted at length into the sun-hazed vistas of October.

Nothing was left but his hands. The rest of the man was dead. But the great hands of the stonecutter, on whose sinewy and bony substance there was so little that disease or death could waste, looked as power-ful and living as ever. Although one of his hands—the right one—had been stiffened years before by an attack of rheumatism, they had lost none of their character of power and massive shapeliness.

In the huge shapely knuckles, in the length and sinewy thickness of the great fingers—which were twice the size of an ordinary man's—and in the whole length and sinewy contour of the hand, there was a quality of sculptural design which was as solid and proportionate as any of the marble hands of love and grace which the stonecutter had so often carved upon the surface of a grave-yard monument.

Thus, as he sat there now, staring dully out across the city, an emaciated and phantasmal shadow of a man, there was, in the appear-ance of these great living hands of power (one of which lay with an enormous passive grace and dignity across the arm of his chair and the other extended and clasped down upon the handle of a walking stick), something weirdly incongruous, as if the great strong hands had been unnaturally attached to the puny lifeless figure of a scarecrow.

Now, wearily, desperately, the old enfeebled mind was trying to grope with the strange and bitter miracle of life, to get some meaning out of that black, senseless fusion of pain and joy and agony, that web that had known all the hope and joy and wonder of a boy, the fury, passion, drunkenness, and wild desire of youth, the rich adventure and fulfilment of a man, and that had led him to this fatal and abominable end.

But that fading, pain-sick mind, that darkened memory could draw no meaning and no comfort from its tragic meditation.

The old man's land of youth was far away in time, yet now only the magic lonely hills of his life's journey, his wife's people, seemed sorrowful, lonely, lost, and strange to him. Now he remembered all places, things, and people in his land of youth as if he had known them instantly and forever!

Oh, what a land, a life, a time was that—that world of youth and no return. What colors of green-gold, magic, rich plantations, and shining cities were in it! For now when this dying man thought about this vanished life that tragic quality of sorrow and loneliness had vanished instantly. All that he had read in books about old wars seemed far and lost and in another time, but when he thought about these things that he had known as a boy, he saw them instantly, knew them, breathed them, heard them, felt them, was there beside them, living them with his own life. He remembered now his wife's people!—tramping in along the Carlisle Pike on that hot first morning in July, as they marched in towards Gettysburg. He had been standing there with his next older brother Gil, beside the dusty road, as they came by.

And he could see them now, not as shadowy, lost, phantasmal figures of dark time, the way they were in books; he saw them, heard them, knew them again as they had been in their shapeless rags of uniforms, their bare feet wound in rags, their lank disordered hair, sometimes topped by stove-pipe hats which they had looted out of stores.

"God!" the old man thought, wetting his great thumb briefly, grinning thinly, as he shook his head, "What a scare-crow crew that was! In all my days I never saw the like of it! A bum-looking lot, if ever there was one!—And the bravest of the brave, the finest troops that ever lived!" —his mind swung upward to its tide of rhetoric—"Veterans all of them, who had been through the bloodiest battles of the war, they did not know the meaning of the word 'fear,' and they would have gone into the valley of death, the jaws of hell, at a word from their Commander!" His mind was alive again, in full swing now, the old voice rose and muttered on the tides of rhetoric, the great hand gestured, the cold-gray, restless eyes glared feverishly about—and all of it began to live for him again.

He remembered how he and Gil had been standing there beside the road, two barefoot farmer boys, aged thirteen and fifteen, and he remembered how the rebels would halt upon their march, and shout jesting remarks at the two boys standing at the road. One shouted out to Gil:

"Hi, there, Yank! You'd better hide! Jeb Stuart's on the way an' he's been lookin' fer you!"

And Gil, older, bolder, more assured than he, quick-tempered, stubborn, fiercely partisan, had come back like a flash:

"He'll be lookin' fer *you* when we get through with you!" said Gil and the rebels had slapped their ragged thighs and howled with laughter, shouting at their crestfallen, grinning comrade:

" 'Y, God! I reckon you'll be quiet now! He shore God put it on ye that time!"

And he was there beside his brother, seeing, hearing, living it again, as he remembered his strange first meeting with the Pentland tribe, the haunting miracle of that chance meeting. For among that ragged crew he had first seen his wife's uncle, the prophet, Bacchus Pentland, and he had seen him, heard him that hot morning, and had never been able to forget him, although it would be twenty years, after many strange turnings of the roads of destiny and wandering, before he was to see the man again, and know his name, and join together the two halves of fated meeting.

Yes, there had been one among the drawling and terrible mountaineers that day who passed there on that dusty road, and paused, and talked, and waited in the heat, one whose face he had never been able to forget— one whose full, ruddy face and tranquil eyes were lighted always by a smile of idiot and beatific saintliness, whose powerful fleshy body gave off a stench that would have put a goat to shame, and who on this account was called by his jesting comrades, "Stinking Jesus." Yes, he had been there that morning, Bacchus Pentland, the fated and chosen of God, the supernatural appearer on roads at nightfall, the harbinger of death, the prophet, chanting even then his promises of Armageddon and the Coming of the Lord, speaking for the first time to the fascinated ears of those two boys, the full, drawling, unctuous accents of the fated, time-triumphant Pentlands.

They came, they halted in the dust before the two young brothers, the lewd tongues mocked and jested, but that man of God, the prophet Bacchus Pentland, was beautifully unmoved by their unfaith, and chanted, with a smile of idiot beatitude, his glorious assurances of an end of death and battle, everlasting peace:

"Hit's a comin'!" cried the prophet with the sweet purity of his saintly smile. "Hit's a comin'! Accordin' to my figgers the Great Day is almost here! Oh, hit's a comin', boys!" he sweetly, cheerfully intoned, "Christ's kingdom on this airth's at hand! We're marchin' in to Armageddon now!"

"Hell, Back!" drawled one, with a slow grin of disbelief. "You said the same thing afore Chancellorsville, an' all I got from it was a slug of canister in my tail!"—and the others slapped their ragged thighs and shouted.

"Hit's a comin'!" Bacchus cried, with a brisk wink, and his seraphic smile, unmoved, untouched, by their derision. "He'll be here a-judgin' an' decreein' afore the week is over, settin' up His Kingdom, an' sortin' us all out the way it was foretold—the sheep upon His right hand an' the goats upon His left."

"An' which side are you goin' to be on, Back, when all this sortin' starts?" one drawled with evil innocence. "Are you goin' to be upon the sheep-side or the goat-side?" he demanded.

"Oh," cried Bacchus cheerfully, with his seraphic smile, "I'll be upon the sheep-side, brother, with the Chosen of the Lord."

"Then, Back," the other slowly answered, "you'd shore God better begin to smell a whole lot better than you do right now, for if the Lord starts sortin' in the dark, Back, He's goin' to put you where you don't belong—He'll have you over thar among the goats!"—and the hot brooding air had rung then with their roars of laughter. Then a word was spoken, an order given, the ragged files trudged on again, and they were gone.

Now this was lost, a fume of smoke, the moment's image of a fading memory, and he could not say it, speak it, find a word for it—but he could see that boy of his lost youth as he sat round the kitchen table with the rest of them. He could see his cold-gray, restless, unhappy eyes, the strange, gaunt, almost reptilian conformation of his staring face, his incredibly thin, blade-like nose, as he waited there in silence, looking uneasily at the others with his cold-gray, shallow, most unhappy eyes. And the old man seemed to be the spy of destiny, to look at once below the roofs of a million little houses everywhere and on the star-shone, death-flung mystery of the silent battlefield.

He seemed to be a witness of the secret weavings of dark chance that threads our million lives into strange purposes that we do not know. He thought of those dead and wounded men upon the battlefield whose lives would touch his own so nearly, the wounded brother that he knew, the wounded stranger he had seen that day by magic chance, whom he could not forget, and whose life, whose tribe, in the huge abyss and secret purpose of dark time would one day interweave into his own.

Oh, he could not find a word, a phrase to utter it, but he seemed to have the lives not only of those people in him, but the lives of millions of others whose dark fate is thus determined, interwove, and beyond their vision or their knowledge, foredone and made inevitable in the dark destiny of unfathomed time. And suddenly it seemed to him that all of it was his, even as his father's blood and earth was his, the lives and deaths and destinies of all his people. He had been a nameless atom in the great family of earth, a single, unknown thread in the huge warp of fate and chance that weaves our lives together and because of this he had been the richest man that ever lived; the power, grandeur, glory of this earth and all its lives of men were his.

And for a moment he forgot that he was old and dying, and pride, joy, pain, triumphant ecstasy that had no tongue to utter it rose like a wordless swelling pæan in his throat, because it seemed to him that this great familiar earth on which his people lived and wrought was his, that all the mystery, grandeur and beauty in the lives of men were his, and that he must find a word, a tongue, a door to utter what was his, or die!

How could he say it! How could he ever find a word to speak the joy, the pain, the grandeur bursting in the great vine of his heart, swelling like a huge grape in his throat—mad, sweet, wild, intolerable with all the mystery, loneliness, wild secret joy, and death, the ever-returning and renewing fruitfulness of the earth!

A cloud-shadow passed and left no light but loneliness on the massed green of the wilderness! A bird was calling in a secret wood! And there was something going, coming, fading there across the sun—oh, there was something lonely and most sorrowful, his mother's voice, the voices of lost men long, long ago, the flowing of a little river in the month of April—and all, all of it was his!

A man had passed at sunset on a lonely road and vanished unknown years ago! A soldier had toiled up a hill at evening and was gone! A man was lying dead that day upon a bloody field!—and all, all, all of it was his!

He had stood beside a dusty road, feet bare, his gaunt boy's face cold-eyed, staring, restless, and afraid. The ragged jesting rebels passed before him in the dusty heat, the huge drowse and cricketing stitch of noon was rising from the sweet woods and nobly swelling, fertile fields of Pennsylvania and all, all, all of it was his!

A prophet passed before him in the road that day with the familiar haunting unction of an unmet, unheard tribe; a wounded prophet lay that night below the stars and chanted glory, peace, and Armageddon; the boy's brother lay beside the prophet bleeding from the lungs; the boy's people grimly waited all night long in a little house not fourteen miles away; and all, all, all of it was his!

Over the wild and secret earth, the lonely, everlasting, and unchanging earth, under the huge tent of the all-engulfing night, amid the fury, chaos, blind confusions of a hundred million lives, something wild and secret had been weaving through the generations, a dark terrific weaving of the threads of time and destiny.

But it had come to this: an old man dying on a porch, staring through the sun-hazed vistas of October towards the lost country of his youth.

This was the end of man, then, end of life, of fury, hope, and passion, glory, all the strange and bitter miracle of chance, of history, fate, and destiny which even a stonecutter's life could include. This was the end, then:—an old man, feeble, foul, complaining and disease-consumed who sat looking from the high porch of a hospital at the city of his youth. This was the sickening and abominable end of flesh, which infected time and all man's living memory of morning, youth, and magic with the death-putrescence of its cancerous taint, and made us doubt that we had ever lived, or had a father, known joy: this was the end, and the end was horrible in ugliness. At the end it was not well.

On the last morning when his sons came, Gant was there on the high porch of the hospital, among the other old men who were sitting there. All of the old men looked very feeble, shrunk, and wasted, their skins had the clear and frail transparency that men get in hospitals, and in the bright tremendous light of morning and October, the old men looked forlorn.

Some looked out wearily and vacantly across the sun-hazed vistas of the city, with the dull and apathetic expression of men who are tired of pain and suffering and disease, and who wish to die. Others, who were in a state of convalescence after operations, looked out upon the sun-lit city with pleased, feeble smiles, awkwardly holding cigars in their frail fingers, putting them in their mouths with the uncertain and unaccustomed manner which a convalescent has, and looking up slowly, questioningly, with a feeble and uncertain smile into the faces of their relatives, wives, or children, as if to ask if it could really be true that they were going to live instead of die.

Their smiles and looks were pitiful in their sense of childish trust, of growing hopefulness, of wondering disbelief, but there was something shameful in them, too. In these feeble smiles of the old men there was something pleased and impotent, as if they had been adroitly castrated in the hospital, and shorn of their manhood. And for some reason, one felt suddenly a choking anger and resentment against some force in life which had betrayed these old men and made them impotent—something unspeakably ruthless, cruel, and savage in the world which had made these old and useless capons. And this anger against this unknown force suddenly took personal form in a blind resentment against doctors, nurses, internes, and the whole sinister and suave perfection of the hospital which, under glozing words and cynical assurances, could painlessly and deftly mutilate a living man.

The great engine of the hospital, with all its secret, sinister, and inhuman perfections, together with its clean and sterile smells which seemed to blot out the smell of rotting death around one, became a hateful presage of man's destined end. Suddenly, one got an image of his own death in such a place as this—of all that death had come to be—and the image of that death was somehow shameful. It was an image of a death without man's ancient pains and old gaunt aging—an image of death drugged and stupefied out of its ancient terror and stern dignities —of a shameful death that went out softly, dully in anesthetized oblivion, with the fading smell of chemicals on man's final breath. And the image of that death was hateful.

Thus, as Gant sat there, his great figure wasted to the bone, his skin yellow and transparent, his eyes old and dead, his chin hanging loose and petulant, as he stared dully and unseeingly out across the great city of his youth, his life seemed already to have been consumed and wasted, emptied out into the void of this cruel and inhuman space. Nothing was left, now, to suggest his life of fury, strength and passion except his hands. And the hands were still the great hands of the stone-cutter, powerful, sinewy, and hairy as they had always been, attached now with a shocking incongruity to the wasted figure of a scarecrow.

Then, as he sat there staring dully and feebly out upon the city, his great hairy hands quietly at rest upon the sides of his chair, the door opened and his two sons came out upon the porch.

"W-w-w-well, Papa," Luke sang out in his rich stammering tones. "Wy-wy, wy, wy, I f'ought we'd just c-c-c-come by for a m-m-m-moment to let Gene say g-g-good-bye to you." In a low tone to his younger brother he added nervously, "Wy, I f'ink, I f'ink I'd m-m-make it short and snappy if I were you. D-d-don't say anyf'ing to excite him, wy, wy, wy, I'd just say good-bye."

"Hello, son," said Gant quietly and dully, looking up at him. For a moment his great hand closed over the boy's, and he said quietly:

"Where are you going?"

"Wy, wy, wy, he's on his way up Norf . . . wy . . . he's g-g-going to Harvard, Papa."

"Be a good boy, son," Gant said gently. "Do the best you can. If you need anything let your mother know," he said wearily and indifferently, and turned his dead eyes away across the city.

"Wy . . . wy . . wy he'd like to tell you——"

"Oh, Jesus. . . . I don't want to hear about it," Gant began to sniffle in a whining tone. . . . "Why must it all be put on me . . . sick and old as I am? . . . If he wants anything let him ask his mother for it . . . it's fearful, it's awful, and it's cruel that you should afflict a sick man in this way." He was sniffling petulantly and his chin, on which a wiry stubble of beard was growing, trembled and shook like that of a whining child.

"I . . . I . . . I f'ink I'd just say g-g-good-bye now, Gene . . . m-m-make it, wy make it quick if you can: he's not f-f-feeling good today."

"Good-bye, Papa," the boy said, and bending, took his father's great right hand.

"Good-bye, son," Gant now said quietly as before, looking up at him. He presented his grizzled mustache, and the boy kissed him briefly, feeling the wiry bristles of the mustache brush his cheek as they had always done.

"Take care of yourself, son," said Gant kindly. "Do the best you can." And for a moment he covered the boy's hand with one great palm, and gestured briefly across the city: "I was a boy here," Gant said quietly, "over fifty years ago . . . old Jeff Streeter's hotel where I lived was there," he pointed briefly with his great forefinger. ". . . I was alone in this great city like the city you are going to—a poor friendless country boy who had come here to learn his trade as apprentice to a stonecutter . . . and I had come from . . . *there!*" as he spoke these words, a flash of the old power and life had come into Gant's voice, and now he was pointing his great finger strongly towards the sun-hazed vistas of the North and West.

"There!" cried Gant strongly now, his eye bright and shining as he followed the direction of his pointing finger. "Do you see, son? . .

Pennsylvania . . . Gettysburg . . . Brant's Mill . . . the country that
I came from is *there!* . . . Now I shall never see it any more," he said.
"I'm an old man and I'm dying. . . . The big farms . . . the orchards
. . . the great barns bigger than houses. . . . You must go back, son,
someday to see the country that your father came from. . . . I was a boy
here," the old man muttered. "Now I'm an old man. . . . I'll come back
no more. . . . No more . . . it's pretty strange when you come to think
of it," he muttered, "by God it is!"

"Wy, wy, P-p-p-papa," Luke said nervously, "I . . . I f'ink if he's
g-g-going to get his train wy we'd better——"

"Good-bye, son," Gant said quietly again, giving the boy the pressure
of his great right hand. "Be a good boy, now."

But already all the fires of life, so briefly kindled by this memory of
the past, had died away: he was an old sick man again, and he had
turned his dead eyes away from his son and was staring dully out across
the city.

"Good-bye, Papa," the boy said, and then paused uncertainly, not
knowing further what to say. From the old man there had come suddenly the loathsome stench of rotting death, corrupt mortality, and he
turned swiftly away with a feeling of horror in his heart, remembering
the good male smell of childhood and his father's prime—the smell of
the old worn sofa, the chairs, the sitting room, the roaring fires, the plug
tobacco on the mantelpiece.

At the screen door he paused again and looked back down the porch.
His father was sitting there as he had left him, among the other old
dying men, his long chin loose, mouth half open, his dead dull eye fixed
vacantly across the sun-hazed city of his youth, his great hand of power
quietly dropped upon his cane.

Down in the city's central web, the boy could distinguish faintly the
line of the rails, and see the engine smoke above the railroad yards, and
as he looked, he heard far off that haunting sound and prophecy of
youth and of his life—the bell, the wheel, the wailing whistle—and the
train.

Then he turned swiftly and went to meet it—and all the new lands,
morning, and the shining city. Upon the porch his father had not moved
or stirred. He knew that he should never see him again.

BOOK II

YOUNG FAUSTUS

VII

THE train rushed on across the brown autumnal land, by wink of water and the rocky coasts, the small white towns and flaming colors and the lonely, tragic and eternal beauty of New England. It was the country of his heart's desire, the dark Helen in his blood forever burning —and now the fast approach across October land, the engine smoke that streaked back on the sharp gray air that day!

The coming on of the great earth, the new lands, the enchanted city, the approach, so smoky, blind and stifled, to the ancient web, the old grimed thrilling barricades of Boston. The streets and buildings that slid past that day with such a haunting strange familiarity, the mighty engine steaming to its halt, and the great train-shed dense with smoke and acrid with its smell and full of the slow pantings of a dozen engines, now passive as great cats, the mighty station with the ceaseless throngings of its illimitable life, and all of the murmurous, remote and mighty sounds of time forever held there in the station, together with a tart and nasal voice, a hand'sbreadth off that said: "There's hahdly time, but try it if you want."

He saw the narrow, twisted, age-browned streets of Boston, then, with their sultry fragrance of fresh-roasted coffee, the sight of the man-swarm passing in its million-footed weft, the distant drone and murmur of the great mysterious city all about him, the shining water of the Basin, and the murmur of the harbor and its ships, the promise of glory and of a thousand secret, lovely and mysterious women that were waiting somewhere in the city's web.

He saw the furious streets of life with their unending flood-tide of a million faces, the enormous library with its million books; or was it just one moment in the flood-tide of the city, at five o'clock, a voice, a face, a brawny lusty girl with smiling mouth who passed him in an instant at the Park Street station, stood printed in the strong October wind a moment—breast, belly, arm, and thigh, and all her brawny lusti-hood—and then had gone into the man-swarm, lost forever, never found?

Was it at such a moment—engine-smoke, a station, a street, the sound of time, a face that came and passed and vanished, could not be forgot—

89

here or *here* or *here,* at such a moment of man's unrecorded memory, that he breathed fury from the air, that fury came?

He never knew; but now mad fury gripped his life, and he was haunted by the dream of time. Ten years must come and go without a moment's rest from fury, ten years of fury, hunger, all of the wandering in a young man's life. And for what? For what?

What is the fury which this youth will feel, which will lash him on against the great earth forever? It is the brain that maddens with its own excess, the heart that breaks from the anguish of its own frustration. It is the hunger that grows from everything it feeds upon, the thirst that gulps down rivers and remains insatiate. It is to see a million men, a million faces and to be a stranger and an alien to them always. It is to prowl the stacks of an enormous library at night, to tear the books out of a thousand shelves, to read in them with the mad hunger of the youth of man.

It is to have the old unquiet mind, the famished heart, the restless soul; it is to lose hope, heart, and all joy utterly, and then to have them wake again, to have the old feeling return with overwhelming force that he is about to find the thing for which his life obscurely and desperately is groping—for which all men on this earth have sought—one face out of the million faces, a wall, a door, a place of certitude and peace and wandering no more. For what is it that we Americans are seeking always on this earth? Why is it we have crossed the stormy seas so many times alone, lain in a thousand alien rooms at night hearing the sounds of time, dark time, and thought until heart, brain, flesh and spirit were sick and weary with the thought of it; "Where shall I go now? What shall I do?"

He did not know the moment that it came, but it came instantly, at once. And from that moment on mad fury seized him, from that moment on, his life, more than the life of any one that he would ever know, was to be spent in solitude and wandering. Why this was true, or how it happened, he would never know; yet it was so. From this time on—save for two intervals in his life—he was to live about as solitary a life as a modern man can have. And it is meant by this that the number of hours, days, months, and years—the actual time he spent alone—would be immense and extraordinary.

And this fact was all the more astonishing because he never seemed to seek out solitude, nor did he shrink from life, or seek to build himself into a wall away from all the fury and the turmoil of the earth. Rather, he loved life so dearly that he was driven mad by the thirst and hunger which he felt for it. Of this fury, which was to lash and drive him on for fifteen years, the thousandth part could not be told, and what is told may seem unbelievable, but it is true. He was driven by a hunger so literal, cruel and physical that it wanted to devour the earth and all the things and people in it, and when it failed in this attempt, his spirit would drown in an ocean of horror and desolation, smothered below the overwhelming tides of this great earth, sickened and made sterile, hopeless, dead by the stupefying weight of men and objects in the world, the everlasting flock and flooding of the crowd.

Now he would prowl the stacks of the library at night, pulling books out of a thousand shelves and reading in them like a madman. The thought of these vast stacks of books would drive him mad: the more he read, the less he seemed to know—the greater the number of the books he read, the greater the immense uncountable number of those which he could never read would seem to be. Within a period of ten years he read at least 20,000 volumes—deliberately the number is set low—and opened the pages and looked through many times that number. This may seem unbelievable, but it happened. Dryden said this about Ben Jonson: "Other men read books but he read libraries"—and so now was it with this boy. Yet this terrific orgy of the books brought him no comfort, peace, or wisdom of the mind and heart. Instead, his fury and despair increased from what they fed upon, his hunger mounted with the food it ate.

He read insanely, by the hundreds, the thousands, the ten thousands, yet he had no desire to be bookish; no one could describe this mad assault upon print as scholarly: a ravening appetite in him demanded that he read everything that had ever been written about human experience. He read no more from pleasure—the thought that other books were waiting for him tore at his heart forever. He pictured himself as tearing the entrails from a book as from a fowl. At first, hovering over book stalls, or walking at night among the vast piled shelves of the library, he would read, watch in hand, muttering to himself in triumph or anger at the timing of each page: "Fifty seconds to do that one. Damn you, we'll see! You will, will you?"—and he would tear through the next page in twenty seconds.

This fury which drove him on to read so many books had nothing to do with scholarship, nothing to do with academic honors, nothing to do with formal learning. He was not in any way a scholar and did not want to be one. He simply wanted to know about everything on earth; he wanted to devour the earth, and it drove him mad when he saw he could not do this. And it was the same with everything he did. In the midst of a furious burst of reading in the enormous library, the thought of the streets outside and the great city all around him would drive through his body like a sword. It would now seem to him that every second that he passed among the books was being wasted—that at this moment something priceless, irrecoverable was happening in the streets, and that if he could only get to it in time and see it, he would somehow get the knowledge of the whole thing in him—the source, the well, the spring from which all men and words and actions, and every design upon this earth proceeds.

And he would rush out in the streets to find it, be hurled through the tunnel into Boston and then spend hours in driving himself savagely through a hundred streets, looking into the faces of a million people, trying to get an instant and conclusive picture of all they did and said and were, of all their million destinies, and of the great city and the everlasting earth, and the immense and lonely skies that bent above them. And he would search the furious streets until bone and brain and blood could stand no more—until every sinew of his life and spirit was wrung, trembling, and exhausted, and his heart sank down beneath its weight of desolation and despair.

Yet a furious hope, a wild extravagant belief, was burning in him all the time. He would write down enormous charts and plans and projects of all that he proposed to do in life—a program of work and living which would have exhausted the energies of 10,000 men. He would get up in the middle of the night to scrawl down insane catalogs of all that he had seen and done:—the number of books he had read, the number of miles he had travelled, the number of people he had known, the number of women he had slept with, the number of meals he had eaten, the number of towns he had visited, the number of states he had been in.

And at one moment he would gloat and chuckle over these stupendous lists like a miser gloating over his hoard, only to groan bitterly with despair the next moment, and to beat his head against the wall, as he remembered the overwhelming amount of all he had not seen or done, or known. Then he would begin another list filled with enormous catalogs of all the books he had not read, all the food he had not eaten, all the women that he had not slept with, all the states he had not been in, all the towns he had not visited. Then he would write down plans and programs whereby all these things must be accomplished, how many years it would take to do it all, and how old he would be when he had finished. An enormous wave of hope and joy would surge up in him, because it now looked easy, and he had no doubt at all that he could do it.

He never asked himself in any practical way how he was going to live while this was going on, where he was going to get the money for this gigantic adventure, and what he was going to do to make it possible. If he thought about it, it seemed to have no importance or reality whatever—he just dismissed it impatiently, or with a conviction that some old man would die and leave him a fortune, that he was going to pick up a purse containing hundreds of thousands of dollars while walking in the Fenway, and that the reward would be enough to keep him going, or that a beautiful and rich young widow, true-hearted, tender, loving, and voluptuous, who had carrot-colored hair, little freckles on her face, a snub nose and luminous gray-green eyes with something wicked, yet loving and faithful in them, and one gold filling in her solid little teeth, was going to fall in love with him, marry him, and be forever true and faithful to him while he went reading, eating, drinking, whoring, and devouring his way around the world; or finally that he would write a book or play every year or so, which would be a great success, and yield him fifteen or twenty thousand dollars at a crack. Thus, he went storming away at the whole earth about him, sometimes mad with despair, weariness, and bewilderment; and sometimes wild with a jubilant and exultant joy and certitude as the conviction came to him that everything would happen as he wished. Then at night he would hear the vast sounds and silence of the earth and of the city, he would begin to think of the dark sleeping earth and of the continent of night, until it seemed to him it all was spread before him like a map—rivers, plains, and mountains and 10,000 sleeping towns; it seemed to him that he saw everything at once.

VIII

ONE morning, a few days after his arrival in Cambridge, he had received a letter, written on plain but costly paper in a fine but almost feminine hand. The letter read as follows:

"Dear Sir: I should be pleased to have your company for dinner

Wednesday evening at eight-thirty at The Cock Horse Tavern on Brattle Street. In case of your acceptance will you kindly call at my rooms in Holyoke House, opposite the Widener Library, at seven-fifteen?

Sincerely yours,
FRANCIS STARWICK."

He read that curt and cryptic note over and over with feelings mixed of astonishment and excitement. Who was Francis Starwick? Why should Francis Starwick, a stranger of whom he had never heard, invite him to dinner? And why was that laconic note not accompanied by a word of explanation?

It is likely he would have gone anyway, from sheer curiosity, and because of the desperate eagerness with which a young man, alone in a strange world for the first time, welcomes any hope of friendship. But before the day was over, he had learned from another student in Professor Hatcher's celebrated course for dramatists, of which he himself was now a member, that Francis Starwick was Professor Hatcher's assistant; and correctly inferring that the invitation had some connection with this circumstance, he resolved to go.

In this way, his acquaintance began with that rare and tragically gifted creature who was one of the most extraordinary figures of his generation and who, possessing almost every talent that an artist needs, was lacking in that one small grain of common earth that could have saved him, and brought his work to life.

No fatality rested on that casual meeting. He could not have foreseen in what strange and sorrowful ways his life would weave and interweave with this other one, nor could he have known from any circumstance of that first meeting that this other youth was destined to be that triune figure in his life, of which each man knows one and only one, in youth, and which belongs to the weather of man's life, and to the fabric of his destiny: his friend, his brother,—and his mortal enemy. Nor was there, in the boy he met that night, any prefigurement of the tragic fatality with which that brilliant life was starred, the horrible end toward which, perhaps, it even then was directed.

They were both young men, and both filled with all the vanity, anguish and hot pride of youth, and with its devotion and humility; they were both strong in their proud hope and faith and untried confidence; they both had shining gifts and powers and they were sure the world was theirs; they were splendid and fierce and weak and strong and foolish;

the prescience of wild swelling joy was in them; and the goat cry was still torn from their wild young throats. They knew that the most fortunate, good and happy life that any man had ever known was theirs, if they would only take it; they knew that it impended instantly—the fortune, fame, and love for which their souls were panting; neither had yet turned the dark column, they knew that they were twenty, and that they could never die.

Francis Starwick, on first sight, was a youth of medium height and average weight, verging perhaps toward slenderness, with a pleasant ruddy face, brown eyes, a mass of curly auburn-reddish hair, and a cleft chin. The face in its pleasant cast and healthy tone, and spacious, quiet intelligence was strikingly like those faces of young Englishmen which were painted by Hoppner and Sir Henry Raeburn towards the beginning of the nineteenth century. It was an attractive, pleasant immensely sensitive and intelligent face, but when Starwick spoke this impression of warmth and friendliness was instantly destroyed.

He spoke in a strange and rather disturbing tone, the pitch and timbre of which it would be almost impossible to define, but which would haunt one who had heard it forever after. His voice was neither very high nor low, it was a man's voice and yet one felt it might almost have been a woman's; but there was nothing at all effeminate about it. It was simply a strange voice compared to most American voices, which are rasping, nasal, brutally coarse or metallic. Starwick's voice had a disturbing lurking resonance, an exotic, sensuous, and almost voluptuous quality. Moreover, the peculiar mannered affectation of his speech was so studied that it hardly escaped extravagance. If it had not been for the dignity, grace, and intelligence of his person, the affectation of his speech might have been ridiculous. As it was, the other youth felt the moment's swift resentment and hostility that is instinctive with the American when he thinks some one is speaking in an affected manner.

As Starwick welcomed his guest his ruddy face flushed brick-red with the agonizing embarrassment of a shy and sensitive person to whom every new meeting is an ordeal; his greeting was almost repellently cold and formal, but this, too, with the studied affectation of his speech, was protective armor for his shyness.

"A-d'ye-do," he said, shaking hands, the greeting coming from his throat through lips that scarcely seemed to move. "It was good of you to come."

"It was good of you to ask me," the other boy said awkwardly, fumbled desperately for a moment, and then blurted out—"I didn't know who you were at first—when I got your note—but then somebody told me:—you're Professor Hatcher's assistant, aren't you?"

"Ace," said Starwick, this strange sound which was intended for "yes" coming through his lips in the same curious and almost motionless fashion. The brick-red hue of his ruddy face deepened painfully, and for a moment he was silent—"Look!" he said suddenly, yet with a casualness that was very warm and welcome after the stilted formality of his greeting, "would you like a drink? I have some whiskey."

"Why, yes—sure—certainly," the other stammered, almost feverishly grateful for the diversion—"I'd like it."

Starwick opened the doors of a small cupboard, took out a bottle, a siphon, and some glasses on a tray, and placed them on a table.

"Help yourself," he said. "Do you like it with soda—or plain water—or how?"

"Why—any way you do," the other youth stammered. "Aren't you going to drink? I don't want to, unless you do."

"Ace," said Starwick again, "I'll drink with you. I like the soda," he added, and poured a drink for himself and filled it with the siphon. "Go on. Pour your own. . . . Look," he said abruptly again, as the other youth was awkwardly manipulating the unaccustomed siphon. "Do you mind if I drink mine while I'm shaving? I just came in. I'd like to shave and change my shirt before we go out. Do you mind?"

"No, of course not," the other said, grateful for the respite thus afforded. "Go ahead. Take all the time you like. I'll drink my drink and have a look at your books, if you don't mind."

"Please do," said Starwick, "if you find anything you like. I think this is the best chair." He pushed a big chair up beneath a reading lamp and switched the light on. "There are cigarettes on the table," he said in his strange mannered tone, and went into the bathroom, where, after a moment's inspection of his ruddy face, he immediately began to lather himself and to prepare for shaving.

"This is a nice place you have here," the visitor said presently, after another awkward pause, during which the only sound was the minute scrape of the razor blade on Starwick's face.

"Quite," he answered concisely, in his mannered tone, and with that blurred sound of people who try to talk while they are shaving. For a few moments the razor scraped on. "I'm glad you like it," Starwick said presently, as he put the razor down and began to inspect his work in the mirror. "And what kind of place did you find for yourself? Do you like it?"

"Well, it will do, I guess," the other boy said dubiously. "Of course, it's nothing like this—it's not an apartment; it's just a room I rented."

"Ace," said Starwick from the bathroom. "And where is that?"

"It's on a street called Buckingham Road. Do you know where that is?"

"Oh," said Starwick coldly, and he craned carefully with his neck, and was silent a moment as he did a little delicate razor-work around the Adam's apple. "Ace," he said at length as he put the razor down again. "I think I do. . . . And how did you happen to go out there?" he inquired coldly as he began to dry his face on a towel. "Did some one tell you about the place?"

"Well—yes. I knew about it before I came. It's a room in a house that some people I know have rented."

"Oh," said Starwick coldly, formally again, as he thrust his arms into a fresh shirt. "Then you do know people here in Cambridge?"

"Well, no: they are really people from home."

"Home?"

"Yes—from my own state, the place I came from, where I went to school before I came here."

"Oh," said Starwick, buttoning his shirt, "I see. And where was that? What state are you from?"

"Catawba."

"Oh. . . . And you went to school down there?"

"Yes. To the State University."

"I see. . . . And these people who have the house where you are living now—what are they doing here?"

"Well, the man—he's a professor at the State University down there—he's up here getting some sort of degree in education."

"In what?"

"In education."

"Oh. I see. . . . And what does his wife do; has he got a wife?"

"Yes; and three children. . . . Well," the other youth said uncertainly, and then laughed suddenly, "I haven't seen her do anything yet but sit on her tail and talk."

"Ace?" said Starwick, knotting his tie very carefully. "And what does she talk about?"

"Of people back home, mostly—the professors at the University, and their wives and families."

"Oh," said Starwick gravely, but there was now lurking in his voice an indefinable drollery of humor. "And does she say nice things about them?" He looked out towards his guest with a grave face, but a sly burble in his voice now escaped him and broke out in an infectious chuckling laugh. "Or is she—" for a moment he was silent, trembling a little with secret merriment, and his pleasant face reddened with laughter—"or is she," he said with sly insinuation—"bitter?"

The other, somehow conquered by the sly yet broad and vulgar humor in Starwick's tone, broke out into a loud guffaw, and said:

"God! she's bitter—and nothing but! That's just the word for it."

"Has any one escaped yet?" said Starwick slyly.

"Not a damned one of them," the other roared. "She's worked her way from the President and his family all the way down to the instructors. Now she's started on the people of the town. I've heard about every miscarriage and every dirty pair of drawers that ever happened there. We've got a bet on, a friend of mine from home who's also staying there—he's in the Law School—whether she's going to say anything good about any one before the year is over."

"And which side have you?" said Starwick.

"I say she won't—but Billy Ingram says she will. He says that the last time she said anything good about any one was when some one died during the influenza epidemic in 1917; and he claims she's due again."

"And what is the lady's name?" said Starwick. He had now come out into the living room and was putting on his coat.

"Trotter," the other said, feeling a strange convulsive humor swelling in him. "Mrs. Trotter."

"What?" said Starwick, his face reddening and the sly burble appearing in his voice again. "Mrs.—who?"

"Mrs. Trotter!" the other choked, and the room rang suddenly with their wild laughter. When it had subsided, Starwick blew his nose vigorously, and his pleasant face still reddened with laughter, he asked smoothly:

"And what does Professor Trotter say while this is going on?"

"He doesn't say anything," the other laughed. "He can't say anything. He just sits there and listens. . . . The man's all right. Billy and I feel sorry for him. He's got this damned old shrew of a wife who sits there talking ninety to the minute, and three of the meanest, dirtiest, noisiest little devils you ever saw falling over his feet and raising hell from morning to night, and this sloppy nigger wench they brought up with them from the South—the place looks like an earthquake hit it, and the poor devil is up here trying to study for a degree—it's pretty hard on him. He's a nice fellow, and he doesn't deserve it."

"God!" said Starwick frankly and gravely, "but it sounds dreary! Why did you ever go to such a place?"

"Well, you see, I didn't know any one in Cambridge—and I had known these people back home."

"I should think that would have made you anxious to avoid them," Starwick answered. "And it's most important that you have a pleasant place to work in. It really is, you know," he said earnestly and with a note of reproof in his mannered tone. "You really should be more careful about that," he said.

"Yes, I suppose it is. You certainly have a good place here."

"Ace," said Starwick. "It is very pleasant. I'm glad you like it."

He came out, with his drink in his hand, put the drink down on a table and sat down beside it, crossing his legs and reaching for one of the straw-tipped cigarettes in a small and curiously carved wooden box. The impression he made on the other youth was one of magnificence and luxury. The boy's rooms seemed to fit his sensuous and elegant personality like a glove: he was only twenty-two years old but his distinctive and incomparable quality was everywhere about him in these two rooms.

To the unaccustomed eyes of the younger boy, these modest rooms seemed to be the most magnificent apartment he had seen. For a moment he thought that Starwick must be an immensely wealthy person to live in such a way. The fact that a man so young should live in such splendid and luxurious independence—that he should "have his own place," an apartment of his own, instead of a rented room, the thrilling solitudes of midnight privacy to himself, the freedom to come and go as he pleased, to do as he wished, to invite to his place whoever he chose, "to bring a girl there" whenever he wanted, without fear or the need for stealth—all these simple things which are just part of the grand and hopeful joy of youth, which the younger boy had never known, but to which he had aspired, as every youth aspires, in many a thrilling fantasy—now made Starwick's life seem almost impossibly fortunate, happy and exciting.

And yet it was not merely his own inexperience that made Starwick seem so wealthy. Starwick, although he had no regular income save a thousand dollars a year which he received for his work as Professor

Hatcher's assistant, and small sums he got from time to time from his family—he was, incredibly enough, the youngest of a middle-western family of nine children, small business and farming people in modest circumstances—gave the impression of wealth because he really was a wealthy person: he had been born wealthy, endowed with wealth by nature. In everything he did and said and was, in all he touched, in the whole quality of his rare and sensuous personality there was an opulence of wealth and luxury such as could not be found in a hundred million-aires. He had that rare and priceless quality that is seldom found in any one, and almost never in Americans, of being able to give to any simple act or incident a glamour of luxury, pleasure, excitement. Thus, when he smoked a cigarette, or drank a drink, or invited some one to go with him to the theatre, or ordered a meal in a shabby Italian restaurant, or made coffee in his rooms, or talked of something he had read in a book, or tied his neck-tie—all these things had a rare, wonderful and thrilling quality in them that the richest millionaire in the world could not have bought for money. And for this reason, people were instantly captivated by the infinite grace and persuasiveness of Starwick's personality: he had the power, as few people in the world have ever had the power, instantly to conquer and command the devotion of people because, while they were with him, everything in the world took on a freshness, wonder, joy and opulence it had never had before, and for this reason people wanted to be near him, to live in this thrilling enhancement that he gave to everything.

Even as he sat there smoking, drinking and talking with his guest, he did a simple and characteristic thing that yet seemed wonderful and thrilling to the other boy.

"Look," said Starwick suddenly, getting up, going over to one of his bookshelves and switching on a light. "Look," he said again, in his strangely fibred voice, "did you ever read this?"

As he uttered these words he took a book from one of the shelves and put on his spectacles. There was something strange and wonderful about the spectacles, and in the way he put them on, quietly, severely, plainly; the spectacles had thick old-fashioned silver rims, and silver handles. Their plain, honest and old-fashioned sobriety was somehow remarkable, and as he put them on, with a patient and quiet movement, and turned his attention to the pages of the book, the gravity and maturity of quiet and lonely thought in the boy's face and head was remarkably evident.

"Did you ever read this?" he said quietly, turning to the other youth, and handing him the book. It was a copy of George Moore's *Confessions of a Young Man:* the other replied he had not read it.

"Then," said Starwick, "why don't you take it along with you? It's really quite amusing." He switched off the light above the book shelves, took off his glasses with a quiet tired movement, and folding them and putting them in his breast pocket, came back to the table and sat down.

"I think it may interest you," he said.

Alhough the other boy had always felt an instinctive repulsion towards books which some one else urged him to read, something in Starwick's simple act had suddenly given the book a strange rare value: he felt a strange and pleasurable excitement when he thought about it, and was instantly eager and curious to read it. Moreover, in an indefinable way, he had understood the moment that Starwick turned to him, that he was *giving,* and not *lending* him the book; and this act, too, instantly was invested with a princely and generous opulence. It was this way with everything that Starwick did: everything he touched would come instantly to life with grace and joy; his was an incomparable, an enslaving power—a Midas-gift of life and joy almost too fortunate and effortless for one man to possess and in the end like all his other gifts of life and joy, a power that would serve death, not life, that would spread corruption instead of health, and that finally would turn upon its owner and destroy him.

Later, when they left his rooms and went out on the street, the sensuous quickening of life, the vital excitement and anticipation which Starwick was somehow able to convey to everything he did and give to every one he knew and liked, was constantly apparent. It was a fine clear night in early October, crispness and an indefinable smell of smoke were in the air, students were coming briskly along the street, singly or in groups of two or three, light glowed warmly in the windows of the book-shops, pharmacies, and tobacco stores near Harvard Square, and from the enormous library and the old buildings in the Harvard Yard there came a glow of lights, soft, rich, densely golden, embedded in old red brick.

All of these things, vital, exciting, strangely, pleasurably stirring as they were, gained a curious enhancement from Starwick's presence until they gave to the younger boy not only a feeling of sharp, mounting, strangely indefinable excitement, but a feeling of power and wealth—a sense of being triumphant and having before him the whole golden and unvisited plantation of the world to explore, possess and do with as he would—the most fortunate and happy life that any man had ever known.

Starwick went into a tobacco shop to cash a check and the whole place, with its pungent smells of good tobacco, its idling students, its atmosphere of leisure and enjoyment, became incomparably wealthy, rich, exciting as it had never been before.

And later, when the two young men had gone into the Cock Horse Tavern on Brattle Street, the prim and clean little rooms of the old house, the clean starched waitresses and snowy table cloth, the good food, and several healthy and attractive-looking girls of the New England type all gained an increased value. He felt a thrill of pleasurable anticipation and a feeling of unlimited wealth, simply because Starwick was there ordering the meal, conferring on everything around him the sense of wealth and ease and nameless joy which his wonderful personality with its magic touch instantly gave to anything on earth.

Yet during the meal the feeling of hostile constraint between the two young men was not diminished, but grew constantly. Starwick's impeccable cold courtesy—really the armor of a desperately shy person—his mannered tone, with its strange and disturbing accent, the surgical precision of his cross-examination into the origin, experience, and training of the other youth sharpened a growing antagonism in the other's spirit, and put him on his guard. Moreover, failure to give any information about himself—above all his complete reticence concerning his association with Professor Hatcher and the reason for his curt and brusquely-worded invitation to dinner—all this began to bear now with oppressive weight upon the other's spirit. It seemed to him there was a deliberate arrogance in this cold reticence. He began to feel a sullen resentment because of this secretive and mysterious conduct. And later that evening when the two young men parted, the manner of each of them was cold and formal. They bowed stiffly, shook hands with each other coldly, and marched away. It was several months before the younger would again talk to Starwick, and during that period he thought of him with a feeling of resentment, almost of dislike.

IX

THAT first impact of the city had stunned him with its huge and instant shock, and now, like a swimmer whelmed in a raging storm, he sought desperately among that unceasing flood of faces for one that he knew, one that he could call his own, and suddenly he thought of

Uncle Bascom. When his mother had told him he should go to see his uncle and his family as soon as he could he had nodded his head mechanically and muttered a few words of perfunctory assent, but so busy were his mind and heart with his shining vision of the city and all the magic he was sure to find there that it had never seriously occurred to him that he would turn eagerly to the old man for companionship and help.

But now, the day after his arrival in the city, he found himself pawing eagerly through the pages of the phone book for his uncle's business address: he found it—the familiar words, "Bascom Pentland" stared up out of the crowded page with a kind of unreal shocking incandescence, and in another moment he heard himself speaking across the wire to a puzzled voice that came to him with its curious and unearthly remoteness as if from some planetary distance—and suddenly the howling recognition of the words—words whose unearthly quality now came back to him in a searing flash of memory, although he had not heard his uncle's voice for eight years, when he was twelve years old:

"Oh, hello! hello! hello!" that unearthly voice howled faintly at him. "How are you, my boy, how are you, how are you, how are you! . . . And say!" the voice yelled with a sudden comical transition to matter-of-factness—"I had a letter from your mother just this morning. She told me you were on your way. . . . I've been expecting you."

"Can I come over to see you now, Uncle Bascom?"

"Oh, by all means, by all means, by all means!" that unearthly and passionate voice howled back at once enthusiastically. "Come over at once, my boy, at once! Oh, by all means, by all means, by all means! . . . And now, my boy!" the voice became faintly and comically precise, and he could hear his uncle smacking his large rubbery lips with pedantical relish as he pronounced the words: "Know-ing you are a young man alone in this great city for the first time, I shall give you a few brief—and, I trust, reasonably clear, di-rections," again Bascom smacked his lips with audible relish as he pronounced this lovely word—"concerning your i-tin-er-ary"—his joy as he smacked his lips over this last word was almost indecently evident, and he went on with meticulous elaboration through a bewildering labyrinth of instructions until even he was satisfied at the confusion he had caused. Then he said goodbye, upon the assurance of his nephew that he would come at once. And it was in this way, after eight years of absence, that the boy again met his uncle.

He found the old man hardly changed at all. He was, indeed, a member of that race of men who scarcely vary by a jot from one decade to another; he was a trifle grayer, the stringy gauntness of his tall stooped frame was perhaps a little more pronounced, his eccentric tricks of speech and manner a little more emphatic—but this was all. In dress, speech, manner and appearance he was to an amazing degree the same as he had been the last time that his nephew saw him.

It is doubtful, in fact, if he had changed appreciably in thirty years. And certainly during the first twenty-five years of this century, business people who had their offices in or near State Street, Boston, and who had grown very familiar with that cadaverous and extraordinary figure, could have testified that he had not changed at all. His daily appearances, indeed, had become so much a part of the established process of events in that crowded street, that they had attained a kind of ritualistic dignity, and any serious alteration in their pattern would have seemed to hundreds of people to whom his gaunt bowed figure had become familiar, almost to constitute a serious disruption of the natural order.

Shortly before nine o'clock of every working-day he would emerge from a subway exit near the head of the street and pause vaguely for a moment, making a craggy eddy in the tide of issuing workers that foamed swiftly about him while he stood with his enormous bony hands clutched comically before him at the waist, as if holding himself in, at the same time making the most horrible grimaces with his lean and amazingly flexible features. These grimaces were made by squinting his small sharp eyes together, widening his mouth in a ghastly travesty of a grin, and convolving his chin and cheek in a rapid series of pursed lips and horrible squints as he swiftly pressed his rubbery underlip against a few enormous horse teeth that decorated his upper jaw. Having completed these facial evolutions, he glanced quickly and, it must be supposed, blindly, in every direction; for he then plunged heedlessly across the street, sometimes choosing the moment when traffic had been halted, and pedestrians were hurrying across, sometimes diving into the midst of a roaring chaos of motor cars, trucks, and wagons, through which he sometimes made his way in safety, accompanied only by a scream of brake bands, a startled barking of horns, and the hearty curses of frightened drivers, or from which, howling with terror in the centre of a web of traffic which he had snarled hopelessly and brought to a complete standstill, he was sometimes rescued by a red-faced and cursing young Irishman who was on point duty at that corner.

But Bascom was a fated man and he escaped. Once, it is true, a bright mindless beetle of machinery, which had no thought for fated men, had knocked him down and skinned and bruised him; again, an uninstructed wheel had passed across the soft toe-end of his shoe and held him prisoner, as if he were merely some average son of destiny—but he escaped. He escaped because he was a fated man and because the providence which guides the steps of children and the blind was kind to him; and because this same policeman whose simian upper lip had once been thick and twisted with its curses had long since run the scale from anger to wild fury, and thence to madness and despair and resignation, and had now come to have a motherly affection for this stray sheep, kept his eye peeled for its appearance every morning or, failing this, at once shrilled hard upon his whistle when he heard the well-known howl of terror and surprise, plunged to the centre of the stalled traffic snarl, plucked Bascom out to safety under curse and shout and scream of brake, and marched him tenderly to the curb, gripping his brawny hand around the old man's arm, feeling his joints, testing his bones, massaging anxiously his sinewy carcass, and calling him "bud"—although Bascom was old enough to be his grandfather. "Are you all right, bud? You're not hurt, are you, bud? Are you O. K.?"—to which Bascom, if his shock and terror had been great, could make no answer for a moment save to pant hoarsely and to howl loudly and huskily from time to time "Ow! Ow! Ow! Ow!"

At length, becoming more coherent, if not more calm, he would launch into an ecclesiastical indictment of motor cars and their drivers delivered in a high, howling, and husky voice that suggested the pronouncements of a prophet from a mountain. This voice had a quality of strange remoteness and, once heard, would never be forgotten. It actually had a howling note in it, and carried to great distances, and yet it was not loud: it was very much as if Mr. Bascom Pentland were standing on a mountain and shouting to some one in a quiet valley below—the sounds came to one plainly but as if from a great distance, and it was full of a husky, unearthly passion. It was really an ecclesiastical voice, the voice of a great preacher; one felt that it should be heard in churches, which was exactly where it once was heard, for Bascom had at various times and with great conviction, in the course of his long and remarkable life, professed and preached the faith of the Episcopalians, the Presbyterians, the Methodists, the Baptists, and the Unitarians.

Quite often, in fact, as now, when he had narrowly escaped disaster in the streets, Bascom still preached from the corner: as soon as he recovered somewhat from his shock, he would launch forth into a sermon of eloquent invective against any driver of motor cars within hearing, and if any of them entered the fray, as sometimes happened, a very interesting performance occurred.

"What happened to *you?*" the motorist might bitterly remark. "Do the keepers know you're out?"

Mr. Pentland would thereupon retort with an eloquent harangue, beginning with a few well-chosen quotations from the more violent prophets of the Old Testament, a few predictions of death, destruction and damnation for the owners of motor cars, and a few apt references to Days of Judgment and Reckoning, Chariots of Moloch, and Beasts of the Apocalypse.

"Oh, for God's sake!" the exasperated motorist might reply. "Are you *blind?* Where do you think you are? In a cow-pasture? Can't you read the signals? Didn't you see the cop put his hand up? Don't you know when it says to 'Stop' or 'Go'? Did you ever hear of the traffic law?"

"The *traffic* law!" Bascom sneeringly exclaimed, as if the mere use of the word by the motorist evoked his profoundest contempt. His voice now had a precise and meticulous way of speech, there was something sneering and pedantical in the way he pronounced each word, biting it off with a prim, nasal and heavily accented enunciation in the manner of certain pedants and purists who suggest by their pronunciation that language in the mouths of most people is vilely and carelessly treated, that each word has a precise, subtle, and careful meaning of its own, and that they—*they* alone—understand these matters. "The *traffic* law!" he repeated again: then he squinted his eyes together, pursed his rubbery lip against the big horsey upper teeth, and laughed down his nose in a forced, sneering manner, "The *traffic* law!" he said. "Why, you pit-i-ful ig-no-*ram*-us! You il-*lit*-ter-ate ruffian! You dare to speak to me—to *me!*" he howled suddenly with an ecclesiastical lift of his voice, striking himself on his bony breast and glaring with a majestical fury as if the word of a mighty prophet had been contradicted by an upstart—"of the traffic law, when it is doubtful if you could *read* the law if you saw it,"—he sneered—"and it is obvious to any one with the perception of a school-boy that you would not have intelligence enough to understand it, and"—here his voice rose to a howling emphasis and he held one huge bony finger up to command attention—"*and* to interpret it, if you could read."

"Is *that* so!" the motorist heavily remarked. "A *wise* guy, eh? One of these guys who knows it all, eh? You're a *pretty* wise guy, aren't you?" the motorist continued bitterly, as if caught up in the circle of his refrain and unable to change it. "Well, let me tell *you* something. You think you're pretty smaht, don't you? Well, you're not. See? It's wise guys like you who go around looking for a good bust on the nose. See? That's how smaht you are. If you wasn't an old guy I'd give you one, too," he said, getting a moody satisfaction from the thought.

"Ow-w! Ow-w! Ow-w!" Bascom howled in sudden terror.

"If you know so much, if you're so smaht as you think you are, what *is* the traffic law?"

Then, assuredly, if there was a traffic law, the unfortunate motorist was lost, for Uncle Bascom would deliver it to him verbatim, licking his lips with joy over all the technicalities of legal phrasing and pronouncing each phrase with a meticulous and pedantical enunciation.

"And furthermore!" he howled, holding up his big bony finger, "the Commonwealth of Massachusetts has decreed, by a statute that has been on the books since 1856, by a statute that is irrevocably, inexorably, ineluctably plain that any driver, director, governor, commander, manager, agent or conductor, or any other person who shall conduct or cause to be conducted any vehicular instrument, whether it be of two, four, six, eight or any number of wheels whatsoever, whether it be in the public service, or in the possession of a private individual, whether it be—" but by this time, the motorist, if he was wise, had had enough, and had escaped.

If, however, it had been one of his more fortunate mornings, if he had blindly but successfully threaded the peril of roaring traffic, Uncle Bascom proceeded rapidly down State Street, still clutching his raw bony hands across his meagre waist, still contorting his remarkable face in its endless series of pursed grimaces, and presently turned in to the entrance of a large somewhat dingy-looking building of blackened stone, one of those solid, unpretentious, but very valuable properties which smell and look like the early 1900's, and which belong to that ancient and enormously wealthy corporation across the river known as Harvard University.

Here, Uncle Bascom, still clutching himself together across the waist, mounted a flight of indented marble entry steps, lunged through revolving doors into a large marble corridor that was redolent with vibrating waves of hot steamy air, wet rubbers and galoshes, sanitary disinfectant, and serviceable but somewhat old-fashioned elevators and, entering one of the cars which had just plunged down abruptly, banged open its door, belched out two or three people and swallowed a dozen more, he was finally deposited with the same abruptness on the seventh floor, where he stepped out into a wide dark corridor, squinted and grimaced uncertainly to right and left as he had done for twenty-five years, and then went left along the corridor, past rows of lighted offices in which one could hear the preliminary clicking of typewriters, the rattling of crisp papers, and the sounds of people beginning their day's work. At the end of the corridor Bascom Pentland turned right along another corridor and at length paused before a door which bore this inscription across the familiar glazed glass of American business offices: The John T. Brill Realty Co.—Houses For Rent or Sale. Below this bold legend in much smaller letters was printed: Bascom Pentland— Att'y at Law—Conveyancer and Title Expert.

The appearance of this strange figure in State Street, or anywhere else, had always been sufficient to attract attention and to draw comment. Bascom Pentland, if he had straightened to his full height, would have been six feet and three or four inches tall, but he had always walked with a stoop and as he grew older, the stoop had become confirmed: he presented a tall, gnarled, bony figure, cadaverous and stringy, but tough as hickory. He was of that race of men who seem never to wear out, or to grow old, or to die: they live with almost undiminished vitality to great ages, and when they die they die suddenly. There is no slow wastage and decay because there is so little to waste or decay: their mummied and stringy flesh has the durability of granite.

Bascom Pentland clothed his angular figure with an assortment of odd garments which seemed to have the same durability: they were immensely old and worn, but they also gave no signs of ever wearing out, for by their cut and general appearance of age, it seemed that his frugal soul had selected in the 'nineties materials which it hoped would last forever. His coat, which was originally of a dark dull pepper-and-salt gray, had gone green at the seams and pockets, and moreover it was a ridiculously short skimpy coat for a gaunt big-boned man like this: it was hardly more than a jacket, his great wristy hands burst out of it like lengths of cordwood, and the mark of his high humped narrow shoulders cut into it with a knife-like sharpness. His trousers were also tight and skimpy, of a lighter gray and of a rough woolly texture from which all fuzz and fluff had long ago been rubbed; he wore rough country brogans with raw-hide laces, and a funny little flat hat of ancient black felt, which had also gone green along the band. One understands now why the policeman called him "Bud": this great bony figure seemed ruthlessly to have been crammed into garments in which a country fledgling of the 'eighties might have gone to see his girl, clutching a bag of gumdrops in his large red hand. A stringy little necktie, a clean but dilapidated collar which by its bluish and softly mottled look Bascom Pentland must have laundered himself (a presumption which is quite correct since the old man did all his own laundry work, as well as his mending, repairing, and cobbling)—this was his costume, winter and summer, and it never changed, save that in winter he supplemented it with an ancient blue sweater which he wore buttoned to the chin and whose frayed ends and cuffs projected inches below the scanty little jacket. He had never been known to wear an overcoat, not even on the coldest days of those long, raw, and formidable winters which Boston suffers.

The mark of his madness was plain upon him: intuitively men knew he was not a poor man, and the people who had seen him so many times in State Street would nudge one another, saying: "You see that old guy? You'd think he was waitin' for a handout from the Salvation Army, wouldn't you? Well, he's not. He's *got* it, brother. Believe me, he's *got* it good and plenty: he's *got* it salted away where no one ain't goin' to touch it. That guy's got a sock full of dough!"

"Jesus!" another remarks. "What good's it goin' to do an old guy like that? He can't take any of it with him, can he?"

"You said it, brother," and the conversation would become philosophical.

Bascom Pentland was himself conscious of his parsimony, and although he sometimes asserted that he was "only a poor man" he realized that his exaggerated economies could not be justified to his business associates on account of poverty: they taunted him slyly, saying, "Come on, Pentland, let's go to lunch. You can get a good meal at the Pahkeh House for a couple of bucks." Or "Say, Pentland, I know a place where they're havin' a sale of winter overcoats: I saw one there that would just suit you—you can get it for sixty dollars." Or "Do you need a good laundry, Reverend? I know a couple of Chinks who do good work."

To which Bascom, with the characteristic evasiveness of parsimony, would reply, snuffling derisively down his nose: "No, sir! You won't catch me in any of their stinking restaurants. You never know what you're getting: if you could see the dirty, nasty, filthy kitchens where your food is prepared you'd lose your appetite quick enough." His parsimony had resulted in a compensating food mania: he declared that "in his young days" he "ruined his digestion by eating in restaurants," he painted the most revolting pictures of the filth of these establishments, laughing scornfully down his nose as he declared: "I suppose you think it tastes better after some dirty, nasty, stinking *nigger* has wiped his old hands all over it" (phuh-phuh-phuh-phuh-phuh!)—here he would contort his face and snuffle scornfully down his nose; and he was bitter in his denunciation of "rich foods," declaring they had "destroyed more lives than all the wars and all the armies since the beginning of time."

As he had grown older he had become more and more convinced of the healthy purity of "raw foods," and he prepared for himself at home raw revolting messes of chopped-up carrots, onions, turnips, even raw potatoes, which he devoured at table, smacking his lips with an air of keen relish, and declaring to his wife: "You may poison *yourself* on your old roasts and oysters and turkeys if you please: you wouldn't catch *me* eating that stuff. No, sir! Not on your life! I think too much of my stomach!" But his use of the pronoun "you" was here universal rather than particular because if that lady's longevity had depended on her abstinence from "roasts and oysters and turkeys" there was no reason why she should not have lived forever.

Or again, if it were a matter of clothing, a matter of fencing in his bones and tallows against the frozen nail of Boston winter, he would howl derisively: "An overcoat! Not on your life! I wouldn't give two cents for all the old overcoats in the world! The only thing they're good for is to gather up germs and give you colds and pneumonia. I haven't worn an overcoat in thirty years, and I've never had the *vestige*—no! not the *semblance*—of a cold during all that time!"—an assertion that was not strictly accurate since he always complained bitterly of at least two or three during the course of a single winter, declaring at those times that no more hateful, treacherous, damnable climate than that of Boston had ever been known.

Similarly, if it were a question of laundries he would scornfully declare that he would not send "*his* shirts and collars to let some dirty old Chinaman spit and *hock* upon them—*yes!*" he would gleefully howl, as some new abomination of nastiness suggested itself to his teeming brain— "*yes!* and iron it *in,* too, so you can walk around done up in old Chinaman's spit!"—(Phuh-phuh-phuh-phuh-phuh!)—here he would grimace, contort his rubbery lip, and laugh down his nose in forced snarls of gratification and triumph.

This was the old man who, even now, as his nephew sped to meet him, stood in his dusty little office clutching his raw and bony hands across his waist.

In spite of the bewildering elaboration of his uncle's direction, the boy found his offices without much trouble. He went in and a moment later, his hand was being vigorously pumped by his uncle's great stiff paw, and he heard that instant howling voice of welcome—the voice of a prophet calling from the mountain tops—coming to him without preliminary or introduction, as he had heard it last eight years before.

"Oh, hello, hello, hello. . . . How are you, how are you, how are you. . . . say!" his uncle turned abruptly and in a high howling tone addressed several people who were staring at the young man curiously, "I want you all to meet my sister's youngest son—my nephew, Mr. Eugene Gant . . . and say!" he bawled again, but in remoter tone, in a strangely confiding and insinuating tone— "would you know he was a Pentland by the look of him? . . . Can you see the family resemblance?" He smacked his rubbery lips together with an air of relish, and suddenly threw his great gaunt arms up and let them fall with an air of ecstatic jubilation, squinted his small sharp eyes together, contorted his rubbery lips in their amazing and grotesque grimace, and stamping ecstatically at the floor with one long stringy leg, taking random ecstatic kicks at any object that was within reach, he began to snuffle with his strange forced laughter, and howled deliriously, "Oh, *my* yes! . . . The thing is evident. . . . He is a Pentland beyond the shadow of a vestige of a doubt! . . . Oh, by all means, by all means, by all means!" and he went on snuffling, stamping, howling, and kicking at random objects in this way until the strange seizure of his mirth had somewhat subsided. Then, more quietly, he introduced his nephew to his associates in the curious business of which he was a partner.

And it was in this way that the boy first met the people in his uncle's office—an office and people who were, during the years that followed, and in the course of hundreds of visits, to become a part of the fabric of his life—so hauntingly real, so strangely familiar that in the years that followed he could forget none of them, remember everything just as it was.

These offices, which he saw for the first time that day, were composed of two rooms, one in front and one behind, L-shaped, and set in the elbow of the building, so that one might look out at the two projecting wings of the building, and see lighted layers of offices, in which the actors of a dozen enterprises "took" dictation, clattered at typewriters, walked back and forth importantly, talked into telephones or, what they did with amazing frequency, folded their palms behind their skulls, placed their feet restfully on the nearest solid object, and gazed for long periods dreamily and tenderly at the ceilings.

Through the broad and usually very dirty panes of the window in the front office one could catch a glimpse of Faneuil Hall and the magnificent and exultant activity of the markets.

These dingy offices, however, from which a corner of this rich movement might be seen and felt, were merely the unlovely counterpart of millions of others throughout the country and, in the telling phrase of Baedeker, offered "little that need detain the tourist": a few chairs, two scarred roll-top desks, a typist's table, a battered safe with a pile of thumb-worn ledgers on top of it, a set of green filing cases, an enormous green, greasy water-jar always half filled with a rusty liquid that no one drank, and two spittoons, put there because Brill was a man who chewed and spat widely in all directions—this, save for placards, each bearing several photographs of houses with their prices written below them—8 rooms, Dorchester, $6500; 5 rooms and garage, Melrose, $4500, etc.— completed the furniture of the room, and the second room, save for the disposition of objects, was similarly adorned.

Such then was the scene in which the old man and his nephew met again after a separation of eight years.

X

THE youth was drowned in the deepest sea—an atom bombarded, ignorant of all defense in a tumultuous world. The shell of custom, the easy thoughtless life which had sucked pleasure from the world about, these four years past, crumbled like caked mud. He was nothing, nobody—there was no heart or bravery left in him; he was conscious of unfathomable ignorance—the beginning, as Socrates suggested, of wisdom—he was lost.

He had wanted to cut a figure in the world—he had simply never imagined the number of people that were in it. And like most people who hug loneliness to them like a lover, the need of occasional companionship, forever tender and forever true, which might be summoned or dismissed at will, cut through him like a sword.

There was, of course, among the members of the play-writing class an energetic and calculated sociability. The supposed advantages of discussion with one another, the interplay of wit, and so on, above all what was called "the exchange of ideas," but what most often was merely the exchange of other people's ideas,—all these were mentioned often; they were held in the highest esteem as one of the chief benefits to be derived from the course.

Manifestly, one could write anywhere. But where else could one write with around one the constant stimulus of other people who also wrote? Where could one learn one's faults so well as before a critical and serious congress of artists? They were content with it—they got what they wanted. But the lack of warmth, the absence of inner radial heat which, not being fundamental in the structure of their lives, had never been wanted, filled him with horror and impotent fury.

The critical sense had stirred in him hardly at all, the idea of questioning authority and position had not occurred to him.

He was facing one of the oldest—what, for the creative mind, must be one of the most painful—problems of the spirit—the search for a standard of taste. He had, at seventeen, as a sophomore, triumphantly denied God, but he was unable now to deny Robert Browning. It had never occurred to him that there was a single authoritatively beautiful thing in the world that might not be agreed on, by a community of all the enlightened spirits of the universe, as beautiful. *Every one,* of course, *knew* that *King Lear* was one of the greatest plays that had ever been written. Only, he was beginning to find, every one didn't.

And now for the first time he began to worry about being "modern." He had the great fear young people have that they will not be a part of the most advanced literary and artistic movements of the time. Several of the young men he knew had contributed stories, poems, and criticisms to little reviews, published by and for small groups of literary adepts. They disposed of most of the established figures with a few well-chosen words of contempt, and they replaced these figures with obscure names of their own who, they assured him, were the important people of the future.

For the first time, he heard the word "Mid-Victorian" applied as a term of opprobrium. What its implications were he had no idea. Stevenson, too, to him hardly more than a writer of books for boys, books that he had read as a child with interest and delight, was a symbol of some vague, but monstrously pernicious influence.

But he discovered at once that to voice any of these questionings was to brand oneself in the esteem of the group; intuitively he saw that their jargon formed a pattern by which they might be placed and recognized; that, to young men most of all, to be placed in a previous discarded pattern was unendurable disgrace. It represented to them the mark of intellectual development, just as in a sophomore's philosophy, the belief that God is an old man with a long beard brings ridicule and odium upon the believer, but the belief that God is an ocean without limit, or an allpervasive and inclusive substance, or some other equally naive and extraordinary idea, is regarded as a certain sign of bold enlightenment. Thus, it often happens, when one thinks he has extended the limits of his life, broken the bonds, and liberated himself in the wider ether, he has done no more than to exchange a new superstition for an old one, to forsake a beautiful myth for an ugly one.

The young men in Professor Hatcher's class were sorry for many things and many people.

"Barrie?" began Mr. Scoville, an elegant and wealthy young dawdler from Philadelphia, who, by his own confession, had spent most of his life in France, "Barrie?" he continued regretfully, in answer to a question. For a moment, he drew deeply on his cigarette, then raised sad, languid eyes. "I'm sorry," he said gently, with a slight regretful movement of his head—"I can't read him. I've tried it—but it simply can't be done." They laughed, greatly pleased.

"But it is a pity, you know, a *great* pity," Francis Starwick remarked languidly, using effectively his trick of giving a tired emphasis to certain words which conveyed a kind of sad finality, a weary earnestness to what he said. He turned to go.

"But—but—but—how—how—how very interesting! Why *is* it, Frank?" Hugh Dodd demanded with his earnest stammering eagerness. He was profoundly respectful of Starwick's critical ability.

"Why is what?" said Starwick in his curiously mannered voice, his air of languid weariness.

"Why is it a great pity about Barrie?" knitting his bushy brows together, and scowling with an air of intense concentration over his words as he spoke. "Because," said the appraiser of Values, as he prepared to depart, arranging with feminine luxuriousness the voluptuous folds of his blue silk scarf, "the man really had something one time. He really did. Something strange and haunting—the genius of the Kelt." Swinging his cane slowly, acutely and painfully conscious that he was being watched, with the agonizing stiffness that was at the bottom of his character, he strolled off across the Yard, stark and lovely with the harsh white snow and wintry branches of bleak winter.

"You know—you know—you know—that's very interesting," said Dodd, intent upon his words. "I'd—I'd—I'd never thought of it in *just* that way."

"Barrie," drawled Wood, the maker of epigrams, "is a stick of taffy, floating upon a sea of molasses."

There was laughter.

He was forever making these epigrams; his face had a somewhat saturnine cast, his lips twisted ironically, his eyes shot splintered promises of satiric wisdom. He looked like a very caustically humorous person; but unhappily he had no humor. But they thought he had. No one with a face like that could be less than keen.

So he had something to say for every occasion. He had discovered that the manner counted for wit. If the talk was of Shaw's deficiencies as a dramatist, he might say:

"But, after all, if one is going in for all that sort of thing, why not have lantern slides and a course of lectures."

Thus he was known, not merely as a subtle-souled and elusive psychologist but also as a biting wit.

"Galsworthy wrote something that looked like a play once," some one remarked. "There were parts of *Justice* that weren't bad."

"Yes. Yes," said Dodd, peering intently at his language. "*Justice*—there were some interesting things in that. It's—it's—it's rather a *pity* about him, isn't it?" And as he said these words he frowned earnestly and intently. There was genuine pity in his voice, for the man's spirit had great charity and sweetness in it.

As they dispersed, some one remarked that Shaw might have made a dramatist if he had ever known anything about writing a play.

"But he *dates* so—how he *dates!*" Scoville remarked.

"Those earlier plays——"

"Yes, I agree"—thus Wood again. "Almost Mid-Victorian. Shaw:—a prophet with his face turned backwards." Then they went away in small groups.

XI

To reach his own "office," as Bascom Pentland called the tiny cubicle in which he worked and received his clients, the old man had to traverse the inner room and open a door in a flimsy partition of varnished wood and glazed glass at the other end. This was his office: it was really a very narrow slice cut off from the larger room, and in it there was barely space for one large dirty window, an ancient dilapidated desk and swivel chair, a very small battered safe buried under stacks of yellowed newspapers, and a small bookcase with glass doors and two small shelves on which there were a few worn volumes. An inspection of these books would have revealed four or five tattered and musty law books in their ponderous calf-skin bindings—one on *Contracts,* one on *Real Property,* one on *Titles*—a two-volume edition of the poems of Matthew Arnold, very dog-eared and thumbed over; a copy of *Sartor Resartus,* also much used; a volume of the essays of Ralph Waldo Emerson; the Iliad in Greek with minute yellowed notations in the margins; a volume of the *World Almanac* several years old; and a very worn volume of the Holy Bible, greatly used and annotated in Bascom's small, stiffly laborious, and meticulous hand.

If the old man was a little late, as sometimes happened, he might find his colleagues there before him. Miss Muriel Brill, the typist, and the eldest daughter of Mr. John T. Brill, would be seated in her typist's chair, her heavy legs crossed as she bent over to undo the metal latches of the thick galoshes she wore during the winter season. It is true there were also other seasons when Miss Brill did not wear galoshes, but so sharply and strongly do our memories connect people with certain gestures which, often for an inscrutable reason, seem characteristic of them, that any frequent visitor to these offices at this time of day would doubtless have remembered Miss Brill as always unfastening her galoshes. But the probable reason is that some people inevitably belong to seasons, and this girl's season was winter—not blizzards or howling winds, or the blind skirl and sweep of snow, but gray, grim, raw, thick, implacable winter: the endless successions of gray days and gray monotony. There was no spark of color in her, her body was somewhat thick and heavy, her face was white, dull, and thick-featured and instead of tapering downwards, it tapered up: it was small above, and thick and heavy below, and even in her speech, the words she uttered seemed to have been chosen by an automaton, and could only be remembered later by their desolate banality. One always remembered her as saying as one entered: "... Hello! ... You're becoming quite a strangeh! ... It's been some time since you was around, hasn't it? ... I was thinkin' the otheh day it had been some time since you was around. ... I'd begun to think you had forgotten us. ... Well, how've you been? Lookin' the same as usual, I see. ... Me? ... Oh, can't complain. . Keepin' busy? *I'll* say! I manage to keep goin'. ... Who you lookin' for? Father? He's in *there*. ... Why, yeah! Go right on in."

This was Miss Brill, and at the moment that she bent to unfasten her galoshes, it is likely that Mr. Samuel Friedman would also be there in the act of rubbing his small dry hands briskly together, or of rubbing the back of one hand with the palm of the other in order to induce circulation. He was a small youngish man, a pale somewhat meagre-looking little Jew with a sharp ferret face: he, too, was a person who goes to "fill in" those vast swarming masses of people along the pavements and in the subway—the mind cannot remember them or absorb the details of their individual appearance but they people the earth, they make up life. Mr. Friedman had none of the richness, color, and humor that some members of his race so abundantly possess; the succession of gray days, the grim weather seemed to have entered his soul as it enters the souls of many different races there—the Irish, the older New England stock, even the Jews—and it gives them a common touch that is prim, drab, careful, tight and sour. Mr. Friedman also wore galoshes, his clothes were neat, drab, a little worn and shiny, there was an odor of thawing dampness and warm rubber about him as he rubbed his dry little hands saying: "Chee! How I hated to leave that good wahm bed this morning! When I got up I said, '*Holy* Chee!' My wife says, 'Whatsa mattah?' I says, 'Holy Chee! You step out heah a moment where I am an' you'll see whatsa mattah.' 'Is it cold?' she says. 'Is it cold! I'll tell the cock-eyed wuhld!' I says. Chee! You could have cut the frost with an axe: the wateh in the pitchehs was frozen hahd; an' she has the nuhve to ask me if it's cold! 'Is it cold!' I says. 'Do you know any more funny stories?' I says. Oh, how I do love my bed! Chee! I kept thinkin' of that guy in Braintree I got to go see today an' the more I thought about him, the less I liked him! I thought my feet would tu'n into two blocks of ice before I got the funniss stahted! 'Chee! I hope the ole bus is still workin',' I says. 'If I've got to go thaw that damned thing out,' I says, 'I'm ready to quit.' Chee! Well, suh, I neveh had a bit of trouble: she stahted right up an' the way that ole moteh was workin' is nobody's business."

During the course of this monologue Miss Brill would give ear and assent from time to time by the simple interjection: "Uh!" It was a sound she uttered frequently, it had somewhat the same meaning as "Yes," but it was more non-committal than "Yes." It seemed to render assent to the speaker, to let him know that he was being heard and understood, but it did not commit the auditor to any opinion, or to any real agreement.

The third member of this office staff, who was likely to be present at this time, was a gentleman named Stanley P. Ward. Mr. Stanley P. Ward was a neat middling figure of a man, aged fifty or thereabouts; he was plump and had a pink tender skin, a trim Vandyke, and a nice comfortable little pot of a belly which slipped snugly into the well-pressed and well-brushed garments that always fitted him so tidily. He was a bit of a fop, and it was at once evident that he was quietly but enormously pleased with himself. He carried himself very sprucely, he took short rapid steps and his neat little paunch gave his figure a movement not unlike that of a pouter pigeon. He was usually in quiet but excellent spirits, he laughed frequently and a smile—rather a subtly amused look—was generally playing about the edges of his mouth. That smile and his laugh made some people vaguely uncomfortable: there was a kind of deliberate falseness in them, as if what he really thought and felt was not to be shared with other men. He seemed, in fact, to have discovered some vital and secret power, some superior knowledge and wisdom, from which the rest of mankind was excluded, a sense that he was "chosen" above other men, and this impression of Mr. Stanley Ward would have been correct, for he was a Christian Scientist, he was a pillar of the church, and a very big church at that—for Mr. Ward, dressed in fashionable striped trousers, rubber soles, and a cut-away coat, might be found somewhere under the mighty dome of the Mother Church on Huntington Avenue every Sunday suavely, noiselessly, and expertly ushering the faithful to their pews.

This completes the personnel of the first office of the John T. Brill Realty Company, and if Bascom Pentland arrived late, if these three people were already present, if Mr. Bascom Pentland had not been defrauded of any part of his worldly goods by some contriving rascal of whom the world has many, if his life had not been imperilled by some speed maniac, if the damnable New England weather was not too damnable, if, in short, Bascom Pentland was in fairly good spirits he would on entering immediately howl in a high, rapid, remote and perfectly monotonous tone: "Hello, Hello, Hello! Good-morning, Good-morning, Good-morning!"—after which he would close his eyes, grimace horribly, press his rubbery lip against his big horse teeth, and snuffle with laughter through his nose, as if pleased by a tremendous stroke of wit. At this demonstration the other members of the group would glance at one another with those knowing, subtly supercilious nods and winks, that look of common self-congratulation and humor with which the more "normal" members of society greet the conduct of an eccentric, and Mr. Samuel Friedman would say: "What's the mattah with you, Pop? You look happy. Some one musta give you a shot in the ahm."

At which, a coarse powerful voice, deliberate and rich with its intimation of immense and earthy vulgarity, might roar out of the depth of the inner office: "No, I'll tell you what it is." Here the great figure of Mr. John T. Brill, the head of the business, would darken the doorway. "Don't you know what's wrong with the Reverend? It's that widder he's been takin' around." Here, the phlegmy burble that prefaced all of Mr. Brill's obscenities would appear in his voice, the shadow of a lewd smile would play around the corner of his mouth: "It's the widder. She's let him have a little of it."

At this delicate stroke of humor, the burble would burst open in Mr. Brill's great red throat, and he would roar with that high, choking, phlegmy laughter that is frequent among big red-faced men. Mr. Friedman would laugh drily ("Heh, heh, heh, heh, heh!"), Mr. Stanley Ward would laugh more heartily, but complacently, and Miss Brill would snicker in a coy and subdued manner as became a modest young girl. As for Bascom Pentland, if he was really in a good humor, he might snuffle with nosey laughter, bend double at his meagre waist, clutching his big hands together, and stamp at the floor violently several times with one stringy leg; he might even go so far as to take a random ecstatic kick at objects, still stamping and snuffling with laughter, and prod Miss Brill stiffly with two enormous bony fingers, as if he did not wish the full point and flavor of the jest to be lost on her.

Bascom Pentland, however, was a very complicated person with many moods, and if Mr. Brill's fooling did not catch him in a receptive one, he might contort his face in a pucker of refined disgust, and mutter his disapproval, as he shook his head rapidly from side to side. Or he might rise to great heights of moral denunciation, beginning at first in a grave low voice that showed the seriousness of the words he had to utter: "The lady to whom you refer," he would begin, "the very charming and cultivated lady whose name, sir," here his voice would rise on its howling note and he would wag his great bony forefinger, "whose name, sir, you have so foully traduced and blackened——"

"No, I wasn't, Reverend. I was only tryin' to whiten it," said Mr. Brill, beginning to burble with laughter.

"—Whose name, sir, you have so foully traduced and blackened with your smutty suggestions," Bascom continued implacably, "—that lady is known to me, as you very well know, sir," he howled, wagging his great finger again, "solely and simply in a professional capacity."

"Why, hell, Reverend," said Mr. Brill innocently, "I never knew she was a perfessional. I thought she was an amatoor."

At this conclusive stroke, Mr. Brill would make the whole place tremble with his laughter, Mr. Friedman would laugh almost noiselessly, holding himself weakly at the stomach and bending across a desk, Mr. Ward would have short bursts and fits of laughter, as he gazed out the window, shaking his head deprecatingly from time to time, as if his more serious nature disapproved, and Miss Brill would snicker, and turn to her machine, remarking: "This conversation is getting too rough for me!"

And Bascom, if this jesting touched his complex soul at one of those moments when such profanity shocked him, would walk away, confiding into vacancy, it seemed, with his powerful and mobile features contorted in the most eloquent expression of disgust and loathing ever seen on any face, the while he muttered, in a resonant whisper that shuddered with passionate revulsion: "Oh, *bad!* Oh, *bad!* Oh, *bad, bad, bad!*"—shaking his head slightly from side to side with each word.

Yet there were other times, when Brill's swingeing vulgarity, the vast coarse sweep of his profanity not only found Uncle Bascom in a completely receptive mood, but evoked from him gleeful responses, counter essays in swearing which he made slyly, craftily, snickering with pleasure and squinting around at his listeners at the sound of the words, and getting such stimulus from them as might a renegade clergyman exulting in a feeling of depravity and abandonment for the first time.

To the other people in this office—that is, to Friedman, Ward, and Muriel, the stenographer—the old man was always an enigma; at first they had observed his peculiarities of speech and dress, his eccentricity of manner, and the sudden, violent, and complicated fluctuation of his temperament, with astonishment and wonder, then with laughter and ridicule, and now, with dull, uncomprehending acceptance. Nothing he did or said surprised them any more, they had no understanding and little curiosity, they accepted him as a fact in the gray schedule of their lives. Their relation to him was habitually touched by a kind of patronizing banter—"kidding the old boy along" they would have called it—by the communication of smug superior winks and the conspiracy of feeble jests. And in this there was something base and ignoble, for Bascom was a better man than any of them.

He did not notice any of this, it is not likely he would have cared if he had, for, like most eccentrics, his thoughts were usually buried in a world of his own creating to whose every fact and feeling and motion he was the central actor. Again, as much as any of his extraordinary family, he had carried with him throughout his life the sense that he was "fated" —a sense that was strong in all of them—that his life was pivotal to all the actions of providence, that, in short, the time might be out of joint, but not himself. Nothing but death could shake his powerful egotism, and his occasional storms of fury, his railing at the world, his tirades of invective at some motorist, pedestrian, or laborer occurred only when he discovered that these people were moving in a world at cross-purposes to his own and that some action of theirs had disturbed or shaken the logic of his universe.

It was curious that, of all the people in the office, the person who had the deepest understanding and respect for him was John T. Brill. Mr. Brill was a huge creature of elemental desires and passions: a river of profanity rushed from his mouth with the relentless sweep and surge of the Mississippi, he could no more have spoken without swearing than a whale could swim in a frog-pond—he swore at everything, at every one, and with every breath, casually and unconsciously, and yet when he addressed Bascom his oath was always impersonal, and tinged subtly by a feeling of respect.

Thus, he would speak to Uncle Bascom somewhat in this fashion: "God-damn it, Pentland, did you ever look up the title for that stuff in Malden? That feller's been callin' up every day to find out about it."

"Which fellow?" Bascom asked precisely. "The man from Cambridge?"

"No," said Mr. Brill, "not him, the other son of a bitch, the Dorchester feller. How the hell am I goin' to tell him anything if there's no goddamn title for the stuff?"

Profane and typical as this speech was, it was always shaded nicely with impersonality toward·Bascom—conscious to the full of the distinction between "damn *it*" and "damn *you*." Toward his other colleagues, however, Mr. Brill was neither nice nor delicate.

Brill was an enormous man physically: he was six feet two or three inches tall, and his weight was close to three hundred pounds. He was totally bald, his skull was a gleaming satiny pink; above his great red moon of face, with its ponderous and pendulous jowls, it looked almost egg-shaped. And in the heavy, deliberate, and powerful timbre of his voice there was always lurking this burble of exultant, gargantuan obscenity: it was so obviously part of the structure of his life, so obviously his only and natural means of expression, that it was impossible to condemn him. His epithet was limited and repetitive—but so, too, was Homer's, and, like Homer, he saw no reason for changing what had already been used and found good.

He was a lewd and innocent man. Like Bascom, by comparison with these other people, he seemed to belong to some earlier, richer and grander period of the earth, and perhaps this was why there was more actual kinship and understanding between them than between any of the other members of the office. These other people—Friedman, Brill's daughter Muriel, and Ward—belonged to the myriads of the earth, to those numberless swarms that with ceaseless pullulation fill the streets of life with their gray immemorable tides. But Brill and Bascom were men in a thousand, a million: if one had seen them in a crowd he would have looked after them, if one had talked with them, he could never have forgotten them.

It is rare in modern life that one sees a man who can express himself with such complete and abundant certainty as Brill did—completely, and without doubt or confusion. It is true that his life expressed itself chiefly by three gestures—by profanity, by his great roar of full-throated, earth-shaking laughter, and by flatulence, an explosive comment on existence which usually concluded and summarized his other means of expression.

Although the other people in the office laughed heartily at this soaring rhetoric of obscenity, it sometimes proved too much for Uncle Bascom. When this happened he would either leave the office immediately, or stump furiously into his own little cupboard that seemed silted over with the dust of twenty years, slamming the door behind him so violently that the thin partition rattled, and then stand for a moment pursing his lips, and convolving his features with incredible speed, and shaking his gaunt head slightly from side to side, until at length he whispered in a tone of passionate disgust and revulsion: "Oh, *bad! Bad! Bad!* By every *gesture,* by every *act,* he betrays the *boor,* the *vulgarian!* Can you imagine"—here his voice sunk even lower in its scale of passionate whispering repugnance—"can you for one *moment* imagine a man of *breeding* and the social graces breaking wind publicly?—And before his own daughter. Oh, *bad! Bad! Bad! Bad!*"

And in the silence, while Uncle Bascom stood shaking his head in its movement of downcast and convulsive distaste, they could hear, suddenly, the ripping noise Brill would make as his pungent answer to all the world—and his great bellow of throaty laughter. Later on, if Bascom had to consult him on any business, he would open his door abruptly, walk out into Brill's office clutching his hands together at his waist, and with disgust still carved upon his face, say: "Well, sir, . . . If you have concluded your morning devotions," here his voice sank to a bitter snarl, "we might get down to the transaction of some of the day's business."

"Why, Reverend!" Brill roared. "You ain't heard nothin' yet!"

And the great choking bellow of laughter would burst from him again, rattling the windows with its power as he hurled his great weight backward, with complete abandon, in his creaking swivel-chair.

It was obvious that he liked to tease the old man, and never lost an opportunity of doing so: for example, if any one gave Uncle Bascom a cigar, Brill would exclaim with an air of innocent surprise: "Why, *Reverend,* you're not going to smoke that, are you?"

"Why, certainly," Bascom said tartly. "That is the purpose for which it was intended, isn't it?"

"Why, yes," said Brill, "but you know how they make 'em, don't you? I didn't think you'd touch it after some dirty old Spaniard has wiped his old hands all over it—yes! an' *spit* upon it, too, because that's what they do!"

"Ah!" Bascom snarled contemptuously. "You don't know what you're talking about! There is nothing cleaner than good tobacco! Finest and healthiest plant on earth! No question about it!"

"Well," said Brill, "I've learned something. We live and learn, Reverend. You've taught me somethin' worth knowing: when it's free it's clean; when you have to pay for it it stinks like hell!" He pondered heavily for a moment, and the burble began to play about in his great throat: "And by God!" he concluded, "tobacco's not the only thing that applies to, either. Not by a damned sight!"

Again, one morning when his nephew was there, Bascom cleared his throat portentously, coughed, and suddenly said to him: "Now, Eugene, my boy, you are going to have lunch with me today. There's no question about it whatever!" This was astonishing news, for he had never before invited the youth to eat with him when he came to his office, although the boy had been to his house for dinner many times. "Yes, sir!" said Bascom, with an air of conviction and satisfaction. "I have thought it all over. There is a splendid establishment in the basement of this building—small, of course, but everything clean and of the highest order! It is conducted by an Irish gentleman whom I have known for many years. Finest people on earth: no question about it!"

It was an astonishing and momentous occasion; the boy knew how infrequently he went to a restaurant. Having made his decision, Uncle Bascom immediately stepped into the outer offices, and began to discuss and publish his intentions with the greatest satisfaction.

"Yes, sir!" he said in a precise tone, smacking his lips in a ruminant fashion, and addressing himself to every one rather than to a particular person. "We shall go in and take our seats in the regular way, and I shall then give appropriate instructions, to one of the attendants—" again he smacked his lips as he pronounced this word with such an indescribable air of relish that immediately the boy's mouth began to water, and the delicious pangs of appetite and hunger began to gnaw his vitals—"I shall say: 'This is my nephew, a young man now enrolled at Harvard Un-i-ver-sit-tee!' "—here Bascom smacked his lips together again with that same maddening air of relish—" 'Yes, sir' (I shall say!) —'You are to fulfil his order without *stint*, without *delay*, and without *question*, and to the *utmost* of your ability' "—he howled, wagging his great bony forefinger through the air— "As for myself," he declared abruptly, "I shall take nothing. Good Lord, no!" he said with a scornful laugh. "I wouldn't touch a thing they had to offer. You couldn't pay me to: I shouldn't sleep for a month if I did. But you, my boy!" he howled, turning suddenly upon his nephew, "—are to have everything your heart desires! Everything, everything, everything!" He made an inclusive gesture with his long arms; then closed his eyes, stamped at the floor, and began to snuffle with laughter.

Mr. Brill had listened to all this with his great-jowled face slack-jawed and agape with astonishment. Now, he said, heavily: "He's goin' to have everything, is he? Where are you goin' to take him to git it?"

"Why, sir!" Bascom said in an annoyed tone, "I have told you all along—we are going to the modest but excellent establishment in the basement of this very building."

"Why, Reverend," Brill said in a protesting tone, "you ain't goin' to take your nephew *there,* are you? I thought you said you was goin' to git somethin' to *eat.*"

"I had supposed," Bascom said with bitter sarcasm, "that one went there for that purpose. I had not supposed that one went there to get shaved."

"Well," said Brill, "if you go there you'll git shaved, all right. You'll not only git *shaved,* you'll git *skinned* alive. But you won't git anything to eat." And he hurled himself back again, roaring with laughter.

"Pay no attention to him!" Bascom said to the boy in a tone of bitter repugnance. "I have long known that his low and vulgar mind attempts to make a joke of everything, even the most sacred matters. I assure you, my boy, the place is excellent in every way:—do you suppose," he said now, addressing Brill and all the others, with a howl of fury—"do you suppose, if it were not, that I should for a single moment *dream* of taking him there? Do you suppose that I would for an instant *contemplate* taking my own nephew, my sister's son, to any place in which I did not repose the fullest confidence? Not on your life!" he howled. "Not on your life!"

And they departed, followed by Brill's great bellow, and a farewell invitation which he shouted after the young man. "Don't worry, son! When you git through with that cockroach stew, come back an' I'll take you out to lunch with *me!*"

Although Brill delighted in teasing and baiting his partner in this fashion, there was, at the bottom of his heart, a feeling of deep humility, of genuine respect and admiration for him: he respected Uncle Bascom's intelligence, he was secretly and profoundly impressed by the fact that the old man had been a minister of the gospel and had preached in many churches.

Moreover, in the respect and awe with which Brill greeted these evidences of Bascom's superior education, in the eagerness he showed hen he boasted to visitors, as he often did, of his partner's learning, there was a quality of pride that was profoundly touching and paternal: it was as if Bascom had been his son, and as if he wanted at every opportunity to display his talents to the world. And this, in fact, was exactly what he did want to do. Much to Bascom's annoyance, Brill was constantly speaking of his erudition to strangers who had come into the office for the first time, and constantly urging him to perform for them, to "say some of them big words, Reverend." And even when the old man answered him, as he frequently did, in terms of scorn, anger, and contempt, Brill was completely satisfied, if Uncle Bascom would only use a few of the "big words" in doing it. Thus, one day, when one of his boyhood friends, a New Hampshire man whom he had not seen in thirty-five years, had come in to renew their acquaintance Brill, in describing the accomplishments of his partner, said with an air of solemn affirmation: "Why, hell yes, Jim! It'd take a college perfesser to know what the Reverend is talkin' about half the time! No ordinary son-of-a-bitch is able to understand him! So help me God, it's true!" he swore solemnly, as Jim looked incredulous. "The Reverend knows words the average man ain't never heard. He knows words that ain't even in the dictionary. Yes, sir!—an' uses 'em, too—all the time!" he concluded triumphantly.

"Why, my dear sir!" Bascom answered in a tone of exacerbated contempt, "What on earth are you talking about? Such a man as you describe would be a monstrosity, a heinous perversion of natural law! A man so wise that no one could understand him:—so literate that he could not communicate with his fellow creatures:—so erudite that he led the inarticulate and incoherent life of a beast or a savage!"—here Uncle Bascom squinted his eyes tightly shut, and laughed sneeringly down his nose: "Phuh! phuh! phuh! phuh! phuh!— Why, you con-sum-mate fool!" he sneered, "I have long known that your ignorance was bottomless—but I had never hoped to see it equalled—Nay, surpassed!" he howled, "by your asininity."

"There you are!" said Brill exultantly to his visitor, "What did I tell you? There's one of them words, Jim: 'asserninity,' why, damn it, the Reverend's the only one who knows what that word means—you won't even find it in the dictionary!"

"Not find it in the dictionary!" Bascom yelled. "Almighty God, come down and give this ass a tongue as Thou did'st once before in Balaam's time!"

Again, Brill was seated at his desk one day engaged with a client in those intimate, cautious, and confidential preliminaries that mark the consummation of a "deal" in real estate. On this occasion the prospective buyer was an Italian: the man sat awkwardly and nervously in a chair beside Brill's desk while the great man bent his huge weight ponderously and persuasively toward him. From time to time the Italian's voice, sullen, cautious, disparaging, interrupted Brill's ponderous and coaxing drone. The Italian sat stiffly, his thick, clumsy body awkwardly clad in his "good" clothes of heavy black, his thick, hairy, blunt-nailed hands cupped nervously upon his knees, his black eyes glittering with suspicion under his knitted inch of brow. At length, he shifted nervously, rubbed his paws tentatively across his knees and then, with a smile mixed of ingratiation and mistrust, said: "How mucha you want, eh?"

"How mucha we want?" Brill repeated vulgarly as the burble began to play about within his throat. "Why, how mucha you got? . . . You know we'll take every damn thing you got! It's not how mucha we want, it's how mucha you got!" And he hurled himself backward, bellowing with laughter. "By God, Reverend," he yelled as Uncle Bascom entered, "ain't that right? It's not how mucha we want, it's how mucha you got! 'od damn! We ought to take that as our motter. I've got a good mind to git it printed on our letterheads. What do you think, Reverend?"

"Hey?" howled Uncle Bascom absently, as he prepared to enter his own office.

"I say we ought to use it for our motter."

"Your what?" said Uncle Bascom scornfully, pausing as if he did not understand.

"Our motter," Brill said.

"Not your *motter*," Bascom howled derisively. "The word is *not* motter," he said contemptuously. "Nobody of any refinement would say *motter*. *Motter* is *not* correct!" he howled finally. "Only an igno-*ram*-us would say *motter*. No!" he yelled with final conclusiveness. "That is *not* the way to pronounce it! That is ab-so-lute-ly and em-phat-ic-ally *not* the way to pronounce it!"

"All right, then, Reverend," said Brill, submissively. "You're the doctor. What is the word?"

"The word is *motto*," Uncle Bascom snarled. "Of course! Any fool knows that!"

"Why, hell," Mr. Brill protested in a hurt tone. "That's what I said, ain't it?"

"No-o!" Uncle Bascom howled derisively. "No-o! By no means, by no means, by no means! You said *motter*. The word is *not* motter. The word is motto: m-o-t-t-o! M-O-T-T-O does *not* spell motter," he remarked with vicious decision.

"What does it spell?" said Mr. Brill.

"It spells *motto*," Uncle Bascom howled. "It *has* always spelled motto! It *will* always spell motto! As it was in the beginning, is now, and ever shall be: A-a-men!" he howled huskily in his most evangelical fashion. Then, immensely pleased at his wit, he closed his eyes, stamped at the floor, and snarled and snuffled down his nose with laughter.

"Well, anyway," said Brill, "no matter how you spell it, it's not how mucha we want, it's how mucha you got! That's the way we feel about it!"

And this, in fact, without concealment, without pretense, without evasion, was just how Brill did feel about it. He wanted everything that was his and, in addition, he wanted as much as he could get. And this rapacity, this brutal and unadorned gluttony, so far from making men wary of him, attracted them to him, inspired them with unshakable confidence in his integrity, his business honesty. Perhaps the reason for this was that concealment did not abide in the man: he published his intentions to the world with an oath and a roar of laughter—and the world, having seen and judged, went away with the confidence of this Italian—that Brill was "one fine-a man!" Even Bascom, who had so often turned upon his colleague the weapons of scorn, contempt, and mockery, had a curious respect for him, an acrid sunken affection: often, when the old man and his nephew were alone, he would recall something Brill had said and his powerful and fluent features would suddenly be contorted in that familiar grimace, as he laughed his curious laugh which was forced out, with a deliberate and painful effort, through his powerful nose and his lips, barred with a few large teeth. "Phuh! phuh! phuh! phuh! phuh! . . . Of course!" he said, with a nasal rumination, as he stared over the apex of his great bony hands, clasped in meditation—"of course, he is just a poor ignorant fellow! I don't suppose—no, sir, I really do not suppose that Brill ever went to school over six months in his life!—Say!" Bascom paused suddenly, turned abruptly with his strange fixed grin, and fastened his sharp old eyes keenly on the boy: in this sudden and abrupt change, this transference of his vision from his own secret and personal world, in which his thought and feeling were sunken, and which seemed to be so far away from the actual world about him, there was something impressive and disconcerting. His eyes were gray, sharp, and old, and one eyelid had a heavy droop or ptosis which, although it did not obscure his vision, gave his expression at times a sinister glint, a malevolent humor. "—Say!" here his voice sank to a deliberate and confiding whisper, "(Phuh! phuh! phuh! phuh! phuh!) Say—a man who would—he told me—Oh, vile! vile! vile! my boy!" his uncle whispered, shutting his eyes in a kind of shuddering ecstasy as if at the memory of things too gloriously obscene to be repeated. "Can you *imagine,* can you even *dream* of such a state of affairs if he had possessed an atom, a *scintilla* of delicacy and good breeding! Yes, sir!" he said with decision. "I suppose there's no doubt about it! His beginnings were very lowly, very poor and humble, indeed! . . . Not that that is in any sense to his discredit!" Uncle Bascom said hastily, as if it had occurred to him that his words might bear some taint of snobbishness. "Oh, by no means, by no means, by no means!" he sang out, with a sweeping upward gesture of his long arm, as if he were clearing the air of wisps of smoke. "Some of our finest men—some of the nation's *leaders,* have come from just such surroundings as those. Beyond a doubt! Beyond a doubt! There's no question about it whatever! Say!"—here he turned suddenly upon the boy again with the ptotic and sinister intelligence of his eye. "Was *Lincoln* an aristocrat? Was he the issue of wealthy parents? Was he brought up with a silver spoon in his mouth? Was our *own* former governor, the Vice-President of the United States today, reared in the lap of luxury! Not on your life!" howled Uncle Bascom. "He came from frugal and thrifty Vermont farming stock, he has never deviated a *jot* from his early training, he remains today what he has always been—one of the simplest of men! Finest people on earth, no question about it whatever!"

Again, he meditated gravely with lost stare across the apex of his great joined hands, and the boy noticed again, as he had noticed so often, the great dignity of his head in thought—a head that was highbrowed, lean and lonely, a head that not only in its cast of thought but even in its physical contour, and in its profound and lonely earnestness, bore an astonishing resemblance to that of Emerson—it was, at times like these, as grand a head as the young man had ever seen, and on it was legible the history of man's loneliness, his dignity, his grandeur and despair.

"Yes, sir!" said Bascom, in a moment. "He is, of course, a vulgar fellow and some of the things he says at times are Oh, vile! vile! vile!" cried Bascom, closing his eyes and laughing, "Oh, vile! *most* vile! . . . but (phuh! phuh! phuh!) you can't help laughing at the fellow at times because he is so . . . Oh, I could tell you things, my boy! . . . Oh, *vile! vile!*" he cried, shaking his head downwards. "What coarseness! . . . What in-*vect*-ive!" he whispered, in a kind of ecstasy.

XII

EUGENE was now a member of Professor Hatcher's celebrated course for dramatists, and although he had come into this work by chance, and would in the end discover that his heart and interest were not in it, it had now become for him the rock to which his life was anchored, the rudder of his destiny, the sole and all-sufficient reason for his being here. It now seemed to him that there was only one work in life which he could possibly do, and that this work was writing plays, and that if he could not succeed in this work he had better die, since any other life than the life of the playwright and the theatre was not to be endured.

Accordingly every interest and energy of his life was now fastened on this work with a madman's passion; he thought, felt, breathed, ate, drank, slept, and lived completely in terms of plays. He learned all the jargon of the art-playwriting cult, read all the books, saw all the shows, talked all the talk, and even became a kind of gigantic eavesdropper upon life, prowling about the streets with his ears constantly straining to hear all the words and phrases of the passing crowd, as if he might hear something that would be rare and priceless in a play for Professor Hatcher's celebrated course.

Professor James Graves Hatcher was a man whose professional career had been made difficult by two circumstances: all the professors thought he looked like an actor and all the actors thought he looked like a professor. In reality, he was wholly neither one, but in character and temper, as well as in appearance, he possessed some of the attributes of both.

His appearance was imposing: a well-set-up figure of a man of fifty-five, somewhat above the middle height, strongly built and verging toward stockiness, with an air of vital driving energy that was always filled with authority and a sense of sure purpose, and that never degenerated into the cheap exuberance of the professional hustler. His voice, like his manner, was quiet, distinguished, and controlled, but always touched with the suggestions of great latent power, with reserves of passion, eloquence, and resonant sonority.

His head was really splendid: he had a strong but kindly-looking face touched keenly, quietly by humor; his eyes, beneath his glasses, were also keen, observant, sharply humorous, his mouth was wide and humorous but somewhat too tight, thin and spinsterly for a man's, his nose was large and strong, his forehead shapely and able-looking, and he had neat wings of hair cut short and sparse and lying flat against the skull.

He wore eye-glasses of the pince-nez variety, and they dangled in a fashionable manner from a black silk cord: it was better than going to a show to see him put them on, his manner was so urbane, casual, and distinguished when he did so. His humor, although suave, was also quick and rich and gave an engaging warmth and humanity to a personality that sometimes needed them. Even in his display of humor, however, he never lost his urbane distinguished manner—for example, when some one told him that one of his women students had referred to another woman in the course, an immensely tall angular creature who dressed in rusty brown right up to the ears, as "the queen of the angle-worms," Professor Hatcher shook all over with sudden laughter, removed his glasses with a distinguished movement, and then in a rich but controlled voice, remarked:

"Ah, she has a very pretty wit. A very pretty wit, indeed!"

Thus, even in his agreeable uses of the rich, subtle and immensely pleasant humor with which he had been gifted, Professor Hatcher was something of an actor. He was one of those rare people who really "chuckle," and although there was no doubting the spontaneity and naturalness of his chuckle, it is also probably true that Professor Hatcher somewhat fancied himself as a chuckler.

The Hatcherian chuckle was just exactly what the word connotes: a movement of spontaneous mirth that shook his stocky shoulders and strong well-set torso with a sudden hearty tremor. And although he could utter rich and sonorous throat-sounds indicative of hearty mirth while this chuckling process was going on, an even more characteristic form was completely soundless, the tight lips firmly compressed, the edges turned up with the convulsive inclination to strong laughter, the fine distinguished head thrown back, while all the rest of him, throat, shoulders, torso, belly, arms—the whole man—shook in the silent tremors of the chuckle.

It could also be said with equal truth that Professor Hatcher was one of the few men whose eyes could really "twinkle," and it is likewise true that he probably fancied himself as somewhat of a twinkler.

Perhaps one fact that made him suspect to professors was his air of a distinguished and mature, but also a very worldly, urbanity. His manner, even in the class room, was never that of the scholar or the academician, but always that of the cultured man of the world, secure in his authority, touched by fine humor and fine understanding, able, knowing and assured. And one reason that he so impressed his students may have been that he made some of the most painful and difficult labors in the world seem delightfully easy.

For example, if there were to be a performance by a French club at the university of a French play, produced in the language of its birth, Professor Hatcher might speak to his class in his assured, yet casual and urbanely certain tones, as follows:

"I understand *Le Cercle Français* is putting on De Musset's *Il faut qu'une porte soit ouverte ou fermée* on Thursday night. If you are doing nothing else, I think it might be very well worth your while to brush up on your French a bit and look in on it. It is, of course, a trifle and perhaps without great significance in the development of the modern theatre, but it is De Musset in rather good form and De Musset in good form is charming. So it might repay you to have a look at it."

What was there in these simple words that could so impress and captivate these young people? The tone was quiet, pleasant and urbanely casual, the manner easy yet authoritative, what he said about the play was really true. But what was so seductive about it was the flattering unction which he laid so casually to their young souls—the easy off-hand suggestion that people "brush up on their French a bit" when most of them had no French at all to brush up on, that if they had "nothing else to do," they might "look in" upon De Musset's "charming trifle," the easy familiarity with De Musset's name and the casual assurance of the statement that it was "De Musset in rather good form."

It was impossible for a group of young men, eager for sophistication and emulous of these airs of urbane worldliness, not to be impressed by them. As Professor Hatcher talked they too became easy, casual and urbane in their manners, they had a feeling of being delightfully at ease in the world and sure of themselves, the words "brush up on your French a bit" gave them a beautifully comfortable feeling that they would really be able to perform this remarkable accomplishment in an hour or two of elegant light labor. And when he spoke of the play as being "De Musset in rather good form" they nodded slightly with little understanding smiles as if De Musset and his various states of form were matters of the most familiar knowledge to them.

What was the effect, then, of this and other such-like talk upon these young men eager for fame and athirst for glory in the great art-world of the city and the theatre? It gave them, first of all, a delightful sense of being in the know about rare and precious things, of rubbing shoulders with great actors and actresses and other celebrated people, of being expert in all the subtlest processes of the theatre, of being travelled, urbane, sophisticated and assured.

When Professor Hatcher casually suggested that they might "brush up on their French a bit" before going to a performance of a French play, they felt like cosmopolites who were at home in all the great cities of the world. True, "their French had grown a little rusty"—it had been some time since they were last in Paris—a member of the French Academy, no doubt, might detect a few slight flaws in their pronunciation—but all that would arrange itself by a little light and easy "polishing"—"tout s'arrange, hein?" as we say upon the boulevards.

Again, Professor Hatcher's pleasant and often delightfully gay anecdotes about the famous persons he had known and with whom he was on such familiar terms—told always casually, apropos of some topic of discussion, and never dragged in or labored by pretense— "The last time I was in London, Pinero and I were having lunch together one day at the Savoy"—or "I was spending the week-end with Henry Arthur Jones"—or "It's very curious you should mention that. You know, Barrie was saying the same thing to me the last time I saw him—" or—"Apropos of this discussion, I have a letter here from 'Gene O'Neill which bears on that very point. Perhaps you would be interested in knowing what he has to say about it."— All this, of course, was cakes and ale to these young people—it made them feel wonderfully near and intimate with all these celebrated people, and with the enchanted world of art and of the theatre in which they wished to cut a figure.

It gave them also a feeling of amused superiority at the posturings and antics of what, with a slight intonation of disdain, they called "the commercial producers"—the Shuberts, Belascos, and others of this kind. Thus, when Professor Hatcher told them how he had done some pioneer service in Boston for the Russian Players and had received a telegram from the Jewish producer in New York who was managing them, to this effect: "You are the real wonder boy"—they were instantly able to respond to the sudden Hatcherian chuckle with quiet laughter of their own.

Again, he once came back from New York with an amusing story of a visit he had paid to the famous producer, David Belasco. And he described drolly how he had followed a barefoot, snaky-looking female, clad in a long batik gown, through seven gothic chambers mystical with chimes and incense. And finally he told how he had been ushered into the presence of the great ecclesiastic who sat at the end of a cathedral-like room beneath windows of church glass, and how he was preceded all the time by Snaky Susy who swept low in obeisance as she approached, and said in a silky voice—"One is here to see you, Mahster," and how she had been dismissed with Christ-like tone and movement of the hand—"Rise, Rose, and leave us now." Professor Hatcher told this story with a quiet drollery that was irresistible, and was rewarded all along by their shouts of astounded laughter, and finally by their smiling and astonished faces, lifting disbelieving eyebrows at each other, saying, "Simply incredible! It doesn't seem possible! . . . *Marvellous!*"

Finally, when Professor Hatcher talked to them of how a Russian actress used her hands, of rhythm, tempo, pause, and timing, of lighting, setting, and design, he gave them a language they could use with a feeling of authority and knowledge, even when authority and knowledge was lacking to them. It was a dangerous and often very trivial language—a kind of jargonese of art that was coming into use in the world of those days, and that seemed to be coincident with another jargonese—that of science—"psychology," as they called it—which was also coming into its brief hour of idolatry at about the same period, and which bandied about its talk of "complexes," "fixations," "repressions," "inhibitions," and the like, upon the lips of any empty-headed little fool that came along.

But although this jargon was perhaps innocuous enough when rattled off the rattling tongue of some ignorant boy or rattle-pated girl, it could be a very dangerous thing when uttered seriously by men who were trying to achieve the best, the rarest, and the highest life on earth—the life which may be won only by bitter toil and knowledge and stern living—the life of the artist.

And the great danger of this glib and easy jargon of the arts was this: that instead of knowledge, the experience of hard work and patient living, they were given a formula for knowledge; a language that sounded very knowing, expert and assured, and yet that knew nothing, was experienced in nothing, was sure of nothing. It gave to people without talent and without sincerity of soul or integrity of purpose, with nothing, in fact, except a feeble incapacity for the shock and agony of life, and a desire to escape into a glamorous and unreal world of make believe—a justification for their pitiable and base existence. It gave to people who had no power in themselves to create anything of merit or of beauty—people who were the true Philistines and enemies of art and of the artist's living spirit—the language to talk with glib knowingness of things they knew nothing of—to prate of "settings," "tempo," "pace," and "rhythm," of "boldly stylized conventions," and the wonderful way some actress "used her hands." And in the end, it led to nothing but falseness and triviality, to the ghosts of passion, and the spectres of sincerity, to the shoddy appearances of conviction and belief in people who had no passion and sincerity, and who were convinced of nothing, believed in nothing, were just the disloyal apes of fashion and the arts.

"I think you ought to go," says one. "I really do. I really think you might be interested."

"Yes," says number two, in a tone of fine, puzzled, eyebrow-lifting protest, "but I hear the play is pretty bad. The reviews were rather awful —they really were, you know."

"Oh, the play!" the other says, with a slight start of surprise, as if it never occurred to him that any one might be interested in the play— "the play, the play *is* rather terrible. But my dear fellow, no one goes to see the *play* . . . the play is nothing," he dismisses it with a contemptuous gesture— "it's the *sets!*" he cries— "the *sets* are really quite remarkable. You ought to go, old boy, just to see the *sets!* They're very good—they really are."

"H'm!" the other says, stroking his chin in an impressed manner. "Interesting! In that case, I shall go!"

The *sets!* The *sets!* One should not go to see the play; the only thing that matters is the sets. And this is the theatre—the magic-maker and the world of dreams; and these the men that are to fashion for it—with their trivial ape's talk about "sets." Did any one ever hear such damned stuff as this since time began?

False, trivial, glib, dishonest, empty, without substance, lacking faith —is it any wonder that among Professor Hatcher's young men few birds sang?

XIII

THAT year the youth was twenty, it had been his first year in New England, and the winter had seemed very long. In the man-swarm he felt alone and lost, a desolate atom in the streets of life. That year he went to see his uncle many times.

Sometimes he would find him in his dusty little cubicle, bent over the intricacy of a legal form, painfully and carefully, with compressed lips, filling in the blank spaces with his stiff, angular and laborious hand. Bascom would speak quietly, without looking up, as he came in: "Hello, my boy. Sit down, won't you? I'll be with you in a moment." And for a time the silence would be broken only by the heavy rumble of Brill's voice outside, by the minute scratching of his uncle's pen, and by the immense and murmurous sound of time, which rose above the city, which caught up in the upper air all of the city's million noises, and yet seemed remote, essential, imperturbable and everlasting—fixed and unchanging, no matter what men lived or died.

Again, the boy would find his uncle staring straight before him, with his great hands folded in a bony arch, his powerful gaunt face composed in a rapt tranquillity of thought. At these times he seemed to have escaped from every particular and degrading thing in life—from the excess of absurd and eccentric speech and gesture, from all demeaning parsimonies, from niggling irascibilities, from everything that contorted his face and spirit away from its calmness and unity of thought. His face at such a time might well have been the mask of thought, the visage of contemplation. Sometimes he would not speak for several minutes, his mind seemed to brood upon the lip and edge of time, to be remote from every dusty moment of the earth.

One day the boy went there and found him thus: after a few moments he lowered his great hands and without turning toward his nephew, sat for some time in an attitude of quiet relaxation. At length he said: "What is man that thou art mindful of him?"

It was one of the first days of spring: the spring had come late, with a magical northern suddenness. It seemed to have burst out of the earth overnight, the air was lyrical and sang with it.

Spring came that year like a triumph and like a prophecy—it sang and shifted like a moth of light before the youth, but he was sure that it would bring him a glory and fulfilment he had never known.

His hunger and thirst had been immense: he was caught up for the first time in the midst of the Faustian web—there was no food that could feed him, no drink that could quench his thirst. Like an insatiate and maddened animal he roamed the streets, trying to draw up mercy from the cobblestones, solace and wisdom from a million sights and faces, or he prowled through endless shelves of high-piled books, tortured by everything he could not see and could not know, and growing blind, weary, and desperate from what he read and saw. He wanted to know all, have all, be all—to be one and many, to have the whole riddle of this vast and swarming earth as legible, as tangible in his hand as a coin of minted gold.

Suddenly spring came, and he felt at once exultant certainty and joy. Outside his uncle's dirty window he could see the edge of Faneuil Hall, and hear the swarming and abundant activity of the markets. The deep roar of the markets reached them across the singing and lyrical air, and he drank into his lungs a thousand proud, potent, and mysterious odors which came to him like the breath of certainty, like the proof of magic, and like the revelation that all confusion had been banished—the world that he longed for won, the word that he sought for spoken, the hunger that devoured him fed and ended. And the markets, swarming with richness, joy, and abundance, thronged below him like a living evidence of fulfilment. For it seemed to him that nowhere more than here was the passionate enigma of New England felt: New England, with its harsh and stony soil, and its tragic and lonely beauty; its desolate rocky coasts and its swarming fisheries, the white, piled, frozen bleakness of its winters with the magnificent jewelry of stars; the dark firwoods, and the warm little white houses at which it is impossible to look without thinking of groaning bins, hung bacon, hard cider, succulent bastings and love's warm, white, and opulent flesh.

There was the rustle of gingham by day and sober glances; then, under low eaves and starlight, the stir of the satiny thighs in feather beds, the white small bite and tigerish clasp of secret women—always the buried heart, the sunken passion, the frozen heat. And then, after the long, unendurably hard-locked harshness of the frozen winter, the coming of spring as now, like a lyrical cry, like a flicker of rain across a window glass, like the sudden and delicate noises of a spinet—the coming of spring and ecstasy, and overnight the thrum of wings, the burst of the tender buds, the ripple and dance of the roughened water, the light of flowers, the sudden, fleeting, almost captured, and exultant spring.

And here, within eighty yards of the dusty little room where his uncle Bascom had his desk, there was living evidence that this intuition was not false: the secret people, it was evident, did not subsist alone on codfish and a jug full of baked beans—they ate meat, and large chunks of it, for all day long, within the market district, the drivers of big wagons were standing to their chins in meat, boys dragged great baskets of raw meat along the pavements, red-faced butchers, aproned with gouts of blood, and wearing the battered straw hats that butchers wear, toiled through the streets below with great loads of loin or haunch or rib, and in chill shops with sawdust floors the beeves were hung in frozen regimental rows.

Right and left, around the central market, the old buildings stretched down to the harbor and the smell of ships: this was built-on land, in old days ships were anchored where these cobbles were, but the warehouses were also old—they had the musty, mellow, blackened air and smell of the 'seventies, they looked like Victorian prints, they reeked of ancient ledgers, of "counting houses," of proud, monied merchants, and the soft-spoked rumble of victorias.

By day, this district was one snarled web of chaos: a *gewirr* of deep-bodied trucks, powerful dappled horses, cursing drivers, of loading, unloading, and shipping, of dispatch and order, of the million complicated weavings of life and business.

But if one came here at evening, after the work of the day was done, if one came here at evening on one of those delicate and sudden days of spring that New England knows, if one came here as many a lonely youth had come here in the past, some boy from the inland immensity of America, some homesick lad from the South, from the marvellous hills of Old Catawba, he might be pierced again by the bitter ecstasy of youth, the ecstasy that tears him apart with a cry that has no tongue, the ecstasy that is proud, lonely, and exultant, that is fierce with joy and blind with glory, but yet carries in it a knowledge, born in such a moment, that the intangible cannot be touched, the ungraspable cannot be grasped—the imperial and magnificent minute is gone forever which, with all its promises, its million intuitions, he wishes to clothe with the living substance of beauty. He wishes to flesh the moment with the thighs and breast and belly of a wonderful mistress, he wishes to be great and glorious and triumphant, to distill the ether of this ecstasy in a liquor, and to drink strong joy forever; and at the heart of all this is the bitter knowledge of death—death of the moment, death of the day, death of one more infrequent spring.

Perhaps the thing that really makes New England wonderful is this sense of joy, this intuition of brooding and magic fulfilment that hovers like a delicate presence in the air of one of these days. Perhaps the answer is simple: perhaps it is only that this soft and sudden spring, with its darts and flicks of evanescent joy, its sprite-like presence that is only half-believed, its sound that is the sound of something lost and elfin and half-dreamed, half-heard, seems wonderful after the grim frozen tenacity of the winter, the beautiful and terrible desolation, the assault of the frost and ice on living flesh which resists it finally as it would resist the cruel battering of a brute antagonist, so that the tart, stingy speech, the tight gestures, the withdrawn and suspicious air, the thin lips, red pointed noses and hard prying eyes of these people are really the actions of those who, having to defend themselves harshly against nature, harshly defend themselves against all the world.

At any rate, the thing the boy feels who comes here at the day's end is not completion, weariness, and sterility, but a sense of swelling ecstasy, a note of brooding fulfilment. The air will have in it the wonderful odors of the market and the smell of the sea; as he walks over the bare cobbled pavement under the corrugated tin awnings of the warehouses and produce stores a hundred smells of the rich fecundity of the earth will assail him: the clean sharp pungency of thin crated wood and the citric nostalgia of oranges, lemons, and grapefruit, the stench of a decayed cabbage and the mashed pulp of a rotten orange. There will be also the warm coarse limy smell of chickens, the strong coddy smell of cold fish and oysters; and the crisp moist cleanliness of the garden smells—of great lettuces, cabbages, new potatoes, with their delicate skins loamy with sweet earth, the wonderful sweet crispness of crated celery; and then the melons—the ripe golden melons bedded in fragrant straw—and all the warm infusions of the tropics: the bananas, the pineapples and the alligator pears.

The delicate and subtle air of spring touches all these odors with a new and delicious vitality; it draws the tar out of the pavements also, and it draws slowly, subtly, from ancient warehouses, the compacted perfumes of eighty years: the sweet thin piney scents of packing-boxes, the glutinous composts of half a century, that have thickly stained old warehouse plankings, the smells of twine, tar, turpentine and hemp, and of thick molasses, ginseng, pungent vines and roots and old piled sacking; the clean, ground strength of fresh coffee, brown, sultry, pungent, and exultantly fresh and clean; the smell of oats, baled hay and bran, of crated eggs and cheese and butter; and particularly the smell of meat, of frozen beeves, slick porks, and veals, of brains and livers and kidneys, of haunch, paunch, and jowl; of meat that is raw and of meat that is cooked, for upstairs in that richly dingy block of buildings there is a room where the butchers, side by side with the bakers, the bankers, the brokers and the Harvard boys, devour thick steaks of the best and tenderest meat, smoking-hot breads, and big, jacketed potatoes.

And then there is always the sea. In dingy blocks, memoried with time and money, the buildings stretch down to the docks, and there is always the feeling that the sea was here, that this is built-on earth. A single truck will rattle over the deserted stones, and then there is the street that runs along the harbor, the dingy little clothing shops and eating places, the powerful strings of freight cars, agape and empty, odorous with their warm fatigued planking and the smells of flanges and axles that have rolled great distances.

And finally, by the edges of the water, there are great piers and storehouses, calm and potent with their finished work: they lie there, immense, starkly ugly, yet touched with the powerful beauty of enormous works and movements; they are what they are, they have been built without a flourish for the work they do, their great sides rise in level cliffs of brick, they are pierced with tracks and can engulf great trains; and now that the day is done they breathe with the vitality of a tired but living creature. A single footfall will make remote and lonely echoes in their brooding depths, there will be the expiring clatter of a single truck, the sound of a worker's voice as he says "Good-night," and then the potent and magical silence.

And then there is the sea—the sea, beautiful and mysterious as it is only when it meets the earth in harbors, the sea that bears in swell and glut of tides the odorous savor of the earth, the sea that swings and slaps against encrusted piles, the sea that is braided with long ropes of scummy weed, the sea that brings the mast and marly scent of shelled decay. There is the sea, and there are the great ships—the freighters, the fishing schooners, the clean white one-night boats that make the New York run, now also potent and silent, a glitter of bright lights, of gleaming brasses, of opulent saloons—a token of joy and splendor in dark waters, a hint of love and the velvet belly upon dark tides—and the sight of all these things, the fusion of all these odors by the sprite of May is freighted with unspeakable memories, with unutterable intuitions for the youth: he does not know what he would utter, but glory, love, power, wealth, flight, and movement and the sight of new earth in the morning, and the living corporeal fulfilment of all his ecstasy is in his wish and his conviction.

Certainly, these things can be found in New England, but perhaps the person who finds this buried joy the most is this lonely visitor—and particularly the boy from the South, for in the heart of the Southerner alone, perhaps, is this true and secret knowledge of the North: it is there in his dreams and his childhood premonition, it is there like the dark Helen, and no matter what he sees to cheat it, he will always believe in it, he will always return to it. Certainly, this was true of the gnarled and miserly old man who now sat not far from all this glory in his dingy State Street office, for Bascom Pentland, although the stranger on seeing him might have said, "There goes the very image of a hard-bitten old Down-Easter," had come, as lonely and wretched a youth as ever lived, from the earth of Old Catawba, he had known and felt these things and, in spite of his frequent bitter attacks on the people, the climate, the life, New England was the place to which he had returned to live, and for which he felt the most affection.

Now, ruminant and lost, he stared across the archway of his hands. In a moment, with what was only an apparent irrelevance, with what was really a part of the coherent past, a light plucked from dark adyts of the brain, he said: "Who knoweth the spirit of man that goeth upward, and the spirit of the beast that goeth downward to the earth?"

He was silent and thoughtful for a moment; then he added sadly: "I am an old man. I have lived a long time. I have seen so many things. Sometimes everything seems so long ago."

Then his eye went back into the wilderness, the lost earth, the buried men.

Presently he said, "I hope you will come out on Sunday. O, by all means! By all means! I believe your aunt is expecting you. Yes, sir, I believe she said something to that effect. Or perhaps she intends to pay a visit to one of her children. I do not know, I have not the *remotest*— not the *faintest* idea of what she proposes to do," he howled. "Of course."

he said impatiently and scornfully, "I never have any notion what she has in mind. No, sir, I really could not tell you. I no longer pay any attention to what she says—O! not the slightest!" he waved his great hand through the air— *"Say!"* stiffly and harshly he tapped the boy's knee, grinning at him with the combative glitter of his ptotic eye— *"Say!* did you ever find *one* of them with whom it was possible to carry on a coherent conversation? Did you ever find one of them who would respond to the processes of reason and ordered thought? My dear boy!" he cried, "you cannot talk to them. I assure you, you cannot talk to them. You might as well whistle into the wind or spit into the waters of the Nile, for all the good it will do you. In his youth man will bare the riches of his spirit to them, will exhaust the rich accumulations of his genius—his wisdom, his learning, his philosophy—in an effort to make them worthy of his companionship—and in the end, what does he *always* find? Why," said Uncle Bascom bitterly, "that he has spent his powers in talking to an imbecile"—and he snarled vengefully through his nose. In a moment more, he contorted his face, and nasally whined in a grotesque and mincing parody of a woman's voice, "O, I feel *so* sick! O, deary *me,* now! I think my *time* is coming on again! O, you don't *love* me any mo-o-ore! O, I *wish* I was dead! O, I can't get *up* to-day! O, I wish you'd bring me something *nice* from *ta-own!* O, if you loved me you'd buy me a *new* hat! O, I've got nothing to *we-e-ar!*" here his voice had an added snarl of bitterness—"I'm ashamed to go out on the street with all the other wim-men!"

Then he paused broodingly for a moment more, wheeled abruptly and tapped the boy on the knee again: "The proper study of mankind is —say!" he said with a horrible fixed grimace and in a kind of cunning whisper—"does the poet say—*woman?* I want to ask you: *does* he, now? Not on your life!" yelled Uncle Bascom. "The word is *man, man, man!* Nothing else but *man!*"

Again he was silent: then, with an accent of heavy sarcasm, he went on: "Your aunt likes music. You may have observed your aunt is fond of music——"

It was, in fact, the solace of her life: on a tiny gramophone which one of her daughters had given her, she played constantly the records of the great composers.

"—Your aunt is fond of music," Bascom said deliberately. "Perhaps you may have thought—perhaps it seemed to you that she discovered it—perhaps you thought it was your aunt's own patent and invention—

but there you would be wrong! O yes! my boy!" he howled remotely.
"You may have thought so, but you would be wrong— Say!" he turned
slowly with a malevolent glint of interrogation, a controlled ironic power
—"was the Fifth Symphony written by a woman? Was the object of
your aunt's worship, Richard Wagner, a *female?*" he snarled. "By no
means! Where are their great works—their mighty symphonies, their
great paintings, their epic poetry? Was it in a woman's skull that the
Critique of Pure Reason was conceived? Is the gigantic work upon the
ceiling of the Sistine Chapel the product of a woman's genius?—Say!
did you ever hear of a lady by the name of William Shakespeare? Was
it a female of that name who wrote *King Lear?* Are you familiar with
the works of a nice young lady named John Milton? Or Fräulein
Goethe, a sweet German girl?" he sneered. "Perhaps you have been
edified by the writ-ings of Mademoiselle Voltaire or Miss Jonathan
Swift? Phuh! Phuh! Phuh! Phuh! Phuh!"

He paused, stared deliberately across his hands, and in a moment repeated, slowly and distinctly: "The woman gave me of the tree and I
did eat. Ah! that's it! There, my boy, you have it! There, in a nut-shell,
you have the work for which they are best fitted." And he turned upon
his nephew suddenly with a blaze of passion, his voice husky and tremulous from the stress of emotion. "The tempter! The Bringer of Forbid-
den Fruit! The devil's ambassador! Since the beginning of time that has
been their office—to madden the brain, to turn man's spirit from its
highest purposes, to corrupt, to seduce, and to destroy! To creep and
crawl, to intrude into the lonely places of man's heart and brain, to wind
herself into the core of his most secret life as a worm eats its way into a
healthy fruit—to do all this with the guile of a serpent, the cunning of
a fox—that, my boy, is what she's here for!—and she'll never change!"
And, lowering his voice to an ominous and foreboding whisper, he said
mysteriously, "Beware! Beware! Do not be deceived!"

In a moment more he had resumed his tone and manner of calm deliberation and, with an air of irrelevance, somewhat grudgingly, as if
throwing a bone to a dog, he said, "Your aunt, of course, was a woman
of considerable mentality—considerable, that is, for a female. Of course,
her mind is no longer what it used to be. I never talk to her any more,"
he said indifferently. "I do not listen to her. I think she said something
to me about your coming out on Sunday! But I do not know. No, sir,
I could not tell you what her plans are. I have my own interests, and I
suppose she has hers. Of course, she has her music. . . . Yes, sir, she

always has her music," he said indifferently and contemptuously, and, staring across the apex of his hands, he forgot her.

Yet, he had been young, and full of pain and madness. For a space he had known all the torments any lover ever knew. So much Louise had told her nephew, and so much Bascom had not troubled to deny. For bending toward the boy swiftly, fiercely, and abruptly, as if Bascom was not there, she whispered: "Oh, yes! he's indifferent enough to me now—but there was a time, there was a time, I tell you!—when he was mad about me! The old fool!" she cackled suddenly and bitterly with a seeming irrelevance. Then bending forward suddenly with a resumption of her former brooding intensity, she whispered: "Yes! he was mad, mad, mad! Oh, he can't deny it!" she cried. "He couldn't keep his eyes off me for a minute! He went cwazy if any other man so much as looked at me!"

"Quite true, my dear! Quite true!" said Uncle Bascom without a trace of anger or denial in his voice, with one of his sudden and astonishing changes to a mood of tender and tranquil agreement. "Oh, yes," he said again, staring reminiscently across the apex of his great folded hands, "it is all quite true—every word as she has spoken it—quite true, quite true. I had forgotten but it's all quite true." And he shook his gaunt head gently from side to side, turning his closed eyes downward, and snuffling gently, blindly, tenderly, with laughter, with a passive and indifferent memory.

For a year or two after his marriage, she had said, he had been maddened by a black insanity of jealousy. It descended on his spirit like a choking and pestilence-laden cloud, it entered his veins with blackened tongues of poison, it crept along the conduits of his blood, sweltered venomously in his heart, it soaked into the convolutions of his brain until his brain was fanged with hatred, soaked in poison, stricken, maddened, and unhinged. His gaunt figure wasted until he became the picture of skeletonized emaciation, jealousy and fear ate like a vulture at his entrails, all of the vital energy, the power and intensity of his life, was fed into this poisonous and consuming fire and then, when it had almost wrecked his health, ruined his career, and destroyed his reason, it left him as suddenly as it came: his life reverted to its ancient and imbedded core of egotism, he grew weary of his wife, he thought of her indifferently, he forgot her.

And she, poor soul, was like a rabbit trapped before the fierce yellow eye, the hypnotic stare of a crouching tiger. She did not know whether he would spring, strike forth his paw to maul her, or walk off indifferently. She was dazed and stricken before the violence of his first passion, the unreasoning madness of his jealousy, and in the years that followed she was bewildered, resentful, and finally embittered by the abrupt indifference which succeeded it—an indifference so great that often he seemed to forget her very existence for days at a time, to live with her in a little house as if he were scarcely conscious of her presence, stumping about the place in an intensity of self-absorption while he cursed and muttered to himself, banged open furnace doors, chopped up whatever combinations of raw foods his fantastic imagination might contrive, and answering her impatiently and contemptuously when she spoke to him: "What did you *say-y?* Oh, what are you talk-ing about?"—and he would stump away again, absorbed mysteriously with his own affairs. And sometimes, if he was the victim of conspiracy in the universe—if God had forsaken him and man had tricked and cheated him, he would roll upon the floor, hammer his heels against the wall, and howl his curses at oblivious heaven.

Louise, meanwhile, her children having left her, played Wagner on the gramophone, kept her small house tidy, and learned to carry on involved and animated conversations with herself, or even with her pots and pans, for when she scrubbed and cleaned them, she would talk to them: if she dropped one, she would scold it, pick it from the floor, spank it across the bottom, saying: "No, you don't! Naughty, you bad thing, you!" And often, while he stumped through the house, these solitary conversations were interspersed by fits of laughter: she would bend double over her pots snuffling with soft laughter which was faintly broken at its climax, a long high "Who-o-op." Then she would shake her head pityingly, and be off again, but at what she was laughing she could not have said.

One night, however, she interrupted one of Bascom's stamping and howling tirades by putting on her tiny gramophone *The Ride of the Valkyries,* as recorded by the Philadelphia Symphony Orchestra. Bascom, after the first paralysis of his surprise had passed, rushed furiously toward the offending instrument that was providing such melodious but mighty competition. Then Bascom halted; for suddenly he noticed that Louise was standing beside the instrument, that she was snuffling through her nose with laughter, and that from time to time she looked craftily toward him, and broke into a high piercing cackle.

Bascom also noticed that she held a large carving knife in her hand. With a loud yell he turned and fled toward his room, where he locked the door, crying out strongly in an agony of terror: "O Momma! Momma! Save me!"

All this had amused Louise enormously. She played the record over time after time, forever snuffling with laughter and the high cackle: "Who-oo-oo!" She bent double with it.

And now, as the boy looked at the old man, he had a sense of union with the past. It seemed to him if he would only speak, the living past, the voices of lost men, the pain, the pride, the madness and despair, the million scenes and faces of the buried life—all that an old man ever knew—would be revealed to him, would be delivered to him like a priceless treasure, as an inheritance which old men owed to young, and which should be the end and effort of all living. His savage hunger was a kind of memory: he thought if he could speak, it would be fed.

And for a moment, it seemed, he saw the visages of time, dark time, the million lock-bolts shot back in man's memory, the faces of the lost Americans, and all the million casual moments of their lives, with Bascom blazing at them from a dozen pulpits, Bascom, tortured by love and madness, walking the streets of the nation, stumping the rutted roads, muttering through darkness with clasped bony hands, a gaunt and twisted figure reeling across the continent below immense and cruel skies. Light fell upon his face and darkness crossed it:—he came up from the wilderness, from derbied men and bustled women, from all of the memories of lavish brown, and from time, dark time—from a time that was further off than Saxon thanes, all of the knights, the spearheads, and the horses.

Was all this lost?

"It was so long ago," the old man said.

Bitterly, bitterly Boston one time more: the flying leaf, the broken cloud. Was no love crying in the wilderness?

"—So long ago. I have lived so long. I have seen so much. I could tell you so many things," his uncle said huskily, with weariness and indifference. His eye was lustreless and dead, he looked for a moment tired and old.

All at once, a strange and perplexing vision, which was to return many times in the years that followed, came to the boy. It was this: there was a company of old men and women at dinner, seated together around a table. All of them were very old, older than his uncle; the faces of the old men and women were fragile and delicate like old yellowed china, their faces were frail and sexless, they had begun to look alike. In their youth all these people had known one another. The men had drunk, fought, whored, hated one another, and loved the women. Some had been devoured by the sterile and corrupt fear and envy that young men know. In secret their lips were twisted, their faces livid, and their hearts bitter; their eyes glittered with a reptilian hatred of another man—they dreaded his success, and they exulted in his failure, laughing with a delirious joy when they heard or read of his hurt, defeat, or humiliation. They had been afraid to speak or confess what was in their hearts, they feared the mockery of their fellows; with one another their words were careful, picked, and disparaging. They gave the lie to passion and belief and they said what they knew was false. And yet along dark roads at night they had shouted out into the howling winds their great goat cries of joy, exultancy and power; they had smelled snow in thick brooding air at night, and they had watched it come, softly spitting at the window glass, numbing the footfalls of the earth with its soft silent fall, filling their hearts with a dark proud ecstasy, touching their entrails with impending prophecy. Each had a thousand dark desires and fantasies; each wanted wealth, power, fame and love; each saw himself as great, good and talented; each feared and hated rivals in business or in love—and in crowds they glared at one another with hard hostile eyes, they bristled up like crested cocks, they watched their women jealously, felt looks and glances through their shoulderblades, and hated men with white spermatic necks, amorous hair, and faces proud and insolent with female conquest.

They had been young and full of pain and combat, and now all this was dead in them: they smiled mildly, feebly, gently, they spoke in thin voices, and they looked at one another with eyes dead to desire, hostility, and passion.

As for the old women, they sat there on their yellowed and bony haunches. They were all beyond the bitter pain and ecstasy of youth—its frenzy, its hope, its sinew of bright blood and agony: they were beyond the pain and fear of anything save age and death. Here was a faithful wife, a fruitful mother; here was an adulterous and voluptuous woman, the potent mistress of a dozen men, here was her cuckold husband, who had screamed like a tortured animal when he had first found her in bed with another man, and here was the man he found her with; here was another man in whom the knowledge of his wife's infidelity had aroused only a corrupt inverted joy, he exulted in it, he urged her on into new love affairs, he besought her greedily to taunt him with it, he fed upon his pain—and now they were all old and meagre and had the look of yellowed china. They turned their mild sunken faces toward one another with looks in which there was neither hate nor love nor desire nor passion, they laughed thinly, and their memory was all of little things.

They no longer wanted to excel or to be first; they were no longer mad and jealous; they no longer hated rivals; they no longer wanted fame: they no longer cared for work or grew drunk on hope; they no longer turned into the dark and struck their bloody knuckles at the wall; they no longer writhed with shame upon their beds, cursed at the memory of defeat and desolation, or ripped the sheets between convulsive fingers. Could they not speak? Had they forgotten?

Why could not the old men speak? They had known pain, death and madness, yet all their words were stale and rusty. They had known the wilderness, the savage land, the blood of the murdered men ran down into the earth that gave no answer; and they had seen it, they had shed it. Where were the passion, pain and pride, the million living moments of their lives? Was all this lost? Were they all tongueless? It seemed to the boy that there was something sly and evil in their glances as they sat together, as if they hoarded some cunning and malevolent wisdom in their brains, as if the medicine to all our grief and error was in them, but as if through the evil and conspirate communication of their glance, they had resolved to keep it from us. Or were they simply devoured with satiety, with weariness and indifference? Did they refuse to speak because they could not speak, because even memory had gone lifeless in them?

Yes. Words echoed in their throat but they were tongueless. For them the past was dead: they poured into our hands a handful of dry dust and ashes.

The dry bones, the bitter dust? The living wilderness, the silent waste? The barren land?

Have no lips trembled in the wilderness? No eyes sought seaward from the rock's sharp edge for men returning home? Has no pulse beat more hot with love or hate upon the river's edge? Or where the old wheel and the rusted stock lie stogged in desert sand: by the horsehead a woman's skull. No love?

No lonely footfalls in a million streets, no heart that beat its best and bloodiest cry out against the steel and stone, no aching brain, caught in its iron ring, groping among the labyrinthine canyons? Naught in that immense and lonely land but incessant growth and ripeness and pollution, the emptiness of forests and deserts, the uhearted, harsh and metal jangle of a million tongues, crying the belly-cry for bread, or the great cat's snarl for meat and honey? All, then, all? Birth and the twenty thousand days of snarl and jangle—and no love, no love? Was no love crying in the wilderness?

It was not true. The lovers lay below the lilac bush; the laurel leaves were trembling in the wood.

Suddenly it seemed to the boy, that if he could put his hand upon his uncle, if he could grip his fingers in his stringy arm, his own strength and youth would go into him, and he could rekindle memory like a living flame in him, he could animate for an hour that ancient heart with the exultancy, the power, the joy that pulsed in himself; he could make the old man speak.

He wanted to speak to him as people never speak to one another, he wanted to say and hear the things one never says and hears. He wanted to know what the old man's youth beyond its grim weather of poverty, loneliness, and desperation had been like. His uncle had been over ten years old when the war had ended, and he had seen the men plod home in wreaths of dust and heard their casual voices in a room, he had breathed the air of vanished summers, he had seen cloud shadows floating on the massed green of the wilderness, the twisting of a last lone leaf upon a bough; and he had heard the desolate and stricken voices in the South long, long ago, the quiet and casual voices of lost men, a million vanished footsteps in the streets of life. And he had known the years of brown, dark lavish brown, the lost and hypocritic years, the thunder of the wheels and hooves upon the cobbles, the color of bright blood—the savagery, the hunger and the fear.

Was the memory of all this lost?

The boy touched him—he put his hand upon his uncle's shoulder; the old man did not move. Sunken in what lost world, buried in what incommunicable and tongueless past, he said "So long ago."

Then the boy got up and left him and went out into the streets where the singing and lyrical air, the man-swarm passing in its million-footed weft, the glorious women and the girls compacted in a single music of belly and breasts and thighs, the sea, the earth, the proud, potent, clamorous city, all of the voices of time, fused to a unity that was like a song, a token and a cry. Victoriously, he trod the neck of doubt as if it were a serpent: he was joined to the earth, a part of it, and he possessed it; he would be wasted and consumed, filled and renewed eternally; he would feel unceasingly alternate tides of life and dark oblivion; he would be emptied without weariness, replenished forever with strong joy. He had a tongue for agony, a food for hunger, a door for exile and a surfeit for insatiate desire: exultant certainty welled up in him, he thought he could possess it all, and he cried: "Yes! It will be mine!"

XIV

HE had spells and rhymes of magic numbers which would enable him, he thought, to read all of the million books in the great library. This was a furious obsession with him all the time. And there were other spells and rhymes which would enable him to know the lives of 50,000,000 people, to visit every country in the world, to know a hundred languages, possess 10,000 lovely women, and yet have one he loved and honored above all, who would be true and beautiful and faithful to him.

And by the all-resuming magic of these spells he would go everywhere on earth, while keeping one place to return to; and while driven mad with thirst and hunger to have everything, he would be peacefully content with almost nothing; and while wanting to be a famous, honored, celebrated man, he would live obscurely, decently, and well, with one true love forever. In short, he would have the whole cake of the world, and eat it, too—have adventures, labors, joys, and triumphs that would exhaust the energies of ten thousand men, and yet have spells and charms for all of it, and was sure that with these charms and spells and sorceries, all of it was his.

He would rush out of the great library into the street, and take the subway into Boston. And as the train smashed and rocked along, he would sit there solemnly with his lungs expanded to the bursting point and his chest swollen and stuck out like the breast of a pouter pigeon, while his eyes bulged, the veins on his forehead stuck out, and his face slowly turned an apoplectic purple as he sat there rocking with the agony of his effort.

Then the train would roar into the Central Station, and the breath would come sobbing and soughing out of his tortured lungs like wind out of an organ bellows. And for several seconds, while the train was stopped there at the station (for in these magic formulas these stops at stations "did not count") he would pant and gasp for breath like a fish out of water, gulping a new supply ravenously down into his lungs again, as if he thought he was being shot in a projectile through the terrific vacuum of unmeasured space.

Then, as the train roared out into the tunnel's dark again, he would repeat the effort, sitting as solemn as an owl with his bulging eyes, stuck-out chest, the stolid apoplectic purple of his swollen face, while little children looked at him with frightened eyes, their mothers with a glance of nervous apprehension, and the men in all the various attitudes of gape-jawed astonishment and stupefaction. Yet, at that time, he saw nothing strange or curious in this mad behavior. Rather, to hold his breath there in the tunnel's dark, to make that mystery of rite and number, and to follow it with a maniacal devotion seemed as inevitable and natural to him as the very act of life, of breath itself, and he was sometimes bitterly incensed when people stared at him because of it.

Those faces—the secret dark, unknown, nameless faces, the faces of the million instant casual meetings of these years, in the cars of subway trains or on the swarming streets—returned in later years to haunt him with a blazing, unforgettable intensity of vision, with an overwhelming sense of strangeness, loss and sorrow, a poignancy of familiarity, affection and regret, which was somehow, unbelievably, as wordless, grievous, full of an instant rending and unfathomable pity, as those things a man has known best and loved with all the life and passion in him, and has lost forever—a child's quick laugh of innocence and exultant mirth, a woman's smile, an intonation in her voice, the naked, child-like look remembered in the eyes of simple, faithful people who have gone, or the snatches of the song one's brother sang when he lay drowned in darkness and delirium, as he died.

Why did the unknown faces of these years come back to him? For he could not forget the million obscure faces of those first years of his wandering when for the first time he walked alone the streets of a great city, a madman, a beggar, and a king, feeling the huge joy of the secret world impending over him with all the glory of its magic imminence, and when each furious prowl and quest into the swarming streets of life, each furious journey through the tunnel's depth was living with the intolerable prescience of triumph and discovery—a life more happy, fortunate, golden, and complete than any life before had ever been.

He did not know. He never knew why all those obscure, nameless and unknown faces of a million strangers who passed and vanished in an instant from his sight, or whom he passed a hundred times upon the streets without a word or sign of recognition, should return to haunt him later with a sense of loss, affection, and the familiarity of utter knowledge. But he knew that they came back to him in images of unfading brightness, and that the light of time, dark time, was on them all, and that there was revealed to him, in later years, something strange and mad and lonely in the lives of all of them, which he had accepted instantly, and felt no wonder or surprise at, when he had seen them.

But these images of the past would come back in later years, and with a feeling of bitter loss and longing he would want to find, to see, to know them all again, to ask them what their lives had been, and what had happened to them. It was a weird, strange, assorted crew—that company of memory—on whom the light of time would fall with such a lonely hue, and how they were all got together in that magic consonance, he could never tell, but he could not forget them.

One was an old man, an old man with fierce restless eyes, and bedraggled mustaches of a stained tobacco yellow who kept a lodging house where a student that he knew had rooms, and whose house, from the basement to the attic, was a museum to the old man's single mania. For that house was crowded with old tottering stacks of books, a mountain of junk, uncounted and uncountable, a weariness and desolation of old print, dusty, yellowed, and unreadable—and all were memoirs of a single man, Napoleon.

Another was a woman with a mass of henna hair, piled up in a great crown upon her head, who sat smugly, day after day, like something ageless and embalmed, a presence deathless and hermetic to all the things that change and pass, in a glass cage before a moving-picture house on Washington Street, where people thronged in the dense and narrow line before her all the time, and glass steps and a rotating stairway went steeply up beside her cage, and flashing cascades of bright water foamed and tumbled underneath the glassy stairs, as the woman with piled henna hair sat always in her cage, deathless, smug, hermetic, and embalmed.

Another was an old man with a mad, fierce, handsome face and wild strewn hair of silvery white, who never wore a hat or overcoat, and who muttered through the streets of Cambridge, over the board walks of the Harvard Yard, in every kind of weather: winter was around him always, the rugged skies of wintry sunsets, red and harsh, the frozen desolation of old snow in street and Yard and gutter, the harsh, interminable, weary savagery of gray winter.

One was a waitress in a restaurant on Tremont Street, a woman quiet, decent, and demure in manner, who wore faintly on her lips continually the most sensual, tender, and seductive mystery of a smile that he had ever seen on any woman's face, who drew him back into that place to eat a thousand times, who made him think of her at night, and prowl the streets and think of her, and go back to that restaurant night after night, with a feeling of wild joy and imminent possession when he thought of her, and yet who said, did, promised nothing that was not sedate, decent, and correct, or that could give him comfort, hope, or knowledge of her life.

He never got to know her, he never even knew her name, some secrecy and pride in him prevented him from speaking to her with familiar warmth or curiosity, but he spent thousands of good hours in thinking of her—hours filled with all the passion, dreams, and longing youth can know. The woman was no longer young; the other waitresses were younger, fresher, better-looking, had better legs and finer figures; he had no way at all of knowing the quality of her life, mind, spirit, speech —save that when he heard her speak her voice was a little husky and coarse-fibred—but that woman became the central figure of one of those glittering and impossible fantasies young men have.

It was a great legend of wealth and fame and love and glory in which this woman lived as a creature of queenly beauty, delicacy, intelligence, and grandeur of the soul—and every obstacle of cold and acid fact that interposed itself between him and his vision he would instantly destroy by the wild fantastic logic of desire.

And because of her he prowled a hundred streets, and walked three thousand miles, and ate one thousand sirloin steaks in that one restaurant. He would wait for night to come with furious impatience, and would feel his hands grow weak, his entrails numb, his heart begin to pound, and his throat to swell with this intolerable exultancy of joy as he approached the restaurant. Then when he got inside, and had gone upstairs to where the restaurant was, his whole body would be stirred with such a shifting iridescence of passion, happiness, hunger, triumph, music, and wild exuberant humor that he felt he could no longer hold the swelling power of ecstasy that he felt in him.

Everything in the restaurant would become impossibly good, wonderful, and happy. The beautifully clean, crisply waisted, and voluptuous-looking waitresses would be passing all around him bearing trays of food, the empress of his desire would pass by clean and neat and dainty, sedate and decent and demure, smiling that proud, smoke-like, faint, ghost-phantom smile of maddening tenderness and seduction, the three-piece orchestra would be playing briskly, softly, languorously, strains of popular music, filling his heart with the swelling pæans of another, prouder, grander, more triumphant music; while he listened, some robust, handsome, clear-eyed and lusty-figured New England girls would be sitting at a table, smartly, roughly dressed, their fine legs clothed with woollen stockings, their feet shod with wide-open galoshes, looking almost ripe for love and tenderness if something could be done to them—and all of this spurred his hunger with a kind of maddening relish, and made the food taste better than any he had ever had before.

Everything he saw would fill him with haunting sorrow, hunger, joy, the sense of triumph, glory, and delight, or with a limitless exuberance of wild humor. The motto of the restaurant, fixed on the wall in shields embossed with a flamboyant coat of arms, was written in a scroll beneath the coat of arms, as follows: "Luxuria Cum Economia." The effect these words wrought on his spirit was unbelievable: he could never say what he wished to say, or what he felt about them, and to say that they were "the funniest words he ever saw," would not begin to convey their real effect on him.

For what they did to him was so far beyond mere funniness that he had no name to give to the emotion they evoked. But instantly, when he saw them, the wild wordless surge of a powerful and idiot exuberance of humor would swell up in him and split his features with an exultant grin.

He would want to roar with laughter, to shout out and pound upon the table in his joy, but instead the wild voices of a goat-like exuberance would swell up in his throat until the people at the other tables would begin to stare at him as if he had gone mad. And later, on the streets, or in his room at night, he would suddenly remember them again, and then that idiot, wordless, and exultant glee would burst out of him in one roar of joy.

Yet, the words gave him a strange happiness and content, as well. He felt a feeling of tenderness for the people who had written them, for the owners of the restaurant who had solemnly and triumphantly thought them out, for all the doctrines of "taste," "class," and "refinement" they evoked, for something mistaken and most pitiful that had got into our lives, and that was everywhere, something grotesquely wrong, ridiculous and confused that made one somehow feel a warm, a wordless affection for its victims.

But this was the reason why these things could never be forgotten—because we are so lost, so naked and so lonely in America. Immense and cruel skies bend over us, and all of us are driven on forever and we have no home. Therefore, it is not the slow, the punctual sanded drip of the unnumbered days that we remember best, the ash of time; nor is it the huge monotone of the lost years, the unswerving schedules of the lost life and the well-known faces, that we remember best. It is a face seen once and lost forever in a crowd, an eye that looked, a face that smiled and vanished on a passing train, it is a prescience of snow upon a certain night, the laughter of a woman in a summer street long years ago, it is the memory of a single moon seen at the pine's dark edge in old October—and all of our lives is written in the twisting of a leaf upon a bough, a door that opened, and a stone.

For America has a thousand lights and weathers and we walk the streets, we walk the streets forever, we walk the streets of life alone.

It is the place of the howling winds, the hurrying of the leaves in old October, the hard clean falling to the earth of acorns. The place of the storm-tossed moaning of the wintry mountainside, where the young men cry out in their throats and feel the savage vigor, the rude strong energies; the place also where the trains cross rivers.

It is a fabulous country, the only fabulous country; it is the one place where miracles not only happen, but where they happen all the time.

It is the place of exultancy and strong joy, the place of the darkened brooding air, the smell of snow; it is the place of all the fierce, the bitten colors in October, when all of the wild, sweet woods flame up; it is also the place of the cider press and the last brown oozings of the York Imperials. It is the place of the lovely girls with good jobs and the husky voices, who will buy a round of drinks; it is the place where the women with fine legs and silken underwear lie in the pullman berth below you, it is the place of the dark-green snore of the pullman cars, and the voices in the night-time in Virginia.

It is the place where great boats are baying at the harbor's mouth, where great ships are putting out to sea; it is the place where great boats are blowing in the gulf of night, and where the river, the dark and secret river, full of strange time, is forever flowing by us to the sea.

The tugs keep baying in the river; at twelve o'clock the Berengaria *moans, her lights slide gently past the piers beyond Eleventh Street; and in the night a tall tree falls in Old Catawba, there in the hills of home.*

It is the place of autumnal moons hung low and orange at the frosty edges of the pines; it is the place of frost and silence; of the clean dry shocks and the opulence of enormous pumpkins that yellow on hard clotted earth; it is the place of the stir and feathery stumble of the hens upon their roost, the frosty, broken barking of the dogs, the great barn-shapes and solid shadows in the running sweep of the moon-whited countryside, the wailing whistle of the fast express. It is the place of flares and steamings on the tracks, and the swing and bob and tottering dance of lanterns in the yards; it is the place of dings and knellings and the sudden glare of mighty engines over sleeping faces in the night; it is the place of the terrific web and spread and smouldering, the distant glare of Philadelphia and the solid rumble of the sleepers; it is also the place where the Transcontinental Limited is stroking eighty miles an hour across the continent and the small dark towns whip by like bullets, and there is only the fanlike stroke of the secret, immense and lonely earth again.

I have foreseen this picture many times: I will buy passage on the Fast Express.

It is the place of the wild and exultant winter's morning and the wind, with the powdery snow, that has been howling all night long; it is the place of solitude and the branches of the spruce and hemlock piled with snow; it is the place where the Fall River boats are tethered to the wharf, and the wild gray snow of furious, secret, and storm-whited morning whips across them. It is the place of the lodge by the frozen lake and the sweet breath and amorous flesh of sinful woman; it is the place of the tragic and lonely beauty of New England; it is the place of the red barn and the sound of the stabled hooves and of bright tatters of old circus posters; it is the place of the immense and pungent smell of breakfast, the country sausages and the ham and eggs, the smoking wheat cakes and the fragrant coffee, and of lone hunters in the frosty thickets who whistle to their lop-eared hounds.

Where is old Doctor Ballard now with all his dogs? He held that they were sacred, that the souls of all the dear lost dead went into them. His youngest sister's soul sat on the seat beside him; she had long ears and her eyes were sad. Two dozen of his other cherished dead trotted around the buggy as he went up the hill past home. And that was eleven years ago, and I was nine years old; and I stared gravely out the window of my father's house at old Doctor Ballard.

It is the place of the straight stare, the cold white bellies and the buried lust of the lovely Boston girls; it is the place of ripe brainless blondes with tender lips and a flowery smell, and of the girls with shapely arms who stand on ladders picking oranges; it is also the place where large slow-bodied girls from Kansas City, with big legs and milky flesh, are sent East to school by their rich fathers, and there are also immense and lovely girls, with the grip of a passionate bear, who have such names as Neilson, Lundquist, Jorgenson, and Brandt.

I will go up and down the country, and back and forth across the country on the great trains that thunder over America. I will go out West where States are square; Oh, I will go to Boise, and Helena and Albuquerque. I will go to Montana and the two Dakotas and the unknown places.

It is the place of violence and sudden death; of the fast shots in the night, the club of the Irish cop, and the smell of brains and blood upon the pavement; it is the place of the small-town killings, and the men who shoot the lovers of their wives; it is the place where the negroes slash with razors and the hillmen kill in the mountain meadows; it is the place of the ugly drunks and the snarling voices and of foul-mouthed men who want to fight; it is the place of the loud word and the foolish boast and the violent threat; it is also the place of the deadly little men with white faces and the eyes of reptiles, who kill quickly and casually in the dark; it is the lawless land that feeds on murder.

"Did you know the two Lipe girls?" he asked. "Yes," I said. "They lived in Biltburn by the river, and one of them was drowned in the flood. She was a cripple, and she wheeled herself along in a chair. She was strong as a bull." "That's the girl," he said.

It is the place of the crack athletes and of the runners who limber up in March; it is the place of the ten-second men and the great jumpers and vaulters; it is the place where Spring comes, and the young birch trees have white and tender barks, of the thaw of the earth, and the feathery smoke of the trees; it is the place of the burst of grass and bud, the wild and sudden tenderness of the wilderness, and of the crews out on the river and the coaches coming down behind them in the motorboats, the surges rolling out behind when they are gone with heavy sudden wash. It is the place of the baseball players, and the easy lob, the soft spring smackings of the glove and mit, the crack of the bat; it is the place of the great batters, fielders, and pitchers, of the nigger boys and the white, drawling, shirt-sleeved men, the bleachers and the resinous smell of old worn wood; it is the place of Rube Waddell, the mighty untamed and ill-fated pitcher when his left arm is swinging like a lash. It is the place of the fighters, the crafty Jewish lightweights and the mauling Italians, Leonard, Tendler, Rocky Kansas, and Dundee; it is the place where the champion looks over his rival's shoulder with a bored expression.

I shall wake at morning in a foreign land thinking I heard a horse in one of the streets of home.

It is the place where they like to win always, and boast about their victories; it is the place of quick money and sudden loss; it is the place of the mile-long freights with their strong, solid, clanking, heavy loneliness at night, and of the silent freight of cars that curve away among raw piney desolations with their promise of new lands and unknown distances —the huge attentive gape of emptiness. It is the place where the bums come singly from the woods at sunset, the huge stillness of the watertower, the fading light, the rails, secret and alive, and trembling with the oncoming train; it is the place of the great tramps, Oklahoma Red, Fargo Pete, and the Jersey Dutchman, who grab fast rattlers for the Western shore; it is the place of old blown bums who come up in October skirls of dust and wind and crumpled newspapers and beg, with canned heat on their breaths: "Help Old McGuire: McGuire's a good guy, kid. You're not so tough, kid: McGuire's your pal, kid: How about McGuire, McGuire——?"

It is the place of the poolroom players and the drug-store boys; of the town whore and her paramour, the tough town driver; it is the place where they go to the woods on Sunday and get up among the laurel and dogwood bushes and the rhododendron blossoms; it is the place of the cheap hotels and the kids who wait with chattering lips while the nigger goes to get them their first woman; it is the place of the drunken college boys who spend the old man's money and wear fur coats to the football games; it is the place of the lovely girls up North who have rich fathers, of the beautiful wives of business men.

The train broke down somewhere beyond Manassas, and I went forward along the tracks with all the other passengers. "What's the matter?" I said to the engineer. "The eccentric strap is broken, son," he said. It was a very cold day, windy and full of sparkling sun. This was the farthest north I'd ever been, and I was twelve years old and on my way to Washington to see Woodrow Wilson inaugurated. Later I could not forget the face of the engineer and the words "eccentric strap."

It is the place of the immense and lonely earth, the place of fat ears and abundance where they grow cotton, corn, and wheat, the wine-red apples of October, and the good tobacco.

It is the place that is savage and cruel, but it is also the innocent place; it is the wild lawless place, the vital earth that is soaked with the blood of the murdered men, with the blood of the countless murdered men, with the blood of the unavenged and unremembered murdered men; but it is also the place of the child and laughter, where the young men are torn apart with ecstasy, and cry out in their throats with joy, where they hear the howl of the wind and the rain and smell the thunder and the soft numb spitting of the snow, where they are drunk with the bite and sparkle of the air and mad with the solar energy, where they believe in love and victory and think that they can never die.

It is the place where you come up through Virginia on the great trains in the night-time, and rumble slowly across the wide Potomac and see the morning sunlight on the nation's dome at Washington, and where the fat man shaving in the pullman washroom grunts, "What's this? What's this we're coming to—Washington?"—And the thin man glancing out the window says, "Yep, this is Washington. That's what it is, all right. You gettin' off here?"— And where the fat man grunts, "Who —me? Naw—I'm goin' on to Baltimore." It is the place where you get off at Baltimore and find your brother waiting.

Where is my father sleeping on the land? Buried? Dead these seven years? Forgotten, rotten in the ground? Held by his own great stone? No, no! Will I say, "Father" when I come to him? And will he call me, "Son"? Oh, no, he'll never see my face: we'll never speak except to say——

It is the place of the fast approach, the hot blind smoky passage, the tragic lonely beauty of New England, and the web of Boston; the place of the mighty station there, and engines passive as great cats, the straight dense plumes of engine smoke, the acrid and exciting smell of trains and stations, and of the man-swarm passing ever in its million-footed weft, the smell of the sea in harbors and the thought of voyages—and the place of the goat cry, the strong joy of our youth, the magic city, when we knew the most fortunate life on earth would certainly be ours, that we were twenty and could never die.

And always America is the place of the deathless and enraptured moments, the eye that looked, the mouth that smiled and vanished, and the word; the stone, the leaf, the door we never found and never have forgotten. And these are the things that we remember of America, for we have known all her thousand lights and weathers, and we walk the streets, we walk the streets forever, we walk the streets of life alone.

XV

Now at Cambridge, in the house of the Murphys on Trowbridge Street, he found himself living with the Irish for the first time, and he discovered that the Murphys were utterly different from all the Irish he had known before, and all that he had felt and believed about them. He soon discovered that the Murphys were a typical family of the Boston Irish. It was a family of five: there were Mr. and Mrs. Murphy, two sons and a daughter. Mrs. Murphy ran the house on Trowbridge Street, which they owned, and rented the rooms to lodgers, Mr. Murphy was night watchman in a warehouse on the Boston waterfront, the girl was a typist in an Irish business house in Boston, the older boy, Jimmy, had a clerical position in the Boston City Hall, and the youngest boy, Eddy, whom the youth knew best, was a student at Boston College. In addition there were two Irish lodgers who had lived with them for years: Mr. Feeney, a young man who worked at Raymond's, a department store in Washington Street, Boston, and Mr. O'Doul, a middle-aged man, unmarried, who occupied the front room upstairs just over the boy's own room. Mr. O'Doul was a civil engineer, he drank very heavily, and he would sometimes be confined to his bed for days at a time with terrible attacks of rheumatism which would bend, gnarl, and twist him, and render him incapable of movement.

But in the Murphys the boy discovered none of the richness, wildness, extravagance, and humor of such people as Mike Fogarty, Tim Donovan, or the MacReadys—the Irish he had known at home. The Murphys were hard, sterile, arid, meagre, and cruel: they were disfigured by a warped and infuriated puritanism, and yet they were terribly corrupt. There was nothing warm, rich, or generous about them or their lives: it seemed as if the living roots of nature had grown gnarled and barren among the walls and pavements of the city, it seemed that everything that is wild, sudden, capricious, whimsical, passionate, and mysterious in the spirit of the race had been dried and hardened out of them by their divorce from the magical earth their fathers came from, as if the snarl and jangle of the city streets, the barren and earthless angularity of steel and stone and brick, had entered their souls. Even their speech had become hard, gray, and sterile: the people were almost inarticulate, it is doubtful if one of them had three hundred words in his vocabulary: the boy noticed that the men especially—Murphy, his two sons, Feeney, and O'Doul—made constant use of a few arid words and phrases, which, with the intonation of the voice, and a slight convulsive movement of the arms and hands, filled in enormous vacancies in thought and feeling, and said all that they could say, or wished to say. Chief among these words or phrases was *"You* know? . . . or *"You* know what I mean?"—words which were uttered with a slight protesting emphasis on "You," a slight and painful movement of the hands or shoulders, and an air that the listener must fill in for himself all that they wanted to imply. For epithets of rich resounding rage, for curses thick and opulent with fury, in which he had believed their tongues were apt and their spirits prodigal, he discovered that they had no more to offer than "Chee!" or "Jeez!" or "Ho-ly Jeez!" or "Christ!" or *"Ho-*ly Christ!" or occasionally *"Ho-*ly Mary!" Finally, they made a constant and stupefying use of that terrible gray abortion of a word "guy": it studded their speech with the numberless monotony of paving brick, without it they would have been completely speechless and would have had to communicate by convulsions of their arms and hands and painful croakings from their tongueless throats—the word fell upon the spirit of the listener with the gray weariness of a cold incessant drizzle, it flowed across the spirit like a river of concrete; hope, joy, the power to feel and think were drowned out under the relentless and pitiless aridity of its flood.

At first, he thought these words and phrases were part of a meagre but sufficient pattern which they had learned in order to meet the contingencies of life and business with alien and Protestant spirits, as waiters in European cafés, restaurants, and dining-cars will learn a few words of English in order to serve the needs of British and American tourists—

he thought this because he saw something sly, closed, conspiratorial, mocking and full of hatred and mistrust, in their relations with people who were not members of their race and their religion; he thought they had a warm, secret and passionate life of their own which never could be known by a stranger. But he soon found that this belief was untrue: even in their conversations with one another, they were almost inarticulate—a race which thought, felt, and spoke with the wooden insensitivity of automatons or dummies on whose waxen souls a few banal formulas for speech and feeling had been recorded. He heard some amazing performances: every evening toward six o'clock the family would gather in their dingy living-room at the end of the hall, Mr. Feeney and Mr. O'Doul would join them, and then he could hear the voices of the men raised in argument, protest, agreement, denial, affirmation and belief, or skepticism, evoking a ghastly travesty of all of man's living moments of faith, doubt, and passion, and yet speaking for hours at a time, with the idiot repetitions of a gramophone held by its needle to a single groove, a blunted jargon of fifty meaningless words:

"What guy?"

"*Dat* guy!"

"Nah, nah, nah, not him—duh otheh guy!"

"Wich guy do yuh mean—duh big guy?"

"Nah, nah, nah—yuh got it all wrong!— Not *him*—duh little guy!"

"Guh-*wan!*"—a derisive laugh— "Guh-wan!"

"Watcha tryin' t' do—*kid* me? Dat guy neveh saw de day he could take Grogan. Grogan 'ud bat his brains out."

"Guh-*wan!* Yer full of prunes! . . . Watcha tryin' t' give me? Dat guy 'ud neveh take Tommy Grogan in a million yeahs! He couldn't take Tommy duh best day he eveh saw! Grogan 'ud have him on de floeh in thirty-seconds!"

"*Ho*-ly Chee!"

"Sure he would!"

"Guh-*wan,* Guh-*wan!* Yer *crazy! Grogan! Ho*-ly Chee!"

And this, with laughter, denial, agreement—all the appurtenances of conversation among living men—could go on unweariedly for hours at a time.

Sometimes he would interrupt these conversations for a moment: he would go back to leave a message, to pay the rent, to ask if any one had called.

As soon as he knocked, the voices would stop abruptly, the room would grow suddenly hushed, there would be whispers and a dry snickering laughter: in a moment some one would say "Come in," and he would enter a room full of hushed and suddenly straightened faces. The men would sit quietly or say a word or two of greeting, friendly enough in appearance, but swift sly looks would pass between them, and around the corners of their thin, hard mouths there would be something loose, corrupt and mocking. Mrs. Murphy would arise and come to greet him, her voice filled with a false heartiness, an unclean courtesy, a horrible and insolent travesty of friendliness, and her face would also have the look of having been suddenly straightened out and solemnly compressed, she would listen with a kind of evil attention, but she would have the same loose, mocking look, and the quiet sly look would pass between her and the others. Then, when he had left them, and the door had closed behind him, there would be the same sly silence for a moment, then a low muttering of words, a sudden violence of hard derisive laughter, and some one saying, "*Ho*-ly Jeez!"

He despised them: he loathed them because they were dull, dirty, and dishonest, because their lives were stupid, barren, and ugly, for their deliberate and insolent unfriendliness and for the conspiratorial secrecy and closure of their petty and vicious lives, entrenched solidly behind a wall of violent and corrupt politics and religious fanaticism, and regarding the alien, the stranger, with the hostile and ignorant eyes of the peasant.

All of the men had a dry, meagre, and brutal quality: Mr. Murphy was a little man with a dry, corky figure, he had a gray face, a thin sunken mouth, around which the line of loose mockery was always playing, and a closely cropped gray moustache. The boy always found him in his shirt-sleeves, with his shoes off, and his stockinged feet thrust out upon a chair. Feeney, O'Doul, Jimmy and Eddy Murphy, although of various sizes, shapes, and ages, all had thick tallowy-looking skins, hard dull eyes and a way of speaking meagrely out of the corners of their loose thin mouths. Mrs. Murphy was physically the biggest of the lot, with a certain quality of ripeness and fertility, however blighted, that none of the others had: she was a large slatternly woman, with silvery white hair which gave her somehow a look of sly and sinister haggishness; she had a high, flaming color marked with patches of eczemic red, her voice was hearty and she had a big laugh, but her face also had the false, hostile and conspiratorial secrecy of the others.

Eddy Murphy, the youngest boy, was also the best of the crowd. All decent and generous impulse had not yet been killed or deadened in him, he still possessed a warped and blunted friendliness, the rudiments of some youthful feeling for a better, warmer, bolder, and more liberal kind of life. As time went on, he made a few awkward, shamed, and inarticulate advances toward friendship, he began to come into the young man's room from time to time, and presently to tell him a little of his life at college and his hopes for the future. He was a little fellow, with the same dry, febrile, alert, and corky figure that his father had: he was one of the dark Irish, he had black hair, and black eyes, and one of his legs was badly bowed and bent outward, the result, he said, of having broken it, in a high-school football game. The first time he came into the room, he stood around shyly, awkwardly, and mistrustfully for a spell, blurting out a few words from time to time, and looking at the books and papers with a kind of dazed and stricken stupefaction.

"Watcha do wit all dese books? Huh?"

"I read them."

"Guh-*wan!* Watcha tryin' t' hand me? Y' ain't read all dem books! Dey ain't no guy dat's read dat much."

As a matter of fact, there were only two or three hundred books in the place, but he could not have been more impressed if the entire contents of the Widener Library had been stored there.

"Well, I have read them all," the other said. "Most of them, any way, and a lot more besides."

"Guh-*wan!* No kiddin!" he said, in a dazed tone and with an air of astounded disbelief. "Watcha want to read so much for?"

"I like to read. Don't you?"

"Oh, I don't know. *You* know," he said painfully, with the slightest convulsive movement of his hands and shoulders. ". . . 'S'all right."

"You have to read for your classes at Boston College, don't you?"

"*DO* I?" he cried, with a sudden waking to life. "I'll say I do! . . . *Ho*-ly Chee! Duh way dose guys pile it on to you is a *crime!*"

There was another awkward silence, he continued to stare at the books, and to fumble about in an embarrassed and tongue-tied manner, and suddenly he burst out explosively and triumphantly: "Shakespeare was de greatest poet dat evah lived. He wrote plays an' sonnets. A sonnet is a pome of foihteen lines: it is composed of two pahts, de sextet an' de octrave."

"That's pretty good. They must make you work out there?"

"DO they?" he cried. "I'll tell duh cock-eyed world dey do! . . . Do you know who de greatest prose-writeh was?" he burst out with the same convulsive suddenness.

"No . . . who was it? Jonathan Swift?"

"Guh-*wan!*"

"Addison? . . . Dryden? . . . Matthew Arnold?" the youth asked hopefully.

"Guh-*wan,* Guh-*wan!*" he shouted derisively. "Yuh're way off!"

"Am I? . . . Who was it then?"

"James Henry Cardinal Nooman," he crowed triumphantly. "Dat's who it was! . . . Father Dolan said so. . . . Chee! . . . Dey ain't nuttin' dat guy don't know! He's duh greatest English scholeh livin'! . . . Nooman wrote de *Apologia pro Vita Suo,"* he said triumphantly. "Dat's Latin."

"Well, yes, he *is* a good writer," said the other boy. "But Thomas Carlyle is a good writer, too?" he proposed argumentatively.

"Guh-*wan!*" shouted Eddy derisively. "Watcha givin' me?" He was silent a moment; then he added with a grin, "Yuh know de reason why you say dat?"

"No, why?"

"It's because yuh're a Sout'paw," and suddenly he laughed, naturally and good-naturedly.

"A Southpaw? How do you mean?"

"Oh, dat's duh name de fellows call 'em out at school," he said.

"Call who?"

"Why, guys like you," he said. "Dat's de name we call duh Protestants," he said, laughing. "We call 'em Sout'paws."

The word in its connotation of a life that was hostile, hard, fanatic, and suspicious of everything alien to itself was disgraceful and shameful but there was something irresistibly funny about it too, and suddenly they both laughed loudly.

After that, they got along together much better: Eddy came in to see the other youth quite often, he talked more freely and naturally, and sometimes he would bring his English themes and ask for help with them.

Such were the Boston Irish as he first saw them; and often as he

course. He did not predict a successful career in the professional theatre for every student who had been a member of his class. He did not
even say he could teach a student how to write plays. No. He made, in
fact, no claims at all. Whatever he said about his course was very reasonably, prudently, and temperately put: it was impossible to quarrel
with it.

All Professor Hatcher said about his course was that, if a man had a
genuine dramatic and theatric talent to begin with, he might be able to
derive from the course a technical and critical guidance which it would
be hard for him to get elsewhere, and which he might find for himself
only after years of painful and even wasteful experiment.

Certainly this seemed reasonable enough. Moreover, Professor
Hatcher felt that the artist would benefit by what was known as the
"round table discussion"—that is by the comment and criticism of the
various members of the class, after Professor Hatcher had read them a
play written by one of their group. He felt that the spirit of working
together, of seeing one's play produced and assisting in the production,
of being familiar with all the various "arts" of the theatre—lighting, de-
signing, directing, acting, and so on—was an experience which should
be of immense value to the young dramatist of promise and of talent.
In short, although he made no assertion that he could create a talent
where none was, or give life by technical expertness to the substance of
a work that had no real life of its own, Professor Hatcher did feel that
by the beneficent influence of this tutelage he might trim the true lamp
to make it burn more brightly.

And though it was possible to take issue with him on some of his
beliefs—that, for example, the comment and criticism of "the group,"
and a community of creative spirits was good for the artist—it was impossible to deny that his argument was reasonable, temperate, and conservative in the statement of his purposes.

And he made this plain to every member of his class. Each one was
made to understand that the course made no claims of magic alchemy—
that he could not be turned into an interesting dramatist if the talent
was not there.

But although each member of the class affirmed his understanding
of this fundamental truth, and readily said that he accepted it, most of
these people, at the bottom of their hearts, believed—pitiably and past
belief—that a miracle would be wrought upon their sterile, unproduc-
tive spirits, that for them, for *them,* at least, a magic transformation

would be brought about in their miserable small lives and feeble purposes—and all because they now were members of Professor Hatcher's celebrated class.

The members of Professor Hatcher's class belonged to the whole lost family of the earth, whose number is uncountable, and for this reason, they could never be forgotten.

And, first and foremost, they belonged to that great lost tribe of people who are more numerous in America than in any other country in the world. They belonged to that unnumbered horde who think that some-how, by some magic and miraculous scheme or rule or formula, "something can be done for them." They belonged to that huge colony of the damned who buy thousands of books that are printed for their kind, telling them how to run a tea shop, how to develop a pleasing personal-ity, how to acquire "a liberal education," swiftly and easily and with no anguish of the soul, by fifteen minutes' reading every day, how to perform the act of sexual intercourse in such a way that your wife will love you for it, how to have children, or to keep from having children, how to write short-stories, novels, plays, and verses which are profitably salable, how to keep from having body odor, constipation, bad breath, or tartar on the teeth, how to have good manners, know the proper fork to use for every course, and always do the proper thing—how, in short, to be beautiful, "distinguished," "smart," "chic," "forceful," and "sophisticated"—finally, how to have "a brilliant personality" and "achieve success."

Yes, for the most part, the members of Professor Hatcher's class be-longed to this great colony of the lost Americans. They belonged to that huge tribe of all the damned and lost who feel that everything is going to be all right with them if they can only take a trip, or learn a rule, or meet a person. They belonged to that futile, desolate, and for-saken horde who felt that all will be well with their lives, that all the power they lack themselves will be supplied, and all the anguish, fury, and unrest, the confusion and the dark damnation of man's soul can magically be healed if only they eat bran for breakfast, secure an in-troduction to a celebrated actress, get a reading for their manuscript by a friend of Sinclair Lewis, or win admission to Professor Hatcher's celebrated class of dramatists.

And, in a curious way, the plays written by the people in Professor Hatcher's class, illustrated, in one form or another, this desire. Few of the plays had any intrinsic reality, for most of these people were lacking

year away in the rare ether, among the precious and æsthetic intellects of
Professor Hatcher's celebrated course, a year in which to realize the
dream of a life-time, the vision of his youth—a year in which to write
the plays he had always dreamed of writing. And what kind of plays
did he write?

Alas! Old Seth did exactly what he set out to do, he succeeded perfectly in fulfilling his desire—and, by a tragic irony, his failure lay in
just this fact. The plays which he produced with an astounding and
prolific ease—("Three days is enough to write a play," the old man said
in his sour voice. "You guys who take a year to write a play give me
a pain. If you can't write a play a week, you can't write anything; the
play's no good")—these plays were just the plays which he had dreamed
of writing as a young man, and therein was evident their irremediable
fault.

For Seth's plays—so neat, brisk, glib, and smartly done—would have
been good plays in a commercial way, as well, if he had only done
them twenty years before. He wrote, without effort and with unerring
accuracy, a kind of play which had been immensely popular at the beginning of the twentieth century, but which people had grown tired of
twenty years before. He wrote plays in which the babies got mixed up
in the maternity ward of a great hospital, in which the rich man's child
goes to the family of the little grocer, and the grocer's child grows up
as the heir to an enormous fortune, with all the luxuries and securities
of wealth around him. And he brought about the final resolution of this
tangled scheme, the meeting of these scrambled children and their bewildered parents, with a skill of complication, a design of plot, a dex-
terity that was astonishing. His characters—all well-known types of the
theatre, as of nurse tough-spoken, shop-girl slangy, reporter cynical, and
so on—were well conceived to fret their purpose, their lives well-timed
and apt and deftly made. He had mastered the formula of an older type
of "well-made play" with astonishing success. Only, the type was dead,
the interest of the public in such plays had vanished twenty years before.

So here he was, a live man, writing, with amazing skill, dead plays
for a theatre that was dead, and for a public that did not exist.

"Chekhov! Ibsen!" old Seth would whine sourly with a dismissing
gesture of his parched old hand, and a scornful contortion of his bitter
mouth in his old mummy of a face. "You guys all make me tired the
way you worship them!" he would whine out at some of the exquisite young temperaments in Professor Hatcher's class. "Those guys

can't write a play! Take Chekhov, now!" whined Seth. "That guy never wrote a real play in his life! He never knew how to write a play! He couldn't have written a play if he tried! He never learned the rules for writing a play!—That *Cherry Orchard* now," whined old Seth with a sour sneering laugh, "—that *Cherry Orchard* that you guys are always raving about! That's not a play!" he cried indignantly. "What ever made you think it was a play? I was trying to read it just the other day," he rasped, "and there's nothing there to hold your interest! It's got no *plot!* There's no story in it! There's no suspense! Nothing happens in it. All you got is a lot of people who do nothing but talk all the time. You never get anywhere," said Seth scornfully. "And yet to hear you guys rave about it, you'd think it was a great play."

"Well, what do you call a great play, then, if *The Cherry Orchard* isn't one?" one of the young men said acidly. "Who wrote the great plays that you talk about?"

"Why George M. Cohan wrote some," whined Seth instantly. "That's who. Avery Hopwood wrote some great plays. We've had plenty of guys in this country who wrote great plays. If they'd come from Russia you'd get down and worship 'em," he said bitterly. "But just because they came out of this country they're no good!"

In the relation of the class towards old Seth Flint, it was possible to see the basic falseness of their relation towards life everywhere around them. For here was a man—whatever his defects as a playwright might have been—who had lived incomparably the richest, most varied and dangerous, and eventful life among them; as he was himself far more interesting than any of the plays they wrote, and as dramatists they should have recognized and understood his quality. But they saw none of this. For their relation towards life and people such as old Seth Flint was not one of understanding. It was not even one of burning indignation—of that indignation which is one of the dynamic forces in the artist's life. It was rather one of supercilious scorn and ridicule.

They felt that they were "above" old Seth, and most of the other people in the world, and for this reason they were in Professor Hatcher's class. Of Seth they said:

"He's really a misfit, terribly out of place here. I wonder why he came."

And they would listen to an account of one of Seth's latest errors in good taste with the expression of astounded disbelief, the tones of stunned incredulity which were coming into fashion about that time among elegant young men.

"Not really! ... But he never really said *that*. ... You *can't* mean it."

"Oh, but I assure you, he did!"

"... It's simply past belief! ... I can't believe he's as bad as *that*."

"Oh, but he *is!* It's incredible, I know, but you've no idea what he's capable of." And so on.

And yet old Seth Flint was badly needed in that class: his bitter and unvarnished tongue caused Professor Hatcher many painful moments, but it had its use—oh, it had its use, particularly when the play was of this nature:

Irene (slowly with scorn and contempt in her voice). So—it has come to this! This is all your love amounts to—a little petty selfish thing! I had thought you were bigger than that, John.

John (desperately). But—but, my God, Irene—what am I to think? I found you in bed with him—my best friend! *(with difficulty).* You know— that looks suspicious, to say the least!

Irene (softly—with amused contempt in her voice). You poor little man! And to think I thought your love was *so big.*

John (wildly). But I do love you, Irene. That's just the point.

Irene (with passionate scorn). Love! You don't know what love means! Love is bigger than that! Love is big enough for all things, all people. *(She extends her arms in an all-embracing gesture.)* My love takes in the world—it embraces all mankind! It is glamorous, wild, free as the wind, John.

John (slowly). Then you have had other lovers?

Irene: Lovers come, lovers go. *(She makes an impatient gesture.)* What is that? Nothing! Only love endures—my love which is greater than all.

Eugene would writhe in his seat, and clench his hands convulsively. Then he would turn almost prayerfully to the bitter, mummied face of old Seth Flint for that barbed but cleansing vulgarity that always followed such a scene:

"Well?" Professor Hatcher would say, putting down the manuscript he had been reading, taking off his eye-glasses (which were attached to a ribbon of black silk) and looking around with a quizzical smile, an impassive expression on his fine, distinguished face. "Well?" he would say again urbanely, as no one answered. "Is there any comment?"

"What is she?" Seth would break the nervous silence with his rasping snarl. "Another of these society whores? You know," he continued, "you can find plenty of her kind for three dollars a throw without any of that fancy palaver."

Some of the class smiled faintly, painfully, and glanced at each other with slight shrugs of horror; others were grateful, felt pleasure well in them and said underneath their breath exultantly:

"Good old Seth! Good old Seth!"

"Her love is big enough for all things, is it?" said Seth. "I know a truck driver out in Denver I'll match against her any day."

Eugene and Ed Horton, a large and robust aspirant from the Iowa cornlands, roared with happy laughter, poking each other sharply in the ribs.

"Do you think the play will act?" some one said. "It seems to me that it comes pretty close to closet drama."

"If you ask me," said Seth, "it comes pretty close to water-closet drama. . . . No," he said sourly. "What that boy needs is a little experience. He ought to go out and get him a woman and get all this stuff off his mind. After that, he might sit down and write a play."

For a moment there was a very awkward silence, and Professor Hatcher smiled a trifle palely. Then, taking his eyeglasses with a distinguished movement, he looked around and said:

"Is there any other comment?"

XVII

OFTEN during these years of fury, hunger, and unrest, when he was trying to read all the books and know all the people, he would live for days, and even for weeks, in a world of such mad and savage concentration, such terrific energy, that time would pass by him incredibly, while he tried to eat and drink the earth, stare his way through walls of solid masonry into the secret lives of men, until he had made the substance of all life his own.

And during all this time, although he was living a life of the most savage conflict, the most blazing energy, wrestling day by day with the herculean forces of the million-footed city, listening to a million words and peering into a hundred thousand faces, he would nevertheless spend a life of such utter loneliness that he would go for days at a time without seeing a face or hearing a voice that he knew, and until the sound of his own voice seemed strange and phantasmal to him.

Then suddenly he would seem to awake out of this terrific vision, which had been so savage, mad, and literal that its very reality had a fabulous and dreamlike quality, and time, strange million-visaged time, had been telescoped incredibly, so that weeks had passed by like a single day. He would awake out of this living dream and see the minutes, hours, and days, and all the acts and faces of the earth pass by him in their usual way. And instantly, when this happened, he would feel a bitter and intolerable loneliness—a loneliness so acrid, gray, and bitter that he could taste its sharp thin crust around the edges of his mouth like the taste and odor of weary burnt-out steel, like a depleted storage battery or a light that had gone dim, and he could feel it grayly and intolerably in his entrails, the conduits of his blood, and in all the substance of his body.

When this happened, he would feel an almost unbearable need to hear the voice and see the face again of some one he had known and at such a time as this he would go to see his Uncle Bascom, that strange and extraordinary man who, born like the others in the wilderness, the hills of home, had left these hills forever.

Bascom now lived alone with his wife (for his four children were grown and would have none of him) in a dingy section of one of the innumerable suburbs that form part of the terrific ganglia of Boston, and it was here that the boy would often go on Sundays.

After a long confusing journey that was made by subway, elevated, and street car, he would leave the chill and dismal street car at the foot of a hill on a long, wide, and frozen street lined with tall rows of wintry elms, with smoky wintry houses that had a look of solid, closed and mellow warmth, and with a savage frozen waste of tidal waters on the right—those New England waters that are so sparkling, fresh and glorious, like a tide of sapphires, in the springtime, and so grim and savage in their frozen desolation in the winter.

Then the street car would bang its draughty sliding doors together, grind harshly off with its cargo of people with pinched lips, thin red pointed noses, and cod-fish faces, and vanish, leaving him with the kind of loneliness and absence which a street car always leaves when it has gone, and he would turn away from the tracks along a dismal road or street that led into the district where his uncle had his house. And stolidly he would plunge forward against the gray and frozen desolation of that place, to meet him.

And at length he would pause before his uncle's little house, and as he struck the knocker, he was always glad to hear the approaching patter of his Aunt Louise's feet, and cheered by the brightening glance of her small birdy features, as she opened the door for him, inwardly exultant to hear her confirm in her bright lady-like tones his own prediction of what she would say: "Oh, *theah* you ah! I was wondering what was keeping you."

A moment later he would be greeted from the cellar or the kitchen by his uncle Bascom's high, husky and yet strangely remote yell, the voice of a prophet calling from a mountain:

"Hello, Eugene, my boy. Is that *you?*" And a moment later the old man would appear, coming up to meet him from some lower cellar-depth, swearing, muttering, and banging doors; and he would come toward him howling greetings, buttoned to his chin in the frayed and faded sweater, gnarled, stooped and frosty-looking, clutching his great hands together at his waist; then hold one gaunt hand out to him and howl:

"Hello, hello, hello, sit down, sit down, sit down," after which, for no apparent reason, he would contort his gaunt face in a horrible grimace, convolve his amazing rubbery lips, and close his eyes and his mouth tightly and laugh through his nose in forced snarls: "Phuh! Phuh! Phuh! Phuh! Phuh!"

Bascom Pentland had been the scholar of his amazing family: he was a man of powerful intelligence and disordered emotions. Even in his youth, his eccentricities of dress, speech, walk, manner had made him an object of ridicule to his Southern kinsmen, but their ridicule was streaked with pride, since they accepted the impact of his personality as another proof that theirs was an extraordinary family. "He's one of 'em, all right," they said exultantly, "queerer than any of us!"

Bascom's youth, following the war between the States, had been seared by a bitter poverty, at once enriched and warped by a life that clung to the earth with a root-like tenacity, that was manual, painful, spare and stricken, and that rebuilt itself—fiercely, cruelly, and richly—from the earth. And, because there burned and blazed in him from the first a hatred of human indignity, a passionate avowal of man's highness and repose, he felt more bitterly than the others the delinquencies of his father, and the multiplication of his father's offspring, who came regularly into a world of empty cupboards.

"As each of them made its unhappy entrance into the world," he would say later, his voice tremulous with passion, "I went out into the woods striking my head against the trees, and blaspheming God in my anger. Yes, sir," he continued, pursing his long lip rapidly against his few loose upper teeth, and speaking with an exaggerated pedantry of enunciation, "I am not ashamed to confess that I did. For we were living in conditions un-*worthy*—*unworthy*"—his voice rising to an evangelical yell, "I had almost said—of the condition of animals. And—*say*—what do you think?"—he said, with a sudden shift in manner and tone, becoming, after his episcopal declaration, matter of fact and whisperingly confidential. "Why, do you know, my boy, at one time I had to take my *own* father aside, and point out to him we were living in no way becoming decent people."—Here his voice sank to a whisper, and he tapped Eugene on the knee with his big, stiff finger, grimacing horribly and pursing his lip against his dry upper teeth.

Poverty had been the mistress of his youth and Bascom Pentland had not forgotten: poverty had burned its way into his heart. He took what education he could find in a backwoods school, read everything he could, taught, for two or three years, in a country school and, at the age of twenty-one, borrowing enough money for railway fare, went to Boston to enroll himself at Harvard. And, somehow, because of the fire that burned in him, the fierce determination of his soul, he had been admitted, secured employment waiting on tables, tutoring, and pressing every one's trousers but his own, and lived in a room with two other starved wretches on $3.50 a week, cooking, eating, sleeping, washing, and studying in the one place.

At the end of seven years he had gone through the college and the school of theology, performing brilliantly in Greek, Hebrew, and metaphysics.

Poverty, fanatical study, the sexual meagreness of his surroundings, had made of him a gaunt zealot: at thirty he was a lean fanatic, a true Yankee madman, high-boned, with gray thirsty eyes and a thick flaring sheaf of oaken hair—six feet three inches of gangling and ludicrous height, gesticulating madly and obliviously before a grinning world. But he had a grand lean head: he looked somewhat like the great Ralph Waldo Emerson—with the brakes off.

About this time, he married a young Southern woman of a good family: she was from Tennessee, her parents were both dead, and in the 'seventies she had come North and had lived for several years with an uncle in Providence, who had been constituted guardian of her estate, amounting probably to about $75,000, although her romantic memory later multiplied the sum to $200,000. The man squandered part of her

money and stole the rest: she came, therefore, to Bascom without much
dowry, but she was pretty, bright, intelligent, and had a good figure.
Bascom smote the walls of his room with bloody knuckles, and fell
down before God.

When Bascom met her she was a music student in Boston: she had
a deep full-toned contralto voice which was wrung from her somewhat
tremulously when she sang. She was a small woman, birdlike and
earnest, delicately fleshed and boned, quick and active in her movements
and with a crisp tart speech which still bore, curiously, traces of a
Southern accent. She was a brisk, serious, lady-like little person, without
much humor, and she was very much in love with her gaunt suitor.
They saw each other for two years: they went to concerts, lectures, sermons; they talked of music, poetry, philosophy and of God, but they
never spoke of love. But one night Bascom met her in the parlor of her
boarding house on Huntington Avenue, and with a voice vibrant and
portentous with the importance of the words he had to utter, began as
follows: "Miss Louise!" he said carefully, gazing thoughtfully over the
apex of his hands, "there comes a time when a man, having reached
an age of discretion and mature judgment, must begin to consider one
of the *gravest*—yes! by all means one of the most important events in
human life. The event I refer to is—matrimony." He paused, a clock
was beating out its punctual measured tock upon the mantel, and a
horse went by with ringing hoofs upon the street. As for Louise, she
sat quietly erect, with dignified and lady-like composure , but it seemed
to her that the clock was beating in her own breast, and that it might
cease to beat at any moment.

"For a minister of the gospel," Bascom continued, "the decision is
particularly grave because, for him—once made, it is *irrevocable,* once
determined upon, it must be followed *inexorably, relentlessly*—aye! to
the edge of the grave, to the *uttermost* gates of death, so that the possibility of an error in judgment is *fraught,*" his voice sinking to a boding
whisper—"is *fraught* with the most terrible consequences. Accordingly,"
Uncle Bascom said in a deliberate tone, "having decided to take this
step, realizing to the *full*—to the *full,* mind you—its gravity, I have
searched my soul, I have questioned my heart. I have gone up into the
mount-ings and out into the desert and communed with my *Maker*
until," his voice rose like a demon's howl, "there no longer remains an
atom of doubt, a *particle* of uncertainty, a *vestige* of *disbelief!* Miss
Louise, I have decided that the young lady best fitted in every way to

be my helpmate, the partner of my joys and griefs, the confidante of my dearest hopes, the in-*spir*-a-tion of my noblest endeavors, the companion of my declining years, and the *spirit* that shall accompany me along each step of life's vexed and troubled way, sharing with me whatever God in his *inscrutable* Providence shall will, whether of wealth or poverty, grief or happiness—I have decided, Miss Louise, that that lady must be—yourself!—and, therefore, I request," he said slowly and impressively, "the honor of your hand in mar-ri-age."

She loved him, she had hoped, prayed, and agonized for just such a moment, but now that it had come she rose immediately with lady-like dignity, and said: "Mistah Pentland: I am honuhed by this mahk of yoah esteem and affection, and I pwomise to give it my most *un*nest con-sidahwation without delay. I wealize fully, Mistah Pentland, the gwavity of the wuhds you have just uttuhed. Foh my paht, I must tell you, Mistah Pentland, that if I accept yoah pwoposal, I shall come to you without the fawchun which was *wight*fully mine, but of which I have been depwived and defwauded by the *wascality*—yes! the *wascality* of my gahdian. I shall come to you, theahfoh, without the dow'y I had hoped to be able to contwibute to my husband's fawchuns."

"Oh, my *dear* Miss Louise! My *dear* young lady!" Uncle Bascom cried, waving his great hand through the air with a dismissing gesture. "Do not suppose—do not for one instant suppose, I beg of you!—that consideration of a monetary nature could influence my decision. Oh, not in the slightest!" he cried. "Not at all, not at all!"

"Fawchnatly," Louise continued, "my inhewitance was not *wholly* dissipated by this scoundwel. A pohtion, a vewy small pohtion, re-mains."

"My dear girl! My dear young lady!" Uncle Bascom cried. "It is not of the *slightest* consequence. . . . How much did he leave?" he added.

Thus they were married.

Bascom immediately got a church in the Middle West: good pay and a house. But during the course of the next twenty years he was shifted from church to church, from sect to sect—to Brooklyn, then back to the Middle West, to the Dakotas, to Jersey City, to Western Massachusetts, and finally back to the small towns surrounding Boston.

When Bascom talked, you may be sure God listened: he preached magnificently, his gaunt face glowing from the pulpit, his rather high, enormously vibrant voice husky with emotion. His prayers were fierce solicitations of God, so mad with fervor that his audiences uncomfortably felt they came close to blasphemy. But, unhappily, on occasions his own mad eloquence grew too much for him: his voice, always too near the heart of passion, would burst in splinters, and he would fall violently forward across his lectern, his face covered by his great gaunt fingers, sobbing horribly.

This, in the Middle West, where his first church had been, does not go down so well—yet it may be successful if one weeps mellowly, joyfully—smiling bravely through the tears—at a lovely aisle processional of repentant sinners; but Bascom, who chose uncomfortable titles for his sermons, would be overcome by his powerful feelings on those occasions when his topic was "Potiphar's Wife," "Ruth, the Girl in the Corn," "The Whore of Babylon," "The Woman on the Roof," and so on.

His head was too deeply engaged with his conscience—he was in turn Episcopal, Presbyterian, Unitarian, searching through the whole roaring confusion of Protestantism for a body of doctrine with which he could agree. And he was forever finding it, and later forever renouncing what he had found. At forty, the most liberal of Unitarians, the strains of agnosticism were piping madly through his sermons: he began to hint at his new faith in prose which he modelled on the mighty utterance of Carlyle, and in poetry, in what he deemed the manner of Matthew Arnold. His professional connection with the Unitarians, and indeed with the Baptists, Methodists, Holy Rollers, and Seventh Day Adventists, came to an abrupt ending after he read from his pulpit one morning a composition in verse entitled "The Agnostic," which made up in concision what it lacked in melody, and which ended each stanza sadly, but very plainly, on this recurrence:

> "I do not know:
> It may be so."

Thus, when he was almost fifty, Bascom Pentland stopped preaching in public. There was no question where he was going. He had his family's raging lust for property. He became a "conveyancer"; he acquired enough of the law of property to convey titles; but he began to buy pieces of land in the suburbs of Boston, and to build small cheap houses, using his own somewhat extraordinary designs to save the architect's fees and, wherever possible, doing such odd jobs as laying the foundations, installing the plumbing, and painting the structure.

The small houses that he—no, he did not build them!—he went through the agonies of monstrous childbirth to produce them, he licked, nursed, and fondled them into stunted growth, and he sold them on long, but profitable terms to small Irish, Jewish, Negro, Belgian, Italian and Greek laborers and tradesmen. And at the conclusion of a sale, or after receiving from one of these men the current payment, Uncle Bascom went homeward in a delirium of joy, shouting in a loud voice, to all who might be compelled to listen, the merits of the Jews, Belgians, Irish, Swiss or Greeks.

"Finest people in the world! No question about it!"—this last being his favorite exclamation in all moments of payment or conviction.

For when they paid, he loved them. Often on Sundays they would come to pay him tramping over the frozen ground or the packed snow through street after street of smutty gray-looking houses in the flat weary-looking suburb where he lived. To this dismal heath, therefore, they came, the swarthy children of a dozen races, clad in the hard and decent blacks in which the poor pay debts and go to funerals. They would advance across the barren lands, the harsh sere earth scarred with its wastes of rust and rubbish, going stolidly by below the blank board fences of a brick yard, crunching doggedly through the lanes of dirty rutted ice, passing before the gray besmutted fronts of wooden houses which in their stark, desolate, and unspeakable ugliness seemed to give a complete and final utterance to an architecture of weariness, sterility and horror, so overwhelming in its absolute desolation that it seemed as if the painful and indignant soul of man must sicken and die at length before it, stricken, stupefied, and strangled without a tongue to articulate the curse that once had blazed in him.

And at length they would pause before the old man's little house—one of a street of little houses which he had built there on the barren flatlands of the suburb, and to which he had given magnificently his own name— Pentland Heights—although the only eminence in all that flat and weary waste was an almost imperceptible rise a half mile off. And here along this street which he had built, these little houses, warped, yet strong and hardy, seemed to burrow down solidly like moles for warmth into the ugly stony earth on which they were built and to cower and huddle doggedly below the immense and terrible desolation of the northern sky, with its rimy sun-hazed lights, its fierce and cruel rags and stripes of wintry red, its raw and savage harshness. And then, gripping their greasy little wads of money, as if in the knowledge that all reward below these fierce and cruel skies must be wrenched painfully and minutely from a stony earth, they went in to pay him. He would come up to meet them from some lower cellar-depth, swearing, muttering, and banging doors; and he would come toward them howling greetings, buttoned to his chin in the frayed and faded sweater, gnarled, stooped and frosty-looking, clutching his great hands together at his waist. Then they would wait, stiffly, clumsily, fingering their hats, while with countless squints and grimaces and pursings of the lip, he scrawled out painfully their receipts—their fractional release from debt and labor, one more hard-won step toward the freedom of possession.

At length, having pocketed their money and finished the transaction, he would not permit them to depart at once, he would howl urgently at them an invitation to stay, he would offer long weedy-looking cigars to them, and they would sit uncomfortably, crouching on their buttock bones like stalled oxen, at the edges of chairs, shyly and dumbly staring at him, while he howled question, comment, and enthusiastic tribute at them.

"Why, my dear sir!" he would yell at Makropolos, the Greek. "You have a glorious past, a history of which any nation might well be proud!"

"Sure, sure!" said Makropolos, nodding vigorously. "Beeg Heestory!"

"The isles of Greece, the isles of Greece!" the old man howled, "where burning Sappho loved and sung—" (Phuh! phuh! phuh! phuh! phuh!)

"Sure, sure!" said Makropolos again, nodding good-naturedly but wrinkling his lowering finger's-breadth of brow in a somewhat puzzled fashion. "Tha's right! You got it!"

"Why, my dear sir!" Uncle Bascom cried. "It has been the ambition of my lifetime to visit those hallowed scenes, to stand at sunrise on the Acropolis, to explore the glory that was Greece, to see the magnificent ruins of the noblest of ancient civ-i-*liz*-a-tions!"

For the first time a dark flush, a flush of outraged patriotism, began to burn upon the swarthy yellow of Mr. Makropolos's cheek: his manner became heavy and animated, and in a moment he said with passionate conviction:

"No, no, no! No ruin! Wat you t'ink, eh! Athens fine town! We got a million pipples dere!" He struggled for a word, then cupped his hairy paws indefinitely: "*You* know? *Beeg!* O, ni-ez!" he added greasily, with a smile. "Everyt'ing good! We got everyt'ing good dere as you got here! *You* know?" he said with a confiding and painful effort. "Everyt'ing ni-ez! Not old! No, no, no!" he cried with a rising and indignant vigor. "New! de same as here. Ni-ez! You get good and cheap—everyt'ing! Beeg place, new house, dumbwaiter, elevator—wat chew like!—oh, ni-ez!" he said earnestly. "Wat chew t'ink it cost, eh? Feefateen dollar a month! Sure, sure!" he nodded with a swarthy earnestness. "I wouldn't keed you!"

"Finest people on earth!" Uncle Bascom cried with an air of great conviction and satisfaction. "No question about it!"—and he would usher his visitor to the door howling farewells into the terrible desolation of those savage skies.

Meanwhile, Aunt Louise, although she had not heard a word of what was said, although she had listened to nothing except the periods of Uncle Bascom's heavily accented and particular speech, kept up a constant snuffling laughter punctuated momently by faint whoops as she bent over her pots and pans in the kitchen, pausing from time to time as if to listen, and then snuffling to herself as she shook her head in pitying mirth which rose again up to the crisis of a faint crazy cackle as she scoured the pan; because, of course, during the forty-five years of her life with him she had gone thoroughly, imperceptibly, and completely mad, and no longer knew or cared to know whether these words had just been spoken or were the echoes of lost voices long ago.

And again, she would pause to listen, with her small birdlike features uplifted gleefully in a kind of mad attentiveness as the door slammed and he stumped muttering back into the house, intent upon the secret designs of his own life, as remote and isolate from her as if they had each dwelt on separate planets, although the house they lived in was a small one.

Such had been the history of the old man. His life had come up from the wilderness, the buried past, the lost America. The potent mystery of old events and moments had passed around him, and the magic light of dark time fell across him.

Like all men in this land, he had been a wanderer, an exile on the immortal earth. Like all of us he had no home. Wherever great wheels carried him was home.

As the old man and his nephew talked together, Louise would prepare the meal in the kitchen, which gave on the living-room where they ate, by a swing door that she kept open, in order that she might hear what went on. And, while they waited, Uncle Bascom would talk to the boy on a vast range of subjects, dealing with that literature in which he had once been deep—the poetry of the Old Testament, the philosophy of Hegel, Carlyle, and Matthew Arnold, whom he worshipped, or some question in the daily papers.

Uncle Bascom, seated, his fine gaunt face grave, magnificently composed now above his arched gnarled hands, spoke with eloquent deliberation. He became triumphant reasoning mind: he talked with superb balanced judgment. All the tumult and insanity of his life had been forgotten: no question of money or of self was involved. Meanwhile, from the kitchen Aunt Louise kept up a constant snuffling laughter, punctuated momently by faint whoops. She was convinced, of course, that her husband was mad and all his opinions nonsensical. Yet she had not listened to a word of what he was saying, but only to the sound of his heavily accented, precise, and particular speech. From time to time, snuffling to herself she would look in on Eugene, trembling with laughter, and shake her head at him in pitying mirth.

"*Beyond* a doubt! Beyond a *doubt!*" Uncle Bascom would say. "The quality of the best writing in the books of the Old Testament may take rank with the best writing that has ever been done, but you are right in believing, too, the amount of great writing is less than it is commonly supposed to be. There are passages, nay! *books*"—his voice rising strangely to a husky howl—"of the vilest rubbish—Noah, Shem, Ham and Japheth— O vile! vile!" he cried. . . . "And Azariah begat Amariah and Amariah begat Ahitub (Phuh! Phuh! Phuh!). *Ahitub,*" he sneered. "And Azariah begat Seraiah, and Seraiah begat Jehozadak (Phuh! Phuh! Phuh!) *Jehozadak*"—he sneered with his precise articulation, finally letting out the last syllable with a kind of snarling contempt. "Can you *imagine,* can you even *dream,*" he howled, "of calling any one a name like that! 'And Jehozadak went into captivity'—as, indeed, he ought! (phuh! phuh! phuh!)—his *very* name would constitute a *penal* offense! (Phuh! Phuh! Phuh!) Je*h*ozadak!" Uncle Bascom sneered. "But," he proceeded deliberately in a moment, as he stared calmly over his great arched hands, "—but—the quality of some of the language is God-intoxicated: the noblest poetry ever chanted in the service of eternity."

"The Book of Wevelations," cried Aunt Louise, suddenly rushing out of the kitchen with a carving knife in her hand, having returned to earth for a moment to hear him. "The Book of Wevelations!" she said in a hoarse whisper, her mouth puckered with disgust. "*Eugene!* A *wicked,* bloo-o-edy, kwu-u-el monument to supahstition. Twibute to an avenging and *muh-duh-wous Gawd!*" The last word uttered in a hoarse almost inaudible whisper would find his aunt bent double, clutching a knife in one hand, with her small bright eyes glaring madly at us.

"Oh no, my dear, oh no," said Uncle Bascom, with astonishing, unaccustomed sadness, with almost exquisite gentleness. And, his vibrant passionate voice thrilling suddenly with emotion, he added: "The triumphant music of one of the mightiest of earth's poets: the sublime utterance of a man for whom God had opened the mysteries of heaven and hell."

He paused a moment, then quietly in a remote voice—in that remote and magnificent voice which could thrill men so deeply when it uttered poetry, he continued: " 'I am Alpha and Omega, the first and the last, the beginning and the end'—the mightiest line, my dear boy, the most magnificent poetry, that was ever written." And suddenly Uncle Bascom threw his gaunt hands before his face, and wept in strong hoarse sobs: "Oh, my God, my God!—the beauty, the pity of it all! . . . You must pardon me," he whispered after a moment, drawing his faded sweater sleeve across his eyes. "You must pardon me. It brought back —memories."

Aunt Louise, who had been stricken with a kind of fear and horror when he began to weep, now looked at Eugene with an expression of strong physical disgust, almost of nausea, shaking her head slightly in an affronted and lady-like manner as might one who, having achieved healthy and courageous discipline over all the excesses of emotion, feels only contempt for him who gives way to them.

She retired now with exaggerated dignity to the kitchen, served the meal, and addressed Eugene for some time thereafter with absurd quietness and restraint of manner, and a kind of stiff primness about her backbone. She was an excellent cook; there was magic in her treatment of food, and on the occasions when Eugene was coming out, she insisted that Bascom get her a decent piece of meat to work with.

There would be a juicy fragrant piece of lamb, or a boiled leg of mutton with currant jelly, or perhaps a small crisply browned roast of beef, with small flaky biscuits, smoking hot, two or three vegetables, and rich coffee. Uncle Bascom, quite unperturbed by his outbreak, would stamp into the kitchen, where he could be heard swearing and muttering to himself, as he searched for various things. Later he would appear at the table bearing a platter filled with some revolting mess of his own concoction,—a mixture of raw vegetables, chopped up—onions, carrots, beans, and raw potatoes—for he had the full strength of his family's mania concerning food, violent prejudices about its preparation, and deep-seated distrust of everybody's cleanliness but his own.

"Have some, my boy. Have some!" he would yell huskily, seating himself, and lunging toward Eugene with the awful mess, in a gesture of violent invitation.

"Thank you, no." Eugene would try to keep his eyes averted from the mess, and focus on the good food heaping his plate.

"You may eat that slop if you want to," Uncle Bascom would exclaim with a scornful and sneering laugh. "It would give *me* my death of dyspepsia." And the silence of their eating would be broken by the recurrent snuffling whoops of Aunt Louise, accompanied by many pitying looks and head-shakes as she trembled with laughter and hid her mouth.

Or, suddenly, in the full rich progress of the meal, Eugene would be shocked out of his pleasure in the food by the mad bright eyes of Aunt Louise bearing fiercely down upon him:

"Eugene!—don't bwood, boy! Don't bwood! You've got it in you— it's in the blood! You're one of them. You're one of *them!*—a *Pentland*," she croaked fatally.

"Ah-h—you *don't* know what you're talking about"—thus suddenly in fierce distemper Uncle Bascom. "*Scotch! Scotch*-Irish! Finest people on earth! No question about it whatever."

"Fugitive ideation! Fugitive ideation," she chattered like a monkey over a nut. "Mind goes off in all diwections. Can't stick to anything five minutes at a time. The same thing that's wong with the moduhn decadents. Wead Nordau's book, Eugene. It will open yoah eyes," and she whispered hoarsely again: "You're *ovah-sexed—all* of you!"

"Bosh: Bosh!" growled Uncle Bascom. "Some more of your psychology—the *bastard* of superstition and quackery: the black magic of little minds—the effort of a blind man (phuh! phuh! phuh!) crawling about in a dark room (phuh! phuh!) looking for a *black cat* (phuh! phuh!) that *isn't there*," he yelled triumphantly, and closed his eyes and snarled and snuffled down his nose with laughter.

He knew nothing about it: occasionally he still read Kant, and he could be as deep in absolute categories, moments of negation, and definitions of a concept, as she with all of her complicated and extensive paraphernalia of phobias, complexes, fixations, and repressions.

"Well, Eugene," thus Aunt Louise with light raillery and yet with eager curiosity, "have you found you a nice wosy-cheeked New England gul yet? You had bettah watch *out,* boy! I tell you, you had bettah watch *out!* she declared, kittenishly, wagging her finger at him, before he had time to answer.

"If he has," said Uncle Bascom grimly, "he will find her sadly lacking in the qualities of delicacy, breeding, and womanly decorum that the Southern girl has. Oh, yes! No question about that whatever!" for Uncle Bascom still had the passionate loyalty and sentimental affection for the South that many Southerners have who could not be induced, under any circumstances, to return.

"Take a Nawthun gul, Eugene." Aunt Louise became at once combative. "They're bettah for you! They are *bettah.* They are *bettah!*" she declared, shaking her head in an obdurate manner, as if further argument was useless. "Moah independence! Bettah minds! They won't choke yoah life out by hanging awound yoah neck," she concluded crisply.

"I will tell you a story," Uncle Bascom continued deliberately as if she had not spoken, "that will illustrate admirably what I mean." Here he cleared his throat, as if he were preparing to deliver a set speech, and began in a deliberate and formal tone, "Some years ago I had occasion to go to Portland, Maine, on business. When I arrived at the North Station I found a crowd waiting before the window: it was necessary for me to wait in line. I was carrying a small valise which I placed on the floor between my legs in order to get out the money for my ticket. At this moment, the woman who stood behind me, apparently not given to noticing very well where she was going," he snarled bitterly, "started to move forward and stubbed her toe against the valise. Before I had time to turn around and apologize"—he stopped abruptly, then, leaning forward with a horrible grimace, he tapped Eugene stiffly with his great bony fingers and continued in a lowered voice: "Say! Have you any idea what she did, my boy?"

"No," Eugene said.

"Why I give you my word, my boy," he whispered solemnly, "without so much as 'By your leave,' she lifted her leg and *kicked* me, *kicked* me"—he howled, "in the *stern!* And *she,* my boy, was a New England woman."

"Whoo-o-op!" Aunt Louise was off again, rocking back and forth, holding her napkin over her mouth.

"Can you *imagine,* can you *dream,*" said Bascom, his voice an intense whisper of disgust, "of a Southern lady, the flower of modesty and the old aristocracy, doing such a thing as that?"

"Yes-s," hissed Aunt Louise, her cackle subsiding, leaning intensely across the table and glaring at him, "and it *suhved* you wight! It *suhved* you wight! It *suhved* you wight! These things would nevah happen if you thought of any one's convenience but yoah own. What *wight* did you have to put yoah baggage there? What *wight?*"

"Ah," he replied, with a kind of precise snarl, profoundly contemptuous of her opinion, "you-don't-know-what-you're-talk-ing-about! What *right?* she says—Why all the right in the world," he yelled. "Have you ever read the conditions enumerated upon the back of railway tickets concerning the transportation of baggage?"

"Suttinly not!" she retorted crisply. "One does not need to wead the backs of wailway tickets to learn how to behave like a civilized pusson!"

"Well, I will tell them to you," said Uncle Bascom, licking his lips, and with a look of joy upon his face. And, at great length, with infinite gusto, lip-pursing, and legal pedantry of elocution, he would enumerate them all.

"And say, by the way, Eugene," he would continue without a halt, "there is a very charming young lady who occasionally comes to my office (with her mother, of course) who is very anxious to meet you. She is a musician: she appears quite often in public. They live in Melrose, but they came, originally, I believe, from New Hampshire. Finest people in the world: no question about it," his uncle said.

And suddenly alert, scenting adventure and seduction, the young man got the address from him immediately.

"Yes, my boy," here Uncle Bascom fumbled through a mass of envelopes, "you may call her, without indiscretion, over the telephone at any time. I have spoken to her frequently about you: no doubt you'll find much in common. Or, *say!*" here a flash of inspiration aroused him to volcanic action, "I could call her now and let you talk to her." And he plunged violently toward the telephone.

"No, no, no, no, no!" Eugene sprang after him and checked him. For he wanted to make his own appointment luxuriously in private, sealed darkly in a telephone booth, craftily to feel his way, speculating on the curve of the unseen hip by the sound of the voice; probing, with the most delicate innuendo, the depth and richness of the promise. He loathed all family intercession and interference: they placed, he felt, at the outset, a crushing restraint upon the adventure from which it could never recover.

"I had rather call her myself," he added, "when I have more time. I don't know when I could see her now: it might be awkward calling at just this time."

Later, while Uncle Bascom was poking furiously at the meagre coals of the tiny furnace in the cellar, setting up a clangorous and smoky din all through the house, Aunt Louise would bear down madly upon the boy, whispering:

"Did you hear him! Did you hear him! Still mad about the women at his age! Can't keep his hands off them! The lechewous old fool!" and she cackled bitterly. Then, with a fierce change: "He's *mad* about them, Eugene. He's had one after anothah for the last twenty yeahs! He has spent *faw-chuns* on them! Have you seen that gul in his office yet? The stenographer?"

He had, and believed he had rarely seen a more solidly dull unattractive female than this pallid coarse-featured girl. But he only said: "Yes."

"He has spent thousands on her, Gene! *Thousands!* The old fool! And all they do is laugh at him behind his back. Why even at home heah," her eyes darting madly about the place, "he can hardly keep his hands off me at times! I have to lock myself in my woom to secure pwotection" and her bright old eyes muttered crazily about in her head.

He thought these outbursts the result of frantic and extravagant jealousy: fruit of some passionate and submerged affection that his aunt still bore for her husband. This, perhaps, was true, but later he was to find there was a surprising modicum of fact in what she had said.

During the wintry afternoon, he would sit and smoke one of his uncle's corn-cob pipes, filling it with the coarse cheap powerful tobacco that lay, loosely spread, upon a bread-board in the kitchen.

Meanwhile, his aunt, on these usual Sundays when she must remain at home, played entire operas from Wagner on her small victrola.

Most of the records had been given her by her two daughters, and during the week the voices of the music afforded her the only companionship she had. The boy listened attentively to all she said about music, because he knew little about it, and had got from poetry the kind of joy that music seemed to give to others. Shifting the records quickly, his aunt would point out the melodramatic effervescence of the Italians, the metallic precision, the orderly profusion, the thrill, the vibration, the emptiness of French composition. She liked the Germans and the Russians. She liked what she called the "barbaric splendor" of Rimsky, but was too late, of course, either to have heard or to care much for the modern composers.

She would play Wagner over and over again, lost in the enchanted forests of the music, her spirit wandering drunkenly down vast murky aisles of sound, through which the great hoarse throats of horns were baying faintly. And occasionally, on Sundays, on one of her infrequent excursions into the world, when her daughters bought her tickets for concerts at Symphony Hall—that great gray room lined on its sides with pallid plaster shells of Greece—she would sit perched high, a sparrow held by the hypnotic serpent's eye of music—following each motif, hearing minutely each subtle entry of the mellow flutes, the horns, the spinal ecstasy of violins—until her lonely and desolate life was spun out of her into aerial fabrics of bright sound.

During this time, Uncle Bascom, who also knew nothing about music, and cared so little for it that he treated his wife's passion for it with contempt, would bury himself in the Sunday papers, or thumb deliberately through the pages of an ancient edition of the *Encyclopædia Britannica* in search of arbitrament for some contested point.

"Ah! Here we are, just as I thought," he would declare suddenly, with triumphant satisfaction. " 'Upon the fifth, however, in spite of the heavy rains which had made of the roads quaking bogs, Jackson appeared suddenly from the South, at the head of an army of 33,000 men.' "

Then they would wrangle furiously over the hour, the moment, the place of dead event: each rushing from the room fiercely to produce the document which would support his own contention.

"Your aunt, my boy, is not the woman she once was," Bascom would say regretfully during her absence. "No question about that! At one time she was a very remarkable woman! Yes, sir, a woman of very considerable intelligence—considerable, that is, for a woman," he said, with a slight sneer.

And she, whispering, when he had gone: "You have noticed, of course, Gene?"

"What?"

"His mind's going," she muttered. "What a head he had fifteen years ago! But *now!*—Senile decay—G. Stanley Hall—forgets everything—" she whispered hoarsely, as she heard his returning footsteps.

Or, as the winter light darkened grayly, slashed on the western sky by fierce cold red, his uncle passed sheaf after sheaf of his verse to him, sniggering nosily, and prodding the boy with his great fingers, while his aunt cleared the table, or listened to the music. The great majority of these verses, labored and pedantic as they were, were variations of the motif of agnosticism, the horn on which his ministry in the Church had fatally gored itself—and still a brand that smouldered in his brain—not now so much from an all-mastering conviction, as from some desire to justify himself. These verses, which he asserted were modelled on those of his great hero, Matthew Arnold, were all remarkably like this one:

MY CREED

"Is there a land beyond the stars
Where we may find eternal day,
Life after death, peace after wars?
Is there? I cannot say.
Shall we find there a happier life,
All joy that here we never know,
Love in all things, an end of strife?
Perhaps: it may be so."

And so on.

And sniggering down his nose, Bascom would prod the young man stiffly with his great fingers, saying, as he slyly thrust another verse into his hand:

"Something in a lighter vein, my boy. Just a little foolishness, you know. (Phuh! Phuh! Phuh! Phuh! Phuh!)" Which was:

"Mary had a little calf,
It followed up her leg,
And everywhere that Mary went,
The boys were sure to beg."

And so on.

Uncle Bascom had hundreds of them: *Poems—Chiefly Religious,* he sent occasionally to the morning papers. They were sometimes printed in the Editor's Correspondence or The Open Forum. But *Poems—Chiefly Profane* he kept apparently for his own regalement.

Then, as it darkened, toward five o'clock, the boy would depart leaving them at times bitterly involved in a political wrangle, with the strewn Sunday members of *The Boston Herald* and *The Boston Post*

around them, she parroting intensely the newspaper jargon, assaulting
Borah and "the Senate iwweconcilables," he angrily defending Senator
Lodge as a scholar and a gentleman, with whom he had not always been
in agreement, but from whom he had once received a most courteous
letter—a fact which seemed to distinguish him in Bascom's mind as the
paragon of statesmanship.

And as Eugene left, he would note, with a swift inchoate pang, the
sudden mad loneliness in Aunt Louise's eyes, doomed for another week
to her grim imprisonment. But he did not know that her distended and
exhausted heart hissed audibly each time she ascended from futile labor
on the cold furnace, stoked with cheap slag and coke, and that her thin
blood was fed by gristly butcher's leavings, in answer to the doctor's
call for meat.

And his aunt would go with Eugene to the frost-glazed door, open it,
and stand huddled meagrely and hugging herself together beneath the
savage desolation of the Northern cold; talking to him for a moment and
calling brightly after him as he went down the icy path:

"Come again, boy! Always glad to see you!"

And in the dull cold Sunday light he strode away, his spirit braced by
the biting air, the Northern cold, the ragged bloody sky, which was
somehow prophetic to him of glorious fulfilment, and at the same time
depressed by the gray enormous weight of Sunday tedium and dreariness
all around him.

And yet, he never lost heart that out of this dullness he would draw
some rich adventure. He strode away with quickening pulse, hoping to
see it issue from every warmly lighted house, to find it in the street cars,
the subway or at a restaurant. Then he would go back into the city and dine
at one of the restaurants where the pretty waitresses served him. Later
he would go out on the sparsely peopled Sunday streets, turning finally,
as a last resort, into Washington Street, where the moving-picture places
and cheap vaudeville houses were filled with their Sunday Irish custom.

Sometimes he went in, but as one weary act succeeded the other, and
the empty brutal laughter of the people echoed in his ears, seeming to
him forced and dishonest, as if people laughed at the ghosts of mirth, the
rotten husks of stale wit, the sordidness, hopelessness, and sterility of
their lives oppressed him hideously. On the stage he would see the
comedian again display his red necktie with a leer, and hear the people
laugh about it; he would hear again that some one was a big piece of
cheese, and listen to them roar; he would observe again the pert and

cheap young comedian with nothing to offer waste time portentously, talk in a low voice with the orchestra leader; and the only thing he liked would be the strength and balance of the acrobats.

Finally, drowned in a sea-depth of gray horror, and with the weary brutal laughter of the audience ringing in his ears, he would rush out on the street again, filled with its hideous Sunday dullness and the sterile wink of the chop-suey signs, and take the train to Cambridge.

And there, as the night grew late, his spirit would surge up in him: sunken in books at midnight, with the soft numb prescience of brooding snow upon the air, the feeling of exultancy, joy, and invincible strength would come back; and he was sure that the door would open for him, the magic word be spoken, and that he would make all of the glory, power, and beauty of the earth his own.

XVIII

ONE day the boy telephoned the girl of whom his Uncle Bascom had spoken. She was coy and cautious, but sounded hopeful: he liked her voice. When, after some subtle circumlocutions, he asked her for an early meeting, she countered swiftly by asking him to meet her the following evening at the North Station: she was coming in to town to perform at a dinner. She played the violin. He understood very well that she was really anxious to see him before admitting him to the secure license of a suburban parlor; so, he bathed himself, threw powder under his arm-pits, and put on a new shirt, which he bought for the occasion.

It was November: rain fell coldly and drearily. He buttoned himself in his long raincoat and went to meet her. She had promised to wear a red carnation; the suggestion was her own, and tickled him hugely. As the pink-faced suburbanites poured, in an icy stream, into the hot wait-ing-room, he looked for her. Presently he saw her: she came toward him immediately, since his height was unmistakable. They talked excitedly flustered, but gradually getting some preliminary sense of each other.

She was a rather tall, slender girl, dressed in garments that seemed to have been left over, in good condition, from the early part of the century. She wore a flat but somehow towering hat: it seemed to perch upon her head, as do those worn by the Queen of England. She was covered with a long blue coat, which flared and bustled at the hips, and had screws and curls of black corded ornament; she looked respectable and anti-quated, but her costume, and a naive stupidity in her manner, gave her a quaintness that he liked. He took her to the subway, having arranged a meeting at her home for the following night.

The girl, whose name was Genevieve Simpson, lived with her mother and her brother, a heavy young lout of nineteen years, in a two-family house at Melrose. The mother, a small, full, dumpling-faced woman, whose ordinary expression in repose, in common with that of so many women of the middle class in America who have desired one life and followed another and found perhaps that its few indispensable benefits, as security, gregariousness, decorum, have not been as all-sufficient as they had hoped, was one of sullen, white, paunch-eyed discontent.

It was this inner petulance, the small carping disparagement of every one and everything that entered the mean light of her world, that made absurdly palpable the burlesque mechanism of social heartiness. Looking at her while she laughed with shrill falsity at all the wrong places, he would rock with huge guffaws, to which she would answer with eager renewal, believing that both were united in their laughter over something of which she was, it is true, a little vague.

It was, she felt, her business to make commercially attractive to every young man the beauty and comfort of the life she had made for her family, and although the secret niggling discontent of their lives was plainly described on both her own and her daughter's face, steeped behind their transparent masks in all the small poisons of irritability and bitterness, they united in their pretty tableau before the world—a tableau, he felt, something like those final exhibitions of grace and strength with which acrobats finish the act, the strained smile of ease and comfort, as if one could go on hanging by his toes forever, the grieving limbs, the whole wrought torture which will collapse in exhausted relief the second the curtain hides it.

"We want you to feel absolutely at home here," she said brightly "Make this your headquarters. You will find us simple folk here, without any frills," she continued, with a glance around the living-room letting her eye rest with brief satisfaction upon the striped tiles of the hearth, the flowered vases of the mantel, the naked doll, tied with a pink sash, on the piano, and the pictures of "The Horse Fair," the lovers flying before the storm, Maxfield Parrish's "Dawn," and Leonardo da Vinci's "Last Supper," which broke the spaces of the wall, "but if you like a quiet family life, a welcome is always waiting for you here. Oh, yes—every one is for each other here: we keep no secrets from each other in our little family."

Eugene thought that this was monstrous if it was true; a swift look at Genevieve and Mama convinced him, however, that not everything was being told. A mad exultancy arose in him: the old desire returned again to throw a bomb into the camp, in order to watch its effect; to express murderous opinions in a gentle Christian voice, further entrenched by an engaging matter-of-factness, as if he were but expressing the common-place thought of all sensible people; bawdily, lewdly, shockingly with a fine assumption of boyish earnestness, sincerity, and naïveté. So, in a voice heavily coated with burlesque feeling, he said: "Thank you, thank you, Mrs. Simpson. You have no idea what it means to me to be able to come to a place like this."

"I know," said Genevieve with fine sympathy, "when you're a thou-sand miles from home——"

"A thousand!" he cried, with a bitter laugh, "a thousand! Say rather a million." And he waited, almost squealing in his throat, until they should bite.

"But—but your home is in the South, isn't it?" Mrs. Simpson in-quired doubtfully.

"Home! Home!" cried he, with raucous laugh. "I have no home!"

"Oh, you poor boy!" said Genevieve.

"But your parents—are they *both* dead?"

"No!" he answered, with a sad smile. "They are both living."

There was a pregnant silence.

"They do not live together," he added after a moment, feeling he could not rely on their deductive powers.

"O-o-oh," said Mrs. Simpson significantly, running the vowel up and down the vocal scale. "O-o-oh!"

"Nasty weather, isn't it?" he remarked, deliberately drawing a loose cigarette from his pocket. "I wish it would snow: I like your cold North-ern winters as only a Southerner can like them; I like the world at night when it is muffled, enclosed with snow; I like a warm secluded house, sheltered under heavy fir trees, with the curtains drawn across a mellow light, and books, and a beautiful woman within. These are some of the things I like."

"Gee!" said the boy, his heavy blond head leaned forward intently. "What was the trouble?"

"Jimmy! Hush!" cried Genevieve, and yet they all looked toward Eugene with eager intensity.

"The trouble?" said he, vacantly. "What trouble?"

"Between your father and mother?"

"Oh," he said carelessly, "he beat her."

"Aw-w! He hit her with his fist?"

"Oh, no. He generally used a walnut walking stick. It got too much for her finally. My mother, even then, was not a young woman—she was almost fifty, and she could not stand the gaff so well as she could in her young days. I'll never forget that last night," he said, gazing thoughtfully into the coals with a smile. "I was only seven, but I remember it all very well. Papa had been brought home drunk by the mayor."

"The *mayor?*"

"Oh, yes," said Eugene casually. "They were great friends. The mayor often brought him home when he was drunk. But he was very violent that time. After the mayor had gone, he stamped around the house smashing everything he could get his hands on, cursing and blaspheming at the top of his voice. My mother stayed in the kitchen and paid no attention to him when he entered. This, of course, infuriated him. He made for her with the poker. She saw that at last she was up against it; but she had realized that such a moment was inevitable. She was not unprepared. So she reached in the flour bin and got her revolver——"

"Did she have a revolver!"

"Oh, yes," he said nonchalantly, "my Uncle Will had given it to her as a Christmas present. Knowing my father as he did, he told her it might come in handy sometime. Mama was forced to shoot at him three times before he came to his senses."

There was a silence.

"Gee!" said the boy, finally. "Did she hit him?"

"Only once," Eugene replied, tossing his cigarette into the fire. "A flesh wound in the leg. A trifle. He was up and about in less than a week. But, of course, Mama had left him by that time."

"Well!" said Mrs. Simpson, after a yet longer silence, "I've never had to put up with anything like *that*."

"No, thank heaven!" said Genevieve fervently. Then, curiously: "Is —is your mother Mr. Pentland's sister?"

"Yes."

"And the uncle who gave her the revolver—Mr. Pentland's brother?"

"Oh, yes," Eugene answered readily. "It's all the same family." He grinned in his entrails, thinking of Uncle Bascom.

"Mr. Pentland seems a very educated sort of man," said Mrs. Simpson, having nothing else to say.

"Yes. We went to see him when we were hunting for a house," Genevieve added. "He was very nice to us. He told us he had once been in the ministry."

"Yes," said Eugene. "He was a Man of God for more than twenty years—one of the most eloquent, passionate, and gifted soul-savers that ever struck fear into the hearts of the innumerable sinners of the American Nation. In fact, I know of no one with whom to compare him, unless I turn back three centuries to Jonathan Edwards, the Puritan divine, who evoked, in a quiet voice like the monotonous dripping of water, a picture of hell-fire so near that the skins of the more imaginative fanatics on the front rows visibly blistered. However, Edwards spoke for two and a half hours: Uncle Bascom, with his mad and beautiful tongue, has been known to drive people insane with terror in twenty-seven minutes by the clock. There are still people in the asylums that he put there," he said piously. "I hope," he added quickly, "you didn't ask him why he had left the church."

"Oh, no!" said Genevieve. "We never did that."

"Why did he?" asked Mrs. Simpson bluntly, who felt that now she had only to ask and it would be given. She was not disappointed.

"It was the centuries-old conflict between organized authority and the individual," said Eugene. "No doubt you have felt it in your own lives. Uncle Bascom was a poet, a philosopher, a mystic—he had the soul of an artist which must express divine love and ideal beauty in corporeal form. Such a man as this is not going to be shackled by the petty tyrannies of ecclesiastical convention. An artist must love, and be loved. He must be swept by the Flow of Things, he must be a constantly expanding atom in the rhythmic surges of the Life Force. Who knew this better than Uncle Bascom when he first met the choir contralto?"

"Contralto!" gasped Genevieve.

"Perhaps she was a soprano," said Eugene. "It skills not. Suffice it to say they lived, they loved, they had their little hour of happiness. Of course, when the child came——"

"The child!" screamed Mrs. Simpson.

"A bouncing boy. He weighed thirteen pounds at birth and is at the present a Lieutenant Commander in the United States Navy."

"What became of—her?" said Genevieve.

"Of whom?"

"The—the contralto."

"She died—she died in childbirth."

But—but Mr. Pentland?" inquired Mrs. Simpson in an uncertain voice. "Didn't he—marry her?"

"How could he?" Eugene answered with calm logic. "He was married to some one else."

And casting his head back suddenly he sang: "You know I'm in love with some-boddy else, so why can't you leave me alone?"

"Well, I *never!*" Mrs. Simpson stared dumbly into the fire.

"Well, *hardly* ever," Eugene became allusively Gilbertian. "She hardly ever has a Big, Big B." And he sang throatily: "Oh, yes! Oh, yes, in-deed!" relapsing immediately into a profound and moody abstraction, but noting with delight that Genevieve and her mother were looking at him furtively, with frightened and bewildered glances.

"Say!" The boy, whose ponderous jowl had been sunken on his fist for ten minutes, now at length distilled a question. "What ever became of your father? Is he still living?"

"No!" said Eugene, after a brief pause, returning suddenly to fact. "No! He's still dying."

And he fixed upon them suddenly the battery of his fierce eyes, lit with horror:

"He has a cancer." After a moment, he concluded: "My father is a very great man."

They looked at him in stricken bewilderment.

"Gee!" said the boy, after another silence. "That guy's worse than our old man!"

"Jimmy! Jimmy!" whispered Genevieve scathingly.

There was a very long, for the Simpson family, a very painful, silence.

"Aha! Aha!" Eugene's head was full of *ahas*.

"I suppose you have thought it strange," Mrs. Simpson began with a cracked laugh, which she strove to make careless, "that you have never seen Mr. Simpson about when you called?"

"Yes," he answered with a ready dishonesty, for he had never thought of it at all. But he reflected at the same moment that this was precisely the sort of thing people were always thinking of: suddenly before the embattled front of that little family, its powers aligned for the defense of reputation, he felt lonely, shut out. He saw himself looking in at them through a window: all communication with life grouped and protected seemed forever shut off.

"Mother decided some months ago that she could no longer live with Father," said Genevieve, with sad dignity.

"Sure," volunteered Jimmy, "he's livin' with another woman!"

"Jimmy!" said Genevieve hoarsely.

Eugene had a momentary flash of humorous sympathy with the departed Simpson; then he looked at her white bickering face and felt sorry for her. She carried her own punishment with her.

XIX

SHALL a man be dead within your heart before his rotten flesh be wholly dead within the ground, and before the producing fats and syrup cease to give life to his growing hair? Shall a man so soon be done with that which still provides a nest for working maggotry or shall a brother leave a brother's memory before the worms have left his tissue? This is a pregnant subject: there should be laws passed, and a discipline, which train a man to greater constancy. And suddenly, out of this dream of time in which he lived, he would awaken, and instantly, like a man freed from the spell of an enchantment which has held him captive for many years in some strange land, he would remember home with an intolerable sense of pain and loss, the lost world of his childhood, and feel the strange and bitter miracle of life and have no words for what he wished to say.

That lost world would come back to him at many times, and often for no cause that he could trace or fathom—a voice half-heard, a word far-spoken, a leaf, a light that came and passed and came again. But always when that lost world would come back, it came at once, like a sword thrust through the entrails, in all its panoply of past time, living, whole, and magic as it had always been.

And always when it came to him, and at whatever time, and for whatever reason, he could hear his father's great voice sounding in the house again and see his gaunt devouring stride as he had come muttering round the corner at the hour of noon long years before.

And then he would hear again the voice of his dead brother, and remember with a sense of black horror, dream-like disbelief, that Ben was dead, and yet could not believe that Ben had ever died, or that he had had a brother, lost a friend. Ben would come back to him in these moments with a blazing and intolerable reality, until he heard his quiet living voice again, saw his fierce scowling eyes of bitter gray, his scornful, proud and lively face, and always when Ben came back to him it was like this: he saw his brother in a single image, in some brief forgotten moment of the past, remembered him by a word, a gesture, a forgotten act; and certainly all that could ever be known of Ben's life was collected in that blazing image of lost time and the forgotten moment. And suddenly he would be there in a strange land, staring upward from his bed in darkness, hearing his brother's voice again, and living in the far and bitter miracle of time.

And always now, when Ben came back to him, he came within the frame and limits of a single image, one of those instant blazing images which from this time would haunt his memory and which more and more, as a kind of distillation—a reward for all the savage struggles of his Faustian soul with the protean and brain-maddening forms of life— were to collect and concentrate the whole material of experience and memory, in which the process of ten thousand days and nights could in an instant be resumed. And the image in which Ben now always came to him was this: he saw his brother standing in a window, and an old red light of fading day, and all the strange and tragic legend of his destiny was on his brow, and all that any man could ever see or know or understand of his dead brother's life was there:

Bitter and beautiful, scorn no more. Ben stands there in the window, for a moment idle, his strong, lean fingers resting lightly on his bony hips, his gray eyes scowling fiercely, bitterly and contemptuously over the laughing and exuberant faces of the crowd. For a moment more he scowls fixedly at them with an expression of almost savage contempt. Then scornfully he turns away from them. The bitter, lean and pointed face, the shapely, flashing, close-cropped head jerks upward, backward, he laughs briefly and with pitying contempt as he speaks to that unknown and invisible auditor who all his life has been the eternal confidant and witness of his scorn:

"Oh my God!" he says, jerking his scornful head out towards the crowd again. "Listen to this, will you?"

They look at him with laughing and exuberant faces, unwounded by his scorn. They look at him with a kind of secret and unspoken tenderness which the strange and bitter savor of his life awakes in people always. They look at him with faith, with pride, with the joy and confidence and affection which his presence stirs in every one. And as if he were the very author of their fondest hopes, as if he were the fiat, not the helpless agent, of the thing they long to see accomplished, they yell to him in their unreasoning exuberance: "All right, Ben! Give us a hit now! A single's all we need, boy! Bring him in!" Or others, crying with the same exuberance of faith: "Strike him out, Ben! Make him fan!"

But now the crowd, sensing the electric thrill and menace of a decisive conflict, has grown still, is waiting with caught breath and pounding hearts, their eyes fixed eagerly on Ben. Somewhere, a thousand miles to the North, somewhere through the reddened, slanting and fast-fading light of that October day, somewhere across the illimitable fields and folds and woods and hills and hollows of America, across the huge brown earth, the mown fields, the vast wild space, the lavish, rude and unfenced distances, the familiar, homely, barren, harsh, strangely haunting scenery of the nation; somewhere through the crisp, ripe air, the misty, golden pollenated light of all her prodigal and careless harvest; somewhere far away at the heart of the great sky-soaring, smoke-gold, and enchanted city of the North, and of their vision—the lean right arm of the great pitcher Mathewson is flashing like a whip. A greyhound of a man named Speaker, quick as a deer to run, sharp as a hawk to see, swift as a cat to strike, stands facing him. And the huge terrific stands, packed to the eaves incredibly with mounting tiers of small white faces, now all breathless, silent, and intent, all focused on two men as are the thoughts, the hearts, the visions of these people everywhere in little towns, soar back, are flung to the farthest edges of the field in a vision of power, of distance, space and lives unnumbered, fused into a single unity that is so terrific that it bursts the measures of our comprehension and has a dream-like strangeness of reality even when we see it.

The scene is instant, whole and wonderful. In its beauty and design that vision of the soaring stands, the pattern of forty thousand em-petalled faces, the velvet and unalterable geometry of the playing field, and the small lean figures of the players, set there, lonely, tense and waiting in their places, bright, desperate solitary atoms encircled by that huge wall of nameless faces, is incredible. And more than anything, it is the light, the miracle of light and shade and color—the crisp, blue light that swiftly slants out from the soaring stands and, deepening to violet, begins to march across the velvet field and towards the pitcher's box, that gives the thing its single and incomparable beauty.

The batter stands swinging his bat and grimly waiting at the plate, crouched, tense, the catcher, crouched, the umpire, bent, hands clasped behind his back, and peering forward. All of them are set now in the cold blue of that slanting shadow, except the pitcher who stands out there all alone, calm, desperate, and forsaken in his isolation, with the gold-red swiftly fading light upon him, his figure legible with all the resolution, despair and lonely dignity which that slanting, somehow fatal light can give him. Deep lilac light is eating swiftly in from every corner of the field now, and far off there is a vision of the misty, golden and October towers of the terrific city. The scene is unforgettable in the beauty, intoxication and heroic feeling of its incredible design, and yet, as overwhelming as the spectacle may be for him who sees it, it is doubtful if the eye-witness has ever felt its mystery, beauty, and strange loveliness as did that unseen and unseeing audience in a little town.

But now the crowd, sensing the menaceful approach of a decisive moment, has grown quiet and tense and breathless, as it stands there in the street. In the window, Ben sets the earphones firmly with his hands, his head goes down, the scowl between his gray eyes deepens to a look of listening intensity. He begins to speak sharply to a young man standing at a table on the floor behind him. He snaps his fingers nervously, a card-board placard is handed to him, he looks quickly at it, and then thrusts it back, crying irritably:

"No, no, no! Strike one, I said! Damn it, Mac, you're about as much help to me as a wooden Indian!"

The young man on the floor thrusts another placard in his hand. Ben takes it quickly, swiftly takes out a placard from the complicated frame of wires and rows and columns in the window (for it is before the day of the electric scoreboard, and this clumsy and complicated system whereby every strike, ball, substitution, or base hit—every possible movement and event that can occur upon the field—must be indicated in this way by placards printed with the exact information, is the only one they know) and thrusts a new placard on the line in place of the one that he has just removed. A cheer, sharp, lusty, and immediate, goes up from the crowd. Ben speaks sharply and irritably to the dark and sullen-featured youth whose name is Foxey and Foxey runs outside quickly with another placard inscribed with the name of a new player who is coming in. Swiftly, Foxey takes out of its groove the name of the departing player, shoves the new one into place, and this time the rival partisans in the crowd cheer for the pinch hitter.

In the street now there is the excited buzz and hum of controversy. The people, who, with a strange and somehow moving loyalty, are divided into two groups supporting the merits of two teams which they have never seen, are eagerly debating, denying, making positive assertions of what is likely to happen, which are obviously extravagant and absurd in a contest where nothing can be predicted, and so much depends on fortune, chance, and the opportunity of the moment.

In the very forefront of the crowd, a little to the right as Ben stands facing them, a well-dressed man in the late fifties can be seen excitedly discussing the prospect of the game with several of his companions. His name is Fagg Sluder, a citizen well known to every one in town. He is a man who made a fortune as a contractor and retired from active business several years ago, investing part of his wealth in two or three large office buildings, and who now lives on the income he derives from them.

He is a nervous energetic figure of a man, of middle height, with graying hair, a short, cropped mustache, and the dry, spotted, slightly concave features which characterize many Americans of his age. A man who, until recent years, has known nothing but hard work since his childhood, he has now developed, in his years of leisure, an enthusiastic devotion to the game, that amounts to an obsession.

He has not only given to the town the baseball park which bears his name, he is also president of the local Club, and uncomplainingly makes good its annual deficit. During the playing season his whole time is spent in breathing, thinking, talking baseball all day long: if he is not at the game, bent forward in his seat behind the home plate in an attitude of ravenous absorption, occasionally shouting advice and encouragement to the players in his rapid, stammering, rather high-pitched voice that has a curiously incisive penetration and carrying power, then he is up on the Square before the fire department going over every detail of the game with his cronies and asking eager, rapid-fire questions of the young red-necked players he employs, and towards whom he displays the worshipful admiration of a school-boy.

Now this man who, despite his doctor's orders, smokes twenty or thirty strong black cigars a day, and in fact is never to be seen without a cigar in his fingers or in his mouth—may be heard all over the crowd speaking eagerly in his rapid, stammering voice to a man with a quiet and pleasant manner who stands behind him. This is the assistant chief of the fire department and his name is Bickett:

"Jim," Mr. Sluder is saying in his eager and excited way, "I—I—I—I tell you what I think! If—if—if Speaker comes up there again with men on bases—I—I—I just believe Matty will strike him out—I swear I do. What do you think?" he demands eagerly and abruptly.

Mr. Bickett, first pausing to draw slowly and languorously on a cigarette before casting it into the gutter, makes some easy, quiet and non-committal answer which satisfies Mr. Sluder completely, since he is paying no attention to him anyway. Immediately, he claps the chewed cigar which he is holding in his stubby fingers into his mouth, and nodding his head briskly and vigorously, with an air of great decision, he stammers out again:

"Well—I—I—I just believe that's what he's going to do: I—I—I don't think he's afraid of that fellow at all! I—I—I think he knows he can strike him out any time he feels like it."

The boy knows every one in the crowd as he looks around him. Here are the other boys of his own age, and older—his fellow route-boys in the morning's work, his school companions, delivery boys employed by druggists, merchants, clothiers, the sons of the more wealthy and prominent people of the town. Here are the boys from the eastern part of town from which he comes and in which his father's house is built—the older, homelier, and for some reason more joyful and confident part of town to him—though why he does not know, he cannot say. Perhaps it is because the hills along the eastern borders of the town are near and close and warm, and almost to be touched. But in the western part of town, the great vistas of the soaring ranges, the distant summits of the Smokies fade far away into the west, into the huge loneliness, the haunting desolation of the unknown distance, the red, lonely light of the powerful retreating sun.

But now the old red light is slanting swiftly, the crowd is waiting tense and silent, already with a touch of sorrow, resignation, and the winter in their hearts, for summer's over, the game is ending, and October has come again, has come again. In the window, where the red slant of the sun already falls, Ben is moving quickly, slipping new placards into place, taking old ones out, scowling, snapping his hard, white fingers in command, speaking curtly, sharply, irritably to the busy figures, moving at his bidding on the floor. The game—the last game of the series—is sharp, close, bitterly contested. No one can say as yet which way the issue goes, which side will win, when it will end—but that fatality of red slanting light, the premonitory menace of the frost, the fatal certitude of victory and defeat, with all the sorrow and regret that both can bring to men, are in their hearts.

From time to time, a wild and sudden cheer breaks sharply from the waiting crowd, as something happens to increase their hope of victory.

but for the most part they are tense and silent now, all waiting for the instant crisis, the quick end.

Behind Ben, seated in a swivel chair, but turned out facing toward the crowd, the boy can see the gouty bulk of Mr. Flood, the owner of the paper. He is bent forward heavily in his seat, his thick apoplectic fingers braced upon his knees, his mouth ajar, his coarse, jowled, venously empurpled face and bulging yellow eyes turned out upon the crowd, in their constant expression of slow stupefaction. From time to time, when the crowd cheers loudly, the expression of brutal surprise upon Mr. Flood's coarse face will deepen perceptibly and comically, and in a moment he will say stupidly, in his hoarse and phlegmy tones:

"Who done that? . . . What are they yelling for? . . . Which side's ahead now? . . . What happened that time, Ben?"

To which Ben usually makes no reply whatever, but the savage scowl between his gray eyes deepens with exasperation, and finally, cursing bitterly, he says:

"Damn it, Flood! What do you think I am—the whole damned newspaper? For heaven's sake, man, do you think all I've got to do is answer damn-fool questions! If you want to know what's happening, go outside where the rest of them are!"

"Well, Ben, I just wanted to know how—" Mr. Flood begins hoarsely, heavily, and stupidly.

"Oh, for God's sake! Listen to this, won't you?" says Ben, laughing scornfully and contemptuously as he addresses the invisible auditor of his scorn, and jerking his head sideways toward the bloated figure of his employer as he does so, "Here!" he says, in a disgusted manner. "For God's sake, some one go and tell him what the score is, and put him out of his misery!" And scowling savagely, he speaks sharply into the mouthpiece of the phone and puts another placard on the line.

And suddenly, even as the busy figures swarm and move there in the window before the waiting crowd, the bitter thrilling game is over! In waning light, in faint shadows, far, far away in a great city of the North, the 40,000 small empetalled faces bend forward, breathless, waiting— single and strange and beautiful as all life, all living, and man's destiny. There's a man on base, the last flash of the great right arm, the crack of the bat, the streaking white of a clean-hit ball, the wild, sudden, solid roar, a pair of flashing legs have crossed the rubber, and the game is over!

And instantly, there at the city's heart, in the great stadium, and all across America, in ten thousand streets, ten thousand little towns, the crowd is breaking, flowing, lost forever! That single, silent, most intolerable loveliness is gone forever. With all its tragic, proud and waiting unity, it belongs now to the huge, the done, the indestructible fabric of the past, has moved at last out of that inscrutable maw of chance we call the future into the strange finality of dark time.

Now it is done, the crowd is broken, lost, exploded, and 10,000,000 men are moving singly down 10,000 streets—toward what? Some by the light of Hesperus which, men say, can bring all things that live on earth to their own home again—flock to the fold, the father to his child, the lover to the love he has forsaken—and the proud of heart, the lost, the lonely of the earth, the exile and the wanderer—to what? To pace again the barren avenues of night, to pass before the bulbous light of lifeless streets with half-averted faces, to pass the thousand doors, to feel again the ancient hopelessness of hope, the knowledge of despair, the faith of desolation.

And for a moment, when the crowd has gone, Ben stands there silent, lost, a look of bitter weariness, disgust, and agony upon his gray gaunt face, his lonely brow, his fierce and scornful eyes. And as he stands there that red light of waning day has touched the flashing head, the gaunt, starved face, has touched the whole image of his fiercely wounded, lost and scornful spirit with the prophecy of its strange fatality. And in that instant as the boy looks at his brother, a knife is driven through his entrails suddenly, for with an instant final certitude, past reason, proof, or any visual evidence, he sees the end and answer of his brother's life. Already death rests there on his proud head like a coronal. The boy knows in that one instant Ben will die.

XX

He visited Genevieve frequently over a period of several months. As his acquaintance with the family deepened, the sharpness of his appetite for seduction dwindled, and was supplanted by an ecstatic and insatiable glee. He felt that he had never in his life been so enormously and constantly amused: he would think exultantly for days of an approaching visit, weaving new and more preposterous fables for their consumption, bursting into violent laughter on the streets as he thought of past scenes, the implication of a tone, a gesture, the transparent artifice of mother and daughter, the incredible exaggeration of everything.

He was charmed, enchanted: his mind swarmed daily with monstrous projects—his heart quivered in a tight cage of nervous exultancy as he thought of the infinite richness of absurdity that lay stored for him. His ethical conscience was awakened hardly at all—he thought of these three people as monsters posturing for his delight. His hatred of cruelty, the nauseating horror at the idiot brutality of youth, had not yet sufficiently defined itself to check his plunge. He was swept along in the full tide of his adventure: he thought of nothing else.

Through an entire winter, and into the spring, he went to see this little family in a Boston suburb. Then, he got tired of the game and the people as suddenly as he had begun, with the passionate boredom, weariness, and intolerance of which youth is capable. And now that the affair was ending, he was at last ashamed of the part he had played in it, and of the arrogant contempt with which he had regaled himself at the expense of other people. And he knew that the Simpsons had themselves at length become conscious of the meaning of his conduct, and saw that, in some way, he had made them the butt of a joke. And when they saw this, the family suddenly attained a curious quiet dignity, of which he had not believed them capable and which later he could not forget.

One night, as he was waiting in the parlor for the girl to come down, her mother entered the room, and stood looking at him quietly for a moment. Presently she spoke:

"You have been coming here for some time, now," she said, "and we were always glad to see you. My daughter liked you when she met you —she likes you yet—" the woman said slowly, and went on with obvious difficulty and embarrassment. "Her welfare means more to me than anything in the world—I would do anything to save her from unhappiness or misfortune." She was silent a moment, then said bluntly, "I think I have a right to ask you a question:—what are your intentions concerning her?"

He told himself that these words were ridiculous and part of the whole comic and burlesque quality of the family, and yet he found now that he could not laugh at them. He sat looking at the fire, uncertain of his answer, and presently he muttered:

"I have no intentions concerning her."

"All right," the woman said quietly. "That is all I wanted to know. . . . You are a young man," she went on slowly after a pause, "and very clever and intelligent—but there are still a great many things you do not understand. I know now that we looked funny to you and you have amused yourself at our expense. . . . I don't know why you thought it was such a joke, but I think you will live to see the day when you are sorry for it. It's not good to make a joke of people who have liked you and tried to be your friends."

"I know it's not," he said, and muttered: "I'm sorry for it now."

"Still, I can't believe," the woman said, "that you are a boy who would wilfully bring sorrow and ruin to any one who had never done you any harm. . . . The only reason I am saying this is for my daughter's sake."

"You don't need to worry about that," he said. "I'm sorry now for acting as I have—but you know everything I've done. And I'll not come back again. But I'd like to see her, and tell her that I'm sorry before I go."

"Yes," the woman said, "I think you ought."

She went out and a few minutes later the girl came down, entered the room, and he said good-bye to her. He tried to make amends to her with fumbling words, but she said nothing. She stood very still as he talked, almost rigid, her lips pressed tightly together, her hands clenched, winking back the tears.

"All right," she said finally, giving him her hand. "I'll say good-bye to you without hard feelings. . . . Some day . . . some day," her voice choked and she winked furiously— "I hope you'll understand—oh, good-bye!" she cried, and turned away abruptly. "I'm not mad at you any longer—and I wish you luck. . . . You know so many things, don't you? —You're so much smarter than we are, aren't you? . . . And I'm sorry for you when I think of all you've got to learn . . . of what you're going through before you do."

"Good-bye," he said.

He never saw any of them again, but he could not forget them. And as the years went on, the memory of all their folly, falseness, and hypocrisy was curiously altered and subdued and the memory that grew more vivid and dominant was of a little family, one of millions huddled below the immense and timeless skies that bend above us, lost in the darkness of nameless and unnumbered lives upon the lonely wilderness of life that is America, and banked together against these giant antagonists, for comfort, warmth, and love, with a courage and integrity that would not die, and could not be forgotten.

XXI

ONE afternoon early in May, Helen met McGuire upon the street. He had just driven in behind Wood's Pharmacy on Academy Street, and was preparing to go in to the prescription counter when she approached him. He got out of his big dusty-looking roadster with a painful grunt, slammed the door, and began to fumble slowly in the pockets of his baggy coat for a cigarette. He turned slowly as she spoke, grunted, "Hello, Helen," stuck the cigarette on his fat under-lip and lighted it, and then looking at her with his brutal, almost stupid, but somehow kindly glance, he barked coarsely:

"What's on your mind?"

"It's about Papa," she began in a low, hoarse and almost morbid tone— "Now I want to know if this last attack means that the end has come. You've got to tell me—we've got the right to know about it——"

The look of strain and hysteria on her big-boned face, her dull eyes fixed on him in a morbid stare, the sore on her large cleft chin, above all, the brooding insistence of her tone as she repeated phrases he had heard ten thousand times before suddenly rasped upon his frayed nerves, stretched them to the breaking point; he lost his air of hard professionalism and exploded in a flare of brutal anger:

"You want to know what? You've got a right to be told what? For God's sake,"—his tone was brutal, rasping, jeering—"pull yourself together and stop acting like a child." And then, a little more quietly, but brusquely, he demanded:

"All right. What do you want to know?"

"I want to know how long he's going to last," she said with morbid insistence. "Now, you're a doctor," she wagged her large face at him with an air of challenge that infuriated him, "and you ought to tell us. We've got to know!"

"Tell you! Got to know!" he shouted. "What the hell are you talking about? What do you expect to be told?"

"How long Papa has to live," she said with the same morbid insistence as before.

"You've asked me that a thousand times," he said harshly. "I've told you that I didn't know. He may live another month, he may be here a year from now—how can we tell about these things," he said in an exasperated tone, "particularly where your father is concerned. Helen, three or four years ago I might have made a prediction. I did make them—I didn't see how W. O. could go on six months longer. But he's fooled us all—you, me, the doctors at Johns Hopkins, every one who's had anything to do with the case. The man is dying from malignant carcinoma—he has been dying for years—his life is hanging by a thread, and the thread may break at any time—but when it is going to break I have no way of telling you."

"Ah-hah," she said reflectively. Her eyes had taken on a dull appeased look as he talked to her, and now she had begun to pluck at her large cleft chin. "Then you think—" she began.

"I think nothing," he shouted. "And for God's sake stop picking at your chin!"

For a moment he felt the sudden brutal anger that one sometimes feels toward a contrary child. He felt like taking her by the shoulders and shaking her. Instead, he took it out in words and scowling at her, said with brutal directness:

"Look here! . . . You've got to pull yourself together. You're becoming a mental case—do you hear me? You wander around like a person in a dream, you ask questions no one can answer, you demand answers no one can give—you work yourself up into hysterical frenzies and then you collapse and soak yourself with drugs, patent medicines, corn licker—anything that has alcohol in it—for days at a time. When you go to bed at night you think you hear voices talking to you, some one coming up the steps, the telephone. And really you hear nothing: there is nothing there. Do you know what that is?" he demanded brutally. "Those are symptoms of insanity—you're becoming unbalanced, if it keeps on they may have to send you to the crazy-house to take the cure."

"Ah-hah! Uh-huh!" she kept plucking at her big chin with an air of abstracted reflection, and with a curious look of dull appeasement in her eyes as if his brutal words had really given her some comfort. Then she suddenly came to herself, looked at him with clear eyes, and, her generous mouth touched at the corners with the big lewd tracery of her earthy humor, she sniggered hoarsely, and prodding him in his fat ribs with a big bony finger, she said:

"You think I've got 'em, do you? Well—" she nodded seriously in agreement, frowning a little as she spoke, but with the faint grin still legible around the corners of her mouth,—"I've often thought the same thing. You may be right," she nodded seriously again. "There are times when I do feel off—you know?—*queer*—looney—crazy—like there was a screw loose somewhere— Brrr!" and with the strange lewd mixture of frown and grin, she made a whirling movement with her finger towards her head. "What do you think it is?" she went on with an air of seriousness. "Now, I'd just like to know. What is it that makes me act like that? . . . Is it woman-business?" she said with a lewd and comic look upon her face. "Am I getting funny like the rest of them— now I've often thought the same—that maybe I'm going through a change of life—is that it? Maybe——"

"Oh, change of life be damned!" he said in a disgusted tone. "Here you are a young woman thirty-two years old and you talk to me about a change of life! That has about as much sense to it as a lot of other things you say! The only thing you change is your mind—and you do that every five minutes!" He was silent for a moment, breathing heavily and staring at her coarsely with his bloated and unshaven face, his veined and weary-looking eyes. When he spoke again his voice was gruff and quiet, touched with a burly, almost paternal tenderness:

"Helen," he said, "I'm worried about you—and not about your father. Your father is an old man now with a malignant cancer and with no hope of ever getting well again. He is tired of life, he wants to die— for God's sake why do you want to prolong his suffering, to try to keep him here in a state of agony, when death would be a merciful release for him? . . . I know there is no hope left for your father: he has been doomed for years, the sooner the end comes the better——"

She tried to speak but he interrupted her brusquely, saying:

"Just a minute. There's something that I want to say to you—for God's sake try to use it, if you can. The death of this old man seems strange and horrible to you because he is your father. It is as hard for you to think about his death as it is to think about the death of God Almighty; you think that if your father dies there will be floods and earthquakes and convulsions throughout nature. I assure you that this is not true. Old men are dying every second of the day, and nothing happens except they die——"

"Oh, but Papa was a wonderful man," she said. "I *know!* I *know!* Everybody who ever knew him said the same."

"Yes," McGuire agreed, "he was—he was one of the most remarkable men I ever knew. And that is what makes it all the harder now."

She looked at him eagerly, and said:

"You mean—his dying?"

"No, Helen," McGuire spoke quietly and with a weary patience.

"There's nothing very bad about his dying. Death seems so terrible to you because you know so little about it. But I have seen so much of death, I have seen so many people die—and I know there is really nothing very terrible about it, and about the death of an old man ravaged by disease there is nothing terrible at all. It seems terrible to those looking on—there are," he shrugged his fat shoulders, "there are sometimes—physical details that are unpleasant. But the old man knows little of all that: an old man dies as a clock runs down—he is worn out, has lost the will to live, he wants to die, and he just stops. That is all. And that will happen to your father."

"Oh, but it will be so strange now—so hard to understand!" she muttered with a bewildered look in her eyes. "We have expected him to die so many times—we have been fooled so often—and now I can't believe that it will ever happen. I thought that he would die in 1916, I never expected him to live another year; in 1918, the year that Ben died, none of us could see how he'd get through the winter—and then Ben died! No one had even thought of Ben—" her voice grew cracked and hoarse and her eyes glistened with tears. "We had forgotten Ben—every one was thinking about Papa—and then when Ben died, I turned against Papa for a time. For a while I was bitter against him—it seemed that I had done everything for this old man, that I had given him everything I had—my life, my strength, my energy—all because I thought that he was going to die—and then Ben, who had never been given anything— who had had nothing out of life—who had been neglected and forgotten by us all and who was the best one—the most decent one of the whole crowd—Ben was the one who had to go. For a time after his death I didn't care what happened—to Papa or to any one else. I was so bitter about Ben's death—it seemed so cruel, so rotten and unjust—that it had to be Ben of all the people in the world—only twenty-six years old and without a thing to show for his life—no love, no children, no happiness, cheated out of everything, when Papa had had so much—I couldn't stand the thought of it, even now I hate to go to Mama's house, it almost kills me to go near Ben's room, I've never been in it since the night he died—and somehow I was bitter against Papa! It seemed to me that he had cheated me, tricked me—at times I got so bitter that I thought that he was responsible in some way for Ben's death. I said I was through with him, that I would do nothing else for him, that I had done all that I intended to do, and that somebody else would have to take care of him. . . . But it all came back; he had another bad spell and I was

afraid that he was going to die, and I couldn't stand the thought of it.
. . . And it has gone on now so long, *year* after year, and *year* after
year," she said in a frenzied tone, "always thinking that he couldn't
last and seeing him come back again, that I couldn't believe that it would
ever happen. I can't believe it now. . . . And what am I going to do?"
she said hoarsely and desperately, clutching McGuire by the sleeve,
"what am I going to do now if he really dies? What is there left for me
in life with Papa gone?" Her voice was almost sobbing now with grief
and desperation— "He's all I've got to live for, Doctor McGuire. I've
got nothing out of life that I wanted or expected—it's all been so different
from the way I thought it was—I've had nothing—no fame, no glory,
no success, no children—everything has gone—Papa is all that I have
left! If he dies what shall I do?" she cried frantically, shaking him by
the sleeve. "That old man is all I've got—the only thing I've got left to
live for; to keep him alive, to make him comfortable, to ease his pain, to
see he gets good food and attention—somehow, somehow," she panted
desperately, clasping her big bony hands in a gesture of unconscious
but pitiable entreaty, and beginning to rock unsteadily on her feet as
she spoke—"somehow, somehow, to keep life in him, to keep him
here, not to let him go—that's all I've got to live for—what in the name
of God am I going to do when that is taken from me?"

And she paused, panting and exhausted by her tirade, her big face
strained and quivering, glaring at him with an air of frantic entreaty
as if it was in his power to give the answers to these frenzied questions.
And for a moment he said nothing; he just stood there looking at her
with the coarse and brutal stare of his blotched face, his venous yellowed
eyes, the wet cigarette stuck comically at the corner of one fat lip.

"What are you going to do?" he barked, presently. "You're going to
get hold of yourself—pull yourself together—amount to something,
be somebody!" He coughed chokingly to one side, for a moment there
was just the sound of his thick short breathing, then he flung the cigarette away, and said quietly:

"Helen, for God's sake, don't throw your life away! Don't destroy
the great creature that lies buried in you somewhere—wake it up, make
it come to life. Don't talk to me of this old man's life as if it were
your own——"

"It is, it is!" she said in a brooding tone of morbid fatality.

"It is not!" he said curtly, "unless you make it so—unless you play the
weakling and the fool and throw yourself away. For God's sake, don't

let that happen to you. I have seen it happen to so many people—some of them fine people like yourself, full of energy, imagination, intelligence, ability—all thrown away, frittered away like that," he flung fat fingers in the air—"because they did not have the guts to use what God had given them—to make a new life for themselves—to stand on their own feet and not to lean upon another's shoulder! . . . Don't die the death!" he rasped coarsely, staring at her with his brutal face. "Don't die the rotten, lousy, dirty death-in-life—the only death that's really horrible! For God's sake, don't betray life and yourself and the people who love you by dying that kind of death! I've seen it happen to so many people—and it was always so damned useless, such a rotten waste! That's what I was trying to say to you a few minutes ago—it's not the death of the dying that is terrible, it is the death of the living. And we always die that death for the same reason:—because our father dies, and takes from us his own life, his world, his time—and we haven't courage enough to make a new life, a new world for ourselves. I wonder if you know how often that thing happens—how often I have seen it happen—the wreck, the ruin, and the tragedy it has caused in life! When the father goes, the whole structure of the family life goes with him—and unless his children have the will, the stuff, the courage to make something of their own, they die, too. . . . With you, it's going to be very hard when your father dies; he was a man of great vitality and a strong personality who has left a deep impression on every one who knew him. And for seven years now, your father's death has been your life. . . . It has become a part of you, you have brooded over it, lived with it, soaked in it, been tainted by it—and now it is going to be hard for you to escape. But escape you must, and stand on your own feet—or you are lost. . . . Helen!" he barked sharply, and fixed her with his coarse and brutal stare—"listen to me:—your childhood, Woodson Street, getting your father over drunks, cooking for him, nursing him, feeding him, dressing and undressing him—I know about it all, I saw it all—and now!"—he paused, staring at her, then made a sudden gesture outward, palms downward, of his two thick hands—"over, done for, gone forever! It's no good any more, it won't work any more, it can't be brought back any more—forget about it!"

"Oh, I can't! I can't!" she said desperately. "I can't give him up—I can't let him go—he's all I've got. Doctor McGuire," she said earnestly, "ever since I was a kid of ten and you first came to get Papa over one of his sprees, I've fairly worshipped you! I've always felt down in my heart that you were one of the most wonderful people—the most wonderful doctor—in the world! I've always felt that at the end you could do anything—perform a miracle—bring him back. For God's sake, don't go back on me now! Do something—anything you can—but save him, save him."

He was silent for a moment, and just stared at her with his yellow, venous eyes. And when he spoke his voice was filled with the most quiet and utter weariness of despair that she had ever heard:

"Save him?" he said. "My poor child, I can save no one—nothing—least of all myself."

And suddenly she saw that it was true; she saw that he was lost, that he was done for, gone, and that he knew it. His coarse and bloated face was mottled by great black purplish patches, his yellow weary eyes already had the look of death in them; the knowledge of death rested with an unutterable weariness in his burly form, was audible in the short thick labor of his breath. She saw instantly that he was going to die, and with that knowledge her heart was torn with a rending pity as if a knife had been driven through it and twisted there; all of the brightness dropped out of the day, and in that moment it seemed that the whole substance and structure of her life was gone.

The day was a shining one, full of gold and sapphire and sparkle, and in the distance, toward the east, she could see the sweet familiar green of hills. She knew that nothing had been changed at all, and yet even the brightness of the day seemed dull and common to her. It served only to make more mean and shabby the rusty buildings and the street before her. And the bright light filled her with a nameless uneasiness and sense of shame: it seemed to expose her, to show her imperfections nakedly, and instinctively she turned away from it into the drugstore, where there were coolness, artificial lights and gaiety, the clamor of voices and people that she knew. And she knew that most of them had come here for the same reason—because the place gave them a sort of haven, however brief and shabby, from the naked brightness of the day and their sense of indefinable uncertitude and shame—because "it was the only place there was to go."

Several young people, two girls and a boy were coming down among the crowded tables towards one of the mirrored booths against the wall, where another boy and girl were waiting for them. As they approached, she heard their drawling voices, talking "cute nigger-talk" as her mind contemptuously phrased it, the vapid patter phrased to a monotonous formula of "charm," inane, cheap, completely vulgar, and as if they had been ugly little monsters of some world of dwarfs she listened to them with a detached perspective of dislike and scorn.

One of the girls—the one already in the booth—was calling to the others in tones of playful protest, in her "cute," mannered, empty little voice:

"*Hey,* theah, you all! *Wheah* you been! Come *on,* heah, man!" she cried urgently and reproachfully toward the approaching youth— "We been lookin' up an' down faw you! What you been doin', anyhow?" she cried with reproachful curiosity. "We been *waitin'* heah an' waitin' heah until it seemed lak you nevah *would* come! We wuh about to give you up!"

"Child!" another of the girls drawled back, and made a languid movement of the hand—a move indicative of resignation and defeat. "Don't tawk! I thought we nevah would get away. . . . That Jawdan woman came in to see Mothah just as me an' Jim was fixin' to go out, an' child!"—again the languid movement of exhaustion and defeat— "when that woman gits stahted tawkin' you might as well give up! No one else can git a wuhd in edgeways. I'll declayah!" the voice went up, and the hand again made its languid movement of surrender— "I nevah huhd the lak of it in all mah days! That's the tawkinest woman that evah lived. You'd a-died if you could a-seen the way Jim looked. I thought he was goin' to pass right out befoah we got away from theah!"

"Lady," said Jim, who had as yet taken no part in the conversation, "you *said* it! It sho'ly is the truth! That sho is *one* tawkin' woman— an' I don't mean *maybe,* eithah!" He drawled these words out with an air of pert facetiousness, and then looked round him with a complacent smirk on his young, smooth, empty face to see if his display of wit had been noticed and properly appreciated.

And Helen, passing by, kept smiling, plucking at her chin abstractedly, feeling toward these young people a weary disgust that was tinged with a bitter and almost personal animosity.

"Awful little made up girls . . . funny-looking little boys . . . nothing to do but hang out here and loaf . . . walk up and down the street . . . and drink coca-cola all day long . . . and to think it seemed so wonderful to me when I was a kid, to dress up and go up town and come in here where Papa was. . . . How dull and cheap and dreary it all is!"

XXII

A LITTLE after three o'clock one morning in June, Hugh McGuire was seated at his desk in the little office which stood just to the left of the entrance hall at the Altamont Hospital, of which institution he was chief of staff and principal owner. McGuire's burly bloated form was seated in a swivel chair and sprawled forward, his fat arms resting on the desk which was an old-fashioned roll-top affair with a number of small cubby-holes above and with two parallel rows of drawers below. In the space below the desk and between the surgeon's fat legs there was a gallon jug of corn whiskey.

And on the desk there was a stack of letters which had also been delivered to him the day before. The letters had been written to one of McGuire's own colleagues by a certain very beautiful lady of the town, of whom it is only necessary to say that she was not McGuire's wife and that he had known her for a long time. The huge man—curiously enough, not only a devoted father and a loyal husband, but a creature whose devotion to his family had been desperately intensified by the bitter sense of his one unfaith—had been for many years obsessed by one of those single, fatal and irremediable passions which great creatures of this sort feel only once in life, and for just one woman. Now the obsession of that mad fidelity was gone—exploded in an instant by a spidery scheme of words upon a page, a packet of torn letters in a woman's hand. Hence, this sense now of a stolid, slow, and cureless anguish in the man, the brutal deliberation of his drunkenness. Since finding these letters upon his desk when he had returned at seven o'clock the night before from his visit to Gant, McGuire had not left his office or moved in his chair, except to bend with a painful grunt from time to time, feel between his legs with a fat hand until he found the jug, and then, holding it with a bear-like solemnity between his paws, drink long and deep of the raw, fiery, and colorless liquid in the jug. He had done this very often, and now the jug was two-thirds empty. As he read, his mouth was half open and a cigarette was stuck on the corner of one fat lip, a look that suggested a comical drunken stupefaction. The hospital had long since gone to sleep, and in the little office there was no sound save the ticking of a clock and McGuire's short, thick, and stertorous breathing. Then when he had finished a letter, he would fold it carefully, put it back in its envelope, rub his thick fingers across the stubble of brown-reddish beard that covered his bloated and discolored face, reach with a painful grunt for the glass jug, drink, and open up another letter.

And from time to time he would put a letter down before he had finished reading it, take up a pen, and begin to write upon a sheet of broad hospital stationery, of which there was a pad upon the desk. And McGuire wrote as he read, slowly, painfully, carefully, with a fixed and drunken attentiveness, no sound except the minute and careful scratching of the pen in his fat hands, and the short, thick stertorous breathing as he bent over the tablet, his cigarette plastered comically at the edge of one fat lip.

McGuire would read the letters over and over, slowly, carefully, and solemnly. Burly, motionless and with no sound save for the short and stertorous labor of his breath he stared with drunken fixity at the pages which he held close before his yellowed eyes, his bloated face. He had read each letter at least a dozen times during the course of the long evening. And each time that he finished reading it, he would fold it carefully with his thick fingers, put it back into its envelope, bend and reach down between his fat legs with a painful grunt, fumble for the liquor jug, and then drink long and deep.

It seemed that a red-hot iron had been driven through his heart and twisted there; the liquor burned in his blood and guts like fire; and each time that he had finished reading that long letter, he would grunt, reach for the jug again, and then slowly and painfully begin to scrawl some words down on the pad before him.

He had done this at least a dozen times that night, and each time after a few scrawled lines, he would grunt impatiently, wad the paper up into a crumpled ball and throw it into the waste-paper basket at his side. Now, a little after three o'clock in the morning, he was writing steadily; there was no sound now in the room save for the man's thick short breathing, and the minute scratching of his pen across the paper. An examination of these wadded balls of paper, however, in the order in which they had been written, would have revealed perfectly the successive states of feeling in the man's spirit.

The first, which was written after his discovery of the letters, was just a few scrawled words without punctuation or grammatical coherence, ending abruptly in an explosive splintered movement of the pen, and read simply and expressively as follows:

"You bitch you damned dirty trollop of a lying whore you——"

And this ended here in an explosive scrawl of splintered ink, and had been wadded up and thrown away into the basket.

XXIII

HELEN had lain awake for hours in darkness, in a strange comatose state of terror and hallucination. There was no sound save the sound of Barton's breathing beside her, but in her strange drugged state she would imagine she heard all kinds of sounds. And she lay there in the dark, her eyes wide open, wide awake, plucking at her large cleft chin abstractedly, in a kind of drugged hypnosis, thinking like a child:

"What is that? . . . Some one is coming! . . . That was a car that stopped outside. . . . Now they're coming up the steps. . . . There's some one knocking at the door. . . . Oh, my God! . . . It's about Papa! . . . He's had another attack, they've come to get me . . . he's dead! . . . Hugh! Hugh! Wake up!" she said hoarsely, and seized him by the arm. And he woke, his sparse hair tousled, grumbling sleepily.

"Hugh! Hugh!" she whispered. "It's Papa—he's dying . . . they're at the door now! . . . oh, for heaven's sake, get up!" she almost screamed, in a state of frenzied despair and exasperation. "Aren't you good for anything! . . . Don't lie there like a dummy—Papa may be dying! Get up! Get up! There's some one at the door! My God, you can at least go and find out what it is! Oh, get up, get up, I tell you! . . . Don't leave everything to me! You're a man—you can at least do that much!" —and by now her voice was almost sobbing with exasperation.

"Well, *all* right, *all* right!" he grumbled in a tone of protest, "I'm going! Only give me a moment to find my slippers and my bath-robe, won't you?"

And, hair still twisted, tall, bony, thin to emaciation, he felt around with his bare feet until he found his slippers, stepped gingerly into them, and put on his bath-robe, tying the cord around his waist, and looking himself over in the mirror carefully, smoothing down his rumpled hair and making a shrugging motion of the shoulders. And she looked at him with a tortured and exasperated glare, saying:

"Oh, slow, slow, slow! . . . My God, you're the slowest thing that ever lived! . . . I could walk from here to California in the time it takes you to get out of bed."

"Well, *I'm* going, *I'm* going," he said again with surly protest. "I don't want to go to the front door naked—only give me a minute to get ready, won't you?"

"Then, go, go, go!" she almost screamed at him. "They've been there for fifteen minutes.... They're almost hammering the door down—for God's sake go and find out if they've come because of Papa, I beg of you."

And he went hastily, still preserving a kind of dignity as he stepped along gingerly in his bath-robe and thin pyjamaed legs. And when he got to the door, there was no one, nothing there. The street outside was bare and empty, the houses along the street dark and hushed with their immense and still attentiveness of night and silence and the sleepers, the trees were standing straight and lean with their still young leafage—and he came back again growling surlily.

"Ah-h, there's no one there! You didn't hear anything! . . . You imagined the whole thing!"

And for a moment her eyes had a dull appeased look, she plucked at her large cleft chin and said in an abstracted tone: "Ah-hah! . . . Well, come on back to bed, honey, and get some sleep."

"Ah, get some sleep!" he growled, scowling angrily as he took off his robe—and scuffed the slippers from his feet. "What chance do I have to get any sleep any more with you acting like a crazy woman half the time?"

She snickered hoarsely and absently, still plucking at her chin, as he lay down beside her; she kissed him, and put her arms around him with a mothering gesture:

"Well, I know, Hugh," she said quietly, "you've had a hard time of it, but someday we will get away from it and live our own life. I know you didn't marry the whole damn family—but just try to put up with it a little longer: Papa has not got long to live, he's all alone over there in that old house—and she can't realize—she doesn't understand that he is dying—she'll never wake up to the fact until he's gone! I lie here at night thinking about it—and I can't go to sleep . . . I get funny notions in my head." As she spoke these words the dull strained look came into her eyes again, and her big-boned generous face took on the warped outline of hysteria— "You know, I get queer." She spoke the word in a puzzled and baffled way, the dull strained look becoming more pronounced— "I think of him over there all alone in that old house, and then I think they're coming for me—" she spoke the word "they" in this same baffled and puzzled tone, as if she did not clearly understand who "they" were— "I think the telephone is ringing, or that some one is coming up the steps and then I hear them knocking at the door, and then I hear them talking to me, telling me to come quick, he needs me—

and then I hear him calling to me 'Baby! Oh, baby—come quick, baby, for Jesus' sake!' "

"You've been made the goat," he muttered, "you've got to bear the whole burden on your shoulders. You're cracking up under the strain. If they don't leave you alone I'm going to take you away from here."

"Do you think it's right?" she demanded in a frenzied tone again, responding thirstily to his argument. "Why, good heavens, Hugh! I've got a right to my own life the same as anybody else. Don't you think I have? I married *you!*" she cried, as if there were some doubt of the fact. "I wanted a home of my own, children, my own life—good heavens, we have a right to that just the same as any one else! Don't you think we have?"

"Yes," he said grimly, "and I'm going to see we get it. I'm tired of seeing you made the victim! If they don't give you some peace or quiet we'll move away from this town."

"Oh, it's not that I mind doing it for Papa," she said more quietly. "Good heavens, I'll do anything to make that poor old man happier. If only the rest of them—well, honey," she said, breaking off abruptly, "let's forget about it! It's too bad you've got to go through all this now, but it won't last forever. After Papa is gone, we'll get away from it. Some day we'll have a chance to lead our own lives together."

"Oh, it's all right about me, dear," the man said quietly, speaking the word "dear" in the precise and nasal way Ohio people have. He was silent for a moment, and when he spoke again, his lean seamed face and care-worn eyes were quietly eloquent with the integrity of devotion and loyalty that was of the essence of his life. "I don't mind it for myself—only I hate to see you get yourself worked up to this condition. I'm afraid you'll crack under the strain: that's all I care about."

"Well, forget about it. It can't be helped. Just try to make the best of it. Now go on back to sleep, honey, and try to get some rest before you have to get up."

And returning her kiss, with an obedient and submissive look on his lean face, he said quietly, "Good night, dear," turned over on his side and closed his eyes.

She turned the light out, and now again there was nothing but darkness, silence, the huge still hush and secrecy of night, her husband's quiet breath of sleep as he lay beside her. And again she could not sleep, but lay there plucking absently at her large cleft chin, her eyes open, turned upward into darkness in a stare of patient, puzzled, and abstracted thought.

XXIV

For a long time now, McGuire had sat there without moving, sprawled out upon the desk in a kind of drunken stupor. About half-past three the telephone upon the desk began to ring, jangling the hospital silence with its ominous and insistent clangor, but the big burly figure of the man did not stir, he made no move to answer. Presently he heard the brisk heel-taps of Creasman, the night superintendent, coming along the heavy oiled linoleum of the corridor. She entered, glanced quickly at him, and saying, "Shall I take it?" picked up the phone, took the receiver from its hook, said "hello" and listened for a moment. He did not move.

In a moment, the night superintendent said quietly:

"Yes, I'll ask him."

When she spoke to him, however, her tone had changed completely from the cool professional courtesy of her speech into the telephone: putting the instrument down upon the top of the desk, and covering the mouth-piece with her hand, she spoke quietly to him, but with a note of cynical humor in her voice, bold, coarse, a trifle mocking.

"It's your wife," she said. "What shall I tell her?"

He regarded her stupidly for a moment before he answered.

"What does she want?" he grunted.

She looked at him with hard eyes touched with pity and regret.

"What do you think a woman wants?" she said. "She wants to know if you are coming home tonight."

He stared at her, and then grunted:

"Won't go home."

She took her hand away from the mouth-piece instantly, and taking up the phone again, spoke smoothly, quietly, with cool crisp courtesy:

"The doctor will not be able to go home tonight, Mrs. McGuire. He has to operate at seven-thirty. . . . Yes. . . . Yes. . . . At seven-thirty. . . . He has decided it is best to stay here until the operation is over. . . . Yes. . . . I'll tell him. . . . Thank *you*. . . . Good-bye."

She hung up quietly and then turning to him, her hands arched cleanly on starched hips, she looked at him for a moment with a bold sardonic humor.

"What did she say?" he mumbled thickly.

"Nothing," she said quietly. "Nothing at all. What else is there to say?"

He made no answer but just kept staring at her in his bloated drunken way with nothing but the numb swelter of that irremediable anguish in his heart. In a moment, her voice hardening imperceptibly, the nurse spoke quietly again:

"Oh, yes—and I forgot to tell you—you had another call tonight."

He moistened his thick lips, and mumbled:

"Who was it?"

"It was that woman of yours."

There was no sound save the stertorous labor of his breath; he stared at her with his veined and yellowed eyes, and grunted stolidly:

"What did she want?"

"She wanted to know if the doc-taw was theah," Creasman said in a coarse and throaty parody of refinement. "And is he coming in tonight? Really, I should like to know. . . . Ooh, yaas," Creasman went on throatily, adding a broad stroke or two on her own account. "I simply must find out! I cawn't get my sleep in until I do. . . . Well," she demanded harshly, "what am I going to tell her if she calls again?"

"What did she say to tell me?"

"She said"—the nurse's tone again was lewdly tinged with parody—"to tell you that she is having guests for dinner tomorrow night—this evening—and that you simply *got* to be thöh, you, and your wife, too—ooh, Gawd, yes!—the Reids are comin', don't-cherknow—and if you are not thöh Gawd only knows what will happen!"

He glowered at her drunkenly for a moment, and then, waving thick fingers at her in disgust, he mumbled:

"You got a dirty mouth . . . don't become you. . . . Unlady-like. . . . Don't like a dirty-talkin' woman. . . . Never did. . . . Unbecomin'. . . . Unlady-like. . . . Nurses all alike . . . all dirty talkers . . . don't like 'em."

"Oh, dirty talkers, your granny!" she said coarsely. "Now you leave the nurses alone. . . . They're decent enough girls, most of 'em, until they come here and listen to you for a month or two. . . . You listen to me, Hugh McGuire; don't blame the nurses. When it comes to dirty talking, you can walk off with the medals any day in the week. . . . Even if I am your cousin, I had a good Christian raising out in the country before I came here. So don't talk to me about nurses' dirty talk: after a few sessions with you in the operating room even the Virgin Mary could use language fit to make a monkey blush. So don't blame it on the nurses. Most of them are white as snow compared to you."

"You're dirty talkers—all of you," he muttered, waving his thick fingers in her direction. "Don't like it.... Unbecomin' in a lady."

For a moment she did not answer, but stood looking at him, arms akimbo on her starched white hips, a glance that was bold, hard, sardonic, but somehow tinged with a deep and broad affection.

Then, taking her hands off her hips, she bent swiftly over him, reached down between his legs, and got the jug and lifting it up to the light in order to make her cynical inspection of its depleted contents more accurate, she remarked with ironic approbation:

"My, my! You're doing pretty well, aren't you? ... Well, it won't be long *now,* will it?" she said cheerfully, and then turning to him abruptly and accusingly, demanded:

"Do you realize that you were supposed to call Helen Gant at twelve o'clock?" She glanced swiftly at the clock. "Just three and a half hours ago. Or did you forget it?"

He passed his thick hand across the reddish unshaved stubble of his beard.

"Who?" he said stupidly. "Where? What is it?"

"Oh, nothing to worry about," she said with a light hard humor. "Just a little case of carcinoma of the prostate. He's going to die anyway, so you've got nothing to worry about at all."

"Who?" he said stupidly again. "Who is it?"

"Oh, just a man," she said gaily. "An old, old man named Mr. Gant.— You've been his physician for twenty years, but maybe you've forgotten him. You know—they come and go; some live and others die—it's all right,—this one's going to die. They'll bury him—it'll all come out right one way or the other—so you've nothing to worry about at all.... Even if you kill him," she said cheerfully. "He's just an old, old man with cancer, and bound to die anyway, so promise me you won't worry about it too much, will you?"

She looked at him a moment longer; then, putting her hand under his fat chin, she jerked his head up sharply. He stared at her stupidly with his yellowed drunken eyes, and in them she saw the mute anguish of a tortured animal, and suddenly her heart was twisted with pity for him.

"Look here," she said, in a hard and quiet voice, "what's wrong with you?"

In a moment he mumbled thickly:

"Nothing's wrong with me."

"Is it the woman business again? For God's sake, are you never going to grow up, McGuire? Are you going to remain an overgrown school-boy all your life? Are you going to keep on eating your heart out over a bitch who thinks that spring is here every time her hind end itches? Are you going to throw your life away, and let your work go to smash because some damned woman in the change of life has done you dirt! What kind of man are you, anyway?" she jeered. "Jesus God! If it's a woman that you want the woods are full of 'em. Besides," she added, "what's wrong with your own wife! She's worth a million of those flossy sluts."

He made no answer and in a moment she went on in a harsh and jeering tone that was almost deliberately coarse:

"Haven't you learned yet, with all you've seen of it, that a piece of tail is just a piece of tail, and that in the dark it doesn't matter one good God-damn whether it's brown, black, white, or yellow?"

Even as she spoke, something cold and surgical in his mind, which no amount of alcohol seemed to dull or blur, was saying accurately: "Why do they all feel such contempt for one another? What is it in them that makes them despise themselves?"

Aloud, however, waving his thick fingers at her in a gesture of fat disgust, he said:

"Creasman, you got a dirty tongue. . . . Don't like to hear a woman talk like that. . . . Never liked to hear a dirty-talkin' woman. . . . You're no lady!"

"Ah-h! No lady!" she said bitterly, and let her hands fall in a ges-ture of defeat. "All right, you poor fool, if that's the way you feel about it, go ahead and drink yourself to death over your 'lady.' That's what's wrong with you."

And, muttering angrily, she left him. He sat there stupidly, without moving, until her firm heel-taps had receded down the silent hall, and he heard a door close. Then he reached down between his knees, and got the jug, and drank again. And again there was nothing in the place ex-cept the sound of silence, the rapid ticking of a little clock, the thick short breathing of the man.

XXV

SOMEWHERE, far away, across the cool sweet silence of the night, Helen heard the sound of a train. For a moment she could hear the faint and ghostly tolling of its bell, the short explosive blasts of its hard labor, now muted almost into silence, now growing near, immediate as it labored out across the night from the enclosure of a railway cut down by the river's edge; and for an instant she heard the lonely wailing and receding cry of the train's whistle, and then the long heavy rumble of its wheels; and then nothing but silence, darkness, the huge hush and secrecy of night again.

And still plucking at her chin, thinking absently, but scarcely conscious of her thinking, like a child in revery, she thought:

"There is a freight-train going west along the river. Now, by the sound, it should be passing below Patton Hill, just across from where Riverside Park used to be before the flood came and washed it all away. . . . Now it is getting farther off, across the river from the casket factory. . . . Now it is almost gone, I can hear nothing but the sound of wheels . . . it is going west toward Boiling Springs . . . and after that it will come to Wilson City, Tennessee . . . and then to Dover. . . . Knoxville . . . Memphis—after that? I wonder where the train is going . . . where it will be tomorrow night? . . . Perhaps across the Mississippi River, and then on through Arkansas . . . perhaps to St. Louis . . . and then on to—what comes next?" she thought absently, plucking at her chin—"to Kansas City, I suppose . . . and then to Denver . . . and across the Rocky Mountains . . . and across the desert . . . and then across more mountains and then at last to California."

And still plucking at her chin, and scarcely conscious of her thought —not *thinking* indeed so much as reflecting by a series of broken but powerful images all cogent to a central intuition about life—her mind resumed again its sleepless patient speculation:

"How strange and full of mystery life is. . . . Tomorrow we shall all get up, dress, go out on the streets, see and speak to one another—and yet we shall know absolutely nothing about any one else. . . . I know almost every one in town—the bankers, the lawyers, the butchers, the bakers, the grocers, the clerks in the stores, the Greek restaurant man, Tony Scarsati the fruit dealer, even the niggers down in Niggertown— I know them all, as well as their wives and children—where they came from, what they are doing, all the lies and scandals and jokes and mean stories, whether true or false, that are told about them—and yet I really know nothing about any of them. I know nothing about any one, not even about myself—" and suddenly, this fact seemed terrible and grotesque to her, and she thought desperately:

"What is wrong with people? ... Why do we never get to know one another? ... Why is it that we get born and live and die here in this world without ever finding out what any one else is like? ... No, what is the strangest thing of all—why is it that all our efforts to know people in this world lead only to greater ignorance and confusion than before? We get together and talk, and say we think and feel and believe in such a way, and yet what we really think and feel and believe we never say at all. Why is this? We talk and talk in an effort to understand another person, and yet almost all we say is false: we hardly ever say what we mean or tell the truth—it all leads to greater misunderstanding and fear than before—it would be better if we said nothing. Tomorrow I shall dress and go out on the street and bow and smile and flatter people, laying it on with a trowel, because I want them to like me, I want to make 'a good impression,' to be a 'success'—and yet I have no notion what it is all about. When I pass Judge Junius Pearson on the street, I will smile and bow, and try to make a good impression on him, and if he speaks to me I shall almost fawn upon him in order to flatter my way into his good graces. Why? I do not like him, I hate his long pointed nose, and the sneering and disdainful look upon his face: I think he is 'looking down' on me—but I know that he goes with the 'swell' social set and is invited out to all the parties at Catawba House by Mrs. Goulderbilt and is received by them as a social equal. And I feel that if Junius Pearson should accept me as *his* social equal it would help me— get me forward somehow—make me a success—get *me* an invitation to Catawba House. And yet it would get me nothing; even if I were Mrs. Goulderbilt's closest friend, what good would it do me? But the people I really like and feel at home with are working people of Papa's kind. The people I really like are Ollie Gant, and old man Alec Ramsay, and big Mike Fogarty, and Mr. Jannadeau, and Myrtis, my little nigger servant girl, and Mr. Luther, the fish man down in the market, and the nigger Jacken, the fruit and vegetable man, and Ernest Pegram, and Mr. Duncan and the Tarkintons—all the old neighbors down on Woodson Street—and Tony Scarsati and Mr. Pappas. Mr. Pappas is just a Greek lunchroom proprietor, but he seems to me to be one of the finest people I have ever known, and yet if Junius Pearson saw me talking to him I should try to make a joke out of it—to make a joke out of talking to a Greek who runs a restaurant. In the same way, when some of my new friends see me talking to people like Mr. Jannadeau or Mike Fogarty or Ollie or Ernest Pegram or the Tarkintons or the old Woodson Street crowd, I feel ashamed or embarrassed, and turn it off as a big joke. I laugh about Mr. Jannadeau and his dirty fingers and the way he picks his nose, and old Alec Ramsay and Ernest Pegram spitting tobacco while they talk, and then I wind up by appearing to be democratic and saying in a frank and open manner— 'Well, I like them ... I don't care what any one says' (when no one has said anything!), 'I like them, and always have. If the truth is told, they're just as good as any one else!'—as if there is any doubt about it, and as if I should have to justify myself for being 'democratic.' Why 'democratic'? Why should I apologize or defend myself for liking people when no one has accused me?

"I'm pushing Hugh ahead now all the time; he's tired and sick and worn-out and exhausted—but I keep 'pushing him ahead' without knowing what it is we're pushing ahead toward, where it will all wind up. What is it all about? I've pushed him ahead from Woodson Street up here to Weaver Street: and now this neighborhood has become old-fashioned—the swell society crowd is all moving out to Grovemont—opposite the golf-course; and now I'm pushing him to move out there, build upon the lot we own, or buy a house. I've 'pushed' him and myself until now he belongs to the Rotary Club, and I belong to the Thursday Literary Club, the Orpheus Society, the Saturday Musical Guild, the Woman's Club, the Discussion Group, and God knows what else—all these silly and foolish little clubs in which we have no interest—and yet it would kill us if we did not belong to them, we feel that they are a sign that we are 'getting ahead.' Getting ahead to what?

"And it is the same with all of us: pretend, pretend, pretend—show-off, show-off, show-off—try to keep up with the neighbors and to go ahead of them—and never a word of truth; never a word of what we really feel, and understand and know. The one who shouts the loudest goes the farthest:—Mrs. Richard Jeter Ebbs sits up on top of the whole heap, she goes everywhere and makes speeches; people say 'Mrs. Richard Jeter Ebbs said so-and-so'—and all because she shouts out everywhere that she is a lady and a member of an old family and the widow of Richard Jeter Ebbs. And no one in town ever met Richard Jeter Ebbs, they don't know who he was, what he did, where he came from; neither do they know who Mrs. Richard Jeter Ebbs was, or where she came from, or who or what her family was.

"Why are we all so false, cowardly, cruel, and disloyal toward one another and toward ourselves? Why do we spend our days in doing useless things, in false-pretense and triviality? Why do we waste our lives—exhaust our energy—throw everything good away on falseness and lies and emptiness? Why do we deliberately destroy ourselves this way, when we want joy and love and beauty and it is all around us in the world if we would only take it? Why are we so afraid and ashamed when there is really nothing to be afraid and ashamed of? Why have we wasted everything, thrown our lives away, what is this horrible thing in life that makes us throw ourselves away—to hunt out death when what we want is life? Why is it that we are always strangers in this world, and never come to know one another, and are full of fear and shame and hate and falseness, when what we want is love? Why is it? Why? Why? Why?"

And with that numb horror of disbelief and silence and the dark about her, in her, filling her, it seemed to her suddenly that there was some monstrous and malevolent force in life that held all mankind in its spell and that compelled men to destroy themselves against their will. It seemed to her that everything in life—the things men did and said, the way they acted—was grotesque, perverse, and accidental, that there was no reason for anything.

A thousand scenes from her whole life, seen now with the terrible detachment of a spectator, and dark and sombre with the light of time, swarmed through her mind: she saw herself as a child of ten, hanging on grimly to her father, a thin fury of a little girl, during his sprees of howling drunkenness—slapping him in the face to make him obey her, feeding him hot soup, undressing him, sending for McGuire, "sobering him up" and forcing him to obey her when no one else could come near him. And she saw herself later, a kind of slavey at her mother's boarding house in St. Louis during the World's Fair, drudging from morn to night, a grain of human dust, an atom thrust by chance into the great roar of a distant city, or on an expedition as blind, capricious, and fatally mistaken as all life. Later, she saw herself as a girl in high school, she remembered her dreams and hopes, the pitiably mistaken innocence of her vision of the world; her grand ambitions to "study music," to follow a "career in grand opera"; later still, a girl of eighteen or twenty, amorous of life, thirsting for the great cities and voyages of the world, playing popular songs of the period— "Love Me and the World Is Mine," "I Wonder Who's Kissing Her Now," "Till the Sands of the Desert Grow Cold," and so on—for her father, as he sat, on summer evenings, on his porch; a little later, "touring" the little cities of the

South, singing and playing the popular "rhythm" and sentimental bal-
lads of the period in vaudeville and moving-picture houses. She remembered how she had once been invited to a week-end house party
with a dozen other young men and women of her acquaintance, and of
how she had been afraid to go, and how desperately ashamed she was
when she had "to go in swimming" with the others, and to "show her
figure," her long skinny legs, even when they were concealed by the
clumsy bathing dress and the black stockings of the period. She remembered her marriage then, the first years of her life with Barton,
her tragic failure to have children, and the long horror of Gant's last
years of sickness—the years of sombre waiting, the ever-impending terror of his death.

A thousand scenes from this past life flashed through her mind now,
as she lay there in the darkness, and all of them seemed grotesque, accidental and mistaken, as reasonless as everything in life.

And filled with a numb, speechless feeling of despair and nameless terror, she heard, somewhere across the night, the sound of a train again,
and thought:

"My God! My God! What is life about? We are all lying here in
darkness in ten thousand little towns—waiting, listening, hoping—for
what?"

And suddenly, with a feeling of terrible revelation, she saw the
strangeness and mystery of man's life; she felt about her in the darkness
the presence of ten thousand people, each lying in his bed, naked and
alone, united at the heart of night and darkness, and listening, as she, to
the sounds of silence and of sleep. And suddenly it seemed to her that she
knew all these lonely, strange, and unknown watchers of the night, that
she was speaking to them, and they to her, across the fields of sleep, as
they had never spoken before, that she knew men now in all their dark
and naked loneliness, without falseness and pretense as she had never
known them. And it seemed to her that if men would only listen in the
darkness, and send the language of their naked lonely spirits across the
silence of the night, all of the error, falseness and confusion of their
lives would vanish, they would no longer be strangers, and each would
find the life he sought and never yet had found.

"If we only could!" she thought. "If we only could!"

Then, as she listened, there was nothing but the huge hush of night
and silence, and far away the whistle of a train. Suddenly the phone
rang.

XXVI

A FEW minutes after four o'clock that morning as McGuire lay there sprawled upon his desk, the phone rang again. And again he made no move to answer it: he just sat there, sprawled out on his fat elbows, staring stupidly ahead. Creasman came in presently, as the telephone continued to disturb the silence of the hospital with its electric menace and this time, without a glance at him, answered.

It was Luke Gant. At four o'clock his father had had another hemorrhage, he had lost consciousness, all efforts to awaken him had failed, they thought he was dying.

The nurse listened carefully for a moment to Luke's stammering and excited voice, which was audible across the wire even to McGuire. Then, with a troubled and uncertain glance toward the doctor's sprawled and drunken figure, she said quietly:

"Just a minute. I don't know if the doctor is in the hospital. I'll see if I can find him."

Putting her hand over the mouthpiece, keeping her voice low, she spoke urgently to McGuire:

"It's Luke Gant. He says his father has had another hemorrhage and that they can't rouse him. He wants you to come at once. What shall I tell him?"

He stared drunkenly at her for a moment, and then waving his finger at her in a movement of fat impatience, he mumbled thickly:

"Nothing to do. . . . No use . . . . Can't be stopped. . . . People expect miracles. . . . Over. . . . Done for. . . . Tell him I'm not here . . . gone home," he muttered, and sprawled forward on the desk again.

Quietly, coolly, the nurse spoke into the phone again:

"The doctor doesn't seem to be here at the hospital, Mr. Gant. Have you tried his house? I think you may find him at home."

"No, G-g-g-god-damn it!" Luke fairly screamed across the wire. "He's not at home. I've already t-t-tried to get him there. . . . N-n-n-now you look here, Miss Creasman!" Luke shouted angrily. "You c-c-can't kid me: I know where he is— He's d-d-down there at the hospital right now—wy-wy-wy—stinkin' drunk! You t-t-tell him, G-g-g-god-damn his soul, that if he d-d-doesn't come, wy-wy-wy—P-p-p-papa's in a bad way and and and f-f-frankly, I f'ink it's a rotten shame for McGuire to act this way, wy-wy-wy after he's b-b-been Papa's doctor all these years. F-f-frankly, I do!"

"Nothing to be done," mumbled McGuire. "No use. . . . All over."

"I'll see what I can do, Mr. Gant," said Creasman quietly. "I'll let the doctor know as soon as he comes in!"

"C-c-c-comes in, hell!" Luke stammered bitterly. "I'm c-c-comin' down there myself and g-g-get him if I have to wy wy wy d-d-drag him here by the s-s-scruff of his neck!" And he hung up the receiver with a bang.

The nurse put the phone down on the desk, and turning to McGuire, said:

"He's raving. He says if you don't go, he'll come for you and get you himself. Can't you pull yourself together enough to go? If you can't drive the car, I'll send Joe along to drive it for you—" Joe was a negro orderly in the hospital.

"What's the use?" McGuire mumbled thickly, a little angrily. "What the hell do these people expect anyway? . . I'm a doctor, not a miracle man. . . . The man's gone, I tell you . . . the whole gut and rectum is eaten away . . . he can't live over a day or two longer at the most. . . . It's cruelty to prolong it: why the hell should I try to?"

"All right," she said resignedly. "Do as you please. Only, he'll probably be here for you himself in a few minutes. And since they do feel that way about it, I think you might make the effort just to please them."

"Ah-h," he muttered wearily. "People are all alike. . . . They all want miracles."

"Are you just going to sit here all night?" she said with a rough kindliness. "Aren't you going to try to get a little sleep before you operate?"

He waved fat fingers at her, and did not look at her.

"Leave me alone," he mumbled; and she left him.

When she had gone, he fumbled for the jug and drank again. And then, while time resumed its sanded drip, and he sat there in the silence, he thought again of the old dying man whom he had known first when he was a young doctor just beginning and with whom his own life had been united by so many strange and poignant memories. And thinking of Gant, the strangeness of the human destiny returned to haunt his mind; there was something that he could not speak, a wonder and a mystery he could not express.

He fumbled for the jug again, and holding it solemnly in his bearish paws, drained it. Then he sat for several minutes without moving. Finally, he got up out of his chair, grunting painfully, and fumbling for the walls, lurched out into the hall, and began to grope his way across the corridor toward the stairs. And the first step fooled him as it had done so many time before; he missed his step, even as a man stepping out in emptiness might miss, and came down heavily upon his knees. Then, pushing with his hands, he slid out peacefully on the oiled green linoleum, pillowed his big head on his arms with a comfortable grunt, and sprawled out flat, already half dead to the world. It was in this position—also a familiar one—that Creasman, who had heard his thump when falling, found him. And she spoke sharply and commandingly as one might speak to a little child:

"You get right up off that floor and march upstairs," she said. "If you want to sleep you're going to your room; you'll not disgrace us sleeping on that floor."

And like a child, as he had done so many times before, he obeyed her. In a moment, as her sharp command reached his drugged consciousness, he grunted, stirred, climbed painfully to his knees, and then, pawing carefully before him like a bear, unable or unwilling to stand up, he began to crawl slowly up the stairs.

And it was in this position, half-way up, pawing his burly and cumbersome way on hands and knees, that Luke Gant found him. Cursing bitterly, and stammering with wild excitement, the young man pulled him to his feet, Creasman sponged off the great bloated face with a cold towel and assisted by Joe Corpering, the negro man, they got him down the stairs and out of the hospital into Luke's car.

Dawn was just breaking, a faint glimmer of blue-silver light, with the still purity of the earth, the sweet fresh stillness of the trees, the bird-song waking. The fresh sweet air, Luke's breakneck driving through the silent streets, the roaring motor—finally, the familiar and powerfully subdued emotion of a death chamber, the repressed hysteria, the pain and tension and the terror of shocked flesh, the aura of focal excitement around the dying man revived McGuire.

Gant lay still and almost lifeless on the bed, his face already tinged with the ghostly shade of death, his breath low, hoarse, faintly rattling, his eyes half-closed, comatose, already glazed with death.

McGuire sighted at his shining needle, and thrust a powerful injection of caffeine, sodium, and benzoate into the arm of the dying man. This served partially to revive him, got him through the low ebb of the dark, his eyes opened, cleared, he spoke again. Bright day and morning came, and Gant still lived. And with the light, their impossible and frenzied hopes came back again, as they have always been revived in desperate men. And Gant did not die that day. He lived on.

XXVII

By the middle of the month Gant had a desperate attack; for four days now he was confined to bed, he began to bleed out of the bowels, he spent four sleepless days and nights of agony, and with the old terror of death awake again and urgent, Helen telegraphed to Luke, who was in Atlanta, frantically imploring him to come home at once.

With the arrival of his son and under the stimulation of Luke's vital and hopeful nature, the old man revived somewhat: they got him out of bed, and into a new wheel-chair which they had bought for the purpose, and the day of his arrival Luke wheeled his father out into the bright June sunshine, and through the streets of the town, where he again saw friends, and renewed acquaintances he had not known in years.

The next day Gant seemed better. He ate a good breakfast, by ten o'clock he was up and Luke had dressed him, got him into the new wheel-chair and was wheeling him out on the streets again in the bright sunshine. All along the streets of the town people stopped and greeted the old man and his son, and in Gant's weary old brain there may perhaps have been a flicker of an old hope, a feeling that he had come to life again.

"Wy-wy-wy-wy, he's f-f-f-fine as silk!" Luke would sing out in answer to the question of some old friend or acquaintance, before his father had a chance to answer. "Aren't you, C-C-C-Colonel? Wy-wy-wy-wy Lord God! Mr. P-p-p-parker, you couldn't k-k-k-kill him with a wy wy wy wy wy with a b-b-butcher's cleaver. He'll be here when you and I bofe are p-p-p-pushing daisies." And Gant, pleased, would smile feebly, puffing from time to time at a cigar in the unaccustomed, clumsy, and pitifully hopeful way sick men have.

Towards one o'clock Gant began to moan with pain again, and to entreat his son to make haste and take him home. When they got back before the house, Luke brought the wheel chair to a stop, and helped his father to get up. His stammering solicitude and over-extravagant offers of help served only to exasperate and annoy the old man who, still moaning feebly, and sniffling with trembling lip, said petulantly:

"No, no, no. Just leave me alone to try to get a moment's peace, I beg of you, I ask you, for Jesus' sake."

"Wy-wy-wy-wy, all right, P-p-p-papa," Luke stammered with earnest cheerfulness. "Wy-wy-wy, you're the d-d-d-doctor. Wy-wy, I'll just wheel the chair up on the porch and then I'll c-c-come back to your room and f-f-f-fix you up in a j-j-j-j-jiffy."

. "Oh, Jesus, I don't care what you do. . . . Do what you like," Gant moaned. "I'm in agony. . . . O Jesus!" he wept. "It's fearful, it's awful, it's cruel—just leave me alone, I beg of you," he sniffled.

"Wy-wy-wy, yes, sir, P-p-p-papa—wy, you're the doctor," Luke said. "Can you make it by yourself all right?" he said anxiously, as his father, leaning heavily upon his cane, started up the stone steps toward the walk that led up to the house.

"Why, yes, now, son," Eliza, who had heard their voices and come out on the porch, now said diplomatically, seeing that Luke's well-meant but stammering solicitude had begun to irritate his father. "Mr. Gant doesn't want any help—you put the car up, son, and leave him alone, he's able to manage all right by himself."

And Luke, muttering respectfully, "Wy-wy-wy, yes, sir, P-p-p-papa, you're the d-d-doctor," stopped then, lifted the chair up to the walk, and began to push it toward the house, not however without a troubled glance at the old man who was walking slowly and feebly toward the porch steps. And for a moment, Eliza stood surveying them and then turned, to stand looking at her house reflectively before she entered it again, her hands clasped loosely at her waist, her lips pursed in a strong reflective expression in which the whole pride of possession, her living and inseparable unity with this gaunt old house, was powerfully evident.

It was at this moment while she stood planted there upon the sidewalk looking at the house, that the thing happened. Gant, still moaning feebly to himself, had almost reached the bottom of the steps when suddenly he staggered, a scream of pain and horror was torn from him; in that instant, the walking cane fell with a clatter to the concrete walk, his two great hands went down to his groin in a pitiable clutching gesture and crying out loudly: "O Jesus! Save me! Save me!" he fell to his knees, still clutching at his entrails with his mighty hands.

Even before Eliza got to him, her flesh turned rotten at the sight. Blood was pouring from him; the bright arterial blood was already running out upon the concrete walk, the heavy black cloth of Gant's trousers was already sodden, turning purplish with the blood; the blood streamed through his fingers, covering his great hands. He was bleeding to death through the genital organs.

Eliza rushed toward him at a strong clumsy gait; she tried to lift him, he was too big for her to handle, and she screamed to Luke for help. He came at once, running at top speed across the yard and, scarcely pausing in his stride, he picked up Gant's great figure in his arms—it felt as light and fleshless as a bundle of dry sticks—and turning to his mother, said curtly:

"Call Helen! Quick! I'll take him to his room and get his clothes off."

And holding the old man as if he were a child, he fairly raced up the steps and down the hall, leaving a trail of blood behind him as he went.

Eliza, scarcely conscious of what she did, paused just long enough to pick up Gant's black felt hat and walking stick which had fallen to the walk. Then, her face white and set as a block of marble, she rushed up the steps and down the hall toward the telephone. Now that the end had come, after all the years of agony and waiting, the knowledge filled her with an unbelievable, an incredulous horror. In another moment she was talking to her daughter:

"Oh, child, child," she said in a low tone of utter terror, "come quick! . . . Your father's bleeding to death!"

There was a gasp, a sob of anguish and surprise, half broken in the throat, the receiver was banged on the hook without an answer: within four minutes Helen had arrived, Barton, usually a deliberate and cautious driver, having taken the dangerous hills and curves between at murderous speed.

As she entered the hall, her mother had just finished phoning to McGuire. Without a word of greeting the two women rushed back through the rear hall towards Gant's room; when they got there Luke had already finished undressing him. Gant lay half propped on pillows still holding his great hands clutched around his genitals, the sheet beneath him was already soaked with blood, a red wet blot that spread horribly, sickeningly even as they looked. Gant's cold-gray eyes were bright with terror. As his daughter entered the room, he looked at her with the pitiable entreaty of a child, a look that tore at her heart, that begged her —the only one on earth who could, the only one who through black years of horror actually had—by some miracle of strength and grace to save him. And even as he looked at her with pitiable entreaty, she saw that he was gone, that he was dying, and that he knew it. Cold terror drank her heart; without a word she seized a towel, pulled his great hands away from that fount of jetting blood and covered him. By the time McGuire arrived, they had got a fresh sheet under him: but the spreading horror of the great red blot could not be checked, the sheet was soaking in bright blood the moment that they got it down.

McGuire came in and took one look, then turned toward the window, fumbling in his pocket for a cigarette. Helen came to him and seized him by his burly arms, unconsciously shaking him in the desperation of her entreaty.

"You've got to make it stop," she said hoarsely, "you've got to! You've got to!"

He stared at her for a moment, then stuck the cigarette in the corner of his thick lip, and barked coarsely:

"Stop what? What the hell do you think I am—Jehovah?"

"You've got to! You've got to!" she muttered again, her large gaunt face strained with hysteria—and then, suddenly, abruptly, quietly:

"What's to be done?"

He did not answer for a moment; he stared out the window, his coarse, bloated and brutally good face patched and mottled in late western light.

"You'd better wire the others," he grunted. "That is, if you want them here. Tell Steve and Daisy to come on. They may make it. Where's Eugene?"

"Boston."

He shrugged his burly shoulders and said nothing for a moment.

"All right. Tell him to come on."

"How long?" she whispered.

Again he shrugged his burly shoulders, but made no answer. He lit his cigarette, and turned toward the bed: nothing could be heard except Luke's heavy and excited breathing. Both towel and sheet were red and wet again. Gant remained motionless, his great hands clasped upon the towel, his eyes bright with terror and pitiable entreaty. McGuire opened his old leather case, squinted at the needle, and loaded it. Then, the cigarette still plastered on his fat lip, coiling smoke, he walked over to the bed and even as Gant raised his fear-bright eyes to him, he took him by his stringy arm, and grunting "All right, W. O.," he plunged the needle in above the elbow. Gant moaned a little, and relaxed insensibly after the needle had gone in: in a few minutes his eyes grew dull, and his great hands loosened in their clutch.

XXVIII

He bled incredibly. It was unbelievable that an old cancer-riddled spectre of a man should have so much blood in him. One has often heard the phrase "bled white," and that is literally what happened to him. Some liquid still came from him, but it was almost colorless, like water. There was no more blood left in him. And even then he did not die. Instead, as if to compensate him for all these years of agony and mortal terror, this bitter clutch on life so desperately relinquished, there came now a period of almost total peace and clarity. And Helen, grasping hope fiercely from that unaccustomed tranquillity, tried to hearten him and herself with futile words; she even seized him by his shoulders and shook him a little, saying:

"Why, you're all right! You're going to be all right now! The worst is over—you'll get well now! Don't you know it?"

And Gant covered her fingers with his own great hand and, smiling a little and shaking his head, looked at her, saying in a low and gentle voice:

"Oh, no, baby. I'm dying. It's all right now."

And in her heart, she knew at last that she was beaten; yet she would not give up. The final stop of that horrible flow of blood which had continued unabated for a day, the unaccustomed tranquil clarity of Gant's voice and mind, awakened in her again all the old unreasoning hopefulness of her nature, its desperate refusal to accept the ultimate.

"Oh," she said that night to Eliza, shaking her head with a strong movement of negation—"you can't tell me! Papa's not going to die yet! He'll pull through this just like he's pulled through all those other spells. Why, his mind is as clear and sound as a bell! He knows everything that's going on around him! He hasn't talked in years as he talked to me tonight—he was more like his old self than he's been since he took sick."

"Why, yes," Eliza answered instantly, eagerly catching up the drift of her daughter's talk, and pursuing it with the web-like, invincibly optimistic hopefulness of her own nature.

"Why, yes," she went on, pursing her lips reflectively and speaking in a persuasive manner. "And, see here, now!—Say!—Why, you know, I got to studyin' it over tonight and it's just occurred to me—now I'll tell you what *my* theory is! I believe that that old growth—that awful old thing—that—well, I suppose, now, you might say—that *cancer*," she said, making a gesture of explanation with her broad hand—"whatever it is, that awful old thing that has been eating away inside him there for years—" here she pursed her lips powerfully and shook her head in a short convulsive tremor of disgust—"well, now, I give it as my theory that the whole thing tore loose in him yesterday—when he had that attack—and," she paused deliberately, looked her daughter straight in the eyes, and went on with a slow and telling force—"and that he has simply gone and got that rotten old thing out of his system."

"Then, you mean—" Helen began eagerly, seizing at this fantastic straw as if it were the rock by which her drowning hope might be saved—"you mean, Mama——"

"Yes, sir!" said Eliza, shaking her head slowly and positively. "That's exactly what I mean! I think nature has taken its own course—I think nature has succeeded in doing what all the doctors and hospitals in the world were not able to do—for you can rest assured," and here she paused, looking her daughter gravely in the eyes—"you can rest assured that nature is the best physician in the end! Now, I've always said as much, and all the best authorities agree with me. Why, yes, now!—here! —say!—wasn't I readin' in the paper—oh! here along, you know a week or so ago—Doctor Royal S. Copeland!—yes, sir!—that was the very feller—why, he said, you know—" she went on in explanatory fashion.

"Oh, but, Mama!" Helen said, desperately, unable to make her mind believe this grotesque reasoning, and yet clutching at every word with a pleading entreaty that begged to be convinced.

"Oh, but, Mama, surely Wade Eliot and all those other men at Hopkins couldn't have been wrong! Why, Mama," she cried furiously, yet pleadingly—"you know they couldn't—after all these years—after taking him there for treatment a dozen times or more! Why, Mama, those men are *famous*—the greatest doctors in the world! Oh, surely not! Surely not!" she said desperately, and then gazed at Eliza pleadingly again.

"H'm!" said Eliza, pursing her lips with a little scornful smile. "It won't be the first time that a doctor has been wrong—I don't care how famous they may be! You can rest assured of that! It's always been my opinion that they're wrong about as often as they're right—only you can't prove it on 'em. They *bury* their mistakes." She was silent a moment, looking at her daughter in a sudden, straight and deadly fashion, with a little smile at the corners of her mouth. "Now, child, I want to tell you something. . . . I want to tell you what I saw today." Again she was silent, looking straight in her daughter's eyes, smiling her quiet little smile.

"What? What was it, Mama?" Helen demanded eagerly.

"Did you ever take a good look at that maple tree out front that stands on your right as you come in the house?"

"Why, no," Helen said in a bewildered tone. "How do you mean?"

"Well," said Eliza calmly, yet with a certain triumph in her voice, "you just take a good look at it tomorrow. That's all."

"But why—I can't see—how do you mean, Mama?"

"Now, child—" Eliza pursued her subject deliberately, with a ruminant relish of her strong pursed lips—"I was born and brought up in the country—close to the lap of Mother Earth, as the sayin' goes—and when it comes to *trees*—why, I reckon there's mighty little about 'em that I don't know. . . . Now here," she said abruptly, coming to the centre of her argument—"did you ever see a tree that had a big hollow gash down one side—that looked like it had all been eaten an' rotted out by some disease that had been destroyin' it?"

"Why, yes," Helen said, in a puzzled voice. "But I don't see yet——"

"Well, child, I'll tell you, then," said Eliza, both voice and worn brown eyes united in their portents of a grave and quiet earnestness—"that tree doesn't *always* die! You'll see trees that have had that happen to them—and they *cure* themselves! You can see where some old rotten growth has eaten into them—and then you can see where the tree has got the best of it—and grown up again—as sound and healthy as it *ever* was—around that old rotten growth. And that," she said triumphantly, "that is just exactly what has happened to that maple in the yard. Oh, you can *see* it!" she cried positively, at the same time making an easy descriptive gesture with her wide hand—"you can see where it has lapped right around that old growth—made a sort of fold, you know—and here it is just as sound and healthy as it ever was!"

"Then you mean?——"

"I mean," said Eliza in her straight and deadly fashion—"I mean that if a tree can do it, a *man* can do it—and I mean that if any man alive could do it your daddy is that man—for he's had as much strength and vitality as any man I ever saw—and *more* than a tree!" she cried. "Lord! I've seen him do enough to kill a *hundred* trees—the things *he's* done and managed to get over would kill the strongest tree that ever lived!"

"Oh, but Mama, surely not!" said Helen, laughing, and beginning to pluck at her chin in an abstracted manner, amused ~nd tickled in spite of herself by her mother's extraordinary reasoning. "You know that a man is not built the same way as a tree!"

"Why," Eliza cried impatiently, "why not! They're both Nature's products, aren't they? Now, here," she said persuasively, "just stop and consider the thing for a moment. Just imagine for a moment that *you're* the tree." Here she took her strong worn fingers and traced a line down Helen's stomach. "Now," she went on persuasively, "you've got some kind of growth inside you—call it what you like—a tumor, a growth, a cancer—anything you will—and your *healthy* tissues get to work to get the *best* of that growth—to build up a wall around it—to destroy it—to replace it with sound tissues, weed it out! Now," she said, clenching her fingers in a loose but powerful clasp—"if a *tree* can do that, doesn't it stand to reason that a *man* can do the same! Why, I wouldn't doubt it for a moment!" she cried powerfully. "Not a bit of it."

Thus the two women talked together according to the laws of their nature—the one with an invincible and undaunted optimism that persuaded itself in the octopal pursuit of its own reasonings, the other clutching like a drowning person at a straw.

XXIX

HE had not heard from any of his family in some weeks but late that night, while he was reading in his room on Trowbridge Street, he received the following telegram from home: "Father very ill doctor says cannot live come at once." The telegram was signed by his mother.

He telephoned the railway information offices and was informed that there was a train for New York and the South in about an hour. If he hurried, he could make it. He did not have enough money for the fare, he knew that he might hunt up Starwick, Dodd, Professor Hatcher, or other people that he knew, and get the money, but the delay would make him miss the train. Accordingly, he appealed to the person he knew best in the house, and who would be, he thought, most likely to help him. This was Mr. Wang, the Chinese student.

Mr. Wang was as good-hearted as he was stupid and childlike and now, faced with the need of getting money at once, the boy appealed to him. Mr. Wang came to his door and blinked owlishly; behind him the room was a blur of smoke and incense, and the big cabinet victrola was giving forth for the dozenth time that evening the hearty strains of "Yes, We Have No Bananas."

When Mr. Wang saw him, his round yellow face broke into a fool-

ish crease of merriment, he began to shake his finger at the young man
waggishly, and his throat already beginning to choke and squeak a little
with his jest, he said:

"I s'ink lest night I see you with nice—" Something in the other's
manner cut him short; he stopped, his round foolish face grew wondering and solemn, and in a doubtful and inquiring tone, he said:

"You say——?"

"Listen, Wang: I've just got this telegram from home. My father is
very sick—they think that he is dying. I've got to get money to go
home at once. I need fifty dollars: can you let me have it?"

As Mr. Wang listened, his sparkling eyes grew dull as balls of tar, his
round yellow moon of face grew curiously impassive. When the boy
had finished, the Chinese thrust his hands into the wide flowered sleeves
of his dressing gown, and then with a curious formal stiffness said:

"Will you come in? Please."

The boy entered, and Mr. Wang, closing the door, turned, thrust his
hand in his sleeves again, marched across the room to a magnificent
teak-wood desk and opening a small drawer, took out a roll of bills,
peeled off two twenties and a ten, and coming back to where his visitor
was standing, presented the money to him with a stiff bow, and his
round face still woodenly impassive, said again:

"Please."

The young man seized the money and saying, "Thank you, Wang,
I'll send it to you as soon as I get home," ran back to his room and began
to hurl clothing, shirts, socks, toilet articles, into his valise as hard as he
could. He had just finished when there was a tapping on the door and
the Chinese appeared again. He marched into the room with the same
ceremonious formality that had characterized his former conduct and
bowing stiffly again, presented the boy with two magnificent fans of
peacock feathers of which the lacquered blades were delicately and
beautifully engraved.

And bowing stiffly again, and saying, "Please!" he turned and
marched out of the room, his fat hands thrust into the wide sleeves of
the flowered dressing gown.

Thirty minutes later he was on his way, leaving behind him, in the
care of Mrs. Murphy, most of his belongings—the notebooks, letters,
books, old shoes, worn-out clothes and battered hats, the thousands
of pages of manuscript that represented the accretions of two years—
that immense and nondescript collection of past events, foredone accom-

plishment, and spent purposes, the very sight of which filled him with weariness and horror but which, with the huge acquisitive mania of his mother's blood, he had never been able to destroy.

In this way he left Cambridge and a life he had known for two years; instantly re-called, drawn back by the hand of death into the immediacy of a former life that had grown strange as dreams. It was toward the end of June, just a day or two before the commencement exercises at the university. That year he had been informed of his eligibility for the Master's degree—a degree he had neither sought nor known he had earned and, at the time he had received the telegram, he had been waiting for the formal exercises at which he would receive the degree—a wait prompted more by his total indecision as to his future purpose than by any other cause. Now, with explosive sudden·ness, his purpose had been shaped, decided for him, and with the old feeling of groping bewilderment, he surveyed the history of the last two years and wondered why he had come, why he was here, toward what blind goal he had been tending: all that he had to "show" for these years of fury, struggle, homelessness and hunger was an academic distinction which he had not aimed at, and on which he placed small value.

And it was in this spirit that he left the place. Rain had begun to fall that night, it fell now in torrential floods. The gay buntings and Japanese lanterns with which the Harvard Yard were already decked were reduced to sodden ruin, and as he raced towards the station in a taxi, the streets of Cambridge, and the old, narrow, twisted and familiar lanes of Boston were deserted—pools of wet light and glittering ribbons swept with storm.

When he got to the South station he had five minutes left to buy his ticket and get on his train. In spite of the lashing storm and the lateness of the hour, that magnificent station, which at that time—before the later "improvements" had reduced it to a glittering sterility of tile and marble—was one of the most thrilling and beautiful places in the world, was still busy with the tides of people that hurry forever through the great stations of America, and that no violence of storm can check.

The vast dingy sweep of the cement concourse outside the train-gates was pungent, as it had always been, with the acrid and powerfully exciting smell of engine smoke, and beyond the gates, upon a dozen tracks, great engines, passive and alert as cats, purred and panted softly, with the couched menace of their tremendous stroke. The engine smoke rose up straight in billowing plumes to widen under vaulting arches, to spread foggily throughout the enormous spaces of the grimy sheds. And beside the locomotives, he could see the burly denimed figures of the engineers, holding flaming torches and an oil-can in their hands as they peered and probed through the shining flanges of terrific pistoned wheels much taller than their heads. And forever, over the enormous cement concourse and down the quays beneath the powerful groomed attentiveness of waiting trains the tides of travellers kept passing, passing, in their everlasting change and weft, of voyage and return—of speed and space and movement, morning, cities, and new lands.

And caught up in the vaulting arches of those immense and grimy sheds he heard again the murmurous sound of time—that sound remote and everlasting, distilled out of all the movement, frenzy, and unceasing fury of our unresting lives, and yet itself detached, as calm and imperturbable as the still sad music of humanity, and which, made up out of our million passing lives, is in itself as fixed and everlasting as eternity.

They came, they paused and wove and passed and thrust and vanished in their everlasting tides, they streamed in and out of the portals of that enormous station in unceasing swarm; great trains steamed in to empty them, and others steamed out loaded with their nameless motes of lives, and all was as it had always been, moving, changing, swarming on forever like a river, and as fixed, unutterable in unceasing movement and in changeless change as the great river is, and time itself.

And within ten minutes he himself, another grain of dust borne onward on this ceaseless tide, another nameless atom in this everlasting throng, another wanderer in America, as all his fathers were before him, was being hurled into the South again in the huge projectile of a train. The train swept swiftly down the gleaming rails, paused briefly at the Back-Bay station, then was on its way again, moving smoothly, powerfully, almost noiselessly now, through the outer stretches of the small dense web of Boston. The town swept smoothly past: old blanks of wall, and old worn brick, and sudden spokes of streets, deserted, lashed with rain, set at the curbs with glittering beetles of its wet machinery and empetalled with its wet and sudden blooms of life. The flushed spoke-wires crossed his vision, lost the moment that he saw them, his forever, gone, like all things else, and never to be captured, seen a million times, yet never known before—as haunting, fading, deathless as a dream, as brief as is the bitter briefness of man's days, as lost and lonely as his life upon the mighty breast of earth, and of America.

Then the great train, gathering now in speed, and mounting smoothly to the summit of its tremendous stroke, was running swiftly through the outskirts of the city, through suburbs and brief blurs of light and then through little towns and on into the darkness, the wild and secret loneliness of earth. And he was going home again into the South and to a life that had grown strange as dreams, and to his father who was dying and who had become a ghost and shadow of his father to him, and to the bitter reality of grief and death. And—how, why, for what reason he could not say—all he felt was the tongueless swelling of wild joy. It was the wild and secret joy that has no tongue, the impossible hope that has no explanation, the savage, silent, and sweet exultancy of night, the wild and lonely visage of the earth, the imperturbable stroke and calmness of the everlasting earth, from which we have been derived, wherein again we shall be compacted, on which all of us have lived alone as strangers, and across which, in the loneliness of night, we have been hurled onward in the projectile flight of mighty trains —America.

Then the great train was given to the night and darkness, the great train hurtled through the night across the lonely, wild, and secret earth, bearing on to all their thousand destinations its freight of unknown lives—some to morning, cities, new lands, and the joy of voyages, and some to known faces, voices, and the hills of home—but which to certain fortune, peace, security, and love, no man could say.

The news that Gant was dying had spread rapidly through the town and, as often happens, that news had brought him back to life again in the heart and living memory of men who had known him, and who had scarcely thought of him for years. That night—the night of his death— the house was filled with some of the men who had known him best since he came to the town forty years before.

Among these people were several of the prominent and wealthy business men of the community: these included, naturally, Eliza's brothers, William and James Pentland, both wealthy lumber dealers, as well as one of her younger brothers, Crockett, who was Will Pentland's bookkeeper, a pleasant, ruddy, bucolic man of fifty years. Among the other men of wealth and influence who had been Gant's friends there was Fagg Sluder, who had made a fortune as a contractor and retired to invest his money in business property, and to spend his time seated in an easy creaking chair before the fire department, in incessant gossip about baseball with the firemen and the young professional baseball players whose chief support he was, whose annual deficit he cheerfully supplied, and to whom he had given the local baseball park, which bore his name. He had been one of Gant's best friends for twenty years, he was immensely fond of him, and now, assembled in the broad front hall in earnest discussion with the Pentlands and Mike Fogarty, another of Gant's friends, and armed with the invariable cigar (despite his doctor's orders he smoked thirty or forty strong black cigars every day), which he chewed on, took out of his mouth, and put back again, with quick, short, unconscious movements, he could be heard saying in the rapid, earnest, stammering tone that was one of the most attractive qualities of his buoyant and constantly hopeful nature:

"I-I-I-I just believe he's going to pull right out of this and-and-and-get well! Why-why-why-why-when I went in there tonight he spoke right up and-and-and knew me right away!" he blurted out, sticking the cigar in his mouth and chewing on it vigorously a moment—"why-why-why his mind is-is-is-is just as clear—as it always was—spoke right up, you know, says 'Sit down, Fagg'—shook hands with me—knew me right away—talked to me just the same way he always talked—says 'Sit down, Fagg. I'm glad to see you. How have you been?' he says—and-and-and—I just believe he's going to pull right out of this," Mr. Sluder blurted out,—"be damned if I don't—what do *you* say, Will?" and snatching his chewed cigar butt from his mouth he turned eagerly to Will Pentland for confirmation. And Will, who, as usual, had been paring his stubby nails during the whole course of the conversation, his lips pursed in their characteristic family grimace, now studied his clenched fingers for a moment, pocketed his knife and turning to Fagg Sluder, with a little bird-like nod and wink, and with the incomparable Pentland drawl, at once precise, and full of the relish of self-satisfaction, said:

"Well, if any man alive can do it, W. O. is that man. I've seen him time and again when I thought every breath would be his last—and he's got over it every time. I've always said," he went on precisely, and with a kind of deadly directness in his small compact and almost wizened face, "that he has more real vitality than any two men that I ever knew—he's got out of worse holes than this before—and he may do it again."

He was silent a moment, his small packed face pursed suddenly in its animal-like grimace that had an almost savage ferocity and a sense of deadly and indomitable power.

Even more astonishing and troubling was the presence of these four older members of the Pentland family gathered together in his mother's hall. As they stood there talking—Eliza with her hands held in their loose and powerful clasp across her waist, Will intently busy with his finger-nails, Jim listening attentively to all that was said, his solid porcine face and small eyes wincing from time to time in a powerful but unconscious grimace, and Crockett, gentlest, ruddiest, most easy-going and dreamy of them all, speaking in his quiet drawling tone and stroking his soft brown mustaches in a gesture of quiet and bucolic meditation, Luke could not recall having seen so many of them together at one time and the astonishing enigma of their one-ness and variety was strikingly apparent.

What was it?—this indefinable tribal similarity that united these people so unmistakably. No one could say: it would have been difficult 'o find four people more unlike in physical appearance, more strongly marked by individual qualities. Whatever it was—whether some chemistry of blood and character, or perhaps some physical identity of broad and fleshy nose, pursed reflective lips and flat wide cheeks, or the energies of powerfully concentrated egotisms—their kinship with one another was astonishing and instantly apparent.

XXX

In a curious and indefinable way the two groups of men in the hallway had become divided: the wealthier group of prominent citizens, which was composed of the brothers William, James, and Crockett Pentland, Mr. Sluder and Eliza, stood in a group near the front hall door, engaged in earnest conversation. The second group, which was composed of working men, who had known Gant well, and worked for or with him —a group composed of Jannadeau the jeweller, old Alec Ramsay and Saul Gudger, who were stonecutters, Gant's nephew, Ollie Gant, who was a plasterer, Ernest Pegram, the city plumber, and Mike Fogarty, who was perhaps Gant's closest friend, a building contractor—this group, composed of men who had all their lives done stern labor with their hands, and who were really the men who had known the stone-cutter best, stood apart from the group of prominent and wealthy men who were talking so earnestly to Eliza.

And in this circumstance, in this unconscious division, in the air of constraint, vague uneasiness and awkward silence that was evident among these working men, as they stood there in the hallway dressed in their "good clothes," nervously fingering their hats in their big hands, there was something immensely moving. The men had the look that working people the world over have always had when they found themselves suddenly gathered together on terms of social intimacy with their employers or with members of the governing class.

And Helen, coming out at this instant from her father's room into the hall, suddenly saw and felt the awkward division between these two groups of men, as she had never before felt or noticed it, as sharply as if they had been divided with a knife.

And, it must be admitted, her first feeling was an unworthy one— an instinctive wish to approach the more "important" group, to join her life to the lives of these "influential" people who represented to her a "higher" social level. She found herself walking towards the group of wealthy and prominent men at the front of the hall, and away from the group of working men who had really been Gant's best friends.

But seeing the brick-red face of Alec Ramsay, the mountainous figure of Mike Fogarty, suddenly with a sense of disbelief, and almost terrified revelation of the truth, she thought: "Why-why-why—these men are really the closest friends he's got—not rich men like Uncle Will or Uncle Jim or even Mr. Sluder—but men like Mike Fogarty—and Jannadeau—and Mr. Duncan—and Alec Ramsay—and Ernest Pegram—and Ollie Gant—but—but—good heavens, no!" she thought, almost desperately—"surely these are not his closest friends—why-why —of course, they're decent people—they're honest men—but they're only common people—I've always considered them as just *working* men—and-and-and—my God!" she thought, with that terrible feeling of discovery we have when we suddenly see ourselves as others see us—"do you suppose that's the way people in this town think of Papa? Do you suppose they have always thought of him as just a common working man—oh, no! but of course not!" she went on impatiently, trying to put the troubling thought out of her mind. "Papa's not a working man—Papa is a *business* man—a well thought of business man in this community. Papa has always owned property since he came here—he has always had his own shop"—she did not like the sound of the word shop, and in her mind she hastily amended it to "place"—"he's always had his own place, up on the public square—he's—he's rented places to other people—he's—he's—oh, of course not!—Papa is different from men like Ernest Pegram, and Ollie, and Jannadeau and Alec Ramsay—why, they're just working men—they work with their hands—Ollie's just an ordinary plasterer—and-and—Mr. Ramsay is nothing but a stone-cutter.'

And a small insistent voice inside her said most quietly: "And your father?"

And suddenly Helen remembered Gant's great hands of power and strength, and how they now lay quietly beside him on the bed, and lived and would not die, even when the rest of him had died, and she remembered the thousands of times she had gone to his shop in the afternoon and found the stonecutter in his long striped apron bending with delicate concentration over a stone inscription on a trestle, holding in his great hands the chisel and the heavy wooden mallet the stonecutters use, and remembering, the whole rich and living compact of the past came back to her, in a rush of tenderness and joy and terror, and on that flood a proud and bitter honesty returned. She thought: "Yes, he was a stonecutter, no different from these other men, and these men were his real friends."

And going directly to old Alec Ramsay she grasped his blunt thick fingers, the nails of which were always whitened a little with stone dust, and greeted him in her large and spacious way:

"Mr. Ramsay," she said, "I want you to know how glad we are that you could come. And that goes for all of you—Mr. Jannadeau, and Mr. Duncan, and Mr. Fogarty, and you, Ernest, and you, too, Ollie—you are the best friends Papa has, there's no one he thinks more of, and no one he would rather see."

Mr. Ramsay's brick-red face and brick-red neck became even redder before he spoke, and beneath his grizzled brows his blue eyes suddenly were smoke blue. He put his blunt hand to his mustache for a moment, and tugged at it, then he said in his gruff, quiet, and matter-of-fact voice:

"I guess we know Will about as well as any one, Miss Helen. I've worked for him off and on for thirty years."

At the same moment, she heard Ollie Gant's easy, deep, and powerful laugh, and saw him slowly lift his cigarette in his coarse paw; she saw Jannadeau's great yellow face and massive domy brow, and heard him laugh with guttural pleasure, saying, "Ah-h! I tell you vat! Dat girl has alvays looked out for her datty—she's de only vun dat coult hantle him; efer since she vas ten years olt it has been de same." And she was overwhelmingly conscious of that immeasurable mountain of a man, Mike Fogarty, beside her, the sweet clarity of his blue eyes, and the almost purring music of his voice as he gently laid his mutton of a hand upon her shoulder for a moment, saying,

"Ah, Miss Helen, I don't know how Will could have got along all these years without ye—for he has said the same himself a thousand times—aye! that he has!"

And instantly, having heard these words, and feeling the strong calm presences of these powerful men around her, it seemed to Helen she had somehow re-entered a magic world that she thought was gone forever. And she was immensely content.

At the same moment, with a sense of wonder, she discovered an astonishing thing, that she had never noticed before, but that she must have heard a thousand times;—this was that of all these people, who knew Gant best, and had a deep and true affection for him, there were only two—Mr. Fogarty and Mr. Ramsay—who had ever addressed him by his first name. And so far as she could now remember, these two men, together with Gant's mother, his brothers, his sister Augusta, and a few of the others who had known him in his boyhood in Pennsylvania, were the only people who ever had. And this revelation cast a strange, a lonely and a troubling light upon the great gaunt figure of the stonecutter, which moved her powerfully and which she had never felt before. And most strange of all was the variety of names by which these various people called her father.

As for Eliza, had any of her children ever heard her address her husband as anything but "Mr. Gant"—had she ever called him by one of his first names—their anguish of shame and impropriety would have been so great that they could hardly have endured it. But such a lapse would have been incredible: Eliza could no more have addressed Gant by his first name, than she could have quoted Homer's Greek; had she tried to address him so, the muscles of her tongue would have found it physically impossible to pronounce the word. And in this fact there was somehow, now that Gant was dying, an enormous pathos. It gave to Eliza's life with him a pitiable and moving dignity, the compensation of a proud and wounded spirit for all the insults and injuries that had been heaped upon it. She had been a young country woman of twenty-four when she had met him, she had been ignorant of life, and innocent of the cruelty, the violence, the drunkenness and abuse of which men

are capable, she had borne this man fifteen children, of whom eight had
come to life, and had for forty years eaten the bread of blood and tears
and joy and grief and terror, she had wanted affection and had been
given taunts, abuse, and curses, and somehow her proud and wounded
spirit had endured with an anguished but unshaken fortitude all the
wrongs and cruelties and injustices of which he had been guilty toward
her. And now at the very end her pride still had this pitiable distinction,
her spirit still preserved this last integrity: she had not betrayed her
wounded soul to a shameful familiarity, he had remained to her—in
mind and heart and living word—what he had been from the first day
that she met him; the author of her grief and misery, the agent of her
suffering, the gaunt and lonely stranger who had come into her hills
from a strange land and a distant people—that furious, gaunt, and
lonely stranger with whom by fatal accident her destiny—past hate or
love or birth or death or human error and confusion—had been in-
solubly enmeshed, with whom for forty years she had lived, a wife, a
mother, and a stranger—and who would to the end remain to her a
stranger—"Mr. Gant."

What was it? What was the secret of this strange and bitter mystery
of life that had made of Gant a stranger to all men, and most of all a
stranger to his wife? Perhaps some of the answer might have been
found in Eliza's own unconscious words when she described her meeting with him forty years before:

"It was not that he was old," she said,—"he was only thirty-three—but
he *looked* old—his *ways* were old—he had lived so much among old people.—Pshaw!" she continued, with a little puckered smile, "if any one
had told me that night I saw him sitting there with Lydia and old Mrs.
Mason—that was the very day they moved into the house, the night he
gave the big dinner—and Lydia was still alive and, of course, she was
ten years older than he was, and that may have had something to do with
it—but I got to studying him as he sat there, of course, he was tired and
run down and depressed and worried over all that trouble that he'd had
in Sidney before he came up here, when he lost everything, and he
knew that Lydia was dying, and that was preyin' on his mind—but he
looked old, thin as a rake you know, and sallow and run down, and
with those *old* ways he had acquired, I reckon, from associatin' with
Lydia and old Mrs. Mason and people like that—but I just sat there
studying him as he sat there with them and I said— 'Well, you're an old
man, aren't you, sure enough?'—pshaw! if any one had told me that

night that some day I'd be married to him I'd have laughed at them—
I'd have considered that I was marrying an old man—and that's just
exactly what a lot of people thought, sir, when the news got out that I
was goin' to marry him—I know Martha Patton came running to me,
all excited and out of breath—said, 'Eliza! You're not going to marry
that old man—you know you're not!'—you see, his *ways* were old, he
looked old, *dressed* old, *acted* old—everything he did was old; there was
always, it seemed, something strange and old-like about him, almost
like he had been born that way."

And it was at this time that Eliza met him, saw him first—"Mr. Gant"
—an immensely tall, gaunt, cadaverous-looking man, with a face stern
and sad with care, lank, drooping mustaches, sandy hair, and cold-gray
staring eyes—"not so old, you know—he was only thirty-three—but he
looked old, he *acted* old, his *ways* were old—he had lived so much
among older people he seemed older than he was—I thought of him as
an old man."

This, then, was "Mr. Gant" at thirty-three, and since then, although
his fortunes and position had improved, his character had changed little. And now Helen, faced by all these working men, who had known,
liked, and respected him, and had now come to see him again before he
died—suddenly knew the reason for his loneliness, the reason so few
people—least of all, his wife—had ever dared address him by his first
name. And with a swift and piercing revelation, his muttered words,
which she had heard him use a thousand times when speaking of his
childhood— "We had a tough time of it—I tell you what, we did!"—
now came back to her with the unutterable poignancy of discovery. For
the first time she understood what they meant. And suddenly, with the
same swift and nameless pity, she remembered all the pictures which
she had seen of her father as a boy and a young man. There were a half
dozen of them in the big family album, together with pictures of his
own and Eliza's family: they were the small daguerreotypes of fifty years
before, in small frames of faded plush, with glass covers, touched with
the faint pale pinks with which the photographers of an earlier time
tried to paint with life the sallow hues of their photography. The first
of these pictures showed Gant as a little boy; later, a boy of twelve, he
was standing in a chair beside his brother Wesley, who was seated, with
a wooden smile upon his face. Later, a picture of Gant in the years in
Baltimore, standing, his feet crossed, leaning elegantly upon a marble
slab beside a vase; later still, the young stonecutter before his little shop

in the years at Sidney; finally, Gant, after his marriage with Eliza, standing with gaunt face and lank drooping mustaches before his shop upon
the square, in the company of Will Pentland, who was at the time his
business partner.

And all these pictures, from first to last, from the little boy to the
man with the lank drooping mustaches, had been marked by the
same expression: the sharp thin face was always stern and sad with care,
the shallow cold-gray eyes always stared out of the bony cage-formation
of the skull with a cold mournfulness—the whole impression was always one of gaunt sad loneliness. And it was not the loneliness of the
dreamer, the poet, or the misjudged prophet, it was just the cold and
terrible loneliness of man, of every man, and of the lost American who
has been brought forth naked under immense and lonely skies, to "shift
for himself," to grope his way blindly through the confusion and brutal
chaos of a life as naked and unsure as he, to wander blindly down across
the continent, to hunt forever for a goal, a wall, a dwelling place of
warmth and certitude, a light, a door.

And for this reason, she now understood something about her father,
this great gaunt figure of a stonecutter that she had never understood or
thought about before: she suddenly understood his order, sense of decency and dispatch; his love of cleanness, roaring fires, and rich abundance, his foul drunkenness, violence, and howling fury, his naked
shame and trembling penitence, his good clothes of heavy monumental
black that he always kept well pressed, his clean boiled shirts, wing collars, and his love of hotels, ships, and trains, his love of gardens, new
lands, cities, voyages. She knew suddenly that he was unlike any other
man that ever lived, and that every man that ever lived was like her
father. And remembering the cold and mournful look in his shallow
staring eyes of cold hard gray, she suddenly knew the reason for that
look, as she had never known it before, and understood now why so few
men had ever called him by his first name—why he was known to all
the world as "Mr. Gant."

Having joined this group of working men, Helen immediately felt
an indefinable but powerful sense of comfort and physical well-being
which the presence of such men as these always gave to her. And she
did not know why; but immediately, once she had grasped Mr. Ramsay
by the hand, and was aware of Mike Fogarty's mountainous form and
clear-blue eye above her, and Ollie Gant's deep and lazy laugh, and the

deliberate and sensual languor with which he raised his cigarette to his lips with his powerful plasterer's hand, drawing the smoke deep into his strong lungs and letting it trickle slowly from his nostrils as he talked —she was conscious of a feeling of enormous security and relief which she had not known in years.

And this feeling, as with every person of strong sensuous perceptions, was literal, physical, chemical, astoundingly acute. She not only felt an enormous relief and joy to get back to these working people, it even seemed to her that everything they did—the way Mr. Duncan held his strong cheap cigar in his thick dry fingers, the immense satisfaction with which he drew on it, the languid and sensual trickling of cigarette smoke from Ollie Gant's nostrils, his deep, good-natured, indolently lazy laugh, even the perceptible bulge of tobacco-quid in Alec Ramsay's brick-red face, his barely perceptible rumination of it—all these things, though manlike in their nature, seemed wonderfully good and fresh and living to her—the whole plain priceless glory of the earth restored to her—and gave her a feeling of wonderful happiness and joy.

And later that night when all these men, her father's friends, had gone into his room, filling it with their enormous and full-blooded vitality, as she saw him lying there, wax-pale, bloodless, motionless, yet with a faint grin at the edge of his thin mouth as he received them, as she heard their deep full-fibred voices, Mike Fogarty's lilting Irish, Mr. Duncan's thick Scotch burr, Ollie Gant's deep and lazy laugh, and the humor of Alec Ramsay's deep, gruff and matter-of-fact tone, relating old times—"God, Will!" he said, "at your worst, you weren't in it compared to Wes! He was a holy terror when he drank! Do you remember the day he drove his fist through your plate-glass window right in the face of Jannadeau—and went home then and tore all the plumbing out of the house and pitched the bathtub out of the second-storey window into Orchard Street—God! Will!—you weren't in it compared to Wes"—as she heard all this, and saw Gant's thin grin and heard his faint and rusty cackle, his almost inaudible "E'God! Poor Wes!"—she could not believe that he was going to die, the great full-blooded working men filled the room with the vitality of a life which had returned in all its rich and living flood, and seemed intolerably near and familiar—and she kept thinking with a feeling of wonderful happiness and disbelief: "Oh, but Papa's not going to die! It's not possible! He can't! He can't!"

XXXI

The dying man himself was no longer to be fooled and duped by hope; he knew that he was done for, and he no longer cared. Rather, as if that knowledge had brought him a new strength—the immense and measureless strength that comes from resignation, and that has vanquished terror and despair—Gant had already consigned himself to death, and now was waiting for it, without weariness or anxiety, and with a perfect and peaceful acquiescence.

This complete resignation and tranquillity of a man whose life had been so full of violence, protest, and howling fury stunned and silenced them, and left them helpless. It seemed that Gant, knowing that often he had lived badly, was now determined to die well. And in this he succeeded. He accepted every ministration, every visit, every stammering reassurance, or frenzied activity, with a passive gratefulness which he seemed to want every one to know. On the evening of the day after his first hemorrhage, he asked for food and Eliza, bustling out, pathetically eager to do something, killed a chicken and cooked it for him.

And as if, from that infinite depth of death and silence from which he looked at her, he had seen, behind the bridling brisk activity of her figure, forever bustling back and forth, saying confusedly— "Why, yes! The very thing! This very minute, sir!"—had seen the white strained face, the stricken eyes of a proud and sensitive woman who had wanted affection all her life, had received for the most part injury and abuse, and who was ready to clutch at any crust of comfort that might console or justify her before he died—he ate part of the chicken with relish, and then looking up at her, said quietly:

"I tell you what—that was a good chicken."

And Helen, who had been sitting beside him on the bed, and feeding him, now cried out in a tone of bantering and good-humored challenge:

"What! Is it better than the ones *I* cook for you! You'd better not say it is—I'll beat you if you do."

And Gant, grinning feebly, shook his head, and answered:

"Ah-h! Your mother is a good cook, Helen. You're a good cook, too—but there's no one else can cook a chicken like your mother!"

And stretching out his great right hand, he patted Eliza's worn fingers with his own.

And Eliza, suddenly touched by that word of unaccustomed praise and tenderness, turned and rushed blindly from the room at a clumsy bridling gait, clasping her hands together at the wrist, her weak eyes blind with tears—shaking her head in a strong convulsive movement, her mouth smiling a pale tremulous smile, ludicrous, touching, made unnatural by her false teeth, whispering over and over to herself, "Poor fellow! Says, 'There's no one else can cook a chicken like your mother.' Reached out and patted me on the hand, you know. Says 'I tell you what, there's no one who can cook a chicken like your mother.' I reckon he wanted to let me know, to tell me, but says, 'The rest of you have all been good to me, Helen's a good cook, but there's no one else can cook like your mother.'"

"Oh, here, here, here," said Helen, who, laughing uncertainly had followed her mother from the room when Eliza had rushed out, and had seized her by the arms, and shook her gently, "good heavens! *Here!* You mustn't carry on like this! You mustn't take it this way! Why, he's all right!" she cried out heartily and shook Eliza again. "Papa's going to be all right! Why, what are you crying for?" she laughed. "He's going to get well now—don't you know that?"

And Eliza could say nothing for a moment but kept smiling that false trembling and unnatural smile, shaking her head in a slight convulsive movement, her eyes blind with tears.

"I tell you what," she whispered, smiling tremulously again and shaking her head, "there was something about it—you know, the way he said it—says, 'There's no one who can come up to your mother'—there was something in the way he said it! Poor fellow, says, 'None of the rest of you can cook like her'—says, 'I tell you what, that was certainly a good chicken'— Poor fellow! It wasn't so much what he said as the way he said it—there was something about it that went through me like a knife—I tell you what it did!"

"Oh, here, here, here!" Helen cried again, laughing. But her own eyes were also wet, the bitter possessiveness that had dominated all her relations with her father, and that had thrust Eliza away from him, was suddenly vanquished. At that moment she began to feel an affection for her mother that she had never felt before, a deep and nameless pity and regret, and a sense of sombre satisfaction.

"Well," she thought, "I guess it's all she's had, but I'm glad she's got that much to remember. I'm glad he said it: she'll always have that now to hang on to."

And Gant lay looking up from that sunken depth of death and silence, his great hands of living power quiet with their immense and passive strength beside him on the bed.

XXXII

TOWARDS one o'clock that night Gant fell asleep and dreamed that he was walking down the road that led to Spangler's Run. And although he had not been along that road for fifty years everything was as fresh, as green, as living and familiar as it had ever been to him. He came out on the road from Schaefer's farm, and on his left he passed by the little white frame church of the United Brethren, and the graveyard about the church where his friends and family had been buried. From the road he could see the line of family gravestones which he himself had carved and set up after he had returned from serving his apprenticeship in Baltimore. The stones were all alike: tall flat slabs of marble with plain rounded tops, and there was one for his sister Susan, who had died in infancy, and one for his sister Huldah, who had died in childbirth while the war was on, and one for Huldah's husband, a young farmer named Jake Lentz who had been killed at Chancellorsville, and one for the husband of his oldest sister, Augusta, a man named Martin, who had been an itinerant photographer and had died soon after the war, and finally one for Gant's own father. And since there were no stones for his brother George or for Elmer or for John, and none for his mother or Augusta, Gant knew that he was still a young man, and had just recently come home. The stones which he had put up were still white and new, and in the lower right hand corner of each stone, he had carved his own name: W. O. Gant.

It was a fine morning in early May and everything was sweet and green and as familiar as it had always been. The graveyard was carpeted with thick green grass, and all around the graveyard and the church there was the incomparable green velvet of young wheat. And the thought came back to Gant, as it had come to him a thousand times, that the wheat around the graveyard looked greener and richer than any other wheat that he had ever seen. And beside him on his right were the great fields of the Schaefer farm, some richly carpeted with young green wheat, and some ploughed, showing great bronze-red strips of fertile nobly swelling earth. And behind him on the great swell of the land, and commanding that sweet and casual scene with the majesty of its incomparable lay was Jacob Schaefer's great red barn and to the right the neat brick house with the white trimming of its windows, the white picket fence, the green yard with its rich tapestry of flowers and lilac bushes and the massed leafy spread of its big maple trees. And behind the house the hill rose, and all its woods were just greening into May, still smoky, tender and unfledged, gold-yellow with the magic of young green. And before the woods began there was the apple orchard halfway up the hill; the trees were heavy with the blossoms and stood there in all their dense still bloom incredible.

And from the greening trees the bird-song rose, the grass was thick with the dense gold glory of the dandelions, and all about him were a thousand magic things that came and went and never could be captured. Below the church, he passed the old frame house where Elly Spangler, who kept the church keys, lived, and there were apple trees behind the house, all dense with bloom, but the house was rickety, unpainted and dilapidated as it had always been, and he wondered if the kitchen was still buzzing with a million flies, and if Elly's half-wit brothers, Jim and Willy, were inside. And even as he shook his head and thought, as he had thought so many times "Poor Elly," the back door opened and Willy Spangler, a man past thirty wearing overalls, and with a fond, foolish witless face, came galloping down across the yard toward him, flinging his arms out in exuberant greeting, and shouting to him the same welcome that he shouted out to every one who passed, friends and strangers all alike— "I've been lookin' fer ye! I've been lookin' fer ye, Oll," using, as was the custom of the friends and kinsmen of his Pennsylvania boyhood, his second name—and then, anxiously, pleadingly, again the same words that he spoke to every one: "Ain't ye goin' to stay?"

And Gant, grinning, but touched by the indefinable sadness and pity which that kind and witless greeting had always stirred in him since his own childhood, shook his head, and said quietly:

"No, Willy. Not to-day. I'm meeting some one down the road"—and straightway felt, with thudding heart, a powerful and nameless excitement, the urgency of that impending meeting—why, where, with whom, he did not know—but all-compelling now, inevitable.

And Willy, still with wondering, foolish, kindly face followed along beside him now, saying eagerly, as he said to every one:

"Did ye bring anythin' fer me? Have ye got a chew?"

And Gant, starting to shake his head in refusal, stopped suddenly, seeing the look of disappointment on the idiot's face, and putting his

hand in the pocket of his coat, took out a plug of apple-tobacco, saying:
"Yes. Here you are, Willy. You can have this."

And Willy, grinning with foolish joy, had clutched the plug of tobacco and, still kind and foolish, had followed on a few steps more,
saying anxiously:

"Are ye comin' back, Oll? Will ye be comin' back real soon?"

And Gant, feeling a strange and nameless sorrow, answered:

"I don't know, Willy"—for suddenly he saw that he might never
come this way again.

But Willy, still happy, foolish, and contented, had turned and gal-
loped away toward the house, flinging his arms out and shouting as he
went:

"I'll be waitin' fer ye. I'll be waitin' fer ye, Oll."

And Gant went on then, down the road, and there was a nameless
sorrow in him that he could not understand, and some of the brightness
had gone out of the day.

When he got to the mill, he turned left along the road that went down
by Spangler's run, crossed by the bridge below, and turned from the
road into the wood-path on the other side. A child was standing in the
path, and turned and went on ahead of him. In the wood the sunlight
made swarming moths of light across the path, and through the leafy
tangle of the trees: the sunlight kept shifting and swarming on the child's
gold hair, and all around him were the sudden noises of the wood, the
stir, the rustle, and the bullet thrum of wings, the cool broken sound of
hidden water.

The wood got denser, darker as he went on and coming to a place
where the path split away into two forks, Gant stopped, and turning to
the child said, "Which one shall I take?" And the child did not answer
him.

But some one was there in the wood before him. He heard footsteps
on the path, and saw a footprint in the earth, and turning took the path
where the footprint was, and where it seemed he could hear some one
walking.

And then, with the bridgeless instancy of dreams, it seemed to him that
all of the bright green-gold around him in the wood grew dark and
sombre, the path grew darker, and suddenly he was walking in a strange
and gloomy forest, haunted by the brown and tragic light of dreams.
The forest shapes of great trees rose around him, he could hear no
bird-song now, even his own feet on the path were soundless, but he

always thought he heard the sound of some one walking in the wood before him. He stopped and listened: the steps were muffled, softly thunderous, they seemed so near that he thought that he must catch up with the one he followed in another second, and then they seemed immensely far away, receding in the dark mystery of that gloomy wood. And again he stopped and listened, the footsteps faded, vanished, he shouted, no one answered. And suddenly he knew that he had taken the wrong path, that he was lost. And in his heart there was an immense and quiet sadness, and the dark light of the enormous wood was all around him; no birds sang.

XXXIII

GANT awoke suddenly and found himself looking straight up at Eliza who was seated in a chair beside the bed.

"You were asleep," she said quietly with a grave smile, looking at him in her direct and almost accusing fashion.

"Yes," he said, breathing a little hoarsely, "what time is it?"

It was a few minutes before three o'clock in the morning. She looked at the clock and told him the time: he asked where Helen was.

"Why," said Eliza quickly, "she's right here in this hall room: I reckon she's asleep, too. Said she was tired, you know, but that if you woke up and needed her to call her. Do you want me to get her?"

"No," said Gant. "Don't bother her. I guess she needs the rest, poor child. Let her sleep."

"Yes," said Eliza, nodding, "and that's exactly what you must do, too, Mr. Gant. You try to go on back to sleep now," she said coaxingly, "for that's what we all need. There's no medicine like sleep—as the fellow says, it's Nature's sovereign remedy," said Eliza, with that form of sententiousness that she was very fond of—"so you go on, now, Mr. Gant, and get a good night's sleep, and when you wake up in the morning, you'll feel like a new man. That's half the battle—if you can get your sleep, you're already on the road to recovery."

"No," said Gant, "I've slept enough."

He was breathing rather hoarsely and heavily and she asked him if he was comfortable and needed anything. He made no answer for a moment, and then muttered something under his breath that she could not hear plainly, but that sounded like "little boy."

"Hah? What say? What is it, Mr. Gant?" Eliza said. "Little boy?" she said sharply, as he did not answer.

"Did you see him?" he said.

She looked at him for a moment with troubled eyes, then said:

"Pshaw, Mr. Gant, I guess you must have been dreaming."

He did not answer, and for a moment there was no sound in the room but his breathing, hoarse, a little heavy. Then he muttered:

"Did some one come into the house?"

She looked at him sharply, inquiringly again, with troubled eyes:

"Hah? What say? Why, no, I think not," she said doubtfully, "unless you may have heard Gilmer come in an' go up to his room."

And Gant was again silent for several moments, breathing a little heavily and hoarsely, his hands resting with an enormous passive strength, upon the bed. Presently he said quietly:

"Where's Bacchus?"

"Hah? Who's that?" Eliza said sharply, in a startled kind of tone. "Bacchus? You mean Uncle Bacchus?"

"Yes," said Gant.

"Why, pshaw, Mr. Gant!" cried Eliza laughing—for a startled moment she had wondered if "his mind was wanderin'," but one glance at his quiet eyes, the tranquil sanity of his quiet tone, reassured her——

"Pshaw!" she said, putting one finger up to her broad nose-wing and laughing slyly. "You must have been havin' queer dreams, for a fact!"

"Is he here?"

"Why, I'll vow, Mr. Gant!" she cried again. "What on earth is in your mind? You know that Uncle Bacchus is way out West in Oregon—it's been ten years since he came back home last—that summer of the reunion at Gettysburg."

"Yes," said Gant. "I remember now."

And again he fell silent, staring upward in the semi-darkness, his hands quietly at rest beside him, breathing a little hoarsely, but without pain. Eliza sat in the chair watching him, her hands clasped loosely at her waist, her lips pursed reflectively, and a puzzled look in her eyes: "Now I wonder what ever put that in his mind?" she thought. "I wonder what made him think of Bacchus. Now his mind's not wanderin'— that's one thing sure. He knows what he's doing just as well as I do —I reckon he must have dreamed it—that Bacchus was here—but that's certainly a strange thing, that he should bring it up like this."

He was so silent that she thought he might have gone to sleep again, he lay motionless with his eyes turned upward in the semi-darkness of the room, his hands immense and passive at his side. But suddenly he startled her again by speaking, a voice so quiet and low that he might have been talking to himself.

"Father died the year before the war," he said, "when I was nine years old. I never got to know him very well. I guess Mother had a hard time of it. There were seven of us—and nothing but that little place to live on—and some of us too young to help her much—and George away at war. She spoke pretty hard to us sometimes—but I guess she had a hard time of it. It was a tough time for all of us," he muttered, "I tell you what, it was."

"Yes," Eliza said, "I guess it was. I know she told me—I talked to her, you know, the time we went there on our honeymoon—whew! what about it?" she shrieked faintly, and put her finger up to her broad nose-wing with the same sly gesture—"it was all I could do to keep a straight face sometimes—why, you know, the way she had of talkin'— the expressions she used—oh! came right out with it, you know—some-times I'd have to turn my head away so she wouldn't see me laughin'— says, you know, 'I was left a widow with seven children to bring up, but I never took charity from no one; as I told 'em all, I've crawled under the dog's belly all my life; now I guess I can get over its back.'"

"Yes," said Gant with a faint grin. "Many's the time I've heard her say that."

"But she told it then, you know," Eliza went on in explanatory fash-ion, "about your father and how he'd done hard labor on a farm all his life and died—well, I reckon you'd call it consumption."

"Yes," said Gant. "That was it."

"And," Eliza said reflectively, "I never asked—of course, I didn't want to embarrass her—but I reckon from what she said, he may have been— well, I suppose you might say he was a drinkin' man."

"Yes," said Gant, "I guess he was."

"And I know she told it on him," said Eliza, laughing again, and passing one finger slyly at the corner of her broad nose-wing, "how he went to town that time—to Brant's Mill, I guess it was—and how she was afraid he'd get to drinkin', and she sent you and Wes along to watch him and to see he got home again—and how he met up with some fellers there and, sure enough, I guess he started drinkin' and stayed away too long—and then, I reckon he was afraid of what she'd say to him when he got back—and that was when he bought the clock—it's that very clock upon the mantel, Mr. Gant—but that was when he got the clock, all right—I guess he thought it would pacify her when she started out to scold him for gettin' drunk and bein' late."

"Yes," said Gant, who had listened without moving, staring at the ceiling, and with a faint grin printed at the corners of his mouth, "well do I remember: that was it, all right."

"And then," Eliza went on, "he lost the way comin' home—it had been snowin', and I reckon it was getting dark, and he had been drinkin' —and instead of turnin' in on the road that went down by your place he kept goin' on until he passed Jake Schaefer's farm—an' I guess Wes and you, poor child, kept follerin' where he led, thinkin' it was all right—and when he realized his mistake he said he was tired an' had to rest a while and—I'll vow! to think he'd go and do a thing like that," said Eliza, laughing again—"he lay right down in the snow, sir, with the clock beside him—and went sound to sleep."

"Yes," said Gant, "and the clock was broken."

"Yes," Eliza said, "she told me about that too—and how she heard you all come creepin' in real quiet an' easy-like about nine o'clock that night, when she and all the children were in bed—an' how she could hear him whisperin' to you and Wes to be quiet—an' how she heard you all come creepin' up the steps—and how he came tip-toein' in real easy-like an' laid the clock down on the bed—I reckon the glass had been broken out of it—hopin' she'd see it when she woke up in the morning an' wouldn't scold him then for stayin' out——"

"Yes," said Gant, still with the faint attentive grin, "and then the clock began to strike."

"Whew-w!" cried Eliza, putting her finger underneath her broad nose-wing—"I know she had to laugh about it when she told it to me— she said that all of you looked so sheepish when the clock began to strike that she didn't have the heart to scold him."

And Gant, grinning faintly again, emitted a faint rusty cackle that sounded like "E'God!" and said: "Yes, that was it. Poor fellow."

"But to think," Eliza went on, "that he would have no more sense than to do a thing like that—to lay right down there in the snow an' go to sleep with you two children watchin' him. And I know how she told it, how she questioned you and Wes next day, and I reckon started in to scold you for not takin' better care of him, and how you told her, 'Well, Mother, I thought that it would be all right. I kept steppin' where he stepped, I thought he knew the way.' And said she didn't have the heart to scold you after that—poor child, I reckon you were only eight or nine years old, and boy-like thought you'd follow in your father's footsteps and that everything would be all right."

"Yes," said Gant, with the faint grin again, "I kept stretchin' my legs to put my feet down in his tracks— it was all I could do to keep up with him. . . . Ah, Lord," he said, and in a moment said in a faint low voice, "how well I can remember it. That was just the winter before he died."

"And you've had that old clock ever since," Eliza said. "That very clock upon the mantel, sir—at least, you've had it ever since I've known you, and I reckon you had it long before that—for I know you told me how you brought it South with you. And that clock must be all of sixty or seventy years old—if it's a day."

"Yes," said Gant, "it's all of that."

And again he was silent, and lay so still and motionless that there was no sound in the room except his faint and labored breathing, the languid stir of the curtains in the cool night breeze, and the punctual tocking of the old wooden clock. And presently, when she thought that he might have gone off to sleep again, he spoke, in the same remote and detached voice as before:

"Eliza,"—he said—and at the sound of that unaccustomed word, a name he had spoken only twice in forty years—her white face and her worn brown eyes turned toward him with the quick and startled look of an animal—"Eliza," he said quietly, "you have had a hard life with me, a hard time. I want to tell you that I'm sorry."

And before she could move from her white stillness of shocked surprise, he lifted his great right hand and put it gently down across her own. And for a moment she sat there bolt upright, shaken, frozen, with a look of terror in her eyes, her heart drained of blood, a pale smile trembling uncertainly and foolishly on her lips. Then she tried to withdraw her hand with a clumsy movement, she began to stammer with an air of ludicrous embarrassment, she bridled, saying—"Aw-w, now, Mr. Gant. Well, now, I reckon,"—and suddenly these few simple words of regret and affection did what all the violence, abuse, drunkenness and injury of forty years had failed to do. She wrenched her hand free like a wounded creature, her face was suddenly contorted by that grotesque and pitiable grimace of sorrow that women have had in moments of grief since the beginning of time, and digging her fist into her closed eye quickly with the pathetic gesture of a child, she lowered her head and wept bitterly:

"It was a hard time, Mr. Gant," she whispered, "a hard time, sure enough. . . . It wasn't all the cursin' and the drinkin'—I got used to that. . . . I reckon I was only an ignorant sort of girl when I met you and I guess," she went on with a pathetic and unconscious humor, "I didn't know what married life was like . . . but I could have stood the rest of it . . . the bad names an' all the things you called me when I was goin' to have another child . . . but it was what you said when Grover died . . . accusin' me of bein' responsible for his death because I took the children to St. Louis to the Fair—" and at the words as if an old and lacerated wound had been re-opened raw and bleeding, she wept hoarsely, harshly, bitterly—"that was the worst time that I had—sometimes I prayed to God that I would not wake up—he was a fine boy, Mr. Gant, the best I had—like the write-up in the paper said he had the sense an' judgment of one twice his age . . . an' somehow it had grown a part of me, I expected him to lead the others—when he died it seemed like everything was gone . . . an' then to have you say that I had—" her voice faltered to a whisper, stopped: with a pathetic gesture she wiped the sleeve of her old frayed sweater across her eyes and already ashamed of her tears, said hastily:

"Not that I'm blamin' you, Mr. Gant. . . . I reckon we were both at fault . . . we were both to blame . . . if I had it to do all over I know I could do better . . . but I was so young and ignorant when I met you, Mr. Gant . . . knew nothing of the world . . . there was always something strange-like about you that I didn't understand."

Then, as he said nothing, but lay still and passive, looking at the ceiling, she said quickly, drying her eyes and speaking with a brisk and instant cheerfulness, the undaunted optimism of her ever-hopeful nature:

"Well, now, Mr. Gant, that's all over, and the best thing we can do is to forget about it. . . . We've both made our mistakes—we wouldn't be human if we didn't—but now we've got to profit by experience—the worst of all this trouble is all over—you've got to think of getting well now, that's the only thing you've got to do, sir," she said pursing her lips and winking briskly at him—"just set your mind on getting well—that's all you've got to do now, Mr. Gant—and the battle is half won. For half our ills and troubles are all imagination," she said sententiously, "and if you'll just make up your mind now that you're going to get well—why, sir, you'll do it," and she looked at him with a brisk nod. "And we've both got years before us, Mr. Gant—for all we know, the

best years of our life are still ahead of us—so we'll both go on and profit
by the mistakes of the past and make the most of what time's left," she
said. "That's just exactly what we'll do!"

And quietly, kindly, without moving, and with the impassive and
limitless regret of a man who knows that there is no return, he answered:
"Yes, Eliza. That is what we'll do."

"And now," she went on coaxingly, "why don't you go on back to
sleep now, Mr. Gant? There's nothin' like sleep to restore a man to
health—as the feller says, it's Nature's sovereign remedy, worth all the
doctors and all the medicine on earth," she winked at him, and then
concluded on a note of cheerful finality, "so you go on and get some
sleep now, and tomorrow you will feel like a new man."

And again he shook his head in an almost imperceptible gesture of
negation:

"No," he said, "not now. Can't sleep."

He was silent again, and presently, his breath coming somewhat
hoarse and labored, he cleared his throat, and put one hand up to his
throat, as if to relieve himself of some impediment.

Eliza looked at him with troubled eyes and said:

"What's the matter, Mr. Gant? There's nothing hurtin' you?"

"No," he said. "Just something in my throat. Could I have some
water?"

"Why, yes, sir! That's the very thing!" She got up hastily, and looking
about in a somewhat confused manner, saw behind her a pitcher of
water and a glass upon his old walnut bureau, and saying "This very
minute, sir!" started across the room.

And at the same moment, Gant was aware that some one had
entered the house, was coming towards him through the hall, would
soon be with him. Turning his head towards the door he was conscious
of something approaching with the speed of light, the instancy of
thought, and at that moment he was filled with a sense of inexpressible
joy, a feeling of triumph and security he had never known. Something
immensely bright and beautiful was converging in a flare of light, and
at that instant, the whole room blurred around him, his sight was fixed
upon that focal image in the door, and suddenly the child was standing
there and looking towards him.

And even as he started from his pillows, and tried to call his wife he
felt something thick and heavy in his throat that would not let him
speak. He tried to call to her again but no sound came, then something

wet and warm began to flow out of his mouth and nostrils, he lifted his hands up to his throat, the warm wet blood came pouring out across his fingers; he saw it and felt joy.

For now the child—or some one in the house was speaking, calling to him; he heard great footsteps, soft but thunderous, imminent, yet immensely far, a voice well-known, never heard before. He called to it, and then it seemed to answer him; he called to it with faith and joy to give him rescue, strength, and life, and it answered him and told him that all the error, old age, pain and grief of life was nothing but an evil dream; that he who had been lost was found again, that his youth would be restored to him and that he would never die, and that he would find again the path he had not taken long ago in a dark wood.

And the child still smiled at him from the dark door; the great steps, soft and powerful, came ever closer, and as the instant imminent approach of that last meeting came intolerably near, he cried out through the lake of jetting blood, "Here, Father, here!" and heard a strong voice answer him, "My son!"

At that instant he was torn by a rending cough, something was wrenched loose in him, the death gasp rattled through his blood, and a mass of greenish matter foamed out through his lips. Then the world was blotted out, a blind black fog swam up and closed above his head, some one seized him, he was held, supported in two arms, he heard some one's voice saying in a low tone of terror and of pity, "Mr. Gant! Mr. Gant! Oh, poor man, poor man! He's gone!" And his brain faded into night. Even before she lowered him back upon the pillows, she knew that he was dead.

Eliza's sharp scream brought three of her children—Daisy, Steve, and Luke, and the nurse, Bessie Gant, who was the wife of Gant's nephew Ollie—running from the kitchen. At the same moment Helen, who had taken an hour's sleep—her first in two days—in the little hall-bedroom off the porch, was wakened by her mother's cry, the sound of a screen-door slammed, and the sound of footsteps running past her window on the porch. Then, for several minutes she had no consciousness of what she did, and later she could not remember it. Her actions were those of a person driven by a desperate force, who acts from blind intuition, not from reason. Instantly, the moment that she heard her mother scream, the slam of the screen-door, and the running feet, she knew what had happened, and from that moment she knew only one frenzied desire; somehow to get to her father before he died.

The breath caught hoarse and sharp in her throat in a kind of nervous sob, it seemed that her heart had stopped beating and that her whole life-force was paralyzed; but she was out of her bed with a movement that left the old springs rattling, and she came across the back-porch with a kind of tornado-like speed that just came instantly from nowhere: in a moment she was standing in the open door with the sudden bolted look of a person who has been shot through the heart, staring at the silent group of people, and at the figure on the bed, with a dull strained stare of disbelief and horror.

All the time, although she was not conscious of it, her breath kept coming in a kind of hoarse short sob, her large big-boned face had an almost animal look of anguish and surprise, her mouth was partly open, her large chin hung down, and at this moment, as they turned towards her she began to moan, "Oh-h, oh-h, oh-h, oh-h!" in the same unconscious way, like a person who has received a heavy blow in the pit of the stomach. Then her mouth gaped open, a hoarse and ugly cry was torn from her throat—a cry not of grief but loss—and she rushed forward like a mad woman. They tried to stop her, to restrain her, she flung them away as if they had been rag dolls and hurled herself down across the body on the bed, raving like a maniac.

"Oh, Papa, Papa. . . . Why didn't they tell me? . . . Why didn't they let me know? . . . Why didn't they call me? . . . Oh, Papa, Papa, Papa! . . . dead, dead, dead . . . and they didn't tell me . . . they didn't let me know . . . they let you die . . . and I wasn't here! . . . I wasn't here!"—and she wept harshly, horribly, bitterly, rocking back and forth like a mad woman, with a dead man in her arms. She kept moaning, ". . . They didn't tell me . . . they let you die without me . . . I wasn't here . . . I wasn't here . . ."

And even when they lifted her up from the bed, detached her arms from the body they had held in such a desperate hug, she still kept moaning in a demented manner, as if talking to the corpse, and oblivious of the presence of these living people:

"They never told me . . . they never told me. . . . They let you die here all by yourself . . . and I wasn't here . . . I wasn't here."

All of the women, except Bessie Gant, had now begun to weep hysterically, more from shock, exhaustion, and the nervous strain than from grief, and now Bessie Gant's voice could be heard speaking to them sharply, coldly, peremptorily, as she tried to bring back order and calmness to the distracted scene:

"Now, you get out of here—all of you! . . . There's nothing more any of you can do—I'll take care of all the rest of it! . . . Get out, now . . . I can't have you in the room while there's work to do. . . . Helen, go on back to bed and get some sleep. . . . You'll feel better in the morning."

"They never told me! . . . They never told me," she turned and stared stupidly at Bessie Gant with dull glazed eyes. "Can't you do something? . . . Where's McGuire? Has any one called him yet?"

"No," said the nurse sharply and angrily, "and no one's going to. You're not going to get that man out of bed at this hour of the night when there's nothing to be done. . . . Get out of here, now, all of you," she began to push and herd them towards the door. "I can't be bothered with you. . . . Go somewhere—anywhere—get drunk—only don't come back in here."

The whole house had come to life; in the excitement, shock, and exhaustion of their nerves the dead man still lying there in such a grotesque and twisted position, was forgotten. One of Eliza's lodgers, a man named Gilmer, who had been in the house for years, was wakened, went out, and got a gallon of corn whiskey; every one drank a great deal, became, in fact, somewhat intoxicated; when the undertakers came to take Gant away, none of the family was present. No one saw it. They were all in the kitchen seated around Eliza's battered old kitchen table, with the jug of whiskey on the table before them. They drank and talked together all night long until dawn came.

XXXIV

THE morning of Gant's funeral the house was filled with people who had known him and the air was heavy with the sweet, cloying fragrance of the funeral flowers: the odors of lilies, roses, and carnations. His coffin was banked with flowers, but in the centre there was a curious and arresting plainness, a simple wreath of laurel leaves. Attached to the wreath was a small card on which these words were written: "Hugh McGuire."

And people passing by the coffin paused for a moment and stared at the name with a feeling of unspoken wonder in their hearts. Eliza stood looking at the wreath a moment with hands clasped across her waist, and then turned away, shaking her head rapidly, with a short convulsive pucker of her lips, as she spoke to Helen in a low voice:

"I tell you what—it's pretty strange when you come to think of it—it gives you a queer feeling—I tell you what, it does."

And this expressed the emotion that every one felt when they saw the wreath. For Hugh McGuire had been found dead at his desk at six o'clock that morning, the news had just spread through the town, and now, when people saw the wreath upon Gant's coffin, there was something in their hearts they could not utter.

Gant lay in the splendid coffin, with his great hands folded quietly on his breast. Later, the boy could not forget his father's hands. They were the largest, most powerful, and somehow the most shapely hands he had ever seen. And even though his great right hand had been so crippled and stiffened by an attack of inflammatory rheumatism ten years before that he had never regained the full use of it, and since that time could only hold the great wooden mallet that the stone-cutters use in a painful and clumsy half-clasp between the thumb and the big stiffened fingers, his hands had never lost their character of life, strength, and powerful shapeliness.

The hands had given to the interminable protraction of his living death a kind of concrete horror that it otherwise would not have had. For as his powerful gaunt figure waned and wasted under the ravages of the cancer that was consuming him until he had become only the enfeebled shadow of his former self, his gaunt hands, on which there was so little which death could consume, lost none of their former rock-like heaviness, strength and shapely power. Thus, even when the giant figure of the man had become nothing but a spectral remnant of itself, sunk in a sorrow of time, awaiting death, those great, still-living hands of power and strength hung incredibly, horribly, from that spectral form of death to which they were attached.

And for this reason those powerful hands of life evoked, as nothing else could have done, in an instant searing flash of memory and recognition the lost world of his father's life of manual power, hunger, fury, savage abundance and wild joy, the whole enchanted structure of that lost life of magic he had made for them. Constantly, those great hands of life joined, with an almost grotesque incongruity, to that scarecrow form of wasting death would awake for them, as nothing else on earth could do, all of the sorrowful ghosts of time, the dream-like spell and terror of the years between, the years of phantom death, the horror of unreality, strangeness, disbelief, and memory, that haunted them.

So was it now, even in death, with his father's hands. In their powerful, gaunt and shapely clasp, as he lay dead in his coffin, there seemed to be held and gathered, somehow, all of his life that could never die—a living image of the essential quality of his whole life with its fury and unrest, desire and hunger, the tremendous sweep and relish of its enormous appetites and the huge endowment of its physical and sensual powers.

Thus, one could suppose that on the face of a dead poet there might remain—how, where or in what way we could not tell, a kind of flame, a light, a glory,—the magic and still living chrysm of his genius. And on the face of the dead conqueror we might still see living, arrogant, and proud with all its dark authorities the frown of power, the inflexible tyranny of stern command, the special infinitude of the invincible will that would not die with life, and that incredibly remains, still dark and living in its scorn and mockery of time.

Then, on the face of an old dead prophet or philosopher there would live and would not die the immortality of proud, lonely thought. We could not say just where that spirit rested. Sometimes it would seem to rest upon the temples of the grand and lonely head. Sometimes we would think it was a kind of darkness in the shadows of the closed and sunken eyes, sometimes the marsh fire of a dark and lambent flame that hovered round the face, that could never be fixed, but that we always knew was there.

And just as poet, prophet, priest and conqueror might each retain in death some living and fitting image of his whole life's truth, so would the strength, the skill, all of the hope, hunger, fury, and unrest that had lashed and driven on through life the gaunt figure of a stonecutter be marvellously preserved in the granite power and symmetry of those undying hands.

Now the corpse was stretched out on the splendid satin cushions of the expensive coffin. It had been barbered, powdered, disembowelled, and pumped full of embalming fluid. And as it lay there with its waxen head set forward in its curious gaunt projectiveness, the pale lips firmly closed and with a little line of waxen mucous in the lips, the women came forward with their oily swollen faces, and a look of ravenous eagerness in their eyes, stared at it hard and long, lifted their sodden handkerchiefs slowly to their oily mouths, and were borne away, sobbing hysterically, by their equally oily, ravenous, sister orgiasts in sorrow.

Meanwhile his father's friends, the stonecutters, masons, building contractors, butchers, business men and male relatives were standing awkwardly about, dressed in their good, black clothes which they seemed not to wear so much as to inhabit with a kind of unrestful itchiness, lowering their eyes gravely and regretfully as the women put on their revolting show, talking together in low voices, and wondering when it would all be over.

These circumstances, together with the heavy unnatural languor of the funeral smells, the sweet-sick heaviness of the carnations, the funereal weepy blacks in which the women had arrayed themselves, the satiny sandalwood scent that came from the splendid coffin, and the fragrant faintly acrid odor of embalmed flesh, particularly when blended with the smell of cooking turnip greens, roast pork and apple sauce out in the kitchen, combined to create an atmosphere somewhat like a dinner party in a comfortably furnished morgue.

In all this obscene pomp of burial there was something so grotesque, unnatural, disgusting, and remote from all he could remember of the dead man's life and personality that everything about him—even the physical horror of his bloody death—now seemed so far away he could hardly believe it ever happened. Therefore, he stared at this waxen and eviscerated relic in the coffin with a sense of weird disbelief, unable to relate it to the living man who had bled great lakes of blood the night before.

Yet, even in his death, his father's hands still seemed to live, and would not die. And this was the reason why the memory of those hands haunted him then and would haunt him forever after. This was the reason why, when he would try to remember how he looked when dead, he could remember nothing clearly except the powerful sculptured weight and symmetry of his tremendous hands as they lay folded on his body in the coffin. The great hands had a stony, sculptured and yet living strength and vitality, as if Michelangelo had carved them. They seemed to rest there upon the groomed, bereft and vacant horror of the corpse with a kind of terrible reality as if there really is, in death, some energy of life that will not die, some element of man's life that must persist and that resumes into a single feature of his life the core and essence of his character.

XXXV

STARWICK had now become his best and closest friend. Suddenly, it occurred to him with a strange and bitter sense of loss and lack that Starwick was the only friend of his own age that he had ever known to whom he had fully and passionately revealed his own life, of whose fellowship and comradeship he had never grown weary. Friends he had had—friends in the casual and indifferent sense in which most friendship is understood—but until now he had never held a friend like Starwick in his heart's core.

Why was it? What was this grievous lack or loss—if lack or loss it was—in his own life? Why was it that, with his fierce, bitter, and insatiate hunger for life, his quenchless thirst for warmth, joy, love, and fellowship, his constant image, which had blazed in his heart since childhood, of the enchanted city of the great comrades and the glorious women, that he grew weary of people almost as soon as he met them? Why was it that he seemed to squeeze their lives dry of any warmth and interest they might have for him as one might squeeze an orange, and then was immediately filled with boredom, disgust, dreary tedium, and an impatient weariness and desire to escape so agonizing that it turned his feeling almost into hatred?

Why was it that his spirit was now filled with this furious unrest and exasperation against people because none of them seemed as good as they should be? Where did it come from—this improvable and yet unshakable conviction that grew stronger with every rebuff and disappointment—that the enchanted world was here around us ready to our hand the moment that we chose to take it for our own, and that the impossible magic in life of which he dreamed, for which he thirsted, had been denied us not because it was a phantom of desire, but because men had been too base and weak to take what was their own?

Now, with Starwick, and for the first time, he felt this magic constantly—this realization of a life forever good, forever warm and beautiful, forever flashing with the fires of passion, poetry and joy, forever filled with the swelling and triumphant confidence of youth, its belief in new lands, morning, and a shining city, its hope of voyages, its conviction of a fortunate, good and happy life—an imperishable happiness and joy—that was impending, that would be here at any moment.

For a moment he looked at the strange and delicate face of the young man beside him, reflecting, with a sense of wonder, at his communion with this other life, so different from his own in kind and temper. What was it? Was it the sharp mind, that original and penetrating instrument which picked up the old and weary problems of the spirit by new handles, displaying without labor planes and facets rarely seen? With what fierce joy he welcomed those long walks together in the night, along the quiet streets of Cambridge, or by the marvellous river that wound away small and magical in the blazing moonlight into the sweet, dark countryside! What other pleasure, what other appeasement of his mind and sense had been so complete and wonderful as that which came from this association as, oblivious of the world, they carried on their fierce debate about all things under heaven; his own voice, passionate, torrential, and wild, crying out against the earth, the moon, invoking all the gods of verse and magic while his mind played rivers of lightning across the vast fields of reading and experience!

And how eagerly he waited for the answers of that other voice, quiet, weary, drawling—how angrily he stormed against its objections, how hungrily and gratefully he fed upon its agreement! What other tongue had had the power to touch his pride and his senses as this one had—how cruelly had its disdain wounded him, how magnificently had its praise filled his heart with glory! On these nights when he and Starwick had walked along the river in these vehement, passionate, and yet affectionate debates, he would relive the scene for hours after it had ended, going over their discussion again and again, remembering every gesture, every intonation of the voice, every flash of life and passion in the face. Late in the night he would pace up and down his room, or pause dreaming by his window, still carrying on in his mind the debate with his friend, inventing and regretting splendid things he might have said, exulting in those he had said and in every word of approval or burst of laughter he had provoked. And he would think: Ah, but I was *good* there! I could see how he admired me, how high a place I have in his affection. For when he says a thing he *means* it: he called me a poet, his voice was quiet and full of passion, he said my like had never been, that my destiny was great and sure.

Was this, then, the answer?

Until this period of his life he had drunk very little: in spite of the desperate fear his mother had that each of her children inherited the whiskey disease—"the curse of licker," as she called it—from their father, he felt no burning appetite for stimulant. Alone, he never sought it out, he never bought a bottle for himself: solitary as his life had become, the idea of solitary drinking, of stealthy alley potations from a flask, filled him with sodden horror.

Now, in the company of Starwick, he was drinking more frequently than he had ever done before. Alcohol, indeed, until his twentieth year had been only a casual and infrequent spirit—once, in his seventeenth year, when he had come home from college at the Christmas vacation, he had got very drunk on various liquors which his brother Luke had brought home to his father, and which he had mixed together in a tumbler, and drunk without discretion. And there had been two or three casual sprees during his years at college, but until this time he had never known the experience of frequent intoxication.

But now, in the company of Frank Starwick, he went every week or so to a little restaurant which was situated in the Italian district of the eastern quarter of town, beyond Scollay Square and across Washington Street. The place was Starwick's own discovery, he hoarded his knowledge of it with stern secrecy, yielding it up only to a few friends—a few rare and understanding spirits who would not coarsely abuse the old-world spirit of this priceless place because, he said:

"It would be a pity if it ever got known about. It really would, you know. . . . I mean, the kind of people who would begin to go there would ruin it. . . . They really would. . . . I mean, it's *quite* astonishing to find a place of that sort here in Boston."

It was the beginning of that dark time of blood, and crime, and terror which the years of prohibition brought and which was to leave its hideous mutilation not only upon the soul and conscience of the nation, but upon the lives of millions of people—particularly the young everywhere. At this time, however, the ugly, jeering, open arrogance of the later period—the foul smell of privilege and corruption, the smirk of protection, and the gangster's sneer, were not so evident as they became in the years that followed. At this time, it was by no means easy "to get a drink": the speakeasy had already started on its historic career, but was still more or less what its name suggested—a place to be got at quietly and by stealth, a place of low voices, furtive and suspicious eyes, and elaborate precautions.

The place which Starwick had "discovered," and which he hoarded with such precious secrecy, was a small Italian restaurant known as Posillipo's, which occupied the second floor of an old brick building in an obscure street of the Italian quarter. Frank pronounced the name strongly and lovingly—"Pothillippo's"—in the mannered voice, and with the affected accent which all foreign and exotic names—particularly those that had a Latin flavoring—inspired in him.

Arrived at "Pothillippo's," Frank, who even at this time did all things with the most lavish and lordly extravagance, and who tipped generously at every opportunity, would be welcomed obsequiously by the proprietor and the waiters, and then would order with an air of the most refined and sensual discrimination from his favorite waiter, a suave and fawning servitor named Nino. There were other waiters just as good as Nino, but Frank expressed an overwhelming preference for him above all others because, he said, Nino had the same face as one of the saints in a painting by Giotto, and because he professed to find all of the ancient, grave and exquisite rhythm of the ancient Tuscan nobility composed in the one figure of this waiter.

"But have you noticed the way he uses his hands while talking?" Frank would say in a tone of high impassioned earnestness.—"Did you notice that last gesture? It is the same gesture that you find in the figure of the disciple Thomas in Leonardo's painting of 'The Last Supper.' It really is, you know. . . . Christ!" he would cry, in his high, strange, and rather womanish tone. "The centuries of art, of living, of culture—the terrific knowledge *all* these people have—the kind of thing you'll never find in people in this country, the kind of thing that no amount of college education or books can give you—all expressed in a single gesture of the hands of this Italian waiter. . . . The whole thing's *quite* astonishing, it really is, you know."

The real reason, however, that Frank preferred Nino to all the other waiters in "Pothillippo's" establishment was that he liked the sound of the word "Nino," and pronounced it beautifully.

"Nino!" Frank would cry, in a high, strange, and rather womanish voice—"Nino!"

"Si, signor," Nino would breathe unctuously, and would then stand in an attitude of heavy and prayerful adoration, awaiting the young lord's next commands.

"Nino," Frank would then go on in the tone and manner of a sensuous and weary old-world sophisticate. "Quel vin avez-vous? . . . Quel vin—rouge—du—très—bon. Vous—comprenez? said Frank, using up in one speech most of his French words, but giving a wonderful sense of linguistic mastery and complete eloquence in two languages.

"Mais si, signor!" Nino would answer immediately, skilfully buttering

Frank on both sides—the French and the Italian—with three masterly words.

"Le Chianti est *très, très* bon! . . . C'est parfait, monsieur," he whispered, with a little ecstatic movement of his fingers. "Admirable!"

"Bon," said Frank with an air of quiet decision. "Alors, Nino," he continued, raising his voice as he pronounced these two words, which were among his favorites. "Alors, une bouteille du Chianti—n'est-ce pas——"

"Mais si, signor!" said Nino, nodding enthusiastically. "Si—et pour manger?" he went on coaxingly.

"Pour manger?" Frank began—"Ecoute, Nino—vous pouvez recommander quelque-chose—quelque-chose *d'extraordinaire!*" Frank cried in a high impassioned tone. "Quelque-chose de la *maison!*" he concluded triumphantly.

"Mais, si!" Nino cried enthusiastically. "Si, signor. . . . Permettez-moi! . . . Le spaghetti," he whispered seductively, rolling his dark eyes rapturously aloft, and making a little mincing movement, indicative of speechless ecstasy, of his thumb and forefinger. "Le spaghetti . . . de la . . . maison . . . ah, signor," Nino breathed—"le spaghetti avec la sauce de la maison est merveilleuse . . . merveilleuse!" he whispered.

"Bon," said Starwick nodding. "Alors, Nino—le spaghetti pour deux —vous comprenez?"

"Mais si, signor! Si," Nino breathed. "Parfaitement"—and wrote the miraculous order on his order pad. "Et puis, monsieur," said Nino coaxingly, and with complete humility. "Permettez moi de recommander—le poulet," he whispered rapturously—"le poulet roti," he breathed, as if unveiling the rarest secrets of cookery that had been revealed since the days of Epicurus—"le poulet roti . . . de la maison," again he made the little speechless movement of the finger and the thumb, and rolled his rapturous eyes around—"ah, signor," said Nino, "Vous n'aurez pas de regrets si vous commandez le poulet."

"Bon. . . . Bon," said Starwick quietly and profoundly. "Alors, Nino —deux poulets rotis, pour moi et pour monsieur," he commanded.

"Bon, bon," said Nino, nodding vigorously and writing with enthusiasm—"et pour la salade, messieurs," he paused—looking inquiringly and yet hopefully at both his lordly young patrons.

And so it went, until the menu had all been gone through in mangled French and monosyllabic Italian. When this great ceremony was over, Frank Starwick had done nothing more nor less than order the one-dollar table d'hôte dinner which Signor "Pothillippo" provided for all the patrons of his establishment and whose order—soup, fish, spaghetti, roasted chicken, salad, ice-cream, cheese, nuts and bitter coffee—was unchangeable as destiny, and not to be altered by the whims of common men, whether they would or no.

And yet Frank's manner of ordering his commonplace rather dreary meal was so touched by mystery, strangeness, an air of priceless rarity and sensual refinement, that one would smack his lips over the various dishes with a gourmandizing gusto, as if the art of some famous chêf had really been exhausted in their preparation.

And this element of Frank Starwick's character was one of the finest and most attractive things about him. It was, perhaps as much as anything else, the reason why people of all kinds were drawn to him, delighted to be with him, and why Frank could command the boundless affection, devotion, and support of people more than any one the other boy had ever known.

For, in spite of all Frank's affectations of tone, manner, gesture, and accent, in spite of the elaborately mannered style of his whole life—no! really *because* of them (for what were all these manners and affectations except the evidence of Frank's constant effort to give qualities of strangeness, mystery, rareness, joy and pleasure to common things that had none of these qualities in themselves)—the deep and passionate desire in Frank's spirit to find a life that would always be good, beautiful, and exciting was apparent.

And to an amazing degree, Frank Starwick succeeded in investing all the common and familiar acts and experiences of this world with this strange and romantic color of his own personality.

When one was with him, everything—"le Chianti de la maison," a cigarette, the performance of a play, a poem or a book, a walk across the Harvard Yard, or along the banks of the Charles River—became strange and rare and memorable, and for this reason Frank, in spite of the corrupt and rotten spot which would develop in his character and eventually destroy him, was one of the rarest and highest people that ever lived, and could never be forgotten by any one who had ever known him, and been his friend.

For, by a baffling paradox, these very affectations of Frank's speech and dress and carriage, the whole wrought manner of his life, which caused many people who disbelieved him to dismiss him bitterly as an affected and artificial poseur, really came from something innocent and naive and good in Frank's character—something as innocent and fa-

miliar as the affectations of Tom Sawyer when he told tall stories, invented wild, complicated, and romantic schemes, when none was necessary, or used big words to impress his friends, the nigger Jim, or Huckle-
berry Finn.

Thus, the two young men would stay in "Pothillippo's" until late at
night when the place closed, drinking that wonderful "Chianti de la
maison," so preciously and lovingly described, which was really nothing
but "dago red," raw, new, and instantaneous in its intoxication, filled
with headaches and depression for tomorrow morning, but filled now
with the mild, soaring, jubilant and triumphant drunkenness that only
youth can know.

And they would leave this place of Latin mystery and languor at one
o'clock in the morning, Frank shouting in a high drunken voice before
he left, 'Nino! Nino!—Il faut quelque chose à boire avant de partir—
Nino!—Nino!—Encora! Encora!"—pronouncing his last Italian word
victoriously.

"Mais si, signor," Nino would answer, smiling somewhat anxiously.
"Du vin?"

"Mais non, mais non, Nino" Frank would cry violently. "Pas de vin
—du wis-kee, Nino! Du wis-kee!"

Then they would gulp down drinks of the raw and powerful beverage to which the name of whiskey had been given in that era, and
leaving a dim blur of lights, a few dim blots of swarthy, anxiously smiling faces behind them, they would reel dangerously down the rickety
stairs and out into the narrow, twisted streets, the old grimed web of
sleeping quietness, the bewildering, ancient, and whited streets of
Boston.

Above them, in the cool sweet skies of night, the great moons of the
springtime, and New England, blazed with a bare, a lovely and enchanted radiance. And around them the great city, and its thousand
narrow twisted streets lay anciently asleep beneath that blazing moon,
and from the harbor came the sound of ships, the wasting, fresh, half-
rotten harbor-smells, filled with the thought of ships, the sea, the proud
exultancy of voyages. And out of the cobbled streets and from the old
grimed buildings—yes! from the very breast and bareness of that springtime moon and those lovely lilac skies, there came somehow—God
knows how—all of the sweet wildness of New England in the month
of May, the smell of the earth, the sudden green, the glorious blossoms

—all that was wild, sweet, strange, simple, instantly familiar—that impossible loveliness, that irresistible magic, that unutterable hope for the magic that could not be spoken, but that seemed almost in the instant to be seized, grasped, and made one's own forever—for the hunger, possession and fulfilment—and for God knows what—for that magic land of green, its white and lovely houses, and the white flesh, the moon-dark hair, the depthless eyes and everlasting silence of its secret, dark, and lavish women.

Dark Helen in our hearts forever burning—oh, no more!

Then the two young men would thread that maze of drunken moon-lit streets, and feel the animate and living silence of the great city all around them, and look then at the moon with drunken eyes, and see the moon, all bare and drunken in the skies, the whole earth and the ancient city drunk with joy and sleep and springtime and the enchanted silences of the moon-drunk squares. And they would come at length to Cambridge, to find the moonlight dark upon the sleeping silence of the university and Harvard Square, and exultancy and joy welled up in them forever, wild shouts and songs and laughter were torn from their throats and rang out through the sleeping streets of Cambridge, filling the moon-sweet air with jubilation, for they were drunken, young, and twenty—immortal confidence and victorious strength possessed them—and they knew that they could never die.

Immortal drunkenness! What tribute can we ever pay, what song can we ever sing, what swelling praise can ever be sufficient to express the joy, the gratefulness, and the love which we, who have known youth and hunger in America, have owed to alcohol?

We are so lost, so lonely, so forsaken in America: immense and savage skies bend over us, and we have no door.

But you, immortal drunkenness, came to us in our youth when all our hearts were sick with hopelessness, our spirits maddened with unknown terrors, and our heads bowed down with nameless shame. You came to us victoriously, to possess us, and to fill our lives with your wild music, to make the goat-cry burst from our exultant throats, to make us know that here upon the wilderness, the savage land, that here beneath immense, inhuman skies of time, in all the desolation of the cities, the gray unceasing flood-tides of the manswarm, our youth would soar to fortune, fame, and love, our spirits quicken with the power of mighty poetry, our work go on triumphantly to fulfilment until our lives prevailed.

What does it matter then if since that time of your first coming, magic drunkenness, our head has grown bald, our young limbs heavy, and if our flesh has lain battered, bleeding in the stews?

You came to us with music, poetry, and wild joy when we were twenty, when we reeled home at night through the old moon-whitened streets of Boston and heard our friend, our comrade, and our dead companion, shout through the silence of the moonwhite square: "You are a poet and the world is yours."

And victory, joy, wild hope, and swelling certitude and tenderness surged through the conduits of our blood as we heard that drunken cry, and triumph, glory, proud belief was resting like a chrysm around us as we heard that cry, and turned our eyes then to the moon-drunk skies of Boston, knowing only that we were young, and drunk, and twenty, and that the power of mighty poetry was within us, and the glory of the great earth lay before us—because we were young and drunk and twenty, and could never die!

XXXVI

WHEN Oswald Ten Eyck left his $8000 job on the Hearst Syndicate and came to Cambridge to enroll in Professor Hatcher's celebrated course for dramatists, he had saved a sum rare in the annals of journalism—$700. When he got through paying the tuition, admission, and other accessory fees that would entitle him to a membership in good standing in the graduate school of the university, something less than $500 remained. Oswald got an attic room in Cambridge, in a square, smut-gray frame house which was the home of an Irish family named Grogan. To reach his room, he had to mount a rickety flight of stairs that was almost as steep as a ladder, and when he got there, he had to manage his five feet five of fragile stature carefully in order to keep from cracking his head upon the sloping white-washed walls that followed the steep pitch of the roof with painful fidelity. The central part of Oswald's room, which was the only place in which the little man could stand erect, was not over four feet wide: there was a single window at the front where stood his writing table. He had a couple of straight chairs, a white iron cot pushed in under the eave of the left side, a few bookshelves pushed in under the eave of the right. It could literally be said that the playwright crawled to bed, and when he read he had to approach the poets as a poet should—upon his knees.

For this austere cell, Professor Hatcher's dramatist paid Mrs. Mary Grogan fifteen dollars every month. Therefore, when the primary fees of tuition and matriculation and the cell in Mrs. Grogan's house had been accounted for, Oswald Ten Eyck had all of $300 left to take care of clothing, food, tobacco, books, and plays during the ensuing period of nine months. This sum perhaps was adequate, but it was not grand, and Ten Eyck, poet though he was, was subject to all those base cravings of sensual desire that 100 pounds of five feet five is heir to.

This weakness of the flesh was unhappily reflected in the artist's work. During the brief period of his sojourn in Professor Hatcher's class, his plays were numerous but for the most part low. Ten Eyck turned them out with the feverish haste which only a trained newspaper man can achieve when driven on by the cherished ambition of a lifetime and the knowledge that art is long and $300 very fleeting. He had started out most promisingly in the fleshless ethers of mystic fantasy, but he became progressively more sensual until at the end he was practically wallowing in a trough of gluttony.

The man, in fact, became all belly when he wrote—and this was strange in a frail creature with the large burning eyes of a religious zealot, hands small-boned, fleshless as a claw, and a waist a rubber band would have snapped round comfortably. He seemed compact of flame and air and passion and an agonizing shyness. Professor Hatcher had great hopes for him—the whole atom was framed, Professor Hatcher thought, for what the true Hatcherian called "the drama of revolt," but the flaming atom fooled him, fooled him cruelly. For after the brilliant promise of that first beginning—a delicate, over-the-hills-and-far-away fantasy reminiscent of Synge, Yeats, and the Celtic Dawn—brain bowed to belly, Ten Eyck wrote of food.

His second effort was a one-act play whose action took place on the sidewalk in front of a Childs restaurant, while a white-jacketed attendant deftly flipped brown wheat-cakes on a plate. The principal character, and in fact the only speaker in this play, was a starving poet who stood before the window and delivered himself of a twenty-minute monologue on a poet's life and the decay of modern society, in the course of which most of the staple victuals on the Childs menu were mentioned frequently and with bitter relish.

Professor Hatcher felt his interest waning: he had hoped for finer things. Yet a wise caution learned from errors in the past had taught him to forbear. He knew that out of man's coarse earth the finer flowers of his spirit sometimes grew. Some earlier members of his class had taught him this, some who had written coarsely of coarse things. They wrote of sailors, niggers, thugs, and prostitutes, of sunless lives and evil strivings, of murder, hunger, rape, and incest, а black picture of man's life unlighted by a spark of grace, a ray of hope, a flicker of the higher vision. Professor Hatcher had not always asked them to return—to "come back for a second year," which was the real test of success and future promise in the Hatcherian world. And yet, unknighted by this accolade, some had gone forth and won renown: their grim plays had been put on everywhere and in all languages. And the only claim the true Hatcherian could make of them was: "Yes, they were with us but not of us: they were not asked to come back for a second year."

There were some painful memories, but Professor Hatcher had derived from them a wise forbearance. His hopes for Oswald Ten Eyck were fading fast, but he had determined to hold his judgment in abeyance until Oswald's final play. But, as if to relieve his distinguished tutor from a painful choice, Ten Eyck himself decided it. After his third play there was no longer any doubt of the decision. For that play, which Oswald called "Dutch Fugue," would more aptly have been titled "No Return."

It was a piece in four acts dealing with the quaintly flavored life and customs of his own people, the Hudson River Dutch. The little man was hotly proud of his ancestry, and always insisted with a slight sneer of aristocratic contempt: "Not the Pennsylvania Dutch—Good God, no! *They're* not Dutch but German: the *real* Dutch, the *old* Dutch, *Catskill* Dutch!" And if Ten Eyck's interest in food had been uncomfortably pronounced in his earlier work, in this final product of his curious genius, his sensual appetites became indecent in their unrestraint. It is doubtful if the long and varied annals of the stage have ever offered such a spectacle: the play became a sort of dramatic incarnation of the belly, acted by a cast of fourteen adults, male and female, all of whom were hearty eaters.

The central events of that extraordinary play, which were a birth, a death, a wedding, were all attended by eating, drinking, and the noises of the feast. Scene followed scene with kaleidoscopic swiftness: the jubilant merry-making of the christening had hardly died away before the stage was set, the trestles groaning, with the more sombre, sober and substantial victuals of the funeral; and the wheels of the hearse had hardly echoed away into the distance before the scene burst out in all the boisterous reel and rout and feasting of the wedding banquet. Of no play that was ever written could it be more aptly said that the funeral baked meats did coldly furnish forth the marriage tables, and what is more, they almost furnished forth the casket and the corpse as well. Finally, the curtain fell as it had risen, upon a groaning table surrounded by the assembled cast of fourteen famished gluttons—a scene in which apparently the only sound and action were provided by the thrust of jowl and smack of lip, a kind of symphonic gluttony of reach and grab, cadenced by the stertorous breathing of the eaters, the clash of crockery, and the sanguinary drip of rare roast beef—the whole a prophetic augury that flesh was grass and man's days fleeting, that life would change and reappear in an infinite succession of births and deaths and marriages, but that the holy rites of eating and the divine permanence of good dinners and roast beef were indestructible and would endure forever.

Ten Eyck read the play himself one Friday afternoon to Professor Hatcher and his assembled following. He read in a rapid high-pitched voice, turning the pages with a trembling claw, and thrusting his long fingers nervously through his disordered mop of jet-black hair. As he went on, the polite attention of the class was changed insensibly to a paralysis of stupefaction. Professor Hatcher's firm thin lips became much firmer, thinner, tighter. A faint but bitter smile was printed at the edges of his mouth. Then, for a moment, when the playwright finished, there was silence: Professor Hatcher slowly raised his hand, detached his gold-rimmed glasses from his distinguished nose, and let them fall and dangle on their black silk cord. He looked around the class; his cultivated voice was low, controlled, and very quiet.

"Is there any comment?" Professor Hatcher said.

No one answered for a moment. Then Mr. Grey, a young patrician from Philadelphia, spoke:

"I think," he said with a quiet emphasis of scorn, "I think he might very well get it produced in the Chicago Stock Yards."

Mr. Grey's remark was ill-timed. For the Stock Yards brought to Ten Eyck's mind a thought of beef, and beef brought back a memory of his palmy days with Mr. Hearst when beef was plenty and the pay-checks fat, and all these thoughts brought back the bitter memory of the day before which was the day when he had eaten last: a single meal, a chaste and wholesome dinner of spaghetti, spinach, coffee, and a roll. And thinking, Ten Eyck craned his scrawny neck convulsively along the edges of his fraying collar, looked desperately at Professor Hatcher, who returned his gaze inquiringly; ducked his head quickly, bit his nails and craned again. Then, suddenly, seeing the cold patrician features of young Mr. Grey, his blue shirt of costly madras, his limp crossed elegance of legs and pleated trousers, the little man half rose, scraping his chair back from the table round which the class was sitting, and with an inclusive gesture of his claw-like hand, screamed incoherently:

"These! These! . . . We have the English. . . . As for the Russians. . . . Take the Germans—Toller—Kaiser—the Expressionists. . . . But the Dutch, the Dutch, the *Catskill* Dutch. . . ." Pointing a trembling finger towards Mr. Grey, he shrieked: "The Philadelphia Cricket Club. . . . God! God!" he bent, racked with soundless laughter, his thin hands pressed against his sunken stomach. "That it should come to this!" he said, and suddenly, catching Professor Hatcher's cold impassive eye upon him, he slumped down abruptly in his seat, and fell to biting his nails: "Well, I don't know," he said with a foolish little laugh. "Maybe—I guess . . ." his voice trailed off, he did not finish.

"Is there any other comment?" said Professor Hatcher.

There was none.

"Then," said Professor Hatcher, "the class is dismissed until next Monday."

Professor Hatcher did not look up as Ten Eyck went out.

When Oswald got out into the corridor, he could hear the last footfalls of the departing class echoing away around the corner. For a moment, he leaned against the wall: he felt hollow, weak, and dizzy: his knees bent under him like rubber, and his head, after its recent flood of blood and passion, felt swollen, light, and floating as a toy balloon. Suddenly he remembered that it was Friday. Saturday, the day on which he could next allow himself to take a little from his dwindling hoard—for such was the desperate resolution made at the beginning and adhered to ever since—Saturday shone desperately far away, a small and shining disc of light at the black mouth of an interminable tunnel, and all giddy, weak, and hollow as he was, he did not see how he could wait! So he surrendered. He knew that if he hurried now he would be just in time for old Miss Potter's Friday afternoon. And torn between hunger and disgust, Ten Eyck gave in again to hunger as he had done a score of times before, even when he knew that he must face again that crowning horror of modern life, the art party.

Miss Potter was a curious old spinster of some property, and she lived, with a companion, in a pleasant house on Garden Street, not far from the University. Miss Potter's companion was also an aged spinster: her name was Miss Flitcroft; the two women were inseparable. Miss Potter was massively constructed: a ponderous woman who moved heavily and with wheezing difficulty, and whose large eyes bulged comically out of a face on which a strange fixed grin was always legible.

Miss Flitcroft was a wren of a woman, with bony little hands, and an old withered, rather distinguished-looking face: she wore a band of velvet around her stringy neck. She was not only a companion, she was also a kind of nurse to Miss Potter, and she could give relief and comfort to the other woman as no one else could.

For Miss Potter was really very ill: she had a savage love of life, a desperate fear of death, and she knew that she was dying. But even the woman's sufferings, which were obviously intense, were touched by that grotesque and ridiculous quality that made Ten Eyck want to howl with explosive laughter, even when he felt a rending pity for her. Thus, at table sometimes, with all her tribe of would-be poets, playwrights, composers, novelists, painters, critics, and enfeebled litterateurs gathered around her, putting away the delicious food she had so abundantly provided, Miss Potter would suddenly begin to choke, gasp, and cough horribly; her eyes would bulge out of her head in a fish-like stare, and looking desperately at Miss Flitcroft with an expression of unutterable terror, she would croak: . . . "Dying! Dying! I tell you I'm dying!"

"Nonsense!" Miss Flitcroft would answer tartly, jumping up and running around behind Miss Potter's chair. "You're no such thing! . . . You've only choked yourself on something you have eaten! There!" and she would deliver herself straightway of a resounding whack upon Miss Potter's meaty, mottled back (for on these great Friday afternoons, Miss Potter came out sumptuously in velvet, which gave ample glimpses of her heavy arms and breasts and the broad thick surface of her shoulders).

"If you didn't eat so fast these things would never happen!" Miss Flitcroft would say acidly, as she gave Miss Potter another resounding whack on her bare shoulders. "Now you get over this nonsense!" . . .

whack! "There's nothing wrong with you—do you hear?" . . . whack! "You're frightened half out of your wits," . . . whack! . . . "just because you've tried to stuff everything down your throat at once!" whack! whack!

And by this time, Miss Potter would be on the road to recovery, gasping and panting more easily now, as she continued to look up with a fixed stare of her bulging eyes at Miss Flitcroft, with an expression full of entreaty, dawning hopefulness, apology, and pitiable gratitude.

As for Ten Eyck, his pain and embarrassment when one of these catastrophes occurred were pitiable. He would scramble to his feet, stand helplessly, half-crouched, casting stricken glances toward the most convenient exit as if contemplating the possibility of a sudden and inglorious flight. Then he would turn again toward the two old women, his dark eyes fixed on them in a fascinated stare in which anguish, sympathy, helplessness and horror were all legible.

For several years, in spite of her ill health, Miss Potter had fiddled around on the edges of Professor Hatcher's celebrated course at the university. She had written a play or two herself, took a passionate interest in what she called "the work," was present at the performances of all the plays, and was a charter member of Professor Hatcher's carefully selected and invited audiences. Now, whether by appointment or self-election, she had come to regard herself as a kind of embassadress for Professor Hatcher's work and was the chief sponsor of its social life.

The grotesque good old woman was obsessed by that delusion which haunts so many wealthy people who have no talent and no understanding, but who are enchanted by the glamour which they think surrounds the world of art. Miss Potter thought that through these Friday afternoons she could draw together all the talent, charm, and brilliance of the whole community. She thought that she could gather here not only Professor Hatcher's budding dramatists and some older representatives of the established order, but also poets, painters, composers, philosophers, "radical thinkers," people "who did interesting things," of whatever kind and quality. And she was sure that from this mad mélange every one would derive a profitable and "stimulating" intercourse.

Here, from the great "art community" of Cambridge and Boston, came a whole tribe of the feeble, the sterile, the venomous and inept—the meagre little spirits of no talent and of great pretensions: the people who had once got an essay printed in *The Atlantic Monthly* or published "a slender volume" of bad verse; the composers who had had one dull academic piece performed a single time by the Boston Symphony; the novelists, playwrights, painters, who had none of the "popular success" at which they sneered and which they pretended to despise, but for which each would have sold his shabby little soul; the whole wretched poisonous and embittered crew of those who had "taken" some one's celebrated course, or had spent a summer at the MacDowell Colony—in short, the true philistines of art—the true enemies of the artist's living spirit, the true defilers and betrayers of creation—the impotent fumbling little half men of the arts whose rootless, earthless, sunless lives have grown underneath a barrel, and who bitterly nurse their fancied injuries, the swollen image of their misjudged worth, and hiss and sting in all the impotent varieties of their small envenomed hate; who deal the stealthy traitor's blow in darkness at the work and talent of far better men than they.

Usually, when Ten Eyck went to Miss Potter's house he found several members of Professor Hatcher's class who seemed to be in regular attendance on all these Friday afternoons. These others may have come for a variety of reasons: because they were bored, curious, or actually enjoyed these affairs, but the strange, horribly shy and sensitive little man who bore the name of Oswald Ten Eyck came from a kind of desperate necessity, the ravenous hunger of his meagre half-starved body, and his chance to get his one good dinner of the week.

It was evident that Ten Eyck endured agonies of shyness, boredom, confusion, and tortured self-consciousness at these gatherings but he was always there, and when they sat down at the table he ate with the voracity of a famished animal. The visitor to Miss Potter's reception room would find him, usually backed into an inconspicuous corner away from the full sound and tumult of the crowd, nervously holding a tea-cup in his hands, talking to some one in the strange blurted-out desperate fashion that was characteristic of him, or saying nothing for long periods, biting his nails, thrusting his slender hands desperately through his mop of black disordered hair, breaking from time to time into a shrill, sudden, almost hysterical laugh, blurting out a few volcanic words, and then relapsing into his desperate hair-thrusting silence.

The man's agony of shyness and tortured nerves was painful to watch: it made him say and do sudden, shocking and explosive things that could suddenly stun a gathering such as this, and plunge him back immediately into a black pit of silence, self-abasement and despair. And as great as his tortured sensitivity was, it was greater for other people than for himself. He could far better endure a personal affront, a wounding of his own quick pride, than see another person wounded. His anguish, in fact, when he saw this kind of suffering in other people would become so acute that he was no longer responsible for his acts: he was capable of anything on such an occasion.

And such occasions were not lacking at Miss Potter's Friday afternoons. For even if the entire diplomatic corps had gathered there in suavest mood, that good grotesque old woman with her unfailing talent for misrule, would have contrived to set every urbane minister of grace snarling for the other's blood before an hour had passed. And with that museum collection of freaks, embittered æsthetes and envenomed misfits of the arts, that did gather there, she never failed. Her genius for confusion and unrest was absolute.

If there were two people in the community who had been destined from birth and by every circumstance of education, religious belief, and temperament, to hate each other with a murderous hatred the moment that they met, Miss Potter would see to it instantly that the introduction was effected. If Father Davin, the passionate defender of the faith, and the foe of modernism in all its hated forms, had been invited to one of Miss Potter's Friday afternoons, he would find himself shaking hands before he knew it with Miss Shanksworth, the militant propagandist for free love, sterilization of the unfit, and the unlimited practice of birth control by every one, especially the lower classes.

If the editor of *The Atlantic Monthly* should be present, he would find himself, by that unerring drawing together of opposites which Miss Potter exercised with such accuracy, seated next to the person of one Sam Shulemovitch, who as leader and chief editorial writer of an organ known as *Red Riot* or *The Worker's Dawn,* had said frequently and with violence that the sooner *The Atlantic Monthly* was extinguished, and its writers, subscribers, and editorial staff embalmed and put on exhibition in a museum, the better it would be for every one.

If the radical leader who had just served a sentence in prison for his speeches, pamphlets, and physical aggressions against the police, or members of the capitalist class, should come to one of Miss Potter's Friday afternoons, he would find himself immediately debating the merits of the present system and the need for the swift extinction of the wealthy parasite with a maiden lady from Beacon Street who had a parrot, two Persian kittens, and a Pekinese, three maids, a cook, a butler, chauffeur and motor car, a place at Marblehead, and several thousand shares of Boston and Maine.

And so it went, all up and down the line, at one of Miss Potter's Friday afternoons. There, in her house, you could be sure that if the lion and the lamb did not lie down together their hostess would seat them in such close proximity to each other that the ensuing slaughter would be made as easy, swift, and unadorned as possible.

And as the sound of snarl and curse grew louder in the clamorous tumult of these Friday afternoons, as the face grew livid with its hate, as the eye began to glitter, and the vein to swell upon the temple, Miss Potter would look about her with triumphant satisfaction, seeing that her work was good, thinking with delight:

"How stimulating! How fine it is to see so many interesting people together—people who are really doing things! To see the flash and play of wit, to watch the clash of brilliant intellects, to think of all these fine young men and women have in common, and of the mutual benefits they will derive from contact with one another!—ah-ha! What a delightful thing to see—but who is this that just came—" she would mutter, peering toward the door, for she was very near-sighted—"who? Who?—O-oh! Professor Lawes of the Art Department—oh, Professor Lawes, I'm so glad you could come. We have the most *interesting* young man here today—Mr. Wilder, who painted that picture every one's talking about—"Portrait of a Nude Falling Upon Her Neck in a Wet Bathroom"— Mr. Wilder, this is Doctor Lawes, the author of *Sanity and Tradition in the Renaissance*—I know you're going to find *so* much in common."

And having done her duty, she would wheeze heavily away, looking around with her strange fixed grin and bulging eyes to see if she had left anything or anyone undone or whether there was still hope of some new riot, chaos, brawl, or bitter argument.

And yet there was a kind of wisdom in her too, that few who came there to her house suspected: a kind of shrewdness in the fixed bulging stare of her old eyes that sometimes saw more than the others knew. Perhaps it was only a kind of instinct of the old woman's warm humanity that made her speak to the fragile little man with burning eyes more gently than she spoke to others, to seat him on her right hand at the dinner table, and to say from time to time: "Give Mr. Ten Eyck some more of that roast beef. Oh, Mr. Ten Eyck, *do*—you've hardly eaten anything."

And he, stretched out upon the rack of pride and all the bitter long‐ing of his hunger, would crane convulsively at his collar and laugh with a note of feeble protest, saying "Well—I don't know . . . I really think . . . if you want me to. . . . Oh! all right then," as a plate smoking with her lavish helping was placed before him, and would straight‐way fall upon it with the voracity of a famished wolf.

When Ten Eyck reached Miss Potter's on that final fateful Friday, the other guests were already assembled. Miss Thrall, a student of the woman's section of Professor Hatcher's course, was reading her own translation of a German play which had only recently been produced. Miss Potter's reception rooms—which were two large gabled rooms on the top floor of her house, ruggedly festooned with enormous fishing nets secured from Gloucester fishermen—were crowded with her motley parliament, and the whole gathering was discreetly hushed while the woman student read her play.

It was a scene to warm the heart of any veteran of æsthetic parties. The lights were soft, shaded, quietly and warmly subdued: the higher parts of the room were pools of mysterious gloom from which the Gloucester fishing nets depended, but within the radius of the little lamps, one could see groups of people tastefully arranged in all the atti‐tudes of rapt attentiveness. Some of the young women slouched dream‐ily upon sofas, their faces and bodies leaning toward the reader with a yearning movement, other groups could be vaguely discerned leaning upon the grand piano, or elegantly slumped against the walls with tea-cups in their hands. Mr. Cram, the old composer, occupied a chosen seat on a fat sofa; he drew voluptuously on a moist cigarette which he held daintily between his dirty fingers, his hawk-like face turned meditatively away into the subtle mysteries of the fishing nets. From time to time he would thrust one dirty hand through the long sparse locks of his gray hair, and then draw deeply, thoughtfully on his cigarette.

Some of the young men were strewn about in pleasing postures on the floor, in attitudes of insouciant grace, gallantly near the ladies' legs. Ten Eyck entered, looked round like a frightened rabbit, ducked his head, and then sat down jack-knife fashion beside them.

Miss Thrall sat on the sofa with the old composer, facing her audi‐ence. The play that she was reading was one of the new German Ex‐pressionist dramas, at that time considered one of "the most vital movements in the world theatre," and the young lady's translation of the play which bore the vigorous title of *You Shall Be Free When You Have Cut Your Father's Throat,* ran somewhat in this manner:

Elektra: (advancing a step to the top of the raised dais, her face blue with a ghastly light, and her voice low and hoarse with passion as she addresses the dark mass of men below her.) Listen, man! To you it is now proper that I speak must. Do you by any manner of means know who this woman who now before you speaking stands may be? (With a sudden swift movement she, the purple-reddish silk-stuff of the tunic which she wearing is, asunder in two pieces rips, her two breasts exposing.)

(A low swiftly-growing-and-to-the-outer-edges-of-the-crowd-thunder-becoming mutter of astonishment through the great crowd surges.)

Elektra: (Thunder louder becomes, and even with every moment growing yet) Elektra! (The sound to a mighty roar arisen has, and now from every throat is in a single shout torn.) ELEKTRA!

Elektra: (quietly) Ja! Man, thou hast said it. I am Elektra!

The Crowd: (with from their throats an even-stronger roar yet) E L E K - T R A . It is Elektra !

Elektra: (her voice even lower and more hoarse becoming, her eyes with the red blood-pains of all her heart-grief with still greater love-sorrow at the man-mass gleaming.) Listen, man. Slaves, workers, the of your fathers' sons not yet awakened—hear! Out of the night-dark of your not yet born souls to deliver you have I come! So, hear! (Her voice even lower with the low blood-pain heart-hate hoarse becoming.) Tonight must you your old with-crime-blackened and by-ignorance-blinded father's throat cut! I have spoken: so must it be.

A Voice, Homunculus: (from the crowd, pleadingly, with protest.) Ach! Elektra! Spare us! Please! With the blood-lust malice-blinded your old father's throat to cut not nice is.

Elektra: (raising her arm with a cold imperious gesture of command.) As I have spoken, must it be! Silence!

(Homunculus starts to interrupt: again she speaks, her voice more loud and stern becoming.) Silence! Silence!

At this moment there was a loud and sibilant hiss from the door. Miss Potter, who had been on the point of entering the room, had been halted by the sight of Miss Thrall's arm uplifted in command and by the imperious coldness of her voice as she said "Silence!" Now as Miss Thrall stopped and looked up in a startled manner, Miss Potter, still hissing loudly, tip-toed ponderously into the room. The old woman advanced with the grace of a hydroptic hippopotamus, laying her finger to her lips as she came on, looking all around her with her fixed grin and bulging eyes, and hissing loudly for the silence she had thus violently disrupted every time she laid her finger to her lips.

Every one *stared* at her in a moment of blank and horrible fascination. As for Miss Thrall, she gaped at her with an expression of stupefaction which changed suddenly to a cry of alarm as Miss Potter, tiptoeing blindly ahead, barged squarely into the small crouched figure of Oswald Ten Eyck, and went plunging over him to fall to her knees with a crash that made the fish-nets dance, the pictures swing, and even drew a sympathetic resonant vibration from the polished grand piano.

Then, for one never-to-be-forgotten moment, while every one *stared* at her in a frozen paralysis of horrified astonishment, Miss Potter stayed there on her knees, too stunned to move or breathe, her eyes bulging from her head, her face turned blindly upward in an attitude of grotesque devotion. Then as she began to gasp and cough with terror, Ten Eyck came to life. He fairly bounded off the floor, glanced round him like a startled cat, and spying a pitcher on a tray, rushed toward it wildly, seized it in his trembling hands, and attempted to pour a glass of water, most of which spilled out. He turned, still clutching the glass in his hand, and panting out "Here! Here! . . . Take this!" he rushed toward Miss Potter. Then, terrified by her apoplectic stare, he dashed the contents of the glass full in her face.

A half dozen young men sprang to her assistance and lifted her to her feet. The play was forgotten, the whole gathering broke into excited and clamorous talk, above which could be heard Miss Flitcroft's tart voice, saying sharply, as she whacked the frightened and dripping old woman on the back:

"Nonsense! You're not! You're no such thing! . . . You're just frightened out of your wits, that's all that's the matter with you— If you ever stopped to look where you were going, these things would never happen!"

Whack!

Both Oswald and Miss Potter had recovered by the time the guests were assembled round the table. As usual, Oswald found he had been seated on Miss Potter's right hand: and the feeling of security this gave him, together with the maddening fragrance of food, the sense of ravenous hunger about to be appeased, filled him with an almost delirious joy, a desire to shout out, to sing. Instead, he stood nervously beside his chair, looking about with a shy and timid smile, passing his fingers through his hair repeatedly, waiting for the other guests to seat themselves. Gallantly, he stood behind Miss Potter's chair, and pushed it under her as she sat down. Then, with a feeling of jubilant elation, he sat down beside her and drew his chair up. He wanted to talk, to prove himself a brilliant conversationalist, to surprise the whole gathering with his wit, his penetration, his distinguished ease. Above all, he wanted to eat and eat and eat! His head felt light and drunk and giddy, but gloriously so—he had never been so superbly confident in his life. And in this mood, he unfolded his napkin, and smiling brightly, turned to dazzle his neighbor on his right with the brilliant effervescence of wit that already seemed to sparkle on his lips. One look, and the bright smile faded, wit and confidence fell dead together, his heart shrank instantly and seemed to drop out of his very body like a rotten apple. Miss Potter had not failed. Her unerring genius for calamity had held out to the finish. He found himself staring into the poisonous face of the one person in Cambridge that he hated most—the repulsive visage of the old composer, Cram.

An old long face, yellowed with malevolence, a sudden fox-glint of small eyes steeped in a vitriol of ageless hate, a beak of cruel nose, and thin lips stained and hardened in a rust of venom, the whole craftily, slantingly astare between a dirty frame of sparse lank locks. Cackling with malignant glee, and cramming crusty bread into his mouth, the old composer turned and spoke:

"Heh! Heh! Heh!"—Crunch, crunch— "It's *Mister* Ten Eyck, isn't it? The man who wrote that play Professor Hatcher put on at his last performance—that mystical fantasy kind of thing. That was *your* play, wasn't it?"

The old yellow face came closer, and he snarled in a kind of gloating and vindictive whisper: "Most of the audience *hated* it! They thought it very *bad,* sir—very bad!" Crunch, crunch. "I am only telling you because I think you ought to know—that you may profit by the criticism."

And Ten Eyck, hunger gone now, shrank back as if a thin poisoned blade had been driven in his heart and twisted there. "I—I—I thought some of them rather liked it. Of course I don't know—I can't say—" he faltered hesitantly, "but I—I really thought some of the audience—liked it."

"Well, they *didn't,*" the composer snarled, still crunching on his crust of bread. "Every one that I saw thought that it was terrible. Heh! Heh! Heh! Heh! Except my wife and I—" Crunch, crunch. "We were the only ones who thought that it was any good at all, the only ones who thought there would ever be any *hope* for you. And we found parts of it—a phrase or sentence here and there—now and then a scene—that we *liked*. As for the rest of them," he suddenly made a horrible downward gesture with a clenched fist and pointing thumb, "it was *thumbs down,* my boy! Done for! No good. . . . That's what they thought of *you,* my boy. And that," he snarled suddenly, glaring round him, "*that* is what they've thought of *me* all these years—of *me,* the greatest composer that they have, the man who has done more for the cause of American music than all the rest of them combined—*me! me! me!* the prophet and the seer!" he fairly screamed, "*thumbs down!* Done for! No good any more!"

Then he grew suddenly quiet, and leaning toward Ten Eyck with a gesture of horrible clutching intimacy, he whispered: "And *that's* what they'll always think of you, my boy—of any one who has a grain of talent— Heh! Heh ! Heh! Heh!" Peering into Ten Eyck's white face, he shook him gently by the arm, and cackled softly a malevolent tenderness, as if the evidence of the anguish that his words had caused had given him a kind of paternal affection for his victim. "That's what they said about your play, all right, but don't take it too seriously. It's live and learn, my boy, isn't it—profit by criticism—a few hard knocks will do you no harm. Heh! Heh! Heh! Heh! Heh!"

And turning, satisfied with the anguish he had caused, he thrust out his yellowed face with a vulture's movement of his scrawny neck, and smacking his envenomed lips with relish, drew noisily inward with slobbering suction on a spoon of soup.

As for Ten Eyck, all hunger now destroyed by his sick shame and horror and despair, he turned, began to toy nervously with his food, and forcing his pale lips to a trembling and uncertain smile, tried desperately to compel his brain to pay attention to something that was being said by the man across the table who was the guest of honor for the day, and whose name was Hunt.

Hunt had been well-known for his belligerent pacifism during the war, had been beaten by the police and put in jail more times than he could count, and now that he was temporarily out of jail, he was carrying on his assault against organized society with more ferocity than ever. He was a man of undoubted courage and deep sincerity, but the suffering he had endured, and the brutal intolerance of which he had been the victim, had left its mutilating mark upon his life. His face was somehow like a scar, and his cut, cruel-looking mouth could twist like a snake to the corner of his face when he talked. And his voice was harsh and jeering, brutally dominant and intolerant, when he spoke to any one, particularly if the one he spoke to didn't share his opinions.

On this occasion, Miss Potter, with her infallible talent for error, had seated next to Hunt a young Belgian student at the university, who had little English, but a profound devotion to the Roman Catholic Church. Within five minutes, the two were embroiled in a bitter argument, the Belgian courteous, but desperately resolved to defend his faith, and because of his almost incoherent English as helpless as a lamb before the attack of Hunt, who went for him with the rending and pitiless savagery of a tiger. It was a painful thing to watch: the young man, courteous and soft-spoken, his face flushed with embarrassment and pain, badly wounded by the naked brutality of the other man's assault.

As Ten Eyck listened, his spirit began to emerge from the blanket of shame and sick despair that had covered it, a spark of anger and resentment, hot and bright, began to glow, to burn, to spread. His large dark eyes were shining now with a deeper, fiercer light than they had had before, and on his pale cheeks there was a flush of angry color. And now he no longer had to force himself to listen to what Hunt was saying: anger had fanned his energy and his interest to a burning flame, he listened tensely, his ears seemed almost to prick forward on his head, from time to time he dug his fork viciously into the table cloth. Once or twice, it seemed that he would interrupt. He cleared his throat, bent forward, nervously clutching the table with his claw-like hands, but each time ended up thrusting his fingers through his mop of hair, and gulping down a glass of wine.

As Hunt talked, his voice grew so loud in its rasping arrogance that every one at the table had to stop and listen, which was what he most desired. And there was no advantage, however unjust, which the man did not take in this bitter argument with the young Belgian. He spoke jeeringly of the fat priests of the old corrupt church, fattening themselves on the blood and life of the oppressed workers; he spoke of the bigotry, oppression, and superstition of religion, and of the necessity for the workers to destroy this monster which was devouring them. And when the young Belgian, in his faltering and painful English, would try to reply to these charges, Hunt would catch him up on his use of words, pretend to be puzzled at his pronunciation, and bully him brutally in this manner:

"You think *what?* ... *What?* ... I don't understand what you're saying half the time. . . . It's very difficult to talk to a man who can't speak decent English."

"I—vas—say—ink," the young Belgian would answer slowly and painfully, his face flushed with embarrassment— "—vas—say—ink—zat—I sink—zat you—ex—ack—sher—ate——"

"That I *what?*— *What?* What is he trying to say, anyway?" demanded Hunt, brutally, looking around the table as if hoping to receive interpretation from the other guests. "Oh-h!" he cried suddenly, as if the Belgian's meaning had just dawned on him. *"Exaggerate!* That's the word you're trying to say!" and he laughed in an ugly manner.

Oswald Ten Eyck had stopped eating and turned white as a sheet. Now he sat there, looking across in an agony of tortured sympathy at the young Belgian, biting his nails nervously, and thrusting his hands through his hair in a distracted manner. The resentment and anger that he had felt at first had now burned to a white heat of choking, murderous rage. The little man was taken out of himself entirely. Suddenly his sense of personal wrong, the humiliation and pain he had himself endured, was fused with a white-hot anger of resentment for every injustice and wrong that had ever been done to the wounded soul of man. United by that agony to a kind of savage fellowship with the young Belgian, with the insulted and the injured of the earth, of whatsoever class or creed, that burning coal of five feet five flamed in one withering blaze of wrath, and hurled the challenge of its scorn at the oppressor.

The thing happened like a flash. At the close of one of Hunt's jeering tirades, Ten Eyck jumped from his chair, and leaning half across the table, cried out in a high shrill voice that cut into the silence like a knife:

"Hunt! You are a swine, and every one who ever had anything to do with you is likewise a swine!" For a moment he paused, breathing hard, clutching his napkin in a bony hand. Slowly his feverish eyes went round the table, and suddenly, seeing the malevolent stare of the old composer Cram fixed upon him, he hurled the wadded napkin down and pointing a trembling finger at that hated face, he screamed: "And that goes for you as well, you old bastard! . . . It goes for all the rest of you," he shrieked, gesturing wildly. "Hunt . . . Cram! *Cram!* . . . God!" he cried, shaking with laughter. *"There's* a name for you! . . . It's perfect. . . . Yes, you! You swine!" he yelled again, thrusting his finger at Cram's yellowed face so violently that the composer scrambled back with a startled yelp. "And all the rest of you!" he pointed towards Miss

Thrall— "You—the Expressionist!" And he paused, racked terribly again by soundless laughter— "The Greeks—the Russians— Oh, how we love in Spain!—and fantasy—why, Goddam my soul to hell, but it's delightful!" he fairly screamed, and then pointing a trembling finger at several in succession he yelled "You?—And you?—And you?—What the hell do you know about anything? . . . Ibsen—Chekov—the Celtic Dawn— *Balls!*" he snarled, "Food! Food! Food!—you Goddam fools! . . . That's all that matters." He picked up a morsel of his untouched bread and hurled it savagely upon the table— "Food! Food!—Ask Cram—he knows. . . . Now," he said, panting for breath and pointing a trembling finger at Miss Potter— "Now," he panted, "I want to tell *you* something."

"Oh . . . Mr. . . . Ten . . . Eyck," the old woman faltered in a tone of astonished reproach, "I . . . never . . . believed it possible . . . you could——"

Her voice trailed off helplessly, and she looked at him.

And Ten Eyck, suddenly brought to himself by the bulging stare of that good old creature fixed on him with wounded disbelief, suddenly laughed again, shrilly and hysterically, thrust his fingers through his hair, looked about him at the other people whose eyes were fixed on him in a stare of focal horror, and said in a confused, uncertain tone: "Well, I don't know—I'm always—I guess I said something that—oh, damn it, what's the use!" and with a desperate, stricken laugh, he slumped suddenly into his chair, craned convulsively at his collar, and seizing a decanter before him poured out a glass of wine with trembling haste and gulped it down.

Meanwhile, all around the table people began to talk with that kind of feverish eagerness that follows a catastrophe of this sort, and Hunt resumed his arguments, but this time in a much quieter tone, and with a kind of jeering courtesy, accompanying his remarks from time to time with a heavy sarcasm directed toward Ten Eyck— "If I may say so— since, of course, Mr. Ten Eyck considers me a swine" *or* "if you will pardon such a remark from a swine like me"—or—"as Mr. Ten Eyck has told you I am nothing but a swine," and so on.

The upshot of it was that Ten Eyck gulped down glass after glass of the strong wine, which raced instantly through his frail starved body like a flame.

He got disgracefully drunk, sang snatches of bawdy songs, screamed with maudlin laughter, and began to pound enthusiastically on the

table, shaking his head to himself and shouting from time to time:
"You're right, Hunt! . . . God-damn it, man, you're right! . . . Go on!
. . . Go on! I agree with you! You're right! Everybody else is wrong
but Hunt and Cram! . . . Words by Hunt, music by Cram . . . no one's
right but Hunt and Cram!"

They tried to quiet him, but in vain. Suddenly Miss Potter began to
cough and choke and gasp, pressed both hands over her heart, and
gasped out in a terror-stricken voice:

"Oh, my God, I'm dying!"

Miss Flitcroft jumped to her feet and came running to her friend's
assistance, and then while Miss Flitcroft pounded the old woman on her
back, and the guests scrambled up in a general disruption of the party,
Oswald Ten Eyck staggered to the window, flung it open, and looking
out across one of the bleak snow-covered squares of Cambridge,
screamed at the top of his voice:

"Relentless! . . . Relentless! . . . Juh sweez un art-e-e-este!" Here he
beat on his little breast with a claw-like hand and yelled with drunken
laughter, "And, Goddamn it, I will always be relentless . . . relentless
. . . relentless!"

The cool air braced him with its cleansing shock: for a moment, the
fog of shame and drunkenness shifted in his brain, he felt a vacancy of
cold horror at his back, and turning suddenly found himself confronted
by the frozen circle of their faces, fixed on him. And even in that instant glimpse of utter ruin, as the knowledge of this final castastrophe
was printed on his brain, over the rim of frozen faces he saw the dial-
hands of a clock. The time was seven-fifty-two: he knew there was a
train at midnight for New York—and work, food, freedom, and forgetfulness. He would have four hours to go home and pack: if he hurried
he could make it.

Little was heard of him thereafter. It was rumored that he had gone
back to his former lucrative employment with Mr. Hearst: and Professor
Hatcher smiled thinly when he heard the news; the young men looked
at one another with quiet smiles.

And yet he could not wholly be forgotten: occasionally some one
mentioned him.

"A strange case, wasn't it?" said Mr. Grey. "Do you remember how
he looked? Like . . . like . . . really, he was like some mediæval ascetic.
I thought he had something. I thought he would do something . . I

really did, you know! And then—heavens!—that last play!" He tossed his cigarette away with a movement of dismissal. "A strange case," he said with quiet finality. "A man who looked as if he had it and who turned out—all belly and no brain."

There was silence for a moment while the young men smoked.

"I wonder what it was," another said thoughtfully at length. "What happened to him? I wonder why."

There was no one there who knew the answer. The only one on earth, perhaps, who could have given it was that curious old spinster named Miss Potter. For blind to many things that all these clever young men knew, that good grotesque old empress of confusion still had a wisdom that none of them suspected. But Miss Potter was no longer there to tell them, even if she could. She had died that spring.

Later it seemed to Gene that the cold and wintry light of desolation—the red waning light of Friday in the month of March—shone forever on the lives of all the people. And forever after, when he thought of them, their lives, their faces and their words—all that he had seen and known of them—would be fused into a hopeless, joyless image which was somehow consonant to that accursed wintry light that shone upon it. And this was the image:

He was standing upon the black and grimy snow of winter before Miss Potter's house, saying good-bye to a group of her invited guests. The last red wintry light of Friday afternoon fell on their lives and faces as he talked to them, and made them hateful to him, and yet he searched those faces and talked desperately to see if he could find there any warmth or love or joy, any ring of hope for himself which would tell him that his sick heart and leaden spirit would awake to life and strength again, that he would get his hands again on life and love and labor, and that April would come back again.

But he found nothing in these cold and hateful faces but the lights of desolation, the deadly and corrupt joy that took delight in its own death, and breathed, without any of the agony and despair he felt, the poisonous ethers of its own dead world. In those cold hateful faces as that desolate and wintry light fell on them he could find no hope for his own life or the life of living men. Rather, he read in their pale faces, and in their rootless and unwholesome lives, which had come to have for him the wilted yellow pallor of nameless and unuseful plants such as flourish under barrels, a kind of cold malicious triumph, a momentary gleam in pale fox eyes, which said that they looked upon his desperate life and knew the cause of his despair, and felt a bitter triumph over it. The look on their cold faces and in their fox eyes said to him that there was no hope, no work, no joy, no triumph, and no love for such as he, that there could be nothing but defeat, despair and failure for the living of this world, that life had been devoured and killed by such as these, and had become rat's alley, death-in-life forever.

And yet he searched their hated faces desperately in that cold red light, he sought frantically in their loathed faces for a ray of hope, and in his drowning desolation shameful words were wrenched from him against his will—words of entreaty, pleading, pitiful begging for an alms of mercy, a beggarly scrap of encouragement, even a word of kindly judgment on his life, from these cold and hateful faces that he loathed.

"But my work—this last work that I did—don't you think—didn't it seem to you that there was something good in it—not much, perhaps, but just enough to give me hope? . . . Don't you think if I go on I may do something good some day—for God's sake, tell me if you do?—or must I die here in this barren and accursed light of Friday afternoon, must I drown and smother in this poisonous and lifeless air, wither in this rootless, yellow, barren earth below the barrel, die like a mad-dog howling in the wilderness, with the damned, cold, hateful sneer of your impotent lives upon me?

"Tell me, in God's name, man, is there no life on earth for such as I? Has the world been stripped for such as you? Have all joy, hope, health, sensual love, and warmth and tenderness gone out of life—are living men the false men, then, and is all truth and work and wisdom owned by rat's alley and the living dead such as yourself?—For God's sake, tell me if there is no hope for me! Let me have the worst, the worst, I beg of you. Is there nothing for me now but the gray gut, the sick heart, and the leaden spirit? Is there nothing now but Friday afternoon in March, Miss Potter's parties, and your damned poisonous, sterile, cold, life-hating faces? For God's sake tell me now if I am no good, am false while you, the living dead, are true—and had better cut my throat or blow my brains out than stay on longer in this world of truth, where joy is dead, and only the barren rootless lives of dead men live!—In God's name, tell me now, if this is true—or do you find a rag of hope for me?"

"Ah," the old composer Cram would answer, arranging the folds of his dirty scarf, and peering out malevolently underneath his sparse lank webs of dirty gray, as the red and wintry light fell hopelessly on his poisonous old face. "—Ah-h," he rasped bitterly, "—my wife and I liked some things in that play of yours that Professor Hatcher put on in his Playshop. . . . My wife and I liked one or two speeches in that play," he rasped, "but"—for a moment a fox's glittering of malevolent triumph shone in his eyes as he drove the fine blade home "—no one else did! —No one else thought it was any good at all!" he cackled malevolently. "I heard people saying all around me that they *hated* it," he gloated, "—that you had no talent, no ability to write, and had better go back where you came from—live some other kind of life—or *kill* yourself," he gloated— "That's the way it is, my boy!—Nothing but defeat and misery and despair for such as you in life! . . . That has been my lot, too," he cackled vindictively, rubbing his dry hands in glee. "They've always hated what I did—if I ever did anything good I was lucky if I found two people who liked it. The rest of them *hated* it," he whispered wildly. "There's no hope for you—so *die, die, die,*" he whispered, and cackling with malevolent triumph, he rubbed his dry hands gleefully.

"Meeker, for God's sake," the boy cried, turning to the elegant figure of the clergyman, who would be carefully arranging around his damned luxurious neck the rich folds of a silk blue scarf— "Meeker, do you feel this way about it, too? . . . Is that your opinion? . . . Do you find nothing good in what I do?"

—"You see, old chap, it's this way," Meeker answered, in his soft voice, and drew with languor on one of his expensive straw-tipped cigarettes— "You have lots of ability, I am sure"—here he paused to inhale meditatively again— "but don't you think, old boy, it's critical rather than creative?—now with Jim here it's different," he continued, placing one hand affectionately on Hogan's narrow shoulders— "Jim here's a great genius—like Shelley—with a great gift waiting for the world"— Here Hogan lowered his pale weak face with a simpering smile of modesty, but not before the boy had seen the fox's glitter of vindictive triumph in his pale dull eyes—"but you have nothing of that sort to give. Why don't you try to make the best of what you have?" he said with hateful sympathetic urbanity and put the cigarette to elegant and reflective lips again.

"Hogan," the boy cried hoarsely, turning to the poet,"—is that your answer, too? Have you no word of hope for me?—but no, you damned, snivelling, whining upstart—you are gloating at your rotten little triumph, aren't you? I'd get nothing out of you, would I?"

"Come on, Jim," said Meeker quietly. "He's becoming abusive. . . .

The kind of attack you make is simply stupid," he now said. "It will get you nowhere."

"And so raucous—so raucous," said Hogan, smirking nervously. "It means nothing."

And the three hated forms of death would go away then rapidly, snickering among themselves, and he would turn again, filled with the death of life, the end of joy, again, again, to prowl the wintry, barren, and accursed streets of Friday night.

XXXVII

IT had been almost two years since Eugene had last seen Robert Weaver, but now, by one of those sudden hazards of blind chance that for a moment bring men's lives together, and in an instant show them more than years together could have done, he was to see the other youth again.

One night in his second year at Cambridge he was reading in his room at about two o'clock in the morning, at the heart and core of the brooding silence of night that had come to mean so much to him, and that had the power to stir him as no other time of day could do with a feeling of swelling and exultant joy. The house had gone to sleep long before and there was no sound anywhere: it was late in winter, along in March, and the ice and snow had been packed and frozen on the earth for months with a kind of weary permanence—with a tenacity that gave to winter a harsh and dreary reality, a protraction of gray days and grim gray light which made the memory of other seasons, and particularly the hope of spring, remote and almost unbelievable. The street outside was frozen in this living and animate silence of great cold: suddenly this still perfection of night and darkness was shattered by the engines of a powerful motor which turned into the end of the street from Massachusetts Avenue, and tore along before the house at drunken speed with a roaring explosion of sound. Then, without slacking its speed, the brakes were jammed on, the car skidded murderously to a halt on the slippery pavement, and immediately backed up at full speed until it came before the house again, skidded to a halt and was abruptly silent.

Some one got out with the same violent impatience, slammed the door, and then for a moment, he could hear him hunting along the street, swearing and muttering to himself, at length he came back to the house, started up the steps on which he slipped or stumbled and fell heavily,

after which he heard Robert cursing in a tone of hoarse and feverish discontent: "The God-damnedest place I ever saw. . . . Did they never
hear of a light around here? . . . Who the hell would want to live in a
place like this?"

He began to hammer at the front door and to bawl out Eugene's name
at the top of his voice: then he came up outside his windows and began
to knock on the glass impatiently with his fist. Eugene went to the door
and let him in: he entered the room without a word, and with the intent
driving movement of a man who is very drunk, then he looked at him
scornfully and accusingly, and barked out: "What time do you go to
bed? . . . Do you stay up all night? . . . What do you do, sleep all
morning?" . . . He looked around the room: the floor was strewn with
books he had been reading and littered with pieces of paper on which he
had been writing. Robert broke into his sudden, hoarse, falsetto laugh:
"The damndest place I ever saw!" he said. "Do you sleep on that thing?"
he said contemptuously, pointing to his cot bed which stood along the
wall in one corner of the room.

"No, Robert," he said, "I sleep on the floor. I use that for an ice box."

"What's that in the corner?" Robert asked pointing to some dirty
shirts he had thrown there. "Shirts? . . . How long has it been since you
sent anything to the laundry? . . . What do you do when you want a shirt,
go out and buy one? . . . Do you ever take a bath? . . . Have you had
a bath since you came to Harvard?" He laughed suddenly, hoarsely and
wildly again, hurled himself into a chair, sighed sharply with a weary
and impatient discontent, began to pass his hand across his forehead
with an abstracted and weary movement, and said, "Lord! Lord! Lord!
. . . The things I've done!" he shook his head mournfully. "Why it's
awful," he said, and he started to shake his head again.

"Why don't you try to talk a little louder?" Eugene suggested. "I
think there are a few people over in South Boston who haven't heard
you yet."

He laughed, hoarsely and abruptly, and then resumed his abstracted
and repentant shaking of the head, sighing heavily from time to time
and saying, "Lord!"

It was the first time Eugene had seen Robert in two years. Under the
hard light that he kept burning in his room he now looked closely at him:
he wore a derby hat that became his small lean head well, and he had on
a magnificent fur coat, such as the rich Harvard boys wear, that came
down almost to his shoe-tops. For the rest, he was quietly and ele-

gantly tailored with the distinction he had always seemed to get into
his clothes—there was always, even in his boyhood, a kind of formal
dignity in his dress: he always wore a stiff, starched collar.

Robert's face had grown thinner, he looked haggard and a good deal
older: the lines of his sharp, incisive features were more deeply cut and
his eyes, now injected and bloodshot from heavy drinking, were more
wild and feverish in their restless discontent than they had ever been—he
seemed to be lashed and driven by a savage and desperate hunger which
he could neither satisfy nor articulate: he was being consumed and torn
to pieces by a torment of desire and longing, the cause of which he
could not define, and which he had no means to assuage or quench.

He had a bottle half filled with whiskey in the pocket of his fur coat: he
took it out and offered Eugene a drink and after he had drunk, he put the
bottle to his lips and gulped down all that remained in a single draught.
Then he flung the empty bottle away impatiently on the table: it was
obvious that the liquor, instead of giving him some peace or comfort,
acted as savagely and immediately as oil poured on the tumult of a raging fire—it fed and spurred the madness in him and gave him no release
until he had drunk himself into a state of paralysis and stupefaction.
He was one of those men for whom alcohol was a fatal and uncontrollable stimulant: having once drawn the cork from a bottle and tasted his
first drink he was then powerless to resist or stop: he drank until he
could drink no more, and he would beg, fight, lie, cheat, crawl or walk
or incur any desperate risk or danger to get more drink. Yet, he told
Eugene that until his twenty-first year he had never tasted liquor: he
began to drink during his last year in college, and during the two years
that followed he had gone far on the road toward alcoholism.

Eugene asked him how he had found out where he lived and, still passing his hand across his forehead, he answered in an impatient and abstracted tone: "Oh . . . I don't know. . . . Some one told me, I guess.
. . . I think it was Arthur Kittrell," and then he fell to shaking his head
again, and saying, "Awful! awful! awful! . . . Do you know how much
money I've spent so far this year. . . . Forty-eight hundred dollars. . . .
So help me God, I hope I may die if I'm not telling you the truth! Why
it's awful!" he said, and burst into a laugh.

"Have you travelled around a lot?" Gene asked.

"Have I? My God, I've spent only one week-end in New Haven since
the beginning of the year," he said. "Why it's terrible! . . . Do you
know who I'm rooming with?" he demanded.

"No."

"Andy Westerman," he said impressively and then, as the name communicated none of its significance to Gene, he added impatiently: "Why you've heard of the Westermans, haven't you? . . . My God, what have you been doing all your life? . . . You've heard of the Westerman vacuum cleaners and electric refrigerators, haven't you? . . . Why, he's worth $20,000,000 if he's worth a cent! . . . The craziest man that ever lived!" he said, breaking suddenly into a sharp recollective laugh.

"Who? Westerman?"

"No. . . . My room-mate . . . that damned Andy Westerman. . . . Do you want to meet him?"

"Is he up here with you?"

"Why, that's what I'm telling you," he said impatiently.

"Where is he?"

"I don't know," said Robert with a laugh. "In jail by now, I reckon. . . . I left him down at the Copley Plaza an hour ago stopping every one who came in and asking him if he'd ever been to Harvard. . . . If the man said yes, Andy would haul off and hit him as hard as he could. . . . God! the craziest man!" he said. Then, in a feverish staccato monolog, he continued: "The damnedest story you ever heard. . . . You never heard anything like the way I met him in your life. . . . Passed right out in the gutter on Park Avenue one night. . . . All alone. . . . They'd given me knockout drops in some joint and robbed me. . . . Waked up in the most magnificent apartment you ever saw in your life. . . . Most beautiful woman you ever saw sitting right there on the bed holding my hand. . . . Andy Westerman's sister. . . . God! they've got stuff in that place that cost a fortune. . . . They've got one picture that the old man paid a hundred thousand dollars for. . . . Damned little thing that doesn't take up a foot of space. . . . Twenty million dollars! Yes, sir! . . . And those two get it all. . . . Why, it'll ruin me!" he burst out. "It takes every cent I can get to keep up with 'em. . . . My God! I never saw a place like this in my life! . . . These people up here think no more of spending a thousand dollars than we'd think of fifty cents down home. . . . God! I've got to do something. . . . I've got to get money somehow. . . . Yes, sir, Robert is going to be right up there among them. . . . Apartment on Park Avenue and everything. . . . God! that's the most beautiful woman in the world! All I want is to sleep with her just once. . . . Yes, sir, just once. . . .

"And to think that she'd go and throw herself away on that damned consumptive little . . .!" he fairly ground his teeth together, turned away abruptly, and did not finish.

"Throw herself away on who? Who is this, Robert?"

"Ah-h! that damned little fellow Upshaw that she's married to: been waiting—praying—hoping that he'd die for months—she'll marry me just as soon as he's out of the way—and he knows it! The damned little rat!" He gnashed his teeth savagely. "He's hanging on just as long as he can to spite us!" And he cursed bitterly, with a terrible unconscious humor, against a man who was too stubborn to oblige him by an early death.

Then he jumped up and said abruptly: "Do you want to go to New York with me?"

"When?"

"Right now!" said Robert. "I'm ready to go this very minute. Come on!"—and he started impatiently toward the door.

When Eugene made no move to follow him, he turned and came back, saying in a resentful tone: "Well, are you coming, or are you just trying to bluff about it?"

For a moment, the boy was infected by the other's madness, too near akin to his own ever to be wholly strange to him. The prospect of that reckless, drunken, purposeless flight through darkness towards the magic city held him with hypnotic power. Then, rudely, painfully, he broke the spell and answered curtly:

"I wouldn't go as far as Harvard Square with you tonight, Robert. Not if you're going to drive that car. You're too drunk to know what you're doing and you'll have a smash-up as sure as you live if you try to drive."

He was, in fact, wildly and dangerously drunk by now and Eugene began to think of some way of persuading him to go to sleep and of finding some place where he could spend the night: in his own room there was only a single cot, and it was too late to rouse the Murphys— they had been in bed for hours. Then he remembered that Mr. Wang had an extra couch in one of his rooms: it was a very comfortable one and he did not think that Wang would make any objection to Robert's sleeping there if he explained the situation to him. Therefore, he cautioned Robert to keep quiet, and went to Wang's door and knocked. Presently he appeared sleepily, thrusting out his fat, drowsy, and troubled face to see what the trouble was: when Eugene told him he agreed very generously and readily to let Robert sleep upon the couch and thus the young man got him settled at length although not before the sudden apparition of a dragon with a scaly tail—one of the drawings that hung above the couch—had wrested from him a howl of terror: he had sprung out of bed and rushed out of Wang's apartment and into Eugene's, saying hoarsely, and in a tone of frightened indignation: "Do you expect me to spend the night alone in there with that damned Chinaman and his dragon? . . . How do I know what he'll do? . . . One of those people would cut your throat while you're asleep and think nothing of it. . . . I'm not going to stay in there." Gene finally persuaded him of Wang's innocence and kindness, and at length he went off to sleep after drinking the better part of a bottle of Wang's rice wine.

XXXVIII

One Sunday morning early in the month of May, Starwick and Eugene had crossed the bridge that led to the great stadium, and turned right along a path that followed the winding banks of the Charles River. Spring had come with the sudden, almost explosive loveliness that marks its coming in New England: along the banks of the river the birch trees leaned their slender, white and beautiful trunks, and their boughs were coming swiftly into the young and tender green of May.

That spring—which, for Eugene, would be the second and last of his years in Cambridge—Starwick had become more mannered in his dress and style than ever before. During the winter, much to Professor Hatcher's concern—a concern which constantly became more troubled and which he was no longer able to conceal—the darling protégé on whom his bounty and his favor had been lavished, and to whom, he had fondly hoped, he would one day pass on the proud authorities of his own position when he himself should become too old to carry on "the work," had begun to wear spats and carry a cane and be followed by a dog.

Now, with the coming of spring, Frank had discarded the spats, but as they walked along beside the Charles, he twirled his elegant light stick with an air of languid insouciance, interrupting his conversation with his friend now and then to speak sharply to the little dog that frisked and scampered along as if frantic with the joy of May, crying out to the little creature sharply, commandingly, and in a rather womanish tone from time to time:

"Heel, Tang! Heel, I say!"

And the dog, a shaggy little terrier—the gift of some wealthy and devoted friends of Frank's on Beacon Hill—would pause abruptly in its frisking, turn its head, and look towards its owner with the attentive, puzzled, and wistfully inquiring look that dogs and little children have, as if to say: "What is it, master? Are you pleased with me or have I done something that was wrong?"

And in a moment, in response to Frank's sharper and more peremptory command, the little dog, with a crestfallen and somewhat apologetic look, would scamper back from its wild gaieties along the green banks of the Charles, to trot meekly along the path behind the two young men, until its exuberant springtime spirits got the best of it again.

From time to time, they would pass other students, in pairs or groups, striding along the pleasant path; and when these young men saw Starwick twirling his stick and speaking to the little dog, they would grin broadly at each other, and stare curiously at Starwick as they passed.

Once Starwick paused to call "Heel!" sharply to the little dog at the very moment it had lifted its leg against a tree, and the dog, still holding its leg up, had looked inquiringly around at Starwick with such a wistful look that some students who were passing had burst out in hearty laughter. But Starwick, although the color of his ruddy face deepened a shade, had paid no more attention to these ruffians than if they had been scum in the gutter. Rather, he snapped his fingers sharply, and cried, "Heel!" again, at which the little dog left its tree and came trotting meekly back to its obedient position.

Suddenly, while one of these episodes was being enacted, Eugene heard the bright wholesome tones of a familiar voice, and turning around with a startled movement, found himself looking straight into the broad and beaming countenance of Effie Horton, and her husband Ed.

"*Well!*" Effie was saying in her rich bright voice of Iowa. "Look who's here! I *thought* those long legs looked familiar," she went on in her tone of gay and lightsome, and yet wholesome, banter, "even from a distance! I told Pooly—" this, for an unknown reason, was the affectionate nickname by which Horton was known to his wife, and all his friends from Iowa—"I told Pooly that there was only one pair of legs as long as that in Cambridge. 'It *must* be Eugene,' I said.—Yes, sir!" she went on brightly, shaking her head with a little bantering movement, her broad and wholesome face shining with good nature all the time. "It *is* Eugene —and *my! my! my!*—I just wish you'd look at him," she went on gaily, in her tones of full rich fellowship and banter in which, however, a trace of something ugly, envious, and mocking was evident—"all dressed up in his Sunday-go-to-meeting clothes out for a walk this fine morning just to give the pretty girls a treat! Yes, sir!" she cried again, shaking her head in wondering admiration, and with an air of beaming satisfaction, "I'll *bet* you that's *just* what he's going to do."

He flushed, unable to think of an apt reply to this good-natured banter, beneath whose hearty good-fellowship he felt the presence of something that was false, ugly, jeering and curiously tormented, and while he was blundering out a clumsy greeting, Horton, laughing with lazy good-nature at his confusion, slapped him on the back and said:

"How are yuh, kid? . . . Where the hell have you been keeping yourself, anyway?"

The tone was almost deliberately coarse and robust in its hearty masculinity, but beneath it one felt the same false and spurious quality that had been evident in the woman's tone.

—"And here is *Mister* Starwick!" Effie now cried brightly. "—And I *wish* you'd *look!*" she went on, as if enraptured by the spectacle—"all dressed up with a walking stick and a dog—and yes, *sir!*" she exclaimed ecstatically, after an astonished examination of Frank's sartorial splendor —"wearing a *bee-yew-teeful* brown tweed suit that looks as if it just came out of the shop of a London tailor! . . . *My! My! My!* . . . I tell *you!*" she went on admiringly—"I just wish the folks back home could see us now, Pooly——"

Horton laughed coarsely, with apparent good nature, but with an ugly jeering note in his voice.

"—I just wish they could see us now!" she said. "It's not every one can say they knew two London swells—and here they are—Mr. Starwick with his cane and his dog—and Eugene with his new suit—yes, *sir!*— and talking to us just as if we were their equals."

Eugene flushed, and then with a stiff and inept sarcasm, said:

"I'll try not to let it make any difference between us, Effie."

Horton laughed coarsely and heartily again, with false good nature, and then smote the boy amiably on the back, saying:

"Don't let her kid you, son! Tell her to go to hell if she gets fresh with you!"

"—And how is Mr. Starwick these fine days!" cried Effie gaily, now directing the artillery of her banter at his unworthy person— "Where is that great play we've all been waiting for so eagerly for lo these many

years! I tell *you!*" she exclaimed with rich conviction—"I'm going to be
right there on the front row the night it opens up on Broadway!—I know
that a play that has taken any one so many years will be a masterpiece—
every word pure gold—I don't want to miss a *word* of it."

"Quite!" said Starwick coldly, in his mannered and affected tone. His
ruddy face had flushed crimson with embarrassment; turning, he called
sharply and coldly to the little dog, in a high and rather womanish voice:

"Heel, Tang! Heel, I say!"

He snapped his fingers and the little dog came trotting meekly toward
him. Before Starwick's cold and scornful impassivity, Effie's broad and
wholesome face did not alter a jot from its expression of radiant good-
will, but suddenly her eyes, which, set in her robust and friendly countenance, were the tortured mirror of her jealous, envious, possessive, and
ravenously curious spirit, had grown hard and ugly, and the undernote
of malice in her gay tones was more apparent than ever when she spoke
again:

"Pooly," she said. laughing, taking Horton affectionately by the arm,
and drawing close to him with the gesture of a bitterly jealous and
possessive female, who, by the tortured necessity of her own spirit, must
believe that "her man" is the paragon of the universe, and herself the
envy of all other women, who lust to have him, but must gnash their
teeth in vain—"Pooly," she said lightly, and drawing close to him—"maybe that's what's wrong with us! ... Maybe that's what it takes to make
you write a great play! ... Yes, *sir!*" she said gaily, "I believe that's
it! ... I believe I'll save up all my spending money until I have enough
to buy you a bee-yew-teeful tailored suit just like the one that Mr. Starwick has on. ... Yes, *sir!*" She nodded her head emphatically in a
convinced manner. "That's just *exactly* what I'm going to do! ... I'm
going to get Mr. Starwick to give me the address of his tailor—and have
him make you a *bee-yew-teeful* new suit of English clothes—and then,
maybe, you'll turn into a great genius like Mr. Starwick and Eugene!"

"The hell you will!" he said coarsely and heartily. "What's wrong
with the one I got on? I only had it three years—why, it's as good as the
day I bought it." And he laughed with hearty, robust masculinity.

"Why, Poo-o-ly!" she said reproachfully. "It's turning *green!* And I
do so want you to get dressed up and be a *genius* like Mr. Starwick!"

"Nope!" he said in his tone of dominant finality. "I'll wear this
pair of pants till it falls off me. Then I'll go into Filene's bargain
basement and buy another pair. Nope! You can't make an æsthete out of

me! I can write just as well with a hole in the seat of my britches as not." And laughing coarsely, with robust and manly good nature, he smote Eugene on the back again, and rasped out heartily:

"Ain't that right, kid?"

"Oh, *Pooly!*" cried Effie reproachfully— "And I do *so* want you to be a genius—like Mr. Starwick!"

"Now, wait a minute! Wait a minute!" he rasped, lifting a commanding hand, as he joined with her in this ugly banter. "That's different! Starwick's an artist—I'm nothing but a writer. They don't understand the way we artists work—do they, Starwick? Now an artist is sensitive to all these things," he went on in a jocose explanatory tone to his wife. "He's got to have the right *atmosphere* to work in. Everything's got to be just right for we artists—doesn't it, Starwick?"

"Quite!" said Starwick coldly.

"Now with me it's different," said Horton heavily. "I'm just one of those big crude guys who can write anywhere. I get up in the morning and write, whether I feel like it or not. But it's different with us artists, isn't it, Starwick? Why, with a real honest-to-God-dyed-in-the-wool *artist* like Starwick, his whole life would be ruined for a *month* if his pants didn't fit, or if his necktie was of the wrong shade. . . . Ain't that right, Starwick?"

And he laughed heavily, apparently with robust fellowship, hearty good nature, but his eyes were ugly, evil, jeering, as he spoke.

"Quite!" said Starwick as before; and, his face deeply flushed, he called sharply to his dog, and then, turning inquiringly to Eugene, said quietly: "Are we ready?"

Oh, I *see*, I *see!*" cried Effie, with an air of gay enlightenment. "That's what every one is all dressed up about!—You're out for a walk, aren't you—all among the little birdies, and the beeses, and the flowers! *My! My!* How I wish I could go along! Pooly!" she said coaxingly, "why don't you take *me* for a walk sometime? I'd love to hear the little birdies sing! Come on, dear. Won't you?" she said coaxingly.

"Nope!" he boomed out finally. "I walked you across the bridge and I walked to the corner this morning for a paper. That's all the walking that I'm going to do today. If you want to hear the little birdies sing, I'll buy you a canary." And turning to Eugene, he smote him on the shoulder again, and laughing with coarse laziness, said:

"You know me, kid. . . . You know how I like exercise, don't you?"

"Well, then, if we can't go along to hear the little birdies sing to Mr.

Starwick and Eugene, I suppose we'll have to say good-bye," said Effie regretfully. "We've got no right to keep them from the little birdies any longer—have we, dear? And think what a treat it will be for all the little birdies. . . . And you, Eugene!" she cried out gaily and reproachfully, but now with real warmth and friendship in her voice. "We haven't seen you at our home in a-a-ages! What's *wrong* with you? . . . You come up soon or I'll be mad at you."

"Sure," Horton came out in his broad Iowa accent, putting his hand gently on the boy's shoulder. "Come up to see us, kid. We'll cook some grub and chew the rag a while. You know, I'm not coming back next year—" for a moment Horton's eyes were clear, gray, luminous, deeply hurt, and full of pride and tenderness. "We're going to New Hampshire with Jim Madden. So come up, kid, as soon as you can: we ought to have one more session before I go."

And the boy, suddenly touched and moved, felt the genuine affection, the real friendliness—an animal-like warmth and kindliness and affection that was the truest and most attractive element in Horton's personality.

And nodding his head, suddenly feeling affection for them both again, he said:

"All right, Ed. I'll see you soon. So long, Effie. Good-bye. Good-bye, Ed."

"Good-bye, kid. So long, Starwick," Horton said in a kindly tone. "We'll be looking for you, 'Gene— So long!"

Then they parted, in this friendly manner, and Starwick and Eugene continued their walk along the river. Starwick walked quietly, saying nothing; from time to time he called sharply to the little dog, commanding him to come to "heel" again.

The two young men had not seen each other for two months, save at Professor Hatcher's class, and then their relations had been formal, cold, and strained. Now Starwick, with a quick friendly and generous spontaneity, had broken through the stubborn and resentful pride of the other youth, had made the first advance towards reconciliation, and, as he was able to do with every one when and where he pleased, had instantly conquered his friend's resentful feelings, and won him back with the infinite grace, charm, and persuasiveness of his own personality.

Yet, during the first part of their walk along the river their conversation, while friendly, had almost been studiously detached and casual, and was the conversation of people still under the constraint of embarrassment and diffidence, who are waiting for the moment to speak things in which their lives and feelings are more intimately concerned.

At length, they came to a bending in the river where there was a bank of green turf on which in the past they had often sat and smoked and talked while that small and lovely river flowed before them. Seated here again, and provided with cigarettes, a silence came between them, as if each was waiting for the other one to speak.

Presently when Eugene looked towards his companion, Starwick's pleasant face with the cleft chin was turned towards the river in a set stare, and even as the other young man looked at him, his ruddy countenance was contorted by the animal-like grimace swift and instant, which the other boy had often seen before, and which had in it, somehow, a bestial and inarticulate quality, a kind of unspeakable animal anguish that could find no release.

In a moment, lowering his head, and staring away into the grassy turf, Starwick said quietly:

"Why have you not been in to see me these last two months?"

The other young man flushed, began to speak in a blundering and embarrassed tone and then, angered by his own confusion, burst out hotly:

"Look here, Frank—why have you got to be so damned mysterious and secretive in everything you do?"

"Am I?" said Starwick quietly.

"Yes, you are! You've been that way ever since I met you."

"In what way?" Starwick asked.

"Do you remember the first time I met you?" the other one demanded.

"Perfectly," Starwick said. "It was during your first year in Cambridge, a few days after you arrived. We met for dinner at the Cock Horse Tavern."

"Yes," the other said excitedly. "Exactly. You had written me a note inviting me to dinner, and asking me to meet you there. Do you remember what was in that note?"

"No. What was it?"

"Well, you said: 'Dear Sir—I should be pleased if you will meet me for dinner at seven-thirty Wednesday evening at the Cock Horse Tavern on Brattle Street.' And the note was signed, 'Francis Starwick.'"

"Well?" Starwick demanded quietly. "And what was wrong with that?"

"Nothing!" the other young man cried, his face flushing to a darker

hue, and the excitement of his manner growing. "Nothing, Frank!
Only, if you were going to invite a stranger—some one you had never
met before—to dinner—why the hell couldn't you have told him who
you are, and the purpose of the meeting?"

"I should think the purpose of the meeting was self-evident," said
Starwick calmly. "The purpose was to have dinner together. Does that
demand a whole volume of explanation? No," he said coldly, "I confess I see nothing extraordinary about that at all."

"Of course there wasn't!" the other youth exclaimed with vehement
excitement. "Of course there was nothing extraordinary about it! Why,
then, did you attempt, Frank, to make something extraordinary out of
it?"

"It seems to me that you're the one who's doing that!" Starwick
answered.

"Yes, but, damn it, man," the other cried angrily "—don't you see the
point? You're that way with everything you do! You try to surround the
simplest act with this great air of mystery and secrecy," he said bitterly.
"Inviting me to dinner was all right—it was fine!" he shouted. "I was a
green kid of twenty who knew no one here, and I was scared to death.
It was wonderful to get an invitation from some one asking me to
dinner. But when you sent the invitation, why couldn't you have added
just a word or two by way of explanation? Why couldn't you have
stated one or two simple facts that would have made the reason for
your invitation clear?"

"For example?" Starwick said.

"Why, Frank, simply that you were Professor Hatcher's assistant in
the course, and that this thing of inviting people out to dinner was just
a way you and Professor Hatcher had of getting acquainted with the
new people," the other youth said angrily. "After all, you can't get an
invitation to dinner from some one you don't know without wondering
what it's all about."

"And yet you came," said Starwick.

"Yes, of course I came! I think I would have come if I had never
heard of you before—I was so bewildered and rattled by this new life,
and so overwhelmed by living in a big city for the first time in my life
that I would have accepted any kind of invitation—jumped at the chance
of meeting any one! However, I already knew who you were when
your invitation came. I had heard that a man named Starwick was
Hatcher's assistant. I figured therefore that the invitation had something

to do with your connection with Professor Hatcher and the course—that you were inviting me to make me feel more at home up here, to establish a friendly relation, to give me what information you could, to help the new people out in any way you could. But when I met you, what happened?" he went on indignantly. "Never a word about the course, about Professor Hatcher, about your being his assistant—you pumped me with questions as if I were a prisoner on the witness stand and you the prosecuting lawyer. You told me nothing about yourself and asked a thousand questions about me—and then you shook hands coldly, and departed!—Always this air of secrecy and mystery, Frank!" the boy went on angrily. "That's always the way it is with you—in everything you do! And yet you wonder why people are surprised at your behavior! For weeks at a time I see you every day. We get together in your rooms and talk and argue about everything on earth. You come and yell for me in my place at midnight and then we walk all over Cambridge in the dead of night. We go over to Masillippo's place in Boston and eat and drink and get drunk together, and when you pass out, I bring you home and carry you upstairs and put you to bed. Then the next day, when I come around again," the boy cried bitterly, "what has happened? I ring the bell. Your voice comes through the place as cold as hell— 'Who is it?' you say. 'Why,' I say, 'it's your old friend and drunken companion, Eugene Gant, who brought you home last night.'—'I'm sorry,' you say, in a tone that would freeze a polar bear— 'I can't see you. I'm busy now'—and then you hang up in my face. The season of the great mystery has now begun," he went on sarcastically. "The great man is closeted in his sanctum *composing,*" he sneered. "Not *writing,* mind you, but *composing* with a gold-tipped quill plucked from the wing of a Brazilian condor—so, out, out, damned spot—don't bother me, Gant—begone, you low fellow—on your way, bum!—the great master, Signor Francis Starwick, is upstairs in a purple cloud, having a few immortal thoughts today with Amaryllis, his pet muse——"

"Gene! Gene!" said Starwick laughing, a trace of the old mannered accent returning to his voice again. "You are *most* unfair! You really are, you know!"

"No—but Frank, that's just the way you act," the other said. "You can't see enough of some one for weeks at a time and then you slam the door in his face. You pump your friends dry and tell them nothing about yourself. You try to surround everything you do with this grand

romantic air of mysterious secrecy—this there's-more-to-this-than-meets-
the-eye manner. Frank, who the hell do you think you are, anyway,
with these grand airs and mysterious manners that you have? Is it that
you're not the same as other men?" he jeered. "Is it that like Cæsar you
were from your mother's womb untimely ripped! Is it that you are made
from different stuff than the damned base clay of blood and agony from
which the rest of us have been derived?"

"What have I ever done," said Starwick flushing, "to give you the impression that I think of myself that way?"

"For one thing, Frank, you act sometimes as if the world exists solely
for the purpose of being your oyster. You sometimes act as if friendship,
the affection of your friends, is something that exists solely for your
pleasure and convenience and may be turned on and off at will like a
hot-water faucet—that you can use their time, their lives, their feelings
when they amuse and interest you—and send them away like whipped
dogs when you are bored, tired, indifferent, or have something else it
suits you better to do."

"I am not aware that I have ever done that," said Starwick quietly.
"I am sorry if you think I have."

"No, but, Frank—what can you expect your friends to think? I have
told you about my life, my family, the kind of place and people I came
from—but you have told me nothing. You are the best friend I have here
in Cambridge—I think," the boy said slowly, flushing, and with some
difficulty, "one of the best friends I have ever had. I have not had many
friends—I have known no one like you—no one of my own age to whom
I could talk as I have talked to you. I think I enjoy being with you and
talking to you more than to any one I have ever known. This friendship
that I feel for you has now become a part of my whole life and has got
into everything I do. And yet, at times, I run straight into a blank wall.
I could no more separate my friendship for you from the other acts and
meetings of my life than I could divide into two parts of my body my
father's and my mother's blood. With you it's different. You seem to
have all your friends partitioned off and kept separate from one another
in different cells and sections of your life. I know now that you have
three or four sets of friends and yet these different groups of people
never meet one another. You go about your life with all these different
sets of people in this same secret and mysterious manner that charac-
terizes everything you do. You have these aunts and cousins here in
Cambridge that you see every week, and who, like every one else,

lay themselves out to do everything they can to make your life comfortable and pleasant. You know these swells over on Beacon Hill in Boston, and you have some grand, mysterious and wealthy kind of life with them. Then you have another group here at the university—people like Egan, and Hugh Dodd and myself. And at the end, Frank," the boy said almost bitterly—"what is the purpose of all this secrecy and separation among your friends? There's something so damned arrogant and cold and calculating about it—it's almost as if you were one of these damned, wretched, self-centred fools who have their little time and place for everything—an hour for social recreation and an hour for useful reading, another hour for healthy exercise, and then four hours for business, an hour for the concert and an hour for the play, an hour for "business contacts" and an hour for friendship— Surely to God, Frank, you of all people on earth are not one of these damned, smug, vain, self-centred egotists—who would milk this earth as if it were a great milk cow here solely for their enrichment, and who, at the end, in spite of all their damned, miserable, self-seeking profit for themselves remain nothing but the God-damned smug, sterile, misbegotten set of impotent and life-hating bastards that they are— Surely to God, you, of all people in the world are not one of these," he fairly yelled, and sat there panting, exhausted by the tirade, and glaring at the other youth with wild, resentful eyes.

"Eugene!" cried Starwick sharply, his ruddy features darkened with an angry glow. "You are being most unjust! What you are saying simply is not true." He was silent a moment, his face red and angry-looking, as he stared out across the river— "If I had known that you felt this way," he went on quietly, "I should have introduced you to my other friends—what you call these separate groups of people—long ago. You may meet them any time you wish," he concluded. "It simply never occurred to me that you would be interested in knowing them."

"Oh, Frank, I'm not!" the other boy cried impatiently, with a dismissing movement of the hand. "I don't want to meet them—I don't care who they are—or how rich and fashionable or 'artistic' they may be. The thing I was kicking about was what seemed to me to be your air of secrecy—the mysterious manner in which you go about things: it seemed to me that there was something deliberately calculating and secretive in the way you shut one part of your life off from the people who know and like you best."

Starwick made no answer for a moment, but sat looking out across the river. And for a moment, the old grimace of bestial, baffled pain passed swiftly across his ruddy features, and then he said, in a quiet and weary tone:

"Perhaps you are right. I had never thought about it in that way. Yes, I can see now that you have told me much more about yourself— your family, your life before you came here, than I have told you about mine. And yet it never occurred to me that I was being mysterious or secretive. I think it is easier for you to speak about these things than it is for me. There is a great river of energy in you and it keeps bursting over and breaking loose. You could not hold it back if you tried. With me, it's different. I have not got that great well of life and power in me, and I could not speak as you do if I tried. Yet, Gene, if there is anything you want to know about my life before I came here, or what kind of people I came from I would tell you willingly."

"I have wanted to know more about you, Frank," the other young man said. "All that I know about your life before you came here is that you come from somewhere in the Middle West, and yet are completely different from any one I ever knew who came from there."

"Yes," said Starwick quietly. "From Horton, for example?" his tone was still quiet, but there was a shade of irony in it.

"Well," the other boy said, flushing, but continuing obstinately, "— yes, from Horton. He is from Iowa, you can see, smell, read, feel Iowa all over him, in everything he says and does——"

" 'It's—a—*darn—good—yarn*,' " said Starwick, beginning to burble with laughter as he imitated the heavy, hearty, sonorous robustiousness of Horton's voice when he pronounced his favorite judgment.

"Yes," said Eugene, laughing at the imitation, "that's it, all right—'it's a *darn good yarn*.' Well, Frank, you couldn't be more different from Horton if you had come from the planet Mars, and yet the place you come from out there in the Middle West, the kind of life you knew when you were growing up—could not have been so different from Ed Horton's."

"No," said Starwick quietly. "As a matter of fact, I know where he is from—it's not over fifty miles from the town I was born in, which is in Illinois, and the life in both places is much the same."

He was silent a moment longer, as he stared across the river, and then continued in a quiet voice that had a calm, weary, and almost inert detachment that characterized these conversations with his friend, and that was almost entirely free of mannered speech:

"As to the kind of people that we came from," he continued, "I can't say how different they may be, but I should think it very likely that Horton's people are much the same kind of people as my own——"

"His father is a Methodist minister," the other young man quickly interposed. "He told me that."

"Yes," said Starwick in his quiet and inert voice—"and Horton is the rebel of the family." His tone had not changed apparently in its quality by an atom, yet the quiet and bitter irony with which he spoke was evident.

"How did you know that?" the other youth said in a surprised tone. "Yes—that's true. His wife told me that Ed and his father are scarcely on speaking terms—the old man prays for the salvation of Ed's soul three times a day, because he is trying to write plays and wants to get into the theatre. Effie Horton says Ed's father still writes Ed letters begging him to repent and mend his ways before his soul is damned forever: she says the old man calls the theatre the Devil's Workshop."

"Yes," said Starwick in his quiet and almost lifeless tone that still had curiously the cutting edge of a weary and detached sarcasm—"and Horton has bearded the philistines in their den, hasn't he, and given all for art?"

"Isn't that a bit unjust? I know you don't think very highly of Ed Horton's ability, but, after all, the man must have had some genuine desire to create something—some real love for the theatre—or he would not have broken with his family, and come here."

"Yes. I suppose he has. Many people have that desire," said Starwick wearily. "Do you think it is enough?"

"No, I do not. And yet I think a man who has it is better off—will have a better life, somehow—than the man who does not have it at all."

"Do you?" Starwick answered in a dead tone. "I wish I thought so, too."

"But don't you, Frank? Surely it is better to have some kind of talent, however small, than none at all."

"Would you say, then," Starwick answered, "that it was better to have some kind of child—however puny, feeble, ugly, and diseased—as King Richard said about himself, brought into the world 'scarce half made up'—than to have no child at all?"

"I would not think so. No."

"Have you ever thought, Eugene, that the great enemy of life may not be death, but life itself?" Starwick continued. "Have you never noticed that the really evil people that one meets—the people who are filled with hatred, fear, envy, rancour against life—who wish to destroy the artist and his work—are not figures of satanic darkness, who have been born with a malignant hatred against life, but rather people who have had the seeds of life within themselves, and been destroyed by them? They are the people who have been given just enough to get a vision of the promised land—however brief and broken it may be——"

"But not enough to get there? Is that what you mean?"

"Exactly," Starwick answered. "They are left there in the desert, maddened by the sight of water they can never reach, and all the juices of their life then turn to gall and bitterness—to envy and malignant hate. They are the old women in the little towns and villages with the sour eyes and the envenomed flesh who have so poisoned the air with their envenomed taint that everything young and beautiful and full of joy that lives there will sicken and go dead and vicious and malignant as the air it breathes. They are the lecherous and impotent old men of the world, those foul, palsied creatures with small rheumy eyes who hate the lover and his mistress with the hate of hell and eunuchry—who try to destroy love with their hatred, and the slanderous rumor of their poisoned tongues. And, finally, they are the eunuchs of the arts—the men who have the lust, without the power, for creation, and whose life goes dead and rotten with its hatred of the living artist and the living man."

"And you think that Horton will be one of these?"

Again Starwick was silent for a moment, staring out across the river. When he spoke again, he did not answer his companion's question directly, but in a quiet and inert tone in which the cutting edge of irony was barely evident, he said:

"My *God*, Eugene"—his voice was so low and wearily passionate with revulsion that it was almost inaudible—"if ever you may come to know, as I have known all my life, the falseness in a hearty laugh, the envy and the malice in a jesting word, the naked hatred in a jeering eye, and all the damned, warped, poisonous constrictions of the heart—the horrible fear and cowardice and cruelty, the naked shame, the hypocrisy, and the pretense, that is masked there behind the full hearty tones, the robust manliness of the Hortons of this earth . . ." He was silent a moment longer, and then went on in a quiet, matter-of-fact tone— "I was the youngest in a family of nine children—the same kind of family that you will find everywhere. I was the only delicate flower among them," he went on with a cold impassive irony. "We were not rich people . . . a big family growing up with only a small income to support us. They were all good people," he said quietly. "My father was superintendent of a small farm-machinery plant, and before that they were farming people, but they sent me to school, and after that to college. I was the 'bright boy' of the town"—again the weary irony of his voice was evident—"the local prodigy, the teacher's pet. . . . Perhaps that is my destiny; to have something of the artist's heart, his soul, his understanding, his perceptions—never to have his power, the hand that shapes, the tongue that can express—oh, God! Eugene! is *that* to be my life—to have all that I know and feel and would create rot still-born in my spirit, to be a wave that breaks forever in mid-ocean, the shoulder of a strength without the wall—my God! My God! to come into this world scarce half made up, to have the spirit of the artist and to lack his hide, to feel the intolerable and unspeakable beauty, mystery, loveliness, and terror of this immortal land—this great America—and a skin too sensitive, a hide too delicate and rare—" his voice was high and bitter with his passion—"to declare its cruelty, its horror, falseness, hunger, the warped and twisted soul of its frustration, and lacking hide and toughness, born without a skin, to make an armor, school a manner, build a barrier of my own against its Hortons——"

"And is that why—?" the other boy began, flushed, and quickly checked himself.

"Is that why—what?" said Starwick turning, looking at him. Then as he did not answer, but still remained silent, flushed with embarrassment, Starwick laughed, and said: "Is that why I am an affected person—a poseur—what Horton calls a 'damned little æsthete'—why I speak and act and dress the way I do?"

The other flushed miserably and muttered:

"No, I didn't say that, Frank!"

Starwick laughed suddenly, his infectious and spontaneous laugh, and said:

"But why not? Why shouldn't you say it? Because it is the truth. It really is, you know," and almost mockingly at these words, his voice assumed its murmured and affected accent. Then he said quietly again:

"Each man has his manner—with each it comes for his own reason— Horton's, so that his hearty voice and robust way may hide the hatred in his eyes, the terror in his heart, the falseness and pretense in his pitiable warped small soul. He has his manner, I have mine—his for concealment, mine for armor, because my native hide was tender and my skin too sensitive to meet the Hortons of the earth—and somewhere, down below our manner, stands the naked man." Again he was silent and in a moment he continued quietly:

"My father was a fine man and we never got to know each other very well. The night before I went away to college he 'took me to one side' and talked to me—he told me how they had their hearts set on me, and he asked me to become a good and useful man—a good American."

"And what did you say, Frank?"

"Nothing. There was nothing I could say. . . . Our house stands on a little butte above the river," he went on quietly in a moment, "and when he had finished talking I went out and stood there looking at the river."

"What river, Frank?"

"There is only one," he answered. "The great slow river—the dark and secret river of the night—the everlasting flood—the unceasing Mississippi. . . . It is a river that I know so well, with all my life that I shall never tell about. Perhaps you will some day—perhaps you have the power in you— And if you do—" he paused.

"And if I do?"

"Speak one word for a boy who could not speak against the Hortons of this land, but who once stood above a river—and who knew America as every other boy has known it." He turned, smiling: "If thou did'st ever hold me in thy heart, absent thee from felicity awhile, and in this harsh world draw thy breath in pain, to tell my story."

In a moment he got up, and laughing his infectious laugh, said: "Come on, let's go."

And together they walked away.

BOOK III

TELEMACHUS

XXXIX

OCTOBER had come again, and that year it was sharp and soon: frost was early, burning the thick green on the mountain sides to massed brilliant hues of blazing colors, painting the air with sharpness, sorrow and delight—and with October. Sometimes, and often, there was warmth by day, an ancient drowsy light, a golden warmth and pollenated haze in afternoon, but over all the earth there was the premonitory breath of frost, an exultancy for all the men who were returning, a haunting sorrow for the buried men, and for all those who were gone and would not come again.

His father was dead, and now it seemed to him that he had never found him. His father was dead, and yet he sought him everywhere, and could not believe that he was dead, and was sure that he would find him. It was October and that year, after years of absence and of wandering, he had come home again.

He could not think that his father had died, but he had come home in October, and all the life that he had known there was strange and sorrowful as dreams. And yet he saw it all in shapes of deathless brightness—the town, the streets, the magic hills, and the plain prognathous faces of the people he had known. He saw them all in shapes of deathless brightness, and everything was instantly familiar as his father's face, and stranger, more phantasmal than a dream.

Their words came to him with the accents of an utter naturalness, and yet were sorrowful and lost and strange like voices speaking in a dream, and in their eyes he read a lost and lonely light, as if they were all phantoms and all lost, or as if he had revisited the shores of this great earth again with a heart of fire, a cry of pain and ecstasy, a memory of intolerable longing and regret for all the glorious and exultant life that he had known and which he must visit now forever as a fleshless ghost, never to touch, to hold, to have its palpable warmth and substance for his own again. He had come home again, and yet he could not believe his father was dead, and he thought he heard his great voice ringing in the street again, and that he would see him striding toward him across the Square with his gaunt earth-devouring stride, or find him waiting every time he turned the corner, or lunging toward the house bearing the tremendous provender of his food and meat, bringing to them all the deathless security of his strength and power and passion, bringing to them all again the roaring message of his fires that shook the fire-full chimney throat with their terrific blast, giving to them all again the exultant knowledge that the good days, the magic days, the golden weather of their lives would come again, and that this dream-like and phantasmal world in which they found themselves would waken instantly, as it had once, to all the palpable warmth and glory of the earth, if only his father would come back to make it live, to give them life, again.

Therefore, he could not think that he was dead, and yet it was October, and that year he had come home again. And at night, in his mother's house, he would lie in his bed in the dark, hearing the wind that rattled dry leaves along the empty pavement, hearing far-off across the wind, the barking of a dog, feeling dark time, strange time, dark secret time, as it flowed on around him, remembering his life, this house, and all the million strange and secret visages of time, dark time, thinking, feel-ing, thinking:

"October has come again, has come again.... I have come home again, and found my father dead ... and that was time ... time ... time.... Where shall I go now? What shall I do? For October has come again, but there has gone some richness from the life we knew, and we are lost."

Storm shook the house at night—the old house, his mother's house—where he had seen his brother die. The old doors swung and creaked in darkness, darkness pressed against the house, the darkness filled them, filled the house at night, it moved about them soft and secret, palpable, filled with a thousand secret presences of sorrowful time and memory, moving about him as he lay below his brother's room in darkness, while storm shook the house in late October, and something creaked and rat-tled in the wind's strong blast. It was October, and he had come home again: he could not believe that his father was dead.

Wind beat at them with burly shoulders in the night. The darkness moved there in the house like something silent, palpable—a spirit breath-ing in his mother's house, a demon and a friend—speaking to him its silent and intolerable prophecy of flight, of darkness and the storm, mov-ing about him constantly, prowling about the edges of his life, ever be-side him, with him, in him, whispering:

"Child, child—come with me—come with me to your brother's grave tonight. Come with me to the places where the young men lie whose bodies have long since been buried in the earth. Come with me where they walk and move again tonight, and you shall see your brother's face again, and hear his voice, and see again, as they march toward you from their graves the company of the young men who died, as he did, in October, speaking to you their messages of flight, of triumph, and the all-exultant darkness, telling you that all will be again as it was once."

October had come again, and he would lie there in his mother's house at night, and feel the darkness moving softly all about him, and hear the dry leaves scampering on the street outside, and the huge and burly rushes of the wind. And then the wind would rush away with huge caprice, and he could hear it far off roaring with remote demented cries in the embraces of great trees, and he would lie there thinking:

"October has come again—has come again"—feeling the dark around him, not believing that his father could be dead, thinking: "The strange and lonely years have come again. . . . I have come home again . . . come home again . . . and will it not be with us all as it has been?"—feeling the darkness as it moved about him, thinking, "Is it not the same darkness that I knew in childhood, and have I not lain here in bed before, and felt this darkness moving all about me? . . . Did we not hear dogs that barked in darkness, in October?" he then thought. "Were not their howls far broken by the wind? . . . And hear dry leaves that scampered on the streets at night . . . and the huge and burly rushes of the wind . . . and hear huge limbs that stiffly creak in the remote demented howlings of the burly wind . . . and something creaking in the wind at night . . . and think, then, as we think now, of all the men who have gone and never will come back again, and of our friends and brothers who lie buried in the earth? . . . Oh, has not October now come back again?" he cried. "As always—as it always was?"—and hearing the great darkness softly prowling in his mother's house at night, and thinking, feeling, thinking, as he lay there in the dark:

"Now October has come again which in our land is different from October in the other lands. The ripe, the golden month has come again, and in Virginia the chinkapins are falling. Frost sharps the middle music of the seasons, and all things living on the earth turn home again. The country is so big you cannot say the country has the same October. In Maine, the frost comes sharp and quick as driven nails, just for a week or so the woods, all of the bright and bitter leaves, flare up: the maples turn a blazing bitter red, and other leaves turn yellow like a living light, falling about you as you walk the woods, falling about you like small pieces of the sun so that you cannot say where sunlight shakes and flutters on the ground, and where the leaves.

"Meanwhile the Palisades are melting in massed molten colors, the season swings along the nation, and a little later in the South dense woodings on the hill begin to glow and soften, and when they smell the burning wood-smoke in Ohio children say: 'I'll bet that there's a forest fire in Michigan.' And the mountaineer goes hunting down in North Carolina, he stays out late with mournful flop-eared hounds, a rind of moon comes up across the rude lift of the hills: what do his friends say to him when he stays out late? Full of hoarse innocence and laughter, they will say: 'Mister, yore ole woman's goin' to whup ye if ye don't go home.' "

Oh, return, return!

"October is the richest of the seasons: the fields are cut, the granaries are full, the bins are loaded to the brim with fatness, and from the cider-press the rich brown oozings of the York Imperials run. The bee bores to the belly of the yellowed grape, the fly gets old and fat and blue, he buzzes loud, crawls slow, creeps heavily to death on sill and ceiling, the sun goes down in blood and pollen across the bronzed and mown fields of old October.

"The corn is shocked: it sticks out in hard yellow rows upon dried ears, fit now for great red barns in Pennsylvania, and the big stained teeth of crunching horses. The indolent hooves kick swiftly at the boards, the barn is sweet with hay and leather, wood and apples—this, and the clean dry crunching of the teeth is all: the sweat, the labor, and the plow is over. The late pears mellow on a sunny shelf; smoked hams hang to the warped barn rafters; the pantry shelves are loaded with 300 jars of fruit. Meanwhile the leaves are turning, turning, up in Maine, the chestnut burrs plop thickly to the earth in gusts of wind, and in Virginia the chinkapins are falling.

"There is a smell of burning in small towns in afternoon, and men with buckles on their arms are raking leaves in yards as boys come by with straps slung back across their shoulders. The oak leaves, big and brown, are bedded deep in yard and gutter: they make deep wadings to the knee for children in the streets. The fire will snap and crackle like a whip, sharp acrid smoke will sting the eyes, in mown fields the little vipers of the flame eat past the black coarse edges of burned stubble like a line of locusts. Fire drives a thorn of memory in the heart.

"The bladed grass, a forest of small spears of ice, is thawed by noon: summer is over but the sun is warm again, and there are days throughout the land of gold and russet. But summer is dead and gone, the earth is waiting, suspense and ecstasy are gnawing at the hearts of men, the brooding prescience of frost is there. The sun flames red and bloody as it sets, there are old red glintings on the battered pails, the great barn gets the ancient light as the boy slops homeward with warm foaming milk. Great shadows lengthen in the fields, the old red light dies swiftly, and the sunset barking of the hounds is faint and far and full of frost: there are shrewd whistles to the dogs, and frost and silence—this is all. Wind stirs and scuffs and rattles up the old brown leaves, and through the night the great oak leaves keep falling.

"Trains cross the continent in a swirl of dust and thunder, the leaves fly down the tracks behind them: the great trains cleave through gulch and gulley, they rumble with spoked thunder on the bridges over the powerful brown wash of mighty rivers, they toil through hills, they skirt the rough brown stubble of shorn fields, they whip past empty stations in the little towns and their great stride pounds its even pulse across America. Field and hill and lift and gulch and hollow, mountain and plain and river, a wilderness with fallen trees across it, a thicket of bedded brown and twisted undergrowth, a plain, a desert, and a plantation, a mighty landscape with no fenced niceness, an immensity of fold and convolution that can never be remembered, that can never be forgotten, that has never been described—weary with harvest, potent with every fruit and ore, the immeasurable richness embrowned with autumn, rank, crude, unharnessed, careless of scars or beauty, everlasting and magnificent, a cry, a space, an ecstasy!—American earth in old October.

"And the great winds howl and swoop across the land: they make a distant roaring in great trees, and boys in bed will stir in ecstasy, thinking of demons and vast swoopings through the earth. All through the night there is the clean, the bitter rain of acorns, and the chestnut burrs are plopping to the ground.

"And often in the night there is only the living silence, the distant frosty barking of a dog, the small clumsy stir and feathery stumble of the chickens on limed roosts, and the moon, the low and heavy moon of autumn, now barred behind the leafless poles of pines, now at the pinewoods' brooding edge and summit, now falling with ghost's dawn of milky light upon rimed clods of fields and on the frosty scurf on pumpkins, now whiter, smaller, brighter, hanging against the steeple's slope, hanging the same way in a million streets, steeping all the earth in frost and silence.

"Then a chime of frost-cold bells may peal out on the brooding air, and people lying in their beds will listen. They will not speak or stir, silence will gnaw the darkness like a rat, but they will whisper in their hearts:

" 'Summer has come and gone, has come and gone. And now—?' But they will say no more, they will have no more to say: they will wait listening, silent and brooding as the frost, to time, strange ticking time, dark time that haunts us with the briefness of our days. They will think of men long dead, of men now buried in the earth, of frost and silence long ago, of a forgotten face and moment of lost time, and they will think of things they have no words to utter.

"And in the night, in the dark, in the living sleeping silence of the towns, the million streets, they will hear the thunder of the fast express, the whistles of great ships upon the river.

"What will they say then? What will they say?"

Only the darkness moved about him as he lay there thinking, feeling in the darkness: a door creaked softly in the house.

"October is the season for returning: the bowels of youth are yearning with lost love. Their mouths are dry and bitter with desire: their hearts are torn with the thorns of spring. For lovely April, cruel and flowerful, will tear them with sharp joy and wordless lust. Spring has no language but a cry; but crueller than April is the asp of time.

"October is the season for returning: even the town is born anew," he thought. "The tide of life is at the full again, the rich return to business or to fashion, and the bodies of the poor are rescued out of heat and weariness. The ruin and horror of the summer is forgotten—a memory of hot cells and humid walls, a hell of ugly sweat and labor and distress and hopelessness, a limbo of pale greasy faces. Now joy and hope have revived again in the hearts of millions of people, they breathe the air again with hunger, their movements are full of life and energy. The mark of their summer's suffering is still legible upon their flesh, there is something starved and patient in their eyes, and a look that has a child's hope and expectation in it.

"All things on earth point home in old October: sailors to sea, travellers to walls and fences, hunters to field and hollow and the long voice of the hounds, the lover to the love he has forsaken—all things that live upon this earth return, return: Father, will you not, too, come back again?

"Where are you now, when all things on the earth come back again? For have not all these things been here before, have we not seen them, heard them, known them, and will they not live again for us as they did once, if only you come back again?

"Father, in the night time, in the dark, I have heard the thunder of the fast express. In the night, in the dark, I have heard the howling of the winds among great trees, and the sharp and windy raining of the acorns. In the night, in the dark, I have heard the feet of rain upon the roofs, the glut and gurgle of the gutter spouts, and the soaking gulping throat of all the mighty earth, drinking its thirst out in the month of May—and heard the sorrowful silence of the river in October. The hill-streams foam and welter in a steady plunge, the mined clay drops and melts and eddies in the night, the snake coils cool and glistening under dripping ferns, the water roars down past the mill in one sheer sheet-like plunge, making a steady noise like wind, and in the night, in the dark, the river flows by us to the sea.

"The great maw slowly drinks the land as we lie sleeping: the mined banks cave and crumble in the dark, the earth melts and drops into its tide, great horns are baying in the gulph of night, great boats are baying at the river's mouth. Thus, darkened by our dumpings, thickened by our stains, rich, rank, beautiful, and unending as all life, all living, the river, the dark immortal river, full of strange tragic time is flowing by us—by us—by us—to the sea.

"All this has been upon the earth, and will abide forever. But you are gone; our lives are ruined and broken in the night, our lives are mined below us by the river, our lives are whirled away into the sea and darkness, and we are lost unless you come to give us life again.

"Come to us, Father, in the watches of the night, come to us as you always came, bringing to us the invincible sustenance of your strength, the limitless treasure of your bounty, the tremendous structure of your life that will shape all lost and broken things on earth again into a golden pattern of exultancy and joy. Come to us, Father, while the winds howl in the darkness, for October has come again bringing with it huge prophecies of death and life and the great cargo of the men who will return. For we are ruined, lost, and broken if you do not come, and our lives, like rotten chips, are whirled about us onward in darkness to the sea."

So, thinking, feeling, speaking, he lay there in his mother's house, but there was nothing in the house but silence and the moving darkness: storm shook the house and huge winds rushed upon them, and he knew then that his father would not come again, and that all the life that he had known was now lost and broken as a dream.

XL

DURING the whole course of that last October—the last October he would spend at home—he was waiting day by day with a desperation of wild hope for a magic letter—one of those magic letters for which young men wait, which are to bring them instantly the fortune, fame, and triumph for which their souls thirst and their hearts are panting, and which never come.

Each morning he would get up with a pounding heart, trembling hands, and chattering lips, and then, like a man in prison who is waiting feverishly for some glorious message of release or pardon which he is sure will come that day, he would wait for the coming of the postman. And when he came, even before he reached the house, the moment that Eugene heard his whistle, he would rush out into the street, tear the mail out of his astounded grasp, and begin to hunt through it like a madman for the letter which would announce to him that fortune, fame, and glittering success were his. He was twenty-two years old, a madman and a fool, but every young man in the world has been the same.

Then, when the wonderful letter did not come, his heart would sink down to his bowels like lead, all of the brightness, gold, and singing would go instantly out of the day and he would stamp back into the house, muttering to himself, sick with despair and misery and thinking that now his life was done for, sure enough. He could not eat, sleep, stand still, sit down, rest, talk coherently, or compose himself for five minutes at a time. He would go prowling and muttering around the house, rush out into the streets of the town, walk up and down the main street, pausing to talk with the loafers before the principal drug store, climb the hills and mountains all around the town and look down on the town with a kind of horror and disbelief, an awful dreamlike unreality because the town, since his long absence and return to it, and all the people in it, now seemed as familiar as his mother's face and stranger than a dream, so that he could never regain his life or corporeal substance in it, any more than a man who revisits his youth in a dream, and so that, also, the town seemed to have shrunk together, got little, fragile, toy-like in his absence, until now when he walked in the street he thought he was going to ram his elbows through the walls, as if the walls were paper, or tear down the buildings, as if they had been made of straw.

Then he would come down off the hills into the town again, go home, and prowl and mutter around the house, which now had the same real-unreal familiar-strangeness that the town had, and his life seemed to have been passed there like a dream. Then, with a mounting hope and a pounding heart, he would begin to wait for the next mail again; and when it came, but without the letter, this furious prowling and lashing about would start all over. His family saw the light of madness in his eyes, and in his disconnected movements, and heard it in his incoherent speech. He could hear them whispering together, and sometimes when he looked up he could see them looking at him with troubled and bewildered faces. And yet he did not think that he was mad, nor know how he appeared to them.

Yet, during all this time of madness and despair his people were as kind and tolerant as any one on earth could be.

His mother, during all this time, treated him with kindness and tolerance, and according to the law of her powerful, hopeful, brooding, octopal, and web-like character, with all its meditative procrastination, never coming to a decisive point, but weaving, re-weaving, pursing her lips, and meditating constantly and with a kind of hope, even though in her deepest heart she really had no serious belief that he could succeed in doing the thing he wanted to do.

Thus, as he talked to her sometimes, going on from hope to hope, his enthusiasm mounting with the intoxication of his own vision, he would paint a glittering picture of the fame and wealth he was sure to win in the world, as soon as his play was produced. And his mother would listen thoughtfully, pursing her lips from time to time, in a meditative fashion, as she sat before the fire with her hands folded in a strong loose clasp above her stomach. Then, finally, she would turn to him and with a proud, tremulous, and yet bantering smile playing about her mouth, such as she had always used when he was a child, and had perhaps spoken of some project with an extravagant enthusiasm, she would say:

"Hm, boy! I tell you what!" his mother said, in this bantering tone, as if he were still a child. "That's mighty big talk—as the sayin' goes " here she put one finger under her broad red nose-wing and laughed shyly, but with pleasure—"as the sayin' goes, mighty big talk for poor-folks!" said his mother. "Well, now," she said in a thoughtful and hope-ful tone, after a moment's pause, "you may do it, sure enough. Stranger things than that have happened. Other people have been able to make a success of their writings—and there's one thing sure!" His mother cried out strongly with the loose, powerful and manlike gesture of her hand and index finger which was characteristic of all her family—"there's one thing sure!—what one man has done another can do if he's got grit and determination enough!" His mother said, putting the full strength of her formidable will into these words— "Why, yes, now!" she now said, with a recollective start, "Here, now! Say!" she cried—"wasn't I reading?—didn't I see? Why, pshaw!—yes! just the other day—that all these big writers—yes, sir! Irvin S. Cobb—there was the very feller!" cried his mother in a triumphant tone— "Why, you know," she continued, pursing her lips in a meditative way, "—that he had the very same trials and tribulations—as the sayin' goes—as every one else! Why, yes!—here he told it on himself—admitted it, you know—that he kept writin' these stories for years, sendin' them out, I reckon, to all the editors and magazines—and having them all sent back to him. That's the way it was," she said, "and now—look at him! Why, I reckon they'd pay him hundreds of dollars for a single piece—yes! and be glad of the chance to get it," said his mother.

Then for a space his mother sat looking at the fire, while she slowly and reflectively pursed her lips.

"Well," she said slowly at length, "you may do it. I hope you do. Stranger things than that have happened.—Now, there's one thing sure," she said strongly, "you have certainly had a good education—there's been more money spent upon your schoolin' than on all the rest of us put together—and you certainly ought to know enough to write a story or a play!—Why, yes, boy! I tell you what," his mother now cried in the old playful and bantering tone, as if she were speaking to a child, "if I had *your* education I believe I'd try to be a writer, too! Why, yes! I wouldn't mind getting out of all this drudgery and house-work for a while—and if I could earn my living doin' some light easy work like that, why, you can bet your bottom dollar, I'd do it!" cried his mother. "But, say, now! See here!" his mother cried with a kind of jocose seriousness—"maybe that'd be a good idea, after all! Suppose you write the stories," she said, winking at him,—"and I tell you what I'll do!—Why, I'll *tell* 'em to you!

Now, if I had your education, and your command of language," said his mother, whose command of language was all that any one could wish—"I believe I could tell a pretty good story—so if you'll write 'em out,' she said, with another wink, "I'll tell you what to write—and I'll *bet* you—I'll *bet* you," said his mother, "that we could write a story that would beat most of these stories that I read, all to pieces! Yes, sir!" she said, pursing her lips firmly, and with an invincible conviction—"and I bet you people would buy that story and come to see that play!" she said. "Because I know what to tell 'em, and the kind of thing people are interested in hearing," she said.

Then for a moment more she was silent and stared thoughtfully into the fire.

"Well," she said slowly, "you may do it. You may do it, sure enough! Now, boy," she said, levelling that powerful index finger toward him, "I want to tell you! Your grandfather, Tom Pentland, was a remarkable man—and if he'd had your education he'd a-gone far! And every one who ever knew him said the same! . . . Oh! stories, poems, pieces in the paper—why didn't they print something of his every week or two!" she cried. "And that's exactly where you get it," said his mother. "—But, say, now," she said in a persuasive tone, after a moment's meditation, "I've been thinkin'—it just occurred to me—wouldn't it be a good idea if you could find some work to do—I mean, get you a job somewheres of some light easy work that would give you plenty of time to do your writin' as you went on! Now, Rome wasn't built in a day, you know!" his mother said in the bantering tone, "—and you might have to send that play around to several places before you found the one who could do it right for you! So while you're waitin'," said his mother persuasively, "why wouldn't it be a good idea if you got a little light newspaper work, or a job teachin' somewheres—pshaw! you could do it easy as falling off a log," his mother said contemptuously. "I taught school myself before I got married to your papa, and I didn't have a bit of trouble! And all the schoolin' that I ever had—all the schoolin' that I ever had," she cried impressively, "was six months one time in a little backwoods school! Now if I could do it, there's one thing sure, with all your education you ought to be able to do it, too! Yes, sir, that's the very thing!" she said. "I'd do it like a shot if I were you."

He said nothing, and his mother sat there for a moment looking at the fire. Suddenly she turned, and her face had grown troubled and sorrowful, and her worn and faded eyes were wet with tears. She stretched her strong rough hand out and put it over his, shaking her head a little before she spoke:

"Child, child!" she said. "It worries me to see you act like this! I hate to see you so unhappy! Why, son," his mother said, "what if they shouldn't take it now! You've got long years ahead of you, and if you can't do it now, why, maybe, some day you will! And if you don't!" his mother cried out strongly and formidably, "why, Lord, boy, what about it! You're a young man with your whole life still before you—and if you can't do this thing, why there are other things you can do! . . . Pshaw, boy, your life's not ended just because you find out that you weren't cut out to be a playwriter," said his mother. "There are a thousand things a young man of your age could do! Why, it wouldn't faze me for a moment!" cried his mother.

And he sat there in front of her invincible strength, hope, and fortitude and her will that was more strong than death, her character that was as solid as a rock; he was as hopeless and wretched as he had ever been in his life, wanting to say a thousand things to her and saying none of them, and reading in her eyes the sorrowful message that she did not believe he would ever be able to do the thing on which his heart so desperately was set.

At this moment the door opened and his brother entered the room. As they stared at him with startled faces, he stood there looking at them out of his restless, tormented gray eyes, breathing his large and unhappy breath of unrest and nervousness, a harassed look on his handsome and generous face, as with a distracted movement he thrust his strong, impatient fingers through the flashing mop of his light brown hair, that curled everywhere in incredible whorls and screws of angelic brightness.

"Hah?" his mother sharply cried, as she looked at him with her white face, the almost animal-like quickness and concentration of her startled attention. "What say?" she said in a sharp startled tone, although as yet his brother had said nothing.

"W-w-w-wy!" he began in a distracted voice, as he thrust his fingers through his incredible flashing hair, and his eyes flickered about absently and with a tormented and driven look, "I was just f-f-f-finkin'—" he went on in a dissonant and confused tone, then, suddenly catching sight of her white startled face, he smote himself suddenly and hard upon his

temple with the heel of one large hand, and cried out, "Haw!" in a tone
of such idiot exuberance and exultancy that it is impossible to reproduce
in words the limitless and earthy vulgarity of its humor. At the same
time he prodded his mother stiffly in the ribs with his clumsy fingers, an
act that made her shriek out resentfully, and then say in a vexed and
fretful tone:

"I'll vow, boy! You act like a regular idiot! If I didn't have any
more sense than to go and play a trick like that—I'd be ash-a-a-med—
ash-a-a-a-med," she whispered, with a puckered mouth, as she shook her
head at him in a movement of strong deprecation, scorn, and reproof.
"I'd be *ashamed* to let any one know I was such a fool," his mother
said.

"Whah! *Whah!*" Luke shouted with his wild, limitlessly exuberant
laugh, that was so devastating in its idiot exultancy that all words, reproaches, scorn, or attempts at reason were instantly reduced to nothing by it. "Whee!" he cried, prodding her in her resentful ribs again,
his handsome face broken by his huge and exuberant smile. Then, as if
cherishing something secret and uncommunicably funny in its idiot humor, he smote himself upon the forehead again, cried out, "Whah—
Whah!" and then, shaking his grinning face to himself in this movement of secret and convulsive humor, he said: "Whee! Go-o-d-damn!"
in a tone of mincing and ironic refinement.

"Why, what on earth has got into you, boy!" his mother cried out
fretfully. "Why, you're actin' like a regular simpleton, I'll vow you
are!"

"Whah! *Whah!*" Luke cried exultantly.

"Now, I don't know where it comes from," said his mother judicially,
with a deliberate and meditative sarcasm, as if she were seriously con-
sidering the origin of his lunacy. "There's one thing sure: you never
got it from me. Now, all my people had their wits about them—now,
say what you please," she went on in a thoughtful tone, as she stared
with puckered mouth into the fire, "I never heard of a weak-minded
one in the whole crowd——"

"Whah—*whah!*" he cried.

"—So you didn't get it from any of my people," she went on with
deliberate and telling force—"no, you didn't!" she said.

"*Whah-h!*" he prodded her in the ribs again, and then immediately,
and in a very earnest tone, he said:

"W-w-w-wy, I was just f-f-f-finkin' it would be a good idea if we all w-w-w-went for a little ride. F-f-f-frankly, I fink it would do us good," he said, looking at Eugene with a very earnest look in his restless and tormented eyes. "I fink we need it! F-f-f-frankly, I fink we do," he said, and then added abruptly and eagerly as he thrust his clumsy fingers through his hair: "W-w-w-wy, what do you say?"

"Why, yes!" his mother responded with an instant alacrity as she got up from her chair. "That's the very thing! A little breath of fresh air is just the thing we need—as the feller says," she said, turning to Eugene now and beginning to laugh slyly, and with pleasure, passing one finger shyly underneath her broad red nose-wing as she spoke—, "as the feller says, it costs nothin' and it's Nature's sovereign remedy, good for man and good for beast!—So let's all get out into the light of open day again," she said with rhetorical deliberation, "and breathe in God's fresh air like He intended we should do—for there's one thing sure," his mother went on in tones of solemn warning, which seemed directed to a vast unseen audience of the universe rather than to themselves, "there's one thing sure—you can't violate the laws of God or nature," she said decisively, "or you'll pay for it—as sure as you're born. As sure as you're born," she whispered. "Why, yes, now!"—she went on, with a start of recollective memory— "Here now!—Say!—Didn't I see it—wasn't I readin'— Why, here, you know, the other day," she went on impatiently, as if the subject of these obscure broken references must instantly be clear to every one—"why, it was in the paper, you know— this article written by Doctor Royal S. Copeland," his mother said, nodding her head with deliberate satisfaction over his name, and pronouncing the full title sonorously with the obvious satisfaction that titles and distinctions always gave her—"that's who it was all right, sayin' that fresh air was the thing that every one must have, and that all of us should take good care to——"

"Now, M-m-m-m-mama," said Luke, who had paid no attention at all to what she had been saying, but had stood there during all the time she was speaking, breathing his large, weary, and unhappy breath, thrusting his clumsy fingers through his hair, as his harassed and tormented eyes flickered restlessly about the room in a driven but unseeing stare:— "Now, M-m-m-mama!" he said in a tone of exasperated and frenzied impatience, "if we're g-g-g-going we've g-g-g-got to get started! N-n-n-now I d-d-don't mean next W-w-w-w-Wednesday," he snarled, with exasperated sarcasm, "I d-d-d-don't m-m-m-mean the fifteenth of next July. But—*now—now—now,*" he muttered crazily, coming to her with his large hands lifted like claws, the fingers working, and with a look of fiendish madness in his eyes.

"Now!" he whispered hoarsely. "This week! Today! This afternoon! A-a-a-a-at once!" he barked suddenly, jumping at her comically, then thrusting his hand through his hair again, he said in a weary and exasperated voice:

"M-m-m-mama, will you please get ready! I b-b-b-beg of you. I beseech you—*please!*" he said, in tortured entreaty.

"*All* right! *All* right!" his mother replied instantly in a tone of the heartiest and most conciliatory agreement. "I'll be ready in five minutes! I'll just go back here and put on a coat over this old dress—so folks won't see me," she laughed shyly, "an' I'll be ready before you know it!—Pshaw, boy!" she now said in a rather nettled tone, as if the afterthought of his impatience had angered her a little, "now you don't need to worry about *my* being ready," she said, "because when the time comes —I'll be *there!*" she said, with the loose, deliberate, man-like gesture of her right hand and in tones of telling deliberation. "Now you worry about yourself!" she said. "For I'll be ready before *you* are—yes, and I'm never late for an appointment, either," she said strongly, "and that's more than *you* can say—for I've seen you miss 'em time an' time again."

During all this time Luke had been thrusting his fingers through his hair, breathing heavily and unhappily, and pawing and muttering over a mass of thumbed envelopes and papers which were covered with the undecipherable scrawls and jottings of his nervous hand: "T-t-t-Tuesday," he muttered, "Tuesday . . . Tuesday in Blackstone— B-b-b-b-Blackstone—Blackstone—Blackstone, South Car'lina," he muttered in a confused and distracted manner, as if these names were completely meaningless to him, and he had never heard them before. "Now —*ah!*" he suddenly sang out in a rich tenor voice, as he lifted his hand, thrust his fingers through his hair, and stared wildly ahead of him— "meet Livermore in Blackstone Tuesday morning—see p-p-p-p-prospect in G-g-g-g-Gadsby Tuesday afternoon about—about—about— Wheet!" —here he whistled sharply, as he always did when hung upon a word— "about a new set of batteries for his Model X—Style 37—lighting system —which the cheap p-p-p-penny-pinching South Car'lina bastard w-w-w-wants for nothing—Wednesday m-m-m-morning b-b-b-back to Blackstone—F'ursday . . . w-w-w-wy," he muttered pawing clumsily and confusedly at his envelopes with a demented glare— "F-f-f-f-f'ursday—you —ah—j-j-j-jump over to C-c-c-Cavendish to t-t-t-try to persuade that ignorant red-faced nigger-Baptist son-of-a-bitch that it's f-f-f-for his own b-b-b-best interests to scrap the-the-w-w-w-wy the d-d-d-decrepit pile of junk he's been using since S-s-s-Sherman marched through Georgia and b-b-b-buy the new X50 model T Style 46 transmission——

"M-m-m-mama!" he cried suddenly, turning toward her with a movement of frenzied and exasperated entreaty. "Will you *please* kindly have the g-g-g-goodness and the m-m-m-mercy to do me the favor to b-b-b-begin to commence—w-w-w-w-wy—to start—to make up your mind—to get ready," he snarled bitterly. "W-w-w-w-wy sometime before midnight—I b-b-b-beg of you . . . I beseech you . . . I ask it of you p-p-p-*please*, for *my* sake—for *all* our sakes—for *God's* sake!" he cried with frenzied and maddened desperation.

"*All* right! *All* right!" his mother cried hastily in a placating and reassuring tone beginning to move with an awkward, distracted, bridling movement that got her nowhere, since there were two doors to the parlor and she was trying to go out both of them at the same time. "*All* right!" she said decisively, at length getting started toward the door nearest her. "I'll just go back there an' slip on a coat—and *I'll be with you* in a jiffy!" she said with comforting assurance.

"If you *please!*" Luke said with an ironic and tormented obsequiousness of entreaty, as he fumbled through his mass of envelopes. "If you *please!* W-w-w-wy I'd certainly be m-m-m-m-much obliged to you if you would!" he said.

At this moment, however, a car halted at the curb outside, some one got out, and in a moment more they could hear Helen's voice, as she came towards the house, calling back to her husband in tones of exasperated annoyance:

"All *right,* Hugh! All *right!* I'm coming!"—although she was really going toward the house. "Will you *kindly* leave me alone for just a moment! Good heavens! Will I never get a little peace? All right! All right! I'm coming! For God's sake, leave me *alone* for just five minutes, or you'll drive me crazy!" she stormed, and with a high-cracked note of frenzied strain and exasperation that was almost like hysteria.

"All right, Mr. Barton," she now said to her husband in a more good-humored tone. "Now you just hold your horses for a minute and I'll come on out. The house is not going to burn down before we get there."

His lean, seamed, devoted face broke into a slow, almost unwilling grin, in which somehow all of the submission, loyalty and goodness of his soul was legible, and Helen turned, came up on the porch, opened the hall door, and came into the parlor where they were, beginning to speak immediately in a tone of frenzied and tortured exacerbation of the nerves and with her large, gaunt, liberal features strained to the breaking point of nervous hysteria.

"My *God!*" she said in a tone of weary exasperation. "If I don't get away from them soon I'm going to lose my mind! . . . From the moment that I get up in the morning I never get a moment's peace! Some one's after me all day long from morn to night! Why, good heavens, Mama!" she cried out in a tone of desperate fury, and as if Eliza had contradicted something she had said, "I've got troubles enough of my own, without any one else putting theirs on me! Have they got no one else they can go to? Haven't they got homes of their own to look after? Do I have to bear the burden of it all for every one *all* my life?" she stormed in a voice that was so hoarse, strained and exasperated now that she was almost weeping. "Do I have to be the goat *all* my life? Oh, I want a little peace," she cried desperately. "I just want to be left alone by myself once in a while!—The rest of you don't have to worry!" she said accusingly. "You don't have to stand for it. You can get away from it!" she cried. "You don't know—you don't *know!*" she said furiously, "what I put up with—but if I don't get away from it soon, I'm going all to pieces."

During all the time that Helen had been pouring out her tirade of the wrongs and injuries that had been inflicted on her, Luke had acted as a kind of dutiful and obsequious chorus, punctuating all the places where she had to pause to pant for breath, with such remarks as——

"W-w-w-w-well, you d-d-do too much for every one and they don't appreciate it—that's the trouble," or, "I f-f-f-f-fink I'd tell them all to p-p-p-p-politely step to hell—f-f-frankly I fink you owe it to yourself to do it! W-w-w-wy you'll only w-w-w-wear yourself out doing for others and in the end you d-d-d-don't get so m-m-m-much as one good Goddamn for all your trouble! F-f-f-frankly, I mean it!" he would say with a very earnest look on his harassed and drawn face. "W-w-w-wy hereafter I'd let 'em g-g-g-g-go to hell!"

—"If they'd only show a little appreciation once in a while I wouldn't mind so much," she panted. "But do you think they care? Do you think it ever occurs to them to lift a hand to help me when they see me working my fingers to the bone for them? Why," and here her big-boned generous face worked convulsively, "if I should work myself to death for them, do you think any of them would even so much as send a bunch of flowers to the funeral?"

Luke laughed with jeering scorn: "W-w-w-wy," he said, "it is to laugh! It is to laugh! They w-w-wouldn't send a G-g-g-g-God-damn thing—n-n-n-not even a ten-cent b-b-b-bunch of-of-w-w-w-w-wy—of turnip-greens!" he said.

"All *right!* All *right!*" Helen again cried furiously through the door, as Barton sounded a long imperative blast of protest and impatience on his horn. "All *right,* Hugh! I'm coming! Good heavens, can't you leave me in peace for just five minutes! . . . Hugh, *please!* Please!" she stormed in a tone of frenzied exasperation as he sourly answered her. "Give me a little time alone, I beg of you—or I'll go mad!"—And she turned to them again, panting and with the racked and strained expression of hysteria on her big-boned features. In a moment, her harassed and driven look relaxed somewhat, and the big rough bawdy smile began to shape itself again around the corners of her generous mouth.

"My God, Mama," she said in a tone of quiet and weary despair, but with this faint lewd smile about her mouth and growing deeper as she spoke, "what am I going to do about it? Will you please tell me that? Did you have to put up with that when you and Papa were together? Is that the way it is? Is there no such thing as peace and privacy in this world? Now, I'd like to know. When you marry one of them, does that mean that you'll never get a moment's peace or privacy alone as long as you live? Now, there are some things you like to do alone"—she said, and by this time the lewd smile had deepened perceptibly around her mouth. "Why, it's got so," she said, "that I'm almost afraid to go to the bath-room anymore——"

"Whew-w!" shrieked Eliza, laughing, putting one finger underneath her nose.

"Yes, sir," Helen said quietly, with the lewd smile now deep and loose around her mouth. "I've just got so I'm almost afraid to go, I don't know from one moment to the next whether one of them is going to come in and keep me company or not."

"Whew!" Eliza cried. "Why, you'll have to put up signs! 'No Visitors Allowed!'—that's exactly what you ought to say! I'd fix 'em! I'd do it like a shot," she said.

Helen sniggered hoarsely, and absently began to pluck at her chin.

"But *oh!*" she said with a sigh. "If only they'd leave me alone an hour a day! If only I could get away for just an hour——"

"W-w-w-wy!" Luke began. "Why don't you c-c-come with us! F-f-f-frankly, I fink you ought to do it! I fink the change would do you good," he said.

"Why?" she said rather dully, yet curiously. "Where are you going?"

"W-w-w-wy," he said, "we were just starting for a little ride. . . . Mama!" he burst out suddenly in a tone of exasperated entreaty— "Will you k-k-k-kindly go and get yourself ready? W-w-wy, its g-g-g-going to get d-d-d-dark before we get started," he said bitterly, as if she had kept him waiting all this time. "Now, *please*—I b-b-b-beg of you—to g-g-g-get ready—wy-wy-wy without f-f-f-further delay—now, I ask it of you, for God's sake!" he said, and then turning to Helen with a movement of utter exasperation and defeat, he shuddered convulsively, thrust his fingers through his hair, and moaned "Ah-h-h-h-h-h!" after which he began to mutter "My God! My God! My God!"

"All *right,* sir! All *right!*" Eliza said briskly, in a conciliating tone. "I'll just go right back here and put my coat and hat on and I won't keep you waitin' *five*——"

"Wy, wy, wy. If you p-p-please, Mama," said Luke with a tortured and ironic bow. "If you p-p-please."

At length, they really did get out of the house and were assembled on the curb in the last throes of departure. Luke, breathing stertorously his large unhappy breath, began to walk about his battered little car, casting uneasy and worried looks at it and falling upon it violently from time to time, kicking it in the tires with his large flat feet, smiting it with a broad palm and seizing it by the sides and shaking it so savagely that its instant dissolution seemed inevitable. Meanwhile Eliza stood planted solidly, facing her house, her hands clasped loosely at the waist, and her powerful and delicate mouth pursed reflectively as she surveyed her property—a characteristic gesture that always marked every departure from the house and every return to it, in which the whole power and relish of possession was evident. As for Barton, while these inevitable ceremonies were taking place, he just sat in his car with a kind of sour resigned patience, and waited. And Helen, while this was going on, had taken Eugene by the arm and walked a few paces down the street with him, talking all the time in a broken and abstracted way, of which the reference could only be inferred:

"You see, don't you? . . . You see what I've got to put up with, don't you? . . . You only get it for a little while when you come here, but with me it's *all* the time and *all* the time"— Suddenly she turned to him, looked him directly in the eye, and speaking quietly to him, but with a curious, brooding and disturbing inflection in her voice, she said:

"Do you know what day this is?"

"No."

"Do you realize that Ben died five years ago this morning?—I was thinking of it yesterday when she was talking about getting that room ready for those people who are coming," she muttered, and with a note of weary bitterness in her voice. For a moment her big-boned face was marked with the faint tension of hysteria, and her eyes looked dark and lustreless and strained as she plucked absently at her large chin. "But do you see how she can do it?" she went on in a low tone of brooding and weary resignation. "Do you understand how she can ever bear to go back in there? Do you see how she can rent that room out to any cheap roomer who comes along? Do you realize that she's got the same bed in there he died on," she said morbidly, "the same mattress?—K-k-k-k-k-k!" she laughed softly and huskily, poking at his ribs. "She'll have you sleeping on it next"——

"I'll be damned if she does!"

"K-k-k-k-k-k!"

"Do you think I could be sleeping on it now!" Eugene said with a feeling of black horror and dread around his heart.

"K-k-k-k-k-k!" she snickered. "Would you like that? Would you sleep better if you knew it was? . . . No," she said quietly, shaking her head. "Uh-uh. I don't think so. It's still up there in the same room. She may have painted the bed, but otherwise I don't think she's changed a thing. Have you ever been back up there since he died?" she said curiously.

"My *God,* no! Have you?"

She shook her head: "Not I," she said with weary finality. "I've never even been up-stairs since that morning. . . . Hugh hates the place," she muttered, looking towards him. "He doesn't even like to stop and wait for me. He won't come in."

Then she was silent for a moment as they looked at the gaunt ugly bay of the room upstairs where Ben had died. In the yard the maple trees were thinning rapidly; the leaves were sere and yellow and were floating to the ground. And the old house stood there in all its ugly, harsh, and prognathous bleakness, its paint of rusty yellow scaling from it in patches, and weathered and dilapidated as Eugene had never seen it before, but incredibly near, incredibly natural and familiar, so that all its ghosts of pain and grief and bitterness, its memories of joy and magic and lost time, the thousand histories of all the vanished people it had sheltered, whom all of them had known, revived instantly with an intolerable and dream-like strangeness and familiarity.

And now, as they looked up at the bleak windows of the room in which he died, the memory of his death's black horror passed across their souls a minute, and then was gone, leaving them only with the fatality of weary resignation which they had learned from it. In a moment, with a look of ancient and indifferent weariness and grief in her eyes, Helen turned to him, and with a faint rough smile, around her mouth, said quietly:

"Does he ever bother you at night?—When the wind begins to howl around the house, do you ever hear him walking up there? Has he been in to see you yet?—K-k-k-k-k!" she poked him with her big stiff finger, laughing huskily, and then in a low, sombrely brooding tone, as if the grisly suggestion were his, she shook her head, saying:

"Forget about it! They don't come back, Eugene! I used to think they did, but now I know they never do.—He won't come," she muttered, as she shook her head. "Forget about it. He won't come. Just forget about it," she continued, looking at Eliza with weary resignation. "It's not her fault. I used to think that you could change them. But you can't. Uh-uh," she muttered, plucking at her large, cleft chin. "It can't be done. They never change."

Luke stood distractedly for a moment on the curbstone, breathing his large unhappy breath and thrusting his clumsy fingers strongly through the flashing whirls and coils of his incredible hair:

"Now—ah!" he sang out richly. "Let me see! I—wy—I fink! M-m-m-mama, if you *please!*" he said. "Wy if you *please!*" with an exasperated and ironic obsequiousness.

She had been standing there, planted squarely on the sidewalk, facing her house. She stood with her hands clasped loosely across her stomach, and as she looked at the gaunt weathered shape of the old house, her mouth was puckered in an expression of powerful rumination in which the whole terrible legend of blood and hunger and desperate tenacity— the huge clutch of property and possession which, with her, was like the desperate clutch of life itself—was evident.

What was this great claw in her life—this thing that was stronger than life or death or motherhood—which made her hold on to anything which had ever come into her possession, which made her cling desperately to everything which she had ever owned—old bottles, papers, pieces of string, worn-out gloves with all the fingers missing, frayed cast-off sweaters which some departed boarder had left behind him, postcards, souvenirs, sea-shells, cocoanuts, old battered trunks, dilapidated furniture which could be no longer used, calendars for the year 1906, showing coy maidens simpering sidewise out beneath the crisply ruffled pleatings of a Japanese parasol—a mountainous accumulation of old junk for which the old dilapidated house had now become a fit museum.

Then in the wink of an eye she would pour thousands of dollars after the crazy promises of boom-town real-estate speculation that by comparison made the wildest infatuation of a drunken race-track gambler look like the austere process of a coldly reasoning mind.

Even as she stood there staring at her house with her pursed mouth of powerful and ruminant satisfaction, another evidence of this madness of possession was staring in their face. At the end of the alley slope, behind the house, there was a dilapidated old shed or house of whitewashed boards, which had been built in earlier times as a carriage house. Now through the open entrance of this shed, they could see the huge and dusty relic of Eliza's motor car. She had bought it four years before, and bought it instantly one day before they knew about it, and paid $2000 in hard cash for it—and why she bought it, what mad compulsion of her spirit made her buy it, no one knew, and least of all Eliza.

For from that day to this that car had never left the carriage house. Year by year, in spite of protests, oaths, and prayers, and all their frantic pleading, she had got no use from it herself, and would let no one else use it. No, what is more, she had even refused to sell it later, although a man had made her a good offer. Rather she pursed her lips reflectively, smiled in a bantering fashion, and said evasively: "Well, I'll see now! I'll think it over!—I want to study about it a little—you come back later and I'll let you know! . . . I want to think about it!"—as if, by hanging on to this mass of rusty machinery, she hoped it would increase in value and that she could sell it some day for twice the price she paid for it, if only she "held on" long enough.

And at first they had all wrestled by turns with the octopal convolutions of her terrific character, exhausting all the strength and energy in them against the substance of a will that was like something which always gave and never yielded, which could be grasped, compressed, and throttled in the hard grip of their furious hands, only to bulge out in new shapes and forms and combinations—which flowed, gave, withdrew, receded and advanced, but which remained itself forever, and beat everything before it in the end.

Now, for a moment, as Luke saw the car he was goaded into the old madness of despair. Thrusting his fingers through his hair, and with a look of desperate exasperation in his tortured eyes, he began, "M-m-m-mama—M-m-m-mama—I beg of you, I—wy I entreat you,—w-w-w-wy I *beseech* you either to s-s-s-sell that God-damn thing or—wy—g-g-g-get a little s-s-service out of it."

"Well, now," Eliza said quickly and in a conciliating tone, "we'll see about it!"

"S-s-s-see about it!" he stammered bitterly. "See about it! In G-g-g-God's name, what is there to see about! M-m-m-mama, the car's there—there—there—" he muttered crazily, poking his clumsy finger in a series of jerky and convulsive movements in the direction of the carriage house. "It's *there!*" he croaked madly. "C-c-c-can't you understand that? W-w-w-wy, it's rotting away on its God-damn wheels—M-m-m-mama, will you *please* get it into your head that it's not g-g-going to do you or any one else any good unless you take it out and use it?"

"Well, as I say now"—she began hastily, and in a diplomatic tone of voice.

"M-m-m-m-mama"—he began, again thrusting at his hair—"wy, I beg of you—I beseech you to sell it, g-g-g-give it away, or wy-wy-wy try to get a little use out of it!—Let me take it out and drive you round the block in it—w-w-w-wy—just once! Just once! F-f-f-frankly, I'd like to have the satisfaction of knowing you'd had *that* much out of it!" he said. "Wy, I'll p-p-p-pay for the gas, if that's what's worrying you! Wy, I'll do it with pleasure! . . . But just let me take it out of that G-g-g-g-God-damn place if all—if all—wy if all I do is drive you to the corner! Now, *please!*" he begged, with an almost frantic note of entreaty.

"Why, no, boy!" she cried out in a startled tone. "We can't do that!"

"C-c-c-can't do that!" he stuttered bitterly. "Wy, in G-g-g-g-God's name, why can't we?"

"I'd be *afra-a-id!*" she said with a little troubled smile, as she shook her head. "Hm! I'd be *afraid!*"

"Wy-wy-wy-wy *afraid!*" he yelled. "Wy, what's there to be afraid of, 'n God's name?"

"I'd be afraid you'd *do* something to it," she said with her troubled smile. "I'd be afraid you'd smash it up or run over some one with it. No, child," she said gravely, as she shook her head. "I'd be afraid to let you drive it. You're too nervous."

"Ah-h-h-h-h-h!" he breathed clutching convulsively in his hair as his eyes flickered madly about in his head. "Ah-h-h-h-h! M-m-m-merciful God!" he muttered. "M-m-m-m-m-merciful God!"—and then laughed wildly, frantically, and bitterly.

Now Helen spoke curiously, plucking reflectively at her large chin, but with weariness and resignation in her accent as if already she knew the answer:

"Mama, what are you going to do with your car? It seems a shame to let it rot away back there after you've paid out all that money for it. Aren't you going to try to get any use out of it at all?"

"Well, now, as I say," Eliza began smugly, pursing her lips with ruminative relish as she looked into the air, "I'm just waitin' for the chance—I'm just waitin' till the first fine day to come along—and then, I've got a good notion to take that thing out and learn to run it myself."

"Oh, Mama," Helen began quietly and wearily, "good heavens——"

"Why, yes!" Eliza cried nodding her head briskly. "I could do it! Now, I can do most anything when I make my mind up to it! Now I've never seen anything yet I couldn't do if I had to! . . . So I'm just waitin' until spring comes round again, and I'm goin' to take that car out and drive it all around," she said. "I'm just goin' to sit up there an' enjoy the scenery an' have a big time," said Eliza with her little tremulous smile. "That's what I'm goin' to do," she said.

"All right," Helen said wearily. "Have it your own way. Do as you please: it's your own funeral! Only it seems a shame to let it go to waste after you've spent all that money on it."

But turning to Eugene, and speaking in a lowered tone, she said to him, with the faint tracing of hysteria on her big-decent face, and weariness and resignation in her voice:

"Well, what are you going to do about it? I used to think that you could change her, but now I know she never will. . . . I've given up trying. It's no use," she muttered. "It's no use. I worked my fingers to the bone to help them save a nickel—and you see what comes of it. . . . I did the work of a nigger in the kitchen from the time I was ten years old —and you see what comes of it, don't you? I went off and sang my way around the country in cheap moving-picture shows . . . and came up here and waited on the tables to help feed a crowd of cheap boarders—

and Luke sold *The Saturday Evening Post,* and peddled hot dogs and
toy balloons—and you got up at three o'clock, carried the morning paper
—and they let Ben go to hell until his lungs were gone and it was too
late—and you see what it all comes to in the end, don't you? . . . It's all
given away to real-estate men or thrown away for automobiles they
never use. I've given up worrying," she said. "I don't think about it any
more. . . . They don't change," she muttered. "I used to think they did
but now I know they don't. Uh-uh. They don't change! . . . Well,
forget about it," and she turned wearily away.

The year Eliza bought the car, Eugene had been eighteen years old,
and was a Junior at the State University. When he came home that
year, he asked her if she would let him learn to drive it. It was about the
time when every one in town was beginning to own motor cars. When
he walked up town, every one he knew would drive by him in an auto-
mobile. Every one on earth was beginning to live upon a wheel. Somehow it gave him a naked and desolate feeling, as if he had nowhere to
go, and no door to enter. When he asked her if she would let him take
the car out and learn to drive it, she had looked at him a moment with
her hands clasped loosely at the waist, her head cocked quizzically to
one side, and the little tremulous and bantering smile that had always
filled him with such choking exasperation and wordless shame, and
somehow with a nameless and intolerable pity, too, because behind it
he felt always her high white forehead, and her faded, weak, and child-
like eyes, the naked intelligence, whiteness, and immortal innocence
of the child that was looking straight through the mask of years with
all the deathless hope and faith and confidence of her life and character.

Now, for the last time, he asked her again the question he had asked
with such an earnest hope so many times before. And instantly, as if
he had dreamed her answer, she replied—the same reply that she had
always made, the only reply the invincible procrastination of her soul
could make.

"Hm!" she said, making the bantering and humming noise in her
throat as she looked at him. *"Wha-a-a-t!* Why, you're my *ba-a-a-by!"* she
said with jesting earnestness, as she laid her strong worn hand loosely
on his shoulder. "No, sir!" she said quickly and quietly, shaking her
head in a swift side-ways movement. "I'd be *afra-a-id,* afraid," she
whispered.

"Mama, afraid of what?"

"Why, child," she said gravely, "I'd be afraid you'd go and hurt yourself. Uh-uh," she shook her head quickly and shortly. "I'd be afraid to let you try it—well, we'll see," she said, turning it off easily in an evasive and conciliatory tone. "We'll see about it. I'd like to study about it a little first."

After that, there was nothing to do except to curse and beat their fists into the wall. And after that there was nothing to do at all. She had beaten them all, and they knew it. Their curses, prayers, oaths, persuasions and strangled cries availed them nothing. She had beaten them all, and finally they spoke no more to her or to themselves about her motor car: the gigantic folly of that mad wastefulness evoked for them all memories so painful, desolate and tragic—a memory of the fatality of blood and nature which could not be altered, of the done which could be undone never, and of the web of fate in which their lives were meshed—that they knew there was no guilt, no innocence, no victory, and no change. They were what they were, and they had no more to say.

So was it now as she stood planted there before her house. As she had grown older, her body had grown clumsier with the shapeless heaviness of age: as she stood there with her hands clasped in this attitude of ruminant relish, she seemed to be planted solidly on the pavement, and somehow to own, inhabit, and possess the very bricks she walked on. She owned the street, the pavement, and finally her terrific ownership of the house was as apparent as if the house were living and could speak to her. For the rest of them that old bleak house had now so many memories of grief and death and intolerable, incurable regret that in their hearts they hated it; but although she had seen a son strangle to death in one of its bleak rooms, she loved the house as if it were a part of her own life—as it was—and her love for it was greater than her love for anv one or anything else on earth.

And yet, for her, even if that house, the whole world, fell in ruins around her, there could be no ruin—her spirit was as everlasting as the earth on which she walked, and could not be touched—no matter what catastrophes of grief, death, tragic loss, and unfulfilment might break the lives of other men—she was triumphant over the ravages of time and accident, and would be triumphant to her death. For there was only the inevitable fulfilment of her own destiny—and ruin, loss, and death availed not—she would be fulfilled. She had lived ten lives, and now she was embarked upon another one, and so it had been ordered in the beginning: this was all that mattered in the end.

But now, Luke, seeing her, as she stood planted there in all-engulfing rumination, thrust his hands distractedly through his shining hair again, and cried to her with exasperated entreaty:

"W-w-w-wy, Mama, if you *please!* I b-b-b-beg of you and *beseech* you, if you *please!*"

"I'm *ready!*" Eliza cried, starting and turning from her powerful contemplation of her house. "This very minute, sir! Come on!"

"Wy, if you p-p-p-*please!*" he muttered, thrusting at his hair.

They walked towards his car, which he had halted in the alley-way beside the house. A few leaves, sere and yellow, from the maples in the yard, were drifting slowly to the ground.

XLI

During all that time, when he was waiting with a desperate hope that rose each day to the frenzy of a madman's certitude, and sank each day to the abyss of his despair, for the magic letter which was coming to him from the city, and which would instantly give him all the fortune, fame, and triumph for which his soul was panting, his family looked at him with troubled question in their eyes. His enthusiastic hopes and assurances of the great success that he would have from writing plays seemed visionary and remote to them. Perhaps they were right about this, although the reason that they had for thinking so was wrong.

Thus, although they said little to Eugene at this time about his plans for the future, and what they did say was meant to hearten him, their doubt and disbelief was evident, and sometimes when he came into the house, he could hear them talking in a troubled way about him:

"Mama," he heard his sister say one day, as she sat talking with his mother in the kitchen, "what does Gene intend to do? Have you heard him say yet?"

"Why, no-o-o!" his mother answered slowly, in a puzzled and meditative tone. "He hasn't said. At least he says he's goin' to write plays,—of course, I reckon he's waiting to hear from those people in New York about that play he's written," she added quickly.

"Well, I know," his sister answered wearily. "That's all very fine—if he can do it. But, good heavens, Mama!" she cried furiously—"you can't live on hope like that! Gene's only one out of a million! Can't you realize that?—Why, they used to think I had some talent as a singer"— here she laughed ironically, a husky high falsetto, "I used to think so, myself—but you don't notice that it ever got me anywhere, do you? No, sir!" she said positively. "There are thousands more just like Gene, who are trying to get ahead and make a name for themselves. Why should he think he's any better than the rest of them? Why, it might be years before he got a play produced—and even then, how can he tell that it would be a success?—What's he going to live on? How's he going to keep going until all this happens? What's he going to do?—You know, Mama, Gene's no little boy any more. Please get that into your head," she said sharply, as if her mother had questioned the accuracy of her remark. "No, sir! No, sir!" she laughed ironically and huskily. "Your baby is a grown man, and it's time he waked up to the fact that he's got to support himself from now on.—Mama, do you realize that it has been over four months since Gene left Harvard and, so far as I can see, he has made no effort yet to get a job. What does he intend to do?" she said angrily. "You know, he just can't mope around like this *all* his days! Sooner or later he's got to find some work to do!"

In all these words, there was apparent not so much hostility and antagonism as the driving fury and unrest of Helen's nervous, exacerbated, dissonant, and unhappy character, which could lavish kindness and affection one moment, and abuse and criticism the next. These were really only signs of the frenzy and unrest in her large, tortured, but immensely generous spirit. Thus, she would rage and storm at her husband at one moment for "moping about the house," telling him, "for heaven's sake am I never to be left alone! Am I never to get a moment's peace or quiet? Must I have you around me every moment of my life? In God's name, Hugh—go! go! go!—Leave me alone for a few minutes, I beg of you!"—and by this time his sister's voice would be cracked and strident, her breath coming hoarsely and almost with a sob of hysteria. And yet, she could be just as violent in her sense of wrong and injustice done to her if she thought he was giving too much time to business, rushing through his meals, reading a book when he should be listening to her tirade, or staying away from home too much.

Poor, tortured, and unhappy spirit, with all the grandeur, valor, and affection that Eugene knew so well, it had found, since her father's death, no medicine for the huge and constant frenzy of its own unrest, no guide or savior to work for it the miracle of salvation it must work itself, and it turned and lashed out at the world, demanding a loneliness which it could not have endured for three days running, a peace and quiet from its own fury, a release from its own injustice. And it was for this reason—because her own unrest and frenzy made her lash out constantly against the world, praising one week, condemning the next, accusing life and people of doing her some injury or wrong that she had done herself—it was for this reason, more than for any other, that Helen now lashed out about Eugene to their mother.

And because Eugene was strung on the same wires, shaped from the same clay, cut from the same kind and plan and quality, he stood there in the hall-way as he heard her, his face convulsed and livid, his limbs trembling with rage, his bowels and his heart sick and trembling with a hideous gray nausea of hopelessness and despair, his throat choking with an intolerable anguish of resentment and wrong, as he heard Helen's voice, and before he rushed back into the kitchen to quarrel with her and his mother.

"Well, now," he heard his mother say in a diplomatic and hopeful tone that somehow only served to increase his feeling of rage and exasperation—"well, now—well, now," she said, "let's wait and see! Let's wait and see what happens with this play. Perhaps he'll hear tomorrow that they have taken it. Maybe it's going to be all right, after all!"

"Going to be all right!" Eugene fairly screamed at this juncture, rushing in upon them in the kitchen. "You're God-damned right it's going to be all right. I'll tell you what's all right!" he panted, because his breath was laboring against his ribs as if he had run up a steep hill—"if it was some damned real-estate man, that would be all right! If it's some cheap shyster lawyer, that would be all right! If it was some damned rascal sitting on his tail up here in the bank, cheating you out of all you've got, that would be all right—hey?" he snarled, conscious that his words had no meaning or coherence, but unable to utter any of the things he wished to say and that welled up in that wave of hot and choking resentment. "O yes! The big man! The great man! The big deacon—Mr. Scroop Pegram—the big bank president—that would be all right, wouldn't it?" he cried in a choked and trembling voice. "You'd get down on your hands and knees, and crawl if he spoke to you, wouldn't you?—'O thank you, Mr. Pegram, for letting me put my money in your bank so you can loan it out to a bunch of God-dam real-estate crooks,'" he sneered, in an infuriated parody of whining servility. "'Thank you, sir,'" he said, and in spite of the fact that these words made almost no coherent meaning, his mother began to purse her lips rapidly in an excited fashion, and his sister's big-boned face reddened with anger.

"Now," his mother said sternly, as she levelled her index finger at him, "I want to tell you something! You may sneer all you please, sir, at Scroop Pegram, but he's a man who has worked all his life for everything he has——"

"Yes," Eugene said bitterly, "and for everything *you* have, too—for that's where it's going in the end."

"He has made his *own* way since his childhood," Eliza continued sternly and deliberately—"no one ever did anything for him, for there's one thing sure:—there was no one in his family who was in a position to do it.—What he's done he's done for himself, without assistance and," his mother said in a stern and telling voice, "without education—for he never had three months' schoolin' in his life—and today he's got the respect of the community as much as any man I know."

"Yes! And most of their money, too," Eugene cried.

"You'd better not talk!" Helen said. "If I were you I wouldn't talk! Don't criticize other people until you show you've got it in you to do something for yourself," she said.

"You! You!" Eugene panted. "I'll show you! Talking about me when my back is turned, hey? That's the kind you are! All right! You wait and see! I'll show you!" he said, in a choked and trembling whisper of fury and resentment.

"All right," Helen said in a hard and hostile voice. "I'll wait and see. I hope you do. But you've got to show me that you've got it in you. It's time for you to quit this foolishness and get a job! Don't criticize other people until you show you've got it in you to support yourself," she said.

"No," said Eliza, "for we've done as much for you as we are able to. You've had as good an education as any one could want—and now the rest is up to you," she said sternly. "I've got no more money to pay out on you, so you can make your mind up to it from now on," she said. "You've got to shift for yourself."

And in the warm and living silence of the kitchen, they looked at one another for a moment, all three, breathing heavily, and with hard and bitter eyes.

"Well, Gene," Helen said, "I know. Try to forget about it. You'll change as you grow older," she said wearily. "We've all been like that. We all have these wonderful ambitions to be somebody famous, but that all changes. I had them, too," she said. "I was going to be a great singer, and have a career in opera, but that's all over now, and I know I never

will. You forget about it," she said quietly and wearily. "It all seems
wonderful to you, and you think that you can't live without it, but you
forget about it. Oh, of course you will!" she muttered, "of course! Why
—!" she cried, shaking Eugene furiously, and now her voice had its old
hearty and commanding ring,—"I'm going to beat you if you act like
this! What if they don't take your play! I'll bet that has happened to
plenty of people— Yes, sir!" she cried. "I'll bet that has happened to all
of them when they started out—and then they went on and made a big
success of it later! Why, if those people didn't take my play," she said,
"I'd sit down and write another one so good they'd be ashamed of themselves! Why, you're only a kid yet!" she cried furiously, shaking Eugene, and frowning fiercely but with her tongue stuck out a little and a
kind of grin on her big-boned liberal-looking face. "Don't you know
that! You've got *loads* of time yet! Your life's ahead of you! Of course
you will! Of course you will!" she cried, shaking him. "Don't let a thing
like this get you down! In ten years' time you'll look back on all this
and laugh to think you were ever such a fool! Of course you will!"—
and then as her husband, who had driven up before their mother's
house, now sounded on the horn for her, she said again, in the quiet
and weary tone: "Well, Gene, forget about it! Life's too short! I know,"
she said mysteriously, "I know!"

Then, as she started to go, she added casually, "Honey, come on over
for supper, if you want to.—Now, it's up to you. You can suit yourself!
—You can do exactly as you please," she said in the almost hard, deliberately indifferent tone with which she usually accompanied these invitations:

"What would you like to eat?" she now said meditatively. "How about
a nice thick steak," she said juicily, as she winked at him. "I've got the
whole half of a fried chicken left over from last night, that you can have
if you come over!—Now, it's up to you!" she cried out again in that almost hard challenging tone, as if he had shown signs of unwillingness
or refusal. "I'm not going to urge you, but you're welcome to it if you
want to come.—How about a big dish full of string beans—some mashed
potatoes—some stewed corn, and asparagus! How'd you like some
great big wonderful sliced tomatoes with mayonnaise?—I've got a big
deep peach and apple cobbler in the oven—do you think that'd go good
smoking hot with a piece of butter and a hunk of American cheese?"
she said, winking at him and smacking her lips comically. "Would that
hit the spot? Hey?" she said, prodding him in the ribs with her big

stiff fingers and then saying in a hoarse, burlesque, and nasal tone, in extravagant imitation of a girl they knew who had gone to New York, and had come back talking with the knowing, cock-sure nasal tone of the New Yorker.

"Ah, fine, boys!" Helen said, in this burlesque tone. "Fine! Just like they give you in New York!" she said. Then turning away indifferently, she went down the steps, and across the walk towards her husband's car, calling back in an almost hard and aggressive tone:

"Well, you can do exactly as you like! No one is going to urge you to come if you don't want to!"

Then she got in the car, and they drove swiftly off down hill, turned the corner, and vanished.

The reason, in fact, which argued in Eugene's family's mind against his succeeding in the work he wished to do, was the very thing that should have been all in his favor. But neither he nor his family thought so. It was this: a writer, they thought, should be a wonderful, mysterious, and remote sort of person—some one they had never known, like Irvin S. Cobb. "Now, this boy," they argued in their minds, "our son and brother, is neither wonderful, mysterious, nor remote. We know all about him, we all grew up together here, and there's no use talking— he's the same kind of people that we are. His father was a stone-cutter —a man who was born on a farm and had to work all his life with his hands. And five of his father's brothers were also stone-cutters, and had to earn their living in the same way—by the sweat of their brow. And his mother is a hard-working woman who brought up a big family, runs a boarding house and has had to scrape and save and labor all her life. Every one in this part of the country knows her family: her brothers are respected business men in town here, and there are hundreds of her kins- folk—farmers, storekeepers, carpenters, lumber dealers, and the like— all through this section. Now, they're all good, honest, decent, self-re- specting people—no one can say they're not—but there's never been a writer in the crowd. No—and no doctors or lawyers either. Now there may have been a preacher or two—his Uncle Bascom was a preacher and a highly educated man too, always poking his nose into a book, and went to Harvard, and all,—yes, and now that we remember, always had queer notions like this boy—had to leave the church, you know, for be- ing an agnostic, and was always writing poems, and all such as that. Well, this fellow is one of the same kind—a great book reader but with no practical business sense—and it seems to us he ought to get a job somewhere teaching school, or maybe some newspaper work—which he could do—or, perhaps, he should have studied law."

So did their minds work on this subject. Yet the very argument they made—that he was the same kind of person as the rest of them, and not remote, wonderful, or mysterious—should have been the chief thing in his favor. But none of them could see this. For where they thought there was nothing wonderful or mysterious about them, he thought that there was; and none of them could see that his greatest asset, his greatest advantage, if he had any, was that he was made out of the same earth—the same blood, bone, character, and fury—as the rest of them. For, could they only have known it, the reason he read all the books was not, as they all thought, because he was a bookish person, for he was not, but for the same reason that his mother was mad about property— talked, thought, felt, and dreamed about real estate all the time, and wanted to own the earth just as he wanted to devour it. Again, the fury that had made him read the books was the same thing that drove his brothers and his sisters around incessantly, feeding the huge fury of their own unrest, and making them talk constantly and to every one, until they knew all about the lives of all the butchers, bakers, merchants, lawyers, doctors, Greek restaurant owners, and Italian fruit dealers in the community.

If they had understood this—that he had the same thing in him that they all had in them—they would have understood about his wanting to be a writer, and even the trouble in which presently he would involve himself, and that seemed so catastrophic and disgraceful to him at that time, would not have seemed so bad to them, for his father, one of his brothers, and several of his kinsmen had been in this same trouble —and it had caused no astonishment at all. But now that he had done this thing—now that the one they looked on as the scholar, and the bookish person, had done it—it was as if the leading deacon of the church had been caught in a raid on a bawdy house.

Finally, there was to be some irony for Eugene later in the fact that, had he only known it and grasped it, there was ready to his use in that one conflict all of the substance and energy of the human drama, and that the only thing that was wonderful or important was that they were all full of the passion, stupidity, energy, hope, and folly of living men— fools, angels, guiltless and guilty all together, not to be praised or blamed, but just blood, bone, marrow, passion, feeling—the whole swarming web of life and error in full play and magnificently alive. As for the fancied woes and hardships of the young artist in conflict with the dull and brutal philistines,—that, he saw later, had had nothing to do with it, and was not worth a damn, any more than the plays that had been written in Professor Hatcher's class, and in which a theatrical formula for living was presented in place of life. No; the conflict, the comedy, the tragedy,—the pain, the pride, the folly and the error— might have been just the same had Eugene wanted to be an aviator, a deep-sea diver, a bridge-builder, a professional pall-bearer, or a locomotive engineer. And the stuff of life was there in all its overwhelming richness, was right there in his grasp, but he could not see it, and would not use it. Instead he went snooping and prowling around the sterile old brothels of the stage, mistaking the glib concoctions of a counterfeit emotion for the very flesh and figure of reality. And this also has been true of every youth that ever walked the earth.

The letter came at length one gray day in late October; and instantly, when he had opened it, and read the first words "We regret," his life went gray as that gray day, and he thought that he would never have heart or hope nor know the living joy of work again. His flesh went dead and cold and sick, yet he read the smooth lying phrases in the letter with the stolid face with which people usually receive bad news, and even tried to insinuate a thread of hope, to suck a kind of meagre and hopeless comfort from the hard, yet oily, words, "We are looking forward with great interest to reading your next play, and we hope you will send it to us as soon as it is completed." . . . "Our members were divided in their opinion, four voting to reconsider it, and five for rejection . . . although all were agreed on the freshness and vitality of the writing . . . while the power of some of the scenes is undeniable . . . we must reluctantly. . . . You are one of the young men whose work we are watching with the greatest interest . . ." and so on.

Those on whom the naked weight of shame has rested, who have felt its gray and hideous substance in their entrails, will not smile calmly and with comfort if their memory serves them.

Now a huge, naked, and intolerable shame and horror pressed down on Eugene with a crushing and palpable weight out of the wet, gray skies of autumn. The hideous gray stuff filled him from brain to bowels, was everywhere and in everything about him so that he breathed it out of the air, felt it like a naked stare from walls and

houses and the faces of the people, tasted it on his lips, and endured it
in the screaming and sickened dissonance of ten thousand writhing
nerves so that he could no longer sit, rest, or find oblivion, exhaustion,
forgetfulness or repose anywhere he went, or release from the wild
unrest that drove him constantly about. He went to bed only to get up
and prowl again the wet and barren little streets of night; he ate, and instantly vomited up again all he had eaten, and then, like a dull, distressed and nauseated brute, he would sullenly and wretchedly eat again.

He saw the whole earth with the sick eyes, the sick heart, the sick
flesh, and writhing nerves of this gray accursed weight of shame and
horror in which his life lay drowned, and from which it seemed he could
never more emerge to know the music of health and joy and power
again; and from which, likewise, he could not die, but must live hideously and miserably the rest of his days, like a man doomed to live forever in a state of retching and abominable nausea of heart, brain, bowels,
flesh and spirit.

It seemed to him that all was lost, that he had been living in a fool's
dream for years, and that now he had been brutally wakened and
saw himself as he was—a naked fool—who had never had an ounce of
talent, and who no longer had an ounce of hope—a madman who had
wasted his money and lost precious years when he might have learned
some work consonant with his ability and the lives of average men. And
it now seemed to him, that his family had been terribly and mercilessly
right in everything they had said and felt, and that he had been too great
a fool to understand it. His sense of ruin and failure was abysmal,
crushing, and complete.

XLII

IT was in this temper, after two days of aimless and frenzied wandering about the streets of the town, and over the hills that surrounded it,
during which time he was no more conscious of what he did, said, ate,
thought or felt than a man in a trance, that Eugene started off suddenly
to visit his other married sister, who lived in a little town in South Carolina. He had not seen her since his father's death a year ago, she
had written him a few days before asking him to come down, and now,
driven more by a fury of flight and movement than by any other impulse, he wired her he was coming, and started out in one of the Public
Service motor cars which at that time made the trip across the mountains. Luke had arranged to meet him sixty miles from home at the

town of Blackstone, in South Carolina, and drive him the remainder of the distance to his sister's house.

He set out on a day in late October, wild and windy, full of ragged torn clouds of light that came and went from gray to gold and back to gray again. And everything that happened on that savage day he was to remember later with a literal and blazing intensity.

Autumn had come sharp and quick that year. October had been full of frost and nipping days, the hills were glorious that year as Eugene had never seen them before. Now, only a day or two before, there had been, despite the early season, a sudden and heavy fall of snow. It still lay, light but fleecy, in the fields; and on the great bulk of the hills it lay in a pattern of shining white, stark grays and blacks, and the colors of the leaves, which now had fallen thickly and had lost their first sharp vividness, but were still burning with a dull massed molten glow.

An hour away, and twenty-five miles from home, the car had drawn up before the post-office of a mountain village or resort which lay at the crest of the last barrier of the hills, before the road dropped sharply down the mountain-side to South Carolina.

While they were halted here, another car drove up—an open, glittering, and expensive-looking projectile of light gray—and in it were three young men from home, two of whom Eugene knew. This car drew up abreast, stopped, and he saw that its driver was Robert Weaver. And although he had not seen the other youth since a midnight visit Robert had made to his room in Cambridge, the latter peered over towards him owlishly and without a word of greeting and with that abrupt, feverish, and fragmentary speech that was characteristic of him and was constantly becoming more dissonant and broken, he barked out:

"Who's in there? Who's that sitting up there in the front seat? Is that you, Gene?" he called.

When Gene assured him that it was, Robert asked where he was going. When he told him "Blackstone," he demanded at once that he leave the service car, and come with him.

"We're going there, too," he said. Turning to his comrades, he added earnestly:

"Aren't we? Isn't that where we're going, boys?"

The two young men to whom he spoke now laughed boisterously, crying:

"Yeah! That's right! That's where we're going, Robert," and one of them added with a solemn gravity:

"We're going to—Blackstone," here a slight convulsion seemed to seize his throat, he swallowed hard, hiccoughed, and concluded, "to see a football game"—a statement which again set them off into roars of boisterous laughter. Then they all shouted at Eugene:

"Come on! Come on! Get in! We've lots of room."

Eugene got out of the service car, paid the driver, took the small handgrip he had, and got into the other car with Robert and his two companions. They drove off fast, and almost immediately they were dropping down the mountain, along the sinuous curves and turns of the steep road.

Robert's two companions on this journey were young men whom Eugene had not known in boyhood, with whom he had now only a speaking acquaintance, and both of whom were recent comers to the town. The older of these two was a man named Emmet Blake, and he now sat beside Robert on the front seat of the car.

Emmet Blake was a man of twenty-seven years, a frail and almost wasted-looking figure of medium height, straight black hair, black eyes, and a thin, febrile, and corrupted-looking face which, although almost dead-white in its color, was given a kind of dark and feverish vitality by a faint thin smile that seemed always to hover about the edges of his mouth, and the dark unnatural glitter of his black eyes.

He lived a reckless and dissipated life, and drank heavily: time after time, after a hemorrhage of the lungs, he had been taken to a sanitarium in an ambulance, and his death had seemed to be a matter of only a few hours. And time after time, he had come out again, and immediately started on another wild spree of women and corn whiskey with Robert and others of the same breed. He was well-off as to money, and lived expensively, because he was a nephew of George Blake, the great Middle-western manufacturer of cheap motor cars, which in twenty years' time had created twenty thousand jokes, and glutted the highways of the earth in twenty million tinny and glittering repetitions.

The name of the other youth, who was Eugene's own age, and sat beside him on the back seat, was Kitchin. He was a tall, dark, handsome fellow, with agreeable manners and a pleasant voice, the nephew of a retired physician in the town but not native to the place. Eugene had seen him on the streets, but had never talked to him before. It was evident that both Robert and his two friends had been drinking, although not heavily: there was in their manner the subdued yet wild and mounting elation of young men when they begin to drink. They laughed a

great deal, rather hilariously, and for no good reason: they insisted frequently that they were going to the town of Blackstone to see a football
game, an announcement which would set them off again in roars of
laughter.

Almost as soon as Eugene got in the car, and even as they started off
again, Blake thrust his thin hand into the leather pocket of the door beside him, produced a bottle that was three quarters full of Scotch whiskey, and turning, gave it to Eugene, saying:

"Take a big one, Gant. We're all ahead of you."

He drank long and deep, gulping the fiery liquor down his throat
recklessly, feeling suddenly an almost desperate sense of release from the
gray misery of hopelessness which had crushed him down for days now,
since the letter had come. When he had finished, he handed the bottle
back to Emmet Blake, who took it, looked at it with a thin, evil, specu-
lative smile, and said:

"Well, that's pretty good. What do you say, Robert? Shall we let him
pass on that?"

"Hell, no!" cried Robert hoarsely, looking swiftly around at the bottle. "That's no drink! Make him take a good one, Emmet. You've got to
do better than that if you keep up with us," he cried, and then he burst
out suddenly in his staccato laugh, shaking his head to himself as he bent
over the wheel, and crying out: "Lord! Lord!"

Blake handed Eugene the bottle again, and he drank some more.
Then Kitchin took the bottle and drank; he handed it back to Emmet
Blake, who drank, and Blake handed it to Robert who took it with one
hand, his face turned slightly from the wheel, his eyes still fastened on
the road, and drank until the bottle was empty. Then he flung it away
from him across his arm. The bottle went sailing out across the road
and down the gulch or deep ravine that sloped away beside them far
down: the bottle struck a rock, exploding brilliantly in a thousand glittering fragments, and they all roared happily, and cheered.

They had finished up that bottle in one round of gulps and swallows,
passing it from hand to hand as they rushed down the mountain-side,
and almost instantly they were at work on a beverage of a yet more instant and fiery power—raw, white corn-whiskey, in a gallon jug, clear
as water, rank and nauseous to an unaccustomed throat, strong and instant as the kick of a mule, fiery, choking, formidable, and savage. They
hooked their thumbs into the handle of the jug, and brought the stuff
across their shoulders with a free-hand motion, they let the wide neck

pour into their tilted throats with a fat thick gurgle, and they gulped that raw stuff down with greedy gulpings like water going down a gully drain.

It was a drink that would have felled an ox, a terrific lightning-blast of alcohol that would have thrown Polyphemus to the earth; and yet it was not drink alone that made them drunk that day. For they were all young men, and they had shouted, sung, and roared with laughter, and pounded one another with affectionate delight as they rushed on—and it was not drink alone that made them drunk.

For they felt that everything on earth was good and glorious, that everything on earth was made for their delight, that they could do no wrong and make no error, and that such invincible strength was in them that trees would fall beneath their stroke, the immortal hills bow down before their stride, and that nothing in the world could stop them.

And for Eugene it seemed that everything had come to life for him at once—that he had emerged instantly and victoriously from the horror of shame, the phantasmal and dreamlike unreality that had held him in its spell. It seemed to him that all the earth had come to life again in shapes of deathless and familiar brightness, that he had gloriously re-entered a life he thought he had lost forever, and that all the plain price-less joy and glory of the earth was his, as it had never been before.

And first of all, and with an almost intolerable relief and happiness, he was conscious of the pangs of hunger: his famished belly and his withered guts which had for days shrunk wearily and with disgust from food, now, under the stimulation of a ravenous hunger, fairly pled for nourishment. He thought of food—food in a hundred glorious shapes and varieties: the literal sensual images of food blazed in his mind like paintings from the brush of a Dutch master, and it seemed to him that no one had ever painted, spoken, or written about food before in a way that would do it justice.

Later, these were the things Eugene would remember from that day with a living joy, for it was as if he had been born again, or discovered the world anew in all its glory. And besides all this—a part, an element in all this whole harmonious design of triumphant joy and rediscovery —was the way the hills had looked that day as they came down the mountain, the smell of the air which was mellow and autumnal, and yet had in it the premonitory breath of frost and sharpness, and the wild joy, power, and ecstasy that had filled their hearts, their throats, their lives—the sense of victory, triumph, and invincible strength, and of some rare, glorious, and intolerable happiness that was pending for them, and which seemed to swell the tremendous and exulting music of that magic day.

Around them, above them, below them—from the living and shining air of autumn, from the embrowned autumnal earth, from the great shapes of the hills behind them with their molten mass of color—dull browns, rich bitter reds, dark bronze, and mellow yellow—from the raw crude clay of the piedmont earth and the great brown stubble of the cotton fields—from a thousand impalpable and unutterable things, there came this glorious breath of triumph and delight. It was late October, there was a smell of smoke upon the air, an odor of burning leaves, the barking of a dog, a misty red, a pollenated gold in the rich, fading, sorrowful, and exultant light of the day,—and far off, a sound of great wheels pounding on a rail, the wailing whistle, and the tolling bell of a departing train.

And finally, the immortal visage of the earth itself with the soaring and limitless undulations of its blue ranges, the great bulk of the autumn hills, immense and near, the rugged, homely, and familiar trees—the pines, oaks, chestnuts, maples, locusts—the homely look of the old red clay—the unforgettable and indescribable naturalness of that earth—with its rudeness, wildness, richness, rawness, ugliness, fathomless mystery and utter familiarity, and finally the lonely, haunting, and enchanted music that it made—the strange spirit of time and solitude that hovered above it eternally, and which can never be described, but which may be evoked by a cow-bell broken by the wind in distant valleys, the lonely whistle of a departing train, or simply a sinuous gust of wind that smokes its way across coarse mountain grasses when spring comes—all this, which Eugene had felt and known in his childhood, and yet had never had a tongue to utter, he seemed now to know and understand so well that he had himself become its tongue and utterance, the more its child because he had been so long away from it, the more its eye because he now saw it again as it must have seemed to the first men who ever saw it, with the eyes of discovery, love, and recognition.

And yet, for him all these things spoke instantly, intolerably, exultantly, not of home, return, and settlement, but of one image, which now burned forever in his brain, rose like a triumphant music in his heart. And that image was the image of the enchanted city, in which, it now seemed, all the frenzy and unrest of his spirit would find a certain goal and triumph, and toward which everything on earth, and all the hope and joy now rising in his heart, was tending.

When they got down off the mountain into South Carolina they were very drunk. On a dusty sand-clay road between some cotton fields they stopped the car, and walked out into the fields to piss. The cotton stood stiff and dry and fleecy in its pods, the coarse brown stalks rose up in limitless planted rows, and underneath, he could see the old and homely visage of the red-clay earth.

At one edge of the field, and seeming very far away and lonely-looking, there was a negro shanty, and behind this a desolate wooded stretch of pine. Over all the earth at once, now that the roar of the engine had stopped, there was an immense and brooding quietness, a drowsed autumnal fume and warmth, immensely desolate and mournful, holding somehow a tragic prophecy of winter that must come, and death, and yet touched with the lonely, mournful and exultant mystery of the earth.

Eugene pulled several of the big cotton stalks out of the dry red earth, thrust one through the button-hole of his coat lapel, and tore it through exultantly, although the stalk was two feet long. Then he reeled back toward the car again, holding the other stalks of cotton in his hands, got in the car, and at once began to talk to his companions about the cotton—ending up in a passionate oration about the hills, the fields, the cotton and the earth—trying to tell them all about "the South" and making of the stalks of cotton and "the South" a kind of symbol, as young men will, although they all felt and acted just as young men anywhere would do.

But at that moment, all Eugene was trying to say about his years away from home, and his return, and how he had discovered his own land again and was, "by God," one of them—waving the stalks of cotton as he talked, and finding the whole core and kernel of all he wished to say in these stalks of cotton—all of this, although incoherent, drunken, and confused, seemed so eloquent and beautiful to him, so truthful, passionate, and exact—that he began to weep for joy as he talked to them. And they—they were, of course, delighted: they howled with laughter, cheered enthusiastically, slapped him on the back, and shook hands all around, crying—"By God! Listen to him talk! . . . Give 'em hell, son! We're with you! . . . Hot-damn! Thataway, boy! . . . Stay with 'em! . . Whee!"

Meanwhile, Robert was driving at terrific speed. They had begun to rip and tear along between the cotton fields, and over the dusty sand-clay roads, mistaking the screams of women and the shouts of men, as they swerved by their cars and wagons in a cloud of yellow dust and at a murderous clip, for admiring applause and enthusiastic cheers, an illusion which only spurred them on to greater efforts.

The upshot of it was that they finally tore into town, careening hideously along a central street, and with no slackening of their speed whatever. The excited people in that part of the State had been phoning in about them for the last fifteen miles of their mad journey, and now they were halted suddenly at sight of the police who stood lined up across the street in a double row—big, red-faced, country cops—to stop them.

The first brilliant, sparkling and wildly soaring effects of their intoxication had now worn off and, although they still felt full of power and a savage rending strength, the corn whiskey was now smouldering in their veins more dully and with a sombre and brutal drunkenness. Eugene seemed to see all shapes and figures clearly—the coarse red faces of the country cops and their clumsy lumbering bodies, and the street drowsy and dusty in the warmish autumn afternoon.

The grasses on the lawns of houses were faded, sere and withered-looking, the leaves upon the trees had thinned and hung yellowed, dry and dead, and in the gutters a few dead leaves stirred dryly, a few scampered dryly in the streets before a moment's gust of wind, and then lay still again.

Robert slowed down and stopped before that solid wall of beefy country blue and red: the police surrounded them and clambered heavily over the sides of the car, two standing on the fenders, two on either side of Eugene on the back seat, and one with Robert and Emmet Blake up front.

"All right, boys," said one of them, good-naturedly and casually enough, in the full, sonorous and somewhat howling voice of the country man, "drive on down thar to the station house now."

"Yes, *sir!* Yes, *sir!*" Robert replied at once in a meek and obedient tone, and with a comical drunken alacrity. "How do you get there, Captain?" he said with a cunning and flattering ingratiation.

"Right down this here street to your right," said the policeman in his drawling and countrified tone, "until you come to that 'air second turning where you see that 'air f'ar hydrant. Turn in to the left thar," he said.

"Yes, sir!" said Robert heartily, starting the car again. "We're all strangers here," he lied, as if he hoped this lie might make amends for them. "We don't know our way about yet."

"Well," the policeman drawled with a kind of ugly heartiness, "maybe the next time you come back you'll be better acquainted here," he said, winking at his comrades, and they all guffawed. "We're glad to see you, boys," he continued, still with this ugly falseness of good nature in his tone. "We been hearin' about you," he said, winking at his fellows again, "an' we wanted to git acquainted."

Here the policemen laughed again with sonorous countrified appreciation of their spokesman's wit.

The policemen were all big beefy men, with hearty drawling voices, red countrified faces. They had large square feet, wore dusty-looking black slouch hats with a wide brim, and were dressed in rather gaudy but slovenly-looking uniforms, with stripes of gold braid running up the sides of their baggy trousers, and with the lower brass buttons of their heavy blue coats unbuttoned, exposing areas of soiled shirts and paunchy bellies. Their faces had a look of a slow but powerful energy, a fathomless and mindless animal good nature, and at the same time a fathomless and mindless animal cruelty—instant, volcanic, and murderous—written terribly somehow into their wide, thin and horribly cruel mouths, in which there was legible a vitality that had all the wild and sensual force of nature packed into it, and was therefore beyond nature—almost super-natural—in its savage and mindless qualities.

He had seen them standing idly on the corners of the little towns, huge and slovenly, swinging their thonged clubs in the great muttons of their hands, surveying with their great red faces and their wide thin mouths of fathomless cruelty and good nature the crowds that swarmed around them. He had heard their drawling howling accents of the country, that had all of the moisture and distance of the earth in them, and seen their slow minds wake to a mindless and murderous fury. Once as a child he had seen one of them, a ponderous giant so huge he lurched from side to side when he walked, and seemed to fill the street up with his size, beat a drunken old man—a little howling integument of bone and gristle—to death with his club, smashing the little old man across the skull until the blood rushed out in torrents through his sparse silvery hair, lacing its way in channels of brilliant red across his face and through his beard, until it seemed incredible so small and old a man could have such fountains of bright blood in him.

And these huge creatures evoked for Eugene a whole history of this earth and people, monstrous, savage, and unutterable—a congruent and unspeakable legend which he knew, and all of them knew, down to the roots, and which he could not speak about and had to speak about, somehow, or die. For in these men there was evident not only the savage and mindless energy of the earth itself, with all that was wild, sensual, fecund, cruel and good-natured—the whole weather of life—but there was also evident the fear, the shame, the horror that had crushed them beneath its ocean weight of nameless and cowering dread, and broken or destroyed their souls.

The two policemen who had clambered into the back seat of the car and now sat on each side of Eugene had these mountainous and fleshy figures, heavy, yet with a kind of solid and ugly softness, meaty, and without the muscular and sinewy leanness of young men. The back seat of the car was a narrow one—the car was a new "sports model" designed only for four people—and now the huge fleshy figures of these two policemen, wedged against Eugene, gave him a feeling of disgust and revulsion.

Nevertheless, the feeling of exultant and jubilant power had not yet worn off, and although he had understood at once, when he saw the men lined up across the street, that they were under arrest and would be taken to the city jail, this sordid prospect caused him no uneasiness whatever. Rather, the feeling of drunken joy was still so powerful in him that everything on earth seemed good, and everything that happened wonderful. He hailed the experience of being arrested and taken to jail exultantly as if some fortunate and glorious experience was in store for him, and his exuberant affection for the world was so great that he even liked the policemen.

Eugene howled with laughter, smote them on their broad backs, flung his arms out and around their shoulders, saying, "By God, you're fine fellows, both of you, and you've got to have a drink!"

At this Robert laughed uneasily, saying to the policemen:

"Don't pay any attention to him! We haven't got anything to drink —I swear we haven't."

One of them had been rummaging around, however, and now triumphantly produced the jug from its hiding place beneath Blake's legs.

"Here it is, boys," he cried, as he displayed it. "I've got it."

The glass jug was almost empty, but there was still perhaps an inch of the whiskey at the bottom. Robert's face had a worried look, for the law was such that a capture of this sort might also mean the confiscation of the owner's car.

Blake, meanwhile, had been talking in a low, craftily persuasive tone of drunken insinuation and bribery to the policeman up front, saying: "Now I know you boys don't want to get us into any trouble. We weren't doing anything wrong—just having a drink or two together —and if you fellows will just forget about this thing, we'll fix it up right with you—anything you say," he whispered cunningly, "and get on out of town right now without any one knowing a thing about it. What do you say, now? Come on! You can do it," he said, with a leer of ingratiation.

The policeman to whom he spoke smiled good-naturedly, but said nothing. At this moment they drove up before the station house, a shabby-looking little building of brick, with bars over the window, and which was situated on a side-street.

The shabby street looked warm, faded, sleepy, touched with the ghosts of autumn, but in an instant, as the police got out, opened the doors, and the gay men clambered down drunkenly among them, a rabble-rout of ragged negro boys, grinning, gape-mouthed countrymen with red faces, slouchy-looking barbers in their shirt-sleeves, and wormy-looking loafers, had gathered magically from nowhere, stood in a ring about them and snickered and shuffled about, pressed up to the barred windows and peered in curiously with shaded eyes as the policemen took them into the station.

As they started, Robert held back a little, and said hoarsely, and in a plaintive, troubled voice to the policeman who had him by the arm: "What are you taking us in here for? We weren't doing anything. Honest we weren't. What are you going to do to us?"

The policeman smiled good-humoredly, and then said in a hearty reassuring voice:

"Aw, we're not goin' to do anything to you. We were just afraid you boys might run into something and hurt yourself, that's all. We're just goin' to take you in here, and let you stay here a little while until you feel better," he said, at the same time winking at his fellows.

"Well," said Robert sullenly, casting a troubled and unwilling glance back at his shining car, "—I want to find my car here when I come out. Now if anything happens to that car, there's going to be trouble," he said ominously.

"That car will be right here when you come out the way you left it," the policeman said heartily. "No one is goin' to touch it. No, sir! I'll look after that car myself!" he said, winking again at the others.

"All right, then," said Robert. "That's all I want to know."

Then they marched all of them into the station house.

The room they entered was a large one, and at first, because they had come into it out of the brightness of the sun, and the swimming confusion of drunkenness and arrest, it was so dark Eugene could not distinguish clearly any of its features. Then he saw that it was a square, rather high room with worn wooden floors, wainscoting of a dark varnished brown, and above that rude calcimined walls of white. In the wall along the street, there were, besides the door, two barred windows which were very dirty and not very large, and did not give much light.

At one end of the room, as they came in, there was a row of dull green lockers, probably for the use of the police, and at the other end a high, square, somewhat majestical-looking desk, which was also of a dark maply-brown and which seemed to be built on an elevated rostrum or platform a few inches high. Over this desk a light with a green glass shade was burning, and behind it another large red-faced policeman was sitting. By his look of authority, and the military opulence of his slovenly uniform—for he had epaulets of thick gold braid upon his shoulders that would have glorified the uniform of a general in the Marine Corps—he seemed to be the superior in command.

As for the rest of the room, there was little decoration save for a row of worn and rickety-looking wooden chairs with rounded backs along the wall, and a liberal distribution of large brass spittoons which, to judge from the bare wooden boards around them, were used less frequently as receptacles than as targets, and obviously with uncertain success.

Finally, the whole place had the unforgettable look and smell that police stations everywhere—and particularly those in little towns—have always had. Its stale dark air was impregnated with the odor of cheap cigars and tobacco-juice, of old worn varnished wood, of human sweat and urine and heavy wool, and with the strong tarry odor of a sanitary disinfectant. And somehow, in this stale, dark and weary odor, there was also a quality of terror, menace, and foreboding—as if the huge and dingy chronicle of human tragedy and error which this grim room had witnessed—all the brutal, shabby sinfulness of a little town—that swarming, hideous and tawdry fraternity of poverty, vice and error—dredged from its rat-holes in the dark depths of old brick buildings, hunted out of cheap hotels, pool rooms, greasy little lunch rooms, nigger shacks, and the rickety wooden whore-houses near the railroad tracks, with its vast brotherhood of scarred and battered men and women—chain-gang niggers, drunken country youths and cheap bootleggers, grimy prostitutes and all their furtive bawds and pimps, cutters, sluggers, stabbers, slashers, and brawlers—both those who live by vice and those who are its victims—this whole huge earth of pain and crime and misery had left the terrible imprint of its history so indelibly there that the weary air was impregnated with sorrow and fear, and the wood, walls, floors and ceilings were seasoned and ingrained with the substance of human wretchedness.

When they had come in, the police had lined up Eugene's three companions before the imposing rostrum where the desk officer was sitting, but they had placed him carefully to one side against the wall, like an object too rare and precious for ordinary usage. Now, as the great man behind the desk glowered down gloomily and mistrustfully at them, one of the police spoke to the desk sergeant and, turning toward Eugene with a nod of the head, declared in a full countrified tone:

"This big 'un here's the drunkest of the lot."

And the enthroned law bent his gloomy gaze upon him with a hostile and suspicious look which said as plain as words that it was no more than he had suspected.

Eugene had not realized, in fact, until he felt that wall against his shoulders, how very drunk he was; but he was drunker now than he had ever been in all his life before. He could feel his back slide down along the wall, and then his bending knees would straighten with a jerk, and he would solemnly begin to slide up the wall again. Meanwhile, the room swam and rocked and then was still before his eyes: the shapes of things would melt into a smear, and then resolve into their proper selves once more.

And he was conscious that the police were searching him and his companions, patting their pockets to see if they carried weapons, examining wallets and letters for identifications, taking their watches from them, and arraigning them on a series of formal charges, some of which had no bearing on their case whatever. Drunk, assuredly, they were; disorderly they might have been—although it had not seemed so to them; of driving in a reckless manner they were guilty; but of resisting an officer in the performance of his duty they had been, up to that time, spotlessly innocent.

But such were the charges delivered against them in sonorous and countrified tones. And in the solemn voices of the policemen, the knowing and portentous way in which they searched the young men —as if they were a gang of armed desperadoes, and in a manner that smacked of correspondence-school detective methods—and finally in the solemn countrified tones of the one who had pointed to Eugene, saying: "This big 'un here's the drunkest of the lot," there was something comical and ludicrous.

But in their sense of banded authority, in the stubborn almost conspiratorial way in which they had now hardened in a group against the young men, forsaking the good-humored and jovial manners which had heretofore distinguished them, there was something ugly and revolting—something stupid, provincial, mob-like, and unreasoning, which told the young men plainly that "they had them" now, that they were "foreigners," therefore suspect, and must bow their heads in silence to the obdurate and capricious tyrannies of a local and, for them, impregnable authority.

At length, the sonorous formalities of their arraignment having been completed, the sergeant having scrawled and written in his ledger, the man looked up and ordered sternly:

"All right, boys! Take 'em back and lock 'em up!"

Then the young men were marched back along a corridor into a large two-storied room, which had brick walls and cement floors, two rows of dirty barred windows, a gray and gelid light, and a general feel of raw and clammy dankness. This room, which had a harsh angular steel-and-cement newness that the other did not have, seemed to be of more recent construction, and to have been added on to the front part of the jail. In this room, also, there were several rows of cells, ascending in tiers up to the ceiling When they entered, the place was quiet, but immediately a drunken negress in one of the cells began to bawl and rave and sob, smashing, hammering, and rattling the bars of her cell like a demented ape. There was everywhere a foul rank odor of undrained fecal matter, tempered with the odor of the tarry disinfectant, and cut more sharply with the acrid smell of some ammoniac fluid.

At the first row of cells they paused, and the police in charge of Robert and Emmet Blake (for Eugene now discovered with a sense of shock that Kitchin was not with them) unlocked the doors of cells two and three and thrust Blake and Robert into them. The last, or end, cell in the row, Eugene now saw was intended for his occupancy and he stood waiting obediently, in the relaxed grip of one of the policemen, until his comrade should unlock the door.

Suddenly, as the door swung open, and Eugene stepped forward into the cell, his vision cleared somewhat, and he saw a young negro standing in the cell, beside the iron bed that projected from the wall, looking toward him with a startled expression on his face that suggested he had been asleep upon the cot, and had been rudely wakened by their entrance. Instantly, one fixed and all-obsessing belief began to burn in Eugene's inflamed and drunken brain. He thought that he was being put here with this negro because the jail was crowded and the cell-space scanty, and further—and this was the thing that maddened him and that he found intolerable—because, as the policeman had said when they arraigned the young men, "this big 'un here's the drunkest of the lot," and they thought he was too drunk to notice or to care about the advantage they were taking of him.

For this reason—and this reason only—he now acted as he did. As far as the negro himself was concerned, Eugene bore no grudge against him, and the feeling of shame and degradation which had swept over him in an overwhelming flood when he saw the cell and knew he was to be locked in it like an animal was so great that he would not have cared with whom he had to share that cell, if it had been the custom of the country so to share it. But the custom of the country was not so, he knew, and the belief that he was being put upon, his drunkenness taken advantage of, and that he was being dealt with less fairly than the others, now so stung his maddened pride that he turned and kicked the iron door back in the faces of the two policemen, just as they were closing it.

Then he started to come out of the cell. When he did, the two big red-faced policemen came running forward with a lumbering, panting, and somehow revolting clumsiness and tried to push him back into the cell. When this happened, something dark, gray, and terrible that he had never known before rose up in his soul—and this thing, which now came to him for the first time, was to return often in the savage years that followed.

As the police came rushing towards Eugene his fury and desperation were so great that he felt little or no fear, but the sensations of horror and disgust were so terrible that they drove him mad, and he

seemed to be drowning in them. And the first visible and physical, al·
though perhaps not the basic, causes of these sensations of horror and
disgust came from the mountainous figures of the two policemen, and
the feel of their huge soft-solid bodies as they jammed against him. For,
if they had quelled his rebellion at the outset by smashing him over the
head with their clubs, he might have felt a moment's fear before the club
crashed on his skull, but he would not have felt horror and disgust.

But the sight, the feel, the smell, the look of these huge soft-solid
bodies of mountainous flesh, and the revolting clumsiness of their movements, made the thing horrible. As they rushed towards Eugene and
tried to thrust him back into the cell, he grabbed hold of the bars on
either side of the door, and began to howl at them and curse them
foully, and to butt at them with his head. When this happened the
policemen braced themselves together like turn-squat Buddhas, holding
on to the bars with their huge muttony hands, that had no leanness in
them, and butted back at Eugene with their huge soft-solid stomachs.

They stood, half-squatly, side by side, their muttony hands gripped
around the bars, their great red faces moist and panting, their huge
buttocks somehow obscenely womanish in their fat breadth, as they
butted back clumsily at him with their soft ponderous bellies—all of
this, and the revolting contact of their flesh against his own, filled him
with such an infinite loathing of horror and disgust that he went mad.

Once more he struggled to push his way out, and again the two
big policemen braced themselves clumsily against him and tried to
push him back in. One of the men raised his ponderous fist and
shouted: "Git back in thar now or I'll hit ye." A huge muttony fist
smashed squarely on his nose and mouth: he butted, cursed, amid a
pin-wheel aura of exploding rockets: the fist smashed hard again below
one eye: the boy screamed like a wounded animal and cursing horribly
all the time began to use his head as a battering ram, butting again and
again at the fat red faces.

Meanwhile the other one, grunting and puffing, and with his tongue
between his teeth, began to thump, tug and wrench at the fingers of
one hand, trying to loosen them from the bar, and saying to his fellow:
"You git his other hand, Jim, an' try to make him turn a-loose."

During all this time that Eugene had been cursing and butting at these
men, he had also been shouting "You God-damned red-faced South Car'-
lina bastards, you're not going to lock me up in here with a nigger—no
you ain't!"—and now he felt something rough and wooly scraping un·

derneath his arm. It was the frightened negro's head. He went squirming out below Eugene's arm until he was outside peering with white eyeballs over a policeman's shoulder, and when Eugene saw they would not try to keep the negro there with him, he went back into the cell and was locked up. He felt very sick, and everything was swimming nauseously around him: for a while he leaned over the w. c. and vomited into it. Then he sat down on the edge of the cot, and stared ahead, thinking about nothing, but with something hideous, like a great gray smear, inside him.

XLIII

How long he sat there in this way he did not know, for time would pass in a hideous smear of brownish gray while all things reeled, mixed, and were fused drunkenly and shapelessly around him—and then for a moment time would burn in his mind like a small hard light of brilliant color, and he would see everything with an exact and blazing vividness and hear the voices of his comrades in their cells.

The cell Eugene sat in was a little cubicle of space, perhaps eight feet deep, and four or five feet wide. Its only furnishings were a black iron cot or bed which projected from the wall and could be turned up or out, and which had no springs or mattress on it, and a w. c. of dirty white enamel, which had no seat, and was broken and would not flush, so that it had run over and spilled out upon the cement floor. The walls and ceilings of the cell were made of some hard slate-like substance of black-gray, scrawled with the familiar obscenities and pictures of its former occupants. Because of these solid walls, each cell was cut off from its neighbors and for this reason he could not see Emmet Blake, who had the cell next to him, nor Robert, who had the cell on the other side of Emmet, but now, as his mind swam from the stupor of its drunkenness, he could hear their voices, and began to listen to their conversation.

Both were still quite drunk, and for a while they continued a kind of mournful drunken chant, each responding to the other with a repetition of his own misfortune.

"Yes, sir," Robert would say, heaving a sigh and speaking in a hoarse, mournfully drunken voice, "this is certainly a hell of a way to treat a man who's just been admitted to the bar six weeks ago! A hell of a thing!" he said.

And Blake would answer:

"Yes, sir! And I'll tell *you* what *is* a hell of a thing! This is a hell of a way to treat George Blake's nephew! A hell of a way!" he said. "If my uncle knew about this he'd come down here and tear their damned little jail to pieces! He'd *ruin* their town!" he cried. "Yes, sir! He'd wash 'em out and send 'em to the cleaners! Why!" Blake now said in a tone of drunken boastfulness, "there are 70,000 Blake dealers in the United States *alone*—and if they knew that *I* was here," he said, "every damned one of them would be on his way here in five minutes to get us out!"

"Lord! Lord!" said Robert, in a kind of mournful brooding ululation, as if he had not heard Blake's words at all. "Who'd have thought it? A young attorney just admitted to the bar six weeks ago and here he is in jail! The damnedest thing I ever heard of!" he declared.

"Yes, sir," Blake declared, not by way of response, but with the same self-centred concentration on the indignity which had been visited on him. "If you told any Blake dealer in the country that George Blake's nephew was down here in the Blackstone jail, he wouldn't believe you. Uncle George will carry this thing to the Supreme Court when we get out," he said. "It is certainly a hell of a thing to happen to George Blake's nephew!"

"Yes, sir," Robert answered, "a hell of a thing to happen is *right*—and here I've only had my license to practise, for six weeks. Why, it's awful!" he said solemnly.

"Robert!" Blake cried suddenly, getting to his feet.—"Do you guess these damned Blackstone cops know who I am? Do you guess they realize they've got George Blake's nephew here?" Here he went to the door of his cell, rattled it violently, and yelled: "Hey—y! I'm George Blake's nephew! Do you know you've got George Blake's nephew back here? Come and let me out!" he shouted. No one answered.

Then they would be silent for a while, and mournful, brooding drunken time would pass around them.

Then Blake would say:

"Robert?"

"What do you want?" said Robert mournfully.

"What time is it?"

"Hell, how do I know what time it is," said Robert in a sullen and protesting tone. "You know they took my watch." Then there would be silence for a moment more.

"Emmet?" Robert would then say.

"All right. What is it?"

"Did they take your watch, too?"

"Yes!" Blake shouted suddenly in an angry and excited tone. "And that was an eighteen carat, thirty-two jewel platinum-case watch that Uncle George bought for me in Switzerland. That watch is worth $225 and I'd better get it back when I get out of here!" he shouted rattling the door. "Do you hear? If those sons-of-bitches try to steal my watch, my Uncle George will put 'em *all* in jail! I want it back!" he shouted. No one answered.

Then they were silent for another spell of time, and finally Robert said in a hoarse, brooding, and mournful tone.

"Eugene?"

"Well."

"Are you there?"

"Where the hell do you think I am?" Eugene said bitterly. "You don't see any holes in this place you can crawl out of, do you?"

Robert laughed his hoarse falsetto laugh, and then said with a kind of brooding wonder:

"Lord! Lord! Who'd have thought it? Who'd ever have thought Eugene and I would get put in jail together here in Blackstone, South Carolina. Here I am just out of Yale and admitted to the bar six weeks ago and you—boy!" he laughed suddenly his annoying falsetto laugh, and concluded—"Just got back from three years at Harvard and here you are in jail already! Lord! Lord! What are you going to tell your mother when she sees you? What's she going to say when you tell her you've been in jail?"

"Oh, I don't know!" the other said angrily. "Shut up!"

Robert laughed his annoying falsetto laugh again, and said:

"Boy! I'd hate to have to face her! I'm glad I'm not in *your* shoes!"

"Not in *my* shoes!" the other shouted in an exasperated tone. "You damned fool, you are in my shoes!"

Then they were silent for a spell, and gray time ticked wearily around them the slow remorseless sound of its interminable minutes.

Presently Blake spoke, out of a drunken silence, saying:

"Gant?"

"What is it?"

"What time is it now?"

"I don't know. They have my watch,' he said.

And gray time ticked around them.

"Robert," Eugene said at length, straightening from his dejected stupor on the cot, "did you see that nigger?"

"What nigger?" Robert said stupidly.

"Why the nigger they tried to put in here with me!" he said.

"Why, I didn't see any nigger, Gene," said Robert in a hoarse and drunken tone of mild and melancholy protest. "When was this?"

"Why, Robert!" the other boy now cried in an excited voice, and with a feeling of hideous dread inside him. "You were right here all the time! Didn't you hear us?"

"Why, no, Eugene," Robert answered in a slow protesting voice that had dull wonder and surprise in it. "I didn't hear anything," he said.

"Why, my God, Robert!" Eugene now cried excitedly, and even with a kind of frenzy in his tone. "You must have heard us! Why, we were fighting here for ten minutes!" he said, for the time of the struggle now seemed at least that long to him.

"Who?" said Robert, dully and stupidly.

"Why, me and those two big cops!" he cried. "Good God, Robert, didn't you see us?—didn't you hear us?—butting and kicking like a goat—hitting me over the head, trying to make me turn a-loose!" he cried in an excited, almost incoherent tone.

"Who did?" Robert stupidly inquired.

"Why—those two big cops, Robert—that's who! Good God, do you mean to tell me that you never heard us when we were cursing and butting away there right in front of you!"

"I didn't hear anything—I thought you said a nigger," he said in a stupid and confused tone.

"Why, Robert, that's what I'm telling you!" Eugene shouted. "They had him in here——"

"Where?"

"Why, in the cell! They were trying to put me in here with him! That's what the trouble was about!" he said.

"Why, Eugene," Robert said with an uneasy and troubled laugh, which yet had a note of good-natured derision in it that was maddening, "I didn't see any nigger. Did you, Emmet? I was right here all the time and I didn't hear any trouble. . . . *You've* been dreaming," Robert now said, with a conviction in his tone that goaded the other boy almost past endurance, and yet struck a knife of cold terror into his heart. And he began to laugh hoarsely his annoying and derisive laugh, as he shook his head, and said: "Lord! *Lord!*—He's in there seeing niggers and policemen and I don't know what-all." And here he laughed hoarsely again, his derisive and falsetto laugh, and said: *"Boy!* You've got 'em! You've *got* 'em bad! You've been seeing things!"

"Robert, God-damn it!" Eugene now fairly screamed, "I tell you he was here! I tell you I saw him standing in the cell when I came in! I know what I'm talking about, Robert!—there was a nigger here when I came in!"

"Why, hell, Eugene!" Robert said more kindly, but with a hoarse derisive laugh, "you've just been seeing things, son. There was no one there; you just imagined it. I reckon you just passed out and dreamed it happened!"

"Dreamed! Dreamed!" Eugene shouted, "God-damn it, Robert, don't you think I know when I'm dreaming? I'll show you if it was a dream! I'll prove it to you that it really happened! I can prove it by Blake!" he cried. "Ask Blake! . . . Blake! Blake! Blake!" he shouted.

And gray time slid with its slow sanded drop around them.

Blake did not answer: he had not heard their conversation and now they heard him talking softly, slowly, murderously to himself.

"Yes, sir," he was saying, in a low, quiet, drunkenly intent soliloquy. "Yes, sir, I'll kill him! . . . So help me God, I'll kill him dead, as sure as my name is Emmet Blake! . . . I'll pull out my forty-five. . . . I'll get my forty-five out, when I go home . . . and I'll go Ping! Ping! Ping! the minute that I see him. I'll go Ping! Ping! Ping!" cried Blake. "I'll kill him dead, so help me God, if it's the last thing that I ever do!"

"I'll kill him!" Blake continued in a tone of dogged, drunken repetition, still talking to himself. "When I get home I'll kill him if it's the last thing I ever do!"

"And I'll kill *you,* too," Blake muttered in this same brooding and intent oblivion of drunken soliloquy. "You God-damned whore, I'll kill you, too! I'll kill the two of you together! . . . The bitch! The bitch! The dirty bitch!" the man now screamed, starting to his feet, and now really with a tortured note of agony and desperation in his voice. "I know where you are this minute! I know you're with him! I know you'll sleep with him tonight, you—dirty—lowdown——"

"Emmet, you damned fool, shut up!" Robert now said, with a troubled and protesting laugh. "Do you want every one in the whole damned place to hear you?" The dreadful shame and anguish in the man's desperate life had burst nakedly through his drunkenness, and the hideous mutilation of his soul was suddenly stripped bare— "Don't talk like that," said Robert, with a troubled laugh—"you'll be sorry tomorrow for what you said, you know you will: oh, Emmet, shut up!" Robert said again with a protesting and embarrassed laugh.

For Blake was now sobbing horribly in his cell: as Eugene stood leaning against the wall next to him, he could hear him sobbing, and pounding his thin fist savagely into the gray-slate substance of the wall, while he went on:

"The whore! The dirty whore!" he wept. "I know that she's just waiting for me to die! I know that's what she wants! I know that's all she's waiting for! . . . That's what you want, you bitch, isn't it? You'd like that, wouldn't you? That would just suit you, wouldn't it? . . . Ah, I've fooled you! I've fooled you, haven't I?" he panted, with a savage and vindictive triumph in his voice. "You've been waiting for it for the last two years, haven't you? And I've fooled you every time," he gasped. "And I'll fool you yet—you bitch, you dirty bitch!"

And they sat there, saying nothing, listening with desolation in their hearts to the man's naked shame, and now hearing nothing but his gasping sobs, and the slow gray wear and waste of time around them. And then his sobbing breath grew quieter, they could hear him panting feebly like an exhausted runner, and presently he went over and sat down upon his cot, and there was nothing but time and silence all about them.

Finally Blake spoke again, and now in a voice that was quiet, lifeless, and curiously sober, as if this outlet and easance of his grief had also quenched the drunkenness in him.

"Gant?" he said, in a quiet and lifeless tone that penetrated curiously the gray silence all around them.

"Yes," said Eugene.

"I never met you till today," said Blake, "and I want you to know I've got no grudge against you."

"Why, Eugene never did anything to you, Emmet," said Robert at this point, in a tone of protest. "Why should you have anything against him?"

"Now, *wait* a minute!" said Blake pugnaciously. "Eugene," he went on in a maudlin tone of voice, "I'm friends with every one. I haven't got an enemy in the world, . . . There's just one man in this world I hate," he went on sombrely, "and I hate his guts—I hate his life—God-damn him! I hate the air he breathes!" he snarled, and then was silent for a moment. "Eugene," he went on in a moment, in a low voice, and with a tone of brooding drunken insinuation, "you know the man I mean, don't you?"

Eugene made no answer, and in a moment he repeated the question, in a more insistent and pugnacious tone:

"*Don't* you?" he demanded.

And Eugene said, "Yes."

"You're damned right you do," he said in a low, ruminant, and brooding tone. "Everybody knows who I mean. He's a cousin of yours," said Blake, and then began to mutter to himself:

"I'll kill him! So help me God, I'll kill him!" And suddenly, starting from his cot with a scream of baffled misery and anguish, he began to beat his fist into the hard slate wall again, yelling:

"I'll kill you! I'll kill you! . . . You son-of-a-bitch, I'll kill the two of you! . . . I'll send you both to hell where you belong, if it's the last thing that I ever do!"

And he began to sob horribly and curse foully, and pounded his fist into the wall again until he was exhausted, and went back and sat down on his cot again, muttering his drunken and impotent threats.

And Eugene did not try to answer him, for there was nothing he could say. George Pentland was his cousin, and had taken Blake's wife away from him, and got her love; and Blake was dying, and they knew it. And suddenly, it seemed to Eugene that there was in this whole story something dark, and hideously shameful, which he had never clearly seen in life before, which could not be endured, and which yet suspended over every man who ever lived the menace of its intolerable humiliation and dishonor.

For, to see a man—a manly-looking man, strong of body, fearless and bold of glance, deep of voice—physically humiliated and disgraced, slapped and whipped like a cur before his wife, his mistress, or his children, and forced to yield, retreat and slink away, to see his face turn white and the look of the coward shine through his mask of manhood, is not an easy thing to see.

Presently, they heard steps coming along the corridor again, and they were so certain they belonged to a messenger bringing them release that they all arose instinctively, and stood before the barred doors of the cells, waiting to walk out into the air of freedom again. To their astonishment the visitor was Kitchin. They had forgotten him completely, and now as they saw him doing a gleeful caper before their cells, with a grin of triumphant satisfaction written wide across his face, they looked at him with the astounded recognition of men who see a face which they had known years before, but have forgotten—in the lapse of time and memory.

"Where?—" Robert began hoarsely and accusingly, in a tone of astounded stupefaction. "Where have you been all this time?"

"Out front!" said Kitchin exultantly. "Sitting in your car!"

"Out front!" cried Robert in a bewildered and resentful tone. "Didn't they lock you up, too?"

"Hell, no!" cried Kitchin, fairly dancing about with gleeful satisfaction. "They never touched me! And I'd had as much to drink as any of you. I've been sittin' out front all afternoon reading the paper! I guess they thought I was the only sober one of the crowd," he said modestly. And this apparently was the reason for his astonishing freedom—this and another, more mercenary reason, which will presently be apparent.

"Why, what do they mean by keeping us locked up back here while you're out front there reading the paper? Darnedest thing I ever heard of!" Robert barked. "Kitchin!" he now said angrily. "You go out there and tell them we want out of here!"

"I told 'em! I told 'em!" Kitchin said virtuously. "That's what I've been telling them all afternoon."

"Well, what do they say?" Robert demanded impatiently.

"Boys," said Kitchin now, shaking his head regretfully, but unable to conceal his own elation and sense of triumph, "I've got news for you—and I'm afraid it's not going to be good news, either. How much money you got?"

"Money!" Robert cried, in an astounded tone, as if the uses of this vile commodity had never occurred to him. "What's money got to do with it? We want out of here!"

"I know you do," said Kitchin coolly, "but you're not going to get out unless you've got money enough to pay your fine."

"Fine?" Robert repeated stupidly.

"Well, that's what they call it anyway. Fine or graft, or whatever the hell it is, you've got to pay it if you want to be let out."

"How much is it?" said Robert. "How much do they want?"

"Boys," said Kitchin, slowly and solemnly, "have you got seventy-three dollars?"

"Seventy-three dollars!" Robert shouted. "Kitchin, what are you talking about?"

"Well, don't shout at me," said Kitchin. "I can't help it! I didn't do it! But if you get out of here that's what you've got to pay."

"Seventy-three dollars!" Robert cried. "Seventy-three dollars for what?"

"Well, Robert," said Kitchin patiently, "you've got to pay fifty dollars fine and one dollar costs. That's because you were driving the car. That's fifty-one. And Emmet and Eugene here have to pay ten dollars apiece and one dollar costs—that's twenty-two dollars more. That figures up to seventy-three dollars. Have you got it?"

"Why, the dirty grafting sons-of-bitches!" Blake now cried. "Telling us that everything would be all right and that they had put us in here so we wouldn't hurt ourselves! . . . All right, you cheap grafting bastards!" he shouted at the top of his lungs, rattling the barred door furiously as he spoke. "We'll give you your dirty graft—but wait till I get out of here!" he cried threateningly. "Just wait till I get out! George Blake will tend to you!" he shouted. "It'll be the worst day's work *you've* ever done!"

But no one answered, although Blake and Robert cursed foully and shouted insults at the men. Meanwhile, Kitchin waited patiently before their cells until the furious tumult should subside a little; when they were calmer he suggested that they pool their resources to see if they had enough to pay the total of the fines. But the sum of their combined funds was only a little more than forty dollars, of which Blake and Robert contributed the greater part, and of which Eugene could contribute less than three dollars, which was all he had.

When it was apparent that their total funds would not be adequate to secure their release Blake, still furiously angry, began to talk in a loud and drunken tone of bravado about his famous uncle, scrawling out a check and instructing Kitchin to go at once to the local agent for his uncle's motor cars and get the necessary money:

"Any Blake dealer in the country will cash my personal check for fifty thousand dollars any time I need it!" he cried with extravagant boast, as if he thought this threat of opulence would strike terror to the hearts of the police. "Yes, sir!" he said. "All you got to do is to walk into any Blake agency in the country and tell them George Blake's nephew needs money—and they'll give you everything they've got!" he cried. "Tell 'em you need ten thousand dollars," he said, coming down in scale somewhat, "and they'll have it for you in five minutes."

"Why, Emmet," said Kitchin quietly, and yet with a trace of mockery and ridicule on his dark, handsome, and rather sly face. "We don't need fifty thousand dollars. You know, we're not trying to buy the whole damned jail. Now, I thought," he went on quietly and ironically, "that all we needed was about thirty or forty—say fifty dollars—to make up the fine and get us out of town."

"Yes," said Robert in a quick excited tone of vigorous agreement. "You're absolutely right! That's all we need, all right!"

"All *right!* All *right!* Go to the Blake dealer! Go to the Blake dealer! That's what I'm telling you," cried Blake with an arrogant impatience. "He'll give you anything you want.—What are you waiting for?" he cried furiously. "Go *on!* Go *on!*"

"But Emmet," said Kitchin quietly and reasonably, in his dark low voice, as he looked at the check which Blake had scrawled out for him. "This check you've given me is for five hundred dollars. Hadn't you better make out another one for fifty? You know, we don't need five hundred dollars, Emmet. And besides," he suggested tactfully, "the man might not have that much on hand. Hadn't you better give me one just made out for what we need?"

"He'll have it! He's got it! He's *got* to have it!" said Blake with a dogmatic and unreasoning arrogance. "Tell him I sent you and you'll get the money right away!"

Kitchin did not answer him: he thrust the check into his pocket and turned to Eugene, saying quietly:

"Didn't you say your brother was waiting to meet you here at a hotel?"

"Yes: he expected to meet me at four o'clock when that service car came in."

"At what hotel?"

"The Blackstone—listen, Kitchin," he reached through the bar and grabbed him by the arm, with a feeling of cold horror in his heart. "For Christ's sake, don't drag my brother into this," he whispered. "Kitchin—listen to me! If you can get this money from the Blake agent here, for God's sake, do it! What's the use of bringing my brother in to it," he pleaded, "when it's all between the four of us, and can stay that way? I don't want my family to know I ever got into any trouble like this. Kitchin, look here—I can get the money for my fine: I've got a little money in the bank, and I'll pay Blake every cent I owe him if you get the money from the agent. Now, promise me you won't go and tell my brother!"

He held him hard in the tension of desperation, and Kitchin promised. Then he went swiftly away, and they were left alone in their cells again. Robert, utterly cast down from his high exaltation, now cursed bitterly and morosely against the police, and the injustice of his luck and destiny.

Meanwhile, Blake, whose final and chief resource, it had now become pitifully evident, was nothing in himself, but just the accident of birth that had made him nephew to a powerful and wealthy man, kept declaring in a loud tone of arrogant bravado that "any Blake agent in the United States will cash my personal check for fifty thousand dollars any time I ask for it! Yes, sir, any of them—I don't give a damn where it is! He's on his way here now! You'll see! We'll be out of here in five minutes now!"—a boastful assurance that was hardly out of his mouth before they heard steps approaching rapidly along the corridor and, even as Blake cried out triumphantly, "What did I tell you?" and as Eugene leaped up and ran to the door of his cell, clutching the bars with both hands, and peering out with bloodshot eyes like a caged gorilla, Kitchin entered the cell-room, followed by a policeman, and—Eugene's brother!

Luke looked at him for a moment with a troubled expression and said: "Why, how did you get in here? What's happened to you?" he said, suddenly noticing his battered face. "Are you hurt, Eugene?"

The boy made no reply but looked at him with sullen desperation and jerked his head towards the cells where his two companions were imprisoned—a gesture that pled savagely for silence. And Luke, instantly reading the meaning of that gesture, turned and called out cheerfully:

"Now you boys just hold on a minute and I'll have you out of here."

Then he came up close to the barred door of the cell where his younger brother stood and, his face stern with care, he said in a low voice: "What happened? Who hit you? Did any of these bastards hit you? I want to know."

A policeman was standing behind him looking at them with narrowed eyes, and the boy said desperately:

"Get us out of here. I'll tell you later."

Then Luke went away with the policeman to pay their fines. When he had gone, Eugene turned bitterly on Kitchin, who had remained with the boys, accusing him of breaking his word by going to Luke. Kitchin's dark evasive eyes shifted nervously in his head as he answered:

"Well, what else could I do? I went to the Blake agent here——"

"Did you get the money?" Blake said. "Did he give it to you?"

"Give!" Kitchin said curtly, with a sneer. "He gave me nothing—not a damned cent! He said he'd never heard of you!"

There was silence for a moment.

"Well, I can't understand that," Blake said at length, feebly, and in a tone of dazed surprise. "That's the first time anything like that has ever happened."

At this moment Eugene's brother returned with two policemen who unlocked the cell doors and let them out. The feeling of coming from the cell into free space again was terrific in its physical intensity: never before had Eugene known the physical sensations of release as he knew them at that moment. The very light and air in the space outside the cell had a soaring buoyancy and freshness which, by comparison, gave to that within the cell a material and oppressive heaviness, a sense of walled and mortared space that had pressed upon his heart and spirit with a crushing weight. Now, suddenly, as if a cord that bound him had been cut, or a brutal hand that held his life in its compelling grip had been removed, the sensations of release and escape filled his body with a sense of aerial buoyancy and the power of wing-like flight.

With a desperate eagerness he had never felt before he wanted to feel the free light and air again: even the shocked solicitude of his companions when they saw his puffed lips and his blackened eye was drearily oppressive. He thrust past them, muttering, striding towards the door.

It was the first time in his life that he had ever been arrested and locked up, and for the first time now, he felt and understood the meaning of an immense and brutal authority in life, which he had seen before, but to which he had always believed himself to be immune. Until that day, he had had all the pride and arrogance a young man knows. Since childhood no one had ever compelled him to do anything by force, and although he had seen the million evidences of force, privilege, and compulsion applied to the lives of people around him, so that like every other native of the land in which he lived, he had in his heart no belief in law whatever, and knew that legal justice, where it was achieved, was achieved by fortuitous accident rather than by intent, he had believed, as every young man believes, that his own life and body were fiercely immune to every indignity of force and compulsion.

Now this feeling was gone forever. And having lost it irrecoverably, he had gained something of more value.

For now, he was conscious, even at the moment he came out of the cell, of a more earthly, common, and familiar union with the lives of other men than he had ever known. And this experience was to have another extraordinary effect upon his spirit and its understanding and love of poetry, which may seem ludicrous, but which certainly dated from these few hours of his first imprisonment. Up to this time in his life, the poet who had stirred him by his power and genius more than any other was the poet Shelley.

But in the years that followed, Shelley's poetry came to have so little meaning for him, that all the magic substance which his lines once had was lost, and Eugene seemed to look indifferently at the hollow shells and ghosts of words, from which all enchantment and belief had vanished. And he felt this way not because the words of this great poet now seemed false to him, but because, more than any other poet he had known, Shelley was the poet of that time of life when men feel most strongly the sense of proud and lonely inviolability, which is legible in everything he wrote, and when their spirits, like his, are also "tameless and swift and proud." And this is a time of life and magic that, once gone, is gone forever, and that may never be recaptured save by memory.

But in the years that followed, just as Eugene's physical body grew coarser and more heavy, and his sensual appetites increased enormously, so also did the energy of his spirit, which in childhood had been wing-like, soaring, and direct in its aerial buoyancy, grow darker, slower, heavier, smouldering and slow in its beginning heat, and densely woven and involved in all its web-like convolutions.

And as all the strength and passion of his life turned more and more away from its childhood thoughts of aerial flight and escape into some magic and unvisited domain, it seemed to him that the magic and unvisited domain was the earth itself, and all the life around him—that he must escape not out of life but into it, looking through walls he never had seen before, exploring the palpable and golden substance of this earth as it had never been explored, finding, somehow, the word, the key, the door, to the glory of a life more fortunate and happy than any man has ever known, and which yet incredibly, palpably, is his, even as the earth beneath his feet is his, if he could only take it.

And as he discovered this, Eugene turned more and more for food and comfort to those poets who have found it, and who have left great pieces of that golden earth behind them in their verse, as deathless evidence that they were there:—those poets who wrote not of the air but of the earth, and in whose verse the gold and glory of the earth is treasured—their names are Shakespeare, Spenser, Chaucer, Herrick, Donne, and Herbert.

Their names are Milton (whom fools have called glacial and austere, and who wrote the most tremendous lines of earthly passion and sensuous magic that have ever yet been written), Wordsworth, Browning, Whitman, Keats, and Heine—their names are Job, Ecclesiastes, Homer, and The Song of Solomon.

These are their names, and if any man should think the glory of the earth has never been, let him live alone with them, as Eugene did, a thousand nights of solitude and wonder, and they will reveal to him again the golden glory of the earth, which is the only earth that is, and is forever, and is the only earth that lives, the only one that will never die.

XLIV

When they got out into the street again, night had almost come. It was about six o'clock, the lights in the streets had gone on, and in the figures of the people that went by, and the motor cars that flashed past sparsely, there was something hurried, mournful, and departing, like the breath of autumn and old leaves stirred by wind and driven on.

Neither spoke for some time, nor dared look at the other: the boy walked with lowered head, his hat pulled down across his eyes. His lips were puffed and swollen, and his left eye was now entirely closed, a blind poached swelling of bruised blue. They passed below a street lamp, paused for a minute in the hard white glare, turned as if impelled by sombre instinct, and regarded each other with the stern defenseless eye of shame and sorrow. Luke looked earnestly at his brother for a second and then said gently:

"How's your eye, Eugene?"

The boy said nothing: sullenly, steadily, with his one good eye he returned his brother's look. Luke stared for a minute at the nauseous, fatted purple where the bad eye was, suddenly cursed bitterly, turned, and walked ahead.

"The d-d-dirty bastards!" he said. "I've always f'ought they were a f-f-fairly decent lot till now, but the nice, damned, d-d-d-dirty South

Car'lina—" he ground his teeth together, paused again, and turned towards his younger brother: "What d-d-did they do to you while you were in there? I w-w-w-want to know what happened."

"I guess I got what was coming to me," the boy muttered. "We were all drunk, and we were driving pretty fast. So I want you to know that I'm not making any excuses for that."

"Well," Luke said quietly, "that's all over now, and there's no use to w-w-worry about it. I guess you're not the f-f-f-first one that it's happened to. So let's f-f-forget about that." He was silent for a moment, and then he went on sternly, "But if those b-b-bastards beat you up while you were in there I w-w-w-want to know about it."

"I'm not kicking about it," the boy muttered again, because he was ashamed to tell him of the struggle he had had with the two policemen. "I guess I had it coming—but there was one thing!" he said with a surge of bitter feeling as he remembered it. "They did one thing I don't believe they had any right to do. If it had happened in the North it would have been all right, but, by God, I don't believe they have any right in this State to put a white man in the same cell with a nigger!"

"Did they d-d-d-do that to you?" Luke cried in an excited voice, stopping short and half turning as he spoke.

"Yes, they did, they tried to," and then he told him what had happened.

Luke turned completely, and started back towards the station, cursing bitterly.

"C-c-come on!" he said.

"Where are you going?"

"I'm g-g-g-going down there and tell those b-b-b-bastards what I f'ink of them!"

"No, you're not! Listen!" Eugene seized his brother by the arm. "We'll only get locked up again! They've got us and we've got to take it! We're not going! Let's get out of this damned town quick as we can! I never want to see the place again!"

Luke paused and stood, distractedly thrusting his fingers through his hair.

"All right," he said at last. "We'll go. . . . But by G-g-god," his voice rose suddenly and he shook his fist in the direction of the station, "I'll be back. I've done business in this town for years, I've got f-f-f-friends here who are going goddam well to know the reason why a kid is beaten up and locked up with a n-n-nigger by the Blackstone cops. I'll see this f'ing through now if it t-t-t-takes a life-time!" Then, turning to his brother, he said shortly: "All right, Gene. C-c-come on. We're g-g-getting out of town."

Without further speech, they walked on down the street until they came to the place where Luke's car was parked.

"W-w-w-what do you want to d-d-d-do, Gene?" he said quietly. "Do you want to go over to D-d-Daisy's tonight?"

The boy shook his head: "No," he said thickly. "Home. Home. Let's get out of here. Got to go home now."

Luke said nothing for a moment, thrusting his fingers through his hair. "W-w-w-well," he muttered at length, "perhaps you're right."

XLV

THEY left town at once.

Luke drove savagely going out of town. He kept his big clumsy hands gripped hard upon the rim of the steering wheel, his brow knit and furrowed by its ridge of wrinkles, his face taut and drawn from the tension of his nerves. From time to time he would thrust his clumsy fingers strongly through his flashing mass of hair, laugh a wild jeering "whah-whah" of rage and exasperation, and then say in a voice so packed with sneering bitterness and contempt that it was hard to keep from laughing at him:

"S—t! Resisting an officer in the p-p-p-p-performance of his duties! Now ain't that nice?" he said in a voice of mincing refinement and daintiness. "W-w-w-wy the nice neat nigger-Baptist God-damned sons-of-bitches!" he snarled. "The cheap grafting South Car'lina bastards! D-d-d-d-disorderly conduct! S—t!" he snarled with a savage, dainty, mincing bitterness that was somehow wildly and explosively funny.

Meanwhile, they were speeding along through quiet streets that even in the night-time had the worn and faded dustiness of autumn, past withered lawns, by frame houses which had the same faded dusty look, and under trees on which the dry leaves hung and fluttered: the mournful, worn, weary feeling told of departed summer, evoked sadly the memory of a savage heat, and the sorrowful ghosts and omens of the autumn were everywhere about them. October was there with its strange, brooding presences of sorrow and delight—its sense of something lost and vanished, gone forever, its still impending prescience of something grand and wild to come. Above them the ragged cloudy sky had cleared: it was a night of blazing and magnificent stars, set in the limitless velvet substance of the sky, burning with faint brilliance and without light over the immense, mysterious, and mournful-looking earth.

Twice, going out of town, his brother stopped, and both times with a kind of sudden indecisive after-thought. Once, when they had passed a little corner drug-store, he jammed the breaks on suddenly, bringing the car to such an abrupt and jolting halt that Eugene was flung forward violently against the wind-shield. He turned to him with a nervous and distracted air of indecision, saying:

"Do you f-f-f-fink you could go a dope?" (this was the word in common use for Coca Cola) "W-w-w-would you like a drink?" he said, with a comical thrusting movement of the head, a wild look in his eyes, a restless and stammering indecision and earnestness. The boy told him no, and after a worried and restless look of his flickering gray eyes, in the direction of the drug store, he thrust his large flat foot into the clutch and started the car in motion again, with the same violent and jarring movement as when he had halted.

Again, on the very outposts of the town, where there was nothing but the dusty road, a few cheap frame houses, sparely, flimsily, and carelessly built upon the breast of an immense and formless land, which seemed indifferent to them and with which they seemed to have no union, and with nothing but the road, the stars and the huge mysteries of the earth before them, his brother had halted with another jarring jolt, when they had flashed past a filling station where, so read a sign, soft drinks and barbecued sandwiches were for sale.

"How about a b-b-b-barbecued sandwich?" he demanded, looking at Eugene with a wild and glaring suddenness. "C-c-c-could you go one? Huh?"—he said, almost barking at him, with a comical thrusting movement of the head. But even before the boy could answer, and he saw the sullen and exasperated scowl upon his face, he thrust his fingers wildly through his hair, burst into a wild rich "whah-whah" of crazy laughter —a laughter that was all the more strange and astonishing because even as he laughed, the taut and drawn tension of his face and nerves, and the frenzied unrest of his eyes, were terribly apparent—and then started the car in motion again with a jarring, grinding and convulsive jolt. And Luke could not have said why he had halted at these last two outposts of the town—the drug store and the filling station—but certainly the impulse that had made him halt, had little to do with food or drink, for neither of them was hungry, and they had no need or desire for further nourishment.

But the impulse which had made his brother halt belonged to all the dissonance and frenzied unrest of his whole life, and by thousands of actions such as this, the course and pattern of his life was shaped. And finally, his brother had halted because those two small flares of light—pitiful and shabby as they were—had wakened in him a memory of the vast darkness of the huge and lonely earth before them, and because he gave himself into this dark regretfully, and with some misgiving of his soul.

For his spirit was afraid of solitude and darkness and, like all men in this land, his soul was drawn by the small hard blaze of incandescence —even by those barren bulbous clusters of hard light upon the wintry midnight pavements of a little town—which somehow pitifully and terribly suggest the fear and loneliness in men's souls, the small hard assurances of manufactured light which they have gathered as some beacon of comfort and security against a dark too vast and terrible, an earth too savage in its rudeness, space, and emptiness, for the spirit and the strength of men.

And now his brother and he were given to this earth, this dark, this loneliness again. And as they rushed on into the darkness, held, save for the throbbing motor of the little car, in the immutable silence of the earth and darkness, the flickering headlights of the car would suddenly pierce into the huge surrounding mystery of night, lunging for an instant the flashing finger of their light upon some fugitive and secret presence in the vault of night, where all the million lives of men were held. Sometimes, the flashing light would blaze upon the boarding of a little house at the bend of the road, and then the house would flash behind and be engulfed in darkness.

Sometimes, it would reveal the brown and dusty stubble of the cotton fields, a stretch of ragged pine, a lonely little wooden church, a shack, a cabin, the swift and sinuous forking of another road that spoked into their own, flashed past, and curved away—was gone forever—leaving an instant and intolerable pain and memory—a searing recognition and discovery—a road once seen but never followed and now forever lost with all its promises of a life that they had never known or explored, of faces they had never seen.

And again, out of this huge and mournful earth, out of the limitless mystery of this continent of night, the lights upon his brother's car would for an instant pick out faces, shapes, and people, and they, too, would blaze there for a moment in our vision with an intolerable and lonely briefness, and then be lost forever—and in that moment of instant parting and farewell was written the history of man's destiny—his brother's life, and that of all men living on the earth around him.

Once their lights picked out the figure of a country negro: his weary plodding figure loomed up for an instant dustily—a mournful image of bowed back, shapeless garments stained with red field earth, and clumsy brogans coated with the red dust of the road, plodding along against a terrific and desolate landscape of brown cotton fields, clay, and lonely pine, as much a part of it as the earth he walked upon, fixed instantly into it in a vision of labor, sorrow, and destiny, that was eternal.

And again they passed by negroes coming from a country church, and for a moment saw their white eyes and their black and mournful faces staring towards the light, and lost these, too, forever, and passed into a little town and out again, and saw far-off, and at its edges, a pollen of bright light above a little travelling carnival, and heard the sad wheeling music of the carousel, the mixed and woven clamor of the barker's cries, the shouts, the people's voices, and all far-faint and lost and mournful as a dream; and then the earth again—the two back wheels, clay-caked and rattling, of an ancient buggy, the lifting hooves of an old boneyard nag, that slowly turned away from the road's centre to make way for them, the slow, staring, stupid looks of wonder and astonishment of a young country fellow and his girl as they went by them—and finally, always and forever, nothing but the earth—that mournful, desolate, and lonely earth of cotton fields, and raw red clay and lonely pine, wheeling past forever in rude and formless undulations, immemorable, everlasting, and terrific, above which the great stars blazed their imperturbable and inscrutable messages of deathless calm.

And as they rushed ahead into the dark, he thought of the hundreds of times his brother had hurled himself along this road at night alone, going furiously from nowhere into nowhere, rushing ahead with starlight shining on his knit brows and his drawn face, with nothing but the lonely, mournful, and desolate red-clay earth about him, the immense, the merciless emptiness and calm of the imperturbable skies above him. And he wondered if there was anywhere on earth a goal for all his frenzy and unrest, some final dwelling-place of certitude and love for all his wandering, or if he must hurl furiously along in darkness beneath these stars forever—lost, unassuaged, and driven—until the immense and mournful earth should take him once again.

The ride back up into the hills with Luke was cold, dark, bleak, and desolate—the very painting of his own sick soul. Black night had come when they had reached the mountains. The stars were out, and around them the great bulk of the hills was barren, bleak, and wintry-looking, and there was the distant roaring of demented winds upon the hills, the lonely preludes of grim winter among the barren trees. Already, it seemed, the same landscape which only a day or two before had flamed with all the blazing colors of October, and with the enchantment which his hope and joy had given it, had been sorrowfully transformed by the mournful desolation of coming winter. The earth was no longer beautiful and friendly: it had become a waste, a desert, and a prison bleak and bare.

During the ride up the mountain into Old Catawba, the two brothers spoke seldom to each other. Luke, who had made that dark journey up into the hills a thousand times—for whom, in fact, this ceaseless hurtling along dark roads had become the very pattern of the unrest and fury that lashed his own life on forever—drove hard and raggedly, communicating perfectly to ʰe machine he drove the tension and dissonance of his own tormented spirit. This wordless instrument of steel and brass and leather seemed, in fact, to start, halt, jolt, stammer, and lunge fiercely onward as if it had a brain and spirit of its own that was in anguished sympathy with the tortured nerves that governed it. His brother drove, bent forward tensely, his large clumsy hands gripped hard and nervously upon the steering wheel, as he peered out upon the ribbon of road before him, which bent and twisted in a bewildering serpentine that curved constantly upward along the slopes and flanks of the dark mountainside. The boy sat cold and numb and sick at heart, hands thrust in pockets, his hat pulled low across his eyes, his overcoat turned up around his neck. He glanced at his brother once or twice. He could see his face drawn and taut and furrowed in the dim light, but when he tried to speak to him he could not. The sense of ruin, shame, and failure which filled his spirit seemed so abysmal and complete that there was nothing left to say. And he faced the meeting with his mother and his sister with a sick heart of dread.

Once going up the mountainside his brother stopped, jamming his huge flat foot so rudely onto the brake that the car halted with a jarring shuddering thud. They had just passed a road of unpaved clay which led off from the mountain road towards the right, and towards a farm house and a light or two which were clearly visible.

Now, looking nervously and uncertainly toward this house, Luke muttered, almost to himself, thrusting his hand through his hair with a distracted movement as he spoke: "Wy-wy-wy-I f'ink we could g-g-g-get a drink in here wy—if you'd like one. Wy-wy-I know the old fellow who lives there . . . he's a moonshiner—wy-wy-I f'ink—would you like to stop?" he said abruptly and then, getting no answer from the younger one, he gave another worried and uncertain look in the direction of the house, thrust his fingers through his hair, and muttered to himself "W-w-w-well, perhaps you're right—maybe it's j-j-j-just as well if we g-g-g-get home wy-wy-wy I guess that Mama will be waiting up for us."

When they reached town, the hour was late, the streets had a wintry, barren, and deserted look, and the lights burned dim: from time to time another motor car would flash by them speedily, but they saw few people. As they drove across the Square, it seemed almost to have been frozen in a cataleptic silence, the bulbous clusters of the street lamps around the Square burned with a hard and barren radiance—a ghastly mocking of life, of metropolitan gaiety, in a desert scene from which all life had by some pestilence or catastrophe of nature been extinguished. The fountain in the square pulsed with a cold breezeless jet, and behind the greasy windows of a lunch room he could see a man in a dim light, seated on a stool and drinking coffee, and the swart muscular Greek leaned over the counter, his furrowed inch of brow painfully bent upon the columns of a newspaper.

As they turned into the street where stood his mother's house, and sloped swiftly down the hill toward home, his brother, in a tone that tried in vain to be matter-of-fact, and to conceal the concern and pain which his own generous spirit felt because of the feeling of defeat, failure, and desperation which was now legible in every word and gesture of the younger one, began to speak to him in a nervous, almost pleading voice:

"N-n-now I f'ink," he began, thrusting his big hand through his hair, —"I—wy I f'ink when we get home wy—I just wouldn't say anything to Mama about—wy-wy about that trouble—wy—that we had in Blackstone—wy—at all!" he blurted out. "Wy—f-f-f-frankly, I mean it!" he continued earnestly, as he brought the car to a jolting halt before the

house. "Wy-wy—if I were in your p-p-place, Gene—wy I'd just forget it.
. . . It's all over now—and it would only worry M-m-m-mama if you
t-t-told her about it— Wy-wy—the whole f'ing's over now . . . those—
wy—those cheap Nigger-Baptist South Car'lina sons-of-bitches—wy-wy
—just saw the chance of m-m-making a martyr of you—so I'd j-j-just forget about it— It's all over now— Wy-wy—f-f-f-forget it!" he cried earnestly. "I—I—wy I wouldn't f'ink about it again!"

But the younger one, seeing the light that burned warmly behind the
drawn shades of the parlor, set his sick heart and his grim face desperately towards the light, shook his head silently, and then walked grimly
towards the house.

He found his mother and his sister seated together in the parlor before the fire. In another moment, almost before their first startled
words of greeting were out of their mouths, he was blurting out the
story of his drunkenness, arrest, and imprisonment. As he went on, he
could see his mother's face white, serious, eagerly curious, fixed upon
him, and her powerful, deliberate, and curiously flexible mouth which
she pursed constantly, darting her eyes at him from time to time with
the quick, startled attentiveness of an animal or a bird, as she said
sharply: "Hah? . . . What say? . . . The police, you say? . . . Jail?
. . . Who was with you—hah? Emmet Blake? . . . Weaver? . . .
How much did they fine you—hah?"

Meanwhile his sister sat listening quietly, with an absent yet intent
look in her eyes, stroking her large cleft chin in a reflective manner with
her big hand, smiling a little, and saying from time to time:

"Ah-hah? . . . and what did Blake say then? . . . What did you say
to the nigger when you saw him in the cell? . . . Ah-hah. . . . They
didn't abuse you, did they? . . . Did they hurt you when they hit you?
. . . Ah-hah. . . . And what did Luke say when he saw you looking
through the bars?" She snickered hoarsely, and then taking him by the
hand, turned to her mother and in a kindly yet derisive tone, said:

"Here's your Harvard boy. . . . What do you think of your baby
now?" And seeing the gloomy and miserable look upon his face, she
laughed her high, husky, and derisive falsetto, prodding him in the ribs
with her big finger, saying: "K-k-k-k! . . . This is our Harvard boy!
. . . Hi, hi, hi, hi, hi! . . . Here's your baby son, Miss Eliza!" Then
releasing his hand, and turning to her mother, she said in a good-natured tone, in which yet a kind of melancholy satisfaction was evident:

"Well, you see, don't you? . . . It just goes to show you, doesn't it? . . . I knew it all the time. . . . It just goes to show that we're all the same beneath the skin. . . . We're all alike. . . . We all like the stuff . . . with all his book education and going off to Harvard, he's no different from Papa, when you come down to it," she concluded with a note of sombre brooding satisfaction in her voice.

"Wy-wy-wy—" he could see Luke teetering nervously from one huge flat foot to another, thrusting his huge hand distractedly through his flashing hair as he attempted to stammer out an earnest and excited defense and justification for his disgrace:

"Wy-wy-wy I don't believe that Gene was drunk at all!" he stammered. "Wy I f'ink wy—that he j-j-j-just had the bad luck to wy to f-f-f-fall in with that gang when they were drinking and and and—wy I f'ink those wy those B-B-B-B-Blackstone bastards just saw a chance wy of collecting a wy a little graft and and and wy j-j-just made Gene the goat. Wy f-f-f-frankly I don't believe he was drunk at all. . . . Wy I doubt it very much," he said, thrusting his fingers through his hair. "F-f-f-frankly, I do."

"I was drunk!" the boy muttered sullenly and miserably. "Drunker than any of them. . . . I was the worst of the lot."

"You see, don't you?" his sister said again to her mother in a weary, kindly, yet triumphant tone. "You see what happens, don't you? . . . I've known it. . . . I've known it all the time," she said with sombre satisfaction. ". . . No, sir," she shook her head with a movement of emphatic conviction, as if some one had disputed her argument, "you can't change them! . . . You can't change the leopard's spots. . . . Murder will out. . . . You can't tell me!" she cried again, shaking her head in a movement of denial. "Blood is thicker than water. But you see, don't you?" she said again with this curiously kindly yet triumphant satisfaction; and then added illogically: "This is what comes of going to Harvard."

And his mother, who had been following this broken and almost incoherent discourse of his brother and sister with the quick, startled darting and attentive glances of an animal or a bird, now said nothing. Instead she just stood looking at him, her broad worn hands held at the waist for a moment in a loose strong clasp, her face white and stern, and her mouth pursed in a strong pucker of reproach. For a moment it seemed that she would speak, but suddenly her worn brown eyes were hot with tears, she shook her head at him in a strong, convulsive and almost imperceptible tremor of grief and disappointment, and turning quickly with a rapid awkward movement of her short figure, she went out of the room as fast as she could, slamming the door behind her.

When she had gone, there was silence for a minute, save for the gaseous flare and crumble of the coal-fire in the grate, and the stertorous, nervous and uneasy labor of Luke's breath. Then his sister turned to him, and looking at him with eyes which had grown dead and lustreless, and in a tone that was full of the sombre and weary resignation that was now frequent when she spoke, she said: "Well, forget about it. She'll get over it. . . . You will, too. . . . It's done now, and it can't be helped. . . . So forget it. . . . I know, I know," she said with a sombre, weary, and fatal resignation as she shook her head. "We all have these great dreams and big ambitions when we're twenty. . . . I know. . . . I had them, too. . . . Don't break your heart about it, Gene. . . . Life's not worth it. . . . So forget it. . . . Just forget about it. . . . You'll forget," she muttered, "like I did."

Later that night, when his sister had departed for her home and his brother had gone to bed, he sat with his mother in the parlor looking at the fire. Blundering, stumbling incoherently, he tried desperately to reassure her, to tell her of his resolution to expiate his crime, to retrieve his failure, somehow to justify her in the faith and support she had given him. He spoke wildly, foolishly, desperately, of a dozen plans in progress, promising everything, swearing anything, and sure of nothing. He told her he was ready to go to work at once, to do any work that he could find—like a drowning man he clutched wildly at a dozen straws—he would get a job on the paper as a reporter; he would teach school; there were great sums of money to be made from advertising, he had a friend in that profession, he was sure he would succeed there; he felt sure that Professor Hatcher could get him placed at some small college teaching drama and play-writing courses; some one had told him he could find employment editing the little magazine or "house organ" of a department store in the city; a friend at college had secured employment as librarian of an ocean liner; another made large sums of money selling floor-mops and brushes to the housewives of the Middle West—he blurted out the foolish and futile projects feverishly, clutching at straw after straw, and halted abruptly, baffled by her silence, and by the sudden sickening realization that he no longer had a straw to clutch at—how foolish, futile, feeble all these projects were!

As for his mother, she sat staring straight into the fire, and made no answer. Then, for a long time, he sat there melancholy, saying nothing, while the woman looked straight ahead, hands clasped across her waist, looking into the fire with a fixed stare of her white face and puckered mouth. At length she spoke:

. . . "I have brought them all into the world," she said quietly, "and seen them all grow up . . . and some are dead now . . . and some have done nothing with their lives. . . . You were the youngest, and the last . . . my only hope. . . . Oh, to see them all, all go the same way . . . to hope and pray year after year that there would be one of them who would not fail—and now!" her voice rose strongly, and she shook her head with the old convulsive tremor, "to think that you—the one on whom my hope was set—the one who has had the education and the opportunity that the others never had—should go the way that the others went. . . . It's too bad to bear!" she cried, and suddenly burst into tears. "Too much to ask of me!" she whispered huskily, and suddenly drew the sleeve of the old frayed sweater across her weak wet eyes, with the pathetic gesture of a child—a gesture that tore him with a rending anguish of pity, shame, and inexpiable regret. "Too hard . . . too hard," she whispered. "Surely there's a curse of God upon us if after all the pain and sorrow all are lost."

And he sat there, sick with shame, self-loathing and despair, unable to reply. And then he heard again the remote demented howling of the wind, the creaking of bare boughs, the vast dark prowling of the beast of night about his mother's house. And again he heard, as he had heard a thousand times in childhood, far, faint, and broken by the wind, the wailing whistle of a distant train. It brought to him, as it had brought to him so many times, the old immortal promises of flight and darkness, the golden promises of morning, new lands and a shining city. And to his sick and desperate soul, the cry of the great train now came with a sterner and more desperate hope than he had ever known as a boy. Suddenly he knew that now there was one road, and only one before him— flight from this defeat and failure which his life had come to, redemption by stern labor and grim loneliness, the stern challenge, the sharp peril and the grand reward—the magic and undying image of the city. And suddenly he knew that he would go.

The night before he went away he went out and prowled restlessly about the streets of the town until the hour was very late. A letter from a friend had informed them that there was hope of a teaching appointment at one of the city universities, later, when the spring term began. Meanwhile, a swift exchange of telegrams had promised him temporary employment in New York, soliciting funds from alumni of his university, for a memorial building. And uncertain, specious, and disheartening as this employment seemed to him, he had eagerly seized the offer when it came. He was leaving home the next day.

Now, sick of soul and driven by the unquiet heart, the furious unrest, he prowled the barren night-time streets of his native town. The Square was bleak and lifeless and deserted, with its hard glare of lights: along the main street of the town a few belated citizens hurried past from time to time, faces and voices he remembered from his childhood, driven by like ghosts. Everything he saw and touched was strange and familiar as a dream—a life which he had known utterly and which now vanished from his grasp whenever he approached it—his forever, buried in his blood and memory, never to be made his own again.

When he returned home, it was after midnight, and his mother's old gaunt house was dark. He went quietly up the steps and into the broad front hallway, closing the heavy door quietly behind him. For a minute he stood there in that living dark, the ancient and breathing darkness of that old house which seemed to speak to him with all the thousand voices of its vanished lives—with all the shapes and presences of things and people he had known, who had been there, and who had passed or vanished, or had died.

Then quietly he groped his way along the dark old hallway, and towards the kitchen, and the little room beyond in which his mother slept.

When he got to the kitchen the room was dark, save for the soft flare and crumble of the fading ashes in the old coal range. But the kitchen was still warm, with a curious and recent currency of warmth and silence, as if it were still filled with his mother's life, and as if she had just been there.

He turned on the light and for a minute stood looking at the familiar old table with its sheathing of ragged battered zinc, and at the ironing board with its great stack of freshly ironed and neatly folded linen; and he knew that she had worked there late.

Suddenly, a desperate urge, an overmastering desire to see her, speak to her, awoke in him. He thought that if he could only see her now, he could reveal himself to her, explain the purpose of his failure, the certainty of his success. He was sure that now, if ever, he could speak to ner, and say the things he had always wished to say, but never said—speak the unspeakable, find a tongue for the unspoken language, make her understand his life, his purpose, and his heart's desire, as he had never done before. And filled with this wild hope, this impossible conviction, he strode towards the closed door of her little room to rouse her.

Then abruptly, he paused. Upon an old cupboard, in a glass half-filled with water, he saw, as he had seen a thousand times, grinning at him with a prognathous, a strangely human bleakness, the false teeth she had put there when she went to bed. And suddenly he knew he could not speak to her. For grotesque, ugly, and absurd as they were, those grinning teeth evolved for him, somehow, as nothing else on earth could do, the whole image of his mother's life of grief and toil and labor—the intolerable memories of the vanished and the irrevocable years, the strange and bitter miracle of life. And he knew then that he could not speak, that there was nothing he could say to her.

He rapped gently at the door, and in a moment heard her voice, quick, sharp, and startled, roused from sleep, saying: "Hah? . . . what say? . . . who's there?"

He answered: in a moment she opened the door and stood there, her face startled, curiously small and white and sunken, somehow like a child's. When he spoke to her, she answered incoherently: and then she smiled in an apologetic and embarrassed manner, and covered her mouth shyly with one hand, while she extended her other for the glass that held her teeth. He turned his head away: when he looked again her face had taken on its familiar contour, and she was saying in her usual tone: "Hah? . . . What is it, son?" "Nothing, Mama," he said awkwardly. "I —I didn't know you were asleep . . . I—I—just came in to say goodnight, Mama."

"Good-night, son," she said, and turned her white cheek up to him. He kissed it briefly.

"Now go and get some sleep," she said. "It's late and you've all your packing to do yet when you get up tomorrow."

"Yes," he said awkwardly. ". . . I guess you're right. . . . Well, good-night." And he kissed her again.

"Good-night," she said. "Turn out the lights, won't you, before you go to bed."

And as he turned the kitchen light out, he heard her door close quietly behind him, and the dark and lonely silence of the old house was all around him as he went down the hall. And a thousand voices—his father's, his brothers', and of the child that he himself had been, and all the lives and voices of the hundred others, the lost, the vanished people, were whispering to him as he went down the old dark hall there in his mother's house. And the remote demented wind was howling in the barren trees, as he had heard it do so many times in childhood, and far off, far-faint and broken by the wind, he heard the wailing cry of the great train, bringing to him again its wild and secret promises of flight and darkness, new lands, and a shining city. And there was something wild and dark and secret in him that he could never utter. The strange and bitter miracle of life had filled him and he could not speak, and all he knew was that he was leaving home forever, that the world, the future of dark time, and of man's destiny lay before him, and that he would never live here in his mother's house again.

BOOK IV

PROTEUS: THE CITY

XLVI

As the train was pounding north across New Jersey, another train upon the inside track began to race with it, and for a distance of ten miles the two trains thundered down the tracks in an even, thrilling, and tremendous contest of steel and smoke and pistoned wheel that blotted out everything, the vision of the earth, the thought of the journey, the memory of the city, for all who saw it.

The other train, which was bound from Philadelphia, appeared so calmly and naturally that at first no one suspected that a race was on. It came banging up slowly, its big black snout swaying and bucking with a clumsy movement as it came on, its shining pistons swinging free and loose, and with short intermittent blasts of smoke from its squat funnel. It came up so slowly and naturally, past their windows, that at first it was hard to understand at what terrific speed the train was running, until one looked out of the windows on the other side and saw the flat, formless and uncharactered earth of New Jersey whipping by like pickets on a fence.

The other train came slowly on with that huge banging movement of the terrific locomotive, eating its way up past the windows, until the engine cab was level with Eugene and he could look across two or three scant feet of space and see the engineer. He was a young man cleanly jacketed in striped blue and wearing goggles. He had a ruddy color and his strong pleasant face, which bore on it the character of courage, dignity, and the immense and expert knowledge these men have, was set in a good-natured and determined grin, as with one gloved hand held steady on the throttle, he leaned upon his sill, with every energy and perception in him fixed with a focal concentration on the rails. Behind him his fireman, balanced on the swaying floor, his face black and grinning, his eyes goggled like a demon, and lit by the savage flare of his terrific furnace, was shovelling coal with all his might. Meanwhile, the train came on, came on, eating its way past, foot by foot, until the engine cab had disappeared from sight, and the first coaches of the train drew by.

And now a wonderful thing occurred. As the heavy rust-red coaches of the other train came up and began to pass them, the passengers of both trains suddenly became aware that a race between the trains was taking place. A tremendous excitement surged up in them, working its instant magic upon all these travellers, with their gray hats, their gray, worn city faces, and their dull tired eyes, which just the moment before had been fastened wearily on the pages of a newspaper, as if, having been hurled along this way beneath the lonely skies so many times, the desolate face of the earth had long since grown too familiar to them, and they never looked out windows any more.

But now the faces that had been so gray and dead were flushed with color, the dull and lustreless eyes had begun to burn with joy and interest. The passengers of both trains crowded to the windows, grinning like children for delight and jubilation.

Eugene's train, which for a space had been holding its rival even, now began to fall behind. The other train began to slide past the windows with increasing speed, and when this happened the joy and triumph of its passengers were almost unbelievable. Meanwhile their own faces had turned black and bitter with defeat. They cursed, they muttered, they scowled malevolently, they turned away with an appearance of indifference, as if they had no further interest in the thing, only to come back again with a fascinated and bitter look as their accursed windows slid by them with the inevitability of death and destiny.

Throughout, the crews of the two trains had shown as keen and passionate an interest, as intense a rivalry, as had the passengers. The conductors and porters were clustered at the windows or against the door in the car-ends, and they grinned and jeered just as the rest of them had done; but their interest was more professional, their knowledge more intimate and exact. The conductor on the train would say to the porter —"Whose train is that? Did you see John McIntyre aboard?" And the Negro would answer positively, "No, sah! Dat ain't Cap'n McIntyre. Ole man Rigsby's got her. Dere he is now!" he cried, as another coach moved past, and the grizzled and grinning face of an old conductor came in sight.

Then the conductor would go away, shaking his head, and the Negro would mutter and chuckle to himself by turns. He was a fat enormous darkey, with an ink-black skin, a huge broad bottom, teeth of solid grinning white, and with a big fatty growth on the back of his thick neck. He shook like jelly when he laughed. Eugene had known him for years because he came from his native town, and the Pullman car in which he rode, which was known as K 19, was the car that always made the journey of 700 miles between his home town and the city. Now the Negro sprawled upon the green upholstery of the end seat in the Pullman and grinned and muttered at his fellows in the other train.

"All right, boy. All right, you ole slew-footed niggah!" he would growl at a grinning darkey in the other train. "Uh! Uh!" he would grunt ironically. "Don't you think you's somp'n, dough! You's pullin' dat train yo'self, you is!" he would laugh sarcastically, and then sullenly and impatiently conclude, "Go on, boy! Go on! I sees you! I don't care how soon I loses you! Go on, niggah! Go on! Git dat ugly ole livah-lipped face o' yo'n out o' my way!"

And that grinning and derisive face would also vanish and be gone, until the whole train had passed them, pulled ahead of them, and vanished from their sight. And their porter sat there staring out the window, chuckling and shaking his head from time to time, as he said to himself, with a tone of reproof and disbelief:

"Dey ain't got no right to do dat! Dey ain't got no right to run right by us like we wasn't here!" he chuckled. "Dey ain't nothin' but a little ole Philadelphia local! Dey're not supposed to make de time we is! We's de Limited! We got de outside rail!" he bragged, but immediately, shaking his head, he said: "But Lawd, Lawd! Dat didn't help us none today. Dey've gone right on by us! We'll never ketch dem now!" he said mournfully, and it seemed that he was right.

Eugene's train was running in free light and open country now, and the passengers, resigned finally to defeat, had settled back into their former dozing apathy. But suddenly the train seemed to start and leap below them with a living energy, its speed increased visibly, the earth began to rush by with an ever-faster stroke, the passengers looked up and at one another with a question in their eyes, and an awakened interest.

And now their fortune was reversed, the train was running through the country at terrific speed, and in a moment more they began to come up on the rival train again. And now, just as the other train had slid by them, they began to walk by its windows with the calm imperious stride of their awakened and irresistible power. But where, before, the passengers of both trains had mocked and jeered at one another, they now smiled quietly and good-naturedly, with a friendly, almost affectionate, interest. For it seemed that they—the people in the other train—now felt that their train had done its best and made a manful showing against its mighty and distinguished competitor, and that they were now cheerfully resigned to let the Limited have its way.

And now their train walked up past the windows of the dining-car of the other: they could see the smiling white-jacketed waiters, the tables covered with their snowy-white linen and gleaming silver, and the people eating, smiling and looking toward them in a friendly manner as they ate. And then they were abreast the heavy parlor cars: a lovely girl, blonde-haired, with a red silk dress, and slender shapely legs crossed carelessly, holding an opened magazine face downward in one hand, and with the slender tapering fingers of the other curved inward towards her belly where they fumbled with a charm or locket hanging from a chain, was looking at them for a moment with a tender and good-natured smile. And opposite her, with his chair turned towards her, an old man, dressed elegantly in a thin, finely-woven and expensive-looking suit of gray, and with a meagre, weary, and distinguished face that had brown spots upon it, was sitting with his thin phthisic shanks crossed, and for a moment Eugene could see his lean hands, palsied, stiff, and folded on his lap, and the brown spots on them; and he could see a corded, brittle-looking vein upon the back of one old hand.

And outside there was the raw and desolate-looking country, there were the great steel coaches, the terrific locomotives, the shining rails, the sweep of the tracks, the vast indifferent dinginess and rust of colors, the powerful mechanical expertness, and the huge indifference to suave finish. And inside there were the opulent green and luxury of the Pullman cars, the soft glow of the lights, and people fixed there for an instant in incomparably rich and vivid little pictures of their life and destiny, as they were all hurled onward, a thousand atoms, to their journey's end somewhere upon the mighty continent, across the immense and lonely visage of the everlasting earth.

And they looked at one another for a moment, they passed and vanished and were gone forever, yet it seemed to him that he had known these people, that he knew them better than the people in his own train, and that, having met them for an instant under immense and timeless skies, as they were hurled across the continent to a thousand destinations, they had met, passed, vanished, yet would remember this forever. And he thought the people in the two trains felt this, also: slowly they passed each other now, and their mouths smiled and their eyes grew friendly, but he thought there was some sorrow and regret in what they felt. For, having lived together as strangers in the immense and swarming city, they now had met upon the everlasting earth, hurled past each other for a moment between two points in time upon the shining rails, never to

meet, to speak, to know each other any more, and the briefness of their
days, the destiny of man, was in that instant greeting and farewell.

Therefore, in this way, they passed and vanished, the coaches slipped
away from them until again they came up level with the cab of the
other locomotive. And now the young engineer no longer sat in his high
window with a determined grin, and with his hard blue eyes fixed on
the rail. Rather, he stood now in the door, his engine banging away
deliberately, slowed down, bucking and rocking loosely as they passed.
His attitude was that of a man who has just given up a race. He had
turned to shout something at his fireman who stood there balanced, arms
akimbo, black and grinning, as they moved up by them. The engineer
had one gloved hand thrust out against the cab to support him, he held
the other on his hip and he was grinning broadly at them, with solid
teeth edged with one molar of bright gold—a fine, free, generous, and
good-humored smile, which said more plain than any words could do:
"Well, it's over, now! You fellows win! But you'll have to admit we
gave you a run for your money while it lasted!"

Then, they drew away and lost the train forever. And presently their
own train came in to Newark, where it stopped. And suddenly, as
Eugene was looking at some Negroes working there with picks and
shovels on the track beside the train, one looked up and spoke quietly
to the fat porter, without surprise or any greeting, as casually and naturally as a man could speak to some one who has been in the same room
with him for hours.

"When you comin' back dis way, boy?" he said.

"I'll be comin' back again on Tuesday," said the porter.

"Did you see dat ole long gal yet? Did you tell huh what I said?"

"Not yet," the porter said, "but I'll be seein' huh fo' long! I'll tell yo'
what she says."

"I'll be lookin' fo' you," said the other Negro.

"Don't fo'git now," said the fat black porter, chuckling; and the train
started, the man calmly returned to work again; and this was all. What
that astounding meeting of two black atoms underneath the skies, that
casual incredible conversation meant, he never knew; but he did not
forget it.

And the whole memory of this journey, of this race between the trains,
of the Negroes, of the passengers who came to life like magic, crowding
and laughing at the windows, and particularly of the girl and of the vein

upon the old man's hand, was fixed in Eugene's brain forever. And like everything he did or saw that year, like every journey that he made, it became a part of his whole memory of the city.

And the city would always be the same when he came back. He would rush through the immense and glorious stations, murmurous with their million destinies and the everlasting sound of time, that was caught up forever in their roof—he would rush out into the street, and instantly it would be the same as it had always been, and yet forever strange and new.

He felt as if by being gone from it an instant he had missed something priceless and irrecoverable. He felt instantly that nothing had changed a bit, and yet it was changing furiously, unbelievably, every second before his eyes. It seemed stranger than a dream, and more familiar than his mother's face. He could not believe in it—and he could not believe in anything else on earth. He hated it, he loved it, he was instantly engulfed and overwhelmed by it.

He brought to it the whole packed glory of the earth—the splendor, power, and beauty of the nation. He brought back to it a tremendous memory of space, and power, and of exultant distances; a vision of trains that smashed and pounded at the rails, a memory of people hurled past the window of his vision in another train, of people eating sumptuously from gleaming silver in the dining cars, of cities waking in the first light of the morning, and of a thousand little sleeping towns built across the land, lonely and small and silent in the night, huddled below the desolation of immense and cruel skies.

He brought to it a memory of the loaded box-cars slatting past at fifty miles an hour, of swift breaks like openings in a wall when coal cars came between, and the sudden feeling of release and freedom when the last caboose whipped past. He remembered the dull rusty red, like dried blood, of the freight cars, the lettering on them, and their huge gaping emptiness and joy as they curved in among raw piney land upon a rusty track, waiting for great destinies in the old red light of evening upon the lonely, savage, and indifferent earth; and he remembered the cindery look of road-beds, and the raw and barren spaces in the land that ended nowhere; the red clay of railway cuts, and the small hard lights of semaphores—green, red, and yellow—as in the heart of the enormous dark they shone, for great trains smashing at the rails, their small and passionate assurances.

He brought to it the heart, the eye, the vision of the everlasting

stranger, who had walked its stones, and breathed its air, and, as a
stranger, looked into its million dark and driven faces, and who could
never make the city's life his own.

And finally he brought to it the million memories of his fathers who
were great men and knew the wilderness, but who had never lived in
cities: three hundred of his blood and bone, who sowed their blood and
sperm across the continent, walked beneath its broad and lonely lights,
were frozen by its bitter cold, burned by the heat of its fierce suns,
withered, gnarled, and broken by its savage weathers, and who fought
like lions with its gigantic strength, its wildness, its limitless savagery
and beauty, until with one stroke of its paw it broke their backs and
killed them.

He brought to it the memory and inheritance of all these men
and women who had worked, fought, drunk, loved, whored, striven,
lived and died, letting their blood soak down like silence in the earth
again, letting their flesh rot quietly away into the stern, the beautiful,
the limitless substance of the everlasting earth from which they came,
from which they were compacted, on which they worked and wrought
and moved, and in whose immense and lonely breast their bones were
buried and now lay, pointing eighty ways across the continent.

Above the pounding of the mighty wheels their voices had seemed to
well out of the everlasting earth, giving to him, the son whom they had
never seen, the dark inheritance of the earth and the centuries, which was
his, even as his blood and bone were his, but which he could not fathom:

"Whoever builds a bridge across this earth," they cried, "whoever lays
a rail across this mouth, whoever stirs the dust where these bones lie, let
him go dig them up, and say his Hamlet to the engineers. Son, son," their
voices said, "is the earth richer where our own earth lay? Must you
untwist the vine-root from the buried heart? Have you unrooted man-
drake from our brains? Or the rich flowers, the big rich flowers, the
strange unknown flowers?

"You must admit the grass is thicker here. Hair grew like April on
our buried flesh. These men were full of juice, you'll grow good corn
here, golden wheat. The men are dead, you say? They may be dead,
but you'll grow trees here; you'll grow an oak but we were richer than
an oak: you'll grow a plum tree here that's bigger than an oak, it will
be all filled with plums as big as little apples.

"We were great men and mean men hated us," they said. "We were
all men who cried out when we were hurt, wept when we were sad,

drank, ate, were strong, weak, full of fear, were loud and full of clamor, yet grew quiet when dark came. Fools laughed at us and witlings sneered at us: how could they know our brains were subtler than a snake's? Because they were more small, were they more delicate? Did their pale sapless flesh sense things too fine for our imagining? How can you think it, child? Our hearts were wrought more strangely than a cat's, full of deep twistings, woven sinews, flushing with dull and brilliant fires; and our marvellous nerves, flame-tipped, crossed wires too intricate for their fathoming.

"What could they see," the voices rose above the sound of the wheels with their triumphant boast, "what could they know of men like us, whose fathers hewed the stone above their graves, and now lie under mountains, plains, and forests, hills of granite, drowned by a flooding river, killed by the stroke of the everlasting earth? Now only look where these men have been buried: they've heaved their graves up in great laughing lights of flowers—do you see other flowers so rich on other graves?

"Who sows the barren earth?" their voices cried. "We sowed the wilderness with blood and sperm. Three hundred of your blood and bone are recompacted with the native earth: we gave a tongue to solitude, a pulse to the desert, the barren earth received us and gave back our agony: we made the earth cry out. One lies in Oregon, and one, by a broken wheel and horse's skull, still grips a gunstock on the Western trail. Another one has helped to make Virginia richer. One died at Chancellorsville in Union blue, and one at Shiloh walled with Yankee dead. Another was ripped open in a bar-room brawl and walked three blocks to find a doctor, holding his entrails thoughtfully in his hands.

"One died in Pennsylvania reaching for a fork: her reach was greater than her grasp; she fell, breaking her hip, cut off from red rare beef and roasting-ears at ninety-six. Another whored and preached his way from Hatteras to the Golden Gate: he preached milk and honey for the kidneys, sassafras for jaundice, sulphur for uric acid, slippery-ellum for decaying gums, spinach for the goitre, rhubarb for gnarled joints and all the twistings of rheumatism, and pure spring water mixed with vinegar for that great ailment dear to Venus, that makes the world and Frenchmen kin. He preached the brotherhood and love of man, the coming of Christ and Armageddon by the end of 1886, and he founded the Sons of Abel, the Daughters of Ruth, the Children of The Pentateuch, as well as twenty other sects; and finally he died at eighty-four, a son of the Lord, a prophet, and a saint.

"Two hundred more are buried in the hills of home: these men got land, fenced it, owned it, tilled it; they traded in wood, stone, cotton, corn, tobacco; they built houses, roads, grew trees and orchards. Wherever these men went, they got land and worked it, built upon it, farmed it, sold it, added to it. These men were hill-born and hill-haunted: all knew the mountains, but few knew the sea.

"So there we are, child, lacking our thousand years and ruined walls, perhaps, but with a glory of our own, laid out across three thousand miles of earth. There have been bird-calls for our flesh within the wilderness. So call, please, call! Call the robin red-breast and the wren, who in dark woods discover the friendless bodies of unburied men!

"Immortal land, cruel and immense as God," they cried, "we shall go wandering on your breast forever! Wherever great wheels carry us is home—home for our hunger, home for all things except the heart's small fence and dwelling-place of love.

"Who sows the barren earth?" they said. "Who needs the land? You'll make great engines yet, and taller towers. And what's a trough of bone against a tower? You need the earth? Whoever needs the earth may have the earth. Our dust, wrought in this land, stirred by its million sounds, will stir and tremble to the passing wheel. Whoever needs the earth may use the earth. Go dig us up and there begin your bridge. But whoever builds a bridge across this earth, whoever lays a rail across this mouth, whoever needs the trench where these bones lie, let him go dig them up and say his Hamlet to the engineers."

So had their hundred voices welled up from the earth and called to him, their son and brother, above the pounding of the mighty wheels that roared above them. And the memory of their words, their triumphant tongue of deathless silence, and the full weight of the inheritance they had given him, he brought back again out of the earth into the swarming canyons and the million tongues of the unceasing, the fabulous, the million-footed city.

And all that he had seen, all that he remembered of this earth he brought to the city, and it seemed to be the city's complement—to feed it, to sustain it, to belong to it. And the image of the city, written in his heart, was so unbelievable that it seemed to be a fiction, a fable, some huge dream of his own dreaming, so unbelievable that he did not think that he should find it when he returned; yet it was just the same as he had remembered it. He found it, the instant he came out of the station: the tidal swarm of faces, the brutal stupefaction of the street, the immense and arrogant blaze and sweep of the great buildings.

It was fabulous and incredible, but there it was. He saw again the million faces—the faces dark, dingy, driven, harried, and corrupt, the faces stamped with all the familiar markings of suspicion and mistrust, cunning, contriving, and a hard and stupid cynicism. There were the faces, thin and febrile, of the taxi drivers, the faces cunning, sly, and furtive, the hard twisted mouths and rasping voices, the eyes glittering and toxic with unnatural fires. And there were the faces, cruel, arrogant and knowing of the beak-nosed Jews, the brutal heavy figures of the Irish cops, and their red beefy faces, filled with the stupid, swift, and choleric menaces of privilege and power, shining forth terribly with an almost perverse and sanguinary vitality and strength among the swarming tides of the gray-faced people. They were all there as he remembered them—a race mongrel, dark, and feverish, swarming along forever on the pavements, moving in tune to that vast central energy, filled with the city's life, as with a general and dynamic fluid.

And, incredibly, incredibly! these common, weary, driven, brutal faces, these faces he had seen a million times, even the sterile scrabble of harsh words they uttered, now seemed to be touched by this magic of now and forever, this strange and legendary quality that the city had, and to belong themselves to something fabulous and enchanted. The people, common, dull, cruel, and familiar-looking as they were, seemed to be a part, to comprise, to be fixed in something classic, and eternal, in the everlasting variousness and fixity of time, in all the fabulous reality of the city's life: they formed it, they were part of it, and they could have belonged to nothing else on earth.

And as he saw them, as he heard them, as he listened to their words again, as they streamed past, their stony gravel of harsh oaths and rasping cries, the huge single anathema of their bitter and strident tongues dedicated so completely, so constantly, to the baseness, folly, or treachery of their fellows that it seemed that speech had been given to them by some demon of everlasting hatred only in order that they might express the infamy and vileness of men, or the falseness of women—as he listened to this huge and single tongue of hatred, evil, and of folly, it seemed incredible that they could breathe the shining air without weariness, agony, and labor—that they could live, breathe, move at all among the huge encrusted taint, the poisonous congestion of their lives.

And yet live, breathe, and move they did with a savage and indubitable violence, an unfathomed energy. Hard-mouthed, hard-eyed, and strident-tongued, with their million hard gray faces, they streamed past upon the streets forever, like a single animal, with the sinuous and baleful convolutions of an enormous reptile. And the magical and shining air—the strange, subtle and enchanted weather, was above them, and the buried men were strewn through the earth on which they trod, and a bracelet of great tides was flashing round them, and the enfabled rock on which they swarmed swung eastward in the marches of the sun into eternity, and was masted like a ship with its terrific towers, and was flung with a lion's port between its tides into the very maw of the infinite, all-taking ocean. And exultancy and joy rose with a cry of triumph in his throat, because he found it wonderful.

Their voices seemed to form one general City-Voice, one strident snarl, one twisted mouth of outrage and of slander bared forever to the imperturbable and immortal skies of time, one jeering tongue and rumor of man's baseness, fixed on the visage of the earth, and turned incredibly, and with an evil fortitude, toward depthless and indifferent space against the calm and silence of eternity.

Filled with pugnacious recollection that Voice said, " 'Dis guy,' I says, 'dis friend of yoehs,' " it said, " 'dis bastad who owes me fawty bucks—dat yuh introduced me to—when's he goin' t' giv'it to me?' I says." And derisive, scornful, knowing, it would snarl: *"W'ich guy? W'ich guy do yuh mean? Duh* guy dat used to come in Louie's place?" And bullying and harsh it would reply: *"Yuh* don't know? Watcha mean yuh don't know!" . . . Defiant, *"Who* don't know? . . . *Who* says so? . . . *Who* told yuh so?" And jeering, "Oh *dat* guy! . . . Is *dat* duh guy yuh mean? An' wat t' hell do *I* care wat he t'inks, f'r Chris' sake! . . . To hell wit' him!" it said.

Recounting past triumphs with an epic brag, it said: " 'You're comin' out of dere!' I said. 'Wat do you t'ink of dat?' . . . 'Oh, yeah,' he says, 'who's goin' t' make me?' So I says, 'You hoid me—yeah! . . . You're goin' to take dat little tin crate of yoehs right out of deh! You'll take yoeh chance right on duh line wit' all duh rest of us!' . . . 'Oh, yeah,' he says. . . . 'You hoid me, misteh'—an' he went!" In tones of ladylike refinement, it recounted romance into ravished ears as follows: " 'Lissen,' I says, 'as far as my boss is consoined it's bizness only. . . .

An' as far as Mr. Ball is consoined it's my own bizness' (hah! hah! hah! Y'know that's wat I tol' him. . . . Jeez: it handed him a laugh, y'know!)—'An afteh five o'clock,' I says, 'I'm my own boss. . . . At duh same time,' I says, 'deh's duh psychological side to be considehed.'"

And with the sweet accent of maternal tribulation, it admitted, "Sure! I hit her! I did! Oh, I hit her very hahd! Jeez! It was an awful crack I gave her, honestleh! My hand was boinin' f'r a half-oueh aftehwads! . . . I just blow up, y' know! . . . Dat's my on'y reason f'r dat! I jus' blow up! Dis fellah's in duh bathroom callin' f'r his eggs, duh baby's yellin' f'r his bottle, an' I jus' blow up! . . . Dat's my on'y reason f'r *dat!* Dat's duh on'y reason dat I hit her, see? I'm afraid she'll hoit duh baby, see? She bends its fingehs back. So I says, 'F'r God's sake, please, don't do dat! . . . I gotta headache' . . . an' then, I jus' blow up! Sure! I hit her hahd! . . . Duh trouble is I can't stop wit' one slap, see! . . . Jeez! I hit her! My hand was boining f'r a half-oueh aftehwads!"

Hot with its sense of outraged decency, it said, "I went upstairs an' pounded on dat doeh! . . . 'Come out of dere, you s of a b,' I says— Sure, I'm tellin' yuh! Dat's what I said to her, y' know! . . . 'Come out of dere,' I says, 'before I t'row you out,'" and regretfully it added, "Sure! I hate to do dese t'ings—it makes me feel bad lateh—but I won't have dem in my place. Dat's duh one t'ing I refuse t' do," it said. And with a passionate emotion, it asserted, "Sure! . . . Dat's what I'm tellin' yuh! . . . Yuh know how dat was, don't cha? Duh foist guy—her husban'— was passin' out duh sugah an' duh otheh guy—duh boy-friend—was layin' her. Can yuh ima-a-gine it?" it said.

Amazed, in tones of stupefaction, it would say "No kiddin'! *No!*" And with solemn reprehension it would add, "Oh, yuh know I think that's te-e-ri-bul! I think that's aw-w-ful!"—the voice of unbelieving horror would reply.

Finally, friendly and familiar, the great Voice of the city said, "Well, so long, Eddy. I'm goin' t' ketch some sleep," it said, and answered, "Well, so long, Joe, I'll be seein' yuh." "So long, Grace," it added with an accent of soft tenderness and love, and the huge Voice of the city murmured, "O. K. kid! Eight o'clock—no kiddin'—I'll be deh!"

Such were some of the million tongues of that huge single Voice, as he had heard them speak a thousand times, and as now instantly, incredibly, as soon as he came back to them, they spoke again.

And as he listened, as he heard them, their speech could not have been more strange to him had they been people from the planet Mars

He stared gape-mouthed, he listened, he saw the whole thing blazing in his face again to the tone and movement of its own central, unique, and incomparable energy. It was so real that it was magical, so real that all that men had always known was discovered to them instantly, so real he felt as if he had known it forever, yet must be dreaming as he looked at it; therefore he looked at it and his spirit cried:

"Incredible! Oh, incredible! It moves, it pulses like a single living thing! It lives, it lives, with all its million faces"—and this is the way he always knew it was.

XLVII

THAT year—the first year that he lived there in the city—he was twenty-three years old. After these months of frenzy, drunkenness, and arrest, he was at the last gasp of his resources, and the eighteen hundred dollars a year, which was his salary at the university that had employed him as an instructor, seemed to him a wage of princely munificence—a stroke of incredible good fortune.

And although his position as instructor had been given to him in one of the usual ways, through the recommendation of the teachers' bureau at Harvard University, and the letters of some of the professors there, he was tortured constantly by the thought of his inadequacy and ignorance, and by the horrible fear that his incompetence would be discovered and that one day he would be suddenly, peremptorily, ruinously, and disgracefully discharged.

At night, when he went to bed in his little cell at the cheap little hotel nearby where he lived, the thought of the class he had to meet the next day fed at his heart and bowels with cold poisonous mouths of fear, and as the hour for a class drew nigh he would begin to shake and tremble as if he had an ague; the successive stages of his journey from his room in the Leopold, to the class room at the university a few hundred yards away—from cell to elevator, from the tiled sterility of the hotel lobby to the dusty beaten light and violence of the street outside, thence to the brawling and ugly corridors of the university, which drowned one, body and soul, with their swarming, shrieking, shouting tides of dark amber Jewish flesh, and thence into the comparative sanctuary of the class room with its smaller horde of thirty or forty Jews and Jewesses, all laughing, shouting, screaming, thick with their hot and swarthy body-smells, their strong female odors of rut and crotch and arm-pit and cheap perfume, and their hard male smells that were rancid, stale, and sour—the successive stages of this journey were filled with such dazed numbness, horror, fear, and nauseous stupefaction as a man might feel in the successive stages of a journey to the gallows, the guillotine, or the electric chair: the world swarmed blindly, nauseously, drunkenly about him. He looked at the faces in the hotel lobby, the brawling, furious, and chaotic street, and the swarming and rancid corridors, with dizzy swimming eyes and a constricted heart; a thousand unutterable and horrible premonitions and imaginings of ruin and shame swarmed through his mind—every day he felt the impending menace of some new and fatal catastrophe, some indefinable and crushing disgrace with which each hour was ominously, murderously pregnant.

What these fears and forebodings were he could not have told, but they occasionally found articulate expression in some scene of frightful insubordination and rebellion, in which he found himself faced with forty brawling, mocking, swarthily jeering faces who, like savage and untamed horses that have sensed the fear and incompetence of their driver, have now broken the last feeble thread of restraint and are running free and wild before him. The terror and menace of such a disgrace was heightened by the intrusion into the scene at the apex of such a moment of riot and rebellion, of one of his employers, the Dean, the head of the department, or a creature with a wry lean face, a convulsive Adam's apple, a habit of writhing his lean belly and loins erotically as he spoke, and a mind of the most obscene puritanism, who was employed to oversee the work and methods of the instructors: he could visualize the moment of their fatal entrance into the class-room, and hear their words of stern, curt and immediate dismissal as they drove him out and gathered the reins strongly into their own parched and freckled hands.

A thousand such images of disgrace and terror swarmed through his mind, and at the same time there began to smoulder in his heart a dogged resentment and hatred of this nameless fear, this wordless and sourceless shame, impalpable, causeless, maddening, which pressed upon him from the sky, which hovered in the vast unrest and dissonance of the air he breathed, and which at length crept poisonously through all the rivers of life, corrupting the healthy music of the blood, the sweet exultant music of the heart, curdling men's bowels with fear and withering their loins with sterile impotence. What was this gray lipless shape of fear that stalked their lives incessantly—that was everywhere, legible in the faces, the movements, and the driven frenzied glances of the people who swarmed on the streets. What was this thing that duped men out of joy, tricked them out of all the exultant and triumphant music of the world, drove them at length into the dusty earth, cheated, defrauded, tricked out of life by a nameless phantom, with all their glory wasted?

Already, in the city, he had begun to see how life was duped and menaced by this cheat: a thousand images of cruelty, violence, cowardice and dishonor swarmed about him in the streets. As the sparkling and winey exultancy of October, with its grand and solemn music of death and life, of departure and return, moved on into the harsh, raw, green implacability of winter, one could observe the death of joy and hope, the barometric rise of hate and fear and venom in the city's life: it got into the faces of the people, it wasted their flesh and corrupted their blood, it glittered in the eyes of the instructors at the university, their flesh got green and yellow with its poisons, the air about them was webbed, cross-webbed, and counter-webbed with the dense fabric of their million spites and hatreds. They wasted and grew sick with hate and poison because another man received promotion, because another man had got his poem printed, because another man had eaten food and swallowed drink and lain with women, and lived and would not die; they sweltered with hate and fear against the professors who employed them—they grew pale and trembled, and spoke obsequiously when their employer passed, but when the man had gone, they whispered with trembling lips: "Has he spoken to you yet? . . . Has he said anything to you yet about next year? . . . Are you coming back next year? . . . Did he say anything to you about *me* next year? . . ." They greeted him with sly humility and a servile glance, but they snickered obscenely at him when his back was turned. And they smiled and sneered at one another with eyes that glittered with their hate: they never struck a blow but they spoke lying words of barbed ambiguity, they lied, cheated, and betrayed, and they sweltered in the poisons of their hate and fear, they breathed the weary hatred-laden air about them into their poisoned lungs.

Around him in the streets, again, as winter came, he heard a million words of hate and death: a million words of snarl and sneer and empty threat, of foul mistrust and lying slander: already he had come to see the poisonous images of death and hatred at work in the lives of a million people—he saw with what corrupt and venomous joy they seized on

But if he retreated daily, out of this savage and unequal struggle with the Herculean forces of the city, if he returned trembling, beaten and exhausted to the hermitage of his own small cell, it was with no sense of final defeat, no desire for ultimate escape. His pride and fury grew from every beating that they got, his faith grew stubborn on adversity, his spirit fed upon humiliation, and spat into the face of failure, his soul plunged darkly to the sea-floor of blind horror, swarming desolation, and came up dripping with a snarl of hatred and defiance: daily they beat him with their blind appalling mass, daily they drove him livid, shaking, blind with horror, back into his cell, so stunned and stricken by the savage, obscene, and mindless fury of the streets that he could no longer think, feel, or remember; and hour by hour his soul swam upwards out of the jungles of the sea! And every night, the merciful anodyne of dark restored him; sunk deep, at length, in midnight, beastwise aprowl in all the brooding silence of the night, his spirit swept out through the fields of sleep, he heard the heartbeats of six million men: within their million cells sleep crossed the faces of six million sleepers and in the night-time, in the dark, in all the living silence of the night, the sleeping faces of Snodgrass, Weisberg, and O'Hare were strange and dark as his. He saw the city with the great giant webbing of its thousand streets, he heard the long deep notes of warning and departure, from the great ships in the harbor; and then he saw the city as a whole, six million sleepers celled in sleep and walled in night, and girdled by the bracelet of two flashing sea-borne tides that isled them round: he held them legible as minted gold within his hand, he saw them plain as apples in the adyts of his brain. Exultant certitude and joy welled up in him, and he knew that his hunger could eat the earth, his eye and brain gulp down the vision of ten thousand streets, ten million faces, he knew he should beat and eat them all one day, and that a man was more than a million, stronger than a wall, and greater than a door, and taller than a ninety-storey tower.

They swept around him on the rootless pavements in drowning tides of gray abomination, of numberless depth and horror, and like the memory of a bird-song in the wood, the memory of all his people who had lived and died alone for two hundred years within the wilderness, and whose buried bones were pointing eighty ways across the continent, returned to him in a rush of savage resolution, and he swore that he would beat death and nothingness and all the abominations of a sterile and nameless fear: he swore it with a sick heart, a trembling lip, and

ing of six stori
more simple in
the rough, po
of the new ar
compact, and
how gave the
of its kind, by
speak, how or i
mechanic spirit
"the 'twenties,

It was hard to
how it left one
parent at once
superior to its
combined simp
England do—it
ingless adornm
Moreover, the r
integrity: it wa
one did—the ot
oration, were th

What was it?
new annex" or
was unmistakal
stance which h
sterile, and inh
blind proliferati
number in the
the nameless, fa

The transient
The great tidal
newly wedded c
out for a spree or
in unceasing mo
life of the Leop
little remote fro
largely for its cu
was, in short, th
hotel"—a phrase

a nauseous gut in which the rancid wash of a sour distressful coffee growled and rumbled queasily—for in those months, this sense of nameless fear and dread, impending ruin, disgrace and menace, was so great each time he went to meet a class, its damnable victory over all the clean and healthful music of the flesh, the exultant joy of thirst and hunger, so complete and devastating, that he was unable to touch a mouthful of food for hours in advance.

Thus, while a thousand such images of disgrace and terror swarmed through his mind, he stood before each class on a small raised platform three or four inches in height, trembling on limbs from which every vital essence of blood and bone and marrow had been drained, staring at the faces that seethed and swarmed below him, with dead glazed eyes, nauseous, and sick, and palsied, left only with something clear and small and shining at the bottom of his mind, one pure small note of conviction and belief at the bottom of this horrible sea-depth of phantasmagoric chaos, of desolation and fury. Then, in a voice that was remote, unreal, and hollow in his throat and ears, he would attempt to silence them, he would begin to speak to them, and one by one, each in his accustomed place he would see the dark, ugly, grinning faces in their seats below him and become aware of the pale sweatshop tailors sitting cross-legged on their tables in the buildings just across the street—buildings which the university was acquiring as class-rooms, year by year, and one by one, as the numberless thousands of these dark and brawling hordes, there by God knows what blind fantasticality of purpose, increased.

And then, faint and far, sunken below the furious glare and clamor of the city's life, fantastic and unreal at first in these machine shops of the brain, the old words, the undying words, the deathless bird-song in the city street returned, and he spoke to them again out of the lips of Herrick, Donne, and Shakespeare, of all the things that never change, of all the things that would abide forever.

"When to the sessions of sweet silent thought I summon up remembrance of things past—" Clang—a lang—a lang—a lang a lang! Hard and harsh with the violence of an unexpected blow, the bell that marked the ending of the period rang pat upon the last word of the sentence and as it died, all of his senses rudely shocked out of the potent enchantments of the music, he gave a violent start, as if he had been prodded from behind, stopped reading, and looked up quickly from his book with an angry and bewildered face. The class, which had tittered, now

This d
structor:
his class.
"If any
choked w
for at thi:
slowly th
paused a
legible up
the door,
class wait
opened, a
of the hal
choly and
sagging f
neck, sur
glance fu
come, as
the face
For a r
stupefact
plosive,
welled u
laughter
"Get o
away! L

THE H
and grim
the direc
The L
single bu
block. T
twelve st
seems to
left was
annex."
floor was

This, indeed, seemed to be the truth about them: as they sat together in one corner of the lobby talking, all their conversation seemed made up of dreary dialogs such as these:

"How do you do, Mrs. Grey? I didn't see you in the restaurant to-night."

"No—" the old woman spoke triumphantly, proudly conscious of a sensational adventure—"I ate out tonight at a new place that my son-in-law told me about!—Oh! I had the most *dee*-licious meal—a *won*-derful meal—all any one could eat and only sixty cents. First I had a dish of nice fruit salad—and then I had a bowl of soup—oh-h! *dee*-licious soup, Mrs. Martin—it was vegetable soup, but oh-h! *dee*-licious!—a whole meal in itself—and then—" with a ruminant satisfaction she continued her arid catalogue— "I had some nice lamb chops, and some *dee*-licious green peas—and a nice baked potato—and some salad—and some rolls and butter—and then I had a nice cup of coffee—and a piece of apple pie—oh-h! the apple pie was simply *dee*-licious, Mrs. Martin, I had——"

"I'd think you'd be getting hungry by that time," said another of the group, an old man, who was their humorist, with a wink around him at the others. They all laughed appreciatively, and he continued: "You're sure you didn't miss anything as you went along—" he winked again and they all laughed dryly, with appreciation.

"No, sir!"—firmly, positively, with an emphatic nod of the head—"I ate every bite of it, Doctor Withers—oh-h it was so *dee*-licious, I just couldn't bear to see *anything* go to waste—only," regretfully, "I did have to leave my apple pie—I couldn't finish it——"

"What!" the humorist exclaimed in mock astonishment. "You mean you left something behind! Why you hardly ate enough to feed an elephant! You'll be getting all run down if you starve yourself this way!"—and the jester winked again, and the old women of his audience cackled aridly with appreciative laughter.

"—Well, I know," the glutton said regretfully, "I just hated to see that good apple pie go to waste—oh-h! I wish you could have tasted it, Mrs. Martin,—it was simply *dee*-licious— 'What's the matter?' the girl says to me—the waitress, you know— 'Don't you like your pie?—I'll go get you something else if you don't like it.'—Oh! yes—" with sudden recollection —"oh, yes! she says to me, 'How'd you like some ice cream?—You can have ice cream instead of pie,' she says, 'if you'd rather have it'— 'Oh-h!' I said,"—spoken with a kind of gasp, the withered old hand upon the meagre stomach— " 'Oh-h!' I says, 'I couldn't!'—She had to laugh, you know, I guess the way I said it. 'Well, you got enough?' she said. 'Oh-h!' I said,"—again the faint protesting gasp, " 'if I ate another mouthful, I'd pop open! Oh-h!'—Well, it made her laugh, you know, the way I said it—'I'd *pop* open!' I said 'I *couldn't* eat another mouthful!'—'Well, just so long as you got enough!' she says. 'We like to see every one get enough. We want you to be satisfied,' she said. 'Oh-h!' I said," the faint protesting gasp again, " 'not another *mouthful, my* dear! I *couldn't!'*—But, oh-h! Mrs. Martin, if you could have seen that apple pie! It was *dee*-licious! I was sorry to see it go to waste!"

"Well," said Mrs. Martin, rather tartly, obviously a little envious of the other's rich adventure— "we had a good meal here at the hotel, too. We had some celery and olives to start off with and then we had some good pea soup and after that we had roast beef and mashed potatoes— wasn't the roast beef we had tonight delicious, Doctor Withers?" she demanded of this arbiter of taste.

"Well," he said, smacking his dry lips together drolly, "the only complaint I had to make was that they didn't bring me the whole cow. I had to ask George for a second helping. . . . Yes, sir, if I never fare any worse than that I'll have no kick—it was a very good piece of beef— well-cooked, tender, very tasty," he said with a dry, scientific precision, and again he smacked his leathery lips together with an air of relish.

"—Well, I thought so, too," said Mrs. Martin, nodding her head with satisfaction at this sign of his agreement "—I thought it was delicious— and then," she went on reflectively, "we had a nice lettuce and tomato salad, some biscuit tortoni and, of course," she concluded elegantly, "the demy-tassy."

"Well, I didn't have any of the demy-tassy," said Doctor Withers, the droll wit. "None of your demy-tassy for me! No, sir! I had *coffee*—two big cups of it, too," he went on with satisfaction. "If I'm going to poison myself I'm going to do a good job of it—none of your little demy-tassys for me!"

And the old women cackled aridly their dry appreciation of his wit.

"—Good evening, Mrs. Buckles," Doctor Withers continued, getting up and bowing gallantly to a heavily built, arthritic-looking old woman who now approached the group with a stiff and gouty movement. "We missed you tonight. Did you eat in the restaurant?"

"No," she panted in a wheezing tone, as, with a painful grunt, she lowered her heavily corseted bulk into the chair he offered her. "I didn't go down—I didn't have much appetite and I didn't want to risk it. I had them bring me something in my room—some tea and toast and a little marmalade . . . I didn't intend to come down at all," she went on in a discontented tone, "but I got tired of staying up there all alone and I thought I'd just as well—I'd be just as well off down here as I'd be up in my room," she concluded morosely.

"And how *is* your cold today, Mrs. Buckles?" one of the old women now asked with a kind of lifeless sympathy. "—Do you feel better?"

"—Oh," the old woman said morosely, uncertainly, "I suppose so. . . . I think so. . . . Yes, I think it's a little better. . . . Last night I was afraid it was getting down into my chest but today it feels better— seems to be more in my head and throat— But I don't know," she muttered in a sullen and embittered tone, "it's that room they've given me. I'll always have it as long as I've got to live there in that room. I'll never get any better till I get my old room back."

"Did you do what I told you to do?" asked Doctor Withers. "Did you go and dose yourself the way I told you?"

"—No—well," she said indefinitely, "I've been drinking lots of water and trying a remedy a friend of mine down at the Hotel Gridly told me about—it's a new thing called Inhalo, all you got to do is put it up your nose and breathe it in—she said it did her more good than anything she'd ever tried."

"I never heard of it," said Doctor Withers sourly. "Whatever it is, it won't cure your cold. No, sir!" He shook his head grimly. "Now, I didn't practice medicine for forty years without finding out *something* about colds! Now I don't care anything about your Inhalos or Breathos or Spray-Your-Throatos, or whatever they may call 'em—any of these new-fangled remedies. The only way to get rid of a cold is to have a thorough cleaning-out, and the only way to get a thorough cleaning-out is to dose yourself with castor oil, the way I told you, too.—Now you can do as you please," he said sourly, with a constricted pressure of his thin convex mouth, "it's no business of mine what you do—if you want to run the risk of coming down with pneumonia it's your own affair— but if you want to get over that cold you'll take my advice."

"Well," the old woman muttered in her tone of sullen discontent. "—It's that room I'm in. That's the trouble. I've hated that room ever since they put me in there. I know if I could get my old room back I'd be all right again."

"Then why don't you ask Mr. Betts to give it back to you?" said Mrs.

Martin. "I'm sure if you went to him and told him that you wanted it, he'd let you have it."

"No, he wouldn't!" said Mrs. Buckles bitterly. "I've been to him—I've asked him. He paid no attention to me—tried to tell me I was better off where I was, that it was a better room, a better bargain!—Here I've been living at this place for eight years now, but do you think they show me any consideration? No," she cried bitterly, "they're all alike nowadays—out for everything they can get—it's grab, grab, grab—and they don't care who you are or how long they've known you—if they can get five cents more from some one else, why, out you go! . . . When I came back here from Florida last spring I found my old room taken. . . . I went to Mr. Betts a dozen times and asked to have it back and he always put me off—told me there were some people in there who were leaving soon and I could have it just as soon as they moved out. . . . That was all a put-up job," she said resentfully. "He didn't mean a word of it. I see now that he never had any intention of giving me my old room. . . . No! They've just found that they can get a dollar or two more a week for it from these fly-by-nights than I could afford to pay— and so, of course, I'm the one that gets turned out!" she said. "That's the way it goes nowadays!"

"Well," said Mrs. Martin a trifle acidly, "I'm sure if you went to Mr. Betts in the right way you could get your old room back. He's always done everything I ever asked him to do for *me*. But, of course," she said pointedly, "you've got to approach him in the right way."

"Oh-h!" said old Mrs. Grey rapturously, "I think Mr. Betts is the *nicest* manager they've ever had here—so pleasant, so *good-natured,* so *willing* to oblige! Now that other man they had here before he came— what was his name?" she said impatiently. "—Mason, or Watson, or Clarkson—something like that——"

"Wilson," said Doctor Withers.

"—Oh, yes—Wilson!" said Mrs. Grey. "That's it—Wilson! I never liked him at *all,*" she said with an accent of scornful depreciation. "You could *never* get anything out of Wilson. He never did anything you wanted him to do. But Mr. *Betts!*—oh-h! I think Mr. Betts is a lovely manager!"

"Well, I haven't found him so," said Mrs. Buckles grimly. "I liked Wilson better."

"Oh, I don't agree with you, Mrs. Buckles," Mrs. Gray said with a stony and somewhat hostile emphasis. "I don't ag-*gree* with you at *all!* I think there's no *comparison!* I like Mr. Betts *so* much better than I like Wilson!"

"Well, I like Wilson better," said Mrs. Buckles grimly, and for a moment the two old women glared at each other with bitter hostile eyes.

"—Well," Doctor Withers broke the silence quickly in a diplomatic effort to avert an impending clash, "—what are your plans for the winter, Mrs. Buckles? What have you decided to do? Are you going to Florida again this winter?"

"I don't know what I'll do," old Mrs. Buckles answered in a tone of sullen dejection. "I haven't decided yet. . . . I had planned to go down to Daytona Beach with Mrs. Wheelwright—that's my friend at the Hotel Gridly—she had a daughter living in Daytona, and we had planned to spend the winter there in order to be near them. But now that's all fallen through," she said dejectedly. "Here, at the last moment, when all my plans were made, she decided not to go—says she likes it at the Gridly and it will be cheaper to stay on there than to make a trip to Florida and back. . . . That's the trouble with people nowadays," she said bitterly, "you can't depend on them. They never mean anything they say!" And she lapsed again into a sullen and dejected silence.

"Why aren't you going to St. Petersburg?" said Mrs. Martin curiously after a brief pause. "I thought that's where you always spent the winter."

"It was," said Mrs. Buckles, "until last winter. But I'll never go back there again. It's not the same place any more. I've been going to the same hotel down there for more than twenty years—it used to be a lovely place—when I went back there last winter I found the whole place changed. They had ruined it," she bitterly concluded.

"How was that?" said Doctor Withers curiously. "What had they done to it?"

Mrs. Buckles looked around cautiously and craftily to make sure that in this sinister melting-pot of a million listening ears, she would not be overheard, and then, bending forward painfully, with one old arthritic hand held up beside her mouth, she muttered confidingly to her listeners:

"—I'll tell you what it is. It's the *Jews!* They get in everywhere." she whispered ominously. "They ruin *everything!* When I got down there last winter the whole place was over-run with Jews! They had ruined the place!" she hissed. "The place was *ruined!*"

At this moment, another old woman joined the group. She advanced slowly, leaning on a cane, smiling, and with a movement of spacious benevolence. Everything about this old woman—her big frame, slow movement, broad and tranquil brow, silvery hair parted in the middle, and her sonorous and measured speech, which came deliberately from her mouth in the periods of a cadenced rhetoric, had an imposing and majestical quality. As she approached, every one greeted her eagerly, and with obvious respect, Doctor Withers got up quickly and bent before her with almost obsequious courtesy, she was herself addressed by every one as "Doctor," and her position among them seemed to be one of secure and tranquil authority.

This old woman was known to every one in the hotel as Doctor Thornton. She had been one of the first woman physicians in the country and a few years before, after a long and, presumably, successful practice, she had retired to spend the remaining years of her life in the peaceful haven of the Leopold, and to bestow on man, God, nature and the whole universe around her the cadenced and benevolent reflections of her measured rhetoric. She became, by virtue of this tranquil and majestic authority that emanated from her, the centre of every group, young and old, that she approached. She was known to every one in the hotel, every one referred to her as "a wonderful old woman," spoke of her brilliant mind, her ripe philosophy, and her "beautiful English."

The respect and veneration in which she was held was now instantly apparent as, with a benevolent smile, she slowly approached this company of old people. They greeted her with an eager and excited scraping of chairs, the welcoming tumult of several old voices, speaking eagerly at once: Doctor Withers himself scrambled to his feet, pushed a large chair into the circle and stood by gallantly as, with a slow and stately movement, she settled her large figure into it, and for a moment looked about her over the top of her cane with a tranquil, smiling and benevolent expression.

"*Well,* Doctor!" said Mrs. Grey, almost breathlessly. "Where have you been keeping yourself all day long? We've *missed* you."

The others murmured agreement to this utterance, and then leaned forward with eager attentiveness so as not to miss any of the gems of wisdom which would fall from this great woman's lips.

For a moment Doctor Thornton regarded her interlocutor with an expression of tolerant and almost playful benevolence. Presently she spoke:

"What have *I* been doing all day long?" she repeated in a tone of sonorous deliberation. "Why, my dear, I have been *reading*—reading," she pursued with rhythmical sonority, "in one of my favorite and most cherished volumes."

And instantly there was for all her listeners a sense of some transforming radiance in the universe: an event of universal moment: the Doctor had been reading all day long. They looked at her with an awed stare.

"What," Mrs. Martin nervously began, with a little giggle, "—what was it you were reading, Doctor? It must have been a good book to hold your interest all day long?"

"It was, my dear," said Doctor Thornton sonorously and deliberately. "It *was* a good book. More than that, it was a *great* book—a magnificent work of genius to show us to what heights the mind of man may soar when he is inspired by lofty and ennobling sentiments."

"What was this, Doctor Thornton?" Doctor Withers now inquired. "—Something of Tennyson's?"

"No, Doctor Withers," Doctor Thornton answered sonorously, "it was not Tennyson—much as I admire the noble beauty of his poetry. I was not reading poetry, Doctor Withers," she continued, "I was reading —*prose*," she said. "I was reading—*Ruskin!*" As these momentous words fell from her lips, her voice lowered with such an air of portentous significance that the last word was not so much spoken as breathed forth like an incense of devotion. "*Ruskin!*" she whispered solemnly again.

And although it is doubtful if this name conveyed any definite meaning to her audience, its magical effect upon them was evident from the looks of solemn awe with which they now regarded her.

"—*Ruskin!*" she said again, this time strongly, in an accent of rapturous sonority. "The noble elevation of his thought, the beautiful proportion and the ordered harmony of all the parts, the rich yet simple style, and above all, the sane and wholesome beauty of his philosophy of art—what nobler monument to man's higher genius was ever built, my friends, than he proportioned in *The Stones of Venice*— itself a work of art entirely worthy of the majestic sculptures that it consecrates?"

For a moment after the sonorous periods of that swelling rhetoric had ceased, the old people stared at her with a kind of paralysis of reverent wonder. Then old Mrs. Grey, gasping with a kind of awed astonishment, said:

"Oh-h, Doctor Thornton, I think it's the most *wonderful* thing the way you keep your mind occupied all the time with all these deep and beautiful thoughts you have! I don't see how you do it! I should think you'd get yourself all tired out just by all the *thinking* that you do."

"Tired, my dear?" said Doctor Thornton sonorously, bestowing upon her worshipper a smile of tolerant benevolence. "How can any one grow tired who *lives* and *moves* and *breathes* in this great world of ours? No, no, my dear, do not say *tired*. Rather say *refreshed, rejuvenated,* and *inspired* by the glorious pageant that life offers us in its unending beauty and profusion. Wherever I look," she continued, looking, "I see nothing but order and harmony in the universe. I lift my eyes unto the stars," she said majestically, at the same time lifting her face in a movement of rapturous contemplation toward the ceiling of the hotel lobby, "and feast my soul upon the infinite beauties of God's heaven, the glorious proportion of the sidereal universe. I turn my gaze around me, and everywhere I look I see the noble works that man has fashioned, the unceasing progress he has made in his march upward from the brute, the noble aspiration of his spirit, the eternal labor of his mighty intellect towards a higher purpose, the radiant beauty of his countenance in which all the highest ardors of his soul may be discerned!"

And as she pronounced this sonorous eulogy her glance rested benevolently on old Doctor Withers' soured and wizened features. He lowered his head coyly, as becomes a modest man, and in a moment the rhapsodist continued:

"'What a piece of work is man! How noble in reason! How infinite in faculty! In form, in moving, how express and admirable! In action, how like an angel! In apprehension, how like a God!'"

And having sonorously pronounced Hamlet's mighty judgment, the wonderful old woman, who had herself for thirty years been one of the most prosperous abortionists in the nation, looked benevolently about her at all the specimens of God's choice article who were assembled in the lobby.

Over behind the cigar counter, the vender, a fat Czechish youth with a pale flabby face and dull taffy-colored hair, was industriously engaged in picking his fat nose with a greasy thumb and forefinger. Elsewhere, in another corner of the lobby, three permanent denizens of the Leopold, familiarly and privately known to members of the hotel staff as Crabface Willy, Maggie the Dope, and Greasy Gerty, were sitting where they always sat, in an unspeaking and unsmiling silence.

And at this moment, two more wonder-works of God came in from the street and walked rapidly across the lobby, speaking the golden and poetic language which their Maker had so marvellously bestowed on them:

"Cheezus!" said one of them, a large man with a gray hat and a huge, dead, massive face of tallowy gray which receded in an indecipherable manner into the sagging flesh-folds of his flabby neck— "Cheezus!" he eloquently continued with a protesting laugh that emerged from his tallowy lips in a hoarse expletive mixed with spittle— "Yuh may be right about him, Eddie, but Cheezus!"—again the hoarse protesting laugh. "Duh guy may be all right but Cheezus!—I don't know! If he'd come in dere like duh rest of dem an' let me know about it—but Cheezus!— duh guy may be all right like you say!—but Cheezus! Eddie, I don't know!"

Doctor Thornton bestowed on them the benevolent approval of her glance as they went by and then, turning to her awed listeners again, declared sonorously with a majestic and expressive gesture of her hand:

"Tired? How could one ever grow tired, my friends, in this great world of ours?"

XLIX

AT the end of his classes, the final end, when all had spoken, when that hot wave of life and turbulence had withdrawn, the last clattering foot-falls had echoed away along the corridors, the last loud aggressive voices had faded into silence, leaving, it seemed, an odor of exhaustion, use, and weariness even in the walls, boards and benches of the room, so that the empty classroom had a tired but living presence of fatigue, the indefin-able but sharply felt character of a room with people absent from it, and seemed somehow to relax, settle, and respire with relief and weariness— at this final, fagged, and burned-out candle-end of day, Abraham Jones, as relentless as destiny, would be there waiting for Eugene. He waited there, grim, gray, unsmiling, tortured-looking behind an ominous wink of glasses, a picture of Yiddish melancholy and discontent, and as Eugene looked at him his heart went numb and dead; he hated the sight of him. He sat there now in the front rows of the class like a nemesis of scorn, a merciless censor of Eugene's ignorance and incompetence: the sight of his dreary discontented face, with its vast gray acreage of a pain-ful Jewish and involuted intellectualism, was enough, even at the crest of a passionate burst of inspiration, to curdle his blood, freeze his heart, stun and deaden the fiery particle of his brain, and thicken his tongue to a faltering, incoherent mumble. Eugene did not know what Abe wanted, what he expected, what kind of teaching he thought worthy of him: he only knew that nothing he did suited him, that the story of his inadequacy and incompetence was legible in every line of that gray, dreary, censorious face. He thought of it at night with a kind of horror: the ghoulish head which craned out of a vulture's body swept after him through all the fields of a distressful sleep, a taloned fury filled with croakings of hoarse doom. Never before had Eugene been driven through desperation to such exhausting intensities of work: night by night he sweated blood over great stacks and sheaves of their dull, careless, trivial papers—he read, re-read, and triple-read them, putting in all commas, colons, periods, correcting all faults of spelling, grammar, punctuation that he knew, writing long, laborious comments and criticisms on the back and rising suddenly out of a haunted tortured sleep to change a grade. And at the end, the inexorable end, he was always faced with the menace of Abe's weekly paper: with dread and quaking he tackled it. He wrote the best papers that Eugene got: the grammar was flawless, the spelling impeccable, the vocabulary precise and extensive, the sentences cleanly and forcibly shaped. The thought was sound, subtle, and coherent—by every standard the work was of an extraordinary grade and quality, its merit was unmistakable, and yet Eugene approached a four-page paper with fear and trembling, before he had gone beyond the first paragraph great sobs and groans of weariness and despair were wrung from him, he stamped across the floor with it like a man maddened by an aching tooth; he began again, he flung himself upon the bed, got up and walked again, doused his head in basins of cold water—but it was no use: to read the paper to the end, as he did and must, was weariness and travail of the spirit—it was like eating chalk or trying to suck sweetness out of paving brick, or being drowned in an ocean of dishwater, or forced to gorge oneself on boiled unseasoned spinach. Abe wrote on a great range and variety of subjects and everything he wrote was good: he wrote about the plays of Pirandello, of "Six Characters in Search of an Author," and of "three planes of reality" therein: he estimated and analyzed those three planes with the power of a philosopher, the delicacy of a subtle-souled psychologist, and all of this to Eugene was as weeping and wailing and gnashing of teeth, because it was so good, and he did not know what was wrong, and he could not endure to read it. He could not write upon his papers that he found them intolerably dull unless he knew wherein the reason for that dullness lay, and he did not know the reason: accordingly the highest grade he ever gave to any one—the grade of "A"—was week by week wrung from trembling and reluctant fingers. But no matter what the grade was, or how flattering the comment, Abe protested. Gray, dreary, tortured, discontented, Yiddish, he would be waiting for Eugene at the end of every class, clutching his paper in his impatient fingers, armed and eager for the combat of dispute that was to follow.

The class met at night and they would walk rapidly away together along the empty echoing corridors, and turning clatter down the stairs that led to the main entrance. The vast building was deserted and full of weary echoes: they could hear the solitary clang of an elevator door, and the dynamic hum of its machinery as it mounted. Some one was walking in the big corridor downstairs: they heard the echoing ring of his footsteps on the slick marble flags, and the noisy rattle of a cleaner's bucket on the floor. The whole building was charged with a weary electric quality—with the quality of a light which has gone dim. And the taste and the smell of this weariness was in Eugene's mouth and nostrils; it was as if he had stuck his tongue against a warm but burned-out storage battery; it was like the smell that comes from the wheels of a street car when they have ground around a curve, or like the odor from a smoking hot-box on the fast express. His body also had this feeling of electric weariness, as if the vital currents were exhausted: his flesh felt dry and juiceless, his back was tired, his loins were sterile, the acrid burned-out flavor filled him.

The big ugly building breathed slowly with the fatigue of inanimate objects which have been overcharged with human energy: it was haunted with its tired emptiness, with the absence of the thousands of people who had swarmed through its every part that day with such a clamorous, hot and noisy life. The lifeless air in its passages had been breathed and rebreathed again and again: the walls, the furniture, the floors—every part of the building—seemed to exude this sense of nervous depletion.

As he hurried down the stairs on such an evening with his unshakable companion, his implacable disputant, he hated the building more than he had ever hated any building before: it seemed to be soaked in all the memories of fruitless labor and harsh strife, of fear and hate and weariness, of ragged nerves and pounding heart and tired flesh: the building brooded there, charged with its dreadful burden of human pain, encumbered with its grief; and his hatred for the building was the hatred of a man for the place where he has met some terrible humiliation of the flesh or spirit, or for the room in which a man has seen his brother die, or for the dwelling from which love and the beloved have departed. The ghosts of pain and darkness sat in the empty chairs, the spirits of venom and sterility brooded over the desks: dry hatred and the poison of the brain were seated in the chairs of the instructors; fear trembled in their seats, it made a hateful cold around the heart, it made the bowels queasy, it made swallowing hard, it slithered at the edges of the desk, it fell and crawled and wobbled like a boneless thing. And the gray-faced Jew beside Eugene made the weary lights burn dim: he gave a tongue to weariness, a color to despair.

They hurried down the steps and left the building almost as if they were in flight. The heavy door clanged to behind them making echoes in the halls, they reached the pavement of the Square, and immediately they halted. Here, they were in another world, and their weary bodies drank in a new vitality. Sometimes, on a cold still night in winter, the sky had the peculiarly frosty clarity that comes from a still, biting cold. Above the great vertical radiance and cold Northern passion of New York, it was a-glitter with magnificent stars, it was a-glitter with small pollens, with a jewelled dust of stars that seemed to have been sown drunkenly through heaven, and as Eugene looked his weariness was cleansed out of him at once, he was filled with an overwhelming desire to possess beauty and all things else, and to include all things in him. He would learn to be all things: he would be an artist and he would find a way of living in the maelstrom. The darkness filled him with a sense of power and possession: his spirit soared out over the city, and over the earth, he was no longer afraid of the gray-faced Jew beside him, peace and power and certitude possessed him. He drank the air into his veins in great gulps, he saw the huge walled cliff of the city ablaze with its jewelry of hard sown lights, he knew he could possess it all, and a feeling of joy and victory rushed through his senses.

Under the furious goad of desperation, a fear of failure and disgrace, a sense of loneliness and desolation, and a grim determination to go down into the dust of ruin only when he could no longer lift a hand or draw a breath, he learned his job, and found his life again, he did the labor of a titan, the flesh wasted from his bones, he became a mad, driven zealot, but he was a good teacher, and the day came when he knew he need no longer draw his breath in fear or shame, that he had paid his way and earned his wage and could meet them eye to eye. He took those swarthy swarming classes and looted his life clean for them: he bent over them, prayed, sweated, and exhorted like a prophet, a poet, and a priest—he poured upon them the whole deposit of his living, feeling, reading, the whole store of poetry, passion and belief: he went into the brain of a dullard like a surgeon, and he blew some spark of fire into a glow in even the least and worst of them, but that gray-faced Yiddish inquisitor hung doggedly to his heels, the more he gave, the more Abe wanted; he fed on Eugene's life, enriching his grayness with an insatiate and vampiric gluttony, and yet he never had a word of praise, a sentence of thanks, a syllable of commendation.

Instead he became daily more open in his surly discontent, his sour depreciation; his insolence, unchecked, grew by leaps and bounds, he exulted in a feeling of cruel crowing Jewish mastery over Eugene's bent aching spirit, he walked away with him day by day and his conversation now was one long surly indictment of his class, his teaching, and his competence. Why didn't Eugene give them better topics for their themes? Why didn't they use another volume of essays instead of the one they had, which was no good? Why, in the list of poems, plays, biographies and novels which Eugene had assigned, and which were no good, had he omitted the names of Jewish writers such as Lewisohn and Sholem Asch? Why did he not give each student private "conferences" more frequently, although he had conferred with them until his brain and heart were sick and weary. Why did they not write more expository, fewer descriptive themes; more argument, less narration? Why, in short, did he not do everything in a different way?—the indictment, merciless, insistent, unrelenting, piled up day by day and meanwhile resentment, anger, resolution began to blaze and burn in Eugene, a conviction grew that this could no longer be endured, that no life, no wage, no position was worth this thankless toil and trouble, and that he must make an end of a situation which had become intolerable.

One night, when Abe had accompanied Eugene from the class to the entrance of the hotel, and as he was in the full course and tide of his surly complaint, Eugene stopped him suddenly and curtly, saying: "You don't like my class, do you, Jones? You don't think much of the way I teach, do you?"

Abe was surprised at the question, because his complaint had always had a kind of sour impersonality: it had never wholly dared a final accusatory directness.

"Well," he said in a moment, with a surly and unwilling tone, "I never said that. I don't think we're getting as much out of the class as we should. I think we could get a lot more out of it than we're getting. That's all I said."

"And you have a few thousand suggestions to make, that would improve it? Is that it?"

"Well, I had to tell you how I felt about it," Abe said doggedly. "If you don't like it, I'm sorry. You know we fellows down there have got to pay tuition. And they charge you plenty for it, too! . . . Don't let them kid you!" he said with a derisive and scornful laugh. "That place is a gold mine for some one! The trustees are getting rich on it!"

"Well, I'm not getting rich on it," Eugene said. "I get $150 a month out of it. Apparently you think it's too much."

"Well, we've got a right to expect the best we can get," he said. "That's what we're there for. That's what we're paying out our dough for. You know, the fellows down there are not rich guys like the fellows at Yale and Harvard. A dollar means something to them. . . . We don't get everything handed to us on a silver platter. Most of us have got to work for everything we get, and if some guy who's teaching us is not giving us the best he's got we got a right to kick about it. . . . That's the way I feel about it."

"All right," Eugene said, "I know where you stand now. Now, I'll tell you where I stand. I've been giving you the best I've got, but you don't think it's good enough. Well, it's all I've got and it's all you're going to get from me. Now, I tell you what you're going to do, Jones. You're going out of my class. Do you understand?" he shouted. "You're going now. I never want to see you in my class again. I'll get you transferred, I'll have you put in some other instructor's class, but you'll never come into my room again."

"You can't do that," Abe said. "You've got no right to do that. You've got no right to change a fellow to another class in the middle of the term. I've done my work," he said resentfully, "you're not going to change me. . . . I'll take it to the faculty committee if you do."

Eugene could stand no more: in misery and despair he thought of all he had endured because of Abe, and the whole choking wave of resentment and fury which had been gathering in his heart for months burst out upon him.

"Why, damn you!" he said. "Go to the faculty committee or any other damned place you please, but you'll never come back to any room where

I'm teaching again. If they send you back, if they say I've got to have you
in my class, I quit. Do you hear me, Jones?" he shouted. "I'll not have
you! If they try to force me, I'm through! To hell with such a life! I'll
get down and clean out sewers before I have you in my class again. . . .
Now, you damned rascal," his voice had grown so hoarse and thick he
could hardly speak, and the blind motes were swimming drunkenly before him. ". . . I've had all I can stand from you. . . . Why, you
damned dull fellow. . . . Sitting there and sneering at me day after day
with your damned Jew's face. . . . What are you but a damned dull
fellow, anyway? . . . Why, damn you, Jones, you didn't deserve any
one like me. . . . You should get down on your knees and thank God
you had a teacher half as good as me. . . . You . . . damned . . . *fellow*. . . . You! . . . To think I sweat blood over you! . . . Now, get
away from here!" . . . he yelled. "To hell with you! . . . I never want
to see your face again!"

He turned and started toward the hotel entrance: he felt blind and
weak and dizzy, but he did not care what happened now: after all these
weeks of heavy misery a great wave of release and freedom was coursing
through his veins. Before he had gone three steps Abe Jones was at his
side, clutching at his sleeve, beseeching, begging, pleading: "Say! . . .
You've got the wrong idea! Honest you have! . . . Say! I never knew
you felt like that! Don't send me out of there," he begged earnestly, and
suddenly Eugene saw that his shining glasses had grown misty and that
his dull weak eyes blinked with tears. "I don't want to leave your class,"
he said. "Why, that's the best class that I've got! . . . Honest it is! No
kiddin'! . . . All the fellows feel the same way about it."

He begged, beseeched, and almost wept: finally, when good will had
again been restored between them, he wrung Eugene's hand, laughed
painfully and shyly, and then took off his misted glasses and began to
shine and polish them with a handkerchief. His gray ugly face as he
stood there polishing his glasses had that curiously naked, inept, faded
and tired wistful look that is common to people with weak eyes when
they remove their spectacles; it was a good and ugly face, and suddenly
Eugene began to like Abe very much. He left him and went up to his
room with a feeling of such relief, ease and happiness as he had not
known for months; and that night, unhaunted, unashamed, unpursued
by fears and furies and visions of his ruin and failure for the first time
in many months, he sank dreamlessly, sweetly, deliciously, into the
depths of a profound and soundless sleep.

And from that moment, through every change of fortune, all absence, all return, all wandering, and through the whole progress of his city life, through every event of triumph, ruin, or madness, this Jew, Abe Jones, the first manswarm atom he had come to know in all the desolation of the million-footed city—had been his loyal friend.

It was not the golden city he had visioned as a child, and the gray reptilian face of that beak-nosed Jew did not belong among the company of the handsome, beautiful and fortunate people that he had dreamed about, but Abe was made of better stuff than most dreams are made of. His spirit was as steady as a rock, as enduring as the earth, and like the flash of a light, the sight of his good, gray ugly face could always evoke for Eugene the whole wrought fabric of his life in the city, the whole design of wandering and return, with a thousand memories of youth and hunger, of loneliness, fear, despair, of glory, love, exultancy and joy.

L

ROBERT WEAVER appeared suddenly one night about seven o'clock as Eugene was sitting in the lobby at the Leopold: he had not seen Robert since their arrest. His visit to the hotel was the result of a sudden impulse on Robert's part: immediately, without greeting or any preliminary whatever, he began to ask all sorts of questions about the Leopold —How long had Eugene been there? Did he have a good room and how big was it? How well did he like living at the hotel? Then he insisted that Eugene show him his room. Eugene got his key at the desk and took him up: at the sight of the small room with its piles of books and stacks of student themes Robert burst out laughing. Then he began to ask all manners of questions in a serious and earnest tone— Where was the bathroom?— Eugene showed him— Did they give him plenty of towels?— Eugene told him— How much did he pay?— Eugene said the rent was twelve dollars a week.

He received these answers with an air of astounded surprise, his manner became even more earnest and excited, he began to say, "You don't mean it!" "Well, I'll be damned!" "Well, what do you know about that?"—as if the most astonishing revelations were being made to him. Eugene looked at him with misgiving, because he was obviously caught in the full surge of one of his impulses and, sure enough, all at once he said with an air of complete decision: "Damned if I don't do it! It's the very place I've been looking for all along! Why, look at all you get for

the money! Damnedest bargain I ever heard of! I've just been throwing my money away up there!"—he had been living at the Yale Club—
"Damned if I don't get me a room and move in right away!"

This sudden prospect of having Robert as a neighbor did not attract
the other youth: he was working very hard with his classes and trying
to complete a play he had begun to write, and he had no intention of
becoming the companion or nurse of Robert's drunkenness or the con-
fessor of his fevered despair and unrest: he told him he would not like
the Leopold, that the people were old and stodgy, and the rules of propriety very strict. Further, he made the mistake of emphasizing the difficulty of getting a room there, although there really was no difficulty: he
told him the place was a quiet family hotel, that the management wanted
regular tenants of quiet habits who intended to live there permanently,
that the preference was given to middle-aged married couples, and that
there were no vacancies anyway—that a long list of applicants were
waiting to get in. All this merely whetted Robert's eagerness: he
now said that he fulfilled all the requirements save marriage, and that
this deficiency would soon be remedied: he said he had completely re-
formed his old habits of life, and that a quieter, steadier, more sober and
industrious man did not exist: he said he was determined to live there,
and he demanded that Eugene take him to the manager and plead for
him without delay.

When Eugene saw that he was really determined, he agreed: they
went downstairs to see the manager. He came out of his office with the
habitual defensive look of caution and suspicion on his sour meagre
face, and listened with his usual unwilling and disparaging air, not facing them or directly looking at them, but with his small parsley face
averted and his eyes turned downward, while Eugene praised up Robert
to the skies, said he had known him all his life, that he was the scion
of an ancient and distinguished family in the South, a brilliant young
attorney in a New York firm, and one of the steadiest and most proper
youths that ever lived. Robert also put in from time to time with his
deep voice and impressive manners, and at length Mr. Gibbs began to
shake his head dubiously, to say he didn't know, to tell how difficult it
was to get admitted to the Leopold—until Eugene almost laughed in his
face—but that in a case like this, because it was Eugene and he knew if
he recommended a man he must be all right, and so on—he would see
what he could do: he began to thumb over the pages of a meaningless
ledger, peering at it and squinting along his parched finger as it moved

across the page and chattering and mumbling like a monkey: at length he straightened with an air of decision, took four or five keys from their boxes and gave them to the negro captain with instructions "to show this gentleman these rooms." They all got into the elevator and went upstairs again with Robert and the negro: they looked at several rooms and at length, after great indecision, appeals for advice and guidance, and innumerable questions, Robert selected a room in the old annex—a selection for which the other youth was grateful, since his own room was in the new one.

Robert moved in promptly the next day: they had dinner together; he was in a state of jubilant elation. Then no more was seen or heard of him for a week; when Eugene did get news of him it was neither welcome nor reassuring. The phone in his room rang one morning as he was dressing: a voice from the office asked him curtly to see Mr. Gibbs when he came down. He went downstairs with a sense of ominous misgiving: Mr. Gibbs came toward him with a puckered and protesting face as if he had just tasted something sour and unexpected, he began to speak at once in a tone of shocked and astounded indignation: "In heaven's name!" he rasped; "who is this man Weaver that you brought here? What kind of man is he? *You* brought him here," he said accusingly. "*You* recommended him. We thought he was all right. We took *your* word for it? What's wrong with the man? Is he crazy? Is he out of his head completely?"—his face was soured and wrinkled like a persimmon, his small pinched figure trembled with excitement and indignation, he looked at the boy with an expression of horrified reproof —he was a comical sight, but the boy was in no temper at the moment to appreciate the humor of his appearance.

"What is it, Mr. Gibbs? What's the matter? What has he done?"

"Why," he said, trembling with anger at the very thought of it, "he tried to burn us all up last night. He came in here at three o'clock in the morning, raving and carrying on like a crazy man. Then he went upstairs and set his room on fire."

"On fire!"

"Why, yes!" said Gibbs. "We had to call the fire department to put it out. Why, it's a wonder any of us are left alive—all of these people sleeping in the hotel and this crazy man yelling and screaming at five o'clock this morning that the place is on fire! Why, we can't have anything like that in this hotel," he said with the air of one who describes 'the desecration of a temple. "We can't have a man like that here. Why, he'll drive the other people out, we'll lose all our guests: people aren't going to stay in a place with a crazy man. There's no telling what a man like that is liable to do. Now!" he said with an air of abrupt and pugnacious decision, "he's got to get out: I won't have him here! I'm not going to have a man like that in my hotel a moment longer"—his small jaw hardened meanly, his face shrank, and his eyes narrowed, as he turned away, "and some one's got to pay for all the damage that was done! Now I don't care who pays it"—his face was averted—"but it's not going to be us! Now you can tell him," he snapped curtly, and he left.

Eugene went upstairs at once to Robert's room in a state of choking anger and resentment: he felt that Robert had tricked him and taken advantage of him, that he was being held accountable for Robert's mis-behavior, and that now his own standing in the hotel had been jeopard-ized and he would be forced to leave this delightful and charming estab-lishment at which he had cursed and mocked so bitterly many times, but which now, in his resentful spirit, took on a peaceful and home-like glamour it had never had before. He walked into Robert's room with-out knocking: the room was a wreck, a negro maid was mournfully and sullenly gathering up from the floor the charred and blackened remnants of a pile of bed linen and blankets; the mirror had been smashed by a drinking-glass which Robert had hurled at it, he said, when he saw his image reflected in it, the remnants of a chair lay on the floor, the heavy glass plate upon a writing table had been broken, there was a large brownish stain upon one of the walls where he had hurled a whiskey bottle, and one end of his bed lay tilted on the floor where he had stamped or kicked the slats and boards to splinters. Robert was standing in the midst of all the ruin he had made, with a nervous and rueful ex-pression on his face: when his friend came in he looked at him uneasily and laughed in a feeble and foolish manner, without conviction.

"Now, damn it, don't stand there laughing about it, Robert," the other said. "You may think it's funny as hell, but it's no joke for me. Of course," he went on bitterly, "I'm the goat. I'm the one who's got to suffer for it. I'm the one they hold responsible. Now you've just fixed it so that I can't stay here in the hotel any longer: they're going to put me out!"

"You!" Robert said, in a protesting tone. "Why, it's not your fault. You didn't have anything to do with it."

"You're damned well right I didn't," he answered. "And you're going to tell them so. Now, I was a fool once, but you won't catch me that way again: I begged and pleaded to get you in here and you go and play a dirty trick like this. And you're going to pay for it, too."

"I'll pay, I'll pay," Robert said hastily. "I know it was my fault. I'll pay whatever they ask. Have they said anything to you about it?" he said nervously. "What do they say?"

"They say you've got to pay for all the damage that you've done and get out of the hotel at once."

"Oh, I'll pay!" he said earnestly, and with a pleading note in his voice. "I don't want to leave the hotel. . . . I'll never act like that again. . . . Does Gibbs want to see me?" he said nervously.

"You can just bet your balls he does! And right now!"

"Come on!" said Robert coaxingly. "You go with me. . . . He'll listen to you. . . . Tell him how it was."

"Tell him how it was! Why, he knows damn well how it was! And so do you! You were lousy and crazy-drunk, that's how it was. . . . No, I won't do it: I've been your goat long enough. You'll have to fight it out with him for yourself. . . . And don't you bring my name into it, either, Robert, this was a hell of a thing to do!" Eugene yelled furiously. "In God's name, what's got into you? Have you gone mad?"

"Ah," he said in a brooding, sullen tone, "you know what it is. . . . It's that woman. . . . It's Martha! I can't get her off my mind, I think about her all the time. . . . My God, Eugene, if something doesn't happen soon, I will go crazy, sure enough."

"Happen! What do you want to happen?"

He beat himself, suddenly and savagely, on his breast.

"Christ knows!" he said. "Something's got to break loose . . . here . . . here . . . here!" His eyes were shot with tears and a madness of desperation: in this baffled and infuriated gesture there was something that was really painful, tortured, and deeply moving: all at once Eugene felt sorry for him; he did not know why Robert wanted to stay at the hotel any longer, he did not know what he found there in that shabby and sterile life to attract or interest him, and perhaps it was nothing except a sense in him that he was disgraced, an outcast from the ranks of orderly society: he wanted to stay in order to subdue the fear and shame he felt, and to soothe, in whatever way he could, his lacerated pride. Therefore, Eugene resolved to help him.

"Robert," he said, "if you really want to stay here, why don't you go and see old Gibbs, and talk to him. Tell him you're sorry for all the trouble you made and the damage you did, and that you're willing to pay whatever he says is fair. Then let him rave. He's a sour old bastard and he'll bawl you out, but let him rave. He enjoys it. Then tell him if he'll let you stay, you'll never act like this again. And if I can help out any, I'll do it."

He agreed to this at once, and Eugene left him and went to his own room: when he went downstairs a few minutes later on his way to his first class, Robert was standing at the desk, submissively attentive to the tongue-lashing Gibbs was giving him. The little man was in a state of trembling denunciation, he squinted and peered at Robert's face, and wagged an indignant finger at him; his shrewd, sour, nasal voice carried to all parts of the room, and Robert listened apologetically and sorrow-fully, putting in a word of penitent assent from time to time, in a deep, respectful voice:

"I quite agree with you. . . . You are absolutely right, sir. . . . It was a terrible thing to do. . . . I'll never do it again as long as I live, . . . I'll pay you for every bit of damage that I did"—and he took out his check-book and opened it upon the counter. Eugene went over and joined them: the old man was beginning to simmer down somewhat into occasional howls and blasts of fury, like a hurricane which has spent its fiercest violence and is in process of abatement: Robert began to talk smoothly, entreatingly, and charmingly—he swore to a complete and abject repentance, spoke touchingly and mysteriously of great storms and tragedies in his recent life which had driven him to this mad and violent explosion, and gave his solemn oath never to repeat the experience again if he was only allowed to remain in the hotel: Eugene put in a word of agreement here and there when he thought it might help—the upshot of it was that Gibbs finally began to speak to Robert in a tone of almost paternal affection, a kind of radiance was given off from his meagre soul, he bent towards Robert intimately, he even laughed—and when they departed, to their astonishment, he even gave the repentant sinner a warm squeeze of the hand, and a friendly pat upon the shoulder.

Within a period of three furious months Robert made trips to Colo-rado seven times: he got on trains and was hurled 2000 miles across the continent as casually as a man would make the subway trip from Times Square to Brooklyn Heights. Sometimes he would leave New

York on Friday night and be back within four or five days, after spending ten hours with Martha Upshaw: sometimes he would be gone a week, and once he did not return for three. On this occasion Eugene received a telegram from him when he had been absent about five days: the message curtly bade Eugene to send all his mail to a hotel in Colorado Springs until further notice, and said he would explain on his return.

Eugene was sitting in the lobby one evening two weeks later, when Robert came in. He walked with a limp and his face seemed to have undergone a curious angular distortion: he came toward Eugene with a kind of frozen grin and when he spoke to him he began to mutter something incoherent between set teeth and to point with his finger at his jaw. In a few moments, Eugene was able to decipher his jargon sufficiently to understand that his jaw and nose were broken, that most of the teeth had been extracted, in order that the jaw-bone might be wired together, and that he could not open his mouth now, either to speak or eat, because of wires that bound the fracture. In addition, his nose, which had been strong and straight, now curved sideways in a wide broken arc.

Robert was shockingly thin and wasted, he said he had bled a great deal, and had been unable to eat any solid food since his injury: it was obvious he had about reached the limit of his strength, the whole contour of his skull was visible, his eyes were sunken and burned with a more furious and fatal glow than ever before.

But he laughed at Eugene's look of stupefaction when he saw him, and laughed again, morosely and indifferently, as he told him the cause of his injuries: he said he had been driving with Martha Upshaw the night he got to Colorado Springs, both had been to a roadhouse and were drunk and neither, to use his description of their feeling, "gave a damn." The girl was driving, the hour was late, they had come around a curve in a mountain road at great speed, the car had left the road, plunged down a steep embankment, and turned over three times before it smashed up against a tree. The girl had been badly cut by broken glass and had several stitches taken in wounds on her face and head, but she broke no bones. Robert had been hurled twenty feet from the car, he was unconscious and bleeding horribly, and it had been thought at first his injuries were fatal.

But here he was, at least a vital piece of him, smashed and broken, but still fiercely living. It was obvious, however, that this final catastrophe had hardened his spirit in a resolute desperation: the suicidal fatalism—that hunger for death which all men have in them and which is perhaps as strong a driving-force in man as the hunger for life—and which had been strongly marked in Robert only when he was drunk— had now become the habit of his soul. He no longer cared whether he lived or died, in his inmost heart he had grown amorous of death, and it was evident that living flesh and bone could not much longer endure the cruel beating he had given it. And this fact—this shocking, visible, physical fact—as much as anything—sealed him in fatal desperation, confirmed him in his belief that everything was lost.

LI

MAN'S youth is a wonderful thing: It is so full of anguish and of magic and he never comes to know it as it is, until it has gone from him forever. It is the thing he cannot bear to lose, it is the thing whose passing he watches with infinite sorrow and regret, it is the thing whose loss he must lament forever, and it is the thing whose loss he really welcomes with a sad and secret joy, the thing he would never willingly re-live again, could it be restored to him by any magic.

Why is this? The reason is that the strange and bitter miracle of life is nowhere else so evident as in our youth. And what is the essence of that strange and bitter miracle of life which we feel so poignantly, so unutterably, with such a bitter pain and joy, when we are young? It is this: that being rich, we are so poor; that being mighty, we can yet have nothing, that seeing, breathing, smelling, tasting all around us the impossible wealth and glory of this earth, feeling with an intolerable certitude that the whole structure of the enchanted life—the most fortunate, wealthy, good, and happy life that any man has ever known—is ours—is ours at once, immediately and forever, the moment that we choose to take a step, or stretch a hand, or say a word—we yet know that we can really keep, hold, take, and possess forever—nothing. All passes; nothing lasts: the moment that we put our hand upon it it melts away like smoke, is gone forever, and the snake is eating at our heart again; we see then what we are and what our lives must come to.

A young man is so strong, so mad, so certain, and so lost. He has everything and he is able to use nothing. He hurls the great shoulder of his strength forever against phantasmal barriers, he is a wave whose power explodes in lost mid-oceans under timeless skies, he reaches out to grip a fume of painted smoke; he wants all, feels the thirst and power for everything, and finally gets nothing. In the end, he is destroyed by his own strength, devoured by his own hunger, impoverished by his own wealth. Thoughtless of money or the accumulation of material possessions, he is none the less defeated in the end by his own greed—a greed that makes the avarice of King Midas seem paltry by comparison.

And that is the reason why, when youth is gone, every man will look back upon that period of his life with infinite sorrow and regret. It is the bitter sorrow and regret of a man who knows that once he had a great talent and wasted it, of a man who knows that once he had a great treasure and got nothing from it, of a man who knows that he had strength enough for everything and never used it.

All youth is bound to be "mis-spent"; there is something in its very nature that makes it so, and that is why all men regret it. And that regret becomes more poignant as the knowledge comes to us that this great waste of youth was utterly unnecessary, as we discover with a bitter irony of mirth, that youth is something which only young men have, and which only old men know how to use. And for that reason, in later years, we all look back upon our youth with sorrow and regret— seeing what a wealth was ours if we had used it—remembering Weisberg, Snodgrass, and O'Hare—finally remembering with tenderness and joy the good bleak visage of the pavement cipher who was the first friend we ever knew in the great city—in whose gray face its million strange and secret mysteries were all compact—and who was our friend, our brother, and this earth's nameless man. And so Eugene recalled Abraham Jones.

This ugly, good, and loyal creature had almost forgotten his real name: the "Jones," of course, was one of those random acquisitions which, bestowed in some blind, dateless moment of the past, evoked a picture of those nameless hordes of driven and frightened people who had poured into this country within the last half-century, and whose whole lives had been determined for them by the turn of a word, the bend of a street, the drift of the crowd, or a surly and infuriated gesture by some ignorant tyrant of an official. In such a way, Abe Jones's father, a Polish Jew, without a word of Yankee English in his throat, had come to Castle Garden forty years before and, stunned and frightened by the moment's assault of some furious little swine of a customs inspector, had stood dumbly while the man snarled and menaced him: "What's yer name? . . . Huh? . . . Don't yuh know what yer name is . . . Huh? . . . Ain't yuh got a name? . . . Huh?" To all this the poor Jew had no answer but a stare of stupe-faction and terror: at length a kind of frenzy seized him—a torrent of Polish, Jewish, Yiddish speech poured from his mouth, but never a word his snarling inquisitor could understand. The Jew begged, swore, wept, pleaded, prayed, entreated—a thousand tales of horror, brutal violence and tyranny swept through his terror-stricken mind, the whole vast obscene chronicle of immigration gleaned from the mouths of returned adventurers or from the letters of those who had triumphantly passed the gates of wrath: he showed his papers, he clasped his hands, he swore by all the oaths he knew that all was as it should be, that he had done all he had been told to do, that there was no trick or fraud or cheat in anything he did or said, and all the time, the foul, swollen, snarling face kept thrusting at him with the same maddening and indecipherable curse: "Yer name! . . . Yer name! . . . Fer Christ's sake don't yuh know yer own name? . . . All right!" he shouted sud-denly, furiously, "If yuh ain't got a name I'll give yuh one! . . . If yuh ain't got sense enough to tell me what yer own name is, I'll find one for yuh!" The snarling face came closer: "Yer name's Jones! See! J-o-n-e-s. Jones! That's a good Amurrican name. See? I'm giving yuh a good honest Amurrican name that a lot of good decent Amurricans have got. Yuh've gotta try to live up to it and desoive it! See? Yer in Amurrica now, Jones. . . . See? . . . Yuh've gotta t'ink fer yerself, Jones. In Amurrica we know our own name. We've been trained to t'ink fer ourselves over here! . . . See? Yer not one of them foreign dummies any more! . . . Yer Jones—Jones—Jones!" he yelled. "See!" —and in such a way, on the impulsion of brutal authority and idiot chance, Abe's father had been given his new name. Eugene did not know what Abe's real name was: Abe had told him once, and he re-membered it as something pleasant, musical, and alien to our tongue, difficult for our mouths to shape and utter.

Already, when he had first met Abe Jones in the first class he taught, the process of mutation had carried so far that he was trying to rid himself of the accursed "Abraham," reducing it to an ambiguous initial, and signing his papers with a simple unrevealing "A. Jones," as whales are said to have lost through atrophy the use of legs with which they once walked across the land, but still to carry upon their bodies the rudimentary stump. Now, in the last year, he had dared to make a final transformation, shocking, comical, pitifully clumsy in its effort at concealment and deception: when Eugene had tried to find his name and number in the telephone directory a month before, among the great gray regiment of Joneses, the familiar, quaint, and homely "Abe" had disappeared—at length he found him coyly sheltered under the gentlemanly obscurity of A. Alfred Jones. The transformation, thus, had been complete: he was now, in name, at any rate, a member of the great Gentile aristocracy of Jones; and just as "Jones" had been thrust by violence upon his father, so had Abe taken violently, by theft and rape, the "Alfred." There was something mad and appalling in the bravado, the effrontery, and the absurdity of the attempt: what did he hope to do with such a name? What reward did he expect to win? Was he engaged in some vast conspiracy in which all depended on the *sound* and not the *appearance* of deception? Was he using the mails in some scheme to swindle or defraud? Was he carrying on by correspondence an impassioned courtship of some ancient Christian maiden with one tooth and a million shining dollars? Or was it part of a gigantic satire on Gentile genteelness, country-club Christianity, a bawdy joke perpetrated at the expense of sixty thousand anguished and protesting Social Registerites? That he should hope actually to palm himself off as a Gentile was unthinkable, because one look at him revealed instantly the whole story of his race and origin: if all the Polish-Russian Jews that ever swarmed along the ghettoes of the earth had been compacted in a single frame the physical result might have been something amazingly like Eugene's friend, Abraham Jones.

The whole flag and banner of his race was in the enormous putty-colored nose that bulged, flared and sprouted with the disproportionate extravagance of a caricature or a dill-pickle over his pale, slightly freckled and rather meagre face; he had a wide, thin, somewhat cruel-looking mouth, dull weak eyes that stared, blinked, and grew misty with a murky, somewhat slimily ropy feeling behind his spectacles, a low, dull, and slanting forehead, almost reptilian in its ugliness, that sloped painfully back an inch or two into the fringes of unpleasantly greasy curls and coils of dark, short, screwy hair. He was about the middle height, and neither thin nor fat: his figure was rather big-boned and angular, and yet it gave an impression of meagreness, spareness, and somewhat tallowy toughness which so many city people have, as if their ten thousand days and nights upon the rootless pavement had dried all juice and succulence out of them, as if asphalt and brick and steel had got into the conduits of their blood and spirit, leaving them with a quality that is tough, dry, meagre, tallowy, and somewhat calloused.

What earth had nourished him? Had he been born and grown there among the asphalt lilies and the pavement wheat? What corn was growing from the cobblestones? Or was there never a cry of earth up through the beaten and unyielding cement of the streets? Had he forgotten the immortal and attentive earth still waiting at the roots of steel?

No. Beneath that cone of neat gray felt, behind the dreary, tallowed pigment of his face, which had that thickened, stunned, and deadened look one often sees upon the faces of old bruisers, as if the violent and furious assault of stone and steel, the million harsh metallic clangors, the brutal stupefaction of the streets, at length had dried the flesh and thickened the skin, and blunted, numbed and calloused the aching tumult of the tortured and tormented senses—there still flowed blood as red and wet as any which ever swarmed into the earth below the laurel bush. He was a part, a drop, an indecipherable fraction of these gray tides of swarming tissue that passed in ceaseless weft and counter-weft upon the beaten pavements, at once a typical man-swarm atom and a living man. Indistinguishable in his speech, gait, dress, and tallowy pigmentation from the typical cell-and-pavement article, at the same time, although ugly, meagre, toughened, gnarled and half-articulate, angular as brick and spare as steel webbing, with little juice and succulence, he was honest, loyal, somehow good and memorable, grained with the life and movement of a thousand streets, seasoned and alert, a living character, a city man. In that horrible desperation of drowning and atomic desolation among the numberless hordes that swept along the rootless pavements, in Eugene's madness to know, own, intrude behind the million barriers of brick, to root and entrench himself in the hive, he seized upon that dreary, gray and hopeless-looking Jew.

This was his history:

Abraham Jones was one of the youngest members of a large family. In addition to two brothers, younger than himself, there were three older brothers, and two sisters. The family life was close, complex, and passionate, torn by fierce dislikes and dissensions, menaced by division among some of its members, held together by equally fierce loyalties and loves among the others. Abe disliked his father and hated one of his older brothers. He loved one of his sisters and was attached to the other one by a kind of loyalty of silence.

She, Sylvia, was a woman of perhaps thirty-five years when Eugene first saw her, she had not lived at home for ten years, she was a febrile, nervous, emaciated, highly enamelled city woman—a lover of what was glittering and electric in life, caught up in the surge of a furious and feverish life, and yet not content with it, dissonant, irritable and impatient. Like the rest of her family she had been forced to shift for herself since childhood: she had been first a salesgirl, then a worker in a millinery shop, and now, through her own cleverness, smartness, and ability, she had achieved a very considerable success in business. She ran a hat shop on Second Avenue, which Abe told him was the Broadway of the lower East Side: she had a small, elegant, glittering jewel of a shop there, blazing with hard electric light and smartly and tastefully dressed with windows filled with a hundred jaunty styles in women's hats. She did a thriving business and employed several assistants.

The first time Eugene met her, one day when Abe had taken him home to the flat where he lived with his mother, two of his brothers, and Sylvia's child, he thought she had the look and quality of an actress much more than of a business woman. There was a remarkably electric glitter and unnaturalness about her: it seemed as if the only light that had ever shone upon her had been electric light, the only air she could breath with any certitude and joy, the clamorous and electric air of Broadway. Her face belonged, indeed, among those swarms of livid, glittering, night-time faces that pour along the street, with that mysterious fraternity of night-time people who all seem to speak a common language and to be bound together by some central interest and communication, who live mysteriously and gaudily without discoverable employments, in a world remote and alien. Sylvia was a woman of middling height, but of a dark and almost bird-like emaciation: all the flesh seemed to have been starved, wasted, and consumed from her by this devil of feverish and electric unrest and discontent that glittered with almost a drugged brilliance in her large dark eyes. Every visible portion of her body, hair, eyebrows, lashes, lips, skin and nails was greased, waved, leaded, rouged, plucked, polished, enamelled and varnished with the conventional extravagance of a ritualistic mask until now it seemed that all of the familiar qualities of living tissue had been consumed, and were replaced by the painted image, the varnished mask of a face, designed in its unreality to catch, reflect, and realize effectively the thousand lurid shifting lights and weathers of an electric, nocturnal, and inhuman world. Moreover, she was dressed in the most extreme and sharpest exaggeration of the latest style, her thin long hands, which were unpleasantly and ominously veined with blue, and her fragile wrists, which were so thin and white that light made a pink transparency in them when she lifted them, were covered, loaded— one vast encrusted jewelled glitter of diamond rings and bracelets: a fortune in jewelry blazed heavily and shockingly on her bony little hands.

Her life had been hard, painful, difficult, full of work and sorrow. Ten years before, when she was twenty-five years old, she had had her first—and probably her last—love affair. She had fallen in love with an actor at the Settlement Guild—a little East Side theatre maintained by the donations of two rich æsthetic females. She had left her family and become his mistress: within less than a year the man deserted her, leaving her pregnant.

Her child was a boy: she had no maternal feeling and her son, now nine years old, had been brought up by Abe's mother and by Abe. Sylvia rarely saw her son: she had long ago deserted the orthodoxy of Jewish family life, she had a new, impatient, driving, feverish city life of her own, she visited her family every month or so, and it was then, and only then, that she saw her child. This boy, Jimmy, was a bright, quick, attractive youngster, with a tousled sheaf of taffy-colored hair, and with the freckled, tough, puggish face and the cocky mutilated pavement argot and assurance of the city urchin: he was nevertheless excellently clothed, schooled, and cared for, for the old woman, Abe's mother, watched and guarded over him with the jealous brooding apprehension of an ancient hen, and Sylvia herself was most generous in her expenditures and benefactions, not only for the child, but also for the family.

The relation between Sylvia and her illegitimate child, Jimmy, was remarkable. He never called her "mother"; in fact neither seemed to have a name for the other, save an impersonal and rather awkward "You." Moreover, the attitude of both mother and child was marked by a quality that was hard, knowing, and cynical in its conversation: when she spoke to him her tone and manner were as cold and impersonal as if the child had been a stranger or some chance acquaintance, and this manner was also touched by a quality that was resigned, and somewhat mocking—with a mockery which seemed to be directed toward herself, more than toward any one, as if in the physical presence of the boy she saw the visible proof and living evidence of her folly, the bitter fruit of the days of innocence, love, and guileless belief, and as if she was conscious that a joke had been played on both her and her child. And the boy seemed to understand and accept this feeling with a sharp correspondence of feeling, almost incredible in a child. And yet they did not hate each other: their conversations were cynically wise and impersonal and yet curiously honest and respectful. She would look at him for a moment with an air of cold and casual detachment, and that faint smile of mockery when, on one of her visits home, he would come in, panting and dishevelled, a tough and impish urchin, from the street.

"Come here, you," she would say at length, quietly, harshly. "Whatcha been doin' to yourself?" she would ask, in the same hard tone, as deftly she straightened and re-knotted his tie, smoothed out his rumpled sheaf of oaken-colored hair. "You look as if yuh just crawled out of some one's ash can."

"Ah!" he said in his tough, high city-urchin's voice, "a coupla guys tried to get wise wit' me an' I socked one of 'em. Dat's all!"

"Oh-ho-ho-ho!"—Abe turned his gray grinning face prayerfully to heaven and laughed softly, painfully.

"Fightin', huh?" said Sylvia. "Do you remember what I told you last time?" she said in a warning tone. "If I catch yuh fightin' again there's goin' to be no more ball games. You'll stay home next time."

"Ah!" he cried again in a high protesting tone. "What's a guy gonna do? Do you t'ink I'm gonna let a coupla mugs like dat get away wit' moidah?"

"Oh-ho-ho-ho!"—cried Abe, lifting his great nose prayerfully again: then with a sudden shift to reproof and admonition, he said sternly: "What kind of talk do you call that? Huh? Didn't I tell you not to say 'mugs'?"

"Ah, what's a guy gonna say?" cried Jimmy. "I neveh could loin all dem big woids, noway."

"My God! I wish you'd listen to 'm," his mother said in a tone of hard and weary resignation. "I suppose that's what I'm sendin' him to school for! Loin, woids, noway, t'ink! Is that the way to talk?" she demanded harshly. "Is that what they teach yuh?"

"Say *think!*" commanded Abe.

"I *did* say it," the child answered evasively.

"Go on! You *didn't!* You didn't say it right. I'll bet you can't say it right. Come on! Let's hear you: *think!*"

"T'ink," Jimmy, answered immediately.

"Oh-ho-ho-ho!"—and Abe lifted his grinning face heavenward, saying, "Say! This is rich!"

"Can yuh beat it?" the woman asked.

And, for a moment, she continued to look at her son with a glance that was quizzical, tinged with a mocking resignation, and yet with a cold, detached affection. Then her long blue-veined hands twitched nervously and impatiently until all the crusted jewels on her wrists and fingers blazed with light: she sighed sharply and, looking away, dismissed the child from her consideration.

Although the boy saw very little of his mother, Abe watched and guarded over him as tenderly as if he had been his father. If the child was late in coming home from school, if he had not had his lunch before going out to play, if he remained away too long Abe showed his concern and distress very plainly, and he spoke very sharply and sternly at times to other members of the family if he thought they had been lax in some matter pertaining to the boy.

"Did Jimmy get home from school yet?" he would ask sharply. "Did he eat before he went out again? . . . Well, why did you let him get away, then, before he had his lunch? . . . For heaven's sake! You're here all day long: you could at least do that much—I can't be here to watch him all the time, you know—don't you know the kid ought never to go out to play until he's had something to eat?"

Eugene saw the child for the first time one day when Abe had taken him home for dinner: Abe, in his crisp neat shirt-sleeves, was seated at the table devouring his food with a wolfish and prowling absorption, and yet in a cleanly and fastidious way, when the child entered. The boy paused in surprise when he saw Eugene: his wheaten sheaf of hair fell down across one eye, one trouser leg had come unbanded at the knee and flapped down to his ankle, and for a moment he looked at Eugene with a rude frank stare of his puggish freckled face.

Abe, prowling upward from his food, glanced at the boy and grinned; then, jerking his head sharply toward Eugene, he said roughly:

"Whatcha think of this guy? Huh?"

"Who is he?" the boy asked in his high tough little voice, never moving his curious gaze from Eugene.

"He's my teacher," Abe said. "He's the guy that teaches me."

"Ah, g'wan!" the child answered in a protesting tone, still fixing Eugene with his steady and puzzled stare.

"Whatcha handin' me? He's *not!*"

"Sure he is! No kiddin'!" Abe replied. "He's the guy that teaches me English."

"Ah, he's *not!*" the boy answered decisively. "Yuh're bein' wise."

"What makes you think he's not?" Abe asked.

"If he's an English teacher," Jimmy said triumphantly, "w'y don't he say somet'ing? W'y don't he use some of dose woids?"

"Oh-ho-ho-ho!" cried Abe lifting his great bleak nose aloft. "Say! . . . This is good! . . . This is swell! . . . Say, that's some kid!" he said when the boy had departed. "There's not much gets by *him!*" And lifting his gray face heavenward again, he laughed softly, painfully, in gleeful and tender reminiscence.

Thus, the whole care and government of the boy had been entrusted to Abe and his mother: Sylvia herself, although she paid liberally all her child's expenses, took no other interest in him. She was a hard, feverish, bitter, and over-stimulated woman, and yet she had a kind of harsh loyalty to her family: she was, in a fierce and smouldering way, very ambitious for Abe, who seemed to be the most promising of her brothers: she was determined that he should go to college and become a lawyer, and his fees at the university, in part at any rate, were paid by his sister—in part only, not because Sylvia would not have paid all without complaint, but because Abe insisted on paying as much as he could through his own labor, for Abe, too, had embedded in him a strong granite of independence, the almost surly dislike, of a strong and honest character, of being beholden to any one for favors. On this score, indeed, he had the most sensitive and tender pride of any one Eugene had ever known.

At home, Abe had become, by unspoken consent, the head of a family which now consisted only of his mother, two brothers, and his sister's illegitimate child, Jimmy. Two of his older brothers, who were in business together, had married and lived away from home, as did Sylvia, and another sister, Rose, who had married a musician in a theatre orchestra a year or two before; she was a dark, tortured and sensitive

Jewess with a big nose and one blind eye. Her physical resemblance to Abe was marked. She was a very talented pianist, and once or twice he took Eugene to visit her on Sunday afternoons: she played for them in a studio room in which candles were burning and she carried on very technical and knowing conversations about the work of various composers with her brother. Abe listened to the music when she played with an obscure and murky smile: he seemed to know a great deal about music: it awakened a thousand subtle echoes in his Jewish soul, but for Eugene, somehow, the music, and something arrogant, scornful, and secretive in their knowingness, together with the dreary consciousness of a winter's Sunday afternoon outside, the barren streets, the harsh red waning light of day, and a terrible sensation of thousands of other knowing Jews—the men with little silken mustaches—who were coming from concerts at that moment, awakened in him vague but powerful emotions of nakedness, rootlessness, futility and misery, which even the glorious memory of the power, exultancy and joy of poetry could not conquer or subdue. The scene evoked for him suddenly a thousand images of a sterile and damnable incertitude, in which man groped indefinitely along the smooth metallic sides of a world in which there was neither warmth, nor depth, nor door to enter, nor walls to shelter him: he got suddenly a vision of a barren Sunday and a gray despair, of ugly streets, and of lights beginning to wink and flicker above cheap moving-picture houses and chop-suey restaurants, and of a raucous world of cheap and flashy people, as trashy as their foods, as trivial and infertile as their accursed amusements, and finally of the Jews returning through a thousand streets, in that waning and desolate light, from symphony concerts, an image, which, so far from giving a note of hope, life, and passionate certitude and joy to the wordless horror of this damned and blasted waste of Dead-Man's Land, seemed to enhance it rather, and to give it a conclusive note of futility and desolation.

Abe and his sister did not seem to feel this: instead the scene, the time, the day, the waning light, the barren streets, the music, awakened in them something familiar and obscure, a dark and painful joy, a certitude Eugene did not feel. They argued, jibed, and sneered harshly and arrogantly at each other: their words were sharp and cutting, impregnated with an aggressive and unpleasant intellectualism, they called each other fools and sentimental ignoramuses, and yet they did not seem to be wounded or offended by this harsh intercourse: they seemed rather to derive a kind of bitter satisfaction from it.

Already, the first year Eugene had known him he had discovered this strange quality in these people: they seemed to delight in jeering and jibing at one another; and at the same time their harsh mockery had in it an element of obscure and disquieting affection. At this time Abe was carrying on, week by week, a savage correspondence with another young Jew who had been graduated with him from the same class in high school. He always had in his pocket at least one of the letters this boy had written him, and he was forever giving it to Eugene to read, and then insisting that he read his answer. In these letters, they flew at each other with undisciplined ferocity, they hurled denunciation, mockery, and contempt at each other, and they seemed to exult in it. The tone of their letters was marked by an affectation of cold impersonality and austerity, and yet this obviously was only a threadbare cloak to the furious storm of personal insult and invective, the desire to crow over the other man and humiliate him, which seemed to delight them. "In your last letter," one would write, "I see that the long-expected *débâcle* has now occurred. In our last year at high school I saw occasional gleams of adult intelligence in your otherwise infantile and adolescent intellect, and I had some hope of saving you, but I now see my hopes were wasted—your puerile remarks on Karl Marx, Anatole France, et al, show you up as the fat-headed bourgeois you always were, and I accordingly wash my hands of you. You reveal plainly that your intellect is incapable of grasping the issues involved in modern socialism: you are a romantic individualist and you will find everything you say elegantly embalmed in the works of the late Lord Byron which is where you belong also: your mother should dress you up in a cowboy suit and give you a toy pistol to play with before you hurt yourself playing around with great big rough grown-up men."

Abe would read Eugene one of these letters, grinning widely with Kike delight, lifting his grinning face and laughing softly, "Oh-ho-ho-ho-ho!" as he came to some particularly venomous insult.

"But who wrote you such a letter?" Eugene demanded.

"Oh, a guy I went to school with," he answered, "a friend of mine!"

"A friend of yours! Is that the kind of letter that your friends write you!"

"Sure," he said. "Why not? He's a good guy. He doesn't mean anything by it. He's got bats in the belfry, that's all. But wait till you see what I wrote *him!*" he cried, grinning exultantly as he took his own letter from his pocket. "Wait till you see what I call *him!* Oh-ho-ho-

ho-ho!"—softly, painfully, he laughed. "Say, this is rich!" and gleefully he would read his answer: five closely typed pages of bitter insult
and vituperation.

Another astonishing and disquieting circumstance of this brutal correspondence was now revealed: this extraordinary "friend" of Abe's,
who wrote him these insulting letters, had not gone abroad, nor did he
live in some remote and distant city. When Eugene asked Abe where
this savage critic lived, he answered: "Oh, a couple of blocks from where
I live."

"But do you ever see him?"

"Sure. Why not?" he said, looking at Eugene in a puzzled way.
"We grew up together. I see him all the time."

"And yet you write this fellow letters and he writes you, when you
live only a block apart and see each other all the time?"

"Sure. Why not?" said Abe.

He saw nothing curious or unusual in the circumstance, and yet there
was something disturbing and unpleasant about it: in all these letters
Eugene had observed, below the tirades of abuse, an obscure, indefinable,
and murky emotionalism that was somehow ugly.

Within a few months, however, this strange communication with his
Jewish comrade ceased abruptly: Eugene began to see Abe, in the halls
and corridors of the university, squiring various Jewish girls around
with a sheepish and melancholy look. His lust for letter-writing still
raged with unabated violence, although now the subjects of his correspondence were women. His attitude towards girls had always been
cold and scornful: he regarded their cajoleries and enticements with
a fishy eye, and with a vast Jewish caution and suspiciousness, and he
laughed scornfully at any one who allowed himself to be ensnared.
Like many people who feel deeply, and who are powerfully affected by
the slightest and remotest changes in their emotions, he had convinced
himself that he was a creature whose every action was governed by the
operations of cool reason, and accordingly now that his feelings were
powerfully and romantically involved in thoughts about several of
these warm and luscious-looking Jewish wenches, he convinced himself that he "cared only for their minds" and that what he really sought
from them was the stimulation of intellectual companionship. Accordingly, the love-letters which this great-nosed innocent now wrote to
them, and read to Eugene, were extraordinary and unwitting productions of defense and justification.

". . . I think I observe in your last letter," Abe would write, "traces of that romantic sentimentality which we have both seen so often in these childish lives around us but from which you and I long ago freed ourselves. As you know, Florence, we both agreed at the beginning that we would not spoil our friendship by the intrusion of a puerile and outmoded romanticism. Sex can play no part in our relations, Florence: it is at best a simple biological necessity, the urge of the hungry animal which should be recognized as such and satisfied without intruding on the higher faculties. Have you read Havelock Ellis yet? If not, you must read him without further delay. . . . So Myrtle Goldberg really thought I was in earnest that night of the dance. . . . Ye Gods! It is to laugh! Ha-ha! What fools these mortals be . . . I laugh, and yet I do not laugh . . . I laugh and observe my laughter, and then there is yet another level of reality which observes my laughter at my laughter. . . . I play the clown with an ironic heart and put on the grinning mask these fools wish to see. . . . O tempora! O mores!"—*et cetera.*

And yet these same letters, in which he protested the cold detachment of his spirit, his freedom from the romantic fleshliness which degraded the lives of lesser men, were invariably tagged and embellished by little verses of his own contriving, all of them inspired by the emotion he pretended to despise. He always had a number of these little poems written down in a small note-book of black leather which he carried with him, and in which, at this time, with a precise and meticulous hand, he noted down his rarest thoughts, excerpts from books he had been reading, and these brief poems. At this time Abe was in a state of obscure and indefinable evolution: it was impossible to say what he would become, or what form his life would take, nor could he have told, himself. He walked along at a stooping loping gait, his face prowling around mistrustfully and with a glance full of tortured discontent: he was tormented by a dozen obscure desires and purposes and by a deep but murky emotionalism: his flesh was ugly, bowed, and meagre—conscious of a dreary inferiority (thus, in later and more prosperous years, he confessed to Eugene that he loved to abuse and "order around" brusquely the waiters in restaurants, because of the feeling of power and authority it gave him), but his spirit was sustained by an immense and towering vanity, a gloomy egotism which told him he was not as other men, that his thoughts and feelings were too profound and rare to be understood and valued by the base world about him. At the same time he was secretly and fiercely ambitious, although the energy of his ambition was scattered in a half dozen directions and could fasten on no purpose: by turn, he wanted to be a teacher and a great investigator in the sciences—and in this he might have succeeded, for he showed a brilliant aptness in biology and physics—or an economist, a critic of literature, an essayist, a historian, a poet, or a novelist. His desire was high: at this time he did not want to make money, he regarded a life that was given up to money-making with contempt, and although he sometimes spoke of the study of medicine, he looked at the profession of law, which was the profession his sister and his family wanted him to follow, with horror and revulsion: he shrank with disgust from the prospect of joining the hordes of beak-nosed shysters, poured out of the law school year by year and who were adept in every dodge of dishonorable trickery, in working every crooked wire, or squirming through each rat's hole of escape and evasion the vast machinery of the law afforded them.

Such a man was Abe Jones when Eugene first knew him: dreary, tortured, melancholy, dully intellectual and joylessly poetic, his spirit gloomily engulfed in a great cloud of Yiddish murk, a gray pavement cipher, an atom of the slums, a blind sea-crawl in the drowning tides of the man-swarm, and yet, pitifully, tremendously, with a million other dreary Hebrew yearners, convinced that he was the messiah for which the earth was groaning. Such was he in the state of becoming, an indefinable shape before necessity and his better parts—the hard, savage, tough and honest city sinew, hardened the mould—made a man of him, —this was Abe at this time, an obscure and dreary chrysalis, and yet a dogged, loyal, and faithful friend, the salt of the earth, a wonderfully good, rare, and high person.

LII

"WHERE shall I go now? What shall I do?" A dozen times that year he made these tormented journeys of desire. Why did he make them? What did he expect to find? He did not know: he only knew that at night he would feel again the huge and secret quickening of desire to which all life in the city moved, that he would be drawn again, past hope and past belief, to the huge glare, the swarming avenues of night, with their great tides of livid night-time faces. He only knew that he would prowl again, again, each night, the thronging passages of rat's alley where the dead men were, that the million faces, forms and shapes of ungraspable desire would pass, would weave and throng and vanish from his grasp like evil figures in a dream, and that the old unanswered questions which have foiled so many million lives lost there in the labyrinthine maze and fury of the city's life, would come back again, and that he never found an answer to them.

"What shall I do now? Where shall I go?" They returned to mock his furious prowling of kaleidoscopic night with their unsearchable enigmas and when this happened, instant, mad, and overwhelming the desire to burst out of these canyoned walls that held him in, this Tantalus mocker of a city that duped his hunger with a thousand phantom shapes of impossible desire. And when this blind and furious impulse came to him, he knew only one desire—to escape, to escape instantly from the great well and prison of the city; and he had only one conviction—wild, mad, overmastering in its huge unreason—that escape, fulfilment, a fortunate and impossibly happy fruition lay somewhere out across the dark and lonely continent—was somewhere there in any of its thousand silent sleeping little towns—could be found anywhere, certainly, instantly, by the divining rod of miraculous chance, upon the pounding wheels of a great train, at any random halt made in the night.

Thus, by an ironic twist which at the time he did not see or understand, this youth, who in his childhood, like a million other boys, had dreamed and visioned in the darkness of the shining city, and of the fortunate good and happy life that he would find there was now fleeing from it to find in unknown little towns the thing that he had come to the great city to possess.

A dozen times that year he made these mad and sudden journeys: to New England many times, to Pennsylvania, or Virginia; and more than once at night up the great river towards the secret North.

One night that year, in the month of March he was returning from the wintry North—from one of those sudden and furious journeys of caprice, which were decided on the impulse of the moment, towards which he was driven by the goadings of desire, and from which he would return, as now, weary, famished, unassuaged, and driven to seek anew in the city's life for some appeasement.

Under an immense, stormy, and tempestuous sky the train was rushing across the country with a powerful unperturbed movement; it seemed in this dark and wintry firmament of earth and sky that the train was the only fixed and timeless object—the land swept past the windows of the train in a level and powerful tide of white fields, clumped woodland, and the solid, dark, and warmly grouped buildings of a farm, pierced scarcely by a light. High up, in the immense and tempestuous skies the clouds were driving at furious speed, in an inexhaustible processional, across the visage of a wild and desolate moon, which broke through momently with a kind of savage and beleaguered reprisal to cast upon the waste below a shattered, lost and fiercely ragged light. Here then, in this storm-lost desolation of earth and sky the train hung poised as the only motionless and unchanging object, and all things else—the driving and beleaguered moon, the fiercely scudding clouds, the immense regimentation of heaven which stormed onward with the fury of a gigantic and demoniacal cavalry, and the lonely and immortal earth below sweeping past with a vast fan-shaped stroke of field and wood and house—had in them a kind of unchanging changefulness, a spoke-like recurrence which, sweeping past into oblivion, would return as on the upstroke of a wheel to repeat itself with an immutable precision, an unvarying repetition.

And under the spell of this lonely processional of white field, dark wood and wild driven sky, he fell into a state of strange waking-sleepfulness, a kind of comatose perceptiveness that the motion of the train at night had always induced in him. In this weary world of sleep and wakefulness and all the flooding visions of old time and memory, he was conscious of the grand enchantments of the landscape which is at all times one of the most beautiful and lovely on the continent, and which now, under this wild spell of moon and scudding cloud and moving fields and wintry woods, forever stroking past the windows of the train, evoked that wild and solemn joy—the sense of nameless hope, impossible desire, and man's tragic brevity—which only the wildness, the cruel and savage loveliness of the American earth can give.

Thus, as he lay in his berth, in this strange state of comatose perceptiveness he was conscious first of the vast level snowclad fields of the Canadian boundaries, the lights of farms, the whipping past of darkened little stations; then of a wooded land, the foothills of the Adirondacks, dark with their wintry foresting, wild with snow; the haunting vistas of the Champlain country, strange as time, the noble music of Ticonderoga, with its tread of Indians and old wars, and then the pleasant swelling earth and fields and woods and lonely little towns set darkly in the night with a few spare lights; and pauses in the night at Saratoga, and for a moment the casual and familiar voices of

America, and people crowding in the windows of the train, and old familiar words and quiet greetings, the sudden thrum and starting of a motor car, and then dark misty woods, white fields, a few spare lights and houses, all sweeping past beneath the wild beleaguered moon with the fan-like stroke of the immortal and imperturbable earth, with a wild and haunting loneliness, with tragic brevity and strong joy.

Suddenly, in the middle of the night, he started up into sharp wakefulness. The train had slackened in its speed, it was slowing for a halt at the outskirts of a town: in the distance upon the flanks of low sweeping hills he could see a bracelet of hard bright lights, and presently the outposts of the town appeared. And now he saw the spokes of empty wintry streets, and hard street lamps that cast a barren light upon the grimy façades of old houses; and now old grimy blocks of buildings of brown stone and brick, all strange and close and near and as familiar as a dream.

And now the train was slowing to its halt; the old red brick of station warehouses, the worn rust and grime of factory walls abutting on the tracks with startling nearness, and all of it was as it had always been, as he had always known it, and yet he had not seen the place before.

And now the train had slowed to a full halt; he found himself looking at a wall of old red brick at one of the station's corners. It was one of the old brick buildings that one sees in the station section of almost any town: in the wall beside the tracks, there was a dingy-looking door and above the door a red electric bulb was burning with a dim but sinister invitation. Even as he looked, the door opened, a man stepped quickly out, looked quickly to both sides with the furtive and uneasy look men have when they come out of a brothel, and then, turning up the collar of his overcoat, he walked rapidly away.

And at the corner, in the first floor of the old brick building, he could see a disreputable old barroom, and this, too, had this dream-like, stage-like immediacy, it was so near to him that he could almost have touched the building with his hand, a kind of gigantic theatrical setting, overpowering in its immediacy, as strange and as familiar as a dream.

Without moving in his berth he could look through the windows of the bar, which were glazed or painted half way up, and see everything that was going on inside. Despite the lateness of the hour—the round visage of a clock above the bar told him it was just four o'clock —there were several people in the place, and it was doing an open thriving business. Several men, who by their look were probably railway workers, taxi drivers, and night-time prowlers of the station district— (one even wore black leather leggings, and had the fresh red complexion and healthy robust look of a country man)—were standing at the old dark walnut bar and drinking beer. The bartender stood behind the bar with his thick hands stretched out and resting on the bar, and with a wet cloth in one hand. He wore an apron and was in his shirt-sleeves; he had the dead eyes and heavy sagging night-time face that some bartenders have, but he could be seen talking to the men, responding to their jests, with a ready professional cordiality that was nevertheless warily ready for any situation that might come up. And further down the bar, another man was drinking beer and with him was a woman. She was one of the heavy coarsely friendly and experienced whores that one also finds in railway sections, she was drinking beer, talking to the man amiably and with coarse persuasiveness, and presently she took his arm with a rude persuasive gesture, and jerking her head towards the stairs, pulled him towards her. Grinning rather sheepishly, with a pleased but foolish look, he went along with her, and they could be seen going upstairs. When they were gone, the other men drinking at the bar spoke quietly to the bartender, and in a moment he could see them shaking with coarse guffawing laughter. Behind the bar, in old ornately carved walnut frames, there were big mirrors, and at the top of the central mirror there was an American flag, fluted and spread fan-wise, and below this there was a picture of the beetling eyebrows and nobly Roman features of the President of the United States, Warren G. Harding. The whole place looked very old and shabby, and yet somehow warm; dingy with old lights, and stained with drink and worn with countless elbows, and weary and worn and brutal with its memories of ten thousand nights of brawls and lust and drunkenness—its immeasurable age and dateless weariness of violence and desire.

Then the train moved slowly on, and left this scene forever; it passed the street, and there were lights here, taxis, rows of silent buildings, and then the station, the sight of the baggage room big with trunks, piled with mail sacks, crates and boxes, and there were also a few people, a yardman with a lantern, a conductor waiting with a small case in his hand, a few passengers, the brick sides of the station, and the concrete quays.

Then the train stopped again, and this time it stopped across the street at the other end of the station. And again, from his dark berth, he could see without moving this whole immense and immediate theatre of human event, and again it gripped and held him with its dream-like magic, its unbelievable familiarity. At the corner, in another old brick building there was a little lunchroom of the kind he had seen ten thousand times before. Several taxicabs were drawn up along the curb, and from the lunchroom he could hear the hoarse wrangling voices of the taxi drivers, joined in their incessant and trivial debate, and through the misted window he could see the counterman, young, thin, sallow, wearily attentive, wearing a dirty apron, and in his shirtsleeves, leaning back, his thin white arms humbly folded as he listened.

And on the corner, just below the window of his berth there stood a boy of eighteen or twenty years. The boy was tall, thin, and rather fragile-looking, his face had the sullen, scowling almost feverish intensity that boys have on such occasions, he stood there indecisively, as if trying to make up his mind, resolve himself, towards his next action; he put a cigarette into his mouth and lighted it and as he did so, his hands trembled. He turned up the collar of his overcoat impatiently, glanced grudgingly and nervously about him and stood there smoking.

Meanwhile a young prostitute, still slender and good-looking, came out of the back room, strolled over to the corner and stood there indolently, looking around with an innocent and yet impudent look, appearing not to look directly at the boy, or openly to invite him, but plainly waiting for him to speak to her.

And all the time his efforts to make up his mind, to come to a decision, were comically evident. He kept puffing nervously and rapidly at his cigarette, glancing at the girl out of the corner of his eye from time to time, pretending not to notice her, and all the time steeling himself to a decisive action.

But even as he stood there in this temper, trying to focus his wavering decision on a conclusive act, another man came up and took the girl away from him. The other man was much older than the boy; he was in his middle thirties, he was powerfully built and well, though somewhat flashily dressed. He wore a gray felt hat, set at a smart angle on his head, a well-fitting and expensive-looking overcoat cut in at the waist in the "snappy" Broadway fashion, and he looked like a prosperous Greek; he had a strong, swarthy, brutal face, full of sensual assurance, he came walking along the narrow sidewalk beside the tracks, and when he saw the girl, he approached her instantly, with a swaggering assurance, began to talk to her, and in a moment walked away with her.

And again, the effect of this incident upon the boy was comically, pathetically, apparent. He did not appear to notice the girl and the Greek as they walked off together, but when they had gone, his lean young face hardened suddenly, the scowl deepened, and with a sudden angry movement he flung his cigarette into the gutter, turned, and with the sudden resolution of a man who is ashamed of his cowardly procrastination and indecision, he began to walk rapidly along the dark and narrow little sidewalk that ran down beside the tracks and along a row of shabby station tenements.

And again, that strange and stage-like panorama of human comedy was fantastically repeated: the train began to move, and the boy kept pace with it, below the windows of the berth. Immediately they began to pass the row of shabby old wooden brothels that bordered on the tracks; the windows were closely shuttered, but through the shutters there flamed hot exciting bars of reddish light, and in the doorway entrances the small red lights were burning. At the third house, the boy paused, turned, ran swiftly up the wooden steps and rang the bell, almost instantly a small slot-like peep-hole in the door was opened, an inquiring beak-like nose, a wisp of blondined hair peered out, the door was opened, the boy entered in a glow of reddish light, the door was closed behind him, and the train, gathering rapidly in speed now, went on, past the police station where the night-time cops were sitting, past spokes of brown streets, old buildings, warehouses, factories, station tenements, the sudden barren glare of corner lamps—the grimy façade of old rusty buildings—the single substance and the million patterns of America!

And now the train had left the town, and now there was a vast and distant flare, incredible in loveliness, the enormous train yards of the night, great dings and knellings on the tracks, the flare and sweep of mighty rails, the huge and sudden stirrings of the terrific locomotives.

And then there was just loneliness and earth and night, and presently the river, the great and silent river, the noble, spacious, kingly river sweeping on forever through the land at night to wash the basal cliffs and ramparts of the terrific city, to flow forever round its million-celled and prisoned sleepers, and in the night-time, in the dark, in all the sleeping silence of our lives to go flowing by us, by us, by us, to the sea.

That vision haunted him. He could not forget it. That boy who stood there on the corner in that lonely little town at night became the image of his own desire, of the desire of every youth that ever lived, of all the lonely, secret, and unsleeping desire of America, that lives forever in the little towns at night, that wakes at times, a lively, small, and savage flame, while all the sleepers sleep, that burns there, unimprisoned and alone, beneath immense and timeless skies, upon the dark and secret visage of the continent, that prowls forever past the shuttered façades of the night, and furious, famished, unassuaged and driven as it is, lives alone in darkness and will not die.

That urge held and drew him with a magnetic power. Eight times that spring he made that wild journey of impulse and desire up the river. Eight times in darkness over pounding wheel and rod, he saw the wild and secret continent of night, the nocturnal sweep and flow of the great river, and felt the swelling of the old, impossible and savage joy within him. That little town, seen first with such a charm and dream-like casualness out of the windows of a passing train, became part of the structure of his life, carved upon the tablets of his brain indelibly.

Eight times that year he saw it in every light and weather: in blown drifts of sleeting snow, in spouting rain, in bleak and wintry darkness, and when the first gray light of day was breaking haggardly against its ridge of eastern hills. And its whole design—each grimy brick and edge and corner of its shabby pattern—became familiar to him as something he had known all his life.

He came to know its times, its movements, and its people: its station workers, railway men, and porters; the night-time litter of the station derelicts and vagabonds themselves, as he was blown past this little town in darkness.

And he came to know all the prowlers of the night that walk and wait and wear the slow gray ash of time away in little towns—and this too was like something he had known forever. He came to know them all by sight and word and name: the taxi drivers, lunchroom countermen, the soiled and weary-looking night-time Greeks, and all the others who inhabit the great shambles of the night.

Finally, and as a consequence of these blind voyages, he came to know all the whores that lived there in that little row of wooden tenements beside the tracks. Eight times, at the end of night, he came again into the last commerce of their fagged embrace; eight times he left those shabby, shuttered little houses in gray haggard light; and eight times that year, as morning came, he again made the journey down the river.

And later he could forget none of it. It became part of a whole design —all of its horror and its beauty, its grime and rustiness of stark red brick, its dark and secret loneliness of earth, the thrill and magic of its casual friendly voices, and the fagged yet friendly commerce of the whores, the haggard light of morning at the ridges of the hills, and that great enchanted river greening into May—all this was one and single, woven of the same pattern, and coherent to the same design— and that design was somehow beautiful.

That spring, along the noble sweep of the great river he returned at morning to the city many times. He saw April come, with all its sudden patches of shrewd green, and May, with all its bloom, its lights of flowers, its purity of first light and the bird-song waking in young feathered trees, its joy of morning-gold on the great river's tide.

Eight times that spring, after all the fury, wildness and debauch of night, he rode back at morning towards the city in a world of waking men: they were for the most part railroad men—engineers, firemen, brakemen, switchmen, and train conductors, on their way to work. And their homely, seamed and pungent comradeship filled him with the health of morning and with joy.

And his memory of these journeys of the night, and these wonderful returns at morning, was haunted always by the vision of a single house. It was a great white house, set delicate and gleaming in frail morning light upon a noble hill that swept back from the river, and it was shaded by the silent stature of great trees, and vast swards of velvet lawn swept round it, and morning was always there and the tender purity of light.

That house haunted his memory like a dream: he could not forget it. But he did not know, he could not have foreseen, by what strange and dreamlike chance he would later come to it.

LIII

LAUGHING, and breaking at once into the loud harsh accents of the city, the class scrambled to its feet, and began to gather up its books. Eugene walked rapidly to his table which stood upon a little platform a few inches above the floor and stationing himself behind it, he began feverishly and untidily to stuff away into his brief-case text books and themes and the pile of examination papers in which were written out the results of the short "quiz" he had given them that night. But he knew without looking what those results would be. Miss Feinberg would tell him that "Christabel" had been written by "Keiths," and that "it was sort of an epic or narrative poem of a very romantic nature such as they had in those days." Mr. Katz would assure him that "The Eve of St. Agnes" had been written by "Wadsworth," "and you might say there is something very mysterious and peculiar about the atmosphere of the poem." Mr. Harry Fishbein would explain that a sonnet "is a kind of poetry they have, usually of a short nature. The first part of a sonnet is called the octrave. Shakespeare wrote some sonnets, as did also Wadsworth and Keiths!" Only Abe—Abe alone, the merciless and relentless and unfaltering Abe, Abe with his dull, gray, scornful face would make no errors. As for the others, what difference did it make? Would these garbled renderings of what their ears had dully heard make any change for good or ill in the garbled chaos of their lives, the glare and fury of the streets? Would Herrick sing his sweet bird-song to Mr. Shapiro as he roared down to work each morning in the Bronx Express? Would Miss Feinberg think of Crashaw as she ate her noonday cream-cheese sandwich in the drug store? Would it matter much to Katz whether "Wadsworth" or "Keiths" had written "La Belle Dame," so long as he "got by," so long as he "got his," so long as he "got what was comin' to 'm"?— Eugene could not think it. He had heard all the reasons for this folly, and the words that had been used were very fine—"a larger vision,"—"a sense of the larger life," and so on—but the bewilderment of these turbulent and raucous young people was scarcely greater than his own.

At the end of each class, jostling, thrusting, laughing, shouting, and disputing, they would surge in upon him in a hot, clamorous, and insistent swarm, and again, as Eugene backed wearily against the wall and faced them, he had the maddening sense of having been defeated and overcome.

For the weariness of flesh was like the weariness a man has after a great burst of love with a potent and adored mistress—the back was drawn in, half-broken, toward his trembling, wrung, depleted loins, his limbs faltered and his fingers shook, his breath came heavily, his body respired slowly in a state of languorous exhaustion, but where the weariness of triumphant love brings to a man a sense of completion, victory, and finality, the weariness of the class brought to him only a feeling of sterility and despair, a damnable and unresting exacerbation and weariness of the spirit, a sense of having yielded up and lost irrevocably into the sponge-like and withdrawing maws of their dark, oily and insatiate hunger, their oriental and parasitic gluttony, all of the rare and priceless energies of creation: he thought with a weary and impotent fury of great plans and soaring ecstasies of hope and ambition—of poems, stories, books which once had swarmed exultantly their cries of glory, joy, and triumph through his brain—and now all this seemed lost and wasted, flung riotously and fruitlessly away into the blind maw of a headless sucking mouth, a dark brainless, obscene and insatiate hunger.

As he looked at them, a horrible memory returned of the great fish which once he had caught in deep-sea water outside Boston harbor: he could feel again the sudden heavy living tug, the wriggling vitality, at the end of 200 feet of line, and then the wet line slipping harshly through his fingers as exultantly he drew the great fish upward to the surface. Then he remembered the sense of loss and disgust and horror when he saw it: it swam upward wriggling heavily in a flail of heavy dying protest, through a thickened murk of greenish water, and he saw that to its brain was fastened some blind horror of the sea, a foul snake-like shape a foot or more in length, a headless, brainless mouth, a blind suck and sea-crawl, a mindless abomination, glued implacably, fastened in fatal suck in one small rim of bloody foam against the brain-cage of the great dying fish. How often, in a mad fury of escape and freedom, it had lashed its brain to bloody froth against some razored edge, some coral stype upon the swarming jungle of the sea, he did not know; but the memory of it had returned a thousand times in abominable waking-sleeping visions of the night to haunt him with its blind and mouthless horror, and now he thought of it again, as they drew in on him their sucking glut of dark insatiate desire.

Their dark flesh had in it the quality of a merciless tide which not only overwhelmed and devoured but withdrew with a powerful sucking glut all rich deposits of the earth it fed upon: they had the absorptive quality of a sponge, the power of a magnet, the end of each class left him sapped, gutted, drained, and with a sense of sterility, loss, and defeat, and in addition to this exhaustion of the mind and spirit, there was added a terrible weariness and frustration of the flesh: the potent young Jewesses, thick, hot, and heavy with a female odor, swarmed around him in a sensual tide, they leaned above him as he sat there at his table, pressing deliberately the crisp nozzles of their melon-heavy breasts against his shoulder, slowly, erotically they moved their bellies in to him, or rubbed the heavy contours of their thighs against his legs; they looked at him with moist red lips through which their wet red tongues lolled wickedly, and they sat upon the front rows of the class in garments cut with too extreme a style of provocation and indecency, staring up at him with eyes of round lewd innocence, cocking their legs with a shameless and unwitting air, so that they exposed the banded silken ruffle of their garters and the ripe heavy flesh of their underlegs.

Thus, to all his weariness of mind, the terror and torment of his spirit, a thousand erotic images of an aroused, but baffled and maddened sensuality, were added: they swarmed around him like the embodiment of all the frustrate hunger, desire, and fury he had come to know in the city, with a terrible wordless evocation of men starving in the heart of a great plantation, of men dying of thirst within sight of a shining spring, with a damnable mockery, a nightmare vision of proud, potent and hermetic flesh, of voluptuous forms in hell, forever near, forever palpable, but never to be known, owned, or touched.

The girls, the proud and potent Jewesses with their amber flesh, schooled to a goal of marriage, skilled in all the teasings of erotic trickery, with their lustful caution and their hot virginity pressed in around him in a drowning sensual tide: with looks of vacant innocence and with swift counter-glances of dark mockery, they pressed upon him, breathing, soft and warm and full, as they cajoled, teased, seduced with look or gesture, questioned trivially, aggressively, uselessly—those with a body, and no mind, intent alone upon seduction spurred on perhaps by some belief that promotion and reward in all the business of life could best be got at in this way; and those with minds and bodies both, intent upon some painful mixture of sharp protest, struggle, and seduction which made erotic musings in their soul: "Oh, but I don't—ag-gree with you at aw-ull! That's not the meaning that I saw in it, at aw-ull! I think you're being very supe-er-fish-al. I don't ag-gree with you at aw-ull!"—the rich voices, aggrieved, injured, hen-like and sensual, omened with deep undernotes of ripe hysteria, rose and fell with undulant cluckings of yolky protest—the rich sensual voices of the Jewesses receiving, giving, returning and withdrawing, rose and fell in curved undulance of yolky hen-clucking protest, with omens of a ripe hysteria. Receiving, clucking, and protesting with their warm hen-feathered cries, they seemed to say, "Oh, come and take me, break me, but I don't ag-ree with you at aw-ull; Cluck-cluck-cluck-

cluck-cluck! Oh, do, oh, don't, we will, we won't, but we don't ag-ree
with you at aw-ull!"—the rich injured undulations of aggrieved protest, the omened menace of impending hysteria awoke in an alien spirit
a powerful surge of desire and humor, a wave of wild choking laughter
mixed with love and lust as one listened to the sensual, aggrieved, hen-
clucking protest of their souls.

The Jewish women were as old as nature, and as round as the earth:
they had a curve in them. They had gone to the wailing walls of death
and love for seven thousand years, the strong convulsive faces of the
Jews were ripe with grief and wisdom, and the curve of the soul of the
Jewish women was still unbroken. Female, fertile, yolky, fruitful as
the earth, and ready for the plow, they offered to the famished wanderer, the alien, the exile, the baffled and infuriated man, escape and
surcease of the handsome barren women, the hard varnished sawdust
dolls, the arrogant and sterile women, false in look and promise as a
hot-house peach, who walked the streets and had no curves or fruitfulness in them. The Jewish women waited with rich yolky cries for
him, and the news they brought him, the wisdom that they gave to him
was that he need not strangle like a mad dog in a barren dark, nor perish,
famished, unassuaged, within the wilderness beside a rusted lance—
but that there was still good earth for the plow to cleave and furrow,
deep cellars for the grain, a sheath for the shining sword, rich pockets of
spiced fertility for all the maddened lunges of desire.

They pressed around him at his table with insistent surge, and he
looked at them and saw that they were young; and sometimes they
belonged to the whole vast family of the earth: they were like all the
young people who had ever lived—they seemed clumsy, and noisy and
good, full of hope and loyalty and folly; and sometimes again, it seemed
to him that none of them had ever known youth or innocence, that they
had been born with old and weary souls, that they were born instructed
in the huge dark history of pain, the thousand mad and tortured sick-
nesses of the soul, and that the only thirst and hunger that they knew,
the desire that drove them with an insatiate lust, was for sorrow, grief,
and human misery. Had they ever cried into the howling winds at
night? Had they ever felt the sharp and tongueless ecstasy of spring,
or held their breath at night when great wheels pounded at the rail,
or trembled with a vast dark wave of pain, a wordless cry of joy, when
they heard ships calling at the harbor's mouth and thought of new lands

in the morning? Or had they always been so old and wise, so full of grief and evil?

The girls pressed in on him their sensual wave, and the boys stood farther off, behind them, waiting, and he saw the dark and furtive glances of the men pass slyly, each to each, in swift final looks of cynical communication. They waited for the women to have done, with a kind of hard and weary patience, an old and knowing agreement, a sense of acceptance, as if they had known for thousands of years that their women would betray them with a Gentile lover, and yet with a kind of triumph, as if they also knew they would regain them and be victorious in the end.

They seemed to have gained from life the terrible patience, the old and crafty skill and caution that come from long enduring of pain: as he looked at them he knew that they would never be wild and drunken, or beat their knuckles bloody on a wall, or lie beaten and senseless in the stews, but he knew that with smooth faces they would decant the bottle for some man who did, and that they would read him quietly to his desperate fate with their dark, mocking, and insatiate eyes. They had learned that a savage word would break no bones and that the wound of betrayal or a misprized love is less fatal than the stroke of the sword, the thrust of the knife: in the years that followed he saw that physically they were, for the most part, incorrupt, old and cautious, filled with skill and safety—that they had lived so long and grown so wise and crafty that their subtile, million-noted minds could do without and hold in dark contempt the clumsy imperfections of a fleshly evil—that they could evoke and live completely in a world of cruel and subtle intuitions, unphrased and unutterable intensities of cruelty, shame, and horror, without lifting a finger or turning a hand. Thus, in these years, as his own mind grew mad and twisted with the insane fabrications of a poisonous jealousy—as it immediately and without a bridge or break translated into terms of literal physical actuality an insane picture of cruelty and horror: of daughters who acted as procurers to their mothers, of sons and husbands going unperturbed to sleep in houses where their sisters, wives, and children lay quilted in the lust and evil abominations of an adulterous love, of calm untelling faces, looks and glances of a childlike purity, an air of goodness, faith and morning innocence throughout, while the whole knowledge of an unspeakable evil trembled in their hearts forever with an obscene and soundless laughter —these abominations of his fancy, this vile progeny which his mad brain translated into literal fact, were probably for the most part only images the cruel and subtle minds of the old, wise, patient Jews had evoked and played with in their complex fantasy; and as he looked at the swarm of dark insistent faces round him at the table, an overwhelming sensation of defeat and desolation drowned his spirit—their dark looks read, and ate, and mocked at him, and yet were full of affection and tenderness as if they loved the food they fed upon: it seemed to him that he alone must die; that he must break his heart and smash his bones, lie beaten, drunken, mashed and senseless in the dives, must wreck his reason, lose his sanity, destroy his talent, and die a mad-dog howling in the wilderness while they—they alone—these old, wise, weary, patient, pain-devouring subtle-minded Jews—endured.

LIV

ROBERT's mistress had come to town, and Robert asked Eugene to dine with them. In spite of the fact that Robert had talked constantly of his love for Martha, they snapped and snarled at each other throughout the evening. They went to a restaurant on Sixth Avenue in Greenwich Village for dinner. During the course of the meal several people came in whom Robert knew: the moment he saw them he would call sharply to them, or jump up nervously and go to greet them. Then he would bring them back to the table and, in a tone of dogged and sullen intensity, introduce them to Martha, saying: "I want you to meet my wife." Martha's face would flush with anger and sullen rage, but she would acknowledge the introduction and mutter a few uncordial words of greeting. As for the people to whom he introduced her, they at first received the news that Martha was his wife with a look of blank stupefaction, managing, at length, to stammer: "B-b-but we didn't know you were married, Robert! Why didn't you let some one know about it? When did it happen?"

"About two weeks ago," he said brusquely, obviously getting a fierce and sullen satisfaction from this absurd lie.

"Where are you living?"

"At the Leopold."

"Will you be staying there?"

"No, we're moving out soon."

"Are you going to live in New York?"

"Yes," he said doggedly, "we've taken an apartment. . . . Going to move in Monday."

"Why, Robert!" they cried, having now recovered some fluency of speech, "we're awfully glad to know about this." And the women with some pretense at cordiality would turn to Martha, saying, "You must come to see us when you've settled down," and the men would wring Robert by the hand, slap him on the back, and dig him in the ribs. It was obvious that Robert derived a fierce and perverse pleasure from his stupid lie, but the girl was in a state of smouldering rage which blazed out at him the moment his friends had gone away. "You damn fool," she snapped, "what do you mean by telling a lie like that?"

"It's not a lie," he said, "it's the truth. You're my wife in everything but name!"

"You're a liar! Take that back! Don't you believe him," she said to Eugene, "there's not a word of truth in what he says. . . . You damned fool!" she blazed out at him. "What do you mean by telling your friends a story like that? Don't you know they're going to find out that you lied to them. And then," she added bitterly, "what are they going to say about me? You never thought of that, did you? Oh, no! You don't care if you ruin me or not! All you think of is yourself!"

"I don't care," he said with a sullen fierceness, "you're my wife and that's what I'm going to tell them all!"

"You're not!"

"I am! I'll show you if I don't!"

"I'm not your wife, and you needn't be so sure I ever will be! I got married once to a sick man, and I'll think it over a good long time, I assure you, before I get married again to a crazy man! Now, you'd better not be too sure of yourself, Mr. Weaver! You're not married to me yet by a long shot!"

A bitter quarrel broke out between them: they snarled, snapped, sneered, and wrangled—their voices rose until people at other tables began to look at them and listen curiously, but they paid no attention whatever to any one but themselves. Robert ended the argument suddenly by pushing his chair back from the table, sighing heavily, and saying feverishly and impatiently:

"All right, all right, all right! You're right! I'm wrong! Only, for God's sake, shut up and let me have a little peace!" Then they got into a taxi and went back to the hotel. They had a bottle of whiskey and they all went up to Robert's room, telephoned for ice and ginger ale, and began to drink. It was a little before midnight.

About two o'clock that night, as they sat there, a light, odd step, approaching briskly, came down the corridor and paused outside Robert's door: then some one rapped lightly and sharply at the door, and with this same movement of an odd, light and exuberant vitality. They looked at one another with the sudden startled look of people who feel the interruption of an intense silence around them—for the Leopold for two hours had been steeped in this silence of sleep, and they now experienced its living and animate presence for the first time. A good many sensations of guilt—all but the real one—flashed through their minds: that they had been drinking and making more noise than they should, and that a guest had complained to the office about them; or that some one had discovered that Robert had a woman in his room, and that, in the interests of hotel decorum, she was to be commanded to leave and go to her own quarters. The rapping at the door was repeated, more brisk and loud. They were all very still, Robert looked at Eugene nervously, remembering, perhaps, the sum of his past errors at the hotel and his precarious standing there.

"You go see who it is," he said.

Eugene went to the door and opened it. A man—or rather, the wisp, the breath, the fume of what had been a man—stood there: it was a small figure with nothing on its skeleton of fragile bone which was recognizable as living flesh, with only the covering, it seemed, of a parchment-like skin so tightly drawn over the contours of the face and head that the skull widened and flared with an impression of enormous dome-like width and depth above a face so wizened and shrunken that one remembered it later only as a feverish glint of teeth, an unshaved furze of beard, and two blazing flags of red, darkened and shadowed by the sunken depth of the sockets of the eye, where burned a stare of an incredible size and brilliance—that and the whispering ghost of a voice, the final, dominant, and unforgettable impression.

This wraith was clothed, or rather, engulfed, in garments which, although of good cut and quality, it seemed never to have worn before: they swathed it around and fell away in shapeless folds so that the body was as indecipherable among them as a stick, and the neck emerged from a collar through which it seemed the whole figure of the man might have slipped as easily as through a hoop.

And yet the creature was burning with a savage energy which coursed like an electric current through his withered body: it bore him along at a light, odd step, capricious and buoyant as the bobbing of a cork, and it foamed and bubbled in him now as he stood impatiently rapping at the door, and it blazed in his eyes with a corrupt and fatal glee, a mad flaming exuberance, a focal intensity of triumph, joy, and hate.

He entered the room immediately as soon as Eugene opened the door: he went in briskly at his light corky step and immediately said briskly and jovially in his whispering thread of voice: "Good evening! Are we all here? Is every one well? Did some one say something?"—he looked around inquiringly, then, with a disappointed air, continued — "No? I thought some one spoke. Well, then, come in, Mr. Upshaw. Thank you, I will. Won't you sit down? Yes, indeed!" He seated himself. "Will you have a drink? I should be delighted"—here he took the bottle, poured a stiff shot of whiskey into a glass, and drank it at one gulp. When he had finished, he looked around more quietly until his gaze rested with a kind of evil temperance on his wife: "Hello, Martha," he said casually and quietly. "How are you?" She did not answer and in a minute he repeated, still with his evil calm but with a more vicious intensity of tone, "Listen, you God-damned bitch! . . . When I ask you a question, you answer. How are you?"

"How did you get here?" she said.

"Oh!—Surprised to see me, is she?—Well, I tell you, darling, how it was. I was going to walk—I was going to walk, if necessary—now that just shows you how anxious I was to see you—I was going to walk the whole damned way from Denver, right over mountains and prairies and rivers and everything—but I didn't have to. I found a train all ready to go, darling; it was waiting for me when I got there, so 'Why walk?' I said. When I got to Kansas City I found an airplane waiting there, so I said, 'Why ride when flying's faster?' So that's the way I got here, darling."—He paused and drank again.

"How did you know where to find me?" asked Martha sullenly.

"Oh!" said Upshaw, lightly and gaily, "that was no trouble at all. Where should I find you, my dear? Where did I expect to find you? Why, right in the bedroom of my dear old pal, Mr. Robert Weaver, of course. I knew he'd look after you. I knew he wouldn't leave an innocent young girl like you to wander around all alone in the city. . . . Hi, there, Robert," he said cordially, lifting his hand in a salute of friendly greeting, as if noting Robert's presence for the first time.

"How are you, boy! I'm glad to see you. You've been looking after my wife, haven't you, Robert? You took care of her, didn't you? I'm much obliged to you. . . . You son-of-a-bitch," he added quietly and slowly, and with an accent of infinite loathing.

No one spoke, and after gazing at his wife a moment longer with this same air of evil quietness, he said, in a tone of mock surprise: "Why, what's the matter? You don't look a bit glad to see me, darling. Most men's wives would be wild about a husband who flew across the country in an aeroplane to see them, most women would be crazy about that."

"I wish," the girl said bitterly, "that you had fallen into a river and drowned."

"Now, is *that* nice! Is *that* kind!" said Upshaw in a tone of grieved reproach.

He turned toward Eugene and spoke to him for the first time. . . . "Now, I leave it to you, Mr. ——" he hesitated, "I didn't catch your name, sir, but is it all right if I call you Mr. Whipple?"

"Yes," Eugene said. "It's all right."

"Good!" he cried. "I knew it would be. The reason I say that is I used to have a friend out in Cleveland named Charley Whipple, who was just the same type of fellow that you are—*you* know," he said quietly and sneeringly, "a fine clean-cut fellow, eyes glowing with health, beautiful complexion, broad-shouldered, both feet on the ground, good to his mother.—Oh! he was a prince!—Just the same sort of looking fellow you are—so you won't mind if I call you by his name, will you? You remind me so much of him. Well, now, Mr. Whipple, I ask you if you think it's nice for a man's wife to talk to him like this? Is it kind? Is it fair?"

"She's not your wife," said Robert. "She's my wife."

For the first time Upshaw turned and faced his enemy squarely: he surveyed him slowly, up and down, with eyes which burned and glittered with their hatred. "Did you say something?" he asked.

"You heard me," said Robert.

"Did any one speak to you? Did any one say anything to you?" Upshaw whispered. He was silent a moment; then he leaned forward slightly over the table. "Let me give you some advice," he said. "The only pity about this is that you're not going to be able to use it.—But I'm going to give it to you anyway: here it is—Don't fool with a dying man, Robert. If you're going to play around with any one, play around with the living, and not with the dead. Dead men are bad people to play around with."

"All right! All right!" cried Robert in a hoarse, excited tone. "That constitutes a threat! . . . Martha, Eugene, . . . I call on you to bear witness that he threatened me! We'll just see how that sounds in a court of law."

"Courts! Law!" said Upshaw; and even as he spoke they all felt instantly how preposterous was Robert's threat and how meaningless such terms had become for this wisp of a man.

"Do you think I care one good God-damn now for all the courts and laws that ever were? . . . Do you think there has been a time for the last two years when I gave a damn whether I lived or died?"

"Except to spite Martha and me," said Robert bitterly. "You cared about that, all right!"

"Yes," said Upshaw quietly. "You're right. I would have hung on to life as long as I could gasp a breath of air into what was left of my lung, and I would have lived on without a lung to breathe with in order to spoil your filthy game—that was the way I hated the two of you. You don't understand that, do you, Robert? You don't understand a man being able to hate so hard he can keep alive on it, he can use it instead of a lung to breathe with, he can use it instead of air. You don't know anything about that, do you?"

"Yes, I do," said Robert. "I knew you hated my guts all along!"

"Your guts!" Upshaw snarled. "Why, damn you, I hated the earth you walked upon, the air you breathed, the house you lived in, the places you went to; I hated all the people who saw you or spoke to you or had ever spent an hour in your company—you polluted the atmosphere for me if I even heard the sound of your voice."

"I know you did," said Robert, nodding. "What did I tell you?" he cried to Martha, with a note of triumphant conviction.

"You *know*! You *know*!" cried Upshaw fiercely. "Why, damn you, you poor cheap imitation of a contriving rascal, you damned little drug-store Casanova, you dirty little swine of a country-club snob, you village fortune-teller, you know nothing! . . . For two years I stayed alive with not enough sound lung left in me to cover the size of a silver dollar—and do you think it was because I was afraid to die, or wanted to live? No! No!" he whispered, and his face or rather that eloquence of eye and tooth grew passionate with the bitterest disgust and loathing he had ever seen. "I've had more than thirty years of it, and Christ! it's been enough! I've had my belly full of it. . . . I'm fed up all the way to here!" he whispered, and he struck himself fiercely at the base of the throat. He coughed, suddenly, briefly, terribly, and with a swift impatient movement of his hot corded fingers he snatched a towel from the rack beside the water-basin, pressed his lowered face into it and then stared for a moment with an expression of intent and fascinated disgust into its folds, then he flung the bloodied rag away impatiently.

"You know," he said again more calmly, and for the first time now with a touch of weariness, as if the fierce flame of this incredible energy of passion which had thus far upheld him had now been spent. "Why, you know nothing. It took a *man* to hate like that," he said. . . . "—a better man than you could ever be—yes! . . . with no more lung than a rabbit, I'm still a better man than you could ever be, for you are nothing but a thing without the courage even of your own rotten convictions——

"God!" he looked with weary disgust from one to the other as they sat sullen, dumbly sodden, saying nothing. "The two of you! What a pair! . . . And to think of the time I wasted hating you . . . to think of all the time when I might have been pushing daisies in some quiet spot . . . keeping myself alive by thinking of this moment." His body was shaken again by a horrible soundless laughter. "Christ! . . . To think that I should ever have wanted to kill either of you."

"To kill us!" said Robert hoarsely, not with fear but accusingly, as if he were collecting damning evidence in a trial.

"Yes," Upshaw answered with the same weary tranquillity, "to kill you! . . . I've breathed and drunk and thought it for two years. I've lived just for this moment. I came two thousand miles across the continent to blow your brains out. . . ."

"Did you hear him?" cried Robert, jumping up from the table. "Did you hear what he said, Martha? Did you hear him threaten me?"

"Sit down!" said Upshaw quietly. "I've seen you now and I'm satisfied. I wouldn't touch you. Why, God-damn you, you're not worth it, either of you." Again he surveyed them with slow loathing, and broke into his soundless laughter. "Kill you! Why, I wouldn't do either of you so big a favor. You don't deserve such luck! I'll let you live and rot together. . . . Take her! . . . Take her!" he cried, more strongly, his eyes burning into fury. "Take her! . . . But before you do"—with a swift movement he withdrew from his pocket a small and crumpled wad of dollar bills—"here! I want to give you something!" And he flung them straight at Robert's face, "Take that . . . and go and get yourself a *good* whore while you're at it!"

Robert sat perfectly still for a moment; then he got up slowly, went over to the door, and flung it open and walked back to the table. . . . "Get out of here," he said. Upshaw did not move: he sat regarding him silently, with an intent, contemptuous, catlike stare.

"Did you hear me?" said Robert. . . . "Get out of my room!"

"Sit down," said Upshaw. "You're going to annoy me."

"Annoy you! I'll annoy you, you damned rascal," Robert cried furiously, and suddenly he slapped Upshaw in the face, shouting, "You're going out of here this minute, do you hear? . . . I'll show you if you can insult me in my own place," and he lunged viciously towards him.

What happened then was so sudden and swift that Eugene could never thereafter remember clearly the order in which all of the events occurred: as Robert plunged towards the little man, Martha spoke sharply to him, commanding him to be still, at the same moment the table and two chairs overturned with a crash of glassware . . . and Upshaw, somehow, with an incredible speed of movement was on his feet and moving backward out of the way of Robert's lunging fist. Eugene had a brief and terribly clear sensation of a gesture of catlike speed as Upshaw thrust his hand into the pocket of his coat and then the bright wicked wink of steel. Then Martha was on top of him, clinging frantically to his arm, wrestling him into the wall, and in a moment wrenching the weapon from his grasp.

For a moment there was no sound in the room whatever save the sound of three excited people breathing rapidly and heavily, and another sound, the terrible sound of Upshaw's breathing, hoarse, rattling, painful, breaking suddenly and sharply into a torn gasping cough that was thick with blood. The first words spoken came from Martha:

"Close that door!" she commanded curtly.

Robert, instead of obliging her, turned to Eugene with an awed and quieted light in his eye.

"Did you see that?" he whispered to Eugene.—"Did you see him pull that gun on me? . . . Why!" he cried with a kind of sudden astonishment, "it was assault with a deadly weapon! That's what it was! He tried to murder me!" He was beside himself with astonishment and excitement. "I'm going to get the police," and he rushed out into the hall.

"Go get that damned fool and bring him back here," she said to Eugene. *"And close that door!"*

Eugene ran out into the corridor just in time to see Robert disappear.

ing at his long stiff stride around the corner that led to the elevators in the main building. When Eugene got there Robert was pressing buttons feverishly, but unfortunately, because the hour was so late, and the elevator man was asleep below, his call had not yet been answered. Eugene seized him by the arm and began to pull him along back towards his room.

"Let go of me!" he said.

"You damned fool! . . . Do you want to ruin us all?"

He seemed to sober up and grew calmer after a moment or two of excited prayer and protest. They went back to the room quietly enough. When they got there Martha was supporting Upshaw's body against the basin of the washstand. The man, by this time, was either unconscious or semiconscious: all the savage and unholy energy which had burned for a space so incredibly that it had the power to hurl this diseased and near-dead mite across a continent, had now flared utterly out and the creature which the girl supported in her arms, with a kind of dark and sullen tenderness, seemed to have died and dwindled with it; the body was no longer discernible, it seemed to have faded, a fabric of rotten sticks, into a shapeless heap of clothing; it dangled shapelessly and grotesquely like some deflated figure, and yet from the head, from that death's head of skull and tooth and blazing eyes, there were spurting unbelievable, incredible fountains of blood: it burst simultaneously from the mouth and nostrils in a steady torrent until his skin was laced with it, it filled the basin, it was incredible that such fountains of bright blood should pour out of this withered squirrel of a man.

Robert sat down sullenly in a chair by the table after saying, "Now, this is your last chance. . . . I've had as much as I can stand. You've got to decide between us here and now!" She did not answer him, and he said no more, relapsing into a sullen and half-drunken stupor.

The girl washed the blood away from Upshaw's face with a towel: in a moment more she asked Eugene if he would help her carry him to the bed. Eugene picked him up and put him on the bed, his body felt like a handful of light dry sticks, he weighed no more than a child of ten, already his figure seemed, under the strange and terrible chemistry of death, to shrink and wither visibly from one moment to another but his head rested above that shapeless and grotesque bundle of clothing as if it had been severed from the body—with an immense austerity of line and light, a cold, stiffening, and upthrust calm.

Eugene went down to the office and told them what had happened.

The night clerk, a fat, shuffling old man with a mild, pasty face, and the black African negro who was at the telephone-board, received the news with astonishing calmness, and matter-of-factness, and then acted with an admirable coolness, speed and quiet precision, of which Eugene often thought in the months that followed, because it revealed to him. a kind of secret knowledge, a hidden seriousness in the hotel's working, and it showed, moreover, how much knowledge, ability, and decision may be stored behind the faces of inept and foolish-looking men.

Eugene looked at the clock above the office desk: it was now ten minutes after three o'clock in the morning. Within twenty minutes they had an ambulance, a doctor, and two stretcher-bearers at the hotel; the interne, a young Jew with a little mustache, walked quietly and casually into the room, with the ends of a stethoscope fastened in his ears. Eugene thought that Upshaw was already dead! His face had the upthrust marble rigidity of death, but after a moment's examination, the doctor spoke quietly to the two men with him, they put the stretcher on the floor and laid the withered little figure on it. As they started to move out of the room Upshaw's arms began to flop and jerk stiffly and grotesquely with every step they took: at another word from the doctor they put their burden on the floor again, the interne knelt swiftly, unknotted the cravat in Upshaw's collar and loosely tied his wrists together. Then they all went out, and Martha followed, holding Upshaw's hat. She rode over in the ambulance to the hospital, which was only a few blocks away in Fifteenth Street. Robert and Eugene followed in a taxi, there was no one on the streets, the buildings and the pavements had the hard, bare angularity they have early in the morning: they waited downstairs in a little room until shortly after five o'clock in the morning, when Martha came down to see them and to tell them that Upshaw had just died.

Then Eugene left Robert and Martha there together, and walked back towards the hotel. The streets were still bare, but in the east there was the first width of morning light, cold steel-gray, harsh and sharply clean: day was beginning to break, and he could hear the rumbling jingle of a milk-wagon, and the sound of hoof and wheel behind him in the lonely street.

LV

IF the hard and rugged lineaments of Abe's character had not at this time emerged out of the glutinous paste of obscure yearnings, there was no such indecision and uncertainty in the character of his mother. It was as legible as gold, as solid as a rock.

Abe's mother was an old woman, with the powerful and primitive features of the aged Jewess: she was almost toothless, a solitary blackened tooth stood mournfully in the centre of her strong ruined mouth: she had a craggy worn face, seamed and furrowed by a countless sorrow, a powerful beaked nose, and a strong convulsive mouth, a mask which was like a destiny since it seemed to have been carved and fashioned for the dirge-like wailing of eternal grief. The face of the old woman might have served not only as the painting of the whole history of her race, but as the painting of the female everywhere—not the female with her ephemeral youth, her brief snares of hair and hide, her succulent burst of rose-lips and flowing curve—but the female timeless, ageless, fixed in sorrow and fertility, as savage, as enduring, and as fecund as the earth. The old woman's face was like a worn rock at which all the waves of life had smashed and beaten: it was unmistakably the face of an old Jewess and yet the powerful and craggy features bore an astonishing resemblance to the face of a pioneer woman or of an old Indian chief.

Her life, moreover, had the agelessness of the earth, the timelessness of her race and destiny: she had not been touched at all by the furious and savage life of the city with its sensational brevities, its hard, special, temporal qualities of speech, fashion, and belief, its million ephemeral enthusiasms, briefly held and forgotten, the stunned oblivion of its memory, which, in the brutal stupefaction of a thousand days, can hold to nothing, so that even the memory of love and death cannot endure there and a man may forget his dead brother ere his flesh grow rotten in the grave.

The old woman did not forget: for her, as for the God she worshipped, the passing of seven thousand years was like the passing of a single day; yesterday, tomorrow, and forever, a moment at the heart of love and memory. Thus, once when Eugene had called Abe upon the telephone, a full year after the death of his oldest brother, Jacob, the old woman had answered: the old voice came feebly, brokenly, indecipherably, and was like a wail. He asked for Abe, she could not understand: she began to talk in an excited, toothless mumble—a torrent of Yiddish broken here and there by a few mangled words and scraps of English—all she knew. At length Eugene made her understand he wanted to speak to Abe: suddenly she recognized his voice and remembered him. Then, instantly, as if it had happened only the day before, and as if he had been a friend of her dead son, although he had never known him, the old woman began to wail, faintly and rhythmically, across the wire: "Jakie! . . . My Jakie! . . . Mein Sohn Jakie! . . . He is dead."

A few days later Eugene had gone home with Abe for dinner: he lived with his mother, two brothers, and Jimmy, his sister's illegitimate child, in a flat which occupied the second floor of an old four-storey red-brick house in Twelfth Street, near Second Avenue, on the East Side. The old woman had prepared a good meal for them: a thick rich soup, chopped chicken livers, chicken, cake, and a strong sweet wine: she served them but would not sit and eat with them: she came in briefly and shook hands shyly and awkwardly, mumbling incoherently, a mangled jargon of Yiddish and English. Suddenly, however, as if she had briefly mastered herself by a strong effort her old and sorrowful face was twisted by a convulsion of powerful and incurable grief, and a long, terrible, savagely wailing cry was torn from her throat: she turned blindly, and with a movement of natural and primitive sorrow, she suddenly seized the edges of her apron in her gnarled and worn hands and flung it up over her head and rushed toward the door at a blind, lunging, reeling step. She was like one demented by sorrow: the old woman began to beat her withered breasts and pull at her wispy gray hair, meanwhile running and stumbling blindly around her kitchen in a horrible and savage dementia and drunkenness of grief. Abe followed her out, and Eugene could hear his voice, low, urgent, and tender, as he spoke to her persuasively in Yiddish, and her long wailing cries subsided and he returned. His face was sad and weary-looking and in a moment he said: "Mama's breaking up fast. She's never been able to get over my brother's death. She thinks about it all the time: she can't get it off her mind."

"How long has he been dead, Abe?"

"He died over a year ago," Abe said. "But that doesn't matter: I know her—she'll never forget it now as long as she lives. She'll always feel the same about it."

This terrible and savage picture of grief was carved upon Eugene's memory unforgettably: it became a tremendous and formidable fact, a fact as ancient, timeless, and savage as the earth, a fact which neither the stupefying oblivion of the city's life, the furious chaos of the streets, the savage glare of ten thousand blind and dusty days could touch. The

old woman's grief was taller than their tallest towers, and more enduring than all their steel and stone: it would last forever when all the
city's bones were dust, and it was like the grief of all the women who
had ever beat their breasts and flung their aprons across their heads and
run, wailing, with a demented and drunken step: it filled him with
horror, anger, a sense of cruelty, disgust, and pity.

She was the fertile and enduring earth from which they sprung, and
all of them, transformed so sharply and so curiously by the city's tone
and life, drew in to her with devotion and respect: Abe, with his dreary
gray face of the man-swarm cipher, Sylvia with her feverish, electric
night-time glitter, all of the brothers and sisters, with all that was new,
sharp, alien, flashy, trivial, or material in speech, dress, manner, and
belief—all of them returned to her with love, loyalty, and reverence as
to some great broodhen of the earth. The old woman's life was rooted
in the soil of two devotions: the synagogue and the home, and all that
happened beyond the limits of this devotion was phantom and remote:
this soil was ageless, placeless, everlasting.

Abe loved his mother dearly: whenever he spoke of her, even casually, his voice was touched with a hush of respect and affection. But he
disliked his father: the few times Eugene heard him mention him he
spoke of him in a hard and bitter voice, referring to him as "that guy,"
or "that fellow," as if he were a stranger. Eugene never saw the father:
the children all felt bitterly towards him and had sent him away to room
alone. Abe told Eugene that the man was a shoemaker, and apparently
improvident and thriftless. He had never been able to earn enough
to support his family, and in addition, Abe said, he was a petty family
tyrant. Abe's childhood had been scarred by memories of privation,
tyranny and poverty—the mother and the children had had a
bitter struggle for existence, and Abe had worked since his eighth
year at a variety of hard, gray, shabby and joyless employments: he
had been a newsboy, a grocer's delivery boy, an office boy in a
broker's office, a typist in a collection agency endlessly writing out
form letters, the office man and secretary for the head-professor of
the architectural school, and one of these pallid, swarthy, greasily sweating youths of the fur and garment house districts who ceaselessly
propel through swarming and kaleidoscopic streets of trade small wheel-
trucks piled high with dresses, garments, furs, and clothes or with
the thousand travelling varieties of all that horrible nondescript junk
known under the indecisive name of "novelties." Once, also, he had

spent part of a summer in New Jersey unloading freight cars filled with Georgia watermelons, and for a considerable time he had driven a truck for his two oldest brothers, who had a zinc business in the "gas-house district" of the East Side, between Avenue A and the river and North of Fourteenth Street.

Here, once, Eugene had accompanied him at noon of a flashing day in spring, a glitter of light and flashing waters, a sparkle of gold and blue: in a large bare space near factories they had seen a ring of young thugs throwing dice, and near the river were the immense and ugly turrets of the gas tanks, and then the wharves, the great odorous piers, and the flashing waters—the vast exultant play and traffic of the river life, the powerful little tugs, the ships, and the barges laden with their strings of rusty freight cars.

As they walked away through the powerful ugliness and devastation of that district, with its wasteland rusts and rubbish, its slum-like streets of rickety tenement and shabby brick, its vast raw thrust of tank, glazed glass and factory building, and at length its clean, cold, flashing strength and joy of waters—a district scarred by that horror of unutterable desolation and ugliness and at the same time lifted by a powerful rude exultancy of light and sky and sweep and water, such as is found only in America, and for which there is yet no language—as they walked away along a street, the blue wicked shells of empty bottles began to explode on the pavements all around them: when they looked around to see from what quarter this attack was coming, the street was empty save for a young thug who leaned against the rotting edge of a closed door, hands thrust in pockets, and a look of pustulate and evil innocence upon his thin tough Irish face. The street was evil and silent and empty, but when they turned and went on again, the exploding bottles began to drop around them on the pavement in splinters of sinister blue.

Abe grinned toughly: he did not seem at all surprised or perturbed by the murderous stealth and secrecy of the attack, its obscene and cowardly uselessness. He explained that the district had been one of the worst in the city and the headquarters for one of the most criminal gangs: time and again the gangsters had broken into his brother's zinc shop and robbed it, and Abe and all his brothers, being Jews, had had to fight it out since childhood, foot and fist and tooth and nail, and club and stone, with the young Irish toughs and gangsters who infested the district. Such had been his childhood: he told Eugene many stories of bloody fights waged back and forth across these pavements, of young boys maimed, crippled, or blinded in these savage fights. of one boy who had his eye torn out of his head by his enemy's gouging thumb in a fight to a finish on one of the piers, and of another whose brains had been smashed out on the pavement below the elevated structure by a rock hurled by an enemy's hand in a fight of the neighborhood gangs. Thus, in pier and alley, on street and roof, children had learned the arts of murder, the smell of blood, the odor of brains upon the pavement. Abe told how one of his older brothers, Barney—a thickly set powerful-looking man with short thick hands and a tough meaty-looking fighter's face, gray, square, and good-humored—had to fight it out step by step with the gangsters, who had come to his shop, again and again, with demands for money—money which the merchants of the district paid them meekly and regularly for "protection" —a euphemism for graft and menace, a bribe for being left alone and for the assurance that one's shop would not be entered and one's stock smashed or stolen in the night. Barney had met all these menaces with a hard cold eye and two rock-like fists with which time and again he had beaten into a pulp the thugs who came to threaten him: he was a good man and a savage fighter and he had learned the arts of combat in the sternest and most brutal arena on earth—the city streets.

"And—oh-ho-ho-ho!"—softly, painfully, Abe lifted his widely grinning face and laughed, "how that guy loves it! Say! they picked the wrong one when they picked on him! Oh-ho-ho-ho-ho! *Can* he fight! *Does* he love it! Say! do you know what I saw him do to two of them one time—oh-ho-ho-ho-ho-ho! Gee! it was rich! They came in there to shake him down and— Oh! Ho-ho!—ho! You shoulda seen it! He picks up a keg of zinc that weighs 200 pounds and he *breaks* it—oh-ho-ho-ho!—over the first guy's head."

"And what became of the second guy?"

"Oh-ho-ho-ho! . . . Gee, it was rich! You shoulda seen that other guy get out of there! Say! He almost tore the door down in his hurry—oh-ho-ho-ho!"

Such were the various members of this family as Eugene came to know about them: each of them in his own way was marked by a decisive individuality and independence of spirit which told of their lives of combat, toil and struggle in the city streets, and yet, although indelibly marked, scarred and hardened by his life, none of them had been brutalized by it. In fact, as Eugene thought of all these people later, an extraordinary quality in them became evident. It was this: here was a family of poor East Side Jews, the children of an immigrant and thriftless shoemaker and an old orthodox Jewish woman. These children had all had to make their own way, to fight and struggle bitterly for a living: now some of them were tough, rugged and unlettered merchants, traders and mechanics, some were successful milliners and designers, and some were talented musicians, students of science, people of extraordinary intelligence and ability. And all of them, even the most unlettered, seemed to have a completely natural unaffected interest and respect for the arts, or for scholarly and intellectual attainment. This circumstance—this remarkable fusion in one poor Jewish family of elements which would have seemed almost incredible in the families of poor laboring or country people Eugene had known before—this combination of the manual, the commercial, the artistic and the scholarly in one poor family—seemed so natural both to him and to them that Eugene never found it strange or wonderful until years later.

LVI

JUNE had brought with it a blessed respite from his classes at the university. Now the summer drew on towards its close—the brutal and weary New York summer with its swelter of dead wet heats, its death of hope, its sorrow of a timeless memory. And yet, in the city's summer nights there was a kind of solemn joy, a hush of peace and light and human resignation that was so different from the wild and nameless joy and pain of spring, the sorrow of autumn, the winter's grim and stern protraction of the soul. *Then*—in these nights of waning summer—more than at any other season of the year, the immense and murmurous sound of time was audible. It was above one and around one, it was near and far, it was immense and omnipresent, and it was indefinable. It seemed to hover somewhere in the upper air, above the city's steep canyons, the giant explosions of her thousand towers, the swarming millions of her tortured and uneasy life forever waging their desperate, ugly and unprofitable strife in all her hot and tangled mazes. And that voice of time, above the ugly clamor of that tormented life, was imperturbable; immense, remote and murmurous, it seemed to have resumed into itself all of the rumors of the earth, and to comprise, out of the bitter briefness of man's days, the essence of his own eternity, and to be itself eternal, fixed, and everlasting, no matter what men lived or died.

The people of the city heard this sound of time, and on these evenings of the waning summer, their lives were subject to its spell. For the first time in many months one heard the sounds of quiet laughter in the streets at night, the voices of the people as they passed were strangely hushed, the sounds of life were immense, all murmurous as time itself.

This sense of peace, of resignation, of a quiet and tranquil sorrow and joy was everywhere; it may have been some quality of the summer air that imposed on all the violence of the city's life a kind of muted harmony, but the spirit of this peace seemed to have entered the very flesh and spirit of the city, somehow to have tranquillized the feverish blood and nervous and exacerbated bodies of its people. For the first time in months their eyes were quiet and thoughtful and had lost their look of hatred and suspicion, hostility and mistrust. Their faces had lost their strained, hard, and hurried look, even their tongues had lost some of their strident, rasping, and abusive violence.

That immense and murmurous hush of time and sorrowful acceptance had touched even the life of youth. At night one still saw groups of young men walking through the streets, but even they had somehow been subdued and chastened by this spell of time. And in these bands of youth—these straggling bands of young men who struggle through the city streets at night in groups of six or eight, and who have become so much a part of our familiar experience and the city's life that they no longer seem curious to us—the change that this great spell of time had wrought was perhaps more evident than anywhere else.

Where were the songs of youth upon those city streets? Where the laughter, the wild spontaneous mirth, the passion, warmth and golden poetry of youth? Where was the great boy Jason looking for brothers in the fellowship of that inspired adventure of man's youth—the proud, deathless image of what all of us desire when young, where was it? Where were the noble thoughts and ardors of young men, the fierce and bitter desperation and the proud and foolish hopes, the grand dreams and the music of the fleeting and impossible reveries—all that makes youth lovely and desirable, and that keeps man's faith—where was it among these young men on the city streets?

It was not there. Poor sallow, dark, swarthy creatures that they were, with rasping tongues, loose mouths and ugly jeering eyes, this infamous band of youth was death-in-life itself. It had been brought still-born from its mother's womb into a world of city streets and corners, into all the waning violence of the tenement, bitterly to try to root its meagre life into the rootless rock, meagrely to struggle in its infamous small phlegm along the pavements, feebly to imitate the feeble objects of its base idolatry—of which the most heroic was a gangster, the most sagacious was a pimp, the most witty was some Broadway clown.

How often have we seen them, heard them, turned away from them with weariness and disgust, as they straggled along at night, a meagre shirt-sleeved band of gangling sizes, each fearful and uneasy in the other's eye, kicking the ash-cans over as feats of derring-do, trying for approbation with a hoarse call and a pitiable and mirthless striving after repartee, of which the more glittering fragments ran like this:

"Hey-y . . . Eddy! . . . Holy Jeez! . . . Hey-y, youse guys! . . . Cuh-*mahn!*"

"Ah-h, what's yer hurry? . . . Hey-y! Youse udah guys! . . . Joe's in a hurry . . . Who's goin' t' pay duh taxi-ride?"

"Holy *Jeez!* What's keepin' yuh! . . . Youse guys, cuh-mahn!"

"Ah-h, guh-wahn. . . . What's t' hurry? Where's duh fire?"

Now in these nights of waning summer, even these raucous voices, the pitiable sterility of these feeble jests, that meagre and constricted speech consisting almost wholly of a few harsh cries and raucous imprecations that recurred intolerably, incredibly through all the repercussions of an idiot monotony—all of the rootless, fearful, and horrible desolation of these young pavement lives—was somehow caught up in this great and tragic nush and spell of time, transmuted by it, until even their vast unloveliness of youth was given a sorrowful quality of pity and regret.

August came, and with it already a faint and troubling premonition of the autumn—a breath, a fragrance, and an odor—that somehow spoke of summer's ending, the premonitory thrill and promise of the voyage. What was it? It was one of those very strange and troubling odors known here in America, of which our lives are all compact, which we have lived and breathed and known with our blood, and for which we have no language. It is, somehow—the odor of cities, cities, cities— at the hour of evening, the scorched end of every expiring day—the smell of evening hush and peace and of the sea in harbors. It is the smell of old worn woods, warm, resinous, sultry, getting into our very entrails somehow with its strange and nameless fragrance of sorrow and delight; the smell of the wooden baseball bleachers, of the old worn plankings of an amusement park, passed over by a million feet since morning; and it is the smell of street-cars, car-barns, the faded day-coach plush of trains, the smell of bridges and of old wharves and piers, of hot tarred roofing, and of tar out in the streets, of summer's fatigue, quietness, and summer's ending, the quiet and tranquil sorrow of memory as we remember youth, our father's voice upon the night-time summer porch, the smell of the grape-vines and the ripened grapes, the grinding screech and halt of a street-car on the hill above our father's house, and the knowledge that all this is lost, our father dead, our childhood gone, another year, our first in the great man-swarm of the city, ended—and this, the knowledge of the bitter briefness of our days, is somehow mixed with the smell of the sea in harbors, the freshen-ing breeze of evening, the call of ships, and, somehow, God knows how, with the intolerable thrill and promise of the unknown voyage.

And with this breath of autumn and the promise of the voyage there came to Eugene the news that Starwick was at that moment in the city—would stop there briefly on his way to Europe. At this time also, Joel Pierce turned up and Eugene renewed an acquaintance that had begun in Cambridge and lapsed during the interim.

LVII

HE had never met any of Joel Pierce's family, but one night towards seven o'clock when he had just returned to his room from the university, Joel telephoned him, and, saying that his father was in town, asked him if he would not go to dinner and to the theatre with them. He found Joel and his father waiting for him in the lobby. Mr. Pierce was a man of fifty years, comfortably dressed for the hot weather in a black mohair suit, and with a kind of stately yet spacious dignity of linen that was agreeably old-fashioned and that evoked a picture of an older and more leisurely generation. He was quite deaf—so deaf, in fact, that he made use of a small ear-phone—but his speech and manners, like his dress, were easy, friendly, and yet touched with an air of distinguished au-thority.

He took the two boys to the Lafayette for dinner, and ordered gen-erously and with the easy and comforting assurance of a man of the world who gives every one around him a happy feeling of security and well-being. For Eugene, it was a memorable experience.

The fine restaurant—it was perhaps the finest he had yet seen—the

French waiters, the delicious food, the beautiful women, the well-dressed, prosperous and worldly-looking men and the pleasant weary languor of fading day, the huge nameless thrill and prophecy of on-coming night touched him with a feeling of joy and nameless anticipation. He felt, as he had never felt before, that strange, seductive promise which the city has at evening, at the end of a day of terrible summer's heat, and which is so strangely mixed of sorrow and delight, of desolation and the promise of a wild and nameless joy.

And suddenly, all the horror, heat and desolation of the day was forgotten. He forgot the blind horror of the man-swarm thrusting through the mazes of the furious streets. He forgot the drowning flood of humid flesh, the pale, wet, suffering faces that thrust from nowhere out of sweltering heat, that were engulfed again into the heat-hazed distances of swarming streets in which man's life seemed more uncountable than the sands of the sea, and more blind, lost and horribly forsaken than the lives of those eyeless crawls and gropes that scuttle blindly and forever through murky ooze upon the sea's vast floor.

The old red light of evening filled his heart again with its wild prophecy, its huge and secret joy, and the great stride of oncoming night revived again, in all their magic, his childhood dreams of the enchanted city, the city of great men and glorious women, the city of unceasing joy, of power, triumph and success, and of the fortunate, good, and happy life.

As Mr. Pierce sat there with his air of quiet and urbane authority, studying the menu with a little frowning smile through the lenses of a pince-nez that dangled fashionably and casually from a black silk cord when he was not using it, the boy felt an indescribable sense of wealth and power and prosperous ease. It seemed to him that everything in the world was his for the asking, and the suave service of the waiter, hovering over Mr. Pierce with poised pencil and an attitude of devoted respect, the rich designs of snowy linen, the heavy silver, the thick carpets, the handsome women and distinguished-looking men, all added to this feeling of wealth and happiness.

Mr. Pierce kept studying the menu with an air of good-natured seriousness, quizzing his son from time to time with gruff but genial banter:

"Joel," he would say, "what do you want? Have you any preference of your own or will you leave it to me to decide?"

"Gosh!" Joel answered in his soft, eager tone. "I don't care, Pups. Whatever you say goes with me! You know, it's all the same to me, anyway. I can eat anything you order. Only," he added laughing, "I'd prefer it if there's no meat. I'd like it much better if you ordered vegetables."

Mr. Pierce knocked the pince-nez from his nose, and turning to Eugene with an air of agreeable confidence, said:

"What's wrong with a boy who takes no more interest in his food than that? Can you make it out? It strikes me as the most astonishing thing," he went on in a gruff, distinguished way, "to see a healthy young man who has no interest in his belly. Really, Joel," he went on, turning to his son and regarding him with a kind of quizzical but good-humored sarcasm, "I'd feel so much better about you if you only liked food more. It's really tragic to see a boy of your age deliberately throwing away one of the greatest pleasures in life. Don't you think so?" he demanded, turning to the other boy again with his air of friendly confidence. "Or have you turned vegetarian, too?"

"Gosh, no!" Joel said, laughing his hushed eager, immensely agreeable laugh. "He'll agree with every word you say, Pups. He likes food even more than you do."

"Then I'm glad to hear it!" said Mr. Pierce approvingly. "I had begun to fear that this younger generation had gone utterly to hell. But if the symptoms are only local—" he frowned humorously at his son for a moment—"perhaps it's not as bad as I thought."

"You and Pups should get along together beautifully," said Joel to Eugene. "He loves to eat—he's a wonderful cook—you should come up to Rhinekill sometime and let him cook one of his meals for you."

The ordering of the meal proceeded in this agreeable fashion. Mr. Pierce ordered liberally: small pink-fleshed clams, cold, pungent and exciting in their perfect shells, a thick pea soup with little squares of toast-crust floating in it, young chicken, plump and tender, grilled so succulently that it seemed to melt away the moment that one put it in his mouth, asparagus and potatoes, and a salad of crisp lettuce, beautifully mixed, "fatigued," in a big salad bowl, iced coffee, and a dessert of ripe Camembert and salted crackers. Mr. Pierce and Eugene ate heartily and with obvious relish, but Joel, in spite of all their protests and his father's bantering ridicule, which he took with the beautiful laughing good-nature which was one of the finest traits of his character, stuck to his vegetable diet with the gentle doggedness that was also characteristic of him.

Later, when they had finished dinner, they drove uptown in a taxicab and went to one of the summer musical shows near Broadway, where an English revue was appearing. The comic actress, Beatrice Lillie, was the star of the performance. Eugene had never heard of her before, but it was evident from the fashionable and "smart" look of the audience, and the way in which Joel and other people greeted every word and gesture, that the actress was "all the rage," one of those persons who, in addition to their native talent, have some special quality that for a time makes them the darling of the cult-adepts of the world of fashion.

The revue was a clever and amusing one, but it also had a stylish quality of fashionable smartness that was more and more beginning to mark the productions of the theatre and the responses of the audience. Thus, in later years, when one had almost completely forgotten the scenes of the revue and its songs and jokes, one could still remember it for the brilliant picture of the life it evoked. And the image of that life was implied rather than portrayed. The revue was one of those productions which people were beginning to "wear" as they "wore" books or plays or a dress: people went to the revue more because it was "the thing to do," the thing that every one was talking about, than because they had a genuine desire to go, more because they had been told that it was "amusing" than from any deep conviction that they would find it so.

Thus, not only in the jokes and songs and scenes of the revue, but in the laughter and applause with which the fashionable audience greeted them, there was a quality that was somewhat strained and metallic— a new and disagreeable mirth that was coming into man's life, which seemed to have its sources not in the warm human earth and blood of humor, but to proceed from something sterile, sour and acrid in his soul. In this hard and essentially lifeless merriment there was evident the desire to wound and mock and injure. And this desire came more from fear, a need to divert attention from one's own nakedness and insecurity by an attack upon a common target, than from any real cruelty or scornful hardihood of the soul.

This fear and insecurity was evident even in the fashionable and sophisticated audience which had come to this theatre to see the smart revue. In the interval between the acts, the people streamed up the aisles and out into the lobby, and everywhere one looked, the hostile fear and insecurity of the people were apparent. For the most part the audience was fashionably dressed, the men in evening clothes, the women in expensive evening gowns, that revealed their long white arms, the velvet perfection of their breasts and long backs. It would have been difficult to find a more assured, sophisticated and wealthy-looking group of people, but in spite of this air of complete worldly assurance, their unhappiness and fear were painfully evident. Their bodies seemed to throw off and to fill the air with a feverish electric tension, the texture of their thousand voices rising all together in a braided clamor was almost hysterically high, and remembering suddenly the quiet murmurous drone of voices in a theatre twenty years before, the glamorous spell of enchantment and happiness that surrounded even the performances of some travelling company in its one-night appearance in a little town, one felt poignantly again that something old and pleasant had gone out of life, that something dissonant, painful and unwholesome had changed man's rhythm, spread a poisonous infection through the human chemistries.

One also saw, or rather powerfully felt, among these fashionable and worldly-looking men of the great city, something jaded, puny, sterile, horribly weary; a quality as if their vital energies had been depleted in an unnatural way, as if they were emptied out, dried up, sapped of their juice, and could keep going now only by a kind of lifeless dynamism, a dry electric energy which paced them to the tempo of the city's furious life, which would not let them go until it had burned them hollow to a dry gray shell.

By contrast, the vivid loveliness of the women was astonishing. The differences that distinguished these women from these men, in coloring, in the velvety texture of the skin, in the sparkling eyes, red mouths, voluptuously seductive bodies and general healthiness and glowing elasticity of figure, were so great that one was reminded of those insect species whose females are wonderfully and fatally superior in strength and beauty to their drab mates, and who finally devour them. And yet, even in the faces and figures of these lovely women, the mutilation of that hard, metallic, blunted-out stamp was also evident: one noticed that the general quality of the tone of all these mixed and intermingled voices was feminine rather than masculine, and that the feminine voice was even more assertive, arrogant and incisive in its naked penetration than the voices of the men.

In fact, even as the two young men stood in one corner of the lobby, surveying the keyed pulsations of this brilliant scene, a woman's voice could be heard, speaking with an arrogant and dogmatic assertiveness that instantly quenched denial and left no room for disagreement, however mild:

"*Yes!* I think she is *very* charming, and *very* clever, and *terribly, terribly* amusing. The dancing is *very* bad; they simply *don't know how* to train a chorus. As for the songs, I thought that one she sings about Queen Mary's hats was *awfully* funny; the rest are only fair. Of course, the décor is *abominable*—but what can you expect? That man who sings the song with her is rather good—the other one, the awful little Cockney thing, is *simply horrible!* Where do they ever find these people anyway? . . . No! No!" she said harshly and arrogantly at this point as one of the men put in a mild, low-voiced, and apologetic interjection of his own, "I do *not* agree with you! I *absolutely* do *not* agree with you: you are *absolutely* wrong! The nursemaid scene is *decidedly* the best thing in the show! The restaurant scene is *very* dull, and *very* cheap, and *terribly, terribly* vulgar! And it is *very* stupid of you not to see it!"— And having delivered herself with womanly modesty of these tolerant and generous observations, the lady turned, saw Joel, and instantly addressed him, speaking to him in the same arrogant and assertive tones she had used before, and blurting her words out through lips that she kept perfectly straight and that scarcely seemed to move or open as she spoke:

"*Joel!*" she cried. "What on earth are you doing here? . . . I thought you were at Rhinekill or in Maine? . . . And where's your mother? . . . Did she come down too? . . . No? Too bad!" she said harshly. "I want *very* much to see her. . . . Yes, I shall be in Newport the week-end after next. . . . Yes, yes," she went on with metallic harshness, "—with Alice Mortimer. . . . Is she going, too? . . . Good; then I shall see her!— My *God,* no! . . . We're not staying here. . . . We motored in to see the show. . . . No, No. . . . I've been staying at Sands Point. . . . Jerry's at Southampton. . . . But *God,* no! . . . A whole summer in this hell-hole! . . . The man's *mad!* . . . How d'ya do!" she said curtly and harshly, throwing a cold look and a curt nod towards Eugene as Joel whispered at his name, and instantly dismissing him. . . . "But do you seriously mean you're going to spend the whole summer here? . . . Not *really!* . . . But, my dear child, what in

heaven's name ever prompted you to do an idiotic thing like that?
. . . Oh! I see!" she said coldly. "Painting, eh . . ."

But now the bell for the curtain sounded, and after a few conventional
words of parting they returned to their seats.

LVIII

THE Hudson River joins the harbor. And then the harbor joins the
sea. Always the rivers run.

The Hudson River drinks from out the inland slowly; it is like
vats that well with purple and rich wine. The Hudson River is like
purple depths of evening; it is like the flames of color on the Palisades,
elves' echoes, and old Dutch and Hallowe'en. It is like the Phantom
Horseman, the tossed boughs, and the demented winds, and it is like
the headed cider and great fires of the Dutchmen in the winter time.

The Hudson River is like old October and tawny Indians in their
camping places long ago; it is like long pipes and old tobacco; it is like
cool depths and opulence; it is like the shimmer of liquid green on summer days.

The Hudson River takes the thunder of fast trains and throws a handful of lost echoes at the hills. It is like the calls of lost men in the mountains; and it is like the country boy who is coming to the city with a
feeling of glory in his guts. It is like the green plush smell of the Pullman cars and snowy linen; it is like the kid in upper four and the good-
looking woman down below who stirs her legs slowly in starched sheets:
it is the magic river. It is like coming to the city to make money, to find
glory, fame and love, and a life more fortunate and happy than any we
have ever known. It is like the Knickerbockers and early autumn; it is
like the Rich Folks, and the River People, the Vanderbilts, the Astors,
and the Roosevelts; it is like Robert W. Chambers and the Society Folks;
it is like the younger set and Hilary, and Monica, and Garth; it is like
The Story Thus Far:

The lovely Monica Delavere the beautiful but spoiled daughter of one of
the richest men in the world meets at a party given at her father's Mount
Kisco estate in honor of her approaching marriage to a young architect
Hilary Chedester his friend Garth Montgomery a young artist just returned
from years of study abroad fascinated yet repelled by his dark passionate face
and his slender hands with the longer tapering fingers of the artist and
goaded by something enigmatic and mocking in his eyes in a moment of
mad recklessness spurred on by a twinge of jealousy at the undue attention
which she thinks Hilary is bestowing on Rita Daventry an old flame she

accepts a challenge from Garth to go for a mad dash across the night in his speedster their objective being his hunting lodge in the hills and a return before dawn arrived at the lodge however Garth coolly announces that his car is out of gasoline and that he must phone for assistance to the nearest town somewhat disturbed and reflecting for the first time now on the possible scandal her reckless exploit may cause she enters the lodge now go on with the story:

"Monica's red lips curved in a smile of mocking reproof. She made a *moue*.

" 'Hardly a place I should have chosen to spend the evening, my dear man,' she said. 'But then, perhaps it is the latest Paris fashion to take ladies to deserted places and inform them you are stranded. *C'est comme ça à Paris, hein?'* "

Yes, all these things were like the Hudson River.

And above all else, the Hudson River was like the light—oh, more than anything it was the light, the light, the tone, the texture of the magic light in which he had seen the city as a child, that made the Hudson River wonderful.

The light was golden, deep and full with all rich golden lights of harvest; the light was golden like the flesh of women, lavish as their limbs, true, depthless, tender as their glorious eyes, fine-spun and maddening as their hair, as unutterable with desire as their fragrant nests of spicery, their deep melon-heavy breasts. The light was golden like a golden morning light that shines through ancient glass into a room of old dark brown. The light was brown, dark lavish brown hued with rich lights of gold; the light was rich brown shot with gold like the sultry and exultant fragrance of ground coffee; the light was lavish brown like old stone houses gulched in morning on a city street, brown like exultant breakfast smells that come from basement areas in the brownstone houses where the rich men lived; the light was blue, steep frontal blue, like morning underneath the frontal cliff of buildings, the light was vertical cool blue, hazed with thin morning mist, the light was blue, cold flowing harbor blue of clean cool waters rimed brightly with a dancing morning gold, fresh, half-rotten with the musty river stench, blue with the blue-black of the morning gulch and canyon of the city, blue-black with cool morning shadow as the ferry packed with its thousand small white staring faces turned one way, drove bluntly toward the rusty weathered slips.

The light was amber brown in vast dark chambers shuttered from young light where in great walnut beds the glorious women stirred in sensual warmth their lavish limbs. The light was brown-gold like ground coffee, merchants and the walnut houses where they lived, brown-gold like old brick buildings grimed with money and the smell of trade, brown-gold like morning in great gleaming bars of swart mahogany, the fresh wet beer-wash, lemon-rind, and the smell of angostura bitters. Then full-golden in the evening in the theatres, shining with full golden warmth and body on full golden figures of the women, on fat, red plush, and on rich, faded, slightly stale smell, and on the gilt sheaves and cupids and the cornucopias, on the fleshly, potent softly-golden smell of all the people; and in great restaurants the light was brighter gold, but full and round like warm onyx columns, smooth warmly tinted marble, old wine in dark rounded age-encrusted bottles, and the great blonde figures of naked women on rose-clouded ceilings. Then the light was full and rich, brown-golden like great fields in autumn; it was full swelling golden light like mown fields, bronze-red picketed with fat rusty golden sheaves of corn, and governed by huge barns of red and the mellow winey fragrance of the apples.—Yes, all of this had been the tone and texture of the lights that qualified his vision of the city and the river when he was a child.

Proud, cruel, everchanging and ephemeral city, to whom we came once when our hearts were high, our blood passionate and hot, our brain a particle of fire: infinite and mutable city, mercurial city, strange citadel of million-visaged time—Oh! endless river and eternal rock, in which the forms of life came, passed and changed intolerably before us, and to which we came, as every youth has come, with such enormous madness, and with so mad a hope—for what?

To eat you, branch and root and tree; to devour you, golden fruit of power and love and happiness; to consume you to your sources, river and spire and rock, down to your iron roots; to entomb within our flesh forever the huge substance of your billion-footed pavements, the intolerable web and memory of dark million-visaged time.

And what is left now of all our madness, hunger, and desire? What have you given, incredible mirage of all our million shining hopes, to those who wanted to possess you wholly to your ultimate designs, your final sources, from whom you took the strength, the passion, and the innocence of youth?

What have we taken from you, protean and phantasmal shape of time? What have we remembered of your million images, of your billion weavings out of accident and number, of the mindless fury of your dateless days, the brutal stupefaction of your thousand streets and pavements? What have we seen and known that is ours forever?

Gigantic city, we have taken nothing—not even a handful of your trampled dust—we have made no image on your iron breast and left not even the print of a heel upon your stony-hearted pavements. The possession of all things, even the air we breathed, was held from us, and the river of life and time flowed through the grasp of our hands forever, and we held nothing for our hunger and desire except the proud and trembling moments, one by one. Over the trodden and forgotten words, the rust and dusty burials of yesterday, we were born again into a thousand lives and deaths, and we were left forever with only the substance of our waning flesh, and the hauntings of an accidental memory, with all its various freight of great and little things which passed and vanished instantly and could never be forgotten, and of those unbidden and unfathomed wisps and fumes of memory that share the mind with all the proud dark images of love and death.

The tugging of a leaf upon a bough in late October, a skirl of blown papers in the street, a cloud that came and went and made its shadow in the lights of April. And the forgotten laughter of lost people in dark streets, a face that passed us in another train, the house our mistress lived in as a child, a whipping of flame at a slum's cold corner, the corded veins on an old man's hand, the feathery green of a tree, a daybreak in a city street in the month of May, a voice that cried out sharply and was silent in the night, and a song that a woman sang, a word that she spoke at dusk before she went away,—the memory of a ruined wall, the ancient empty visage of a half-demolished house in which love lay, the mark of a young man's fist in crumbling plaster, a lost relic, brief and temporal, in all the everlasting variousness of your life, as the madness, pain and anguish in the heart that caused it—these are all that we have taken from you, iron-breasted city, and they are ours and gone forever from us, even as things are lost and broken in the wind, and as the ghosts of time are lost, and as the everlasting river that flowed past us in darkness to the sea.

The river is a tide of moving waters: by night it floods the pockets of the earth. By night it drinks strange time, dark time. By night the river drinks proud potent tides of strange dark time. By night the river drains the tides, proud potent tides of time's dark waters that, with champ and lift of teeth, with lapse and reluctation of their breath, fill with a kissing glut the pockets of the earth. Sired by the horses of the sea, maned with the dark, they come.

They come! Ships call! The hooves of night, the horses of the sea, come on below their manes of darkness. And forever the river runs. Deep as the tides of time and memory, deep as the tides of sleep, the river runs.

And there are ships there! Have we not heard the ships there? (Have we not heard the great ships going down the river? Have we not heard the great ships putting out to sea?)

Great whistles blow there. Have we not heard the whistles blow there? Have we not heard the whistles blowing in the river? (A harness of bright ships is on the water. A thunder of faint hooves is on the land.)

And there is time there. (Have we not heard strange time, dark time, strange tragic time there? Have we not heard dark time, strange time, the dark, the moving tide of time as it flows down the river?)

And in the night time, in the dark there, in all the sleeping silence of the earth have we not heard the river, the rich immortal river, full of its strange dark time?

Full with the pulse of time it flows there, full with the pulse of all men living, sleeping, dying, waking, it will flow there, full with the billion dark and secret moments of our lives it flows there. Filled with all the hope, the madness and the passion of our youth it flows there, in the daytime, in the dark, drinking with ceaseless glut the land, mining into its tides the earth as it mines the hours and moments of our life into its tides, moving against the sides of ships, foaming about piled crustings of old wharves, sliding like time and silence by the vast cliff of the city, girdling the stony isle of life with moving waters—thick with the wastes of earth, dark with our stains, and heavied with our dumpings, rich, rank, beautiful, and unending as all life, all living, as it flows by us, by us, by us, to the sea!

LIX

FULL night had come when he got off the train at the town where Joel was to meet him. After the heavy rains of the afternoon, and the stormy sunset, the sky had cleared completely: a great moon blazed in the cloudless bowl of a depthless sky; after the rain, and the sultry swelter of the city streets, the tainted furnace-fumes of city breath, the air was clean and fresh, and marvellously sweet, and the great earth waited, and was still enormously, and one always knew that it was there.

The engine panted for a moment with a hoarse, metallic resonance, in the baggage-car some one threw mail-bags and thick bundles of evening papers off onto the platform, there was the swinging signal of a brakeman's lantern, the tolling of the engine bell, thick, hose-like jets of steam blew out of her, the terrific pistons moved like elbows, caught, bore down, the terrific flanges spun for a moment, the short, squat funnel belched explosive thunders of hot smoke, the train rolled past with a slow, protesting creak of ties, a hard-pressed rumble of the heavy coaches, and was on her way again.

Then the train was gone, and there was nothing but the rails, the earth, the moon, the river, and strong silence—and the haunting and immortal visage of America by night. It was there, and it was there forever, and he had always known it, and it abode there and was still, and there was something in his heart he could not utter. The rails swept northward towards the dark, and in the moon the rails were like two living strands of burning silver, and between the rails the heavy ballast rock was white as lunar marble, and the brown wooden ties were resinous and dry and very still.

Sheer beside the tracks, the low banks of the ballast-fill sloped to the edges of the mighty river. And the river blazed there in the great blank radiance of the moon, cool waters gently lapped small gluts and pockets of the shore, and in the great wink of the moon the river blazed more brightly than elves' gold. And farther off, where darkness met it, the light was broken into scallop-shells of gold, it swam and shimmered in a billion winks of fire like a school of herrings on the water, and beyond all that there was just the dark, the cool-flowing mystery of velvet-hearted night, the silent, soundless surge and coolness of the strange, the grand, the haunting, the unceasing river.

Far, far away in darkness, on the other shore—more than a mile away —the river met the fringes of the land, but where the river ended, or the land began, was hard to say. There was just *there* a greater darkness, perhaps just by a shade, a deeper, dark intensity of night—a dark, perhaps, a shade less lucent, smooth, and fluid, by an indefinable degree more solid.

Yet there were lights there—there were lights—a bracelet of a few, hard lights along the river, a gem-like incandescence, few and hard and bright, and so poignantly lost and lonely in enormous darkness as are all lights in America, sown sparsely on the enormous viewless mantle of the night, and by that pattern so defining it—a scheme of sparse, few lights, hard, bright and small, sown there upon night's enormous darkness, the great earth's secret and attentive loneliness, its huge, abiding mystery.

And forever, beyond the mysterious river's farthest shore, the great earth waited in the darkness, and was still. It waited there with the huge, attentive secrecy of night and of America, and of the wilderness of this everlasting earth on which we live; and its dark visage that we cannot see was more cruel, strange and lonely than the visage of dark death, and its rude strength more savage and destructive than a tiger's paw, and its wild, mysterious loveliness more delicate than magic, more desireful than a woman's flesh, and more thrilling, secret and seductive than a woman's love.

As he stood there, tranced in that powerful spell of silence and of night, he heard swift foot-steps running down the station stairs, he turned and saw Joel Pierce approaching. He ran forward quickly, his tall, thin figure clad in a blue coat and white flannels, alive with the swift boyish eagerness that was one of his engaging qualities.

"Gosh!" he said, in his eager whispered tone, panting a little as he came up, "—I'm sorry that I'm late: we have people staying at the house, I had to drive a woman who's been staying with us to Poughkeepsie—I tried to get you there, but your train had already gone. I drove like hell getting here.— It's good to see you!" he burst out in his eager whispering way—at once so gentle, and so friendly and spontaneous— "It's *swell* that you could come!" he whispered enthusiastically. "Come on! They're all waiting for you!"

And picking up his friend's valise, he walked swiftly across the platform and began to climb the stairs.

Although Joel Pierce would have spoken in this way to any friend—to any one for whom he had a friendly feeling, however casual—and although the other youth knew that he would have spoken this way to many other people—the words filled him with happiness, with an instinctive warmth and affection for the person who had spoken them. Indeed, the very fact that there was in Joel's words—in all his human relationships—this curious impersonality, gave what he said an enhanced value. For in this way Joel revealed instinctively what every one who knew him well felt about him—an enormous decency and radiance in his soul and character, a wonderfully generous and instinctive friendliness towards humanity—that became finer and more beautiful because of its very impersonality.

This warm, instinctive humanity was evident in all he did, it came out somehow in the most casual words and relationships with people. For example, when they went upstairs into the station waiting-room, which was completely empty, Joel paused for a moment at the ticket-seller's window and spoke to a man in shirtsleeves inside.

"Joe," he said casually yet in his eager, whispering way, "if Will comes down will you tell him not to wait? I've got every one: there'll be no one else tonight."

"All right, Mr. Pierce," the man said quietly. "If I see him, I'll tell him."

Joel's car, a small, cheap one of a popular make, was backed up against the station curb: he opened the door and put his friend's suitcase in the back, then they both got in and drove away.

About two miles back from town upon the crest of a hill that gave a good view of the great moon-wink of the noble and haunting river far below, Joel suddenly, and without slackening his reckless speed, swerved from the concrete highway into a dusty and gravel road that went off to the left. And now they were really in the heart of the deep country: on each side of them the moon-drenched fields and dreaming woods of a noble, grand and spacious land slept in the steep, white silence of the moon. From time to time, they would pass cornfields, the high and silent stature, the cool figure of the corn at night, and see a great barn, or small lights burning in some farmer's house. Then there would be only the deep, dark mystery of sleeping woods beside the road and once, in a field, a herd of cows, all faced one way, bedded down upon their forequarters, the mottled colors of their hides showing plainly in the blazing radiance of the moon. When they had gone about a mile their road swept into another one that joined it at right angles: between these roads, in the angle that they formed, there was a pleasant house—a wooden structure of eight or ten rooms, white and graceful in the moon, and surrounded by a trim, well-kept lawn and well laid-out flower-plots and gardens.

A swift and pleasurable conviction told the youth that this was Joel's house: he was therefore surprised when the car shot past without

slackening its speed and then turned left upon the other road. He
turned to Joel and, almost with a note of protest in his voice, said:

"Don't you live there? Isn't that your house?"

"What?" Joel whispered quickly, startled from the focal concentration of his driving. He turned to his companion with a surprised inquiring look. "—Oh, *that* house?" he went on at once. "No," he said
softly. "That's not our house.— That is, it is our house," he corrected
himself, "it belongs to us, but a friend of ours—Margaret Telfair—lives
there now. You'll meet her tonight," he went on casually. "She's at the
house now.—You'll *like* her," he whispered with soft conviction,
"—she's grand! An *incredible* person!" he whispered enthusiastically.

They drove on in silence for some time: more moon-drenched
fields, great barns and little farmhouses, and herds of crouching cattle,
more dreaming and mysterious woods, the mysterious shadows of
great trees against the road, and secrecy, and sweet balsamic scents and
cool-enfolding night.—They were now driving back in the direction of
the river: the new road led that way.

"When do we come to your place, Joel?" the other youth asked,
when they had driven on in silence for a time. "How far is it?"

"What?" Joel whispered quickly, again turning his radiant and inquiring face. "*Our* place? Oh!" he said. "We're on our place now."

"*On* it?" the other stammered, after a moment's bewildered pause.
"But—but—where—I didn't see a gate or anything—when?——"

"Oh," Joel whispered, with an enlightened air. "*That!* We passed
it."

"*Passed* it? Where?"

"When we turned in from the main-road," Joel whispered. "Do you
remember?"

"The—the *main* road?" the other stammered. "You—you mean—that
concrete highway way back there?"

"Yes," Joel whispered. "That was the entrance to our place—one of
them. It's not much of an entrance," he whispered apologetically. "I
don't wonder that you couldn't see it."

"Then—then—everything since then—all we passed—all this—?" the
other stammered.

"Yes," Joel whispered, with his radiant, eager look, "that's it. That's
our place. It's really grand country," he went on matter-of-factly. "I
want to show you around tomorrow."

They swept suddenly around a curve of the gravelled road, bordered with fragrant shrubs. Before them stretched out an immense sward of velvet lawn, darkened by the grand and silent stature of great trees. The car swept forward; through the tree-barred vista of the lawn, the outline of a house appeared. It was a dream house, a house such as one sees only in a dream—the moonlight slept upon its soaring wings, its white purity, and gave the whole enormous structure an aerial delicacy, a fragile loveliness like some enchanted structure that one sees in dreams. And yet, for all this quality of dream-enchantment, there was something hauntingly familiar about it too. The car swept round the drive and halted before the moonlit façade of the house. A back porch level with the ground was flanked by tall, square columns of graceful, slender wood. To one side, far below, beyond the house, and the great moon-sweep of velvet, he could see the wink and glimmer of the Hudson River.

And suddenly that haunting sense of familiarity fused to a blind flash of recognition. The house was the house he had passed a dozen times in darkness, had seen a dozen times at morning from the windows of a speeding train along the river, as he hurtled city-wards again from those blind night passages of desire and fury in a town called Troy.

They got out of the car. Joel took his valise, and like a person walking in a dream, he followed him across the porch, into a large and dimly lit entrance-hall. Joel put his valise down in the hall, and turning, whispered:

"Look. I'll show you your room later. Mums and some other people are waiting for us on the terrace. Let's go and say hello to them first."

He nodded, unable to speak, and in silence followed his guide down the hall and through the house. Joel opened a door: the blazing moonlight fell upon the vast, swarded lawn and sleeping woods of that magic domain known as Far Field Farm. And that haunting and unearthly radiance fell as well upon the white wings of that magic house and on a group of its fortunate inhabitants who were sitting on the terrace.

The two young men went out: forms rose to greet them.

LX

A GROUP of eight or ten people were gathered on the terrace. Joel introduced Eugene swiftly, quietly, in an eager, whispering voice, as always, with his fine, kind intuition, mindful of another person's embarrassment and confusion: the moonlit figures rose, looked toward him, passed and swam and mixed around him in a blur of names and moon-white faces and politely murmured words. Then all the figures resolved themselves again into their former positions, he was standing beside Joel's mother, looking at her with a helpless and bewildered face, she put one hand swiftly, lightly on his arm, and in a kind and quiet voice, said to him: "You sit down here, next to me."

Then she sat down again in her chair—a big, wicker chair with a vast, fan-shaped back, he sat down beside her, and sank gratefully into oblivion while the other people resumed their interrupted conversation:

"No, but—*Polly! Surely* not! You know, she actually did not go through with it?" said a strong, protesting voice, in which yet an eager curiosity was evident. "You know, they stopped the thing before she went the whole way?"

"My dear," said Polly firmly—she had evidently been well named: in the moonlight her face showed sharp and pointed, with a big nose, and the shrewd, witty, and rather malicious features of a parrot— "my dear, I *know* she *did*. I was visiting Alice Bellamy at Newport when it happened: I got the whole story straight from her. The family were perfectly frantic—they were calling Hugh Bellamy up or running in to see him a dozen times a day to find out if something could be done—how to get it annulled— But I tell you," Polly cried, shaking her head obstinately and speaking in a tone of unmistakable conviction, "—I know what I'm talking about! There's no doubt about it whatever —she *married* him—the ceremony was *actually* performed——"

"And she really *lived* with him—with this—this *stable-boy?*"

"*Lived* with him!" Polly cried. "My dear, they'd been living together for almost two weeks before old Dick Rossiter found them. Now, of course," she said piously, but with a faint, malicious smirk, "—I don't know what they'd been doing all that time—perhaps the whole affair had been quite idyllic, but—well, my dear, you can use your own imagination. My own experience with hostlers is rather limited, but I shouldn't think they were particularly renowned for their platonic virtues."

"No," said Mrs. Pierce quietly, but with an unmistakable note of level and obdurate cynicism in her voice, "—nor Ellen Rossiter either— not if I know the breed! . . . After all," she went on in a moment, in a voice that was characterized by its grimly quiet conviction, "what else could you expect out of that crowd! . . . There's bad blood there!

Bad blood in the whole lot of them," her voice rose on a formidable and powerful note of unrelenting judgment. "—Every one in Society knows that old Steve Buchanan, that girl's grandfather, was a thorough-going rotter," she bit the word off almost viciously. "His reputation was so bad that most people wouldn't even have him in their house—that was the reason he spent the last twenty years of his life in France: he had become an outcast over here, no one would speak to him —he had to get out!— But! Heavens! A *stable-boy!*" she laughed again, and this time her laugh was almost hard and ugly. "What a blow to Myra—after all her years of scheming and contriving to get Timmy Wilson and his millions into the family! . . . I knew it! I knew it!" she shook her head with formidable, obstinate conviction. "I could have told them long ago they'd have trouble with that girl before they were done with her! There's bad blood there! Of course, it was *bound* to happen, sooner or later, anyway—Myra's a fool of the first water: she never had the brains of a rabbit. But to think!—Heavens! what a let-down, after all her scheming: a stable-boy! I bet she had a fit!"

"Still," suggested a young man named Howard, at this propitious moment, in his mincing, lisping, and effeminately mannered tone, "—as Irene Cartwright said, it was the only original thing that Ellen Rossiter ever did, and it was rather a pity to break the romance off. . . . I thought," he went on casually, "that the story they told about the hostler was rather touching—asking her to send his letters back, you know?"

"No!" cried Mrs. Pierce in an astounded tone. "Did he? . . . Well!" she went on eagerly. "And did she send them? . . . Go on, Howard!"

"But, of course," said Howard. "And the wedding ring, and everything else that he had given her. . . . I read the letter that he wrote her: it was really *too* pathetic—he said he was going with another girl—a house-maid, I believe—and he didn't want it to get out that he had paid attentions to some one else. . . . 'I have spoke it all over with my mother,' he said," Howard quoted drolly, "'and she thinks the same as me, you ought to let me have them back'"——

"Oh, *Howard!*" Mrs. Pierce shrieked faintly. "You *know* he didn't! Simply *priceless!*"

For a moment her splendid, even teeth flashed brilliantly in the moonlight: she lifted the long cigarette-holder in her hand and took a long, deliberate puff: the fragrant, acrid smoke of Turkish tobacco coiled upward in the moon-light air like filings of light steel. Turning to the young man beside her, she addressed him with the somewhat patient and dutiful kindliness of a person receiving a strange guest in her home for the first time:

"Well," she said, "and how did you find the trip up? Did Joel frighten you out of your wits by his driving? He does every one else."

"Well, he did go pretty fast," the youth admitted. "He had me hanging on once or twice—when we left the main road we took the curve on two wheels, but he seemed to know what he was doing."

"I assure you," said Mrs. Pierce, with a stern laugh, "that he does not. I wish I could share your confidence, but I can't. I don't think he has the faintest notion what he's doing."

"But, after all," the very quiet, pleasant, almost toneless voice of a young man whose name was George Thornton now took up the thread of the discussion—"after all, I should think that any reasonable man would be content with a speed of thirty-five or forty miles an hour. After all," he said very quietly again, "perhaps the most important things in life are not to be got at through speed—perhaps all the things that are most worth living for are not to be had if we always go a mile a minute."

"That's just it, George!" Mrs. Pierce put in with decisive satisfaction. "That's just it! Any reasonable man *would* be content with thirty-five or forty miles an hour—but Joel is not reasonable. When he gets in a car he's like a child that's been given a new toy to play with for the first time."

"The greatest things in life, the highest values," George Thornton went on in his quiet, pleasant, almost toneless voice, which now, despite the air of telling reasonableness with which he spoke—the air of temperance, moderation and control—was, somehow, indefinably tinged by a sombre fatality: the tone of a man whose extreme reasonableness comes from a fear of madness, whose temperance from some fatal impulse to insane excess—"the greatest things in life," he went on in his quiet, toneless voice, almost as if he were talking to himself and had not heard what Mrs. Pierce had said—"are not to be got from machinery or speed, or any material object in the world whatever. . . . Christ," he continued with his quiet, utterly reasonable, and implacable finality, "said that the greatest thing in life is love. Buddha said that the greatest thing in life is the illumination of the human spirit. Socrates found that man's highest duty was obedience to his country's laws. And

Confucius, after weighing life and death against each other, found man's only reason for living in keeping as many of the conventions of society as he could. . . . And that, Joel, perhaps is the real reason, the only reason, why you should not drive your car at reckless speed. . . . You break your country's law by doing so . . . and you cause pain and worry and anxiety to other people who may love you. For that reason, if for nothing else, you ought not to do it."

He delivered this judgment in his quiet and toneless voice, without vanity or arrogance, but with a finality that was almost prophetic, and that left no room for argument. When he was done speaking, there was a deep, impersonal silence for a moment, and then the voice of Joel's sister, Rosalind—a voice that was still the voice of a girl, but that was also sweet and low and womanly, full of noble tenderness and warmth—could be heard in all its affectionate young impulsiveness:

"Oh, but, George!—you're an *angel* about everything! If every one were like you, life would be heaven!" She took his hand between her strong, warm hands and squeezed it—an impulsive and natural gesture with her that revealed, as much as anything else, the deep and true affection of her nature. "—Darling," she said, "—you make all of us— every one else—feel so mean—and small—and—so petty. . . . I mean," she went on with the earnest and naïve sincerity, the spontaneous admiration, of a generous and warm-spirited girl—"the way you live —the way you have spent your whole life, George, in helping other people—the way you have found out all these wonderful things about— about—Buddha and Confucius and Socrates—you *know* so much, George!" she cried enthusiastically—"you have learned so much, while the rest of us were just leading an idle, stupid, empty kind of life— and the way you give it all away to others!—the way you give your money away to any one who needs it—the—the—way," she faltered suddenly, and her voice was choked with tears—"the way you have looked after poor Dick all these years"—she blurted out.

"Rosalind!" Mrs. Pierce cried out sharply and warningly, yet not with reproof so much as with apprehension.

"I don't care!" cried Rosalind impulsively—"I—I think he's wonderful! George, you're a *saint!*" she said, and clasped his hand again.

No one spoke for a moment: George sat quietly on the terrace step, his fine and small, bronzed head, his very still eyes, in whose steady, quiet depths the fatal madness which would destroy him was already legible, turned out across the great sward of moon-drenched lawn towards the shine and wink and velvet mystery of the noble river far below. In the quality of silence that held all these people, there was a sense of profound emotion—the reference to "poor Dick" had touched some sorrowful fact that all of them knew about, and one could sense this deep feeling now in the stony silence that held all of them. It was broken in a moment by Mrs. Pierce, who betrayed, by the studied matter-of-factness of her tone, the emotion which she, too, had felt:

"But it *is* an extraordinary thing, George—a simply astonishing thing —to find a young man of your age who has read and studied—and— and—*prepared* himself for life the way you have. It's, *simply* astonishing!" she concluded, and then did what was perhaps an astonishing thing for her—quickly and vigorously she blew her nose. "But *simply* astonishing!" she said again, as she thrust the handkerchief away, and put a cigarette into her eight-inch holder.

"No, I think not," he said quietly, and without a trace of vanity or false modesty. "It would have been astonishing if I had not done it. After all, my debt to society for all that it has done for me is great enough as it is: I could not with any decency look the world in the face if I knew that I had not made some effort to repay it."

"How few rich young men feel that way about it," said Mrs. Pierce quietly. "I wish more did!"

The conversation was now turned to other, lighter channels of discussion: gossip, spirited but light debate. Mrs. Pierce renewed her conversation with Howard and Polly, farther away upon the steps Rosalind, Seaholm, a dark girl named Ruth, and George Thornton talked, gossiped and laughed together with the charming intimacy of youth, and Joel and Miss Telfair were engaged in eager and excited debate— Joel, for the most part, listening with the eager, respectful, bent-forward attentiveness, the devoted courtesy of reverence, that marked all of his relations with women, and Miss Telfair doing most of the talking. She talked the way she looked and dressed and acted, the way she was: a speech fragile, empty, nervous, brittle, artificial and incisive as one of the precious bits of china, the costly, rare, enamelled little trinkets that filled up her house, her life, her interest:

"No, Joel!" she was saying with a voice that had a curious, shell-like penetration—a positive, brittle, but incisively certain voice—"you are absolutely wrong! You are *completely* mistaken about that! The thing cannot by any stretch of the imagination be called Sienese! It is *pure* Ravenna,—*perfect* Ravenna—*absolutely!*" she cried, shaking her enamelled face with obdurate conviction. "It's nothing else on earth but the *purest* and *most perfect* Ravenna—and Fourteenth Century Ravenna at that! . . . No! No!" she cried incisively, cutting him off shortly, and shaking her head stubbornly as he tried to put in a smiling, whispered word of courteous doubt. "My dear child, you are dead wrong! You don't know what you're talking about! . . . I was an authority on these things before you were born. . . . I've forgotten more about Ravenna than you'll ever know! . . . No! . . . No! . . . Absolutely *not!* . . . You're *all* wrong!"

He received this stubborn, arrogant and almost insulting rebuttal as he always did—with the whispered, gracious humility of his beautiful good nature: laughing softly and enthusiastically over her arrogant and contemptuous denial, as if he were merely the victim of the most tender and high-spirited raillery.

At this moment, however, when, with a sense of resentment and displeasure he was listening to the naked and arrogant penetrations of Miss Telfair's voice, Rosalind Pierce rose from her seat on the terrace step, left the other young people there, came swiftly to where Eugene was seated, and sat down beside him.

"Why are you sitting here all by yourself—so quiet and so alone?" she said in her warm, sweet, lovely, and affectionate young voice. "Can I sit here and talk to you?" she said, and even as she spoke these words, she slipped her arm through his, and clasped him by the hand. The whole life and character of this beautiful, fine and lovely girl was in that simple, natural and spontaneous gesture. That gesture did what words could never do, explained what years of living with many people could not explain: in an instant she communicated to him the whole quality of her life, told him the kind of person she was. And the kind of person she was was unbelievably good and beautiful.

"What have you been thinking of all the time you have been sitting here?" she whispered in her low, sweet voice. "I could see you sitting here, listening, looking at us, and all the time it was just as if you were a million miles away. What were you thinking?—that we are all an idle, shallow lot, with nothing to do except to chatter and gossip about other useless people like ourselves?"

"Why—no—no," he stammered. "Why—not at all—" He looked at her with a red embarrassed face, but there was no guile or mockery in her. She was not clever enough for sarcasm or malice, not witty enough for irony: she was a creature full of innocence and ardor, without profound intelligence, but with a nature full of warmth, generous enthusiasm, and affection.

"I—I—think you're all fine," he blurted out. "I think you're great."

"Do you, darling?" she said softly. "Well, we're not." She pulled him towards her with a gesture of friendly intimacy, and said. "Come on: let's leave them all for a few minutes. I want to talk to you."

They got up, and still with her warm hand clasped in his, they walked along the terrace and around the great, moon-whitened wings of the house on to the road that swept in an oval before it.

"Do you really like us?" she said, as they walked on down the road away from the house under a deep, nocturnal mystery of great trees through which the moonlight shone and swarmed upon the earth in mottles of light. "Don't you like Joel? Don't you think he's grand?"

"I—I think he's the best fellow in the world," he said. "He's—he's just *too* good!"

"Oh, he's a saint," she said in her quiet, sweet voice. "There was never any one like him: he's the loveliest person I've ever known. . . Aren't people wonderful?" she said, and turned and paused in the moonlit road and looked at him. "I mean, there are a lot of mean ones . . . and useless ones . . . and sort of shabby ones like . . . like—well, like some of those people there tonight . . . but there's something good in all of them—even poor little Howard Martin has something sweet and good in him: he has a kind heart—he really has—he wants to be amusing and to entertain people, he wants every one to be happy and have a good time. . . . And when you meet some one like Joel, it makes up for everything else, doesn't it? . . . Or George Thornton—don't you like him? Don't you think he's a grand person, too?"

"He—seems fine," he answered with some difficulty. "I—I never met him till tonight."

"Oh, you'll *love* him when you get to know him," the girl said earnestly. "—Everybody does. . . . He's another saint, just like Joel . . . and he's so brave, and kind, and good—and his life has been so terrible."

"Terrible? I—I thought he said——"

"Oh, he *is,* darling—he *does* have everything *that* way—money, I mean. He's terribly rich: one of the richest young men in the world. . . . Only he doesn't spend it on himself, he gives it all away and then

. . . you see, darling, George has had an unhappy life of it from the beginning. . . . His father died a raving madman, there's been insanity in his family for generations back, his mother was a horrible woman who deserted him when he was a child and ran off with a man, and he was brought up by an aunt—his father's sister—who was half cracked herself. . . . Now he lives all alone on this big place that he's inherited—he has one brother, Dick, who is two years older than he is—and he has spent practically his whole life in looking after Dick."

"Looking after him?"

"Yes," the girl said quietly, "—Dick is insane too—a raving maniac; they have guards for him, they have to watch him every minute of the time—when George comes to see him, Dick tries to kill him. . . . And George loves him, he'd give his life for him, he does everything he can to make Dick happy—and Dick hates him so that he'd kill him if he could. . . . And George has this thing hanging over him all the time, he can't forget about it for a moment, it's made his whole life wretched, and yet you'd never know it when you talk to him: he never mentions it, he's always the same to people,—always kind and good and gentle, never thinking of himself."

"I see. And is that the reason why he studies all these different philosophies—Christ and Socrates and Confucius?—"

"Yes," she said quietly. "—And Buddha. I think so. . . . He would never admit it . . . he has never said so . . . and of course no one *could* ask him. . . . But I think that's the reason. . . . There's something . . . something desperate . . . lost . . . in his eyes sometimes," she said slowly, after a pause. ". . . It's . . . it's not good to look at . . . it's . . . I imagine it's like the look you would see in the eyes of a drowning man."

"And you think that he may be afraid of . . . of insanity?"

She was silent for a moment, and did not answer him directly.

"He's been studying Buddhism for the last two years," she said. "He's had all kinds of people at the house to teach him. . . . Hindus, mystics, scholars—learned people . . . he's . . . he's become more and more . . . I don't know," she said in a puzzled tone. "—I don't know what you'd call it—sort of mystical." Again she was silent, and presently added matter-of-factly: "He's going to India next year."

"To study?"

"Yes, I think so," the girl said, and again was silent. "Somehow—it's a dreadful thought, isn't it?" she said in a low tone after a moment—

"But sometimes I have wondered if George would ever come back. . . . Perhaps," she concluded quietly, ". . . perhaps that is why we all love him so much . . . it's like loving some one who is brave and good and gentle that you know has got to die."

For some time they walked on slowly down the moon-white road without further speech.

"I want you to know Carl, too," she said. "He seems very cold and strange at first—but that is just his foreign way. He is really one of the loveliest, sweetest people that ever lived. . . . You know," she said presently, "we are going to be married in October."

"Yes, I know. Joel told me. . . . Will you live here—in this country?"

"No. I'm afraid not. . . . You see, Carl is in the diplomatic service, and they get moved around a great deal. They have to go where they get sent."

"And where will you go first? Do you know?"

"Yes, I think they are sending him to Paris next."

"Will you like that? Do you think you'll like living in Paris?"

"Of *course*," she said with her rich, warm, easy laugh. "I'm awfully easy to please—I like everything—I'm happy anywhere—wherever I am. Is that very bad of me?" she said with a kind and gently teasing smile.

"No, that's very good of you. . . . Have you ever been to Paris?"

"Yes," she cried in a rich, enthusiastic tone, "and I love it. I adore it. I studied music there. Mother and I lived there for two years before I came out."

"But now you'll have to learn Swedish and German and Italian and Spanish and Russian—all those languages—now that you're getting married to a diplomat. Won't you?"

"Yes," she said with her sweet and careless laugh— "Everything! One must become a regular little walking Berlitz school of languages—only I shan't mind very much: I'm very stupid, but my husband is so kind and clever I'm sure I'll learn in spite of everything."

"And you'll live in Paris and Rome and London and Berlin—all those places? Won't you?"

"Yes, darling," she said in her warm, sweet tone that always had something maternal and tolerantly amused in its humor, "—and in Copenhagen and Stockholm and Bucharest and Madrid—even in Pogo Pogo or in China or Peru—wherever they choose to send us. We'll be two international hoboes, darling—that's the kind of life we'll have to lead."

"God!" he said bluntly. "It sounds wonderful! What a thing to happen to any one!—and to happen to you at your age! . . . But won't it make all this—this place here—seem awfully far away, and very strange—when you think back on it?"

"Yes," the girl said quietly, and added so softly that she seemed to breathe the words—so softly that he could scarcely hear her, "—and quite impossibly lovely!"

He stared at her in blank astonishment for a minute: she had clasped her hands against her breast in a natural and simple gesture, the moon had made an aureole of magic around the silken strands of her brown hair, and suddenly he noticed that her eyes were bright with tears.

"Very, very far away," she said in a low tone, "and enormously beautiful. . . . You see," she said simply, "this is my home. . . . I was born here, and I love it." She was silent for a moment longer, and then she said quietly but in a more matter-of-fact way:

"Don't you think our place—this country here—is beautiful?"

He did not answer her for a moment: at first he was not even conscious that he had heard her. He kept staring at her with a comical expression of gape-jawed and hypnotic fascination. He was conscious of a queer, bewildered and inappropriate feeling of surprise—a kind of numb, absurd wonder that if he had read all the books and poems in the world, and then tried to imagine for himself something as impossibly lovely as this girl and the whole scene around her, he could never, by any soaring stretch of the imagination, have come within a million miles of it.

Behind her head the moon was making its spun aura of enchanted light, the dress she was wearing was of some sweet gossamer stuff of light moon-blue that seemed spun out of the very substance of the moon itself—to float, to move like some aerial fume of magic smoke, but the girl herself was lovely, sweet and strong as the whole earth around her. She was herself no creature of elves' fantasy, she was not lithe and slender, fleeting as a nymph: she was a warm, strong-bodied girl, wide in the hips for children, a nature warm and soft and gentle as a cow, but radiant and lovely with fair girlhood, too, and full of sweetness, strength, and tender, jolly humor.

She stood there in the middle of the white, empty road with the enchanted radiance of the moon upon her, and he stared at her unbelievingly, like a man who meets some vision in a dream, and does not know if he is dreaming or awake, and yet knows all the time that it is real. Then he would take his fascinated gaze away from her, and look down at the moon-white road, and stamp it with his foot, and kick and scurf the ground of the moon-white road to see if it was real, and then lift his head and look at her again, and turn and see the great, sweet fields and meadows dreaming in the moonlight, and cows down upon their knees, facing toward him with their strange and silent stare, or faced one way and grazing towards him through the moon pastures with sweet, wrenching pull of teeth; and then he would see the dark and sleeping woods of night, with all their mystery and loveliness and wild and solemn joy, and secret terror, and all the grand and casual folds and convolutions of the sleeping, moon-enchanted earth, and far away the moon-blaze and wink, the herring glamour, and the dancing scallop fires, and all the darkness, coolness, and the velvet-breasted mystery of the strange and silent river, the haunted river, the great Hudson River, drawing on forever from the dark and secret earth the sources of its depthless tides, and in the night-time, in the dark, with soundless movings of its tide, drawing on forever like time and silence past the strange and secret land, the mysterious earth, the sleeping cities and the lost and lonely little towns of dark America.

It was all so strange, so impossibly lovely, so hauntingly familiar—the grand and casual landscape of America—and it seemed past words and past belief, to be so much a part of this girl's life, and she a part of it, that all the haunting mystery of the secret earth, the silent river, and all its sweetness, fragrance and fertility, its casual homeliness, and its unuttered loveliness had entered into her, had fed her life, had shaped her to its special quality, and like a solemn music was mixed into the conduits of her blood and life and soul forever, so that now he could not bear to see her taken from it, he felt a cruel and ruinous loss and waste in this destructive separation—a loss that touched not only this girl's life, but the life of the great earth and all America as well—a loss as if a rare and glorious flower were brutally uprooted from the only earth that could produce or nurture it and which would henceforth be, by reason of its treasured loss, bereft. And feeling so, a blind and bitter resentment surged up in his heart, his whole life and spirit was set against her going, and in his soul an unforgiving and protesting voice kept saying doggedly:

"Why has she got to go? Why must she be lost? Why does she have to go and marry that damned Swede?"

In the great moon-drenched field beside the road, the cows were moving towards them slowly, grazing, pulling the fragrant meadow grass of night with sweet, cool wrenching, with rustling stir, and with whisking of dry tails.

The girl walked over to the wire fence, and one of the cows, after regarding her with its grave, gentle stare, moved slowly towards her, rattling the fence wires as it thrust its gentle, bending head across the fence and nuzzled her soft palm.

"She seems to know you," said the youth.

"Yes," the girl answered. "I know them all by name, they all know me. I gave them all their names: this one's Brindle. Aren't they lovely creatures?" she said quietly, as she stroked the cow. "Such—such—gentle pets," she said, "with their kind looks and great, soft eyes. They all know me, and will come to me when I call their names."

The other cows, indeed, were now standing still, faced toward her, looking at her with slow, gaunt, and gentle heads. Now, slowly, they started to move toward her, making a cool, sweet rustling through night grasses as they came. The moonlight burst upon their short, curved horns, it burst upon the rich bright patches of their mottled hides, upon their stringy, dung-bespattered rumps, their soft eyes, and the slow, gentle wonder of their long, gaunt heads.

And it was all so wonderful—the sleeping woods, the moon-enchanted fields, the slow, light grazings of the moonlit cows, and all the fragrance of the night, the grass, the clover and the meadow spells, and the magic warmth and loveliness of the girl, and her sweet, low voice beside him in the moonlight—that it seemed to him that all his life had been a prelude and a preparation to this wonder. He did not know what he could say, it came swelling up in a wild flood of tenderness and passion, he felt that he must tell her somehow, and he had no words for saying it; he seized her hands, and stammered:

"Look here—if I live to be a million years I'll never—the way the river was tonight, the moon, and the way Joel met me and then finding you and your mother and your friends there in the moonlight—and the river down below—and now this walk with you—this road—the field—and all these cows there in the field—and you here—why, by God!" he cried thickly, incoherently, "you are the finest girl I ever saw in all my life!—this place—tonight here—the most wonderful——"

"Come on," she said quietly, with her warm, young laugh, and took him by the arm again. "We must be going back:—the others will be waiting for us—but it *has* been lovely, hasn't it?"

"Why," he muttered thickly and seized her hand again, "—why! By God! By God!"

When they got back to the house, the guests had risen for departure, but were standing in an interested group around George Thornton, who was showing them gymnastics.

"Another thing," he was saying, in his very quiet, pleasant, toneless voice, "—another thing that you can try is this." With these words he stretched his slight and graceful figure—which was as tough as hickory and as flexible as a whip—flat out upon the bricked floor of the terrace.

"Try this some time," he continued in his quiet, even tone that had a curiously hushed, still and almost sombre penetration in the deep moon-silence of the night. "Try lying flat out on your back sometime—like this." And he lay there, small, graceful, beautifully lithe, completely relaxed.

"And then what?" said Mrs. Pierce in an interested tone. "What do you do then, George?"

"Nothing," he said with toneless quiet. "You just lie there—it relaxes you: a Hindu showed me how to do it."

"Oh, but any one could do that!" Howard Martin protested, in his mannered and rather effeminate voice. "Even I could do that, George."

"It's not as easy as you think," George said. "You see," he went on quietly, "it's really a greater effort to be relaxed than most of us realize. Most of us are all tied up in a knot—so much more tense than we know we are. The thing you've got to do," he went on with his quiet and fatal tonelessness, "is to relax—utterly relax—just let everything relax. You've got to lie so that everything—the back of your head, your shoulders, your spinal column—the whole thing—lies flat upon the floor. Like this," he said, and just lay there, small, fragile, beautifully lithe and strong, and utterly, quietly, "relaxed"—his voice coming with a quiet and strange penetration from a figure that seemed inanimate. "—It's not easy to do, but you can master it if you try."

"Oh, let me see! I'm going to try!" little Howard Martin cried with the good-natured and unself-conscious eagerness that was really one of his attractive and appealing qualities. And completely unruffled by the laughter of the group, he immediately lay down and stretched himself out beside George, his dapper little figure looking indescribably comical as he tried to follow George's instructions and imitate his posture:

"How's that, George?" he said presently, without moving. "Have I got it?"

George turned and observed him keenly for a moment:

"No," he said quietly, "you haven't got it yet, Howard. You see, you've got to flatten out completely. You've just got to let everything go limp—relax—so that your whole back is flat upon the ground."

"But I *am* flat! I *am* flat!" little Howard protested in such a mincing and comical tone of protest that every one burst out in hearty laughter, and even George smiled his fine, rare, and grave smile. "My *God!*" Howard said in an agonized tone when the laughter had subsided, "if I was any flatter I'd feel like a pancake."

"No, Howard," George Thornton said quietly after another moment of observant silence. "You haven't got it yet. You see, your back is really arched—you're not *relaxed*—your back is not upon the floor—the thing is to make yourself lie out as flat as a board—like this," and with the fingers of his strong, small, bronzed hand he gently but firmly pushed Howard's stomach down towards the floor. Howard grunted protestingly but lay there after George had taken his hand away, and George, after looking at him closely for a moment, nodded approvingly and said:

"Yes, that's better. You're getting it now. But you've really got to practice every day. It looks easy, but it's hard to do."

"But, George," Mrs. Pierce broke in, as Howard scrambled to his feet, "—what I'm interested in knowing is how you keep that beautiful, strong athlete's figure that you've got! And that dancer's *waist!* My dear sir, that is the curse of a woman's life: so if you can tell me what to do to take it off around the waist and hips I'll be eternally grateful to you."—She was, as a matter of fact, herself as lean and well-conditioned as a race-horse, but George, still lying flat upon the floor, answered quietly:

"Did you ever try this, Ida? I think you'll find it very useful for keeping the waist down.—You lie flat on your back—like this. You keep your arms flat at your sides—you mustn't raise them or lift your head. You keep your legs straight—you mustn't bend them at the knees—and then," slowly, and with a sense of infinite, hard-muscled power and lean endurance, he suited the action to the words, "you raise your legs to right angles with your body—straighten out again—raise—straighten—raise—straighten—raise—straighten—if you do that a hundred times a day, when you get up and when you go to bed, I don't think you'll ever be troubled by fat around the waist," he concluded quietly.

"I know," Joel whispered, nodding with vigorous agreement. "I've tried that. That's a good one. But a hundred times is a lot! It's more than most people can do at first."

"Yes," said George quietly. "But you get used to it if you do it every day! I can do it a hundred times with no difficulty whatever," he concluded quietly.

"Oh, of *course!*" Joel whispered instantly. "But then, you're hard as a rock, George. You can do anything."

"But that doesn't look hard," Howard said again with blithe confidence. "Oh, I just *know* that I can do *that* one," he said mincingly. And without further ado, while every one laughed, he stretched himself out again, extended his dapper flannelled legs as George instructed him, and then slowly raised them, lowered them, raised them again with such a painful grunt that every one burst out again in hearty laughter. After the fourth effort he was through, admitting defeat with a painful "Gosh! If I had to do that for a hundred times I'd be ready for the undertaker," and scrambled to his feet again.

"Then," said George in his quiet, pleasant tone, "I think you'll find this one good, Ida, for strengthening the muscles of the back and stomach. You *arch,*" he said, "you arch with the neck and feet—like this," and instantly his strong, frail, beautifully proportioned figure was arched as lithely and gracefully as a bow, "—you come down slow like this," he said, and sank slowly toward the ground, "you arch again like this"—again the light and graceful human bow.

"Oh, but that looks terribly hard to do, George!" Mrs. Pierce protested. "I could never learn to do that: it's a regular circus stunt."

"No," he said in his quiet and toneless fashion, "you could do it, Ida. Of course, it *is* hard at first, but it would come with practice. . . . It makes you very strong," he went on with a completely detached matter-of-factness. "Do you see that?" He arched his whip-cord body again and held it in that posture—"I could keep that up indefinitely—it makes you hard as nails," he went on quietly, and without an atom of vanity or self-consciousness. "I could support the whole weight of a man's body there without any difficulty—and *lift* him, too."

"Not *really!*" Joel whispered in an astounded tone. "Simply incredible!"

"But not at all," said George quietly. "It's the easiest thing on earth if you're used to it. Come here, Howard," he said quietly, without moving from his arched position. "Sit down on me."

"Sit *down* on you?" said Howard, in a comically bewildered tone. "*Where,* George?"

"On my stomach," George replied. "Go on," he said, smiling his fine, grave smile at sight of Howard's hesitation. "It's all right. You won't hurt me at all. Sit down."

"Like—like this?" said Howard, and squatted gingerly and gently, settling down finally upon George's arched stomach and looking about with such a comically troubled and inquiring expression that every one burst out in hearty laughter again. "Is that all right?" he said, turning anxiously and looking down at his supporter.

"Yes, perfectly," said George. "Now draw your knees up and hold them with your arms so that your whole weight is on me. . . . Good! . . . Now! Are you ready? . . . One, two . . . One, two . . . One, two," his lithe, whip-cord figure rose and fell, arched and straightened, with little Howard sitting on top of him, and looking around with the expression of a frightened, huddled mannikin. When the demonstration was finished, both young men got to their feet, and Joel's face could be seen raised in an expression of radiant admiration, his voice could be heard in an astounded whisper, saying:

"*Simply* incredible!"

And Mrs. Pierce, her voice stronger, more powerful, and penetrating, in slow, decisive declaration:

"*George!* I—think—that—is—the—*most—astonishing*—I think—that —is—the—*most*——"

Words failed her, and as she looked at him, standing quietly composed before her, with all his beautiful, lithe grace and stillness, he smiled his grave, rare smile, and displayed his only playful raillery of the evening:

"But really, Ida," he said quietly, as he smiled his fine, slow smile at her, "if you're worried about that girlish figure you ought to try *this* sometime." With these words he bent over backward, as lithe and limber as a whip, and with his fingers arched upon the floor, suddenly, with effortless grace and speed, and without moving an inch from his position, whirled off a dozen brilliant cartwheels that would have done credit to a circus tumbler.

He came gracefully, unweariedly erect again, to standing posture, amid an ovation of breathlessly uttered wonder, frank applause.

But now the time had come for parting: there was the sound of a motor in the drive before the house, in a moment a maid-servant came quietly out upon the terrace and informed Miss Telfair that her car had come. She gathered her evening cloak about her fragile, ivory shoulders—that were somehow like a piece of her own rare porcelain—thrust her hand out towards Mrs. Pierce in swift and firm farewell, and turned saying in her crisp, incisive voice: "Well, children, I'm departing . . . Joel," she said, pausing a moment as she went, "I shall expect you and your young friend at my house for tea tomorrow."

"And are you coming to the pool tomorrow morning, Margaret?" Mrs. Pierce called after her.

"That, my dear, I couldn't tell you," she said, going. "If I do not get a call from town. We shall see what we shall see—good-night, all," and she went through the moonlit door into the house.

LXI

Mrs. Pierce stood at the foot of the stairs surveying this young stranger from the outside world with a tolerant but glacially detached smile of impersonal curiosity:

" . . . Joel tells me that you like to stay up all night and prowl around. What do you do on these prowling expeditions?"

He wanted to answer her with simple eloquence and grace and warmth, he wanted to paint a picture of his midnight wanderings that would hold her there in fascinated interest, but the glacial impersonality of the woman's smile, the proud and haughty magnificence of her person, froze all the ardors of enthusiasm and conviction with which, he felt, he might have spoken, it even seemed to numb and thicken the muscles of his tongue, and he stood there gaping at her awkwardly, cutting a sorry figure, and flushing crimson with anger and vexation at his lame, stupid, halting tongue, and stammered out, replying:

"I—I walk," he mumbled. "I—I take walks."

"You—what?" she said kindly enough, but sharply, with a kind of peremptory authority that told him that she must already be growing weary and impatient of his stammering, incoherent speech, his mumbling awkwardness:

"Oh—*walk!*" she cried, with an air of swift enlightenment, as if her puzzled mind had just succeeded in translating his jargon. "Oh," she said quietly, and looked at him for a moment steadily with her fixed and glacial smile, "you do."

It seemed to him that those brief words were already pregnant with a cold indifferent dismissal: in them he seemed to feel the impregnable indifference of her cold detachment—the yawning gulf that separated her life from his. Already it seemed to him that she had turned away from him, dismissing him as not worthy even of such amused attention as she had given him. But after a moment, as she continued to look at him with her brilliant, glacial, detached, yet not unkindly smile, she continued:

"And what do you do on these walks? Where do you go?"

—Where? Where? Where indeed? His mind groped desperately over the whole nocturnal pattern of the city—over the lean, gaunt webbing of Manhattan with the barren angularity of its streets, the splintered, glacial soar of its terrific buildings, and the silent, frozen harshness of its streets of old brown houses, grimy brick and rusty, age-encrusted stone.

Oh, he thought that he could tell her all that could be told, that youth could know, that any man had ever known about night and time and darkness, and about the city's dark and secret heart, and what lay buried in the dark and secret heart of all America. He thought that he could tell her all that any man could ever know about the huge, attentive secrecy of night, and of man's silent heart of buried, waiting, and intolerable desire, about the thing that waits there in the nighttime in America, that lies buried at the city's secret heart of night, the mute and single tongue of man's intolerable desire, the silence of his single heart in all its overwhelming eloquence, the great tide flowing in the hearts of men, as dark and as mysterious as the great, unceasing river. the thing that waits and does not speak and is forever silent and that knows forever, and that has no words to say, no tongue to speak, and that unites six million celled and lonely sleepers at the heart of night and silence, in the great dark tide of the unceasing river, and of all our buried songs of hope and joy and wild desire that live forever in the heart of night and of America.

Yes, he thought that he could tell her all of this, but when he spoke, with thickened tongue, a numb and desperate constraint, all that he could mutter thickly was: "I—I walk."

"But *where?*" she said, a trifle more sharply, still looking at him with her glacial, curious smile. "That's what I'd like to know. Where do you go? What do you see that's so interesting? What do you find that's worth staying up all night for? Where do you go when you make these expeditions?" she again demanded. "Up to Broadway?"

"Yes," he mumbled thickly, "—sometimes—and—and sometimes—I go down town."

"Down town?" the cool incisive inflection of the voice, the glacial gray-green of the eye bored through him like a steel-blue drill. "Down-town *where?* To the Battery?"

"Y-y-yes—sometimes. . . . And—and along the East Side, too," he mumbled.

"*Where?*" she cried sharply, smiling, but manifestly impatient with his mumbled, tongue-tied answers. "*Oh*—the East Side!" she cried again, with the air of glacial enlightenment. "—In the tenement section!"

"Yes—yes," he stumbled on desperately, "—and along Fourteenth Street and Second Avenue—and Grand Street—and—and Delancey—and—and the Bowery—and all the docks and piers and all," he blurted out, conscious of Joel's eager, radiant smile of hopeful kindness, and the miserable clown he was making of himself.

"But I should think you would find all that dreadfully boring." Mrs. Pierce's voice was now tinged with cool and mild surprise. "And awfully ugly, isn't it? . . . I mean, if you've got to prowl around at night, you might hunt for something a little more attractive than the East Side, couldn't you? . . . After all, we still have Riverside Drive— I suppose even that has changed a great deal, but in my childhood it was quite a lovely place. Or the Park?" she said, a little more kindly and persuasively. "If you want to take a walk before going to bed, why wouldn't it be better to take it in the Park—where you could see an occasional tree or a little grass. . . . Or even Fifth Avenue and around Washington Square—that used to be quite pleasant! But the East *Side!* Heavens! My dear boy, what on earth do you ever find in a place like that to interest you?"

He was absolutely speechless, congealed, actually terrified by the haughty magnificence, the glacial and almost inhuman detachment, of her person. His mouth gaped, he gulped, his lips quivered and made soundless efforts for a moment, and then he stammered:

"You—you find—you find—p-p-p-people there," he said.

"*People?*" Again, her thin eyebrows arched in fine surprise. "But of course you find people there! You find people everywhere you go. . . . Only," she added, "I shouldn't think you'd find many people anywhere at two o'clock in the morning. I should think most of them would be in bed—even on the East Side."

"They—they stay up late over there."

"But why?" she now cried with a good-natured but frank impatience. "That's just what I'm trying to find out! . . . What's it all about? What's all the *shooting* for?" she said humorously, repeating a phrase which was in current use at that time. "—What's the big attraction? What do they find to do that's so interesting that it can keep them out of bed half through the night? . . . Really," she cried, "if it's so amusing as all that, I think I'll go and have a look myself. What do they *do?*" she again insisted. "That's what I want to know."

"They—they sit around and talk."

"But *where? Where?*" she now cried with frank despair. "My dear boy, that's what I want you to tell me."

"Oh, in—in lunch-rooms—and restaurants—and speakeasies—and—and places like that."

"Yes," she nodded, with an air of satisfaction. "Good. At least, we have *that* settled. And you go to these places, too—and sit around—and watch—and listen to them. Is that it?"

"Yes," he said helplessly, nodding, her words suddenly making all this restless and unceasing explanation of the night seem reasonless, foolish, pitifully absurd, "sometimes."

"And what kind of people do you find in those places?" she said curiously. "I've often wondered what kind of people go there."

Kind? He stared at her foolishly with gaping jaw, and gaped and muttered wordlessly, and could not find a word to say to her. Kind? Great God, what word could ever shape them, what phrase could ever utter the huge swarm and impact of just one moment, out of all those million swarming memories of kaleidoscopic night! Kind? Great God, the kind of all the earth, the kind of the whole world, the unnumbered, nameless, swarming, and illimitable kind that make all living! Kind? The mongrel compost of a hundred races—the Jews, the Irish, the

Italians, and the niggers, the Swedes, the Germans, the Lithuanians and the Poles, the Russians, Czechs, and Greeks, the Syrians, Turks and Armenians, the nameless hodge-podge of the Balkans, as well as Chinese, Japs, and dapper little Filipinos—a hundred tongues, a thousand tribes, unnumbered colonies of life, all poured in through the lean gateways of the sea, all poured in upon that rock of life, to join the countless freightage of that ship of living stone, all nurtured and sustained upon the city's strong breast,—a thousand kinds, a single substance, all fused and joined there at the heart of night, all moving with that central, secret and dynamic energy, all wrought and woven in, with all their swarming variousness, into the great web of America— with all its clamor, naked struggle, blind and brutal strife, with all its violence, ignorance, and cruelty, and with its terror, joy, and mystery, its undying hope, its everlasting life.

All he could do was gape and mumble foolishly again, and stammer finally: "There—there are all kinds, I guess," and plunge on desperately, "and then—and then—there are the wharves and piers and docks— the Battery and the City Hall—and then—and then," he stumbled on, "—the Bridge—the Bridge is good."

"The Bridge?" Again the pencilled brows of arched surprise, the glacial curiosity. "What bridge?"

What bridge? Great God, the only bridge, the bridge of power, life and joy, the bridge that was a span, a cry, an ecstasy—that was America. What bridge? The bridge whose wing-like sweep that was like space and joy and ecstasy was mixed like music in his blood, would beat like flight and joy and triumph through the conduits of his life forever. What bridge? The bridge whereon at night he had walked and stood and watched a thousand times, until every fabric of its soaring web was inwrought in his memory, and every stone of its twin terrific arches was in his heart, and every living sinew of its million cabled nerves had throbbed and pulsed in his own spirit like his soul's anatomy.

"The—the Brooklyn Bridge," he mumbled. "The—the Bridge is good."

"Good? How do you mean—good?" The glacial and amused inquiry pierced his consciousness again with confusion, numb paralysis of speech, and incoherence. And at this moment Joel, seeing his agonizing embarrassment, came to his rescue with the exquisite, radiant kindliness that was the constant evidence of his fine character.

"Um. Yes," he could hear Joel whispering in a thoughtful and convinced way. "He's dead right about it, Mums. I've gone with him once or twice—and the Bridge *is* good! . . . And the East Side has good things in it, too," he whispered generously. "I saw some good bits there —street corners, a store front, alleys—there's good color—I'd like to go back sometime and paint it."

For the first time Mrs. Pierce broke into a robust, free and hearty laugh.

"Joel!" she cried. "You can get the most insane notions in your head of any boy I ever knew! If I didn't watch you, I believe you'd be painting ash-cans! . . . My dear boy," she said, laughing, "you'd better stick to what you're doing. I don't think you've had much experience with low-life—if that's what you want I'll find plenty of it for you right here in Rhinekill or on the farm. . . . If you want low-life," here she paused and laughed heartily again, "go down to Granny's tomorrow and paint the expression of those nine maids of hers when she tells them she's decided to bob their hair because it fits in so nicely with the new decoration—Hah! Hah! Hah! Hah! Hah!"—Mrs. Pierce cast back her head and laughed again, a full free hearty laugh of robust humor, in which Joel joined enthusiastically, almost suddenly, with a face radiant with glee— "I'd just like to be there when she tells them, that'll be low-life enough," she said.

"*Simply* incredible!" Joel whispered, his face still radiant with its gleeful merriment.

"But no," his mother went on more casually, and with humorous tolerance. "—You finish up what you're doing first—finish those screens you're doing for Madge Telfair—then we'll talk about low-life. . . . But I hardly think your talent lies in that direction," she said good-humoredly but with an ironically knowing smile. "I haven't been your mother all these years without finding out something about your abilities—and I hardly think they lie in that direction. So you just stick to what you're doing for the present—and if there's any low-life to be done, just let *me* do the choosing. . . . Well, then, good-night," she said quietly, kindly, and good-naturedly to the young man, as she turned to go upstairs. "Joel has told me so much about your nocturnal habits that I was curious to meet you and find out what you did. I'm glad to get the mystery cleared up. . . . I suppose," she said, with an idle and detached curiosity, "that when one is all alone and knows no one in the city, he is driven to do almost anything for amusement. . . . Where are you from?" she said curiously.

"From—from the South," he answered.

"Oh," she stared at him a moment longer with her cold, fixed smile. "Yes," she said, "I can see you are. I thought so. . . . Well, children," she said with an air of finality, "you can burn the candle at both ends if that's what you want to do—go out and bay the moon, if you like—but not too near the house," she said good-naturedly. "Your *mother's* going to bed. . . . Joel," she said quietly, "you'll be in to see me, of course, before you turn in."

"Yes, Mums," he whispered, eager, radiant, his tall, thin figure bent forward reverentially as he looked up at her, his eyebrows arching with their characteristic expression of fine surprise.—"But of course!" he said.

"Very well," she said quietly. "And now good-night to all of you."

Turning, she went swiftly up the stairs, a tall, magnificently haughty figure of a woman, holding rustling and luxurious skirts.

"And now," Joel whispered, when his mother had departed, "I'll show you your room—and how to find the kitchen—and tell you anything you want to know—and after *that,*" he whispered, laughing and stroking his head, "you can do as you please, stay up as long as you like—but *I'm* going to bed."

With these words he took his guest's valise and started up the stairs. The young man followed him: he had been given a room on the second floor on the river side of the house. It was a magnificent spacious room so richly, softly carpeted that the foot sank down with velvet firmness to a noiseless tread. The quality of the room was the quality of the whole house—a kind of château-like grandeur and solidity, combined with the warmth, comfort and simplicity of a country house. Joel pressed buttons, flooding the great room with light. The wide and snowy covers of the great bed had been drawn back for the night. It was a bed fit for a king, and long and spacious enough for a man of seven feet: it waited there with a kind of still embrace, a silent and yet animate invitation that was eloquent with the promise of a strange and sweet repose.

Joel opened the door of the bathroom—it was a miracle of shining tile and creamy porcelain and gleaming silver and heavy, robe-like towels. Then Joel raised the shades, drew the curtains apart and opened the window: the fragrance of the night came in slowly, sustaining gauzy curtains on its breath of coolness like a cloud of gossamer.

And through the opened window was revealed anew the haunting loneliness of that enchanted landscape: the vast sweep of velvet-rounded lawn that slept in moonlight, and the sleeping and moon-haunted woods below and to each side, and down below them in the distance the great wink and scallop-dance and dark unceasing mystery of the lovely and immortal river—a landscape such as one might see in dreams, in dreams forever haunted by the thought of home.

The feeling of happiness that filled the youth was so grand, so wonderful and so overpowering that he could not speak. It seemed that all his life he had dreamed of one day finding such a life as this, and now that he had found it, it seemed to him that all he had dreamed was but a poor and shabby counterfeit of this reality—all he had imaged as a boy in his unceasing visions of the shining city, and of the glamorous men and women, the fortunate, good, and happy life that he would find there, seemed nothing but a shadowy and dim prefigurement of the radiant miracle of this actuality.

It was not merely the wealth, the luxury and the comfort of the scene that filled his heart with a sense of joy and victory. Far more than this, it was the feeling that this life of wealth, and luxury and comfort was so beautiful and right and good. At the moment it seemed to him to be the life for which all men on the earth are seeking, about which all men living dream, toward which all the myriads of the earth aspire; and the thing, above all, which made this life seem so beautiful and good was the conviction that filled him at that moment of its essential incorruptible righteousness. It seemed to him to be the most wonderful and beautiful life on earth, not only because it existed for the comfort and the soul-enrichment of its choice few, but because it stood there as a beacon and a legend in the hearts of all men living—a symbol of what all life on earth should be, a promise of what every man on earth should have.

In that blind surge of youth and joy, the magic of that unbelievable discovery, he could not estimate the strange and bitter chance of destiny, nor ravel out that grievous web, that dense perplexity. He could not see how men had groped and toiled and mined, and grown blind and bent and gray, deep in the dark bowels of the earth, to wreak this moonlight loveliness upon a hill; nor know how men had sweat and women worked, how youth had struck its fire and grown old, how hope and faith and even love had died, how many nameless lives had labored, grieved, and come to naught in order that this fragile image of compacted night, this priceless distillation of its rare and chosen loveliness, should blossom to a flower of moonlight beauty on a hill.

Joel took him downstairs to the kitchen before telling him good-night. They crossed the hall, and passed through the great dining-room. It was also a noble gleaming room of white, as grand and spacious as a room in a château, but warm, and familiar, comforting as home. Then they passed through a service corridor that connected the kitchen and the pantry with the dining-room, and instantly he found himself in another part of this enchanted world—the part that cooked and served and with viewless grace, and magic stealth and instancy— performed the labors of this enchanted house.

It was such a kitchen as he had never seen before—a kitchen such as he had never dreamed possible. In its space, its order, its astounding cleanliness, it had the beauty of a great machine—a machine of tremendous power, fabulous richness and complexity—which in its ordered magnificence, its vast readiness, had the clear and glittering precision of a geometric pattern. Even the stove—a vast hooded range as large as those in a great restaurant—glittered with the groomed perfection of a racing motor. There was, as well, an enormous electric stove that was polished like a silver ornament, the pots and pans were hung in gleaming rows, in vast but orderly profusion ranging from great copper kettles big enough to roast an ox to little pans and skillets just large enough to poach an egg, but all hung there in regimented order, instant readiness, shining like mirrors, scrubbed and polished into gleaming disks, the battered cleanliness of well-used copper, seasoned iron and heavy steel.

The great cupboards were crowded with huge stacks of gleaming china ware and crockery, enough to serve the needs of a hotel. And the long kitchen table, as well as the chairs and woodwork of the room, was white and shining as a surgeon's table: the sinks and drains were blocks of creamy porcelain, clean scrubbed copper, shining steel.

It would be impossible to describe in detail the lavish variety, the orderly complexity; the gleaming cleanliness of that great room, but the effect it wrought upon his senses was instant and overwhelming. It was one of the most beautiful, spacious, thrilling, and magnificently service-able rooms that he had ever seen: everything in it was designed for use, and edged with instant readiness; there was not a single thing in the room that was not needed, and yet its total effect was to give one a feeling of power, space, comfort, rightness and abundant joy.

The pantry shelves were crowded to the ceiling with the growing treasure of a lavish victualling—an astounding variety and abundance of delicious foods, enough to stock a grocery store, or to supply an Arctic expedition—but the like of which he had never seen, or dreamed of, in a country house before.

Everything was there, from the familiar staples of a cook's necessities to every rare and toothsome dainty that the climates and the markets of the earth produce. There was food in cans, and food in tins, and food in crocks, and food in bottles. There were—in addition to such staple products of the canning art as corn, tomatoes, beans and peas, pears, plums and peaches, such rarer relishes, as herrings, sardines, olives, pickles, mustard, relishes, anchovies. There were boxes of glacéd crystalline fruits from California, and little wickered jars of sharp-spiced ginger fruit from China: there were expensive jellies green as emerald, red as rubies, smoother than whipped cream, there were fine oils and vinegars in bottles, and jars of pungent relishes of every sort, and boxes of assorted spices. There was everything that one could think of, and everywhere there was evident the same scrubbed and gleaming cleanliness with which the kitchen shone, but here there was as well, that pungent, haunting, spicy odor that pervades the atmosphere of pantries—a haunting and nostalgic fusion of delicious smells whose exact quality it is impossible to define, but which has in it the odors of cinnamon, pepper, cheese, smoked ham, and cloves.

When they got into the kitchen they found Rosalind there: she was standing by the long white table drinking a glass of milk. Joel, in the swift and correct manner with which he gave instructions, at once eager, gentle and decisive, began to show his guest around.

"And look," he whispered with his soft, and yet incisive slowness, as he opened the heavy shining doors of the great refrigerator—"here's the icebox: if you find anything there you like, just help yourself——"

Food! Food, indeed! The great icebox was crowded with such an assortment of delicious foods as he had not seen in many years: just to look at it made the mouth begin to water, and aroused the pangs of a hunger so ravenous and insatiate that it was almost more painful than the pangs of bitter want. One was so torn with desire and greedy gluttony as he looked at the maddening plenty of that feast that his will was rendered almost impotent. Even as the eye glistened and the mouth began to water at the sight of a noble roast of beef, all crisp and crackly in its cold brown succulence, the attention was diverted to a plump broiled chicken, whose brown and crackly tenderness fairly seemed to beg for the sweet and savage pillage of the tooth. But now a pungent and exciting fragrance would assail the nostrils: it was the smoked pink slices of an Austrian ham—should it be brawny bully beef, now, or the juicy breast of a white tender pullet, or should it be the smoky pungency, the half-nostalgic savor of the Austrian ham? Or that noble dish of green lima beans, now already beautifully congealed in their pervading film of melted butter; or that dish of tender stewed young cucumbers; or those tomato slices, red and thick and ripe, and heavy as a chop; or that dish of cold asparagus, say; or that dish of corn; or, say, one of those musty fragrant, deep-ribbed cantaloupes, chilled to the heart, now, in all their pink-fleshed taste and ripeness; or a round thick slab cut from the red ripe heart of that great watermelon; or a bowl of those red raspberries, most lucious and most rich with sugar, and a bottle of that thick rich cream which filled one whole compartment of that treasure-chest of gluttony, or——

What shall it be now? What shall it be? A snack! A snack!— Before we prowl the meadows of the moon to-night, and soak our hearts in the moonlight's magic and the visions of our youth—what shall it be before we prowl the meadows of the moon? Oh, it shall be a snack, a snack—hah! hah!—it shall be nothing but a snack because— hah! hah!—you understand, we are not hungry and it is not well to eat too much before retiring—so we'll just investigate the icebox as we have done so oft at midnight in America—and we are the moon's man, boys—and all that it will be, I do assure you, will be something swift and quick and ready, something instant and felicitous, and quite delicate and dainty—just a snack!

I think—now let me see—h'm, now!—well, perhaps I'll have a slice or two of that pink Austrian ham that smells so sweet and pungent and looks so pretty and so delicate there in the crisp garlands of the parsley leaf!—and yes, perhaps, I'll have a slice of this roast beef, as well— h'm now!—yes, I think that's what I'm going to do—say a slice of red rare meat there at the centre—ah-h! there you are! yes, that's the stuff, that does quite nicely, thank you—with just a trifle of that crisp brown crackling there to oil the lips and make its passage easy, and a little of that cold but brown and oh—most—brawny gravy—and, yes, sir!

I think I *will*, now that it occurs to me, a slice of that plump chicken—some white meat, thank you, at the breast—ah, there it is!—how sweetly doth the noble fowl submit to the swift and keen persuasion of the knife—and now, perhaps, just for our diet's healthy balance, a spoonful of those lima beans, as gay as April and as sweet as butter, a tomato slice or two, a speared forkful of those thin-sliced cucumbers—ah! what a delicate and toothsome pickle they do make—what sorcerer invented them, a little corn perhaps, a bottle of this milk, a pound of butter and that crusty loaf of bread—and even this moon-haunted wilderness were paradise enow—with just a snack—a snack—a snack——

He was aroused from this voluptuous and hypnotic revery by the sound of Rosalind's warm sweet laugh, her tender and caressing touch upon his arm, and Joel's soundless and astonished mouth, the eager incandescence of his gleeful smile, his whole face uplifted in its fine and gentle smile, his voice cast in its frequent tone of whispering astonishment:—

"*Simply* incredible!" he was whispering to his sister. "I've never seen such an expression on *any* one's face in all my life! It's simply diabolical! When he sees food, he looks as if he's just getting ready to rape a woman!"

"Do you, darling?" said the girl, with her warm, sweet tolerance of humor. "I'm so glad to know that some one else likes food. I like it, too," she said with a warm plainness, "when I am married and start having babies I shall eat and eat and eat to my heart's content—as much as I want to, all the things I ever wanted, till I'm satisfied. . . . It's so wonderful to find some one who will eat! You don't know how hard it is to have a brother who's a vegetarian—and who tells me that I'm getting disgustingly fat—and what a horrible thing it is to eat dead animals—like eating corpses. . . . Wouldn't Joel be wonderful if he ate roast beef," she added with her warm and gentle humor, as she put her arm around her brother's waist—"he looks so thin and starved, poor thing—like a religious ascetic—doesn't he?—But then, he's such a saint as he is—isn't he?—if he liked food, as well, he'd just have everything—he'd be too perfect."

"No, sir," Joel whispered, shaking his head and laughing with his curiously boyish, almost clumsily naïve, but beautifully engaging good nature—"Not I! . . . The rest of you can eat all the dead animals you like—but you don't catch me doing it! . . . I'll stick to spinach," he whispered radiantly. "That's good enough for me."

"I know, darling," she said with a gentle and tolerant sarcasm. "You and Bernard Shaw: if he said baled hay was good for you, you'd believe him, wouldn't you?"

He laughed in his soundless, enthusiastic and beautifully generous way, his gaunt starved face lighting up with the gleeful almost diabolically brilliant radiance of his wonderful selfless good-nature.

Then, turning swiftly to his firmer manner of incisive severity—the direct and earnest concision with which he whispered his instructions —he said abruptly:

"And look, Gene . . . when you finish eating put the lights out: the switch is on the right hand by the door as you go out. ... And stay up as long as you like, go wherever you like, do as you please— you'll bother no one," he whispered, ". . . and a good walk," he continued abruptly after a moment's pause, "—is down the road—the way you went with Ros' tonight—except that you keep on——"

"Past the cows, darling," said Rosalind gently. "Past all the lovely cows and barns and meadows of the moon."

LXII

THE two young people stopped talking instantly as Eugene came in, Joel got up and shut the door behind him, indicated an easy leather chair, where the author could read his play most comfortably, and sitting down again beside his sister, waited for the play to begin.

Eugene began to read haltingly, with the difficulty and embarrassed constraint of a young man just beginning to test his powers, exhibiting his talents to the public for the first time, and torn by all the anguish, hope, and fear, the proud incertitude, of youth.

It was a play called "Mannerhouse," a title which itself might reveal the whole nature of his error—and its subject was the decline and fall and ultimate extinction of a proud old family of the Southern aristocracy in the years that followed the Civil War, the ultimate decay of all its fortunes and the final acquisition of its proud estate, the grand old columned house that gave the play its name, by a vulgar, coarse and mean, but immensely able member of the rising "lower class."

This theme—which, in its general form and implications, was probably influenced a good deal by *The Cherry Orchard* of Chekhov— was written in a somewhat mixed mood of romantic sentiment, Byronic irony, and sardonic realism. The hero was a rather Byronic character, a fellow who concealed his dark and tender poetry under the mask of a sardonic humor; the love story was colored by defeat and error and departure, and the hero's final return "years later," a lonely and nameless wanderer, battered by the world and the wreckage of his life, to the old ruined house in which already the rasping note of the wrecker's crew was audible, was tempered by the romantic gallantry of Cyrano. The final meeting with the girl—the woman that he loved —their ultimate gallant resignation to fate and age and destiny—was wholly Cyranoic; and the final scene, in which the gigantic faithful negro slave—now an old man, almost blind, but with the savage loyalty and majesty of a race of African kings from whom he is descended— wraps his great arms around the rotting central column of the old ruined house, snaps it in two with a last convulsion of his dying strength, and brings the whole ruined temple thundering down to bury his beloved master, his hated "poor white" enemy the new owner, and himself, beneath its ruins—was obviously a product of the Samson legend.

In spite of this, there was good stuff in the play, dramatic conflict, moving pageantry. The character of the hard, grasping but immensely able materialist of "the lower class," the newer South, was well realized —and had been derived from the character of the youth's own uncle, William Pentland. The scenes between the hero and his father—the leonine and magnificently heroic "General"—were also good; as were those between the hero and Porter, the poor-white capitalist. Even in these romantic, grandly-mannered scenes, he had already begun to use some of the powerful and inimitable materials of life itself and of his own experience: the speech of Porter was the plain, rich, pungent, earthly, strongly colored speech of his mother, of his uncle William Pentland, and of the Pentland tribe.

But the scenes between the hero and the girl were less successful: the character of the girl was shadowy and uncertain—a kind of phantasmal combination of the characters of Roxane in *Cyrano,* and Ophelia— and her sweet romantic loveliness, the yearning tenderness of her pure love, did not provide a convincing foil and balance for the sardonic humor, the hard and almost brutal violence of wit, with which the hero masked his pain and love and bitterness and repulsed her advances. (This scene, by the way, was undoubtedly influenced a great deal by the Hamlet and Ophelia situation.)

Likewise—in various and interesting ways, what he had read and seen and actually experienced had shaped the tone and temper of his play: the character of the pompous and banal old "Major"—the "General's" contemporary and friend and the father of the heroine— and his conversations with the hero, in which his conventional and pompous character is made the butt for the biting and sardonic gibes of the latter, were also evidently strongly colored with the influence of Polonius and Hamlet. But there was good stuff in these scenes as well, considerable originality and naturalness was shown in the characterization of the old "Major": he was, for example, trying to support the tottering fortune of a small military school, which his family had established several generations before, and whose gigantic futility, amid this decline of a ruined order and a vanquished system was, in the years after the war, ironically apparent. There was, in fact, much telling satire in this situation, and on the whole it was well managed. Moreover, its "modern" implications were evident: it suggested, for example, the Southerner's pitiable devotion to a gaudy uniform and military trappings, the profusion of ugly, trivial, cheap and brutal little "military schools" that cover the whole South, even to the present day, like an ugly rash, and whose "You furnish the boy—we send back the man" philosophy is nauseous in its hypocrisy, dishonesty, and cheap pretense.

There was much more that was good and pungent and original in these scenes between the "Major" and the hero: a great deal of the falseness, hypocrisy and sentimentality of the South was polished off in these episodes, and "the war"—the Civil War—was used effectively as a stalking horse to satirize the great World War of modern times. There was, for example, a good, and original—on the whole, a very true—variation of the Youth-and-Age, Old Man-Young Man conflict that was evident at that period, and that provided the material of so many books and plays and poems of the time.

In these scenes, it was very forcefully and amusingly shown that the conflict between youth and age had in it an element of mutual hypocrisy, a kind of mutual acceptance of a literary game about youth and age which both young and old knew in their hearts was false, but which both played.

Thus, when the old "Major" would heave a melancholy sigh, and shaking his head with a doleful and hypocritical regret, would say:

"Ah yes, my boy! . . . We old men have made a sad mess of this world. . . . We have betrayed our trust, and showed ourselves unworthy of the confidence you young men have reposed in us. . . . We were given the opportunity of making the world a better place in which to live and we have left nothing but ruin, poverty, and misery wherever we went—we have left the world in ashes. . . . Now it is for you young men of the world—for youth—glorious, brave and noble-hearted youth——"

"Ah, youth, youth," the hero would murmur at this point with a sardonic humor that of course went unnoticed by the pompous old fool to whom it was uttered—and the Major would nod his head in agreement and go on——

"Yes, youth—brave, generous and devoted youth—it remains for youth to repair the damage that we old men have done, to bind up the nation's broken wounds, to see to it that the world be made into a fit place for their children to live in, to see that——"

"Government of the people, by the people and for the people," the hero would sardonically supply.

"Yes," the old Major would agree, "—and that the children of the coming generation may not look at you, as you can look at us, and say—'What have you done, old men, with your inheritance? What kind of world are you leaving behind you for us *young* men to inherit? How can you look us in the eyes, old men, when you know that you have been unworthy of your sacred trust—that the young men of the world have been foully tricked, betrayed, dishonored by you old men'——"

"Why, Major!" the hero would now cry, in mock astonishment, as he ironically applauded. "—This is eloquence! Hear, hear! . . . And you are right! Major, you are right! The young men of the world have been betrayed and tricked! Not only tricked—but tr-r-ricked! . . . And by whom?" he would inquire with sardonic rhetoric. "Why, by these false, lying, greedy, hypocritical old men who have had the whole world in their keeping and who have reduced it to a shambles for our inheritance! . . . Major, who made the war? Who *sent* us forth to war? . . . Why, these old, false, lying, greedy men, of course! . . . And who fought the war? . . . Why, these brave, gallant, devoted, noble-spirited young men, of course! . . . And why did you old men send us forth to war, Major? . . . Why, to further your own rapacity, to protect your own ill-gotten wealth, to conquer, ravage, and invade for your own enrichment. . . . And how did we go to war, Major? Why, with faith and trust and the purity of a high conviction. . . . And how did we come back from war? With hell in our eyes. . . . We young men always go to war with faith and trust and the purity of a high conviction. . . . And we always come back with hell in our eyes! Why, Major? . . . Why, because you false, lying, greedy, selfish, and hypocritical old men of the world have lied to us. . . . You always lie to us. And how, Major, in what way do you lie to us? . . . Why, Major," he said solemnly, "you tell us that war is beautiful, ideal, and heroic—that we are going forth to fight for pure ideals, noble faith, . . . And what do we find, Major? Why," he said, as his voice sank to an ironically solemn whisper—"we find that war is really *ugly*— is really cruel—horrible—base. . . . Why, Major, do you know what we young men find when we go to war? We find that men in war actually *kill* one another. . . . Yes, sir," he would whisper solemnly, ". . . they *shoot* one another—they blow one another's brains out— *that's* what they do—why, it's murder, Major—sheer cold-blooded murder—it's not what you said it was at all—and all of it because you old greedy, lying, selfish men who make the wars have lied to us and tr-r-ricked us all along!"

"Ah, my boy," the old "Major" would answer sorrowfully—"it is a grievous charge you make against us—but I fear—I fear," here his voice would sink to a dejected whisper—"I fear that it is just."

In this way, a telling and satiric irony was derived from this scene, which was well-handled and might have been effective on the stage.

But the most effective scene of all, perhaps, was in the prologue of this play: here the scene was really splendid, thrilling in its dramatic pageantry, and undoubtedly would have been a very good and moving one upon a stage. The scene was on a hill and showed the building of the great white house—really the founding of a whole society. Before the unfinished house, a gun held cocked and ready in his hands, was standing the stern and silent figure of its founder. And before him, up and down the hill, and in and out of the unfinished house, and past its great unfinished columns, were moving two silent and unceasing files of slaves, powerful black men stripped naked to the waist, bearing upon their heads the heavy burdens of material that would go into the house. And from the house there comes a sound of constant hammering, and night comes, there are the flares of watchfires and the swift and cat-like passing of the great black forms. A moment's flare of insurrection, the spring of a great negro at the stern and lonely figure of the man, the flash of a knife, and the rebel falls, knocked senseless by a blow from the stock of the master's gun.

Then, another white man from the neighboring town—the minister:

the minister's low persuasive voice urging the man to see the crime of slavery, quoting the Scriptures with a telling aptness, urging him to repent, to join the life of town and church, to "come to God" . . . And the quiet and inflexible answer of the master: "I must build my home."

And nothing finally but night and darkness; the great figures of the slaves pad past in darkness, as noiseless as cats, and from the mystery of night there rises now the wailing chant of all the jungle, the lamentation of man's life of toil and grief and bitter labor, the chant of the slave.

This was a fine scene, and should have been beautiful and moving on a stage.

From this description, it will be seen how the young man's play was made up both of good and bad, how strongly it was marked by the varied influence of his reading and idolatry—by Shakespeare, Chekhov, Shaw, Rostand, the Bible—and how he had also already begun to use some of the materials of his own life and feeling and experience, how even in this groping and uncertain play, some of the real grandeur, beauty, terror, and unuttered loveliness, of America, was apparent.

Thus the play, with all its faults and imitations, really did illustrate, as few things else could do, the confused incertitude and the flashes of blind but powerful intuition, which mark the artist's early life here in America, and for this reason chiefly the play was interesting.

And feeling this incertitude as he sat down to read the play— that feeling mixed of hope, of fear, of quivering apprehension which the artist feels when for the first time he releases his work from the lonely prison of creation and lets it go then, irrevocably, to stand upon its own feet, meet the naked eye of the great world without protection, and stand or fall upon its own merits—feeling this fatality of release, this irrevocable finality of action, he began to read the play in a halting, embarrassed, and almost inaudible tone, full of the proud and desperate hope, the trembling apprehension, the almost truculent hostility towards imaginary detractors which every young man feels at such a time.

He sensed quickly that his fears were groundless. No man ever had a more generous, enthusiastic and devoted following than he had that morning in the presence of these two fine young people—Joel Pierce and his sister Rosalind.

He saw—or rather *felt* at once—their rapt and fascinated attentiveness. Joel sat, his gaunt figure hinged forward on his knees, in an
attitude of tense, motionless and utterly silent interest: from time to
time as the young dramatist glanced up from his great sheaf of written
manuscript, he could see Joel's lean gaunt face fixed on him, uplifted,
with its strangely pure and radiant eagerness, and Rosalind, her warm
and strong young hands clasped quietly, folded in her lap, her warm
and lovely face flushed with excitement, her eyes luminous, vague and
tender, as if she were really in a theatre seeing the figures in the play pass
before her invested in all the magic that the stage could give to them,
displayed an interest that was more relaxed and more abstracted than
her brother's, but none the less absorbed.

The sense and sight and assurance of these things acted like a powerful and gloriously intoxicating liquor on his heart and mind and spirit.
He felt an overpowering surge of warm affection, proud and tender
gratefulness towards Joel and his sister. It seemed to him that they were
the finest people he had ever known—the most generous, the truest,
highest, and the loyalest—and the knowledge that they liked his play—
were in fact conquered and possessed, brought out of themselves and
laid under the play's power and magic—his *own* power and magic—
overwhelmed him for a moment with a feeling of the purest, highest,
and most glorious happiness that life can yield—the happiness that is
at once the most selfish and the most selfless—the happiness of the artist
when he sees that his work has been found good, has for itself a place
of honor, glory, and proud esteem in the hearts of men, and has
wrought upon their lives the spell of its enchantment. At that instant
he saw, in one blaze of light, an image of unutterable conviction, the
reason why the artist works and lives and has his being—the reward
he seeks—the only reward he really cares about, without which there
is nothing. It is to snare the spirits of mankind in nets of magic, to
make his life prevail through his creation, to wreak the vision of his
life, the rude and painful substance of his own experience, into the
congruence of blazing and enchanted images that are themselves the
core of life, the essential pattern whence all other things proceed, the
kernel of eternity. This is the reason that the artist lives and works
and has his being: that from life's clay and his own nature, and from
his father's common earth of toil and sweat and violence and error
and bitter anguish, he may distill the beauty of an everlasting form,
enslave and conquer man by his enchantment, cast his spell across the

generations, beat death down upon his knees, kill death utterly, and fix eternity with the grappling-hooks of his own art. His life is soul-hydroptic with a quenchless thirst for glory, and his spirit tortured by the anguish of possession—the intolerable desire to fix eternally in the patterns of an indestructible form a single moment of man's living, a single moment of life's beauty, passion, and unutterable eloquence, that passes, flames and goes, slipping forever through our fingers with time's sanded drop, flowing forever from our desperate grasp even as a river flows and never can be held. This is the artist, then—life's hungry man, the glutton of eternity, beauty's miser, glory's slave—and to do these things, to get the reward for which he thirsts, with his own immortality to beat and conquer life, enslave mankind, utterly to possess and capture beauty he will do anything, use anything, destroy anything—be ruthless, murderous and destructive, cold and cruel and merciless as hell to get the thing he wants, achieve the thing he values and must do or die.

He is at once life's monstrous outcast and life's beauty-drunken lover, man's bloody, ruthless, pitiless and utterly relentless enemy, and the best friend that mankind ever had: a creature compact of the most selfish, base, ignoble, vicious, cruel and unrighteous passions that man's life can fathom or the world contain, and a creature whose life with all its toil and sweat and bitter anguish is the highest, grandest, noblest, and the most unselfish, the most superbly happy, good and fortunate life that men can know, or any man attain. He is the tongue of his unuttered brothers, he is the language of man's buried heart, he is man's music and life's great discoverer, the eye that sees, the key that can unlock, the tongue that will express the buried treasure in the hearts of men, that all men know and that no man has a language for—and at the end, he is his father's son, shaped from his father's earth of blood and sweat and toil and bitter agony: he is at once therefore the parent and the son of life, and in him life and all man's nature are compact, he is most like man in his very differences, he is what all men are and what not one man in a million ever is; and he has all, knows all, sees all that any man on earth can see and hear and know.

This knowledge came to him that morning as he read the play that he had written to his two friends: as he went on with his reading, and felt with a proud triumphant joy and happiness the sense of their devotion, his voice grew strong and confident, the scenes and words and people of the play began to flame and pulse and live with his own passion—the whole play moved across his vision in flaming images of beauty, truth and loveliness, his spirit rose on the powerful wings of a jubilant conviction, a tremendous happiness, his heart beat like a hammer-stroke and seemed to ring against his ribs with every blow the music of this certitude.

It took him about two hours to read the play: when he finished he felt a sense of triumphant finality, an immense and joyful peace within him, and he waited for them to speak. For a moment there was utter stillness: Joel sat bent forward in the same position, his head supported by his lean hand; Rosalind sat quietly; neither moved an inch. In a moment Joel spoke, nodding his head and speaking with a kind of matter-of-fact assertiveness that was far more wonderful and thrilling than any idolatrous warmth of praise could have been:

"Yes," he whispered, nodding his head thoughtfully,—"it's as good as *The Cherry Orchard*—I like it better, myself—but it's as good." His manner now did take on an electric energy: he straightened sharply, and speaking almost sternly, with a blazing earnestness of conviction, he looked his friend in the eyes, and cried: "Eugene! . . . It's simply magnificent! . . . It's *easily* the greatest play any one in this country ever wrote. . . . There's nothing else to touch it . . . it's *miles* ahead of O'Neill . . . it's . . . it's as good as *Cyrano,* and you've got to admit," he said, nodding his head decisively, ". . . that's pretty great. . . . *Cyrano's* pretty swell," he whispered, ". . . And those scenes between the boy and the old 'Major' . . . they're simply grand," he whispered. "I mean, I didn't know you had it in you . . . that kind of writing, the satiric kind. . . . But it's . . . it's," his face flushed, he nodded his head doggedly, and almost grimly, as if willing to stand up for his conviction against the whole world, "it's . . . it's as good as *Shaw!*" And he laughed suddenly his radiant, soundless laugh and whispered drolly, ". . . And when I say anything's as good as Shaw . . . you've got to admit that's going pretty far for me. . . . Ros'," he said quietly, turning to the girl, "what do you think? . . . Don't you think it's pretty grand?"

For a moment she did not answer; her eyes were luminous as stars and far away.

"Oh," she said presently in her low and sweet and lovely young voice, "it's wonderful. . . . It's the most gloriously beautiful thing I ever heard. . . . Darling," she said, and took his hand between her strong, warm and living hands, as she had done the night before, ". . . you are a great man . . . a great writer. . . . I am so proud and happy to have known you . . . to be allowed to hear your play."

He felt the overpowering, thrilling happiness and joy, the blind speechless gratefulness, and the helpless and agonizing embarrassment that a young man feels at a moment like this. He did not know what to say, what to do, how to express the gratefulness, the affection, the tenderness that he felt towards them; he turned to Joel, his mouth moving wordlessly and helplessly, and could say nothing, he made a baffled and inarticulate movement of the hands, and ended up by putting his arms around Rosalind and hugging her in a clumsy, helpless fashion, which was perhaps as good a thing as he could do, and said all he wished to say.

It was not what these two young people had said to him that gave the moment a strange imperishable loveliness. Even in the blind surge of joy and happiness that swept over him and made him passionately want to believe that his play was as good as Joel and his sister said it was, that he was really the great man, the great writer they had called him, a grain of judgment remained and saved him from an utter self-deception. And curiously, for that very reason, his joy was somehow greater, his feeling of triumphant happiness sweeter than if what they had said were true. For in the very idolatry of their devotion, the enthusiastic exaggeration of their praise, there was all the blind but noble loyalty of youth, the beautiful and generous admiration of youth, that is so fine, so good, so high, so proud with faith and confidence and loyalty, and because of this, so right. It was for this reason that, even after years had passed and he had perhaps accomplished better work, earned more valid praise, he would yet remember that morning with a peculiar sense of proud and tender gratefulness. It brought back to him, as nothing else on earth could do, the beauty and the innocence of youth, the extravagance of its blind devotion that is so mistaken and so wonderful, the generous enthusiasm of its loyal faith that is so wrong and yet so right, its noble sincerity that burns brightly even in its grievous error, and that is somehow more true than fact, more real than glory, and more lasting and more precious than man's fame.

LXIII

WHEN they came out on the verandah, Joel's mother, Howard Martin, and Joel's cousin, Ruth, had just driven up before the entrance and were

getting out. They had been to the swimming pool—a small but delightful one a half mile away in a green hollow, tree-embowered—and
all three were in bathing costume. Howard Martin trod gingerly across
the drive and on to the warm brick flooring of the porch, on white
wincing well-kept feet; Mrs. Pierce and the girl wore light bathing-
robes and walked firmly, with assurance. Mrs. Pierce's figure was as
slender and as well-conditioned as the girl's—her ankles and her legs
were wonderfully graceful, strong and slender—but in comparison to her
niece's black and white voluptuousness—her dark and sullen, almost
brooding, face and her swelling creamy thighs, her lavish belly and
her melon-heavy breasts—the figure of Mrs. Pierce was lacking in
seduction: it had the strength and slenderness of youth without youth's
warmth and freshness, it had, like everything about her, a chilled and
glacial perfection that spoke of stern regimen, grim watchfulness, and
unflagging effort—"keeping fit."

As the two young men came up, Mrs. Pierce turned gracefully, her
hand upon the screen-door, and with a smile awaited them. Her teeth
were so solid, white, and perfect in their alignment that it was difficult to see where they joined together, and they sometimes suggested
twin rows of solid gleaming ivory more than individual teeth: this
circumstance also contributed to the glacial, detached and almost inhuman quality of her smile. She greeted her son's friend with a kindly
but detached "Good-morning," and without altering the rigid brilliance of her smile a jot, turned to her son, and said:

"I thought you were coming to the pool. What happened to you
and Ros'?"

These words were spoken quietly and matter-of-factly: nevertheless,
the suggestion of strong displeasure and annoyance was somehow unmistakable.

Joel answered quickly, whispering a swift concerned explanation, his
thin figure slightly bent forward, his gaunt face lifted, eagerly, radiantly
concerned, in that attitude of devoted and solicitous respect that characterized his relations with every woman, but that was extremely marked
when he spoke or listened to his mother:

"I know, Mums," he whispered swiftly, apologetically,—"I'm *terribly*
sorry—but he promised to read his play to us and that took all morning.
. . . *Mums!*" he went on in his astounded and enthusiastic whisper, "it's
simply magnificent—I wish you could have been there to hear it."

"Oh," said Mrs. Pierce quietly, and turning, for a moment she regarded her son's friend with that glacially brilliant smile of her thin and faintly carmined lips that never changed or altered in expression by an atom. "Oh," she said, "I should like to—perhaps you will read it to me sometime."

"*Simply* superb," Joel whispered, "it really is."

"And now you boys had better get ready for lunch," she said in a more warm and friendly tone. "You know how Granny hates it if people get there late."

With these words she went into the house and mounted the stairs. The young men followed her: at the foot of the stairs Joel turned and said to his visitor:

"Look—I'd hurry as much as I could! . . . We've only twenty minutes: you've just got time to bathe and dress."

Bathe and dress! The youth looked at his young host with a bewildered, uncomprehending face, and with a sinking feeling in his heart. What did they expect him to do—what, according to the formula of these strange rare people, was one supposed to do when one was invited out to lunch? He had bathed that morning when he got up, it seemed to him that he must still be very clean, and as for dressing, he had just one suit of clothes in all the world, and that was the suit he was wearing at that moment. And just one day before, when he had left New York to come to this magical, unbelievably glorious place, he had thought, in his miserable naïve ignorance, that this one suit of clothes, three shirts, three pairs of socks, and a change of underwear were abundantly sufficient to all the demands that fashion and a week-end visit could possibly make on him. At that moment, as he stared at his friend with a gaping mouth, unable to reply, the terrific impact of this new world which had stunned him the night before with its magnificence and beauty exploded in his brain in a flare of stars and rockets. And for a moment now he felt a lost, sickening desperate terror, and curiously, a feeling of blind resentment against his friend. For a moment he felt tricked and deceived—deceived by Joel's modesty, his exquisite humility, by the frayed and shabby clothes he had worn in Cambridge and New York, by the over-refinement of his breeding, which had caused him to conceal utterly his true state of life, never to suggest by a word or reference the kind of life that he came from, the wealth, the luxury, the magnificence of the world in which he had been born and lived.

"D-d-dress! . . . But . . . how—," his face reddened, he craned his neck doggedly, and suddenly blurted out:

"Dress? In what? This is the only suit I've got!"

"But of *course!*" Joel whispered, arching his eyebrows in astounded surprise. "What's wrong with that? . . . You can wear a dark coat anywhere—all that I meant was that you could wear white flannels with it."

"Flannels!" the other said, "I have no flannels, Joel. . . . This suit is all I've got to wear; if I can't wear this, I can't go."

"But of course you can wear it!" Joel cried, concealing any surprise he may have felt with the instant impatient agreement of his tone. "It's *perfectly* all right—only," his eyes were thoughtful for a moment, he considered swiftly—"Look here!" he said abruptly, "would you like to wear a pair of mine? I'm not as tall as you are, but perhaps you can make them fit. . . . And if you can't," he said quickly, "it's *perfectly* all right—it doesn't matter in the slightest—it's only," and his eyes for an instant had a faintly perturbed expression, "—it's only that Grandfather belongs to the old school—oh, he's *swell, simply* magnificent; you'll like him the moment you see him—the only reason I dress when going there is that he's got old-fashioned standards—and he's so *grand* —I do everything I can to please him— But come on!" he whispered quickly, 'I'll give you a pair of mine, and you can wear them if they fit —and if they don't—it doesn't matter in the slightest."

They went upstairs then to Joel's room; he gave his friend a pair of striped flannel trousers, and the other departed dutifully to bathe, put on a clean shirt and collar and the flannel trousers—which proved, indeed, a very tight precarious fit, but which were made to do—and thus correctly garmented, he joined the family and the other guests, and they drove away to Mr. Joel's house.

The great rambling old house which had been so lovely in the moon-enchantment of the night before was no less beautiful by day. It sat there in the hollow of the hill, embowered in rich green and shaded by the leafy spread of its great maples, with the homely, pure, and casual loveliness that the old houses of New England have.

Old Mr. Joel himself was just as grand and imposing a personality as Joel had indicated. He was, indeed, in Joel's word, "stupendous"; a figure of leonine magnificence and gallant gentility, who might have stepped forth from a page of Thackeray. He was already past his seventieth year, but his body was still strongly, vigorously set: he was somewhat above the middle height, but his neck and shoulders had a kind of massive strength that suggested he had been a powerfully built man in his prime. His white mane of hair was soft as silk and gave his wide brow and ruddy, pleated old man's face a kind of noble lion-like fierceness, and this impression was enhanced by his grizzled mustache and his old, rather growling, voice, which had in it nothing surly or ill-tempered, but rather a kind of old and noble masculinity, an aristocratic kind of growl that seemed perfectly adjusted to a kind of Pendennis-like language, a "Dammit-all,-sir,-it's-not-the-fellow's-drinking-that-I-mind,-it's-only-that-he's-proved-himself-incapable-of-holding-his-liquor-like-a-gentleman" kind of voice.

The inference was warranted: even as they stood there in a spacious, airy big room, the guests standing and talking in groups, drinking small glasses of a fine dry sherry, the youth could hear Joel's eager whispering voice engaged in earnest, but respectful, debate, with his leonine grandsire, and Mr. Joel's nobly growled out answers. The conversation was about books—about the artist's right to use the materials of his own experience and conversation—and it hinged particularly upon a certain book in which the writer had apparently made use of personal letters and private documents that people he knew, a woman chiefly, had written him.

"No, sir," Mr. Joel growled, "I do not care what the circumstances may be or what the nature of the work. If I had a friend, sir, who would deliberately make public letters which a woman had written him, why, sir, I should drop him from my acquaintance—I should be forced to conclude, sir," here the old growling voice fell to an ominous whisper of irrevocable judgment, and he looked out at his grandson with a fierce glint of his old eyes under bushy brows—"I should be forced to conclude, sir, that he was nothing but a cad," old Mr. Joel whispered, and with a suddenly fierce glint of his old eyes, a sudden movement of his leonine head, he growled out in a low and savage tone: "And I should tell him so, sir. I should be compelled to tell him that he was nothing but a cad!"

"Yes, grandfather," Joel whispered eagerly, his thin figure bent forward in an attitude of devoted and attentive reverence— "But after *all,* some pretty great people have done it—Rousseau did it, and *The Confessions* are pretty great, you know— You've got to admit that.—And Byron did it in his poems—at least, every one knew who he was talking about, and then there was De Musset and George Sand."

"It makes no difference, sir," growled Mr. Joel implacably, "it makes no difference who they were or how great they may be considered in the realm of art, or how great the work they did may be—if I knew a man who did a thing like that, I should be forced to consider him a low cad—no matter how great a poet or a writer, or how great his work might be—I should consider him a cad,—and," his old growling voice fell to a whisper of boding and implacable judgment—"I should tell him so, sir. I should let him know that I considered him a cad."

Such was Joel's grandsire, Mr. Joel, and surely he was a specimen of which any group or class could well be proud: of all that Hudson River aristocracy he was justly venerated and esteemed as one of its noblest and proudest adornments. He had lived a long, honorable, and successful life; and now in his old age he had retired to the bosom of his paternal earth to spend his last years in dignity and simple ease and in calm but fruitful reflection on his rich experience. He was writing a book, and in advance it could be solemnly averred that he would make no use in it of any letters that a woman ever wrote to him.

What man, therefore, could speak with greater weight about the duties, codes and principles of man? What man was better qualified to know the rules of honor and the standards of a gentleman—and to assert a truth that might have gone unnoticed by a person of a baser spirit and a lower quality—that Rousseau was a scoundrel and De Musset and Lord Byron a couple of low cads—"because, sir, they made public letters that a woman wrote them."

It was indeed delightful to find such Thackerayan gallantry, such Olympian scorn for knavish genius and for the lives of mighty poets dead and gone, who illuminated mankind with their radiance but had their own light put out—must dwell forevermore "a couple of low cads," in outer darkness, never again to be received, acknowledged, given gracious pardon by the chivalric flower of the Hudson River rich. How wretched that stern judgment must have made Rousseau! What bitter news for Byron! What misery for De Musset!

But now a woman servant entered and announced that lunch was served. The chattering groups of people turned, and formed instinctively, and by a kind of native respect, into files of deferential waiting. until Mr. Joel had passed. He led the way, a grand and leonine old man, superbly garmented in a coat of soft, rich blue, wide loose white flannels, wound at the waist by a great sash of yellow silk—an adornment that seemed in no way inappropriate but superbly fitting the noble dignity of the old man.

At the door he paused and stood aside, with a grizzled majesty of courtesy, for his wife and the other ladies of the group to pass. Then he entered the dining room followed by his grandson and the other young men. The dining room was another light, spacious, and graciously beautiful room in the old New England style: through the open windows one saw the deep green and gold of trees and flowers in the embowered magic of the setting, and the fragrance of sweet drowsy air breathed on the curtains and flowed through the room.

The snowy table had a great bowl of fresh-cut wood flowers in the centre: the food was also native, plain old American, and superbly cooked: there was a thick pea-soup, fried chicken, plump and tender, done superbly to a juicy, delicately encrusted brown: there were candied sweet potatoes, string beans, cooked the Southern way with the succulent sweet seasoning of pork, stewed golden corn, and creamy mashed potatoes, a deep smooth gravy, rich and brown and thick, sliced tomatoes and sliced cucumbers, no alcoholic beverages, but iced tea, cold and tall and fragrant in high tinkling glasses rimed with ice, flaky biscuits, smoking hot, and for dessert, fresh apple-pie, hot and crusty, hued with cinnamon and flanked by thick fresh squares of pungent yellow cheese.

It was, in short, a plain but wholesome and most appetizing meal, completely American in its flavor and abundance, and superbly cooked, most fitting to this house; the simple green and natural, casual beauty of the place, the life, the people, the homely gracious hospitality of democracy.

It is true, the meal was also rather Southern in its cooking, and its quality—a fact that was not surprising, however, when one remembered that Mr. Joel's present wife had been a famous Southern belle from the bluegrass region of Kentucky.

One not only remembered this fact, it was difficult for one not to remember it; Mrs. Joel herself made her romantic origins evident. Although she was a woman in her early sixties with white hair, she was still remarkably preserved, and her manners, graces, dimpled smiles, her roguish glances and her languishing soft drawl were still the familiar stock in trade of the Dixieland coquette.

She was certainly what is called "a fine figure of a woman"; her figure was tall, spacious, amply proportioned, her face, although beginning to show the signs of age—a slightly wrinkled plumpness like the skin of a full but slightly withered apple—was still almost as soft and white and tender as a child's: she had almost all her natural teeth and they were white and pearly, her hands were white and plump and fine, her voice had the refined and throaty burble that is familiar in the majestic American female of the upper crust, and she dimpled beautifully when she smiled.

It was rather uncomfortably evident at once that there was a strong, if suppressed, hostility between Mrs. Joel and her step-daughter, Joel's mother.

The struggle between the two was for the possession of something that neither of them any longer had—youth. Both were obviously enamored of youth—of the freshness of youth, the warmth, the charm, the grace, the vitality of youth. Both hated the idea of growing old: both bitterly and desperately refused to admit the possibility of growing old. Mrs. Joel was able to cast over her soul a spell of hypnotic deception, and by absurdly flaunting around the graces, airs and manners of a coquette, to convince herself that she was young and beautiful, able to enslave every man she met under the domination of her captivating charm.

And Mrs. Pierce felt bitterly that the older woman had had her day, that she should be willing to admit her years, gracefully submit, and take a back seat. This ugly rivalry was now apparent in almost everything they said, and gave every one at the table a feeling of tension, embarrassment and discomfort. Thus, Mrs. Joel, speaking to her step-daughter, and including the whole company, in a reference to Mrs. Pierce's strenuous pursuit of youth, her grim devotion to youth's figure and its vigorous gymnastics, now remarked in a tone of sugared venom, a malicious gaiety of fine surprise:

"But really, I do, I think it's the most astonishing thing to see a woman of your age take part in all these sports and games that only the *young* people of my generation played. ... After all, if you were twenty—the age of Joel or this young man—I could understand it better—but at *your* age, my dear,"—she drew a fine breath of astonishment, "—really, I marvel that you don't collapse."

"Do you?" said Mrs. Pierce, smiling her glacial and inflexible smile, and in a tone of cold, impassive irony— "I confess, Mother, I see nothing at all to marvel at. ... Please set your mind at rest—I assure you I'm not in the slightest danger of collapse. ... I can do everything," she went on grandly, "that I could do at twenty—and I can do it better now, with less fatigue and greater skill. ... I can hold my own with any of these young people around here, no matter what it is—whether swimming, golfing, playing tennis, or going for a walk. So you can save your sympathy, Mother," she concluded with a laugh which seemed casual and friendly enough, but which showed plainly the hard inflexibility of her antagonism, "—when I need your condolences I'll let you know."

"But, my *dear,*" said Mrs. Joel with sweet gushing malice—"I think it's ma-a-rvellous! I only wonder how you do it at your age! . . . Why, no girl of my time and generation would have *thought* of doing all the things you do every day without turning a hair— Why!" she breathed, looking around her with an air of fine amazement, "I hear Ida plays *five* sets before breakfast every morning and thinks nothing of it—but in *my* day and time, if a girl—a *young* girl, mind you—played a *single* set—she'd be positively exhausted—done up for a week."

"Perhaps, Mother," Mrs. Pierce coolly suggested, "that is why the young girls of your time were such a soft and grubby lot—and why they turned out to be such dowdy frumps later on."

Mrs. Joel's dimpled smile did not lose a single atom of its saccharine benevolence, nor did her voice alter by a shade its honied drip, but for a moment something bright and adderous passed across her eyes, and she gave her step-daughter a swift and poisonous glance that would have done credit to a snake. "—And then, of course," she went on sweetly, taking the young men at the table into her confidence with her dimpled smile—"we had such old-fashioned notions in those days, too—you boys, I know, would be amused if you could know what some of our quaint notions were—but—hah! hah! hah!"—she laughed a gay and silvery little laugh of envenomed hatred, "—my dear," she said to Joel, "—you'll have to laugh when I tell you—but do you know it was actually considered *immodest—unwomanly*—for a young girl of my time to take part in sports—*compete* in sports—against men—and as for a woman of Ida's age doing it—why, it was *unthinkable! unheard* of!—a middle-aged woman," she pronounced the words with obvious relish and for a moment there was a swift hard flexion of the muscles in Mrs. Pierce's jaw—"but a middle-aged woman in *my* day who had attempted such a thing would have been *ostracized*—an *outcast*—decent people would have had nothing to do with her!"

"Yes, I know, Mother," Mrs. Pierce said with a swift and glacial urbanity. "We've all heard about that—I think it's generally conceded now by most intelligent people that women of that generation were a pretty worthless, dull and barbarous lot."

"Ah-hah-hah!" Mrs. Joel laughed sweetly, and dimpled at her best—
"*terribly* old-fashioned, of course—but," she turned graciously to her
grandson's young guest and lavished on him her most dimpled smile,—
"*frightfully* amusing, don't you think?"

He reddened like a beet, looked helplessly at the two contesting
women, craned his neck nervously along the edges of his collar, and
finally said nothing.

Joel relieved the painful situation with his swift whispering grace of
tact and kindliness. "But really, Granny," he whispered courteously and
eagerly, "—Mums is awfully good at it, she really is. . . . She can beat
me two sets out of three in tennis, and give me ten strokes in golf—and
when it comes to *swimming*——"

"Oh," said little Howard Martin in his mincing, languishing, and
effeminate tone—"she's ma-a-rvellous! . . . Ida," he gushed, in a kind of
over-ripe ecstasy—"your diving is simply divine! . . . If you could only
show me—oh-h," he said, with gushing effeminacy—"if you could only
teach *me* how you do it—but it's *simply* perfect—*marvellous*——"

The meal now proceeded more smoothly. Mr. Joel seemed to take
small notice of the feud between the two women—his daughter and his
wife—he talked to Joel, Rosalind, and to the other young men in his
grand growling way, expressed his opinion on the candidacies of Davis
and Coolidge, and said he would vote for Davis.

"If John Davis gets in," said Mrs. Pierce with that positive worldly
assurance that characterized her opinions, "Charles Dana Gibson will
get the ambassadorship to England—oh, but *that's* settled!" she said
positively, "I happen to know that Dana Gibson can have the ambassadorship any time he wants it——"

"Providing Davis gets elected," Joel whispered, laughing. Turning to
his grandfather, he whispered respectfully, "What do you think, Grandfather? Do you think that Davis will get in?"

"No, sir," Mr. Joel growled, "I do not. I think his chances of getting
elected are *very* slight—unless some sudden upheaval turns the tide in
his direction before election day."

"And who will you vote for, sir?" Joel whispered.

"I shall vote for Davis, sir," growled Mr. Joel. "I have known him for
many years, he is a very able lawyer, a very *able* man—but, sir," his old
growling voice sank to a whisper, and he peered out fiercely from under
his grizzled eyebrows at his grandson—"his chances of election are **very**

slight indeed. I should not be surprised to see Coolidge win by a land-slide."

"Did you hear what Alice Longworth said about him?" said Mrs. Pierce laughing, "—that he looked as if he had been weaned upon a pickle."

Every one laughed, even Mr. Joel joining with a kind of growling chuckle. As for Joel, he bent double, radiantly, gleefully convulsed with soundless laughter, snapping his fingers softly as he did so. His own humorous invention was not fertile, but his love of a good story—particularly when his mother or one of his friends told it, or quoted one of their own group—was enthusiastic. Now for a moment he bent double with this convulsed, whispering laughter: when he recovered somewhat he said softly and slowly:

"*Simply* swell . . . Gosh!" he whispered admiringly. "What a wit she's got! It's a swell story," he whispered.

"By the way, Ida," Mr. Joel growled, tugging at his short and griz-zled mustache, "how is Frank? Have you been over to see them, lately?"

"Yes, Father," she answered, "we drove over last Tuesday and spent the evening with them. . . . He looks very well," she added, in answer to his question, "but, of *course*," she said decisively, "he's *never* going to be any better—they all say as much——"

"Hm," old Mr. Joel growled, tugged reflectively at his short and grizzled mustache for a moment longer, and then said: "Has he been taking any part in the campaign this summer?"

"Very little," she answered—"of course, the man has gone through hell these last few years—he's suffered agonies! He seems a little better now, but," her voice rose again on its tone of booming finality as she shook her head—"he'll never get back the use of his legs again—the man is a *permanent* cripple," she said positively—"there's no getting around it—and he himself is reconciled to it."

"Hm," growled old Mr. Joel again, as he tugged at his short mus-tache—"Pity! Nice fellow, Frank! Always liked him! . . . A little on the flashy order, maybe—like all his family . . . too easy-going, too agree-able . . . but great ability! . . . Pity!"

"Yes, isn't it!" Joel whispered with soft eager sympathy. "And, Grandfather," he went on with an eager enthusiasm, "—his charm is *simply* stupendous! . . . I've never known anything like it! . . . The mo-ment that he speaks to you he makes you his friend forever—and he *knows* so much—he has such interesting things to say—really, the amount he knows is *simply* stupendous!"

"Hm, yes," old Mr. Joel agreed with a consenting growl, as he tugged thoughtfully at his grizzled gray mustache, "—but a little superficial, too. . . . The whole lot is like that . . . go hell-for-leather at everything for three weeks at a time—and then forget it. . . . Still," he muttered, ". . . an able fellow—very able. . . . Pity this thing had to happen to him just at the start of his career."

"Still, Father," Mrs. Pierce put in, "—don't you think he'd gone about as far as he was going when this thing hit him? . . . I mean, of course, he *is* a charming person—every one agrees on that. I never knew a man with more native charm than Frank— But for all his charm, don't you think there's something rather weak in his character? . . . Do you think he would have had the stamina and determination to go much further if this disease hadn't forced him to retire?"

"Um," Mr. Joel growled, as he tugged thoughtfully at his short cropped mustache. ". . . Hard to say. . . . Hard to tell what would have happened to him. . . . A little soft, perhaps, but great ability . . . great charm . . . and great opportunists, every one of them. . . . Have instinctive genius for seizing on the moment when it comes. . . . Never know what's going to happen to a man like that——"

"Well," said Mrs. Pierce, politely, but with an accent of conviction— "he might have kept on going—but I think he was through—that he'd gone as far as he could—I don't think he could have stood the gaff—I don't believe he had it in him."

"Um," Mr. Joel growled, "perhaps you're right. . . . But great pity just the same. . . . Always liked Frank. . . . Very able fellow——"

The conversation proceeded in these channels for some time, the guests discussing politics, ambassadorships, using the names of the great and celebrated people of the earth with the casual and familiar intimacy of people talking about life-long friends whom they had last seen at dinner Tuesday evening. It was the "inside" of the great world of wealth and fame and fashion—the world that the youth had read and heard about all his life—but that he had thought about, had visioned, as Olympus, mantled in celestial clouds, and forever remote from the intruding gaze of common men. Now, to hear these great names, these celestial personages, bandied about on the tip of the tongue just as familiarly as one spoke of one's own friends—to hear these people speak of the habits, the health, the conversation, and the personal home-life of this august parliament in just the same way that people spoke of their friends, acquaintances and familiars the whole world over, gave the youth a sense of living in a dream, of hearing incredible things—things incredible because of their very casual familiarity—of being the witness of an incredible event.

In this way, the meal drew to its close: Mrs. Pierce and her step-mother managed to avoid further friction, although once it threatened, when Mrs. Pierce, observing the retreating figure of one of the maid-servants—a robust and plain-featured country woman of middle age—noticed from the cropped and unnaturally white texture of her neck and skull that her hair had been cut, "bobbed" in the fashion that was to grow so popular and that was just then coming into style, and turned and questioned her step-mother about it:

"What has happened to that woman's hair, Mother?" she said. "What did she do to it?"

"Why," cried Mrs. Joel eagerly, beginning to beam and dimple around at her guests with an air of delighted satisfaction—"I had it cut off."

"*You* had it cut off?" cried Mrs. Pierce in an astounded tone.

"Why, yes, my dear," chirped Mrs. Joel eagerly, "I sent all the girls into the village one morning last week and had the barber cut their hair."

"*What!*" Mrs. Pierce boomed out in an astounded tone, and then sank back against her chair, and for a moment returned her son's stare incredulously, "you mean you herded all these girls together and *whacked* their hair off at one stroke?"

"Why, of course, my dear," said Mrs. Joel eagerly, in a rather excited and disturbed tone, "—or rather, I told them that they'd have to do it—that that was what I wanted."

"What *you* wanted?" Mrs. Pierce boomed out in the same astounded and incredulous tone.

"Why, yes"—Mrs. Joel rushed on eagerly, excitedly, taking the whole table in now with a look of beaming explanation. "—You see, I had the whole house done over this spring—redecorated—I told the decorator the *effect* I wanted," she said gushingly—"I told him everything must be done for—for—*lightness!*" she said triumphantly, "—*coolness!* . . . to do everything in light cool colors . . . get *that* effect. . . . So last week," she went on happily, "when we had that spell of *frightful* hot weather, I noticed suddenly how—how *hot*—and disagreeable all the girls looked with their long hair—how—how *out of place*," she said triumphantly, "they looked in this new scheme of things. . . . Ugh," she shuddered with a little gesture of discomfort and distaste, "—the very *sight* of them made me uncomfortable—I couldn't *bear* them! So all of a sudden it occurred to me how nice it would be—how much it would improve the —the—the general *atmosphere* of the whole house if I made them bob their hair. . . . So," she concluded, beaming around at every one with dimpled satisfaction—"that's how I came to do it—I called them all together one morning last week—Friday I think it was—and told them what I wanted—and then sent them all into the village to get it done."

There was a moment's pause while Mrs. Joel beamed at her guests with a dimpled smile of triumphant finality that seemed to say—"There! Behold my work and marvel at it! That is the way the thing was done." Her obvious satisfaction was suddenly disturbed, however, by Mrs. Pierce, who, after staring at her in astounded silence for a moment, boomed out incredulously:

"*Mother!* You *know* you didn't do a thing like *that!*"

"But—but, of course I did it, Ida," Mrs. Joel returned in a surprised and nettled tone of voice— "That's what I'm telling you. . . . What's the matter with it? . . . Don't you think the girls look nice?"

"I—think," said Mrs. Pierce slowly, after a moment's stunned reflection—"I—think—that—is—the—most—preposterous—the—most—high-handed—the—most—*God!*" she cried, and throwing her head back she fairly made the room ring with her hearty, booming, and astonished laughter: "I've heard of Catherine the Great and Marie Antoinette and the days of the Medicis—and the things they did—but I never thought I'd live to see the day their methods were adopted here in free America —Why! hah! hah! hah! hah! hah!" she fell back in her chair and fairly rocked with booming and incredulous laughter—"*whacking* the hair off those eight girls at one fell stroke because—because—" her voice choked speechlessly—"because it made you *hot* to look at them . . . because —because," her voice rose to a rich choked scream and presently she said in an almost inaudible squeak—"because she's had the house— *redecorated,*" she panted— "Why, *Mother!*" she cried strongly at last, her shoulders shaking, and her face still red with laughter, "—the King of Siam is not in it compared to you—you make absolute tyranny look like free democracy—hah! hah! hah! hah! hah!—Strike off their heads!" cried Mrs. Pierce, "—the very *sight* of them makes me perspire!" And leaning back again she surrendered herself to free, ringing, and whole-hearted laughter, in which every one save Mrs. Joel joined. When the laughter had somewhat subsided, Mrs. Joel, her plump white cheeks red with open anger, cried out in a furious voice:

"I don't agree with you! . . . I don't agree with you at all. . . . And I must say it seems very stupid of you, Ida, to take such a childish point of view."

"Childish!" Mrs. Pierce cried in a challenging tone, "you're the one who's childish! . . . If I did a thing like that to *my* girls—if I for one moment thought I had a right to take such liberties as that with other people, I'd feel like a fool! . . . Why, Mother," she cried in a strong protesting tone, "wake up! . . . What kind of a world do you live in, anyway? . . . What ever gave you the notion that you have a right to do things like that to other people—and all because you're fortunate enough to be able to keep servants and pay them wages. . . . Wake up! Wake up!" she cried in a tone of almost furious indignation, "—You're not living in the dark ages, Mother. . . . Slavery has been abolished! . . This is the twentieth century! . . . Why, it's absurd!" she cried scornfully, and with two spots of angry color in her cheeks—"the most arrogant and high-handed thing I ever heard in all my life— The whole thing's preposterous—I only hope that no one hears about it."

"If you feel that way about it," Mrs. Joel began in a voice choked with fury, and at this moment Joel came to the rescue, and saved what really threatened to develop into an ugly, open, painful quarrel between the two women——

"Oh, but Granny," he whispered—"I'm sure the girls don't mind a bit! . . . And they look *much* nicer—and *much* cooler—without their hair than when they had it—I'm sure they feel that way about it, too."

"Well," Mrs. Joel began, still very angry but somewhat placated by her grandson's tactful intervention—"I'm glad to see that some one still has a little common sense."

And in this way the trouble was finally smoothed out by Joel's quick diplomacy, and the guests, eager to avert another painful scene between the two women, rose to go. And it was in this way that they departed, not without a final explosion of booming and astounded laughter from Mrs. Pierce as she walked out towards her car, a final hilarious reference to "redecoration," *and* the King of Siam, and the modern prototype of Catherine the Great.

LXIV

JOEL and his friend did not return immediately to the house with
Joel's mother, and her other guests. Instead, leaving old Mr. Joel's house,
they turned left, and struck out for a walk through the fields and slopes
and wooded country of the great estate. The day was hot, the broad
fields brooded in the powerful and fragrant-clovered scent of afternoon, the woods were dense with tangled mystery, immensely still and
green, yet dark incredibly, and filled with drowsy silence, brooding
calm, ringing with the lovely music of unnumbered birds, alive with
the swift and sudden bullet-thrum of wings, and haunted with the cool
and magical incantation of their hidden waters.

It was the wild, sweet, casual, savage, and incredibly lovely earth of
America, and of the wilderness, and it haunted them like legends, and
pierced them like a sword, and filled them with a wild and swelling
prescience of joy that was like sorrow and delight.

They toiled upward through the tangled forest-jungle of a wooded
slope, and down again into the cool green-gladed secrecies of a hollow,
and up through the wild still music of the woods again and out into the
great rude swell of unmown fields, alive with all their brooding potency,
their powerful and silent energy of the hot and fragrant earth of three
o'clock, the drowsy and tremulous ululation of afternoon.

Their feet trod pathways in the hot and fragrant grasses, where they
trod, a million little singing things leaped up to life, and hot dry stalks
brushed crudely at their knees: the earth beneath their feet gave back a
firm and unsmooth evenness, a lumpy resiliency.

Once in a field before them they saw a tree dense-leaved and burnished
by hot light: the sun shone on its leaves with a naked and un-green
opacity, and Joel, looking towards it, whispered thoughtfully:

". . . Hm . . . It's nice, that—I mean the way the light falls on it— It
would be hard to paint: I'd like to come out here and try it."

And the other assented, not, however, without a certain nameless
desolation in his heart that broad and naked lights, the white and glacial
opacity of brutal day aroused in him,—and wanting more the wooded
grove, the green-gold magic of a wooded grass, the woodland dark and
thrum and tingled mystery, and the sheer sheeting silence of the hidden
water.

It was a swelling, casual, nobly lavish earth, forever haunted by a
drowsy spell of time, and the unfathomed mystery of an elfin enchant-

ment, the huge dream-sorcery of the mysterious and immortal river.

It was what he had always known it to be in his visions as a child, and he came to it with a sense of wonder and of glorious discovery, but without surprise, as one who for the first time comes into his father's country, finding it the same as he had always known it would be, and knowing always that it would be there.

And finally the whole design of that earth, with the casual and powerful surveys of its great fields, its dense still woods of moveless silence ringing with the music of the birds, its far-off hills receding into time as haunting as a dream, and the central sorcery of its shining river —that enchanted thread which ran through all, from which all swept away, and towards which all inclined—was unutterably the language of all he had ever thought or felt or known of America: the great plantation of the earth abundant to the sustenance of mighty men, and enriching all its glamorous women with the full provender of its huge compacted sweetness, an America that was so casual and rich and limitless and free, and so haunted by dark time and magic, so aching in its joy with all the bitter briefness of our days, so young, so old, so everlasting, and so triumphantly the place of man's good earth, his ripe fulfillment and of the most fortunate, good, and happy life that any man alive had ever known.

It changed, it passed, it swept around him in all its limitless surge and sweep and fold and passionate variety, and it was more strange in all its haunting loveliness than magic or a dream, and yet more near than morning, and more actual than noon.

It was a hot day: the two young men walked along with their coats flung back across their shoulders: towards five o'clock as they were coming home again, and coming down into the wooded hollow where Mr. Joel lived, Joel turned, and with a slight flush of embarrassment on his gaunt face, said:

"Look—do you mind wearing your coat when we go by Grandfather's house—you can take it off again when we get out of sight."

He said nothing, but silently did as his friend requested, and thus correctly garmented they passed the old man's great white house and crossed the little wooden bridge and stared up again out of the hollow, taking a foot-path through the woods that would lead them out into the road near Miss Telfair's house: she had invited them to tea.

And curiously, inexplicably, of all that they had said and talked about together on that walk, these two things were later all he could remember:—his friend's eyes narrowed with professional appraisal as he looked at the hot opacity of the sun-burnished tree and said, "—hm ... It's nice, that—the light is interesting—I'd like to do it;" and the embarrassed but almost stubbornly definite way in which Joel had asked him to put on his coat as he went past "Grandfather's place." He did not know why, but that simple request aroused in him a feeling of quick and hot resentment, a desire to say,

"Good God! What kind of idol-worship is this, anyway? Surely that old man has been made of the same earth as all the rest of us—surely he's not so grand and rare and fine that he can't stand the sight of two young men in shirt-sleeves going by his house! ... Surely there is something false, inhuman, barren in this kind of reverence—no real respect, no decent human admiration, but something cruel, empty, worthless and untrue, and against the real warmth and worth and friendliness of man!"

For a moment hot resentful words rose to his lips: that act of empty reverence seemed to him, somehow, to be arrogant and disdainful of humanity; he felt a sudden blind resentment, a choking anger against old Mr. Joel and his grand manners and his growling and magnificent old age: he wanted to bring back again the conversation he had overheard at lunch, to ask Joel bitterly who the hell he thought this old man was that he could grandly dispose of man according to his judgment as "low cads," as "gentlemen"—to inquire savagely who the hell this damned contriving, cunning old custodian of the treasures of the rich thought he was that he could arrogate unto himself the power to pronounce banishment on his betters—to call Rousseau a rascal, and De Musset and Lord Byron "a couple of low cads."

And childish, foolish as this anger was in all its blind unreason, he was to remember these two trifling episodes in later years with a feeling of regret and nameless loss. These two acts on Joel's part—the one an act of barren interest—a joyless empty interest in the blind opacity of light—and the other an act of barren joyless reverence to old age and an inhuman state—seemed to mark for him the beginning of his gradual separation from his friend, a dumb, inexplicable and sorrowful acceptation of their fatal severance. It seemed to him that here began that slow, and somehow desperately painful recognition that the enchanted world of wealth and love and beauty, of living fulfillment and of fruitful power, which he had visioned as a child in all his dreams about the fabled rich along the Hudson River—did not exist; and that he must look for that grand life in ways stranger, darker, and more painful in their labyrinthine complications than any he had ever dreamed of as a child; and that, like Moses, he must strike water from the common stone of life, and like Samson, take honey from the savage lion's maw of the great world, find all the joy of living that he lusted for in the blind swarm, the brutal stupefaction of the streets; goodness and truth in the mean hearts of common men; and beauty in the only place where it can ever be found—inextricably meshed, inwrought, and interwoven in that great web of horror, pain and sweat and bitter anguish, that great woven fabric of blind cruelty, hatred, filth and lust and tyranny and injustice, of joy, of faith, of love, of courage and devotion—that makes up life, and that resumes the world.

It was a desolating loss, a hideous acknowledgment, a cruel discovery —to know that all the haunted glory of this enchanted world, which he thought he had discovered the night before, had been just what it now seemed to him to be—moon-magic—and to know that it was gone from him forever. It was a bitter pill to know that what had seemed so grand, so strong, so right, and so inevitable at the moment of discovery was now lost to him—that some blind chemistry of man's common earth, and of his father's clay, and of genial nature, had taken from him what he seemed to possess, and that he could never make this enchanted life his own again, or ever again believe in its reality. It was a desperate and soul-sickening discovery to know that not alone through moonlight, magic, and the radiant images of their heart's desire could men find America, but that somewhere there, and far darklier and strangelier than the river, lay the thing they sought, in all the blind and brutal complications of its destiny—buried there in the grimy and illimitable jungles of its savage cities—a-prowl and raging in the desert and half-mad with hunger in the barren land, befouled and smutted with the rust and grime of its vast works and factories, warped and scarred and twisted, stunned, bewildered by the huge multitude of all its errors and blind gropings, yet still fierce with life, still savage with its hunger, still broken, slain and devoured by its terrific earth, its savage wilderness—and still, somehow, God knows how, the thing of which he was a part, that beat in every atom of his blood and brain and life, and was indestructible and everlasting, and that was America!

Miss Telfair's house, which they now entered, was just the sort of house that one would expect a woman like Miss Telfair to live in. Everywhere one looked, one saw the image of the woman's personality—and that personality was fragile, exquisite, elegant, and elaborately minute In spite of its graceful, plain proportions, that house was not wholly a comfortable place to be in. It was filled with ten thousand little things —ten thousand little, fragile, costly, lovely and completely useless little things, and their profusion was so great, their arrangement so exquisitely right, their proximity so immediate and overwhelming that one instantly felt cramped, uneasy, and uncomfortable, fearfully apprehensive lest a sudden free and spacious movement should send a thousand rare and terribly costly little things crashing into shattered bits, the treasure of a lifetime irretrievably lost, and one's own life and work and future irretrievably mortgaged, blighted, wrecked, in one shattering instant of blind ruin. In short, in Miss Telfair's lovely, exquisite and toy-becluttered house, one felt very much like a delicate, sensitive, intelligent and highly organized bull in a horribly expensive china-shop, and this feeling was cruelly enhanced if one was twenty-three years old and six and a half feet tall, and large of hand and foot, and long of arm and leg in just proportion, and painfully embarrassed, and given to sudden and convulsive movements, and keyed and strung on the same wires as a racehorse.

It was an astonishing place, about as exquisitely feminine a place as one could imagine. One had only to take a look around to feel that no man had ever lived here, that the only man who ever came here had come as a visitor; and somehow one felt at once he knew the reason why Miss Telfair had not married—she simply did not want to have "a man about the place," a disgusting, clumsy brute of a man who would go plunging around like a wild bull, sending her vases crashing to the floor, upsetting her fragile little tables and all the precious little bric-a-brac that crowded them, sprawling out upon the voluptuously soft but elegantly arrayed cushions of the sofa, reaching for matches on the mantel and sweeping it clear of a half dozen dainty eighteenth-century clocks and plates and china shepherds with one swingeing blow, barging into dainty little stools of painted china and sending it a-teeter while Miss Telfair watched and prayed and waited with a smile of frozen apprehension, raising hell with the Wedgewood plates, the vases of Dresden and of Delft, and making the buried kings of the old Ming dynasty turn over in their graves with groans of anguish every time some brute of a bull of a man came lumbering near the dearest and most priceless treasures of their epoch.

Miss Telfair, herself the most dainty, fragile, and exquisitely inviolable ornament of the collection, was waiting for them at the centre of this fabulous clutter. She gave each of the young men a quick cool clasp of her small, frail, nail-bevarnished hand, a few crisp words of greeting, and a quick light smile, as brittle, frail, and painted as a bit of china—a smile curiously like that of Mrs. Pierce in its glacial rigidity but, like everything else about the woman, more fragile, delicate, and shell-like.

Then she turned and led the way through the house out into the sun-porch. The two young men picked their way carefully between the frail and crowded complications of a thousand costly relics and around great bowls and vases filled with flowers—great bouquets of roses, lilies and carnations, which were everywhere—and which filled the air with the clinging, dense, and overpowering sweetness of their perfumes.

The sun-parlor was a great, light place, alive and golden with bright sunlight—a magnificent room with comfortably padded wicker chairs and tables and settees, but here, as elsewhere in the house, the fabulous complication of small useless ornaments was overwhelming, and one walked with care. This room also was filled with great bowls of roses, lilies and carnations, the air was dense and heavy with their scent, and through the windows of the place one could see the smooth velvet of the lawns, trimly patterned with designs of flowers aflame with all their glorious polychrome of color, and at the end the flower-garden, which was alive with many rich and costly blooms growing in geometric designs. It was just the kind of flower-garden, just the kind of flowers, that a woman like Miss Telfair would have: their orderly, exotic and unnatural profusion suggested the cultivation of a hot-house; even the wild and lyric growth of sweet unordered nature had been made to conform to the elegant and fragile pattern of Miss Telfair's life.

She led the way to a wicker table where there were easy chairs and a comfortable settee and great flaming fragrant lights of flowers. They seated themselves and tea was brought in by a maid-servant. The service of the tea was fragile, costly, elegant, like everything else about the woman; but it was also wonderful, rich, and generous in its abundance, and this was probably like her, too. There were delicate little pastries, cubes, and crusts of things that were so flaky, rich and succulent that they melted away in the mouth; and there were little cubes and squares of sandwiches, as well, all dainty, elegant, and small, but wonderfully good. She asked them if they wanted hot-tea or iced-tea or some whiskey: the day was hot and Joel took iced-tea, refusing whiskey; the other youth took iced-tea too—she poured it for them in marvellous tall frail glasses filled with slivers of bright ice, and put in mint and lemon, doing all things deftly, beautifully, with her small, swift, china-lovely hands, and then turning to Joel's guest, with her light cool smile, her crisp incisive inquiry, in which there was somehow something good and generous, she said:

"And won't you have some whiskey, too?" and as he hesitated, and looked dubious yet consenting, added: "In your iced-tea—if you like it that way?"

He looked at her, perplexed, and said uncertainly:

"I—don't know... Does it go that way?"

Miss Telfair bent back her head—her cheeks had the delicate color of rose-tinted china, and she was pretty in the rose-tinted-china way—and laughed a thin, metallic, and yet musical and friendly laugh:

"Oh, yes!" she cried briskly and gaily, "it goes that way! . . . It goes very well that way." More seriously, she added: "Yes, it's really very good that way"—and crisply, yet encouragingly, with her fire-bright china-smile—"why don't you try it?"

He looked at Joel dubiously, not certain what to do, and not wishing to embarrass his friend, and Joel looked back, with his radiant eager smile, shaking his head in droll refusal, whispering:

"Not for me. But go on if you like. Do as you like——"

"Well, then—" he said consentingly—and Miss Telfair, smiling lightly, took a bottle of Scotch liquor off the tray, uncorked it, and poured a drink into the tea—a good stiff shot it was, too—and when he had finished the drink, she poured him out another, adding another liberal potation of the Scotch.

Thus animated and released, he felt more at ease: they talked together quickly and easily, he had a good time. She was a bright, quick, cool, inquiring kind of woman, at once detached yet friendly, coolly amused yet curious: she asked him about his work at the university, the kind of classes that he taught and the kind of people that attended them, the kind of life he had in the city, and about the play that he was writing. The detached coolness of her curiosity was much like that of Mrs. Pierce, and suggested the curiosity of a woman of a separate and privileged world hearing about the creatures who lived in the great nameless world of dust and noise and strife and swelter "down below"—and yet it was also a more friendly and eager curiosity than Mrs. Pierce had shown: it had a certain warmth of human interest in it, too.

She was obviously very fond of Joel: her relation to him was that of an old-maid friend of the family, who is so intimate and close to all the family's history that she is practically a part of it herself, and who feels for the children and all their lives and actions as much affection and interest as she could feel for her own blood. Now she turned to Joel, and began to talk to him about some decorative screens which he was painting for her: as one might expect, she knew all about decorative screens and their respective merits; she spoke of them with the exact authority, the assured conviction of the expert, she spoke her mind about them crisply, plainly, incisively, and Joel listened to her eagerly, his gaunt face lifted, turned towards her in an attitude of rapt attention and respect, while she was talking.

"The central one is excellent, Joel—really first rate, the best one you've ever done—and *decidedly* the best of the lot. The one on the right is also good—not as good as the first, it swings off-balance in the foreground. I'll show you what I mean tomorrow—but it is good, and will do."

"What about the other one—the one on the left?" he whispered eagerly. "What did you think of that?"

"I think it's very, very bad," she said coolly and incisively. "I think you've fallen down on it, and that you're going to have to do the whole thing over."

For a moment his gaunt face winced, but not with pain and disappointment, rather with swift, concerned interest, eager attentiveness: he hitched his long thin figure forward unconsciously, his large well-boned hands splayed out upon his knees, and he whispered eagerly:

"But why, Madge? . . . Tell me. Where do you think I've fallen down?"

"Well," said Miss Telfair, "in the first place, Joel, you've lost out on your design— It falls all to pieces now, you've let the whole thing get away from you: you were trying to follow it out from the one in the middle and bring it to an end, but you didn't know how to finish it— and so you put in that pavilion or summer house or whatever it is— because you didn't know what else to do."

"Don't you like that?" he whispered, smiling.

"I think it's perfectly god-awful," she answered quietly, "utterly mean-

ingless—simply terrible! It has no relation to anything else in the whole
design—it stands out like a sore thumb—and the color is atrocious
. . . No, Joel, the whole thing is out of key, it upsets the whole design,
it has no place there."

"And what about the background?" he whispered. "What did you
think of that?"

"I think that's bad, too," she replied without a moment's hesitation.
"You've used *far, far* too much gold—almost twice as much as you did
in the other two—the proportion is very bad."

"Hm," he muttered, stroking his chin thoughtfully. "Yes," he whispered, "I see what you mean. . . . I hadn't thought about the pavilion
being out of key—perhaps you're right. . . . But," he whispered, smiling his radiantly gentle and good-natured smile, "I *don't* agree with you
about the background, Madge. . . . I think you're wrong: I'd like to
argue with you about that."

"All right," she answered crisply and good-naturedly. "I'll come over
tomorrow and we'll have it out. . . . But," she shook her head, and
spoke with a crisp but obstinate conviction, "Joel, I *know* I'm right!
. . . That whole screen is out of proportion. It *won't* do. . . . You'll
have to do the whole thing over again."

They debated in this fashion of art-talk for some time, and presently
the young men rose to go. As they departed, Miss Telfair returned to
her former tone of crisp and casual friendliness, saying:

"What is Ida doing tonight? Is she going to the Pastons' for the fireworks?"

"Yes," Joel whispered. "We're all going; can't you come along?"

"No, thank you," she said, smiling. "Not this time. They're very
lovely—and very awe-inspiring—and all that—but about once every five
years is my limit. I would *not* get into that mob tonight, as hot as it is,
for a million dollars. . . . Tell Ida I expect her here for lunch tomorrow: Irene will be here. . . . And now, goodbye," she said, turning to
the other young man, and giving him a bright china smile, a swift cool
pressure of her little china hand. . . . "Come up again to see us, won't
you? . . . And bring your play along. And try going to bed some
night at ten o'clock. . . . Really!" she said with a crisp cool irony,
"—you miss very little by doing so."

As they walked away along the road towards Joel's house, Joel whispered with his radiant and admiring astonishment:

"She's *simply* incredible! . . . Don't you *think* so? . . . She *knows* everything," he went on, without defining more exactly that large specification. "It's simply *stupendous* the things she knows! . . . And she's *such* a nice person," he said quietly. "One of the *nicest* people that I ever knew—just what an old maid ought to be—don't you think so?"

"Yes. But why is she an old maid? Why did she never get married?"

"Hm," said Joel thoughtfully, looking down the road with a detached, abstracted stare. "I can't say. . . . She's *awfully* rich," he whispered. "*Enormously* rich—she has loads of money—she's been able to do *just* as she pleased all her life—she's *been* everywhere—all over the world— and I suppose that's the reason that she never married. She never found any one that she liked well enough to give up the kind of life she had. . . . But she's an amazing person. . . . Don't you think so?"

"Yes," the other said.

They walked on down the road, and presently they saw the great white shape of Joel's house, framed in the trees before them, and below them in the light and distance of a westering sun, the shine and wink of the great river. They entered the house.

LXV

THE Paston estate, like the Pierce estate, was situated upon the river, but several miles farther north. To reach it, they drove through the eastern entrance of the Pierce place and through the little Dutch Colonial village of Leydensberg, of which Joel's father was the mayor and which the Pierce family largely owned.

"It's a pity Pups never went into politics," Joel whispered, as they drove through the old leafy village, with its pleasant houses among which a few of the lonely white houses of the Colonial period still remained. "The people around here worship him: he could have anything he wanted if he ran for office."

It was the first time he had spoken of his father: with a feeling of sharp surprise, the other youth now remembered that he had not seen Mr. Pierce since his arrival: he wondered where he was, but did not ask. He also now remembered that Joel's references to his father had often been marked by a note of resignation and regret—the tone a person uses when he speaks of some one who has possessed talents and wasted opportunities, and whose life has come to nothing.

Their road led northward from the village: they sped swiftly along a paved highway bordered by trees and fields and woods, by houses here and there, and presently by the solid masonry of a wall that marked the boundaries of another great estate. It was the Paston place, and presently they turned in to an entrance flanked by stone markers, and began to drive along a road arched by tall leafy trees. Night had come, the moon was not yet well up, but from time to time, there was beside the road the gleam of steel, and at times as they passed a cleared space he could plainly see the rail pattern of a tiny railway, complete in all respects—with roadbed, rock-ballast, grades, and cuts, embankments, even tunnels, but all so small in scale that it suggested a gigantic toy more than anything else. He asked what it was and Joel answered:

"It's Hunter's railway."

"*Hunter's* railway?" he asked in a puzzled tone. "But why does he need a railway here? What does he use it for?"

"Oh, he really doesn't need it for anything," Joel whispered. "It's of no use to any one. He just likes to play with it."

"Play with it? But—but what is it? . . . Isn't it a real railway?"

"Yes, of course," Joel answered, laughing at his astonishment. "It's really quite marvellous—complete in every way—with tunnels, stations, bridges, signals, round-houses, and everything else a regular railway has. Only everything is on a very small scale—like a toy."

"But the engine—the locomotive? . . . How does that run? Do you wind it up, as you do a toy, or run it by electricity, or how?"

"Oh, no," Joel answered. "It's a regular locomotive—not over two or three feet high, I should say—but runs by steam, just like a real locomotive. . . . It's really quite a fascinating thing," he whispered. "You ought to see it some time."

"But—but how does he run it? Is he able to get into anything as small as that?"

"He can, yes," said Joel, laughing again. "But usually he just runs along by the side. It's pretty cramped quarters for a grown man."

"A grown *man!* . . . Do you mean that Mr. Paston built this little railway for himself?"

"But, of *course!*" Joel turned, and looked at his friend with a surprised stare. "Who did you think I was talking about?"

"Why, I—I thought when you said—'Hunter' you meant one of his children—a boy—some child in his family who——"

"No, not at all," Joel whispered, laughing again at the astonished and bewildered look upon his companion's face. "It may be for a child, but the child is Hunter Paston himself. . . . You see," he said more quietly and seriously after a brief pause, "he's crazy about all kinds of machinery—locomotives, airplanes, motor-boats, automobiles, steam-yachts—he loves anything that has an engine in it—he always has been that way since he was a boy—and it's such a pity, too," he whispered, in the same regretful tone he had used when speaking of his father— "It's a shame he was never able to do anything with it. . . . If he hadn't had all this money, he would have made a *swell* mechanic —he really would."

But now there was a row of lights through the trees, the murmurous hum of many voices, the glittering shapes of parked machinery. They were approaching the Paston house: it was a rather gloomy-looking mansion of old brown stone, square in shape and immensely solid and imposing in its grimy magnificence, and of that style of architecture which was borrowed from France, but which went through curious and indefinable transformations on the way, so that any native grace and lightness which the style may once have had was lost: it was lumpish, ugly and involved, and somehow looked like one of the children of the New York Post Office.

A broad verandah ran around the house on all four sides, and on the side that faced the river, a large number of the friends and guests of the Paston family were now assembled. Seated on the great lawns that swept away before the house on the river side there was another larger audience composed of the people of the near-by town, and people employed on the Paston estate and the other great estates in the vicinity.

But over both groups, not only the wealthier and smaller group upon the porch, but the larger one spread out upon the lawn, there was evident a spirit of gay, happy, eager and child-like elation and expectancy that united every one in a curiously moving and high-hearted way. From the dark sweep and mystery of the lawn there rose the murmur of hundreds of excited and happy voices, all talking at once, and little bursts of laughter, sudden stirs and flurries of eager and mysterious interest.

The same spirit, the same feeling—a spirit and a feeling of plain democracy, warm friendliness, simple, eager hope and expectancy—animated the people on the porch. They were, as a group, fine-looking people: many of the young men were tall, handsome, strong and comely-looking, the girls were lovely, and many of the women were beautiful. Most of them also had a look of dignity, assurance, and character. They represented, he knew, that small group of the fabulously

wealthy whose names were household words throughout the nation—
and yet, whether it was due to the innate democracy of the occasion,
the almost childish pleasure and anticipation which the Fourth of
July and its fireworks renewed in them, and the grand and natural
warmth and spaciousness of the scene—their native earth, or whether
the quality of their lives was really warm and free and friendly, there
was nothing at all arrogant, haughty, cold or insolently "societified"
about these people. Their gathering together here upon the front porch
of this gloomy old Victorian house had exactly the same quality that
these summer front-porch gatherings had always had for him everywhere in little towns; with a feeling of incredulous recognition he found
that the scene was instantly familiar to him, and he almost expected
to hear old familiar voices—his father's voice among them, as he
had heard it on the porch at home so many times, and now so long
ago.

Every one in the crowd knew the Pierce family and instantly welcomed them in an eager, laughing, and excited babel of affectionate
greeting. Rosalind and Joel and Mrs. Pierce went about among the
crowd shaking hands and greeting people all about them, and when the
greetings were over, simply and naturally found their place among
those persons to whom each was most akin by virtue of friendship,
age, or temperament—Mrs. Pierce among men and women of her own
generation and among the older people, and Joel, Rosalind, George
Thornton, and Carl Seaholm among the younger people of the gathering.

Joel introduced him quickly, casually, with his infinite grace and consideration, to several people—to several of his younger friends and
to certain of the older ones who were obviously among the best-liked
and most respected people there. He was introduced to Mrs. Paston, a
tall and beautiful young woman, very slender, blonde, and lovely-look-
ing: a kind of exquisite blonde icicle, and with no more human
warmth or passion than an icicle of any sort would have. She gave him
a few cool words of greeting, a swift cool clasp of her swift cool hand,
a swift, glacial, yet not unfriendly smile, and so dismissed him, not
unkindly, turning with the same cool, smiling and glacial detachment
to her other guests.

Suddenly the fireworks started. Far away, at the end of the great
lawn, in the obscuring darkness of the night, and among the obscuring
shadows of the shrubs and trees above the hill that swept down towards

the river, there was a terrific detonation—the deafening bang and flare of a gigantic rocket that whizzed up into the air in a small hurtling point of light, and exploded, illuminating heaven with a constellation of enchanted falling stars. There was a long-drawn "Oh-h!" of excitement, eagerness, and expectant joy from the crowd gathered on the lawn, the same from the people gathered on the porch, who quickly scrambled into chairs; and instantly from all the people there was utter silence, a thrilled and fascinated attentiveness, broken now and then by gasps of wonder, joy, surprise and rapture, as one giant rocket followed another in unending series, in constantly growing magnificence, until the whole universe of night was blooming with flowers of fire, alive with constellations of enchanted stars—green, red, and yellow, blue and violet and gold, that burst softly in the night with spreading glory, falling slowly to the earth like some great parachuted blossom, and cracking, puffing, bursting softly, to flower, spread, again develop in great blooms of star-enchanted fire.

Everything had the same familiar quality of America that he had always remembered, and known as a child. It brought back to him again the quiet voices of people on their summer porches, the street-car grinding to a halt on the corner of the hill above his father's house, his father's voice in darkness on the porch, and the red lifted flare of his cigar, and those Thursday nights in summer when his father took him on the street-car to the little park along the river three miles away, where there were outdoor moving-pictures on an island; later, fireworks and across the river the great flare, the receding thunder of a train. Now, curiously, that whole memory came back to him with all its vivid and unutterable poignancy: he could remember the little artificial lake there at the park—that lake just three feet deep that had seemed so vast and thrilling to him, and the boat-house with lake-water lapping at the piers, the clank of oarlocks and the dull bump and dry knocking of the boats together as they collided in the darkness, and the people, gathered there in darkness, with their dim faces upturned to the great silver dance and flicker of the moving-picture screen which was set on a little island on the lake—an island that was dense with trees and foliage, and that had seemed to him as mysterious and illimitable as the jungle. And opposite the island, on the shore, looking over the heads of the people in the boats, the greater part of the audience sat on wooden benches, all thirsty, silent, and insatiate, the petals of five hundred dim white faces all lifted to the flickering magic of the screen.

It all came back to him now as he sat there on the porch of this splendid mansion with Mrs. Pierce and Joel and the other guests, and though the place was splendid, wealthy and luxurious beyond dreams, the happy, warm, and friendly gaiety of the people, their eager looking-forward to fireworks and the Fourth of July, something free and warm and simple in their relation, recalled again those glorious expeditions of his youth to the little park upon the river, and the crowded street-cars going home, and friendly voices, laughter, and the slamming of a door, and then his father's voice upon the porch and sleep and silence —it all came back now in tones of unutterable brightness, and the Hudson River lay below him in the great fall and hush of evening light that fell across America, and even as he thought these things, a train rushed by below them on the bank of the river, was hurled instantly past in a projectile flight—a thunderbolted speed, was hurled past them citywards, and was gone at once, leaving nothing behind it but the sound of its departure, a handful of lost echoes in the hills, and the river, the mysterious river, the Hudson River in the great fall and hush of evening light, and all somehow was just as it had always been, and just as he had known he would find it, as it would always be.

LXVI

LATER that night, when the other people in the house had gone up-stairs to bed, and as he was in the quiet library, making a final, longing, hungrily regretful survey of the treasure-hoard of noble books that walled the great room in their rich and mellow hues from floor to ceiling, Joel came in.

"Look," he whispered, in his abrupt and casual way, "I'm going to bed now: stay up as long as you please and sleep as late as you like to-morrow morning. . . . And look," he whispered casually—and quickly again—"what are you going to do? Do you think you have to go back to the city tomorrow?"

"Yes, Joel: I think I'll have to—I have an early class the first thing Monday morning, and if I'm going to meet it, I ought to be back by tomorrow night: I think that will be best."

"It's been nice having you," Joel whispered. "It was swell that you could come. And if you really like the place," he said simply, "I'm glad. . . . I think it's a grand place, too. . . . And Look!" he whispered

quickly, casually, looking away "—I meant what I said yesterday—about
that house, the gatekeeper's lodge, I mean— If you like the place, and
think you'd care to live there, or come up whenever you feel like
it, I wish you'd take it," he whispered. "I really do— It's no use to
any one the way it stands, and we'd all be delighted if you'd come and
live in it. . . . Just let me know when you are coming, just say the
word, and I'll have everything ready for you— And we *wish* you would,"
he whispered earnestly, with his radiant smile, as if asking the other
youth to do him a favor—"it would be swell."

"It's—it's pretty fine of you, Joel, too——"

"All right, sir," Joel whispered quickly, hastily, with a smile, avoiding
skilfully the embarrassment of thanks: "And look, Eugene—of course
I'll see you Tuesday when I get back to town—I'll be right there at the
hotel the rest of the summer—except for week-ends when I come up
here—but I wanted to ask you if you had made up your mind yet about
going to Europe?"

"Yes, I have, Joel. At least, that's what I want to do—what I'd like
to do. If I can manage it, I intend to set sail—" the two words had a
glorious magic sound to him, and his pulse beat hot and hard with joy
and hope as he spoke them—"to set sail in September when my work
at the university is over!"

"Gosh! That's swell!" Joel whispered enthusiastically, his face lighting with radiant eagerness as if the news had given him some great and
unexpected happiness— "And Frank Starwick will be glad to hear it,
too. You know he's going over at the end of August; I had a letter from
him just the other day."

"Yes, I know: he wrote me too."

"And he'll want to see you when he comes to town: we must all
try to get together before he goes. . . . And look," he said quickly,
abruptly, casually again—"if you go, how long will you be gone? How
long do you intend to stay away?"

"I don't know, Joel. I'd like to go for a whole year, but I don't know
if I can manage it. They've offered me an appointment for another year
at the university. They want me to come back for the new term that
begins in February, and maybe that's what I'll have to do. But I'd like
to stay away a year!"

"I hope you can," Joel whispered. "You ought to spend a whole
year over there! It would be a swell thing if you could."

"Yes; I think so, too. But I don't know how I'm going to manage it:

at the present time I don't quite see how I can. . . . You see, all I've got to live on at the present time is what I earn as an instructor at the university—they pay me eighteen hundred dollars a year——"

"Gosh!" Joel whispered, arching his eyebrows in polite astonishment—"That's a lot, isn't it?"

"It's not much, Joel: it amounts to $150 a month, you can get along on that but you're not going to paint New York red on it, the way things are to-day, especially if you've got a healthy appetite and love to eat, the way I do."

"Yes," Joel whispered, laughing his beautiful, radiant, and almost soundless laugh. "I can see that—that belly of yours is going to cost you a lot of money before you get through with it. A man who loves food the way you do ought to be a millionaire. But you see, don't you," he said, with a flash of his rare and gentle malice—"that's what you get for not being a vegetarian like Bernard Shaw and me. . . . Eugene," he cried softly, laughing, after a moment's brief reflection, "—you'll love France—the food is wonderful—but Lord!" and he laughed again his radiant soundless laugh "—how you're going to hate England!"

"Why? Is the food bad?"

"It's unspeakable!" Joel whispered—"that is for any one who loves food the way you do: they go through the tortures of the damned . . . of course, for me it doesn't matter. I can eat anything—anything, that is, so long as it's vegetables—it all tastes alike to me—but *you'll* hate it . . . of course," he whispered earnestly, "you really won't: you'll love the country and you'll like the English. They're swell."

"Have you been there much, Joel?"

"Only once," he whispered. "When Mums and Rosalind were there. We had a house out in the country and we stayed there for fifteen months. And it was grand! You'll love it. . . . Gosh! I hope you can stay over there a whole year!" he went on eagerly. "Don't you think you can?"

"I don't think so: you see, as I was telling you, I have only $150 a month; when I finish up in September I'll have about five pay-checks coming to me: that's only $750. So I figure I can get over there on that and live for several months, but unless I can get money from my mother —I think perhaps she'll help me—I don't see how I can get along for a whole year."

"Then look," said Joel, speaking swiftly, and casually, and looking

away as if he were making the most matter-of-fact proposal in the world
—"Why don't you let me help you? . . . I mean," he went on hastily,
and showing his embarrassment only by two spots of color in his
gaunt face— "I'd love to do it if you'd let me—it'd be no trouble at all—
and you could pay it back whenever you like—just as soon as your play
goes on: you'll have plenty of money then, so I wish you'd take it now
when you need it. . . . You see," he whispered quickly, with a smile,
"I have loads of money—more than I can ever *possibly* use—I have no
need for it—I was twenty-one this spring, you know,—and now I'm
awfully rich," he whispered humorously, and then concluded in a
quickly apologetic whisper—"not *really,* of course—not compared to
most people—but rich, for *me,*" he whispered, smiling. "—I've got *much*
more than I need—so I really wish you'd let me help you if you need
it—Frank said he'd let me know if he needed anything and I wish you'd
do the same. . . . I think you ought to go for a whole year since you're
going—it's your first trip and *gosh!*" he whispered enthusiastically, "how
I envy you! How I wish *I* were going for the first time! It's going to be
a swell thing for you, you're going to have a grand time—and you've
simply *got* to stay for a whole year—so I wish you'd let me help you if
I can."

He had made this astoundingly generous proposal with a quick, hurried matter-of-factness that seemed to be eagerly begging for a favor,
instead of magnificently and nobly giving it. And for a moment, the
other could not answer, and when he did he did not know the reason for
his reply, for his refusal. It was as generous, as selfless, and spontaneous
an act of liberal and noble friendship as he had ever known or experienced, and for a moment, as he thought of his longed-for trip, his dire
need of money, it all seemed so magically easy, good, and wonderfully
right to him that there seemed nothing to do except instantly, gratefully and jubilantly to accept. Yet, when he opened his mouth to
speak, he found himself to his surprise refusing this miraculous and generous good-fortune. And he never knew exactly the reason why: there
was, perhaps, the growing sense of something alien and irreconcilable
in the design and purpose of their separate lives, a growing feeling of
regret, a conviction enhanced by his conversation with Joel in the studio
that morning that their lives would be lived out in separate worlds,
wrought to separate purposes, and shaped by separate beliefs, and with
that knowledge a feeling—a feeling of loneliness and finality and fare-

well—as if a great door had swung forever closed between them, as if there was something secret, buried, and essential, in the soul of each, which now could never be revealed. And, to his surprise, he heard himself saying:

"Thanks, Joel—it's mighty fine of you—about as fine as anything I ever heard—but I don't need help now. If I need it later——"

"If you do," said Joel very quickly, "I wish you'd let me know— I'd like it if you would. . . . And gosh! it's great to know that you are going," he whispered again with radiant enthusiasm. "I envy you!"

"Then I wish to God you'd come along! . . . Joel," the other burst out excitedly, with a sudden surge of eager warm conviction. "Why can't you? We'd have a great time of it—go everywhere—see everything! It would be a wonderful thing—a great experience—for you and me both. You've never seen Europe that way before, have you?—the way that you and I could see it?—-you've always been with your family, your mother, haven't you?— Come on!" he cried, seizing his friend by the arm, as if they were ready to go that instant. "Let's go! We'll have the grandest trip you ever heard about!"

But Joel, laughing his radiant soundless laugh, and shaking his head with gentle but inflexible denial, said:

"No, Eugene! . . . Not for me! . . . I can't do it! I'm going to stay right here and keep on with the work I'm doing . . . besides," he added gravely, "Mums needs me. No one knows what's going to happen here in the family," he said quietly— "I mean—that thing tonight—you saw —about Mums and Pups"—he said with painful difficulty. The other nodded, and Joel concluded simply: "I've got to stay." For a moment he was silent, and suddenly the other youth noticed something starved and lonely, and almost desperately forsaken and resigned, that he had never observed in the boy's gaunt face and eyes before, and when Joel spoke again, although there was a faint smile on his face, there was something old and sad and weary in his voice that the other youth had never heard before. He said quietly:

"Perhaps you're right. . . . Perhaps you and I do belong in different worlds . . . must go different ways. . . . If that is true," Joel turned and looked directly at his friend and in his eyes there was an infinite quiet depth of regret and acceptance "—if that is true, I'm sorry. . . . At any rate, it was good to have known you. . . . And now, good-bye, Eugene—Good-night, I mean," he hastily concluded, in his former whispered, quick and casual tones, "I'll see you in the morning."

With these words he turned quickly and left him.

He stayed there long into the night in that rich room, while the great house sank to sleep and silence all around him. And at first he moved there quietly like a man living in an enchanted dream, almost afraid to draw a breath lest he dispel the glory and the magic of enchantment, and all the time the voices of the living books around him seemed to speak to him, to say to him: "Now it is night and silence and the sleep-time of the earth, the all-exultant time of youth and loneliness, and of your spirit's proud accession. Now take us, plunder us and take us, for you are alone and living in the world to-night while all the sleepers sleep, immortal knowledge will be yours to-night, the secrets of an everlasting and triumphal wisdom; the huge compacted treasure of the earth speaks to you from these storied shelves, and it is yours, you are the richest man in all the earth if you will take us, only take us, we have waited for you long, dear friend, tonight the world is yours, and will be yours for-ever, if you will only take us, take us, take us."

And like a man drunk with joy, half through the night he plun-dered the living treasure of those shelves. They were all there—the great chroniclers and recorders, the marvellous and enchanted lies of old Herodotus, and Sir Thomas Malory, and the voyages of Hakluyt and of Purchas, the histories of Mandeville and Hume. There was Bur-ton's marvellous *Anatomy,* his staggering erudition never smelling of the dust or of the lamp, his lusty, pungent ever-rushing-onward style, and the annihilating irony of Gibbon's latinized sonority, and the sav-age, burning, somehow magic plainness of Swift's style. There was the dark tremendous music of Sir Thomas Browne, and Hooker's sounding and tremendous passion made great by genius and made true by faith, and there was the giant dance, the vast storm-rounding cadence, now demented and now strong as light, of great Carlyle; and beside the haunting cadences of this tremendous piece, there was the pungent worldliness of life-loving men; the keen diaries of John Evelyn, the lusty tang and calculation and sensual rumination of old Pepys, the writ-ing bright as noon, natural as morning, and the plain and middle-magic of the eighteenth century, the flawless grace and faultless clearness of Addison and Steele, and then all the pageantry of living character, the pages crowded with the immortal flesh of Sterne, Defoe, and Smollett, the huge comic universe of Fielding, the little one of Austen, and the immortal and extravagant one of Charles Dickens, the magnificent proliferation of Sir Walter Scott's tremendous gallery—and Thackeray's sentimental gallantry and magic, and all the single magics of Nathaniel Hawthorne, of Meredith, and Melville, of Landor, Peacock, Lamb, and of De Quincey, of Hazlitt, and of Poe.

There were as well, the works of all the poets, the Kelmscott Chaucers, the Dove editions, the doe-skin bindings, white and soft and velvet to the touch, the splendid bodies in all their royal pageantry of blue and gold and dense rich green—the Greek anthologies, and all the poets of antiquity, and the singing voices of the great Elizabethans—of Wyatt, Surrey, Sidney, and of Spenser, Webster, Ford and Massinger, of Kyd and Greene and Marlowe, of Beaumont, Lyly, Nash and Dekker, of Jonson, Shakespeare, Herrick, Herbert, Donne.

They were all there, from thundering Æschylus to the sweet small voice of perfect singing Herrick, from grand plain Homer to poignant Catullus, from acid and tart-humored Horace, from the lusty, vulgar and sweet-singing voice of Geoffrey Chaucer, the great bronze ring and clangorous sonority of John Dryden, to the massy gold, the choked-in richness, the haunting fall and faery, of John Keats.

They were all there—each stored there in his little niche upon the living shelves, and at first he looted them, he plundered through their golden leaves as a man who first discovers a buried and inestimable treasure, and at first is dumb with joy at his discovery, and can only plunge his hands in it with drunken joy, scoop handfuls up and pour it over him and let the massy gold leak out again in golden ruin through his spread hands; or as a man who discovers some enchanted spring of ageless youth, of ever-living immortality, and drinks of it, and can never drink enough, and drinks and feels with every drink the huge summation of earth's glory in his own enrichment, the ageless fires of its magic youth.

Then, as the night wore on, another feeling crept across his heart, the living voices of the books spoke to him with another tone. From those great tongues of life and power and soaring immortality there had now departed all the sonorous conviction of their overwhelming, all-triumphant chant. The grand and ringing tongue and joy now spoke the language of a quiet and illimitable despair, confided the legend of an inevitable defeat, an inexorable fatality.

From those high storied shelves of dense rich bindings the great voices of eternity, the tongues of mighty poets dead and gone, now seemed to speak to him out of the living and animate silence of the room. But in that living silence, in the vast and quiet spirit of sleep which filled the great house, out of the grand and overwhelming stillness of that proud power of wealth and the impregnable security of its position, even the voices of those mighty poets dead and gone now seemed somehow lonely, small, lost, and pitiful. Each in his little niche of shelf securely stored—all of the genius, richness, and whole compacted treasure of a poet's life within a foot of space, within the limits of six small dense richly-garnished volumes—all of the great poets of the earth were there, unread, unopened, and forgotten, and were somehow, terribly, the mute small symbols of a rich man's power, of the power of wealth to own everything, to take everything, to triumph over every-. thing—even over the power and genius of the mightiest poet—to keep him there upon his little foot of shelf, unopened and forgotten, but possessed.

Thus, for the first time in his life, even the voices of the mighty poets seemed lost and small and pitifully defeated. Their great voices, which had given to the heart of youth the added fire of their triumphant magic, had borne his spirit high upon the wings of the soaring and invincible belief that no might on earth was equal to the might of poetry, no immortality could equal the immortality of a poet's life and fame, no glory touch his glory, or no strength his strength—now seemed to speak to him the mute and small and lonely judgment of defeat:

"Child, child," they said to him, "look at us and reflect: what shall it profit you to feed upon the roots of all-engulfing night, desiring glory? Do not the rats of death and age and dark oblivion feed so forever at the roots of sleep, and can you tell us where a man lies buried now, whose substance they have not devoured? Oh, child, forever in the dark old house of life to go alone, to prowl the barren avenues of night, and listen while doors swing and creak in the old house of life, and ponder on the lids of night, and ruminate the vast heart of sleep and silence and the dark, and so consume yourself—desiring what? Poor child, you son of an unlettered race, you nameless atom of the nameless wilderness, how have you let us dupe you with our fictive glories? What power is there on earth, in sea or heaven, what power have you in yourself, you son of your unuttered fathers, to find a tongue for your unuttered brothers, and to make a frame, a shape, a magic and eternal form out of the jungle of the great unuttered wilderness from which you came, of which you are a nameless and unuttered atom? What can you hope to do, poor nameless child, and would-be chronicler of the huge unhistoried morass of the dark wilderness of America, when we, who were the children of a hundred gold-recorded centuries and the heirs of all the rich accumulations of tradition, have really done so little—and have come to this? What profit do you hope to gain—what reward could you achieve that would repay you for all the anguish, hunger, and the desperate effort of your life? At its rare infrequent best, out of your blind and famished gropings in the jungle depths, you may pluck out a shining word—achieve a moment's flash of grace and intuition—a half-heard whisper of the vast unuttered language that you seek—perhaps a moment's taste of fame, a brief hour's flash of the imagined glory that you thirst for. For just a moment, you, like other men, will play the lion, will feed upon the older lion's blood, will triumph for a moment through his defeat, will taste joy for a moment through the blood of his despair—and then, like him, you too will be thrown to the mercy of the coming lion, the wilderness will rise again to engulf you, your little hour of glory for which your soul thirsts and your life is panting will be over before it has well begun, and the myriad horde of all your thousand mongrel races will rise with snarl and jeer and curse and lie and mocking to do your life to death, with all the hatred of their mongrel rancor and their own self-loathing, to kill the lion they have crowned for just a day, to hurl you back into a nameless and dishonor- able oblivion, drowned down beneath the huge mock and jibe of the old scornmaker's pride. Therefore, short-lived, your life will soon be ended; your youth, but just begun, will shortly be consumed, and all the labor of your anguish and your hunger will be mocked to scorn by the same mongrel fools who praised it, and forgotten by the very knaves who gave it fame. Such is the infrequent good, the flash of brief fame, to which you may aspire, the huge oblivion of failure, misery and dishonor which will follow. But if, by miraculous good chance, you should escape from this—be not devoured and slain and drowned out and forgotten in the brutal swarming shades of jungle time—what greater glory is there that you can achieve? Some such as ours, per- haps—then look at us, and see the state to which we've come. To lie forgotten on the rich shelves of a rich man's library—to be a portion of his idle wealth—the evidence of his arrogant possession—to rise, as all the earth must rise—these dreaming hills and haunted woods, the mighty river and this great moon-haunted hill where stands this house— shout the tributes of a rich man's glory—to bow before him—to lie bought, owned, forgotten and possessed—the greatest poets that ever walked the earth or built, like you, great dreams of glory—to be obsequious tributes to a rich man's fame. Yes, you, even you—poor naked child —may come to this—to reach this state, to be entombed here, bought and idle and among the forgotten huge encumbrance of a rich man's arrogant possession—and to know at last that all the glory, genius, and magic of a poet's life may lie condensed in six rich bindings, forgotten, purchased and unread—and finally defeated by the only thing in life that lasts and will triumph forever—the all-consuming tyranny of wealth that makes a slave of its great poets—that makes us the barren whores of fame, the pimps of wealth—unused and empty on a rich man's shelf."

So did that great treasure of unread, purchased, and forgotten books speak to him in the silent watches of the night, as they stood there, lonely, small and bought, on a rich man's shelf.

Towards morning, as he sat there with a great book propped upon his knees, his mind filled with the thought of those dead, forgotten, and still-living voices and of his rich young friend and the strange and bitter enigma of the fatal severance which had seemed that day to close a great door between their lives forever, he turned the pages of the book idly, and suddenly the blurred characters on the page before him swam legibly to view. And what those words upon the page before him said was this:

"The young man saith unto him, All these things have I kept from my youth up: what lack I yet?

"Jesus said unto him, If thou wilt be perfect, go and sell that thou hast, and give to the poor, and thou shalt have treasure in heaven: and come and follow me.

"But when the young man heard that saying, he went away sorrowful: for he had great possessions."

LXVII

As he and Joel drove to the station it seemed to Eugene that he was returning to a world from which he had been absent for years. And the return was not a pleasant one. As they entered the little town, and began to drive swiftly down a street that led to the station, the little frame houses with their new architectures—their faded little strips of "front yard" grass, cement walks, and cement yard walls, looked cheap, flimsy, new and dreary—the image of a life that was itself as rootless, insecure, and drearily pretentious as the little painted frames it lived in.

It was Sunday, and as they drove up to the station, he saw before a Greek confectionery and newspaper store a group of the town sports. They were dressed up in their cheap Sunday finery, and their faces wore a smirk. As Joel got out of the car, the sports tried to look nonchalant and easy in their relations with one another, but a kind of uneasy constraint had fallen upon them, and held them until he had gone. And yet he had not noticed them or done anything that might have caused them this discomfort.

In the gravelled parking space before the station several cars were drawn up. Their shining bodies glittered in the hot sunlight like great beetles of machinery, and in the look of these great beetles, powerful and luxurious as most of them were, there was a stamped-out quality, a kind of metallic and inhuman repetition that filled his spirit, he could not say why, with a vague sense of weariness and desolation. The feeling returned to him—the feeling that had come to him so often in recent years with a troubling and haunting insistence—that "something" had come into life, "something new" which he could not define, but something that was disturbing and sinister, and which was somehow represented by the powerful, weary, and inhuman precision of these great, glittering, stamped-out beetles of machinery. And consonant to this feeling was another concerning people themselves: it seemed to him that they, too, had changed, that "something new" had come into their faces, and although he could not define it, he felt with a powerful and unmistakable intuition that it was there—that "something" had come into life that had changed the lives and faces of the people, too. And the reason this discovery was so disturbing—almost terrifying, in fact—was first of all because it was at once evident and yet indefinable; and then because he knew it had happened within the years of his own life, few and brief as they were—had happened, indeed, within "the last few years," had happened all around him while he lived and breathed and worked among these very people to whom it had happened, and that he had not observed it at the "instant" when it came. For, with an intensely literal, an almost fanatically concrete quality of imagination, it seemed to him that there must have been an "instant" —a moment of crisis, a literal fragment of recorded time in which the transition of this change came. And it was just for this reason that he now felt a nameless and disturbing sense of desolation—almost of terror;

it seemed to him that this change in people's lives and faces had occurred right under his nose, while he was looking on, and that he had not seen it when it came, and that now it was here, the accumulation of his knowledge had burst suddenly in this moment of perception—he saw plainly that people had worn this look for several years, and that he did not know the manner of its coming.

They were, in short, the faces of people who had been hurled ten thousand times through the roaring darkness of a subway tunnel, who had breathed foul air, and been assailed by smashing roar and grinding vibrance, until their ears were deafened, their tongues rasped and their voices made metallic, their skins and nerve-ends thickened, calloused, mercifully deprived of aching life, moulded to a stunned consonance with the crashing uproar of the world in which they lived. These were the dead, the dull, lack-lustre eyes of men who had been hurled too far, too often, in the smashing projectiles of great trains, who, in their shining beetles of machinery, had hurtled down the harsh and brutal ribbons of their concrete roads at such a savage speed that now the earth was lost forever, and they never saw the earth again: whose weary, desperate ever-seeking eyes had sought so often, seeking *man,* amid the blind horror and proliferation, the everlasting shock and flock and flooding of the million-footed crowd, that all the life and lustre and fire of youth had gone from them; and seeking so forever in the man-swarm for man's face, now saw the blind blank wall of faces, and so would never see man's living, loving, radiant, and merciful face again.

Such were the faces that he now saw waiting on the station platform of this little Hudson River town—two dozen faces from the mongrel and anonymous compost of like faces that made up America—and with a sudden blinding flash of horror and of recognition, it now came to him that they were just the faces he had seen everywhere, at a thousand times and places in "the last few years."

He had seen them in their last and greatest colony—the huge encampment of the innumerable submerged, the last and largest colony of the great mongrel and anonymous compost that makes up America: he had seen them there, hurtling forever, from the roaring arch of the great bridge, with their unceasing flight, projectile roar, unnumbered flood, in their great and desolate beetles of glittering machinery—boring forever through the huge and labyrinthine horror of that trackless jungle of uncounted ways, beneath the grime and rust

and swarm and violence and horror of Fulton Street, past all the vast
convergences, the threat and menace of the empty naked corners, the
swarming and concentric chaos of Borough Hall, and with beetling and
unceasing flight through Clinton Street, on Henry Street, through the
Bedford section, out through the flat and limitless swelter known as
"the Flatbush section," beneath the broad and humid light of solid
skies, through ten thousand rusty, grimy, nameless streets that make
up that huge and trackless swelter—and most horrible of all, a
flood of nameless faces, rootless and unnumbered lives, hurtling
blindly past forever in hot beetles of machinery along those broad,
wide, and splendidly desolate "avenues," that were flanked upon each
side by the cheap raw brick, the gaudy splendor, of unnumbered new
apartment houses, the brick and stucco atrocities of unnumbered new
cheap houses, and that cut straight and brutal as a spoke across the
labyrinthine chaos of the Brooklyn jungle—and that led to God knows
where—to Coney Island, to the beaches, to the outer districts of that
trackless web, the unknown continent of Long Island—but that, no matter where or how they led, were always crowded, with the blind horror
of those unnumbered, hurtling faces, the blind horror of those great
glittering beetles of machinery drilling past forever in projectile flight,
unceasing movement and unending change, the blind horror of these
unknown nameless lives hurtling on forever, lost forever, going God
knows where!

Yes, this was the thing—blindly, desperately, unutterably though he
felt it—this was the thing that had put this look—the "new look"—
the horrible, indefinable, and abominably desolate and anonymous
look into the face of people. This was the thing that had taken all the
play and flash of passion, joy, and instant, lovely and mercurial life
out of their living faces, and that gave their faces the look of something blunted, deadened, stunned, and calloused.

This was the thing that had given people "the new look"—that
had made man what he had become—that had made all these people
waiting on the platform for the train, what they were—and now that
he had to face this thing again, now that he had to be thrust back in
it, now that, after these three days of magic, and enchantment, he must
leave this glorious world that he had just discovered—and be thrust
brutally back again into the blind and brutal stupefaction, the nameless agony and swelter of that life from which he came—it seemed to
him he could not face it, he could not go back to it again, it was too

hard, too full of pain and sweat and agony and terror, too ugly, cruel, futile, and horrible, to be endured.

No more! No more! And not be be endured! To discover for three days—three magic swift-winged days—that enchanted life that had held all his visions as a child in fee—to be for just three brief and magic days a lord of life, the valued friend, the respected and well-loved companion of great men and glorious women, to discover and possess for three haunting and intolerably lovely days the magic domain of his boyhood's "America"—the most fortunate, good and happy life that men had ever known—the most true and beautiful, the most *right*—and now to have it torn from him at the very instant of possession—and to come to this:—a nameless cipher hurtled citywards in the huge projectile of a train, with all his fellow ciphers, towards this blind and brutal stupe-faction. A voice sounded far off, thundering in his ears through the battle-roar and rock of that stunned universe, as he cried:

"Joel! Joel! It was good to be here with you—Joel——"

And suddenly saw his friend's tall form recoil, shrink back, the look of something instant, startled, closed and final in his face and eye, and heard the swift incisive whisper saying quickly——

"Yes! . . . It was good that you could come! . . . And now, good-bye! . . . I shall see you——"

And so heard no more, and knew that that good-bye was final and irrevocable and could not be altered, no matter now how much or how often they should "see" each other in the future.

And at the same moment, as that door swung shut between them, and he saw that it never could be opened any more, he felt, with the knowledge of that irrevocable loss, a moment's swift and rending pity for his friend. For he saw somehow that he was lost—that there was nothing for him now but shadows on the wall—Circean make-believe —that world of moonlight, magic and painted smoke that "the river people" knew. For three days, he himself had breathed the poppied fumes of all its glorious unreality, and in those three short days the world from which he came—his father's earth of blood and sweat and stinking clay and bitter agony—this world of violence and toil and strife and cruelty and terror, this swarming world of nameless lives and mongrel faces, with all its ugliness—had become phantasmal as an evil dream, until now he could scarcely endure the hot and savage swelter, the savage fury, of the unceasing city. To grope and sweat and thrust and curse his way again among the unceasing flood-tides of the grimy swarming pavements; to be buffeted, stunned, bewildered, deadened, and exhausted by the blind turmoil, the quenchless thirst and searching, the insatiate hunger and the black despair of all that bleak and fruitless struggle, that futile and unceasing strife—and to come to this! To come to this!

It was too hard, too painful, too much to be endured, he could not go!—and even as his life shrank back in all the shuddering revulsion and loathing of his desolate discovery—he heard the great train thunder on the rails—and he knew that he *must* go!

For a moment, as the train pulled out, he stood looking out the window, waved good-bye to Joel standing on the platform, and for a moment watched his tall retreating form. Then the train gained speed, was running swiftly now along the river's edge, swept round a bend, the station and the town were left behind him, and presently, just for a few brief moments as it swept along below the magic and familiar hill, he caught a vision of the great white house set proudly far away up on the hill and screened with noble trees. Then this was gone: he looked about him, up and down the grimy coach, which was dense with smoke and pungent with the smell of cheap cigars and strong tobacco.

They were all there, and instantly he knew that he had seen each one of them a million times, and had known all of them forever; the Greek from Cleveland with his cheap tan suit, his loud tan shoes, his striped tan socks, his cheap cardboard suitcase with its tan shirts and collars and its extra pair of pants, and with his hairy, seamed and pitted night-time face, his swarthy eyes, his lowering finger-breadth of forehead bent with painful patient furrowed rumination into the sensational mysteries of tabloid print. They were all there—two deaf-mutes talking on their fingers; a young Harlem negro and his saffron wench, togged to the nines in tan and lavender; two young Brooklyn Jews and their two girl friends grouped on turned seats; a little chorus girl from the burlesque, with dyed hair of straw-pale falseness, a false, meagre, empty, painted little whore's face, and a costume of ratty finery false as all the rest of her; a young Italian with grease-black hair sleeked back in faultless patent-leather pompadour, who talked to her, eyes leering and half-lidded, with thick pale lips fixed in a slow thick smile of sensual assurance, the jaws slow-working on a wad of gum; a man with the strong, common, gaunt-jawed and anonymous

visage of the working man, wearing neat, cheap, nameless clothing, and
with a brown paper parcel on the rack above him; and a young dark
Irishman, his tough face fierce with drink and truculence, his eyes
glittering with red points of fire, his tongue snarling curses, threats,
and invitations to the fight that rasped and cut with naked menace
through the smoke-blue air.

The young Jews slouched with laughter, filled the car with noisy
clamor, sparred glibly, swiftly, with quick, eager, and praise-asking
repartee, with knowing smirk, and cynic jest, with acrid cynic wit that
did not hit the mark. The little blondined whore listened to the hypnotic, slit-eyed, thick-lipped seductions of the young Italian with a
small coy-bawdy smirk upon her painted face: she did not know what
he meant, she had no idea what he was talking about, and with coy-
bawdy smirk she rose, edged past his slow withdrawn knees and
minced down the aisle towards the little cupboard at the end that
housed the women's toilet, while with lidded sly eyes, and thick, slow-
chewing and slow-smiling lips his calculating glance pursued her. The
lady entered, closed the door upon a stale reek, and was gone some time.
When she emerged, she arranged her clothing daintily, smoothed out her
rumpled dress across her hips and came mincing down the aisle again
with faint coy-bawdy smirk, and was greeted again by her gallant
suitor, who welcomed her in the same manner, with lidded eyes, thick,
pallid and slow-chewing lips, and slow withdrawn knees. The two
deaf-mutes surveyed the scene with loathing: one was large and heavy,
with the powerful shoulders of the cripple, a brutal face, a wide and
cruel mouth; the other small and dark and ferret-faced—but both surveyed the scene with loathing. They looked at each and all the passengers and they dismissed each in turn upon their fingers. As they did so,
their faces writhed in vicious snarls, in sneering smiles, in convulsions
of disgust and hatred; they looked upon the objects of their hate and
jerked cruel thumbs towards earth in gestures eloquent of annihilation
and destructive sudden-death, and they drew swift fingers meaningly
across their gullets with the deadly move of men who slit a throat—
and all was as he had known it would be.

The working man with the strong and common face, the cheap, neat
clothes, sat quietly, and looked quietly out the window, with seamed
face and quiet worn eyes, and the young Irishman sweltered in strong
drink and murder; the taste of blood was thick in him, his little eyes
glittered with red points of fire, and ever as the train rushed on, be

sowed that smoke-blue air with rasping curse, and snarling threat, with all the idiot stupefaction of a foul and idiot profanity, an obscene but limited complaint:—

"Yuh f—kin' Kikes! . . . Yuh f—kin' Jews! . . . I'll kick duh f—kin' s—t outa duh f—kin' lot of yuh, yuh f—kin' bastards, you. . . . Hey-y! You! . . . Yuh f—kin' dummies up deh talkin' on yer f—kin' fingers all duh time. . . . Hey-y! You! Inches! You f—kin' bastard, I don't give a s—t for duh whole f—kin' lot of yuh."

It was all as it had always been, as he had known it would be, as he never could have foreseen it: the young dark Irishman sowed the air with threats and foulness, he finished up his bottle, and the foulness and the old red light of murder grew. And the mongrel compost laughed and snickered as they always did, and at length grew silent when he lurched with drunken menace towards them, and the old conductor with the sour, seamed face then stopped the Irishman, and he cursed him.

And the slant light steepened in the skies, the old red light of waning day made magic fire upon the river, and the train made on forever its tremendous monotone that was like silence and forever—and now there was nothing but that tremendous monotone of time and silence and the river, the haunted river, the enchanted river that drank forever its great soundless tides from out the inland slowly, and that moved through all man's lives the magic thread of its huge haunting spell, and that linked his life to magic kingdoms and to lotus-land and to all the vision of the magic earth that he had dreamed of as a child, and that bore him on forever out of magic to all the grime and sweat and violence of the city, the unceasing city, the million-footed city, and into America.

The great river burned there in his vision in that light of fading day and it was hung there in that spell of silence and forever, and it was flowing on forever, and it was stranger than a legend, and as dark as time.

BOOK V

JASON'S VOYAGE

LXVIII

SMOKE-GOLD by day, the numb exultant secrecies of fog, a fog-numb air filled with the solemn joy of nameless and impending prophecy, an ancient yellow light, the old smoke-ochre of the morning, never coming to an open brightness—such was October in England that year. Sometimes by night in stormy skies there was the wild, the driven moon, sometimes the naked time-far loneliness, the most-oh-most familiar blazing of the stars that shine on men forever, their nameless, passionate dilemma of strong joy and empty desolation, hope and terror, home and hunger, the huge twin tyranny of their bitter governance—wandering forever and the earth again.

They are still-burning, homely particles of night, that light the huge tent of the dark with their remembered fire, recalling the familiar hill, the native earth from which we came, from which we could have laid our finger on them, and making the great earth and home seem near, most near, to wanderers; and filling them with naked desolations of doorless, houseless, timeless, and unmeasured vacancy.

And everywhere that year there was something secret, lonely, and immense that waited, that impended, that was still. Something that promised numbly, hugely, in the fog-numb air, and that never broke to any open sharpness, and that was almost keen and frosty October in remembered hills—oh, there was something there incredibly near and most familiar, only a word, a stride, a room, a door away—only a door away and never opened, only a door away and never found.

At night, in the lounging rooms of the old inn, crackling fires were blazing cheerfully, and people sat together drinking small cups of the black bitter liquid mud that they called coffee.

The people were mostly family groups who had come to visit their son or brother in the university. They were the most extraordinary, ugly, and distinguished-looking people Eugene had ever seen. There was the father, often the best looking of the lot: a man with a ruddy weathered face, a cropped white mustache, iron gray hair—an open, driving, bull-dog look of the country carried with tremendous style. The mother was very ugly with a long horse face and grimly weathered cheek flanks that seemed to have the tough consistency of well-tanned

601

leather. Her grim bared smile shone in her weathered face and was nailed forever round the gauntness of her grinning teeth. She had a neighing voice, a shapeless figure, distinguished by the bony and angular width of the hip structure, clothed with fantastic dowdiness—fantastic because the men were dressed so well, and because everything they wore, no matter how old and used it might be, seemed beautiful and right.

The daughter had the mother's look: a tall gawky girl with a bony, weathered face and a toothy mouth, she wore an ill-fitting evening or party dress of a light unpleasant blue, with a big meaningless rosette of ruffles at the waist. She had big feet, bony legs and arms, and she was wearing pumps of dreary gray and gray silk stockings.

The son was a little fellow with ruddy apple-cheeks, crisp, fair, curly hair, and baggy gray trousers; and there was another youth, one of his college friends, of the same cut and quality, who paid a dutiful but cold attention to the daughter, which she repaid in kind, and with which every one was completely satisfied.

They had to be seen to be believed, but even then, one could only say, like the man who saw the giraffe: "I don't believe it." The young men sat stiffly on the edges of their chairs, holding their little cups of coffee in their hands, bent forward in an attitude of cold but respectful attentiveness, and the conversation that went on among them was incredible. For their manner was impregnable, they were cold, remote, and formal almost to the point of military curtness, and yet Eugene felt among them constantly an utter familiarity of affection, a strange secret warmth, past words or spoken vows, that burned in them like glacial fire.

When you got ten or fifteen feet away from them, their language could not have been more indecipherable if they had spoken in Chinese; but it was fascinating just to listen to the sounds. For there would be long mounting horse-like neighs, and then there would be reedy flute-like notes, and incisive cold finalities and clipped ejaculations and sometimes a lovely and most musical speech. But the horse-like neighs and clipped ejaculations would predominate; and suddenly Eugene understood how strange these people seemed to other races, and why Frenchmen, Germans, and Italians would sometimes stare at them with gape-mouthed stupefaction when they heard them talking.

Once when he passed by them they had the family vicar or some clergyman of their acquaintance with them. He was a mountain of a man, and he too, was hardly credible: the huge creature was at least six and a half feet tall, and he must have weighed three hundred pounds. He had a flaming moon of face and jowl, at once most animal and delicate, and he peered out keenly with luminous smoke-gray eyes beneath a bushy hedge-growth of gray brows. He was dressed in the clerical garb and his bulging grossly sensual calves were encased in buttoned gaiters. As Eugene went by, he was leaning forward with his little cup of muddy coffee held delicately in the huge mutton of his hand, peering keenly out beneath his beetling bush of brow. And what he said was this:

"Did you ever read—that is, in recent yöhs—the concluding chaptahs in 'The Vicah of Wakefield'?" Carefully he set the little cup down in its saucer. "I was reading it just the other day. It's an extraordinary thing!" he said.

It is impossible to reproduce the sound of these simple words, or the effect they wrought upon Eugene's senses.

For first, the words "Did you ever" were delivered in a delicate rising-and-falling neigh, the word "read" really came out with a long reedy sound, the words "that is, in recent yöhs," in a parenthesis of sweetly gentle benevolence, the phrase "the concluding chaptahs in 'The Vicah of Wakefield,'" in full, deliberate, satisfied tones of titular respect, the phrase "I was reading it just the other day," thoughtfully, reedily, with a subdued, gentle, and mellow reminiscence, and the final decisive phrase, "It's an extraordinary thing," with passionate conviction and sincerity that passed at the end into such an unction of worshipful admiration that the words "extraordinary thing" were not spoken, but breathed out passionately, and had the sound " 'strawd'n'ry thing!"

"Ow!" the young man answered distantly, and in a rather surprised tone, with an air of coldly startled interest, "Now! I can't say that I have—not since my nursery days, at any rate!" He laughed metallically.

"You should read it again," the mountainous creature breathed unctuously. "A 'strawd'n'ry thing! A 'strawd'n'ry thing." Delicately he lifted the little cup of muddy black in his huge hand again and put it to his lips.

"But frightfully sentimental, down't you think?" the girl neighed sharply at this point. "I mean all the lovely-woman-stoops-to-folly sawt of thing, you now. After all, it is a bit thick to expect people to swallow that nowadays," she neighed, "particularly after all that's happened in the last twenty yöhs. I suppose it mattuhed in the eighteenth centureh but after all," she neighed with an impatient scorn, "who cares today? Who cares," she went on recklessly, "*what* lovely woman stoops to? I cawn't see that it makes the *slightest* difference. It's not as if it mattuhed any longah! No one cares!"

"Ow!" the young man said with his air of coldly startled interest. "Yes, I think I follow you, but I don't entirely agree. How can we be certain what *is* sentimental and what's not?"

"But it seems to me he misses the whole point!" the girl exclaimed with one full, mouth-like rush. "After all," she went on scornfully, "no one is interested in woman's folly any longah—the ruined-maiden broken-vows sawt of thing. If that was what she got she should have jolly well known what she wanted to begin with! *I'll* not waste any pity on her," she said grimly. "The greatest folly is not knowin' what you want to do! The whole point today is to live as cleveleh as possible! That's the only thing that mattahs! If you know what you want and go about it cleveleh, the rest of it will take care of itself."

"Um," the mother now remarked, her gaunt bare smile set grimly, formidably, on her weathered face. "That takes a bit of doin', *doesn't* it?" And as she spoke these quiet words her grim smile never faltered for an instant and there was a hard, an obdurate, an almost savage irony in her intonation, which left them all completely unperturbed.

"Oh, a *'strawd'n'ry* thing! A *'strawd'n'ry* thing!" the huge clerical creature whispered dreamily at this point, as if he had not heard them. And delicately he set his little cup back on the saucer.

Eugene's first impulse when he saw and heard them was to shout with an astounded laughter—and yet, somehow, one never laughed. They had a formidable and impregnable quality that silenced laughter: a quality that was so assured in its own sense of inevitable rightness that it saw no other way except its own, and was so invincibly sure in its own way that it was indifferent to all others. It could be taken among strange lands and alien faces, and to the farthest and most savage colonies on earth, and would never change or alter by a jot.

Yes, they had found a way, a door, a room to enter, and there were walls about them now, and the way was theirs. The mark of dark time and the architecture of unnumbered centuries of years were on them, and had made them what they were; and what they were, they were, and would not change.

Eugene did not know if their way was a good way, but he knew it was not his. Their door was one he could not enter. And suddenly the naked empty desolation filled his life again, and he was walking on beneath the timeless sky, and had no wall at which to hurl his strength, no door to enter by, and no purpose for the furious unemployment of his soul. And now the worm was eating at his heart again. He felt the slow interminable waste and wear of gray time all about him and his life was passing in the darkness, and all the time a voice kept saying: "Why? Why am I here now? And where shall I go?"

When Eugene got out into the High Street after dinner, the dark air would be thronging with the music of great bells, and there would be a smell of fog and smoke and old October in the air, the premonitory thrill and menace of some intolerable and nameless joy. Often at night, the visage of the sky would by some magic be released from the thick grayness that had covered it by day, and would shine forth barely, blazing with flashing and magnificent stars.

And, as the old bells thronged through the smoky air, the students would be passing along the street, singly or in groups of two or three, briskly, and with the eager haste that told of meetings to come, appointments to be kept, the expectation of some good fortune, happiness, or pleasure toward which they hurried on.

The soft glow of lights would shine from the ancient windows of the colleges, and one could hear the faint sounds of voices, laughter, sometimes music.

Then Eugene would go to different pubs and drink until the closing time. Sometimes the proctors would come into a pub where he was drinking, speak amicably to every one, and in a moment more go out again.

Somehow he always hoped that they would take him for a student. He could see them stepping up to him, as he stood there at the bar, saying courteously, yet gravely and sternly:

"Your name and college, sir?"

Then he could see the look of astonished disbelief on their grim red faces when he told them he was not a student, and at last, when he had convinced them, he could hear their crestfallen muttered-out apologies, and would graciously excuse them.

But the proctors never spoke to him, and the bar-man, seeing him look at them as they went out one night, misunderstood the look, and laughed with cheerful reassurance:

"You've nothing at all to worry about, sir. They won't bother you. It's only the gentlemen at the university they're after."

"How do they know I'm not there?"

"That I couldn't tell you, sir," he answered cheerfully, "but they 'ave a way of knowin'! Ah, yes!" he said with satisfaction, slapping a wet cloth down upon the bar. "They 'ave a way of knowin', right enough! They're a clever lot, those chaps. A very clever lot, sir, and they always 'ave a way of knowin' when you're not." And smiling cheerfully, he made a vigorous parting swipe across the wood, and put the cloth away below the counter.

Eugene's glass was almost empty and he looked at it, and wondered if he ought to have another. He thought they made them very small, and kept thinking of the governors of North and South Carolina. It was a fine, warm, open sort of pub, and there was a big fire-place just behind him, crackling smartly with a fire of blazing coals: he could feel the warmth upon his back. Outside, in the fog-numb air, people came by with lonely rapid footsteps and were lost in fog-numb air again.

At this moment the bar-maid, who had bronze-red hair and the shrewd, witty visage of a parrot, turned and called out in a cheerful, crisply peremptory tone: "Time, please, gentlemen. Closing time."

Eugene put the glass down empty on the bar again. He wondered what the way of knowing was.

It was October, about the middle of the month, at the opening of the Michaelmas term. Everywhere there was the exultant thrill and bustle of returning, of a new life, a new adventure beginning in an ancient and beautiful place that was itself enriched by the countless lives and adventures of hundreds of years which had come and gone. In the morning there was the smoky old-gold yellow of the sun, the numb excitement of the foggy air, a smell of good tobacco, beer, grilled kidneys, ham and sausages, and grilled tomatoes, a faint nostalgic smell of tea, and incredibly, somehow, in that foggy old-gold light, a smell of coffee—an intolerable, maddening, false, delusive smell, for when one went to find the coffee it would not be there: the coffee was black liquid mud, bitter, lifeless, and undrinkable.

Everything was very expensive and yet it made you feel rich yourself just to look at it. The little shops, the wine shops with their bay windows of small leaded glass, and the crusty opulence of the bottles of old port and sherry and the burgundies, the mellow homely warmth and quietness of the interior, the tailor shops, the tobacco shops with their selected grades of fine tobacco stored in ancient crocks, the little bell that tinkled thinly as you went in from the street, the decorous, courteous, yet suavely good-natured proprietor behind the counter, who had the ruddy cheeks, the flowing brown mustache and the wing-collar of the shopkeeper of solid substance, and who would hold the crock below your nose to let you smell the moist fragrance of a rare tobacco before you bought, and would offer you one of his best cigarettes before you left— all of this gave somehow to the simplest acts of life and business a ritualistic warmth and sanctity, and made you feel wealthy and secure.

And everywhere around Eugene in the morning there was the feeling of an imminent recovery, a recapture of a life that had always been his own. The buildings seemed to come from some essence of reality he had always known, but had never seen, and could scarcely believe in now, even when he put his hand upon the weathered surface of the stone.

And this look kept shining at him through the faces of the people. Sometimes it was in the faces of the college boys but more often he saw it in the people of the town. It was in the faces of tradesmen—people in butcher shops, wine shops, clothing stores—and sometimes it was in the faces of women, at once common, fine, familiar, curiously delicate and serene, going to the markets, in the foggy old-bronze light of morning, and of men who passed by wearing derby hats and with wing collars. It was in the faces of a man and his son, good-humored little red-faced bullocks, packed with life, who ran a pub in the Cowley Road near the house where, later, he went to live.

It was a look round, full, ruddy, and serene in its good-nature and had more openness and mellow humor in it than Eugene had found in the faces of the people in New England. It was more like the look of country people and small-town people in the South. Sometimes it had the open tranquil ruddiness, the bovine and self-satisfied good humor of his uncle, Crockett Pentland, and sometimes it was like Mr. Bailey, the policeman, whom the negro killed one winter's night, when snow was on the ground and all the bells began to ring. And then it was full and hearty like the face of Mr. Ernest Pegram, who was the City Plumber and lived next door to Eugene's father, or it was plump, common, kindly, invincibly provincial, ignorant and domestic, like the face of Mrs. Higginson, who lived across the street, and had herself been born in England, who had a family of eight children and three baking days a week, and was a praying, singing, and fanatic Baptist; yet on her common kindly face was the same animal, gentle, smoke-like delicacy of expression round the mouth that some of these men and women had.

It was a life that seemed so near to Eugene that he could lay his hand on it and make it his at any moment. He seemed to have returned to a room he had always known, and to have paused for a moment, without any doubt or perturbation of the soul, outside the door.

But he never found the door, or turned the knob, or stepped into the room. When he got there he couldn't find it. It was as near as his hand if he could only touch it, only as high as his heart and yet he could not reach it, only a hand's breadth off if he would span it, a word away if he would speak it. Only a stride, a move, a step away was all the peace, the certitude, the joy—and home forever—for which his life was panting, and he was drowning in the darkness.

He never found it. The old smoke-gold of morning would be full of hope and joy and imminent discovery but afternoon would come and the soft gray humid skies pressed down on him with their huge numb waste and weight and weariness of intolerable time, and the empty naked desolation filled his guts.

He would walk that legendary street past all those visible and enchanted substances of time, and see the students passing through the college gates, the unbelievable velvet green of college quads, and see the huge dark room of peace and joy that time had made, and he had no way of getting into it.

Each day he walked about the town and breathed the accursed languid softness of gray foreign air, that had no bite or sparkle in it, and went by all their fabulous age-encrusted walls of Gothic time, and wondered what in the name of God he had to do with all their walls or towers, or how he could feed his hunger on the portraits of the Spanish king, and why he was there, why he had come!

Sometimes it was just a word, the intonation of a phrase—the way they would say *"very"* or "American," which chilled and withered all the ardours of the heart, or the way they would say "Thank *you!*" when you paid for something, crisply, courteously, yet with a quick, cautious, and obdurate finality, as if some one had swiftly and firmly closed a door lest you should try to enter it. Eugene could listen to them talk and hear all the words, the moods and tones of life and humor that he had known all his life, until it seemed that he could foresee the very stories they were going to tell, the very situations they were going to describe—

and then in an instant all the familiar pattern of their speech would vanish, and their words could not have been stranger to him had they spoken in a foreign tongue.

Thus, as Eugene looked at the young college fellows playing in the fields below the house, their shouts and cries, the boyish roughness of their play, their strong scurfed knees, and panting breath, evoked the image of a life so familiar to him that he felt all he had to do to enter it again was to walk across the velvet width of lawn that separated him from it. But if he passed these same people two hours later in the High Street, their lives, their words were stranger than a dream, or they seemed to have an incredible fictitious quality that made everything they did or said seem false, mannered, and affected, so that when he listened to them he had a feeling of resentment and contempt for them, as if they spoke and moved with the palpable falseness of actors.

Eugene would see two young fellows before a college gate, and one, fragile of structure, with a small lean head, a sheaf of straight blonde hair and thin, sensitive features which were yet sharply and strongly marked, would be talking to another youth, his hands thrust jauntily into the pockets of his baggy gray trousers as he talked and the worn elegance of his baggy coat falling across his hands in folds of jaunty well-worn smartness.

"I say!" the youth would be saying in his crisp, rapid, sharply blurred inflections that seemed to come out of lips that barely moved. "Where *were* you last night? We missed you at the party in old Lambert's rooms, you know. Every one wondered why you didn't turn up."

"Oh," the other said (but the way he said this word sounded almost like "Ow" to Eugene). "Did they? I'm frightfully sorry to have missed it, but I simply couldn't get thöh. Had dinner with a chap I know at Magdalen. His sister's down for a day or so, and later on I simply couldn't break away.—How was the party?"

"Ow!" the other cried, casting his head back with a strong quick movement and an exultant little laugh. "Ripping! Simply ripping! What a shame you had to miss it! Old Fenton got quite squiffed along towards ten o'clock," he went on affectionately and with his exultant little laugh, "and really it was priceless! He insisted on doing an imitation of Queen Victoria sitting down to read *The Times* upon her w. c. just after modern plumbing was installed—Ow!" he cried exultantly again, casting his head up with a sharp strong movement, "the whole thing was convulsing!—To see old Fenton *settle* down!"

he cried, "to see him *look* around *suspiciously*," he whispered, still maintaining the perfect dramatic sharpness of his inflection as he looked around with a descriptive gesture, "to see him wait *uneasily* to see what's going to happen—finally to see the look of *blissful* satisfaction and contentment gradually *stealing* over his face," he whispered rapturously, "as he settles back to read *The Times* in peace—*ow!*" he cried again, as he cast back his small lean head with an exultant laugh, "—the whole thing was really *too* superb!—it really was, you know! Old Lambert was quite convulsed! We had to lift him up and stretch him out upon the bed before he got his breath again."

In conversations such as these, in the choice and accent of the words, the sharp crisp and yet blurred inflections of the speech, even in the jaunty nonchalance of hands in pockets, the hang and fold of the coat, in the exultant little laugh and the sharp strong upward movement of the small lean head, there was something alien, suave, and old. To Eugene it seemed to be the style of a life that was far older, more suavely knowing and mature, than any he had ever known, so that at such a time as this, these young boys who on the playing fields had almost the appearance of tousled overgrown urchins, now seemed far more assured and sophisticated than he could ever be.

At the same time, the sound and inflection of their words—their assured exercise of a style of language that knew exactly where to use and how to inflect such words as "very," "quite," "superb," "priceless," "terribly," "marvellous," and so on—this style and use seemed to Eugene almost false, fictional, affected, and theatrical.

He felt this way chiefly because he had read about such people all his life in books and for the most part had heard them speak in this manner only in smart plays upon the stage. He was always connecting these young Englishmen with actors in the theatre, and for a moment his mind would resentfully accuse them of being nothing but cheap and affected actors themselves and, bitterly, of "trying to talk with an English accent"—a phrase which obviously had no meaning, since they were only speaking their own language in the way they had been taught to speak it.

But then, at tea-time, Eugene would see these youths again in Buol's, flirting, with the clumsy naïveté of a grubby schoolboy, with a leering rawboned hag of a waitress, and obviously getting the thrill of their lives from the spurious grins which this dilapidated strumpet flashed at them through her artificial teeth. Or, as he went up the road towards his house at night, he would pass them standing in the dark shadows of the stormy trees, with their arms clumsily clasped around the buttocks of a servant girl, and their lives seemed unbelievably young, naked, and innocent again.

Around Eugene was the whole structure of an enchanted life—a life hauntingly familiar and just the way he had always known it would be —and now that he was there, he had no way of getting into it. The inn itself was ancient, legendary, beautiful, elfin, like all the inns he had ever read about, and yet all of the cheer, the warmth, the joy and comfort he had dreamed of finding in an inn was lacking.

Upstairs the halls went crazily up and down at different levels, one mounted steps, went down again, got lost and turned around in the bewildering design of the ancient added-on-to structure—and this was the way he had always known it would be. But the rooms were small, cold, dark, and dreary, the lights were dim and dismal, you stayed out of your room as much as possible and when you went to bed at night you crawled in trembling between clammy sheets, and huddled there until the bed was warm. When you got up in the morning there was a small jug of warm water at your door with which to shave, but the jug was too small, you poured it out into the bowl and shaved yourself and added cold water from the pitcher then in order to get enough to wash your face and hands. Then you got out of the room and went downstairs as quickly as you could.

Downstairs it would be fine. There would be a brisk fire crackling in the hearth, the old smoke-gold of morning and the smell of fog, the crisp cheerful voices of the people and their ruddy competent morning look, and the cheerful smells of breakfast, which was always liberal and good, the best meal that they had: kidneys and ham and eggs and sausages and toast and marmalade and tea.

But at night there would come the huge boiled-flannel splendor of the dinner, the magnificent and prayerful service of the waiter, who served you with such reverent grace from heavy silver platters that you felt the food must be as good as everything looked. But it never was.

Eugene ate at a large table, in the centre of the dining-room, provided by a thoughtful management for such isolated waifs and strays as himself. The food looked very good, and was, according to the genius of the nation, tasteless. How they ever did it he could never tell: everything was of the highest quality and you chewed upon it mournfully, wearily, swallowing it with the dreary patience of a man who has been condemned forever to an exclusive diet of boiled unseasoned spinach. There was a kind of evil sorcery, a desolate and fathomless mystery in the way they could take the choicest meats and vegetables and extract all the succulence and native flavor from them, and then serve them up to you magnificently with every atom of their former life reduced to the general character of stewed hay or well-boiled flannel.

There would be a thick heavy soup of dark mahogany, a piece of boiled fish covered with a nameless, tasteless sauce of glutinous white, roast beef that had been done to death in dish-water, and solid, perfect, lovely brussels sprouts for whose taste there was no name whatever. It might have been the taste of boiled wet ashes, or the taste of stewed green leaves, with all the bitterness left out, pressed almost dry of moisture, or simply the taste of boiled clouds and rain and fog. For dessert, there would be a pudding of some quivery yellow substance, beautifully moulded, which was surrounded by a thin sweetish fluid of a sticky pink. And at the end there would be a cup of black, bitter, liquid mud.

Eugene felt as if these dreary ghosts of food would also come to life at any moment, if he could only do some single simple thing—make the gesture of an incantation, or say a prayer, or speak a magic word, a word he almost had, but couldn't quite remember.

The food plagued his soul with misery, bitter disappointment, and bewilderment. For Eugene liked to eat, and they had written about food better than any one on earth. Since his childhood, there had burned in his mind a memory of the food they wrote about. It was a memory drawn from a thousand books (of which *Quentin Durward,* curiously, was one), but most of all it came from that tremendous scene in *Tom Brown at Rugby,* which described the boy's ride with his father through the frosty darkness, in an English stage-coach, the pause for breakfast at an inn, and the appearance of the host, jolly, red-faced, hospitable, who had rushed out to welcome them.

Eugene could remember with a gluttonous delight the breakfast which that hungry boy had devoured. It was a memory so touched with the magic relish of frost and darkness, smoking horses, the thrill, the ecstasy of the journey and a great adventure, the cheer, the warmth, the bustle of the inn, and the delicious abundance of the food they gave the boy, that the whole thing was evoked with blazing vividness, and now it would almost drive Eugene mad with hunger when he thought of it.

Now it seemed to him that these people had written so magnificently about good food not because they always had it, but because they had it rarely and therefore made great dreams and fantasies about it, and it seemed to him that this same quality—the quality of *lack* rather than of *possession,* of desire rather than fulfilment—had got into everything they did, and made them dream great dreams, and do heroic acts, and had enriched their lives immeasurably.

They had been the greatest poets in the world because the love and substance of great poetry were so rare among them. Their poems were so full of the essential quality of sunlight because their lives had known sunlight briefly, and so shot through with the massy substance of essential gold (a matchless triumph of light and color and material, in which they have beaten the whole world by every standard of comparison) because their lives had known so much fog and rain, so little gold. And they had spoken best of April because April was so brief with them.

Thus from the grim gray of their skies they had alchemied gold, and from their hunger, glorious food, and from the raw bleakness of their lives and weathers they had drawn magic. And what was good among them had been won sternly, sparely, bitterly, from all that was ugly, dull, and painful in their lives, and, when it came, was more rare and beautiful than anything on earth.

But that also was theirs: it was another door Eugene could not enter.

LXIX

Later, Eugene could remember everything except the way he found the house and came to live there. But a man named Morison, who was staying at the Mitre when Eugene got there, found the house and gave him the address. He was a man of twenty-eight or thirty years, but he constantly seemed younger, much younger, no older than the average college youth, an illusion that was never permanent, however, and never for a moment convincing, because one felt constantly that everything about the man was spurious.

He had been, he said, a lieutenant in the flying corps, and had just the month before resigned his commission. And he said he had resigned his commission because he had received an appointment from the government in the African colonial service, and had been sent up to the university to take a special six months' course in Colonial Administration, after which he would be "sent out" to assume his new duties in the Colonies. Finally, he was, he said, by birth, an Edinburgh Scotchman, although his family were by blood more English than Scotch, and he had lived most of his life in England. His references to his family were casual, easy, and indefinite, but carried with them, somehow, the connotations of aristocratic distinction.

He referred to his father often, but always in this casual and easy manner, as "the governor," and to his mother as "the mater," flinging in parenthetically with his easy nonchalance such a statement as "of course, my whole crowd came from Devonshire"—a statement which was unadorned and meaningless enough but that somehow—God knows how —carried with it a wonderful evocation of an ancestral seat, an ancient and distinguished name, the quiet but impregnable position of one of the "old county families."

And yet, God knows how he did it: the man said nothing about his people that might not be said of any modest little family, and probably everything he said was true. He made no open pretenses to great name or wealth or ancient lineage, but in these swift, casual, half-blurted-out references to "the governor," "the mater," and so on, he projected perfectly a legend of prestige and family that was most engaging in its sense of style and dash and recklessness.

The design of this legend was perfectly familiar to every one: Eugene had read it a thousand times in the pages of books, but he had never known any one who could evoke it so perfectly, so tellingly, and with such a non-committal economy of means, as Morison. In this casual, charming, almost nakedly simple picture of his life which he could suggest in a blurted-out phrase without giving a shred of real information about himself, or making a single admission of fact, the characters were few in number, their lineaments broadly and forcibly outlined, and their setting a familiar one.

In this setting, Morison himself played the part of the dashing young aristocrat, wild, reckless, and impetuous, always ready for fun, fight, or frolic, a bottle of Scotch, or a pretty woman, a roaring drunk, or a hot seduction—a mad hare-brained sort of fellow who plunged impetuously forward into everything, but who was somehow always saved from the odium that attaches itself to a baser sort of drunkard, brawler, or seducer, because he had in him those mysterious qualities of blood and character that made of him "a gentleman," and therefore gave his acts a faultless style, a whole immunity.

And the figure that he stroked in of his father was also a pleasant one. For "the governor," although he existed chiefly for the purpose of admonishment and reproof, as a curb upon the wild spirits of his son, was neither a sour Puritan, nor a grim-visaged household tyrant, but really a very good and understanding sort of fellow, and, within reasonable limits, as tolerant as any one could ask. The old boy, in fact, had been "a bit of a buck himself" in his younger days, and had seen his share of the flesh and the devil, and was quite willing to make allowances for the wilder escapades of youth, so long as a reasonable decorum and moderation were observed.

But there, alas, was the rub—as Morison himself would ruefully admit. He was himself such a mad, scape-grace sort of fellow that his acts sometimes passed all the bounds of decorum and propriety, and for that reason "the governor" was always "having him in upon the carpet."

There, in fact, was the whole setting. The governor existed for the sole purpose of "having him in upon the carpet"—one never saw them in any other way, but when Morison spoke about it one saw them in *this* way with blazing vividness. And this picture—the picture of Morison going in "upon the carpet"—was a very splendid one.

First, one saw Morison pacing nervously up and down in a noble and ancient hall, puffing distractedly on a cigarette and pausing from time to time in an apprehensive manner before the grim, closed barrier of an enormous seventeenth-century door which was tall and wide enough for a knight in armor to ride through without difficulty, and before whose gloomy and overwhelming front Morison looked very small and full of guilt. Then, one saw him take a last puff at his cigarette, brace his shoulders in a determined manner, knock on the panels of the mighty door, and in answer to a low growl within, open the door and advance desperately into the shadowed depths of a room so immense and magnificent that Morison looked like a single little sinner walking forlornly down the nave of a cathedral.

At the end of this terrific room, across an enormous space of carpet, sat "the governor." He was sitting behind a magnificent flat desk of ancient carved mahogany, in the vast shadowed depths behind him storied rows of old bound volumes climbed dizzily up into the upper darkness and were lost. And men in armor were standing grimly all around, and the portraits of the ancestors shone faintly in the gloom, and the old worn mellow colors of the tempered light came softly through the colored glass of narrow Gothic windows which were set far away in recessed depths of the impregnable mortared walls.

Meanwhile, "the governor" was waiting in grim silence as Morison advanced across the carpet. The governor was a man with beetling bushy eyebrows, silver hair, the lean, bitten and incisive face, the cropped mustache of a man who has seen service in old wars, and commanded garrisons in India, and after clearing his throat with a low menacing growl, he would peer fiercely out at Morison beneath his bushy brows, and say: "Well, young man?"—to which Morison would be able to make no answer, but would just stand there in a state of guilty dejection.

And the talk that then passed between the outraged father and the prodigal son was, from Morison's own account, astonishing. It was a talk that was no talk, a talk that was almost incoherent but that each understood perfectly, another language, not merely an economy of words so spare that one word was made to do the work of a hundred, but a series of grunts, blurts, oaths and ejaculations, in which almost nothing was said that was recognizable as ordered thought, but in which the meaning of everything was perfectly conveyed.

The last outrageous episode that had brought Morison in to his present position of guilt "upon the carpet" was rarely named by name or given a description. Rather, as if affronted decency and aristocratic delicacy could not endure discussion of an unmentionable offense, his fault was indicated briefly as "that sort of thing" (or simply "sort of thing," spoken fast and slurringly)—and all the other passions and emotions of anger, contrition, stern condemnation and reproof, and, at length, of exhausted relief and escape, were conveyed in a series of broken and jerky exclamations, such as: "After *all!*" "It's not as if it were the first time you had played the bloody fool!" "What I mean to say is!" "Damn it all, it's not that I mind the wine-woman-song sort of thing—young myself once—no plaster saint—never pretended that I was—man's own business if he keeps it to himself—never interfered —only when you do a thing like this and make a bloody show of yourself—you idiot!—sort of thing men can understand but women!—it's your mother I'm thinking of!" and so on.

Morison's own speech, in fact, was largely composed of phrases such as these: he blurted them out so rapidly, scarcely moving his lips and slurring his words over in such a broken and explosive way, that when one first met him it was hard to understand what he was saying:— his speech seemed to be largely a series of blurted-out phrases, such as "sort of thing," "after *all!*" "what I mean to say is!" and so on. And yet this incoherent and exclamatory style was curiously effective, for it seemed to take the listener into its confidence in rather an engaging manner which said: "of course there's no need to go into detail about all this, because I can see you are a man of the world and the same kind of fellow as I am. I know we understand each other perfectly, and the truth of what I am saying must be so self-evident that there's no point in discussing it."

In stature, he was a little below the middle height, and rather fleshy. In fact, although his jaunty and impetuous manners gave him an air of boyishness, he was already getting fat around the waist, and his neck was fat and there was a fold of flesh beneath his chin. His face was very ruddy, smooth, a little alcoholic, and he had a small blonde mustache with waxed ends. Finally, his hair was thick, sleek, of a dark taffy-colored blond which shaded off into roots of fine silken blond-ish white at the edges of his temples.

He could almost have passed for the average Oxford youth if it had not been for the roll of fat beneath his chin, and the blurred, veinous, and yellowed look of his eyes, and he could almost have passed for the dashing gentleman whose lineaments he could so deftly and cleverly sketch in a few boldly casual strokes had it not been that there was something spurious in his character that gave him away in everything he did or said.

And yet Eugene never knew just what this spurious quality was. He felt at once that the man was fraudulent and unfortunate, and that all he told about himself was fraudulent, and yet everything he told was not only natural and credible enough but even plausible. All he said was that he had been a lieutenant in the flying corps, and had recently resigned, and had been given an appointment in the Colonies and been sent to Oxford for a course in Colonial Administration, and that later he would be sent to Africa.

Later on, Eugene understood that all of this was probably true, but at the time it sounded like a lie. Or, if it was not a lie, he thought that there was something discreditable and shameful behind it. He thought that if Morison had been in the army flying service, as he said, he had resigned not from choice, but because he had to—because he had been caught cheating at cards, or had not paid his debts, or had been mixed up in some unwholesome mess with a woman. And he thought that if Morison was now going out to Africa it was not so much from choice as by compulsion—because he had to go. In the years that followed Eugene saw that these suspicions were probably unfounded and unjust, but that was the way Morison made him feel.

There was about him somehow the look of the ruined adventurer—
shabby and run-down—the face of the actor shining through its mask
of deft gentility, the face of the charlatan looking through its visage of
sincerity, and the old veined yellow eyes of ruin, hopelessness, and
loss looking through all his attitudes of youth, infectious spontaneity,
and grace. And for this reason, somehow, the man seemed pitiably
gallant, and Eugene liked him.

He and Morison would go to different pubs and drink until the
closing time. Morison was using him vilely, and Eugene knew it, and
did not care. Not only was he paying for three drinks of every four
they drank, but he knew that Morison also sought his companionship
because he thought it gave him some immunity from the college proctors, when they made their visits to a pub. And this, in fact, he admitted
very frankly, and with a disarming gleefulness.

"You see," he said, "if I came in here by myself I'd get progged, but
as long as I'm with you I'm probably all right."

"Why?"

"Oh," he said, with an exultant little chuckle, "because they don't
know what to make of it! They've got their eye on *me,* all right," he
laughed. "They've been giving me some very fishy looks—but when
they see *you* here, they can't be sure—they don't know what to make
of it!"

"Why don't they?"

"Oh," he said, "they're puzzled about me, but they *know* about
you—they don't dare to bother you because they know you're not in the
university."

"How do they know it?" he said resentfully. "I look as much like a
student as these Rhodes scholars that you see—yes, and a damned sight
more than most of them!"

"Yes, I know," he said tolerantly. "Still, they know you're not.
They've got a way of telling."

"A way of telling! Good God, Morison, how have they got a way of
telling? Do you mean to say they memorize the names and faces of all
the students here, the day the term commences?"

"No, it isn't that. You see, old boy, you don't *belong* to them—I
don't know what it is, but they have a way of their own of knowing."

"Do you mean that there's some damned mystery about it?—that they've got some supernatural gift of intuition that tells them when you're a student and when you're not."

"Quite!" he said. "That's just it. That's just the way they do it!" And he looked at Eugene for a moment with his blurred, veinous eyes, and laughed softly, good-naturedly, a little mockingly. "Curious, isn't it?"

"It's more than curious. It's a miracle!"

But it seemed that he was right. For sometimes the proctors would come into a pub where they were drinking, speak amicably to every one, and in a moment more go out again, but Morison would grow very quiet while they were there, and lean upon the bar, and look down at his drink until they left. And as they left they would look curiously at both men again, and their eye would pass Eugene swiftly and indifferently, and for a moment fix on Morison with a fishy and suspicious look. When they were gone he would look up again at the grinning bar-tender and, his ruddy face suffused with laughter, say exultantly:

"Oh, *priceless!* Did you see him when he looked at me?"

"I did," the man behind the counter said. "He didn't half know what to make of it, did he? The other gentleman is not a student, *is* he?"

"No!" Morison fairly shouted, his face crimson, as he pounded on the bar. "That's just the point! And they don't know what to make of it when they see me with him! They can't be sure!" he choked. "They can't be sure!"

And it was Morison who found the house out on the Ventnor road, took lodgings there himself, and gave Eugene the address.

LXX

In the fall that year, Eugene lived about a mile out from town in a house set back from the Ventnor Road. The house was called a "farm" —Hill-top Farm, or Far-end Farm, or some such name as that— but it was really no farm at all. It was a magnificent house of the weathered gray stone they have in that country, as if in the very quality of the wet heavy air there is the soft thick gray of time itself, sternly yet beautifully soaking down forever on you—and enriching everything it touches—grass, foliage, brick, ivy, the fresh moist color of the people's faces, and old gray stone, with the incomparable weathering of time.

The house was set back off the road at a distance of several hundred yards, possibly a quarter of a mile, and one reached it by means of a road bordered by rows of tall trees which arched above the road, and which made Eugene think of home, at night when the stormy wind howled in their tossed branches. On each side of the road were the rugby fields of two of the colleges and in the afternoon he could look out and down and see the fresh moist green of the playing fields, and watch young college fellows, dressed in their shorts and jerseys, and with their bare knees scurfed with grass and turf as they twisted, struggled, swayed, and scrambled for a moment in the scrimmage-circle, and then broke free, running, dodging, passing the ball as they were tackled, filling the moist air with their sharp cries of sport. They did not have the desperate, the grimly determined, the almost professional earnestness that the college teams at home have; their scurfed and muddy knees, their swaying scrambling scrimmages, the swift breaking away and running, their panting breath and crisp clear voices gave them the appearance of grown-up boys.

Once when Eugene had come up the road in afternoon while they were playing, the ball got away from them and came bounding out into the road before him, and he ran after it to retrieve it, as he used to do when passing a field where boys were playing baseball. One of the players came over to the edge of the field and stood there waiting with his hands upon his hips while Eugene got the ball: he was panting hard, his face was flushed, and his blond hair tousled, but when Eugene threw the ball to him, he said "Thanks very much!" crisply and courteously—getting the same sound into the word *"very"* that they got in *"Amer-ican,"* a sound that always repelled Eugene a little because it seemed to have some scornful aloofness and patronage in it.

For a moment Eugene watched him as he trotted briskly away on to the field again: the players stood there waiting, panting, casual, their hands upon their hips; he passed the ball into the scrimmage, the pattern swayed, rocked, scrambled, and broke sharply out in open play again, and everything looked incredibly strange, near, and familiar.

Eugene felt that he had always known it, that it had always been his, and that it was as familiar to him as everything he had seen or known in his childhood. Even the texture of the earth looked familiar, and felt moist and firm and springy when he stepped on it, and the stormy howling of the wind in that avenue of great trees at night, was wild and desolate and demented as it had been when he was eight years old and would lie in his bed at night and hear the great oaks howl-ing on the hill above his father's house.

The name of the people in the house was Coulson: he made arrangements with the woman at once to come and live there: she was a tall, weathered-looking woman of middle age, they talked together in the hall. The hall was made of marble flags and went directly out onto a gravelled walk.

The woman was crisp, cheerful, and worldly-looking. She was still quite handsome. She wore a well-cut skirt of woollen plaid, and a silk blouse: when she talked she kept her arms folded because the air in the hall was chilly, and she held a cigarette in the fingers of one hand. A shaggy brown dog came out and nosed upward toward her hand as she was talking and she put her hand upon its head and scratched it gently. When Eugene told her he wanted to move in the next day, she said briskly and cheerfully:

"Right you are! You'll find everything ready when you get here!" Then she asked if he was at the university. He said no, and added, with a feeling of difficulty and naked desolation, that he was a "writer," and was coming there to work. He was twenty-four years old.

"Then I am sure that what you do will be *very, very* good!" she said cheerfully and decisively. "We have had several Americans in the house before and all of them were very clever! All the Americans we have had here were very clever people," said the woman. "I'm sure that you will like it." Then she walked to the door with him to say good-bye. As they stood there, there was the sound of a small motorcar coming to a halt and in a moment a girl came swiftly across the gravel space outside and entered the hall. She was tall, slender, very lovely, but she had the same bright hard look in her eye that the woman had, the same faint, hard smile around the edges of her mouth.

"Edith," the woman said in her crisp curiously incisive tone, "this young man is an American—he is coming here tomorrow." The girl looked at Eugene for a moment with her hard bright glance, thrust out a small gloved hand, and shook hands briefly, a swift firm greeting.

"Oh! How d'ye do!" she said. "I hope you will like it here." Then she went on down the hall, entered a room on the left, and closed the door behind her.

Her voice had been crisp and certain like her mother's, but it was also cool, young, and sweet, with music in it, and later as Eugene went down the road, he could still hear it.

That was a wonderful house, and the people there were wonderful people. Later, he could not forget them. He seemed to have known them all his life, and to know all about their lives. They seemed as familiar to him as his own blood and he knew them with a knowledge that went deep below the roots of thought or memory. They did not talk together often, or tell any of their lives to one another. It is very hard to tell about it—the way they felt and lived together in that house—because it was one of those simple and profound experiences of life which people seem always to have known when it happens to them, but for which there is no language.

And yet, like a child's half-captured vision of some magic country he has known, and which haunts his days with strangeness and the sense of imminent, glorious re-discovery, the word that would unlock it all seemed constantly to be almost on their lips, waiting, just outside the gateway of their memory, just a shape, a phrase, a sound away, the moment that they chose to utter it—but when they tried to say the thing, something faded within their minds like fading light, and something melted within their grasp like painted smoke, and something went forever when they tried to touch it.

The nearest Eugene could come to it was this: In that house he sometimes felt the greatest peace and solitude that he had ever known. But he always knew the other people in the house were there. He could sit in his sitting-room at night and hear nothing but the stormy moaning of the wind outside in the great trees, the small gaseous flare and jet from time to time of the coal fire burning in the grate—and silence, strong living lonely silence that moved and waited in the house at night—and he would always know that they were there.

He did not have to hear them enter or go past his door, nor did he have to hear doors close or open in the house, or listen to their voices: if he had never seen them, heard them, spoken to them, it would have been the same—he would have known they were there.

It was something he had always known, and he had known it would happen to him, and now it was there with all the strangeness and dark mystery of an awaited thing. He knew them, felt them, lived among them with a familiarity that had no need of sight or word or speech. And the memory of that house and of his silent fellowship with all the people there was somehow mixed with an image of dark time. It was one of those sorrowful and unchanging images which, among all the blazing stream of images that passed constantly their stream of fire across his mind, was somehow fixed. detached, and everlasting, full of a sorrow, certitude, and mystery that he could not fathom, but that wore forever on it the old sad light of waning day—a light from which all the heat, the violence, and the substance of furious dusty day had vanished, and which was itself like time, unearthly-of-the-earth, remote, detached, and everlasting.

And that fixed and changeless image of dark time was this: In an old house of time Eugene lived alone, and yet had other people all around him, and they never spoke to him, or he to them. They came and went like silence in the house, but he always knew that they were there. He would be sitting by a window in a room, and he would know then that they were moving in the house, and darkness, sorrow, and strong silence dwelt within them, and their eyes were quiet, full of sorrow, peace, and knowledge, and their faces dark, their tongues silent, and they never spoke. Eugene could not remember how their faces looked, but they were all familiar to him as his father's face, and they had known one another forever, and they lived together in the ancient house of time, dark time; and silence, sorrow, certitude, and peace were in them. Such was the image of dark time that was to haunt his life thereafter, and into which, somehow, his life among the people in that house had passed.

In the house that year there lived, besides Eugene and Morison, the Coulsons, father and mother, and their daughter, and three men who had taken rooms together, and who were employed in a factory where motor-cars were made, two miles from town.

Perhaps the reason that Eugene could never forget these people later and seemed to know them all so well was that there was in all of them something ruined, lost, or broken—some precious and irretrievable quality which had gone out of them and which they could never get back again. Perhaps that was the reason that he liked them all so much, because with ruined people it is either love or hate: there is no middle way. The ruined people that we like are those who desperately have died, and lost their lives because they loved life dearly, and had that grandeur that makes such people spend prodigally the thing they love the best, and risk and lose their lives because life is so precious to them, and die at length because the seeds of life are in them. It is only the people that love life who die in this way—and these are the ruined people that we like.

The people in the house were people who had lost their lives because they loved the earth too well, and somehow had been slain by their hunger. And for this reason Eugene liked them all, and could not forget them later: there seemed to have been some magic which had drawn them all together to that house, as if the house itself were a magnetic centre for lost people.

Certainly, the three men who worked at the motor-car factory had been drawn together for this reason. Two were still young men in their early twenties. The third man was much older. He was a man past forty, his name was Nicholl, he had served in the army during the war and had attained the rank of captain.

He had the spare, alert, and jaunty figure that one often finds in army men, an almost professional military quality that somehow seemed to set his figure upon a horse as if he had grown there, or had spent a lifetime in the cavalry. His face also had the same lean, bitten, professional military quality: his speech, although good-natured and very friendly, was clipped, incisive, jerky, and sporadic, his lean weather-beaten face was deeply, sharply scarred and sunken in the flanks, and he wore a small cropped mustache, and displayed long frontal teeth when he smiled—a spare, gaunt, toothy, yet attractive smile.

His left arm was withered, shrunken, almost useless, part of his hand and two of the fingers had been torn away by the blast or explosion which had destroyed his arm, but it was not this mutilation of the flesh that gave one the sense of a life that had been ruined, lost, and broken irretrievably. In fact, one quickly forgot his physical injury: his figure looked so spare, lean, jaunty, well-conditioned in its energetic fitness that one never thought of him as a cripple, nor pitied him for any disability. No: the ruin that one felt in him was never of the flesh, but of the spirit. Something seemed to have been torn away from his life—it was not the nerve-centres of his arm, but of his soul, that had been destroyed. There was in the man somewhere a terrible dead vacancy and emptiness, and the spare, lean figure that he carried so well seemed only to surround this vacancy like a kind of shell.

He was always smartly dressed in clothes that sat well on his trim spruce figure. He was always in good spirits, immensely friendly in his clipped spare way, and he laughed frequently—a rather metallic cackle which came suddenly and ended as swiftly as it had begun. He seemed, somehow, to have locked the door upon dark care and worry, and to have flung the key away—to have lost, at the same time that he lost more precious things, all the fretful doubts and perturbations of conscience that most men know.

Now, in fact, he seemed to have only one serious project in his life. This was to keep himself amused, to keep himself constantly amused, to get from his life somehow the last atom of entertainment it could possibly yield, and in this project the two young men who lived with him joined in with an energy and earnestness which suggested that their employment in the motor-car factory was just a necessary evil which must be borne patiently because it yielded them the means with which to carry on a more important business, the only one in which their lives were interested—the pursuit of pleasure.

And in the way in which they conducted this pursuit, there was an element of deliberate calculation, concentrated earnestness, and focal intensity of purpose that was astounding, grotesque, and unbelievable, and that left in the mind of one who saw it a formidable and disquieting memory because there was in it almost the madness of desperation, the deliberate intent to seek oblivion, at any cost of effort, from some hideous emptiness of the soul.

Captain Nicholl and his two young companions had a little motor-car so small that it scuttled up the road, shot around and stopped in the gravel by the door with the abruptness of a wound-up toy. It was astonishing that three men could wedge themselves into this midge of a car, but wedge themselves they did, and used it to the end of its capacity, scuttling away to work in it in the morning, and scuttling back again when work was done, and scuttling away to London every Saturday, as if they were determined to wrest from this small motor, too, the last ounce of pleasure to be got from it.

Finally, Captain Nicholl and his two companions had made up an orchestra among them, and this they played in every night when they got home. One of the young men, who was a tall fellow with blond hair which went back in even corrugated waves across his head as if it had been marcelled, played the piano, the other, who was slight and dark, and had black hair, performed upon a saxophone, and Captain Nicholl himself took turns at thrumming furiously on a banjo, or rattling a tattoo upon the complex arrangement of trap drums, bass drums, and clashing cymbals that surrounded him.

They played nothing but American jazz music or sobbing crooner's rhapsodies or nigger blues. Their performance was astonishing. Although it was contrived solely for their own amusement, they hurled themselves into it with all the industrious earnestness of professional musicians employed by a night-club or dance hall to furnish dance music for the patrons. The little dark fellow who played the saxophone would bend and weave prayerfully with his grotesque instrument, as the fat gloating notes came from its unctuous throat, and from time to time he would sway in a half circle, or get up and prance forward and back in rhythm to the music, as the saxophone players in dance orchestras sometimes do.

Meanwhile the tall blond fellow at the piano would sway and bend above the keys, glancing around from time to time with little nods and smiles as if he were encouraging an orchestra of forty pieces or beaming happily at a dance floor crowded with paying customers.

While this was going on, Captain Nicholl would be thrumming madly on the strings of a banjo. He kept the instrument gripped some how below his withered arm, fingering the end strings with his two good fingers, knocking the tune out with his good right hand, and keeping time with a beating foot. Then with a sudden violent movement he would put the banjo down, snatch up the sticks of the trap drum, and begin to rattle out a furious accompaniment, beating the bass drum with his foot meanwhile, and reaching over to smash cymbals, chimes, and metal rings from time to time. He played with a kind of desperate fury, his mouth fixed in a strange set grin, his bright eyes burning with a sharp wild glint of madness.

They sang as they played, bursting suddenly into the refrain of some popular song with the same calculated spontaneity and spurious enthusiasm of the professional orchestra, mouthing the words of negro blues and jazz with an obvious satisfaction, with an accent which was remarkably good, and yet which had something foreign and inept in it that made the familiar phrases of American music sound almost as strange in their mouths as if an orchestra of skilful patient Japanese were singing them.

They sang:

> "Yes, sir! That's my baby
> Yes, sir! Don't mean maybe
> Yes, sir! That's my baby now!"

or:

> "Oh, it ain't gonna rain no more, no more
> It ain't gonna rain no more"

or:

> "I got dose blu-u-ues"—

the young fellow at the piano rolling his eyes around in a ridiculous fashion, and mouthing out the word "blues" extravagantly as he sang it, the little dark fellow bending forward in an unctuous sweep as the note came gloating fatly from the horn, and Captain Nicholl swaying sideways in his chair as he strummed upon the banjo strings, and improvising a mournful accompaniment of his own, somewhat as follows: "I got dose blu-u-ues! Yes, suh! Oh! I got dose blues! Yes, suh! I sure have got 'em—dose blu-u-ues—blu-u-ues—blu-u-ues!—" his mouth never relaxing from its strange fixed grin, nor his eyes from their bright set stare of madness as he swayed and strummed and sang the words that came so strangely from his lips.

It was a weird scene, an incredible performance, and somehow it pierced the heart with a wild nameless pity, an infinite sorrow and regret.

Something precious, irrecoverable had gone out of them, and they knew it. They fought the emptiness in them with this deliberate, formidable, and mad intensity of a calculated gaiety, a terrifying mimicry of mirth, and the storm-wind howled around them in dark trees, and Eugene felt that he had known them forever, and had no words to say to them—and no door.

LXXI

Once or twice a week Eugene went into town and had tea in the rooms of a boyhood friend whom he had known at school and who was now a Rhodes scholar at Merton College. The name of this youth was Johnny Park: he was a good-natured, industrious, and rather plodding boy, and thus far that patient, diligent and well-ordered plan of life which he had followed since his childhood had brilliantly succeeded. Formed in a native air, and followed out beneath familiar skies, that plan had never been interrupted by any doubt or strangeness, by any serious difficulty, or dark confusion of the soul, or by any of the unforeseen surprises, shocks, or bewilderments of chance which break upon our lives with storm-like fury and twist our precious plans awry.

Therefore, when he had been awarded the Rhodes scholarship a few months before, during his last year at the university, it seemed that Johnny's plan of life was marching on to its inevitable fulfilment. Every one had known he would be appointed, it came to pass with an ordained precision, and Johnny had announced, just as he should, that he would study "International Law," and everything was right and proper as it ought to be, and now he was here to march onward toward his shining goal, as he had always done.

But, for the first time in his life, something had gone wrong, something had gone terribly, appallingly amiss, and Johnny did not yet know what it was. Perhaps he never would, but now he was in the greatest trouble and confusion of his life, and he knew it. His voice was still slow, drawling, and good-natured, he was full of kindly warmth and friendliness as he had always been, he had responded quickly, dutifully, to all the customs and observances of the new life—had had gray baggy trousers and tweed coats made at the tailor's shop, had made arrangements for trips and walking-tours upon the Continent with his fellows in vacation time, had met his tutors, found out about the proctors and the penalties, learned the system of the college bills and battels, joined the Union and learned to go out dutifully for sports in the afternoon— he had even learned the mysterious ceremonial of tea and had it in his rooms each afternoon—all this he had learned and done with a punctilious thoroughness, but something had gone wrong.

Everything about Johnny was just as it had always been—his smile, his slow, good-natured voice, his amiable warmth and modesty and friendliness—all was the same with him except his eyes. But the quiet, thoughtful, tranquilly assured expression of his eyes had changed: he had in them the stunned, bewildered look, full of pain and a groping confusion, of a man who has been brutally slugged at the base of the brain, and is not yet certain what has happened to him.

His was an impossible situation, a tragic ordeal of loneliness, strangeness, and bewilderment among all the complex and alien forms of a new life for which nothing in the old had prepared him. Born in a small town in the South, going to school there and at his own State University, he had all his life breathed and lived in a familiar air, heard the familiar words of well-known voices all around him, known and seen nothing but assurance, certitude and success, in everything he planned.

And now all this, even the earth beneath his feet, had melted from him like a wisp of smoke, and he was wandering blindly about in a life as strange to him as Asia, as far as the moon, and knew nowhere to turn, nothing to grasp, no door to enter. In his whole life he had never seen or visited a great city, and then had seen New York just for a day or two, and then for seven days had known for the first time the mystery of the sea and a great ship, and now was here in the green English country, in an ancient town, hurled cruelly, suddenly, naked and unprepared for it as he was, into a life more subtle, complex and confusing than his placid soul had ever dreamed a life could be.

When Eugene asked him if he had stopped in London on his way to Oxford, the look of pain and bewilderment in his eyes had deepened, and he had answered in a slow confused voice:

"We stopped there over night but we never got to see much of it. We came on out here the next morning."

The boy was silent a moment, then he laughed good-naturedly with a troubled and uncertain note:

"It sure looked big enough from what I could see of it. I want to get down there sometime to see what it is like. I guess I've got a lot to learn," he said.

He could remember London like a man who is whirled blindly at night through a huge, limitless, smoky kaleidoscope of sound and sight and moving objects, and this memory of that enormous terrifying age-encrusted web of life—that web without end or measure, which seems blackened, soaked, and saturated not only in the gray light that falls upon it with its weight of eight million lives, but also by the gray light of compacted centuries and all the countless men who lived there and have died—that great gray web appropriately known to seafaring men as "The Smoke" had added measurably to the sense of bewilderment, terror, and naked desolation in him.

And it was pitifully the same with all the rest of them—the little group of Rhodes scholars that gathered together in Johnny's rooms every afternoon, and who seemed to huddle and cling together desperately as if they would try to shape, to resurrect, or to create some little pattern of familiar life, some small oasis of warmth and friendliness and familiar things to which they turned with desperate relief from all the alien and hostile loneliness of a life which they had never entered, which they could never make their own, which stood against them like a wall they could not pass, closed against them like a door they could not open.

Curiously, among this group of five or six Rhodes scholars, which formed the nucleus of the group which met in Johnny's rooms, only two—Johnny and his room-mate, a youth name Price—were first-year men. The others were either in the second or the final year of their appointments, but they seemed to have made no friendships with any one save with a few of the other Rhodes men, to have no other place to go, and to welcome the hospitality of these two boys with a desperate unspoken gratefulness.

There were, besides Johnny and his room-mate Price, three others who came there every day. One was a chunky, red-faced fellow, with coarse undistinguished features, who parted his short crinkly hair in the middle and had come there from Brown University, where he had been a member of the football team. He was in his second year abroad, and no longer wore his little golden football, but a good deal of his self-satisfied complacency was intact: he was thicker of hide and sense than any of the others, and evidently felt that his three years at Oxford were going to give him a kind of pick-and-choose freedom with any kind of employment when he got back home.

He asked Eugene how much he had been paid by the university in New York City where he had been employed as an instructor, and when Eugene told him, smiled tolerantly saying that he wouldn't mind "trying it for a year after I get back until I have a chance to look around." He then informed Eugene graciously that he was open to an offer, and would even be willing to work for no more than they paid *him,* while he "looked around." He added with a little smile:

"I don't imagine that I'll have much trouble: a man with an Oxford degree gets snapped up pretty quick over there, doesn't he? Still," he went on magnanimously, "I wouldn't mind living in New York a year or two until I settle down—so you can give my name to them, if you don't mind."

The other two in the group that came to Johnny's rooms were both third-year men. One was a frail, sensitive, and æsthetic-looking youth named Sterling. Although he came from one of the Western states—Arizona or New Mexico—there was nothing in him to suggest the wildness, openness, and grandeur of his native scenery. Rather, he was a most precious, a most subtle, elegantly sad, quietly bitter and disdainful fellow: he was quietly, fervently, subtly a devoted follower of Mr. T. S. Eliot, and although he revealed his theories sparely, cautiously, and by evasive indirectness, there was in all he said a quiet air of more-in-this-than-meets-the-eye, as if he were saying: "If you want to follow me you've got to learn to read between the lines and get my meaning by what is implied rather than by what is said—since there's no language that can say exactly what my meaning, which is too subtle and exact for any language, is."

He wore about him always this air of elegant, cold, and slightly disdainful restraint, and he had a habit of looking across his thin arched hands with a faint disdainful smile, and listening coldly, saying nothing, while the others talked, as if the waste-land chatter of their tongues, the waste-land vacancy of their lost waste-land souls was something that he knew he must endure, but would endure with his cold faint disdainful smile, his soul steeped in cold and patient weariness till death should mercifully release him.

The other man was a Jew named Fried and that man Eugene could never forget. Eugene didn't know where he came from, how he got there, who made him a Rhodes scholar, but he knew that of them all, save Johnny, he was the only one who had maintained his integrity, the only one who did not have a spurious, fearful, uneasily evasive quality, the only one who came out with it, the whole packed load of bitterness and hate within him, the only one who had remained himself.

Perhaps it was a bad self to remain: it was certainly a self that was lacking in charm, that had the aggressive, abusive, curiously unrighteous quality of his race—but there he was, terrifically himself and unashamed of it—with a naked formidable integrity of self that blazed with a hard and naked light of a cut jewel, and that Eugene could never forget even when the characters of the rest of them had grown blurred and shapeless and obscure.

Eugene didn't know where he came from, but he was sure it was from one of the great cities of the Atlantic seaboard—from New York, Boston, Baltimore or Philadelphia. He had seen his face, his figure, and his kind a million times upon the pavements of those cities and incredibly now, that dark unhappy face which never before had seemed to him to be a face at all, nothing but a tidal flood of nameless faces, that strident and abusive tongue which had never before seemed to him to be a single tongue, but just a common, nameless, and unnumbered ugliness of rasping voices, an anathema of bitter cries and harsh derisions— a constant phrase, a dissonance, a weather of the city's life—all that had been nameless, faceless, characterless and obscure—the look, the sound, the smell of the man-swarm ciphers of the city as dark-eyed, dark-faced, and bitter-tongued they swarmed along the pavements of the cities—all this, in that strange place, was suddenly, weirdly, resumed into a single character—a character that was hard, bitter, unforgettably itself, and that no change of sky or land or custom, nor the huge impact of all the alien and formidable pageantry of the earth, could ever alter by a jot.

Theirs was a wretched, hopeless, lonely life, a futile, feeble, barren life, an impossible, groping, wretched insecure life—and Fried was the only one of them to meet it, to admit it, to denounce it with all the bitterness of his bitter soul, and to remain himself against it. The rest were frightened, bitter, lonely, homesick, and afraid—afraid of everything, afraid of their own loneliness and their own dismal unsuccess, afraid to confess the desolation of their souls, the bitter disappointment of their hopes, afraid to laugh too loud, to show too much exuberance or enthusiasm for anything, lest some one should consider them a "hearty," and pin that feared and hated label on them.

They were afraid to express any native extravagance in dress, speech or manner lest they be branded as "bounders," afraid to talk their natural speech in their own manner lest they seem too crudely, raucously and offensively American, and afraid to imitate too studiously the language of the nation for fear that their own fellows would sneer at them for servile snobbishness, for "speaking with an English accent." Thus, caught in the web of a thousand fears, the meshes of a thousand impossible restraints, trying to maintain their lives, their characters, their native dignities even while they tried to subdue them by a thousand small half-mimicries, to be themselves even while they tried to shape themselves to something else, their characters finally, strained through the impossible weavings of this mad design, teetering frantically to maintain a crazy balance on a thousand wires, were reduced at last to the consistency of blubber—and trying to be everything, they succeeded finally in being nothing.

Oh, it was a wretched, futile, hopeless kind of life, and in their hearts they knew it, but could only speak casually, smile feebly, speak falsely, yet never lay their hearts bare boldly, and admit the truth. None of them liked Fried, they were ashamed of him, they turned on him at times in force, argued with him, denounced him, jeered at him, but at the bottom of their hearts they had a strange, secret, and unwilling respect for him, and finally grew silent and listened when he talked.

It was astonishing to watch the effect of that man's bitter tirades on that forlorn group. For where at first they would protest, remonstrate, sharply caution him, laugh uneasily and look fearfully toward the door as his harsh rasping voice mounted and grew high and snarling with its packed anathema of bitterness and hate, they would at length grow silent and look at him with fascinated eyes, and listen to that snarling and savage indictment with a kind of feeding gluttony of satisfaction, as if into that single naked and abusive tongue had been packed the whole huge weight of misery that had sweltered in their hearts, but to which they had never dared, themselves, to give utterance.

Eugene had asked Sterling how much longer he would remain abroad, and he had answered:

"Just ten months more. This is my last year. I am going home next August." He was silent for a moment, then he added with a faint, regretful smile: "In another year, I suppose, I'll be wondering if all this has ever happened. It will seem strange and beautiful," he said softly, "like some impossible dream!"

"Yeah!" snarled Fried, with a harsh interruption at this point. "An impossible dream! Jesus! An impossible nightmare!—that's what you'd better say!"

Sterling looked at him silently for a moment over his thin arched hands. He smiled faintly, disdainfully, and made no answer. In a moment he turned quietly to Eugene again, and dismissing the other man with the cold contempt of silence, continued:

"Sometimes it's hard for me to realize I ever lived there. Can there be such a place as America, I wonder?" he said with a sad faint smile. "After all this," he gestured slightly, pausing, "it will seem so strange to be a part of," he paused carefully "—*that* again. . . . Skyscrapers, subways, elevated trains—" he paused again, with a faint smile— "Tell me," he said, turning toward Eugene, "do such things *really* exist?"

"Do they *really* exist!" Fried now snarled with a jeering laugh. "Do they *really* exist! I'll tell the cock-eyed world that they exist!" he rasped. "You can bet your —— that they exist! . . . Do they exist!" he snorted to himself derisively, "Jesus!"

Sterling stared coldly at him and said nothing. For a moment Fried's hard, dark, embittered face, the feverish eyes, stared balefully at the fragile and sensitive face of the other youth, set disdainfully against him over his arched hands.

"Where do you get that stuff?" Fried said at length with harsh contempt. "You may kid these guys who never saw the place until a week ago, but you don't kid me, Sterling. Christ! I know what kind of a dream it's been—and so do you!"

Sterling did not deign to answer, but continued to look at him with cold faint disdain, and after another baleful and disgusted stare, Fried rasped out bitterly again:

"I suppose it was a dream your first term here when you tried to suck around those English guys and you thought they were going to take you right into the family, didn't you?" he sneered. "You thought you were sittin' pretty, didn't you? You were goin' to pal around with the Duke of What's-His-Name and get invited home wit' him for the Christmas holidays and make a big play for his sister, weren't you! Yes, you were!" He jeered, "You saw how far it got you, didn't you? Those guys took you for a ride and played you for a sucker, an' when they'd had all the fun wit' you they could, they dropped you like a ton of bricks! You thought that you were pretty wise, didn't you?" he snarled bitterly. "You thought that you were goin' places, didn't you? You were goin' to do something big, you were! Well, I'll tell you what you did! You handed them a laugh—see? You handed those guys a great big laugh—yes! a laugh!" he shouted violently. "And, I'll tell you something else! They're still laughin' at you! I saw you, Sterling. I know what you did. But you didn't see me, did you? Couldn't see me in those days, could you?"

"I can't see you now," said Sterling coldly. "I never could see you!"

"Is that so!" the Jew said bitterly. "Now isn't that too bad! . . . Well, I'll tell you one time that you saw me, Sterling. . . . That's when those guys had left you flat. . . . You could see me then, couldn't you? You don't remember, do you?" he jeered. "Well, I'll tell you when it was. . . . It was when you came back here that year for the spring term and you found they didn't know you when you went around. It was when your tail was dragging the ground and you didn't have a friend in the world—you could see me then, all right. Couldn't you? . . . I wasn't good enough before when you were trying to break into High Society—but I was good enough to see, after they gave you the big go-by, wasn't I? . . . Sure! Sure!" he said with an air of derision, addressing himself more quietly now to the rest of the group. "I usta go by this guy when he was running around wit' his English friends— and did he see me?" he jibed savagely. "Not so you could notice it! . . . 'Who is that common person who just spoke to you, Mr. Sterling?' 'O, that! O, I cannot say, old chap—some low fellow that was on the boat wit' me when I came ovah! . . . Really cawn't recall his name! A beastly boundah, I believe!' . . . Sure! Sure!" he nodded. "That was it! High-hattin' me, you know! I wasn't good enough! And all the time these English guys were laughin' up their sleeve at him!"

They had been stunned by the snarling fury of his assault, silenced by the hypnotic compulsion of his dark, hard face, his feverish eyes, the rasping bitterness of his voice that at the end grew strident, high, and gasping from his effort to release in one explosive tirade the whole packed weight of misery, disappointment, and defeat that sweltered poisonously in his heart. Now, however, as he paused there, dark and hard and full of bitterness, surveying them balefully with toxic eyes, silenced by lack of breath rather than by lack of further curses, they gathered themselves together and went for him in a mass.

In another moment the last vestige of restraint, gentlemanly decorum, urbane and tolerant sophistication with which they had clothed themselves had vanished, and they were yelping, snarling, shouting, accusing and denying, inextricably mixed-up in one general and inglorious dog-fight; taunts, curses, insults, and indictments filled the air, all of them were shouting at the same time, and out of that roaring brawl all one could decipher was the ragged barbs and ends of their abuse—a tumult of bitter and strident voices characterized by such phrases as—"You never belonged here in the first place!" "It's fellows like you who give all the rest of us a bad name!" "Why the hell should the rest of us have to suffer for it because you talk and act like an East Side gangster?" "They think all Americans are a bunch of roughnecks because they meet a few like you." "Ah, g'wan! youse guys! You give me a pain. You all feel the same way as I do but none of you has guts enough to say so!" "You're just sore because these English boys never had anything to do with you —that's all you're sore about!" "Yeah? They had a hell of a lot to do wit' you, didn't they?—even if you did try to talk wit' an English accent." "You're a damned liar! I never tried to talk with an English accent!" "Sure you did! Everybody hoid you! You coulda cut yoeh accent wit' a hatchet! You were tryin' to suck aroun' that gang at Christ's the first year you were here!" "Who says I was?" "I say so—that's who! You an' Tommy Woodson both—" "Don't mix my name with Tommy Woodson, now! You're not going to include me with that horse's neck!" "Oh, yeah? Since when did you staht callin' him a horse's neck?" "I always called him one! He *is* one!" "Sure he is—but you didn't think so, did you, that first year that you was heah? You was pallin' around wit' him an' wouldn't have anything to do wit' the rest of us! You thought it was goin' to get you somewhere, didn't you? You saw how quick he dropped you after he got in wit' those guys at Christ's! He gave you the big go-by then, didn't he? That's when you stahted callin' him a horse's neck!" "It's a lie! I didn't!" "Sure you did!"

The snarling medley of bitter tongues rose, mounted; they vented their weight of insult, misery, and reproach on one another and at length subsided, checked by exhaustion rather than by some more charitable cause. And as the tumult died away Sterling, two spots of color burning on his pallid face, goaded completely from his former affectation of coldly elegant disdain, could be heard saying to Fried in a high, excited, almost hysterical tone:

"The kind of attack you make is simply stupid! It doesn't get you anywhere! And it's so crude! So raucous! After all, there's no reason why you've always got to be so raucous!"—the way he said the word was "raw-kus," his thin hands were trembling, and the two spots of color burned fiercely in his thin pale face; in this and the bitter way in which he said "raucous" there was finally something pitiable and futile.

And at the end, when all their strident cries had died away, the dark embittered visage of the Jew surveyed them wearily, and held them in its sway again. For as if conceding now what was most evident—that his savage, disappointed spirit had a hard integrity, an unashamed conviction, an ugly, snarling but most open courage which they lacked, they sat there, and looked at him in silence, somehow conveying by that silence a sense of bitter and unwilling respect for him, a final admission of agreement and defeat.

And he, too, when he spoke now, spoke wearily, with a bitter resignation, as if he realized the futility of his victory over them, the futility of hurling further insults, oaths, and accusations at people who knew the bitter truth of his complaint as well as he.

"Nah!" he said quietly in a moment, with this same note of bitter, weary resignation in his voice. "To hell wit' it! W'at t' hell's the use of tryin' to pretend it isn't so? You guys all know the way things are! You come over here and you think you're sittin' pretty right on top of the world! You think these guys are goin' to throw their ahms around your neck and kiss you, because they love Americans so much! And what happens?" He laughed bitterly. "Are you telling *me*? Christ! You can stay here for three years and none of them will ever give a tumble to you! You can eat your heart out for all they care, and when you leave here you'll know no more about them than when you came. And what does it getcha? What's it all about? W'at t' hell do you get out of it that's so wonderful?"

"I thought," one of the first-year men suggested mildly, and a trifle piously, as if he were quoting one of the articles of faith, "that you were supposed to get out of it a better understanding of the relations between the two great English-speaking nations."

"The two great English-speaking nations," Fried answered harshly with a jeering laugh. "Jesus! That's a good one! *What* two English-speaking nations do you mean?" he went on belligerently. "England and what other country?" he demanded. "You don't think *we* speak the same language as *they* do, do you? Christ! The first year I was here they might have been talkin' Siamese so far as I was concerned! It wasn't any language that I'd evah hoid before. . . . Yeah, I know," he went on wearily in a moment, "they fed me all that bunk, too, before I came over. . . . English-speakin' nations! . . . Goin' back to your old home! our old home. For Christ's sake!" he said bitterly. "Christ! It never was a home to me! I'd have felt more at home if they had sent me to Siberia! . . . Home! The rest of you guys can make believe it's home if you want to! . . . I know what you'll do," he muttered. "You'll stick it out and hate it like the rest of them. . . . Then you'll go back home an' high-hat every one and tell them all how wonderful it was, and what a fine time you had when you were here, and how you hated to leave it! . . . Not for me! I'm goin' home where I can see some one that I know sometime who's not too good to talk to me. . . and talk to some one who understands what I'm tryin' to say once in a while . . . and pay my little nickel for the big ride in the subway . . . and listen to the kids playin' in the street . . . an' go to sleep wit' the old elevated bangin' in my ears! . . . That's home!" he cried. "That's home enough for me."

"A hell of a home," said some one quietly.

"Don't I know it!" snarled the man. "But it's the only home I got! It's better than no home at all!"

And for a moment he smoked darkly, bitterly, in silence.

"Nah! To hell wit' it!" he muttered. "To hell wit' it! I'll be glad when it's all over! I'm sorry that I ever came!"

And he was silent then, and the others looked at him, and had no more to say, and were silent.

LXXII

THERE were four in the Coulson family: the father, a man of fifty years, the mother, somewhere in the middle forties, a son, and a daughter, Edith, a girl of twenty-two who lived in the house with her parents. Eugene never met the son: he had completed his course at Oxford a year or two before, and had gone down to London where he was now employed. During the time Eugene lived there the son did not come home.

They were a ruined family. How that ruin had fallen on them, what it was, Eugene never knew, for no one ever spoke to him about them. But the sense of their disgrace, of a shameful inexpiable dishonor, for which there was no pardon, from which there could never be redemption, was overwhelming. In the most astonishing way Eugene found out about it right away, and yet he did not know what they had done, and no one ever spoke a word against them.

Rather, the mention of their name brought silence, and in that silence there was something merciless and final, something that belonged to the temper of the country, and that was far more terrible than any open word of scorn, contempt, or bitter judgment could have been, more savage than a million strident, whispering, or abusive tongues could be, because the silence was unarguable, irrevocable, complete, as if a great door had been shut against their lives forever.

Everywhere Eugene went in town, the people knew about them, and said nothing—saying everything—when he spoke their names. He found this final, closed, relentless silence everywhere—in tobacco, wine, and tailor shops, in book stores, food stores, haberdashery stores—wherever he bought anything and gave the clerk the address to which it was to be delivered, they responded instantly with this shut finality of silence, writing the name down gravely, sometimes saying briefly, "Oh! Coulson's!" when he gave them the address, but more often saying nothing.

But whether they spoke or simply wrote the name down without a word, there was always this quality of instant recognition, this obdurate, contemptuous finality of silence, as if a door had been shut—a door that could never again be opened. Somehow Eugene disliked them more for this silence than if they had spoken evilly: there was in it something ugly, knowing, and triumphant that was far more evil than any slyly whispering confidence of slander, or any open vituperation of abuse, could be. It seemed somehow to come from all the vile and uncountable small maggotry of the earth, the cautious little hatreds of a million nameless ciphers, each puny, pallid, trivial in himself, but formidable because he added his tiny beetle's ball of dung to the mountainous accumulation of ten million others of his breed.

It was uncanny how these clerk-like faces, grave and quiet, that never spoke a word, or gave a sign, or altered their expression by a jot, when

Eugene gave them the address, could suddenly be alive with something secret, foul, and sly, could be more closed and secret than a door, and yet instantly reveal the naked, shameful, and iniquitous filth that welled up from some depthless source. He could not phrase it, give a name to it, or even see a certain sign that it was there, any more than he could put his hand upon a wisp of fading smoke, but he always knew when it was there, and somehow when he saw it his heart went hard and cold against the people who revealed it, and turned with warmth and strong affection towards the Coulson family.

There was, finally, among these grave clerk-like faces, one face that Eugene could never forget thereafter, a face that seemed to resume into its sly suave surfaces all of the nameless abomination of evil in the world, for which he had no name, for which there was no handle he could grasp, no familiar places or edges he could get his hands upon, which slid phantasmally, oilily, and smokily away whenever he tried to get his hands upon it. But it was to haunt his life for years in dreams of hatred, madness, and despair that found no frontal wall for their attack, no word for their vituperation, no door for the shoulder of his hate—an evil world of phantoms, shapes, and whispers that was yet as real as death, as ever-present as man's treachery, but that slid away from him like smoke whenever he tried to meet, or curse, or strangle it.

This face was the face of a man in a tailor shop, a fitter there, and Eugene could have battered that foul face into a bloody pulp, distilled the filthy refuse of that ugly life out of the fat swelling neck and through the murderous grip of his fingers if he could only have found a cause, a logic, and a provocation for doing it. And yet he never saw the man but twice, and briefly, and there had been nothing in his suave, sly careful speech to give offense.

Edith Coulson had sent Eugene to the tailor's shop: he needed a suit and when he asked her where to go to have it made, she had sent him to this place because her brother had his suits made there and liked it. The fitter was a heavy shambling man in his late thirties: he had receding hair, which he brushed back flat in a thick pompadour; yellowish, somewhat bulging eyes; a coarse heavy face, loose-featured, red, and sensual; a sloping meaty jaw, and large discolored buck-teeth which showed unpleasantly in a mouth that was always half open. It was, in fact, the mouth that gave his face its sensual, sly, and ugly look, for a loose and vulgar smile seemed constantly to hover about its thick coarse edges, to be deliberately, slyly restrained, but about to burst at any moment into

an open, evil, foully sensual laugh. There was always about his mouth
this ugly suggestion of a loose, corrupt, and evilly jubilant mirth, and
yet he never laughed or smiled.

The man's speech had this same quality. It was suave and courteous,
but even in its most urbane assurances, there was something non-committal, sly, and jeering, something that slid away from you, and was
never to be grasped, a quality that was faithless, tricky and unwholesome. When Eugene came for the final fitting it was obvious that he
had done as cheap and shoddy a job as he could do; the suit was vilely
botched and skimped, sufficient cloth had not been put into it, and
now it was too late to remedy the defect.

Yet, the fitter gravely pulled the vest down till it met the trousers,
tugged at the coat, and pulled the thing together where it stayed until
Eugene took a breath or moved a muscle, when it would all come apart
again, the collar bulging outward from the shoulder, the skimpy coat
and vest crawling backward from the trousers, leaving a hiatus of shirt
and belly that could not now be remedied by any means.

Then, gravely he would pull the thing together again, and in his suave,
yet oily, sly, and non-committal phrases say:

"Um! Seems to fit you very well."

Eugene was choking with exasperation, and knew that he had been
done, because he had foolishly paid them half the bill already, and now
knew no way out of it except to lose what he had paid, and get nothing
for it, or take the thing, and pay the balance. He was caught in a trap,
but even as he jerked at the coat and vest speechlessly, seized his shirt,
and thrust the gaping collar in the fitter's face, the man said smoothly,

"Um! Yes! The collar. Should think all that will be all right. Still
needs a little alteration." He made some chalk marks on Eugene.
"Should think you'll find it fits you very well when the tailor makes the
alterations."

"When will the suit be ready?"

"Um. Should think you ought to have it by next Tuesday. Yes. I
think you'll find it ready by Tuesday."

The sly words slid away from the boy like oil: there was nothing to
pin him to or grasp him by, the yellowed eyes looked casually away and
would not look at Eugene, the sensual face was suavely grave, the discolored buck-teeth shone obscenely through the coarse loose mouth, and
the suggestion of the foul loose smile was so pronounced now that it
seemed that at any moment the man would have to turn away with

heavy trembling shoulders, and stifle the evil jeering laugh that was
welling up in him. But he remained suavely grave and non-committal
to the end, and when Eugene asked him if he should come again to try
it on, he said, in the same oily tone, never looking at him:

"Um. Shouldn't think that would be necessary. Could have it delivered to you when it's ready. What is your address?"

"The Far End Farm—it's on the Ventnor Road."

"Oh! Coulson's!" He never altered his expression, but the suggestion
of the obscene smile was so pronounced that now it seemed he would
have to come out with it. Instead, he only said:

"Um. Yes. Should think it could be delivered to you there on
Tuesday. If you'll just wait a moment I'll ask the tailor."

Gravely, suavely, he took the coat from Eugene and walked back
towards the tailor's room with the coat across his arm. In a moment,
the boy heard sly voices whispering, laughing slyly, then the tailor saying:

"Where does he live?"

"Coulson's!" said the fitter chokingly, and now the foul awaited laugh
did come—high, wet, slimy, it came out of that loose mouth, and
choked and whispered wordlessly, and choked again, and mingled then
with the tailor's voice in sly, choking, whispering intimacy, and then
gasped faintly, and was silent. When the man came out again his coarse
face was red and swollen with foul secret merriment, his heavy shoulders
trembled slightly, he took out his handkerchief and wiped it once
across his loose half-opened mouth, and with that gesture wiped the
slime of laughter from his lips. Then he came toward Eugene suave,
grave, and courteous, evilly composed, as he said smoothly:

"Should think we'll have that for you by next Tuesday, sir."

"Can the tailor fix it so it's going to fit?"

"Um. Should think you'll find that everything's all right. You ought
to have it Tuesday afternoon."

He was not looking at Eugene: the yellowish bulging eyes were
staring casually, indefinitely, away, and his words again had slid away
from the boy like oil. He could not be touched, approached, or handled:
there was nothing to hold him by, he had the impregnability of smoke
or a ball of mercury.

As Eugene went out the door, the tailor began to speak to some one in
the shop, Eugene heard low words and whispered voices, then, gasping,
the word "Coulson's!" and the slimy, choking, smothered laughter as

the street-door closed behind him. He never saw the man again. He never forgot his face.

That was a fine house: the people in it were exiled, lost, and ruined people, and Eugene liked them all. Later, he never knew why he felt so close to them, or remembered them with such warmth and strong affection.

He did not see the Coulsons often and rarely talked to them. Yet he felt as familiar and friendly with them all as if he had known them all his life. The house was wonderful as no other house he had ever known because they all seemed to be living in it together with this strange speechless knowledge, warmth, and familiarity, and yet each was as private, secret, and secure in his own room as if he occupied the house alone.

Coulson himself Eugene saw least of all: they sometimes passed each other going in or out the door, or in the hall: Coulson would grunt "Morning," or "Good Day," in a curt blunt manner, and go on, and yet he always left Eugene with a curious sense of warmth and friendliness. He was a stocky well-set man with iron-gray hair, bushy eyebrows, and a red weathered face which wore the open color of the country on it, but also had the hard dull flush of the steady heavy drinker.

Eugene never saw him drunk, and yet he was never sober: he was one of those men who have drunk themselves past any hope of drunkenness, who are soaked through to the bone with alcohol, saturated, tanned, weathered in it so completely that it could never be distilled out of their blood again. Yet, even in this terrible excess one felt a kind of grim control—the control of a man who is enslaved by the very thing that he controls, the control of the opium eater who cannot leave his drug but measures out his dose with a cold calculation, and finds the limit of his capacity, and stops there, day by day.

But somehow this very sense of control, this blunt ruddy style of the country gentleman which distinguished his speech, his manner, and his dress, made the ruin of his life, the desperate intemperance of drink that smouldered in him like a slow fire, steadily, nakedly apparent. It was as if, having lost everything, he still held grimly to the outer forms of a lost standard, a ruined state, when the inner substance was destroyed.

And it was this way with all of them—with Mrs. Coulson and the girl, as well: their crisp, clipped friendly speech never deviated into intimacy, and never hinted at any melting into confidence and admission. Upon the woman's weathered face there hovered, when she talked, the same faint set grin that Captain Nicholl had, and her eyes were bright and hard, a little mad, impenetrable, as were his. And the girl, although young and very lovely, sometimes had this same look when she greeted any one or paused to talk. In that look there was nothing truculent, bitter, or defiant: it was just the look of three people who had gone down together, and who felt for one another neither bitterness nor hate, but that strange companionship of a common disgrace, from which love has vanished, but which is more secret, silent, and impassively resigned to its fatal unity than love itself could be.

And that hard bright look also said this plainly to the world: "We ask for nothing from you now, we want nothing that you offer us. What is ours is ours, what we are we are, you'll not intrude nor come closer than we let you see!"

Coulson might have been a man who had been dishonored and destroyed by his women, and who took it stolidly, saying nothing, and drank steadily from morning until night, and had nothing for it now but drink and silence and acceptance. Yet Eugene never knew for certain that this was so, it just seemed inescapable, and was somehow legible not only in the slow smouldering fire that burned out through his rugged weathered face, but also in the hard bright armor of the women's eyes, the fixed set grin around their lips when they were talking—a grin that was like armor, too. And Morison, who had referred to Coulson, chuckling, as a real "bottle-a-day-man," had added quietly, casually, in his brief, indefinite, but blurted-out suggestiveness of speech:

"I think the old girl's been a bit of a bitch in her day. . . . Don't know, of course, but has the look, hasn't she?" In a moment he said quietly, "Have you talked to the daughter yet?"

"Once or twice. Not for long."

"Ran into a chap at Magdalen other day who knows her," he said casually. "He used to come out here to see her." He glanced swiftly, slyly at Eugene, his face reddening a little with laughter. "Pretty hot, I gather," he said quietly, smiling, and looked away. It was night: the fire burned cheerfully in the grate, the hot coals spurting in small gaseous flares from time to time. The house was very quiet all around them. Outside they could hear the stormy wind in the trees along the road. Morison flicked his cigarette into the fire, poured out a drink of whiskey into a glass, saying as he did so: "I say, old chap, you don't mind if I take a spot of this before I go to bed, do you?" Then he shot some seltzer in the glass, and drank. And Eugene sat there, without a word, staring sullenly into the fire, dumbly conscious of the flood of sick pain and horror which the casual foulness of the man's suggestion had aroused, stubbornly trying to deny now that he was thinking of the girl all the time.

LXXIII

ONE night, as Eugene was coming home along the dark road that went up past the playing field to the house, and that was bordered on each side by grand trees whose branches seemed to hold at night all the mysterious and demented cadences of storm, he came upon her suddenly standing in the shadow of a tree. It was one of the grand wild nights that seemed to come so often in the autumn of that year: the air was full of a fine stinging moisture, not quite rain, and above the stormy branches of the trees he could see the sky, wild, broken, full of scudding clouds through which at times the moon drove in and out with a kind of haggard loneliness. By that faint, wild, and broken light, he could see the small white oval of the girl's face—somehow even more lovely now just because he could not see it plainly. And he could see as well the rough gleaming bark of the tree against which she leaned.

As he approached, he saw her thrust her hand into the pocket of her overcoat, a match flared, and for a moment he saw Edith plainly, the small flower of her face framed in the wavering light as she lowered her head to light her cigarette.

The light went out, he saw the small respiring glow of her cigarette before the white blur of her face, he passed her swiftly, head bent, without speaking, his heart filled with the sense of strangeness and wonder which the family had roused in him.

Then he walked on up the road, muttering to himself. The house was dark when he got there, but when he entered his sitting-room the place was still warmly and softly luminous with the glow of hot coals in the grate. He turned the lights on, shut the door behind him, and hurled several lumps of coal upon the bedded coals. In a moment the fire was blazing and crackling cheerfully, and getting a kind of comfort and satisfaction from this activity, he flung off his coat, went over to the sideboard, poured out a stiff drink of scotch from a bottle there, and coming back to the fire, flung himself into a chair, and began to stare sullenly into the dancing flames.

How long he sat there in this stupor of sullen and nameless fury, he did not know, but he was sharply roused at length by footsteps light and rapid on the gravel, shocked into a start of surprise by a figure that appeared suddenly at one of the French windows that opened directly from his sitting-room onto the level sward of velvet lawn before the house.

He peered through the glass for a moment with an astonished stare before he recognized the face of Edith Coulson. He opened the doors at once, she came in quickly, smiling at his surprise, and at the glass which he was holding foolishly, half-raised, in his hand.

He continued to look at her with an expression of gape-mouthed astonishment and in a moment became conscious of her smiling glance, the cool sweet assurance of her young voice.

"I say!" she was saying cheerfully, "what a lucky thing to find you up! I came away without any key—I should have had to wake the whole house up—so when I saw your light!" she concluded briskly, "—what luck! I hope you don't mind."

"Why no-o, no," Eugene stammered foolishly, still staring dumbly at her. "No—no-o—not at all," he blundered on. Then suddenly coming to himself with a burst of galvanic energy, he shut the windows, pushed another chair before the fire, and said:

"Won't you sit down and have a drink before you go?"

"Thanks," she said crisply. "I will—yes. What a jolly fire you have." As she talked she took off her coat and hat swiftly and put them on a chair. Her face was flushed and rosy, beaded with small particles of rain, and for a moment she stood before the mirror arranging her hair, which had been tousled by the wind.

The girl was slender, tall, and very lovely with the kind of beauty they have when they are beautiful—a beauty so fresh, fair, and delicate that it seems to be given to just a few of them to compensate for all the grimly weathered ugliness of the rest. Her voice was also lovely, sweet, and musical, and when she talked all the notes of tenderness and love were in it. But she had the same hard bright look in her eye that her mother had, the faint set smile around her mouth: as they stood there talking she was standing very close to him, and he could smell the fragrance of her hair, and felt an intolerable desire to put his hand upon hers and was almost certain she would not draw away. But the hard bright look was in her eye, the faint set smile around her mouth, and he did nothing.

"What'll you have?" Eugene said. "Whiskey?"

"Yes, thank you," she said with the same sweet crisp assurance with which she always spoke, "and a splash of soda." He struck a match and held it for her while she lit the cigarette she was holding in her hand, and in a moment returned to her with the drink. Then she sat down, crossed her legs, and for a moment puffed thoughtfully at her cigarette as she stared into the fire. The storm wind moaned in the great trees along the road, and near the house, and suddenly a swirl of rain and wind struck the windows with a rattling blast. The girl stirred a little in her chair, restlessly, shivered:

"Listen!" she said. "What a night! Horrible weather we have here, isn't it?"

"I don't know. I don't like the fog and rain so well. But this—the way it is tonight—" he nodded toward the window— "I like it."

She looked at him for a moment.

"Oh," she said non-committally. "You do." Then, as she sipped her drink, she looked curiously about the room, her reflective glance finally resting on his table, where there was a great stack of the ledgers in which he wrote.

"I say," she cried again, "what are you doing with all those big books there?"

"I write in them."

"Really?" she said, in a surprised tone. "I should think it'd be an awful bother carrying them around when you travel?"

"It is. But it's the best way I've found of keeping what I do together."

"Oh," she said, as before, and continued to stare curiously at him with her fair, lovely young face, the curiously hard, bright, and unrevealing glance of her eye. "I see. . . . But why do you come to such a place as this to write?" she said presently. "Do you like it here?"

"I do. As well as any place I've ever known."

"Oh! . . . I should think a writer would want a different kind of place."

"What kind?"

"Oh—I don't know—Paris—London—some place like that, where there is lots of life—people—fun—I should think you'd work better in a place like that."

"I work better here."

"But don't you get awfully fed up sitting in here all day long and writing in those enormous books?"

"I do, yes."

"I should think you would . . . I should think you'd want to get away from it sometimes."

"Yes. I do want to—every day—almost all the time."

"Then why don't you?" she said crisply. "Why don't you go off some week-end for a little spree? I should think it'd buck you up no end."

"It would—yes. Where should I go?"

"Oh, Paris, I suppose. . . . Or London! London!" she cried. "London is quite jolly if you know it."

"I'm afraid I don't know it."

"But you've *been* to London," she said in a surprised tone.

"Oh, yes. I lived there for several months."

"Then you know London," she said impatiently. "Of course you do."

"I'm afraid I don't know it very well. I don't know many people there—and after all, that's the thing that counts, isn't it?"

She looked at Eugene curiously for a moment, with the faint hard smile around the edges of her lovely mouth.

"—Should think that might be arranged," she said with a quiet, an enigmatic humor. Then, more directly, she added. "That shouldn't be difficult at all. Perhaps I could introduce you to some people."

"That would be fine. Do you know many people there?"

"Not many," she said. "I go there—whenever I can." She got up with a swift decisive movement, put her glass down on the mantel and cast her cigarette into the fire. Then she faced Eugene, looking at him with a curiously bold, an almost defiant directness, and she fixed him with this glance for a full moment before she spoke.

"Good-night," she said. "Thanks awfully for letting me in—and for the drink."

"Good-night," Eugene said, and she was gone before he could say more, and he had closed the door behind her, and he could hear her light swift footsteps going down the hall and up the steps. And then there was nothing in the house but sleep and silence, and storm and darkness in the world around him.

Mrs. Coulson came into Eugene's room just once or twice while he was there. One morning she came in, spoke crisply and cheerfully, and walked over to the window, looking out upon the velvet lawn and at the dreary, impenetrable gray of foggy air. Although the room was warm, and there was a good fire burning in the grate, she clasped her arms together as she looked, and shivered a little:

"Wretched weather, isn't it?" she said in her crisp tones, her gaunt weathered face, and toothy mouth touched by the faint fixed grin as she looked out with her bright hard stare. "Don't you find it frightfully depressing? Most Americans do," she said, getting a sharp disquieting sound into the word.

"Yes. I do, a little. We don't have this kind of weather very often. But this is the time of year you get it here, isn't it? I suppose you're used to it by now?"

"Used to it?" she said crisply, turning her gaze upon him. "Not at all. I've known it all my life but I'll never get used to it. It is a wretched climate."

"Still, you wouldn't feel at home anywhere else, would you? You wouldn't want to live outside of England?"

"No?" she said, staring at him with the faint set grin around her toothy mouth. "Why do you think so?"

"Because your home is here."

"My home? My home is where they have fine days, and where the sun is always shining."

"I wouldn't like that. I'd get tired of sunlight all the time. I'd want some gray days and some fog and snow."

"Yes, I suppose you would. But then, you've been used to having fine days all your life, haven't you? With us, it's different. I'm so fed up with fog and rain that I could do without it nicely, thank you, if I never saw it again. . . . . I don't think you could ever understand how much the sunlight means to us," she said slowly. She turned, and for a moment looked out the window. "Sunlight—warmth—fine days forever! Warmth everywhere—in the earth, the sky, in the lives of the people all around you, nothing but warmth and sunlight and fine days!"

"And where would you go to find all that? Does it exist?"

"Oh, of course!" she said crisply and good-naturedly, turning to him again. "There's only one place to live—only one country where I want to live."

"Where is that?"

"Italy," she said. "That's my real home. . . . I'd live the rest of my life there if I could." For a moment longer she looked out the window, then turned briskly, saying:

"Why don't you run over to Paris some week-end? After all, it's only seven hours from London: if you left here in the morning you'd be there in time for dinner. It would be a good change for you. I should think a little trip like that would buck you up tremendously."

Her words gave him a wonderful feeling of confidence and hope: she had travelled a great deal, and she had the casual, assured way of speaking of a voyage that made it seem very easy, and filled one with a sense of joy and adventure when she spoke about it. When Eugene tried to think of Paris by himself it had seemed very far away and hard to reach: London stood between it and him, and when he thought of the huge smoky web of London, the soft gray skies above him, and the enormous weight of lives that were hidden somewhere in that impenetrable fog, a gray desolation and weariness of the spirit filled him. It seemed to him that he must draw each breath of that soft gray air with heavy weary effort, and that every mile of his journey would be a ghastly struggle through some viscous and material substance, that weighted down his steps, and filled his heart with desolation.

But when Mrs. Coulson spoke to him about it, suddenly it all seemed wonderfully easy and good. England was magically small, the channel to be taken in a stride, and all the thrill, the joy, the mystery of Paris his again—the moment that he chose to make it his.

He looked at her gaunt weathered face, the hard bright armor of her eyes, and wondered how anything so clear, so sharp, so crisp, and so incisive could have been shaped and grown underneath these soft and humid skies that numbed him, mind and heart and body, with their thick dull substance of gray weariness and desolation.

A day or two before he left, Edith came into his room one afternoon bearing a tray with tea and jam and buttered bread. He was sitting in his chair before the fire, and had his coat off: when she came in he scrambled to his feet, reached for the coat and started to put it on. In her young crisp voice she told him not to, and put the tray down on the table, saying that the maid was having her afternoon off.

Then for a moment she stood looking at him with her faint and enigmatic smile.

"So you're leaving us?" she said presently.

"Yes. Tomorrow."

"And where will you go from here?" she said.

"To Germany, I think. Just for a short time—two or three weeks."

"And after that?"

"I'm going home."

"Home?"

"Back to America."

"Oh," she said slowly. "I see." In a moment, she added, "We shall miss you."

He wanted to talk to her more than he had ever wanted to talk to any one in his life, but when he spoke, all that he could say, lamely, muttering, was:

"I'll miss you, too."

"Will you?" She spoke so quietly that he could scarcely hear her. "I wonder for how long?" she said.

"Forever," he said, flushing miserably at the sound of the word, and yet not knowing any other word to say.

The faint hard smile about her mouth was a little deeper when she spoke again.

"Forever? That's a long time, when one is young as you," she said.

"I mean it. I'll never forget you as long as I live."

"We shall remember you," she said quietly. "And I hope you think of us sometime—back here, buried, lost, in all the fog and rain and ruin of England. How good it must be to know that you are young in a young country—where nothing that you did yesterday matters very much. How wonderful it must be to know that none of the failure of the past can pull you down—that there will always be another day for you—a new beginning. I wonder if you Americans will ever know how fortunate you are," the girl said.

"And yet you couldn't leave all this?" Eugene said with a kind of desperate hope. "This old country you've lived in, known all your life. A girl like you could never leave a place like this to live the kind of life we have in America."

"*Couldn't* I?" she said with a quiet but unmistakable passion of conviction. "There's nothing I'd like better."

Eugene stared at her blindly, dumbly for a moment; suddenly all that he wanted to say, and had not been able to say, found release in a movement of his hands. He gripped her by the shoulders and pulled her to him, and began to plead with her:

"Then why don't you? I'll take you there!—Look here—" his words were crazy and he knew it, but as he spoke them, he believed all he said

—"Look here! I haven't got much money—but in America you can make it if you want to! I'm going back there. You come, too—I'll take you when I go!"

She had not tried to free herself; she just stood there passive, unresisting, as he poured that frenzied proposal in her ears. Now, with the same passive and unyielding movement, the bright armor of her young eyes, she stepped away, and stood looking at him silently for a moment. Then slowly, with an almost imperceptible movement, she shook her head. "Oh, you'll forget all about us," she said quietly. "You'll forget about our lives here—buried in fog—and rain—and failure—and defeat."

"Failure and defeat won't last forever."

"Sometimes they do," she said with a quiet finality that froze his heart.

"Not for you—they won't!" Eugene said, and took her by the hand again with desperate entreaty. "Listen to me—" he blundered on incoherently, with the old feeling of nameless shame and horror. "You don't need to tell me what it is—I don't want to know—but whatever it is—for you, it doesn't matter—you can get the best of it."

She said nothing, but just looked at him through that hard bright armor of her eyes, the obdurate finality of her smile.

"Good-bye," she said, "I'll not forget you either." She looked at him for a moment curiously before she spoke again. "I wonder," she said slowly, "if you'll ever understand just what it was you did for me by coming here?"

"What was it?"

"You opened a door that I thought had been closed forever," she said, "a door that let me look in on a world I thought I should never see again—a new bright world, a new life and a new beginning—for us all. And I thought that was something which would never happen to any one in this house again."

"It will to you," Eugene said, and took her hand again with desperate eagerness. "It can happen to you whenever you want it to. It's yours, I'll swear it to you, if you'll only speak."

She looked at him, with an almost imperceptible movement of her head.

"I tell you I know what I'm talking about."

Again she shook her head.

"You don't know," she said. "You're young. You're an American. There are some things you'll never be old enough to know.—For some of us there's no return.—Go back," she said, "go back to the life you know—the life you understand—where there can always be a new beginning—a new life."

"And you—" Eugene said dumbly, miserably.

"Good-bye, my dear," she said so low and gently he could scarcely hear her. "Think of me sometimes, won't you—I'll not forget you." And before he could speak she kissed him once and was gone, so light and swift that he did not know it, until the door had closed behind her. And for some time, like a man in a stupor, he stood there looking out the window at the gray wet light of England.

The next day he went away, and never saw any of them again, but he could not forget them. Although he had never passed beyond the armor of their hard bright eyes, or breached the wall of their crisp, friendly, and impersonal speech, or found out anything about them, he always thought of them with warmth, with a deep and tender affection, as if he had always known them—as if, somehow, he could have lived with them or made their lives his own had he only said a word, or turned the handle of a door—a word he never knew, a door he never found.

LXXIV

THE day before he went away, the Rhodes scholars invited Eugene to lunch. That was a fine meal: they ate together in their rooms in college, they had opened their purses to the college chef, and had told him not to spare himself but to go the limit. Before the meal they drank together a bottle of good sherry wine, and as they ate they drank the college ale, strong, brown, and mellow, and when they came to coffee, they all finished off on a bottle of port apiece.

There was a fine thick seasonable soup, of the color of mahogany, and then a huge platter piled high with delicate brown-golden portions of filet of sole, and a roast of mutton, tender, fragrant, juicy and delicious as no other mutton that Eugene had ever eaten, with red currant jelly, well-seasoned sprouts, and boiled potatoes, to go with it, and at the end a fine apple-tart, thick cream, sharp cheese, and crackers.

It was a fine meal, and when they finished with it they were all happy and exultant. They were beautifully drunk and happy, with that golden, warm, full-bodied and most lovely drunkenness that can come only from good rich wine and mellow ale and glorious and abundant food—a state that we recognize instantly when it comes to us as one of the rare, the priceless, the unarguable joys of living, something stronger than philosophy, a treasure on which no price can be set, a sufficient reward for all the anguish, weariness, and disappointment of living, and a far better teacher than Aquinas ever was.

They were all young men and when they had finished they were drunk, glorious, and triumphant as only young men can be. It seemed to them now that they could do no wrong, or make no error, and that the whole earth was a pageantry of delight which had been shaped solely for their happiness, possession, and success. The Rhodes scholars no longer felt the old fear, confusion, loneliness, and bitter inferiority and desolation of the soul which they had felt since coming there.

The beauty, age, and grandeur of the life about them were revealed as they had never been before, their own fortune in living in such a place seemed impossibly good and happy, nothing in this life around them now seemed strange or alien, and they all felt that they were going to win, and make their own, a life among the highest and most fortunate people on the earth.

As for Eugene, he now thought of his departure exultantly, and with intolerable desire, not from some joy of release, but because everything around him now seemed happy, glorious, and beautiful, and a token of unspeakable joys that were to come, a thousand images of trains, of the small rich-colored joy and comfort and precision of their trains, of England, lost in fog, and swarming with its forty million lives, but suddenly not dreary, but impossibly small, and beautiful and near, to be taken at a stride, to be compassed at a bound, to enrich him, fill him, be his forever in all its joy and mystery and magic smallness.

And he thought of the huge smoky web of London with this same joy: of the suave potent ale he could get in one place there, of its squares, and ancient courts, and age-grimed mysteries, and of the fog-numb strangeness of ten million passing men and women. He thought of the swift rich projectile of the channel train, the quays, the channel boats, and darkness, night, the sudden onslaught of the savage choppy seas outside the harbor walls, and England fading, and the flashing beacon lights of France, the quays again, the little swarming figures, the excited tongues, the strange dark faces of the Frenchmen, the always-alien, magic, time-enchanted strangeness of the land, the people, and the faces; and then Paris, the nostalgic, subtle and incomparably exciting fabric of its life, its flavor, and its smell, the strange opiate of its time, the rediscovery of its food, its drink, the white, carnal, and luxurious bodies of the whores.

They were all exultant, wild, full of joy and hope and invincible belief as they thought of all these things and all the glory and the mystery that the world held treasured for their taking in the depths of its illimitable resources; and they shouted, sang, shook hands and roared with laughter, and had no doubts, or fears, or dark confusions, as they had done in other, younger, and more certain times.

Then they started out across the fields behind the colleges, and the fields were wet and green, the trees smoky-gray and blurred in magic veils of bluish mist, and the worn path felt, looked, and seemed incredibly familiar, like a field they had crossed, a path they had trod, a million times. And at length they came to their little creek-wise river, their full, flowing little river of dark time and treasured history, their quiet, narrow, deeply flowing little river, uncanny in the small perfection of its size, as it went past soundlessly among the wet fresh green of the fields that hemmed it with a sweet, kept neatness of perfection.

Then, having crossed, they went up along the river path until they came to where the crews were waiting—the Merton crew before, another college crew behind, and the students of both colleges clustered eagerly on the path beside their boats, exhorting their comrades in the shell, waiting for the signal that would start the race.

Then, even as the Rhodes scholars pounded on Eugene's back and roared at him with an exuberant affection that "You've got to run with us! You've got to root for us! You belong to Merton now!" the starting-gun cracked out, the crews bent furiously to their work, the long blades bit frantically the cold gray water, and the race was on. And they were racing lightly, nimbly now, two packs of young men running on the path, each yelping cries of sharp encouragement to his crew as he ran on beside it.

At first, as Eugene ran, he felt strong and lithe and eager. He was aware of an aerial buoyancy: his step was light, his stride was long and easy, his breath came softly, without labor, and the swift feet of the running boys thudded before, behind, around him, on the hard path, pleasantly, and he was secure in his strength and certitude again, and thought that he was one of them, and could run with them to the end of the world and back, and never feel it.

He thought he had recovered all the lean sinew and endurance of a boy, that the storm-swift flight, the speed, the hard condition, and resilient effort of a boy were his again, that he had never lost them, that they had never changed. Then a leaden heaviness began to steal along his limbs, he felt the weariness of effort for the first time, a thickening slowness in the muscles of his legs, a numb weight-like heaviness tingling at his finger-tips, and now he no longer looked so sharply and so smartly at the swinging crew below him, the nimbly running boys around him.

He began to pound ahead with dogged and deliberate effort, and his heart was pounding like a hammer at his ribs, his breath was laboring hoarsely in his throat and his tongue felt numb and thick and swollen in his mouth, and blind motes were swimming drunkenly before his eyes. He could hear his voice, unfamiliar and detached, weirdly unreal, as if some one else were speaking in him, as it panted hoarsely:

"Come on, Merton! . . . Come on, Merton! . . . Come on, Merton!"

And now the nimbler running footsteps all around him had passed, had gone ahead of him, had vanished. He could no longer see the crews nor know if they were there. He ran on blindly, desperately, hearing, seeing, saying nothing any longer, an anguished leaden creature, weighted down with a million leaden hours and weary efforts, pounding heavily, blindly, mindlessly along, beneath gray timeless skies of an immortal weariness, across the gray barren earth of some huge planetary vacancy—where there was neither shade nor stay nor shelter, where there would never be a resting place, a room, nor any door which he could enter, and where he must pound blindly, wearily along, alone, through that huge vacancy forever.

Then voices swarmed around him once again, and he could feel strong hands on him. They seized him, stopped him, and familiar faces swarmed forward at him through those swimming motes of blind gray vacancy. He could hear again the hoarse ghost-unreality of his own voice panting: "Come on, Merton!" and see his friends again, now grinning, laughing, shouting, as they shook him. "Stop! The race is over! Merton won!"

LXXV

THEIR names were Octave Feuillet, Alfred Capus, and Maurice Donnay; their names were Hermant, Courteline, and René Bazin; their names were Jules Renard, Marcelle Tinayre, and André Theuriet; and Clarétie, and Frapié and Tristan Bernard; and de Régnier and

Paul Reboux, and Lavedan; their names were Rosny, Gyp, Boylesve, and Richepin; their names were Bordeaux, Prévost, Margueritte, and Duvernois—their names, Great God, their names were countless as the sands upon the shore—and in the end, their names were only names and names and names—and nothing more.

Or, if their names were something more than names—if they sometimes shaped themselves in his mind as personalities—these personalities were faded, graceful, and phantasmal ones—each talented and secure in his position, and curiously alike—each brave and good and gentle in his trade, like lesser-known knights of the Round Table. He knew that few of them had been the hero of a generation, the leader of a century; he knew that none of them had rivalled Balzac, surpassed Stendhal, out-done Flaubert. And for this reason, their vague, phantasmal company became more haunting-strange to him than if they had.

He knew, as well, that there must be among them great differences of talent, great differences of style. His reason told him that some were good, and some were fair, and some were only cheap; even his meagre understanding of their tongue showed him that there was a great range, every kind of difference in their choice and treatment of a subject—a range that swept from the gracefully ironic sentiment of *Les Vacances d'un Jeune Homme Sage* to the stern earth-and-peasant austerity of *Le Blé qui lève;* from the dream nostalgia of *Le Passé Vivant* to the salty and difficult drolleries of *Messieurs les Ronds-de-Cuir* or *Le Train de 8h 47.*

He knew that each of these men must have had his own style, his special quality which would instantly be discerned and appraised by a French reader—he knew that some had written of the quiet life of the provinces, and that others wrote of the intrigue, the love affairs, the worldly and sophisticated gentry, of Paris; he knew that some were writers of a graceful sentiment, some delicately ironic, some drolly comic, some savagely satiric, and some grimly tragic.

But all of them seemed to come from the same place, to have the same quality, to evoke the same perfume. They were the vague and shadowy figures of a charming, beautiful, and legendary kind of life—a life that was all the more legendary to him because he was constantly groping with half-meanings, filling in his faulty understanding of the language with painful intuitions, tearing desperately at the contents of unnumbered volumes, with a tortured hunger of frustration, an aching brain, a dictionary in one hand, and one of these slick and flimsy little volumes in another.

And for this reason, perhaps, as much as any other—because óf this savage struggle with an alien tongue, this agonizing, half-intuitive effort by which he groped his way to understanding through a book— the books themselves, and these graceful and shadowy figures who produced them, took on a quality that was as strange as the whole experience of these first weeks in Paris had become. Indeed, in later years, the legendary quality of his savage conflict with this world of print became indistinguishably mixed with the legendary quality of the life around him. Perhaps, even the swift, graceful, and fascinating little drawings and illustrations which dotted the pages of these books were in some measure responsible for this illusion: the pictures gave to the hard and difficult pages of a thousand fictions the illusion of an actual reality: in these little pictures he could see and recognize a thousand things that had already grown familiar to him—the narrow sidewalks and the tall and ancient houses of the Latin Quarter, the bridges of the Seine, the interior of a railway compartment, the great grilled gate of a château, people sitting at the tables in a café or on the terrace, the walls, the roofs, the chimney-pots of Paris which, no matter what changes had come about in human costume, feminine fashions, top-hats, frock-coats, or facial whiskerage, had themselves changed very little.

The most extraordinary and vividly imagined phenomenon of his desperate struggle to understand these innumerable fictions was this: Although his reason told him that all these men—all these phantasmal and haunting names—Feuillet, Capus, Donnay, Tinayre, Boylesve, Bazin, Theuriet—and all the rest of them—must have known all the sweat and anguish of hard labor, the solicitude, the grinding effort, and the desperate patience, that every artist knows, he became obsessed, haunted with the idea that the works of all this graceful, strange, and fortunate company were written without effort, with the most superb casualness and ease. It was his strange delusion that all of them were not only of an equal talent—could do all kinds of writing equally well and with equal ease—but that the reason for this marvellous endowment lay somehow in the fact that they were "French"—that by the fortunate accident of race and birth each one had somehow been constituted an artist who could do all things gracefully and well, and could do nothing wrong. Favored at birth by the great inheritance of their language, blood, and temperament, they grew up as children of a beautiful, strange, and legendary civilization whose very tongue was a guaranty of style, whose very tradition an assurance of form. These men could write nothing badly because it was not within the blood and nature of their race to do so: they must do everything gracefully, easily, and with an impeccable sense of form, because grace and ease and form were innate to them.

Finally, the most extraordinary fact of this curious obsession was his belief that all these books had been written by their authors not in the stern and lonely solitude of some midnight room, but swiftly, casually, and easily, as one might write a letter at the table of a café.

The obsession was so strong that he could see them writing at such a place—Feuillet, Capus, Donnay, Bazin—all the rest of them, each seated in the afternoon at his own inviolable table in his favorite café, each with a writing pad, a pen and ink before him, a half-emptied bock or glass of wine beside him, an adoring and devoted old waiter hovering anxiously near him—each writing steadily, rapidly, and gracefully the pages of some new and faultless story, some graceful, perfect book, filling up page after page of manuscript in their elegant, fine handwriting. without erasures or deletions, pausing thoughtfully from time to time to stare dreamily away, stroking their lank, disordered hair, their elegant French whiskers with a thin white hand, and so far from being distracted by the gaiety, the noise and clatter of the café crowd around them, deriving a renewed vitality from its sparkling stimulation, and returning to fill up page after page again.

And he could see them meeting every afternoon—that band of Bohemian immortality, that fortunate and favored company of art that could do no wrong—in some café on the Boulevards, or in some quiet, gracious old place hallowed by their patronage, in the Latin Quarter, in Montparnasse, or on the Boul St. Mich or in Montmartre.

He saw the whole scene with a blazing imagery, an exact detail, as if he had himself been present and seen and heard it all. He could hear the spirited light clamor of their conversation—like everything they did, gracious, faultless, full of ease—could see them rise to greet their famous comrades—whoever they might be—Feuillet, Capus, or Donnay, all the rest of them—could see them shake hands with the swift, firm greeting, so graceful, worldly, and so French, and hear them saying:

"Ah, my dear Maurice—how goes it with you? But—I see that I disturb you—pardon, my friend!—I see that you are busy with another of

your admirable tales—Ah-h, my old one, not for the world would I
disturb the flow of your so admirable genius. Parbleu! Do I wish my
wretched name to become infamous to all posterity, to be heard with
execration—ah, the devil! Non! The black forgetfulness of the grave is
better! Eh, well, then, old comrade, till tomorrow—*Then* I hope——"

"Ah, but no, but no, but no, but no, but no! My dear Octave, you
shall remain! These pages here!—Pouf! it is nothing! I am already
done—Attend!" Swiftly he scrawls a line or two, and then triumphantly:
"Voilà! C'est fini, old cock! A trifle I was finishing for my scoundrel of
a publisher, who demands it for tomorrow.—But, tell me, my dear boy
—what the devil kept you in the provinces for so long a time—so long
away from this dear Pa-ree? Ah, how we have missed you: my dear
fellow, Paris really never is the same unless you are here to give it grace!
Tiens! Tiens! Poor Courteline has been quite inconsolable! Capus has
sworn daily he would go and fetch you back! Tinayre is grouchy as a
bear! My dear fellow, we have all lamented you! De Régnier was certain you had got another mistress! Boylesve insisted that she was at
least a duchess—Bazin, a milkmaid——"

"And you, my old one?"

"I? My dear fellow—I knew it must be chicken-pox or measles: I was
certain you would not have to stir a foot out of Pa-ree to find a wench."

"But tell me, Octave, how are all our friends? I am starved for news,
I have read nothing. First of all—René——?"

"Has published another admirable work—an excellent study of life
in the provinces."

"Ah, good. And Duvernois?"

"His latest comedy has been produced and is un succès fou—a charming thing—witty, naughty, quite in his best vein, my dear boy."

"Renard?"

"A comedy, a book of stories, a romance—all excellent, all doing well."

"And Courteline?"

"Une chose incomparable, my boy: a book of dialogues in his drollest
vein—the public is convulsed: the police are in a towering rage about
Le Gendarme est sans Pitié——"

"And Abel?"

"A formidable book, my lad—just what you would expect, a powerful
tragedy, exact psychology, brilliant—but here he comes, all smiles—ah-h!
I thought so! He sees you—My dear Abel, welcome: behold, our prodigal has come home again——"

Yes, it was so that it was done, without anguish, error, or maddening of the soul.

And far, far away from all this certain grace, this ease of form, this assured attaining of expression—there lay America—and all the dumb hunger of its hundred million tongues, its unfound form, its unborn art. Far, far away from this enchanted legend of a city—there lay America and the brutal stupefaction of its million streets, its unquiet heart, its vast incertitude, the huge sprawled welter of its life—its formless and illimitable distances.

And Great God! Great God! but it was farther, stranger than a dream —he noted its cruelty, savagery, horror, error, loss and waste of life, its murderous criminality, and its hypocritic mask of virtue, its lies, its horrible falseness, and its murderous closure of a telling tongue—and Great God! Great God! with every pulse and fibre in him, with the huge, sick ache of an intolerable homelessness, he was longing with every beating of his anguished heart for just one thing—*return!*

Day by day, hour by hour, and minute by minute, the blind hunger tore at his naked entrails with a vulture's beak. He prowled the streets of Paris like a maddened animal, he hurled himself at the protean complexities of its million-footed life like a soldier who hurls himself into a battle: he was baffled, sick with despair, wrung, trembling and depleted, finally exhausted, caught in the toils of that insatiate desire, that terrible devouring hunger that grew constantly from what it fed upon and that drove him blindly to madness. The hopeless and unprofitable struggle of the Faustian life had never been so horribly evident as it now was— the futility of his insane efforts to memorize every stone and paving brick in Paris, to burn the vision of his eyes through walls and straight into the lives and hearts of a million people, to read all the books, eat all the food, drink all the wine, to hold the whole gigantic panorama of the universe within his memory, and somehow to make "one small globe of all his being," to compact the accumulated experience of eternity into the little prism of his flesh, the small tenement of his brain, and somehow to use it all for one final, perfect, all-inclusive work—his life's purpose, his heart's last pulse and anguish, and his soul's desire.

As a result of all this anguished and frustrated struggle he began now to go about with a small notebook in his pocket, the worn stub of a chewed pencil in his hands.

And because everything went into this mad mélange, because by every one of these scrawls of notes and sometimes incoherent words—even by the thousands of crude drawings, swift designs which he scrawled down in a thousand towns and places, to get the texture of a wall, the design of a door, the shape of a table, even the sword-cut on a man's scarred face— because in all of these shells and splinters that were thrown off from his tormented and uneasy brain the terrible Faustian fever of his tortured spirit was evident—no better image of his life—the life of a young man of that period—of modern man caught in the Faustian serpent-toils of modern life—can be given than the splintered jottings in these battered little books afford.

Here then, picked out at random from the ferment of ten thousand pages, and a million words—put down just as they were written, in fragments, jots, or splintered flashes, without order or coherence—here, with all its vanity, faith, despair, joy, and anguish, with all its falseness, error and pretension, and with all its desperate sincerity, its incredible hope, its insane desire, is a picture of a man's soul and heart— the image of his infuriate desire—caught hot and instant, drawn flaming from the forge of his soul's agony.

Monday, November 17, 1924: Worked over 5 hours up to present (9:40) Cigarets and coffee—Very tired.

Tuesday: Worked 4 hours yesterday. Very tired today only an hour —more tonight——

Wednesday: Good week's work last week—Four or five hours *actual* writing every day—I may succeed ultimately because I'm not content with what I do.

I was born in 1900—I am now 24 years old. During that period I think the best writing in English has been done by James Joyce in "Ulysses"—I think the best writing in the ballad has been done by G. K. Chesterton in "Lepanto." The best writing in sustained narrative verse by John Masefield—particularly in "The Dauber," "The River" and "The Widow in The Bye Street." Who produce copiously—Arnold Bennet— The best practitioners of the Essay—Belloc—the most gigantically thorough realist—Theodore Dreiser—The most sparing selection and unfailingly competent—Galsworthy—The best play for Poetry—"The Playboy of Western World"—The best journalist—Sinclair Lewis. The critic with the greatest subtlety—T. S. Eliot—The critic with the

greatest range and power—H. L. Mencken—The best woman writer—
May Sinclair—The next best—Virginia Woolf—The next best—Willa
Cather.

Wednesday Night—November 26, 1924: At midnight eating at Chez
Marianne—First day I have not worked for two weeks but am going
home to work after eating. Up at 12:30 today after last night felt sick—
walked to bank—found no mail—wrote and sent letters to Mama and
to University. Talked to young fellow in bank about Switzerland—had
lunch at Taverne Royale—Took taxi to Place des Vosges—Went to
Victor Hugo Museum—Walked around Square—then back to Carnavalet—at National Archives—The narrow streets, the narrow sidewalks, the great busses, taxis, autos, bicycles, trucks and the catty people
jabbering and squalling got me in a stew—Looked over distressing tons
of books at a bookshop, and went on feeling crushed—Bought two
books—Then got taxi Rue du Temple and so home through the jam of
Rue de Rivoli—Women outside pawing cheap articles at Samaritaine.
Then home to hotel where bathed went out to Deux Magots two
Apéritifs then to Apollo Revue!—Not as bad as some—one or two good
songs—but of course, on whole quite stupid.

Thursday—November 27, 1924: At one, after working till five
this morning. Dining at Drouant's—very rich, red restaurant filled with
business men talking of Les Anglais, Les Américaines, et cinq cent
mille francs—at Drouant's—a cold consommé, a rumpsteak grille—
avec des pommes soufflées—a fond d'artichaut mornay (a cheese and
cream dressing and the ends of artichokes—delicious) a coffee and a
half bottle of Nuit St. Georges couvert 4 fr. total 44 frs.

At one table three Frenchmen of 50 or more—one of 40—one with
black beard—coal black, neatly trimmed, naked around jaws—another
a heavy distinguished man—grey beard pompadoured—grey close-
cropped moustache—high colored—nervous grey eyes shot with red—
hands white, taut and tapping constantly, while the face smiles—talks
politely—another a red gnarled satanic face—fierce with rich foods and
wines—smooth shaven—and the youngest—black hair, a black moustache—a quiet smiling, well-fleshed type. He had rich color—red shot
with richness, the satanic yet not unpleasant cast of face—the cropped
brown moustache and such pompadoured brownish hair—a Gallic type.
LATER: Seated at the café in front of Magasin du Louvre and Palais

Royale—Heard a high even monotone that tickles the ear like a dynamo
—It made me think of a great locomotive in the yards at Altamont—
steam shut off (perhaps) and the high small ear-tickling dynamic noise
they make.

Tuesday—December 2, 1924:

MOCK LITERARY ANECDOTES:

Young mannered voice of Harvard johnny: "Oh! Simply *priceless!*
Don't you *l-o-o-ve* that?
. . . *Marvellous!*" etc.—telling what Oscar said to Whistler, and what
Whistler answered him.

A certain kind of mind collects these—pale, feeble, rootless, arty, hopeless, lost—Joel Pierce tells them, too. First time I heard them at Harvard what sophisticated raconteurs I thought them!—God, how green
I was! "You will, Oscar, you will," and all the rest of it!—Today, sitting on terrace at Taverne Royale, I made some of my own. Here they
are:

One day as Whistler was standing before a window in St. James Street
observing some prints of Battersea Bridge, he was accosted by Oscar
Wilde coming in the opposite direction. "You will, James, you will,"
said Wilde with generous impulsiveness.

"Gad," remarked the inimitable James, imperturbably adjusting his
monocle, "I wish I had said that!"

One day in June, Anatole France went to Rodin's studio for luncheon.
The talk having turned to early Greek primitives, Rodin remarked:

"Some writers have a great deal to say and an atrocious style. But
you, dear Master, have a delicious style."

"And you, Master?" queried France ironically, allowing his eyes to
rest upon the torso of The Thinker, "since when did you become a
critic?"

In the burst of laughter that followed the thrust, Rodin had to admit
himself floored for once.

A young actor who had, it must be confessed, more ambition than
talent, one day rushed excitedly up to Sir Henry Irving during the
rehearsal of "Hamlet":

"It seems to me, sir," he burst out without preliminaries, "that some
actors ruin their parts by overplaying them."

"And some," remarked Sir Henry, after an awful pause, "don't."

One day Sir James Barrie discovered Bernard Shaw while he was lunching at the Atheneum, staring somewhat disconsolate at an unsavory mess of vegetables that adorned his plate.

"I hear you are working on a new play," remarked Barrie, whimsically eyeing the contents of the platter.

For once G. B. S. had no answer ready.

Why won't these do?

(Suggestion to Young American writing Book Reviews for *New York Times* in classical, simple, god-like manner of Anatole France.)

"The new book of Monsieur Henry Spriggins, which lies before me on my desk, fills me with misgivings. The author is young and intolerant of simple things. He is full of talent, but he is proud, and has not a simple heart. What a pity!" (etc.)

Wednesday—December 3, 1924: Comédie Française tonight Les Plaideurs—and Phèdre—Respect for play grew and for actors diminished and went on—The French applauded loudly when Madame Weber ended a long declamation on a screech.

LATER: To Régence and Harry's—Bought some books along the quays—Saw Mrs. Martin at hotel today—Story of how she had been robbed—The picture galleries and antique shops of Rue des Saints Pères.

Saturday—December 6,
Young Icarus lies drowned, God knows where.

Oxford in pursuit of a woman—one of the most dreary spectacles God hath given—Buol's in the afternoon——

Foolish Question: Why are the Tories so eager to say Democracy has failed?

Hair like a copper cloud—feather and flame come back again.

The gutted plums bee-burrowed.

The poisoned inch around the heart.

The cancerous inch.

The burning inch of tongue.

The hairy grass.

The long sea-locks.

The hairy seas.

The other gate of ivory——

Ida—Cadmus—blunt drummed woodenly with blunt fingers. Sir Leoline the baron rich—Thunder-cuffing Zeus—Erasmus fed on rotten eggs—what a breath—Has an angel local motion or "The goose-soft snow."

Feathery snow—The feather-quilted snow.

Freckled eyes.

Wild Ceres through the wheat.

The slow dance of dancers.

The gull swerves seaward like hope—September full of departing leaves and wings.

He sat alone four thousand miles from home—the lonely death of seas at dawn.

The decent and untainted eyes that look on spattered death—Myself dreaming of old battles—For a child the spear goes clearly through— The musical horns beg and the battles press—The phantasy of bloody death: The cloven brain-pan—the one lost second near enough to touch its brother life, but infinitely far.

The wind-blown lights of the town.

A branch of stars.

A hen and a pig.

Quills—frills.

Mired—feathers.

The vast low stammer of the night.

By the rim—the geese go waddling to the Fair.

The minute-winning flies buzz home to death.

"Old England will muddle through, my lads"——

She has muddled and she's through: but she's not through muddling.

Gull-cry and gull are gone.

Shadow and hawk are gone.

Shadow and hawk are gone.

Shadow and hawk are——

Friday Night—December 12, 1924:. The Fratellini Brothers: How in his rich robe I saw him—the younger brother—waiting for the act—the waiting is all over—The burlesque musical act—They were great, sad, epic—what clowns should be.

Salle Rubens with all the *meat*—All the people clustered about—dull.

Mona Ugly Lisa.

The Virgin with Saint Anne—a great picture.

Guido Reni—the sainted and sugared faces.

The Italians—Veronese—The Cana—The Gigantic three-storey canvases.

Zurberan—Goya and the Grey—Picture of a Gentleman on horseback —Nicolas Maes—Rembrandt's picture of his brother.

Sam's—The man from San Francisco with the loud, dark, debauched face.

"We had ham and eggs for lunch across at Ciro's, Anne"—the two barkeepers in Harry's, "Chip" and Bob—names of dogs and horses.

Velasquez in the Louvre.

Vetzel's again 12:30 Apéritif (X365) The arch of the opera I have never seen before, things sit like this.

(here follows drawing)

Remember Faust at The Opera.

The Promenoirs—The vast stage—click-clack of feet in the music.

I awoke this morning in a crucifixion of fear and nervousness—What if they hadn't written? What? What? What?

My agony as I approached the place—My distrust of Paris in peril— City of light disloyalties. Sun never shines more than two days (for me) here—Went to American Express—Harry's Bar—The men at Vetzel's eating——

The French are not bad but children—old men too wise and kind for hatred—but French French French and Suspicious.

How beautiful the Fratellini are! How fine a thing is a French circus! Their enormous interest in children—The lion-taming act—by far the best and finest I have ever seen—and I felt sorry for the lions—Savoir is right in this.

Monday—December 15, 1924: I am getting a new sense of control— millions of books don't annoy me so much—went along the Seine today after Louvre—most of it worthless old rubbish I must begin to put up my fences now—I can't take the world or this city with me.

Things in Paris I must see at once—*Père Lachaise—Also* investigate old quarter again around *Place des Vosges*—Go *there* first thing tomorrow—Go to Cluny Musée again—And up and down Rue de la Seine— Also Isle St. Louis.

Books I want: Julien Benda—New one by Soupault (?) Charles Derennes—L'Education Sexuelle. Read one of the Vautel things.

Get for inspection—and at random Le Petit Livre—Mon Livre Favori
—Bibl. Nationale—Livre Epatant—go into Court of Palais Royale—
Investigate there——

Louvre today—Mantegnas picture of St. Sebastian C.

Giotto's great picture of St. Francis D'Assisi receiving stigma from
Christ——

Gros—Pictures of Napoleon at war—The one of the leper's house at
Jaffa a good one—Huge naked leper held in kneeling position—Weight
of body.

Books I want—Go to bookstalls in Seine for books on Paris twenty
or thirty years ago with naughty illustrations.

Tuesday—December 16, 1924: Along Seine again—Looked at thousands of books and bought one—a critique on Julien Benda—Miles and
miles of books—but also, miles and miles of repetitions——

The pictures—cavaliers seducing pretty ladies; one of women half
naked embracing pillow—called Le Rêve—People in old French stage-
comedies—Then 1000's of La Chimie, La Physique, La Géologie,
L'Algèbre, Le Géometrie——

Letters—Morceaux Choisis of XVIII S. All the authors I have never
heard of—but *that* is the same at home.

Wednesday—December 17, 1924: Today bought books—Bookshop
on Rue St. Honoré—Stock's.

Bought Benda there—Along the river—Tons of Trash—L'Univers—
The Miracle of France—4 mos. in the United States, etc. etc.—Les
Cicéron, Ovide, Sénèque, etc.

Bought *Confessions of Alfred Musset*—Stall at Pont Neuf with dirty
books—*Journal d'une Masseuse.*

*Sadie Blackeyes—Lovers of The Whip—The Pleasures of Married
Life—The Galleries of The Palais Royale* where the bookshops are—
Whole series edited by Guillaume Apollinaire——

Pictures, stamps, coins—Daumier-like picture of man having tooth
pulled—Then the near dirty ones of ladies with silver wings—Silhouette-
like—Then the near XVIII Century ones.

Old Books—Seem to be millions of these too—*Essais de L'Abbé Chose
sur la Morale,* etc.

The Faustian hell again!

At La Régence: Semaine de Noël, 1924:

The people who say they "read nothing but the best," are not, as some people call them, snobs. They are fools. The battle of the Spirit is not to read and to know the best—it is to find it—The thing that has caused me so much toil and trouble has come from a deeprooted mistrust in me of all cultured authority. I hunger for the treasure that I fancy lies buried in a million forgotten books, and yet my reason tells me that the treasure that lies buried there is so small that it is not worth the pain of disinterment.

And yet nearly everything in the world of books that has touched my life most deeply has come from authority. I have not always agreed with authority that all the books called great *are* great, but nearly all the books that have seemed great to me have come from among this number.

I have not discovered for myself any obscure writer who is as great a novelist as Dostoievsky, nor any obscure poet with the genius of Samuel Taylor Coleridge.

But I have mentioned Coleridge, and although my use of his name will not, I believe, cause any protest, it may cause surprise. Why not Shelley, or Spenser, or Milton?—It is here that my war with Authority —to which I owe everything—begins again.

There are in the world of my spirit certain gigantic figures who, although great as well in the world of authority, are yet overshadowed, and in some places, loom as enormous half-ghosts—hovering upon the cloudy borderland between obscurity and living remembrance.

Such a man is Samuel Taylor Coleridge. To me, he is not one of the great English poets. He is The Poet. To me he has not to make obeisance at the throne of any other monarch—he is there by Shakespeare and Milton and Spenser.

At La Régence: Remembering the whore with rotten teeth that I talked to last night on Rue Lafayette:

My dirt is not as dirty as your dirt. My clean-ness is cleaner than your clean-ness.

If I have a hole in my sock that is cunning.

If you have a hole in your stocking love flies out of the window. Why are we like this? Boredom is the bedfellow of all the Latin peoples—the English, in spite of the phrase "bored Englishman," are not bored.

The Germans are eager and noisy about everything they are told they should be interested in.

The Americans are interested in everything for a week—a week at a time—except Sensation: they are interested in that all the time.

I have heard a great deal of the "smiling Latins," the "gay Latins," etc. I have seen few indications that the Latins are gay. They are noisy —they are really a sombre and passionate people—the Italian face when silent is rather sullen.

In New York the opportunities for learning, and acquiring a culture that shall not come out of the ruins, but belong to life, are probably greater than anywhere else in the world.

This is because America is young and rich and comparatively unencumbered by bad things.

Tradition, which saves what is good and great in Europe, also saves what is poor, so that one wades through miles of junk to come to a great thing.

In New York books are plentiful and easy to get. The music and the theatre are the best in the world.

The great trouble with New York is that one feels uncomfortable while enjoying these things—In the daytime a man should be making money. The time to read is at night before one goes to bed. The time to hear music or go to the theatre is also at night. The time to look at a picture is on Sunday.

Another fault comes from our lack of independence. I am sure some of the most knowing people in the world, about the arts, are in America. I cannot read a magazine like *The Dial,* or *The Nation* and *The New Republic* without getting frightened. One man wrote a book called *Studies in Ten Literatures*—which of course, is foolish. We want to seem knowing about all these things because we have not enough confidence in ourselves.

We have had niggers for 300 years living all over the place—but all we did about it was to write minstrel shows, and 'coon stories, until two or three years ago when the French discovered for us how interesting they are. We let Paul Morand, and the man who wrote *Batouala,* and Soupault do it for us—Then we began to write stories about Harlem, etc.

Instead of whining, that we have no traditions, or that we must learn by keeping constantly in touch with European models, or by keeping away from them, we should get busy telling some of the stories about America that have never been told.

A book like *Main Street,* which made such a stir, is like Main Street. It is like "I've seen all Europe" tourists, who have spent two days in each country in a round-the-town bus.

In a magazine like *The American Mercury* the stories are also too much of a pattern—they're all about how the "Deacon Screwed the Methodist Minister's Wife," and how the "Town Prostitute Was Put in Jail for Coming to Church on Sunday and Mixing with the Good Folks."

When you hear people saying about *Babbitt*—that it is not the whole story and that much more can be said, you agree with them. Then they begin to talk about "the other side" and you lose hope. You see they mean by other side, Dr. Crane and Booth Tarkington.

So far from these being "the other side," there are a million other sides. And so far from *Babbitt* being too strong, the stories that may be written about America will make *Babbitt* an innocent little child's book to be read at the Christmas School entertainment along with *The Christmas Carol and* "Excelsior." The man who suggests the strangeness and variety of this life most is Sherwood Anderson. Or was. I think, he's got too fancy since he wrote *Winesburg, Ohio.*

A French writer who said there was no real variety in the life of the French because they all had red wine on the table, sat at little tables in cafés to gossip, and had mistresses, would be called a fool. Yet an American will criticize his country for standardization on no better grounds—namely that most of them are Methodists or Baptists, Democrats or Republicans, Rotarians or Kiwanians.

Babbitt is a very interesting book. But I believe it would be possible for a German writer with a talent similar to Sinclair Lewis to write a book called *Schmidt* or *Bauer* which would be just as sweeping a portrait.

Do you want to know what the gentleman looks like? He is much easier to describe than Babbitt.

Tuesday—December 23, 1924: The mystery explained! Today, at American Library, found out what it is:

"Time—that dimension of the world which we express in terms of before and after—the temporal sequence pervades mind and matter alike."

Time the form of the internal sense, and space the form of the external sense.

Theory of Relativity—the time-units of both time and space are neither points nor moments—but moments in the history of a point.

W. James—Within a definite limited interval of duration known as the specious present there is a direct perception of the temporal relations.

After an event has passed beyond the specious present it can only enter into consciousness by reproductive memory.

James "The Object of Memory is only an object imagined in the past to which the emotion of belief adheres."

Temporal experience divided into three qualitatively distinct intervals: the remembered past, the perceived specious present, and the anticipated future—By means of the tripartite division we are able to inject our present selves into the temporal stream of our own experience.

By arrangement of temporal orders of past with temporal orders of future—we can construct a temporal order of our specious presents and their contents.

Thus time has its roots in experience and yet appears to be a dimension in which experiences and their contents are to be arranged.

Thus the stuff from which time is made is of the nature of experienced data.

The Zenonian paradoxes: Achilles cannot catch up with the almost here save by occupying an infinity of positions.

A flying arrow canot remain where it is, nor be where it is not.

These things do not deal with space or time but with the properties of infinite assemblages and dense series (Americana).

Weber's at midnight: The waiters in Weber's standing in a group in their black coats and white boiled shirts——

All around the great mirrors reflecting them—for a moment a *strange* picture I thought of TIME!

The horrible monotony of the French—Weber's at midnight some Frenchmen in evening dress—the heavy eyelids—the dangling legs—the look of weary vitality——

Then in come some "Parisiennes"—God! God! All sizes and shapes and all the same—Unfit for anything else in the world, and not good for what they are—The texture of enamelled tinted skin, the hard avaricious noses, the chic style of coats, hair, eyebrows, etc.

The great myth that the Latins are romantic people. The Latins have qualities and standards that we do not possess—Hence we overvalue them.

There are many places in the world where life attains a greater variety, interest or profundity than in Paris (viz., New York, London, Vienna, Munich). Yet a great many Americans make their homes in Paris because they are sure it is the centre of the world's intellectual and cultural reputations.

It is easier for a writer to secure a reputation in France than in any other country. Many French writers have very respectable reputations who would be laughed at in other countries. For example, Henri Bordeaux—Some Americans who study French literature think he is a distinguished writer. His name has a solid, respectable sound to it. On the cover of all his books is printed "Member of the French Academy." But you could hardly find an intellectual in America who would say a kind word for Harold Bell Wright. Yet Harold Bell Wright—poor as he may be—is a better writer than Henri Bordeaux. If you don't believe it, read them. Americans are very unfair about this.

The way things go: At 6:10 A.M. the street lights of Paris go off. I sit at a little all-night café in Grand Boulevard opposite Rue Faubourg de Montmartre and watch light widen across the sky behind Montmartre. At first a wide strip of blue-grey—a strip of violet light. You see the line of the two clear and sharp. The paper trucks of Hachette, *Le Petit Parisien*, etc., go by.

In the bar a rattling of leaden, hole-y coins—the five, ten and twenty-five centime pieces. Taxi-drivers drinking café rhum, debating loudly in hoarse sanguinary voices. A whore, the blonde all-night antiquity of the quarter streets, drinking rich hot chocolate, crunching crusty croissants at the bar. The veteran of a million loves, well known and benevolently misprized, hoarse with iniquity and wisdom. A pox upon you, Marianne: You have made Monsieur Le Président très triste; the third leg of the Foreign Legion wears a sling because of you! A swart-eyed fellow, oiled and amorous, sweetly licks with nozzly tongue his whore's rouge-varnished face: with choking secret laughter and with kissy, wetty talkie he cajoles her; she answers in swart choked whisperings with her sudden shrill whore's scream of merriment.

A morning rattle of cans and ashes on the pavements. With rich jingle-jangle and hollow clitter-clatter a Paris milk wagon passes. Suddenly, a screak of brakes: all over the world the moaning screak of brakes, and racing, starting motors.

Across the street in faint grey-bluish light the news kiosque is opening up.

"Est-ce que vous avez *Le New York 'Erald?*"

"Non, monsieur. Ce n'est pas encore arrivé."

"Et *Le Tchicago Treebune?*"

"Ça pas plus, monsieur. C'est aussi en retard ce matin."

"Merci. Alors: *Le Matin.*"

"Bien, monsieur."

Passage of leaden sous: the smell of ink-worn paper, dear to morning throughout the world. A big Hachette truck swerves up, an instant halt, the flat heavy smack of fresh-corded ink-warm paper on the pavement, a hoarse cry and instant loud departure!

Ça aussi, monsieur. Sing ye bi-i-i-rds, sing! Lift up your heart, O son of man!

Sweet is the breath of morn, her rising sweet, with charm of earliest birds!

Some things will never change: some things will always be the same: brother we cannot die, we must be saved; we are united at the heart of night and morning.

A good time now, just before dawn and morning. Surfeit of sterile riches: harvests of stale bought love: the burnt-out candle-end of night, the jaded blaze of crimson light, in shuttered bars; numb weary lust—which one, which one?

The whores at daybreak, the dead brilliance of electric smiles.

Tired, tired, tired.

Tuesday: Woman who sang tonight at Concert Mayol—She was near 50—magnificent teeth—so good they made me uneasy—Those things in her head—but how? They keep them so. This comes to me—that they spend all their time looking after them: there is something filthy about this.

On the Boulevards—3.20 du matin. Reading the *Sourire* for whore-house items—I want to find me a Ballon of Champagne—First of all—préservatif right to my left around corner Rue Faubourg de Montmartre; all-night pharmacy.

Along the quais again this afternoon to the bookstalls—Made afraid by the junk—Bought a dozen books or so, but no "prints" or "etchings" —Countless old-fashioned prints—pictures of Versailles—the Palais Royale, the Revolution—Sentimental and cheap pictures—Florid ones— "La Courtisane Passionée," etc. Stage-coach pictures, etc. Works of Eugène Scribe—The little books bound or tied, so you can't look—nothing in them—*Vie à la Campagne*—countless cheap books—ah, I have a little of it all!—Strasbourg.

Christmas Week—Colmar, Alsace-Lorraine—Written on the Spot.
The Isentheimer Altar of Mathias Grunewald in the Cloisters of the Unterlinden Museum at Colmar:
There is nothing like it in the world. I have spent over 4 months getting here—it is much more wonderful than one imagines it will be. The altar is set up *not in one piece* but in three sections in a big room with groined ceilings, a long groined room like a Dominikaner Cloister.
The first two "volets" of the altar—Everything is distorted and out of perspective. The figure of the Christ is twice as big as the other figures—the pointing finger of Saint Antoine is much too big for his body—but everything in this figure points along the joints and elbows of that arm and ends in the pointing finger.
The Lamb with its straight brisk feet, its dainty right foreleg bent delicately about the Cross and red blood spouting from its imperturbable heart into a goblet of rich gold, is a masterpiece of symbolic emotion that strikes far beyond intelligence.
The body of Christ, and its agony, are indescribable. The hands and the feet are enlarged to meet the agony—the hands are tendons of agony, the feet are not feet but lengths of twisted tendons driven through by a bolt and ending in bent, broken, bleeding toes. A supernatural light falls upon the immense twisted length of the body (a grey-white-green) and yet *completely solid light*—you can count the ribs, the muscles, (the head falling to the right), full of brutal agony—it is crowned with long thorns and rusty blood—it droops over, it is too big, Christ is dead.
The great figure of the woman in white comes up and breaks back-

ward at the middle and is caught in the red arms of the pitiful Saint. The fingers of the Magdalen are bent in eloquent supplication.

The blackness of hell's night behind—the unearthly greenish supernatural light upon the figures—on Christ's dead, sinewed, twisted, riven gigantic body and on the living flesh of the other figures.

The sly face of the Virgin in the wing of The Annunciation—the eyes slanting up under lowered lids in a sly leer—the fat loose sensual mouth half open, with the tongue visible—a look of sly bawdiness over all.

The enormous and demoniac intelligence that illuminates the piece in Grunewald's Altar—the angels playing instruments in "La Vierge Glorifiée par les Anges"—the faces have a *sinister golden light*—an almost unholy glee. You can hear *mad heavenly music*. This is not true with Italians—syrup and sugar.

This is the greatest and also the most "modern" picture I have ever seen.

Christmas Week—1924: Returning to Paris from Strasbourg: The approach to Paris through the Valley of the Marne—Winter—The very magnificent rainbow—the rocking clacketing train.

The suburbs of Paris—Dark—The little double-deckers rattling past loaded with people—The weary approaches to a great city—Endless repetition—monotonous endlessness—The sadness of seeing people pass you in a lighted train or subway. Why is this?

PARIS: There is nothing that I do not know about Paris—That sounds like the foolishest boast but that is true—I am sitting on the Terrace of The Taverne Royale—Rue Royale—It is winter—it is cold—but it is the same—to one hand the Madeleine—to the other the Place de la Concorde—to the right that of the Champs-Elysées—the Arc—the Bois—the fashionable quarters—the whore-houses of that district—the rue—the Troc—the Tower—the Champs de Mars—the Montparnasse section—the Latin-Quarter—the bookshops—the cafés—the Ecole—the Institute—the St. Mich—the Ile—the Notre Dame—The Old Houses—the Rue de Rivoli—the Tour St. Jacques—the Carnavalet—the Hugo—Vosges—the Bastille—the Gare de Lyon—the Gare de l'Est—Du Nord—the Montmartre—the Butte—the cafés—houses—the Rue Lepic—the Port Clignancourt—the La Villette—The Parc Monceau—the Bois—Great circle, unending universe of life, huge legend of dark time!

But unannealed by water the gaunt days sloped into the grots of time.

Paris, Saturday Night: Today has been a horrible one—I was able to sleep only the most diseased and distressed sleep (the worst sort of American-in-Europe sleep) last night after leaving Mrs. Morton. I was sick with my loss (the loss of the picture and several letters Helen sent me) and I got up sick and with the *shakes* this morning—I came to the Abiga bar—I went to the Am Ex Co—I went to Wepler's in Montmartre —At each place, as I knew they would, with mean and servile regret cut by mocking, they were sorry, sorry, sorry.

The day was of the most horrible European sort—Something that passes understanding—the wet heavy air, that deadens the soul, puts a lump of indigestible lead in the solar plexus, depresses and fatigues the flesh until one seems to lift himself leadenly through the thick wet steaming air with a kind of terrible fear—an excitement that is without hope, that awaits only the news of some further grief, failure, humiliation, and torture. There is a lassitude that enters the folds and lappings of the brain, that makes one hope for better things and better work tomorrow, but hope without belief or conviction.

The grey depression of the wet buildings—the horrible nervous pettiness of the French, swarming, honking, tooting along the narrow streets and the two-foot sidewalks, while the heavy busses beetle past——

A chapter called PARIS or So You're Going to "Paris"? (Perhaps a piece for a magazine in This.)

The fear always of the corners—you are coming out into the open, there will be waiting to thrust at you, the heavy grinding busses, the irritation of the horns, etc.

A chapter to be called "The Arithmetic of the Soul."

The music deepened like a passion.

All of our hearts are fulfilled of you, all of our souls are growing warm with you, all of our lives are beating out their breath for you, and the strange feel of our pulses is playing through our blood for you, immortal and unending living.

Sunday—Up at noon, bathed, etc. Lunch at Casenave's—Went to

Delacroix and Louvre—Something over-rich and bloody about it.—
Note how French love to paint blood (Delacroix)—then along Seine
bookstalls—found only junk—then to Lipp's for beer and *cervelas*—then
back to hotel where worked from 6:30-10.30—Then out to eat at
Taverne Royale—Walk back through Vendôme and Rue St. Honoré—
Read a little and worked from *one* to 3:00—6 hours today.

Sunday Night: I feel low—discouraged by the mass of things again
tonight. I must make some decisive action—the new web of streets
behind the dome has depressed me.

The mind grows weary with such a problem as mine, by constantly
retracing its steps, by constantly feeling around the same cylinder from
which there seems *at present* to be no escape.

The European temper is one that has learned control—that is it has
learned indifference—Each man writes his own book without worrying
very much about what the other has written—he reads little or if he
reads much, it is only a trifle—a spoonful of the ocean of print that
inundates everything—Picture Anatole France—with a reputation for
omniscience—picking daintily here and there among the bookstalls of
the Seine. To go by them affects me with horror and weariness—as it
does Paul Valéry—but I lack his power to resist. I must go by there—
and if I do again and again I cannot keep away from them.

More and more I am convinced that to be a great writer a man must
be something of an ass. I read of Tolstoi that he read no newspapers,
that he went away and lived among peasants for 7 years at a time, and
that for six years he read nothing except the novels of Dumas. Yet such
a man could write great books. I almost think it is because of this that
he did.

Bernard Shaw, one of our prophets at the present time, is worshiped
past idolatry by many people who consider that he knows everything
or practically everything.

From what I have been able to discover of his reading from his writing, I can be sure that he has read Shakespeare—not very carefully, Ibsen
very carefully, a book by Karl Marx, which made a deep impression on

him, the tracts of the Fabian Society, and the writings of Mr. and Mrs. Sidney Webb.

There is always the moment when we must begin to write. There are always the hundreds, the thousands, of struggle, of getting up, of pacing about, of sitting down, of laborious uneven accomplishment. During the time of actual work, what else besides ourselves, can help us? Can we call to mind then the contents of 20,000 books? Can we depend on anything other than ourselves for help?

At La Régence:

How certain trivial words and phrases haunt the brain—cannot be forgotten—come back again even when years have passed. Today, have been hearing old voices, old songs, fleeting forgotten words of twenty years ago—my mother's—my father's—the voices of the summer boarders on the porches—most of all, Dinwood Bland, sitting in pleasant backyard of his house in Norfolk, a drink in his hand, his blind eyes blindly fixed upon the flashing sparkling waters of Hampton Roads, blindly on a white ship passing—his thin, senile, evil, strangely attractive face touched with bitterness, revulsion, and his weary disgust with life as he said:

"My father was an educated loafer."

And now, all day long, "the sound of these words rings and echoes in my mind until I can listen to nothing else." And sitting here I feel like Coleridge when the rhyme for Youth and Age came to him (10 Sept. 1823 Wed. morning 10 o'clock)—"An Air," he says, "that whizzed *dia engkefalou*" (right across the diameter of my brain) exactly like a Hummel Bee—etc.

So, too, with me, all afternoon—and Dinwood Bland's haunting phrase about his father has now become:

"My father was an educated loafer,
My mother was an alcoholic bum,
My sister's name was Nelly, she had a lovely belly,
Aside from that she was a lousy scum.

"My brother Pete, he went and joined the navy,
My brother Hank, he went and caught the clap,
My little sister Anny, fell down and bruised her fanny——.

Because we had an educated Pap,"—etc.

Obscure, ridiculous—but old words, old phrases, and forgotten sayings—why do they come back to haunt our meaning?

At La Régence:
On quotations—The practice of nineteenth century "good" writers was to decorate their compositions with neat little patterns of quotations. That practice still persists in a great deal of the correct writing of the present —viz., the essays and leading articles of *The Atlantic Monthly, The Spectator, Harpers, The Century, The London Mercury,* etc.—The quotation habit is generally a vicious one, often it has not even so worthy a design as to borrow from stronger and greater people an energy and clearness that we do not have, but rather serves as a sort of diploma to certify our culture—said culture consisting in our ability to quote scraps from Lamb, Dickens, John Keats, Browning, Doctor Johnson, and Matthew Arnold. The distortion this works upon the original sinew of the mind is incalculable—writing becomes a meeting of pseudo-courtliness neatly designed to arrive before Lamb with a bow and to be handed by Dickens to Lord Tennyson with a graceful flourish. The phrase "apt quotation" is one of the most misleading phrases ever invented. Most quotations so far from being apt to any purpose, are distinguished by all the ineptitude a politician displays when having spoken for twenty minutes on the Nicaraguan question, he says: "That reminds me of a little story I heard the other day. It seems there were two Irishmen whose names were Pat and Mike"—then proceeds to a discussion of the Prohibition issue, after his convulsed audience is somewhat recovered.

Europe and America are still too far apart—the "interminable" day is far too long—six days is far too long—for the intense impression— to compare and observe their essential difference——
Results: We must have them closer together—as the English and the French—as Dover and Calais—things that matter in our life cannot be recalled so easily. I have lived deeply, intensely, vividly, on the whole unhappily, for six months. Some people say that is all that matters. I do not think it is. But things cannot be called up so easily.

I am wondering in a vast *vague* about her. I love her, I think of seeing her again with a sense of strangeness and wonder; but I have no sort of

idea what it will be like, or what has happened. Why can we not remember the faces of those we love? This is true: Their faces melt into
a thousand shades and shapes and images of faces, the moment that we
try to fix them in our memory. It is only the face of a stranger we
remember there. Why?

Never has the many-ness and the much-ness of things caused me
such trouble as in the past six months. But never have I had so firm a
conviction that our lives can live upon only a few things, that we must
find them, and begin to build our fences.

All creation is the building of a fence.

But deeper study always, sharper senses, profounder living; *never* an
end to curiosity!

The fruit of all this comes later. I must think. I must mix it all
with myself and with America. I have caught much of it on paper. But
infinitely the greater part is in the wash of my brain and blood.

Shaw makes a fool of himself when he writes of Napoleon, because he
hates Napoleon and wants to make him ridiculous. But Shaw makes a
hero of himself when he writes of Cæsar; Shaw's Cæsar is the best
Cæsar I know of. It beats Shakespeare. It is as Cæsar looks (Naples
Museum) I am sure. I am sure Cæsar was like this.

But it is a mistake to suppose that Napoleon got his hair in the soup.

Dirge: Why are we unhappy?—I have no need to envy this man's
fame—nor skill to cloak myself in that man's manner—I am as naked
now as sorrow—and all I ask is, Why are we so unhappy?

Why are we unhappy?

In my father's country there are yet men with quiet eyes and slow,
fond, kindly faces.

LXXVI

ABOUT four o'clock on the afternoon of New Year's Eve, 1924, as
Eugene was entering the Louvre, he met Starwick. Starwick was
elegantly dressed, as always, in casual, beautifully tailored, brown tweed
garments. He still carried a cane and twirled it indolently as he came
down the steps. He was the same old picture of bored, languorous, almost feminine grace, but instead of a shirt he was wearing a Russian
blouse of soft blue wool which snuggled around his neck in voluptuous

folds and had a kind of diamond-shaped design of crimson threads along the band.

For a moment, half-way down the gray stone steps, worn and hollowed as ancient European steps are worn and hollowed by the soft incessant eternity of feet, as the other people thronged past him, he paused, his pleasant ruddy face and cleft chin turned vaguely up towards those soft skies of time, already fading swiftly with the early wintry light.

As always, Frank looked magnificent, and with his Russian blouse, and the expression of inscrutable sorrow on his face, more mysterious and romantic than ever. Even in this foreign scene, he seemed to take possession of his surroundings with a lordly air. So far from looking like an alien, a foreigner, or a common tourist, Frank seemed to belong to the scene more than anybody there. It was as if something very frail and rare and exquisite and weary of the world—Alfred de Musset or George Moore, or the young Oscar, or Verlaine—had just come out of the Louvre, and it all seemed to belong to him.

The enormous central court of the Louvre, the soaring wings of that tremendous and graceful monument, the planned vistas of the Tuileries before him, fading into the mist-hazed air and the soft graying light— the whole tremendous scene, with all its space and strength and hauntingly aerial grace—at once as strong as ancient battlemented time, and as delicate and haunting as music on a spinet—swept together in a harmonious movement of spaciousness and majesty and graceful loveliness to form a background for the glamorous personality of Francis Starwick.

Even as he stood there, the rare and solitary distinction of his person was evident as it had never been before. People were streaming out of the museum and down the steps past him—for already it was the closing hour—and as they went by they all looked common, shabby and drearily prosaic by comparison. A middle-aged Frenchman of the middle-class, a chubby, ruddy figure of a man, dressed in cloth of the hard, ugly, ill-cut black that this class of Frenchmen wear, came by quickly with his wife, his daughter and his son. The man was driven along by the incessant, hot sugar of that energy which drives the race and which, with its unvaried repetition of oaths, ejaculations, denials, affirmations, and exactitudes, lavished at every minute upon the most trivial episodes of life, can become more drearily tedious than the most banal monotone. Compared with Starwick, his figure was thick, blunt, common in its clumsy shapelessness, and his wife had the same common, swarthy, blunted look. An American came down the steps with his wife: he was neatly dressed in the ugly light-grayish clothes that so many Americans wear, his wife was also neatly turned out with the tedious and metallic stylishness of American apparel. They had the naked, inept and uneasy look of tourists, everything about them seemed troubled and alien to the scene, even to the breezy quality of the air, and the soft thick skies about them. When they had descended the steps, they paused a moment in a worried and undecided way, the man pulled at his watch and peered at it with his meagre prognathous face, and then said nasally:

"Well, we told them we'd be there at four-thirty. It's about that now."

All of these people, young and old, French, American, or of whatever nationality, looked dreary, dull and common, and uneasily out of place, when compared with Starwick.

After a moment's shock of stunned surprise, a drunken surge of impossible joy, Eugene ran towards him shouting, "Frank!"

Starwick turned, with a startled look upon his face: in a moment the two young men were shaking hands frantically, almost hugging each other in their excitement, both blurting out at once a torrent of words which neither heard. Finally, when they had grown quieter, Eugene found himself saying:

"But where the hell have you been, Frank? I wrote you twice: didn't you get any of my letters?—what happened to you?—where were you? —did you go down to the South of France to stay with Egan, as you said you would?"

"Ace," said Starwick—his voice had the same, strangely mannered, unearthly quality it had always had, only it was more mysterious and secretive than ever before—"Ace, I have been there."

"But why—?"—the other began, "why aren't you?—" He paused, looking at Starwick with a startled glance. "What happened, Frank?"

For, by his few quiet and non-committal words, Starwick had managed to convey perfectly the sense of sorrow and tragedy—of a grief so great it could not be spoken, a hurt so deep it could not be told. His whole personality was now pervaded mysteriously by this air of quiet, speechless and incommunicable sorrow; he looked at the other youth with the eyes of Lazarus returned from the tomb, and that glance said more eloquently than any words could ever do that he now knew and understood things which no other mortal man could ever know or understand.

"I should prefer not to talk about it," he said very quietly, and by these words Eugene understood that some tragic and unutterable event had now irrevocably sundered Starwick from Egan—though what that event might be, he saw it was not given him to know.

Immediately, however, in his old, casual, and engaging fashion, speaking between lips that barely moved, Starwick said:

"Look! What are you doing now? Is there any place you have to go?"

"No. I was just going in here. But I suppose it's too late now, anyway."

At this moment, indeed, they could hear the bells ringing in the museum, and the voices of the guards, crying impatiently:

"On ferme! On ferme, messieurs!"—and the people began to pour out in streams.

"Ace," said Starwick, "they're closing now. Besides," he added wearily, "I shouldn't think it would matter to you, anyway. . . . God!" he cried suddenly, in a high, almost womanish accent of passionate conviction, "what junk! What mountains and oceans of junk! And so bad!" he cried passionately, in his strange, unearthly tone. "So incredibly and impossibly bad. In that whole place there are just three things worth seeing—but *they!*"—his voice was high again with passionate excitement —"*they* are *unspeakably* beautiful, Eugene! God!" he cried, high and passionate again, "how *beautiful* they are! How utterly, impossibly beautiful!" Then with a resumption of his quiet, matter-of-fact tone he said, "You must come here with me some time. I will show them to you. . . . Look!" he said, in his casual tone again, "will you come to the Régence with me and have a drink?"

The whole earth seemed to come to life at once. Now that Starwick was here, this unfamiliar world, in whose alien life he had struggled like a drowning swimmer, became in a moment wonderful and good. The feeling of numb, nameless terror, rootless desolation, the intolerable sick anguish of homelessness, insecurity, and homesickness, against which he had fought since coming to Paris, and which he had been ashamed and afraid to admit, was now instantly banished. Even the strange dark faces of the French as they streamed past no longer seemed strange, but friendly and familiar, and the moist and languorous air, the soft thick grayness of the skies which had seemed to press down on his naked sides, to permeate his houseless soul like a palpable and viscous substance of numb terror and despair, were now impregnated with all the vital energies of living, with the intoxication of an unspeakable, nameless, infinitely strange and various joy. As they walked across the vast court of the Louvre towards the great arched gateway and all the brilliant traffic of the streets, the enormous dynamic murmur of the mysterious city came to him and stirred his entrails with the sensual premonitions of unknown, glamorous and seductive pleasure. Even the little taxis, boring past with wasp-like speed across the great space of the Louvre and through the sounding arches, now contributed to this sense of excitement, luxury and joy. The shrill and irritating horns sounded constantly through the humid air, and filled his heart with thoughts of New Year: already the whole city seemed astir, alive now with the great carnival of New Year's Eve.

At the Régence, they found a table on the terrace of the old café where Napoleon had played dominoes, and among the gay clatter of the crowd of waning afternoon, they drank brandy, talked passionately and with almost delirious happiness, drank brandy again, and watched the swarming and beautiful life upon the pavements and at the crowded tables all around them.

The streams of traffic up and down the whole Avenue de l'Opéra and the Place de la Comédie Française, the delicate, plain, and beautiful façade of the Comédie across the Square from them, the statue of frail De Musset, half-fainting backwards in the arms of his restoring muse —all this seemed not only part of him, but now that Starwick was here, to gain an enormous enhancement and enchantment, to be the total perfume of an incredibly good and lovely and seductive life, the whole of which, in all its infinite ramifications, seemed to be distilled into his blood like a rare liquor, and to belong to him. And so they drank and talked and drank until full dark had come, and tears stood in their eyes, and the brandy saucers were racked up eight deep upon their table.

Then, gloriously sad and happy and exultantly triumphant, and full of nameless joy and evil, they stepped into one of the shrill, exciting little taxis, and were charioted swiftly up that thronging noble street, until the great soaring masses of the Opera stood before them and the Café de la Paix was at one side.

And they were young, all-conquering and exultant, and all the magic life of strange million-footed Paris belonged to them, and all its strange and evil fragrance burned fierce and secret in their veins, and they knew that they were young and that they would never die, that it was New Year's Eve in Paris, and that that magic city had been created for them. By this time they had between them about 400 francs.

Then followed the huge kaleidoscope of night: at one o'clock, leaving a café, they got into a taxi, and vociferously demanded of the ruddy driver, in French made eloquently confident by alcohol and joy, that they be taken to the resorts most frequented by "nos frères—vous comprenez—les honnêtes hommes—les ouvriers."

He smilingly assented, and from that time on until dawn they made a madman's round of little vile cafés, so mazed, so numerous, so inextricably confused in the vast web-like slum and jungle of nocturnal Paris, that later they could never thread their way back through that labyrinth of crooked alley-ways, and drunkenness and confusion. Their driver took them to a region which they later thought was somewhere in that ancient, foul and tangled quarter between the Boulevard de Sébastopol and Les Halles. And all that night from one o'clock to dawn, they threaded noxious alleys, beside the shuttered façades of ancient, evil, crone-like houses, and stopped at every blaze of garish light to enter dirty little dives, where sullen evil-visaged men surveyed them sullenly over bistro bars, and gave them with a slimy hand cheap vile cognac in greasy little glasses. In these places there was always the evil, swelling, fatly unctuous and seductive music of accordions, the hoarse bravos of applause. Here one bought metal slugs, a dozen for five francs, and gave them to sluttish sirens with no upper teeth for the favor of a dance; and here also there were many soldiers, Colonial negroes, black as ebony, were most in favor; and here were men with caps and scarves and evil, furtive eyes, who watched them steadily.

From place to place, from dive to dive, all through that huge and noxious labyrinth of night, their wild debauch wore on. And presently they noticed that wherever they went, two gendarmes followed them, stood quietly at the bar, and courteously and genially took the drinks they always bought for them, and were always there when they entered the next place. And the ruddy and good-natured taxi-man was always there as well, and he too always drank with them, and always said, with robust satisfaction: "Mais, oui! Parbleu! A votre santé, messieurs!"

The gray haggard light of daybreak showed the cold gray waters of the Seine, ancient, narrowed, flowing on between huge stone walls, the haggard steep façades of the old shuttered houses in the Latin Quarter, the narrow angularity of the silent streets. In Montparnasse, they got out

LXXVII

THAT was a fine life that he had that year. He lived in a little hotel in the Rue des Beaux Arts. He had a good room there which cost him twelve francs a day. It was a good hotel, and was the place where Oscar Wilde had died. When any one wanted to see the celebrated death-room, he would ask to see "le chambre de Monsieur Veeld," and Monsieur Gely, the proprietor, or one of his buxom daughters, would willingly show it.

At nine o'clock in the morning the maid would come in with chocolate or coffee, bread and jam and butter, which was included in the price of the room. She put it down on a little cabinet beside his bed, which had a door and a chamber pot inside. After she went out he would get up and move it to the table, and drink the chocolate and eat some bread and jam. Then he would go back to bed and sleep until noon and sometimes later: at one o'clock, Starwick and the two women would come to take him to lunch. If they did not come, they would send him a *pneumatique* telling him where to meet them. They went to a great many different places, but the lunch was always good. Sometimes they would send a *pneumatique* telling him to meet them at the Dome or the Rotonde. When he got there, they would be sitting at a table on the terrace, and already very gay. Starwick would have a stack of saucers racked up before him on the table. On each saucer would be a numeral which said 3:50, or 5:00, or 6:00, or 7:50 francs, depending on what he had been drinking.

Usually it was cognac, but sometimes Starwick would greet him with a burble of laughter, saying in his sensuous and voluptuous voice: "Did you ever drink Amer Picon?"

"No," he would say.

"Well," said Starwick. "You ought to try it. You really ought, you know." And the soft burble would come welling up out of his throat again, and Elinor, looking at him tenderly, smiling, would say:

"Francis! You idiot! Leave the child alone!"

Then they would go to lunch. Sometimes they went to a place near by called Henriettes which Elinor had known about when she was an ambulance driver in the war. Again, they would cross the river and eat at Prunier's, Weber's, the Café Régence, Fouquet's, or at a place half way up the hill in Montmartre, which was in a Square called the Place des Martyrs, and which was called L'Ecrevisse, probably because of a little shell-fish which they sold there, and which was a specialty. That was a fine place: they always ate out on the terrace where they could see everything that was going on in the little Square, and Elinor, who had known the place for years, said how lovely it would be in spring.

Often they would eat at little places, which were not very expensive and which Elinor also knew about. She knew about everything: there was nothing about Paris she did not know. Elinor did the talking, rattling off her French like a native—or, anyway, like a native of Boston who speaks French well—trippingly off the tongue, getting the same intonations and gestures the French got, when she argued with them, saying:

"Mais non—mais non mais non mais non mais non mais non!" so rapidly that we could hardly follow her, and she could say: "Oui. C'est ça!—Mais parfaitement!—Entendu! . . . Formidable!" etc., in the same way a Frenchman could.

Yet there was a trace of gaiety and humor in everything she said and did. She had "the light touch" about everything, and understood just how it was with the French. Her attitude toward them was very much the manner of a mature and sophisticated person with a race of clamoring children. She never grew tired of observing and pointing out their quaint and curious ways: if the jolly proprietor of a restaurant came to the table and proudly tried to speak to them his garbled English, she would shake her head sharply, with a little smile, biting her lower lip as she did so, and saying with a light and tender humor:

"Oh, *nice!* . . . He wants to speak his English! . . . *Isn't* he a dear? . . . No, no," she would say quickly if any one attempted to answer him in French. "Please let him go ahead—poor dear! He's so proud of it!"

And again she would shake her head, biting her lower lip, with a tender wondering little smile, as she said so, and "Yes!" Francis would say enthusiastically and with a look of direct, serious, and almost sorrowful earnestness. "And how *grand* the man is about it—how *simple* and *grand* in the way he does it! . . . Did you notice the way he used his hand—I mean like some one in a painting by Cimabue—it really is, you know," he said earnestly. "The centuries of living and tradition that have gone into a single gesture—and he's quite unconscious of it. It's grand—I mean like some one in a painting by Cimabue—it really is, you know," he said with the sad, serious look of utter earnestness. "It's really *quite* incredible."

"Quite," said Elinor, who with a whimsical little smile had been look-ing at a waiter with sprouting mustaches, as he bent with prayerful reverence, stirring the ingredients in a salad bowl—"Oh, Francis, dar-ling, look—" she whispered, nodding toward the man. "Don't you *love* it? . . . Don't you simply *adore* the way they do it! . . . I *mean,* you know! Now where? Where?" she cried, with a gesture of complete surrender—"*where* could you find anything like that in America? . . . I mean, you simply couldn't find it—that's all."

"*Quite!*" said Francis concisely. And turning to Eugene, he would say with that impressive air of absolute sad earnestness, "And it's really *most* important. It really is, you know. It's astonishing to see what they can put into a single gesture. I mean—the Whole Thing's there. It really is."

"Francis!" Elinor would say, looking at him with her gay and tender little smile, and biting her lip as she did so—"You *kid,* you! I *mean!*——"

Suddenly she put her hand strongly before her eyes, bent her head, and was rigid in a moment of powerful and secret emotion. In a moment, however, she would look up, wet-eyed, suddenly thrust her arm across the table at Eugene, and putting her hand on his arm with a slight gal-lant movement, say quietly:

"O, I'm sorry—you poor child! . . . After all, there's no reason why you should have to go through all this. . . . I mean, darling," she ex-plained gently, "I have an adorable kid at home just four years old—sometimes something happens to make me think of him—you under-stand, don't you?"

"Yes," he said.

"Good," she said briskly and decisively, with a swift and gallant smile, as she patted his arm again. "I knew you would!"

She had left her husband and child in Boston, she had come here to join Francis, fatality was in the air, but she was always brave and gallant about it. As Francis would say to Eugene as they sat drinking alone in a café:

"It's *mad*—Boston! . . . Perfectly *mad*—Boston! . . . I mean, the kind of thing they do when they ride a horse up the steps of the State House. . . . I mean, perfectly *grand,* you know," he cried with high enthusiasm. "They stop at nothing. It's simply *swell*—it really is, you know."

Every one was being very brave and gallant and stopping at nothing, and the French were charming, charming, and Paris gave them just the background that they needed. It was a fine life.

Elinor took charge of everything. She took charge of the money, the making of plans, the driving of bargains with avaricious and shrewd-witted Frenchmen, and the ordering of food in restaurants.

"It's really astonishing, you know," said Starwick—"the way she walks in everywhere and has the whole place at her feet in four minutes. . . . Really, Gene, you should have been with us this afternoon when she made arrangements with the man at the motor agency in the Champs Elysées for renting the car. . . . Really, I felt quite sorry for him before the thing was over. . . . He kept casting those knowing and rather *bitter* glances of reproach at me," said Starwick, with his burble of soft laugher, "as if he thought I had betrayed him by not coming to his assistance. . . . There was something *very* cruel about it . . . like a great cat, playing with a mouse . . . there really was, you know," said Starwick earnestly. "She can be completely without pity when she gets that way," he added. "She really can, you know . . . which makes it all the more astonishing—I mean, when you consider what she really is—the way she let me go to sleep on her shoulder the night we were coming back from Rheims, and I was so horribly drunk and got so disgustingly sick," he said with a simple, touching earnestness. "I mean, the *compassion* of it—it was *quite* like that Chinese goddess of the Infinite Compassion, they have in Boston—it *really* was, you know. It's quite astonishing," he said earnestly, "when you consider her back-ground, the kind of people that she came from—it really *is,* you know . . . she's a grand person, simply terrific . . . it's utterly *mad*—Boston . . . it really is."

Certainly it was very pleasant to be in the hands of such a captain. Elinor got things done with a beautiful, serene assurance that made everything seem easy. There was no difficulty of custom or language, no weird mystery and complication of traffic, trade, and commerce, so maddening and incomprehensible to most Americans, that Elinor did not understand perfectly. Sometimes, she would just shake her head and bite her lip, smiling. Sometimes she would laugh with rich astonishment, and say: *"Perfectly* insane, of course—but then, that's the way the poor dears are, and you can't change them. . . . I *know!* I *know!* . . . It's quite incredible, but they'll *always* be that way, and we've simply got to make the best of it."

She was a heavily built woman about thirty years old who seemed older than she was. She dressed very plainly and wore a rather old hat with a cockade, which gave her a look of eighteenth-century gallantry. And the impression of maturity was increased by her heavy and un-youthful figure, and the strong authority of her face which, in spite of her good-humored, gay, and whimsical smile, her light Bostonian air of raillery, indicated the controlled tension and restraint of nerves of a person of stubborn and resolute will who is resolved always to act with aristocratic grace and courage.

In spite of her heavy figure, her rough and rather unhealthy-looking skin, she was a distinguished-looking woman, and in her smile, her tone, her play of wit, and even in the swift spitefulness and violence which could flash out and strike and be gone before its victim had a chance to retort or defend himself, she was thoroughly feminine. And yet the woman made no appeal at all to sensual desire: although she had left her husband and child to follow Starwick to France, and wa. thought by her own family to have become his mistress, it was impos sible to imagine her in such a rôle. And for this reason, perhaps, there was something ugly, dark, and sinister in their relation, which Eugene felt strongly but could not define. He felt that Elinor was lacking in the attraction or desire of the sensual woman as Starwick seemed to be lack-ing in the lust of the sensual man, and there was therefore something in their relation that came from the dark, the murky swamp-fires of emotion, something poisonous, perverse and evil, and full of death.

Just the same, it was fine to be with Elinor when she was gay and deft and charming, and enormously assured, and taking charge of things. At these times, everything in life seemed simple, smooth, and easy; there were no dreary complications, the whole world became an enor-mous oyster ready to be opened, Paris an enormous treasure-hoard of unceasing pleasure and delight. It was good to be with her in a restaurant, and to let her do the ordering.

"Now, children," she would say in her crisp, gay, and yet authoritative tone, staring at the menu with a little frowning smile of studious yet whimsical concentration—"The rest of you can order what you like, but Mother's going to start with fish and a bottle of Vouvray—I seem to re-member that it's very good here—Le Vouvray est bon ici, n'est-ce pas?" she said turning to the waiter.

"Mais, oui, madame!" he said with just the right kind of earnest enthusiasm, "C'est une spécialité."

"Bon," she said crisply. "Alors, une bouteille du Vouvray pour commencer—does that go for the rest of you, mes enfants?" she said, looking around her. They nodded their agreement.

"Bon—bon, madame," the waiter said, nodding his vigorous approval, as he put the order down. "Vous serez bien content avec le Vouvray—et puis?"—He looked at her with suave respectful inquiry. "Pour manger?"

"Pour moi," said Elinor, "le poisson—le filet de sole—n'est-ce pas—Marguery?"

"Bon, bon," he said with enthusiastic approval, writing it down. "Un filet de sole—Marguery—pour Madame—et pour Monsieur?" he said turning suavely to Eugene.

"La même chose," said that linguist recklessly and even as the waiter was nodding enthusiastically, and saying:

"Bon. Bon—parfaitement! La même chose pour monsieur," and writing it down, the others had begun to laugh at him. Starwick with his bubbling laugh, Elinor with her gay little smile of raillery and even Ann, the dark and sullen beauty of her face suddenly luminous with a short and almost angry laugh as she said:

"He hasn't said his other word yet—why don't you tell him that you want some 'mawndiawnts' "—ironically she imitated his pronunciation of the word.

"What's wrong with 'mendiants'?" he said, scowling at her. "What's the joke?"

"Nothing," said Starwick bubbling with laughter. "They're very good. They really are, you know," he said earnestly. "Only we've been wondering if you wouldn't learn another word some day and order something else."

"I know lots of other words," he said angrily. "Only, how am I ever going to get a chance to use them when the rest of you make fun of me every time I open my mouth—I don't see what the great joke is," he said resentfully. "These French people understand what I want to say," he said. "Ecoute, garçon," he said appealingly to the attentive and smiling waiter.—"Vous pouvez comprendre——"

"Cawmprawndre," said Ann mockingly.

"Vous pouvez comprendre—ce-que-je-veux-dire," he blundered on painfully.

"Mais, oui, monsieur!" the waiter cried with a beautiful reassuring smile. "Parfaitement. Vous parlez très bien. Vous êtes ici à Paris depuis longtemps?"

"Depuis six semaines," he said proudly.

The waiter lifted arms and eyebrows eloquent with astounded disbelief.

"Mais c'est merveilleux!" the waiter cried, and as the others jeered Eugene said with bitter sarcasm:

"Every one can't be a fine old French scholar the way you are; after all, I'm not travelled like the rest of you—I've never had your opportunities. And even after six weeks here there are still a few words in the French language that I don't know. . . . But I'm going to speak the ones I do know," he said defiantly, "and no one's going to stop me."

"Of course you are, darling!" Elinor said quickly and smoothly, putting her hand out on his arm with a swift movement. "Don't let them tease you! . . . I think it's mean of you," she said reproachfully. "Let the poor dear speak his French if he wants to—I think it's sweet."

He looked at her with a flushed and angry face while Starwick bubbled with laughter, tried to think of something to say in reply, but, as always, she was too quick for him, and before he could think of something apt and telling, she had flashed off as light and quick as a rapier blade:

"—Now, children," she was studying the card again—"what shall it be after the fish—who wants meat—?"——

"No fish for me," said Ann, looking sullenly at the menu. "I'll take—" suddenly her dark, sullen, and nobly beautiful face was transfigured by her short and almost angry laugh again—"I'll take an 'awmlet,'" she said sarcastically, looking at Eugene.

"Well, take your 'awmlet,'" he muttered. "Only I don't say it that way."

"Pas de poisson," she said quietly to the waiter. "I want an omelette."

"Bon, bon," he nodded vigorously and wrote. "Une omelette pour Madame. Et puis après—?" he said inquiringly.

"Rien," she said.

He looked slightly surprised and hurt, but in a moment, turning to Eugene, said:

"Et pour monsieur?—Après le poisson?"

"Donnez-moi un Chateaubriand garni," he said.

And again Ann, whose head had been turned sullenly down towards the card, looked up suddenly and laughed, with that short and almost angry laugh that seemed to illuminate with accumulating but instant radiance all of the dark and noble beauty of her face.

"God!" she said. "I knew it!—If it's not mendiants, it's Chateaubriand garni."

"Don't forget the Nuits St. George," said Starwick with his bubbling laugh, "that's still to come."

"When he gets through," she said, "there won't be a steak or raisin left in France."

And she looked at Eugene for a moment, her face of noble and tender beauty transfigured by its radiant smile. But almost immediately, she dropped her head again in its customary expression that was heavy and almost sullen, and that suggested something dumb, furious, and silent locked up in her, for which she could find no release.

He looked at her for a moment with scowling, half-resentful eyes, and all of a sudden, flesh, blood, and brain, and heart, and spirit, his life went numb with love for her.

"And now, my children," Elinor was saying gaily, as she looked at the menu—"what kind of salad is it going—" she looked up swiftly and caught Starwick's eye, and instantly their gaze turned upon their two companions. The young woman was still staring down with her sullen, dark, and dumbly silent look, and the boy was devouring her with a look from which the world was lost, and which had no place in it for time or memory.

Dark Helen in my heart forever burning.

"L'écrevisse," Eugene said, staring at the menu. "What does that mean, Elinor?"

"Well, darling, I'll tell you," she said with a grave light gaiety of tone, "an écrevisse is a kind of crawfish they have over here—a delicious little crab—but *much much* better than anything we have."

"Then the name of the place really means *The Crab?*" he asked.

"*Stop* him!" she shrieked faintly. "You barbarian, you!" she went on with mild reproach. "It's not at *all* the same."

"It's really not, you know," said Starwick, turning to him seriously. "The whole quality of the thing is different. It really is. . . . Isn't it astonishing," he went on with an air of quiet frankness, "the genius they have for names? I mean, even in the simplest words they manage to get the whole spirit of the race. I mean, this Square here, even," he gestured briefly, "La Place des Martyrs. The whole thing's there. It's really quite incredible, when you think of it," he said somewhat mysteriously. "It really is."

"Quite!" said Elinor. "And, oh, my children, if it were only spring and

I could take you down the Seine to an adorable place called La Pêche Miraculeuse."

"What does that mean, Elinor?" Eugene asked again.

"Well, darling," she said with an air of patient resignation, "if you *must* have a translation I suppose you'd call it *The Miraculous Catch*— a fishing catch, you know. Only it *doesn't* mean that. It would be sacrilege to call it that. It means *La Pêche Miraculeuse* and nothing else —it's *quite* untranslatable—it really is."

"*Yes,*" cried Starwick enthusiastically, "and even their simplest names —their names of streets and towns and places: L'Etoile, for example— how grand and simple that is!" he said quietly, "and how perfect—the whole design and spatial grandeur of the thing is in it," he concluded earnestly. "It really is, you know."

"Oh, absolutely!" Elinor agreed. "You couldn't call it *The Star,* you know. That means nothing. But *L'Etoile* is perfect—it simply *couldn't* be anything else."

"*Quite!*" Starwick said concisely, and then, turning to Eugene with his air of sad instructive earnestness, he continued: "—And that woman at Le Jockey Club last night—the one who sang the songs—you know?" he said with grave malicious inquiry, his voice trembling a little and his face flushing as he spoke—"the one you kept wanting to find out about— what she was saying?—" Quiet ruddy laughter shook him.

"*Perfectly* vile, of course!" cried Elinor with gay horror. "And all the time, poor dear, he kept wanting to know what it meant. . . . I was going to throw something at you if you kept on—if I'd had to translate *that* I think I should simply have passed out on the spot——"

"I know," said Starwick burbling with laughter—"I caught the look in your eye—it was really *quite* murderous! And *terribly* amusing!" he added. Turning to his friend, he went on seriously: "But really, Gene, it *is* rather stupid to keep asking for the meaning of everything. It *is,* you know. And it's so extraordinary," he said protestingly, "that a person of your quality—your *kind* of understanding—should be so dull about it! It really is."

"Why?" the other said bluntly, and rather sullenly. "What's wrong with wanting to find out what's being said when you don't understand the language? If I don't ask, how am I going to find out?"

"But not at *all!*" Starwick protested impatiently. "That's not the point at all: you can find out nothing that way. Really you can't," he said reproachfully. "The whole point about that song last night was not the words—the meaning of the thing. If you tried to translate it into English, you'd lose the spirit of the whole thing. Don't you see," he went on earnestly, "—it's not the *meaning* of the thing—you can't translate a thing like that, you really can't—if you tried to translate it, you'd have nothing but a filthy and disgusting jingle——"

"But so long as it's French it's beautiful?" the other said sarcastically.

"But *quite!*" said Starwick impatiently. "And it's very stupid of you not to understand that, Gene. It really is. The whole spirit and quality of the thing is *so* French—so *utterly* French!" he said in a high and rather womanish tone—"that the moment you translate it you lose everything. . . . There's nothing disgusting about the song in French —the words mean nothing, you pay no attention to the words; the extraordinary thing is that you forget the words. . . . It's the whole design of the thing, the *tone,* the *quality.* . . . In a way," he added deeply, "the thing has an *enormous* innocence—it really has, you know. . . . And it's so disappointing that you fail to see this. . . . Really, Gene, these questions you keep asking about names and meanings are becoming tiresome. They really are. . . . And all these books you keep buying and trying to translate with the help of a dictionary . . . as if you're ever going to understand anything—I mean, *really* understand," he said profoundly, "in that way."

"You may get to understand the language that way," the other said.

"But not at *all!*" cried Starwick. "That's just the point—you really find out nothing: you miss the whole spirit of the thing—just as you missed the spirit of that song, and just as you missed the point when you asked Elinor to translate La Pêche Miraculeuse for you. . . . It's extraordinary that you fail to see this. . . . The next thing you know," he concluded sarcastically, a burble of malicious laughter appearing as he spoke, "you will have enrolled for a course of lessons—" he choked suddenly, his ruddy face flushing deeply with his merriment—"for a course of lectures at the Berlitz language school."

"Oh, but he's entirely capable of it!" cried Elinor, with gay conviction. "I wouldn't put it past him for a moment. . . . My *dear,*" she said drolly, turning toward him, "I have never known such a glutton for knowledge. It's simply amazing. . . . Why, the child wants to know the meaning of everything!" she said with an astonished look about her—"the confidence he has in my knowledge is rather touching—it really is—and I'm so unworthy of it, darling," she said a trifle maliciously. "I don't deserve it at all!"

"I'm sorry if I've bored you with a lot of questions, Elinor," he said.

"But you *haven't!*" she protested. "Darling, you *haven't* for a moment! I *love* to answer them! It's only that I feel *so*—so *incompetent.* . . . But listen, Gene," she went on coaxingly, "couldn't you try to forget it for a while—just sort of forget all about these words and meanings and enter into the spirit of the thing? . . . Couldn't you, dear?" she said gently, and even as he looked at her with a flushed face, unable to find a ready answer to her deft irony, she put her hand out swiftly, patted him on the arm, and nodding her head with an air of swift satisfied finality, said:

"Good! I knew you would! . . . He's really a darling when he wants to be, isn't he?"

Starwick burbled with malicious laughter at sight of Eugene's glowering and resentful face; then went on seriously:

"—But their genius for names is quite astonishing!—I mean, even in the names of their towns you get the whole thing. . . . What could be more like Paris," he said quietly, "than the name of Paris? . . . The whole quality of the place is in the name. Or Dijon, for example. Or Rheims. Or Carcassonne. The whole spirit of Provence is in the word: what name could more perfectly express Arles than the name it has—it gives you the whole place, its life, its people, its peculiar fragrance. . . . And how different we are from them in that respect. . . . I mean," his voice rose on a note of passionate conviction, "you could almost say that the whole difference between us—the thing we lack, the thing they have —the whole thing that is wrong with us, is evident in our names. . . . It really is, you know," he said earnestly, turning toward his friend again. "The whole thing's most important. . . . How harsh and meaningless most names in America are, Eugene," he went on quietly. "Like addresses printed on a thousand envelopes at once by a stamping machine —labels by which a place may be identified but without meaning. . . . Tell me," he said quietly, after a brief pause, "what was the name of that little village your father came from? You told me one time—I remember because the whole thing I'm talking about—the thing that's wrong with us—was in that name. What was it?"

"Brant's Mill," the other young man answered.

"Quite!" said Starwick with weary concision. "A man named Brant had a mill, and so they called the place Brant's Mill."

"What's wrong with that?"

"Oh, nothing, I suppose," said Starwick quietly. "The whole thing's quite perfect. . . . *Brant's* Mill," there was a note of bitterness in his voice and he made the name almost deliberately rasping as he pronounced it. "It's a name—something to call a place by—if you write it on a letter it will get there. . . . I suppose that's what a name is for. . . . Gettysburg—I suppose a man named Gettys had a house or a farm, and so they named the town after him. . . . And your mother? What was the name of the place she came from?"

"It was a place called Yancey County."

"Quite," said Starwick as before—"and the name of the town?"

"There wasn't any town, Frank. It was a kind of cross-roads settlement called The Forks of Ivy."

"No!" Elinor's light Bostonian accent of astounded merriment rang gaily forth. "Not *really!* You *know* it wasn't!"

"But not at *all!*" said Starwick in a tone of mild and serious disagreement. "The Forks of Ivy is not bad. It's really surprisingly good, when you consider most of the other names. It even has," he paused, and considered carefully, "a kind of quality. . . . But Yancey," he paused again, the burble of sudden laughter came welling up, and for a moment his pleasant ruddy face was flushed with laughter—"*Ya-a-ancey* County" —with deliberate malice he brought the word out in a rasping countrified tone—"God!" he said frankly, turning to the other boy, "isn't it awful! . . . How harsh! How stupid! How banal! . . . And what are some of the names, where you come from, Gene?" he went on quietly after a brief pause. "I'm sure you haven't yet done your worst," he said. "There must be others just as sweet as Ya-a-ancey."

"Well, yes," the boy said grinning, "we've got some good ones: there's Sandy Mush, and Hooper's Bald, and Little Hominy. And we have names like Beaverdam and Balsam, and Chimney Rock and Craggy and Pisgah and The Rat. We have names like Old Fort, Hickory, and Bryson City; we have Clingman's Dome and Little Switzerland; we have Paint Rock and Saluda Mountain and the Frying Pan Gap——"

"Stop!" shrieked Elinor, covering her ears with her shocked fingers— "The Frying Pan Gap! Oh, but that's *horrible!*"

"But how perfect!" Starwick quietly replied. "The whole thing's there. And in the great and noble region where I come from—" the note of weary bitterness in his tone grew deeper—"out where the tall caw-r-n grows we have Keokuk and Cairo and Peoria." He paused, his grave eyes fixed in a serious and reflective stare: for a moment his pleasant ruddy face was contorted by the old bestial grimace of anguish and

confusion. When he spoke again, his voice was weary with a quiet bitterness of scorn. "I was born," he said, "in the great and noble town of
Bloomington but—" the note of savage irony deepened—"at a very
tender age I was taken to Moline. And now, thank God, I am in Paris";
he was silent a moment longer, and then continued in a quiet and almost
lifeless tone: "Paris, Dijon, Provence, Arles . . . Yancey, Brant's Mill,
Bloomington." He turned his quiet eyes upon the other boy. "You see
what I mean, don't you? The whole thing's there."

"Yes," the boy replied, "I guess you're right."

LXXVIII

THEY were sitting at a table in one of the night places of Montmartre.
The place was close and hot, full of gilt and glitter, heavy with that
unwholesome and seductive fragrance of the night that comes from
perfumery, wine, brandy and the erotic intoxication of a night-time
pleasure place. Over everything there was a bright yet golden blaze of
light that wrought on all it touched—gilt, tinsel, table linen, the natural
hue and coloring of the people, the faces of men, and the flesh of the
women—an evil but strangely thrilling transformation.

The orchestra had just finished playing a piece that every one in
Paris was singing that year. It was a gay jigging little tune that Mis-
tinguette had made famous; its name was Ça, c'est Paris, and one heard
it everywhere. One heard lonely wayfarers whistling it as they walked
home late at night through the silent narrow streets of the Latin Quarter,
and one heard it hummed by taxi-drivers, waiters, and by women in
cafés. It was played constantly to the tune of flutes and violins by dance
orchestras in the night-clubs of Montmartre and Montparnasse. And,
accompanied by the swelling rhythms of the accordion, one heard it at
big dance-halls like the Bal Bullier, and in the little dives and stews and
café-brothel-dancing places along noisome alleyways near the markets
and the Boulevard de Sébastopol.

In spite of its gay jigging lilt, that tune had a kind of mournful fatality.
It was one of those songs which seem to evoke perfectly—it is impossible
to know why—the whole color, life, and fragrance of a place and time
as nothing else on earth can do. For the boy, that song would haunt
him ever after with the image of Paris and of his life that year, with
the memory of Starwick, Elinor, and Ann.

The song had for him the fatality of something priceless, irrecoverably lost, full of that bitter joy and anguish we can feel at twenty-four, when the knowledge of man's brevity first comes to us, when we first know ruin and defeat, when we first understand what we have never known before: that for us, as for every other man alive, all passes, all is lost, all melts before our grasp like smoke; when we know that the moment of beauty carries in it the seeds of its own instant death, that love is gone almost before we have it, that youth is gone before we know it, and that, like every other man, we must grow old and die.

The orchestra had finished playing this tune, and the dancers were going to their tables from the polished little square of floor; in a moment Starwick called the leader of the orchestra over to the table and asked him to play Starwick's favorite song. This was a piece called My Chile Bon Bon; it was not new, Starwick had first heard it several years before in Boston, but like the other piece this tune was pregnant with the mournful fatality of a place and period; in its grotesque words and haunting melody there was the sense of something irrevocable, an utter surrender and a deliberate loss, a consciousness of doom. These two pieces together evoked the whole image and quality of that year, and of the life of these four people: for Starwick, in fact, this Chile Bon Bon song somehow perfectly expressed the complete fatality that had now seized his life, the sensual inertia of his will.

The orchestra leader nodded smilingly when Starwick asked him to play the song, went back and conferred with his musicians for a moment, and, himself taking up a violin, began to play. As the orchestra played, the leader walked toward their table, and, bending and swaying with the infinite ductile grace which a violin seems to give to all its performers, he stood facing the two women, seeming to offer up the wailing, hauntingly mournful and exciting music as a kind of devotion to their loveliness.

Elinor, tapping the tune out with her fingers on the table cloth, hummed the words lightly, absently, under her breath; Ann sat quietly, darkly, sullenly attentive; Starwick, at one end of the table, sat turned away, his legs indolently crossed, his ruddy face flushed with emotion, his eyes fixed in a blind stare, and a little wet.

Once, while the piece was being played, Starwick's pleasant ruddy face was contorted again by the old bestial grimace of nameless anguish and bewilderment which Eugene had seen so many times before, and in which the sense of tragic defeat, frustration, the premonition of impending ruin, was legible.

When the orchestra leader had finished with the tune, Starwick turned wearily, thrust his arm indolently across the table towards Ann and wiggling his fingers languidly and a trifle impatiently, said quietly: "Give me some money."

She flushed a little, opened her purse, and said sullenly: "How much do you want?"

The weary impatience of his manner became more evident, he wiggled his languid fingers in a more peremptory command, and, burbling a little with laughter at sight of her sullen face, he said in a low tone of avaricious humor:

"Give, give, give. . . . Money, money, money," he said in a low gloating tone, and burbled again, with a rich welling of humor, as he looked at her.

Red in the face, she flung a wad of bank notes down upon the table with almost vicious force, he accepted them languidly, stripped off 300 franc notes and handed them indolently to the orchestra leader, who responded with a bow eloquent with adoration; and then, without pausing to count them, Starwick thrust the remainder carelessly in his pocket.

"Ann!" he said reproachfully. "I am *very* hurt!" He paused a moment; the flow and burble of soft laughter came quickly, flushing his ruddy face, and he continued as before, with a mock gravity of reproachful humor.

"I had hoped—" his shoulders trembled slightly—"that by this time your *finer* nature—" he trembled again with secret merriment—"your *finer* nature would be ready to reveal itself."

"My finer nature be damned!" Ann said angrily. "Whether you like it or not, I think it's disgraceful the way you fling money around! Three hundred francs to a man for playing that damned song! And you've done the same thing at least a dozen times! God, I'm sick of hearing about your Chile Bon Bon!" she concluded bitterly. "I wish the damned thing had never been written."

"Ann!" again the soft mockery of sounded reproach. "And this is the way you repay us, after all we've done for you! It's not that I'm angry but I'm *very very* hurt," he said gently. "I really am, you know."

"Ah-h!" She made a sudden exasperated movement as if she was going to push the table away from her and get up, and then said with angry warning: "Now, look here, Frank, don't you start that again about how much you've done for me. Done for me!" she said furiously.

"Done for me!" She laughed, short and hard, with angry exasperation, and was unable to find words to continue.

Starwick's burble of soft laughter answered her:

"I *know!*" he said, his face reddening a little as he spoke—"But, after all, you *are* a little *tight,* Ann"—his shoulders trembled slightly, and his ruddy face grew deeper with its hue of humor. "I think," he said gently, and paused again, trembling with quiet laughter—"I think it may be what is known as the Beacon Hill influence. And really," he continued seriously, looking at her with grave eyes, "you really ought to try to get it out of you."

"Now, Frank," cried Ann angrily, half rising from the table, "if you start that again about my being stingy—" She sat down again abruptly, and burst out with bitter resentment, "I'm not stingy and you know it! . . . It's not that I mind spending the money, giving it to you when I've got it. . . . It's only that I think every one ought to try to bear his own share. . . . If you think that's my New England stinginess you're welcome to your opinion. . . . But I've always felt that way and always will! . . . Stingy!" she muttered, "I'm not. . . . I'm just tired of being the goat all the time. . . . It seems to me the rest of you ought to share in the expense sometime!"

"But not at *all!*" cried Starwick in a tone of astonished protest. "I can't see that that makes the *slightest* difference," he went on gently. "After all, Ann, it's not as if we were four old maids from Boston doing the grand tour and putting down every cent we spend in a mutual account book," he said a trifle sarcastically. "It's not that kind of thing at all. When four people know each other the way we do, the last thing in the world that could *possibly* be of value is money. What belongs to one belongs to all. Really," he said a trifle impatiently, "I should think you'd understand that. It's *quite* astonishing to see a person of your quality with such a material—rather *grasping*—view of money. I shouldn't think it would make the *slightest* difference to you. You really ought to get it out of your system, Ann," he said quietly. "You really must. Because you *are* a *grand* person—you really are, you know."

She flushed, and then muttered sullenly:

"Ah! Grand person my eye! I've heard all that before! You can't get around it that way!"

"But you *are!*" he said, with earnest insistence. "You are a *very* grand person—that's what makes the whole thing such a pity."

She flushed again, and then sat staring at the table in sullen embarrassment.

"And, Ann," said Starwick gently, beginning to burble with his soft flow of wicked laughter, "you are really *very* beautiful in that red dress—" his sensuous mannered tone trembled again with its burble of wicked humor—"and *very* seductive—and *very*," his shoulders trembled and his face trembled as he spoke—"You are really *quite* voluptuous," he said with sensual relish, and suddenly choked with laughter. When he had composed himself, he turned his still laughter-reddened face towards Eugene, and said earnestly: "It's *quite* astonishing! She really is, you know! She's *gloriously* beautiful!"

"Frank!" she looked at him for a moment with an expression of baffled exasperation. Then, suddenly she laughed her short and angry laugh: "God!" she cried sarcastically. "It's a high price to pay for compliments, isn't it?"

But that laugh, short and angry as it was, had made radiant, as it always did, her dark and noble beauty. Instantly her face had been lifted, transfigured from its customary expression of dark and almost heavy sullenness, her cheeks, which in repose had the pendulous sagging quality of a plump child, were suffused with rose, her sweet red mouth and white teeth suddenly shone with a radiant and lovely smile, and Eugene noticed now, as he had begun to notice, that her gray eyes when she looked at Starwick were no longer hard and angry, but smoky, luminous with a depthless tenderness.

"You *are*," Starwick concluded quietly, seriously, his pleasant face still a trifle flushed with laughter. "You are one of the most *gloriously* beautiful creatures that ever lived."

What he said was the simple truth. The girl's beauty that night was almost unbelievable. She had put on a new evening dress which had been made for her by a famous designer. The dress was a glorious red, that seemed almost to float with an aerial buoyancy of filmy gauze; no dress in the world could have suited her dark beauty, or revealed the noble proportions of her figure half so well. Her hair, which was black, coarse, and fragrant, was parted simply in the middle: Eugene noted that there were already a few streaks of coarse gray in it, but her face had the dignity of her grand and honest character—the sullen plumpness of a child and the radiant sudden sweetness and happiness of her smile, combined.

And in every other respect, Ann showed this strange and lovely union of delicacy and grandeur, of the child and the woman. Her hands were long, brown, and narrow, the fingers long and delicate, the bones as fine and small as a bird's, and yet they were strong, sensitive, able-looking hands as well. Her arms were long and slender, as firm and delicate as a young girl's, but Eugene noted that her breasts were not round and firm, but the long heavy sloping breasts of a big woman. When she got up to dance with Starwick she topped him by a head, and yet, radiant with a joy and happiness she had never known before, she seemed to float there in his arms, an Amazonian figure, great of thigh and limb and breast, and a creature of a loveliness as delicate and radiant as a child's.

They danced superbly together: in deference to Starwick, the orchestra played his Chile Bon Bon song again; when they returned to the table Starwick's ruddy face was flushed with the emotion the song always aroused in him, his eyes looked wet, and in a high, passionate, almost womanish tone, he cried to Eugene:

"God! Isn't it grand! Isn't it simply superb! It's one of the great songs of the world, it really is, you know! The thing has the same quality as a great primitive—the same quality as a primitive Apollo or Cimabue's Madonna, in the Louvre. Christ!" he cried in a high womanish tone, "the whole thing's there—it really is! I think it's the greatest song that was ever written!"

He poured out a glass of champagne, cold and sparkling, and drank it thirstily, his eyes wet, his face flushed deeply with his feeling.

LXXIX

In the dull gray light of the short and swiftly waning winter's day, the two young men were leaving the museum, to spend the rest of the afternoon until the time of their appointed meeting with the women, in drink and talk at one of the innumerable and seductive cafés of the magic city. Outside the Louvre, they hailed a taxi and were driven swiftly over one of the bridges of the Seine, through the narrow streets of the Latin Quarter, and at length stopped and got out before La Closerie des Lilas, where they were to meet the two women later on.

They spent the remainder of the afternoon in the chill wintry air of the terrace, warm with drink, with argument or discussion, and with the gaiety of life and voices of people all around them, the pageant of life that passed forever on the street before them—all that priceless, rare, and uncostly pleasure and excitement of café life which seemed unbelievable and magical to these two young Americans. The dull gray air, which was at once chill and wintry, and yet languorous, filled them with the sense of some powerful, strange, and inhuman excitement that was impending for them.

And the bright gaiety of the colors, the constant flash and play of life about them and along the pavements, the smell and potent intoxication of the cognac, gave them the sensation of a whole world given over without reserve or shame to pleasure. All these elements, together with that incomparable fusion of odors—at once corrupt and sensual, subtle and obscene—which exudes from the very texture of the Paris life—odors which it is impossible to define exactly, but which seem in the dull wintry air to be compacted of the smells of costly perfumes, of wine, beer, brandy, and of the acrid and nostalgic fumes of French tobacco, of roasted chestnuts, black French coffee, mysterious liquors of a hundred brilliant and intoxicating colors, and the luxurious flesh of scented women—smote the two young men instantly with the sensual impact of this strange and fascinating world.

But in spite of all the magic of the scene, and the assurance and security which Starwick's presence always gave to him, the ghost of the old unquiet doubt would not wholly be laid at rest, the ache of the old hunger stirred in Eugene. Why was he here now? Why had he come? The lack of purpose in this present life, the dozing indolence of this existence in which no one worked, in which they sat constantly at tables in a café, and ate and drank and talked, and moved on to sit at other tables, other cafés—and, most of all, the strange dull faces of the Frenchmen, the strange and alien life of this magic city which was so seductive but so unalterably foreign to all that he had ever known—all this had now begun to weigh inexplicably upon a troubled spirit, to revive again the old feelings of naked homelessness, to stir in him the nameless sense of shame and guilt which an American feels at a life of indolence and pleasure, which is part of the very chemistry of his blood, and which he can never root out of him. And feeling the obscure but powerful insistence of these troubled thoughts within his mind, he turned suddenly to Starwick, and, without a word of explanation said:

"But do you really feel at home here?"

"What do you mean by 'feeling at home'?"

"Well, I mean don't you ever feel out of place here? Don't you ever feel as if you didn't belong to this life—that you are a foreigner?"

"But not at all!" said Starwick a trifle impatiently. "On the contrary, I think it is the first time in my life that I have *not* felt like a foreigner. I never felt at home in the Middle-West where I was born; I hated the place from my earliest childhood, I always felt out of place there, and wanted to get away from it. But I felt instantly at home in Paris from the moment I got here:—I am far closer to this life than to any other life I've ever known, for the first time in my life I feel throughly at home."

"And you don't mind being a foreigner?"

"But of course not!" Starwick said curtly. "Besides, I am *not* a foreigner. You can only be foreign in a place that is foreign to you. This place is not."

"But, after all, Frank, you are not a Frenchman. You are an American."

"Not at all," Starwick answered concisely. "I am an American only by the accident of birth; by spirit, temperament, inclination, I have always been a European."

"And you mean you could continue to lead this kind of life without ever growing tired of it?"

"What do you mean by this kind of life?" said Starwick.

His friend nodded towards the crowded and noisy terrace of the café.

"I mean sitting around at café's all day long, going to night-clubs—eating, drinking, sitting,—moving on from one place to another—spending your life that way?"

"Do you think it's such a bad way to spend your life?" said Starwick quietly. He turned, regarding his friend with serious eyes. "Don't you find it very amusing?"

"Yes, Frank, for a time. But after a while, don't you think you'd get tired of it?"

"No more tired," said Starwick, "than I would of going to an office day after day at nine o'clock and coming away at five, doing useless and dreary work that some one else could do as well. On the contrary—this kind of life—" he nodded towards the crowded tables—"seems to me much more interesting and amusing."

"But how can you feel that you belong to it?" the other said. "I should think that would make a difference to you. It does to me—the feeling that I am a stranger here, that this is not my life. that I know none of these people."

"Are you getting ready to tell me now that an American never really gets to know any French people?" said Starwick, repeating the banal phrase with a quiet sarcasm that brought a flush to the other's face.

"Well, it's not likely that he will, from what I've heard."

Starwick cast a weary look around him at the chattering group of people at the other tables.

"God!" he said quietly. "I shouldn't think he'd want to. I imagine most of them are about as dull a lot as you could find."

"If you feel that way about them, what is the great attraction Paris holds for you? How can you possibly feel that way about the people and still say you feel at home here?"

"Because Paris belongs to the world—to Europe—more than it belongs to France. One does not come here because he wants to know the French: he comes because he can find here the most pleasant, graceful and civilized life on earth."

"Yes, but there are other things that may be more important than leading a graceful and pleasant life."

"What, for instance?" said Starwick, looking at him.

"Getting your work done is one of them. For you, I should think that would be a great deal more important."

Starwick was again silent; the old bestial grimace, image of an unutterable anguish and confusion in his soul, for a moment contorted his pleasant ruddy face, developed, passed, was gone; he said quietly and with the infinite weariness of despair that had now become the image of his life:

"Getting my work done! My God, as if it mattered."

"There was a time when you thought it did, Frank."

"Yes, there was a time when I did think so," he said lifelessly.

"And now you no longer feel that way about it?"

Starwick was silent; when he spoke again, it was not to answer directly.

—"Always the old unquiet heart," he said wearily and sadly; he turned and looked silently at his friend for a moment. "Why? Since I first knew you, you have been like that, Eugene—wanting to devour the earth, lashing your soul to frenzy in this useless, hopeless and impossible search for knowledge."

"Why useless or hopeless, Frank?"

"Because it is a kind of madness in you that grows worse all the time; because you cannot cure it, or ever satisfy this hunger of yours while you have it; because it will exhaust you, break your heart, and drive you mad; and because, even if you could gratify this impossible desire to absorb the whole sum of recorded knowledge and experience in the world, you would gain nothing by it."

"There I can't agree with you."

"Do you really think," said Starwick wearily, "that if you could achieve this hopeless ambition of reading all the books that were ever printed—of knowing all the people—seeing all the places—that you would be any better off than you now are? Now, day after day, you go prowling up and down along the book-stalls on the Seine, pawing through tons of junk and rubbish until your very heart is sick with weariness and confusion. When you are not with us, you sit alone in a café with a dictionary beside you trying to decipher the meaning of some useless and meaningless book. You no longer enjoy what you read, because you are tortured by a consciousness of the vast number of books you have not read; you go to the museums—to the Louvre—and you no longer enjoy the pictures, because you torture your brain and exhaust your energy in a foolish effort to see and remember all of them. You no longer enjoy the crowd, you go out on the streets of Paris, you sit here in this crowded café—and instead of taking pleasure in all this gaiety and life about you, you are tortured by the thought that you know none of these people, that you know nothing about their lives, that there are four million people here in Paris and you do not know a dozen of them. . . . Eugene, Eugene," he said sadly, "this thing in you is growing worse all the time; if you do not master it, it is a disease that will some day drive you mad and destroy you."

"And yet, Frank, many people on this earth have had the same disease. Because of it, in order to get knowledge, Doctor Faust sold his soul to the devil."

"Alas," said Starwick, "where is the devil?" In a moment he continued quietly, as before: "Do you think that you will really gain in wisdom if you read a million books? Do you think you will find out more about life if you know a million people rather than yourself? Do you think you will get more pleasure from a thousand women than from two or three—see more if you go to a hundred countries instead of six? And finally, do you think you'll get more happiness from life by 'getting your work done' than by doing nothing? My God, Eugene—" his voice was weary with the resigned fatality of despair that had now corrupted him—"you still feel that it is important that you 'do your work,' as you call it, but what will it matter if you do or don't? You want to lead the artist's life, to do the artist's work, to create out of the artist's materials—what will it matter in the end if you do this, or nothing?"

"You did not always feel so, Frank."

"No," said Starwick wearily, "there was a time when I felt differently. There was a time when I felt that the artist's life was the finest life on earth—the only life I would care to lead."

"And now?"

"Now—nothing—nothing," he spoke so quietly that his words were scarcely audible. "It no longer matters. . . . I go to the Louvre and look at that colossal mountain of junk—up and down those endless corridors hung with the dull or worthless work of thousands of dead men who once felt as I did—that they must create, express the image of their soul—that art and the artist's life were all that mattered. Now they are dead, their dreary works have been left behind as a kind of use-less relic of their agony: in that whole gigantic storage-plant of worth-less art—there are just three pictures I should have cared to paint—and I know it's not in me to paint any of them. I thought I wanted to write plays, but now I feel the same about that, too; among all the thousands of plays I have read or seen, I doubt that there are a dozen which I should have cared to write—and I know now that I could have written none of them. . . . What does it matter? Why do you goad your spirit and exhaust your mind with these frantic efforts, these useless desires to add another book or play to the mountains of books and plays that have already been written? Why should we break our hearts to add to that immense accumulation of dull, fair, or trivial work that has already been done?" He was silent a moment longer, and then the color in his ruddy face deepening with excitement, he said in a high, passionate tone: "What is great—what is priceless—what we would give our lives to do —is so impossible—so utterly, damnably impossible! And if we can never do the best—then why do anything?"

For a moment, there returned to the other a memory of the moonlit streets of Cambridge, and of a night when Starwick, drunk with wine and the generous and extravagant enthusiasm of youth, had turned to him and in a voice that rung along the sleeping street, had called him a mighty poet. And he remembered how his own heart had beat hot with hope and joy at the sound of those proud and foolish words, and how he had grasped Starwick's hand and wrung it with a hard grip of passionate conviction, and told Frank what he believed at that moment with all the ardor of his heart—that Starwick was the greatest young man of his time and generation.

And remembering now those two drunk and happy boys who stood there in the moon-still streets, and spoke to each other the compact of their devotion and belief, he wanted to ask Frank if this weary acquiescence in defeat, that had now become the very color of his life, was a better thing than the proud and foolish vision of a boy.

But he said nothing, and after a moment's silence, Starwick looked at his watch and called the waiter, saying that it was already time for their meeting with the two women at a café in Montparnasse. Therefore, they paid the bill, and departed; but what Frank had said to him that day would live in his memory in years to come. For in Frank's words were implicit every element of the resignation, despair, and growing inertia and apathy of his will.

LXXX

THE relations between these four people had now been strained to the breaking point. That month of debauch had exacted a stern tribute from them. Their exhausted bodies and frayed nerves cried out for rest, a period of curative repose when the well of their drained energy could be filled up again. But like creatures hopelessly addicted to a drug, they could not break the bonds of this tyranny of pleasure which held them. Starwick seemed to be completely enslaved by this senseless and furious quest, this frantic seeking after new sensations, this hopeless pursuit of a happiness, a fulfilment, that they never found. He seemed unable or unwilling to break the evil spell. Rather, as if a poisonous hunger was feeding on his vitals—a hunger that grew constantly from the food it fed upon, and that could not be assuaged by any means—the evil inertia of his will, the ugly impassivity of his resignation became every day more marked.

Of all of them, he alone preserved the appearance of calm. And that cold, impassive calm was maddening: he met the storms of anger, protests, reproaches, and persuasions of the others with an air of sad humility, a kind of sorrowful acceptance, a quiet agreement to every accusation or indictment, a grand manner of sweet, sorrowful contrition that was more hateful than any deliberate insult could have been. For behind this impenetrable armor of humility, this air of mysterious fatality, there was evident a hateful arrogance which said that words were useless because no words could express the fatal wisdom of his soul, and which, with a stubborn and abominable perversity, seemed deliberately resolved on ruin.

His conduct became daily more absurd, extravagant, ridiculous. He was acting like a melodramatic fool, but it was impossible to laugh at his folly because of the desperate fatality that attended it. He did unbelievable things, contrived unbelievable situations that seemed fitting only in a world of opera but were shamefully unreal and unnecessary in the real one. What was really shameful and unworthy in his conduct was this—his fatality served no purpose, his reckless and deliberate pursuit of danger did no good except to dignify the melodramatic unreality of a comic opera situation with the realities of blood and death.

He was constantly and deliberately involving himself and others in these ridiculous but perilous situations. One night, in one of the Montmartre resorts, he had a quarrel with a man that would have been farcical save for the ugly consequences it produced, the painful and shameful memory it would later evoke. The man, an unpleasant, wizened-looking little Frenchman, a creature of the night, with obscene eyes, a yellowed skin, and a pointed beard half covering the features of a rodent, had not been able to keep his ugly eyes off Ann, had measured the noble proportions of her beauty with a kind of foul leering appraisal that had in it something almost as palpable and sensual as a naked touch, and now, as the orchestra struck up another tune, he approached the table, bowed, and asked her, courteously enough, for a dance.

Ann reddened furiously in the face, looked down sullenly at the tablecloth and, before she was able to think of a reply, Starwick said:

"Mademoiselle does not care to dance. Please go away."

The cold arrogance of Starwick's tone, and his curt dismissal, enraged the Frenchman. When he replied, his lips were bared in an ugly smile that showed unpleasant fangs of yellowed teeth; he said:

"Is the lady not allowed to speak for herself?—Is Monsieur perhaps her guardian?"

"Will you please go away now?" Starwick said again, with a cold and weary impassivity. "You are boring us."

"But, it's marvellous!" The little Frenchman cast back his yellowed face and bared his fangs in a laugh of envenomed mockery. "It's Monsieur D'Artagnan come to life again, and a lady so shy and modest that she can't speak for herself! But, it's superb!" he cried again, and with an ironic bow, concluded: "Monsieur, with all my heart I thank you for this wonderful diversion! You are very droll!"

Starwick's reply to this was to pick up the seltzer bottle on the table and, without for a moment altering his air of cold impassivity, to squirt the siphon straight in the little Frenchman's yellow face.

In a moment, the place was a seething maelstrom of excitement. People all over sprang up from their tables, the dancers stopped dancing, the orchestra stopped with a crash, and the proprietor and the waiter came towards them on the run.

In a moment, they were surrounded by an excited group of gesticulating, chattering people, all trying to talk at once. Starwick was standing up now, facing his antagonist, cold and impassive save for a deeper flush of excitement on his ruddy face. As for the little Frenchman, the look of murderous hatred on his face was horrible. Without stopping to dry his dripping face with the napkin which an excited and persuasive waiter was offering him, he thrust aside the manager, who was trying to restrain him, and coming close to Starwick, snarled:

"Your name, monsieur? I demand to know your name. My representatives will call upon you in the morning."

"Good," said Starwick coldly. "I shall wait for them. Monsieur shall have whatever satisfaction he desires."

And taking a card from his purse, he wrote the studio address below his name and gave it to the man.

"Ah, good!" the Frenchman cried harshly, glancing at it. "Until tomorrow!"

And calling for his bill, and silent to all the apologies and cajoleries of the proprietor, he departed.

"But Frank, darling!" Elinor cried, when they had seated themselves again. "What do you intend to do? Surely you're not going to—" She did not finish, but stared at him with a troubled and astonished face.

"Yes," said Starwick coldly and quietly. "He has asked me to fight a duel, and if he wants it, I shall meet him."

"Oh, but don't be absurd!" cried Elinor with an impatient laugh. "What on earth do you know about fighting duels! My poor child, how can you be so ridiculous! This is the twentieth century, darling. Don't you know that people don't act that way any more?"

"Quite!" said Starwick, with a stony calm. "Nevertheless, I shall meet him if he wants me to." He looked at her with quiet eyes for a moment, and then said gravely: "I've *got* to do that. I really have, you know."

"Got to!" Elinor cried impatiently. "Why, the child is *mad!*" Her tone immediately became crisp, incisive, authoritative: she began to speak to him quietly, kindly, but in a peremptory tone, as one might speak to a child:

"Francis," she said quietly. "Listen to me! Don't be an idiot! What does it matter about that wretched little man? It's all over now! A duel! Good heavens! Don't be such a child! Who ever heard of such a thing?"

His face reddened a little from her ridicule, but he answered, in a cold impassive tone:

"Quite! Nevertheless, I shall meet him if he wants it!"

"Meet him!" Elinor cried again. "Oh, Francis, how can you be so stupid! Meet him with what?"

"With whatever weapon he wants to use," Starwick replied. "Pistols or swords—it doesn't matter!"

"Pistols or swords!" Elinor shrieked faintly, and began to laugh. "Why, you idiot, what do you know about pistols or swords? You've never had a sword in your hand in your life—and as for pistols, you wouldn't even know how to point the thing and press the trigger!"

"It doesn't matter," he said in a very quiet and fatal way. "I shall fire into the air."

In spite of the ridiculous and melodramatic quality of these foolish words, no one laughed. They saw suddenly what fatal consequences this farcical situation might have, and having felt the desperation of his soul—that terrible despair which now seemed to be driving him on to seek ruin everywhere—they knew he would do exactly as he said, if given the opportunity.

Elinor started to go: she beckoned to a waiter and called for the bill, and said persuasively:

"Come on! Let's get out of this place! You've had too much to drink! I think your head needs clearing—a little fresh air will do you good. You'll feel different about all this tomorrow!"

"But not at all!" he said patiently, and then, as she started to get up: "Will you please sit down. We're not going yet."

"But why, darling? Aren't you ready? Haven't you raised enough hell for one evening—or do you want to fight a duel with some one else? Besides, I do think you might think of Ann. I know she's wanted to go for some time."

"But why?" he said, turning to Ann with an air of fine surprise. "Aren't you enjoying yourself? It's a very good place, and the music is awfully good—it really is, you know."

"Oh, charming, charming!" she muttered sarcastically. She had been staring at the tablecloth sullenly, with a flaming face, ever since the quarrel had begun, and now looking up suddenly, with a short and angry laugh, she said:

"God! I don't know whether to walk out of here or *crawl!* I feel all—*undressed!*"

At these words, his face really did flush crimson with embarrassment. He looked at her for a moment, and then said sharply, with a note of stern reproof and anger in his voice:

"Ann! It's *very* bad and *very* wrong—and—and—very *mean* of you to talk like that."

"That's how I feel," she muttered.

"Then," he said quietly, but with two deep and angry spots of color flaming in his cheeks, "I'm *thoroughly* ashamed of you. It's *quite* unworthy of you. At a time like this, a person of your quality has got to show more—" he paused, choosing the word carefully, "more *fibre*. You really must, you know!"

"Oh, fibre my eye!" she flared up, looking at him with flushed, lovely and angry eyes. "You don't lack fibre simply because you don't want to be made a fool of! Frank, you make me tired, the way you talk! Everywhere we go now some one's always showing 'fibre'—and every one is having a rotten, awful time. For God's sake, let's not talk so much about showing fibre and let's try to enjoy ourselves and get some pleasure and some happiness from life, and act like decent, natural people for a change. I had looked forward so much to coming on this trip with Elinor—and now—" Tears of anger and disappointment glittered in her eyes, she looked down at the table sullenly in an effort to conceal them, and then muttered: "Playing the fool and making scenes and starting rows everywhere we go! Getting into trouble everywhere, making people hate us, never having any fun! Squirting siphons at some wretched little man——" she made a sudden impulsive gesture of disgust and turned away. "God! It makes me sick!"

"I'm sorry to know you feel that way," he said quietly. "I'll try to see it doesn't happen again—but, after all, Ann—the reason it did happen is because I like you so *very* much, and have so much respect for you and won't stand for any one insulting you!"

"Ah-h! Insulting me!" she said angrily. "Good heavens, Francis, do you think I need protection from a wretched little man like that? When I've been a nurse, and had to go alone to every rotten slum in Boston, and learned to handle people twice his size! Protect me!" she said bitterly. "Thank you for nothing! I didn't come over here to be protected —I don't need it. I can take care of myself. Just try to act and feel like a decent human being—let's try to be friends together and to show some consideration for each other—and don't worry about protecting me!"

LXXXI

EUGENE slept little that night. The quarrel in the night-club and its consequences seemed fantastic, incredible, like a nightmare. At daybreak he got up and went to the window and stared out at the gray light just breaking on the roofs and chimney-pots of Paris. The old buildings emerged haggard, pale, lemony, with all the wonderful, homely practicality of dawn and morning, and looking at them, Montmartre, the blaze of lights, the music and the drunken voices, and the quarrel with the Frenchman—the whole strange and evil chemistry of night—seemed farther away, more unreal and dream-like than ever. Could it have happened? Had Starwick really been challenged to a duel? Was he going through with it?

He got up and dressed, and with dry lips and a strange, numb lightness in his limbs, descended to the street and hailed a passing taxi in the Rue Bonaparte. The sounds of morning, shutters being rolled up, scrubwomen and maids down on their knees at entrances, shops being opened —all this made the night before seem more unreal than ever.

When he got to the studio he found everybody up. Ann was already at work making coffee, scrambling eggs for breakfast. Elinor was just combing up her hair, Starwick was in the balcony and had not yet come down. Elinor kept talking as she arranged her hair, and from the balcony Starwick answered her:

"But Frank!" she was saying, "you know you wouldn't be fool enough to do such a thing! Surely you don't mean you intend to go through with it?"

"Ace," he said coldly from above, "I do mean to. Quite!"

"But—oh! Don't be an ass!" she cried impatiently. Turning to Ann, with a little, frowning smile, she bit her lips, and shaking her head slightly, cried in an astounded tone:

"Isn't it *incredible!* Did you ever hear of such an *insane* thing in all your life!"

But in the set of her jaw, the faint smile around the corner of her mouth, there was the look of grim decision they had all seen before.

As Eugene entered, Ann turned from the stove, and spoon in hand, stood looking at him sullenly for a moment. Suddenly she laughed her short and angry laugh, and turned away toward Elinor, saying:

"God! Here's the second! Don't they make a pair!"

"But my *dear!*" cried Elinor with a light, gay malice. "Where is the top hat? Where are the striped trousers and the morning coat? Where is the duelling case with the revolvers? . . . All right, Monsieur D'Artagnan," she called up towards the balcony ironically. "Your friend, Monsieur Porthos has arrived . . . and breakfast is ready, darling! What's that they say about an army?" she innocently inquired, "—that it ought not to fight on an empty stomach? . . . Ahem!" she cleared her throat. "Will Monsieur D'Artagnan condescend to have the company of two frail women for breakfast on the morning of the great affair . . . or does Monsieur prefer to be left alone with his devoted second to discuss—ahem! ahem! . . . the final arrangements?"

Starwick made no reply, until he had come down the steps:

"You can stay, if you want to," he said indifferently. "I shall have nothing to say to them anyway." Turning to Eugene, he said with magnificent, bored weariness: "Find out what they want. Let me know what they want to do."

"B—but, what do you want me to say to them, Frank? What shall I tell them?"

"Anything," said Starwick indifferently. "Anything you like. Say that I will meet him anywhere—on any terms—whatever they like. Let them settle it their own way."

He picked up a spoon and started to eat his orange.

"Oh, Frank, you idiot!" cried Elinor, seizing him by the hair, and shaking his head. "Don't be stupid! You know you're not going on with this farce!"

He lifted quiet, wearily patient eyes and looked at her:

"Sorry!" he said. "But I've *got* to. If that's what he wants, I really must. I owe the man that much—I really do, you know!"

Breakfast then proceeded in a painful and uneasy silence, broken only by Elinor's malicious thrusts, and maintained by Starwick's weary and impassive calm.

At ten o'clock, there were steps along the alley-way outside, some one mounted the stoop, and the studio bell jangled. The two women exchanged uneasy looks, Starwick got up quietly and turned away, and in a moment Elinor called out sharply: "Entrez."

The door opened and a man entered the room. He wore striped

trousers that were in need of pressing, a frayed and worn-looking frock coat, and he carried a briefcase under his arm. He was bald, sallow, about forty-five years old, and had a little mustache and furtive eyes. He looked at each person in the room quickly, sharply, and then said inquiringly:

"Monsieur Star-*week?*"

"Ace," said Starwick quietly, and turned.

"Ah, bon!" the little Frenchman said briskly, and smiled, showing yellow fangs of teeth. He had been bent slightly forward, holding his briefcase with thin, eager fingers, as he waited. Now he came forward swiftly, took a card out of his wallet, and presenting it to Starwick with something of a flourish, said:

"Monsieur, permettez-moi. Ma carte."

Starwick glanced at the card indifferently, and was about to put it down upon the table when the little Frenchman interrupted him. Stretching out his thin and rather grimy hand, he said courteously yet eagerly:

"S'il vous plaît, monsieur!"—took the card again, and put it back into his wallet.

Starwick indicated a chair and said:

"Won't you sit down?"

From that time on, the conversation proceeded in mutilated French and English. The little Frenchman sat down, hitched up his striped trousers carefully and with his arched fingers poised upon his bony knees, bent forward and, with another ingratiating and somewhat repulsive smile, said:

"Monsieur Star-week ees Américain, n'est-ce pas?"

"Ace," said Starwick.

"And was at Le Rat Mort last night?"

"Ace," said Starwick again.

"Et Monsieur?" He nodded inquiringly toward Eugene, "vas also zere?"

"Ace," Starwick answered.

"Et Mademoiselle . . . et Mademoiselle," he turned with courteous inquiry towards the two young women—"zey vere also zere?"

"Ace," said Starwick as before.

"Ah, bon!" the little Frenchman cried, nodding his head vigorously, and with an air of complete satisfaction. Then, rubbing his bony, little hands together dryly and briskly, he took up his thin and battered old

briefcase, which he had been holding firmly between his knees, swiftly
unfastened the straps and unlatched it, and took out a few sheets of
flaming, yellow paper covered with notations in a fine, minute hand:

"Monsieur—" he began, clearing his throat, and rattling the flimsy
sheets impressively—"Monsieur, I s'ink"—he looked up at Starwick
ingratiatingly, but with an air of sly insinuation, "—Monsieur, I s'ink,
perhaps, vas"—he shrugged his shoulders slightly, with an air of deprecation—"Monsieur vas—drink-*ing?*"

Starwick made no answer for a moment: his face reddened, he inclined his head, and said coldly, but unconcedingly:

"Oui! C'est ça, monsieur!"

"Ah-h!" the little Frenchman cried again with a dry little cackle of
satisfaction— "—an' ven one drink—espeecial*ee,* monsieur, ven ve are
yong," he laughed ingratiatingly again, "—he sometime do an' say some
t'ings zat he regret—eh?"

"But of course!" cried Elinor at this point, quickly, impatiently,
eagerly. "That's just the point! Frank was drinking—the whole thing
happened like a flash—it's all over now—we're sorry—every one is sorry:
—it was a regrettable mistake—we're sorry for it—we apologize!"

"But not at all!" cried Starwick reddening angrily, and looking resentfully towards Elinor. "Not at all! I do *not* agree with you!"

"Oh, Frank, you idiot, be quiet! Let me handle this," she cried.
Turning to the little Frenchman, she said swiftly, smoothly, with all her
coaxing and formidable persuasiveness:

"Monsieur, what can we do to remedy this regrettable mistake?"

"Comment?" said the Frenchman, in a puzzled tone.

"Monsieur Starwick," Elinor went on with coaxing persuasion, "—
Monsieur Starwick—comme vous voyez, monsieur—est très jeune. Il
a toutes les fautes de la jeunesse. Mais il est aussi un homme de grand
esprit; de grand talent. Il a le tempérament d'un artiste: d'un homme
de génie. Comme un Français, monsieur, vous," she went on flatter-
ingly, "—*vous* connaissez cette espèce d'hommes. Vous savez qu'ils
ne sont pas toujours responsables de leurs actes. C'est comme ça avec
Monsieur Starwick. Il est de bon cœur, de bon volonté: il est honnête,
généreux et sincère, mais il est aussi plein de tempérament—impulsif:—
il manque de jugement. Hier soir nous avons tous—comme on dit—
fait la noçe ensemble. Monsieur Starwick a bu beaucoup—a bu trop
—et il a été coupable d'une chose regrettable. Mais aujourdhui il se
repent très sincèrement de sa conduite.

"Il vous offre ses apologies les plus profondes. Il a déjà souffert assez. Dans ces circonstances, monsieur," she concluded, with an air of charming persuasiveness, "on peut excuser le jeune homme, n'est-ce pas?—on peut pardonner une faute si honnêtement et sincèrement regrettée."

And she paused, smiling at him with an air of hopeful finality, as if to say: "There! You agree with me, don't you? I knew you would!"

But the Frenchman was not to be so easily persuaded. Waving thin fingers sideways in the air, and shaking his head without conviction, he laughed a dry, dubious laugh, and said:

"Ah-h! I don't know—mademoiselle! Zese apologies!—"—again he waved thin dubious fingers—"eet ees all ver-ree well to meck apologies bot ze—vat you say?—ze dom-mage!—ze dom-mage is done. . . . Monsiur," he said gravely, turning to Starwick, "you have been coupable of a ver-ree gret offense. Ze—ze—vay you say?—*ze assault,* monsieur—ze assault ees 'ere in France—une chose très sérieuse! Vous comprenez?"

"Ace," said Starwick coldly.

"Mon client," the little Frenchman cleared his throat portentously—"—mon client, Monsieur Reynal, 'as been terriblement blessé—insulté! monsieur!" he cried sharply. "Eeet ees necessaree zu meck des réparations, n'est-ce pas?"

"Ace," said Starwick coldly. "Whatever reparation you desire."

The Frenchman stared at him a moment in an astonished way and then, in an excited and eager tone, cried:

"Ah, bon! Zen you agree?"

"Perfectly," said Starwick.

"Bon! Bon!" the little man said eagerly, rubbing his hands together with greedy satisfaction. "Monsieur est sage—ees, vat you say?—ees ver-ree wise. Monsieur est Américain—n'est-ce pas?—un étranger—comme vous, mademoiselle . . . et vous, monsieur . . . et vous, mademoiselle—you are 'ere zu meck ze tour—zu be libre—free—n'est-ce pas —zu avoid ze complications——"

"But," said Elinor, in a bewildered tone, "—what is—I don't understand——"

"Alors," the Frenchman said, "eet ees bettaire to avoid ze complications—oui! Ah," he said, with an arching glance at Starwick, "mais Monsieur est sage . . . est très, très sage! C'est toujours mieux de faire des réparations . . . et éviter les conséquences plus sérieuses."

"But!" cried Elinor again, her astonishment growing, "I don't understand. What reparations are you talking about?"

"Zese, madame!" the Frenchman said, and coughing portentously, he rattled the flimsy sheets of paper in his hand, held them up before his eyes, and began to read:

"Pour l'endommagement d'un veston du soir—trois cents francs!"

"What? *What?*" said Elinor in a small, chilled tone. "For—*what?*"

"Mais, oui, madame!" the Frenchman now cried passionately, for the first time rising to the heights of moral indignation, "—un veston du soir complet—ruiné, madame!—*complètement, absolument* ruiné! . . . Trois cents francs, monsieur," he said cunningly, turning to Starwick, "—c'est pas cher! . . . Pour moi, oui!—c'est cher—mais pour vous— ah-h!" he waved his dirty fingers and laughed with scornful deprecation, "—c'est rien! Rien du tout." He rattled the flimsy paper in his hands, cleared his throat, and went on:

"Pour l'endommagement d'une chemise—une chemise, n'est-ce pas, du soir?" he looked up inquiringly, "—cinquante francs"——

"But this," gasped Elinor, "this is—" She looked at Starwick with an astounded face. Starwick said nothing.

"Pour l'angoisse mentale"—the Frenchman continued.

"What?" Elinor gasped and looked at Ann. "What did he say?"

"Mental anguish," Ann answered curtly. "All right," she turned to the Frenchman, "how much is the mental anguish?"

"C'est cinq cent francs, mademoiselle."

"But this man?" cried Elinor, turning to Ann with an air of astounded enlightenment—"this man is——"

"He's a shyster lawyer, yes!" Ann said bitterly. "Couldn't you see it from the first?"

"Ah, mademoiselle,"—the Frenchman began with a reproachful grimace, and a little, deprecating movement of his fingers, "—you are——"

"How much?" Ann answered in her level, toneless French. "How much do you want?"

"Vous comprenez, mademoiselle——"

"How much?" she said harshly. "How much do you want?"

His furtive eyes gleamed with a sudden fox-glint of eager greed.

"Mille francs!" he said eagerly. "Mille francs pour tout ensemble! . . . Pour vous, mademoiselle"—he laughed again with scornful deprecation as he waved his grimy fingers—"c'est rien—pour moi——"

She got up abruptly, went over to the shelf that ran around the wall and got her purse. She opened it, took out a roll of bills, and coming back tossed them on the table before him.

"But mademoiselle"—he stammered, unable to believe his good luck, his eyes glued upon the roll of bills in a stare of hypnotic fascination.

"Give me a receipt," she said.

"Comment?" he looked puzzled for a moment, then cried, "Ah-h! Un reçu! Mais oui, mais oui, mademoiselle! Tout de suite!"

Trembling with frantic haste he scrawled out a receipt on a sheet of yellow paper, gave it to her, clutched the banknotes with a trembling claw, and stuffed them in his wallet.

"Now get out," said Ann.

"Mademoiselle?" he scrambled hastily to his feet, clutched his brief-case and his hat, and looked nervously at her—"vous dites?"

"Get out of here," she said, and began to move slowly towards him.

He scrambled for the door like a frightened cat, stammering:

"Mais oui . . . mais parfaitement . . . mais"—he almost stumbled going down the steps, glancing back with nervous apprehension as he went. She shut the door behind him, came back, sat down in her chair, and stared sullenly at her plate, saying nothing. Starwick was crimson in the face, but did not look at any one and did not speak. Elinor was busy with her napkin: she had lifted it to her face and was holding it firmly across her mouth. From time to time her breast and stomach and her heavy shoulders trembled in a kind of shuddering convulsion, smothered and explosive snorts and gasps came from her.

It got too much for her: they heard a faint, choked shriek, she rose and rushed blindly across the room, entered the bathroom and slammed the door behind her. And then they heard peal after peal of laughter, shrieks and whoops and yells of it, and finally a dead silence, broken at times by exhausted gasps. Ann continued to look sullenly and miserably at her plate. As for Starwick, he sat there wearily detached, impassive, magnificent as always, but his face had the hue and color of boiled lobster.

LXXXII

One night, in a small bar or *bistro* upon the hill of Montmartre, Starwick met a young Frenchman who was to become the companion of his adventures in many strange and devious ways thereafter. It was about four o'clock in the morning: after the usual nightly circuit of the gilded pleasure resorts, cafés and more unsavory dives and stews of the district, Starwick had become very drunk and unruly, had quarrelled with Elinor and Ann when they tried to take him home, and since that time had been wandering aimlessly through the district, going from one cheap bar to another.

The women hung on doggedly; Starwick had refused to let them accompany him, and they had asked Eugene to stay with him and try to keep him out of trouble. Eugene, in fact, was only less drunk than his companion, but fortified by that sense of pride and duty which a trust imposed by two lovely women can give a young man, he hung on, keeping pace with Starwick, drink for drink, until the whole night fused into a drunken blur, a rout of evil faces, the whole to be remembered later as jags of splintered light upon a chain of darkness, as flying images, fixed, instant, and intolerably bright, in the great blank of memory. And out of all these blazing pictures of the night and the wild reel of their debauch, one would remain forever after, to haunt his vision mournfully. It was the memory—or rather the *consciousness*—of the two women, Ann and Elinor, waiting in the dark, following the blind weave of their drunken path, all through the mad kaleidoscope of night, never approaching them, but always there. He had not seemed to look at them, to notice them, and yet later he had always known that they were there. And the memory fused to one final mournful image that was to return a thousand times to haunt him in the years to come. He and Starwick had come out of one of the bars that broke the darkness of the long steep hill, and were reeling down past shuttered stores and old dark houses towards the invitation of another blaze of light.

Suddenly he knew that Ann and Elinor were behind them. For a moment he turned, and saw the two women pacing slowly after them, alone, patient, curiously enduring. The image of that long silent street of night, walled steeply with old houses and shuttered shops, and of the figures of these two women pacing slowly behind them, in the darkness, seemed in later years to bear the sorrowful legend of what their lives—of what so much of life—was to become. And for this reason it burned forever in his memory with a mournful, dark and haunting radiance, became in fact, detached from names and personalities and identic histories—became something essential, everlasting and immutable in life. It was an image of fruitless love and lost devotion, of a love that would never come to anything, and of beautiful life that must be ruinously consumed in barren adoration of a lost soul, a cold and unresponding heart. And it was all wrought mournfully there into the scheme of night, made legible in the quiet and gracious loveliness of these two women, so strong, so patient, and so infinitely loyal, pacing slowly down behind two drunken boys in the slant steep street and emptiness of night.

Suddenly the image blazed to the structure of hard actuality: another bar, and all around hoarse laughter, high sanguinary voices, a sudden scheme of faces scarred with night, and livid with night's radiance—whores, taxi drivers, negroes, and those other nameless unmistakable ones—who come from somewhere—God knows where—and who live somehow—God knows how—and who recede again at morning into unknown cells—but who live here only, brief as moths, and baleful as a serpent's eye, in the unwholesome chemistry of night.

He found himself leaning heavily on the zinc counter of the bar, staring at a pair of whited, flabby-looking arms, the soiled apron and shirt, the soiled night-time face and dark, mistrustful eyes of night's soiled barman. The blur of hoarse voices, shouts and oaths and laughter fused around him, and suddenly beside him he heard Starwick's voice, drunken, quiet, and immensely still:

"Monsieur," it said—its very stillness cut like a knife through all the fog of sound about him—"monsieur, du feu, s'il vous plaît."

"But sairtainlee, monsieur," a droll and pleasant-sounding voice said quietly. "W'y not?"

He turned and saw Starwick, a cigarette between his lips, bending awkwardly to get the light from a proffered cigarette which a young Frenchman was holding carefully for him. At last he got it; puffing awkwardly, and straightening, he slightly raised his hat in salutation, and said with drunken gravity:

"Merci. Vous êtes bien gentil."

"But," said the young Frenchman again, drolly, and with a slight shrug of his shoulder, "not at all! Eet ees noz-zing!"

And as Starwick started to look at him with grave drunken eyes, the Frenchman returned his look with a glance that was perfectly composed, friendly, good-humored, and drolly inquiring.

"Monsieur?" he said courteously, as Starwick continued to look at him.

"I think," said Starwick slowly, with the strangely mannered and almost womanish intonation of his voice, "I think I like you *very* much.

You are *very* kind, and *very* generous, and altogether a *very* grand person. I am *enormously* grateful to you."

"But," the Frenchman said, with droll surprise, and a slight astonished movement of his shoulders, "I 'ave done noz-zing! You ask for du feu—a light—and i geev to you. I am glad eef you like—bot—" again he shrugged his shoulders with a cynical but immensely engaging humor—"eet ees not so ver-ree grand."

He was a young man, not more than thirty years old, somewhat above the middle height, with a thin, nervously active figure, and thin, pointedly Gallic features. It was a pleasant, most engaging face, full of a sharply cynical intelligence; the thin mouth was alive with humor—with the witty and politely cynical disbelief of his race, and his tone, his manner—everything about him—was eloquent with this racial quality of disbelief, a quality that was perfectly courteous, that would raise its pointed eyebrows and say politely, "You s'ink so"—but that accepted without assent, was politely non-committal without agreement.

He was dressed as many young Frenchmen of that period dressed:—a style that served to combine the sinister toughness of the Apache with a rather gaudy and cheap enhancement of the current fashions. His clothes were neat but cheaply made; he wore a felt hat with a wide brim, creased, French fashion, up the sides, an overcoat with padded shoulders, cut in sharply at the waist, his trousers had a short and skimpy look, and barely covered the tops of his shoes. He wore spats, and a rather loud-colored scarf which he knotted loosely, cravat-fashion, and which thus concealed his collar and his shirt. Finally, when he smoked a cigarette, he drew the smoke in slowly, languorously, knowingly, with lidded eyes, and a cruel and bitter convulsion of his thin lips that gave his sharp face a sinister Apache expression.

Starwick was now crying out in a high drunken tone of passionate assurance:

"But yes! Yes! Yes!—You are a *grand* person—a *swell* person—I like you *enormously*. . . ."

"I am glad," said the Frenchman politely, with another almost imperceptible movement of the shoulders.

"But yes! You are my friend!" Starwick cried in a high passionate tone. "I like you—you must drink with me."

"Eef you like—of course!" the Frenchman politely agreed. Turning to the soiled barman who continued to look at them with dark mistrustful eyes, he said, in a hard, sharp voice, "Une fine. . . . And you, monsieur?" he turned inquiringly toward Eugene, "I s'ink you have another drink?"

"No, not now"—his glass was not yet empty. "We—we have both already had something to drink."

"I can see," the Frenchman said politely, but with a swift flicker of cynical mirth across his thin mouth, that needed no translation. Raising his glass, he said courteously:

"A votre santé, messieurs," and drank.

"Look!" cried Starwick. "You are our friend now, and you must call us by our names. My name is Frank; his is Eugene—what is yours?"

"My name ees Alec," said the young Frenchman smiling. "Zat ees w'at zey call me."

"But it's perfect!" Starwick cried enthusiastically. "It's a *swell* name— a *wonderful* name! Alec!—Ecoute!" he said to the soiled barman with the ugly eye, "Juh pawnse qu'il faut—encore du cognac," he said drunkenly, making a confused and maudlin gesture with his arm. "Encore du cognac, s'il vous plaît!" And as the barman silently and sullenly filled the three glasses from a bottle on the bar, Starwick turned to Alec, shouting with dangerous hilarity: "Cognac forever, Alec!— Cognac for you and me and all of us forever!—Nothing but drunkenness—glorious drunkenness—divine poetic drunkenness forever!"

"Eef you like," said Alec, with a polite and acquiescent shrug. He raised his glass and drank.

It was four o'clock when they left the place. Arm in arm they reeled out into the street, Starwick holding onto Alec for support, and shouting drunkenly:

"Nous sommes des amis!—Nous sommes des amis éternels! Mais oui! Mais oui!"

The whole dark and silent street rang and echoed with his drunken outcry. "Alec et moi—nous sommes des frères—nous sommes des artistes! Nothing shall part us! Non—jamais! Jamais!"

A taxi, which had been waiting in the darkness several doors away, now drove up swiftly and stopped before them at the curb. Ann and Elinor were inside: Elinor opened the door and spoke gently:

"Frank, get in the taxi now, we're going home."

"Mais jamais! Jamais!" Starwick yelled hysterically. "I go nowhere without Alec!—We are brothers—friends—he has a poet's soul."

"Frank, don't be an idiot!" Elinor spoke quietly, but with crisp authority. "You're drunk; get in the taxi; we're going home."

"Mais oui!" he shouted. "Je suis ivre! I am drunk! I will always be drunk—nothing but drunkenness forever for Alec and me!"

"Listen!" Elinor spoke quietly, pleasantly to the Frenchman. "Won't you go away, please, and leave him now? He is drunk, he does not know what he is doing, he really must go home now."

"But, of course, madame," said Alec courteously, "I go now." He turned to Starwick and spoke quietly, with his thin, engaging smile: "I s'ink, Frank, eet ees bettaire eef you go home now, non?"

"But no! But no!" cried Starwick passionately. "I will go nowhere without Alec. . . . Alec!" he cried, clutching him with drunken desperation. "You cannot go! You must not go! You cannot leave me!"

"Tomorrow, perhaps," said Alec, smiling. "Ees eet not bettaire eef we go to-gezzer tomorrow?—I s'ink zen you feel motch bettaire."

"No! No! Starwick cried obstinately. "Now! Now! Alec, you cannot leave me! We are brothers, we must tell each other everything. . . . You must show me all you know, all you have seen—you must teach me to smoke opium—take me where the opium smokers go—Alec! Alec! J'ai la nostalgie pour la boue . . ."

"Oh, Frank, quit talking like a drunken idiot! Get in the car, we're going home . . ."

"But no! But no!" Starwick raved on in his high drunken voice. "Alec and I are going on together—he has promised to take me to the places that he knows—to show me the dark mysteries—the lower depths . . ."

"Oh, Frank, for God's sake get in the car; you're making a damned fool of yourself!"

"—But no! I will not go without Alec—he must come with us—he is going to show me . . ."

"But I show you, Frank," said Alec smoothly. "Tonight, non!" He spoke firmly, waved a hand. "Eet ees impossible. I wet 'ere for some one. I must meet, I 'ave engagement—yes. Tomorrow, eef you like, I meet you 'ere! Tonight, non!" His voice was harsh, sharp with irrevocable refusal. "I cannot. Eeet ees impossible."

By dint of infinite prayers and persuasions, and by Alec's promises that he would meet him next day to take him on a tour of "the lower depths," they finally got Starwick into the taxi. All the way down the hill however, as the taxi sped across Paris, through the darkened silent streets, and across the Seine into the Latin Quarter, Starwick raved on madly about his eternal friendship with Alec, from whom he could never more be parted. The taxi turned swiftly into the dark and empty little Rue des Beaux Arts and halted before Eugene's hotel. The two women waited in nervous and impatient haste for Eugene to get out, Elinor giving his arm a swift squeeze and saying:

"Good-night, darling. We'll see you tomorrow morning. Don't forget our trip to Rheims."

When he got out, however, Starwick followed him, and began to run drunkenly towards the corner, smashing at the shutters of the shops with his cane and screaming at the top of his voice:

"Alec! Alec! Où est Alec? Alec! Alec! Mon ami Alec! Où êtes-vous?"

Eugene ran after Starwick and caught him just as he was disappearing around the corner into the Rue Bonaparte, headed for the Seine. By main strength and pleading he brought him back, and managed to get him into the taxi again, which had followed his pursuit in swift watchful reverse. He slammed the door upon that raving madman, and as the taxi drove off, he heard, through a fog of drunkenness, Elinor's swift "Thank you, darling. You behaved magnificently—tomorrow—" and Starwick raving:

"Alec! Alec! Where is Alec?"

They sped off up the silent empty street, a narrow ribbon lit sparsely by a few lamps, and walled steeply with its high old shuttered houses Eugene walked back to his hotel, rang the night bell, and was let in. As he stumbled up the circuitous and perilous ascent of five flights, he caught a moment's glimpse of the little concierge and his wife, startled from their distressful sleep, clutching each other together in a protective embrace, as they peered out at him from the miserable little alcove where they slept—a moment's vision of their pale, meagre faces and frightened eyes.

He climbed the winding flights of stairs, and let himself into his room, switching on the light, and flinging himself down upon the bed immediately in a stupor of drunken exhaustion.

It seemed to him he had not lain there five minutes before he heard Starwick smashing at the street door below, and shouting drunkenly his own name and that of Alec. In another minute he heard Starwick stumbling up the stairs; he went to the door, opened it, and caught him just as he came stumbling in. Starwick was raving, demented, no longer conscious of his acts: he began to smash and beat at the bed with his stick, crying:

"There!—And there!—And there!—Out, out, damned spot, and make an end to you. . . . The stranger—the one I never knew—the stranger you have become—out! Out! Out!"

Turning to Eugene then, he peered at him with drunken bloodshot eyes, and said:

"Who are you?—Are you the stranger?—Are you the one I never knew?—Or are you . . .?" His voice trailed off feebly, and he sank down into a chair, sobbing drunkenly.

And getting to his feet at length, he looked about him wildly, smote the bed again with his stick, and cried out loudly:

"Where is Eugene? Where is the Eugene that I knew?—Where?—Where?—Where?" He staggered to the door and flung it open, screaming: "Alec! Where are you?"

He reeled out into the hall, and for a moment hung dangerously against the stair rail, peering drunkenly down into the dizzy pit five flights below. Eugene ran after him, seized him by the arm and together, they fell or reeled to the bottom. It was a journey as distorted and demented as a dream— a descent to be remembered later as a kind of corkscrew nightmare, broken by blind lurchings into a creaking rail, by the rattling of Starwick's stick upon the banisters, by blind sprawls, and stumblings, and by blobs and blurs of frightened faces at each landing, where Monsieur Gely's more sober patrons waited in breath-caught silence at their open doors. They reached the bottom finally amid such universal thanksgiving, such prayers for their safety, as Gely's hotel had never known before.

A vast sigh, a huge and single respiration of relief rustled up the steep dark pit of the winding stairs. But another peril lay before them. At the foot of the stairs there stood a monstrous five-foot vase which, by its lustre and the loving care with which it was polished every day by Marie, the maid, must have been the pride of the establishment. Starwick reeled blindly against it as he went past, the thing rocked sickeningly, and even as it tottered slowly over, Eugene heard Madame Gely's gasp of terror, heard her low "Mon Dieu! Ça tombe, ça tombe!" and a loud united "Ah-h-h!" of thankfulness as he caught it in his hands, and gently, safely, with such inner triumph as a man may feel who leaps through space and lands safely hanging to a flying trapeze, restored it to its former position. As he looked up he saw old Gely and his wife peering from their quarters with fat perturbed faces, and the little concierge and his wife still clutched together, peering through their curtains in a covert of bright frightened eyes.

They got out into the street at last. In the Rue Bonaparte they stopped a taxi drilling through. When they reached Montmartre again the night was breaking in gray light behind the church of Sacré-Cœur. After further drinks of strong bad cognac, they piled out of the place into another taxi, and went hurtling back through Paris. By the time they arrived at the studio full light had come.

The women were waiting up for them. Starwick mumbled something and, holding his hand over his mouth, rushed across the room into the bathroom and vomited. When he was empty, he staggered out, reeled towards the couch where Ann slept, and toppled on it, and was instantly sunk in senseless sleep.

Elinor regarded him for a while with an air at once contemplative and amused. "And now," she said cheerfully, "to awake the Sleeping Beauty from his nap." She smiled her fine bright smile, but the lines about her mouth were grimly set, and her eyes were hard. She approached the couch, and looking down upon Starwick's prostrate and bedraggled form, she said sweetly: "Get up, darling. It's breakfast-time."

He groaned feebly, and rolled over on his side.

"Up, up, up, my lamb!" Her tone was dulcet, but the hand that grasped his collar and pulled him to a sitting position was by no means gentle. "We are waiting for you, darling. The day's at morn, the hour draws close, it's almost time. Remember, dear, we're starting out for Rheims at nine o'clock."

"Oh God!" groaned Starwick wretchedly. "Don't ask me to do that! Anything, anything but that. I can't! I'll go anywhere with you if you just leave me alone until tomorrow." He flopped back on the bed again.

"Sorry, precious," she said in a light and cheerful tone, as hard as granite, "but it's too late now! You should have thought of that before. Our plans are made, we're going—and *you,*" suddenly her voice hardened formidably, "*you're* coming with us." She looked at him a moment longer with hard eyes, bent and grasped him by the collar, and roughly jerked him up to a sitting position again.

"Francis," she said sternly, "pull yourself together now and get up! We're going to have no more of this nonsense!"

He groaned feebly, and staggered to his feet. He seemed to be on the verge of collapse, his appearance was so pitiable that Ann, coming from the bathroom at this moment, flushed with hot sympathy as she saw him, and cried out angrily, accusingly, to Elinor:

"Oh, leave him alone! Let him sleep if he wants to. Can't you see he is half dead? Why should we drag him along to Rheims if he doesn't feel like going? We can put the trip off until tomorrow, anyway. What does it matter when we go?"

Elinor smiled firmly and shook her head with a short inflexible movement. "No, sir," she said quietly. "Nothing is going to be put off. We are going today, as we planned. And Mr. Starwick is going with us! He may go willingly or against his will, he may be conscious or unconscious when he gets there, but, alive or dead, he's going!"

At these unhappy tidings, Starwick groaned miserably again. She turned to him and, her voice deepening to the authority of indignation, she said:

"Frank! You've *got* to see this through! There's no getting out of it now! If you don't feel well, that's just too bad—but you've got to see this thing through anyway! You've known about this trip for the past week—if you chose to spend last night making the rounds of every joint in Montmartre you've no one to blame for it but yourself! But you've *got* to go. You're not going to let us down this time!"

And steeled and wakened by the challenge of her tone—that challenge which one meets so often in people who have let their whole life go to hell, and lacking stamina for life's larger consequences insist on it for trivialities—he raised his head, looked at her with angry, bloodshot eyes, and said quietly:

"Very well, I'll go. But I resent your asking it *very* much!"

"All right, my dear," she said quietly. "If you resent it, you resent it —and that's that! Only, when you make a promise to your friends they expect you to live up to it."

"Ace," said Starwick coldly. "Quite."

"And now," she spoke more kindly, "why don't you go into the bathroom, Frank, and straighten up a bit? A little cold water across your head and shoulders would do you no end of good." She turned to Ann and said quietly: "Did you finish in there?"

"Yes," said Ann curtly, "it's all right now. I've cleaned it up." For a minute she stared sullenly at the older woman, and suddenly burst into her short and angry laugh:

"God!" she said, with a rich, abrupt, and beautifully coarse humanity. "I never saw the like of it in my life! I don't see where he put it all!" Her voice trembled with a full, rich, infuriated kind of humor. "Everything was there!" she cried, "except the kitchen sink!"

Starwick flushed deeply, and looking at her, said, quietly, gravely: "I'm sorry, Ann. I'm *terribly, terribly* sorry!"

"Oh, it's all right," she said shortly, yet with a kind of tenderness. "I'm used to it. Don't forget that I served three years' training in a hospital once. You get so you don't notice those things."

"You are a *very* swell person," he said slowly and distinctly. "I'm *terribly* grateful."

She flushed, and turned away, saying curtly: "Sit down, Frank. You'll feel better when you have some coffee. I'm making it now." And in her silent and competent way she set to work.

In these few commonplace words, all that was strong, grand, and tender in Ann's soul and character was somehow made evident. Brusque and matter-of-fact as her words had been when she referred to the disgusting task just performed, their very curtness, and the rich and coarse humanity of her sudden angry laugh, had revealed a spirit of noble tenderness and strength, a spirit so strong and sweet and full of love that it had risen triumphant not only over the stale, dead and snobbish little world from which she came, but also over the squeamishness which such a task would have aroused in most of the people who made up that world.

To Starwick, she symbolized certain divinities known to his art and his experience: Maya, or one of the great Earth-Mothers of the ancients, or the goddess of Compassionate Mercy of the Chinese, to whom he often likened her.

But to the other youth, her divinity was less mythical, more racial and mundane. She seemed to fulfill in part his vision of the grand America, to make palpable the female quality of that fortunate, good, and happy life of which he had dreamed since childhood—to evoke the structure of that enchanted life of which every American has dreamed as a child. It is a life that seems forever just a hand's-breadth off and instantly to be grasped and made our own, the moment that we find the word to utter it, the key to open it. It is a world distilled of our own blood and earth, and qualified by all our million lights and weathers, and we know that it will be noble, intolerably strange and lovely, when we find it. Finally, she was the incarnation of all the secret beauty of New England, the other side of man's dark heart, the buried loveliness that all men long for.

LXXXIII

THE car which they had chartered for a four months' tour was brought around from a garage at nine o'clock. A few minutes later they were on their way to Rheims.

Elinor drove; Eugene sat beside her; Ann and Starwick were in the rear seat. The car was a good one—a Panhard—and Elinor drove swiftly, beautifully, with magnificent competence, as she did all things, getting ahead of everybody else, besting even the swerve of the taxi drivers in their wasp-like flight, and doing it all with such smooth ease that no one noticed it.

They seemed to get through the great dense web, the monumental complication of central Paris by a kind of magic. As always, Elinor communicated to every one and everything the superb confidence of her authority. In her presence, and under her governance, the strange and alien world about them became instantly familiar as the Main Street of one's native town, making even the bewildering and intricate confusion of its swarming mass wonderfully natural and easy to be grasped. Paris, in fact, under the transforming magic of this woman's touch, became curiously American, the enchantment beautifully like Eugene's own far-off visions as a child.

It was astounding. The whole city had suddenly taken on the clear and unperplexing proportions of a map—of one of those beautifully simple and comforting maps which are sold to tourists, in which everything is charming, colorful, and cosy as a toy, and where everything that need be known—all the celebrated "points of interest"—the Eiffel Tower, the Madeleine, and Notre Dame, the Trocadéro, and the Arc de Triomphe, are pictured charmingly, in vivid colors.

Paris, in fact, had this morning become a brilliant, lovely, flashing toy. It was a toy which had been miraculously created for the enjoyment of brilliant, knowing and sophisticated Americans like Elinor and himself. It was a toy which could be instantly understood, preserved and enjoyed, a toy that they could play with to their hearts' content, a toy which need confuse and puzzle none of them for a moment, particularly since Elinor was there to explain the toy and make it go.

It was incredible. Gone was all the blind confusion, the sick despair, the empty desolation of his first month in Paris. Gone was the old blind and baffled struggle against the staggering mass and number of a world too infinitely complex to be comprehended, too strange and alien to be understood. Gone were all the old sensations of the drowning horror, the feeling of atomic desolation as he blindly prowled the streets among alien and uncountable hordes of strange dark faces, the sensation of being an eyeless, grope-thing that crawled and scuttled blindly on the sea-depths of some terrible oceanic world of whose dimensions, structure, quality and purpose it could know nothing. Gone were all those feelings of strife, profitless, strange and impotent futility—those struggles that wracked the living sinews of man's life and soul with quivering exhaustion and with sick despair, the hideous feeling of being emptied out in planetary vacancy, of losing all the high hope of the spirit's purpose, the heart's integrity—of being exploded, emptied out and dissipated into hideous, hopeless nothingness where all the spirit of man's courage turned dead and rotten as a last year's apple, and all his sounding plans of work and greatness seemed feebler than the scratchings of a dog upon a wall—a horror that can seize a man in the great jungle of an unknown city and a swarming street and that is far more terrible than the unknown mystery of any Amazonian jungle of the earth could be.

It was all gone now—the devouring hunger, and the drowning horror, and the blind confusion of the old, swarm-haunted mind of man—the fruitless struggle of the Faustian life—and in its place he had the glittering toy, the toy of legend and enchantment and of quick possession.

The French, they were a charming race—so gay, so light, and so incorrigible—so childlike and so like a race of charming toys.

Elinor made their relation to all these good people swarming in the streets around them wonderfully easy, clear, and agreeable. There was nothing strange about them, their ways were unpredictable, since they were French, but they were perfectly understandable. Her attitude, expressed in a rapid, gay and half-abstracted chatter—a kind of running commentary on the life around her as she drove—made the whole thing plain. They were a quaint lot, a droll lot, an incomparable lot—they were charming, amazing, irresponsible, a race of toys and children—they were "French."

"All right, my dear," she would murmur to herself as a fat taxi driver snaked recklessly in ahead of her and came to a triumphant stop—"have it your own way, my darling—have it your own way—I shan't

argue with you—God!" she would cry, throwing her head back with a
sudden rich burst of laughter—"look at the old boy with the whiskers
over there at the table—did you see him twirl his gay mustachios and
roll his roguish eyes at that girl as she went by? *Simply* incredible!"
she cried with another laugh, and bit her lips, and shook her head in fine
astonishment. "Thank you!" she murmured politely, as the gendarme
shrilled upon his whistle and beckoned with his small white club.
"Monsieur l'Agent, vous êtes bien gentil"—as she smoothly shifted
gears and shot past him.

In this wonderful and intoxicating way all of Paris defiled past them
like a great glittering toy, a splendid map of rich, luxurious shops and
great cafés, an animated and beautiful design of a million gay and
fascinating people, all bent on pleasure, all filled with joy, all with something so vivid, bright, particular and incomparable about them that the
whole vast pattern resolved itself into a thousand charming and brilliant
pictures, each wonderful and unforgettable, and all fitting instantly into
the single structure, the simple and magnificent clarity of the whole
design.

They swept through the huge central web of Paris, and were passing
through the great shabby complication of the Eastern Quarters, the
ragged, ugly sprawl of the suburbs.

And now, swift as dreams, it seemed, they were out in open country,
speeding along roads shaded by tall rows of poplars, under a sky of
humid gray, whitened with a milky and soul-troubling light.

Elinor was very gay, mercurial, full of sudden spontaneous laughter,
snatches of song, deep gravity, swift inexplicable delight. Ann maintained a sullen silence. As for Starwick, he seemed on the verge of collapse all the time. At Château-Thierry he announced that he could go
no farther; they stopped, got him into a little café, and fortified him with
some brandy. He sank into a stupor of exhaustion, from which they
could not rouse him. To all their persuasions and entreaties he just
shook his head and mumbled wearily:

"I can't!—Leave me here!—I can't go on!"

Three hours passed in this way before they succeeded in reviving him,
getting him out of the café—or estaminet—and into the car again. Ann's
face was flushed with resentful anger. She burst out furiously:

"You had no right to make him come along on this trip! You knew
he couldn't make it; he's dead on his feet. I think we ought to take
him back to Paris now."

"Sorry, my dear," said Elinor crisply, with a fine bright smile, "but there'll be no turning back! We're going on!"

"Frank can't go on!" Ann cried angrily. "You know he can't! I think it's a rotten shame for you to insist on this when you see what shape he's in."

"Nevertheless, we're going on," said Elinor with grim cheerfulness. "And Mr. Starwick is going with us. He'll see it through now to the bitter end. And if he dies upon the way, we'll give him a soldier's burial here upon the field of honor. . . . Allons, mes enfants! Avancez!" And humming gaily and lightly the tune of Malbrouck, she shifted gears and sent the car smoothly, swiftly forward again.

It was a horrible journey. One of those experiences which, by the grim and hopeless protraction of their suffering, leave their nightmare image indelibly upon the memories of every one who has experienced them. The gray light of the short winter's day was already waning rapidly when they drove out of Château-Thierry. As they approached Rheims, dark had almost come, the lights of the town had begun to twinkle, sparsely, with provincial dismalness, in the distance. No one knew the purpose of their visit; no one knew what the trip was for, what they were coming to see—no one had enquired.

It was almost dark when they entered the town. Elinor drove immediately to the cathedral, halted the car, and got out.

"Voilà, mes amis!" she said ironically. "We are here!"

And she made a magnificent flourishing gesture towards the great ruined mass, which, in the last faint gray light of day, was dimly visible as a gigantic soaring monument of shattering arches and demolished buttresses, a lacework of terrific stone looped ruggedly with splinters of faint light, the demolished façades of old saints and kings and shell-torn towers—the twilit ruins of a twilight world.

"Magnificent!" cried Elinor enthusiastically. "Superb!—Frank! Frank! You must get out and feast your eyes upon this noble monument! I have heard you speak so often of its beauty. . . . But, my dear, you *must!*" she said, answering with fine persuasion his feeble and dispirited groan. "You'd never forgive yourself, or me either, if you knew you'd come the whole way to Rheims without a single look at its cathedral."

And, despite his wearily mumbled protests, she took him by the arm and pulled him from the car. Then, for a moment, as he stared drunkenly, with blind, unseeing eyes, at the great gray twilit shape, she propped him up and held him between herself and Eugene.

Then they all got back into the car, and she drove them to the best café, the best hotel in town. Starwick almost collapsed getting out of the car. His knees buckled under him, and he would have fallen if Ann had not caught him, put her arm around him, and held him up. His condition was pitiable. He could no longer hold his head up; it lolled and wobbled drunkenly on his neck like a flower too heavy for its heavy stalk. His eyes were glazed and leaden, and as they started into the café, he had to be held up. He lifted his feet and dragged them after him like leaden weights. The café was a large and splendid one. They found a table to one side. Starwick staggered towards the cushioned seat against the wall and immediately collapsed. From that time on, he was never wholly conscious. Ann sat down beside him, put her arm around him and supported him. He sank against her shoulder like a child. The girl's face was flushed with anger, she stared at Elinor with resentful eyes, but by no word or gesture did Elinor show that she noticed anything amiss either in Ann's or Starwick's behavior.

Rather, she chatted gaily to Eugene, she kept up a witty and high-spirited discourse with every one around her, she had never been more mercurial, quick, gay and charming than she was that evening. And announcing gaily that she was the hostess that was "giving the party," she ordered lavishly—a delicious meal, with champagne from the celebrated cellars of the establishment. And every one, spurred to hunger by the cold air and their long journey, ate heartily——every one save Ann, who ate little and sat in angry silence, with one arm around Starwick's shoulders, and Starwick, who could not be roused from his deep stupor to eat anything.

It was after nine o'clock before they got up to go. Elinor paid the bill, and still chatting as gaily and as lightly as if the whole wretched expedition had brought nothing but unqualified joy to all her guests, started for the door. Starwick had to be half-carried, half-dragged out by Ann and Eugene, under the prayerful guidance of several deeply troubled waiters. They put him in the car and got in themselves. Elinor looking around lightly, and crying out cheerfully: "Are we ready, children?" started the motor for the long drive back to Paris.

That was a hideous and unforgettable journey. Before they were done

with it, they thought that it would never end. Under the protraction of
its ghastly horror, time lengthened out interminably, unbelievably, into
centuries. It seemed to them at last that they would never arrive,
that they were rolling through a spaceless vacancy without progression,
that they were hung there in the horrible ethers of some planetary
emptiness where their wheels spun futilely and forever in moveless
movement, unsilent silence, changeless change.

From the very beginning they did not know where they were going.
By the time they got out of Rheims they were completely lost. It was a
cold night, late in February; a thick fog-like mist that grew steadily
more impenetrable as the night wore on, had come down and blanketed
the earth in white invisibility. And through this mist there were diffused
two elements: the weird radiance of a submerged moon which gave to
the sea of fog through which they groped, the appearance of an endless
sea of milk, and the bitter clutch of a stealthy, raw, and cruelly penetrating cold which crept into man's flesh and numbed him to the bone
of misery.

All through that ghastly and interminable night, they groped their
way across France in the milky ocean of antarctic fog. It seemed to them
that they had travelled hundreds of miles, that Paris had long since been
passed, lost, forgotten in the fog, that they were approaching the outer
suburbs of Lyons or Bordeaux, that presently they would see the comforting lights of the English Channel or that they had turned north-
wards, had crossed Belgium, and soon would strike the Rhine.

From time to time the road wound through the ghostly street of some
old village; the white walls of village houses rose sheer and blank beside
the road, sheeted in phantasmal mist like ghosts, and with no sound
within. Then they would be groping their way out through the open
countryside again—but where or in what country, no one knew, none
dared to say—and suddenly, low and level, beside them to the left, they
would see the moon. It would suddenly emerge in some blind hole that
opened in that wall of fog, and it was such a moon as no man living ever
saw before. It was an old, mad, ruined crater of a moon, an ancient,
worn, and demented thing that smouldered red like an expiring coal,
and that was like the old ruined moon of a fantastic dream. It hung
there on their left, just at the edge of a low ridge of hills, and it was so
low, so level, and so ghostly-near, it seemed to them that they could
touch it.

Towards midnight they groped their way into a whited ghostly phantom of a town which Elinor at length, with the sudden recognition of a person who revisits some old scene of childhood, discovered to be Soissons. She had known the town well during the War: the ambulance unit, in which she had been for eighteen months a driver, had been stationed here. Starwick was half conscious, huddled into Ann's shoulder on the dark rear seat. He groaned pitiably and said that he could go no farther, that they must stop. They found a hotel café that was still open and half-carried, half-dragged him in. They got brandy for him, they tried to revive him; he looked like a dead man and said that he could go no farther, that they must leave him there. And for the first time Elinor's grave tone showed concern and sharp anxiety, for the first time her hard eye softened into care. She remained firm; gently, obdurately, she refused him. He collapsed again into unconsciousness; she turned her worried eyes upon the others and said quietly:

"We can't leave him here. We've got to get him back to Paris somehow."

After two ghastly hours in which they tried to revive him, persuade him to gird up his fainting limbs for final effort, they got him back into the car. Ann covered him with blankets and held him to her for the remainder of the night, as a mother might hold a child. In the faint ghostgleam of light her face shone dark and sombre, her eyes were dark, moveless, looking straight ahead.

Armed with instructions from an anxious waiter, they set out again on the presumptive road to Paris. The interminable night wore on; the white blanket of the fog grew thicker, they passed through more ghostvillages, sheer and sudden as a dream, sheeted in the strange numb silence of that ghostly nightmare of a fog. The old red crater of the moon vanished in a ruined helve at length behind a rise of earth. They could no longer see anything, the road before was utterly blotted out, the carlights burned against an impenetrable white wall, they groped their way in utter blindness, they crawled at a snail's pace.

Finally, they felt their way along, inch by inch and foot by foot. Eugene stood on the running-board of the car, peering blindly into that blank wall of fog, trying only to define the edges of the road. The bitter penetration of raw cold struck through the fog and pierced them like a nail. From time to time Elinor stopped the car, while he stepped down and stamped numb feet upon the road, swung frozen arms and lustily blew warmth back into numb fingers. Then that infinite groping patience of snail's progress would begin again.

Somewhere, somehow, through that blind sea of fog, there was a sense of morning in the air. The ghosts of towns and villages grew more frequent—the towns were larger now, occasionally Elinor bumped over phantom curbs before the warning shouts of her look-out could prevent her. Twice they banged into trees along unknown pavements. There was a car-track now, the bump of cobbles, the sense of greater complications in the world about them.

Suddenly, they heard the most thrilling and evocative of all earth's sounds at morning—the lonely clopping of shod hooves upon the cobbles. In the dim and ghostly sheeting of that light, they saw the horse, the market cart balanced between its two high creaking wheels, laden with sweet clean green-and-gold of carrot bunches, each neatly trimmed as a bouquet.

They could discern the faint ghost-glimmer of the driver's face, the big slow-footed animal, dappled gray, and clopping steadily towards the central markets.

They were entering Paris, and the fog was lifting. In its huge shroud of mist dispersing, the old buildings of the city, emerged ghostly, haggard, pallidly nascent in the dim gray light. A man was walking rapidly along a terraced pavement, with bent head, hands thrust in pockets—the figure of the worker since the world began. They saw at morning, in gray waking light, a waiter, his apron ends tucked up, lifting racked chairs from the tables of a café, and on light mapled fronts of bars and shops, the signs *Bière—Pâtisserie—Tabac*. Suddenly, the huge winged masses of the Louvre swept upon them, and it was gray light now, and Eugene heard Elinor's low, fervent "Thank God!"

And now the bridge, the Seine again, the frontal blank of the old buildings on the quays, faced haggardly towards light, the narrow lane of the Rue Bonaparte, and in the silent empty street at length, his own hotel.

They said good-bye quickly, hurriedly, abstractedly, as he got out; and drove away. The women were thinking of nothing, no one now, but Starwick, life's fortunate darling, the rare, the precious, the all-favored one. In the gray light, unconscious, completely swaddled in the heavy rugs, Starwick still lay pillowed on Ann's shoulder.

LXXXIV

ALL day Eugene slept the dreamless, soundless sleep of a man who has been drugged. When he awoke, night had come again. And this concatenation of night to night, of dreamless and exhausted sleep upon the strange terrific nightmare of the night before, the swift kaleidoscope of moving action which had filled his life for the past two days, now gave to that recent period a haunting and disturbing distance, and to the events that had gone before the sad finality of irrevocable time. Suddenly he felt as if his life with Ann, Elinor, and Starwick was finished, done; for some strangely troubling reason he could not define, he felt that he would never see them again.

He got up, dressed, and went downstairs. He saw old Gely and his wife, his daughters, Marie the maid, and the little concierge: it seemed to him that they looked at him strangely, curiously, with some sorrowful sad knowledge in their eyes, and a nameless numb excitement gripped him, dulled his heart. He felt the nameless apprehension that he always felt—that perhaps all men feel—when they have been away a day or two. It was a premonition of bad news, of some unknown misfortune: he wanted to ask them if some one had come for him—without knowing who could come—if they had a message for him—not knowing who might send him one—an almost feverish energy to demand that they tell him at once what unknown calamity had befallen him in his absence. But he said nothing, but still haunted by what he thought was the strange and troubling look in their eyes—a look he had often thought he observed in people, which seemed to tell of a secret knowledge, an inhuman chemistry, a communion in men's lives to which his own life was a stranger—he hurried out into the street.

Outside the streets were wet with mist, the old cobbles shone with a dull wet gleam, through the mist the lamps burned dimly, and through the fog he heard the swift and unseen passing of the taxi-cabs, the shrill tooting of their little horns.

Yet everything was ghost-like and phantasmal—the streets of Paris had the unfamiliar reality of streets that one revisits after many years of absence, or walks again after the confinement of a long and serious illness.

He ate at a little restaurant in the Rue de la Seine, and troubled by the dismal lights, the high old houses, and the empty streets of the Latin Quarter sounding only with the brief passage of some furious little taxi drilling through those narrow lanes towards the bridge of the Seine and the great blaze and gaiety of night, he finally forsook that dark quarter, which seemed to be the image of the unquiet loneliness that beset him, and crossing the bridge, he spent the remainder of the evening reading in one of the cafés near Les Magasins du Louvre.

The next morning when he awoke, a *pneumatique* was waiting for him. It was from Elinor, and read:

"Darling, where are you? Are you still recovering from the great debauch, or have you given us the go-by, or what? The suspense is awful —won't you say it ain't so, and come to lunch with us today at half-past twelve? We'll be waiting for you at the studio.—Elinor"—Below this, in a round and almost childish hand, was written: "We want to see you. We missed you yesterday.—Ann."

He read this brief and casual little note over again and again, he laughed exultantly, and smote his fist into the air, and read again. All of the old impossible joy was revived in him. He looked about the room and found everything in it good and homely. He went to the window and looked out: a lemony sunlight was falling on the old pale walls and roofs and chimney-pots of Paris: everything sparkled with health and hope and work and morning—and all because two girls from Boston in New England had written him a note.

He held the flimsy paper of the *pneumatique* tenderly, as if it were a sacred parchment too old and precious for rough handling; he even lifted it to his nose and smelled it. It seemed to him that all the subtle, sensuous femininity of the two women was in it—the seductive and thrilling fragrance, impalpable and glorious as the fragrance of a flower, which their lives seemed to irradiate and to give to everything, to every one they touched, a sense of triumph, joy and tenderness. He read the one blunt line that Ann had written him as if it were poetry of haunting magic: the level, blunt and toneless inflexibility of her voice sounded in the line as if she had spoken, he read into her simple words a thousand buried meanings—the tenderness of a profound, simple and inarticulate spirit, whose feelings were too deep for language, who had no words for them.

When he got to the studio he found the two women waiting, but Starwick was not there. Ann was quietly, bluntly matter-of-fact as usual; Elinor almost hilariously gay, but beneath her gaiety he sensed at once a deep and worried perturbation, a worn anxiety that shone nakedly from her troubled eyes.

They told him that on their return from Rheims, Starwick had left the studio to meet Alec and had not been seen since. No word from him had they had that night or the day before, and now, on the second day since his disappearance, their anxiety was evident.

But during lunch—they ate at a small restaurant in the neighborhood, near the Montparnasse railway station—Elinor kept up a gay and rapid conversation, and persisted in speaking of Starwick's disappearance as a great lark—the kind of thing to be expected from him.

"*Perfectly* insane, of course!" she cried, with a gay laugh. "But then, it's typical of him: it's just the kind of thing that kind would do. Oh, he'll turn up, of course," she said, with quiet confidence, "—he'll turn up in a day or two, after some wild adventure that no one in the world but Francis Starwick could have had. . . . I *mean!*" she cried, "picking that Frenchman—Alec—up the way he did the other night. *Utterly* mad, of course!" she said gaily. "—But then, there you *are!* It wouldn't be Frank if he didn't!"

"I see nothing very funny about it," said Ann bluntly. "It looks like a pretty rotten mess to me. We know nothing at all about that Frenchman —who he is, what he does; we don't even know his name. For all you know he may be one of the worst thugs or criminals in Paris."

"Oh, I know, my dear—but don't be absurd!" Elinor protested. "The man's all right—Frank's always picking up these people—it always turns out all right in the end—oh, but of course!" she cried, as if dispelling a troubling thought from her mind—"Of course it will! It's too ridiculous to allow yourself to be upset like this!"

But in spite of her vigorous assurance, her eyes were full of care, and of something painful and baffled, an almost naked anguish.

He left them after lunch, promising to meet them again for dinner. Starwick had not come back. When they had finished dinner, the two women went back to the studio to wait for Starwick's possible return, and Eugene went to look for him in Montmartre, promising to let them know at once if he found Starwick or got news of him. When he got to Montmartre, he made a round first of all the resorts which Starwick had liked best and frequented most, as Eugene remembered them, of course; but no one had seen him since they had last been there all together. Finally, he went to the bistro in the Rue Montmartre, where they had first encountered Alec, and asked the soiled barman with the dark mistrustful eye, if he had seen either Alec or Starwick in the past three days. The man eyed him suspiciously for a moment before answering. Then he surlily replied that he had seen neither of them. In spite of the man's denial, he stayed on, drinking one cognac after another at the bar, while it filled up, ebbed and flowed, with the mysterious rout and rabble of the night. He waited until four o'clock in the morning: neither Starwick nor Alec had appeared. He got into a taxi and was driven back across Paris to Montparnasse. When he got to the studio, the two women were still awake, waiting, and he gave them his disappointing news. Then he departed, promising to return at noon.

All through that day they waited: the apprehension of the two women was now painfully evident, and Ann spoke bluntly of calling in the police. Towards six o'clock that evening, while they were engaged in vigorous debate concerning their course of action, there were steps along the alley-way outside, and Starwick entered the studio, followed by the Frenchman, Alec.

Starwick was in excellent spirits, his eyes were clear, his ruddy face looked fresh, and had a healthy glow. In response to all their excited greetings and inquiries, he laughed gleefully, teasingly, and refused to answer. When they tried to find out from Alec where Starwick had been, he too smiled an engaging but malicious smile, shrugged his shoulders politely, and said: "I do not know, I s'ink he tells you if he v'ants - - if not!" again he smiled, and shrugged politely. And this moody and secretive silence was never broken. Starwick never told them where he had been. Once or twice, during dinner, which was an hilarious one, he made casual and mysteriously hinting references to Brussels, but, in response to all of Elinor's deft, ironic cross-examination, he only laughed his burbling laugh, and refused to answer.

And she, finally defeated, laughed suddenly, a laugh of rich astonishment, crying: "*Perfectly* insane, of course! But then, what did I tell you? It's just the sort of thing that Frank *would* do!"

But, in spite of all her high light spirits, her gay swift laughter, her distinguished ease, there was in the woman's eyes something the boy had never seen before: a horrible, baffled anguish of torment and frustration. And although her manner towards the Frenchman, Alec, was gracious, gay, and charming—although she now accepted him as "one of us," and frequently said with warm enthusiasm that he was "a *perfectly* swell person—I like him *so* much!" there was often something in her eyes when she looked at him that it was not good to see.

Alec was their guest, and Starwick's constant companion, everywhere they went thereafter. And everywhere, in every way, he proved himself to be a droll, kind, courteous, witty and urbanely cynical person: a man of charming and engaging qualities, and delightful company. They never asked his name, nor inquired about his birth, his family, or his occupation. They seemed to accept his curious fellowship with Starwick as a matter-of-course: they took him on their daily round of cafés, restaurants, night-clubs, and resorts, as if he were a life-long friend of the family. And he accepted all their favors gracefully, politely, with wit and grace and charm, with a natural and distinguished dignity and ease. He, too, never asked disturbing questions; he was a diplomat by nature, a superb tactician from his birth. Nevertheless, the puzzled, doubting and inquiring expression in his eyes grew deeper day by day; his tongue was eloquently silent, but the question in his puzzled eyes could not be hidden, and constantly sought speech.

As for Eugene, he now felt for the first time an ugly, disquieting doubt: suddenly he remembered many things—words and phrases and allusions, swift, casual darts and flashes of memory that went all the way back to the Cambridge years, that had long since been forgotten— but that now returned to fill his mind. And sometimes when he looked at Starwick, he had the weird and unpleasant sensation of looking at some one he had never seen before.

LXXXV

AT the last moment, when it seemed that the argosy of their battered friendship was bound to sink, it was Elinor who saved it again. Ann, in a state of sullen fury, had announced that she was sailing for home the next week; Eugene, that he was going South to "some quiet little place where"—so did his mind comfortably phrase it—"he could settle down and write." As for Starwick, he remained coldly, wearily, sorrowfully impassive; he accepted this bitter dissolution of their plans with a weary resignation at once sad and yet profoundly indifferent; his own plans were more wrapped in a mantle of mysterious and tragic secretiveness than ever before. And seeing the desperate state which their affairs had come to, and that she could not look for help from these three gloomy secessionists, Elinor instantly took charge of things again, and became the woman who had driven an ambulance in the war.

"Listen, my darlings," she said with a sweet, crisp frivolity, that was as fine, as friendly, as comforting, and as instantly authoritative as the words of a capable mother to her contrary children—"no one is going away; no one is going back home; no one is going anywhere except on the wonderful trip we've planned from the beginning. We're going to start out next week, Ann and I will do the driving, you two boys can loaf and invite your souls to your hearts' content, and when you see a place that looks like a good place to work in, we'll stop and stay until you're tired of working. Then we'll go on again."

"Where?" said Starwick in a dead and toneless voice. "Go on where?"

"Why, my dear child!" Elinor cried in a gay tone. "Anywhere! Wherever you like! That's the beauty of it! We're not going to be bound down by any program, any schedule: we shall stay where we like, and go anywhere our sweet selves desire.

"I thought, however," she continued in a more matter-of-fact way, "that we would go first to Chartres and then on to Touraine, stopping off at Orléans or Blois or Tours—anywhere we like, and staying as long as we care to. After that, we could do the Pyrenees and all that part of France: we might stop a few days at Biarritz and then strike off into the Basque country. I know *incredible* little places we could stop at."

"Could we see Spain?" asked Starwick, for the first time with a note of interest in his voice.

"But, of *course!*" she cried. "My dear child, we can see anything, everything, go anywhere your heart desires. That's the beauty of the whole arrangement. If you feel like writing, if you want to run down to Spain to get a little writing done—why, presto! chango! Alacazam!" she said gaily, snapping her fingers, "—the thing is done! There's nothing simpler!"

For a moment, no one spoke. They all sat entranced in a kind of unwilling but magical spell of wonder and delight. Elinor, with her power to make everything seem delightfully easy, and magically simple and exciting, had clothed that fantastic program with all the garments of naturalness and reason. Everything now seemed not only possible, but beautifully, persuasively practicable—even that ludicrous project of "running down to Spain to do a little writing," that hopeless delusion of "stopping off and working, anywhere you like, until you are ready to go on again"—she gave to the whole impossible adventure not only the thrilling colors of sensuous delight and happiness, but also the conviction of a serious purpose, a reasonable design.

And in a moment, Starwick, rousing himself from his abstracted and fascinated reverie, turned to Eugene and, with the old gleeful burble of laughter in his throat, remarked simply in his strangely fibred voice:

"It sounds swell, doesn't it?"

And Ann, whose sullen, baffled look had more and more been tempered by an expression of unwilling interest, now laughed her sudden angry laugh, and said:

"It *would* be swell if every one would only act like decent human beings for a change!"

In spite of her angry words, her face had a tender, radiant look of joy and happiness as she spoke, and it seemed that all her hope and belief had returned to her.

"But of course!" Elinor answered instantly, and with complete conviction. "And that's just exactly how every one *is* going to act! Eugene will be all right," she cried—"the moment that we get out of Paris! You'll see! We've gone at a perfectly *killing* pace this last month or two! No one in the world could stand it! Eugene is tired, our nerves are all on edge, we're worn out by staying up all night, and drinking, and flying about from one place to another—but a day or two of rest will fix all that. . . . And that, my children, is just exactly what we're going to do—now—at once!" She spoke firmly, kindly, with authority. "We're getting out of Paris today!"

"Where?" said Starwick. "Where are we going?"

"We're all going out to St. Germain-en-Laye to rest up for a day or two before we leave. We'll stay at your pension, Francis, and you can pack your things while we're out there, because you won't be going back again. After that we'll come back to Paris to spend the night—we won't stay here over a day at the outside: Ann and I will clear our things out of the Studio, and Eugene can get packed up at his hôtel—that should mean, let's see," she tapped her lips lightly with thoughtful fingers— "we should be packed up and ready to start Monday morning, at the latest."

"Hadn't I better stay in town and do my packing now?" Eugene suggested.

"Darling," said Elinor softly, with a tender and seductive humor, putting her fingers on his arm—"you'll do nothing of the sort! You're driving out with us this afternoon! We all love you so much that we're going to take no chance on losing you at the last minute!"

And for a moment, the strange and almost noble dignity of Elinor's face was troubled by a faint smile of pleasant, tender radiance, the image of the immensely feminine, gracious, and lovely spirit which almost grotesquely seemed to animate her large and heavy body.

Thus, under the benevolent and comforting dictatorship of this capable woman, hope had been restored to them, and in gay spirits, shouting and laughing and singing, feeling an impossible happiness when they thought of the wonderful adventure before them, they drove out to St. Germain-en-Laye that afternoon. The late sun was slanting rapidly towards evening when they arrived: they left their car before an old café near the railway station, and for an hour walked together through the vast aisles of the forest, the stately, sorrowful design of that great planted forest, so different from anything in America, so different from the rude, wild sweep and savage lyricism of our terrific earth, and so haunted by the spell of time. It was the forest which Henry the Fourth had known so well, and which, in its noble planted colonnades, suggested an architecture of nature that was like a cathedral, evoked a sense of time that was ancient, stately, classical, full of sorrow and a tragical joy, and haunted forever by the pacings of noble men and women now long dead.

When they came out of the forest at the closing hour—for in this country, in this ancient noble place, even the forests were controlled, and closed and opened by the measurements of mortal time—the old red sun of waning day had almost gone.

For a time, they stood on the great sheer butte of St. Germain, and looked across the space that intervened between themselves and Paris. Below them in the valley, the Seine wound snakewise through a series of silvery silent loops, and beyond, across the fields and forests and villages, already melting swiftly into night, and twinkling with a diamond dust of lights, they saw the huge and smoking substance that was Paris, a design of elfin towers and ancient buildings and vast inhuman distances, an architecture of enchantment, smoky, lovely as a dream, seeming to be upborne, to be sustained, to float there like the vision of an impossible and unapproachable loveliness, out of a huge opalescent mist. It was a land of far Cockaigne, forever threaded by the eternity of its silver, silent river; a city of enfabled walls, like Carcassonne, and never to be reached or known.

And while they looked it seemed to them that they heard the huge, seductive, drowsy murmur of that magic and eternal city—a murmur which seemed to resume into itself all of the grief, the joy, the sorrow, the ambitions, hopes, despairs, defeats and loves of humanity. And though all life was mixed and intermingled in that distant, drowsy sound, it was itself detached, remote, eternal and undying as the voice of time. And it hovered there forever in the timeless skies of that elfin city, and was eternally the same, no matter what men lived or died.

They turned, and went into the old café near the station for an apéritif before dinner. It was one of those old, pleasantly faded cafés that one finds in little French towns. The place had the comfortable look and feel of an old shoe: the old, worn leather cushions, the chairs and tables, the mirrors in their frames of faded gilt, the old stained woods conveyed a general air of use, of peace, of homely shabby comfort, which suggested the schedule of generations of quiet people who had come here as part of the ordered ritual of a day, and which was so different from the feverish pulse, the sensual flash and glitter of the cafés of Paris. The noble peace and dignity of the great forest, and the magic vision of the time-enchanted city in the evening light, the silver, shining loops of its eternal river, still haunted their spirits, and filled their hearts with wonder and a tranquil joy. And the old café seemed to possess them, to make them its own, with its homely comfort: it was one of those places that one thinks of at once, instinctively, by a powerful intuition, as being a "good" place, and yet they could not have said why. As they came in, the proprietor smiled and spoke to them in a quiet, casual, and friendly manner as if he had always known them and, in a moment, when they were seated in the comfortable old leathers against the wall, their waiter came, and smilingly waited for their order. He was one of those waiters that one often sees abroad: an old man with a sharp, worn face, full of quiet humor and intelligence, an old, thin figure worn in service, but still spry and agile, a decent "family man" with wife and children, a man seasoned in humanity, whose years of service upon thousands of people had given him a character that was wise, good, honest, gentle, and a trifle equivocal. Each ordered an apéritif, the two women a cassis-vermouth, the two young men, Pernod: they talked quietly, happily, and with the weary, friendly understanding that people have when all their passion of desire and grief and conflict is past. The world that they had lived in for the last two months—that world of night and Paris and debauch—seemed like an evil dream, and the way before them now looked clear and plain.

When they left the café, full dark had come: they got in the car and drove to the pension at the other end of town, where Elinor had already engaged rooms for all of them. It now turned out that Elinor had taken rooms for Starwick at this pension three months before, upon his arrival in Paris, but after the first two weeks he had not lived in them, although most of his clothing, books, and other belongings were still there. It was one more of his costly, wrong, and tragically futile efforts to find a place—some impossibly fortunate and favorable place that never would be found—where he could "settle down and get his writing done."

When the four friends got to the pension, dinner had already begun. A table had been reserved for them, and as they entered the dining-room, every one stopped eating—two dozen pairs of old dead eyes were turned mistrustfully upon the young people, and in a moment, all over the room, at every table, the old heads bent together eagerly in conspiratorial secrecy, a low greedy whispering went up.

Starwick and Elinor were apparently already well and unfavorably known to the old pensionnaires. The moment they entered, in the vast and sibilant whispering that went around the room, envenomed fragments of conversation could be heard:

"Ah, c'est lui! . . . Et la dame aussi! . . . Ils sont revenus ensemble. . . . Mais, oui, oui!" At the next table to them an old hag with piled masses of dyed reddish hair, dressed in an old-fashioned dress bedecked with a thousand little gauds, peered at them for a moment with an expression of venomous and greedy curiosity, and then, leaning half across the table towards an old man with a swollen apoplectic face and thick white mustaches, and a little wizened old hag with the beady eyes of a reptile—possibly his wife—she hissed:

"Mais oui! . . . Oui! . . . C'est lui, le jeune Américain! . . . Personne ici ne l'a pas vu depuis trois mois." The old man here muttered something in a choked and phlegmy sort of voice, and the old parrot-visaged hag straightened, struck her bony hand sharply on the table, and cried out in a comical booming note:

"Mais justement! . . . Justement! . . . C'est comme vous voyez!" . . . Here she lowered her voice again, and peering around craftily at Elinor and Frank, who were shaking with laughter, she muttered hoarsely:

"Il n'est pas son mari! . . . Il est beaucoup plus jeune. . . . Mais non, mais non, mais non, mais non, mais non!" she cried with a rapid and violent impatience as the old man muttered out a question to her greedy ear.—"Elle est déjà mariée! . . . Oui! Oui!" This last was boomed out positively, with an indignant glance at Elinor. "Mais justement! Justement! . . . C'est comme vous voyez!"

That night Elinor was instant, swift, and happy as a flash of light. There was nothing that she did not seem to apprehend immediately, to interpret instantly, to understand before a word could be spoken, and to translate at once into a mercurial hilarity which swept every one along with it, and made all share instantly in its wild swift gaiety, even when it would have been impossible to say why one was gay. The soup was served: it was a brown disquieting liquid in which were floating slices of some troubling and unknown tissue—a whitish substance of an obscenely porous texture. It was probably tripe: Eugene stared at it with a sullen and suspicious face, and as he looked up, Elinor rocked back in her chair with a gust of wild hilarity, placed her fingers across her mouth and laughed a rich and sudden laugh. Then, before he could speak, she placed light fingers swiftly on his arm, and said swiftly, gravely, in a tone of commiserating consent:

"Yes, I know darling! I quite agree with you!——"

"What is it?" he said dumbly, in a bewildered tone. "It looks like——"

"Exactly! Exactly!" Elinor cried at once, before he could finish, and was swept by that wild light gale of merriment again—"That's exactly what it looks like—and don't say another word! We all agree with you!" She looked drolly at the uneasy liquid in the soup-plate, and then said, firmly and positively: "No, I think not! . . . If you don't mind, I'd rather not!"—and then seeing his face again, was rocked with rude and sudden laughter. "God!" she cried. "Isn't it marvellous! Will you look at the poor kid's face!"—And put light fingers gravely, swiftly, tenderly upon his arm again.

The great wave of this infectious gaiety swept them along: it was a wonderful meal. Starwick's burble of gleeful, rich humorous and suggestive laughter was heard again; Ann laughed her short and sudden laugh, but her face was radiant, happy, lovelier than it had ever been, everything seemed wonderfully good and pleasant to them. Elinor called the waitress and quietly sent the troubling soup away, but the rest of the meal was excellent, and they made a banquet of it with two bottles of the best Sauterne the pension afforded. Their hilarity was touched somewhat by the scornful patronage of bright young people among their dowdy elders, and yet they did not intend to be unkind: the whole place seemed to them a museum of grotesque relics put there for their amusement, they were determined to make a wonderful occasion of it, the suspicious eyes, greedy whisperings and conferring heads of the old people set them off in gales of laughter, and Elinor, after a glance around and a sudden peal of full rich laughter, would stifle her merriment with her fingers, and say:

"Isn't it marvellous! . . . God! Isn't it wonderful! . . . Could any one have imagined it! . . . Frank. . . . Frank!" she said quietly in a small stifled tone, "will you *look!* . . . Will you *kindly* take one look at the old girl with the dyed hair and all the thingumajigs, at the next table. . . . And the major! . . . And oh! If looks could *kill!* The things they are saying about *us!* . . . I'm sure they think we're *all* living in sin together. . . . Such *goings* on!" she cried with a gay pretense of horror. "Such open barefaced goings on, my friends, right in the face of decent people! . . . Now, is that terrible or not, Monsieur Duval, I ask you! . . . Darling," she said, turning to Starwick, and speaking in a tone of droll reproach, "don't you feel a sense of guilt? . . . Do you intend to do the right thing by a girl or not? . . . Are you going to make an honest woman of me, or aren't you? . . . Come on, now, darling," she said coaxingly, bending a little towards him, "set my tortured heart at rest! Just tell me that you intend to do the right thing by me! Won't you?" she coaxed.

"Quite!" said Starwick, his ruddy face reddening with laughter as he spoke. "But what—" the burble of gleeful and malicious laughter began to play in his throat as he spoke—"just what is the right thing? . . . Do you mean?—" he trembled a little with soundless laughter, and then went on in a gravely earnest but uncertain tone—"do you mean that you want to live?"—he arched his eyebrows meaningly, and then said in a tone of droll impossibly vulgar insinuation—"you know what I mean— *really* live, you know?"

"Frank!" she shrieked, and rocked back in her chair, covering her mouth with her fingers—"But not at *all,* darling," she went on with her former ironic seriousness, "—you're talking to an innocent maid from Boston, Mass., who doesn't know what you *mean—*you *beast!*" she cried. "Don't you know we Boston girls cannot begin to really live until you make an honest woman of us first?"

"In that case," Starwick said quietly, his face reddening again with laughter, "I should think we could begin to live at once. It seems to me that another man has already taken care of making you an honest woman!"

"God!" shrieked Elinor, falling back in her chair with another burst of rich and sudden laughter. "Poor Harold! . . . I had forgotten him! . . . That's all this place needs to make it perfect—Harold walking in right now to glare at us over the tops of his horn-rimmed spectacles——"

"Yes," said Starwick, "and your father and mother bringing up the rear and regarding me," he choked, "—with very *bitter* looks—you know," he said, turning to Eugene, "they feel *quite* bitterly towards me —they really do, you know. It's obvious," he said, "that they regard me as an unprincipled seducer who has defiled," his voice trembled uncertainly again, "—who has defiled the virtue of their only *darter!*" he brought this word out with a droll and luscious nasality that made them howl with laughter.

"But really," he went on seriously, turning to Elinor as he wiped his laughter-reddened face with a handkerchief, "I'm sure that's how they feel about it. When your mother and father came to the Studio the other day and found me there,"—Elinor's parents were at that time in Paris—"your father *glared* at me in much the same way that Cotton Mather would look at Casanova. But *quite!* He really did, you know. I'm sure he thought you had become my concubine."

"But, darling," Elinor replied, in her playful coaxing tone, "can't I be your concubine? . . . Oh, how *mean* you are!" she said reproachfully. "I do *so* want to be somebody's concubine." She turned to Eugene protestingly. "Now is that mean or not, I ask you! Here I am, a perfectly good well-meaning female thirty years old, brought up in Boston all my life, and with the best advantages. I've been a good girl all my life and tried to do the best I could for every one, but try as I will," she sighed, "no one will help me out in my life-long ambition to be somebody's concubine. Now is that fair or not—I ask you!"

"But not at all!" said Starwick reprovingly. "Before you can realize your ambition you've got to go out first and get yourself a reputation! . . . And," he added, with a swift exuberant glance at the crafty whispering old heads and faces all around them, "—I think you're getting one very fast."

They went upstairs immediately to the rooms that Elinor had engaged. Starwick had two comfortable big rooms in one wing of the pension; in his living-room a comfortable wood-fire had been laid and was crackling away lustily. Elinor had taken a small bedroom for Eugene, and a larger room for herself and Ann. In Ann's room, a good wood-fire was also burning cheerfully. Elinor and Starwick obviously wanted to be alone to talk together—they conveyed this by a kind of mysterious more-to-this-than-meets-the-eye quietness that had been frequent with them during all these weeks. They announced that they were going for a walk.

LXXXVI

WHEN they had gone, Eugene went to Ann's door and knocked. She showed no surprise at seeing him, but stood aside sullenly until he had come in, and then closed the door behind him. Then she went back, sat down in a chair before the fire, and leaned forward upon her knees, and for some time stared dumbly and sullenly into the crackling flames.

"Where are the others?" she said presently. "Have they gone out?"

"Yes," he said. "They went for a walk. They said they'd be gone about an hour."

"Yes," she said cynically, "and they thought it would be good for me if you and I were left alone for a while. I'm such a grand person that something just *has* to be done for me. God!" she concluded bitterly, "I'm getting tired of having people do me good! I'm fed up with it!"

He made no reply to this and she said nothing more. Her big body supported by her elbows, she continued to lean forward and stare sullenly into the flames.

He had taken a seat in another chair, and at length the silence, and his position in the chair, and the girl's sullen expression became painfully awkward, unhappy and embarrassing. He got up abruptly, took a pillow from the bed, threw it upon the floor, and lay down flat beside her chair, stretched out comfortably with his head to the dancing flames. The feel of the fire, its snap and crackle, the soft flare and fall of burned wood ash, and the resinous piny smell, together with the broad old wooden planking of the floor, the silence of the house and the feel of numb silent night outside, something homelike in the look of the room—these things, together with Ann's big New England body leaned forward towards the fire, the sullen speechless integrity of her grand and lovely face, and the smell of her, which was the smell of a big healthy woman warmed by fire—all of these things filled his senses with something immensely strong, pleasant, and familiar, something latent in man's blood, which he had not felt in many years, and that now was quiet but powerfully reawakened. It filled his heart, his blood, his senses with peace and certitude, with drowsy sensual joy, and with the powerful awakening of an old perception, like the re-discovery of an ancient faith, that the sensuous integument of life was everywhere the same, that the lives of people in this little town in France were the same as the lives of people in the town he came from, the same as the lives of people everywhere on earth. And after all the dark and alien world of night, of Paris, and another continent, which he had known now for several months, this re-discovery of the buried life, the fundamental structure of the great family of earth to which all men belong, filled him with a quiet certitude and joy.

Ann did not move; bent forward, leaning on her knees, she continued to stare into the fire, and looking up at her warm, dark, sullen face, he fell asleep—into a sleep which, after all the frenzy and exhaustion of the last weeks, was as deep and soundless as if he were drugged.

How long he lay asleep there on the floor he did not know. But he was wakened by the sound of her voice—a sullen monotone that spoke his name—that spoke his name quietly with a toneless, brooding insistence and that at first he thought he must have dreamed. It was repeated, again and again, quietly, insistently, without change or variation until he knew there was no doubt of it, that he no longer was asleep. And with something slow and strange and numb beating through him like a mighty pulse, he opened his eyes and looked up into her face. She had bent forward still more and was looking down at him with a kind of slow, brooding intensity, her face smoldering and drowsy as a flower. And even as he looked at her, she returned his look with that drowsy, brooding stare, and again, without inflection, spoke his name. .

He sat up like a flash and put his arms around her. He was beside her on his knees and he hugged her to him in a grip of speechless, impossible desire: he kissed her on the face and neck, again and again; her face was warm with the fire, her skin as soft and smooth as velvet; he kissed her again and again on the face, clumsily, thickly, with that wild, impossible desire, and with a horrible feeling of guilt and shame. He wanted to kiss her on the mouth, and he did not dare to do it: all the time that he kept kissing her and hugging her to him with a clumsy, crushing grip, he wanted her more than he had ever wanted any woman in his life, and at the same time he felt a horrible profanity in his touch, as if he were violating a Vestal virgin, trying to rape a nun.

And he did not know why he felt this way, the reason for these senseless feelings of guilt and shame and profanation. He had been with so many whores, and casual loose promiscuous women, that he would have thought it easy to make love to this big, clumsy, sullen-looking girl, but now all he could do was to hug her to him in an awkward grip, to mutter foolishly at her, and to kiss her warm sullen face again and again.

He tried to put his clumsy hand upon her breast, but the feeling of shame and profanation swept over him, and he could not keep it there. He put his hand upon her knee, and thrust it under the skirt: the warm flesh of her leg stung him like an electric shock and he jerked his hand away. And all the time the girl did nothing, made no attempt to resist or push him away, just yielded with a dumb sullen passiveness to his embraces, her face smoldering with a slow sullen passion that he could not fathom or define. He did not know why she had wakened him, why she had called his name, what meaning, what emotion lay behind her brooding look, her dumb and sullen passiveness, whether she yielded herself willingly to him or not.

He did not know why he should have this sense of shame and guilt and profanation when he touched her. It may have come from an intrinsic nobility and grandeur in her person and in her character that made physical familiarity almost unthinkable; it may even have come in part from a feeling of social and class inferiority—a feeling which may be base and shameful, but to which young men are fiercely sensitive—the feeling which all Americans know and have felt cruelly, even those who scornfully deny that it exists and yet have themselves done most to foster it. Certainly he had at times been bitterly conscious of the girl's "exclusiveness"—the fact that she was a member of "an old Boston family"—a wealthy, guarded, and powerfully entrenched group; he knew that a beautiful and desirable woman like Ann would have had many opportunities to pick and choose among wealthy men of her own class, and that he himself was just the son of a working-man.

But most of all, he knew that, more than anything else, the thing that checked him now, that overpowered him with its loveliness, that filled his heart with longing and impossible desire, and at the same moment kept him from possession—was the passionate and bitter enigma of that strange and lovely thing which had shaped itself into his life and could never be lost, could never be forgotten, and was never to be known: the thing he knew by these two words—"New England."

And as the knowledge came to him he felt the greatest love and hatred for this thing that he had ever known. A kind of wild cursing anger, a choking expletive of frustration and despair possessed him. He took her by the arms and jerked her to her feet, and cursed her bitterly. And she came dumbly, passively, sullenly as before, neither yielding nor resisting, as he shook her, hugged her, cursed her incoherently in that frenzy of desire and frustrate shame:

"Look here," he panted thickly, shaking her. "Say something! . . . Do something! . . . Don't stand there like a God-damned wooden Indian! . . . Who the hell do you think you are, anyway? . . . Why are you any better than any one else? . . . Ann! Ann! Look at me! . . . Speak! What is it? . . . Oh, God-damn you!" he said with a savagely unconscious humor that neither of them noticed, "—but I love you! . . . Oh, you big, dumb, beautiful Boston bitch," he panted amorously, "—just turn your face to me—and look at me—and by God! I will! I will!" he muttered savagely, and for the first time, and with a kind of desperation, kissed her on the mouth, and glared around him like a madman and, without knowing what he was doing, began to haul and drag her along toward the bed, muttering —"By God, I'll do it!—Oh, you sweet, dumb, lovely trollop of a Back Bay—Ann!" he cried exultantly. "Oh, by God, I'll thaw you out, I'll melt your ice, my girl— by God, I'll open you!—Is it her arm, now?" he began gloatingly, and lifted her long arm with a kind of slow, rending ecstacy and bit into her shoulder haunch, "or her neck, or her warm face and sullen mouth, or the good smell of her, or that lovely belly, darling—that white, lovely, fruitful Boston belly," he gloated, "good for about a dozen babies, isn't it?—or the big hips and swelling thighs, the long haunch from waist to knee—oh, you fertile, dumb, unplowed plantation of a woman—but I'll plant you!" he yelled exultantly—"and the big, dumb eyes of her, and her long hands and slender fingers—how did you ever get such slender, graceful hands, you delicate, big—here! give me the hands now —and all the fine, long lady-fingers"—he said with gentle, murderous desire, and suddenly felt the girl's long fingers trembling on his arm, took them in his hands and felt them there, and all her big, slow body trembling in his grasp, and was suddenly pierced with a wild and nameless feeling of pity and regret.

"Oh, Ann, don't," he said, and seized her hand, and held it prayerfully. "Don't look like that—don't be afraid—oh, look here!" he said desperately again, and put his arms around her trembling shoulders and began to pat her soothingly. "—Please don't act like that—don't tremble so—don't be afraid of me!—Oh, Ann, please don't look at me that way— I didn't mean it—I'm so God-damned sorry, Ann—Ah-h! it's going to be all right! It's going to be all right! I swear it's going to be all right!"

he stammered foolishly, and took her hand, and pleaded with her, not knowing what he was saying, and sick with guilt and shame and horror at the profanation of his act.

Her breath was fluttering, coming uncertainly, panting short and quick and breathless like a frightened child; this and her slender hands, her long trembling fingers, the sight of her hands so strangely, beautifully delicate for such a big woman, filled him with an unspeakable anguish of remorse. She began to speak, a breathless, panting, desperate kind of speech, and he found himself desperately agreeing with everything she said, even though he did not hear or understand half of it!

". . . Mustn't stay here," she panted. "Let's get out of here . . . go somewhere . . . anywhere . . . I've got to talk to you. . . . Something I've got to tell you!" she panted desperately. ". . . You don't understand . . . awful, horrible mistake!" she muttered. ". . . Got to tell you, now! . . . Come on! Let's go."

"Oh, yes—sure—anywhere, Ann. Wherever you say," he agreed eagerly to everything she said: they put on their hats and coats with trembling haste, and were preparing to leave just as Starwick and Elinor returned.

Starwick asked them where they were going: they said they were going for a walk. He said, "Oh!" non-committally. Both he and Elinor observed their flushed, excited manner, and trembling haste, with a curious and rather perturbed look, but said nothing more, and they departed.

The pension was silent: every one had already gone to bed, and when they got out into the street, it was the same. It was a night of still, cold frost, and everywhere around them there were the strange, living presences of silence and of sleep. The houses had the closed, shuttered and attentive secrecy that houses in a small French town have at night, no one else seemed to be abroad: they strode rapidly along in the direction of the railway station, saying nothing for a time, their feet sounding sharply on the frozen ground as they walked.

At length, beneath one of the sparse, infrequent street lamps, Ann paused, turned to him, and in a rapid, excited tone which was so different from her usual sullen curtness, began to speak:

"Look here!" she said, "we've got to forget about all that tonight— about everything that happened! . . . It was my fault," she muttered, with a kind of dumb, spinsterly agony of conscience which, in its evocation of the straight innocence and integrity of her kind and person, was somehow pitiably moving—"I didn't mean to lead you on," she said naïvely. "I shouldn't have let you get started."

"Oh, Ann," he said, "you didn't do anything! It wasn't your fault! You couldn't help it—I was the one who started it."

"No. No," she muttered, with a kind of sullen, miserable doggedness. "It was all my fault. . . . Could have stopped it." She turned abruptly, miserably, and began to stride on again.

"But Ann," he began, with a kind of desperate persuasiveness, as he caught up with her, "don't take it this way. . . . Don't worry about it like this! . . . We didn't do anything bad, honestly we didn't!"

"Oh," she muttered without turning her head, "it was an awful thing—an awful thing to do to you! . . . I'm *so* ashamed," she muttered. "It was a rotten thing to do!"

"But you did nothing!" he protested. "I'm the one!"

"No, no," she muttered again—"I started it . . . I don't know why. . . . But I had no right . . . there's something you don't understand."

"But what? What is it, Ann?" He didn't know whether to laugh or cry over this dumb, spinsterly integrity of New England conscience which, it seemed to him, was taking the episode so bitterly to heart.

She paused in her long stride below another street lamp, and turning, spoke sternly, desperately, to him:

"Listen!" she said. "You've got to forget everything that happened tonight. . . . I never knew you felt that way about me. . . . You've got to forget about me. . . . You must never think of me that way again!"

"Why?" he said

"Because," she muttered, "it's wrong . . . wrong."

"Why is it wrong?"

She did not answer for a moment, and then, turning, looked him straight in the eye:

"Because," she said, with quiet bluntness, "nothing can come of it. . . . I don't feel that way about you."

He could not answer for a moment, and it seemed to him that a thin film of ice had suddenly hardened round his heart.

"Oh," he said presently; and, after a moment, added, "and don't you think you ever could?"

She did not answer, but began to walk rapidly ahead. He caught up with her again, took her by the arm and pulled her around to face him. He said sharply:

"Answer me! Don't you think you ever could?"

Her face was full of dumb, sullen misery; she muttered:

"There's something you don't understand—something you don't know about."

"That's not what I asked you. Answer me."

"No," she muttered sullenly. "I can't feel that way about you. . . . I never will." She turned with a miserable look in her face and began to walk again. The ring of ice kept hardening round his heart all the time; he caught up with her again, and again stopped her.

"Listen, Ann. You've got to tell me why. I've got to know."—She shook her head miserably and turned away, but he caught her, and pulled her back, saying in a sharper, more peremptory tone:

"No, now—I've got to know. Is it because—you just never could feel that way about a fellow like me—because you could never think about me in that way——?"

She didn't answer for a moment; she just stood looking at him dumbly and miserably; and finally she shook her head in a movement of denial:

"No," she said. "It's not that."

The ring of ice kept getting thicker all the time, it seemed he would not be able to speak the words, but in a moment he said:

"Well, then, is it—is it some one else?"

She made a sudden tormented movement of anguish and despair, and turning, tried to walk away. He seized her, and jerked her back to him, and said:

"Answer me, God-damn it! Is that the reason why?"

He waited a long moment before the answer came, and then she muttered it out so low he could scarcely hear it.

"Yes," she said, and wrenched her arm free. "Let me go."

He caught her again, and pulled her back. The ring of ice seemed to have frozen solid, and in that cold block he could feel his heart throbbing like a trip-hammer.

"Who is it?" he said.

She did not answer, and he shook her roughly. "You answer me. . . . Is it some one you knew back home——?"

"Let me go," she muttered. "I won't tell you."

"By God, you will," he said thickly, and held her. "Who is it? Is it some one you met back home, or not?"

"No!" she shouted, and wrenched free with a kind of stifled sob, and started ahead, almost running: "Leave me alone now! I won't tell you!"

A sudden flash of intuition, an instant flash of recognition and horror went through him like a knife. His heart seemed to have frozen solid, his breath to have stopped: he jumped for her like a cat, and whisking her around towards him, said:

"Ann! Look at me a moment!" He put his fingers underneath her chin and jerked her face up roughly: "Are you in love with Starwick?"

A long wailing note of dumb anguish and despair was torn from her; she tried to break from his grasp, and as she wrenched to get free, cried pitiably, in a terror-stricken voice:

"Leave me alone! Leave me alone!"

"Answer, God-damn you!" he snarled. "Is it Starwick or not?"

With a last frenzied effort, she wrenched free, and screamed like a wounded animal:

"Yes! Yes! . . . I've told you now! Are you satisfied? Will you leave me alone?" And with a sobbing breath, she began to run blindly.

He ran after her again, and caught up with her and took her in his arms, but not to embrace her, but just to hold her, stop her, somehow quiet, if he could, the wild, dumb, pitiable anguish of that big creature, which tore through the ventricles of his heart like a knife. He himself was sick with horror, and a kind of utter, paralyzing terror he had never felt before; he scarcely knew what he was doing, what he was saying, but the sight of that great, dumb creature's anguish, that locked and inarticulate agony of grief, was more than he could bear. And cold with terror, he began to mumble with a thickened tongue: "Oh, but Ann, Ann!—Starwick, Starwick!—it's no use! It's no use!—Christ, what a shame! What a shame!" For suddenly he knew what Starwick was, what he had never allowed himself to admit that Starwick had become, and he kept mumbling thickly, "Christ! Christ! What a pity! What a shame!" not knowing what he was saying, conscious only, with a kind of sickening horror, of the evil mischance which had with such a cruel and deliberate perversity set their lives awry, and of the horrible waste and loss which had warped forever this grand and fertile creature's life and which now would bring all her strength, her love, the noble integrity of her spirit, to barren sterile nothing.

At the moment he had only one feeling, overwhelming and intolerable, somehow to quiet her, to stop, to heal this horrible wound of grief

and love, to bring peace to her tormented spirit somehow, to do anything, use his life in any way that would give her a little peace and
comfort.

And he kept holding her, patting her on the shoulders, saying foolishly over and over again, and not knowing what he said:

"Oh, it's all right! . . . It's all right, Ann! . . . You mustn't look
like this, you mustn't act this way . . . it's going to be all right!" And
knowing miserably, horribly, that it was not all right, that the whole
design and fabric of their lives were ruinously awry, that there was a
hurt too deep ever to heal, a wrong too cruel, fatal, and perverse ever
to be righted.

She stayed there in his arms, she turned her face into his shoulder,
she put her slender, strong and lovely hands upon his arms and held on
to him desperately, and there, in the frozen, sleeping stillness of that
street in a little French town, she wept hoarsely, bitterly, dreadfully, like
some great creature horribly wounded; and all he could do was hold on
to her until the last torn cry of pain had been racked and wrenched out
of her.

When it was all over, and she had grown quiet, she dried her eyes,
and looking at him with a dumb, pleading expression, she whispered
miserably:

"You won't tell them? You won't say anything to Frank about this,
will you? You'll never let him know?"

And stabbed again by wild, rending pity, sick with horror at her
devastating terror, he told her he would not.

They walked home in silence through the frozen, sleeping streets.
It was after midnight when they got back to the pension: the whole
house was long ago asleep. As they went up the stairs a clock began to
strike.

LXXXVII

He did not see her the next morning until it was time for lunch. She
had gone out early with the big Alsatian dog, and had spent the morning walking in the forest. During the morning he told Elinor and
Starwick that he was going back to Paris. Starwick said nothing at all,
but Elinor after a moment's silence, said coldly, and with a trace of
sarcasm:

"Very well, my dear. You're the doctor. If the lure of the great city has proved too much for you, go you must." She was silent for a moment, and then said ironically, "Does this mean that we are not to have the honor of your distinguished company on our trip? . . . Really," she said curtly, "I wish you'd try to make up your mind what you're going to do. . . . The suspense, darling, is growing *quite* unbearable. If you're trying to break it to us gently," she went on poisonously, "I beg of you to let the blow fall now, and not to spare us any longer. After all," she said with a kind of evil drollery, "we may manage to survive the shock. . . . Really, I should like to know," she said sharply, as he did not answer. "If you're not going, we'll get some one else to take your place—we wanted a fourth party to help share in the expenses," she added venomously, "and I'd like to know at once what your intentions are."

He stared at her with a smoldering face and with a swelter of hot and ugly anger in his heart, but as usual, her envenomed attack was too quick and sudden for him. Before he could answer, even as his tongue was blundering at a hot reply, she turned swiftly away, and with an air of resignation, said to Starwick:

"Will you try to find out what his intentions are? I can't find out what he wants to do. *Apparently,*" she concluded in a rich, astounded voice, "—apparently, your young friend is tongue-tied." She walked away, contained and beautifully self-possessed as ever, save for two angry spots of color in her face.

When she had gone, Starwick turned to him, and said with quiet reproof:

"You ought to let her know. You really ought, you know."

"All right!" he said quickly and hotly, "I'm letting you know right now. I'm not going."

Starwick said nothing for a moment, then with a quiet, weary, and sorrowful resignation, he said:

"I'm sorry, Gene."

The other said nothing, but just stood looking at Starwick with eyes which were cold and hard and ugly with their hate. Starwick's quiet words, the almost Christ-like humility with which he uttered them, now seemed to him to be nothing but the mask of a sneering arrogance of pride and contemptuous assurance, the badge of his immeasurable good fortune. With cold, measuring eyes of hate he looked at Starwick's soft and graceful throat, the languid indolence of his soft, voluptuously graceful figure, and with murderous calculation he thought: "How easy it would be for me to twist that damned, soft neck of yours off your shoulders! How easy it would be to take that damned, soft body in my hands and break it like a rotten stick across my knees! Oh, you damned, soft, pampered makeshift of a human being—you thing of cunning tricks and words and accents—you synthetic imitation of a living artist —you dear, damned darling of æsthetic females—you Boston woman's lap-dog, you——"

The foul words thickened to a swelter of blind hate and murder in his heart, and would not give him ease, or phrase the choking and intolerable burden of his hate; the light of hate and murder burned in his naked eye, curled his hands into two rending paws of savage power in which he seemed to feel the substance of that warm, soft throat between the strangling grip of his long fingers; and all the time he felt hopelessly tricked, outwitted, beaten by the very nakedness of his surrender to his hate, beaten by something too subtle, soft and cunning for him ever to grasp, by something which, for so it now seemed, would always beat him, by something whose impossible good fortune it would always be to take from him the thing he wanted most.

A thousand times he had foreseen this thing. A thousand times, he had foreseen, as young men will foresee, the coming of the enemy— and always he had pictured him in a definite form and guise. Always he had come, armed in insolence and power, badged with the open menace of the jeering word, the sneering tongue, the brandished fist. Always he had come to strike terror to the heart with naked threat and open brag, to try to break the heart and courage of another man, to win his jeering domination of another's life, by violence and brutal courage. He had never come by stealth but always by the frontal attack, and the youth, like every youth alive, had sworn that he would be ready for him when he came, would meet him fiercely and without retreat, and would either conquer him or most desperately lie dead before he yielded to the inexpiable shame of foul dishonor.

And now the enemy had come, but in no way that he had ever known, in no guise that he had ever pictured. The enemy had come, not armed in brutal might and open brag and from the front, but subtle, soft, and infinitely cunning, and from a place, and in a way that he had never foreseen. The enemy had come behind the mask of friendship, he had come with words of praise, with avowals of proud belief and noble confidence, in an attitude of admiration and humility—had come in such a way, and even as he spoke the words of praise and proud belief in him, had taken from him what he wanted most in life, and had not seemed to take it, or to want it, or to care.

Starwick and Elinor had quarrelled again: this time it was because he too had decided to go back to Paris that afternoon. No one but Elinor knew the purpose of his going; and that purpose, whatever it was, did not please her. When Eugene entered the dining-room for his last meal with them, they were at it hammer and tongs, totally oblivious of the sensation they were causing among the whispering and conspiring old men and women all about them. Or, if not oblivious, they were indifferent to it: even in their quarrels they kept their grand and rare and special manner—a manner which more and more conceived the universe as an appropriate backdrop for the subtle and romantic complications of their own lives, and which, in its remote and lofty detachment from the common run of man, said that here was an intercourse of souls that was far too deep and rare for the dull conscience of the world to apprehend.

Elinor was talking earnestly, positively, an accent rich, yet sharp, cultivated, yet formidably assured, a well-mannered authority, positive with denial and the conviction of experience.

"You cannot do it! I tell you that you cannot *do* it! You will come a cropper if you do!"

Starwick's face was flushed deeply with anger; he answered quietly in a mannered tone filled with a sense of outrage and indignation:

"I resent that *very* much," he said. "It is *very* wrong, and *very* unfair of you to speak that way! I *resent* it!" he said quietly, but with stern reproof.

"Sorry!" she clipped the word out curt and brusque, the way the English say it. "If you resent it, you resent it—and that's *that!* But after *all,* my dear, what else do you expect? If you insist on bringing any little cut-throat you pick up in a Montmartre bistro along with you everywhere you go, your friends are going to complain about it! And they've a right to!"

"I *resent* that *very* much!" he said again, in his mannered tone.

"Sorry!" she said crisply, curtly, as before. "But that's the way I feel about it!" She looked at him for a moment, and then, suddenly shaking her head in a short and powerful movement, she said in a whispering shudder of revulsion and disgust:

"No good, Frank! . . . I'm willing to make all the allowances I can

"I—I guess I spent it," he stammered.

The answer came, and buried itself in his heart, as quick, as cold, as poisonous as a striking snake:

"You did?" she said curtly. "I wonder where. I'm sure you didn't spend any of it while you were with *us*."

He could have strangled her. The veins stood out upon his forehead like cords, his face was brick-red, and for a moment he went blind with the rush of hot, choking blood to his head. He tried to speak, his throat worked convulsively, but no words came: he just stood there goggling at her stupidly with an inflamed face, uttering a few incoherent croaks. Before he could think of anything to say, she had escaped again: Starwick and Ann were coming out of the pension, and she was speaking to them swiftly, telling them to make haste.

No one spoke during the ride to the station. He sat on the back seat beside Ann and the big Alsatian dog; Starwick and Elinor were in front. When they got to the station, the clock still lacked more than five minutes to train-time. He and Starwick bought third-class fares, and went outside where the women were still waiting for them. Starwick and Elinor walked away a few yards and began their quarrel again; Ann said nothing, but looked at him dumbly, miserably, a look that tore at him with pity and wild regret, and that made him weak and hollow with his blind, impossible desire.

They looked at each other with angry, sullen eyes, tormented with the perverse and headstrong pride of youth, unwilling to make concessions or relent, even when each desperately wanted the other to do so.

"Good-bye," he said, and held out his hand. "Good-bye, Ann."

"What do you mean—?" she began angrily. "What are you going to do?"

"I'm saying good-bye," he said doggedly.

"You mean you're not coming with us?"

For a moment he did not answer and then, nodding towards Elinor, he said bitterly:

"Your lady friend there doesn't seem to want me very much. She doesn't seem to think I bear my fair share of the expense."

"What did she say to you?" the girl asked.

"Oh, nothing," he said in a quiet, choking tone of fury. "Nothing in particular. Just one of those friendly little things I've come to look for. She just said she didn't know what I'd done with my money—that I hadn't spent any of it while I was with you."

Her face got brick-red with a heavy, smoldering flush, she looked towards Elinor with angry eyes, and then muttered:

"It was a rotten thing to say!" Turning towards him again, she said in a low tone:

"Do you mean then that you've given up the trip? You're not coming with us?"

"That's what I've told you, isn't it?" he said harshly. "What else do you expect?"

She looked at him sullenly, angrily, a moment longer; and suddenly her eyes were wet with tears.

"It's going to be a fine trip for me, isn't it?" she muttered. "I've got a lot to look forward to, haven't I?"

"Oh, you'll get along, I guess," he jeered. "I don't think you're going to miss *my* company very much." And felt a desperate hope that she would.

"Oh, it's going to be charming, charming, isn't it!" she said bitterly. "Nothing to do but hold down the back seat alone with the dog—while *they*," she nodded towards Elinor and Starwick—"are up there having their wonderful talks together—leaving me alone to watch the dog while they stay out all night together—oh, it's going to be simply wonderful, isn't it!" she said with an infuriated sarcasm.

"So that's the reason I was wanted?" he said. "To keep you company on the back seat! To take the place of the dog! To make it look good, eh—to make the party look a little more respectable back in Boston when they hear of Mr. Starwick and his two lady friends! That's why you wanted me, is it? To fill in extra space—to be a kind of damned male nurse and chaperon to you and Elinor and Frank Starwick——"

She took a step towards him and stopped, her hands clenched beside her, her eyes shot with tears, her big body trembling for a moment with baffled anger and despair:

"God-damn you!" she said in a small, choked voice; and, her hands still clenched, she turned away abruptly to hide her tears.

At this moment Starwick approached and, his ruddy face flushing as he spoke, he said quietly, casually:

"Ann, look! Will you let me have a thousand francs?"

She turned around, glared at Starwick for a moment with angry, reddened eyes and then, to his astonishment and her own, boomed out comically, and in an enraged tone:

"No—o!"

His face went crimson with embarrassment, but after looking at her steadily for a moment, he turned, and walked back to Elinor. In a moment she could be heard saying coldly, positively:

". . . I am sorry, Francis, but I cannot! . . . You should have thought about all that before! . . . If you won't stay out here and go in with us tomorrow, you'll have to do the best you can by yourself. . . . No, sir, I cannot . . . if you want to put it that way, yes; I *won't,* then! . . . I do not *like* the man. . . . I *thoroughly* disapprove of what you're doing. . . . I *will* not help you!"

Some low, excited words passed between them, and in a moment Starwick said:

"You have no right to say that! I *resent* that *very* much!"

His ruddy face was deeply flushed with anger and humiliation; he turned abruptly on his heel and walked away without farewell. At this moment the guards could be heard calling, "En voiture! En voiture, messieurs!" and Elinor, glancing towards Ann and Eugene, said curtly:

"If you're going to catch that train, you'll have to hurry!"

Eugene turned to say good-bye to Ann; she paid no attention to his outstretched hand but stood, her hands clenched, glaring angrily at him with wet eyes.

"Good-bye!" he said roughly. "Aren't you going to say good-bye?"

She made no answer, but just stood glaring at him, and then turned away.

"All right," he said angrily. "Do as you like!"

Without a word to Elinor, he picked up his valise, ran into the station and got through the gates just as the little suburban train began to move. Starwick was climbing up into a compartment, Eugene followed him, flung his valise inside, and clambered in, breathless, just as a guard with a remonstrant face slammed the door behind him.

LXXXVIII

DURING the journey back to Paris, Eugene and Starwick said little. The two young men were the sole occupants of the compartment, they sat facing each other, looking out through the windows with gloomy eyes. The gray light of the short, winter's day was fading rapidly: when they entered Paris dusk had come; as the train rattled over the switchpoints in the yard-approaches to the Gare St. Lazare, they could see lights and life and sometimes faces in the windows of the high, faded buildings near the tracks. Through one window, in a moment's glimpse, Eugene saw a room with a round table with a dark cloth upon it, and with the light of a shaded chandelier falling on it, and a dark-haired boy of ten or twelve leaning on the table, reading a book, with his face propped in his hands, and a woman moving busily about the table, laying it with plates and knives and forks. And as the train slackened speed, he saw, high up in the topmost floor of an old house that rose straight up from the tracks, a woman come to the window, look for a moment at a canary-bird cage which was hanging in the window, reach up and take it from its hook. She had the rough, blowsy, and somewhat old-fashioned look of a whore of the Renoir period; and yet she was like some one he had known all his life.

They passed long strings of silent, darkened railway compartments, and as they neared the station, several suburban trains steamed past them, loaded with people going home. Some of the trains were the queer little double-deckers that one sees in France: Eugene felt like laughing every time he saw them and yet, with their loads of Frenchmen going home, they too were like something he had always known. As the train came into the station, and slowed down to its halt, he could see a boat-train ready for departure on another track. Sleek as a panther, groomed, opulent, ready, purring softly as a cat, the train waited there like a luxurious projectile, evoking perfectly, and at once, the whole structure of the world of power and wealth and pleasure that had created it. Beyond it one saw the whole universe of pleasure—a world of great hotels, and famed resorts, the thrilling structure of the huge, white-breasted liners, and the slanting race and drive of their terrific stacks. One saw behind it the dark coast of France, the flash of beacons, the gray, fortressed harbor walls, the bracelet of their hard, spare lights, and beyond, beyond, one saw the infinite beat and swell of stormy seas, the huge nocturnal slant and blaze of liners racing through immensity, and forever beyond, beyond, one saw the faint, pale coasts of morning and America, and then the spires and ramparts of the enfabled isle, the legendary and aerial smoke, the stone and steel, of the terrific city.

Now their own train had come to a full stop, and he and Starwick were walking up the quay among the buzzing crowd of people.

Starwick turned and, flushing painfully, said in a constrained and mannered tone:

"Look! Shall I be seeing you again?"

Eugene answered curtly: "I don't know. If you want to find me, I suppose I shall be at the same place, for a time."

"And after that?—Where will you go?"

"I don't know," he answered brusquely again. "I haven't thought about it yet. I've got to wait until I get money to go away on."

The flush in Starwick's ruddy face deepened perceptibly, and, after another pause, and with obvious embarrassment, he continued as before:

"Look! Where are you going now?"

"I don't know, Francis," he said curtly. "To the hotel, I suppose, to leave my suitcase and see if they've still got a room for me. If I don't see you again, I'll say good-bye to you now."

Starwick's embarrassment had become painful to watch; he did not speak for another moment, then said:

"Look! Do you mind if I come along with you?"

He did mind; he wanted to be alone; to get away as soon as he could from Starwick's presence and all the hateful memories it evoked, but he said shortly:

"You can come along if you like, of course, but I see no reason why you should. If you're going to the studio we can take a taxi and you can let me off at the hotel. But if you're meeting somebody over on this side later on, why don't you wait over here for him?"

Starwick's face was flaming with shame and humiliation; he seemed to have difficulty in pronouncing his words and when he finally turned to speak, the other youth was shocked to see in his eyes a kind of frantic, naked desperation.

"Then, look!" he said, and moistened his dry lips. "Could you let me have some—some money, please?"

Something strangely like terror and entreaty looked out of his eyes: "I've *got* to have it," he said desperately.

"How much do you want?"

Starwick was silent, and then muttered:

"I could get along with 500 francs."

The other calculated swiftly: the sum amounted at the time to about thirty dollars. It was almost half his total remaining funds but—one look at the desperate humiliation and entreaty of Starwick's face, and a surge of savage, vindictive joy swept through him—it would be worth it.

"All right," he nodded briefly, and started to walk forward again.

"You come with me while I leave this stuff at the hotel and later on we'll see if we can't get these checks cashed."

Starwick consented eagerly. From that time on, Eugene played with him as a cat plays with a mouse. They got a taxi and were driven across the Seine to his little hotel, he left Starwick below while he went upstairs with his valise, promising to "be down in a minute, after I've washed up a bit," and took a full and leisurely three-quarters of an hour. When he got downstairs, Starwick's restless manner had increased perceptibly: he was pacing up and down, smoking one cigarette after another. In the same leisurely and maddening manner, they left the hotel. Starwick asked where they were going: Eugene replied cheerfully that they were going to dinner at a modest little restaurant across the Seine. By the time they had walked across the bridge, and through the enormous arches of the Louvre, Starwick was gnawing his lips with chagrin. In the restaurant, Eugene ordered dinner and a bottle of wine; Starwick refused to eat, Eugene expressed regret and pursued his meal deliberately. By the time he had finished, and was cracking nuts, Starwick was almost frantic. He demanded impatiently to know where they were going, and the other answered chidingly:

"Now, Frank, what's the hurry? You've got the whole night ahead of you: there's no rush at all. . . . Besides, why not stay here a while? It's a good place. Don't you think so? I discovered it all by myself!"

Starwick looked about him, and said:

"Yes, the place is all right, I suppose, the food looks good—it really does, you know—but *God!*" he snarled bitterly, "how dull! how dull!"

"*Dull?*" Eugene said chidingly, and with an air of fine astonishment. "Frank, Frank, such language—and from *you!* Is this the poet and the artist, the man of feeling and of understanding, the lover of humanity? Is this *grand,* is this *fine,* is this *swell?*" he jeered. "Is this the lover of the French—the man who's more at home here than he is at home? Why, Frank, this is unworthy of you: I thought that every breath you drew was saturated with the love of France. I thought that every pulse-beat of your artist's soul beat in sympathy with the people of this noble country. I thought that you would love this place—find it *simply swell,*" he sneered, "and *very* grand and *most* amusing—and here you turn your nose up at the people and call them dull—as if they were a lot of damned Americans! *Dull!* How can they be *dull,* Frank? Don't you see they're *French?* . . . Now this boy here, for example," he pointed to a bus-boy

"He is profoundly moved. . . . What you have said has touched him deeply!"

"Ah-h!" the boy cried, with an air of sudden, happy enlightenment, and thus inspired, began with renewed ardor, and many a vigorous wag of his thick and earnest beak, to proclaim:

"Mais c'est vrai! C'est comme je dis! . . . La France et l'Amérique—" he intoned anew.

"Oh, God!" groaned Starwick without turning, and waved a feeble and defeated arm. "Tell him to go away!"

"He is deeply moved! He says he can stand no more!"

The boy cast an earnest and immensely gratified look at Starwick's dejected back, and was on the point of pushing his triumph farther, when the proprietor angrily called to him, bidding him be about his work and leave the gentlemen in peace.

He departed with obvious reluctance, but not without vigorously nodding his thick head again, proclaiming that "La France et l'Amérique sont comme ça!" and shaking his thick, clasped fingers earnestly in a farewell gesture of racial amity.

When he had gone, Starwick looked around wearily, and in a dispirited tone said:

"God! What a place! How did you ever find it! . . . And how do you manage to stand it!"

"But look at him, Frank . . . I mean, don't you just *lo-o-ve* it?" he jibed. "I mean, there's something so *grand* and so *simple* and so *unaffected* about the way he did it! It's really *quite* astonishing! It really is, you know!"

The poor bus-boy, indeed, had been intoxicated by his sudden and unaccustomed success. Now, as he continued his work of clearing tables and stacking dishes on a tray, he could be seen nodding his thick head vigorously and muttering to himself: "Mais oui, mais oui, monsieur! . . . La France et l'Amérique. . . . Nous sommes de vrais amis!" and from time to time he would even pause in his work, to clasp his thick fingers together illustrating this, and to mutter: "C'est toujours comme ça!"

This preoccupied elation soon proved the poor boy's undoing. For even as he lifted his loaded tray and balanced it on one thick palm, he muttered "C'est comme ça," again, making a recklessly inclusive gesture with his free hand; the mountainously balanced tray was thrown off balance, he made a desperate effort to retrieve it, and as it crashed upon the floor, he pawed frantically and sprawled after it, in one general ruinous smash of broken crockery.

There was a maddened scream from the proprietor. He came running clumsily, a squat, thick figure of a bourgeois Frenchman, clothed in black, and screaming imprecations. His mustaches bristled like the quills of an enraged porcupine, and his ruddy face was swollen and suffused, an apoplectic red:

"Brute! Fool! Imbecile!" he screamed as the frightened boy clambered to his feet and stood staring at him with a face full of foolish and helpless bewilderment. ". . . Salaud! . . . Pig! . . . Architect!" he screamed out this meaningless curse in a strangling voice, and rushing at the boy, cuffed him clumsily on the side of the face, and began to thrust and drive him before him in staggering lunges.

"—And what grace, Frank!" Eugene now said cruelly. "How *grand* and *simple* and how *unselfconscious* they are in everything they do! I *mean,* the way they use their hands!" he said ironically, as the maddened proprietor gave the unfortunate boy another ugly, clumsy shove that sent him headlong. "I *mean,* it's like a fugue—like Cimabue or an early primitive—it really is, you know——"

"Assassin! Criminal!" the proprietor screamed at this moment, and gave the weeping boy a brutal shove that sent him sprawling forward upon his hands and knees:

"Traitor! Misérable scélérat!" he screamed, and kicked clumsily at the prostrate boy with one fat leg.

"Now where?—where?" Eugene said maliciously, as the wretched boy clambered to his feet, weeping bitterly, "—where, Francis, could you see anything like that in America?"

"God!" said Starwick, getting up. "It's unspeakable!" And desperately: "Let's go!"

They paid the bill and went out. As they went down the stairs, they could still hear the hoarse, choked sobs of the bus-boy, his thick face covered with his thick, blunt fingers, crying bitterly.

He didn't know what Starwick wanted the money for, but it was plain he wanted it for something, badly. His agitation was pitiable:— the bitter exasperation and open flare of temper he had displayed once or twice in the restaurant was so unnatural to him that it was evident his nerves were being badly rasped by the long delay. Now, he kept consulting his watch nervously: he turned, and looking at Eugene with a quiet but deep resentment in his eyes, he said:

"Look. If you're going to let me have the money, I wish you'd let me have it now—please. Otherwise, I shall not need it."

And Eugene, touched with a feeling of guilt at the deep and quiet resentment in his companion's face, knowing he had promised him the money, and feeling that this taunting procrastination was ungenerous and mean, said roughly:

"All right, come on. You can have it right away."

They turned into the Rue St. Honoré, turned again, and walked to the Place Vendôme, where there was a small exchange office—or "all-night bank"—where travellers' checks were cashed. They entered, he cashed his three remaining checks: the amount was something over 900 francs. He counted the money, kept out 500 francs for Starwick, stuffed the rest into his pocket, and, turning, thrust the little sheaf of banknotes into Starwick's hand, saying brutally:

"There's your money, Frank. And now, good-bye to you. I needn't detain you any longer."

He turned to go, but the implication of his sneer had not gone unnoticed:

"Just a minute," Starwick's quiet voice halted him. "What did you mean by that?"

He paused, with a slow thick anger beating in his veins:

"By what?"

"By saying you needn't detain me any longer?"

"You got what you wanted, didn't you?"

"You mean the money?"

"Yes."

Starwick looked quietly at him a moment longer, then thrust the little roll of banknotes back into his hand:

"Take it," he said.

For a moment the other could not speak. A murderous fury choked him: he ground his teeth together, and clenched his fist, he felt a moment's almost insane desire to grip that soft throat with his strangling hand, and beat the face into a bloody jelly with his fist.

"Why, God-damn you—" he grated between clenched teeth. "God-damn you for a—!"—he turned away, saying harshly: "To hell with you! . . . I'm through!"

He began to walk away across the Square at a savage stride. He heard footsteps following him: near the corner of the Rue St. Honoré, Starwick caught up with him, and said doggedly:

"No, but I'm going with you! . . . I really *must,* you know!" His voice rose and became high, almost womanish, with his passionate declaration: "If there's anything between you and me that has to be settled before you go away, you can't leave it like this . . . we've got to have it out, you know . . . we really must!"

The other youth stood stock still for a moment. Every atom of him —blood, bone, the beating of his heart, the substance of his flesh— seemed to congeal in a paralysis of cold murder. He licked his dry lips, and said thickly:

"Have it out!"—The blood swarmed through him in a choking flood, it seemed instantly to rush down through his hands and to fill him with a savage, rending strength, the curse was torn from him in a bestial cry and snarling:

"Have it out! Why, you damned rascal, we'll have it out, all right! We'll have it out, you dirty little fairy—" The foul word was out at last, in one blind expletive of murderous hate, and suddenly that tortured, impossibly tangled web of hatred, failure, and despair found its release. He reached out, caught Starwick by the throat and collar of his shirt, and endowed with that immense, incalculable strength which hatred and the sudden lust to kill can give a man, he lifted the slight figure from the ground as if it were a bundle of rags and sticks, and slammed it back against the façade of a building with such brutal violence that Starwick's head bounced and rattled on the stone. The blow knocked Starwick senseless: his hat went flying from his head, his cane fell from his grasp and rattled on the pavement with a hard, lean clatter. For a moment, his eyes rolled back and forth with the wooden, weighted movement of a doll's. Then, as Eugene released his grip, his legs buckled at the knees, his eyes closed and his head sagged, and he began to slump down towards the pavement, his back sliding all the time against the wall.

He would have fallen if Eugene had not caught him, held him, propped him up against the wall, until he could recover. And at that moment, Eugene felt an instant, overwhelming revulsion of shame, despair, and sick horror, such as he had never known before. For a moment all the blood seemed to have drained out of his heart and left it a dead shell. He thought he had killed Starwick—broken his neck or fractured his skull: even in death—or unconsciousness—Starwick's frail body retained its languorous dignity and grace. His head dropped heavily to one side, the buckling weight of the unconscious figure slumped in a movement of terrible and beautiful repose—the same movement that one sees in a great painting of Christ lowered from the cross, as if, indeed, the whole rhythm, balance and design of that art which Starwick had observed with such impassioned mimicry had left its image indelibly upon his own life, so that, even in death or senselessness, his body would portray it.

At that moment, the measure of ruin and defeat which the other young man felt was overwhelming. It seemed to him that if he had deliberately contrived to crown a ruinous career by the most shameful and calamitous act of all, he could not have been guilty of a worse crime than the one he had just committed. It was not merely the desperate, sickening terror in his heart when he thought that Starwick might be dead—that he had killed him. It was even more than this, a sense of profanation, a sense of having done something so foul and abominable that he could never recover from it, never wash its taint out of his blood. There are some people who possess such a natural dignity of person— such a strange and rare inviolability of flesh and spirit—that any famil- iarity, any insult, above all any act of violence upon them, is unthink- able. If such an insult be intended, if such violence be done, the act returns a thousandfold upon the one who does it: his own blow returns to deal a terrible revenge; he will relive his crime a thousand times in all the shame and terror of inexpiable memory.

Starwick was such a person: he had this quality of personal inviolabil- ity more than any one the other youth had ever known. And now, as he stood there holding Starwick propped against the wall, calling him by name, shaking him and pleading with him to recover consciousness, his feeling of shame, despair, and bitter ruinous defeat was abysmal, irremediable. It seemed to him that he could have done nothing which would more have emphasized his enemy's superiority and his own defeat than this thing which he had done. And the feeling that Starwick would always beat him, always take from him the thing he wanted most, that by no means could he ever match the other youth in any way, gain even the most trifling victory, was now overpowering in its horror. With a sick and bitter heart of misery, he cursed the wretched folly of his act. He would willingly have cut off his hand—the hand that gave the blow —if by so doing he could undo his act, but he knew that it was now too late, and with a feeling of blind terror he reflected that this knowledge of his defeat and fear was now Starwick's also, and that as long as Starwick lived, he would always know about it, and realize from this alone the full measure of his victory. And this feeling of shame, horror, and abysmal, inexpiable regret persisted even after, with a feeling of sick relief, he saw Starwick's eyes flutter, open, and after a moment of vague, confused bewilderment, look at him with a quiet consciousness.

Nevertheless, his feeling of relief was unspeakable. He bent, picked up Starwick's hat and cane, and gave them to him, saying quietly:

"I'm sorry, Frank."

Starwick put on his hat, and took the cane in his hand.

"It doesn't matter. If that's the way you felt, you had to do it," he said in a quiet, toneless and inflexible voice. "But now, before we leave each other, we must see this through. We've got to bring this thing into the open, find out what it is. That *must* be done, you know!" His voice had risen with an accent of inflexible resolve, an accent which the other had heard before, and which he knew no fear of death or violence or any desperate consequence could ever alter by a jot. "I've got to understand what this thing is before I leave you," Starwick said. "That must be done."

"All right!" Eugene said blindly, desperately. "Come on, then!"

And together, they strode along in silence, along the empty pavements of the Rue St. Honoré, past shuttered shops, and old, silent buildings which seemed to abide there and attend upon the anguish of tormented youth with all the infinite, cruel, and impassive silence of dark time, the unspeakable chronicle of foredone centuries, the unspeakable anguish, grief, and desperation of a million vanished, nameless, and forgotten lives.

And thus, in bitter shame and silence and despair, the demented, drunken, carnal, and kaleidoscopic circuit of the night began.

LXXXIX

ABOUT ten o'clock the next morning some one knocked at Eugene's door, and Starwick walked in. Without referring to the night before Starwick immediately, in his casual and abrupt way, said:

"Look. Elinor and Ann are here: they came in this morning."

"Where are they?" Excitement, sharp and sudden as an electric shock, shot through him. "Here? Downstairs?"

"No: they've gone shopping. I'm meeting them at Prunier's for lunch Ann said she might come by to see you later on."

"Before lunch?"

"Ace," said Starwick. "Look," he said again, in his casual, mannered tone, "I don't suppose you'd care to come to lunch with us?"

"Thanks," Eugene answered stiffly, "but I can't. I've got another engagement."

Starwick's face flushed crimson with the agonizing shyness and embarrassment which the effort cost him. He leaned upon his cane and looked out the window as he spoke.

"Then, look," he said, "Elinor asks to be remembered to you." He was silent a moment, and then continued with painful difficulty, "We're all going to the Louvre after lunch: I want to see the Cimabue once more before we leave."

"When are you leaving?"

"Tomorrow," Starwick said. "—Look!" he spoke carefully, looking out the window, "we're leaving the Louvre at four o'clock. . . . I thought . . . if you were going to be over that way. . . . I think Elinor would like to see you before she goes. . . . We'll be there at the main entrance." The anguish which the effort had cost him was apparent: he kept looking away out the window, leaning on his cane, and for a moment his ruddy face was contorted by the old, bestial grimace of inarticulate pain and grief which the other had noticed the first time they had met, in Cambridge, years before. Then Starwick, without glancing at Eugene, turned towards the door. For a moment he stood, back turned, idly tapping with his cane against the wall.

"It would be nice if you could meet us there. If not——"

He turned, and for the last time in life the two young men looked squarely at one another, and each let the other see, without evasion or constraint, the image of his soul. Henceforth, each might glimpse from time to time some shadow-flicker of the other's life, the destiny of each would curiously be interwoven through twinings of dark chance and tragic circumstance, but they would never see each other face to face again.

Now, looking steadily at him before he spoke, and with the deep conviction of his spirit, the true image of his life, apparent in his face, his eyes, his tone and manner, Starwick said:

"If I don't see you again, good-bye, Eugene." He was silent for a moment and, the color flaming in his face from the depth and earnestness of his feeling, he said quietly: "It was good to have known you. I shall never forget you."

"Nor I, you, Frank," the other said. "No matter what has happened —how we feel about each other now—you had a place in my life that no one else has ever had."

"And what was that?" said Starwick.

"I think it was that you were young—my own age—and that you were my friend. Last night after—after that thing happened," he went on, his own face flushing with the pain of memory, "I thought back over all the time since I have known you. And for the first time I realized that you were the first and only person of my own age that I could call my friend. You were my one true friend—the one I always turned to, believed in with unquestioning devotion. You were the only real friend that I ever had. Now something else has happened. You have taken from me something that I wanted, you have taken it without knowing that you took it, and it will always be like this. You were my brother and my friend——"

"And now?" said Starwick quietly.

"You are my mortal enemy. Good-bye."

"Good-bye, Eugene," said Starwick sadly. "But let me tell you this before I go. Whatever it was I took from you, it was something that I did not want or wish to take. And I would give it back again if I could."

"Oh, fortunate and favored Starwick," the other jeered. "To be so rich—to have such gifts and not to know he has them—to be forever victorious, and to be so meek and mild."

"And I will tell you this as well," Starwick continued. "Whatever anguish and suffering this mad hunger, this impossible desire, has caused you, however fortunate or favored you may think I am, I would give my whole life if I could change places with you for an hour—know for an hour an atom of your anguish and your hunger and your hope. . . . Oh, to feel so, suffer so, and live so!—however mistaken you may be! . . . To have come lusty, young, and living into this world . . . not to have come, like me, still-born from your mother's womb—never to know the dead heart and the passionless passion—the cold brain and the cold hopelessness of hope—to be wild, mad, furious, and tormented—but to have belief, to live in anguish, but to live,—and not to die." . . . He turned and opened the door. "I would give all I have and all you think I have, for just one hour of it. You call me fortunate and happy. *You* are the most fortunate and happy man I ever knew. Good-bye, Eugene."

"Good-bye, Frank. Good-bye, my enemy."

"And good-bye, my friend," said Starwick. He went out, and the door closed behind him.

Eugene was waiting for them at four o'clock that afternoon when they came out from the Louvre. As he saw them coming down the steps together he felt a sudden, blind rush of affection for all of them, and saw that all of them were fine people. Elinor came towards him instantly, and spoke to him warmly, kindly, and sincerely, without a trace of mannerism or affectation or concealed spitefulness. Starwick stood by quietly, while he talked to Elinor: Ann looked on sullenly and dumbly and thrust her hands in the pockets of her fur jacket. In the dull, gray light they looked like handsome, first-rate, dignified people, who had nothing mean or petty in them and with whom nothing but a spacious, high and generous kind of life was possible. By comparison, the Frenchmen coming from the museum and streaming past them looked squalid and provincial; and the Americans and other foreigners had a shabby, dull, inferior look. For a moment the bitter and passionate enigma of life pierced him with desperation and wild hope. What was wrong with life? What got into people such as these to taint their essential quality, to twist and warp and mutilate their genuine and higher purposes? What were these perverse and evil demons of cruelty and destructiveness, of anguish, error and confusion that got into them, that seemed to goad them on, with a wicked and ruinous obstinacy, deliberately to do the things they did not want to do—the things that were so shamefully unworthy of their true character and their real desire?

It was maddening because it was so ruinous, so wasteful and so useless; and because it was inexplicable. As these three wonderful, rare and even beautiful people stood there telling him good-bye, every movement, look, and word they uttered was eloquent with the quiet but passionate and impregnable conviction of the human faith. Their quiet, serious, and affectionate eyes, their gestures, their plain, clear, and yet affectionate speech, even the instinctive tenderness that they felt towards one another which seemed to join them with a unity of living warmth and was evident in the way they stood, glanced at each other, or in swift, instinctive gestures—all this with a radiant, clear, and naked loveliness seemed to speak out of them in words no one could misunderstand, to say:

"Always there comes a moment such as this when, poised here upon the ledge of furious strife, we stand and look; the marsh-veil shifts from the enfevered swamp, the phantoms are dispersed like painted smoke, and standing here together, friend, we all see clear again, our souls are tranquil and our hearts are quiet—and we have what we have, we know what we know, we are what we are."

It seemed to him that all these people now had come to such a moment, that this clear peace and knowledge rested in their hearts, and spoke out of their eyes; it seemed to him that all his life, for years, since he had first gone to the dark North and known cities—since he had first known Starwick—was now a phantasmal nightmare—a kaleidoscope of blind, furious days, and drunken and diverted nights, the measureless sea-depth of incalculable memory, an atom lost and battered in a world of monstrous shapes, and deafened in a world of senseless, stupefying war and movement and blind fury. And it seemed to him now that for the first time he—and all of them—had come to a moment of clarity and repose, and that for the first time their hearts saw and spoke the truth that lies buried in all men, that all men know.

Elinor had taken him by the hand, and was saying quietly:

"I am sorry that you will not go with us. We have had a strange and hard and desperate time together, but that is over now, Eugene: we have all been full of pain and trouble, and all of us are sorry for the things we've done. I want you to know that we all love you, and will always think of you with friendship, as our friend, and will hope that you are happy, and will rejoice in your success as if it were our own. . . . And now, good-bye, my dear; try to think of us always as we think of you—with love and kindness. Do not forget us; always remember us with a good memory, the way we shall remember you. . . . Perhaps," for a moment her face was touched with her gay, rueful smile —"perhaps when I'm an old Boston lady with a cat, a parrot, and a canary, you will come to see me. I will be a nice old lady, then—but also I will be a ruined old lady—for they don't forget—not in a life-time, not in Boston—and this time, darling, I have gone too far. So I shan't have many callers, I shall leave them all alone—and if you're not too rich, too famous, and too proper by that time, perhaps you'll come to see me. . . . Now, good-bye."

"Good-bye, Elinor," he said. "And good luck to you."

"Look," said Starwick quietly, "we're going on—Elinor and I . . . I

thought . . . if you're not doing anything else . . . perhaps you and
Ann might have dinner together."

"I'm—I'm not," he stammered, looking at Ann, "but maybe you . . ."

"No," she muttered, staring sullenly and miserably at the ground.
"I'm not either."

"Then," Starwick said, "we'll see you later, Ann. . . . And good-bye,
Eugene."

"Good-bye, Frank."

They shook hands together for the last time, and Starwick and Elinor
turned and walked away. Thus, with such brief and casual words, the
bond of friendship—all of the faith, belief and passionate avowal of their
youth—was forever broken. They saw each other once thereafter; by
chance their lives would have strange crossings; but they never spoke
to each other again.

They waited in awkward silence for a moment until they saw Starwick and Elinor get into a taxi and drive off. Then they walked away
together across the great quadrangle of the Louvre. A haze of bluish
mist, soft, smoky as a veil, hung in the air across the vistaed sweep of
the Tuileries and the Place de la Concorde. The little taxis drilled across
the great space between the vast wings of the Louvre and through the
arches, filling the air with wasp-like drone and menace, the shrill excitement of their tootling horns. And through that veil of bluish haze,
the vast mysterious voice of Paris reached their ears: it was a sound
immense and murmurous as time, fused of the strident clamors of its
four million subjects, and yet, strangely muted, seductive, sensuous,
cruel and thrilling, filled with life and death. The mysterious fragrance of that life filled Eugene with the potent intoxication of its magic.
He drew the pungent smoky air into his lungs, and it seemed freighted
with the subtle incense of the great city's hope and secret promise, with
grief and joy and terror, with a wild and nameless hunger, with intolerable desire. It numbed his entrails and his loins with sensual prescience, and it made his heart beat hard and fast; his breath came
quickly: it was mixed into the pulses of his blood and gave to grief and
joy and sorrow, the wild mixed anguish beating in his heart, its single
magic, its impalpable desire.

They walked slowly across the great Louvre court and through the
gigantic masonries of the arch into the Rue de Rivoli. The street was
swarming with its dense web of afternoon: the sensuous complications

of its life and traffic, the vast honeycomb of business and desire; the street was jammed with its brilliant snarl of motors, with shout and horn and cry, and with the throbbing menace of machinery, and on the other side, beneath arched colonnades, the crowd was swarming in unceasing flow.

They crossed the street and made their way through a thronging maze into the Place de la Comédie Française, and found a table on the terrace of La Régence. The pleasant old café was gay with all its chattering groups of afternoon, and yet, after the great boil and fury of the streets, it was strangely calm, detached, and pleasant, too. The little separate verandahs of its terrace, the tables and the old settees and walls, gave the café an incredibly familiar and intimate quality, as if one were seated in a pleasant booth that looked out on life, a box in an old theatre whose stage was the whole world.

In one of the friendly booth-like verandahs of this pleasant old café, they found a table in a corner, seats against the wall, and sat down and gave their order to the waiter. Then, for some time, as they drank their brandy, they looked out at the flashing pulsations of the street, and did not speak.

Presently Ann, without looking at him, in her level, curt, and almost grimly toneless speech, said:

"What did you and Frank do last night?"

Excitement caught him; his pulse beat faster; he glanced quickly at her, and said:

"Oh—nothing. We went out to eat—walked around a bit—that was all."

"Out all night?" she said curtly.

"No. I turned in early. I was home by twelve o'clock."

"What happened to Frank?"

He looked at her sharply, startled. "Happened? What do you mean—'what happened to him?'"

"What did he do when you went home?"

"How should I know? He went back to the studio, I suppose. Why do you want to know?"

She made no answer for a moment, but sat looking sullenly into the street. When she spoke again, she did not look at him, her voice was level, hard, and cold, quietly, grimly inflectionless.

"Do you think it's a very manly thing for a big hulking fellow like you to jump on a boy Frank's size?"

Hot fury choked him, passed before his vision in a blinding flood. He ground his teeth, rocked gently back and forth, and said in a small, stopped voice:

"Oh, so he told you, did he? He had to come whining to you about it, did he? The damned little . . . !"

"He told us nothing," she said curtly. "Frank's not that kind; he doesn't whine. Only, we couldn't help noticing a lump on the back of his head the size of a goose egg, and it didn't take me long to figure out the rest." She turned and looked at him with a straight, unrelenting stare, and then said harshly:

"It was a wonderful thing to do, wasn't it? I suppose you think that settles everything. You can be proud of yourself, now, can't you?"

The thin fine blade of cruel jealousy pierced him suddenly, and was twisted in his heart. In a voice trembling with all the sweltering anguish and defeat that packed his overladen heart, he sneered in bitter parody:

"Come now, Frankie, dear!—Did bad naughty mans crack little Frankie's precious head?—There, there, dearie!—Mamma kiss and make it well . . . let nice big nursey-worsey kiss-um and make-um well!—Next time Frankie-pankie goes for a walk, big Boston nursey Ann will go wiv-ems, won't she, pet, to see that wuff, wuff man leave poor little Frankie be."

She reddened angrily, and said:

"No one's trying to be Frankie's nurse. He doesn't need it, and he doesn't want it. Only, I think it's a rotten shame that a big hulking lout like you should have no more decency than to maul around as fine a person as Frank is. You ought to be ashamed of yourself; it was a rotten thing to do!"

"Why, you bitch!" he said slowly, in a low, strangled tone. "You nice, neat, eighteen-carat jewel of a snobby Boston bitch!—Go back to Boston where you came from!" he snarled. "That's where you belong; that's all you're worth. . . . So I'm a big, hulking lout, am I? And that damned little affected æsthete's the finest person that you ever knew!—Why, God-damn the lot of you for the cheap, lying, fakey Boston bitches that you are!—with your 'he's a *swell* person, he really is, you know,'—'Oh, *grand!* Oh, *swell!* Oh, *fine!*'" he jeered incoherently. "Why, damn you, who do you think you are, anyway?—that you think I'm going to stand for any more of your snobby Boston backwash!—So I'm a big, hulking lout, am I?"—the words rankled bitterly in his memory. "And dear, darling little Francis is too fine, too fine—oh, dearie me, now, yes—to have

his precious little head cracked up against a wall by the likes of me. . . .
Why, damn you, Ann!" he said in a grating voice, "what are you, anyway, but a damned dull lummox of a girl from Boston? Who the hell
do you think you are, anyway, that I should sit here and take your
snobby backwash and play second fiddle while two cheap Boston women
praise Starwick up to the skies all day long, and tell me what a great
genius he is and how much finer than any one else that ever lived? By
God, it is to laugh!" he raved incoherently, blind with pain and passion,
hindering his own progress by his foolish words of wounded pride.
"—To see the damned affected æsthete get it all! You're not worth it!
You're not worth it!" he cried bitterly. "—You call me a big hulking
lout—and I feel more, know more, see more, have more life and power
and understanding in me in a minute than the whole crowd of you will
ever have—why, I'm so much better than the rest of you that—that
—that—there's no comparison!" he said lamely; and concluded, "Oh,
you're not worth it! You're not worth it, Ann! Why should I get down
on my knees to you this way, and worship you, and beg you for just one
word of love and mercy—when you call me a big, hulking lout—and
you are nothing but a rich, dull Boston snob—and you're not worth it!"
he cried desperately. "Why has it got to be like this, when you're not
worth it, Ann?"

Her face flushed, and in a moment, laughing her short and angry
laugh, she said:

"God! I can see this is going to be a pleasant evening, with you raving
like a crazy man and passing out your compliments already." She
looked at him with bitter eyes, and said sarcastically, "You say such nice
things to people, don't you? Oh, charming! Charming! Simply delightful!" She laughed her sudden angry laugh again. "God! I'll never
forget some of the nice things that you said to me!"

And already tortured by remorse and shame, the huge, indefinable
swelter of anguish in his heart, he caught her hand, and pleaded miserably, humbly.

"Oh, I know! I know!—I'm sorry, Ann, and I'll do better—so help
me God, I will!"

"Then why must you carry on like this?" she said. "Why do you
curse and revile me and say such things about Francis, who is one of
the finest people that ever lived, and who has never said a word against
you?"

"Oh, I know!" he groaned miserably, and smote his brow. "—I

don't mean to—it just gets the best of me—Ann, Ann! I love you so!"

"Yes," she muttered, "a funny kind of love, when you can say such things to me!"

"And when I hear you praise up Starwick, it all comes back to me— and Christ! Christ!—why did it have to be this way? Why did it have to be Starwick that you——?"

She got up, her face flaring with anger and resentment.

"Come on!" she said curtly. "If you can't behave yourself—if you're starting in on that—I'm not going to stay——"

"Don't go! Don't go!" he whispered, grabbing her hand and holding it in a kind of dumb anguish. "You said you'd stay! It's just for a few hours longer—oh, don't go and leave me, Ann! I'm sorry! I promise I'll do better. It's only when I think of it—oh, don't go, Ann! Please don't go! I try not to talk about it but it gets the best of me! I'll be all right now. I'll not talk about it any more—if you won't go. If you'll just stay with me a little longer—it will be all right. I swear that everything will be all right if you don't go."

She stood straight and rigid, her hands clenched convulsively at her sides, her eyes shot with tears of anger and bewilderment. She made a sudden baffled movement of frustration and despair, and cried bitterly:

"God! What is it all about? Why can't people be happy, anyway?"

They made a furious circuit of the night. They went back to all the old places—to the places they had been to with Elinor and Starwick. They went to Le Rat Mort, to Le Coq et l'Ane, to Le Moulin Rouge, to Le Bal Tabarin, to La Bolée, to the Jockey Club, to the Dome and the Rotonde,—even to the Bal Bullier. They went to the big night resorts and to the little ones, to great cafés and little bars, to dive and stew and joint and hole, to places frequented exclusively by the rich and fashionable—the foreigners, the wealthy French, the tourists, the expatriates— and to other places where the rich and fashionable went to peer down into the cauldrons of the lower depths at all those creatures who inhabited the great swamp of the night—the thieves, the whores, the rogues, the pimps, the lesbians and the pederasts—the human excrement, the damned and evil swarm of sourceless evil that crawled outward from the rat-holes of the dark, lived for a period in the night's huge blaze of livid radiance, and then were gone, vanished, melted away as by an evil magic into that trackless labyrinth from which they came.

Where had it gone? That other world of just six weeks before, with all its nocturnal and unholy magic, now seemed farther off and stranger than a dream. It was impossible to believe that these shabby places of garish light, and tarnished gold, and tawdry mirrors, were the same resorts that had glowed in all their hot and close perfumes just six weeks before, had burned there in the train of night like some evil, secret and unholy temple of desire. It was all worn off now: cheap as Coney Island, tawdry, tarnished as the last year's trappings of a circus, bedraggled, shabby as a harlot's painted face at noon. All of its sinister and intoxicating magic had turned dull and pitiably sordid: its people were pathetic, and its music dead—serving only to recall the splendid evil people and the haunting music of six weeks before.

And they saw now that this was just the way it was, the way it had always been. Places, people, music—they were just the same. All that had changed had been themselves. And all through the night they went from place to place, drinking, watching, dancing, doing just the things they had always done, but it was no good—it had all gone stale— it would never be any good again. They sat there sullenly, like people at a waning carnival, haunted by the ghosts of memory and departure. The memory of Elinor and Starwick—and particularly of Starwick— haunted each place they went to like a deathshead at a feast. And again Eugene was filled with the old, choking, baffled, and inchoate anger, the sense of irretrievable and certain defeat: Starwick in absence was even more triumphantly alive than if he had been there—he alone, by the strange, rare quality in him, had been able to give magic to this sordid carnival, and now that he was gone, the magic had gone, too.

The night passed in a kaleidoscope of baffled fury, of frenzied search and frustrate desire. All night they hurtled back and forth between the two blazing poles of Montmartre and Montparnasse: later he was to remember everything like the exploded fragments of a nightmare—a vision of dark, silent streets, old shuttered houses, the straight slant and downward plunge out of Montmartre—the sudden blaze of lights at crossings, boulevards, in cafés, night-clubs, bars and avenues, the cool plunge and shock of air along dark streets again, the taxis' shrill horn tootling at space, empty reckless corners, the planted stems of light across the Seine, the bridges and the sounding arches and dark streets, the steep slant of the hill, the livid glare of night and all the night's scarred faces over again.

They did not know why they stayed, why they hung on, why they continued grimly at this barren hunt. But something held them there together: they could not say good-bye and part. Ann hung on sullenly, angrily, in a kind of stubborn silence, saying little, ordering brandy at the bars and cafés, champagnes in the night resorts, drinking little herself, sitting by him in a sullen, angry silence while he drank.

He was like a maddened animal: he raved, stormed, shouted, cursed, implored, entreated, reviled her and made love to her at once—there was no sense, or reason, or coherence in anything he said: it came out of him in one tortured expletive, the urge of the baffled touch, that conflict of blind love and hate and speechless agony, in his tormented spirit: "Oh, Ann! . . . You lovely bitch! . . . You big, dark, dumb, lovely, sullen Boston bitch! . . . Oh, you whore! You whore!" he groaned, and seizing her hand, he caught it to him, and said desperately, "Ann, Ann, I love you! . . . You're the greatest . . . grandest . . . best . . . most beautiful girl that ever lived . . . Ann! Look at me—you big, ox-dumb brute. . . . Oh, you bitch. . . . You Boston bitch. . . . Will it never come out of you? . . . Won't you ever let it come? . . . Can't it be thawed, melted, shaken loose? . . . Oh, you dumb, dark, sullen, lovely bitch . . . is there nothing there? . . . is this all you are? . . . Oh, Ann, you sweet, dumb whore, if you only knew how much I love you——"

"God!" she cried, with her quick, short, and angry laugh that gave her face its sudden, radiant tenderness, its indescribable loveliness and purity, "—God! But you're the gallant lover, aren't you? First you love me, then you hate me, then I'm a dumb, sullen Boston bitch, and then a whore, and then the grandest and most beautiful girl that ever lived! God, you're wonderful, you are!" She laughed bitterly. "You say such charming things."

"Oh, you bitch!" he groaned miserably. "You big, sweet, dumb, and lovely bitch—Ann, Ann, for God's sake, speak to me, talk to me!" He seized her hand and shook it frantically. "Say just one word to show me you're alive—that you've got one, single atom of life and love and beauty in you. Ann, Ann,—look at me! In God's name, tell me, what are you? Is there nothing there? Have you nothing in you? For Christ's sake, try to say a single, living word—for Christ's sake, try to show me that you're worth it, that it's not all death and codfish, Boston, Back Bay, and cold fishes' blood"—he raved on incoherently:

"Oh! Boston and cold fishes' blood, my eye!" she muttered, with an angry flush in her face.

"And you?—What are you?" he jeered. "For God's sake, what kind of woman are you? I never heard you speak a word that a child of ten could not have spoken. I never heard you say a thing that ought to be remembered. The only things I know about you are that you are a Boston spinstress—thirty—no longer very young—a few gray hairs already on your head—comfortably secure on dead investments—over here on a spree—away from father and the family and *The Boston Evening Transcript*—but never losing them: always knowing that you will return to them—in God's name, woman, is that all you are?"

She laughed her sudden, short and angry laugh, and yet there was no rancor in it.

"That's what Frank would call a brief but masterly description, isn't it? I suppose I should be grateful." She looked at him with quiet eyes, and said simply: "What of it? Even if what you say is true, what of it? As you say, I'm just a dull, ordinary kind of person, and until you and Francis came along, no one thought me anything else, or thought any the less of me for being like that. Listen," her voice was hard and straight and sullen, "what do you expect people to be, anyway? Do you think it's fair and decent to talk about how beautiful I am, when I'm not beautiful, and then to turn and curse me because I'm just an ordinary girl?" She was silent a moment, with an angry flush upon her face, and then she said: "As for my intellect, I went to Bryn Mawr, and I got through without flunking, with a C average. That's about the kind of brain I've got." She turned and looked at him with straight, angry eyes, now shut a little with tears:

"What of it?" she said. "You say that I am dull and dumb and ordinary—well, I never pretended to be anything else. You know, we all can't be great geniuses, like you and Francis," she said, and suddenly her eyes were wet, and tears began to trickle down across her flushed face.— "—I'm just what I am, I've never pretended to be any different—if you think I'm dull and stupid and ordinary, you have no right to insult me like this.—Come on, I'm going home."—She started to get up, he seized her, pulled her to him:

"Oh, you bitch! . . . You big, dumb, lovely bitch! . . . Oh, Ann, Ann, you sweet whore, how I love you—I can never let you go—oh, God-damn you, Ann——"

It ended at last, at daybreak in a bistro near Les Halles, where they had often gone at dawn with Elinor and Starwick for rolls and chocolate or coffee. Outside they could hear the nightly roar and rumble of the market, the cries of the venders, and smell all the sweet smells of earth and morning, of first light, health, and joy, and day beginning.

When they left the bistro full light had come, and they at length had fallen silent. They realized that it was useless, hopeless, and impossible, that nothing could be said.

He left her at the gate outside the studio. She pressed the bell, the gate swung open, and for a moment before she left him she stood looking at him with a flushed, angry face, wet angry eyes—a look of dumb, sullen misery that tore at his heart, and for which he had no word.

"Good-bye," she said, "if I don't see you again—" She paused and clenched her fists together at her side, closed her eyes, tears spurted out, and in a choking voice she cried out:

"Oh, this will be a fine thing for me all right! This trip has just been wonderful. God! I'm sorry that I ever saw any of you——"

"Ann! Ann!"

"If you need money—if you're broke——"

"Ann!"

"God!" she cried again. "Why did I ever come!"

She was weeping bitterly, and with a blind, infuriated movement she rushed through the gate and slammed it behind her.

BOOK VI
ANTÆUS: EARTH AGAIN

XC

WHEN he awoke in Chartres he was filled with a numb excitement. It was a gray wintry day with snow in the air, and he expected something to happen. He had this feeling often in the country, in France: it was a strange, mixed feeling of desolation and homelessness, of wondering with a ghostly emptiness why he was there—and of joy, and hope, and expectancy, without knowing what it was he was going to find.

In the afternoon he went down to the station and took a train that was going to Orléans. He did not know where Orléans was. The train was a mixed train, made up of goods cars and passenger compartments. He bought a third-class ticket and got into one of the compartments. Then the shrill little whistle blew, and the train rattled out of Chartres into the countryside, in the abrupt and casual way a little French train has, and which was disquieting to him.

There was a light mask of snow on the fields, and the air was smoky: the whole earth seemed to smoke and steam, and from the windows of the train one could see the wet earth and the striped, cultivated pattern of the fields, and now and then, some farm buildings. It did not look like America: the land looked fat and well kept, and even the smoky wintry woods had this well-kept appearance. Far off sometimes one could see tall lines of poplars and knew that there was water there.

In the compartment he found three people—an old peasant and his wife and daughter. The old peasant had sprouting mustaches, a seamed and weather-beaten face, and small rheumy-looking eyes. His hands had a rock-like heaviness and solidity, and he kept them clasped upon his knees. His wife's face was smooth and brown, there were fine webs of wrinkles around her eyes, and her face was like an old brown bowl. The daughter had a dark sullen face and sat away from them next the window as if she was ashamed of them. From time to time when they spoke to her she would answer them in an infuriated kind of voice without looking at them.

The peasant began to speak amiably to him when he entered the compartment. He smiled and grinned back at the man, although he did not understand a word he was saying, and the peasant kept on talking then, thinking he understood.

The peasant took from his coat a package of the cheap, powerful tobacco—the 'bleu—which the French government provides for a few cents for the poor, and prepared to stuff his pipe. The young man pulled a package of American cigarettes from his pocket, and offered them to the peasant.

"Will you have one?"

"My faith, yes!" said the peasant.

He took a cigarette clumsily from the package and held it between his great, stiff fingers, then he held it to the flame the young man offered, puffing at it in an unaccustomed way. Then he fell to examining it curiously, revolving it in his hands to read the label. He turned to his wife, who had followed every movement of this simple transaction with the glittering intent eyes of an animal, and began a rapid and excited discussion with her.

"It's American—this."

"Is it good?"

"My faith, yes—it's of good quality."

"Here, let me see! What does it call itself?"

They stared dumbly at the label.

"What do you call this?" said the peasant to the young man.

"Licky Streek," said the youth, dutifully phonetical.

"L-l-leek-ee—?" they stared doubtfully. "What does that wish to say, in French?"

"Je ne sais pas," he answered.

"Where are you going?" the peasant said, staring at the youth with rheumy little eyes of fascinated curiosity.

"Orléans."

"How?" the peasant asked, with a puzzled look on his face.

"Orléans."

"I do not understand," the peasant said.

"Orléans! Orléans!" the girl shouted in a furious tone. "The gentleman says he is going to Orléans."

"Ah!" the peasant cried, with an air of sudden illumination. *"Orléans!"*

It seemed to the youth that he had said the word just the same way the peasant said it, but he repeated it.

"Yes, Orléans."

"He is going to Orléans," the peasant said, turning to his wife.

"Ah-h!" she cried knowingly, with a great air of illumination, then both fell silent, and began to stare at the youth with curious, puzzled eyes again.

"What region are you from?" the peasant asked presently, still intent and puzzled, staring at him with his small eyes.

"How's that? I don't understand."

"I say—what region are you from?"

"The gentleman is not French!" the girl shouted furiously, as if exasperated by their stupidity. "He is a foreigner. Can't you see that?"

"Ah-h!" the peasant cried, after a moment, with an air of astounded enlightenment. Then, turning to his wife, he said briefly, "He is not French. He is a stranger."

"Ah-h!"

And then they both turned their small, round eyes on him and regarded him with a fixed, animal-like curiosity.

"From what country are you?" the peasant asked presently. "What are you?"

"I am an American."

"Ah-h! An American. . . . He is an American," he said, turning to his wife.

"Ah-h!"

The girl made an impatient movement, and continued to stare furiously and sullenly out the window.

Then the peasant, with the intent, puzzled curiosity of an animal began to examine his companion carefully from head to foot. He looked at his shoes, his clothes, his overcoat, and finally lifted his eyes in an intent and curious stare to the young man's valise on the rack above his head. He nudged his wife and pointed to the valise.

"That's good stuff, eh?" he said in a low voice. "It's real leather."

"Yes, it's good, that."

And both of them looked at the valise for some time and then turned their curious gaze upon the youth again. He offered the peasant another cigarette, and the old man took one, thanking him.

"It's very fine, this," he said, indicating the cigarette. "That costs dear, eh?"

"Six francs."

"Ah-h! . . . That's very dear," and he began to look at the cigarette with increased respect.

"Why are you going to Orléans?" he asked presently. "Do you know some one there?"

"No, I am just going there to see the town."

"How?" the peasant blinked at him stupidly, uncomprehendingly. "You have business there?"

"No. I am going just to visit—to see the place."

"How?" the peasant said stupidly in a moment, looking at him. "I do not understand."

"The gentleman says he is going to see the town," the girl broke in furiously. "Can't you understand anything?"

"I do not understand what he is saying," the old man said to her. "He does not speak French."

"He speaks very well," the girl said angrily. "I understand him very well. It is you who are stupid—that's all."

The peasant was silent for some time now, puffing at his cigarette, and looking at the young man with friendly, puzzled eyes.

"America is very large—eh?" he said at length—making a wide gesture with his hands.

"Yes, it is very large. Much larger than France."

"How?" the peasant said again with a puzzled, patient look. "I do not understand."

"He says America is much larger than France," the girl cried in an exasperated tone. "I understand all he says."

Then, for several minutes, there was an awkward silence: nothing was said. The peasant smoked his cigarette, seemed on the point of speaking several times, looked puzzled and said nothing. Outside, rain had begun to fall in long slanting lines across the fields, and beyond, in the gray blown sky, there was a milky radiance where the sun should be, as if it were trying to break through. When the peasant saw this, he brightened, and leaning forward to the young man in a friendly manner, he tapped him on the knee with one of his great, stiff fingers, and then pointing towards the sun, he said very slowly and distinctly, as one might instruct a child:

"Le so-leil."

And the young man obediently repeated the word as the peasant had said it:

"Le so-leil."

The old man and his wife beamed delightedly and nodded their approval, saying, "Yes. Yes. Good. Very good." Turning to his wife for confirmation, the old man said:

"He said it very well, didn't he?"

"But, yes! It was perfect!"

Then, pointing to the rain, and making a down-slanting movement with his great hands, he said again, very slowly and patiently:

"La pluie."

"La pluie," the young man repeated dutifully, and the peasant nodded vigorously, saying:

"Good, good. You are speaking very well. In a little time you will speak good French." Then, pointing to the fields outside the train, he said gently:

"La terre."

"La terre," the young man answered.

"I tell you," the girl cried angrily from her seat by the window, "he knows all these words. He speaks French very well. You are too stupid to understand him—that's all."

The old man made no reply to her, but sat looking at the young man with a kind, approving face. Then, more rapidly than before, and in succession, he pointed to the sun, the rain, the earth, saying:

"Le soleil . . . la pluie . . . la terre."

The young man repeated the words after him, and the peasant nodded vigorously with satisfaction. Then, for a long time, no one spoke, there was no sound except for the uneven rackety-clack of the little train, and the girl continued to look sullenly out the window. Outside, the rain fell across the fertile fields in long slanting lines.

Late in the afternoon, the train stopped at a little station, and every one rose to get out. This was as far as the train went: to reach Orléans it was necessary to change to another train.

The peasant, his wife and his daughter collected their bundles and got out of the train. On another track another little train was waiting, and the peasant pointed to this with his great, stiff finger, and said to the young man:

"Orléans. That's your train there."

The youth thanked him, and gave the old man the remainder of the package of cigarettes. The peasant thanked him effusively and before they parted he again pointed rapidly towards the sun, the rain, and the earth, saying with a kind and friendly smile:

"Le soleil . . . la pluie . . . la terre."

And the young man nodded to show that he understood, repeated what the old man had said. And the peasant shook his head with vigorous approval, saying:

"Yes, yes. It's very good. You will learn fast."

At these words, the girl, who with the same sullen, aloof, and shamed look had walked on ahead of her parents, now turned, and cried out in a furious and exasperated tone:

"I tell you, the gentleman knows all that! . . . Will you leave him alone now! . . . You are only making a fool of yourself!"

But the old man and old woman paid no attention to her, but stood looking at the young man, with a friendly smile, and shook hands warmly and cordially with him as he said good-bye.

Then he walked on across the tracks and got up into a compartment in the other train. When he looked out the window again, the peasant and his wife were standing on the platform looking towards him with kind and eager looks on their old faces. When the peasant caught his eye, he pointed his great finger at the sun again, and called out:

"Le so-leil."

"Le so-leil," the young man answered.

"Yes! Yes!" the old man shouted, with a laugh. "It's very good."

Then the daughter looked toward the young man sullenly, gave a short and impatient laugh of exasperation, and turned angrily away. The train began to move, then, but the old man and woman stood looking after him as long as they could. He waved to them, and the old man waved his great hand vigorously and, laughing, pointed towards the sun. And the young man nodded his head and shouted, to show that he had understood. Meanwhile, the girl had turned her back angrily and was walking away around the station.

Then they were lost from sight, the train swiftly left the little town behind, and now there was nothing but the fields, the earth, the smoky and mysterious distances. The rain fell steadily.

XCI

FULL dark had come—the wintry darkness of a gray wet day in early March—before he got to Orléans. The train was of the variety known in France as omnibus, one of those dingy little locals that are made up of third-class compartments and that stop at every country station. As the train neared Orléans, there was a noticeable increase in the travelling public: at every station there was a noisy traffic of arriving and departing passengers. For the most part the people had the look of the country: they came stamping in and out with muddy shoes, with a great banging of compartment doors, with a great tumult of voices, with the vigorous excitement of robust and talkative people.

They were a good-natured crowd, and seemed to know one another, if not actually by name, with the even completer familiarity of race and kind and region. At the sudden pauses at dim-lit country stations, one could hear them shouting greetings and farewells, and see them streaming away along a muddy road towards the dim light and shine of a little town with all the utter, common, and dreary familiarity of March. And the train, in those abrupt and sudden halts and pauses, seemed to be almost as casual a means of transportation as a street-car: it would rattle up to a station, halt, the people would stamp in and out with a banging of doors, and with many shouts, cries, greetings, and farewells, then the shrill little whistle would make its fifing note, and the train would rattle out into the wet and wintry countryside again.

In the compartments the lights were very low and dim, and cast flickering shadows on the faces of the passengers. Somewhere in the train, in another compartment, there was a noisy and jolly crowd of soldiers and robust country people. One man in particular dominated the whole train with his jolly energy, his vulgar and high-spirited good nature. The man's rich voice was charged indescribably with the high, sanguinary vitality of the Frenchman. The voice, to a foreigner, was at once inimitably strange in accent, quality and intonation, and yet familiar as all life, all living. It was packed with the juice of life, and had the full rich qualities of a good wine.

For the youth, that voice heard there in the flickering shadows of the little train, heard with all its robust and full-blooded penetration at the casual and abrupt halts and pauses at little stations, was to be a strangely haunting one. A thousand times thereafter the tone of that rich voice would return to him and reverberate in his memory with the haunting, strange and wonderful recurrence with which the "little" things of life —a face seen one time at a window, a voice that passed in darkness and was gone, the twisting of a leaf upon a bough—come back to us out of all the violence and savage chaos of the days—the "little" things that persist so strangely, vividly, and inexplicably when the more sensational and "important" events of life have been forgotten or obscured.

So, now, the jolly voice of this unseen Frenchman, as it shouted out good-natured but derisive comments on the customs, the appearance, and the inhabitants of every little town at which they stopped, as it was answered in like fashion by the people on the station platforms, brought back to him instantly the memory of a little country town in the South at which, on his way to and from college, he had stopped a dozen times at just this hour. The name of the town was Creasman, there was a small sectarian school there which was known as Creasman College, and it had become traditional with the university students, who crowded the train on their journeys home or back to college, to thrust their heads out of the windows and howl with the derisive arrogance of youth: "Whoopee, girls! Creasman College!"

And this sally was usually answered by similar jibes and jeers from the group of students, townsfolk and country people, who crowded the platform of the station "to see the train come through."

In this Frenchman's taunts and jeers, and in the way the people at the stations answered him, as well as in all the traffic of noisy, muddy, talking and gesticulating people who streamed in and out of the train at every halt, there was, in spite of all the local differences, the same essential quality that had characterized the halts at the little town set there upon the vast, raw Piedmont of the South.

Moreover, there was in the tone and texture of the Frenchman's voice —at once so actual, living, and familiar in its high, sanguinary energy, and so foreign, alien, and troubling to a stranger's ear—the whole warmth and vitality of centuries of living, a quality which brought the ancient past of Europe, and of France, to life, as the pages of history could never do.

In the same way, the boy had long ago discovered that a single tone or shading in his mother's or his father's voice could touch the lost past of America—the past of the Civil War, the strange mysteries of Garfield, Arthur, Harrison, and Hayes, which is, for most Americans, more far and strange in time than the Crusades—and bring it instantly into life.

Thus, he had never gained a living image of the Civil War until he heard his mother speak of it one day. Until that time, all his efforts to recapture that lost time out of the pages of books had been futile; the men, the battles, the generals, and the lives of all the people existed in a world of legendary unreality, and seemed, in fact, as different from the world he knew as if they had existed on a separate planet. And then one day he heard his mother—who had been only five years old when the war ended—describe the return of the troops along a country road near home. She told how the dust rose from the ragged feet of weary marching men, and of how she sat upon her father's shoulder as the troops went by, and of all her friends and kinsmen who were standing near her, and of the return of a cousin—a boy of sixteen years —starved, ragged, wearing a stove-pipe hat, and without shoes, of how the women wept and of the boy's words of jesting and good-natured greeting, as he came to meet them.

Now, with the full rich accents of this unseen Frenchman, at once so strange and so familiar, all of the ancient life of France—her wars and histories, the great chronicles of her battles, and the brilliant and indestructible fabric of her life and energy through so many hundred years of victory and defeat, triumph and catastrophe—began to pulse with such a living and familiar warmth that it seemed to him as if the whole thing from the beginning had been compacted and resumed into the rich and sanguinary energies of this one Frenchman's voice.

The man's speech, a kind of furious and high-spirited repartee, carried on against all comers with an instant's readiness, an animal vigor, that was almost like a national intoxication, was penetrated constantly by the exclamation "Parbleu!"

And more than anything else, it seemed to the youth, it was the tone and quality of that ancient exclamation, delivered with such a buoyant and animal vitality, that united the Frenchman to the distant past of his nation's history, to millions of buried and forgotten lives, and through him, made that distant past blaze instantly with all the warmth and radiance of life again.

The Frenchman's speech was lewd and ribald with the open and robust vulgarity of healthy country people; his broad jests were published without affectation in a tone loud enough for all the world to hear, and it was evident from the roars of hearty, sensual laughter with which his remarks were received by the soldiers, provincials, and strapping peasant women who were with him, that his audience was not a squeamish one.

The chief target for this robust fellow's humor, to which he loudly returned with unwearied pertinacity, was that unfortunate man, the station master, whose calling, for some reason, is provocative of unlimited mirth in France. Now, at every station, the Frenchman would publish to the world, amid roars of laughter, his narration of the station master's unhappy lot. In particular, he sang snatches of a ribald song entitled "Il est cocu le chef de gare"—which described movingly the trials of a station master's life, the cuckoldries to which the nature of the work exposes him, the conduct of his wife when he is away from home dispatching trains. And the Frenchman would garnish this ditty with certain pointed speculations of his own, directed at the station master of each town, concerning the probable whereabouts, at that moment, of the station master's wife.

Sometimes, the answer to this ribald banter would be curses, oaths and maddened imprecations from the station master; sometimes, the answer would be a good-natured one, as rough and ready in its coarse spontaneity as the Frenchman's own, but whatever the result, the Frenchman was always ready with a reply.

"Are you speaking from your own experience?" one of the station masters yelled ironically. "Is that the way your old woman behaves when you leave home?"

"Parbleu! Oui!" the Frenchman roared back cheerfully. "Why not? The meat is all the sweeter for a little extra seasoning."

This sally was rewarded by a scream of delighted laughter from the peasant women, and the jester, thus encouraged, continued:

"Parbleu! Do you think I'd play the miser with the old girl, when I've had so much myself? But, no, my friend! What the devil! My old girl's no rare canary who'll fade away the first time that you look at her. The devil, no! There's good stuff there, sound and solid as an ox, old boy, and lots more where the last batch came from!"

At this delicate sally there were roars and screams of delighted laughter from the peasant women in the train, and when the commotion had somewhat subsided, one could hear the voice of the station master from the platform, yelling back ironically:

"Good! Since there's enough for every one, I'll come around to get my share!"

"Parbleu! Why not?" the high, sanguinary voice responded instantly. "Turn about's fair play, as the saying goes—I've played the cock to many a station master's hen——"

Roars of laughter.

"And I'd be the last fellow in the world to begrudge him now—" he would conclude triumphantly, and the train would move off to the accompaniment of roars of laughter, ribaldry, and lusty and derisive banter, above which the high, rich, energy of the Frenchman's voice, crying out,—"Parbleu! Oui! Why not?" was always dominant.

He left the train at one of the little stations near Orléans, departing amid a rough but good-natured chorus of jeers, jibes, and derisive yells which followed him as he walked away along the platform, and to all of which he instantly responded with his ribald vitality of coarse humor, that in its lusty ebullience was somehow like the intoxication of a sound, rich wine.

The boy saw him for an instant as he passed by the window of the compartment. He was a strong, stocky figure of a man, wearing leggings, with blue eyes, a brown mustache, and a solid face full of dark, rich color. But even after he had disappeared from sight, the boy could hear him shouting to the other people, the sanguinary vitality of his instant, ribald—"Parbleu! Why not!"—a tone, a voice, a word that had evoked the past of France, in all the living textures of her earth and blood, and that, in future years, would bring this scene to life again—all of the faces, voices, lives of these people—as no other single thing could do.

At one of the little stations near Orléans, a girl opened the door and climbed up into the compartment, which was already crowded. The country people, however, made room for her, crowding a little closer together on the wooden bench, and telling her to wedge herself in, with the rough but good-natured familiarity that characterized their conduct towards one another.

The girl sat down opposite the boy, beside the window, and put the market basket which she was carrying, on her knees. She was cleanly but plainly dressed, a very lovely and seductive girl with a slender figure which seemed, however, already to have attained a languorous and sensual maturity. She was wearing a broad-brimmed hat of blue that shaded her face, from which her eyes looked out with a luminous, troubling, and enigmatic clarity. She said nothing, but sat silently listening to the rude jovialities of the peasant people around her, and to the ribald shouts and yells and roars of laughter that came from the nearby compartment.

All the time, the girl gazed directly at the young man, her lovely face traced faintly with a tender, enigmatic smile. It seemed certain to him that if he spoke to her she would not rebuff him. The sensation of an impossible good fortune, of some vague and unutterable happiness that was impending for him in this strange and unknown town, returned. Desire, slow, sultry, began to beat, throbbing in his pulses and through the conduits of his blood. He felt certain that the girl would not rebuff him if he spoke to her. And yet he did not speak.

And presently the little train came puffing in to Orléans, all of the people got out and streamed away towards the station along the platform. He took the girl's basket and helped her down out of the train, and with the old bewildered indecision in his heart stood there looking after her as she walked away from him with a graceful, slow, and sensual stride in which every movement that she made seemed to imply reluctance to depart, an invitation to follow. And he looked after her numbly, with hot desire pounding slow and thick in pulse and blood. And he told himself, as he had told himself so many times before, that he would certainly find her again, knowing in his heart he never would.

Already the girl had been lost among the crowds of people streaming through the station, engulfed again in the everlasting web and weaving of this great earth, to leave him with a memory of another of those brief and final meetings, so poignant with their wordless ache of loss and of regret, in which, perhaps more than in the grander, longer meetings of our life, man's bitter destiny of days, his fatal brevity, are apparent.

And again the boy found himself walking along the platform towards the station after the departing people, whom he had met so briefly, and now lost forever. Again he had sought the mysterious promises of a new land, new earth, and a shining city. Again he had come to a strange place, not knowing why he had come.

Why here?

XCII

THE Grand Hôtel du Monde et d'Orléans, which was situated opposite the railway station on one of the corners of the station square, was, despite its sounding title, a modest establishment of forty or fifty rooms, constructed in that style at once grandiose and solid which is peculiar to French hotel architecture. When he entered, he found two women seated in the *bureau* carrying on an animated conversation in fluent English, of which the startling substance ran somewhat as follows:

"But yes, madame. I assure you—you need have no—kalms?—kalms?" —the younger and larger of the two women said in a doubtful tone, lifting puzzled eyebrows at her older companion—"*kalms,* Comtesse, je ne comprends pas *kalms.* Qu'est-ce-que ça veut dire?"

"Mais, non, chérie," the other answered patiently. "Pas *kalms—qualms—qualms.*" She pronounced the word slowly and carefully several times, until the other woman succeeded in saying it after her, at which the little woman nodded her meagre little head emphatically with a movement of bird-like satisfaction, and said:

"Oui! Oui! Bon! C'est ça! *Qualms.*"

"Mais ça veut dire?" the other said inquiringly in a puzzled tone.

"Ça veut dire, chérie—you need have no qualms, madame—" the little wren-like woman considered carefully before she spoke—"Vous n'avez pas besoin de perturbation—n'est-ce pas?" she cried, with an eager look of triumph.

"Ah-h!" the other cried, with an air of great enlightenment. "Oui! Je comprends. . . . I assure you, madame, that you need have no qualms about the plumbing arrangements."

"Bon! Bon!" the little woman nodded her head approvingly. *"Plumbing,* chérie. *Plumbing,"* she added gently as an afterthought.

"You will find everyt'ing t'oroughly modairne——"

"Thoroughly—" the other said, slowly and carefully. *"Thoroughly—* you pronounce it this way, my dear—*th—th—"* She leaned forward, inserting her tongue illustratively between her false teeth.

"Thoroughly," the other said, with evident difficulty, and repeated— "thoroughly modairne——"

"Modern, dear! *Modern!"* the little wren-like woman said slowly and carefully again, but then, nodding her head with a movement of swift decision, she went on sharply: "Mais non! Ça va! Ça va bien!" She nodded her head vigorously. "Laissez comme ça! Les Américains aiment mieux comme ça—un peu d'accent, n'est-ce pas?" she said craftily. "Pour les Américains."

"Ah, oui!" the other woman responded at once, nodding seriously. "Vous avez raison. Ce n'est pas bon de parler trop correctement. Un peu d'accent est mieux. Ils aiment ça—les Américains."

They nodded wisely at each other, their faces comically eloquent with that strange union of avarice, hard worldliness, and provincial naïveté which qualifies a Frenchman's picture of the earth. Then, looking up at the young man, who was standing awkwardly before the *bureau,* the younger of the two women said coldly:

"Monsieur?——"

The young woman was perhaps twenty-eight years old, but her cold, dark face, which was lean and sallow and cleft powerfully by a large strong nose, had a maturity of cold mistrustfulness and unyielding avarice which was incalculable. It was as if from birth her spirit had been steeped in the hard and bitter dyes of man's iniquity, as if she had sucked the acid nutriment of mistrust and worldly wisdom out of her mother's breast—as if her hard heart and her cold, dark eyes had never known youth, remembered innocence, or been blinded by romantic fantasies—as if, in short, she had sprung full-armored from her cradle, versed in all grim arts of seeking for one's self, clutching her first sous in a sweating palm, learning to add by numbers before she could prattle a child's prayer.

Seen so, the woman's face had a cold and stern authority of mistrust that was impregnable. The face, indeed, might have been the very image of a hotel-keeper's soul, impeccable in its perfection of bought courtesy, but hard, cold, lifeless, cruel as hell, obdurate as a block of granite, to any warming ray of mercy, pardon, or concession where another's loss and its own gain might be concerned.

And yet, for all its cold and worldly inhumanity, the face was a passionate one as well. Her strong, black brows grew straight and thick in an unbroken line above her eyes, her upper lip was dark with a sparse but unmistakable mustache of a few black hairs, her face, at once cold and hard in its mistrust, and smouldering with a dark and sinister desire, was stamped with that strange fellowship of avarice and passion he had seen in the faces of women such as this all over France.

He had seen these women everywhere—behind the cashier's desk in restaurants, shops, and stores, behind the desks in cafés, theatres, and brothels, or in the bureau of a hotel such as this. Sometimes they were alone, sometimes they were seated together behind one of those enormous tall twin desks, enthroned there like the very magistrates of gain, totting up the interminable figures in their ledgers with the slow care and minute painfulness of greed. They sat there, singly, or two abreast, behind their tall desks near the door, casting their hard eyes in a glance of cold mistrust upon the customers and at each other, conspiring broodingly together as they checked and compared each other's ledgers— seeming to be set there, in fact, not only as a watch upon the cheats and treasons of the world, but as a watch upon their own, as well.

And yet, haired darkly on their upper lips, cold, hard, mistrustful in their grasping avarice as they might be, he had always felt in them the complement of a sinister passion. He felt that when all the day's countings were over, the last entry made in the enormous ledger, the last figure added up, and the last drops of sweat wrung from the leaden visage of the final sous—then, *then,* he felt, they would pull down the shutters, bare their teeth in smiles of savage joy, and go to their appointed meeting with their lover, Jack the Ripper. Upon faces such as these, even during their day-light impassivity of cold mistrust, the ardor of their nocturnal secrecies was almost obscenely articulate; it required little effort of the imagination to see these women quilted in a vile, close darkness, a union of evil chemistries, locked in the grip of a criminal love, with teeth bared in the bite and shine of a profane and lawless ecstasy, and making savage moan.

Such, in fact, was the face of the young woman in the bureau of the hotel, who now looked up at him with the cold inquiry of mistrust, and said:

"Monsieur?——"

"I—I'd like to get a room," he stammered awkwardly, faltering before her hard, impassive stare, and speaking to her in her own language.

"Comment?" she said sharply, a little startled at being addressed so immediately in the language wherein she had just been holding—studious practice. "Vous désirez?——"

"Une chambre," he mumbled—"pas trop chère."

"Ah-h—a room! He says he wants a room, my dear," the little woman now put in, quickly and eagerly. She hopped up briskly and came towards him with an eager gleam in her sharp old eyes, an anticipating hope in her meagre face.

"You are a stranger?" she inquired, peering sharply at him. "An American?"—with a look of eager hope.

"Yes," he said.

"Ah-h!" her breath went in with a little intake of greedy satisfaction. "I thought so! . . . Yvonne! Yvonne!" she cried sharply, turning to the other woman in a state of great excitement. "He's an American— he wants a room—he must have something good—an American," she babbled, "the best you've got——"

"But yes!" cried Yvonne rising. "To be sure. At vunce!" she cried, and struck a bell, calling: "Jean! Jean!"

"But not—not," the youth stuttered, "not the best—it's just for me— I'm all alone," he appealed to the smaller woman—"something not very expensive," he said desperately.

"Ah—hah—hah!" she said, emitting a little chuckling laugh of gloating satisfaction and continuing to peer craftily up at him. "An American! And young, too.—How old are you, my boy?"

"T-t-twenty-four," he stuttered, staring at her helplessly.

"Ah—hah—hah!" Again the little gloating laugh. "I thought so—

and why are you here? . . . What are you doing here in Orléans, eh?" she said imperatively, yet coaxingly. "What brings you here, my boy?"

"Why—why—" he stammered confusedly, and then finding no adequate reason (since there was none) for being there, he blurted out— "I'm—a writer—a—a—journalist," he stammered, feeling this made his lie the less.

"Ah—hah—hah," she chuckled softly again with a kind of abstracted gluttony of satisfaction—"a journalist, eh, my boy?" in her ravenous eagerness she had begun to pat and stroke his arm with a claw-like hand, as a cook might stroke a fat turkey before killing it. "A journalist, eh? . . . Yvonne! Yvonne!" suddenly she turned to the other woman again, speaking rapidly in a burst of high excitement. "The young man is a journalist . . . an American journalist . . . he writes for *The New York Times,* Yvonne . . . the greatest newspaper in America."

"Well, not exactly that," he blundered, red in the face from confusion and embarrassment. "I never said——"

"Ah—hah—hah," the little old woman said again with her little gloating laugh, peering up at him with a crafty gleam in her sharp old eyes, and stroking his arm in her unconscious eagerness. ". . . And you've come to write about us, eh? . . . Joan of Arc, eh?" she said seducingly, with a little crafty laugh of triumph. "—The Cathedral . . . the Maid of Orléans . . . ah, my boy, you have come to the right place. . . . I will show you everything. . . . I will take care of you. . . . You are in good hands now. . . . Ah-h, we love the Americans here. . . . Yvonne! Yvonne!" she cried again, her excitement growing all the time. "He says he is here to write about Orléans for *The New York Times* . . . he will put it all in . . . the Cathedral . . . Joan of Arc . . . the hotel here . . . the greatest paper in America . . . millions of people will come here when they read it——"

"Well, now, I never said—" he began again.

"Ah—hah—hah," again she was peering up at him craftily, with old eyes of eager greed, chortling her little laugh of gloating triumph, as she stroked his arm. "Twenty-four, eh? . . . And where are you from, my boy? . . . Where is your home?"

"Why—New York, I suppose," he said hesitantly.

"Yes, yes, I know," she said impatiently—"but before that? Where were you born? . . . What State are you from?"

He stared at her for a moment with bewildered face.

"Why, I don't think you'd know where it is," he said at length. "I'm from Catawba."

"Catawba—yes!" the old woman pressed on eagerly. "And what part of Catawba? What town?"

"Why"—he stared at her, gape-jawed with amazement—"a place called Altamont."

"Altamont!" she crowed jubilantly. "Altamont—yes! Altamont—of course!"

"You *know* it?" he said incredulously. "You've *heard* of it?"

"*Heard* of it! Why, my boy, I've been there seven times!" She chuckled with triumph, then went on with a wild and incoherent eagerness. "Little Mother, they call me . . . I am known everywhere. . . . Letters . . . cablegrams . . . the Governor of Arkansas . . ." she babbled. "I gave up everything . . . spent my fortune. . . . Ah, my boy, I love the Americans. . . . They call me Little Mother. . . . Altamont! . . . A beautiful town! . . . Do you know Doctor Bradford and his family? . . . And how is Harold? . . . What's Alice doing now—has she married . . . a lovely girl. . . . And how is George Watson? . . . What's he doing, eh? . . . Is he still secretary of the Chamber of Commerce? . . . And Mrs. Morgan Hamilton. . . . And Charles McKee— ah, how I should like to see all my dear old friends in Altamont again."

"You—you know them—all those people?" he gasped, hearing as in a dream the great cathedral bells throng out upon the air of night.

"*Know* them! . . . I know every one in the town. . . . I always stay with Doctor Bradford and his family. . . . Ah, what lovely people, my boy. . . . How good they have been to me. . . . I love Americans! . . . Little Mother, they call me," she went on in a strange, tranced tone, her eyes burning feverishly as she spoke—" 'As the brave little woman who is known to thousands of Our Boys as the Little Mother of the Stars and Stripes stood before the great audience that packed the City Auditorium last night as it has never been packed before in its whole history, it is safe to say there was not a dry eye in the great'—Yvonne!" She broke sharply away from her mysterious recitation, and again addressed herself excitedly to the hotel woman—"I know his town . . . I know his family . . . I know his father and his mother . . . I have stayed at their house! . . . They are all dear friends of mine! . . . Quick! Tell Madame Vatel that an American friend of mine is here. . . . Tell her it is going to be a great thing for her . . . for Orléans . . . for all of us. . . . Tell her he is going to write about the hotel in *The New York*

Times . . . you will give him a good room . . . a good price, eh?" she
said cunningly. "He will bring hundreds of people here to the hotel——"

"But yes, Countess," said Yvonne. "Perfectly."

"The best! The best!" the old woman cried. "He comes from one
of the most prominent families in America—ah—hah—hah! You will
see!" She chuckled with mysterious cunning. "I shall make you all rich
and famous before I'm through . . . I know all the rich Americans.
. . . Hah—hah. . . . They will all come here now when he has written
about us. . . . *The New York Times,* Yvonne," she whispered gloatingly, "the paper all the rich Americans read. . . . Tell Madame Vatel
what has happened. . . . Ah, a great thing, Yvonne. . . . a great thing
for us all—see!" she whispered mysteriously, pointing towards the
bewildered youth—"the head, Yvonne! The head! You can tell by the
head, Yvonne," she whispered. "*What* a clever head, Yvonne. . . .
The New York Times, eh? . . ." she chuckled craftily, "that all the
clever writers write for! . . . Tell Vatel!" she whispered gloatingly,
rubbing her little claw-like hands together. "Tell Madame. . . . Tell
every one. . . . He must have the best," she muttered with conspiratorial secrecy. "The best."

"But yes, Countess," Yvonne said smoothly. "Monsieur shall have
nothing but the best. Number Seven, I think," she said reflectively.
"Oui! Number Seven!" She nodded her head decisively with satisfaction. "I am sure Monsieur will like the room. . . . Jean! Jean!" She
clapped her hands sharply to the attentive porter, who now sprang forward nimbly. "Apportez les baggages de Monsieur au Numéro Sept."

"But—but—the price?" the youth said awkwardly.

"The price," said Yvonne, "to Monsieur is—twelve francs. To others
—that is deeferent, eh?" she said with a significant smile and an expressive shrug. "But since Monsieur is a friend of the Countess, the price
will be twelve francs."

"Cheap! Cheap!" the Countess muttered. "And now, my boy," she
said coaxingly, taking him by the arm, "you must take your meals
here, too. . . . The cuisine! . . . Ah-h! Merveilleuse!" she whispered,
making a small rhapsodic gesture with one hand. "You will eat here,
too, my boy—eh?"

He nodded dumbly, and the old woman turned immediately to
Yvonne with a look of cunning triumph, saying: "Did you hear,
Yvonne? . . . Do you see? . . . He will take his meals here, too. . . . Tell
Vatel . . . Tell Madame . . . I know all the rich Americans. . . . They will

all come now, Yvonne," she whispered. "You will see. . . . And now, my boy," she said with an air of decision, turning to him again, "have you had dinner yet? . . . No? . . . Good!" she said with satisfaction. "I shall eat with you," she took him by the arm possessively. "We shall eat together here in the hotel. . . . I shall have Pierre set a table for us . . . we shall always eat together there—just you and I. . . . Ah, you have come to the right place . . . I shall look after you and watch you like your own mother, my boy. . . . There are so many bad places here in Orléans . . . so many low resorts. I shall tell you where they are so that you can keep out of them . . . it is so easy for a young man to go astray. . . . So many young Americans who come over here get into trouble, meet with bad companions, because they have no one to guide them. . . . But have no fear, my boy . . . I will watch over you while you are here like your own mother. . . . They call me Little Mother."

He cast a distressed and perplexed glance towards Yvonne, and that capable person came instantly and suavely to his rescue.

"Perhaps, Countess," she said smoothly, "Monsieur would like to see his room and brosh up a beet after ze fatigue of his journey—eh?"

He looked at her gratefully, and the Countess, nodding her head vigorously, said instantly:

"Oui! Oui! C'est ça! . . . By all means, my boy, go up to your room and wash up a bit. . . . Ah, a lovely room! He will like it, eh, Yvonne? . . . New furnishings, hot and cold water, beautiful plumbing."

"I can assure Monsieur," said Yvonne dutifully, "that he need have no—kalms——"

"Qualms, Yvonne, qualms," the Countess corrected her gently—"a lovely room, my boy! And when you have finished come on down and we will dine together. . . . You will find me here. I will wait for you. And while you eat," she said enticingly, "I shall let you read my clippings—ah-h, I have a great book full of them. . . . You shall read it all, everything—what it says about their Little Mother," she said tenderly. "And I shall keep you company. I shall talk to you and tell you what to do in Orléans. . . . No, no, I shall eat nothing," she said hastily, as if to allay some economic apprehension on his part. "It will cost you nothing. . . . A little of your coffee, perhaps. . . . Perhaps a glass of wine—no more. Ah, my dear," the old woman went on sadly, "the food here is so lovely, and I cannot eat it . . . I can eat nothing——"

"Nothing?" he said, staring at her.

"Rien, rien, rien," she cried, waving her hand sidewise.

"The Countess is on—what you say—a diet?" said Yvonne sympathetically. "Eet ees the doctor's orders—she cannot eat."

"Rien du tout," the Countess said again. "Nothing but horse's blood,
my dear," the Countess said in a sad voice. "That's all I live on now."

"*Horse's* blood!" he stared at her unbelievingly.

"Oui!" she nodded. "Sang de cheval! You see, my dear," she went
on in an explanatory tone, "I have anæmia—and by the doctor's orders
I take horse's blood. . . . But the food here is so lovely. Lovely. I shall
wait for you, my boy, and watch you eat."

"Jean!" cried Yvonne sharply, giving the youth his freedom by one
brisk act. "Les baggages de Monsieur. Numéro Sept."

She handed the key to the porter.

"Oui, monsieur," the porter said cheerfully, picking up the youth's
valise. "Par ici, s'il vous plaît."

They went back and got into the little ascenseur, just big enough for
two. It mounted slowly, creakingly, with slatting rope. They got off
at the first flight: he followed the porter down a thickly-carpeted hall
and then, while the man switched on lights, turned down the coverlet
of the bed, and pulled the heavy curtains together in order to assure that
atmosphere of stale nocturnal confinement without which sleep in
France seems impossible, he examined the room.

The place easily lived up to all the rapturous prophesies which the
Countess had made of it. It was astonishingly luxurious—with that almost indecent luxury that is characteristic of a French hotel room, and
that is disquietingly similar to the luxury of a brothel. The bed was a
lavish, canopied affair with crimson hangings; the floor was covered with
a thick crimson carpet, completely noiseless to the tread; there was a
sensually fat sofa and several fat chairs covered with fat, red plush and
painted with gilt, a great gilt-rimmed mirror above the mantel, a wash-
bowl of deep and heavy porcelain with glittering nickel fixtures, a lavish
bidet the inevitable provision of a French woman's needs, and curtains
of a fat, silk, quilted material whose sensual folds were now closely
drawn together, completing the effect of bordello secrecy and luxury
previously described.

And this oriental luxury was being provided to him for seventy
cents a day on the recommendation of a mad old woman who drank
horse's blood and whom he had never seen until a half hour ago. As
he stood there bewildered by this new, strange turn of chance and

destiny, he felt the stillness of the old town around him, and heard again the vast, sweet thronging of the cathedral bells through the dark and silent air, and felt again, as he had felt so many times, the strange and bitter miracle of life. And there was something in his heart he could not utter.

When he went downstairs again, he found the old woman waiting for him, with an eager and cunning gleam at once comical and pathetic in her sharp old eyes, and a great book of newspaper clippings in her arms.

With an air of complete possession, she took him by the arm, and thus linked, they entered the hotel restaurant together. As they went in, it was at once evident that the fame of the young journalist had preceded him. There was a great scraping of chairs around the family table and Madame Vatel, her husband, their comely married daughter, and the daughter's little girl, rose from the family soup in unison, and received him with a chorus of smiles, bows, and enchanted murmurs of greeting that alarmed him by their profuse respectfulness, and that became almost fawningly obsequious as the Countess began to publish the merits of his power and influence in a torrential French of which he could only capture occasional glittering fragments, the chief of which was the proud name of *The New York Times*—"le grand journal Américain."

Then, having muttered out a few desperate words of thanks for the overwhelming and unexpected warmth of their reception, he and the Countess were escorted by a bowing waiter to the table which had been prepared for them at the other end of the restaurant, near the street entrance. The food—a savory and wholesome country soup, broiled fish, succulent thick slices of roast beef, tender, red, and juicy as none he had ever tasted before, a crisp and tender salad of endive, and camembert and coffee—was as delicious as the Countess had predicted; the wine—a Beaujolais, of which the old woman drank half a glass—both cheap and good; the service of the old waiter suave, benevolent, and almost unctuously attentive; and his own mixed feelings of alarm, astonishment, embarrassment at the position in which he had been placed, resentment at the imposture into which the old woman had compelled him, and wild, helpless, mounting, and astounded laughter—were explosive, indescribable.

He would look up uneasily from the delicious food to see the Vatel family, heads together around their table in a congress of whispering secrecy, and with the imprint of conspiratorial greed and cunning on their faces. Then they would catch his eye, nudge one another, and bow and smile at him with fawning graciousness, and he would return to his food savagely, not knowing whether to curse or howl with laughter.

During the whole course of the meal, the Countess sat opposite him, watching like a hawk every move he made, her old eyes gleaming cunningly, and a strange, fixed smile, which he had come to recognize as being at once crafty and naïve, shrewd with guile and yet pathetically inquiring, hovering faintly upon her sharp and meagre face.

All the time while he was eating, the old woman kept up her strange, fragmentary monologue—a semi-coherent discourse which mirrored forth the very image of her soul and seemed to be addressed to herself as much as to any listener. With a ravenous attentiveness she watched him devour his food, exhorted him to waste none of it, and to sop up the sauce as well, demanded of the old waiter second helpings of the delicious roast beef, accompanying her command with a glittering account of the prosperity that would accrue to him and the hotel as a result of this solicitude; plied the boy with questions concerning his friends, his work, his future prospects, and his travels—in short, pried, probed, wormed and insinuated her way into every corner of his history, and appointed herself guide and censor of his life and conduct from this moment on.

"How long have you been over here, my boy?"—she said in her low but vibrant monotone, which had that curious, dead resonance, an almost bodiless energy that seems to come from indestructible vitality of mind or spirit when the vitality of flesh has been exhausted. It was an energy at once as bitterly tenacious as man's clutch on life, yet marked all the time by the brooding fatality of people who have lived too long and seen all things go—"How long have you been in Europe? . . . And where were you first? . . . England, yes. . . . And after England. . . . Paris? Where did you stay there? . . . How much did they charge you for your room? . . . Twelve francs. . . . Yes, but you could do better, my boy. . . . You could do much better. . . . You should find a place for eight francs a day. . . . All the Americans spend too much money," she said sadly. "They come over here and waste their money. . . . I have seen so many Americans get stranded here. . . . During the war I had to help so many out. . . . Tell me, my boy," she leaned over and clutched his arm with her claw-like hand, "you are not going to get stranded here like other Americans, are you?" her voice had a low, hoarse, and fatal note in it. "Promise me you won't get stranded here."

He promised her.

"How much money have you got, my boy—eh?" she said, her old eyes lighted with an avaricious gleam. A sudden apprehension shocked her; she started forward, saying quickly—"You've got enough to pay your bill? You've got enough to get you out of Orléans? . . . You won't get stranded here at the hotel?"

He reassured her, and with a look of relief she continued:

"You must tell me every day how much you spend. . . . You must let me watch your money for you. . . . So few young men in America understand the value of money. . . . They throw it away as if it were dirt. . . . There are so many ways to waste your money here in France. . . . We have so many things to spend money on—it's gone before you know it—restaurants, hotels, liquor, wine, cafés—Ah, cafés, cafés!" she sighed with dead fatality. "Cafés everywhere you go," she said. "They are the curse of France. Cafés and women. . . . Have you met the women yet?" she demanded sharply. He told her that he had.

"Yes, I know," she said, her voice sad with its note of resigned fatality. "You meet them in cafés—bad women, waiting there to prey upon the young Americans. . . . Tell me—" the eager gleam awakened in her eyes again—"have you given them much of your money?"

He told her that he had.

"Ah, I know," she answered sadly. "All the young Americans waste their money in that way. . . . Don't do it, my boy," her claw-like hand went out and grasped his arm. "Promise me you will not give any more money away to those women. . . . They are *bad,* bad . . . the shame of France. . . . Get yourself a nice girl, my boy. . . . I know some nice girls here in Orléans. . . . I will introduce you—But don't go to the cafés, my boy—Or, if you go, don't talk to any of the women there. . . . No nice woman here in Orléans goes to the café . . . all the women that you meet there are bad, bad. . . . The best café," she concluded irrelevantly, "is on the Place Martroi. You will find the women there. . . . If you go, tell me tomorrow about the music. . . . They have good music there. . . . I love good music. . . . One hears so little music here in Orléans. . . . There are so few amusements for a decent woman here. . . . Sometimes I want to go to the café to hear the music, but if I did I would no longer be a decent woman. . . . I suppose you'll go to

the café tonight?" she said sadly, fatally, but with an eager glint of inquiry in her old eyes. "All the Americans go to the cafés. It's the only
place there is to go to here."

Towards ten o'clock, which was her hour of retiring, he escaped from
her, and went to the café of which she had spoken. There was an
orchestra of three pieces playing the kind of music that is played in
French cafés; and many mirrors, and long seats of old worn leather
around the walls; and several young whores sitting singly at tables, patiently ogling the sporting males of Orléans, who stroked their mustaches
and ogled back, but spent no money on them. And there was one
extremely lovely, blonde, seductive and experienced-looking whore from
Paris, who ogled no one, but sat by herself at a table, frowning reflectively
with half-closed eyes and with a cigarette in her mouth, studiously involved in solitaire, and completely indifferent to the gallantries of the
ogling males of Orléans, although many a languishing look was cast in
her direction. The men played cards or dominoes together, held their
secret, sly, and whispered conversations, and then roared with laughter;
the café orchestra played the music that a French café orchestra always
plays; the waiters went back and forth with trays and glasses; the proprietor went from table to table talking to his regular patrons; the
whores sat patiently at tables, and smiled and ogled when they caught
somebody's eye; and somehow the whole scene was instantly, poignantly
familiar, like something he had known all his life.

And he did not know why this was true. But something essential in
the substance and the structure of the scene—the beautiful and sophisticated prostitute from Paris, the seducers and gallants of the town of
Orléans, the feeling of silence, secrecy, and darkness all around him in
the old sleeping town—in which this place was now the only spot of
warmth and gaiety and lightness—even the occasional shrill fife and
piping whistle at the railway station not far away—all these things and
people had their counterpart, somehow, in the life of small towns
everywhere and in the life he had known in a small town as a child,
when he had lain in his bed in darkness and had heard the distant wail
and thunder of a departing train, and had seen then in the central core
and vision of his heart's desire, his image of the distant, the shining, the
fabulous, thousand-spired, magic city, and had thought then of a lovely
and seductive red-haired woman named Norah Ryan, who had that
year come from the great city to live there in his mother's house, and

whose coming and whose going would always be a thing of mystery and wonder to them all; and felt, then, as now, all around him the numb nocturnal stillness of the town, the impending prescience of wild joy, the heartbeats of ten thousand sleeping men.

And this feeling of unutterable loss and familiarity, of strangeness and reality, remained with him later when he left the closing café and walked home towards his hotel through a silent, cobbled street, between rows of old, still houses, the shuttered secrecy of the shops.

And later, the feeling was more strong and strange than ever, as he lay in his sumptuous bed in the hotel, reading the clippings in the Countess' books—those incredible explosions of Yankee journalese that this old woman had inspired in a thousand little towns across America—brought back here, read here now, in the midnight stillness of this ancient town as the great cathedral bells thronged through the air—the miraculous weavings of dark chance and destiny, all near as his heart and farther off than heaven, familiar as his life, and stranger than a dream.

XCIII

In the weeks that followed, the boy discovered in the totally absurd, yet curiously persuasive illogic of the woman's mind a revealing illustration of the psychology of fraud, the self-hypnosis of the impostor. When he would protest to her at the effrontery of her representations, the staggering fiction she had now woven about him, his family, his wealth, his power, his influence, and his profession, which made an open, bare-faced use of great names and institutions of which he had no knowledge, and to which he could make no claim, the old woman would answer him at once with a series of arguments so ingeniously persuasive that for a moment he would find himself almost conquered by their hypnotic power, absurdly false though he knew them to be.

"Look here," he would say resentfully. "What do you mean by telling all these people that I represent *The New York Times?* What if *The New York Times* should hear about it and have me thrown in jail for fraud—for using their name when I had no right to do it?—You'd be safe—you would," he said bitterly. "I'd be the one to suffer—*you* could always get out of it by saying that you acted in good faith, that you really thought I *did* work for *The Times.*"

"But you *do,* don't you?" She looked at him with a surprised and puzzled face.

"No!" he shouted. "Of course I don't! And I never told you so, either! It's something you made up out of your own head five minutes after I met you, and nothing I could say would stop you.—Now you've told people all over town that I'm writing stories about Orléans for *The New York Times,* and am going to put *them* in the stories. We've accepted favors, got things at reduced prices and been entertained by these people all because you told them I am working for *The Times* and that they are going to get some free publicity out of it. Don't you realize what that is?" he said angrily, glaring at her. "That's fraud. That's getting something by false pretense. You can be put in jail for that! . . . Why the next thing I know you'll be getting money from them—collecting a commission from them for getting me to write them up. Perhaps you have already, for all I know," he concluded bitterly.

"But you did tell me that you were a journalist, my boy," the old woman said gently. "You told me that, you know."

"Well—yes," he sullenly admitted. "I did tell you that. I said that, because I want to be a writer, and I've done nothing yet—and somehow it didn't seem so big to say I was a journalist. . . . Besides," he blundered on uncertainly, "I thought the word had a kind of different meaning here from what it has at home——"

She nodded her head briskly with a satisfied air:

"Exactly. . . . A journalist is one who contributes articles and sketches on timely subjects to current publications. . . . And you've done that, haven't you?"

"Well," he conceded, "I wrote some pieces for the university magazine when I was at college——"

"Ah-h! Exactly!"—this with an air of triumph.

"And I was editor of the college newspaper."

"But of course! Just as I say!"

"And I suppose I did write news stories about the university once in a while and send them to the paper back home."

"Of course you did, my boy! Of course!"

"And I did write what they call a feature article one time and sold it to a paper. . . . And I wrote a one-act play and it was published in a book and I've had so far eight dollars royalty on it," he concluded his recital with a meagre glow of hope, a lame belief that his journalistic pretensions were not wholly fraudulent.

"But—" the Countess lifted astounded eyebrows, and looked about her with a fine gesture of the hands expressive of bewilderment—"just as I *say,* my boy! Just as I *say.* From what you tell me there's no doubt of it! You are a journalist."

"Well," he conceded gloomily, "I guess if you can establish my reputation from that, I could swear to what I've told you. . . . Oh, yes," he added ironically, "and I forgot to tell you that I got up early in the morning and carried papers, when I was a kid."

"Exactly! Exactly!" she nodded seriously—"you showed a talent for your present work right from the start. You have been trained in your profession since childhood."

"Oh, my God!" he groaned. "What's the use? Have it your own way, then. I can't argue with you. . . . Only, for God's sake, Countess, stop telling people around here that I am working for *The New York Times.*"

"Now, my boy, see here; you mustn't be so modest about things. If you don't learn to blow your own horn a little no one else will do it for you. As clever and brilliant as you are, you mustn't be so self-effacing. What if you are not yet editor of *The New York Times*——?"

"Editor! Editor, hell! I'm not even office boy!"

"But, of *course,* my dear!" she said patiently. "You will be some day. But at the present time you are a rising young journalist of great gifts, for whom all of your confrères on *The Times* are expecting a brilliant career——"

"Now, Countess, you look here——"

She waved her hand tolerantly with a dismissing gesture, and went on:

"All that will come," she said. "You are still young—no one expects you to be editor yet."

"You'll have me editor if you talk much longer," he said sarcastically. "I wouldn't put it past you. But if you're determined to tell people I'm a journalist, why drag in *The New York Times?* After all, I could pretend to be a journalist without feeling an utter fraud. So why drag in *The Times?*"

"Ah," she said. *"The Times* is a great newspaper. People have heard of *The Times.* To say you are connected with *The Times* means something, carries prestige."

"Well, if it's prestige you want, why don't you tell them I'm a college professor? You know, I did work as an instructor for a year in New York. If you told them I'm a professor I could at least feel a little less guilty."

"Oh," she said seriously, "but no one here would believe such a story as that. You are too young to be a professor. Besides," she added practically, "it is much better anyway to tell them you are working for *The Times*."

"Why?"

"Because," she patiently explained, "they can see some value in that. The power of the press is great. A professor could do nothing for them. A clever young man writing articles for *The Times* might do much."

"But, damn it," he cried, in an exasperated tone, "I've never written articles for *The Times*. Can't you understand that?"

"Now, see here, my boy," she said quietly. "Try to be reasonable about this thing. What's the use of confusing these people here with needless explanations? What does it matter if you haven't written articles for *The Times*? You *are* writing them now——"

"Oh, hell, Countess!"

"You are going to write these very brilliant and interesting articles about Orléans," she went on calmly, "and they will be published in *The New York Times,* because they will be so very clever that *The New York Times* will want to publish them. So why tell these simple people here anything more than that? It would only confuse them. I have told them nothing but the truth," she said virtuously, "I have told them you are writing a series of articles about Orléans for the great newspaper, *The New York Times,* and that, my boy, is all they need to know." She smiled tranquilly at him. He gave up.

"All right," he said. "You win. Have it your own way. I'm anything you like—the white-haired boy, the prize performer, the crown jewel of *The New York Times*."

She nodded with approval.

The farce grew more extravagant day by day. And because this fantastic chance had somewhat dulled the smothering ache that had been almost constant since his parting with Ann, Elinor, and Starwick, he stayed on from day to day, not knowing why he stayed or why he should depart, but held with a kind of hypnotic interest by this web of absurd circumstance in which he had so swiftly been involved.

In the morning, when he came downstairs, the old woman would be waiting for him and would sharply and eagerly catechize him about his conduct the night before.

"Did you go to the café last night, my dear? . . . How much did

you have to drink? Eh? . . . A Pernod, four cognacs, coffee, a package
of cigarettes. . . . What did that come to, eh? . . . How much did you
spend? . . . Twenty-one francs! . . . Ah, my dear, too much, too
much!" she clucked sadly and regretfully. "You will spend all your
money in cafés and have nothing to go on with! . . . Tell me, now, my
dear," her old eyes had an eager glint of curiosity, "were there many
people there? . . . Was the place crowded? . . . Were there many
women? . . . You didn't talk to any of the girls, did you?" she said
sharply.

He said that he had.

"You should not have done that!" she said reproachfully. "And
what did she want? She wanted you to come with her, eh?"

"No; we didn't get that far. She asked me for a cigarette."

"And did you give it to her?"

"Yes, of course."

"But no money! You didn't give her any money?" she said feverishly.

"No."

"Did you buy her a drink? . . . Was that what all the cognac was
for?"

"No. It was for me."

"How much money have you left, my boy? . . . Are you keeping
track of your expenses? . . . Did you get another of those express
checks cashed yesterday?"

"Yes, I did."

"What kind? A ten-dollar one?"

"Yes."

"Ah, you shouldn't have done that," she said regretfully. "Once you
cash it, it goes quickly." She snapped her fingers, "like that! Ça file!
Ça file!—You do not watch your money as you should. You do not
keep track of what you spend. . . . My boy, promise me something,
will you?" she went on in a low, earnest tone. "Promise me you won't
spend all your money and get stranded here. . . . You won't do that,
will you? . . . How much money have you left? . . . Tell me," she
said eagerly. "How many of those express checks have you left . . .
Count it, count it," she demanded greedily. "Take the book out and
let me see what you have left."

He took out the little leather folder of express checks and opened it.
It was getting very thin. Then he thumbed rapidly through the little

sheaf of checks, trying to get it over as quickly as he could because of
its distasteful reminder of a harsh reality he wanted to forget. He not
only lacked by nature the sense of money, he was also at the blissful
period in a young man's life when one hundred dollars is as good as a
million. In fact, with twenty dollars in bright, flimsy fifty-franc notes in
his pocket, the pleasant terrace of a good café, a drink, the knowledge of
delicious food and wine within, and the slow, sensual meditations of
desire, he felt as rich as any millionaire on earth. At such a time, the
whole earth lay before him in winding vistas of pleasure, joy, and mystery: in the huge unreason of this enchantment he was sure that there
was nothing ahead of him but a beautiful and fortunate life, filled with
success and happiness, and if by any chance he thought of money, it
was only to dismiss the thought impatiently with the irrational conviction that it would always be ready when he needed it, that it would
come to him miraculously and wonderfully like manna out of heaven,
that he could get great sums of money in many strange, delightful ways,
at any time he wanted it.

Now the Countess, by the harsh worldliness of her insistence, had
jarred him back to a disquieting reality for which he had no relish.
While the old woman followed every movement with greedy, avaricious
eyes glued on the checks, he thumbed them over quickly and sullenly,
told her curtly their amount, and thrust the book brusquely back into
his pocket.

When he had finished, she shook her head at him with sad reproach:

"Ah!" she said, "what extravagance! A French family could have
lived comfortably for a month on what you have spent here in the last
week."

He winced, and stirred restlessly, pierced suddenly with a nameless
sense of guilt and shame, and personal unworthiness, a sudden evocation
of the infinite toil and minute saving of his mother's life. And he felt
this despite the fact that his mother had now acquired a considerable
estate, a large sum of money, and, in spite of her parsimonious economies in innumerable small ways, displayed in her real estate investments a riotous extravagance that far surpassed any of his own on the
sensual pleasures of food and drink and books, on voyages and women.
And this curious and irrational sense of guilt and shame was, he knew,
not peculiar to himself, but rooted somehow in the structure of the lives
of most of the Americans ne had known. It was something that went
back almost past time and memory, that they had always had, that was

distilled out of their blood, and drawn from the very air they breathed:— a feeling that any life not based on gainful labor, any life devoted openly and nakedly to pleasure, idleness and leisure, and the gratification of one's own desires, was, somehow, an ignoble and shameful life.

Now, suddenly torn with this old and irremediable sense of guilt, he scowled suddenly, fidgeted restlessly in his chair, and then spoke sharply and angrily to the old woman, who sat with her sad, reproachful gaze upon him:

"Well, it's spent now, it's gone, it can't be helped. What do you expect people to do with money, anyway?" he said irritably. "Count it and kiss it and say good-night to it every time they go to sleep—and kiss it and count it over again every time they wake up, to see none of it has got away from them in the night? What's it for anyway if it's not to spend? What are you living for?" he said bitterly. "What are you waiting for? Are you saving your money so you can have a nice coffin when they bury you?"

"Yes, my boy, but you spend so much on food and drink and on the girls," the old woman said in a sad tone. "So much of it goes on things like that."

"And why not?" he said resentfully. "Will you please tell me what else I should spend it on? Is there anything better than that to spend it on?"

"Don't spend it on those girls in the café," she said. "They are bad—bad—they will bring you nothing but misfortune and trouble. Come," she said, getting up briskly. "I shall take you with me this morning and introduce you to two nice girls. You will be better off with them than with those women in the café."

They went out, and walked along the streets of the old town, brisk with morning life, cheerful with the thin, musty yellow of a wintry sun. As they walked along those streets of morning, many people recognized the old woman and spoke respectfully to her. Sometimes shopkeepers spoke to her from doorways, smiling good-naturedly at the sight of the little old woman trotting briskly along beside the towering height of the young man. Sometimes she would hear their laughter and bantering comment among themselves about the ludicrous disproportion of the pair, and then, turning to the young man, she would laugh in an abstracted and yet pleased way, saying:

"Ah—hah—hah! They are laughing at you and me, my boy. They think it is very funny, the way we look together. . . . Un grand garçon, eh?" she called out to a man standing in the doorway of a shop, who was measuring the boy up and down with a look of good-natured astonishment.

"Mon Dieu!" the man cried. "Qu'il est grand! Il mange beaucoup de soupe!"

At length, they stopped before a small millinery shop, where the old woman was having a hat made, and went in. A small bell tinkled thinly as they entered, and the milliner and her assistant came out from behind some curtains to greet them. The milliner was a competent-looking woman of thirty years, dark, with a wide face, and a strong, compact, and yet seductive figure. The assistant was younger, taller, and fair in coloring. Both were attractive girls, and both greeted him with smiles and the exclamation of good-natured astonishment that he had heard upon the street. Then, for several minutes, the little shop was gay with the light, rapid French of the three women. All seemed to be talking and laughing at the same time, in excited tones; he saw that the Countess was eagerly publishing his merits to the two girls, he caught the magic phrase *The New York Times* now and then, the two girls kept glancing at him with smiling faces, and presently the older one, who was the proprietor, walked towards him, measured her height against his shoulder, and then with a little laugh of astonishment, said:

"Mon Dieu! Qu'il est grand!"

The younger of the two girls, laughing, made a reply in rapid French which he could not follow, and the Countess, with a little chuckle of satisfaction, turned towards him, saying in an explanatory manner:

"They say they need you here, my dear, to get boxes down from the top shelf. It's too tall for them."

"Mon Dieu, oui!" the younger, taller girl, who had picked up the hat she had been making for the old woman and was shaping it in her hands, now answered instantly. "He can help Hélène now with the box while you try this on. Hélène," she called to the other girl, "show Monsieur where the boxes are and have him get one down for you."

He followed Hélène back through the curtains to the rear of the shop, pursued by the laughter and chattering comment of the other two women. Upon a shelf in the rear a number of hat-boxes were stacked up, but when he looked inquiringly at Hélène, she smiled good-naturedly, and kindly said:

"Mais non, monsieur. Nous ne sommes pas sérieuses. Attendez," and got up briskly on a chair, reaching for a box herself. It was, in fact, almost out of reach; she touched it with her outstretched finger-tips, dislodged it, it came tumbling down, and he caught it as it fell. And Hélène herself came close to falling. She teetered uncertainly on her unsteady balance, swayed towards him, and he lifted her down. For a moment, her weight was strong and palpable in his arms. He put her down reluctantly, and for a moment she stood flat against him, her hands gently resting on his arms. Then, with a pleasant litttle laugh, she said:

"Oh, la, la! Qu'il est fort!"

They went out front again, the Countess finished trying on the hat, and presently, after another burst of gay and rapid talk, he and the old woman departed. As he went out, the little bell tinkled thinly and pleasantly again; he had to stoop to go through the door. He turned to say good-bye again, the two girls were looking towards him with gay and friendly smiles; he was sorry to go, and wanted some excuse for staying. Hélène looked strong and competent and desirable, she smiled at him a friendly farewell: he thought if he came back again she would be glad to see him, but he never saw her after that.

Later, the two girls stayed in his memory with a vivid, pleasant warmth: he thought of Hélène many times, her strong seductive figure, and her wide, dark face, and he wondered what her life had been, if she had married, and what time had brought to her.

XCIV

THE crowning extravagance of the Countess' misrepresentation was revealed one morning when he found a letter addressed to him in a firm, feminine, and completely unfamiliar handwriting. The Countess had spoken to him several times of a great noblewoman in the neighborhood, who lived in a magnificent château, and with whom, it was obvious, the Countess wished to improve her slight acquaintance. Now, upon opening the letter, the following message greeted his astounded eye:

Le Château de Mornaye
February 23, 1925

My dear Mr. Gant:

My old friend, La Comtesse de Caux, informs me that you are spending some time in Orléans, preparing a series of articles for the great journal you represent, *The New York Times.*

It will be a great pleasure to me if you, together with La Comtesse, will give me the honor of your presence at Mornaye for luncheon on Thursday, the twenty-sixth. La Comtesse de Caux informs me that you became acquainted with my son Paul when he visited America with Le Maréchal Foch in 1922, and that a warm friendship grew up between you at that time. I have often heard my son speak of his American tour, and of the dear friendships he made there, and I know how keen will be his regret when he hears that you were here and that he missed you. He is at present, I regret to say, at Paris, but I have written informing him of your presence here.

At any rate, it will give me great pleasure to welcome one of my son's American friends to Mornaye, and I am looking forward to your visit with the most eager anticipation. La Comtesse de Caux has already informed me of your acceptance, and my motor will be waiting for you at the village station Thursday the twenty-sixth at noon.

Until then, ever sincerely yours,
MATHILDE, MARQUISE DE MORNAYE.

He read the letter a second time, anger swelling in a hot flood as its full significance was revealed to him. When he at length found the Countess, he was so choked with exasperation that for a moment he could not speak but stood glaring at her with infuriated eyes, holding the crumpled letter in one clenched fist.

"Now, you look here," he said at length in a smothered tone, "you look here—" he held the letter out and shook it furiously under her nose. "What do you mean by a thing like this?"

She returned his furious gaze with a glance of bright inquiry, took the letter from his hand, and immediately, after looking at it, said cheerfully:

"Oh, yes! La Marquise has written you, as she said she would. Did I not tell you I had great things in store for you?" she said triumphantly. "Ah, my boy, how fortunate you were in finding me the way you did! Do you realize how few Americans ever have the opportunity you are getting? Here you are, a boy of twenty-four, being received with open arms into one of the greatest families in France. Why, there are American millionaires who would pay a fortune for the privilege!"

"Now, you see here," he said again in a choking tone. "What do you mean by doing a thing like this behind my back?"

She raised puzzled eyebrows inquiringly:

"Behind your back? What do you mean, my boy?"

"What right have you got to tell this woman I had accepted her invitation, when you never spoke to me about it?"·

"But!" she said, with a small protesting gasp—"I was sure you would be delighted! It never occurred to me that you wouldn't be! I felt sure you'd jump at the opportunity!"

"Opportunity!" he jeered. "Opportunity for what? Opportunity to let you tell this woman a pack of lies about me, and try to work her with some trick or dodge that you've got up your sleeve!"

"I have no idea what you're talking about," she said, with quiet dignity.

"Oh, yes you have!" he snarled. "You know very well what I'm talking about. You've told these lying stories and misrepresented things to people ever since I met you, but you've gone too far this time. What the hell do you mean by telling this woman that I am a good friend of her son's and met him in America?" He picked up the letter and shook it in her face again. "What do you mean by telling her such a lie as that?"

"Lie!" Her brows were lifted with an air of pained surprise. "Why, my boy, you told me that you did know her son."

"*I* told you!" he fairly screamed. "I told you nothing! I never knew the woman had a son until I got this letter."

"Listen, my friend," the Countess spoke gently and patiently as she would speak to a child. "Think back a little, won't you——?"

"Think back my eye!" he said rudely. "There's nothing to think back about. It's another lying story you made up on the spur of the moment, and you know it!"

"Don't you remember," she went on in the same quiet and patient voice, "—don't you remember telling me you were a student at Harvard University?"

"Yes, I did tell you that. And that was true. What has that got to do with knowing this woman's son?"

"Wait!" she said quietly. "Don't you remember telling me that you were there at Harvard when Marshal Foch made his visit to America?"

"Yes, I did tell you that."

"And that you saw him when he visited the university? You told me that, you know."

"Of course I did! I did see him. Every one else saw him, too. He stood on the steps of the library with his aides, and saluted while they fired the cannon off!"

"Ah!—With his aides, you say?" she said eagerly.

"Yes, of course, what's wrong with that?"

"But nothing is wrong! It's all just as I said!—Among his aides, now," she said persuasively, "did you not notice a young man, with a little mustache, about twenty-five years old, dressed in the uniform of a captain in the French army?—Think now, my boy," she went on coaxingly —"a young man—much younger than the other officers on the Marshal's staff?"

"Perhaps I did," he said impatiently. "How should I remember now? What difference does it make?"

"Because that young man, my dear," the Countess patiently explained, "that you saw standing there with the Marshal is the young Marquis— this woman's son."

He stared at her with fascinated disbelief:

"And do you mean to tell me," he said presently, "that because I may have seen some one like that standing in a great crowd of people three years ago, you had the gall to tell that woman that I knew her son— that we were friends?"

"No, no," the Countess said evasively, a little nervously. "I didn't tell her that, my dear. I'm sure I didn't tell her that. She must have misunderstood me. All I said was that you *saw* her son when he was in America. I'm sure that was all I said. And that was true, wasn't it? You *did* see him, didn't you?" she said triumphantly.

He stared at her, with mouth ajar, unable for a moment to comprehend the full enormity of such deception. Then he closed his jaws with a stubborn snap, and said:

"All right. You got yourself into this, now you get out of it. I'm not going with you."

The old woman's eyes were suddenly sharp with apprehension. She leaned forward, clutched him by the arm, and said pleadingly:

"Oh, my boy, you wouldn't do a thing like that to me, would you? Think what it means to me—the humiliation you would cause me now if you refused to go."

"I can't help that. You had no right to make arrangements with the woman in the first place, before you spoke to me. Even that wouldn't matter so much if you hadn't told her that other story about her son and me. That's the reason she's inviting me—because she thinks her son and I were friends. How can I accept such an invitation—take advantage of the woman's hospitality because you told her a story that had no truth in it?"

"Oh, that doesn't matter," the Countess spoke quickly, eagerly. "If you want me to, I shall explain to her that there was a mistake—that you really do not know her son. But it makes no difference, anyway. She would want you to come just the same. —You see," she spoke carefully, and for a moment there was a gleam of furtive, cunning understanding in her eye—the wisdom of fox for fox—"I don't think it's exactly for that reason she is inviting you."

"What other reason could there be? The woman does not know me. What other interest could she have in me?"

"Well, my boy—" the Countess hesitated, and spoke carefully—"you see, it's this way. I think she wants to speak to you," she paused carefully again before she spoke—"about a certain matter—about something she's interested in—When she heard that you were connected with *The New York Times*——"

"*What!*" He stared at her again, and suddenly exploded in a short angry laugh of resignation and defeat—"Are the whole crowd of you alike? Is there a single one of you who doesn't have some scheme, some axe to grind—who doesn't hope to get something out of Americans——"

"Then you'll go?" she said eagerly.

"Yes, I'll go!" he shouted. "Tell her anything you like. It'll serve both of you right! I'll go just to see what new trick or scheme you and this other woman are framing up. All right, I'll go!"

"Good!" she nodded briskly, satisfied. "I knew you would, my boy. La Marquise will tell you all about it when she sees you."

This final grotesque episode had suddenly determined his decision to leave Orléans. For a short time, his chance meeting with this strange old woman, his instant inclusion in the curious schemes, designs and stratagems of her life, with all that it evoked of the strange and the familiar, its haunting glimpse of the million-noted web and weaving of dark chance and destiny, had struck bright sparks of interest from his mind, had fused his spirit to a brief forgetfulness and wonder.

Now, as suddenly as it had begun, that wonder died: the life of the town, the people, the old Countess and her friends, which had for a few days seemed so new, strange, and interesting, now filled him with weariness and distaste. He was suddenly fed up with the provincial tedium of the town, he felt the old dislike and boredom that all dark bloods and races could awake in him an importunate and unreasonable desire, beneath these soft, dull skies of gray, for something bright, sharp, Northern, fierce, and wild, in life—for something gold and blue and shining, the lavish flesh of great blonde women, the surge of savage drunkenness, the fatal desperation of strong joy. The dark, strange faces of the Frenchmen all around, and all the hard perfection of that life, at once so alien and so drearily familiar, the unwearied energies of their small purposes fixed there in the small perfection of their universe, so dully ignorant of the world, so certain of itself, filled him suddenly with exasperation and dislike. He was tired suddenly of their darkness, their smallness, their hardness, their cat-like nervousness, their incessant ebullience, their unwearied and yet joyless vitalities, and the dreary monotony of their timeless greed.

He was tired of Orléans, tired of the Vatels, most of all tired, with a feeling of weary disgust and dislike, of the old Countess, and all the small tricks and schemings of her life.

And with this sudden weariness and distaste, this loss of interest in a life which had for a week or two devoured his interest, the old torment and unrest of spirit had returned. Again, the old question had returned in all its naked desolation: "Why here? And where shall I go now? What shall I do?" He saw, with a return of the old naked shame, in a flash of brutal revelation, the aimless lack of purpose in his wandering. He saw that there had been no certain reason, no valid purpose, for his coming here to Orléans, and with a sense of drowning horror, as if the phial of his spirit had exploded like a flash of ether, and emptied out into the formless spaces of a planetary vacancy, he felt that there was no purpose and no reason for his going anywhere.

And yet, the demons of unrest and tortured wandering had returned with all their fury: he knew that he must leave, that he must go on to some other destination, and he knew nowhere to go. Like a drowning man who clutches at a straw, he sought for some goal or purpose in his life, some justification for his wanderings, some target for his fierce desire. A thousand plans and projects suggested themselves to him, and each one seemed more futile, hopeless, barren than the rest. He would return to Paris and "settle down and write." He would go back to England, get a room in London, go to Oxford, the Lake District, Cornwall, Devon—a thousand towns and places, evoked by a thousand fleeting memories, returned to argue some reasonable purpose for his blind wandering. Or he would go to the South of France, "to some quiet place," or to Switzerland, "to some quiet place," or to Germany, Vienna, Italy, Spain, Majorca,—always "to settle down in some quiet place"— and for what? for what? Why, always, of course, "to write," "to write" —Great God, "to write," and even as he spoke the words the old dull shame returned to make him hate his life and all these sterile, vain pretensions of his soul. "To write"—always to seek the magic skies, the golden clime, the wise and lovely people who would transform him. "To write"—always to seek in the enchanted distances, in the dreamy perspectives of a fool's delusions, the power and certitude he could not draw out of himself. "To write"—to be that most foolish, vain, and impotent of all impostors, a man who sought the whole world over "looking for a place to write," when, he knew now with every naked, brutal penetration of his life "the place to write" was Brooklyn, Boston, Hammersmith, or Kansas—anywhere on earth, so long as the heart, the power, the faith, the desperation, the bitter and unendurable necessity, and the naked courage were there inside him all the time.

Now, having agreed to accompany the Countess on her visit to the Marquise, he suddenly decided to leave Orléans at the same time, spend the night at Blois, and go on to Tours the next day, after visiting Mornaye. And with this purpose, he packed his bag, paid his bill at the hotel, and set out on the appointed day with the old woman who for two weeks now had been his self-constituted guide and keeper.

XCV

THE village of Mornaye was a small and ancient setttlement, similar to thousands of others, situated near the gate of the château from which it got its name. A man was waiting for them at the station with a motor car: they got in and were driven swiftly through the town —a dense cluster of old gray-lemon buildings with tiled roofs, a thatched one here and there, the shops of the village grocer, cobbler, baker, visible through small dormer windows, some farm buildings, a fleeting glimpse of the old cobbled court-yard of a barn, some wagons, and farm implements—a little universe of life, compact, unbroken, built up to the edge of the road—and then, almost immediately, the gates of the château.

They drove through the gates and down a long and stately aisle of noble trees, and presently came to a halt before the great entrance of the château. As they approached, a footman came swiftly down the steps, opened the door of the car, and bowed, and in another moment, led by the man, they had entered the hall and were being escorted into the great salon where their hostess was awaiting them.

La Marquise de Mornaye was a woman of about sixty, but from the energy and vigor of her appearance, she seemed to be in the very prime of life. She was an extraordinary figure of a woman, as tall and strong-looking as a man, with a personal quality that was almost mountainously impressive in its command. The image of the boy's recent discontent had so shaped the French as a dark and swarthy people of mean stature that it was now startling to be confronted by a woman of this grand proportion.

She had a wide, round face, smooth, brown and unwrinkled, such as one often finds in peasant people, her eyes were round, bright, and shrewd, webbed minutely by fine wrinkles at the corners. She had strong, coarse hair of gray, brushed vigorously back from a wide, low forehead. She was big in foot and limb and body, everything about the woman was strong, large and vigorous except her hands. And her hands were plump, white, tiny, as useless-looking as a baby's, shockingly disproportionate to the power and vigor of the rest of her big frame.

The woman had on a long, brown dress that completely covered her from neck to toe: it was a strangely old-fashioned garment—or rather it did not seem to have any fashion or style whatsoever—but it was nevertheless a magnificent garment, in its plain and homely strength perfectly appropriate to the extraordinary woman who wore it.

In every respect—in word, tone, gesture, look, and act—the woman showed a plain, forceful, and immensely able character. Her strong, brown face was friendly, yet shrewd and knowing; she greeted the Countess cordially, but it was evident from the humor in her round, bright eyes that she was no fool in the ways of the world, and perfectly able to hold her own in any worldly encounter.

She was waiting for them, erect and smiling, as they entered the great salon, a magnificent room at least forty feet in length, warmly, luxuriously, yet plainly furnished, and with nothing cold or repellent in its grand proportions. She greeted the Countess immediately and cordially, extending her plump little white hand in a friendly greeting, and bending and kissing the little wren-like woman on her withered cheek. La Marquise, in deference to her young American guest, spoke English from the beginning. And her English, like everything else about her, was plain, forceful, and direct, completely fluent, although marked with a heavy accent.

" 'Ow are you, my dear?" La Marquise said, as she kissed the other woman on the cheek. "It is good to see you again after these so many years. 'Ow long 'as it been since you were last at Mornaye?"

"Almost seven years, Marquise," the Countess answered eagerly. "The last time—do you remember?—was in the spring of 1918."

"Ah, yes," the other answered benevolently. "Now I can remember. You were here when many of our so brave Américains were quartered here at Mornaye—Monsieur," she said, using this reference as an introduction, and turning to the boy with her plump little hand extended in a movement of kindly greeting, "I am delighted. I meck apologies for my son. I know he will so much regret not seeing you."

He flushed, and stammered out his thanks: she seemed to take no notice of his embarrassment and, having completed her friendly welcome, she turned smilingly to the Countess again, and said:

"And 'ow 'ave you been, my dear? You are looking very well," she said approvingly, "and no older dan you were de lest time you were here. I s'ink," she said smilingly, including the young man now in her friendly humor—"I s'ink la Comtesse must 'ave discover—wat you call it, eh?" she shrugged—"ze se-*cret* of ze fountain of yout', eh?"

"Ah, Marquise," the Countess fawned greedily upon the grand woman, obviously elated by these signs of intimacy—"ah—hah—hah! it is so kind of you to say so—but I fear I have grown much older since I saw you last. I have known great trouble," she said sadly, "and, as you know, Marquise, my health has not been good."

"Non?" the other said with an air of solicitous inquiry. "I am so sor-*ree*," she continued in a tone of unimpeachable regret, which neverthe-less showed that the Countess' health or lack of it was really of no moment to her whatever. "Perhaps, my dear, it is ze wretchet cleemat here. I s'ink perhaps you should go Sout' in vintaire—ah, monsieur," she continued regretfully turning to the youth, "you see Mornaye at a bat season of ze year—I fear you may be disappointed by our coun-*tree*. I 'ope you vill come beck some time in sprink. Zen, I s'ink you vill agree la France is beautiful."

"I should like to," he replied.

"But oh zis vintaire! Zis *vintaire!*" La Marquise cried with passionate distaste, folding her arms and drawing herself together in a movement of chilled ardor as she looked through a tall French door across one of those magnificent and opulent vistas that one finds in France, an architecture of proud, comely space into whose proportionate dimensions even nature herself has been compelled. It was a tremendous sweep of velvet sward, that faded into misty distances and that was cut cleanly on each side by the smoky denseness of her forest parks. Her shrewd eyes ranged across this noble prospect for a moment in an expression of chilled distaste. Then, with a slight contracted shudder of her folded arms, she turned, and said wearily:

"Ah, zis vintaire! Zis *vintaire!* Sometimes I s'ink it vill nevaire end. Every day," she went on indignantly, "it rain, rain, rain! All vintaire lonk I see noz-*zing* but rain! I get up in ze mornink and look out—and it rain! I turn my beck and zen look out again—it rain! I take a nep, I get up, I go to bet—always it rain!" She shrugged her shoulders comically, and turning to the boy with a glint of shrewdly cynical humor, she said, "I s'ink if it keep on ve 'ave again—vat you call it—Noah's Floot, eh?"

The Countess clucked sympathetically at this watery chronicle of woe, and said:

"But have you been here by yourself all winter? I should think you would get awfully lonely, my dear," she went on in a tone of ingratiating commiseration. "I know how you must miss your son."

"No. I vas in Paris for two veeks in Decembaire," said La Marquise. "But it rain zere too," she said, with another shrug of comic despair, and then added vigorously, "No! I do not get lonely if it do not rain. But ven it rains—zen it is tereeble. . . . Come," she said brusquely, almost curtly, turning away from the gray prospect through the window, "let us seet here vere eet ees varm." Still clasping her arms across her breast, she led them towards a coal fire which was crackling cheerfully in a hearth at one end of the great room; they seated themselves comfortably around the fire, La Marquise rang a bell, and spoke a few words to a butler, and presently he returned, bringing glasses and a decanter of old Sherry on a tray.

They sat talking amiably then of many things. La Marquise questioned the boy about America, his stay in France, the places he had seen, referred regretfully again to the absence of her son, and of the great friendship he cherished for America and Americans as a result of his travels there with Marshal Foch. And from time to time, the Countess, with a cunning that was comically naïve in its bare-faced self-exposure, would prod him with a skinny finger, and whisper hoarsely:

"Ask her some questions, my dear. You should ask her more questions and write more in your little book. It will make a good impression."

And, although he saw from the glint of shrewd humor in the sharp eyes of La Marquise, that none of this clumsy by-play had been lost on her, and that the other woman's design was perfectly apparent to her, he responded dutifully, if awkwardly, asking respectful questions about the age and history of the château, the extent of its estate, and so on. At length, emboldened by the modest success of these beginnings, and feeling that a clever young journalist should display an intelligent curiosity about the current affairs of the nation to which he is a visitor, he asked a question about the government of the period, of which Herriot was the leader, and which was dominantly socialist.

It was, he saw, an unfortunate move; the Countess poked him sharply with a warning finger, but it was too late. He saw instantly that his question had produced a bad impression on La Marquise: for the first time, her manner of amiable and cordial friendliness vanished, her face hardened, there was an angry glint in her shrewd eyes, and in a moment she said harshly, and in a tone of arrogant impatience:

"I know nozzing about zose pipple! I pay no attention to anys'ing zey say! Zey are fools! fools!" she cried violently. "You must not believe anys'ing zey say! Zose men are traitors! . . . Charlatans! . . . Zey are ze pipple who have ruined and betrayed France!" In her agitation she got up and walked across the room. "Here!" she cried, picking up a newspaper on a table and returning with it. "Here is what you should reat if you want ze trut!" She thrust a copy of *L'Action Française* into his hands. "Zat paper—and zat alone—will tell you ze trut about ze way s'ings are in France today. Ah, monsieur!" she cried earnestly, "you do not know—ze world does not know—no one outside of France can know ze trut, because zese wretched men control ze press—and make it print vatever lies zey tell it to. But you **reat** *zis,* monsieur—you reat *zis,"* she struck the paper with the back of her hand as she spoke, "and you will get ze trut! Ah, zat man!" she said with a grim chuckle of admiration. "Ze rédacteur—ze—vat you say?—ze *editor* of zat paper, Léon Daudet—ah, zat man is *right!"* she said with a chuckle of satisfaction. "Zat man is sometimes coarse—he call zem bat names—he is not always très gentil—but," again she chuckled grimly "he iss *right!* He tells ze trut—he calls zem vat zey are—ze traitors and creemi*nals* who 'ave ruined France." She was silent for a moment, and then in a voice harsh with passion, she said violently: "La France, monsieur, is a royaume—a—vat you call it?—a monarchy —a kinkdom. Ze French people must have a kink—zey are lost vitout a kink—zey cannot govern zemselves vitout a kink! . . . Zere can be no France, monsieur, vitout a kink!" she almost shouted. "Zere has been no France since ze monarchy vas destroyed by zese scélérats who 'ave betrayed La France—zere vill never be a France until ze kink is restored to his rightful office and zese creeminals and traitors 'ave been sent to ze guillotine vere zey belonk. . . . So do not ask me anys'ink about zese men, monsieur," she said with arrogant passion. "I know nozzing about zem. I pay no attention to zem! Zey are fools . . . traitors . . . creeminals," she shouted, "you reat zat paper, you vill get ze trut."

She was breathing hoarsely and her eyes glinted with hard fires of passion. At this moment, fortunately, the butler entered, bowed, and, speaking in a quiet voice, informed his mistress that luncheon was served. The words recalled the angry woman to her duties as a hostess: with an almost comical suddenness, she assumed her former manner of gracious cordiality, smiled amiably at her guests, and saying with benevolent good-nature, "After our lonk journey and our so much talk, ve are 'ongry—yes?" led the way into the dining-room.

As they went in, the little old Countess nudged her young companion again with a stealthy warning, and whispered with nervous reproach:

"You should not have asked her that, my dear. Please do not say anything more to her about the government."

The dining-room of the château was another magnificent chamber, like everything else about the château nobly harmonious with those elements of strength and grace, splendor and simplicity, warmth and delicacy united with princely dignity, which are the triumphs of this period of French architecture. In spite of the chill air of the room—for it was poorly heated—one felt its living and noble warmth immediately.

The boy, who had looked forward to this meeting with considerable awe and apprehension, now felt himself completely at home, stirred by a profound, tranquil and lovely joy at the noble beauty and simplicity of the château. Even in the sense of retrenchment, the worn uniforms of the servants, the knowledge that they served their mistress in various offices, there was something pleasant, homely, and familiar: he discovered, to his surprise, that he now felt none of the constraint and uneasiness which he experienced when Joel Pierce had taken him to his great estate upon the Hudson River, and he had for the first time seen the lives of the great American millionaires.

With La Marquise de Mornaye he was not conscious of that exactly mannered style—most mannered in its very affectation of simplicity— that vulgar arrogance which he had felt among the rich Americans of Joel Pierce's class. La Marquise was plain as an old shoe, vigorous and lusty as a peasant, and completely an aristocrat—magnificently herself, without an ounce of affectation—a woman Joel Pierce's people would have fawned upon, and to whom they would have given a king's ransom if by so doing they could have bought for son or daughter an alliance with her family.

La Marquise seated him beside her, the Countess opposite her, and at once they began to eat. The food was magnificent, there was a different wine of royal vintage (brought up from the famous cellar of the château) with every course. La Marquise left no doubt at all about the robust nature of her appetite, and by everything she did and was—the plain shrewdness, warmth, and sensible humanity of her nature—she made it plain that she expected her guests to eat heartily also, and not to be too nice and dainty about it, either.

"Ven vun is younk as you are," she said, turning with a smile to her young guest, "he is 'ongry often—non?" she inquired. She put her soupspoon to her mouth, swallowed some soup, and smacking her lips with an air of relish, turned to the youth again, and said plainly and positively:

"Eet ees good! Oui! I s'ink you will like it, too." Turning to the Countess, who had tasted nothing, she said severely:

"Vy do you vait, my dear? Are you not 'ongry? You must eat."

"Ah—hah—hah!" the Countess said with a little undecided laugh, her eyes greedily fixed upon the smoking soup. "—You know, my dear, I am on a diet by the doctor's orders—sang de cheval, you know," she chattered in a distracted tone as her greedy eyes went ravenously along the table—"I eat almost nothing—really, my dear, I don't think I should." She snatched up a piece of bread in one greedy little claw, broke it with an appetizing crackle, and began to cram it into her mouth like a starved animal—"Ah—hah—hah!" The poor starved old woman laughed with almost hysterical delight, and tried to speak with a mouth full of bread—"I know I shouldn't—but you always have such delicious food, my dear." She lifted the soup-spoon, and drew in with a long slob-

bering suction. "Ah, mon Dieu! mon Dieu!" she gurgled rapturously—
"quel potage!"

And so the meal progressed. With such a lusty trencher-woman as La
Marquise beside one, it was not hard to follow suit; they polished off
the soup, which was a delicious, savory, peasant-like brew, in record
time, and, as if their hunger mounted from the delicious food it fed
on, they turned then to the chicken. The chicken, which was almost
all fat and juicy breast, was so young, crisp, tender, plump and succulent
that it seemed almost to melt in the mouth, the boy took two or three
rhapsodic swallows and the chicken was gone, at which La Marquise,
lifting her voice over his feeble and half-hearted protests, said to the
butler: "Encore du poulet pour Monsieur."

A second chicken, even plumper, crisper and more tender than the
first, was instantly provided, after which the roast and vegetables were
served. He had never tasted better food in his life—everything, haricots,
peas, beef, seemed to melt like an ambrosial ether the moment that he
put it in his mouth; there was a new wine with every course, each wine
rarer, older, richer and more delicious than the last, the butler kept
filling up their glasses, and he kept drinking the grand wine until
heart, mind, and soul, and every conduit of his life seemed infused by
its glorious warmth and fragrance. They talked little as they ate: for
some time there were no sounds except the crisp crackle of the bread,
the ring of heavy silver, the sound of wine gulped down, the delicate
chime of glasses, and the low, quiet orders of the butler speaking to
his helper, as swiftly, expertly, and noiselessly they moved around the
table, seeming to be there at one's elbow, and to read the gastronomic
hopes and wishes of each guest before he had time to open his mouth
and utter them.

La Marquise ate with robust concentration, putting down her knife
from time to time to pick up her wine-glass and take a generous swallow, after which she would put the glass down and wipe a napkin
deliberately across her mouth and pause, for a moment, breathing a little
heavily, with an air of hearty satisfaction.

As for the Countess, she ate like a famished wolf: where the movements of La Marquise were hearty and deliberate, those of the Countess
were almost frantically swift and eager. Her sharp and greedy little
eyes glittered with an almost delirious joy, she would seize a glass of
wine and drain it in one greedy gulp; at times she was so excited by
the variety and abundance of the dishes that she seemed unable to decide

what to reach for next. She reached out greedily in all directions, her eyes darting avaricious glances to and fro, chicken, meat, vegetables, salad, wine disappeared as if by magic, and were replenished, and all the time the poor old woman chuckled craftily to herself, and muttered to herself in broken monologue:

"Ah—hah—hah!"—crunch, crunch, crunch! And away went the chicken. "Mon Dieu!—But it's good!—Ah—hah—hah!" gulp, gulp, gulp; down would go the wine. "Mon Dieu! mon Dieu! Such food! Such wine!—Mais oui! Mais oui! . . . Un peu encore, s'il vous plaît! Quel boeuf! Quel boeuf!"

At which La Marquise would put down her glass, wipe her mouth, look across the table at the Countess, and say:

" 'Ow you like, eh? Good? Mais oui! Il faut manger," she said coarsely, and applied herself again to knife and fork.

By the time they got down to the cheese—which was a ripe, delicious Brie—La Marquise de Mornaye was at last fortified for conversation. Putting down her empty wine-glass with a deliberate movement, she straightened in her chair, wiped her mouth, sat upright for a moment in an attitude of solid satisfaction, and then, turning to her American guest, said:

"Do you know Patterson T. Jones—eh? 'E is an officer—a vat you call it?—a major in ze Américain army." She pronounced these words with an air of naïve confidence, as if Patterson T. Jones must be a name instantly familiar to every American. When the boy told her, however, that he did not know Major Patterson T. Jones and confessed, further, that he had never heard of him, La Marquise looked slightly astonished and disappointed; and in a moment, her shrewd eyes narrowing slightly as she spoke, she said rather grimly:

"I should like verree verree motch to see zat gentleman again. I should like verree verree motch to know vere he now iss. . . . Attendez!" she said sharply, as inspiration struck her. "Perhaps if I show you this—vat you say?—his photographie—you vill know ze man. . . . Guillaume!" she raised her voice a little in command. "Apportez-moi les photographies des officiers Américains."

"Oui, madame," the butler answered, and went swiftly and silently out of the room.

"Yes," La Marquise continued with an air of grim meditation, "I should verree verree motch like to know vere Major Patterson T. Jones iss to be found."

The butler returned with several large square photographs, bowed, and gave them to his mistress.

" 'Ere, you see," she said, taking one of them and pointing with her finger, "zis vas taken here—in zis verree room at a great ban*quet* vitch I have made for ze Americains in 1918. Zis," she said proudly, and pointing with a plump white finger—"zis is me—c'est moi, La Marquise!" she cried in a jolly tone, and laughed with satisfaction as she pointed to her own beaming likeness at the head of a long table, sumptuously adorned with fine silver, china, linen, and a forest thicket of dark, crusty-looking bottles of old wine—obviously the relics of a memorable feast. "And zis," La Marquise said more grimly, pointing again with her plump white finger, "zis is Major Patter*son* T. Jones—You know him, eh?" she said.

The boy looked at the picture for a moment and then handed it back to La Marquise, telling her that he did not recognize the face of Patterson T. Jones.

"Patter*son* T. Jones," La Marquise answered, slowly, and with an air of grim deliberation, "is a gentleman I vant verree verree motch to see. Zat is ze man," she said, "who took my picture—who told me he vould get for me oh! soch huge soms of mon-nee if he could teck my picture to America," she laughed ironically—"and so I let him teck ze picture, and I have heard nozzing from him since."

"Was—was it your own picture, Marquise? A portrait of yourself?"

"Mais non, mon ami," she said impatiently. "Dat's vat I tell you—eet vas a picture, a photographie—of Le Maréchal. Zere vas only seex sotch pictures of Le Maréchal in existence—I say to Madame Foch vun time ven I am at Paris—I see ze picture in her house—I say—'Oh, my dear, zat so lovely picture of Le Maréchal—I must have vun for myself,' I say. 'Ah,' she say, 'I do not know, Mathilde—he do not like to give away zese pictures—I have only t'ree,' she say, 'but vait. I see vat I can do—' Zen, vun night I go to dinnaire at zere house. 'Mathilde,' he say, 'for vat you vant my picture? I give it to you,' he say, 'and zen all ze ozzer girls vill vant vun, too. I meck my vife jalouse, and zen zere is no peace. I have enough of var,' he say. 'I am too old to start anozzer vit my vife!' 'You give to me zat picture,' I say. 'I am no young leddy in ze chorus,' I say, 'to meck your vife jalouse. She vant you to give it to me, too.' 'Bon,' he say. 'Here it is, zen.' . . . And he give to me ze so beautiful photographie vit his name below written out to me: 'To Mathilde, old comrade, fet'ful friend'—I bring ze picture beck ven I come beck to Mornaye,"

La Marquise continued, "and Major Patter*son* T. Jones he see it ven he iss here. 'How motch you vant for zat picture of Le Maréchal?' he say. 'Oh,' I say, 'I cannot say. Already I have an offer of ten s'ousand francs,' I say, 'but I vould not sell it because ze Maréchal himself, he give to me.' 'Vell,' say Major Patter*son* T. Jones, 'you lett me teck zat picture vit me ven I go beck to America, and I sell it for you.' 'How motch you get for me, eh?' I ask him. 'Oh,' he say, 'I get twent' s'ousand francs for you— mebbe more.' 'You sure?' I say. 'Mais oui!' say Major Patter*son* T. Jones. 'Absolument'—'All right,' I say. 'I give to you. If you get twenty s'ousand francs I give you five,' I say. And so he teck my picture and he go avay, and since den," La Marquise bitterly conclued, "I nevaire hear from him."

"Ah!" the Countess cried indignantly. "Le scélérat!"

"Mais oui!" the other woman now said passionately. "It is infâme! Zis man have my picture, I have nozzing—Ze lest time Madame Foch is here, she look around, she say, 'But vere, my dear,—vere iss ze picture zat Le Maréchal give you? I do not see it,' she say. What can I do?" La Marquise went on in a despairing tone. "I cannot say to her 'I lose it!' I cannot say to her 'I give it away to an Américain who sell it for me.' I don't know vat to say, all I can say is, 'I leave it, my dear, in Paris vit my son Paul ven I vas zere. He have it, **but ze next** time zat he come to Mornaye he vill bring it.' But ven she come again, vat story can I tell her zen?" La Marquise demanded. "Ah! Zat scélérat! Zat Patter*son* T. Jones! If ever I get my fingers on zat gentleman I s'ink he vill remember me!" she said, with a glint in her eye, and a grim note in her voice, that left no doubt of her intention—"But is it not infâme, monsieur," she said with a virtuous indignation that was now ludicrous after her naïve exposure of her own avarice and greed—"is it not infâme zat somevun teck avay a picture zat a friend give to you—and promise you motch monnee for it—and zen to hear from him no more? Scélérat! T'ief!" she muttered, "I like to get my hands on him!—But now, monsieur," she said, turning to him abruptly, with a smile of winning ingratiation, "I meck a leetle speech to you. You are—la Comtesse tells me—a younk journalist—eh?"

"Well, Marquise," he flushed, and began to blunder out an explanation —"I can't exactly say——"

"Mais oui!" the Countess swiftly interposed. "He has written many clever articles—pour les grands journaux Américains, n'est-ce pas—la tête, vous voyez?" she whispered craftily, bending over the table and nodding towards him as she spoke—"C'est très intelligent, n'est-ce pas?"

"Et pour *Le Times?*" La Marquise demanded. "Il écrit tout ça pour *Le New York Times?*"

"Mais oui," the Countess said glibly, before he could object. "Il est déjà bien connu. Moi—j'ai lu beaucoup de choses de sa main——"

"Now, look here," he began, glaring angrily across the table at the lying old woman. "You have no right——"

"Ah, oui!" La Marquise broke in, with a vigorous nod of satisfaction, after a brief inspection of him. "C'est très évident! Il est intelligent! Bon!" she said decisively, and turned to him with the air of a person whose mind is made up, and whose course of action determined—"Now, monsieur," she said, "I tell you vat I have in mind. I have beeg 'ospital—non?" she said, smiling a little at his puzzled look. "I am—vat you call it?—le prés*ident*—le directeur, n'est-ce pas?—of beeg 'ospital in de Nort'—ve have zere ze soldats, n'est-ce pas—ze oh so many blessés—les pauvres!" she said in a tone of pity—"les mutilés de la guerre. . . . Ve have old building—eet ees no good, eet ees not beeg enough—not *moderne*—and so," she added simply, "ve build anozzer—beeg, moderne—and"—the conclusion of the matter—"ve need monnee." She was silent for a moment, beaming hopefully at him. "Monsieur," she said presently, in an ingratiating tone, and with an air of naïve confidence that was astounding—"I s'ink ven I tell you vat ve need—'ow much monnee," her voice sank craftily, "you vill get for us—eh?"

He stared at her for a moment with a bewildered face, unable to reply.

"But how," he stammered at length—"how do you think—what do you think I can do?" he said bluntly.

"Ah!" La Marquise cried triumphantly. "C'est facile!" Again her voice became low, confiding, crafty. "You are a journalist—eh? You write for ze grand journal Américain—ze *New York Times*—yes? . . . Vell, I tell you vat to say," she went on placidly. "You write ze article for ze *Times*—you spick of zis beeg 'ospi*tal*—you tell of ze grand vork of restauration—you tell of ze poor soldats—les blessés—les mutilés—you say La France have nozzing—zey have no monnee—ze poor pipples 'ave lose everys'ink—you say, ve 'ave so motch—ze rich Américains—ve must not let zis great vork die—ve must help ze poor soldats—ve must give ze monnee for ze 'ospital. . . . You see—I show you," she cried with a confident chuckle—"if you like I write eet out myself—and zen all you have to do is meck—vat do you say?—la traduction."

"How—how much do you want?"

"Un million de francs," she said, dismissing this bagatelle airily. "—For ze Américains vat ees dat? Pouf! Nozzing! Mais pour les Français—ah!" she said sadly, "for ze French eet ees too motch. Un millionaire Américain—he see your story—he say 'Ve cannot let zis grand vork die' —he write vun check out for ze whole amount—and zen," her smile of satisfaction deepened, "he send to me, eh?—He meck out check to Marquise—he never miss eet—and he send to me." For a moment she was silent, smiling triumphantly at him. When she spoke again, she bent towards him, her voice became low, confiding, craftily conspiratorial—"And I tell you vat I do. . . . You write ze piece and get for me ze mon-nee . . . and I give you a fourt'—twenty-five per cent—non?"

In a moment, as he continued to stare at her with an expression of gape-mouthed astonishment, she straightened, with an air of satisfied finality, nodded her head, and then said with business-like decision:

"Bon. Eet ees settled zen." She rose decisively from the table, and her guests followed her—"You come vit me," she said, as she led the way out of the dining-room, "and I give you—vat you say?—ze fects."

She was already gone, before he could blurt out a few words of bewildered protest; the Countess was at his side, prodding him sharply with a skinny finger, and muttering in a tone of reproachful entreaty:

"Go on, my dear! Go on! And you should ask more questions! Don't sit there, saying nothing. It will make a good impression. And use your little book more often," the Countess whispered cunningly. "You should write more in it when she speaks to you."

"Now you see here," he burst out furiously, "I'm not going to write down anything. I'm tired of this foolishness—I'm not going to be a party any longer to your damned schemes or for this woman's, either. I'm going to tell her once and for all that I'll write no article—not for *The Times* nor any place else!"

"Oh, my boy," the old woman whispered imploringly. "You wouldn't do that! Please don't say a thing like that, I beg of you! . . . Think what it means to me," she whispered—"I am so poor, so miserable—for years I have waited for an opportunity to see this woman—it means so much to me, so little to you. Please be polite, my dear—it's only for a little time. You'll be going soon. What can it matter to you? She has her schemes like everybody else . . . keep silent if you feel you must, but be polite to her, for God's sake; pretend to listen—don't ruin everything for me now."

"All right," he muttered grimly. "I'll listen, but I'm damned if I'll write anything down in the little book."

When they returned to the salon, La Marquise had provided herself with various letters, folders, and descriptive circulars about the institution for which she was now soliciting aid. They seated themselves around the fire again, with coffee and liqueurs; by the time La Marquise had finished the description of her hospital project, the gray light of the brief wintry afternoon was fading rapidly, and the time for their departure had approached.

Before they left, she took them on a brief tour of inspection of the château, showing them the portraits of her ancestors, the great room with the huge, gold-canopied bed where King Henri IV had slept, on one of his visits to the château—unoccupied since, now closed save for museum visits such as this.

Their last visit, before departure, was to the library: it was a pleasant, warm-looking room adjacent to the grand salon, and had the appearance of being seldom used. La Marquise smiled at the eager curiosity with which the young man looked over the storied rows of books, the costly elegance and rich color of their bindings.

"You like to reat, eh?"

He told her that he did. She smiled, and said indifferently :

"I do not like so motch. It bore me ven I reat so long."

He asked her a few questions about some of the modern French writers—Proust, Gide, Romains, and Cocteau, among others—for a moment her face was hardened by the arrogant look it had worn when he had asked her about the government, and she said rather impatiently:

"I know nozzing about zose pipple. Yes, I have heard of some of zem. But I never reat zem. Zere is no good writing in France any more. Ze latest s'ing I have here,"—she nodded towards the shelves of books—"is Paul Bourget. But I never reat him, eizer."

In a few moments, they had said farewell, and were being driven away from the château. Rain had begun to fall again, the dull, gray light was almost gone and, since there was no convenient train, La Marquise had instructed her driver to take them back to Blois in the car.

During the ride back to town, he spoke seldom to the Countess. And she, as if recognizing the impatience, weariness and dislike he had come to feel towards her, the approaching end of their brief and curious relationship, was silent, too. When they got back to the hotel, he told her rather curtly he was tired and was going to his room to wash up and take a brief rest before dinner.

"But yes, my dear," she said instantly. "Of course you should. I can see that you are tired. Perhaps," she added quietly, "I shall see you again when you come down."

"Of course you will," he said shortly, almost angrily, in a tone that showed the irritable exasperation which too long association with the woman had now caused him to feel.

"Good-bye, my dear. Get some rest now. You need it."

When he got to his room, he took off his coat and shoes, lay down on his bed, and instantly fell asleep. When he awoke, he discovered he had slept almost three hours, that it was eight o'clock. Already late for dinner, washing and dressing hastily, he went down-stairs to find no one but the proprietor's wife in the *bureau*. Even before he could ask her where the Countess was, the woman had smilingly informed him that the old woman had gone, had already taken a train back to Orléans.

"Mais elle vous a remis de très affectueux adieux," the woman said with a smile. "Elle vous a fait des grands compliments."

And for a moment, when he realized that she was gone, he was conscious of a strange, mixed feeling of pity, loss and regret. He remembered suddenly the curt exasperation of his parting and something lonely, sad, and silent in the eyes of the old woman as she had said good-bye. The old loneliness had closed in around him again, he felt the sense of loss and sorrow that one feels when some one he has known a long time has gone.

BOOK VII

KRONOS AND RHEA: THE DREAM OF TIME

BOOK IV

KRONOS AND RHEA; THE DREAM OF TIME

PLAY us a tune on an unbroken spinet, and let the bells ring, let the bells ring! Play music now: play us a tune on an unbroken spinet. Do not make echoes of forgotten time, do not strike music from old broken keys, do not make ghosts with faded tinklings on the yellowed board; but play us a tune on an unbroken spinet, play lively music when the instrument was new, let us see Mozart playing in the parlor, and let us hear the sound of the ladies' voices. But more than that; waken the turmoil of forgotten streets, let us hear their sounds again unmuted, and unchanged by time, throw the light of Wednesday morning on the Third Crusade, and let us see Athens on an average day. Let us hear the sound of the voices of the Greeks, and observe closely if they were all wise and beautiful at ten o'clock in the morning; let us see if their limbs were all perfect, and their gestures grave and stately, also let us smell their food and observe them eating, and hear, if only once, the sound of a wheel in a street, the texture of just four forgotten moments.

Give us the sounds of Egypt on a certain day; let us hear the voice of King Menkaura and some of the words of the Lady Sennuwy; also the voices of the cotton-farmers. Let us hear the vast and casual sound of life, in these old peoples: their greetings in the street, the voices of the housewives and the merchants. And let us hear the laughter of a woman in the sixteenth century.

The cry of the wolf would always be the same; the sound of the wheel will always be the same; and the hoof of the horse on the roads of every time will be the same. But play us a tune on an unbroken spinet; and let us hear the voices of the knights at dinner. The cry of a man to his dog, and the barking of the dog; the call of the plow-driver to his horse, and the sound of the horse; the noise of the hunt, and the sound of the flowing water, will always be the same.

By the waters of life, by time, by time, play us a tune on an unbroken spinet, and let us hear the actual voices of old fairs; let us move backward through our memories, and through the memory of the race, let us relive the million forgotten moments of our lives, and let us see poor people sitting in their rooms in 1597, and let us see the rich man standing with his back before the fire, in the Middle Ages, and his wife knitting by the table, and let us hear their casual words.

Let us see the men who built the houses of Old Frankfort; let us see how they worked, and let us see them sitting on hewn timbers when they ate their lunches; let us hear their words, the sound of their voices. Unwind the fabric of lost time out of our entrails, repair the million little threads of actual circumstance until the seconds grow gray, bright and dusty with the living light, and we see the plain unfabled faces of the people; let us awake, and hear the people in the streets, and see Tobias Smollett pass our window.

Then, play us a tune on the unbroken spinet, let time be as the road to London and we a traveller on it; and let us enter London and find out what year it is there in the Mile End Road; let it be dark, and let us enter London in the dark, and hear men's voices, and let us see if we could understand them; and let us then find out what year it is, a lodging for the night, and see if they read mystery on us, or would fly away from us.

But there are times that are stranger yet, there are times that are stranger than the young knights and the horses, and the sounds of the eating taverns. The far time is the time of yesterday: it is the time of early America, it is the voices of the people on Broadway in 1841, it is the sounds of the streets in Des Moines in 1887, it is the engines of the early trains at Baltimore in 1853, it is the faces and voices of the early American people, who are lapped up in the wilderness, who are hid from us, whose faces are in mystery, whose lives are more dark and strange than the lives of the Saxon thanes.

The time that is lovely is the time of the fatness and of the bright colors; it is the elfin time of the calendars, and the sad and mysterious time of the early photographs. It is the time of the early lithographs, it is the time when the world was green and red and yellow. It is the time of the red barn and the windmill, and the house of the seven thousand gables; it is the time of the green lawn and the blue sky and the white excursion-steamer in the river, and the flags, the streamers, and gay brown-and-white buntings, the brass bands and the tumult of all the people who cry out Hurray, hurray!

It is the time of the boy rolling his hoop down the pink path, and of Mama in a bonnet and with a muff, and a stuck-out bottom, and Papa with a derby; it is the time of peace and plenty and the fair stripes of color, and the iron stag. It is the time of the lightning-rod salesman and the summer boarder, it is the time of Farmer Hayseed and of Dusty Rhodes the tramp, it is the time when boys started on the downward path through cigarettes; it is a lovely time. It is the time of the lures and snares of the wicked city and of the Great White Way; it is the time of pitfalls that await the innocent country girl with a whaleboned collar and a small waist; it is the time of Palaces of Sin or the Devil in Society; it is the time of the Tenderloin, of the nests of vice; it is the time of the gilded resorts with mirrors and soft carpets, where the mechanical piano played and you bought champagne, and of the High Class places and the Madam who would not stand for any ungentlemanly behavior, the time of the girls who wore evening dresses and were Perfect Ladies.

It is the time of the opera and theatre parties, and the Horse Show, and of late jolly suppers in the walnut dining-rooms; it is the time of elegant ladies with long gloves on naked arms, and Welsh rarebit in the chafing-dish; it is the time of the Four Hundred, and the great names of the millionaires—the Vanderbilts, the Astors, and the Goulds —it is the time of the powdered flunkies and the twenty-dollar favors; it is the time of Newport, and the canopied red-carpeted sidewalks, and the great mansions on Fifth Avenue, and the splendid gilt and plush marble halls, and the time of the fortune-hunting foreign noblemen (London papers please copy).

It is the time of the effeminate fop, and the lisping ass (Oh, Percy! I'll slap you on your wrist, you rough, rude thing, you!); it is the time of the Damned Dude who wears English clothes and has cuffs on his trousers (Hey, mister! Is it raining in London?), and he never did anything in his life but spend his old man's money, he never did an honest lick of work in his life, he's not worth powder enough to kill him, and if the son-of-a-bitch comes fooling around any sister of mine I'll beat the everlasting tar out of him.

When the songs that they sang were old and sweet, when the songs that they sang were like beauty's from afar, and when people sitting on their porches in the dusk could hear (O sweet and low!) the corner quartette sing, "Sweet Adeline"; when the songs that they sang were "Daisy, Daisy, Give Me Your Answer True."

It is the time of the wharves and the tangled shipping, the horse-cars by the docks, of piled-up casks and kegs of rum and molasses. There are forgotten fume-flaws of bright smoke above Manhattan; where are the lost faces that came towards us over Brooklyn bridge, where are the parted ripples and the proud forgotten ships?

By the waters of life, before we knew that we must die, before we had seen our father's face, before we had sought the print of his foot: by the waters of time (the tide! the tide!), before we had seen the shadows in the haunted woods, before lost moments lived again, before the shades were fleshed. Who are we, that must follow in the footsteps of the king? Who are we, that had no kings to follow? We are the un-kinged men. Have we left shadows on forgotten walls? Have we crossed running water and lived for seven timeless years with the en-chantress, and shall we find our son who is ourself, and will he know us?

Shall your voices unlock the gates of my brain? Shall I know you, though I have never seen your face? Will you know me, and will you call me "son"? Father, I know that you live, though I have never found you.

In the old town of Tours he quickly found lodging in an ancient hotel or tavern—really a congeries of old, whited buildings with separate doors, looking out on a cobbled courtyard through whose gate, in former times perhaps, the horses and post-chaise of weary travellers had often clat-tered. In a cold, little room in one of the buildings facing on the court, he now settled down, and there began for him one of the most extraor-dinary and phantasmal time-experiences of his life. Day passed into night, night merged into day again like the unbroken weaving of a magic web, and he stayed on, week after week, plunged in a strange and legendary spell of time that seemed suspended and detached from the world of measurable event, fixed in unmoving moment, unsilent silence, changeless change.

Later, it seemed to him that that strange revery and dream of time, in which his life was now so strangely fixed, had been induced by a series of causes, easy to understand in the light of experience, and almost logical in their consequence. It was five months since he had left America. After the overwhelming impact of impression and event which a new world, a new life, had brought to him in so many varied, chance, and unexpected ways—after the ship, the voyage, the enormous isolation, the whole earth-detachment of the sea (itself a life, a world, a universe of new experience), after the weeks in England, the huge web of London, the brief but poignantly illuminating days in Bris-tol, Bath, and Devonshire, with fleeting glimpses of something so strange, yet so familiar, so near, yet never to be touched, that it seemed to him he was looking in through a lighted window at a life which he had always known, but which he could never make his own; after the terrific impact of France and Paris—the month of bewildered, desperate and almost terror-stricken isolation in a new and hostile world—an atom, wordless, tongueless, almost drowned among the strange, dark faces of the Frenchmen; after all the confusion, grief, and error of that month—the night-time kaleidoscope of cafés, brothels, alcohol, and women, the frenzied day-time prowling through museums, bookstalls, thronging streets—the thousand monuments of an alien culture, the million faces of an alien race, until every atom of him was wrung, trembling, maddened and exhausted, sick with loss and hopelessness, weary with despair—after the huge first shock and flood-tide of immersion in an alien life—had come his meeting with Starwick, Elinor, and Ann, the brief, fatal, furious weeks of their relation, the bitter loss and waste and rankling pain of parting; and finally the sweltering and incurable ache, the blind and driven aimlessness of wandering, the chance encounter with the Countess, and the brief interlude of forgetfulness and oblivion that had come to him while he was with her—and now, blank, silent loneliness again, the blind fortuity of chance, the arbitrary halt and desperate entrenchment of his spirit in this town of Tours.

Now, after the savage kaleidoscope of these months of hope and grief and ecstasy, of desolation and despair, of passion, love, and suffering, of maddened hunger and infuriate desire, after all the restless and insatiable seeking of his goaded, driven, and unresting soul, he had come at last to a place of quietness and pause; and suddenly he was like a desperate and bewildered man who has come in from the furious street of life to seek sanctuary and repose in the numb stillness of a tomb.

Day and night now, from dawn to dark, from sleeping until waking, in that strange spell of time and silence that was neither dream nor sleep nor waking vision, but that like an enchantment was miraculously composed of all, obsessed as a man exiled, banished, or condemned by fate to live upon a desert island without possibility of escape or return—he thought of home.

In that enchanted spell of time and silence, as men who gaze in visions across misty and illimitable seas, with the terrible homelessness of a man for whom there can never be return, with the terrible homelessness of a man who longs for home and has no home—with the impossible, hopeless, incurable and unutterable homesickness of the American, who is maddened by a longing for return, and does not know to what he can return, whose brain burns night and day with the maddened hope, whose heart aches night and day with the smothering and incurable ache of the houseless, homeless, and forsaken atom of the earth who has no goal or ending for his hunger, no final dwelling-place for his desire—he thought of home.

What was it? It was the furious desire, unceasing, unassuaged, of wandering and forsaken man—the lost American—who longs forever for return—and who has no door to enter, no room to dwell in, no single handsbreadth of certain, consecrated earth upon that continent of wild houseless space, to which he can return.

An astounding—an almost incredible thing—now happened. He had come to Tours, telling himself that now at last, at last, he was going "to settle down and write," that he was going to justify his voyage by the high purpose of creation. In his mind there swarmed various projects, cloudy, vague, and grandiose in their conception, of plays, books, stories, essays he must write: with desperate resolve he sat down grimly now to shape these grand designs into the stern and toilsome masonry of words. A few impatient, fragmentary beginnings. the opening pages of a story, the beginning speeches of a play—all crumpled in a wad and impatiently tossed aside—were the final results of this ambitious purpose.

And yet, write he did. Useless, fragmentary, and inchoate as were these first abortive efforts, he began to write now like a madman—as only a madman could write—driven by an insanity of sense and soul and feeling which he no longer could master or control, tranced in a hypnosis by whose fatal and insatiate compulsions he was forced, without will, to act. Gripped by that ungovernable desire, all ordered plans, designs, coherent projects for the work he had set out to do went by the board, were burned up in the flame of a quenchless passion, like a handful of dry straw. Seated at a table in his cold, little room that overlooked the old cobbled court of the hotel, he wrote ceaselessly from dawn to dark, sometimes from darkness on to dawn again— hurling himself upon the bed to dream, in a state of comatose awareness, strange sleeping-wakeful visions, dreams mad and terrible as the blinding imagery that now swept constantly across his brain its blaze of fire.

The words were wrung out of him in a kind of bloody sweat, they poured out of his finger tips, spat out of his snarling throat like writhing snakes; he wrote them with his heart, his brain, his sweat, his guts;

he wrote them with his blood, his spirit; they were wrenched out of the last secret source and substance of his life.

And in those words was packed the whole image of his bitter homelessness, his intolerable desire, his maddened longing for return. In those wild and broken phrases was packed the whole bitter burden of his famished, driven, over-laden spirit—all the longing of the wanderer, all the impossible and unutterable homesickness that the American, or any man on earth, can know.

They were all there—without coherence, scheme, or reason—flung down upon paper like figures blasted by the spirit's lightning stroke, and in them was the huge chronicle of the billion forms, the million names, the huge, single, and incomparable substance of America.

XCVII

At morning, in a foreign land, whether upon the mournful plains of Hungary, or in some quiet square of Georgian houses, embedded in the immensity of sleeping London, he awakes, and thinks of home; or in some small provincial town of France, he starts up from his sleep at night, he starts up in the living, brooding stillness of the night, for suddenly he thinks that he has heard there the sounds of America and the wilderness, the things that are in his blood, his heart, his brain, in every atom of his flesh and tissue, the things for which he draws his breath in labor, the things that madden him with an intolerable and nameless pain.

And what are they? They are the whistle-wail of one of the great American engines as it thunders through the continent at night, the sound of the voices of the city streets—those hard, loud, slangy voices, full of violence, humor, and recklessness, now stronger and more remote than the sounds of Asia—the sounds that come up from the harbor of Manhattan in the night—that magnificent and thrilling music of escape, mystery, and joy, with the mighty orchestration of the transatlantics, the hoarse little tugs, the ferryboats and lighters, those sounds that well up from the gulf and dark immensity of night and that pierce the entrails of the listener.

For this will always be one of the immortal and living things about the land, this will be an eternal and unchanging fact about that city whose only permanence is change: there will always be the great rivers flowing around it in the darkness, the rivers that have bounded so many nameless lives, those rivers which have moated in so many changes, which have girdled the wilderness and so much hard, brilliant, and sensational living, so much pain, beauty, ugliness, so much lust, murder, corruption, love, and wild exultancy.

They'll build great engines yet, and grander towers, but always the rivers run, in the day, in the night, in the dark, draining immensely their imperial tides out of the wilderness, washing and flowing by the coasts of the fabulous city, by all the little ticking sounds of time, by all the million lives and deaths of the city. Always the rivers run, and always there will be great ships upon the tide, always great horns are baying at the harbor's mouth, and in the night a thousand men have died while the river, always the river, the dark eternal river, full of strange secret time, washing the city's stains away, thickened and darkened by its dumpings, is flowing by us, by us to the sea.

He awakes at morning in a foreign land, and he thinks of home. He cannot rest, his heart is wild with pain and loneliness, he sleeps, but then he knows he sleeps, he hears the dark and secret spell of time about him; in ancient towns, thick tumbling chimes of the cathedral bells are thronging through the dark, but through the passages of his diseased and unforgetful sleep the sounds and memory of America make way: now it is almost dawn, a horse has turned into a street and in America, there is the sound of wheels, the lonely clop-clop of the hooves upon deserted pavements, silence, then the banging clatter of a can.

He awakes at morning in a foreign land, he draws his breath in labor in the wool-soft air of Europe: the wool-gray air is all about him like a living substance; it is in his heart, his stomach, and his entrails; it is in the slow and vital movements of the people; it soaks down from the sodden skies into the earth, into the heavy buildings, into the limbs and hearts and brains of living men. It soaks into the spirit of the wanderer; his heart is dull with the gray weariness of despair, it aches with hunger for the wilderness, the howling of great winds, the bite and sparkle of the clear, cold air, the buzz, the tumult and the wild exultancy. The wet, woolen air is all about him, and there is no hope. It was there before William the Conqueror; it was there before Clovis and Charles "the Hammer"; it was there before Attila; it was there before Hengist and Horsa; it was there before Vercingetorix and Julius Agricola.

It was there now; it will always be there. They had it in Merry England and they had it in Gay Paree; and they were seldom merry, and they were rarely gay. The wet, woolen air is over Munich; it is over

Paris; it is over Rouen and Madame Bovary; it soaks into England; it gets into boiled mutton and the Brussels sprouts; it gets into Hammersmith on Sunday; it broods over Bloomsbury and the private hotels and the British Museum; it soaks into the land of Europe and keeps the grass green. It has always been there; it will always be there. His eyes are mad and dull; he cannot sleep without the hauntings of phantasmal memory behind the eyes; his brain is overstretched and weary, it gropes ceaselessly around the prison of the skull, it will not cease.

The years are walking in his brain, his father's voice is sounding in his ears, and in the pulses of his blood the tom-tom's beat. His living dust is stored with memory: two hundred million men are walking in his bones; he hears the howling of the wind around forgotten eaves; he cannot sleep. He walks in midnight corridors; he sees the wilderness, the moon-drenched forests; he comes to clearings in the moonlit stubble, he is lost, he has never been here, yet he is at home. His sleep is haunted with the dreams of time; wires throb above him in the whiteness, they make a humming in the noonday heat.

The rails are laid across eight hundred miles of golden wheat, the rails are wound through mountains, they curve through clay-yellow cuts, they enter tunnels, they are built up across the marshes, they hug the cliff and follow by the river's bank, they cross the plains with dust and thunder, and they leap through flatness and the dull scrub-pine to meet the sea.

Then he awakes at morning in a foreign land, and thinks of home.

For we have awaked at morning in a foreign land and heard the bitter curse of their indictment, and we know what we know, and it will always be the same.

"One time!" their voices cried, leaning upon a bar the bitter weight of all their discontent. "One time! I've been back one time—just once in seven years," they said, "and Jesus that was plenty! One time was enough! To hell with that damned country! What have they got now but a lot of cheap spaghetti joints and skyscrapers?" they said. "If you want a drink, you sneak down three back-alleyways, get the once-over from a couple of ex-prize fighters, and then plank down a dollar for a shot of varnish that would rot the guts out of a goat! . . . And the women!"—the voices rose here with infuriated scorn—"What a nice lot of cold-blooded gold-digging bastards *they've* turned out to be! . . . I spent thirty dollars taking one of 'em to a show, and to a night-club

afterward! When bedtime came do you think I got anything out of it?
. . . 'You may kiss my little hand,' she says. . . . 'You may kiss my
little—that's what you may do,' " the voices snarled with righteous bitterness. "When I asked her if she was goin' to come through she started
to yell for the cops! . . . A woman who tried to pull one like that over
here would get sent to Siberia! . . . A nice country, I don't think! . . .
Now, get this! *Me,* I'm a Frenchman, see!" the voice said with a convincing earnestness. "These guys know how to *live,* see! This is my
country where I belong, see! . . . Johnny, luh même chose pour mwah
et m'seer! . . . Fill 'em up again, kid."

"Carpen-*teer!*" the voices then rose jeeringly, in true accents of French
pugnacity. "Sure, I'm a Frenchman—but Carpen-*teer!* Where do yuh
get that stuff? Christ, Dempsey could 'a' took that frog the best day that
he ever saw! . . . An accident!" the voices yelled. "Whattya mean—an
accident? Didn't I see the whole thing with my own eyes? Wasn't I
back there then? . . . Wasn't I talkin' t' Jack himself an hour after the
fight was over? . . . An accident! Jesus! The only accident was that
he let him last four rounds. 'I could have taken him in the first if I
wanted to,' Jack says to me. . . . Sure, I'm a Frenchman!" the voice
said with belligerent loyalty. "But Carpen*teer!* Jesus! Where do you
get that stuff?"

And, brother, I have heard the voices you will never hear, discussing
the graces of a life more cultured than any you will ever know—and I
know and I know, and yet it is still the same.

Bitterly, bitterly Boston one time more! the flying leaf, the broken
cloud—"I think," said they, "that we will live here now. I think," they
said, "that we are running down to Spain next week so Francis can do a
little writing. . . . And really," their gay yet cultivated tones continued,
"it's wonderful what you can do here if you only have a little money.
. . . *Yes,* my dear!" their refined accents continued in a tone of gay conviction. "It's really quite incredible, you know. . . . I happen to know
of a real honest-to-goodness château near Blois that can be had for
something less than $7000! . . . It's all rather incredible, you know,"
those light, half-English tones went on, "when you consider what it takes
to live in Brookline! . . . Francis has always felt that he would like to
do a little writing, and I feel somehow the atmosphere is better here for
all that sort of thing—it really is, you know. Don't you think so?" said
those gay and cultivated tones of Boston which you, my brother, never
yet have heard. "And after all," those cultivated tones went on in accents

of a droll sincerity, "you see all the people here you really *care* to see, I *mean,* you know! They all come to Paris at one time or another—I *mean,* the trouble really is in getting a little time alone for yourself. . . . Or do you find it so?" the voices suavely, lightly, asked. . . . "Oh, look! look at that—there!" they cried with jubilant elation, "I mean that boy and his girl there, walking along with their arms around each other! . . . Don't you just a-do-o-re it? . . . Isn't it too *ma-a-rvelòus?*" those refined and silvery tones went on, with patriotic tenderness. "I mean, there's something so perfectly sweet and un-self-conscious about it all!" the voices said with all the cultivated earnestness of Boston! "Now *where?*—where?—would you see anything like that at home?" the voices said triumphantly.

(Seldom in Brookline, lady. Oh, rarely, seldom, almost never in the town of Brookline, lady. But on the Esplanade—did you ever go out walking on the Esplanade at night-time, in the hot and sultry month of August, lady? They are not Frenchmen, lady: they are all Jews and Irish and Italians, lady, but the noise of their kissing is like the noise the wind makes through a leafy grove—it is like the great hooves of a hundred thousand cavalry being pulled out of the marshy places of the earth, dear lady.)

". . . I *mean*—these people really understand that sort of thing so much better than we do. . . . They're so much *simpler* about it. . . . I mean, so much more graceful with that kind of thing. . . . Il faut un peu de sentiment, n'est-ce pas? . . . Or do you think so?" said those light, those gay, those silvery, and half-English tones of cultivated Boston, which you, my brother, never yet have heard.

(I got you, lady. That was French. I know. . . . But if I felt your leg, if I began by fondling gracefully your leg, if in a somewhat graceful Gallic way I felt your leg, and said, "Chérie! Petite chérie!"—would you remember, lady, this is Paris?)

Oh, bitterly, bitterly, Boston one time more: their silvery voices speak an accent you will never know, and of their loins is marble made, but, brother, there are corn-haired girls named Neilsen out in Minnesota, and the blonde thighs of the Lundquist girl could break a bullock's back.

Oh, bitterly, bitterly, Boston one time more: the French have little ways about them that we do not have, but brother, they're still selling cradles down in Georgia, and in New Orleans their eyes are dark, their white teeth bite you to the bone.

Oh, bitterly, bitterly, Boston, one time more, and of their flesh is cod-

fish made. Big Brother's still waiting for you with his huge, red
fist, behind the barn up in the State of Maine, and they're still having
shotgun marriages at home.

Oh, brother, there are voices you will never hear—ancestral voices
prophesying war, my brother, and rare and radiant voices that you
know not of, as they have read us into doom. The genteel voices of
Oxenford broke once like chimes of weary, unenthusiastic bells across
my brain, speaking to me compassionately its judgment on our corrupted lives, gently dealing with the universe, my brother, gently and
without labor—gently, brother, gently, it dealt with all of us, with easy
condescension and amused disdain:

"I'm afraid, old boy," the genteel voice of Oxenford remarked, "you're
up against it over thöh. . . . I really am. . . . Thöh's no place thö faw
the individual any longah,"—the genteel voice went on, un-individual
brother. "Obviously," that tolerant voice instructed me, "obviously,
thöh can be no cultuah in a country so completely lackin' in tradition as
is yoähs. . . . It's all so objective—if you see what I main—thöh's no
place left faw the innah life," it said, oh, outward brother! ". . . We
Europeans have often obsöhved (it's *very* curious, you know) that the
*Amer*ican is incapable of any real feelin'—it seems quite impawsible faw
him to distinguish between true emotion an' sentimentality—an' he in-
vayably chooses the lattah! . . . *Curious, isn't it?*—or do you think so,
brother? Of co'se, thöh is yoäh beastly dreadful sex-prawblem. . . .
Yoäh women! . . . Oh, deah, deah! . . . Perhaps we'd bettah say no
moah . . . but, thöh you *ah!*"—right in the eye, my brother. "Yoäh
country is a matriahky, my deah fellah . . . it really is, you know."
. . . if you can follow us, dear brother. "The women have the men in a
state of complete subjection . . . the male is rapidly becomin' moah
sexless an' emasculated"—that genteel voice of doom went on—"No!—
Decidedly you have quite a prawblem befoah you. . . . Obviously thöh
can be no cultuah while such a condition puhsists. . . . *That* is why
when my friends say to me, 'You ought to see *America*, . . . you really
ought, you know.' . . . I say, 'No, thanks. . . . If you don't mind, I'd
rathah not. . . . I think I'll stay at home . . . I'm sorry,'" the compassionate tones of Oxenford went on, "but that's the way I feel—it
really is, you know. . . . Of co'se, I know you couldn't undahstand my
feelin'—faw aftah all, you ah a Yank—but thöh you ah! Sorry!" it said
regretfully, as it spoke its courteous but inexorable judgments of eternal

exile, brother, and removed forever the possibility of your ever hearing it. "But that's the way I feel! I hope you don't mind," the voice said gently, with compassion.

No, sir, I don't mind. We don't mind, he, she, it, or they don't mind. Nobody minds, sir, nobody minds. Because, just as you say, sir, oceans are between us, seas have sundered us, there is a magic in you that we cannot fathom—a light, a flame, a glory—an impalpable, indefinable, incomprehensible, undeniable something-or-other, something which I can never understand or measure because—just as you say, sir—with such compassionate regret, I am—I am—a Yank.

'Tis true, my brother, we are Yanks. Oh, 'tis true, 'tis true! I am a Yank! Yet, wherefore Yank, good brother? Hath not a Yank ears? Hath not a Yank lies, truths, bowels of mercy, fears, joys, and lusts? Is he not warmed by the same sun, washed by the same ocean, rotted by the same decay, and eaten by the same worms as a German is? If you kill him, does he not die? If you sweat him, does he not stink? If you lie with his wife or his mistress, does she not whore, lie, fornicate and betray, even as a Frenchman's does? If you strip him, is he not naked as a Swede? Is his hide less white than Baudelaire's? Is his breath more foul than the King of Spain's? Is his belly bigger, his neck fatter, his face more hoggish, and his eye more shiny than a Munich brewer's? Will he not cheat, rape, thieve, whore, curse, hate, and murder like any European? Aye—Yank! But wherefore, wherefore Yank—good brother?

Brother, have we come then from a fated stock? Augured from birth, announced by two dark angels, named in our mother's womb? And for what? For what? Father-less, to grope our feelers on the sea's dark bed, among the polyped squirms, the blind sucks and crawls and sea-valves of the brain, loaded with memory that will not die? To cry our love out in the wilderness, to wake always in the night, smiting the pillow in some foreign land, thinking forever of the myriad sights and sounds of home?

"While Paris Sleeps!"—By God, while Paris sleeps, to wake and walk and not to sleep; to wake and walk and sleep and wake, and sleep again, seeing dawn come at the window-square that cast its wedge before our glazed, half-sleeping eyes, seeing soft, hated foreign light, and breath-ing soft, dull languid air that could not bite and tingle up the blood, seeing legend and lie and fable wither in our sight as we saw what we saw, knew what we knew.

Sons of the lost and lonely fathers, sons of the wanderers, children of hardy loins, the savage earth, the pioneers, what had we to do with all their bells and churches? Could we feed our hunger on portraits of the Spanish king? Brother, for what? For what? To kill the giant of loneliness and fear, to slay the hunger that would not rest, that would not give us rest.

Of wandering forever, and the earth again. Brother, for what? For what? For what? For the wilderness, the immense and lonely land. For the unendurable hunger, the unbearable ache, the incurable loneliness. For the exultancy whose only answer is the wild goat-cry. For a million memories, ten thousand sights and sounds and shapes and smells and names of things that only we can know.

For what? For what? Not for a nation. Not for a people, not for an empire, not for a thing we love or hate.

For what? For a cry, a space, an ecstasy. For a savage and nameless hunger. For a living and intolerable memory that may not for a second be forgotten, since it includes all the moments of our lives, includes all we do and are. For a living memory; for ten thousand memories; for a million sights and sounds and moments; for something like nothing else on earth; for something which possesses us.

For something under our feet, and around us and over us; something that is in us and part of us, and proceeds from us, that beats in all the pulses of our blood.

Brother, for what?

First for the thunder of imperial names, the names of men and battles, the names of places and great rivers, the mighty names of the States. The name of The Wilderness; and the names of Antietam, Chancellorsville, Shiloh, Bull Run, Fredericksburg, Cold Harbor, the Wheat Fields, Ball's Bluff, and the Devil's Den; the names of Cowpens, Brandywine, and Saratoga; of Death Valley, Chickamauga, and the Cumberland Gap. The names of the Nantahalahs, the Bad Lands, the Painted Desert, the Yosemite, and the Little Big Horn; the names of Yancey and Cabarrus counties; and the terrible name of Hatteras.

Then, for the continental thunder of the States: the names of Montana, Texas, Arizona, Colorado, Michigan, Maryland, Virginia, and the two Dakotas; the names of Oregon and Indiana, of Kansas and the rich Ohio; the powerful name of Pennsylvania, and the name of Old Kentucky; the undulance of Alabama; the names of Florida and North Carolina.

In the red-oak thickets, at the break of day, long hunters lay for bear— the rattle of arrows in laurel leaves, the war-cries round the painted buttes, and the majestical names of the Indian Nations: the Pawnees, the Algonquins, the Iroquois, the Comanches, the Blackfeet, the Seminoles, the Cherokees, the Sioux, the Hurons, the Mohawks, the Navajos, the Utes, the Omahas, the Onondagas, the Chippewas, the Crees, the Chickasaws, the Arapahoes, the Catawbas, the Dakotas, the Apaches, the Croatans, and the Tuscaroras; the names of Powhatan and Sitting Bull; and the name of the Great Chief, Rain-In-The-Face.

Of wandering forever, and the earth again: in red-oak thickets, at the break of day, long hunters lay for bear. The arrows rattle in the laurel leaves, and the elmroots thread the bones of buried lovers. There have been war-cries on the Western trails, and on the plains the gunstock rusts upon a handful of bleached bones. The barren earth? Was no love living in the wilderness?

The rails go westward in the dark. Brother, have you seen starlight on the rails? Have you heard the thunder of the fast express?

Of wandering forever, and the earth again—the names of the mighty rails that bind the nation, the wheeled thunder of the names that net the continent: the Pennsylvania, the Union Pacific, the Santa Fé, the Baltimore and Ohio, the Chicago and Northwestern, the Southern, the Louisiana and Northern, the Seaboard Air Line, the Chicago, Milwaukee and Saint Paul, the Lackawanna, the New York, New Haven and Hartford, the Florida East Coast, the Rock Island, and the Denver and Rio Grande.

Brother, the names of the engines, the engineers, and the sleeping-cars: the great engines of the Pacific type, the articulated Mallets with three sets of eight-yoked driving-wheels, the 400-ton thunderbolts with J. T. Cline, T. J. McRae, and the demon hawk-eyes of H. D. Campbell on the rails.

The names of the great tramps who range the nation on the fastest trains: the names of the great tramps Oklahoma Red, Fargo Pete, Dixie Joe, Iron Mike, The Frisco Kid, Nigger Dick, Red Chi, Ike the Kike, and The Jersey Dutchman.

By the waters of life, by time, by time, Lord Tennyson stood among the rocks, and stared. He had long hair, his eyes were deep and sombre, and he wore a cape; he was a poet, and there was magic and mystery in his touch, for he had heard the horns of Elfland faintly blowing. And by the waters of life, by time, by time, Lord Tennyson stood among the cold, gray rocks, and commanded the sea to break—break—break! And the sea broke, by the waters of life, by time, by time, as Lord Tennyson commanded it to do, and his heart was sad and lonely as he watched the stately ships (of the Hamburg-American Packet Company, fares forty-five dollars and up, first-class) go on to their haven under the hill, and Lord Tennyson would that his heart could utter the thoughts that arose in him.

By the waters of life, by time, by time: the names of the mighty rivers, the alluvial gluts, the drains of the continent, the throats that drink America (Sweet Thames, flow gently till I end my song). The names of the men who pass, and the myriad names of the earth that abides for-ever: the names of the men who are doomed to wander, and the name of that immense and lonely land on which they wander, to which they return, in which they will be buried—America! The immortal earth which waits forever, the trains that thunder on the continent, the men who wander, and the women who cry out, "Return!"

Finally, the names of the great rivers that are flowing in the darkness (Sweet Thames, flow gently till I end my song).

By the waters of life, by time, by time: the names of great mouths, the mighty maws, the vast, wet, coiling, never-glutted and unending snakes that drink the continent. Where, sons of men, and in what other land will you find others like them, and where can you match the mighty music of their names?—The Monongahela, the Colorado, the Rio Grande, the Columbia, the Tennessee, the Hudson (Sweet Thames!); the Kennebec, the Rappahannock, the Delaware, the Penobscot, the Wabash, the Chesapeake, the Swannanoa, the Indian River, the Niagara (Sweet Afton!); the Saint Lawrence, the Susquehanna, the Tombigbee, the Nantahala, the French Broad, the Chattahoochee, the Arizona, and the Potomac (Father Tiber!)—these are a few of their princely names, these are a few of their great, proud, glittering names, fit for the im-mense and lonely land that they inhabit.

Oh, Tiber! Father Tiber! You'd only be a suckling in that mighty land! And as for you, sweet Thames, flow gently till I end my song: flow gently, gentle Thames, be well-behaved, sweet Thames, speak softly and politely, little Thames, flow gently till I end my song.

By the waters of life, by time, by time, and of the yellow cat that smites the nation, of the belly of the snake that coils across the land—of the terrible names of the rivers in flood, the rivers that foam and welter in the dark, that smash the levees, that flood the lowlands for two thousand miles, that carry the bones of the cities seaward on their tides: of the awful names of the Tennessee, the Arkansas, the Missouri, the Mississippi, and even the little mountain rivers, brothers, in the season of the floods.

Delicately they dive for Greeks before the railway station: the canoe glides gently through the portals of the waiting-room (for whites). Full fathom five the carcass of old man Lype is lying (of his bones is coral made) and delicately they dive for lunch-room Greeks before the railway station.

Brother, what fish are these? The floatage of sunken rooms, the sodden bridal-veils of poverty, the slime of ruined parlor plush, drowned faces in the family album; and the blur of long-drowned eyes, blurred features, whited, bloated flesh.

Delicately they dive for Greeks before the railway station. The stern, good, half-drowned faces of the brothers Trade and Mark survey the tides. Cardui! Miss Lillian Leitzell twists upon one arm above the flood; the clown, half-sunken to his waist, swims upward out of swirling yellow; the tiger bares his teeth above the surges of a river he will never drink. The ragged tatters of the circus posters are plastered on soaked boards. And delicately they dive for Greeks before the railway station.

Have we not seen them, brother?

For what are we, my brother? We are a phantom flare of grieved desire, the ghostling and phosphoric flicker of immortal time, a brevity of days haunted by the eternity of the earth. We are an unspeakable utterance, an insatiable hunger, an unquenchable thirst; a lust that bursts our sinews, explodes our brains, sickens and rots our guts, and rips our hearts asunder. We are a twist of passion, a moment's flame of love and ecstasy, a sinew of bright blood and agony, a lost cry, a music of pain and joy, a haunting of brief, sharp hours, an almost captured beauty, a demon's whisper of unbodied memory. We are the dupes of time.

For, brother, what are we?

We are the sons of our father, whose face we have never seen, we are the sons of our father, whose voice we have never heard, we are the sons of our father, to whom we have cried for strength and comfort in our agony, we are the sons of our father, whose life like ours was lived in solitude and in the wilderness, we are the sons of our father, to whom only can we speak out the strange, dark burden of our heart and spirit, we are the sons of our father, and we shall follow the print of his foot forever.

XCVIII

How long he had remained at Tours he scarcely knew: suspended in this spell of time and memory, he seemed to have detached himself not only from the infinite connections that bound him to the past, but from every project and direction that he had considered for the future. Day after day he stayed in his little room above the cobbled court of the hotel; he ate his meals there, going out at nightfall to eat and drink in a café, to walk about the streets, once or twice to go home with a woman of the town, and finally to come back to his room, to write furiously for hours, and then, stretched out in bed, nailed to the rock of a furiously wakeful sleep, to live again through the immense and spaceless images of night, in an alert but comatose hypnosis of the will.

One morning he awoke with a shock of apprehension, the foreboding of calamitous mischance. It was the first time in weeks that he had taken thought of the state of his resources, or felt any care or worry for the future. He counted his money with feverish haste, and discovered that less then 250 francs remained. For a moment he sat on the edge of the bed, holding the little wad of franc notes in his hand, stunned and bewildered by this sudden realization that his funds were exhausted, and for the moment not knowing what to do. His hotel bill for the week was due; he went at once to the bureau and asked for it; a hasty calculation assured him that when he had paid it, less than twenty francs would be left.

He knew no one in Tours to whom he could appeal for aid; one glance at the impeccable, cold courtesy of the female face, hard, dark and gallic, in the bureau of the hotel—the basalt of the eyes, the line of hair across the brows—told him that he could as soon wring milk and honey from the cobblestones as extract an ounce of charitable relief from the granite coffers of her soul. The brows drew in, the black eyes hardened with a cold narrowing of mistrust: even before he spoke he saw she had read the story of his profligate extravagance, and that from that moment the hard propriety of her suspicious soul had been turned against him with that virtuous dislike which such people feel for unmonied men. When he spoke, therefore, it was to tell her he was leaving that day: she inclined her dark, hard face impassively, saying: "Oui, monsieur," and asked if he would have his room vacated by twelve o'clock.

He went to the railway station and looked up rates and distances. During the whole period of his stay in Tours—in fact, during the whole course of his wanderings since leaving Paris—he had been vaguely assured that he was moving in the general direction of Provence, Marseilles, and the South. He now discovered, on consulting a map, that he was off this course by some hundreds of kilometers, and on the southwest road to Bordeaux, the Pyrenees, and Spain. For a moment, he was decided to take the train for Bordeaux—a post-card from Ann had been mailed from Carcassonne, and she had informed him that they were on their way to Biarritz. A brief inquiry, however, convinced him that his funds were by no means sufficient to get him even as far as Bordeaux and, over there, he felt, his case was more desperate than ever. He knew no one there and had no hope of meeting any one he knew. He discovered also that the lowest fare back to Paris—the third-class fare— was about thirty-four francs, almost twice as much as he possessed.

Finally, with a feeling of malevolent joy—for, curiously, a growing realization of his plight, and the dark, hard eyes of the Frenchmen fixed on him in an expression of avaricious mistrust, had now wakened in him a jubilant indifference, a desire to roar with laughter—he thought of Orléans and the Countess.

He found that his funds were sufficient for third-class fare to Orléans, which was about seventeen francs, and that a train was leaving in an hour. Returning to the hotel, he packed his valise with frenzied haste, throwing his clothing in and stamping it down with his feet, rode to the station in the hotel's horse-drawn bus, and an hour later was on his way back to Orléans.

Late March had come: the day was overcast with thin, gray clouds, an uncertain milky radiance of light; the fields and earth and forests, still bare, had a moist, thawed fertility that spoke of spring. On the way up, snow began to fall, a brief flurry of large, wet flakes that melted as they fell: it was soon over, and the sun broke through in thin, wavering gusts of light.

There were no other passengers in his compartment; he sat looking

out the window across the wet fields, and from time to time, as he
visualized the look of startled, crafty apprehension on the Countess' face
when she saw him, he burst into wild, sudden whoops and yells of
laughter that echoed loudly above the steady pounding of the wheels.

It was noon when he reached Orléans: he took his heavy bag and
went limping out across the station square, pausing once to rest his
aching arm and change his grip. On entering the hotel he found Yvonne
in the *bureau*. She looked up from her ledger as he entered, her dark
face hardening with a mistrust of cold surprise as she saw him.

"Monsieur has returned to stay?" she inquired, and looked towards
his valise. "You wish a room?"

"I do not know yet," he said easily. "I shall let you know in a few
minutes. At present, I should like to speak to the Countess. Is she here?"

She did not answer for a moment, her black brows gathered in a line,
and her eyes grew perceptibly harder, colder, more mistrustful as she
looked at him.

"Yes. I s'ink she is in her room," she said at length. "I vill see. . . .
Jean!" she called sharply, and struck a bell.

The porter appeared, started with surprise when he saw the youth,
and then smiled cordially and greeted him in friendly fashion. Then he
turned inquiringly to Yvonne. She spoke curtly:

"Dites à Madame la Comtesse que Monsieur, le jeune Américain, est
revenu. Il attend."

"Mais oui, monsieur," the porter said briskly, turning towards him.
"Et **votre bagage?" he looked inquiringly** at the valise. "Vous restez
ici?"

"Je ne sais pas. Je vous dirai plus tard. Merci," he said, as the porter
took the valise, and put it away behind the office desk.

The porter departed with his message. Yvonne returned to her books,
and he waited, pacing the hall in a state of nervous elation, until he
heard the old woman's voice, sharp, startled, excited, speaking to the
porter on the floor above. Then he heard her coming down the stairs,
turned and faced her sharply-inquiring, apprehensive face as she came
down, and was vigorously pumping her uncertain and unwilling little
claw, before she had time to stammer out a greeting:

"But what—why—what brings you here?" she said. "I thought you
had returned to Paris by now. Where have you been?" she asked
sharply.

"In Tours," he answered.

"Tours! But what were you doing there all this time? . . . What happened to you?" she asked suspiciously.

"Ah, Countess," he said solemnly, "it is a long story." Then, with a deliberate burlesque of portentous gravity, he lowered his voice and whispered hoarsely, "I fell among thieves."

"What—?" she said in a faltering tone. "What are you saying? . . . You mean you have come back here . . . that you have no . . . how much money have you left?" she demanded sharply.

He thrust his hand into his trousers pocket, fished around and pulled out a few small coins: four two-franc pieces, a franc, two twenty-five-centime coins, a ten- and a five-centime piece——

"That's all," he said, counting them over. "Nine francs sixty-five."

"W-w-w-w-what?" she stammered. "Nine francs sixty-five—do you mean that's all you have left?"

"That's all," he said cheerfully, "but now that I'm here at last it doesn't matter."

"Here!" she gasped. "Do you mean you are going—what do you intend to do?" she said sharply.

"Oh," he said easily, "I shall wait here until I get money from America."

"And—and how long do you think that will take?" the old woman was twisting her skinny fingers with feverish apprehension.

"Oh, not long," he said airily. "I wrote my mother yesterday, and it ought not to take over four or five weeks to get an answer."

"Four or five weeks!" the old woman said hoarsely. "What are you saying? Four or five weeks, and you have nine francs sixty-five in your pockets! My God! the man is mad!"

"Oh, that part of it will be all right, I guess," he said with an easy laugh. "I told my mother all about you and Monsieur and Madame Vatel, and all my other friends here, and how good you had been to me, and how you were always befriending Americans, and how they call you Little Mother. I told her you couldn't have been kinder to me if you'd been my own mother, and that she didn't need to worry about me at all. So I guess that part of it's all right," he concluded comfortably. "I told her that I'd just put up here at the hotel, and that you and the Vatels would take good care of me until the money comes from home."

"Put up here! . . . For four or five weeks! . . . Hush, my boy! Hush!" she whispered, clutching him feverishly with her bony little claw, and casting an apprehensive glance towards Yvonne whose dark head was lowered studiously above her ledger, but who suggested, by a certain strained attentiveness of posture, that she was missing none of the conversation.

"Come," the Countess whispered feverishly again, pulling him towards the stairway as she spoke. "You come with me, my boy. I want to talk to you alone."

They went upstairs to a parlor on the first floor, deserted, closed, a little stale with its sumptuous bordello furnishings of gilt and crimson plush. There the Countess turned to him, and said directly:

"See here, my boy. What you want to do is out of the question. It will be impossible for you to stay here for four or five weeks! Impossible!" she cried, twisting her bony little hands with growing agitation. "It cannot be done!"

He looked surprised, a little pained.

"Why?" he said.

"Because," she said, and now at last her tone was simple and direct in its quiet assertion, "the Vatels will not keep you here—they will not give you credit for so long a time——"

"And you?" he said quietly.

"My friend," the old woman answered simply, "I have not got it." She raised her bony little shoulders in a shrug. "At the present moment I have nothing—not a sou! I get a little money from America on the first and fifteenth of each month—if I had it, I would give it to you, but I have nothing now. And what I get would not be nearly enough to pay your expenses here for five weeks. It cannot be done."

For the first time since his return he felt respect and sympathy for her; in face of the plain and honest directness of her confession all of his former humor of cynical mockery had vanished. He said:

"In that case, it cannot be done. You are right. I must try to get help elsewhere."

"You nave friends in Paris, haven't you? You know people there—Americans?"

"Yes—I think I could get help from some one if I were in Paris."

"Then I shall try to help you to get there," she said quickly. "How much will you need?"

"I think the third-class fare from here is about seventeen francs," he said.

"And you have—how much? Nine sixty-five?" She calculated

swiftly, was silent a moment, and then with an air of decision, marked by a faint flush of painful embarrassment on her withered cheek as she thought of the unpleasant task before her, she said: "If you will wait here, I will go below and see what I can do with these people. . . . I do not know," she said shortly, the faint flush deepening as she spoke, "but I will try."

She left him, and presently he heard voices below, mixed in rapid and excited argument. In ten minutes the old woman returned. In her hand she held a ten-franc note.

"Here," she said, giving it to him. "With what you have, it will be enough to get you to Paris. I have inquired. There is a train in twenty minutes. Now, my boy," she said quickly, taking him by the arm, "you must go. You will just have time to buy your ticket and get on the train. You have no time to lose."

He had been surprised and disappointed at the meagre exactness of her loan: he had eaten nothing all day long and suddenly, with no funds to spare and the prospect of a continued and indefinite fast before him, he felt ravenously hungry. And now it was his turn to redden with embarrassment; he found it difficult to speak, and in a moment said hesitantly:

"I wonder if these people here would let me have a sandwich. . . . I've had nothing to eat."

She did not answer; he saw the faint flush deepen on her sallow cheeks again and, already sorry for the additional distress his request had caused her, he said quickly:

"No, it doesn't matter. I'll get something when I get to Paris. Besides, there's not time now, anyway. I'll have to get that train."

"Yes," she said quickly, with relief. "I think you should. That is best. . . . And now, my boy, make haste. You have no more time to lose."

"Good-bye, Countess," he said, taking her by the hand, and suddenly feeling for the old, lonely, and penniless woman the deepest affection and respect he had ever felt for her. "You have really been my friend. I'm sorry that I've had to cause you this trouble. I'll send you the money when I get to Paris. Good-bye, now, and good-luck to you."

When she answered, her voice was quiet and her old eyes were sad and tranquilly resigned:

"Ah," she said, "I was afraid that this would happen to you. I have known so many Americans—they are so reckless, so extravagant, they do not watch their money. . . . Good-bye, my boy," she now said quietly, clasping his hand. "Take care of yourself and do not get into any more trouble. . . . Let me know if all goes well with you. . . . Good-bye, good-bye. . . . Ah, you are so young, aren't you? Some day you will learn. . . . Good-bye, God bless you—you must hurry now— good-bye. Good-bye."

She followed him as he went quickly down the stairs, and stood on the stairs watching him as he departed. His valise had been put out before the *bureau,* where he could get it easily: Yvonne and Madame Vatel were waiting silently in the office. Yvonne did not speak at all; when he spoke to Madame Vatel, she cocked her head a little, and said coldly: "Monsieur."

He seized the grip and started for the door with it at a rapid limping stride. At the door he paused, turned, and saw the Countess, still stand- ing on the stairs, and looking at him with old, sad eyes.

"Good-bye," he cried in jubilant farewell. "Good-bye, Countess."

"Good-bye, my boy," her voice was so weary, old, and sad he could scarcely hear her.

Then he limped rapidly away from the hotel, across the square, and towards the station and the train.

All through the afternoon the train roared up across the fat and fertile countryside towards Paris. A late sun broke through ragged clouds of torn gold: the light was wild and radiant with a prophecy of spring. In the compartment, his only companion was a young soldier: a boy of eighteen, tall, gawky, big of hand and foot and limb, looking even clumsier than he really was in his thick-soled army shoes, his blue- olive uniform—his long shanks coarsely wound with bands of olive cloth.

The boy had a friendly, olive-colored face, a little marred by pimples and fuzzy unshaved hair; he talked constantly, amiably indifferent to his companion's foreign speech and manner, garrulously friendly in a hoarse boy voice.

In the middle of the afternoon he began to unpack various bundles from the staggering impedimenta of military equipment with which he was surrounded. From a pocket of his overcoat he solemnly fished out an enormous tin of sardines. From another package he took out a gigantic bottle of red wine, and with the same gravity, began to unfold from its wrapping in a newspaper a three-foot loaf of crusty bread.

Then, with the same deliberate concentration, he opened the sardine tin, uncorked the wine-bottle and took a hearty preliminary swig, pulled out a clasp-knife with an evil-looking six-inch blade and, holding the loaf gripped firmly between his knees, began with a backward motion to carve a crisp and liberal slab out of the crusty loaf. This done, he put the bread aside, solemnly impaled a huge sardine upon the point of his gleaming knife, smacked it down upon the slab of bread and, furnishing himself with another hearty swig of the red wine, began to poke the sandwich happily away towards its intended destination, carrying on a choked but completely unperturbed conversation with his companion as he did so.

And his fellow traveller, gazing on that coarse but appetizing fare, felt the pangs of hunger awake in him again with such maddening insistence, that the whole legend of his starved desire must have been written on his yearning face and greedy eyes. At any rate, the young soldier, his mouth still crammed with food, uttered some inarticulate but friendly sounds, in which the word "Mangez" alone was intelligible, suddenly thrust loaf, bottle, knife, and sardine tin towards his starved companion, and with a gesture of rude encouragement, hoarsely spattered forth again:

"Mangez!"

The fellow traveller required no second bidding. He fell to ravenously on sardines, wine, and crusty loaf; they sat there cramming themselves enthusiastically, uttering choked and muffled sounds from time to time, and grinning at each other amiably.

Nothing he had ever eaten tasted as good as that coarse fare; the strong, plain wine was pulsing warmly in his veins, the food made a warm glow in his grateful belly; outside, the sun had broken through in stripes of ragged gold and bronze, above the wheels he could hear great roars of hearty country laughter from another compartment, the high, rich, sanguinary voice of a Frenchman as he cried "Parbleu!"

And he was going back to Paris again, without a penny, a prospect, or a plan, and he felt no care nor pain nor trouble any longer—nothing but wild joy and jubilant happiness such as he had never felt before. He did not know why.

XCIX

EARLY in April, money came from home, and he was on his way again. This time he started South in true earnest, hurtling southward on one of the crack trains of the P. L. M., his nose flattened against the window of the compartment, and his eyes glued on the landscape with such an unwinking intensity, a desperate and insatiate greed, that his fellow passengers stared at him curiously, and then looked at one another with quiet smiles and winks.

As it had always done, the movement and experience of the train filled him with a sense of triumph, joy, and luxury. The crack express, with its gleaming cars, its richly furnished compartments, its luxurious restaurant, warm with wine and food and opulence and suave service, together with the appearance of the passengers, who had the look of ease and wealth and cosmopolitan assurance that one finds among people who travel on such trains, awoke in him again the feeling of a nameless and impending joy, the fulfilment of some impossible happiness, the feeling of wealth and success which a train had always given him, even when he had only a few dollars in his pocket, and that now, in the groomed luxury of this European express, was immeasurably enhanced.

On such a train, indeed, the compact density of the European continent became thrilling in its magical immediacy: one felt everywhere around him—in the assured and wealthy-looking men, the lovely and seductive-looking women—even in the landscape that stretched past with its look of infinite cultivation, its beautifully checkered design of fields, its ancient scheme of towns and villages and old farm buildings—the sense of a life rich with the maturity of centuries, infinitely various and fascinating in its evocation of a world given without reserve to pleasure, love, and luxury—in short, the American's dream of "Europe," a world with all the labor, pain, and fear, the rasping care and fury of his own harsh world, left out.

At Lyons, mid-way on his journey to the South, he left the train. And again, he did not know the reason for his stopping: he had been told that "there was nothing to be seen," but the place was a great city; his old hunger for new cities conquered him, he paused to stay a day, and stayed a week.

Later, he could remember just four things that had held him there in that great provincial town. They were a river, two restaurants, and a girl. The river was the Rhône; it came foaming out of the Alps to form at Lyons its juncture with the Saône. Day after day he sat on a café terrace looking at the river; it foamed past bright and glacial, green as emerald, cold and shining, bearing in forever its message of the Alps. the thaw of crystal ice, the coming on of spring. All of the coming of the spring was somehow written in the cold, sparkling and unforgettable green loveliness of that shining water; it haunted him like something he had always known, like something he had found, like something he would one day discover.

The food in the town was incomparable. It was a native cookery, a food belonging to the region—plain, pungent, peasant-like and nobly good, there is in all the world no better cooking than can be found in the great provincial town of Lyons.

At two places there, La Mère Guy's, and La Mère Filliou's, they call their best cooks by the name of "mother." They offer eating fit for kings, yet all so reasonable and plain that almost any man can afford it. La Mère Guy's establishment is in an old house with various old rooms all used as restaurants. The floor is sanded, there are no suave carpets, no low murmuring of refined voices, no thin tinkle of musical glasses, none of the suave, worldly luxury that one finds in the great restaurants of Paris. It is a place not made for tourists—for Lyons is not a tourist town, and what tourist before ever came there to eat?—It is a place made for the Lyonnais—according to their taste—and one will find them there at Mother Guy's and Filliou's, in all their robust, straightforward eating earnestness. Mother Filliou's is a more open sort of place than Mother Guy's; it is across the river, away from the central part of Lyons, which is on an island formed by the green girdling of the Rhône and Saône. At Mother Filliou's one can look inside; when the weather permits, most people eat outside on a terrace: Mother Filliou's has more sunlight, open air, and gaiety, but the rooms at Mother Guy's have a more convenient, closed, and homely appearance. Both places are crowded with solid-looking Lyonnais of both sexes, their faces filled with sanguinary life, their voices loud and robust, their napkins tucked in under their chins, as they set heartily to work.

The food is largely chicken, beef, and fish, superbly cooked. One will never forget the chicken at Mother Guy's or Mother Filliou's: the chicken is plump and tender country chicken, fresh from the lovely countryside near Lyons, it is so crisp and succulent it almost melts away in your mouth. The beef is thick and juicy and tender, everything is cooked plainly, but with all the peasant spice and pungency; they like spicy and robust relishes, and one eats whole onions, pickled in a kind of brine. There, people drink only one wine, but that is Beaujolais, a plain, grand wine that in this town is cheaper than mineral water, and seems made by nature to wash down such victuals as these people eat.

On the opposite side of the central isle of Lyons, which is the side bounded by the Saône, there is a steep hill surmounted by the church of Notre-Dame-de-Fourvière, a famous place of pilgrimage for the devout. And there, one day, while pilgrims filed in to see the relics, and pay devotion to their saint, and while some monks were chanting from their sonorous and reverberating litany through the great spaces, he saw a girl he could not forget: she sat down across the aisle from him, looked at him, smiled drowsily. She was small, plump; her figure was erotically seductive; she raised her head, and seemed to listen drowsily to chanting monks, and he saw that in her neck, a warm, slow pulse was beating— slowly, slowly, richly, warmly beating. She turned her eyes, which were gray and smoky with a cat-like potency, and looked at him again, smiled drowsily, and slowly crossed her heavy legs with a slow, sensual sliding of warm silk. And all the time, the pulse beat slowly, richly, with a drowsy warmth of maddening and hot desire—and that was the last of the four things he saw, remembered, and could not forget of Lyons.

A shining river, emerald green, and magic with its Alpine prescience of spring, of known, undiscovered loveliness; the noble cooking of Mother Guy and Mother Filliou; a pulse in the throat of an unknown girl, that beat its slow, warm promise of fulfilled desire—these, of a town of more than six hundred thousand lives and faces, were all that later clearly would remain.

The rest was smoke and silence—some faces here and there, a scheme of streets, an enormous square, a hill crowned with a pilgrim's church, a priest, broad-hatted, with slit mouth and gimlet eyes, some museum relics out of ancient Gaul—all fugitive and broken, gone like smoke.

. . . An emerald river, and a shining light; some glorious cookery and drink; the pulse-beat in the warm throat of a girl—these would remain. Smoke! Smoke! has it been otherwise with any man?

And again, he was hurtling southward in a train.

C

Time, please, time. . . . What time is it? . . . Gentlemen, it's closing time. . . . Time, gentlemen . . . that time of year thou may'st in me behold. . . . In the good old summer-time. . . . I keep thinking of you all the time . . . all the time . . . and all the time. . . . A long time ago the world began. . . . There goes the last bell, run, boy, run: you'll just have time. . . . There are times that make you ha-a-ap-py, there are times that make you sa-a-ad. . . . Do you remember the night you came back to the University: it was that time right after your brother's death, you had just come back that night, I know I was coming across the campus before Old East when I saw you coming up the path with a suitcase in your hand. It was raining but we both stopped and began to talk there—we stepped in under one of the oak-trees because it was raining. I can still remember the old, wet, shining bark of the tree—the reason I can remember is that you put your hand out and leaned against the tree as you talked to me and I kept thinking how tall you were—of course you didn't notice it, you weren't conscious of it but you had your head up and it must have been about eight feet above the ground. But I can remember everything we said that night—it was that time when you came back just after your brother's death: that's when it was all right, I guess that's why I can remember it so well. . . . It's time all little boys were in bed. . . . Now, boy, I'll tell you when it was: it was that time your Papa made that trip to California—the reason that I know is I had just got a letter from him that morning written from Los Angeles telling me how he had seen John Balch and old Professor Truman, and how they had both gone into the real-estate business out there, and both of them getting rich by leaps and bounds —but that's just exactly when it was, sir, the time he made that trip out there in 1906, along towards the end of February, and I had just finished reading his letter when—well as I say now . . . Garfield, Arthur, Harrison and Hayes . . . time of my father's time, life of his life. "Ah, Lord," he said, "I knew them all—and all of them are gone. I'm the only one that's left. By God, I'm getting old." . . . In the year that the locusts came, something that happened in the year the locusts came, two voices that I heard there in that year. . . . Child! Child! It seems so long ago since the year the locusts came, and all of the trees were eaten bare: so much has happened, and it seems so long ago. . . .

"To keep time with!"—To Eugene Gant, Presented to Him on the Occasion of His Twelfth Birthday, by His Brother, B. H. Gant, Oct. 3, 1912. . . . "To keep time with!" . . . Up on the mountain, down in the valley, deep, deep in the hill, Ben, cold, cold, cold.

"Ces arbres——"

"Monsieur?" a thin, waxed face of tired Gaul, professionally attentive,

the eyebrows arched perplexedly above old tired eyes, the waiter's
fatigued napkin on the arm.

"—Monsieur——?"

"Ces arbres—" he stammered, pointing helplessly— "J'ai—j'ai—mais
je les ai vu—avant——"

"Monsieur?"—the eyebrows still more patient, puzzled and concerned,
the voice wrought with attention—"vous dites, monsieur?"

"J'ai dit que—ces arbres—je les ai vu—" he blundered helplessly, and
suddenly muttered with a face gone sullen and ashamed— "Ça ne fait
rien—l'addition, s'il vous plaît."

The waiter stared at him a moment with courteous, slightly pained
astonishment, then smiled apologetically, shrugged his shoulders slightly in a movement of defeat, and saying, "Bien, monsieur," took the ten-
franc note upon the table, counted the racked saucers, and made change
for him.

When the waiter had gone, he sat for a moment staring at the trees.
It was in the month of April, it was night, he was alone on the café
terrace, and yet the chill air was touched with a fragrance that was soft,
thrilling and mysterious—a citrous fume, the smell of unknown flowers,
or perhaps not even this—but only the ghost of a perfume, the thrilling,
barren, and strangely seductive odor of Provence.

It was a street in the little town of Arles, at night—an old, worn,
rutted, curiously dirty-looking street, haunted by the trunks of immense
and dusty-looking trees. He had never been here before, the scene was
strange and haunting as a dream, and yet it was instantly and intolerably
familiar. It was, somehow, he thought, like a street he had been to in
some small town in the hot South at the faded end of summer—a South
Carolina town, he thought it must be, and he was sure that he would
hear the sound of familiar, unknown voices, the passing of feet, the
rustling of quiet, tired leaves. And then he saw again how strange it
was, and could see the tired waiter racking chairs and tables for the
night, and in the café tired lights and emptiness, and the white, tired
light upon the old dusty street, the huge haunting boles of the great
trees; and he knew that he had never been along that way before.

Then he got up and walked away, and put his hand upon the trunk
of one of the old trees: it was white and felt smooth to the touch, and
was somewhat like the sycamores at home—and yet it was not this that
haunted him with troubling memory. He felt, intolerably, that the place,
the scene, the great wreathed branches of the trees, were something he

had seen before—that he had seen it here from the same spot where now he sat—but *when, when, when?*

And suddenly, with a thrill of recognition that flashed across his brain like an electric spark, he saw that he was looking at the same trees that Van Gogh had painted in his picture of the roadmenders at their work in Arles, that the scene was the same, that he was sitting where the painter had sat before. And he noted that the trees had tall, straight, symmetrical trunks, and remembered that the trees that Vincent had painted had great, tendoned trunks that writhed and twisted like creatures in a dream—and yet were somehow more true than truth, more real than this reality. And the great vinelike trunks of these demented trees had wound and rooted in his heart, so that now he could not forget them, nor see this scene in any other way than that in which Van Gogh had painted it.

When he got up, the waiter was still racking chairs upon the tables, and the white and quiet light from the café fell like a tired stillness on the dusty street, and he walked away, haunted by unfathomed memories of home, and with something in his heart he could not utter.

In all the dreams and visions that now swarmed across his sleep, dreams and visions which can only be described as haunted fatally by the sense of time—his mind seemed to exercise the same complete control it ever had shown in all the operations of its conscious memory. He slept, and knew he slept, and saw the whole vast structure of the sleeping world about him as he slept; he dreamed, and knew he dreamed, and like a sorcerer, drew upward at his will, out of dark deeps and blue immensities of sleep, the strange, dark fish of his imagining.

Sometimes they came with elvish flakings of a hoary light, sometimes they came like magic and the promise of immortal joy, they came with victory and singing and a shout of triumph in his blood, and again he felt the strange and deathless joy of voyages: he was a passenger upon great ships again, he walked the broad, scrubbed decks exultantly, and smelled the hot, tarred roofs of powerful and ugly piers, he smelled the spermy sea-wrack of the harbor once again, the wastes of oil, the sharp, acrid and exultant smoke from busy little tugs, the odor of old, worn plankings, drenched with sunlight, and the thousand strange compacted spices of the laden piers. Again he felt the gold and sapphire loveliness of a Saturday in May, and drank the glory of the earth into his heart, and heard in lucent and lyrical air the heavy shattering "baugh" of the great ship's whistle, as it spoke gloriously, of springtime, new lands and departure. Again he saw ten thousand faces, touched with their strange admixture of sorrow and joy, swarm past the openings of the pier, and again he saw the flashing tides that girdled the city, whitened around the prows of a hundred boats, and gleaming with a million iridescent points of light. Again the great walled cliff, the crowded isle, the fabulous spires and ramparts of the city, as delicate as the hues of light that flashed around them, slid away from him, and one by one, the great ships, with the proud sweep of their breasts of white, their opulent storied superstructure, their music of power and speed, fell into line at noon on Saturday. And now, like bridled horses held in rein, with princely chafe and curvetings, they breach the mighty harbor, nose the narrows, circle slowly to brief pauses at the pilot's boat, and then, like racers set loose from the barriers, they are sent away, their engines tremble to a mighty stroke, the ships are given to the sea, to solitude, and to their proper glory once more.

And again he walked the decks, he walked the decks alone, and saw the glittering sea-flung city melt within his sight, and watched the sandy edges of the land fade away, and felt the incredible gold and sapphire glory of the day, the sparkle of dancing waters, and smelled salt, seaborne air again, and saw upon the decks the joyful and exultant faces of the passengers, their looks of wonder, hope, and speculation, as they looked into the faces of strange men and women, now by the miracle of the voyage and chance isled with them in the loneliness of water, upon the glorious prison of a ship. And again he saw the faces of the lovely women, and saw the lights of love and passion in their eyes, and again he felt the plangent and depthless undulance, the unforgettable feeling of the fathomless might of the sea beneath a ship; a wild cry was torn from his throat, and a thousand unutterable feelings of the voyage, of white coasts and sparkling harbors and the creaking, eerie cries of gulls, of the dear, green dwelling of the earth again, and of strange, golden cities, potent wines, delicious foods, of women, love, and amber thighs spread amorously in ripe golden hay, of discovery and new lands, welled up in him like deathless song and certitude.

But just as these visions of delight and joy thronged upward through the deep marine of sleep, so, by the same fiat, the same calm order of an imperial will, the visions of a depthless shame, a faceless abomination of horror, an indefinable and impalpable corruption, returned to haunt his brain with their sentences of inexpiable guilt and ruin: under their evil spell he lay tranced upon his bed in a hypnosis of acquiescent horror, in a willing suspension of all his forces of resistance, like some creature held captive before the hypnotic rhythm of a reptile's head, the dull, envenomed fascination of its eye.

He moved on ceaselessly across a naked and accursed landscape and beneath a naked and accursed sky, an exile in the centre of a planetary vacancy that, like his guilt and shame, had neither place among things living nor among things dead, in which there was neither vengeance of lightning, nor mercy of burial, in which there was neither shade nor shelter, curve nor bend, nor hill, nor tree, nor hollow, in which—earth, air, sky, and limitless horizon—there was only one vast naked eye, inscrutable and accusing, from which there was no escape, and which bathed his naked soul in its fathomless depths of shame.

And then the vision faded, and suddenly, with the bridgeless immediacy of a dream, he found himself within the narrow canyon of a street, pacing interminably along on endless pavements where there was neither face nor footfall save his own, nor eye, nor window, nor any door that he might enter.

He thought he was walking through the harsh and endless continuity of one of those brownstone streets of which most of the city was constructed fifty years ago, and of which great broken lengths and fragments still remain. These streets, even if visited by some one in his waking hours, by some stranger in the fulness of health and sanity, and under the living and practical light of noon or, more particularly, by some man stunned with drink, who came there at some desolate and empty hour of night, might have a kind of cataleptic horror, a visionary unreality, as if some great maniac of architecture had conceived and shaped the first, harsh, ugly pattern of brown angularity, and then repeated it, without a change, into an infinity of illimitable repetition, with the mad and measureless insistence of an idiot monotony.

And forever he walked the street, under the brown and fatal light that fell upon him. He walked the street, and looked for a house there that was his own, for a door he knew that he must enter, for some one who was waiting for him in the house, and for the merciful dark wall and door that would hide and shelter him from the immense and naked eye of shame that peered upon him constantly. Forever he walked the street and searched the bleak, untelling façades for the house he knew and had forgotten, forever he prowled along before the endless and unchanging façades of the street, and he never found it, and at length he became aware of a vast sibilant whispering, of an immense conspiracy of subdued and obscene laughter, and of the mockery of a thousand evil eyes, that peered in silence from these bleak façades, and that he could never find or see; and forever he walked the streets alone, and heard the immense and secret whisperings and laughter, and was bathed in the bottomless depths of a wordless shame, and could never find the house he had lost, the door he had forgotten.

He was sitting in Marseilles, at a table on the terrace of a café on the Canebière, when he saw them. Suddenly, above the rapid and vociferous animation of the café crowd, he heard Starwick's strangely timbred voice, and turning, saw them seated at a table not a dozen feet away. Starwick had just turned to Elinor and was saying something quietly, in his tone of grave yet casual seriousness that often introduced his drolleries, and then he could see Starwick's ruddy face suffuse and deepen with his laughter, and Elinor's heavy shoulders begin to tremble, and then heard her shriek of high, astounded, and protesting merriment. Ann was seated listening, dark, silent, sullenly intent, with one long, slender hand resting upon the neck of the big dog, who crouched quietly beside her, and suddenly her dark and sullen face was lighted by its rare and radiant smile that gave her features the instant configuration of noble beauty.

The world rocked before him as if shattered by the force of an explosion: all the life seemed to have been blown out of him, and he sat there staring at them, blind, numb, hollow, emptied to a shell, and conscious of only one sensation—a kind of horrible fear that they would turn and see him, a kind of horrible fear that they would not. They did not turn or notice him: completely absorbed in one another, it seemed to him that they had forgotten him as completely as if they had never known him, and he was suddenly stabbed with a horrible chagrin at sight of their free gaiety, a bitter anguish of despair because of the triumph of their laughter. Then he was conscious of a single, blind and overpowering desire—to get away from them, to get away unseen, to get away somewhere—anywhere—so long as he could escape the agony of meeting, the naked shame of revelation. He signalled to a waiter, paid his bill, and quickly made his way out among the tables into the noisy crowd that thronged forever past upon the pavement. He set his face blindly away from them, and plunged ahead: it seemed to him that he could hear Starwick's shout of recognition, his voice calling to him above the thousand mixed vociferations of the crowd—and like a man pursued by devils, he set his head down blindly, and fled.

His life had passed into a state which, if not insane, was distinguished from insanity chiefly by a kind of quiescent understanding which surveyed the passage of time and his own actions with the powerless detachment of a spectator in a dream. Now, after this encounter with his three lost friends, even this sense of valuation was taken from him. In the weeks that followed, he was caught in a spell of time in which his life passed in a kind of evil dream, and later he was no more able to recall what he had done, how he had lived, where he had gone during this period, than if he had been the subject of a powerful and complete hypnosis. He was only vaguely conscious of what had happened, he felt a numb sense of horrible catastrophe, such as a drowning man might feel, or an anæsthetized patient who is bleeding to death under the surgeon's knife. He had a blind consciousness that some central governance of his life and reason had been exploded, that he was spinning down out of control like a shattered airplane—and that there was nothing he could do to save himself, that he could not get control again, that he could not "get back."

He lost the time-sense utterly—and it was his consciousness of this that filled him with numb terror. He would return to his room at night telling himself that he must work, then sleep, then rise by day and work again, and suddenly his room would be filled with light, the street below his window would be loud with all the noisy business of noon, and he would be seated at his table, with no knowledge how the time had passed.

He was now haunted constantly by a sense of the overwhelming nearness of his three lost friends. This feeling, indeed, would become so overpowering that at times the living presences of Starwick, Elinor, and Ann seemed invisibly to be with him, beside him. And the knowledge that they were here—for his conviction had become the obsession of an unshakable belief—seemed to give to the strange and sinister life of the evil and mysterious city an unutterable magic, to infect the very air he breathed with an intolerable anguish and delight. His whole life—heart and mind and spirit, and every nerve and sense and sinew of his body—was now passionately, indefatigably on the search for them. If he slept, it only brought to him an unbelievable ecstasy, an unbearable pain.

When he went out into the streets now it was only with the thought that he would find them—with an overwhelming conviction of his impending meeting with them. It seemed to him that every step he took was bringing him nearer to them, that he would meet them face to face around every corner that he turned—and this knowledge palsied his flesh with excitement, joy, and terror.

The two priests had finished eating, and provided with small cups of black coffee and small glasses of green chartreuse, they had settled back against the wall to enjoy in relaxed comfort the peace that passeth understanding. Both of the priests were Franciscans, they were on their way to Rome for the Holy Year, and apparently they had come well bestowed. Beside their table a frosty silver bucket, over the rim of which floated the gold necks of two empty champagne bottles, gave evidence of a meal from which nothing had been lacking. A waiter brought a box of Coronas and offered them prayerfully. The priests selected their cigars with an appeased and drowsy air: they bit the ends and grunted slightly at the flame the waiter offered them, then collapsing slowly against the cushioned wall, they meditated the ceiling in silence for several minutes through a blue, fragrant mist of dreamful ease.

It was a fine evening towards the end of May, and the two priests were in the best place to observe it. They had the first table on the right as you entered the café, and at this season of the year there was no door: the front was open. Just outside, the priests could see all the gaily painted little chairs and tables of the terrace, which was empty, and just beyond, the sidewalk and the Avenue de la Victoire, the chief thoroughfare of Nice. The street itself was quiet: from time to time a motor car flashed past or an old nag with clopping hooves, pulling a dilapidated-looking Victoria and urged on by a driver hunting for a fare. The trees along the street were in their full green leaf now and the air was sweet with the smell of the trees, the fragrance of earth and gardens and of unknown flowers. From time to time people came by with the strolling movement which a fine evening of this sort always seems to induce; and sometimes there would be young couples, lovers with arms around each other's waist, the women walking with a movement of voluptuous and languorous appeasement as if they were just coming from the act of love. But probably all they felt was the sensuous mystery, beauty and fragrance of the night, the smell of the trees and the earth and the flowers, which seemed to impregnate the whole continent of dark with the thrilling promises of desire almost made palpable, of unknown joys about to be realized.

It was a wonderfully seductive scene that opened from the entrance of the café, and all the more exciting because of its homely familiarity, its small framed limits into which life passed briefly with a ring of jaunting hooves, a sudden casual nearness and loudness of passing voices, and then—the fading and lonely recession of these homely sounds, a woman's burst of low and sensual laughter in the dark, the far-off dying-out of jaunting hooves—and silence.

The two priests missed nothing of the quiet scene: they drank it in with the air of men who have eaten nobly and who, fumed to contentment with the drugs of good tobacco and an old liqueur, are enormously pleased with life.

They were a strangely sorted pair and, once seen, would never be forgotten. The larger of the two was a huge tub and belly of a man, a kind of mammoth creature out of Rabelais, whose great moon of face flared fiercely, from the excess of his eating and his drinking. His fat neck and triple chin exuded over the neck-band of his robe, so that the garment he wore seemed to be stained and larded with the man's own grease. Everything about the great priest cried out with swingeing openness: his whole nature seemed to be permeated by a good humor so mountainously all-engulfing that nothing in the world could stop it: the huge red face would swell, suffuse, and purple with its choking laughter, the whole huge torso—the shoulders, arms and breast, and the great heaving belly—would shake and tremble like a hogshead full of jelly. And so far was he from being troubled by a thought of judgment, by fear of censure or the world's reproving eye, that the sight of a shocked or unconceding face was enough to send him off in a renewed paroxysm of volcanic mirth. There was no concealment in the man, there was even a kind of mountainously good-natured contempt for what the world might say or think of him, and for this reason his association with his fellow priest was all the more grotesquely humorous—a humor which was certainly not lost on this great modern Friar John of the Funnels, but which he relished to the full. For, by contrast to this great flaring, heaving, roaring, full moon of a man, it would be impossible to imagine a more cautious and hypocritic figure than the other priest cut. The second priest was a little man with a gray, bleak, meagre and incredibly sly kind of face in which his native caution and fear of self-exposure were constantly waging a grotesque and open warfare with the sly cunning, avaricious greed and sensual desire obscenely legible in his countenance. At the present moment, this tormented struggle between lust and caution was comically evident: the fellow's face was a grotesque painting of desire, and his furtive little eyes kept darting around in his head like rodents and he peered slyly right and left all around the café to see if any one had noticed the naked exposure of his passions. The reason for his confusion, the very sight of which set his huge companion off in great breast and belly-heavings of tremendous laughter, was not hard to find: at the table next to the two priests were seated two comely young whores, who had ogled and enticed the two holy men all through the evening, and whose seductive cajoleries, encouraged by the great priest's explosions of mountainous belly-gushing laughter, had now become naked, open, and outrageous. The little fellow was in a cold, gray sweat of fear and longing: afraid to look at the two women, he could yet hardly keep his eyes off them; and terrified lest his conduct be observed and followed, he was nevertheless unable to conceal the feverish eagerness of desire which held him fascinated in a kind of trance.

So, the indecent comedy proceeded: the two women, emboldened by the huge priest's mountainous heavings of laughter, passed swiftly from flirtatious raillery to proposals of a more serious character: at the end, something certain, swift and serious passed between the women and the huge fat priest: one of them spoke to him in a low hoarse tone, he lowered his great moon of face a trifle, and without looking at her, answered. In a moment the two girls rose with an elaborate casualness, the priest paid their bill, and the women sauntered out, turned left, moved slowly towards the corner and, crossing to the other side, advanced a few yards down the quiet intersecting street, where they paused and turned, waiting, in the obscuring shadow of a tree.

In a moment the huge priest called for the bill, paid it, tipped the waiter generously, and rising with a mountainous grunt, deliberately launched his huge bulk towards the street, closely followed by the sly and terror-stricken figure of the little priest. Outside the café, the great priest paused deliberately, looking both ways with a kind of huge and rotund benevolence; then turning left in the direction the girls had gone, he set out again in leisurely, imperturbed pursuit. And the little priest trotted along beside him like a frightened puppy beside an elephant; in every step, in every stride and movement that they made, the separate characters of the two men were grotesquely and powerfully evident. The huge priest barged along with a tremendous and deliberate majesty, swinging his great belly right and left before him as an elephant swings its trunk, and magnificently indifferent to what any one might think or say. But the little man trotted along in a state bordering on terror; he tried desperately to look casual and unconcerned, but his shifting eyes darted furtive glances right and left, and beneath the hem of his rough gown, his sandalled feet kept slatting up and down in a movement that was somehow comically sly and that revealed the man's whole character. At the corner the big priest paused deliberately again, turned, surveyed the scene and then, espying the white of the girls' dresses below the trees across the street, set out in deliberate pursuit. And the little priest trotted along beside, his head lowered, his eyes darting furtive glances right and left, his sandalled feet slatting slyly up and down. Then they caught up with the girls below the trees and, half obscured in darkness, they stood for a moment talking in low voices. Then each of the girls took one of the priests by the arm and they all walked off together down the street and soon were lost in leafy darkness and the mystery of the night. Then the waiter, who had served the priests and who, standing in the entrance, had observed the meeting across the street, turned and glaring at the youth, said quietly:

"C'est très joli, eh? . . . Moi," he continued, after a brief pause, "je n'ai pas le sentiment religieux." And having delivered himself without rancor or surprise of that devastating statement, he dismissed the subject from his mind completely and, turning to the table that the priests had left, he racked the saucers up, and wiped the table clean.

From a distance there came suddenly a woman's low, rich burst of sensual laughter, the receding hoof-beats of a horse, and then all around there was silence, the overpowering fragrance of the earth, the huge thrill and mystery of night, and the sense of an intolerable desire, close and palpable and lovely, and never to be grasped or found: and from the huge and haunting familiarity of all these things, a thousand receding and unuttered memories of time arose, a feeling of bitter loss, wild joy and pain—of a door that closed, a cloud-shadow that had gone forever. He thought of home.

Among the dreams that returned to haunt his waking, watchful sleep during the strange, living vision of that green spring, as he lay hearted at the pulse of time, there was one which remained ever after in his memory.

He was striding along a wide and sandy beach and by the side of a calm and tranquilly flowing sea. The waves broke quietly and evenly in a long, low roll upon the beach, rushing up the sand in small hissing eddies of foam and water. Below his feet the firm, brown sand sprang back with an elastic vitality, a warm and vital wind was blowing, and he drew into his lungs exultantly the smell of the sea, and of the warm, wet, fragrant beach, ribbed evenly with braided edges of brown seaweed.

He did not recognize the scene as one which he had ever visited before, and yet he felt an instant and complete familiarity with it, as if he had known it forever. Behind him, drumming evenly upon the hard, elastic sand, and fading away into the distance with a hard, wooden thunder of wheels, he heard the furious rhythm of pounding hooves of driven horses. He knew that he had just descended from a ship, and that he was living in one of the antique and early ages of the earth; and all of this he knew with joy and wonder, and without surprise, with the thrill of recovering something he had always known and had lost forever.

It was a scene out of the classic period of the earth, and yet it was wholly different from every image he had ever had about this earth, in his imagination. For where, in every vision of his mind and reading, that earth had come to him in a few sharp and radiant colors, in a structure of life as glowing and proportionate as one of its faultless temples, as remote from the world he lived in as all its fables, myths, and legends, this earth he now walked on was permeated with the living tones and weathers of life.

The world of Homer was the world of first light, sunlight, and of morning: the sea was wine-dark, a gold and sapphire purity of light fell on the walls of Troy, a lucent depthless purity of light welled from the eyes of Helen, as false, fatal, and innocently corrupt a woman as ever wrought destruction on the earth. The light that fell on Nausicaa and her maidens was all gold and crystal like the stream they bathed in, as lucent in purity as their limbs, as radiant as joy and morning on the earth; and even the lights of vengeance and the rout of the dread furies that fell upon the doomed and driven figure of Orestes were as fatal as blood, as relentless as an antique tragedy, as toneless as a destiny.

And in his pictures of a later time, of Athens in the period of recorded history, of Pericles and Plato and the time of the wars with Sparta, the scenes of history were bathed in these radiant and perfect lights and weathers. He knew these men were made of living, breathing flesh and subject to the errors and imperfections of mortal men, and yet when he tried to think of a slum in Athens, of people with bad teeth, blemished skins, muddy complexions—of disease, filth, and squalor among them, and of the million weary, beaten, dusty, sweating moments of their lives, he could not. Even human grief, pain, and trouble took on a color of classical perfection, of tragic grandeur, and the tortured and distressful skein of human life, with all that is ugly, trivial, and disgusting in it, took on the logical pattern of design and ordered destiny.

The light that fell upon them was of gold and sapphire, and of singing, or as ominous and fatal as a certain and inexorable doom; but now he walked this beach in one of the classical periods of the earth, and nothing was as he had tried to picture it, and yet all was as familiar as if he had known it forever.

There was no gold nor sapphire in the air: it was warm and sultry, omened with some troubling, variable and exultant menace, fraught with the sulphurous promise of a storm, pregnant with mystery and discovery, touched with a hundred disturbing elements and weathers of man's soul, and scented with a thousand warm and spermy odors of the land and sea, that touched man's entrails with delight and prophecy.

And the sea also was neither lyrical with gold and blue, or wine-dark in its single harmony: the sea was dark and sultry as the sky that bent above it; murked greenly, thickly, milkily, as it rolled quietly and broke upon the beach; as omened with impalpable prophecy as the earth and air.

He did not know the reason for his being there, and yet he knew beyond a doubt that he had come there for a purpose, that some one was waiting for him there, that the greatest joy and triumph he had ever known was impending in this glorious meeting.

CI

THAT year, in June, he was sitting one day at a table before a little café that looked out across a quiet, cobbled square in the ancient city of Dijon. He was on his way to Paris from Italy and Switzerland and he had stopped here on impulse, remembering that the town was the capital of the old kingdom of Burgundy—a name which, in some way, since childhood, had flourished in his mind with a green magic, evoking images of a fair, green country, noble wine and food, a golden, drowsy legendry of old wars and heroes, women, gallantry, and knightly acts.

And he had not been disappointed. The old town with its ancient palaces—the worn and age-grimed façades of a forgotten power, a storied architecture—and the fair, green earth, the deep, familiar green of the intimate and yet enchanted hills, awoke in him all the old drowsy gold of legendry, the promise of a fair and enfabled domain, fat with plenty.

He had been here three days now, flooded with living green and gold, a willing captive in the spell of time, drinking the noblest wine, eating some of the noblest cookery he had ever known. After the dull Swiss food, the food and wine of Burgundy were good beyond belief; and everything—old town, the fair, green country and the hills—made a music in him again which was like all the green-gold magic of his child-hood dream of France.

Now, he sat there at a table before a little café, already meditating with slow, lustful revery his noon-day meal at an ancient, famous inn where for eighteen francs one was served a stupendous meal—a succession of succulent native dishes such as he had dreamed about but had never thought that he would find outside of dreams or legends, in a town so small as this.

As he thought of this gourmet's heaven with a feeling of wonder and disbelief, the memory of a hundred little towns and cities in America returned to him, with the hideous and dyspeptic memory of their foods —the greasy, rancid, sodden, stale, dead, and weary foods of the Greek restaurants, of the lunchrooms, coffee shops and railroad cafeterias— hastily bolted and washed down to the inevitable miseries of dyspepsia with gulping swallows of sour, weak coffee.

Yes, even the noble food and wine had made a magic in this ancient place, and suddenly he was pierced again by the old hunger that haunts and hurts Americans—the hunger for a better life—an end of rawness, newness, sourness, distressful and exacerbated misery, the taking from the great plantation of the earth and of America our rich inheritance of splendor, ease, and abundance—good food, and sensual love, and noble cookery—the warmth of radiant color and of wine—pulse of the blood —an end of misery, bitterness, hunger and unrest upon the breast of everlasting plenty—the inheritance of exultancy and joy forever, which some foul, corrosive poison in our lives—bitter enigma that it is!—has taken from us.

Now, as he thought these things, sitting before the café and looking across the quiet square of whitened cobbles, a bell struck, and noon came. Slowly a great clock began to strike in the old town. In a cool, dark church, which he had seen the day before, a bell-rope, knotted at the ends, hung down before the altar-steps from an immense distance in the ceiling. The moment the town bell had finished its deep reverberation, a sexton walked noisily across the old flagged church-floor and took the bell-cord in his hands. Slowly, with a gentle rhythm, he began to swing upon the rope, and one could hear at first an old and heavy creaking from the upper air, but as yet no bell.

Then the sexton's body stiffened in its rhythm, he hung hard upon the knotted rope in punctual sway, and there began, far up in the church, the upper air of that old place, a sweet and ponderous beating of the bells. At first they beat in threes—ding-dong-dong; ding-dong-dong; then swiftly the man changed his rhythm, and the bells began to beat a faster double measure.

And now the youth remembered old, distant chimes upon a street at night; and the memory of his own bells came back into his heart. He remembered the great bell at college that rang the boys to classes, and how the knotted bell-rope came down into the room of the student who rang it; and how often he had rung the bell himself, and how at first there was the creaking noise in the upper air of the bell tower, there as here; and how, as the great bell far above him swung into its rhythm, he would be carried off the floor by that weight of thronging bronze; and he remembered still the lift and power of the old college bell, as he swung at the knotted rope, and the feeling of joy and power that surged up in him as he was lifted on the mighty upward stroke, and heard above him in the tower, the dark music of the grand old bell and the students running on the campus paths below the window, and then the loose rope, the bell tolling brokenly away to silence, the creaking sound again, and finally nothing but silence, the day's green spell and golden magic of the drowsy campus in the month of May.

And now the memory of that old bell, with all its host of long-forgotten things, swarmed back with living and intolerable pungency, as he sat there at noon in the old French town, and heard the sexton swinging on the bell of the old church.

He thought of home.

And now, with the sound of that old bell, everything around him burst into instant life. Although the structure of that life was foreign to him, and different from anything he had known as a child, everything instantly became incredibly living, near, and familiar, like something he had always known.

The little café before which he was sitting, was old and small, and had a warm, worn look of use and comfort. Inside, in the cool, dark depth of the place, were two old men sitting at a table playing cards—with a faded, green cloth upon the table; and two waiters. One of the old men had long, pointed mustaches, and a thin, distinguished face; the other was more ruddy and full-fleshed and had a beard. They played quietly, bending over the old, green cloth with studious deliberation, making each play slowly. Sometimes they spoke quietly to each other, only a few words at a time; sometimes the ruddy old man's thick shoulders would heave and tremble, and his face would flush rosily, with satisfaction; but the other one laughed thinly, quietly, in a more gentle, weary way.

The two waiters were polishing up the silverware, and getting the tables set and put in order for the mid-day meal. One of the waiters was an old man with the sprouting, energetic mustaches one sees so often in France, and with the weary, hawk-like, cynical, yet not ill-natured face that one often sees on old waiters. The other—really just a bus-boy— was a young, clumsy, thick-fingered and thick-featured country lad, with the wine-dark, vital, sanguinary coloring some Frenchmen have.

The young fellow was full of exuberant good spirits; he was polishing up the knives and forks and spoons with enthusiastic gusto, humming the snatches of a song as he did so, and slamming each piece of silver down into a drawer with such vigor, when he had finished, that it was obvious that he got great pleasure from the musical jingle thus created.

Meanwhile the old waiter moved quietly, softly, and yet wearily about, setting the tables. At length, however, at the end of a particularly violent and enthusiastic jingle of silverware from his polishing companion, he looked up, with a slight cynical arching of his eyebrows, and then, without ill-nature but with perfect urbanity, he said ironically:

"Ah! On fait la musique!"

This was all, but one saw the young fellow's face flush and redden with exuberant laughter; his thick shoulders rose and for a moment trembled convulsively, then he went on polishing, singing to himself, and hurling the noisy silverware into the drawer with more enthusiasm than ever.

And that brief, pleasant, and somehow poignantly unforgettable scene now seemed, like everything else, to be intolerably near and familiar to the youth, and something he had always known.

Before him, the quiet, faded, strangely pleasant square was waking briefly to its moment of noon-day life. Far off he could hear the little shrill fifing whistle of a French locomotive, and the sound of slow trains; an ice-wagon, with a tin interior and large, delicately carved cakes of ice, clattered across the cobbles of the square; and he remembered how he had seen, the day before, some barge people eating on a barge beneath the trees. From where he sat he could see workmen, wearing shapeless caps and baggy corduroy trousers streaked with lime and cement, and talking in hoarse, loud, disputatious voices as they leaned above their drinks on the zinc bar of a little bistro on the corner.

Some young, dull-looking women, wearing light-colored stockings, and light, gray-tannish overcoats, came by, with domesticity written in every movement that they made, looking, somehow, their wedded propriety, and the stern dullness of provincial places everywhere.

And then the lost, the irrevocable, the lonely sounds which he had not heard for fifteen years awoke there in the square, and suddenly he was a child, and it was noon, and he was waiting in his father's house to hear the slam of the iron gate, the great body stride up the high porch steps, knowing his father had come home again.

At first, before him, in that little whitened square, it was just the thring of the bicycle bells, the bounding of the light-wired wheels. And at first he could see some French army officers riding home upon their bicycles. They were proper and assured-looking men, with solid, wine-dark faces, and they rode solidly and well, driving the light-wired wheels beneath them with firm propulsions of their solid legs.

Then, with a thring of bells, an army sergeant came by, riding fast and smoothly on his way home to dinner. And then, with sudden rush, the thring of bells, the thrum of wheels increased: the clerks, the bank clerks, the bookkeepers—the little proper and respectable people of all sorts—were riding home across the quiet little square at noon.

On the other side of the square he could see two workmen who were still at work upon a piece of stone; one was holding an iron spike, and one a sledge, and they worked slowly, with frequent pauses.

A young buck, with a noisy, sporty little car, sped over the square, and vanished; and the youth wondered if he was one of the daring blades of Dijon, and what young women of the town's best families he had taken out in the car, and if he boasted to other young town blades in cafés of his prowess at seduction, as did the bucks before Wood's Pharmacy at home.

Then, for a moment there was a brooding silence in the square again, and presently there began the most lonely, lost and unforgettable of all sounds on earth—the solid, liquid leather-shuffle of footsteps going home one way, as men had done when they came home to lunch at noon some twenty years ago, in the green-gold and summer magic of full June, before he had seen his father's land, and when the kingdoms of this earth and the enchanted city still blazed there in the legendary magic of his boyhood vision.

They came with solid, lonely, liquid shuffle of their decent leather, going home, the merchants, workers, and good citizens of that old town of Dijon. They streamed across the cobbles of that little square; they passed, and vanished, and were gone forever—leaving silence, the brooding hush and apathy of noon, a suddenly living and intolerable memory, instant and familiar as all this life around him, of a life that he had lost, and that could never die.

It was the life of twenty years ago in the quiet, leafy streets and little towns of lost America—of an America that had been lost beneath the savage roar of its machinery, the brutal stupefaction of its days, the huge disease of its furious, ever-quickening and incurable unrest, its flood-tide horror of gray, driven faces, stolid eyes, starved, brutal nerves, and dull, dead flesh.

The memory of the lost America—the America of twenty years ago, of quiet streets, the time-enchanted spell and magic of full June, the solid, lonely, liquid shuffle of men in shirt-sleeves coming home, the leafy fragrance of the cooling turnip-greens, and screens that slammed, and sudden silence—had long since died, had been drowned beneath the brutal flood-tide, the fierce stupefaction of that roaring surge and mechanic life which had succeeded it.

And now, all that lost magic had come to life again here in the little whitened square, here in this old French town, and he was closer to his childhood and his father's life of power and magnificence than he could ever be again in savage new America; and as the knowledge of these strange, these lost yet familiar things returned to him, his heart was filled with all the mystery of time, dark time, the mystery of strange, million-visaged time that haunts us with the briefness of our days.

He thought of home.

BOOK VIII

FAUST AND HELEN

CII

Immense and sudden, and with the abrupt nearness, the telescopic magic of a dream, the English ship appeared upon the coasts of France, and approached with the strange, looming immediacy of powerful and gigantic objects that move at great speed: there was no sense of continuous movement, of gradual and progressive enlargement, rather the visages of the ship melted rapidly from one bigness to another as do the visages of men in a cinema, which, by a series of fading sizes, brings these kinematic shapes of things, like genii unstoppered from a wizard's bottle, to an overpowering command above the spectator.

At first there was only the calm endlessness of the evening sea, the worn headlands of Europe, and the land, with its rich, green slopes, its striped patterns of minutely cultivated earth, its ancient fortresses and its town—the town of Cherbourg—which, from this distance, lay like a solid pattern of old chalk at the base of the coastal indentation.

Westward, a little to the south, against the darkening bulk of the headland, a long riband of smoke, black and low, told the position of the ship. She was approaching fast, her bulk widened: she had been a dot, a smudge, a shape—a tiny, hardly noticed point in the calm and immense geography of evening. Now she was there, sliding gently in beyond the ancient breakwater, inhabiting and dominating the universe with the presence of her 60,000 tons, so that the vast setting of sky and sea and earth, in which formerly she had been only an inconspicuous but living mark, were now a background for her magnificence.

At this very moment of her arrival the sun rested upon the western wave like a fading coal: its ancient light fell over sea and land without violence or heat, with a remote, unearthly glow that had the delicate tinging of old bronze. Then, swiftly, the sun sank down into the sea, the uninhabited sky now burned with a fierce, an almost unbearable glory; the sun's old light had faded; and the ship was there outside the harbor, sliding softly through the water now, and quartering, in slow turn, upon the land as she came up for anchor.

The sheer wall of her iron plates scarcely seemed to move at all now in the water, it was as if she were fixed and founded there among the tides, as implacable as the headlands of the coast; yet, over her solid bows the land was wheeling slowly. Water foamed noisily from her sides in thick, tumbling columns: the sea-gulls swarmed around her, fluttering greedily and heavily to the water with their creaking and unearthly clamor. Then her anchors rushed out of her, and she stood still.

Meanwhile the tenders, bearing the passengers who were going to board the ship, had put out from the town even before the ship's arrival, and were now quite near. They had, in fact, cruised slowly for some time about the outer harbor, for the ship was late and the commander had wirelessed asking that there be as little delay as possible when he arrived.

Now the light faded on the land: the fierce, hard brilliance of the western sky, full of bright gold and ragged flame, had melted to an orange afterglow, the subtle, grapy bloom of dusk was melting across the land; the town, far off, was half immersed in it, its moving shadow stole across the fields and slopes, it moved upon the waters like a weft. Above the land the sky was yet full of light—of that strange, phantasmal light of evening which reveals itself to people standing in the dusk below without touching them with any of its radiance: the material and physical property of light seems to have been withdrawn from it, and it remains briefly in the sky, without substance or any living power, like the ghost of light, its soul, its spirit.

In these late skies of France, this late, evening light of waning summer had in it a quality that was high and sad, remote and full of classic repose and dignity. Beneath it, it was as if one saw people grave and beautiful move slowly homeward through long aisles of planted trees: the light was soft, lucent, delicately empearled—and all great labor was over, all strong joy and hate and love had ended, all wild desire and hope, all maddening of the flesh and heart and brain, the fever and the tumult and the fret; and the grave-eyed women in long robes walked slowly with cut flowers in their arms among the glades of trees, and night had come, and they would go to the wood no more.

Now, in this light, all over the land of France the men were coming from the fields: they had used preciously the last light of day, summer was almost over, the fields were mown, the hay was raked and stacked, and in a thousand places, along the Rhine, and along the Marne, in Burgundy, in Touraine, in Provence, the wains were lumbering slowly down the roads.

In the larger towns the nervous and swarming activity of evening had begun: the terraces of the cafés were uncomfortably crowded with noisy people, the pavements were thronged with a chattering and gesticulating tide, the streets were loud with traffic, the clatter of trams, the heavy grinding of buses, the spiteful little horns of innumerable small taxis. But over all, over the opulence of the mown fields, and the untidy and distressful throngings of the towns, hung this high, sad light of evening.

A stranger, a visitor from some newer and more exultant earth—an American, perhaps—had he seen this coast thus for the first time, might have imagined the land as inhabited by a race far different from the one that really lived here: he would have felt the opulent austerity of this earth under its dying light, and he would have been deeply troubled by it.

For such a visitor, disturbed by the profound and subtle melancholy of this scene, for which his own experience had given him no adequate understanding or preparation, because it was steeped in peace without hope, in beauty without joy, in tranquil and brooding resignation without exultancy, the sight of the ship, as she lay now, immense and immovable at her anchor, would have pierced him suddenly with a thrill of victory, a sudden renewal of his faith and hope, a belief in the happy destiny of life.

She lay there, an alien presence in those waters; she had the reality of magic, the reality that is so living and magnificent that it seems unreal. She was miraculous and true—as one looked at her, settled like some magic luminosity upon that mournful coast, a strong cry of exultancy rose up in one's throat: the sight of the ship was as if a man's mistress had laid her hand upon his loins.

The ship was now wholly anchored: she lay there in the water with the living stillness of all objects that were made to move. Although entirely motionless, outwardly as fixed and permanent as any of the headlands of the coast, the story of her power and speed was legible in every line. She glowed and pulsed with the dynamic secret of life, and although her great sides towered immense and silent as a cliff, although the great plates of her hull seemed to reach down and to be founded in the sea's bed, and only the quietly flowing waters seemed to move and eddy softly at her sides, she yet had legible upon her the story of a hundred crossings, the memory of strange seas, of suns and moons and many different lights, the approach of April on far coasts, the change of wars and histories, and the completed dramas of all her voyages, charactered by the phantoms of many thousand passengers, the life, the hate, the love, the bitterness, the jealousy, the intrigue of six-day worlds, each one complete and separate in itself, which only a ship can have, which only the sea can bound, which only the earth can begin or end.

She glowed with the radiance of all her brilliant and luminous history; and besides this, she was literally a visitant from a new world. The stranger from the new world who saw the ship would also instantly have seen this. She had been built several years after the war and was entirely a product of European construction, engineering, navigation, and diplomacy. But her spirit, the impulse that communicated itself in each of her lines, was not European, but American. It is Europeans, for the most part, who have constructed these great ships, but without America they have no meaning. These ships are alive with the supreme ecstasy of the modern world, which is the voyage to America. There is no other experience that is remotely comparable to it, in its sense of joy, its exultancy, its drunken and magnificent hope which, against reason and knowledge, soars into a heaven of fabulous conviction, which believes in the miracle and sees it invariably achieved.

In this soft, this somewhat languid air, the ship glowed like an immense and brilliant jewel. All of her lights were on, they burned row by row straight across her 900 feet of length, with the small, hard twinkle of cut gems: it was as if the vast, black cliff of her hull, which strangely suggested the glittering night-time cliff of the fabulous city that was her destination, had been sown with diamonds.

And above this, her decks were ablaze with light. Her enormous superstructure with its magnificent frontal sweep, her proud breast which was so full of power and speed, her storied decks and promenades as wide as city streets, the fabulous variety and opulence of her public rooms, her vast lounges and salons, her restaurants, grills, and cafés, her libraries, writing-rooms, ballrooms, swimming-pools, her imperial suites with broad beds, private decks, sitting-rooms, gleaming baths—all of this, made to move upon the stormy seas, leaning against eternity and the gray welter of the Atlantic at twenty-seven knots an hour, tenanted by the ghosts, impregnated by the subtle perfumes of thousands of beautiful and expensive women, alive with the memory of the silken undulance of their long backs, with the naked, living velvet of their shoulders as they paced down the decks at night—all of this, with the four great funnels that in the immense drive and energy of their slant were now cut sharp and dark against the evening sky, burned with a fierce, exultant vitality in the soft melancholy of this coast.

The ship struck joy into the spinal marrow. In her intense reality she became fabulous, a visitant from another world, a creature monstrous and magical with life, a stranger, seeming strange, to these melancholy coasts, for she was made to glitter in the hard, sharp air of a younger, more exultant land.

She was made also to quarter on the coasts of all the earth, to range powerfully on the crest and ridge of the globe, sucking continents towards her, devouring sea and land; she was made to enter European skies like some stranger from another world, to burn strangely and fabulously in the dull, gray air of Europe, to pulse and glow under the soft, wet European sky. But she was only a marvellous stranger there; she was a bright, jewelled thing; she came definitely, indubitably, wonderfully from but one place on earth, and in only that one place could she be fully seen and understood, in only that one place could she slide in to her appointed and imperial setting.

That place was America: that place was the reaches to the American coast: that place was the approaches to the American continent. That place, finally, and absolutely, was the port whither she was bound—the fabulous rock of life, the proud, masted city of the soaring towers, which was flung with a lion's port into the maw of ocean. And as the Americans who were now approaching the ship in the puffing little tender saw this mark upon her, they looked at her and knew her instantly; they felt a qualm along their loins, their flesh stirred.

"Oh, look!" cried a woman suddenly, pointing to the ship whose immense and glittering side now towered over them. "Isn't that lovely! God, but she's big! How do you suppose we're ever going to find the ocean?"

"The first thing I'm going to do, darling, is find my bed," said her companion, in a tone of languorous weariness. A tall and sensual-looking Jewess, she was seated on a pile of baggage, smoking a cigarette, her long legs indolently crossed: indifferently, with smouldering and arrogant glances, she surveyed the crowd of passengers on the tender.

The other woman could not be still: her rosy face was burning with the excitement of the voyage, she kept slipping the ring on and off her finger nervously, and moving around at her brisk little step among the heaped-up piles of baggage.

"Oh, here!" she cried out suddenly in great excitement, pointing to a bag buried at the bottom of one of the piles. "Oh, here!" she cried again to the general public. "This one's mine! Where are the others? Can't you find the others for me?" she said in a sharp, protesting voice to one of the porters, a little, brawny man with sprouting mustaches. "Hey?" she said, lifting her small hand complainingly to her ear as he answered her in a torrent of reassuring French. She turned to her companion protestingly:

"I can't get them to do anything. They don't pay a bit of attention to what I say! I can't find my trunk and two of my bags. I think it's the most dreadful thing I ever heard of. Don't you? Hey?" again she lifted her little hand to her ear, for she was somewhat deaf: her small, rosy face was crimson with excitement and earnestness—in her tone, her manner, her indignation, there was something irresistibly comic, and suddenly her companion began to laugh.

"Oh, Esther!" she said. "Lord!" and then paused abruptly, as if there were no more to say.

Esther was fair; she was fair; she had dove's eyes.

Now the woman's lovely face, like a rarer, richer, and more luminous substance, was glowing among all the other faces of the travellers, which, as the tender circled and came in close below the ship, were fixed with a single intentness upon the great hull that loomed over them with its overpowering immensity.

The great ship cast over them all her mighty spell: most of these people had made many voyages, yet the great ship caught them up again in her magic glow, she possessed and thrilled them with her presence as if they had been children. The travellers stood there silent and intent as the little boat slid in beside the big one, they stood there with uplifted faces; and for a moment it was strange and sad to see them thus, with loneliness and longing in their eyes. Their faces made small, lifted whitenesses; they shone in the gathering dark with a luminous glimmer: there was something small, naked and lonely in the glimmer of those faces, around them was the immense eternity of sea and death. They heard time.

For if, as men be dying, they can pluck one moment from the darkness into which their sense is sinking, if one moment in all the dark and mysterious forest should then live, it might well be the memory of such a moment as this which, although lacking in logical meaning, burns for an instant in the dying memory as a summary and a symbol of man's destiny on earth. The fading memory has forgotten what was said then

by the passengers, the thousand tones and shadings of the living moment
are forgotten, but drenched in the strange, brown light of time, the
scene glows again for an instant with an intent silence: darkness has
fallen upon the eternal earth, the great ship like a monstrous visitant
blazes on the waters, and on the tender the faces of the travellers are
lifted up like flowers in a kind of rapt and mournful ecstasy—they are
weary of travel, they have wandered in strange cities among strange
tongues and faces, and they have left not even the print of their foot in
any town.

Their souls are naked and alone, and they are strangers upon the
earth, and many of them long for a place where those weary of travel
may find rest, where those who are tired of searching may cease to
search, where there will be peace and quiet living, and no desire. Where
shall the weary find peace? Upon what shore will the wanderer come
home at last? When shall it cease—the blind groping, the false desires,
the fruitless ambitions that grow despicable as soon as they are reached,
the vain contest with phantoms, the maddening and agony of the
brain and spirit in all the rush and glare of living, the dusty tumult, the
grinding, the shouting, the idiot repetition of the streets, the sterile
abundance, the sick gluttony, and the thirst which goes on drinking?

Out of one darkness the travellers have come to be taken into another,
but for a moment one sees their faces, awful and still, all uplifted towards the ship. This is all: their words have vanished, all memory of the
movements they made then has also vanished: one remembers only their
silence and their still faces lifted in the phantasmal light of lost time; one
sees them ever, still and silent, as they slide from darkness on the river of
time; one sees them waiting at the ship's great side, all silent and all
damned to die, with their grave, white faces lifted in a single supplication to the ship, and towards the silent row of passengers along the deck,
who for a moment return their gaze with the same grave and tranquil
stare. That silent meeting is a summary of all the meetings of men's
lives: in the silence one hears the slow, sad breathing of humanity, one
knows the human destiny.

"Oh, look!" the woman cried again. "Oh, see! Was ever anything
more beautiful?" The ship's great beetling cliff swept sheer above her.
She turned the small, flushed flower of her face and saw the slant and
reach and swell of the great prow, and music filled her. She lifted the
small, flushed flower of her face and saw the many men, so little, so

lonely, silent, and intent, that bent above her, looking from the ship's steep rail. She turned and saw the people all around her, the swift weave and patterned shifting of the forms, and she saw light then, ancient fading light, that fell upon the coasts of evening, and quiet waters reddened by fading day, and heard the unearthly creakings of a gull; and wonder filled her. And the strange and mortal ache of beauty, the anguish to pronounce what never could be spoken, to grasp what never could be grasped, to hold and keep forever what was gone the moment she put her hand upon it——

"Oh, these people here," she cried in a high tone—"The ship! . . . My God, the things that I could tell you all!" she cried indignantly. "The things I know—the things I have inside me here!"—she struck herself upon the breast with one clenched hand—"the way things are, the way they happen, and the beauty of the clear design—and no one ever asks me!" she cried out indignantly. "This wonderful thing is going on inside me all the time—and no one ever wants to know the way it happens!"—and stood staring at her friend accusingly a moment, a little figure of indignant loveliness until, becoming aware of people's smiles and her companion's laughter, her own face was suddenly suffused, and, casting back her head, she was swept with gale-like merriment—a full, rich, woman's yell of triumph and delight.

And yet, even as she laughed, she was pierced again by the old ache of wonder, the old anguish of unspoken desire, and saw the many men, so lonely, silent, and intent, the ship immense and sudden there above her in old evening light, and so—remembering, "Canst thou draw out leviathan with an hook? or his tongue with a cord which thou lettest down?"—was still with wonder.

Ah, strange and beautiful, the woman thought, how can I longer bear this joy intolerable, the music of this great song unpronounceable, the anguish of this glory unimaginable, which fills my life to bursting and which will not let me speak! It is too hard, too hard, and not to be endured, to feel the great vine welling in my heart, the wild, strange music swelling in my throat, the triumph of that final perfect song that aches forever there just at the gateway of my utterance—and that has no tongue to speak! O magic moment that are so perfect, unknown, and inevitable, to stand here at this ship's great side, here at the huge last edge of evening and return, with this still wonder in my heart and knowing only that somehow we are fulfilled of you, oh time! And see how gathered there against the rail high over us, there at the ship's great side, are all the people, silent, lonely, and so beautiful; strange brothers of this voyage, chance phantoms of the bitter briefness of our days—and you, oh youth—for now she saw him there for the first time —who bend there, lone and lean and secret, at the rail of night, why are you there alone while these, your fellows, wait? . . . Ah secret and alone, she thought—how lean with hunger, and how fierce with pride, and how burning with impossible desire he bends there at the rail of night—and he is wild and young and foolish and forsaken, and his eyes are starved, his soul is parched with thirst, his heart is famished with a hunger that cannot be fed, and he leans there on the rail and dreams great dreams, and he is mad for love and is athirst for glory, and he is so cruelly mistaken—and so right! . . . Ah, see, she thought, how that wild light flames there upon his brow—how bright, how burning and how beautiful—Oh passionate and proud!—how like the wild, lost soul of youth you are, how like my wild lost father who will not return!

He turned, and saw her then, and so finding her, was lost, and so losing self, was found, and so seeing her, saw for a fading moment only the pleasant image of the woman that perhaps she was, and that life saw. He never knew: he only knew that from that moment his spirit was impaled upon the knife of love. From that moment on he never was again to lose her utterly, never to wholly re-possess unto himself the lonely, wild integrity of youth which had been his. At that instant of their meeting, that proud inviolability of youth was broken, not to be restored. At that moment of their meeting she got into his life by some dark magic, and before he knew it, he had her beating in the pulses of his blood—somehow thereafter—how he never knew—to steal into the conduits of his heart, and to inhabit the lone, inviolable tenement of his one life; so, like love's great thief, to steal through all the adyts of his soul, and to become a part of all he did and said and was—through this invasion so to touch all loveliness that he might touch, through this strange and subtle stealth of love henceforth to share all that he might feel or make or dream, until there was for him no beauty that she did not share, no music that did not have her being in it, no horror, mad-ness, hatred, sickness of the soul, or grief unutterable, that was not somehow consonant to her single image and her million forms—and no final freedom and release, bought through the incalculable expendi-ture of blood and anguish and despair, that would not bear upon its brow forever the deep scar, upon its sinews the old mangling chains, of love.

After all the blind, tormented wanderings of youth, that woman would become his heart's centre and the target of his life, the image of immortal one-ness that again collected him to one, and hurled the whole collected passion, power and might of his one life into the blazing certitude, the immortal governance and unity, of love.

"Set me as a seal upon thine heart, as a seal upon thine arm: for love is strong as death; jealousy is cruel as the grave: the coals thereof are coals of fire, which hath a most vehement flame."

And now all the faces pass in through the ship's great side (the tender flower face among them). Proud, potent faces of rich Jews, alive with wealth and luxury, glow in rich, lighted cabins; the doors are closed, and the ship is given to the darkness and the sea.